THE POWER TRIP

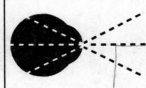

This Large Print Book carries the
Seal of Approval of N.A.V.H.

THE POWER TRIP

JACKIE COLLINS

THORNDIKE PRESS
A part of Gale, Cengage Learning

GALE
CENGAGE Learning·

Detroit • New York • San Francisco • New Haven, Conn • Waterville, Maine • London

GALE
CENGAGE Learning®

Thorndike Press® Large Print Core.
The text of this Large Print edition is unabridged.
Other aspects of the book may vary from the original edition.
Set in 16 pt. Plantin.

LIBRARY OF CONGRESS CATALOGING-IN-PUBLICATION DATA

Collins, Jackie.
   The Power Trip / by Jackie Collins. — Large Print edition.
      pages cm. — (Thorndike Press Large Print Core)
   ISBN-13: 978-1-4104-5549-9 (hardcover)
   ISBN-10: 1-4104-5549-1 (hardcover)
   1. Rich people—Fiction. 2. Cruise ships—Fiction. 3. Yachts—Fiction. 4. Large type books. I. Title.
PR6053.O425P69 2013b
823'.914—dc23   2012045016

Published in 2013 by arrangement with St. Martin's Press, LLC

Printed in the United States of America
1 2 3 4 5 6 7 17 16 15 14 13

To all my readers across the world.
Love . . .
Passion . . .
Friendship . . .
and
Power! Live it!

PROLOGUE

The couple on the bed had sex as if it were their final act.

And for one of them it was.

Neither of them heard the door slowly open.

Neither of them observed the shadowy figure enter the room.

They were too caught up in the throes of passionate lovemaking.

Until . . . one single gunshot.

The blood flowed.

And for one of them, death and orgasm happened at the exact same moment.

Life has a strange way of taking you on an unexpected trip.

This was one of those times.

■ ■ ■ ■

BOOK ONE:
THE INVITATION

■ ■ ■ ■

CHAPTER ONE

DATELINE: MOSCOW

The Russian billionaire Aleksandr Kasianenko admired his supermodel girlfriend as she stepped, unabashedly naked, out of the indoor swimming pool in his luxurious Moscow mansion. Her name was Bianca, and she was known across the world.

God, she is a beautiful creature, Aleksandr thought. *Beautiful and sleekly feline — she moves like a panther. And in bed she is a wild tigress. I am a very fortunate man.*

Bianca was of mixed race: her mother was Cuban, her father black. There was no doubt that Bianca had inherited the best of both her parents' looks.

She'd been raised in New York, was discovered at seventeen, and now, at age twenty-nine, she was the most sought-after supermodel on the planet. Tall, lean, and agile, with coffee-colored skin, fine features, full natural lips, piercing green eyes, and waist-length glossy black hair, Bianca captivated both men and women. Men found her irresistibly sexy, while women admired her sense of style and raunchy humor, which she exhibited every time she appeared on the late-night talk shows.

Bianca knew how to handle herself in front of the cameras, and she certainly knew how to plug her brand. Over the years, she'd created a mini empire that included a fine-jewelry line, exotic sunglasses, a stunning makeup collection for women of color, and several bestselling scents.

Bianca had mastered the art of the sell, making a fortune doing so. But recently, she'd decided that rather than be a one-woman band who worked hard for her money, she was looking for more. She was looking for a powerful man who would take care of her and parlay the money she'd earned into super-rich status.

Aleksandr Kasianenko was just such a man, because Aleksandr was not only a powerful, super-rich businessman, he was also tough and rugged, with a steely reserve.

Bianca was sick of the long list of pretty boys she'd dated over the years. Movie stars, a clutch of rock stars, a half dozen sports heroes, and a politician or two. None of them had really satisfied her — in bed or out. She'd always been the dominant force in whatever relationship she'd been trapped in. The movie stars were all insecure and fixated on their public image. Rock stars were mostly into drugs and getting fucked up, not to mention totally vain. The sports stars were publicity crazy and never faithful. And as for the politicians — sexually incorrect. All horn and no blow.

Then, at exactly the right time, she'd met Aleksandr. And she'd fallen for his silent strength.

Only one problem.

He was married.

They'd met on Aleksandr's home turf. She was in Moscow doing a cover shoot for Italian *Vogue,* and since it happened to be her twenty-ninth birthday, the flamboyant photographer, Antonio — an Italian gay man who knew absolutely everyone who was anyone in Moscow — had decided to throw her a massive party.

The party was a blast. Until she was introduced to Aleksandr.

The moment she saw him, he took her breath away with his brooding dark looks and aura of control and power. He was big and strong, and there was something magnetic about him, something incredibly masculine. One look and she was hooked.

He didn't tell her he was married.

She didn't ask.

An hour after their first encounter, they were making fast, ferocious love on the floor in her hotel suite. Their lovemaking was

13

animalistic in its intensity, so overpowering that they'd never made it as far as the bedroom. It was all clothes off and straight at it.

After their night of unbridled passion, they were both swept up and addicted to each other. And so began their steamy affair, an affair that had them meeting all over the world.

Now, after one year, and in spite of Aleksandr's marital status, they were still very much together.

Aleksandr had assured Bianca that he was in the throes of divorcing his wife, but due to several massive business deals that could affect his wife's settlement, it still had not happened. He also had children to consider. Three daughters. "The timing has to be right," he'd informed her. "However, it *will* happen, and it will happen soon. You have my word."

Bianca believed him. He was separated from his wife, so that was a promising beginning. Still, she couldn't help wanting more. She wanted to be Mrs. Aleksandr Kasianenko, and the less time wasted, the better.

In the meantime, Aleksandr wished to celebrate his love's upcoming thirtieth birthday in a big way. He'd recently taken delivery of a new, luxurious four-hundred-foot superyacht, and to christen their maiden voyage, he planned on throwing Bianca a once-in-a-lifetime special event she would never forget.

14

The celebrations would include inviting several of their friends on a weeklong cruise to enjoy the best of everything. What could be better?

When he informed Bianca of his plan, she was excited, and immediately started thinking about whom they would invite on this very exclusive trip.

"How many can your new yacht accommodate?" she inquired.

"Many," Aleksandr replied with a dry laugh. "But I feel we should invite only five couples."

"Why only five?" Bianca asked, slightly disappointed.

"It's enough," Aleksandr replied. "You make your list, I make mine. Then we will compare and decide who gets invited."

Bianca grinned. "This is gonna be fun," she said, already planning her list.

"Indeed it will," Aleksandr agreed.

CHAPTER TWO

DATELINE: LONDON

Ashley Sherwin stared at her image in the ornate mirror above the vanity for a full ten minutes before her husband, Taye, entered their streamlined bathroom with the marble counters and fancy rock-crystal chandeliers — designed by Jeromy Milton-Gold, one of London's most sought-after interior designers.

"Whatcha lookin' at, toots?" Taye asked cheerfully, taking the opportunity to lean over her shoulder and check out his own image, which was, as usual, totally fine.

"New makeup," Ashley muttered sulkily, annoyed that he'd caught her, wishing she'd locked the door.

Taye had no concept of the word *privacy.* Well, he wouldn't, would he? He was a superstar footballer used to stripping off and basking in all the glory (not to mention the women) that came his way. Cheap nasty little tarts, ready and willing to chase any famous man. She hated them all.

"Well," Taye said, stretching his arms above his head. "You look hot an' horny."

Ashley had no desire to look hot and horny; her aim was to look like an elegant fashion icon, a fashionista with style to spare. Taye simply didn't get it. He thought he was tossing her a compliment, but as far as she was concerned, it was exactly the opposite.

She sighed. After six years of marriage, Taye still had no clue who the person was that she aspired to be. Didn't he realize that she was no longer the pretty, blond, twenty-two-year-old TV presenter he'd married? She was now the mother to their six-year-old twins, Aimee and Wolf. She was older, more mature. She knew what she wanted, and it was certainly not enough to be known as Taye Sherwin's trophy wife.

They'd gotten married because she was pregnant — never the best of ideas, but better than being knocked up without a husband. And Taye was a major catch. Black and beautiful. A sports hero. A moneymaking machine, what with all his various endorsement deals and superstar status.

They'd met on a TV show she'd been co-hosting with Harmony Gee, a former member of the girl group Sweet. Harmony was all over Taye, but it soon became obvious to everyone that he only had eyes for Ashley.

Before long, they were a staple in the U.K.

newspapers, billed as *the* new hot couple. They were even given a nickname by the press: Tashley. It had a ring to it.

Ashley was thrilled; she basked in the attention. For six months she'd been pushed into the background while Harmony scored most of the big interviews, but with all her newfound PR, her bosses at the TV station were suddenly regarding her with new respect, while Harmony was staring at her with daggers in her eyes.

Then Taye had managed to impregnate her, and that was that.

Good-bye, career.

Hello, marriage.

Taye was a superstar in all respects. The moment he found out she was pregnant, he'd insisted they get married. Never mind about his playboy past; Taye was all about doing the right thing. Besides, he loved Ashley. She was perfect for him — a true English peach with her widely spaced blue eyes, flawless skin, long blond hair, and curvy figure.

Taye's mother, Anais, a heavyset Jamaican woman, was not so pleased. "You should be marryin' one of ya own kind," Anais had complained, her accent heavy with disapproval. "This Ashley gal's nothin' but a fancy show pony. She not gonna make ya a satisfyin' wife."

"Your mama's right, son," Taye's dad had agreed. "Ya wanna grab yourself an island

18

woman — more meat on them bones. Juicy dark meat. Delicious!"

The last time Taye's parents had visited Jamaica was forty years ago, so Taye chose to ignore their sage advice. Instead, he forged ahead with elaborate wedding plans.

Ashley's mom, Elise — a faded blonde who worked behind the makeup counter in a department store — was torn. The good news was that Taye was rich and famous. The bad news was that he was black.

Elise tried not to think in a racist way, but, unfortunately, she'd been raised to regard the black race as inferior beings.

Fortunately, Ashley had never harbored any hang-ups about Taye being black. He loved her more than any man ever had; in fact, he kind of worshipped her, which she didn't mind at all. Being worshipped by a very famous man whom every other woman lusted after was quite a kick.

Their lavish marriage made headline news. So did the birth of their twins three months later. Taye bought them all a magnificent house near Hampstead Heath, and everything was well in the world. Except shortly after moving into their new home, Ashley suffered from a bad bout of postpartum depression and refused to go near the twins for the first six months of their lives. This forced Taye to move his parents and Ashley's mother into their house, which turned out to be a most unhappy situation, because the two women soon discovered that they loathed each other — especially when Anais accused the thrice-divorced Elise of making a play for her husband, an accusation Elise hotly denied.

The Sherwin household was not a happy one, with Ashley locked up in the master bedroom refusing to come out, the twins demanding attention day and night, and the mothers-in-law at war.

Taye attempted to keep the peace, but it wasn't easy. And since Ashley shied away from any sexual contact, he was becoming increasingly frustrated, not to mention horny.

So it came to pass that Taye cheated. And as luck would have it, the girl he cheated with (a Page 3 model with outrageous boobs) couldn't wait to run to the tabloids and sell her story for a ridiculous amount of money.

The headlines were relentless:

MY ENDLESS NIGHT OF LUST WITH TAYE SHERWIN

HE'S A STAR IN BED TOO!

IS TASHLEY OVER?

Oh, the humiliation! The fury! The shock that Ashley experienced.

She'd hauled herself out of hiding and confronted her husband in a simmering rage.

His excuses were weak: No sex for months. A depressed wife. Crying babies. Warring mothers-in-law. And a buxom babe throwing herself at him during an aftershave commercial he was shooting.

Taye wasn't made of stone. He'd fallen into those giant tits like a man starved for sustenance. He'd wallowed in them. Then, after wallowing, he'd screwed the random girl, immediately regretted it, and run for his life.

The newspaper story shocked Ashley into action. She'd hurriedly hired two maternity nurses, banished both mothers-in-law to their own homes, and set about getting herself back in shape.

Meanwhile, Taye presented her with a ten-carat diamond ring, assured her his indiscretion would never happen again, paid for the boob job she demanded, and normal life resumed.

Only it wasn't that normal. Ashley forgave; the problem was that she had no intention of ever forgetting.

As the twins grew, Ashley began to think about her future, and what she could do to become more than just another footballer's wife. She'd started by informing Taye that any ads or endorsements he did in the future should include her. He'd agreed. Having rocked the boat once, he was damn sure that he wasn't allowing it to happen again. Ashley meant everything to him, and he wasn't about to risk losing her.

So, ad-wise, they gradually became a team. The Taye and Ashley show. He with the shaved head, muscled body, and killer smile.

She with the baby-blue eyes, lush body, amazing boobs, and tumbling blond curls. They got together with the best photographers, and soon created a partnership brand.

Ashley worked hard on her body, toning and tanning, losing any excess fat and gaining muscle, until she looked almost as fit as Taye, only in a womanly way.

She adored her new breasts; they gave her so much more confidence, and Taye loved them too.

Would he ever cheat again?

He'd better not, because if there *was* a next time, she'd leave him, take the twins, and make his life pure hell.

Eighteen months previously, Ashley had decided that appearing in ads with Taye was not enough for her — it was time she had her own career. The twins were getting older, and she'd been thinking about doing something that was all hers. Since she'd always fancied herself an interior designer, she'd approached Jeromy Milton-Gold, the designer who'd worked on their house. Jeromy was the older boyfriend of Latin singing star Luca Perez. She'd asked Jeromy if she could be part of his team. Jeromy, who was always looking for ways to up his profile, told her it was a fabulous idea, and that if Taye was prepared to invest in his business, they could definitely work something out.

Ashley went to Taye and asked him to put up some money.

To keep Ashley happy, he'd obliged, in spite of his business manager telling him he was nuts.

Ashley was delighted that Jeromy wanted her to work alongside him.

Before long, there was a *new* hot show in town. The Ashley and Jeromy show. Interior designers to the stars. Both with famous partners. Both with endless ambition.

It started out as a winning combination. Lately, things had not been so good.

"Got somethin' to show you," Taye said, waving a large cream envelope in the air.

"What?" Ashley asked, moving away from the mirror and drifting into the bedroom.

"Wouldn't *you* like t' know," Taye teased, following her.

Taye enjoyed teasing his wife; it gave him a feeling of power. And he was holding power in his hand, for in the envelope with the embossed gold border and exquisite calligraphy was an invitation that, if he knew his wife, she would positively cream over.

"Don't mess about," Ashley said, still slightly irritated.

"Give us a kiss, then," Taye said, putting his arms around her from behind.

"Not now," she said, wriggling out of his grasp.

"What's wrong with you?" Taye complained. "The kids are at me mum's. Nobody's around. It's the perfect time."

"No it's not," Ashley argued. "We're about to go out to dinner, and I don't want to ruin my makeup or my hair."

"I'll make it a quickie," Taye promised.

"Don't be disgusting," Ashley responded. "If we're going to do it, then we should do it in our bed like normal people."

Taye shook his head. Sometimes Ashley acted like a total prude. "Normal" people! What was *that* all about? Made her sound like her racist mother, whom he barely tolerated.

"I suppose a blow job's out of the question, then?" he ventured, edging closer.

Ashley's look of disapproval informed him that indeed it was.

Whatever happened to the girl he'd married? Free and easy, up for all kinds of sexual adventures. They'd had sex here, there, and everywhere. Now he had to practically plead to get any sex at all. It wasn't right. He still loved her, though; she was his wife, and nothing would ever change that.

"Later?" he asked hopefully.

"We'll see," she responded. "Go get changed, and hurry up. We're meeting Jeromy. He's off to Miami tomorrow, and we can't be late. You know how prompt *he* always is."

"Jeromy's such a borin' wanker. Do we *have* to go?"

"Yes, Taye. In case you've forgotten, I work with him, so stop bitching and go get ready."

"Okay, okay."

Since she appeared to have forgotten about the envelope, Taye decided not to show it to her until they came home. He knew it would put her in an excellent mood. That and a couple glasses of wine, and he'd have no trouble getting a piece of what was rightfully his.

Yes, Taye knew how to handle his wife.

Carefully.

That was the secret.

Chapter Three

DATELINE: PARIS

There was never enough time in the day for Flynn Hudson to achieve all the things he wished to accomplish. As a respected, somewhat maverick freelance journalist and writer, he was always on the move, traveling wherever the latest disaster took him. Over the last year alone, he'd been in Ethiopia, Haiti, Indonesia, Japan, and Afghanistan. He'd covered tsunamis, earthquakes, floods, wars.

Flynn was always front and center of the action, reporting on events, government corruption, human rights. He was an activist who answered to no one except himself, with a Web site that had almost a million followers, because when Flynn wrote one of his essays, his faithful readers knew they were getting the real deal, not the fake bullshit that most news stations fed the gullible public.

Yet Flynn preferred to keep a low profile. He turned down TV interview requests, avoided being photographed. Home was a small apartment in Paris, where he lived alone.

He did have girlfriends. Several. Although none of them had ever gotten close.

Flynn Hudson was a loner. That's the way he liked it.

Born in England thirty-six years ago to an American mother and British father, he'd been educated across the world, as his father was a diplomat. They'd traveled extensively, until at the age of twelve he'd witnessed his parents killed by a terrorist car bomb in Beirut. Miraculously, he'd survived the tragedy, and he had the scars to prove it.

After the death of his parents, he'd led a double life — spending half his time with his American grandparents in California, and the other half with his British kin, who resided in the English countryside. He didn't mind flying back and forth; it was an adventure.

After attending a U.K. university for a year, he'd switched to UCLA in California, before dropping out when he was twenty-one and setting out to roam the world.

And roam the world he did. He backpacked across Asia, mountain climbed in Nepal, learned martial arts in China, joined a fishing boat in Marseilles, worked as a bodyguard for a Colombian billionaire who turned out to be a drug lord, until finally, at the age of twenty-five, he'd sat himself down and written a successful book about his travels.

Flynn could have been a media star; he was certainly handsome enough. Six feet two, strong and athletic, with longish dark hair, intense ice-blue eyes, and ever-present stubble on his sharp jawline.

Women loved Flynn. And he loved them back, as long as they expected nothing permanent.

Once upon a time, he'd made a lifetime commitment. It hadn't turned out the way he'd expected. No more commitments for Flynn. He was done.

As an alpha male, he respected women, enjoyed their company on a short-term basis, and never tried to control them. He wanted what was best for them, especially women in Third World countries who had to fight every day for their very survival. He helped out when he could, writing about the places he went, exposing corruption, using whatever resources he could get his hands on to assist the not so fortunate.

Money had one meaning to Flynn, and that was helping others.

The girl crawled on top of Flynn like a particularly energetic spider monkey, all long gangly legs and arms, small breasts, cropped hair, and enormous kohl-outlined eyes. He thought her name was Marta; he wasn't sure. Sometimes he felt he wasn't sure of anything anymore, not after some of the atrocities he'd

28

witnessed. He'd recently returned from Afghanistan, where he'd watched a photographer colleague of his caught in the crossfire between border guards and a car carrying two suicide bombers. The guy had gotten his head blown off — literally by getting too close to the bombers simply to catch the best shot.

The image of the car blowing up, and that of the headless body of his friend lying in the mud, was embedded in Flynn's mind. It was a photograph he couldn't erase.

After returning to Paris, he, who didn't drink much, had gotten hopelessly drunk two nights in a row. Marta — or whatever her name was — happened on night two, and he wished he'd never picked her up and brought her home.

After reaching an unsatisfactory orgasm, he managed to slide her off him.

"Et moi?" she said indignantly.

"Not tonight," he mumbled, feeling the onslaught of a major hangover. "Go home."

So she did. Reluctantly.

In the morning, nursing a massive hangover, he discovered she'd taken his wallet with her.

No more drinking.

No more slutting around.

It was his own fault. He should've known better.

Lately, things were getting on top of him: his recent visit to China, where in some places it was deemed acceptable to drown baby girls at birth. Another trip to Bosnia, attempting to give aid to women who'd been raped. And then to Pakistan to write a story for *The New York Times* about an American citizen who'd been drugged by a prostitute and had his kidney cut out and stolen.

Flynn needed a break.

Sorting through his mail, mostly bills, he came across a fancy envelope addressed to "Mr. Flynn Hudson & Guest."

Extracting the invitation, he scanned it quickly.

It wasn't his kind of thing, but then the thought occurred to him — why the hell not?

Maybe this was exactly the break he'd been looking for.

CHAPTER FOUR

DATELINE: LOS ANGELES
Being the girlfriend of a huge movie star did not sit well with Lori Walsh's ego. Oh yes, in one respect it was all strawberries and cream: her name was out there, and people were exceptionally nice to her — important people. All the magazines featured photos of her frolicking on the beach in Malibu, or walking her significant others, two large black Labradors. She was always included in the endless red-carpet interviews at premieres and award shows, hovering beside the famous one, looking like the adoring, albeit slightly awkward, girlfriend.

But *why* was her name out there? *Why* were influential and powerful people nice to her?

Because . . .

Because she was the live-in girlfriend of Cliff Baxter. *The* Cliff Baxter — the man with George Clooney's charm, Jack Nicholson's acting chops, and irresistible good looks. Mister Movie Star. No mistake about *that*.

Mister "I get my ass kissed every time I fart."

Mister "Everyone wants to be my friend."

Mister "Even when I'm full of shit you're still gonna love me."

Lori — an actress herself, although much to her chagrin she was constantly referred to as "former waitress" — had been Mister Movie Star's girlfriend for the past year. "A record," his friends had informed her, as if she'd won some kind of amazing race. "You must have something special," his friends' wives had whispered in her ear with slightly puzzled expressions, because in their minds surely Cliff could do better.

Yes, she had something special, all right. Patience. And the knack for pretending not to know when her famous boyfriend ordered in a call girl for a midnight snack in his pool house office, or spent time on his computer watching porn.

Apparently his former girlfriends *had* objected, and with the objections came banishment. After they were gone, it was on to the next.

However, Lori was smarter than all of them. She was going for the prize. The ring on her finger. She was one canny girlfriend who was sticking it out.

Cliff Baxter was heading full-tilt toward fifty, and he'd never been married.

Lori was twenty-four — half his age, which

was the perfect Hollywood age difference. Besides, she loved him, in a kind of screwed-up way. He reminded her of the father who'd dumped her and her mom when she was only twelve, leaving the two of them with no money, no home, and a ton of bills to pay. Lori felt safe with Cliff; she felt protected, and sometimes she even felt loved.

The truth was that she wanted to be Mrs. Cliff Baxter even more than she wanted a career, and that was saying something, as she'd been harboring an ambition to be the next Emma Stone. She and Emma even looked a little alike, with the same athletic body and slightly toothy grin, although Lori considered herself to be a sexier version of the talented actress. Cliff was very into Lori's amazing mane of red hair, but what *really* turned him on was her matching pubes. She'd offered to do a Brazilian for him, but he was having none of it. "I like a woman to be natural," he'd told her. "Enough with the shaved pussies, they're not sexy. Keep it real, babe."

So be it. Whatever Cliff wanted, Cliff got. It was quite a relief not to have to go through the agony of having the hair ripped from her crotch by a bad-tempered Polish woman with a penchant for inflicting pain.

However, being just the girlfriend was risky. A year was a long time. What if Cliff got bored with her? What if he discovered that

33

the porn and the call girls were enough to keep him satisfied?

She didn't care to think about it. She dreaded going back to being just another Hollywood starlet begging for a job. Oh no, that was not about to be her future.

To protect herself, she'd made it her mission to find out all of Cliff's dirty little secrets — facts that nobody knew about him. She was determined to discover the real Cliff Baxter, not the adored icon with the starry image and self-deprecating charm.

Lori was extremely adept at underground activities. She'd learned from her mom, Sherrine, at an early age that it was useful to dig out people's secrets and use them to your advantage. That's how they'd gotten by after her dad had done a midnight runner. They'd survived because Sherrine had known how to manipulate people — such as their randy landlord, who was cheating on his wife, the supermarket checkout clerk who was padding customers' bills and pocketing the cash, and the cable guy who was into making money on the side.

Free rent. Free food. Free cable. They got by. Her mom juggled a series of boyfriends who also contributed to their survival.

Lori hadn't spoken to her mom in eight years, ever since Sherrine had caught her making out with one of her transient boyfriends. At the time, Lori was sixteen. Sherrine's boyfriend was twenty-five and a total stud. And Sherrine was thirty-five and beyond pissed. She'd thrown Lori out, along with the boyfriend, who'd allowed Lori to camp out at his place for a few weeks until she'd run into Stanley Abbson, an elderly gentleman who drove a Bentley and was very partial to underage girls.

Stanley Abbson was seventy-five years old, but thanks to Viagra, he was still able to get it up. They'd met on the boardwalk in Venice when Lori had skateboarded into him and almost knocked him flat. He hadn't minded at all, and after a couple of lunches, he'd invited her to move into an apartment where he kept two other teenage girls. It was a decent apartment overlooking the ocean; Lori could hardly believe her luck.

Stanley — who, she'd found out, lived elsewhere in a large house — gave the girls a generous allowance, and all he asked in return was the occasional girl-on-girl show, which was doable, until he started bringing along a few of his pervy old business acquaintances to watch and sometimes participate. That's when Lori decided it was not the life for her, so she'd packed up and left, taking with her Stanley's solid-gold watch and the stash of cash he'd kept hidden in the apartment. The money was enough to pay six months' rent on a run-down beach shack in Venice, where she lived for the next four years, taking acting classes, working as an extra, waitressing, doing some escort jobs that did not involve sex, and generally getting by.

Boyfriends came and went. A car salesman. A burned-out comedian. Several out-of-work actors. And a low-rent showbiz manager who offered her a career in porn, which she politely declined.

At twenty-two, Lori had realized she was getting nowhere fast, so she'd decided to move to Vegas.

Because she was a pretty, fresh face, with luxuriant red hair, long legs, and a winning smile, she immediately scored a job at the Cavendish Hotel as a cocktail waitress. The pay wasn't great, but the lavish tips made up for it.

The customers loved Lori, and so did the manager, because she could persuade almost anyone to order the best champagne, the most expensive cocktails, and the high-priced caviar hors d'oeuvres.

It wasn't long before the manager promoted her to chief cocktail hostess in the VIP lounge, and that's where she met Cliff. He'd come in one night pleasantly drunk, accompanied by an entourage of six and a skinny, model-type girlfriend, who kept crawling into his lap and tongue-kissing his ear.

Lori tried not to look impressed at the sight of such a famous man, although she remembered Sherrine taking her to see one of his movies when she was eleven, and she clearly recalled Sherrine stating at the time that Cliff Baxter was the sexiest man on two legs. Lori reckoned that even though he must be in his forties now, he still looked pretty hot.

She played it cool.

He flirted.

His girlfriend gave her the stink-eye.

She ignored the skank.

When Cliff and his entourage left, he slipped her a thousand-dollar cash tip.

She shoved the money down the neckline of her skimpy outfit and didn't share with the other staff, even though she was supposed to.

He came back two weeks later, sober and alone. He sought her out and asked if she had a boyfriend. She said no, although at the time, she was living with a hunky barman who worked at The Keys.

He invited her to dinner.

She said no.

He invited her to visit him in L.A.

She said no.

He invited her upstairs to his suite.

She said no.

Instinctively, she'd known that Cliff Baxter could be her big break, and that to make it happen she had to play hard to get. So she'd strung him along for several months, and each time he made the Vegas trip she'd continued to play it cool. Then just when she'd sensed he was about to give up on her, she'd accepted his dinner invitation.

That night they'd ended up in his suite, where she'd given him the blow job of his dreams.

Just a blow job. Nothing else.

Two weeks later, she was living with him in his L.A. mansion.

"Mr. Baxter, they're ready for you on the set," the young second AD called out, peering into Cliff Baxter's trailer after knocking on the door twice.

When the star didn't respond, she tentatively ventured inside and saw that he was asleep on the comfortable couch, snoring loudly, wearing nothing but a robe that had fallen open to reveal solid tanned thighs and chocolate-colored underwear.

The girl squinted at the sleeping movie star and wondered what she should do. She was new on the job and intimidated by being in the presence of such a big star. Fortunately, she was saved by the arrival of Enid, Cliff Baxter's personal assistant, a fierce older woman clad in a no-nonsense Hillary Clinton–style pantsuit and Nurse Ratched running shoes.

"What's going on here?" Enid inquired, taking in the nervous young girl and her boss's half-exposed lower half.

"Mr. Baxter is needed on the set," the girl

said, an agitated quiver in her voice. "I'm supposed to tell him."

"Then I suggest you wake him," Enid said briskly, placing a large messenger bag filled with papers on the table.

"Uh . . . uh . . . how should I do that?" the girl stammered.

"Like this, dear," Enid said, leaning over and giving Cliff a vigorous shake on his shoulder.

The girl took a hurried step back as Cliff sat up. "What the fuck . . ." he mumbled. "Where am I?"

"You're at the studio," Enid announced. "You're wanted on set, so shift your ass."

"For a rehearsal, Mr. Baxter," the girl said, bravely joining in.

"Must've dozed off," Cliff announced with a big yawn. "Friend's bachelor party last night. It ended late, so I had my driver bring me straight here."

"And how did Little Miss Live-In like *that*?" Enid questioned caustically.

"*C'mon,* Enid," Cliff said, standing up and laughing. "What did Lori ever do to you? She's a sweet kid. Why do you always have to put her down?"

Enid pulled a face, and began extracting papers and mail from her messenger bag and piling them on the table.

"Shall I tell Mr. Sterling you're on your way?" the young AD asked, trying to avert her eyes from Cliff's open robe.

"Yeah, yeah, tell Mac I'll be there in five. And next time, I'd appreciate a fifteen-minute warning. You can go get me coffee now. Black. Plenty of sugar. Have it waiting on the set."

"Yes, Mr. Baxter."

Cliff threw her a jaunty wink. "Run along, unless you're planning to witness me bare-assed naked."

The girl blushed, and hurriedly backed out of the trailer.

Cliff chuckled. "They get younger every day," he ruminated, shrugging off his robe. "And you know what, Enid? Here's the crap part — *I* get older."

"We all do," Enid said crisply. "Stop feeling sorry for yourself, and for God's sake, put some clothes on. I've seen better packages at the post office."

"You can be such a mean old bag," Cliff said, seemingly unfazed. "Mean and ornery. Dunno why I put up with you."

"Because," Enid answered matter-of-factly, "I have worked for you for almost twenty years, and I am one of the few people who can break your balls without getting fired. And speaking of balls, yours are hanging out."

Cliff grinned. "Surely you know that hanging out's my thing?"

"If you're not careful, your *thing* will be out too."

Cliff grabbed his pants from the back of the couch and pulled them on. "Don't you wish," he said, still grinning.

"No, Cliff," Enid said sternly. "I am one of the few women in this world who has no desire to see your cock, your balls, or anything else you might have to offer."

"Dyke!"

"Yes, dear. And I'm proud to say that I enjoy pussy almost as much as you do."

"Except for Lori's."

"She's not pussy, she's a predator," Enid said sharply. "Not good enough for you."

Cliff shook his head. "For crissakes . . ."

"Just don't marry her, that's all."

"Marry her!" Cliff exclaimed with a throaty chuckle. "When did the *m* word raise its ugly head?"

"You should get going," Enid said, folding her arms across her chest. "It's unprofessional to keep people waiting."

"No shit?"

"And when you have time, there are a few things I need your answers on," Enid added, waving an expensive-looking envelope in his face. "This is an invitation you might like."

"Not another black-tie event," he groaned. "I've attended enough of those to last me a lifetime. This is award-show city. No more. I'm over it."

"This invite is something different," Enid said. "I'll show you when you get back. Now it's your turn to run along."

"And she talks to me as if I'm twelve," Cliff said, shaking his head again.

"And sometimes he acts as if he is," Enid retorted.

"I might be forced to fire you when I return," he threatened, reaching for a shirt and putting it on. "You have no respect."

"Later, *Mr.* Baxter," she drawled sarcastically. "Is *that* enough respect for you?"

"Fuckin' A!" And with another wide grin, Cliff exited his trailer.

CHAPTER FIVE

DATELINE: MIAMI

Luca Perez stretched out on a striped lounger wearing a barely-there powder-blue Speedo, his well-toned thirty-year-old body oiled to perfection, not an inch of flesh spared. On the table next to him stood a tall glass containing a mojito. Next to his drink was a Lalique dish filled with ripe red cherries, a pile of the latest entertainment magazines, his iPhone, his platinum diamond-encrusted Chanel watch, and several crucifixes attached to thin leather cords.

Luca, his eyes covered by Dolce & Gabbana shades, was almost asleep, but not quite. He enjoyed lying there in a drowsy state, allowing his mind to run riot. Nothing to disturb him. No one to bother him. Just a lazy day of doing nothing except perfecting his tan. And what a beautiful day it was: hazy sunshine, a light breeze. He'd recently returned from a demanding world tour, so life at his Miami mansion was good.

Tomorrow, his significant other, Jeromy Milton-Gold, would arrive from London, which meant good-bye to peace and quiet. Jeromy was a social animal; he always wanted to go out and be seen at leather bars and gay clubs — something Luca preferred not to do, even though they'd met at a notorious rubber fetish club in London two years ago. Meeting Jeromy had changed Luca's life. Before Jeromy, he'd been firmly closeted, living a secret gay life lest his legions of female fans find out, because Luca was a huge Latin heartthrob, a singer women worshipped and adored.

And he was married. And he had a son.

At the time.

He still had a son, Luca Junior, who was now nine years old. But he was no longer married to the larger-than-life Latin superstar Suga — the woman who'd discovered him as a teenager, nurtured his talent, married him, had his baby, and made him the star he was today.

Suga was twenty years older than Luca, yet still a voluptuous beauty with a huge following in South America. She'd accepted the fact that her husband was gay with humor and understanding. Divorce — no problem. "Ah, but Suga had you at your best," she'd joked. "Go do what makes you happy, Luca. My heart goes with you."

Suga was an amazing woman, and to Luca's delight, they'd remained best friends, sharing custody of their handsome young son, who'd inherited the best of both his parents.

So, against the advice of everyone else — his agents, managers, record producers, and label bosses — Luca had made the leap into gaydom. If Ricky Martin could do it and survive, why couldn't he?

And survive he did. His fans were fiercely loyal; they adored him. Gay or straight, it didn't matter to them. He was Luca Perez. He was their god. Now he was their gay god.

Still, Luca didn't wish to flaunt his coming-out. No threesomes or kinky goings-on in public, although once in a while he allowed Jeromy to throw a wild party at the mansion — no cameras allowed.

Jeromy Milton-Gold was not the partner people would expect Luca to choose. Jeromy was a tall, slim, very English old Etonian, with patrician features, a longish nose, floppy brown hair, and a somewhat snobbish attitude. At forty-two, he was twelve years older than his sun-kissed, blond, buff-bodied, famous boyfriend. They made an incongruous couple; however, it seemed to work for them.

The envelope addressed to Luca Perez and Jeromy Milton-Gold looked like it contained something interesting. It was of excellent stock, with intricate embossed gold calligraphy, and it appeared tasteful and expensive.

Sitting at his David Armstrong-Jones desk in his London showroom adjacent to Sloane Square, Jeromy Milton-Gold pried open the envelope with a silver letter opener and extracted the enclosed invitation.

He read it carefully. Twice.

A satisfied smile crossed his face. This was one invitation they were *not* turning down.

He slid open the center drawer of his desk, carefully placed the invitation back in its envelope, and put it next to his passport. Tomorrow he would show it to Luca and insist that they accept.

Sometimes Luca could be stubborn, only this time Jeromy refused to take no for an answer. This time it was a done deal.

CHAPTER SIX

DATELINE: NEW YORK

The politician and his lovely wife were invited everywhere; they were one of the most popular couples in the city. He, so honest-looking and upstanding with his regular features, well-cut brown hair, and "I will do everything I can for my people" attitude. She, both delicate and strong at the same time, slender, with shoulder-length honey-coppery hair, a beautiful face, and widely spaced, warm brown eyes.

Her name was Sierra Kathleen Snow. His name was Hammond Patterson Jr., although — much to his father's chagrin — shortly after getting into politics, he'd dropped the *Jr.* "It doesn't sound right," he'd muttered.

"I'll tell you what sounds right," his father had raged. "Using the family name and the family reputation. *That's* what sounds right to me."

Hammond Patterson Jr. wasn't so sure. His father had been a congressman for many years, and that was not the role Hammond was planning to play. Instead, after college he'd gone straight to law school, then pursued a career as an attorney, and in time he'd parlayed that career into becoming, at thirty-six, one of the youngest senators in Congress.

Representing New York as the junior senator, he was full of ambition. He had high hopes that eventually he would become governor of the state, then, after that, possibly make a run for the White House.

Why not? He had all the right credentials. And, most of all, he had supreme confidence.

Hammond was an extremely driven man. Nothing was about to stop him.

Sierra, on the other hand, possessed a warmth and candor that attracted men and women alike. She was smart and compassionate, with a generous soul. As far as Hammond was concerned, she was the perfect political wife, an asset to have by his side at all times, which is exactly why he'd picked her.

Recently, Hammond's climb to the top had come across an unexpected stumbling block. And that stumbling block was the disturbing realization that he'd fathered a child in his younger years. Apparently, he'd gotten some girl pregnant, and that girl had gone ahead and given birth to a daughter, named Radical.

Radical had arrived at his office one day,

fifteen years old and determined to meet her father.

Hammond was furious and shocked. When the girl finally got in to see him and announced she was his daughter, he didn't believe her. This couldn't be happening to him. It was impossible.

But Radical produced a birth certificate with his name on it and informed him that her mom had died from a drug overdose, and that she had nowhere else to go.

Two paternity tests later, Hammond was forced to admit that this strange, unruly teenager with streaks of green in her dyed black hair, multiple piercings, and a snotty attitude was indeed his.

Sierra, being the kind and thoughtful person that she was, had insisted that Radical join the family.

"We have to take her in," Sierra had lectured him. "She's your daughter. You have no choice. Think of your public image if you don't."

Finally, Hammond had agreed, terrified that the sudden appearance of an illegitimate teenage daughter would wreak havoc with his carefully projected image.

The public still loved Hammond and Sierra. They were accepting of his youthful transgression. Sexual scandals involving politicians were nothing new, and with Sierra next to him, Hammond could do no wrong.

Radical turned out to be a nightmare. Rude and willful, she caused trouble wherever she went. She hated her father, and he hated her right back.

Angry that he was stuck with her, Hammond soon packed her off to boarding school in Switzerland, even forcing Sierra to agree that it was for the best.

Radical went. But not without a fight.

When Hammond's assistant, Nadia, entered his office and showed him the fancy invitation, he didn't hesitate. Without checking with Sierra, he instructed Nadia to accept immediately.

Hammond smelled big money, major campaign contributions when the time came for him to run, and Hammond was well aware that important connections were everything. Plus this was a fine chance for him to start planting the seeds of his unstoppable ambition.

Yes, Hammond knew a viable opportunity when it came his way. He was no fool.

Sierra Kathleen Snow was born into great privilege. Her father was the respected Pulitzer Prize winner Archibald Snow, an academic and a renowned writer of history tomes, while her mother, Phoebee, was a true New York society beauty whose family dated back to the founding fathers.

Sierra had an older sister, Clare, who was married to a pediatrician and had written a series of bestselling books about parenting. Clare and her husband had three young children and resided in Connecticut. Sierra also had a brother, Sean, who lived in Hawaii with a woman he'd picked up on the beach.

Clare was the darling of the family, while Sean was the dark side. Sierra was somewhere in the middle.

At thirty-two, Sierra was still not sure where she fit in.

She was Archibald and Phoebee Snow's daughter. She was Hammond Patterson's wife. She was Clare Snow's sister. But who was she really?

Every morning, upon waking, she asked herself that question.

Who am I today?
Am I the politician's wife?
The dutiful daughter?
The loving, supportive sister?
Who am I?

It was a question that haunted her, because she honestly didn't know the answer.

Her illustrious parents disapproved of Hammond. Although they'd never actually said it out loud, she knew that they did. When Radical had appeared on the scene, the expression on her mother's face had said it all. *We always suspected that Hammond was a rogue. Now we know for sure.*

A rogue who harbored aspirations to eventually become president of the United States. With her by his side.

The very thought made Sierra shudder. She'd been married to Hammond for eight years, and she didn't love him. She'd started off thinking that she did, but after a while, she'd realized that she'd married him to get over a broken heart, and he'd married her because of her impeccable pedigree and family connections. Hammond was not the man he'd pretended to be.

He was a psychopath. A very clever psychopath.

To the world, he presented a smiling, honest face, was seemingly a nice-looking man filled with empathy and caring. With his brown hair, regular features, and captivating smile, he seemed like such an open book. However, Hammond's public persona was a far cry from how he was in private. Sierra knew for a fact that he was a bigot and a misogynist and hated gays. He had a cruel tongue and a nasty, sadistic streak. He talked about everyone in a disparaging way, including her family, and he loathed his own father. He was forever voicing his wishes that the man would drop dead of a sudden heart attack.

At first she'd tried to dig into his psyche, to discover where all this anger came from, but it was a lost cause. The charming, attentive man she'd married had turned into a secret monster who actually scared her, which was why she hadn't left him.

Two years into their marriage, she'd realized what a fraud he was, and she'd threatened to divorce him. Very calmly, he'd informed her that if she ever left him, he'd arrange to have her entire family killed, and that he would make sure she was maimed for life.

Shocked and horrified, she'd considered going to the police. Then she'd realized that nobody would believe her. She was Sierra Patterson, wife of the up-and-coming politician Hammond Patterson, a man who fought for everyone's rights — including gays and women.

It was an impossible situation, and to make it even worse, Hammond was continually unfaithful, sleeping with any woman he could get his hands on.

When she'd confronted him about his indiscretions, he'd sneered at her. "What am I supposed to do?" he'd said with cold indifference. "Fucking you is like fucking a dead fish."

Sierra knew she should leave, but Hammond's threats were all too real, and she simply couldn't summon the courage to get out. What if he went through with his foreboding words and actually harmed her family? She knew without a doubt that he was capable of anything.

So Sierra stayed and threw herself into helping people. She visited children's hospitals, formed a rape prevention group, rallied for battered women, and did everything she could to take her mind off her miserable home life.

Hammond was pleased. He'd been right about Sierra: she was the perfect politician's wife. A beautiful and gracious woman who was also a do-gooder.

What could be better for a man on his way to the top?

CHAPTER SEVEN

Bianca reached for a towel, wrapping it around her smooth, gleaming body as she moved closer to Aleksandr.

He seized a corner of the towel and roughly pulled it away from her. The towel fluttered to the ground.

"You are so beautiful," he said, his voice a throaty growl as he began rubbing his thick fingers against her extended nipples. "Such a fine woman, and all mine."

Bianca experienced a shiver of delight and responded accordingly. Whenever Aleksandr wanted her, she was ready.

Early on in their relationship, she'd learned from Aleksandr that his wife was a sexually cold woman who'd informed him shortly after they were married that his very touch repulsed her.

Apparently his money hadn't.

Bianca didn't care that he was so enormously rich. She genuinely cared about the man, and she loved the way he was able to turn her on with nothing more than a glance. His dark eyes were deeper than a glacier; she could never tell what he was thinking. His touch was strong and manly. As for his equipment — perfection. Long and thick and solid, the best she'd ever experienced. Plus he knew what to do with it, a true bonus after a series of famous men who considered erectile dysfunction totally normal.

Aleksandr pushed her to the ground and dropped his pants. He never wore underwear, something they had in common.

The cold tile against her skin made her shiver even more as she spread her long legs for her lover. Glancing up, she noticed the red light on the security camera and wondered if they were being watched or filmed.

It didn't matter. Aleksandr controlled everything, and he would never allow anyone to use her or anything bad to happen.

His solid body crushed her beneath him as he entered her. He was a big man, big and powerful. She took a deep breath, inhaling his overpowering masculine scent.

"Oh . . . my . . . God . . ." she murmured. "You feel so amazing, so damn hard."

"Only for you, my little *kotik*. Only for you."

"Yes," she sighed, shifting her body to accommodate him. "You know, Aleksandr, you're the only man who has ever truly satisfied me."

He was heavy on top of her. She didn't

care, the sex was that exciting. She got off on the way he thrust himself inside her as if he was determined to own her.

Nobody had ever owned Bianca. She was a free spirit. With Aleksandr, she had no desire to be free. She yearned for him to possess her in every way, and possess her he did with his strong arms, full body weight, and hard penis.

At the beginning of their relationship, she'd tried to assert herself in the bedroom, but Aleksandr would have none of it. He expected total control. Sex would take place his way or not at all.

Bianca was cool with that. She was so used to calling the shots with men, it made a refreshing change to allow someone else to be in charge.

Groaning with pleasure, she flexed her thigh muscles, causing Aleksandr to grunt his appreciation.

He made her feel like a little girl, a naughty little girl. It turned her on in a big way.

CHAPTER EIGHT

Sometimes Taye Sherwin's mind wandered, especially when Ashley was in one of her haughty moods — a personality trait that seemed to emerge every time they had dinner with Jeromy Milton-Gold. It pained Taye to watch his wife try so hard to act as if she'd been born in Mayfair as opposed to in the modest seaside town of Brighton. Ashley tried desperately to shrug off her roots, even though everyone knew she was not to the manner born. On the other hand, Taye was proud of where he came from, the Elephant and Castle. He was a true Cockney lad who'd done well for himself, and he was happy to tell anyone and everyone about his not-so-fancy beginnings.

Taye had no clue where Jeromy Milton-Gold had originally sprung from, but he was well aware that Jeromy was not averse to dropping names and carrying on as if he were the king of the castle. Or queen. *Yeah,* Taye thought with a wicked grin. *Shouldn't that be queen?*

"What are *you* smirking at?" Ashley asked, catching him mid-smirk.

"Just thinkin' about a joke one of the lads came up with today," Taye said, quick as a flash.

"Do share," Jeromy said, tapping the side of his wineglass with long, elegant fingers.

"You wouldn't find it funny," Taye replied, wishing they could get the hell out of the fancy restaurant and head for home, where he planned on showing his wife the coveted invitation before banging her brains out. Man, he was feeling way horny.

"I can't stand jokes," Ashley said with a slight sniff of distaste. "They're always so sexist and never funny."

"I must say I'm forced to agree with you," Jeromy drawled. "Unamusing, and yet some people feel as if they're obliged to laugh."

"I think people only tell jokes when they run out of conversation," Ashley said, shooting Taye a snarky look. "It's as if they have nothing else to say."

"That'll never happen to you, toots," Taye retorted. "You're a world-class gossiper." He nudged Jeromy. "Never off the freakin' phone, this one. Always got a girl chat goin' on."

Jeromy curled his lip, a habit he'd developed when he wasn't quite sure what to say.

59

Ashley glared at her husband.

"Luca and I are going on a simply marvel-ous trip," Jeromy said at last, filling the sud-den silence.

"That's nice," Ashley said, taking out her compact and applying more lipstick. "Where to?"

"Somewhere hot and exotic, I suspect," Jeromy said with an airy wave of his hand. "We've been invited by Aleksandr Kasian-enko on the maiden voyage of his new yacht."

Ashley's eyes widened. "How fabulous," she sighed. "Lucky you."

Taye was speechless. Dammit, Jeromy was messing with his surprise. What was he sup-posed to do now? Blurt out that they were invited too, and risk a tongue-lashing from Ashley, who'd be livid that he hadn't told her?

"I can certainly use the break," Jeromy said with a patronizing smirk. "I'm expecting that you'll keep an eye on things in the London showroom, won't you, dear?"

Ashley bobbed her head and turned to her husband. "*You* know Aleksandr whatever-his-name is, don't you?"

Taye nodded. "Yeah, we met a coupla times. He's a big football fan. There's a rumor goin' around that he's thinkin' of buyin' one of the clubs."

"Bianca is a dear friend of Luca's," Jeromy allowed, once more sipping his wine. "They met years ago at a fashion show in Milan. Luca was singing for a paltry million dinero, and Bianca was busy strutting her stuff. They have a history."

"Nice," Ashley said wistfully. "I bet it'll be a fab trip."

"Yes," Jeromy agreed. "I am sure it will be."

Taye and Ashley left the restaurant and drove home in silence — an uncomfortable silence, finally broken by Taye, who couldn't stand it when Ashley slipped into one of her moods.

"What's up, toots?" he said, one hand on the steering wheel, the other patting her on the knee. "You've gone all broody on me."

"Why do you always try to put me down in front of Jeromy?" she complained, her cheeks flaming. "I'm in business with the man, and you do your best to make me look like a fool."

"What're you talkin' about?"

"You know full well." And then, attempting to imitate him, she added in a mock-up of his voice, "This one's always on the phone gossiping."

"I'm not makin' it up," Taye said, withdrawing his hand from her knee. "You *are* always on the blower carrying on 'bout this an' that."

"I am so not," she said in an uptight voice. "I *do not* gossip. And even if I did, that's no reason for you to announce it to the world."

"C'mon, toots," he pleaded. "Let's not make this into a fight."

61

"No. *You* come on, Taye," she said crossly. "I hate it when you disrespect me. It's not right. I'm upset."

"Don't be, sunshine," Taye said, eager to placate her. " 'Cause I got a big surprise waitin' for you when we get home."

"I'm not interested in surprises," she said, staring out the window.

"You will be in this one," Taye assured her.

"You're so annoying," she said irritably. "Why do you always have to try and get me off track?"

" 'Cause I love you, toots. You know that. An' I can't stand seein' you upset."

Ashley seized the opportunity to say something that was always lurking in the back of her mind. "I suppose you *really* loved me when you were *fucking* that big-titted tramp," she spat, her voice filled with venom.

"Ashley," he said, groaning. "That was freakin' years ago. How many times I gotta say I'm sorry? That bird meant nothin' to me. I've told you a million times."

"A million times isn't enough," Ashley muttered, still holding on to a major grudge. "How'd you like it if that'd been *me* in bed with some bloke? How would *that* grab you?"

"You wouldn't do it. Anyway, I trust you."

"Yes," she snorted. "And *I* trusted you, and look where *that* got me."

How had their conversation veered so off track? Every so often, Ashley brought up the one time he'd been unfaithful, but why was she doing it tonight?

Best to stay silent and let her vent.

Which she did.

Nonstop.

All the way home.

CHAPTER NINE

Flynn had a few things to take care of, two or three hard-hitting pieces to write, several follow-up calls, and a decision to make.

Aleksandr Kasianenko, an old friend from back in the day, had invited him on what seemed like it might be a spectacular trip. He'd been invited with a guest, and therein lay the problem. Who to bring with him? And, even more important, did he want to bring anyone at all?

Certainly not one of his casual girlfriends who were available for light relief and nothing else, which was one thing he always made clear up front *before* he slept with them. Flynn did not care to have any broken hearts on *his* conscience. He knew what a broken heart felt like only too well. He'd experienced the pain, abandonment, and downright misery that came with heartbreak, albeit a long time ago, but the feeling of loss had never really left him.

Yes. True heartbreak existed. And Flynn

knew all about it, so he was always careful to warn women that if they were after anything more than a casual fling, he was not the man for them.

As he thought about who to take, one name came to mind: Xuan, an exquisite Asian who was beautiful, strong-minded, and conveniently more into women than men.

Xuan would definitely get a kick out of such a trip, and he would enjoy her company — he always did.

Xuan was a fellow journalist who'd escaped from a Communist regime when her parents were accused of being spies, then brutally taken away and murdered for their supposed crimes.

Xuan had arranged to get herself smuggled out of Communist China eleven years previously, and like Flynn, her special talent was writing about the injustices in a world gone crazy. They'd bumped into each other over the years in many different countries, and formed a close, nonsexual friendship, a friendship that suited both of them.

Flynn knew many of her stories: how she'd been gang-raped on her way out of China, then rescued by a man who'd kept her locked up and beaten; how after a devastating miscarriage, she'd made another daring escape, going months with hardly any food, begging for sustenance along the way, until eventually she'd reached Hong Kong, where she'd been taken in by distant relatives.

The difficulties of trying to make a life for herself and discover her own identity had not been easy. But Xuan was strong; she'd prevailed and finally forged a career for herself as a fearless journalist.

After mulling it over, Flynn sent her a text inviting her. Together, exploring the extraordinary lifestyles of the rich and overly privileged could be an extremely memorable experience, one they might both benefit from.

Or not.

It didn't matter. At least it would be a welcome change from the horrors of the world they'd both seen up close.

Flynn waited for Xuan to respond; he hoped her answer would be a resounding yes.

In a small hotel room in Saigon, Xuan and her sometime lover, Deshi, lay on the bed fully sated, a ceiling fan whirling noisily above them. The sex had been satisfying, although not mind-blowing by any means. However, Xuan found Deshi to be an intelligent man with interesting tidbits of information about government activity that he let slip her way. Conveniently, Deshi happened to work for the government.

Sexually, Xuan preferred women, although when the occasion called for it, she was not averse to bedding down with a man. Information was information, and Xuan gathered it any way she could.

Her cell phone bleeped, indicating a text.

She leaned across Deshi to reach it, her small breasts grazing his chest.

Deshi took this as an indication that maybe there was more sex in his future. To his disappointment, it was not to be.

Xuan read Flynn's message. She was pleased to hear from her friend. Of all the knowledgeable and attractive men she knew, Flynn was number one. A solid guy with admirable values and an adventurous spirit.

The first time they'd run into each other, she'd told him she was bisexual, leaning toward the female sex. She was determined there would be no sexual tension messing up a friendship that she'd sensed could be quite precious. She was right. Sex had never interfered with their close relationship.

Now Flynn was inviting her on a trip.

How nice.

With rich people. Insanely rich people, because she knew who Aleksandr Kasianenko was. *Everyone* knew who Aleksandr Kasianenko was — the Russian billionaire steel magnate with the famous supermodel girlfriend, Bianca.

How intriguing.

To go or not to go? She would have to think about it.

"Anything important?" Deshi inquired.

"Nothing that cannot wait until later,"

Xuan said.

In a few hours, she would respond. It was not something she felt obliged to make an instant decision about.

CHAPTER TEN

Cliff Baxter happened to be a much-loved movie star. He had his faults, but overall he was the consummate professional, very aware of the people who worked on his movies, always making sure they were well taken care of. He considered his stand-in, Bonar, a loyal friend — they'd worked together for a solid twenty-five years, ever since Cliff's first big break in the 1987 movie *Fast Times on the Fast Track,* a film about a marathon runner and his dysfunctional family.

Cliff had hit pay dirt on that one. At the time, he was young, virile, and hot — *very* hot. Plus he could really act. The director had liked him and pushed him to do some great work. To Cliff's delight and surprise, he'd gotten his first Oscar nomination. He hadn't won, but what else was new?

He'd been nominated three times since then, and only won once. Better than not winning at all.

He and Bonar were the same age, both

creeping close to fifty. But Bonar had a wife and three kids, while all Cliff had was an amazing career.

He didn't mind. He had no desire to be trapped in an institution called marriage, a soulless place where there was no escape unless you were prepared to part with half of your hard-earned assets.

Cliff liked knowing that, basically, he was a free man who could go wherever he wanted and do anything he cared to do, and that there was no one around to stop him. Only his agent and his manager could tell him what to do, and usually he didn't listen.

Cliff considered most of his male friends totally pussy-whipped, or if not whipped, miserable divorced fathers paying alimony and only getting to see their kids every other weekend.

He was well aware that they all envied him. They *should* envy him. In their eyes, he was the one living the life.

Over the years, he'd had a series of live-in girlfriends, and he'd learned exactly when it was time to move them out. There was always that moment in time when they started becoming overly clingy and needy. He knew the signs only too well. Suddenly they started talking marriage, and marriage was strictly not on his agenda; it never had been.

So far, Lori had lasted longer than the others. She was a fun girl, and he was quite fond of her. Plus she gave the best head ever. He often thought that she must've studied at the famed Academy of Deep Throat — if there was such a place. And if there wasn't, there should be.

The truth was, he couldn't get enough of Lori's expert oral skills.

Usually he counted on professionals to do the things his girlfriends balked at, but since Lori, the midnight call-girl visits were getting fewer and fewer, and Internet porn failed to grab him.

Lori, it seemed, was up for anything.

Lori had a thing about running, and not through the staid streets of Beverly Hills. No, she liked exploring the hills, finding a hiking trail, and hitting it hard.

There were no paparazzi where she went. No spying eyes with cameras affixed to them.

Sometimes she took the dogs, sometimes she didn't.

Today she was on her own, high up in the mountains, running like a crazy woman, ear-buds and iPod in place, Drake and Pitbull keeping her well entertained.

Then it happened. She went flying over a log and hit the ground with a sharp thud.

She sat there stunned, feeling like a fool, finally realizing that, fortunately, there was no one around to witness her embarrassment.

After a few moments of pure dizziness, she

attempted to stand. Her ankle immediately gave way, and she fell back down with a yelp of pain.

Now what was she supposed to do? Call her movie-star boyfriend to rush to her rescue? He wouldn't come. He was currently on the set, filming, which meant he'd send people. One of them might tip off the paps, and then she'd be trapped not looking her best. Wouldn't want that.

Her eyes filled with tears. Why was this happening to her?

She fished out her cell phone from her shorts pocket, and just as she was about to call for help, she saw it and froze. "It" was a raggedy coyote emerging slyly from the bushes, standing stock-still and staring at her with haunted red eyes.

She met the animal's malevolent stare right on and felt fear course through her body. Recently, she'd read about a pack of coyotes savaging a couple of German shepherds. If *they* couldn't defend themselves, how could she?

Then a second coyote came loping out of the bushes, and she knew for sure that she was done for.

After rehearsing his upcoming scene, Cliff returned to his trailer, where Enid had made herself quite comfortable: stretched out on his couch, shoes off, TV on, soap opera in full swing.

"Make yourself at home," Cliff said caustically. "Can I get you anything? Coffee? A drink?"

Unfazed, Enid sat up, slipped on her Nurse Ratched shoes, and said, "It took you long enough. I almost fell asleep."

"So sorry my rehearsal kept you waiting," Cliff said, full of sarcasm.

"I've got to get back to the office," Enid said, thrusting a sheaf of papers at him. "Sign these."

"What am I signing?"

"For God's sake, if you want me to explain, I'll be here all day. Your business manager sent them over. They're for your recent real-estate acquisitions."

Cliff knew he could trust Enid; she would never try to put anything past him.

"If I sign, will you give me my couch back?"

"My pleasure," Enid snorted. "This trailer smells like feet."

"You're not supposed to speak to movie stars like that. Our feet do not stink. Besides, you're the one who had her shoes off."

"Oh, please!" Enid said, waving an invitation at Cliff. "What do you want me to do about this?"

Cliff took the elaborate invitation and scanned it quickly. "Hey," he said. "Wouldn't miss it. Go ahead and accept."

"Just for you?"

"Put your bitch back in the bag, Enid," he said. "Answer for me *and* Lori. She'll get a kick out of a trip like this."

Enid sighed. This one was lasting longer than the others; Lori must have hidden talents that only Cliff knew about.

"Whatever pleases my lord and master."

Cliff chuckled. "Get the fuck outta here before I kick your crusty old ass to the curb."

Enid packed up her papers and left.

After a few minutes, Cliff put his head outside his trailer to see who was around. Sometimes he was able to pull together a bunch of the guys to play softball.

Today there was nobody around. Except . . . who was that approaching?

Oh shit, it was his costar in the movie, Billy Melina, a hot young actor with naked ambition eating away at him. A ready-to-rock stud at the top of his game. *Exactly like I used to be,* Cliff thought wryly.

They had only a few scenes together, so they were hardly friends.

Cliff watched Billy approach. He couldn't help wondering if Billy was headed for an almost thirty-year career like his. He doubted it. Everything was different today. The paparazzi ruled. The magazines printed anything they felt like. There were no rules left. No studio heads and powerful managers to protect their clients. TMZ ran riot on any star who left the sanctuary of their home.

No. In ten years, when Billy hit forty, he'd be long forgotten, while Cliff would still be in the game, because he had no plans to retire. He was an up-and-at-'em kind of guy. Like Redford and De Niro, he had no intention of ever quitting; he was in the race until the end.

"Hey," Billy said, all bronzed hard body and dirty-blond surfer hair. "Wassup?"

"Nothing much," Cliff responded. "You?"

"Same old crap," Billy said, flexing his muscles. "Just tryin' t' stay outta the rags."

"Yeah," Cliff said, thinking that Billy Melina was one handsome son of a bitch. "I know the feeling." He hesitated for a moment. Should he invite the younger actor into his trailer to shoot the shit, or should he let it go?

Let it go, his inner voice warned him. *Do you really want to hear all about Billy's divorce from the very famous Venus? Or the Vegas murder scandal Billy was vaguely involved in?*

No. He had better things to do.

"See you on the set," he said, retreating back into his trailer.

"Yeah, man," Billy said. "Later."

Cliff hit the couch again and reached for his cell. Might as well see what Lori was up to. Maybe even invite her to visit him on set.

Yes, he'd do that, tell her about the invitation.

Little Lori was going to be so excited.

CHAPTER ELEVEN

"Aha!" Suga exclaimed, descending on Luca like a full-blown cyclone, all mountains of blond curls, bouncy breasts and jiggling hips encased in a bright-orange-and-green low-cut jumpsuit, with sky-high gold Louboutins on her tiny feet — the only small thing about her. "How's my favorite baby daddy?"

Suga was an over-the-top voluptuous diva with a steamroller personality. She looked exactly like her fans would expect her to look, and they adored her for it.

Luca rolled off his sun-bed and stood up, allowing his ex-wife to envelop him in her generous curves. He got a whiff of her strong signature perfume, and many fond memories came flooding back. Ah yes, the day she'd discovered him and plucked him from obscurity. The day they'd first made love. And, most important of all, the day he'd stood in her recording studio and cut his first single.

Suga hugged him so tightly he could barely breathe, showering him with wet jammy kisses, as was her way.

Luca was glad Jeromy wasn't around to witness his ex-wife's display of affection. He knew it pissed Jeromy off that Suga was still such a big part of his life. Too bad — as far as Luca was concerned, it was something that would never change. He owed everything to Suga. Without her, there was no way he would have risen to become the star he was today. The blond, blue-eyed Latin singing sensation that Suga had introduced to the world.

"You're back early," he remarked, gently extricating himself from her clutches. "Thought you weren't due home until next week. What happened?"

Suga pulled a face. "My manager — he canceled the São Paulo concert. The ticket sales were not so fantastic."

"Must be the economy," Luca said without taking a beat. "Ticket sales are down across the board."

Suga patted his cheek affectionately. "Not for you, *mi amor*."

"For everyone," Luca assured her, although he suspected it wasn't true. On *his* last concert tour, ticket sales had hit an all-time high.

He hated the fact that Suga's star was starting to fade. What could he do about it?

"Where is my other *tesoro*?" Suga demanded, hands on ample hips. "I have to hug

77

my little Luca Junior."

"He's out playing soccer with some of his friends."

"Too bad," she said, pursing her lips. "I must go fetch him."

"No way," Luca said, hurriedly shaking his head. "The kid's nine — he'll be embarrassed if you descend on him. You know what he's like."

"Embarrassed! Ha!" Suga snorted. "I am his mama. I could *never* embarrass my little baby."

"Let's get together for dinner tonight, just the three of us," Luca suggested, knowing that Luca Junior would be mortified if Suga turned up at his soccer game in all her glory. "We'll have fun."

"*Sí?*" she said, raising an artfully penciled eyebrow. "And where is Mister Stick Up His Ass?"

"If you're talking about Jeromy, he's in London, back tomorrow."

"Ah." Suga sighed. "*Me vuelves loco!* You have so many beautiful boys to choose from, an' yet you stay with someone so . . . dry."

"You need to get to know him better," Luca said calmly. "We should hang out, spend more time together."

"I don't think so, *mi amor,*" Suga said, shaking her curls. "He doesn't like me. I don't like him."

"Why can't you two get along?"

"Because Jeromy is *not* the man for you." After a meaningful pause, she added, "You will see. You will learn."

Luca shrugged. "Nothing to learn. I know everything there is to know about him."

Suga smiled before leaning over and lightly caressing her ex-husband's package. "Do not waste what you have, *cariño.* You are far too young and far too beautiful."

Luca couldn't help grinning. "You think?"

"Ah, *mi tesoro,* Suga knows," she cooed. "An' *you* know that Suga is always right."

Jeromy Milton-Gold groaned as he reached orgasm. When he was done, he roughly shoved the boy's head away from his crotch.

The boy, a sulky eighteen — if that — wondered aloud if Jeromy would now like to blow *him.*

"No," Jeromy snapped, as if the very thought disgusted him. "You can take your money and go."

"But I thought —"

"Don't think," Jeromy said sharply. "I am not paying you to think. Pick up your filthy money and get the hell out."

"Fucker!" the boy muttered under his breath.

Unfortunately, Jeromy heard him. "What did you say?" he asked, narrowing his eyes.

The boy grabbed his money from the table and made a run for the door.

Jeromy thought about chasing him and roughing him up, then thought, *Why bother?* The kid might be a fighter, and the last thing he needed was to arrive in Miami with a nasty black eye.

If only he could curb his desire for random satisfaction.

No, that would be asking the impossible. Besides, after a night out with Ashley and her boring (although admittedly gorgeous) husband, surely he was entitled to some light relief?

And what Luca didn't know . . .

Jeromy was excellent at burying any guilt he might feel. Besides, he'd never promised Luca that he would be faithful, and allowing some random boy he'd ordered off the Internet to give him oral was hardly being a slut. It was more like he was taking care of business in a purely uninvolved way.

Yes, that was it. No emotion. No connection. Merely a swift sexual transaction for money. In the morning, he'd be on a plane to Miami, then straight back into the arms of his superstar boyfriend.

He hoped that Luca's fat ex-wife, Suga, wasn't around. The woman was a joke with her huge floppy breasts, loud voice, and ridiculous blond curls. It was surely time that Luca disassociated himself from her.

The thought of his young partner ever having been with Suga made Jeromy physically sick. He tried not to think about it; however, there were times he couldn't stop himself from imagining them together. Suga rolling on top of Luca, crushing his perfect body with her outrageous tits, opening her legs for him, sucking his delicious cock. The images were unbearable.

What he couldn't understand was why Luca encouraged the cow to still be in his life. True, they had a son together, Luca Junior, but why couldn't Luca start putting some distance between them? Suga's Miami mansion was five minutes away from Luca's mansion. In Jeromy's eyes, it was not a happy situation.

Jeromy had made up his mind that when they were on the Kasianenko yacht, he would insist that they sell the Miami mansion and move far away from Miss Suga Tits, the title he'd bestowed on Luca's ex.

Ah yes, perhaps a house in London's Belgrave Square, a house that he could decorate and transform into an amazing palace for his young lover.

Jeromy gave a thin smile at the thought of how envious all his London acquaintances would be if he persuaded Luca to move to London. With his prince in tow, he could lord it over everyone. He could certainly lord it over the affluent gay brigade who'd dismissed him as an old man when he'd hit forty.

Old man indeed! Meeting up with Luca

had been a lifesaver. He'd shown every one of his so-called friends that Jeromy Milton-Gold still had it.

Jeromy had scored the perfect prize, and they could all go fly a kite. He had a rich, famous boyfriend, a revitalized business, and he was on top of the world. So fuck 'em all.

Chapter Twelve

Hammond waved the invitation in Sierra's face as if it were a weapon. "We're taking this trip," he said brusquely. "And you'd better be sure to look your best. Aleksandr Kasianenko is an extremely rich and influential man. In case you're too stupid to realize it, I need to have people like him on my side. Aleksandr can help us a lot."

"You mean he can help *you*," Sierra muttered, wishing she were somewhere else. She hadn't wanted to visit Hammond at his office; however, he'd insisted she come, and as usual she'd complied.

She had a dull, throbbing headache, which lately was becoming a daily occurrence.

"You're such a miserable bitch," Hammond snarled. "My God, you're starting to look your age too. For crissakes, get yourself together."

"Maybe you should get rid of me," Sierra replied with a flash of her former self. "Find yourself a newer model — I'm sure there's plenty of fresh meat around to accommodate you. How about the young intern I saw in the office when I came in? She seems a likely candidate."

"Shut the fuck up," Hammond said with an icy glare. "You're my wife. Try to act as if you deserve the position."

Sierra was about to respond when Hammond's chief aide, Eddie March, entered the office. Eddie was the complete opposite of Hammond. A genuinely nice man, excellent at his job, and full of boyish enthusiasm. Eddie was the real deal.

As soon as Eddie appeared, Hammond's attitude changed. Suddenly he became Hammond Patterson, the smooth and charming man of the people.

"You should run along now, darling," he said, turning to his wife and kissing her on the cheek. "I want you to buy anything it takes for you to be the most beautiful woman on our upcoming trip. Here," he added, fishing in his pocket and producing a black American Express card. "Buy whatever you deem suitable. I know your taste is impeccable."

Sierra nodded. She was married to Jekyll and Hyde. She was married to a man of many faces.

"That's generous of you," Eddie said with an admiring chuckle. "If I gave my girlfriend a card like that, she'd zip out of town and never come back!"

Sierra smiled politely, while thinking, *I wish I could leave town and never come back.* But she knew that escaping from Hammond's clutches was impossible. Somehow or other he'd make good on his threats; she had no doubt at all about how far he would go.

"You look beautiful, as always," Eddie said, smiling at Sierra. "Morning, noon, and night. How do you do it?"

"You'd be wise to stop flattering her," Hammond said with an affectionate glance at his wife. "Too many compliments will go straight to her head. And that'll cost me."

Sierra couldn't take any more. Hammond's Mister Nice Guy act in front of people sickened her.

"I'd better get going," she said.

"Always a pleasure," Eddie said.

Sierra plastered on an empty smile and exited. She'd taken two Xanax in the morning to dull the pain of her false existence. Now she needed another pill to get her through the day.

The outer offices were full of people who worked for Hammond. His supporters, his team, most of whom had helped get him elected.

She wondered what they'd think if they knew the real man who lurked beneath the facade. Would they ever find out?

No. Because Hammond was too adept at

concealing his real self.

Nadia, Hammond's assistant, stopped her on the way out. "Mrs. Patterson," Nadia said. "Our newest intern is such a huge fan. Would you mind if I introduced you? It would absolutely make her day."

"Not at all," Sierra said graciously as Nadia ushered the girl over to her.

The girl was ripe and young, slightly overweight with large breasts and a toothy smile.

"This is Skylar," Nadia said. "She's joining the team for the summer."

Yes, Sierra thought, *exactly the way Hammond likes them: enthusiastic and naive. He'll soon ruin all her illusions.*

"Hello, Skylar," she said with a warm smile. "Welcome."

"Thank you, Mrs. Patterson," Skylar replied, totally thrilled to be meeting the senator's popular wife. "It's an honor to be working for Senator Patterson. I feel so lucky."

I'm sure, Sierra thought. *And will it still he an honor when he grabs your ass and asks you to go down on him? Will you fall in love with him like a legion of foolish girls before you?*

"Enjoy your summer," Sierra murmured. *Enjoy giving the senator head and getting nothing in return. It's inevitable. A fact of life. Poor little girl, you'll be powerless to resist his honest brown eyes and ready smile. Tread carefully, for he will use you and then abandon you like he did all the others.*

She made it outside and fell into the town car waiting for her, Hammond's black AmEx card still clutched in her hand. What to do with that?

Go shopping, of course. Infuriate him by spending more money than he intended. He'd only handed her the card to look like the generous husband in front of Eddie; it was all for show.

"Barneys," she said to the driver. "After that we'll make a stop at Bergdorf."

"Yes, Mrs. Patterson," the driver said, starting the car.

Sierra leaned back against the leather upholstery. What was she going to do about her life? How was she ever going to get away from Hammond?

The answer always escaped her.

CHAPTER THIRTEEN

The invitations had been sent, and Bianca waited impatiently for the replies to come in. She'd left Moscow and Aleksandr for a *Vanity Fair* cover shoot in Madrid. It wasn't the perfect situation leaving her man by himself, but the *Vanity Fair* photos were to accompany a lengthy story commemorating her successful career and her thirtieth birthday. Such excellent and prestigious coverage was very special.

Bianca had been a top model for almost thirteen years, ever since being discovered at the age of seventeen by a legitimate modeling agent, who'd noticed her waitressing at her parents' deli in Queens, New York. The man had told her she had potential, then slipped her his card.

It had taken her two months to get up the courage to phone him. And when she'd set off for her initial interview, she'd asked her Latino gang-banger boyfriend to go with her. This did not please the agent, who'd insisted her boyfriend stay in the waiting room, a move that didn't sit well with her boyfriend at all. He'd scowled all the way back to Queens, and they'd broken up a few weeks later.

The day she did her first test shots, she'd taken her mom with her. Her mom was an attractive if slightly work-worn Cuban woman who'd always kept secret her own ambition to be a model.

Bianca was a natural in front of the camera. Instinctively, she had it down, posing this way and that, making love to the camera.

And so began her brilliant career. A career that hadn't been without its ups and downs.

When Bianca started modeling, she was young and striking, with a strong personality. It didn't take long before she became the favorite of several top designers. This infuriated some of the older models, who felt she was a pushy girl with way too much attitude for such a newcomer.

Her rise especially angered the small but tight group of ethnic models. One in particular, Willow, did everything she could to sabotage Bianca's photo shoots and modeling gigs. Willow was a great beauty herself, also of mixed race, and she didn't feel there was room for the two of them. However, the more Willow tried to sabotage her, the more Bianca fought back. Eventually, when Willow realized that Bianca was not going away anytime soon, they reached a truce, and after a while they became friends, even doing a cover shoot for *Vogue* together, posing side by side.

Along with Naomi Campbell, Tyra Banks, and Beverly Johnson, they were the most famous women of color in the modeling world.

Bianca embraced her new life. She soon got into drugs and men and parties, sleeping with whomever she felt like, doing whatever she pleased. They were fun times that included snorting cocaine for breakfast and clubbing the night away.

It didn't affect her work. She was a star in her own world, and she enjoyed every minute of the decadent lifestyle she'd so readily embraced.

Her various affairs with rich, powerful, famous, and sometimes titled men were the stuff the tabloids loved. She used men for her own pleasure, and when she was bored with them, she moved on.

In her late twenties she'd gotten hooked on heroin thanks to a world-famous rock-star boyfriend who didn't give a damn about anyone or anything. Her family and friends — including Willow — conducted an intervention, and she'd ended up in rehab for a torturous six months.

It was while she was in rehab that she'd taken a long, hard look at her life and decided it was time to think about what would really make her happy. It wasn't fame — she had that in spades. It wasn't money — she was quite comfortable in that respect. It was something more. She finally desired a real relationship that didn't take place on the front pages of the tabloids.

Yes. She needed someone who cared about Bianca the person, not the fantasy image.

Then along came Aleksandr, and it was as if she'd been reborn.

Ah . . . Aleksandr. She smiled every time she thought of him.

Aleksandr had never touched drugs, and he couldn't care less about seeing his photo in a magazine; in fact, he hated it. He preferred staying out of the limelight, although he'd had to get used to the fact that being with Bianca meant constant attention.

Aleksandr was a man in every way. He cared about her for her own self, not the icon she'd created.

Now he'd invited a select group of people to join him on his new luxurious state-of-the-art yacht for a trip to celebrate her upcoming birthday, and she was excited.

Of course, they'd argued about whom to invite, until eventually she'd given way to Aleksandr's suggestions. He didn't want any of what he referred to as "trashy people." He insisted that they invite only the crème de la crème.

So be it. Whatever Aleksandr wanted, he got. Although she had insisted on inviting her best gay friend from way back, Latin singing sensation Luca Perez. And she'd also invited Ashley Sherwin, who'd helped decorate her London apartment.

Aleksandr hadn't argued about Ashley, for he was a longtime admirer of her footballer husband, the very handsome Taye Sherwin.

With a slight flash of guilt, Bianca remembered hooking up with Taye some time ago, long before he'd met and married Ashley. It was a one-nighter at an out-of-control party in London. She doubted if Taye would even remember, and she'd certainly never mentioned it to Ashley or Aleksandr. God forbid!

Aleksandr's choice of guests was more sedate. They included the movie star Cliff Baxter and his current girlfriend; renowned Senator Hammond Patterson and his wife, Sierra; and Flynn Hudson, a writer whom Bianca had never met, although Aleksandr spoke highly of him.

It promised to be a stellar group. Bianca was all set to make this a trip to remember.

CHAPTER FOURTEEN

Ashley could not stop gazing at the invitation. It was so elegant and simple, yet at the same time it reeked of money and class. She couldn't wait to tell Jeromy that they too were on the guest list. Mr. and Mrs. Taye Sherwin. Jeromy had tried to one-up them, as was his way, but now they had a legitimate invitation of their own.

She wished Taye had given her the invitation before they'd had dinner with Jeromy. For some unknown reason, he'd held back, not showing it to her until they got home. Then he'd had the nerve to expect sex.

Too bad. She wasn't in the mood.

Sometimes Taye could be too demanding when it came to sex. She'd discussed it with some of her girlfriends, and to her surprise they'd all said the same thing: "You're lucky he gets it up at all." It seemed that most men who'd been married for over five years allowed their sex life to slip. Or at least their sex life with their wife.

Ashley did not consider herself lucky at all. Taye's never-ending pawing at her in bed was an irritant, one she could well do without.

Actually, Ashley did not find sex that appealing. It was messy and dirty, a chore she forced herself to do every so often simply to satisfy her husband. As far as she was concerned, Taye was insatiable. However, he was also a famous footballer, so she knew that if *she* didn't oblige, there were plenty of slutty girls who would.

Football groupies. Slags. They were everywhere, with their shorter-than-short skirts skimming their tight little bottoms, skimpy tops, ridiculously high heels, over-the-top makeup, and a burning desire to hop into bed with one of "the boys," as they referred to their prey.

Yes, Taye was one of the boys, all right. He was top boy. The big prize.

Ashley sincerely doubted he'd cheat on her again, not after the last time. The incident with the Page 3 girl had almost cost him his marriage, and one thing she was sure of: he adored her and the twins, and he wouldn't risk it, because she'd warned him countless times that if he ever cheated again, they were over. *Finito.* Goodbye. She'd take the twins and half his money too. She meant it. Oh yes, she certainly meant it.

After turning the invitation over in her hands, she decided that it must've cost a pretty penny to print. She wondered how many people were invited, and who they were other than Luca Perez and Jeromy.

Royalty might be on the list. Kate and William. What a coup *that* would be, sailing the high seas with bloody royalty!

Perhaps she'd text Bianca and inquire who was going. Or was that bad manners?

Probably.

There was a reply card enclosed, stamped and ready to go. No cheesy Evite for *this* couple.

Bianca had landed herself a winner, and Ashley was pleased for her. They'd become vaguely friendly when she'd been involved in helping to decorate Bianca's London penthouse a couple of years ago. They'd found that they had something in common. Bianca was famous, while Ashley was married to fame.

Over a few gossipy lunches, Bianca had regaled her with stories about some of the men she'd bedded. It was exciting stuff, and although Ashley hadn't seen Bianca since the supermodel had hooked up with the Russian billionaire, she was obviously still on her radar, hence the invitation.

Ashley picked up the phone and called her mum. She had to tell *someone* about the invite. Besides, she didn't want Taye's annoying parents moving into the house while they were away; it was better that her own mother was in residence to keep an eye on the twins, even though they had a live-in nanny.

Elise was less than thrilled to hear from her. "You only call me when you need something," she whined.

So? Ashley thought. *Isn't that what mums are for?*

"Take a look at this," one of Taye's fellow players said, thrusting a cell phone at him. "Feast your eyes an' get a load of *those* knockers."

Taye took the phone and stared longingly at the photo of a naked, extremely busty brunette, sitting in a chair facing the camera with her legs spread. She was pretty in a slutty way, but it was her tits that caught his attention. They were huge with dark extended nipples, so very different from Ashley's. Although since she'd had the boob job, Ashley's were pretty spectacular; he couldn't complain.

Taye felt the rise of Mammoth (a name he'd given his penis when he was twelve) and attempted to hide his embarrassment at getting a hard-on simply from checking out some random slag's tits.

"Who is she?" he muttered.

"A fan," his fellow player replied. "Sends me a new filthy photo every week. Nice pair of bazangers, right?"

"Better not let your wife see 'em."

96

"My wife wouldn't give a fast shit. *You're* the one who's pussy-whipped."

"Watch it," Taye warned.

"C'mon, mate," his teammate said with a knowing chuckle. "Everyone an' their dog knows Ashley's got you by the bojangles."

"Do me a favor an' give it a rest," Taye mumbled, glaring at him.

"Go have a wank," his teammate sniggered. "Looks like you're gonna need it."

Mammoth was definitely on course. Taye made it into the men's toilet, locked himself in a stall, and helped Mammoth do its thing.

Balls! This wouldn't be happening if Ashley ever let him within ten feet of her precious pussy. She was depriving him of his conjugal rights, and that wasn't fair. He needed sex. He craved sex, but what was a guy supposed to do when his wife's thighs were locked together tighter than David Blaine's handcuffs?

Fuck! It was a shitty situation.

He loved his wife, that was for sure. But did she honestly think that he was going to sit back and accept her once-a-month sex rule?

Bullshit. He was Taye Sherwin. Women lusted after him. They wrote him adoring and explicit letters, flooded his fan Facebook page and Twitter account, hung around outside every match hoping to get lucky. He could get laid twenty times a day if he so desired.

Things would have to change, and what better time and place to sort everything out than on the upcoming Kasianenko trip?

Yeah, it was confrontation time, and Taye was finally ready.

CHAPTER FIFTEEN

Xuan sent Flynn a terse text. *Of course,* her text read. *Where and when?*

In ten days, he texted back. *Meet me in Paris. We'll go together.*

Flynn was pleased that Xuan had agreed to accompany him on the trip. He found her company to be stimulating, and he had a feeling that Aleksandr would too.

For once he had something to look forward to that didn't involve work, and it made for a welcome change; he needed the break.

He'd first crossed paths with Aleksandr several years previously when he was in Moscow investigating a notorious criminal gang. The mastermind of the group, Boris Zukov, resided in a luxury apartment just outside Moscow with his French stripper girlfriend, who wasn't averse to giving anonymous interviews in exchange for money to feed her secret drug habit. Flynn had a contact who put him in touch with her, and during the course of an extremely interesting

99

and informative one-on-one, he'd discovered that apart from drugs and arms running, there was a plot afoot to abduct one of Aleksandr Kasianenko's three daughters for an enormous ransom. Six months earlier, another rich man's daughter had been kidnapped, and even though that ransom was paid, the child had ended up brutally murdered.

Flynn absorbed the information, and instead of going to the police, he'd done what he considered to be the right thing and gone straight to Kasianenko. It was the smart thing to do, and it turned out to be a wise move, because the Russian oligarch had handled things in his own way and no kidnapping had taken place.

Twenty-four hours later, Boris Zukov had accidently fallen to his death from a fourteenth-floor window in his tony apartment building.

Nobody seemed too concerned about the "accident"; nobody except Boris's younger brother, Sergei, who'd been outraged that the police had done nothing. It appeared that they didn't care. To them the death of Boris Zukov was a bonus. One less vicious criminal to deal with.

It occurred to Flynn that although Aleksandr was a legitimate businessman, he was also a man who knew how to take care of things in a don't-fuck-with-me kind of way.

Flynn admired him for that.

They'd met several times over the following years, and bonded as only two strong men can. Neither wanted anything from the other, and that suited them fine.

It had been a couple of years since they'd last gotten together, and Flynn was looking forward to seeing Aleksandr again. He still admired the man. Ruthless but honest. An interesting mix.

He'd been surprised when he'd read about Aleksandr hooking up with the famous supermodel Bianca, since he'd been under the impression that Aleksandr was a happily married man. Apparently things were different now.

The last time he'd seen Aleksandr, the Russian had taken him to a fancy club around the corner from his hotel, and offered to buy him one of the gorgeous women lounging on barstools and sitting at tables. The place was full of stunning women and very few men.

"Is this a brothel?" Flynn had asked, faintly amused.

Aleksandr had chuckled. "If it was, it would've been shut down years ago," he'd said. "This is a private club, and if a man should want to rent a room upstairs for the night, then it's between him and the lady in question."

Flynn had laughed. "I've never paid for it, and I'm not about to start now," he'd said.

"But you go ahead."

"Me?" Aleksandr had replied, stony-faced. "I am a happily married man, Flynn. I do not cheat. Too expensive. Too complicated."

And now it wasn't so complicated anymore.

Spending half her life on a plane was nothing new for Xuan. Besides, she enjoyed flying. One of her unfulfilled ambitions was to take flying lessons and obtain her pilot's license; it was something she had promised herself she would do sometime in the future.

Martha, a Dutch woman who resided in Amsterdam, had offered Xuan anything she wanted if only she would give up traveling the world and move in with her.

"Including flying lessons," Martha had promised.

"When I am seventy-five," Xuan had joked.

Martha was fifty, divorced, affluent, and attractive, with acceptable bedroom skills. Xuan was not tempted — she relished her independence too much.

Finished with Deshi, she hailed a taxi and visited a group of impoverished women and their children who lived in nothing more than a jumble of run-down shacks on the edge of town. She took food and clothes and as much money as she could spare, then spent several hours with them, playing with the children, laughing and chatting with the women, who were — in spite of their circumstances —

surprisingly upbeat.

Back at her hotel, she thought seriously about Flynn and their trip. It was bound to be excessive and over-the-top. Spoiled rich people vacationing knee-deep in luxury.

Would she be able to stand it?

For Flynn's sake, she'd try. And if it all got too much, she'd simply take off.

That was the cool thing about having no roots — when it was time to go, there was no one and nothing to stop her.

CHAPTER SIXTEEN

Lori made a firm decision: she was not allowing herself to give in to fear. She was a survivor — she could deal. It wasn't like she hadn't dealt with enough crap in her life. Why be frightened of two mangy, red-eyed wild animals?

She stared the coyotes down with a purpose, then, when they didn't move, she started yelling and frantically waving her arms in the air like a crazy person.

"Fuck off, you little monsters!" she screamed. "Get the fuck outta here!"

It was as if she had an angel watching over her, for the two coyotes suddenly turned around and slunk back into the bushes. Just like that.

"Holy shit!" she marveled. "I did it!"

Then, as she was about to use her cell phone to call for help, a young jogger appeared. He was wearing board shorts, a cutoff UCLA tee, and a sweatband to keep his blondish hair from falling into his eyes.

For a brief moment she was mesmerized by his legs standing over her, tanned and strong, athlete's legs. He couldn't be more than eighteen, so she forced herself to shift her gaze.

"I heard yelling," he said, jogging in place. "You okay?"

"I am now," she said, relieved to see him. "Damn coyotes looked about ready to eat me for breakfast."

"Bummer," he said, scratching his chin. "You hurt?"

"It's only my ankle. I'll live."

"You need help?"

"I guess so," she said tentatively, attempting to stand.

"Right," he said, holding out his hand to help her up. "You shouldn't jog by yourself. I tell my mom that all the time."

His mom! Lori was twenty-four, for crap's sake. Why was he comparing her to his mom? Maybe Cliff's advanced age was rubbing off on her.

"I jog by myself all the time," she said, enjoying the intense smell of fresh sweat emanating from his armpit. "Usually I bring my dogs."

"Big dogs or little dogs?" he inquired. " 'Cause if they're little, the coyotes're gonna wolf 'em down."

"Big dogs," she said, leaning on him.

"Big is good," he said.

She wondered how many girls had uttered those words to him, for his package in board shorts left little to the imagination.

"Yes," she managed, holding on to his arm and wincing as her foot hit the ground.

"I could carry you if you can't make it," he offered.

Nice one. She wouldn't mind at all. She could sniff his armpit all the way down to the parking area.

"You're sweet," she said. "If you don't mind me hanging on to your arm, I think I can do it."

"Gotcha," he said.

"Are you *sure* you don't mind?"

"Naw," he said casually. "I was about to turn around anyway."

"What's your name?"

"Chip. You?"

"Uh . . . Lori."

"Okay, Lori," he said, placing her arm around his neck, and getting a grip on her waist. "Let's do this thing."

Lori did not answer her phone. Voice mail picked up. Cliff was not about to tell her that they'd been invited on the Kasianenko yacht until he could watch her quiver with excitement. She'd be so thrilled.

Where was she? What did she do all day when he was busy working?

Girl things, he supposed. Shopping, mani-pedis, Pilates, spinning, shit like that.

He knew she was desperate for him to get her a job as an actress, but it didn't seem right for the star to put his girlfriend in the movie. Although he could've if he'd wanted to. He didn't; he had to be careful that she wasn't using him in that way. Besides, what were actresses? Nothing but egomaniacs with tits and stylists. He'd had a few, and they always ended up causing hysterical scenes and running to the tabloids with a totally made-up story.

No more actresses for Cliff Baxter. Hell, no.

He called Enid and told her to book him a garden booth at the Polo Lounge for tonight. He'd tell Lori then, and later she could show him her appreciation in her own very special way.

Yes, Cliff Baxter didn't do anything unless it suited him.

CHAPTER SEVENTEEN

Once Jeromy was in the house, the staff scuttled around on red alert. Jeromy was a fierce taskmaster; he expected perfection at all times. He was also a stickler for rules — *his* rules. Everything had to be just so, even the way the pots and pans were laid out in the kitchen. Every single thing had to be spotless, not a speck of dust anywhere.

On the other hand, Luca was totally laidback. He couldn't care less if the outdoor cushions weren't arranged just so. It didn't bother him if a painting was crooked or the bed wasn't made to Jeromy's strict specifications.

When Jeromy was away, all was mellow. When he was in residence — look out!

The staff adored Luca.

The staff loathed Jeromy.

After arriving from London and enjoying a mojito on the terrace with his younger boyfriend, Jeromy flashed the coveted invitation, and informed Luca that they simply had to go.

Luca checked it out and inquired who else would be on the trip.

"How would I know?" Jeromy said with a casual shrug. "Although you can rest assured that they will be people of quality."

Luca wrinkled his nose. There were times Jeromy said things that didn't make any sense. What did "people of quality" mean, exactly? It must be one of Jeromy's strange English expressions.

"Sure, we can go," he said, leaning back on his lounger. "I'm not in the recording studio until September, so it works for me."

Jeromy was delighted. "We should go shopping," he announced, eyes gleaming at the thought of an entire new wardrobe. "The Valentino leisure wear this year is divine. We must both get fitted out. Perhaps matching white tuxedos?"

"Why not?" Luca said.

Jeromy nodded, fantasizing about how hot they'd look in matching tuxedos.

"Maybe I'll call Bianca an' see who else is going," Luca said. "Could be they'll have room for Suga and Luca Junior."

Jeromy sat up ramrod straight, almost spilling his drink. Had he heard correctly? Was Luca mad? Did he honestly think he could inveigle an invitation for Suga Tits and the child?

No. It simply wasn't right. Luca had to be stopped immediately.

"That's not acceptable," he said, the words almost sticking in his throat. "It would . . . ah . . . make me most uncomfortable."

"Uncomfortable?" Luca questioned, trying to ignore the fact that Jeromy couldn't stand Suga. "How's that?"

"You were *married* to the woman," Jeromy said with a supercilious sneer. "Her presence on the trip would definitely be awkward. Besides, it's not proper etiquette to start adding guests. This is obviously a very special trip, and I am sure everyone who's been invited was hand-picked by our host."

Luca shrugged. "I thought it would be a welcome surprise for Suga," he said, not thrilled by Jeromy's attitude. "She needs cheering up."

Cheering up, my English arse, Jeromy thought with a bitter twist. *The bitch could light up Times Square with her phony cheeriness.*

"Exactly why does she need cheering up?" he asked through clenched teeth.

"Her ticket sales are down," Luca explained. "Kinda a blow to her ego."

Ha! Jeromy thought. *It would take more than a blow to crash Suga's enormous ego. It would take a nuclear explosion.*

"I'm sorry about that," Jeromy said tightly.

"Surely you can think of something else to lift her spirits?"

"Like what?" Luca said blankly.

Like who gives a damn.

"I don't know," Jeromy admitted. "We should think about it. Between us we'll come up with something."

Luca nodded, although he wasn't sure he trusted Jeromy to do the right thing.

Meanwhile, Jeromy had no intention of coming up with anything; the annoying diva wasn't *his* problem.

Then, deciding a change of pace was in order, he leaned over, gently tweaking Luca's nipple. "Did you miss me?" he cooed. "Were you a well-behaved boy?"

"Were you?" Luca retorted. He might be the superstar in this relationship, but he more than suspected that Jeromy was the slut. It didn't bother him, because he knew that Jeromy was into things he wasn't. He simply hoped that Jeromy was careful and never came home with any kind of disease to pass on.

"I would *never* cheat on you, my little pumpkin," Jeromy crooned, completely out of character, his long thin fingers caressing Luca's oiled abs.

"Sure you would," Luca said mildly, feeling the beginning of a hard-on.

He stood up. It wouldn't be cool to have Jeromy suck him off while there were staff lurking around. "Let's go inside," he suggested.

"I'm right behind you," Jeromy said, thinking of the young boy in London, the young boy with the talented tongue and surly attitude.

In his relationship with Luca, Jeromy had found that it was always *him* who had to perform fellatio on Luca, it was always *him* in the subservient position.

But that's what Luca was into. And since the one with all the money held all the power, then ultimately it was Luca who called the shots.

Jeromy had yet to challenge him.

CHAPTER EIGHTEEN

"Surely you realize that you have it all?" Clare, Sierra's sister, said with an envious sigh. She was a pretty woman, but nowhere near as lovely as Sierra. Clare's hair was brown, not golden copper. Her eyes were quite close together, not widely spaced like Sierra's. Clare had compensated by honing her intellectual skills, and creating a warm and wonderful family life. "And on top of everything," Clare added, "you're about to take off on an incredible trip."

Sure, Sierra thought. *Incredible.*

"I wish *I* was going," Clare said wistfully. "You have to tell me all about it. Oh yes, and be sure to keep a daily journal. I need to know *everything,* all the details." She let out a long, drawn-out sigh. "You're *so* lucky."

No, you're the lucky one, Sierra thought. *You with your comfortable house in Connecticut. Your teddy bear of a husband and your three terrific kids. Not to mention a successful writing career.*

113

"Um, yes," Sierra murmured. "I will."

"Do you have any idea who else is going?" Clare inquired, leaning across the restaurant table, agog for some juicy news.

"Not a clue," Sierra said, taking a sip of her martini. A bold move for lunch, but what the hell — getting drunk could be exactly what she needed.

Oh yes, Hammond would *love* that, she thought, stifling an inane giggle. A drunken wife on his arm. A wife dressed to impress and totally loaded.

"What are you laughing at?" Clare wanted to know.

The insanity of my so-called perfect life, Sierra thought.

"I don't know," she answered vaguely. "Nothing. Everything."

"For God's sake, please do not drift off into one of your weird moods," Clare begged. "And why are you drinking in the middle of the day? What's *that* about?"

"Because I am a political wife," Sierra retorted grandly. "We shop. We drink. We shake hands. We pick up babies. That's what we do."

Clare shook her head disapprovingly. "I don't know what's up with you today," she said, frowning. "You're not yourself."

"I wish," Sierra murmured sotto voce.

"Excuse me?"

"Nothing," Sierra said, taking another sip

of her martini.

"Any news on the baby front?" Clare asked. It was the same question she'd been asking ever since Sierra had married Hammond.

"I guess I'm just not fertile," Sierra said, unwilling to tell her sister that she and Hammond never had sex. He didn't want her in that way, and she certainly didn't want him.

"Or maybe *he* isn't," Clare suggested. "Sometimes it's the man's fault."

"Might I remind you, he already has a child."

"That doesn't matter," Clare said, intent on getting her point across. "He should still get tested."

"I'm not sure I even want a family," Sierra murmured, gulping down the rest of her martini.

"That's ridiculous," Clare said firmly. "Of course you do."

Sierra felt herself losing it. Why couldn't Clare leave the subject alone? "You know what?" she said.

"What?"

"I wish you'd do me a big favor and stop bringing it up all the time."

Clare knew when to change the subject. "I got a text from Sean," she said, lowering her voice and glancing furtively around as if the middle-aged waiter standing nearby was even remotely interested.

"What did he want?" Sierra asked, thinking about her twenty-nine-year-old dropout brother who lived in a run-down beach shack with a forty-two-year-old Puerto Rican divorcée in Hawaii.

"What do you *think* he wanted?" Clare said pointedly. Then, answering her own question, she added, "Money, of course."

Actually, on reflection, Sierra realized that she quite envied Sean. How relaxing to do nothing but sit on a beach all day and beg for handouts from your family.

"I sent him five hundred two weeks ago," she said.

Clare's frown deepened. "I thought we agreed that we weren't sending him any more money."

"He told me that he had a dental problem and was in horrible pain. I couldn't ignore him. What was I supposed to do?"

"Oh my God, Sierra, you're *so* gullible," Clare scoffed. "How could you fall for that? You know he's a blatant liar."

"Yes, I do know, but show some heart, Clare. He's also our brother."

"I am not sending him one more red cent," Clare said, with a stubborn shake of her head. "I don't care how much he begs. He's a grown man, and it's about time he started acting like one. Furthermore, *you* should stop enabling him, because that's exactly what you're doing."

"I'm not enabling him," Sierra objected. "I'm helping him."

"No, you're not helping him at all," Clare argued.

Sierra was too tired to fight with her sister. She had a strong urge to go home, crawl into bed, and sleep. Depression was creeping over her like a black cloud; she could feel it coming on. Once life had held such shining promise. No more.

How had she allowed herself to reach such a miserable place?

Was it because she'd married Hammond?

They were all questions she could answer if she wanted to. However, it was simply easier to forget.

"How old are you, dear?" Hammond asked, leaning back in the chair behind his desk, his eyes inspecting every inch of the latest intern to join the staff.

Skylar blinked rapidly. She couldn't believe that she was in Senator Patterson's presence, that he actually knew she existed. It was all so exciting. Earlier that day she'd been introduced to Mrs. Patterson, and now this!

"Uh . . . I'm going to be nineteen next week," she said, fidgeting nervously. "And uh . . . may I say that it's such an honor to be working here. I am a big admirer of yours, Senator, and of course of your wife too."

"That's nice," Hammond said, his honest

brown eyes shifting into X-ray mode as he skillfully removed her clothes. He noted that she had large real breasts and wide hips. She wasn't perfect like Sierra. Not a beauty, but attractive enough.

And she was young. He preferred them young.

As he sat behind his desk, he imagined placing his penis between her big breasts, then slowly moving up and coming all over her startled face.

After the initial shock, she would love it. They all did.

"Well, Skylar," he said, pressing his fingers together, forming a little arc, "welcome to the team. We all believe in working together here. Sometimes late into the night." He took a long beat. "Does that bother you?"

"Excuse me?" Skylar said, still blinking.

"Does working late bother you?" Hammond asked patiently, thinking this one seemed a little slow.

"No, no, not at all," Skylar said, full of enthusiasm. "That's what I'm here for."

No, Hammond thought. *What you're here for is to satisfy me sexually. And you will. Oh yes, you will. Your turn will come. And soon.*

CHAPTER NINETEEN

Divorce is never easy, but Aleksandr Kasian-enko was prepared to give Rushana, his wife of seventeen years and the mother of his three daughters, whatever she wanted. Unfortunately, what Rushana wanted was to stay married to him, so she and her lawyer were making things as difficult as possible, unnecessarily so.

Aleksandr was beyond irritated. He had offered Rushana everything she could desire, and yet there always seemed to be another roadblock.

The divorce wasn't his fault. He hadn't planned on falling in love with Bianca, only it *had* happened, and Rushana should simply accept it.

Aleksandr was determined that on the forthcoming yacht trip, he would propose to Bianca. He was doing it whether he was free or not. He'd already purchased the ring, a two-million-dollar rare emerald surrounded by diamonds. It was a ring fit for the woman he planned to marry. Bianca would love it, just as she loved him.

He'd never met a woman like Bianca before. So beautiful and yet so independent and strong. And passionate. In the bedroom, she was a roaring tigress; she fulfilled him in every way.

Yes, Aleksandr enjoyed everything about her, although he could do without her fame. The pesky photographers who followed her everywhere. The annoying fans who had no sense of keeping their distance. The hangers-on who often surrounded her. And the Internet, where people made up ridiculous stories every single day.

After a year with his love, he'd learned to ignore the chaos around her. Bianca was his, and nothing could ever change that.

However, he would be lying if he said he didn't relish the peace when Bianca was in another country. He could walk down the street unmolested and be happy that there were no photographers trailing him.

His faithful bodyguard was always in attendance. Kyril, a solid brick of a man who watched his every move, for one could never be too careful. Aleksandr was well aware that he had enemies; it came with the territory. He was a billionaire businessman who along the way had attracted his fair share of haters. People who were jealous of his wealth. Business rivals. His wife's needy two brothers, who felt that he should've done more for them. It wasn't enough that he'd bought them both houses and given them jobs at which they'd both failed. Was he supposed to support their lazy asses forever?

No. With the divorce came freedom from Rushana's clingy family.

The only regret that Aleksandr had was that he was no longer living with his three daughters. They'd remained with their mother, and rightly so. He could see them whenever he wished to, but since they resided in his former home fifteen miles outside of Moscow, it wasn't that easy to make the time.

He had yet to introduce them to Bianca, although in the following months he hoped to do so. It didn't help that the last time he'd seen them, Mariska, his youngest, had said, "Mama told us you have an American whore girlfriend. What's a whore, Papa?"

Aleksandr was furious. Rushana had better learn to control her mouth. He would not stand for her insulting the love of his life.

After Madrid, Bianca headed for Paris and a full-out spending spree. She knew all the designers, and they were delighted to accommodate her, because whenever Bianca was photographed in one of their outfits, sales soared. Bianca was adept at negotiating outrageous discounts, plus she also managed to get many things for free.

121

Her excitement about the trip was building. She had a feeling that something special was going to take place. She had no clue what, but knowing Aleksandr, it would be major.

Bianca had legions of friends in Paris — mostly in the fashion business and mostly gay. She planned on flying on to Moscow the next day, but in the meantime, she called several of her friends, and they all met up for drinks at the Plaza Athenée, before moving on to a decadent dinner at her favorite dining bistro, the well-established L'Ami Louis, where everyone pigged out on the heavenly potato cakes sautéed in duck fat, and the amazingly tender grilled beef. For dessert they indulged in dishes of wild strawberries piled high and topped with crème fraîche. It was a decadent feast.

Bianca ate everything. Usually she watched her diet, but tonight she felt like letting go.

After dinner, her sometime hairstylist Pierre suggested they move on to a club. So they ended up at Amnesia, a mostly gay bar with incredible sounds.

Bianca danced the night away with no inhibitions. When she was out with Aleksandr, she felt as if she had to behave herself, keep her wild side strictly for the bedroom. Tonight it was all systems go, and since the ever-lurking paparazzi had no idea she was in Paris, she was free to be herself.

Ah . . . freedom from prying photo lenses! Oh, how Bianca embraced it.

What she didn't take into account was so-called friends with cell phones. And while she was letting it all hang loose, one of them was capturing images that would soon be for sale.

Her friend Pierre might be gay, but did the rest of the world know it?

Absolutely not. So photos of Bianca hugging and kissing him, dancing in a skirt so short anyone could see she was not wearing panties, grinding on a stripper pole, and generally cavorting . . . well, those photos were pure gold. Soon they would hit the Internet with a vengeance.

Bianca was blissfully unaware of the clandestine shots being taken. She danced the night away with a smile on her face, and had herself a fine old time.

CHAPTER TWENTY

If there was one thing Ashley hated, it was when her mother spewed forth a mouthful of dumb advice, as if Elise had any clue what she was talking about. Three failed marriages and a job in a department store at her age. Exactly who would listen to her?

Certainly not Ashley, because she considered herself way smarter than her mum. She'd moved up in life, far far away from her humble beginnings. Not only was she married to a famous footballer, she was part of a successful interior design team. Partnering with Jeromy had been a clever move on her part. Jeromy had a stellar reputation, and so did she now that they were working side by side.

Well, kind of side by side, because they weren't exactly equal partners, even though Taye had put money into the business. When she'd first started working with Jeromy, he had bestowed the title of creative consultant on her. She'd been a bit miffed, but so far it had worked out. Whenever Jeromy had a celebrity client, he allowed her input. It was fun at first, but then she'd begun noticing that he always introduced her as Ashley Sherwin, Taye Sherwin's wife.

It pissed her off. Wasn't being Ashley Sherwin enough? Did Jeromy have to tack on that she was Taye's wife? What was *that* about?

When this had happened a couple of times, she'd brought it to his attention, pointing out that it certainly wasn't necessary to give Taye billing.

Jeromy had gone all confused and gay on her. "I'm so sorry, sweet thing," he'd purred. "I would *never* do *anything* to upset you."

After that he'd stopped bringing up Taye's name in front of her, although somehow or other all the clients seemed to know she was Taye's wife.

Eventually she'd complained a second time, causing Jeromy to adopt a more frosty attitude. "Is it my fault that you and Taye are photographed wherever you go?" he'd said with an imperious curl of his lip. "People recognize you, dear. Besides, it's good for business. Get used to it, or may I suggest that you stay out of the magazines."

It was true; she couldn't argue with Jeromy's logic. She and Taye *were* a staple in every magazine. *Heat* and *Closer* often featured them on the cover. And *Hello* and *OK!* had done numerous "at home" pictorials with

125

her, Taye, and the twins. As for the Internet, their photos were everywhere. Taye's Facebook page had millions of followers, plus he insisted on tweeting, and occasionally posting intimate family shots he'd taken with his favorite Nikon camera — a birthday gift she regretted giving him. He was always trying to catch her unaware, then posting the stupid photos of her asleep or half dressed.

The problem was that Jeromy was right; she *was* in all the magazines, and that *was* good for business, so eventually she'd stopped complaining.

The moment Ashley invited Elise to stay at their house while they went on their trip, Elise had moved in, even though Ashley had insisted it was way too soon. "We don't leave for another week," she'd pointed out. "No need for you to be here this early."

"I know," Elise had responded, thrilled to get out of her tiny apartment. "I want the twins to get used to having me around. And *you* don't mind, do you, Taye?" she'd added, simpering at her handsome son-in-law, who — once she'd gotten over the fact that he was black — she quite adored.

Taye had nodded. Anything for a peaceful life.

Now they were sitting at dinner in their dining room, and Elise was droning on and on about how they should conduct themselves

126

on their upcoming trip.

"You have to change outfits three times a day," Elise instructed. "Breakfast, lunch, and dinner. I read that's what these fancy people do on their yachts."

"Really?" Ashley drawled sarcastically. "Where did you read that?"

"On the Internet," Elise said, then, spitting up further gems, she added, "And don't be taking any ripped or torn knickers. They have people to do your washing, and you wouldn't want them talking about you behind your back."

"Bloody hell, they'll have a right old time with *my* drawers," Taye joked, letting forth a ribald chuckle. "Skid marks galore."

Ashley threw him a disapproving glare. "Don't encourage her," she said sharply. "And stop being vulgar."

"Lighten up, toots. I'm only jokin'," Taye said, wondering if there was any chance of him getting a leg over tonight.

"Well she's *not,*" Ashley hissed. "She believes every word of it."

"Fine," Elise said grandly. "*Don't* take me seriously, but I know of what I speak. I read all about it."

"Where exactly?" Ashley demanded.

"I Googled 'yacht etiquette,' " Elise replied, straight-faced. "Are you aware that you're supposed to tip the staff at the end of the trip?"

"Good to know," Taye said cheerfully. "I'd better go raid me piggy bank."

"It's no joke," Elise said, wagging a stern finger at the two of them. "The staff talk, and the last thing you need is getting a reputation as a cheapskate."

"Watch it, missus," Taye said. "Nobody's ever accused me of bein' cheap."

Ashley had heard enough. "I'm going to bed," she announced.

"It's not even nine, toots," Taye objected.

"I'm tired."

Too tired for a quick shag?

Maybe.

Maybe not.

"I'll join you, then," Taye said, rising from the table.

"What am *I* supposed to do?" Elise whined.

"I dunno," Ashley said. "Why don't you go Google some more useless information?"

"All I'm trying to do is help," Elise said. "Although if you don't appreciate my help —"

"You're right," Ashley said, before abruptly exiting the room.

Elise turned to Taye. "What've I done now?" she asked plaintively.

Taye felt a bit sorry for her, because when Ashley was in one of her bitchy moods, there was no stopping her.

"I think she's got one of her headaches," he said, making an excuse for his wife's bad

128

behavior.

"I don't know why she thinks she can take it out on me," Elise grumbled. "I've done everything for that girl, made sacrifices you wouldn't believe. When her father walked out on us, Ashley was six, and I didn't give up. I kept on going for her sake." Elise's lower lip began to tremble. "My little girl never lacked for anything. Singing lessons, dancing, piano — she had it all. I used to drive her to all the auditions. And look how it paid off. If she hadn't married you, she could've been a big star."

"I bet," Taye said, wondering how to make a quick getaway before Elise continued her story of sacrifice. "Anyway, you know what, luv? Ashley's a big star to me, so that's all that matters — right?"

And with those words he was out the door.

CHAPTER TWENTY-ONE

I'm coming to Paris early, Xuan texted Flynn. *Please book me a hotel.*

No way, he texted back. *You'll stay with me. Send details of your arrival.*

Which is how he found himself at the airport waiting for her flight to arrive. He got there early, spent some time perusing the magazine stands, picked up a copy of *Newsweek,* and settled back to wait.

Xuan's plane was an hour late. She emerged from the gate with a purposeful stride, attracting attention wherever she went. She might be petite, but she was certainly a beauty with her almond-shaped eyes, full cherry lips, and sweep of straight black hair that fell way below her compact bottom.

Men paid attention. So did women.

Well they would, wouldn't they? Flynn thought, waving at her. *Lesbian signals are surely wafting in the air.*

Xuan headed toward him with just an oversized shoulder bag filled with everything she might need.

"Any more luggage?" Flynn asked, giving her a perfunctory kiss on the cheek.

"Nope," Xuan replied, indicating her bag. "This is it."

Flynn attempted to take it from her.

She shrugged him away with a caustic "What? You think I can't carry my own bag?"

He shook his head, amused. When it came to Xuan, nothing ever changed. She was fiercely independent. Whenever they'd been chasing a story in war zones or other dangerous places, she'd always insisted on being treated like one of the boys.

So be it.

They took a cab back to his apartment. Flynn didn't own a car; he was never in one city long enough to be bothered with the responsibility.

His apartment was a small one-bedroom. He'd already decided that Xuan could have the bed, and he'd bunk down on the couch.

When he told her, she laughed in his face. "No, Flynn. You can keep your bed; the couch suits me fine."

"Still as stubborn as ever."

"This is true," she answered with a slight smile.

Later they left the apartment and dined at a nearby bistro Flynn frequented when he was in town. Xuan drank red wine and regaled him with stories of her adventures in

Vietnam. She told him about the children she'd visited and the women who had to put up with so many incredible hardships.

Flynn listened sympathetically. He understood. There was so much misery in the world, and it never saw the light of day unless someone dedicated — like Xuan or even himself — grabbed a platform to write about it.

"Maybe you should write a book," Xuan announced, devouring a plate of spaghetti, the tomato sauce dribbling down her delicate pointed chin.

"I wrote a book," Flynn reminded her, although he couldn't remember if he'd ever mentioned it before.

Apparently not, because Xuan looked surprised. "What book?" she asked.

"Bullshit stories," he replied, slightly embarrassed. "When I was younger."

"I want to read it."

"It's not your style."

"Excuse me?"

"You wouldn't like it."

"Why not?"

"I wrote it when I was very young."

"Ah . . ." Xuan said, her eyes shining bright. "And now you're so ancient."

Flynn laughed. "*You're* the one who should write a book," he said, leaning across the table and dabbing the sauce from her chin with his napkin.

She stiffened, and snatched the napkin from him.

"Okay, okay," he said, throwing up his hands. "I know you don't like to be touched unless it's sexual."

"You and I, we're never going there," Xuan stated, as if it were a well-known fact.

"You're so right," he retorted.

The bistro owner's daughter, Mai, who was waitressing, approached their table. Mai was a pretty girl who could not understand why Flynn had never invited her out. Tonight she was not pleased to see him with a woman, for he usually dined alone.

"Can I get you anything?" Mai asked, shooting Xuan a dirty look.

"More wine," Flynn said. "And maybe a look at the dessert menu."

"Oui, monsieur," Mai said, suddenly going all French and formal on him. *"Immédiatement."*

Flynn caught her attitude. So did Xuan.

"She likes you," Xuan said with a knowing smile as Mai walked away.

"And I like her," Flynn responded. "What's not to like?"

"Ah, yes," Xuan added. "Only *you* like her as simply another girl. *She* likes you to jump into bed with."

"No way," Flynn objected. "We're friends."

"You're so naïve when it comes to women," Xuan said, shaking back her long hair.

"Not naïve, merely careful," Flynn replied. "Haven't you heard the expression 'don't crap where you eat'?"

"You mean 'shit,' " Xuan said succinctly.

"I'm being polite."

She gave him another knowing smile. "After all we've been through together, you're being *polite*? I'm one of the boys, remember?"

"Sure," Flynn said, deftly switching subjects. "However, has it occurred to you that maybe she likes *you*?"

"Don't be ridiculous."

"Why? You're not feeling the vibe?" Flynn teased.

"No," Xuan said with a casual shrug. "I am not."

"I told you," Flynn said, continuing to tease, "feel free to take the bedroom whenever you want. It's all yours."

"It seems to me that you're very evasive when it comes to women," Xuan said.

"How's that?" Flynn answered vaguely.

"I've observed that wherever we are in the world, you might allow yourself one night with a woman, but never more than one night."

"And *you're* so different?" he retaliated.

"I'm a loner, Flynn. I always have been."

"So am I."

Mai returned and thrust menus at them.

As Flynn studied the menu, he realized it was the most personal conversation he'd ever had with Xuan, and he didn't like it. He didn't like anyone poking around in his so-called love life. It was nobody's business but his.

"Dessert?" he said stiffly.

"Coffee," Xuan replied. "Black. Nothing fancy."

"It'll keep you awake," he pointed out.

"My problem, not yours."

Standing by the table, Mai tapped her foot impatiently.

"One black coffee, Mai," Flynn said, glancing up at her. "And do you have any of that delicious tart you keep for special customers?"

Mai softened as she sensed there was nothing going on between Flynn and the Asian woman. "For you," she said softly, *"bien sûr."*

"Thanks, Mai." And he couldn't help imagining what it would be like to sleep with the young Frenchwoman. She was certainly pretty enough, and from what he could tell, she had a nice personality.

No — it wouldn't work out. After a few weeks, he'd end it and she'd be upset and hurt. Random hookups were not worth the trouble. Besides, he planned on still frequenting the bistro when he was in town, and like he'd told Xuan, do not shit where you eat. A firm rule to believe in.

CHAPTER TWENTY-TWO

"Did you come?" Cliff asked as he rolled over to his side of the bed. He wasn't that concerned; on the other hand, he was not averse to a rave review.

"Oh my God, *did* I!" Lori responded, full of fake enthusiasm. She didn't believe in lying unless it was absolutely necessary, but why tell one of the biggest movie stars in the world that, once again, he hadn't hit a home run?

Cliff was okay in bed, although he was certainly no superman. He was almost fifty years old and a textbook lover. Five minutes of foreplay, followed by a quick fuck, followed by her going down on him until he came in her mouth. And woe betide her if she didn't swallow — that really pissed him off.

She knew why. He'd once relayed the story of a famous tennis player who'd allowed a random date in a restaurant to slip under the table and suck him off. But the random date was smart. She hadn't swallowed, she'd spat his sperm into a paper cup and rushed it to a friendly doctor, who'd inseminated her. And voilà! One successful paternity suit.

Cliff Baxter had to know exactly where his precious sperm was headed. And actually, who could blame him?

It was almost a week after the coyote/ sprained ankle incident. Lori was fully recovered, because that's all it had been, a light sprain.

Cliff had filled her in about the amazing trip they were to take; he'd even sent her out with his personal stylist to purchase a few suitable outfits.

The thought of the Kasianenko yacht intimidated her. Everyone would either be very old, obscenely rich, or at the very least horribly famous. And there she'd be, just the girlfriend, for it was common knowledge that Cliff Baxter was a confirmed bachelor who had no intention of ever getting married. He said so in every interview he ever gave, hammering the point home.

Being just the girlfriend was starting to get old. It occurred to Lori that he could dump her anytime, exactly like he'd done with the string of girls before her.

It was a scary thought. What would she do? Where would she go?

Although Cliff paid for anything she wanted, he didn't give her actual money. He *had* given her a Visa card with a five-thousand-dollar limit, and knowing Cliff, if they split, he'd cancel it immediately. Basically that meant she'd be as broke as when she'd entered the relationship. He'd presented her with a few pieces of jewelry; nothing too expensive. Even the car she drove was only leased — registered in his company's name.

What could she do to secure her position?

Nothing much, except continue to please him.

Lately, she'd been thinking about the young man who'd rescued her on the hike. Chip, with his strong thighs and rippling muscles. What a hunk. Was it wrong to fantasize about him while Cliff was on top of her?

Funny, really: here she was getting boned by a man whom millions of women lusted after, a man she'd once thought she'd loved, and her excitement level hovered at zero. What was wrong with her?

Nothing. She simply wasn't into a man who was almost twenty-six years older than her and treated her like an accessory.

Why didn't anyone ever mention the age gap when they were busy writing about them?

Because nobody wanted to get on Cliff Baxter's bad side, that's why.

It occurred to Cliff that Lori had not been as thrilled about going on a magnificent yacht as he'd expected her to be. He'd been prepared for fireworks and raging excitement.

Instead, he'd gotten a halfhearted "Sounds great."

Hmm . . . was Lori starting to take the good life for granted?

Was she getting blasé?

No. Impossible. She was living a life she could only have dreamed about. She was with him, and he knew without a doubt that most women would give their left tit to be with him. After all, he'd been voted Sexiest Man Alive in *People* two years in a row. He had an Oscar and an Emmy. A red-hot, long-standing career. Three cars. A New York apartment. A mansion in Beverly Hills. A house in Tuscany. No ties to hold him down.

In short, he had the perfect life.

Or did he?

Yes. Yes. Yes.

A resounding trio of yeses. He had enough married friends to convince him that staying single was the only way to go. He'd worked hard for his money, and how many poor schmucks had he seen lose half of what they'd earned to some greedy soon-to-be ex who demanded everything?

He could understand if there were kids involved; child support was a given. Other than that, forget it.

Was Lori reaching that all-too-familiar stage in a relationship where a woman wanted more?

Commitment.

The dreaded word.

No thank you.

Cliff made a decision. He'd take her on the trip, make sure she had a wonderful time, and then when they returned to L.A., he'd ever so gently cut her loose.

Cliff Baxter would soon be back out there. Single and ready for the next adventure.

CHAPTER TWENTY-THREE

They went shopping. They spent a lot of money. Or rather, Luca spent and Jeromy encouraged. They bought clothes and shoes and luggage from the designer stores, then finally they stopped by Cartier, where Luca gifted Jeromy with a black Pasha Seatimer watch for everyday use. At nighttime they both wore their gold Rolexes, but Jeromy had his eye on a more expensive model.

Luca didn't get the hint. Instead, he bought Suga a diamond-encrusted bracelet as a consolation prize for her cut-short tour.

Jeromy tried not to look pissed off, although he was. When would Luca stop spending money on the fat cow? Would that magical day ever come?

The previous night they'd had dinner with Suga and Luca Junior. Today Jeromy's facial muscles hurt from the big phony smile he'd had plastered on his face all night. Luca Junior was boring, and Suga was an embarrassment. Jeromy hated being seen out in public with her.

Of course the photographers and lurking paparazzi were all over them. Since Luca had emerged from the closet, he was more popular than ever. His superstar ex-wife and bright-eyed young son added spice to a story that everyone loved to read about. Photos of them together were gold dust.

When it came to attention, Luca lapped it up. He was so good-looking and charming. A blond Latin god who'd risen from nothing and conquered it all. His music reached out to everyone, and he'd never forgotten his roots and the sensual salsa sounds that were so much a part of his past. He recorded his songs in both Spanish and English, and they were always worldwide hits. His lyrics inspired people.

Because Suga was still so much in the picture, Jeromy found himself the odd one out. The magazines, newspapers, and gossip sites seemed to overlook the fact that he and Luca were partners; they rarely mentioned him, and he was nearly always cut out of press photographs. It infuriated him. How come David Furnish was always pictured alongside Elton John? How come everyone knew who David Furnish was? And how about Ellen and Portia de Rossi? Never apart in the press.

Then it struck Jeromy.

Of course. They were married. They were legal.

So *that's* what he had to do — persuade Luca marry him.

One thing he knew for sure: it would not be easy.

When Luca had come out to Suga, she had not been surprised. She'd always suspected that he preferred boys to girls. In spite of this, she'd married him anyway. Why not? He was a beauty, and he had a generous soul. Plus he was extraordinarily talented, and she'd decided it was her calling to nurture that talent and make him into a star. Which she'd done, very successfully.

Getting pregnant was a bonus. Giving birth to Luca Junior was the best day of her life. Forget about all the accolades and the gold records and the fan worship; having a healthy baby boy was the pinnacle. She'd relished sharing parenthood with Luca, while also watching his career rise.

Then one day he'd come to her and told her he was living a lie, that he was a gay man and could no longer keep it to himself. She'd understood and immediately set him free.

Only he wasn't free, was he? Slimy English Jeromy had somehow or other inveigled his way into Luca's life, and he appeared to be here to stay.

Suga did not like Jeromy. She did not trust

him. And she sure as hell knew that he resented her as only an angry, jealous gay man can.

Unbeknownst to Luca, she'd had Jeromy investigated, and the results of said investigation were not great. Jeromy's design business was in trouble, in spite of the fact that he constantly boasted about how well he was doing. His personal life was also suspect. He was not at all faithful to Luca. In London he was a well-known figure at fetish and leather clubs, and he often used the Internet to trawl for fresh meat.

Did Luca know any of this? Was it up to her to tell him? Or if she did, would he resent her forever?

She knew that she had to tread carefully, and perhaps come up with a plan to get Jeromy out of Luca's life once and for all.

But how? It was something she had to think about.

CHAPTER TWENTY-FOUR

"Thank you, dear," Hammond said as Skylar placed a mug of coffee on his desk. "I warned you there would be late nights."

"Yes, you did," she said sweetly.

"And are you absolutely certain you're okay with it?"

"Of course I am, Senator," Skylar replied, flattered that she was the only one he'd chosen to stay late. She'd been working for him for just a few days, and already she felt special. The offices were deserted except for a couple of cleaners who were busying themselves outside. Even his two assistants had left for the night.

"I'll be needing some papers copied shortly," he said, all business.

"I'll wait," Skylar offered.

"Then you may as well wait in here," Hammond said, indicating the leather couch across from his desk. "Make yourself comfortable."

"Are you sure, Senator?" Skylar asked

tentatively. "I could wait outside."

"No, no, dear. Sit yourself down. I'm expecting a call, and until it comes through, I'm stuck here."

"You work so hard," Skylar ventured, her tone full of admiration as she settled on the couch and crossed her legs.

"Yes," Hammond agreed. "I suppose I do."

He noted that her thighs were a tad too heavy and her skirt was much too short. She had on a pair of wedge-heeled shoes that all the young girls seemed to favor, not at all sexy. Her legs were bare, though, which made up for the clumsy shoes. He imagined running his hands up her legs, starting at the ankle and slowly traveling all the way up until he reached her meaty thighs, then plunging his fingers into what lay beyond.

"My wife doesn't understand why I have to work so late," Hammond said, playing the sympathy card. "The truth is, she doesn't get it."

"Oh," Skylar said, thrilled that Senator Hammond Patterson was actually confiding in her, making her feel even more special.

"Relationships have their ups and downs," Hammond continued, taking a sip of his coffee. He paused for a moment and gave her a long, lingering look. "And how about you, dear? Are you in a relationship?"

"Uh . . . um . . ." Skylar faltered, thinking of her football-playing boyfriend with whom

146

she was always breaking up. "Sort of," she managed.

Hammond's honest brown eyes twinkled. "Sort of?" he said. "What does *that* mean?"

"Well, uh . . . sometimes we're together and sometimes we're not," Skylar admitted, nervously tugging at her short skirt, wishing she'd worn something a little more circumspect. But how was she supposed to know that she'd end the day sitting in Senator Patterson's private office? It was an honor she had not expected.

"Boys," Hammond said with a meaningful chuckle. "Can't live with 'em, can't live without 'em."

"I totally agree," Skylar said, starting to feel more at ease.

"This sometime boyfriend of yours," Hammond continued, "does he push you to do things you might not feel comfortable doing?"

"Excuse me?" Skylar said, startled.

"I'm sure you understand what I'm saying."

"Uh . . . n-no, I don't," Skylar stammered.

"Sexual things," Hammond said, feeling a rising hard-on as he watched the girl squirm and blush beet red. "No need to be embarrassed," he added, adopting his best fatherly voice. "I have a teenage daughter, you know. She tells me what goes on between boys and girls. She listens to me and I give her advice."

147

"Oh," Skylar said, filled with relief. For a moment she'd thought the esteemed senator was about to come on to her, and how would she handle *that?*

"Boys are only after one thing," Hammond said evenly. He was tempted to yell *Pussy! Young juicy pussy!* However, he controlled himself. This one wasn't quite ready, and it wouldn't do to have her screaming rape if he touched her. "Anyway, Skylar — it is Skylar, isn't it?"

"Uh . . . yes, Senator."

"You can go now."

"But I thought —"

Don't think, you stupid little girl. Simply get out of my office before I change my mind and jam my cock into your dumb mouth.

"That's all right," he said easily. "Everything can wait until the morning."

Skylar jumped to her feet. "If you're sure . . ." she said hesitantly.

"I'm sure," Hammond replied, busying himself with some papers on his desk. "Good night, dear."

Slightly disappointed that she was being dismissed, Skylar slunk out.

Hammond immediately hurried into his private bathroom and masturbated, staring at his well-put-together reflection in the mirror while thinking of how it would feel the first time he came in Skylar's mouth, the first time he stuck it into her, the rubbing and fondling of her big breasts naked against his bare chest.

He could wait.

Why not?

He'd done so many times before.

Sierra had shopped. Reluctantly. She'd bought clothes she knew would please her husband. Although why the hell she wanted to please him was beyond her comprehension.

Oh yes. Of course. She'd given up. Given in to the threats and insults he hurled at her. She was his docile arm-piece. She was — to the general public — the perfect wife.

Hammond had caught her in a trap, and the only way out would be to end it all.

Or . . . she could run to her parents and tell them what a terrible monster her husband was, and hope and pray that he would not carry out any of his dire threats.

However, that would be taking too big a risk. Hammond was a dangerous man, and as long as she went along with what he wanted, everyone would be safe.

As each day, week, month passed, Sierra sought solace in a variety of pills. They kept her calm. They kept her going.

They were gradually sucking the life out of her.

■ ■ ■ ■

BOOK TWO:
THE TRIP

■ ■ ■ ■

CHAPTER TWENTY-FIVE

Six months after the murder of his older brother, Boris, Sergei Zukov had moved to Mexico City, where over the years Boris had built many solid connections in the arms and drugs world. Sergei was finished with Russia. Even though the Zukov gang supposedly had people in high places on their payroll, those people had done nothing about finding and prosecuting his brother's murderer. It seemed to be too sensitive a subject, with no one prepared to do a damn thing.

And why was that?

Because Boris Zukov was a known criminal, and even though he'd never spent more than one night in jail, it was a well-known fact that Boris was capable of monstrous crimes. Kidnapping, murder, torture, drug dealing, arms.

Neither the authorities nor the public cared that a violent criminal had been thrown from a fourteenth-floor window to his certain death.

Sergei cared. Sergei cared deeply. His brother had been everything to him. Boris had raised him when their mother had run off with a local car salesman, leaving them with their drunken, violent father, Vlad.

When their mother left, Boris was sixteen and tough as an old boot. Sergei was six, and scared.

Over the years, Boris had protected him from everything, making sure that he attended school, watching out that nothing bad happened to him. Boris had acted more like his father than Vlad had.

Vlad was a heavyset lazy oaf of a man who couldn't care less about raising his two sons, although he certainly didn't mind living off the money Boris brought home, never once asking where it came from.

Boris hated him, and he taught Sergei to feel the same.

When Sergei was ten, Vlad had arrived home one afternoon and flown into a drunken rage when he'd discovered that Sergei had finished the paltry amount of milk left in the empty fridge. He'd beaten the boy badly, cut his cheek with a razor blade, then settled back to watch TV, nursing a full bottle of vodka.

That night, Boris returned to their small apartment late. He was already creating a fierce reputation selling street drugs and making sure he was available for any other jobs that might come his way.

Collecting debts.

No problem.

Stealing cars.

A pleasure.

Even a little murder on the side if the price was right.

Yes, at twenty, Boris Zukov was a man on the come.

When he got home (having had a night of rough sex with a randy local girl), he walked in to check on his younger brother, only to find Sergei crouched in a corner, whimpering and covered in blood from the gash on his cheek, his eyes blackened, his nose broken, and his skinny body covered in welts from his father's heavy belt.

It wasn't necessary to ask who'd done it. Boris had no doubt that it was Vlad.

With a masklike face, he'd marched into the bedroom all three of them shared, taken a pillow from Vlad's bed, and returned to the living room.

His father was passed out in an armchair in front of the TV, still clutching the bottle of vodka he'd been swigging from earlier. It was empty.

Stealthily, Boris positioned himself behind the chair, placing the pillow firmly over his father's face, ignoring the old man's muffled cries of shock.

Boris kept the pillow in place until there

was no breath left in him.

Suffocation. Vlad deserved it. He was a sorry excuse for a father; they were better off without him.

When Sergei was eighteen, Boris packed him off to a college in the U.K. Sergei had liked it, what with all the pretty girls and available sex. Mastering the English language had been easy for him, and learning economics and bookkeeping was also a breeze. When he'd returned to Moscow, Boris had put him to work organizing the financial records of his various so-called legitimate businesses, most of which were merely a front for his criminal activities.

It was tricky. Two sets of books, sometimes three. Sergei had turned out to be a master at manipulating numbers.

Everything was going smoothly until Boris's untimely death. It was then that the problems had started. Sergei had attempted to take over, but there were men in the organization who did not want him seizing control. Men who were older and more experienced. Men with more clout, who thought *they* were entitled to take over. These men blocked Sergei at every turn, although they were happy to keep using his book-manipulating skills.

Sergei had burned with fury — as Boris's brother, *he* was the one who should've been in charge.

But no — he was deemed not worthy to fill his brother's boots.

It was disappointing, because Boris had been so proud of him. "My brother, the smart one," he'd often boast to whoever would listen.

Yes, Sergei was smart, all right. He'd never stolen from his brother, but with Boris gone he began siphoning money from the businesses, then moving it out of the country. After a while, he'd amassed enough to make an overnight exit.

Fuck the men who claimed to be Boris's partners. He'd taken what he considered to be his rightful inheritance and fled to Mexico, where it wasn't long before he reconnected with the people Boris had done business with in the past.

Now, at thirty-two, five years after Boris's murder, he had a new life and more money than he could ever hope to spend.

Input Denim Inc. was a clothing company he'd purchased, a line of clothes that sold all across the U.S., Europe, and the Middle East. He'd also taken over a worldwide medical supply and waste company. Both businesses were savvy fronts for his real business: the drug trade.

Over a short period of time, Sergei had managed to turn himself into a drug kingpin, with major ties to the Mexican drug cartels.

He was a natural at covering his tracks and making new friends.

Apart from his crooked nose, which had never set properly, and the vicious scar on his cheek, Sergei wasn't bad-looking. He was not tall, but his build was quite muscular. He smothered his face and body in fake tan, and exhibited shining white teeth — all capped. Sergei particularly enjoyed the company of women, and they seemed to like him back. Cocaine was his drug of choice. His special kick was snorting it off the body of whatever woman or women he might be with, then packing a fair amount of coke into their vaginas before sucking it out. Good times.

His ex-wife, a Ukrainian model who'd divorced him when she'd found out he was into four-way sex, now lived in New York and headed the legitimate part of his clothing company. Their marriage had lasted barely six months.

He had no children — or at least not any that he knew of, because fucking was one of his favorite pastimes, second only to making money.

He resided in a penthouse in Mexico City. Weekends he spent at the villa he owned on the water in Acapulco, complete with helicopter pad.

Sergei made sure he was always surrounded by half a dozen faithful and dedicated henchmen. In business, a man could never be too careful.

Boris would be so proud if he could see him now. He'd seized control of his destiny, exactly as his big brother would have wanted him to do.

The one thing that continued to bother Sergei was finding out who had arranged the hit on Boris. And exactly who had carried out the plan. For it *was* a plan; he was sure of that.

Sergei wanted that person, and he wanted them badly.

Over the years, he'd never been able to find out. Not knowing ate away at him, because revenge was essential for his peace of mind.

Boris would expect him to exact revenge. Indeed, Boris would demand it.

There had been only one witness to the crime, and that was the whore Boris had been living with at the time, a young French slut who went by the name of Nona. The girl had taken off with the contents of Boris's safe the day after his demise. Sergei had been trying to find her ever since, but she'd managed to disappear.

Over the five years she'd been missing, he'd hired several detectives to locate her, and it was only in the last month that he'd received any results. She was in Arizona, living with a divorced businessman.

Sergei was currently on his way to pay her

a long overdue visit.

The conniving bitch owed him the money she'd stolen from Boris's private safe. And more than that — she owed him the information about who had set up the murder of his brother.

Sergei was convinced she knew.

And he *would* get it out of her, one way or the other.

CHAPTER TWENTY-SIX

Sleek, sensuous, powerful, and fast, Aleksandr's new yacht was all that and more. His orders had been to create an elegant state-of-the-art yacht that could take him anywhere in the world, and that's exactly what he'd ended up with.

Luxury abounded. There were several sundecks on three levels, all with their own bars and spacious dining areas. Plus a spiral staircase leading to all levels. There was a counterflow swimming pool, a Jacuzzi, and a fully equipped gym with a Pilates retreat. On the lower deck was an authentic Finnish sauna, a steam room, a hair salon, a movie theater, and even a small medical room for any emergency that might occur. There were also many toys, from water skis and Jet Skis to snorkeling and sport fishing equipment, kayaks, WaveRunners, and scuba-diving gear. Everything was available.

The interior of the yacht was classy — all imported Italian marble, pale woods, soft beige leathers, and flattering lighting.

A giant Buddha presided over the marble entryway to the master stateroom, leading into the interior, which was more like a luxury apartment. A huge California king bed covered in exotic fur throws dominated the space, and there were rich Oriental fabrics on the walls. En suite were his-and-hers marble bathrooms, a feature Aleksandr had insisted on for Bianca's pleasure; the master also had its own private terrace, lap pool, and Jacuzzi, where Bianca could sunbathe and swim nude if she so desired.

The six other staterooms were also luxurious; however, nothing lived up to the master, which was located on the sky deck, allowing spectacular ninety-degree views.

Aleksandr had ordered the yacht three years earlier, before meeting Bianca. Then Bianca had entered his life and he'd changed the plans and also the name — the yacht was now christened the *Bianca*. He hadn't told her. It would be one of the many surprises he had in store for her.

During the course of the boat's construction at the Hakvoort shipyard in Holland, Aleksandr had visited several times to make sure everything was exactly as he'd envisioned. Later, he'd worked with a team of talented interior designers to fulfill his vision of pure opulence.

The yacht had been finished two months

previously, and the captain and crew had taken it for a series of sea trial runs, finally ending up in Cabo San Lucas, where the big trip would begin.

Aleksandr had decided that rather than make the usual South of France/Sardinia/Italy run, they would embark on a different kind of voyage. They would explore the beautiful Sea of Cortez and the various small Mexican seaside towns and deserted islands along the way.

The Sea of Cortez — sometimes known as the aquarium of the sea because of its bountiful plant species, different kinds of fish, and other marine mammals — offered everything for a fantastic vacation. Aleksandr and his guests would visit uninhabited white sand beaches, experience jungle adventures, and sail far away from the ties of civilization.

Aleksandr was determined that this would be a trip to remember.

To be doubly sure everything was to his liking, he'd made one final visit to speak with Captain Harry Dickson, a ruddy-faced Englishman in his fifties. There were to be no screwups; everything had to be perfect. Captain Dickson assured him that it would be.

Flying back to Moscow, Aleksandr was fully satisfied that the captain was a man in charge, and that none of his guests, especially Bianca, would be disappointed.

Aleksandr was proud to say that he had created the perfect yacht for the perfect woman.

Bianca felt like crap as she sat on the British Airways plane taking her to Moscow. She had a horrible feeling that at any moment she was going to throw up all over the man sitting next to her. It seemed as if the plane was flying one way, and she was flying in the opposite direction. Wow! Talk about the mother of all hangovers.

Her overweight neighbor suddenly leaned over and said, "Excuse me, miss."

"Miss"! Was he fucking kidding?

"Yes," she said, backing away from his garlic breath, lowering her copy of *OK!* magazine. "What?"

"Aren't you that famous model?"

What a dumb question. Either he knows who I am or he doesn't.

"Um, yes, I am a model," she said grudgingly, glad she'd worn her blackout shades so that no one could see her eyes.

"The famous one?" the man said. "I mean if you are, then I have to tell you that my daughter loves you, but, er . . . ." He hesitated for a moment before continuing. "Unfortunately, I can't seem to recall your name . . . ?"

Really? For God's sake, get a life and leave me alone.

"Bianca," she muttered, not pleased and regretting that she hadn't insisted that Alek-

164

sandr send his private plane for her.

"Oh," the man said with a note of disappointment. "I thought it was Naomi."

Please God save me from morons and tell this fucker to leave now!

"Bianca," she repeated, unclipping her seat belt, then abruptly getting up and heading for the galley, where Teddy, a languid gay cabin attendant, was discussing the size of Beyoncé's thighs with an agitated blond flight attendant who could think of nothing but her Russian boyfriend — the one with the massive appendage — who was waiting for her in a hotel room in Moscow.

"You know what?" Bianca said with an *I am very famous so kindly pay attention* scowl. "The guy in the seat next to mine is really bothering me. Do you think you can move him somewhere else?"

Teddy had attitude; this passenger was interrupting his discourse on Beyoncé's thighs, and he didn't care who *she* was or what she wanted.

Then all of a sudden he did care, because the moment she removed her ridiculously large sunglasses, he found himself staring into the feral cat-eyes of Bianca.

"Oh my!" he gasped. Why hadn't anyone alerted him that the super-famous supermodel was aboard? He glared at his lovesick coworker and snapped, "What can we do, Heidi?"

Heidi managed to put on a suitably concerned expression. "We have a full flight," she said apologetically. "Would you like me to have a word with the gentleman?"

"A word's not about to shut him up," Bianca said sharply. "The man's a freaking pest."

"Oh dear!" Teddy exclaimed, waving his arms in the air. "I can't stand pests, or AP's as I call them."

Bianca frowned. "AP's?" she questioned.

"Annoying passengers," Teddy responded. "We get them all the time."

"I could ask the lady sitting across the aisle if she'd swap seats with you," Heidi suggested. "That might solve our dilemma."

"And how can you guarantee that I won't end up sitting next to another moron?" Bianca demanded.

Heidi lowered her voice to a conspiratorial whisper. "The man in the window seat is a well-known English politician recently involved in a big scandal. I doubt if he'll be interested in making conversation."

"Once they know it's me, they're *all* interested in making conversation," Bianca said with a weary sigh. Sometimes it was tough being famous and having to deal with the general public. "But I guess anything is better than Mister Chatty," she added, putting her sunglasses back on.

"I'll go see what I can do," Heidi said, while

166

Teddy envisioned telling his hunky Polish partner all about his encounter with the very famous Bianca. Of course he would embellish, make out that they'd swapped e-mail addresses and would definitely stay in touch.

"You're gorgeous," he managed, staring at her with envy and admiration. "More beautiful than your magazine covers."

Bianca shrugged. "Good genes," she murmured, giving him hope that maybe they *could* become friends, that it wasn't all simply a wild fantasy.

Heidi returned with the news that the woman in the aisle seat had agreed to move.

Bianca nodded; she was so used to getting her own way that it didn't surprise her. And then, because she couldn't help herself, she said, "And who exactly *is* the politician? And what was the scandal?"

Heidi and Teddy exchanged looks. Gossiping about the passengers was a definite rule breaker, but since they were now both suitably impressed that they were conducting an actual conversation with Bianca, what the hell.

"He texted pictures of his *you know what* to seven random women," Heidi whispered. "Sort of like that American politician last year — the Weiner man. Only what this one did was worse."

"Yes," said Teddy, happily joining in. "The pervert sent his texts from the men's room in

Parliament, *and* he perma-marked messages on his piece of man meat."

" 'Man meat'?" Bianca said, suppressing a giggle. "That's a new one."

Teddy lowered his voice even more. "Apparently he has a huge penis."

Bianca squashed an urge to burst out laughing. What was up with these guys who thought that photographing their junk was a fine old idea? Were they the new-age flashers? Or merely horny old hound dogs with nothing better to do?

"Hmm . . ." she said thoughtfully. "Well, as long as he's not gonna show *me* the goods."

"I think we can guarantee that he's learned his lesson," Teddy said, wondering if her small but quite perfect boobs were real.

"Then let's do it," Bianca decided. "But one move from the asshole, and all bets are off."

A few minutes later, she was settled in her new seat. The politician, a thin-faced gentleman, was curled up in his window seat under a blanket, apparently asleep.

Bianca took out her iPod, tuned into Jay-Z and Kanye, leaned back, and daydreamed about Aleksandr, the yacht, and her future.

Everything was set, and if all went according to plan, one of these days in the not-too-distant future she could become Mrs. Aleksandr Kasianenko.

CHAPTER TWENTY-SEVEN

Frantically packing, throwing clothes into several open suitcases, Ashley didn't know what to take because she didn't know where they were going. She wished she did, because surely it made a difference? If it was the French Riviera or Sardinia, then only the fanciest of resort clothes would do. Chanel, Valentino, maybe even Dolce & Gabbana. However, for Greece or Sicily, she would pack differently.

"Take everything," Taye assured her. "Or take nothin'," he added with a ribald chuckle. "You'll look like a right old sexy bird in nothin'."

" 'Old'?" Ashley said, turning on him, nostrils flaring. "I'm twenty-nine, for God's sake. That's hardly old."

"Just f-ing with you, toots," he said good-naturedly, sitting on the edge of the bed, watching her pack. "You'll be the best-lookin' girl on the boat. I'd bet me left ball on that."

"I wish we knew *who* was going," Ashley

169

grumbled, throwing in a leopard-print bikini with a matching cover-up.

"I thought you was gonna give Bianca a buzz, find out."

"I tried. She's changed her cell number."

"Text her, then," Taye suggested.

"Aren't you listening, Taye?" Ashley said, irritably. "I just told you, she's changed her number."

"Oh yeah, right," Taye answered vaguely, wishing his wife would snap out of her never-ending bad mood. It was starting to piss him off.

Ashley held a skimpy white sundress up in front of her and turned to seek her husband's approval. "You like?" she questioned.

"Here's the deal, toots," Taye said, stretching. "I like anything *you* like."

"For God's sake!" Ashley snapped. "Have an opinion for once."

"Okay, okay, don't go gettin' your panties snaggled up your arse," Taye said quickly. "It's nice. Virginal."

"Who wants to look bloody virginal?" Ashley exploded. "What's *wrong* with you?"

I could tell her, Taye thought. *I could tell her that what's wrong with me is an acute case of blue balls, and no amount of whacking off seems to solve the problem.*

"How do you *wanna* look, then?" he asked.

"Sexy. Hot," Ashley said, pouting. "Like I

used to before I had the twins and ruined my figure."

For a second he thought she might burst into tears, and quick as a flash he was on his feet, holding her, comforting her, feeling her boobs pressing up against his chest and liking it a lot.

Then Mammoth intruded and she hurriedly shoved him away. "Is sex all you ever think about?" she said crossly.

"Maybe," he confessed. " 'Cause y' know what, toots? We haven't done it in weeks."

"Oh my God!" she said, glaring daggers. "Are you *counting* now?"

"Not counting," he said, careful not to piss her off further. "Just frustrated."

"The problem with you, Taye," she said grandly, "is that all you can think about is yourself."

Trouble loomed. There was no getting Ashley out of her usual pissy mode, and they were leaving the next day. He didn't want to set off with Ashley all uptight; maybe if he backed down, he could bring her around. Anything for a bit of peace. "Okay, okay," he said soothingly. "I'm sorry, luv, I get it — you're wound up. Me too. We both need this break."

"I know *I* certainly do," Ashley said pointedly.

Saved by the twins, who came bounding into the room, followed by a fussy Elise, who was quite enamored with being in charge. She'd sent the nanny out on a series of errands and was in full control.

The six-year-old twins, Aimee and Wolf, were looking picture-perfect. For some reason known only to Elise, the two children were both dressed as if they were on their way to a party or a photo shoot.

"Daddy!" Aimee flung herself at Taye, wrapping her sturdy little body around his legs, clinging to him tightly. "Don't wantchoo t' go 'way!"

Wolf, a miniature version of his father, hovered in the doorway scowling and kicking at the rug.

"It's only for a week, baby girl," Taye assured Aimee. "And Daddy an' Mummy gonna buy you lotsa presents."

"Don't promise them that," Ashley hissed. "They're spoiled enough as it is."

"I wanna Ferrari," Wolf piped up.

"An' *I* wanna princess castle," Aimee said, joining in.

"Only if you're good, mind your manners, an' listen to Grandma," Taye said.

"Please do *not* call me Grandma," Elise said, throwing him a dirty look. "The children call me Moo-Moo. I've told you both dozens of times. Doesn't anyone listen?"

"Moo-Moo sounds like a cow," Ashley snickered.

"No, it doesn't," Elise objected. "It's an

adorable nickname. Isn't it, children?"

"Wanna get Princess Barbie too," Aimee announced.

"You're stupid," Wolf said with a great deal of authority. "All girls are stupid idiots."

"Don't be rude to your sister," Ashley snapped.

"Yes, you heard your father — mind your manners, young man," Elise interjected.

"*Manners! Manners! Manners!*" Aimee chanted, sticking her tongue out at Wolf, who retaliated by spitting in her direction.

"Oh my *God*!" Ashley screamed. "The two of you are disgusting! Take them away, Mother. I can't stand to look at them."

"We're going for dinner at Nando's," Elise said, unfazed by the children's bad behavior. "The little ones love the chicken burgers there."

"Why're they so dressed up?" Taye asked, attempting to disentangle Aimee from his legs.

"In case they're photographed," Elise responded matter-of-factly. "You never know."

"They only get photographed when they're out with us," Ashley pointed out.

"Not so," Elise argued. "Celebrities' children are quite the vogue. Gwen Stefani's little ones are almost as famous as their mother. And Suri Cruise is simply everywhere."

"That's in America," Ashley stated.

"It's starting here too," Elise said. "And I'm sure you want Aimee and Wolf to look their adorable best."

"Whatever," Ashley muttered, more interested in getting back to her packing.

"Okay then," Taye said, finally freeing himself from his little daughter's clutches. "We'll see you all later."

Elise threw him a pointed stare.

What? Taye said, realizing she wanted something.

"Money," Elise said. "For dinner."

"Oh yeah," Taye said, digging in his pocket and coming up with a crumpled wad of bills. "How much you need?"

"Stop being a cheapskate and give her everything," Ashley said, eager to get rid of them.

"Sure, toots," Taye said, handing over a bundle of cash.

The family departed, and once more Taye found himself alone with his bad-tempered wife. He couldn't wait to get the hell out of England and into sunnier climes. Maybe a change of scenery would put Ashley in a better mood.

A man could only hope.

CHAPTER TWENTY-EIGHT

Xuan did not need to be entertained. She took off on her own every morning, not returning until late at night. When Flynn suggested another dinner, she demurred, saying that she was finishing up work on a thesis she was writing about women who become prostitutes and their reasons. He had plenty of work of his own to get to before they took off, so he didn't mind. But he couldn't help thinking that Xuan was a difficult woman to figure out. Even though he thought he knew her, he soon realized that he actually didn't know her at all. She was an enigma.

The Kasianenko plan was to meet up in Cabo San Lucas at the boat, so he was surprised to get a call from Aleksandr himself.

"I have to stop in Paris for a meeting tomorrow," Aleksandr said briskly. "So we will pick you up and we will fly to Cabo together."

It was as if they'd spoken yesterday instead of almost two years previously.

"Sounds good," Flynn responded, pleased with the change of plan. It certainly beat getting on and off a series of planes to reach their destination.

"I'll have my people call with the arrangements," Aleksandr stated.

And that was that. Aleksandr was a man of few words.

Later, Flynn told Xuan the new plan, and she nodded. "Perhaps I can write a piece about this man with his big plane, his supermodel, and his enormous yacht," she said coolly. "Does he give back to the world, or is everything simply a prize for him?"

"No writing anything," Flynn warned. "Aleksandr's one of the good guys."

"How do you know that?" Xuan asked with a skeptical expression.

"Because I do," he retorted, experiencing doubts about whether inviting Xuan on this journey was such a smart thing to do.

"I will judge for myself," Xuan said, her beautiful face turning inscrutable.

"Don't embarrass me," he warned. "Just remember that Aleksandr is my friend."

"You think I would embarrass you?" Xuan said, amusement lighting her eyes.

"If you could," Flynn said. "Only I'm sure you wouldn't do that to me, would you?"

"We'll see," Xuan answered mysteriously.

Shit! he thought. *I've made a mistake. She's gonna try and break his balls because he's rich and powerful.*

Then he thought, *Well, at least it won't be boring. Let the games begin.*

That night he had dinner alone at his neighborhood bistro, feasting on all his favorite foods.

Mai attended to his table, and when he was finished, he invited her to sit with him while he drank his coffee.

Mai accepted his invitation, and they chatted for a while. She was beguiling and sweet in a very French way.

It occurred to him that he had the apartment to himself tonight; Xuan had informed him she would be staying with a friend and would not be back until morning. So against his better judgment, he ended up asking Mai if she would care to join him for a drink.

She accepted, and they strolled the three blocks to his place.

When they arrived, he poured her a Pernod on the rocks, and they sat around sipping their drinks and talking politics — which surprised him, because Mai was far more knowledgeable than he'd expected.

Eventually they ended up in bed. Somehow it was inevitable.

Being with Mai was not the experience he'd thought it would be. Mai was no spider-monkey girl — she was a gentle lover with a warm and welcoming body. She smelled of lavender and roses, while the Pernod on her breath added a tangy sharpness to their kisses.

He found himself making love to her with more feeling than he'd known in a long time.

She murmured that she'd been wanting to sleep with him ever since he'd first come into her family's restaurant, but she'd felt that he wasn't at all interested.

He was taken by her lilting accent, the way she touched the back of his neck, the smoothness of her hands. Mai was the first woman in a long time who was actually getting through to him.

And did he want that?

No.

Feelings only led to heartbreak.

Eventually they fell asleep, entwined in each other's arms.

When he awoke at dawn, she was gone.

For a moment he was relieved, then he was pissed. Had he not pleased her? What was the deal with walking out without so much as a good-bye?

Suddenly the realization struck him that he was actually experiencing real feelings.

It was a shocker.

Xuan arrived later in the morning, carrying a shopping bag of warm baguettes, a jar of homemade jam, and a tub of thick creamy butter.

"Breakfast," she announced, placing everything on the small kitchen counter. She paused for a moment and sniffed the air. "You had a woman here," she said matter-of-factly. "Will she be joining us for breakfast?"

"No," Flynn said evenly. "She will not. How did you know?"

"Ah . . . I smell her fragrance in the air. *And* I notice the smile on your face."

"I'm not smiling."

"Enjoy it for once."

"I am *not* smiling," he insisted.

Xuan shrugged. "Too bad she isn't here. However, that means all the more for us."

Flynn nodded; his mind was elsewhere.

"Can you make coffee while I take a shower?" Xuan asked. "I was out on the streets all night. It was worth it, because I gathered some very interesting material."

"I'm sure you did," Flynn said, finding himself thinking that he wished he'd invited Mai on the trip as opposed to Xuan. He was already looking forward to seeing the French-woman again, which was a positive sign that maybe he *was* finally ready for more than a two- or three-week stand.

"It's good that you're happy," Xuan said. "This woman, she pleased you?"

"None of your fucking business," Flynn replied, finding himself trying to suppress the stupid grin that seemed to bubble up from nowhere.

"Ah yes," Xuan said with an all-knowing smile. "She pleased you."

"Are you packed and ready to go?" Flynn said, quickly changing the subject. "We're supposed to meet Aleksandr at the Plaza Athenée at three. Then we'll head straight on to the airport."

"Me? Packed?" Xuan said with a gesture of surprise. "I never unpacked. Or didn't you notice?"

"Right."

"It's nice to know that you can still summon up feelings," Xuan remarked. "Unfortunately for me, that is not possible."

He didn't need to ask why. Xuan had shared with him some of the horrors she'd experienced, and for her own peace of mind, it was best not to dredge up the past.

"I don't know about you, but I'm starving," he said, keeping it casual. "Let's eat."

"Ah yes," Xuan said. "Making love always gives one a hearty appetite."

"Will you quit?" he said, slathering butter on a baguette.

Xuan allowed herself another mysterious smile. "Of course," she said. "Only I so enjoy seeing you like this."

"Like what?" he said, attempting a frown.

"Vulnerable."

"Come *on*," he said, almost choking. "Let's not get carried away."

Yet he knew she was right. Maybe he was finally giving himself permission to move on.

And maybe that wasn't such a bad thing.

CHAPTER TWENTY-NINE

Even though he was a major movie star and had been for many years, Cliff Baxter did not own a plane. It wasn't necessary, because whenever he wished to go anywhere, there was always a studio plane available for his use; all he had to do was ask. So he did, and a company jet was on hand to fly him and Lori to Cabo San Lucas the following day. In the meantime, he had his valet pack his clothes, and he had Enid come to his house to go over any last-minute business.

Enid was her usual cryptic self. "I hope and pray you're not planning any surprises for me on this little jaunt you're taking off on," she said, giving him a piercing look.

"Now what kind of surprises did you have in mind, Enid?" Cliff asked, his eyes crinkling.

One thing about Cliff Baxter: he had not succumbed to the Botox and plastic surgery some of the older male stars had dipped into. He was of the George Clooney/Clint Eastwood school. You are what you are, take it or leave it. But he did look fabulous for a man approaching fifty. He had just the right amount of lines and wrinkles, and only a fleck of gray in his lustrous head of hair. Not to mention the devastating smile that had women across the world swooning.

"The marriage surprise," Enid said bluntly. "You know exactly what I mean."

Cliff roared with laughter. Perhaps his laughter wouldn't have been quite so hearty if he'd known that Lori was lurking outside the door to his study, listening to every word.

"Are you *kidding* me?" he blurted. "You better than anyone should know how I feel about marriage. Not for me. Nope. No marriage. No whiny kids. Not anytime soon or indeed ever."

"That's a relief," Enid said. "Because Lori is not for you, yet she seems to have stayed around longer than the others. I really don't understand why."

"They stay because I *want* them to stay," Cliff stated. "They leave when it suits me."

Enid could certainly believe that. "And this one?" she asked.

"Between us?" Cliff said, giving her one of his serious looks.

"No, Cliff," Enid said with a sarcastic edge. "I plan on selling everything you tell me to the tabloids."

"In that case I should be truthful with you."

"Please do."

"Okay, here's the scoop: the truth is that Lori's sell-by date is almost up."

Hovering in the hallway, Lori could not believe what she was hearing. Sell-by date. Fucking *sell-by* date. What did he think she was, a tub of yogurt on the supermarket shelf?

Bastard! Prick! How could he be so cavalier about their relationship? It hurt, it *really* hurt.

She stood there fighting back angry tears, suppressing a burning desire to march into the room and tell him exactly what she thought of him.

But forewarned was forearmed, and Lori began to formulate a plan.

Dinner was a casual affair at a megaproducer's Bel Air mansion. Cliff and the producer had worked together on several movies and were planning a franchise starring a renegade detective, a character Cliff was dying to play. He spoke about the detective all the time as if he were a real person.

Lori was sick of hearing about his upcoming movie. If there wasn't a role in it for her, why would she be remotely interested?

The two men were friends from way back. They had a wish list of leading ladies — everyone from Angelina Jolie to Scarlett Johansson.

What about me? Lori wanted to yell. *How about giving* me *a chance*?

Reality check. She knew that was not about

to happen, especially now with her exit visa waiting to be stamped.

She wondered how Cliff would deal with getting rid of her. Perhaps he'd manufacture a big fight — bad enough that she'd be forced to walk.

Hmm . . . She was smart enough to realize that it takes two to make an argument work, and now that she was aware of the situation, there was no way she'd play into that scenario.

Maybe he'd be brutally honest and simply tell her that it wasn't working for him.

Did that mean a severance package? Money and an apartment?

She felt like calling a couple of his exes and checking out the deal.

Meanwhile, they were still going on the trip, so that was something. Could she salvage their relationship? It was possible.

"You're looking very girlish tonight," said the producer's wife, a Hollywood social blonde with large overplumped lips and an unsatisfied expression. "I simply adore your dress — Kitson?"

No, Target, Lori was tempted to reply. *It cost me twenty-five bucks as opposed to the two hundred twenty it would've been at Kitson. And that's a conservative estimate.*

"The ruffles are such fun," the producer's wife continued. Then, without taking a beat, she added sotto voce, "How are things going

184

between you and Cliff?"

Did she know something? Had Cliff confided in his producer friend?

All the wives were insanely jealous of Lori because they all secretly lusted after a piece of the famous Cliff Baxter cock. Only *she* was the one getting it and *they* weren't.

Too bad, bitches.

"Actually," Lori answered evenly, "things couldn't be better. Cliff is such a sweetheart, so generous and thoughtful." She paused, then added, "Why would you ask something like that?"

The producer's wife was flustered, but only for a moment. "Well," she said. "Cliff *does* have a reputation for moving on. Of course we all love him dearly, and we'd like nothing better than to see him settle down, but you know that our Cliff is totally anti-marriage."

Yes, I do know, bitch. Thank you for reminding me.

"That's why we're so good together," Lori said sweetly. " 'Cause I'm too young to even consider marriage. I plan on having a career first, marriage much much later." *Make sure you tell that to your horny balding husband so he can relay the message to my boyfriend.*

"Oh," the producer's wife said, pursing her wormy lips. "Then you are indeed the perfect girl for Cliff."

Across the room, Cliff and the producer were discussing the advantages of shooting in

185

New York as opposed to L.A. "Better tax breaks in New York," the producer proclaimed, adding with a ribald chuckle, "and better strip clubs."

Cliff shook his head. "Can't show my face at a strip club," he said. "It'd be all over the Internet the next day. Who needs that shit?"

"Why should you care? You're not married."

"It's not right for my image. Besides, I have a girlfriend."

The producer glanced across the room. "How's it hangin' with Lori?" he asked. "Seems like she's a keeper. She's stayed around longer than most."

Cliff nodded. His private life was all his, and only Enid was privy to certain information. However, that didn't mean he couldn't reveal a little something. "Lori gives the best head I've ever had," he confided, knowing it would drive his friend crazy. "Better than a porn star any day."

The producer's mouth quivered slightly as he digested the information. It wasn't enough that Cliff Baxter was a fucking matinee idol, and single too. Now he had a girlfriend who gave the greatest blow jobs ever. Sometimes life just wasn't fair.

Later, the producer and his wife were getting ready to show a first-run movie in their private home theater.

Cliff decided they wouldn't stay. "We're leaving early tomorrow," he explained. Then, winking at the producer, he added, "Gotta take care of a couple of things before bed."

The producer stared hungrily at Lori before moving in for a good-night hug, while the producer's wife managed to kiss Cliff full on his lips.

In the Bentley on the way home, Cliff suggested to Lori that she might like to give him head while he was driving.

"What if we're pulled over?" she asked, thinking of the consequences.

"It'll be worth it," he replied, obviously in the mood for his own particular style of lap dance.

Lori gave in and went to work, her head in his lap as he negotiated the winding roads of Bel Air, one hand on the steering wheel, the other making sure she stayed down.

Lori gave it her best shot, and he came within minutes.

Let's see if you can find a new girlfriend who'll tend to your needs the way I do, she thought. *Lotsa luck, Mister Movie Star. You're gonna find me harder to replace than you can possibly imagine.*

CHAPTER THIRTY

Because Suga had a concert in Mexico City, Luca decided it would be supportive and maybe even fun to attend her show before flying on to Cabo San Lucas the following day.

It was an arrangement that did not sit well with Jeromy. Watching Suga perform was akin to having a thousand sharp knives stuck in his eyes. The woman pranced across the stage like an oversized Barbie doll in ridiculous outfits that she obviously considered insanely sexy. They were insane, all right, suitable only for a five-foot-ten-inch, skinny, flat-chested model, not a short, overweight, fifty-something diva with big hair, huge bosoms, and way too much makeup.

The fans who crowded the arena obviously appreciated her over-the-topness. Jeromy certainly didn't; her voice sent shivers up his spine, and not in a pleasant way.

The most excruciating part of the evening was when she dragged Luca up onstage with her and the crowd erupted into a frenzy of whoops, screams, and orgasmic sighs at the sight of their idol.

Luca. Jeromy's blond Latin god. Onstage with the she-wolf. Not a pretty sight. Jeromy was mortified that he had to witness such a scene.

Afterward there were celebratory drinks in Suga's overcrowded dressing room. Hangers-on abounded. Young fans, old fans, managers, promoters, a couple of photographers.

Jeromy slid into a corner and stayed there. He was an observer at a freak show, certainly not a participant.

Luca didn't seem to notice or care about Jeromy's lack of interest; he was too busy making sure that Suga received the full dazzle of his attention.

Damn the woman! The more time Jeromy spent in her company, the more he loathed her. She was easy to hate.

Looking around, he soon made eye contact with one of Suga's backup dancers, a tall, thin man clad in ass-baring leather pants, his head shaved. Jeromy had noticed him onstage, and now, in close proximity, he felt that old familiar stirring. They continued making eye contact until, with a slight tilt of his eyebrow, Jeromy indicated the door.

Luca was still busy playing nice with Suga; he did not notice Jeromy slipping out, or the dancer following close behind him.

Without exchanging a word, they both headed for the men's room, where they crowded into a stall together.

Jeromy reached out and touched the man's shaven head while feverishly unzipping his own pants.

The dancer fell to his knees and accepted Jeromy's engorged cock into his mouth.

Still no words were spoken.

The sexual excitement was intense as Jeromy realized that at any moment they could be discovered.

He shuddered out an orgasm, hurriedly stuffed his member back into his pants, and rejoined the dressing-room group.

Ten minutes later, Luca finally remembered he was alive, and approached him.

"You getting bored?" Luca asked.

Getting bored! What planet did Luca live on?

"I'm perfectly fine," Jeromy said, noticing his partner in sex across the crowded room. "But since we have such an early flight tomorrow, perhaps we should think about leaving."

"Sure," Luca agreed. "I'll go say good-bye to Suga. Come with me. She adores you."

Blatant lie.

Jeromy followed Luca across the room to where Suga held court. Her elaborate eye makeup was smudged, her lip gloss caked on her obviously enhanced lips. *Vagina lips,* Jeromy thought. *Big old vagina lips.*

"Thank you for coming," Suga said to Jeromy, all fake warmth and cloying perfume.

Ah, she should only know . . .

"It was my pleasure," Jeromy lied. "And you were . . ." He searched for the right word. "Amazing."

"Of course," Suga said, adding a rather grand, "I never let my fans down." Then dismissing him, because she was well aware that he didn't mean a word he said, she turned to Luca and threw her arms around his neck, kissing him full on the lips and whispering something in Spanish in his ear.

Jeromy did not speak Spanish. His young lover spoke perfect English, so there had never been the need to learn. Right now he wished he knew what the annoying cow had said. English, Spanish — it didn't matter. It was one of those intimate whispers that put a big smile on Luca's handsome face.

Dammit. Why did the fat bitch cast such a spell over Luca? It had to be broken, that was for sure. And he was the one to do it.

CHAPTER THIRTY-ONE

Sierra dreaded the forthcoming trip. She loathed the thought of being stuck in a cabin on a boat, however luxurious, with Hammond in close proximity. It wasn't as if she even knew Aleksandr Kasianenko. She'd met him once — briefly — at a political event in Washington. They'd exchanged pleasantries for a moment, and that was it. Hammond had then proceeded to pursue him like a dog chasing a particularly juicy bone.

It was the night before their departure, and as usual, Hammond was once again working late. Earlier in the day, they'd attended a lunch together, and she'd acted as the perfect political wife in a St. John suit, her copper hair neatly coiffed, smile firmly in place. Oh yes, she would make an outstanding first lady, and didn't Hammond know it. That's the *only* reason he wanted her. She understood that, and it sent chills down her spine.

Hammond had a dream. And that dream was to be standing on the steps of the White

House, with her on his arm.

May I present President Hammond Patterson and his lovely wife, Sierra Kathleen Snow Patterson.

The perfect wife. The perfect husband. What a couple. They would put the Kennedys to shame.

Or so Hammond thought.

Sierra was confident that day would never come. Someone would eventually expose Hammond for the phony he was. Maybe it would be her. But she didn't think so. She couldn't risk it.

No. She had to depend on someone else to take him down.

And who that someone was, she didn't yet know.

"Am I working you too hard?" Hammond inquired, pressing his fingers together as Skylar entered his office carrying a stack of papers.

"Not at all, Senator," Skylar said, quite pleased with herself, because out of all the interns, she was obviously his favorite. This was the fourth night in a row he'd asked her to work late. "I'm here to be of service."

Indeed you are, Hammond thought. *And tonight I'm going to test that theory out.*

"How's that boyfriend of yours?" he asked.

"Oh, y'know," Skylar said, gesturing vaguely with her left hand.

"Together? Not together?" Hammond pressed.

"We . . . uh . . . had a bit of a fight."

"About what?"

"I'm not sure," Skylar confessed. "Sometimes he seems so . . . inexperienced."

Hammond jumped at the opening. "Sexually?" he questioned, standing up from behind his desk.

Skylar's face reddened.

"Don't be embarrassed," Hammond continued, walking around the desk toward her. "I told you before, I discuss everything with my teenage daughter. Sex . . . well, naturally, because boys *are* inexperienced. They mature much later than girls, therefore they have no idea how to treat a woman." He took a long, meaningful pause. "And that's what you are, Skylar, a young, beautiful woman."

Skylar blushed beet red. Such a compliment! From such an important man! That very morning her brother had called her a fat-ass, and her mom had told her to clean up her room and stop acting like a twelve-year-old.

They should only know that the esteemed senator had just called her a beautiful woman. *Take that, Mom. I'm a woman. Not a freaking twelve-year-old.*

"Thank you, Senator," she murmured.

He moved closer to her, placing both his hands on her shoulders.

194

She didn't dare move. He reminded her of a teacher she'd had in high school. Older, nice-looking in a very buttoned-up, all-American way.

He had lovely brown eyes. Honest eyes. Eyes she could trust.

He lowered his voice and said, "Did you hear what I told you, Skylar? You are very beautiful."

Hammond had learned over the years that if you told any woman, old or young, that she was beautiful, be she rabid dog or true beauty, she would always believe you. There were no exceptions.

"Uh . . . yes . . . uh . . . thank you," Skylar muttered, flattered, yet at the same time wishing he'd remove his hands from her shoulders. It was creeping her out. She remembered hearing stories in history class about an intern at the White House way back when Bill Clinton was president — apparently he'd come on to the intern or vice versa, Skylar couldn't remember which, but whatever it was, it had gotten him impeached. Not that she thought Senator Patterson was about to do anything, but still — she wished he'd remove his hands.

He didn't.

He moved a tad closer.

He slid his hands down until they cupped both her breasts.

Skylar was mortified. This couldn't be happening. The senator was a married man. She was a teenager, and he had to be somewhere in his late thirties. This wasn't right.

She froze, unable to move.

"You have beautiful breasts," he said. "I noticed them the first time I saw you."

She opened her mouth to object, but nothing came out.

He maneuvered his hands under her sweater, and expertly lifted her bra so that it rested above her breasts. Then his fingers began tweaking her nipples.

She was so confused, fully aware that she should stop him. But suddenly new feelings began flooding her body. The way he was touching her was making her feel excited and breathless. The senator's touch was so different from the furtive fumblings of her on-again, off-again boyfriend, whom she'd never allowed beyond second base — the reason they were always fighting.

"Do you like this?" the senator questioned, circling her nipples with his fingertips. "Does it make you excited?"

She managed a strangled yes, imagining her mom's face if her mom ever found out.

The senator raised her sweater, and bent his head to suck on one of her erect nipples. He stopped for just a moment to ask, "And this?"

Her throat was dry, and she knew she should object, but the way he was making her feel was too good. She didn't want him to stop what he was doing. Never. Ever.

Hammond experienced a moment of triumph. Skylar was primed. Enough action on big-breasted girls and they were all yours. Nothing like a little nipple-play to get them creamed up and ready to go. Hammond knew this for sure.

"I cannot resist you," he crooned, seducing her with his words. "You're like a delicious candy. Your breasts are incredible."

Compliments were an important part of the initial seduction. Compliments and foreplay — a winning combination.

Sierra checked her watch. It was late, and still no sign of Hammond. She ate a solitary dinner without him and finally retired to bed.

Tomorrow they would be on their way, and who knew what would happen?

Maybe she could push him overboard in the middle of the night, and then her problems would be over.

She smiled grimly to herself.

If only . . .

Chapter Thirty-Two

"I dunno what you're talking about," the girl muttered, sitting stiffly in a chair in the living room of the house she shared with her boyfriend in Arizona.

"No?" Sergei Zukov questioned, a nerve in his left cheek twitching out of control. He stood in front of her, angry and disgusted that she was trying to deny who she was. They'd met only once before, when Boris had taken her to a cousin's wedding in Moscow. Five long years ago. She'd had long black hair then and dressed like a Goth. He remembered asking Boris what he was doing with such an odd creature. Boris had chuckled and muttered something about getting off on strange-looking women. After Boris's death, Sergei had discovered that the girl was a heroin addict, and unbeknownst to Boris, had been selling information about him to feed her habit. Boris had always gone for females who walked a dangerous path. It had turned out to be his downfall.

Now the girl had cropped bleached hair. She wore denim shorts, a tank top, and a long green cardigan. She had thin lips and bad skin and spoke with a fake American accent.

It was her, no doubt about it.

Sergei hated the sight of her.

"So what you are telling me is that your name is not Nona, and that you never lived with my brother in Moscow?" he said, circling her chair. "Is that correct?"

She scowled at him, vigorously shaking her head. "My name's Margie," she spat. "I'm an American citizen, an' I know my rights, so get the fuck outta my house."

He'd arrived ten minutes earlier. She'd opened the door thinking it was a delivery. He'd had two of his men with him, and they'd grabbed her and placed her in the chair like a puppet. She hadn't screamed; instead, she'd glared willfully at him, her eyes full of hatred. She knew why he was there.

"I am Boris's brother," he'd said. "And you *are* Nona."

She'd said nothing.

"You know why I am here, don't you?" he'd continued. "I can see it in your face."

That's when she'd denied knowing what he was talking about.

"My husband will be home soon," she said, her eyes darting furtively toward the door. "He has a gun, and he's not afraid to use it."

"The man you live with is not your husband, and you are not Margie," Sergei stated coldly.

"Screw you," she said in a low angry voice. "You don't scare me, so like I said, get the fuck out."

"I will when I recover the money you stole, and get the information I require," Sergei said, quite calm apart from the giveaway muscle twitch in his left cheek.

"Whistle for it, asshole," she said, full of defiance. "The money's long gone."

Sergei was a patient man when he had to be; however, he was not about to play word games with this tough bitch all day.

It took two hours, but after a certain amount of physical persuasion, she'd finally cracked, revealing that she'd sold information to an American journalist about Boris's plans to kidnap one of Aleksandr Kasianenko's daughters, and that the journalist must have gone straight to Kasianenko with the information, because twenty-four hours later Boris was dead and Nona had taken flight, afraid for her own life.

Sergei was finally satisfied; he now had everything he needed.

The fat-cat billionaire Aleksandr Kasianenko was the man responsible for his brother's death.

It was enough knowledge to set Sergei on a vengeful path.

Chapter Thirty-Three

Sitting next to Aleksandr on his plane, Bianca regaled her boyfriend with tales of her commercial flight to Moscow and the many indignities she'd had to endure. "I should've stayed in Paris," she said with a rueful laugh. " 'Cause here I am, twenty-four hours later, on my way *back* to the city I only just left! This is crazy time! *And* like I said, I flew commercial. What a nightmare! I don't know how people do it. It's so inconvenient."

Aleksandr seemed preoccupied, and although she was making light of it, Bianca was not thrilled that she'd traipsed all the way to Moscow to find Aleksandr quite distant. He'd been immersed in business meetings and she'd hardly seen him. Now they were stopping off in Paris to pick up friends of his she'd never met. This wasn't exactly how she'd expected her big birthday trip to start off.

"Are you all right?" she asked Aleksandr, leaning closer to him. "You seem like you've got something on your mind."

"Something on my mind," he repeated, turning and fixing her with a steady gaze.

"That's what I said."

"And how *was* your previous trip to Paris?" he inquired. "Tell me more."

"I told you everything," she said, wondering why he was suddenly so interested. "Dinner with friends, all delightfully gay, so you would've hated it. We had a ton of laughs, and I missed you madly. I always do when we're apart."

"My wife's lawyer seems to be under a different impression," Aleksandr said evenly, tapping his fingers on the side of his seat.

"Excuse me?" Bianca said, frowning. "What's your wife's lawyer got to do with anything?"

"He sent me over some very interesting printouts from various Internet sites."

"What printouts?"

Aleksandr picked up his briefcase, opened it, and laid out various photos of Bianca dancing the night away and grinding on a stripper pole, and — oh, the humiliation — crotch shots that clearly showed she was not wearing underwear.

"Oh crap!" she gasped, reviewing the photos. "I . . . I don't get it."

"Neither do I," Aleksandr said, his face grave. "You surely understand that I am going through an extremely difficult divorce, and visitation with my daughters is of paramount importance to me. Now my wife is saying she will not allow our children to be around a woman of such low character."

"Low character!" Bianca exclaimed, her humiliation turning to anger. "Low fucking *character*. How dare she! It wasn't as if I was *posing* for those shots. Somebody took them without my knowledge."

"However, you *were* in a club," Aleksandr said accusingly. "You *were* dancing on a pole like a cheap stripper. And you were not wearing underwear."

"Something you've never complained about before."

Aleksandr's face darkened. "Do not forget that you are my woman, Bianca. Your behavior reflects on *me*, and this kind of behavior is beyond disrespectful."

"Your *woman*!" Bianca burst out, stunned that Aleksandr was carrying on as if she were his personal property. He was revealing a side of him she'd never seen before, and she didn't like it. "Who the *hell* do you think you are?" she demanded, her temper rising. "An Arab with a fucking harem? 'Cause, baby, I ain't into that game."

"Bianca," Aleksandr said, fixing her with another steady gaze. "This is serious."

"Well, *fuck* serious," she said, still full of anger. "Nobody tells *me* what I can and cannot do. I'm sorry I got photographed, but it comes with the fucking territory of being a star. You should know that."

Their first fight. They glared at each other, neither prepared to back down.

"I loathe it when you swear," Aleksandr said coldly. "It's unfeminine. It does not become you."

"Really?" Bianca retorted, furious at the way he was speaking to her.

"It makes you sound common, using the words of a streetwalker."

"And I bet you've had a few of those," Bianca snapped, unable to help herself.

"Excuse me, Mr. Kasianenko," Olga, his personal flight attendant, said, hovering because she really didn't want to interrupt. "The pilot has asked that you fasten your seat belts in preparation for our landing."

"Thank you, Olga," Aleksandr said with a curt nod.

Bianca turned away from him and grappled with her seat belt. She was seething. This was some shitty start to what was supposed to be a memorable trip.

It suddenly occurred to her that maybe she was making a big mistake.

Flying commercial was not Ashley's favorite thing to do. Going through Heathrow Airport was inconvenient, to say the least. Everyone wanted Taye's autograph, and there was no escaping the hordes of paparazzi who trailed them all the way until they passed through security.

Some of the paparazzi shouted mean things at her. "Give us a smile, luv. You always look so bloody miserable." "Taye gettin' a leg over with any other bird?" "C'mon, Ashley, try not to look as if you're constipated!"

Rude bastards. She hated them all.

It wasn't *her* fault that Taye always managed a big shit-eating grin; she simply couldn't do it. He was mister personality. She was not.

The truth was that she wasn't miserable, merely cool. Better to look cool than to look like a fool.

Once they were through security, things calmed down, although she wasn't too happy about having to remove her shoes, her jacket, and all her jewelry as they passed through the scanner. Damn, why didn't Taye get priority treatment? He was a British football hero, a bona fide star, and stars weren't meant to suffer the indignities of ordinary people.

Sometimes she wondered if it was because he was black that he didn't get the Beckham treatment.

Hmm . . . food for thought.

Sitting in the VIP lounge, Taye chatted amiably with other passengers. Ashley settled herself at a table, sipping an early-morning coffee while leafing through a copy of *Hello* magazine, pausing to study a photo of herself at a fashion event in an extremely chic outfit. She was pleased with the image, pleased enough to tear the page out of the magazine and stash it in her Birkin purse.

Taye was dragging over someone to introduce to her, which was annoying because she wasn't in the mood for company. She soon perked up when she realized it was American movie star Billy Melina, and he was smokin' hot.

Ashley put on her animated face and began plying Billy with questions about his next movie and where he was flying to. Billy was totally charming in an all-American way, and when he left, Ashley fantasized about what it would be like to be married to an actual movie star. A handsome movie star who looked exactly like Billy Melina. So hot and sexy, *and* he'd just finished making a movie with Cliff Baxter — another of her crushes.

Idly, she wondered what Billy was like in bed.

"What you thinkin', luv?" Taye asked.

"Oh," she said cheekily, "I was thinking about what you're gonna do to me once you get me on that boat." Her husband was right; they hadn't had sex in a while, and suddenly she was experiencing quite a tingle.

"You were?" Taye said, startled.

"Boats are sexy, aren't they?" Ashley said, tugging on his arm.

Christ! Was his wife finally feeling horny?

"Dead sexy," he managed. "Let's put it this way, toots. You an' I are gonna rock the boat from stem to stern. Be prepared."

She smiled, then glanced down and noticed the erection growing in his pants.

Taye was so damn easy, and he was all hers.

In the large black SUV on their way to the airport, Lori was on her best behavior. Cliff was thinking of dumping her, and she was having none of it. She was determined to make him see the error of his ways. A perfect blow job in the car while he was driving was merely the beginning of all the exciting things she had in store for him. Their sex life was about to heat up. On their upcoming trip, she had plans to take it to an entirely new level.

Yes, Cliff Baxter was about to see a whole other side of her. By the time she was finished with him, he'd be *begging* her to stay.

Cabo San Lucas was at its glorious, shimmering best. The sun was shining, palm trees swaying; a vacation atmosphere prevailed.

Luca and Jeromy were staying overnight with the Luttmans, acquaintances who owned a magnificent villa overlooking the bay. The Luttmans were a New York power couple whom they'd met on the social circuit several times, a couple Jeromy had been desperately trying to cultivate. So when the yacht trip had come up, Jeromy had quickly discovered the Luttmans would be in residence at their vacation home, and he'd suggested to Luca that they might stay the night. Luca had agreed, and the Luttmans had been thrilled to say yes.

Lanita Luttman, a former showgirl, now a jewelry designer and a well-known lesbian, was a true social butterfly. And her husband, Sydney, an absurdly rich investment banker and a well-known homosexual, couldn't have been happier to welcome Luca and his English partner into their home.

A uniformed driver and two eager assistants met Luca and Jeromy at the airport and whisked them to the gated villa, where Lanita waited to greet them wearing a flowing purple caftan and multiple strands of long diamond necklaces. A flamboyant woman, she had dyed-black hair and turquoise contacts and was decidedly overweight.

Servants abounded. Lanita snapped her fingers, and trays of canapés and Bellinis appeared in the hands of ridiculously handsome young waiters clad in tight shorts, with only colorful braces covering their well-defined abs and pecs.

Jeromy was in heaven. He glanced around and wished that they were spending more than one night; he could get very used to this kind of life.

Luca was already admiring Lanita's array of sparkling necklaces, while various maids and house keepers peered from the windows and behind the bushes, desperate to get a peek at their idol, the fabulous Luca Perez.

So gorgeous, so blond, and what a voice! They were all in a state of hero worship.

Meanwhile, Jeromy was in his element. Who would have thought that his life would take such an amazing turn? The London gays in high places had written him off when he'd turned forty and didn't have a permanent boyfriend, let alone a successful business. However, since hooking up with Luca and bringing Ashley in, he'd managed to achieve it all. With Luca's backing and connections and Taye's investment, his design business had taken off, and now here he was in Cabo San Lucas with one of the richest couples in America, about to set off on an exclusive trip with a Russian oligarch and his supermodel girlfriend.

Not too shabby. Not too shabby at all.

Hammond climbed into the marital bed stinking of sex.

Sierra cowered on her side of the bed, pretending to be asleep. The bastard hadn't even bothered to wash the smell of another woman off his body.

Sierra continued to wonder how she'd allowed herself to sink to such a low point in her life.

Because of Hammond's diabolical threats, that's how. Threats she had no doubt he would manage — somehow or other — to carry out.

You have to get out of this marriage, a voice screamed in her head.

I can't, another voice replied. *I don't have the courage.*

Once she would have fought back, stood up for herself. But now she couldn't summon the strength. Playing along was the only way to go.

She closed her eyes tightly shut and prayed for oblivion.

This was her life, and there was nothing she could do about it.

CHAPTER THIRTY-FOUR

As Flynn and Xuan entered the spacious lobby of the Plaza Athenée hotel, Aleksandr rose to his feet and enveloped Flynn in a hearty bear hug. "It is great to see you, my friend," he said warmly. "It has been far too long. I have missed your company."

Flynn extricated himself and introduced Xuan. Aleksandr gave her an appraising once-over and nodded approvingly. "You have done well," he said.

Flynn realized that he had probably failed to make it clear that he and Xuan were not a couple, merely platonic friends.

He'd have to deal with that.

Xuan proffered her hand, gave Aleksandr a firm handshake and a steady gaze. "I have heard much about you," she said briskly. "And your lady too. Where is she?"

Nothing like getting straight to the point, Flynn thought. But he had to admit he'd been thinking the same thing. Aleksandr appeared to be by himself, apart from a burly

211

bodyguard hovering a few feet away. Where *was* the extraordinary Bianca?

"My lady is waiting for us on my plane," Aleksandr said. "She did not feel like coming into the city."

He omitted to mention that Bianca had refused to accompany him. She was in a full sulk and had locked herself in the bedroom on the plane, much to Aleksandr's chagrin. He was hoping that by the time they got back, she would have had time to think things through and realize that he was right.

"It's great to see you too," Flynn said. "It was quite a surprise hearing from you, though I can assure you it was a welcome one. Your timing was right on — I needed a break."

"Sit," Aleksandr said, indicating a comfortable banquette. "We'll take tea before we return to the plane."

"How very civilized," Xuan murmured, sitting down. Aleksandr sat himself beside her, while Flynn settled on an upholstered chair opposite them.

"Tell me, Mr. Kasianenko," Xuan said, "do you use your plane for humanitarian efforts, or is it merely for your own convenience?"

Aleksandr gave her a long, penetrating look. "So personal, so soon," he said at last, sounding vaguely amused. "Please, *do* call me Aleksandr; there is no need to be so formal."

"Aleksandr it is," Xuan said, twisting a thin gold bangle on her delicate wrist. "You haven't answered my question."

Oh shit, Flynn thought. *She's determined to score points, and she's doing it with the wrong guy.*

Aleksandr didn't seem to mind. "You tell me about *your* humanitarian efforts, and I'll tell you about mine," he said, still sounding amused.

Flynn quickly interjected. "Let's get into it later," he said, determined to avert trouble, because once Xuan got going, she *really* got going. "I heard a rumor you're in talks to buy an English football team," he continued. "Now *that's* what I'm interested in hearing. Want to tell me all about it?"

"Didja fancy him then?" Taye asked, snuggling close to his wife on their British Airways flight to L.A., where they were to make a connection to Cabo San Lucas.

"Fancy who?" questioned Ashley, all wide-eyed and giggly because she'd been taking full advantage of the free champagne.

"You know who," Taye teased. "That American movie-star bloke."

"Dunno what you're talkin' about," Ashley said, letting forth a most unladylike hiccup.

"Billy Melina."

"Oh, *him,*" Ashley said dismissively. "He's not so hot."

"Thought you fancied him."

"Not me," she said innocently.

213

"Is that so?"

"Yes, Taye," she said, fluffing out her blond curls. "He isn't my type."

"Glad to hear it."

"Are you?" she said coyly.

"You bet your pretty little arse," Taye said, reaching over for a quick grope of her left breast, pleased to hear that she didn't fancy the movie star. "Can't wait t' get you on the boat," he added. "We're gonna have a fine old time."

"Stop feeling me up." She giggled. "Try to be patient for once."

"Can't do it, toots. I'm too turned on."

"At least wait until the cabin lights are off," she insisted, impulsively running her hands over his shaved head, something she did only when she was feeling horny.

Holy shit! It looked like little wifey was letting her guard down and he was about to get lucky.

Mile-high club, here I come!

To Flynn's surprise, Aleksandr and Xuan appeared to hit it off. Flynn had expected fireworks, but all he got was a heated discussion between the two of them about why politicians were not doing enough to end wars, world hunger, atrocities, inhumane treatment of prisoners, and urban crime.

It turned out that Aleksandr was quite a do-gooder in his own way. He wasn't a boastful man; however, Xuan managed to pry all kinds of information out of him. She soon discovered that he supported several charitable institutions, that he'd financed a school for uneducated teenagers in Ukraine, and that on occasion he did indeed use his plane to transport food and supplies to disaster areas.

Flynn had not been aware of any of this, and it made him respect Aleksandr a hell of a lot more. The man wasn't simply a rich tycoon looking to sleep with beautiful models and throw decadent parties; he was the real deal. A billionaire with a social conscience. Surprising. Refreshing.

Xuan had her own particular way of making people talk, and by the time they'd had tea in the lobby of the Plaza Athenée and then helicoptered to the airport, she and Aleksandr were carrying on like old friends.

Bianca — not so much. She greeted them with a frosty demeanor as they boarded the plane, practically ignoring Aleksandr when he attempted to give her a kiss. She hurriedly turned away from him, announced that she had a killer of a headache, and flounced off into the bedroom, slamming the door behind her.

"Sorry about that," Aleksandr said, obviously uncomfortable. "Bianca has been working too hard lately."

"Really?" Xuan said with a sarcastic edge.

215

"Posing for pretty photographs all day long must be extremely tiring."

Flynn threw her a warning look, which she ignored. Xuan was not one to back down; like it or not, she always said what was on her mind.

Aleksandr appeared unfazed. He ordered shots of vodka and a large silver bowl piled high with caviar. "We shall drink," he announced. "And we shall eat. Bianca will feel better later. You will see."

The studio corporate jet was luxurious by anyone's standards. Cliff joked with the two attractive flight attendants, and even visited the pilots before takeoff for a manly chat. Everyone loved Cliff Baxter. He was an American classic: handsome, smooth, and a damn fine actor. His movies made billions worldwide, and why not? He always gave his adoring public exactly what they wanted.

"This is quite an adventure for you," he informed Lori as they settled into their seats. "One I hope you'll always remember."

You patronizing shit, she thought, remaining calm on the outside, furious on the inside. She knew exactly how Cliff wanted her to behave. He required her to be the grateful girlfriend who was so very lucky to be given the opportunity to go on such a fabulous trip with her famous movie-star boyfriend. Well, screw him. She could play the crap out of that role.

"How could I *not* be excited?" she said, all bright-eyed and eager, just the way he expected her to be. "Thank you so much, Cliff, for including me."

"That's okay, sweetie," he said, nodding at her reassuringly. "You deserve it."

I do? she was dying to say. *How come? I thought you were preparing to dump me. Isn't that the next item on your agenda?*

But of course the dumping was to take place *after* the trip, *after* he'd used her as his sexual plaything and adorable arm candy, *after* a week of sex Cliff Baxter–style.

Yes, Cliff was that most dangerous of men. An attractive, famous, charming, talented, rich user of women.

We'll see, Mr. Baxter, she thought. *We'll damn well see.*

The Luttmans invited a dozen or so friends over to show off their famous star guest. Luca wasn't thrilled; he'd been looking forward to lying back and relaxing, not being put on display.

Jeromy was one happy camper. The more important people he met, the better for his design business. It seemed everyone had a second home in London, so what could be better? He flung himself into being socially adept, while Luca sat at a table surrounded

217

by predatory, overly tanned, bored women, all married to incredibly rich men who were at least thirty years older than them, and all anxious to capture Luca's full attention.

Jeromy glanced over. Foolish women. Didn't they know Luca was gay? Didn't they get it?

Apparently the message hadn't reached them.

By the end of the evening, Jeromy had acquired three new clients, and an offer for him and Luca to join Lanita and Sydney in their luxurious bedroom later that night.

Jeromy knew Luca would decline, but there was nothing wrong with being curious. What did Lanita and Sydney have in mind?

Sex, of course. But what combination? And where did Lanita fit in?

Jeromy couldn't resist. As soon as Luca was asleep in the guest suite, he took himself to the master bedroom, where incense candles burned and Sydney lay spread-eagled on the middle of the bed with a healthy Viagra-inspired erection and an even healthier gut, which Jeromy found quite exciting in a totally repulsive way.

Lanita was also present, clad head to toe in a Day-Glo purple latex bodysuit, wielding a lethal whip with a sinister Vampira mask covering her eyes. "Welcome," she purred. "Where is Luca?"

Naturally they wanted the star. Who didn't?

But tonight they'd have to make do with him.

Fortunately for them, he was *far* better at participating in games than Luca.

Nobody played a more beguiling man of the people than Senator Hammond Patterson. He had it down to a fine art. Smile at everyone, pose with their children, pick up babies, wave when appropriate, always appear amicable and approachable. He came across as idealistic and full of hope, when in point of fact he was rife with ambition and harbored a deceptive personality.

As Hammond's closest personal aide, Eddie March had yet to discover the real man who lurked beneath the façade of decency and truth. All he saw was an upstanding man who always spoke up for what he believed in. A future candidate for the U.S. presidency. A compassionate man with high standards.

Eddie also saw the very beautiful, classy, and serene wife of the senator, Sierra Hammond. Every time he was in her presence, she took his breath away. He had a schoolboy crush, and there was nothing he could do about it except worship her from afar.

Eddie March was catnip to women. An attractive single man working next to an esteemed senator. At thirty-four he had his own boyish charm; only his was genuine.

Eddie elected to accompany Hammond and Sierra to the airport on the pretext that he had a few things to tie up before the senator's short vacation.

He sat opposite Hammond in the limousine discussing final decisions on several matters pending.

Sierra curled into her seat and gazed blankly out the window.

Eddie couldn't help sending a few furtive glances her way. She was so damn beautiful with her porcelain skin and exquisite cheekbones. How the hell had Hammond gotten so lucky?

There was a mini press conference outside the airport, not planned, but Hammond handled it with his usual style. Everyone was anxious to know when and if he was planning to run — rumors abounded.

Hammond gave them the standard well-thought-out noncommittal answers; he had no intention of revealing his strategy to announce his candidacy. When the time came, he'd decided, he would make his announcement on Jay Leno's *The Tonight Show,* just like several other important politicians before him.

After all, he was a man of the people — what could be more fitting?

CHAPTER THIRTY-FIVE

It was Sergei's way to do things fast. Fast and thorough, with an obsessive attention to detail. Possessing a steel-trap mind, a lack of conscience, and a knack for picking the right business partners was an asset, because when he required something to be done, he expected instant gratification or there would be consequences.

So when Sergei discovered that Aleksandr Kasianenko was the man responsible for his brother's murder, he immediately had his people find out everything he needed to know about his fellow Russian. Sergei had numerous contacts, and since information was a currency he dealt in every day, it didn't take long.

Sergei was reminded that way back in the early nineties, after the fall of the Soviet Union, Boris and Aleksandr Kasianenko had been involved in some kind of business dispute over shares in an oil company that Boris had claimed he was entitled to. Sergei had no memory of how the issue was resolved, but he did recall that Boris had always held a grudge, and after brooding about it for years, he'd made plans to kidnap one of Kasianenko's daughters and hold her for ransom. "That motherfucking *pizda still* owes me money," Boris had raged. "It's been years now, and I have waited long enough. It is time to claim what's mine."

Boris's plan had never materialized because of his untimely death.

Finally, Sergei understood why. Aleksandr Kasianenko must've heard about the kidnapping plot and taken steps to prevent it from happening. Aleksandr Kasianenko had murdered Boris, taken his life as if it meant nothing. And he would pay for that.

When Sergei heard about Aleksandr's new yacht and his upcoming trip, it was like a gift laid out in all its glory for him to salivate over and relish.

Sergei could almost taste the ultimate revenge.

Could anything be more perfect?

Aleksandr Kasianenko.

One rich, lucky motherfucker.

Not so lucky anymore.

Sergei would see to that.

Chapter Thirty-Six

When Bianca caught sight of her name emblazoned across the side of the gleaming white super-yacht, she forgot all about her fight with her lover and melted. She turned to Aleksandr and hugged him tightly. "You didn't!" she squealed.

"Yes, my dear, I did," he said, finally breaking a smile. Their flight to Cabo had been most uncomfortable. Bianca had spent the majority of the time locked in the bedroom, which was an embarrassment, considering they had guests. At times she could be a willful woman, and it infuriated him.

"Why didn't you tell me?" she demanded, green eyes gleaming with delight.

"I decided to surprise you," Aleksandr said. "I know how you love surprises."

"Now I feel so selfish for not helping you with our guests," Bianca said, pouting. "I'm such a bad, bad girl."

"It's all right, my dear," he assured her. "Our guests slept."

"And you?"

"I fell asleep for a minute or two," he replied. "Not as comfortably as if I'd been in my own bedroom, but it was acceptable."

"Why didn't you come in and join me?" Bianca asked, experiencing waves of guilt. "I wouldn't've kicked you out."

"I was under the impression that you were in no mood to be disturbed."

"I'm so sorry," she said, truly meaning it.

"Good enough," he replied, relieved to put their argument to rest. Fighting with Bianca was not his favorite pastime.

"I'm also sorry for flashing my cooch," Bianca added with an embarrassed giggle. "You *know* it wasn't intentional. I wouldn't do that."

"I'm sure it wasn't."

"Damn cell-phone cameras," she grumbled. "They should be banned!"

"I expect my wife will eventually get over it," Aleksandr said, quite certain that Bianca's indiscretion would cost him dearly.

"You think?" she asked hopefully.

"I know," Aleksandr said, taking her arm. "Come, my dear. Let us go board the *Bianca*. The magnificent lady awaits our presence."

Away from London, their large house, the irascible twins, her interfering mother, and her design obligations — which as far as Taye could tell consisted of nothing more than picking out fancy fabrics for rich clients — Ashley was like a different person. She'd suddenly turned all giggly and girlish, groping him on the plane, even suggesting they might do it in the bathroom. His wife was actually happy *and* randy! Exactly like the girl he'd married six years ago, the girl who couldn't get enough, the fun-loving Ashley he'd knocked up in the back of his roller one drunken night after a party.

Ah yes, he remembered that night well. Ashley in a Stella McCartney dress and no knickers, high heels and bare legs. He'd actually gone down on her in the back of the car before jamming it into her sweet wetness.

It was the night they'd conceived Aimee and Wolf. What a night!

"Oh," Ashley said, fanning herself as they got off the plane. "This place is bloody hot."

"Yeah," Taye agreed, "an' it'll get even hotter tonight when I'm givin' you exactly what you want."

"You mean what *you* want." She giggled.

They had not done it on the plane due to the fact that Ashley had complained that the bathroom was too gross. "There's three inches of pee on the floor," she'd moaned in disgust. "Why can't men ever aim straight?"

"I can," Taye had retorted with a lascivious grin.

"Oh, I know *that*," she'd replied.

And *he'd* known without a doubt that

225

tonight he was definitely getting lucky.

Watching Xuan grill Aleksandr was quite entertaining. It wasn't until Xuan had started her inquisition that Flynn realized the charitable deeds the rich Russian was capable of. The man was full of surprises. Now that he was aware Aleksandr had a charitable side, there were many things Flynn thought he might discuss with him. For instance, would Aleksandr be prepared to sponsor the building of a school in Ethiopia for orphans who'd lost their parents in the ongoing war? It was a project that had been on Flynn's mind for a while, but raising the money was almost impossible. He was in weekly contact with people who were prepared to build and organize everything, but lack of funds was the big holdup. One school. Surely that wasn't too much for Aleksandr to manage?

Flynn decided that before the trip was over, it was his duty to ask.

Aleksandr was obviously intrigued by Xuan; they hadn't stopped talking on the flight. Finally — after they'd landed — Bianca had emerged from the bedroom, and she and Aleksandr had left the plane together, followed by Aleksandr's ever-present bodyguard, Kyril.

"I wish to take Bianca to the yacht first," Aleksandr had said. "A car will come for you and Xuan shortly."

So Flynn was left with Xuan, who couldn't wait to inform him that Aleksandr Kasianenko was a far more interesting man than he'd led her to believe.

"I didn't lead you to believe anything," Flynn objected.

"Yes, you did," Xuan insisted. "You told me he was an obscenely rich oligarch with no conscience."

"Bullshit," Flynn said, laughing. "I never said that."

"Well . . . that's the impression I got."

"Then you should listen more carefully."

"Anyway," Xuan said, smoothing back her long hair, "I find him to be an extremely knowledgeable man."

Flynn raised a skeptical eyebrow. "You do?"

"Yes, I do. Although I cannot imagine what he sees in that rude, spoiled creature he's with," Xuan said, seemingly puzzled that Aleksandr Kasianenko was bedazzled by such an exotic woman.

Flynn felt argumentative. "What makes you think Bianca's spoiled?"

"Did you *see* the way she behaved?" Xuan said. "Pouting and sulking like a teenager. I can't stand that kind of woman. They imagine their beauty excuses them from everything."

"I kinda think we caught them mid-fight," Flynn noted.

"Perhaps. But in my opinion, a man like Aleksandr deserves better."

Flynn broke a smile. "I do believe my little Xuan has a crush," he teased.

"Don't be ridiculous!" she snapped.

"These things happen," he said lightly. "Even to you."

"My goodness, Flynn. Having sex with someone you like has taken away your better sense of judgment."

"And so she turns the tables," Flynn said.

"And so he starts speaking in clichés," Xuan shot back.

"I gotta say that you and Aleksandr *would* make an interesting couple," Flynn observed.

"Oh, *please*," Xuan said, dismissing his comments with a shake of her head. "The man is taken, in case you hadn't noticed."

So she *did* like him. Flynn was amused at the thought of Xuan and Aleksandr together. It would be the mismatch of the century. The Russian oligarch and the militant Asian girl. What a fun combination *that* could turn out to be.

Guy, the entertainment director from the yacht, personally met Cliff Baxter and his girlfriend at the airport. A gay, personable Australian, Guy was used to dealing with celebrities; it was his wish to make them feel as comfortable as possible from the get-go.

"The name's Guy," he said, offering Cliff a firm handshake. "It's a pleasure to welcome you, Mr. Baxter."

"It's a pleasure to be welcomed," Cliff responded, his famous movie-star smile thrilling every woman who hovered within ten feet of him.

"I'm Lori," Lori said, asserting herself.

"Welcome, ma'am," Guy said, reaching for her carry-on bag. "Allow me to help you with that."

"Thank you," Lori said, trying to decide if he was gay or not. He was certainly nice-looking: tall and muscular with bleached white hair worn in a spikey cut, crinkly pale blue eyes, and a deep suntan.

"Follow me," Guy said, attempting not to stare at Cliff Baxter, who was just as handsome in person as he was on the screen. "Your luggage will be taken care of. I have a car waiting. And Mr. Kasianenko wanted me to tell you that he is delighted you are here."

The Luttmans supplied a white Bentley to take Luca and Jeromy to the Kasianenko yacht. After his nighttime sexual adventures with the Luttmans, Jeromy was quite hungover. He hadn't drunk *that* much. Was there such a thing as a sexual hangover? Yes. And Jeromy was proof that it existed.

Between the two of them and their sexual perversions, the Luttmans had worn him out. Jeromy had always been partial to a walk on the wild side, but the Luttmans were something else. He almost blushed at the memory.

Luca was his usual handsome, cheerful, blond-god self. Jeromy wondered what Luca would say if he ever found out about the sexual shenanigans that had taken place the previous evening. Luca would probably be shocked; he might be gay, but in Jeromy's world, he was an innocent gay with very limited experience. *You suck my cock, I'll suck yours.* Plus a certain amount of mild penetration on special occasions.

It was no wonder that Jeromy had to venture elsewhere to get real satisfaction.

"I can't wait to relax and get away from everything," Luca said. "How about you?"

"I must say that being on the Kasianenko yacht sounds like the perfect getaway," Jeromy agreed, adjusting his dark glasses so they hid what surely must be hideous bags under his eyes. He longed to pat on some hemorrhoid cream before falling into a deep and most welcome sleep.

Alas, that would have to wait until later, because right now he had the role of attentive boyfriend to play, and nobody played it better than Jeromy Milton-Gold.

"We're here." Hammond nudged his wife awake as the plane landed. "Try to look a little less miserable, and for crissakes, put on a smile," he said, his tone a sharp command. "Do not forget, these people are all future contributors to my campaign, so attempt to sparkle."

Had Hammond just instructed her to sparkle? Was that what he expected?

Yes.

Or what?

Or he'd regale her with his threats again. Threats against her family. Threats he assured her on an almost daily basis he could definitely arrange to have carried out.

Sierra plastered on a fixed smile and prepared herself for the inevitable.

She was the senator's wife.

A good wife.

CHAPTER THIRTY-SEVEN

After exploring the luxurious yacht and falling in love with every aspect of it, especially the opulent master suite, Bianca settled on the main deck with Aleksandr by her side, and a glass of champagne in her hand, ready to greet their guests.

"This is paradise," she commented, taking in her surroundings and realizing how lucky she was to have found a man like Aleksandr. Not only was he a fantastic lover, but he was so very good to her and rich rich rich! Not that his money mattered — she had plenty of her own. However, it made a welcome change to be with a man who did not expect *her* to pick up the check.

"It certainly is," Aleksandr agreed. "And there will be more surprises to come."

"I can't wait," she said, clinging to his arm. "Tell me everything."

"Be patient, my love," he said, lifting his glass to clink it with hers.

"I'll try."

"Try hard."

"You shouldn't keep me waiting," Bianca said with a captivating smile.

"Ah, but that's exactly what I should do," Aleksandr responded. He knew how to keep Bianca interested.

Ashley and Taye were the first guests to arrive. Bianca was pleased; she and Ashley were sometime friends, and she couldn't wait to show off the glamorous yacht. She gave Taye a quick kiss on the cheek and hoped that he'd forgotten about their one night of lust many years ago.

Apparently he had, for he never said a word, not that he would in front of his wife.

"This is amazing!" Ashley squealed, taking in her surroundings. "Your name is on the boat and everything! How fantastic is *that*?"

"My gift to my lady," Aleksandr said with an enigmatic smile. "Bianca deserves only the best."

Some gift, Ashley thought as she quickly checked Aleksandr out. She found him to be a somewhat imposing man with his close-cropped dark hair, gray at the temples, and heavy features. He was attractive in a very manly way. A bit frightening really, like the mysterious villain in a Hollywood action movie.

"This is so exciting!" Ashley said, continuing to enthuse as she and Bianca sipped champagne.

"I know," Bianca agreed, smoothing down her Azzedine Alaïa tighter-than-tight dress. "The whole yacht thing was all Aleksandr's idea, and I'm here to tell you that I'm loving every single minute!"

"Who wouldn't?" Ashley said, experiencing a sharp stab of envy.

"I know," Bianca agreed. "It's quite overwhelming."

"Can I ask who else is coming?" Ashley asked, plucking a smoked salmon canapé from a passing stewardess.

Before Bianca could reveal who the other guests were, Luca and Jeromy were escorted aboard.

Spotting her old friend Luca, Bianca flung herself at him with screams of excitement. "Look at *you*!" she yelled. "Big fuckin' star! And don't we love it!"

Luca was as delighted to see her as she was to see him. He'd known Bianca long before he was famous, and she'd always been a loyal friend to him, especially when he'd come out. He embraced her energy and spirit, and he considered her to be very special, even though they never got to spend as much time together as they would like.

"You look outrageous," he said, taking a step back to admire her. "Could your dress be any tighter?"

"You know what they say," Bianca responded with a cheeky wink. "If you got it, flaunt it!"

"I'm all over that!" Luca said, grinning.

Ashley sauntered over to Jeromy. "Bet you never expected to see *me* here," she said with a distinct note of triumph.

"Lord, no," Jeromy exclaimed, hardly able to conceal his surprise. "When did *you* get invited?"

"The same time as you," Ashley retorted, delighted to stick it to him. "Taye had the invite in his pocket all through that dinner we had. He thought if he kept it hidden he'd get a b.j. out of it."

"And did he?" Jeromy asked caustically, not thrilled with the caliber of guests. He'd expected so much more than Ashley and Taye, although he soon changed his opinion when Cliff Baxter and a vibrant young red-head appeared. Aha! A full-blown movie star. Nice one. Jeromy launched into full smarm.

Lori stood back and checked out the other guests, while a tall, skinny, anonymous Englishman played kiss-ass with Cliff.

She noticed Luca Perez and was immediately smitten. He was so gorgeous with his quiff of blond hair and golden tan. Then there was supermodel Bianca with her deep cara-mel skin and delicious green cat-eyes. The Russian man, their host, was an overpower-ing presence in a very quiet, almost sinister way. And Taye Sherwin, the famous Brit foot-baller. What a hunk, although his wife wasn't

exactly Miss Friendly. When they were introduced, Ashley Sherwin had sniffed out a hello
as if it were giving her a migraine.

Bitch! Lori thought. *I'm not good enough for
you, but I bet my boyfriend is.*

And bingo! Lori was right. Ashley cracked
a big smile when introduced to Cliff. "I love
all your movies," she simpered, tossing her
long blond curls and sticking out her boobs.
"I'm such a big fan."

You should see his cock, Lori thought. *Or
maybe not.* She'd often taken note of Taye
Sherwin's print commercials in all the best
magazines, and he was certainly not lacking
in the big dick department. Either that or he
was stuffing socks.

Lori grinned. Fun with the rich and famous.
Little Lori Walsh was doing well for herself.
Maybe the Russian had a billionaire friend
she could hook up with. After all, she was the
soon-to-be ex of a major movie star; that had
to count for something.

Flynn and Xuan were almost the last to arrive. Flynn might not have been famous, but
every woman's eyes swiveled to check him
out. He was dead sexy in an edgy way. Not
perfect by any means, but he had the look.
The two-day stubble, intense ice-blue eyes,
lean body, and longish hair. Cliff Baxter was
classically handsome. Taye Sherwin, boyish.
Luca, gorgeous but gay. Aleksandr, an over-

powering presence. And then there was Flynn. The most attractive man on the boat.

Hot, Lori thought.

Delicious, Ashley thought.

Damn! Bianca thought.

And while everyone was lusting after Flynn and wondering exactly who he was, Hammond Patterson made his entrance, trailed by the lovely Mrs. Patterson.

Flynn glanced over and suddenly felt his world spin out of control, for to his shock and surprise he was staring straight into the eyes of the love of his life.

Fifteen Years Earlier

By the time he was twenty, Flynn Hudson had been with more girls than he could remember or even count. It wasn't that he chased them; it seemed that they were always coming on to him — and he had no logical reason to turn them down. What the hell, he was young, fit, and enjoying himself while studying economics, journalism, and world affairs at UCLA in Los Angeles.

Flynn lived in a house on Westholm Avenue with several other guys. They were a rowdy bunch who liked to use Flynn as the bait to get girls. It always worked. Flynn took the prize, and they shared the leftovers. They all joked about it, except Hammond Patterson — commonly known as Ham — who often argued that he was the main at-

237

traction, considering that his dad was an important congressman, and that he too was going into politics.

Ham was the peacock of the group, forever boasting about his conquests and insisting on sharing graphic sexual details whenever he got a girl into bed.

Flynn and Ham did not get along at all. Ham was jealous of Flynn, and it showed. Flynn considered Ham to be a major asshole.

Flynn's American grandparents lived in a large house in Brentwood, and sometimes he'd spend the weekends hanging out there.

One memorable weekend while his grandparents were safely in Palm Springs, his buddies persuaded him to throw an openhouse party. It wasn't Flynn's idea, but he got talked into it by Arnie, one of his best friends.

The party started out as a sedate gettogether, but as word spread, it soon turned into a major rave. The beer began flowing, naked girls couldn't wait to jump into the swimming pool, and the smell of pot wafted in the air.

"Jeez, Arnie," Flynn complained after the cops had visited twice. "My grandparents are gonna go ape shit. Help me close this thing down."

And as he watched, Arnie dissolved into a useless stoned heap.

Flynn shook his head, and then he glanced up and saw her. The girl with the heart-shaped face, honey coppery hair, and large brown eyes. Pretty did not describe her; she exuded warmth and compassion. She was a showstopper, and she was busy fighting off Ham, who was trying to persuade her to take a swig from the beer bottle he was holding. Ham had her in a neck lock.

Flynn didn't hesitate; he quickly moved in. "Easy," he warned Ham. "Looks to me like she doesn't want a drink, so get your hands off her."

"Y' can fuck off," Ham slurred, hanging on to the girl with the intent to keep her. "None of your fuckin' business."

Flynn stared at the girl. "Are you with this guy?" he asked.

"No way," she said, suddenly shaking herself free and starting to run off, but not before yelling, "You know something? You're all a bunch of drunken slobs!"

And that was that. Until three weeks later, when he saw her again. She was standing outside a fast-food restaurant in Westwood with another girl, and as luck would have it, he knew the girl she was with.

The good news was that he was acquainted with her friend.

The bad news was that he was on a date, and his date was a clinger who refused to let go of him.

Flynn did not allow this to stop him. He walked over to the girl he knew, said hello, and waited for her to introduce him to her friend. Which she did.

Then he had her name. Sierra Snow. A name as beautiful as the girl herself.

Sierra barely looked at him, but it didn't matter; he was finished, gone, helplessly, hopelessly in love or lust or whatever.

Somehow he knew that Sierra and he were destined to be together. It was fate, karma, whatever you want to call it.

But most of all, it was inevitable.

CHAPTER THIRTY-EIGHT

Women were Sergei's playthings. Like new toys, he only kept them around for so long, trifling with them until they were broken or he got bored.

His current paramours were Ina Mendoza, a former Mexican beauty queen who lived at his Acapulco villa, and Cookie, a ratty blond American D-list actress who'd once starred in a successful comedy where she'd flashed her fake boobs. Since then she'd done nothing of note.

He kept Cookie stashed in his Mexico City penthouse, where she spent her days shopping, always accompanied by a female bodyguard on the vague chance that she might be kidnapped.

"Kidnapped? You?" Sergei had sneered when she'd mentioned her fears. "Nobody would dare to fuck with Sergei Zukov. Any kidnapping to be done is done by *me*." But to placate her, he'd assigned one of his bodyguards to watch over her.

Cookie was thrilled that she had finally landed a powerful boyfriend. Finally. Her Hollywood career had not been stellar, so Sergei was her last chance of hitting the big time. She knew he had plenty of money, and she was hoping that she might get him to finance a movie — starring her. What a coup *that* would be.

Her ex-husband, a nightclub bouncer back in L.A., had written a banging script, and all she had to do was get Sergei interested, which was no easy job. He had the attention span of a gnat.

Lately, he'd had something else on his mind, something that seemed to be taking all his attention.

Cookie hoped it wasn't the fat Mexican so-called beauty queen he kept in Acapulco. She seethed with jealousy over that one. What could Ina do that she couldn't?

She'd raised the subject of Ina once with Sergei, and he'd slapped her across the face so hard that she'd lived with the imprint of his hand for days.

Bastard! He'd pay for that.

Or maybe not. Cookie knew better than to cross boundaries. Sergei was her ticket back to the big time — if only he'd read the fucking script.

"How *is* your American *puta*?" Ina sneered, her Latin eyes filled with jealousy, hands on voluptuous hips — she'd put on twenty pounds since winning her title.

Sergei silenced her with a grim look. He did not appreciate being questioned, and certainly not by a woman. Didn't they realize that they were interchangeable? However sexy and pretty they thought they were, there was always a younger, prettier model creeping up behind.

He had an urge to slap Ina, leave the imprint of his hand on her smooth cheek, exactly as he'd done with Cookie. Women needed discipline.

He couldn't do it because Ina's brother, Cruz, was in the house, and Sergei needed Cruz, for he was an important part of Sergei's plan. In fact, Ina's brother was one of the main reasons he kept Ina around. Family connections were important.

Sergei had conducted business with Cruz before. There were many deals to be brokered when it came to drugs, and Cruz had turned out to be a reliable and useful contact for moving shipments when Sergei needed him.

How fortuitous was it that Ina had a brother who'd spent the last seven years in Somalia, amassing a fortune from pirating small ships and yachts — any vessel he and his team could hold for ransom. Anything to do with the high seas, and Cruz had it down. Therefore he was just the asset Sergei needed right now, and when Sergei needed something, things always fell into place.

He'd made Cruz an offer he couldn't resist, and now Ina's brother was living in his house, and Cruz's men were ensconced in a downtown hotel, ready to move when Cruz gave them the word.

Plans were in motion.

Soon Mr. Big Shot Aleksandr Kasianenko would find out how real men did business.

Chapter Thirty-Nine

Once all the guests were aboard, Aleksandr instructed Captain Dickson to set sail. The captain obliged, aware he had precious cargo, and delighted to add the list of esteemed guests to his résumé. He was particularly chuffed that Taye Sherwin was on the trip. The man was a brilliant footballer — right up there with the best of them. Twice picked as the BBC's sports personality of the year, a former captain of the national English team, a brilliant player, Taye Sherwin had an illustrious career. Captain Dickson was honored to have him aboard. Of course it was not too shabby that movie star Cliff Baxter was also with them, *and* Senator Hammond Patterson and his lovely wife.

The *Bianca* had a crew of eighteen, which included everyone from an executive chef to a barman, stewardesses, engineers, a valet, a head housekeeper, deckhands, maids, and Guy, the entertainment director, whose job was to keep the guests contented and entertained at all times.

Captain Dickson was not as happy with his crew as he should have been. He'd had to say yes to the hiring of a few replacement crew members when three of his regulars dropped out at the last minute. This did not please him, as he preferred working with a crew who knew exactly how he expected them to behave.

One of the new hires was a Mexican girl, Mercedes, that Guy had seen fit to hire as a stewardess. Captain Dickson considered her too attractive for her own good. He didn't want any of the female guests getting annoyed or jealous; he'd seen that happen before. He instructed Guy to keep a close eye on her.

"No worries," Guy had assured him. "Checked out her references. Not one complaint. I'll watch her."

"You'd *better*," Captain Dickson had warned. "Her kind are inclined to give us problems."

Her kind, Guy thought, convinced that Captain Dickson was some sort of racist. Apart from one African-American engineer, the rest of the crew were all white. Besides, Mercedes wasn't *that* attractive. For a start, she was on the short side, and was it his imagination or was her left eye slightly squinty? And could he detect the beginning of a very faint mustache? However, he had to admit that she gave off a sexier vibe than most of the fresh-faced girls he usually worked with. Anyway, it was all last-minute, so he'd hired her. Big deal — he kind of liked the idea of introducing a bit of flavor to the trip. As long as she did her job, he was cool with it.

Over the last year, Guy had worked several high-profile cruises — one with a famous female talk-show host, another with a dominating captain of industry, and then there was the trip with the two NBA players.

The female talk-show titan had turned out to be a secret lesbian. The captain of industry had turned out to be a raging pervert. And the two NBA players had turned out to be hooker hounds with libidos that never quit.

Guy figured if he could handle that lot, then he was certainly well equipped to deal with one sexy little Mexican stewardess.

"Nice!" Taye exclaimed, exploring their accommodations, which consisted of a large, stylishly decorated VIP stateroom — color scheme pale blue — with a king-sized bed, plenty of closet space, a small private terrace, and an all-marble en-suite bathroom.

"Not bad," Ashley agreed, trying to conceal her excitement at actually being on the same trip as Cliff Baxter. *The* Cliff Baxter. *People* magazine's Sexiest Man Alive. *GQ*'s man of the year. *Rolling Stone*'s actor of the decade. Not to mention hundreds of other accolades.

Ashley had a major crush. And was it her imagination or had Cliff given her a long, lingering look — a look rife with sexual promise?

Ashley was full of expectations. What if Cliff Baxter came on to her? What would she do? How would she handle it?

Such delicious questions! She felt quite light-headed.

Was she capable of cheating on Taye? She never had, but this was Cliff Baxter, every woman's fantasy, so surely a quick fling was allowed?

The very thought made her tingle with the anticipation of the forbidden.

She'd relished the expression of shock on uptight Jeromy's face when he'd discovered that she and Taye were guests on the yacht. Jeromy could be such an annoying snob at times, so her and Taye being included kind of evened out the playing field.

In the meantime, she couldn't wait to have a girls' gossip with Bianca, get the scoop on everyone. She'd already decided that Cliff Baxter's girlfriend was no big deal. The girl had a nice body and flaming red hair — probably dyed — but Lori wasn't drop-dead Hollywood gorgeous. Kind of ordinary, really. Ashley had thought Cliff would have a raving beauty on his arm, someone of the Angelina Jolie caliber.

"What're you thinkin'?" Taye asked, plopping himself down on the bed and patting a spot beside him.

"I'm wondering what I should wear for dinner," Ashley mused, fluffing out her blond curls. "Do you think we're eating outside?"

"I expect so," Taye responded. "Heard someone mention dinner is on one of the decks. It's all go, ain't it, toots?"

"Cool it with the 'toots,' " Ashley said irritably. "We wouldn't want to sound like the poor relatives, would we?"

Taye shot her a dirty look. "Poor *what?*"

She'd hit a sensitive spot. Taye hated it when she intimated that they weren't good enough. She suspected it had something to do with him being black. Not that it mattered to her; she wasn't her mother's daughter when it came to racist thoughts.

"Nothing," she said, sitting on the bed beside him.

The bed was soft, welcoming. They'd been traveling all day, so she was entitled to be tired, what with the time change and all. And it was important that she look her best for cocktails at five-thirty. Yes, she wouldn't mind a nap before dinner.

Cocktails first, then dinner in the company of Cliff Baxter. If she was lucky, maybe she'd be seated next to him at the table.

Ashley couldn't wait.

"I can't believe how Taye and Ashley managed to get themselves invited," Jeromy fumed. "I should never have told them about the trip. It's quite obvious they solicited their own invitation once they heard about it."

"I thought you liked Ashley," Luca remarked. "Didn't you bring her in as your partner?"

"Only for the name value." Jeromy sniffed. "And do not forget that Taye invested money in the business too. You could say she bought her way in."

Luca stripped off his shirt and threw it on the bed, then dropped his pants.

"What are you doing?" Jeromy asked, alarmed — because after the sex marathon with the Luttmans the previous evening, he was not in the mood for more of the same. Although with Luca it would be oral and that was about it.

"I'm off to the pool," Luca said, opening a drawer and trying to discover where the valet who'd unpacked for them had put his swimming shorts.

"Oh," Jeromy said. "I was thinking perhaps a nap might be more of a plan."

Luca located his colorful Versace shorts and slipped them on. "Not for me," he said cheerfully. "I'm catching up with Bianca. Promised I'd meet her by the pool."

"Should I come with you?"

"Not necessary," Luca said, running a hand through his thick blond hair. "We'd probably bore you with our reminiscences."

Reminiscences? Luca and Bianca? Yes, he *would* be bored listening to the stories of how the two of them first met.

"Then I shall stay here and rest," Jeromy decided.

"See you later," Luca said, and he was gone, leaving Jeromy to stew over the fact that he wasn't being included.

"Impressed?" Cliff questioned, gesturing around their luxurious stateroom.

"With what?" Lori retorted, opening up her carry-on bag.

"You know what," he said, a tad irritable.

"No, I don't," she said, being purposefully obtuse.

"Oh come *on*," Cliff said, stifling a yawn. "The yacht. The other guests. This whole incredible setup."

She turned on him. "Are *you* impressed, Cliff?"

"Why would *I* be impressed?" he said, laughing and shaking his head.

"Then why would I?" she countered, taking out her makeup case.

" 'Cause you're twenty-four, sweetie," he pointed out. "You've got to admit that you've never seen anything like this yacht before. You shouldn't forget that you're one very, *very* lucky girl."

"Am I?" she said, giving him a piercing look.

"For fuck's sake, what's the matter with you?" Cliff said, his handsome face suddenly scowling. "You've been acting like a petulant little bitch ever since we left L.A."

She was tempted to tell him exactly what she was pissed about. *Excuse me, Mister Big Fucking Movie Star. Correct me if I'm wrong, but aren't you just about getting ready to dump my ass? So why shouldn't I be pissed off?*

"It was a long journey," she said, deciding that backing down was probably the best way to go. "And yes, Cliff, this *is* a once-in-a-lifetime trip. Thanks so much for including me."

"That's better," Cliff said, satisfied.

And before she knew it, he was unzipping, readying himself for the inevitable blow job.

Guy personally escorted Senator Hammond and his wife to their stateroom.

Hammond glanced around and said, "This'll do."

"Is there anything at all I can get for you, Senator?" Guy asked. He was impressed with Sierra Patterson; she was quite lovely, even more so than the photos of her he'd seen in magazines and newspapers.

"A bottle of Grey Goose vodka would be very welcome," Hammond said, winking at Sierra. "Right, darling?"

Sierra summoned a weak smile. She was in shock. Total shock. Never in her wildest dreams had she ever imagined she would run into Flynn again.

Yet here he was. Flynn Hudson. The love of her life.

It was all too much.

Fifteen Years Earlier

Sierra would never forget the first time she saw Flynn. It was at a party, and he came racing over to rescue her from the man who would one day in the far-off future become her husband.

What a joke! What a travesty! Marriage to Hammond should have never happened.

But it had. Unfortunately.

She remembered getting a quick look at Flynn. Tall, with longish hair and the most incredible steely-blue eyes. She'd run off yelling that they were both drunken assholes, and then she hadn't stopped talking about him to her girlfriends. "Who is he?" she'd wanted to know.

"Give us a clue," they'd all replied. "We don't know who you're carrying on about."

She'd shrugged. She had no idea who he was or where she could track him down. A few weeks later she was sitting in Hamburger Hamlet in Westwood when she spotted him through the window.

"Quick!" she'd shouted at her friend. "It's

him! Do something!"

They hurriedly made it outside and tried to appear casual.

The good news was that her friend knew him.

The bad news was that he had a girl clinging to him like a magnet.

But they exchanged names and discovered that they both attended UCLA, and Sierra knew it was the start of something special.

Flynn Hudson was her future. There was no doubt about it.

CHAPTER FORTY

Lying out by the pool located on the middle deck, Bianca and Luca indulged in a major gossip fest as the sleek yacht navigated the shimmering blue waters of the Sea of Cortez.

Aleksandr had wasted no time in instructing the captain to take off. The moment everyone was aboard, he'd announced it was time to go.

"What do you think of the group we've gathered?" Bianca asked, sunning herself in a barely-there Brazilian bikini that hardly covered any of her assets, her dark skin gleaming in the sunlight.

"It's some crazy mix," Luca observed.

"Isn't it just," Bianca agreed, stretching one leg above her head. "I only know half the people."

"That's more than me. And stop flashing."

Bianca lowered her leg and grinned. "Anyway, all I can say is thank God *you're* here."

"Who's the tall guy with the two-day

stubble?" Luca asked, reaching for the bronzing oil.

"Oh, you must mean Aleksandr's writer friend, Flynn. Sexy, isn't he? I just met him for the first time."

"There's something kinda cool yet so hot about him," Luca observed, rubbing oil on his legs.

"Hmm," Bianca murmured knowingly. "Could be you fancy him?"

"Maybe," Luca said with a wide grin. "Don't you?"

"I think just about everyone does," Bianca said. "Only we may as well forget it, 'cause according to Aleksandr he's totally straight. And anyway, he's with that pretty little Asian piece."

"Ah," Luca said knowingly. "Men are like spaghetti — they're all straight until they hit hot water."

"Luca!" Bianca exclaimed, giggling. "I thought you were happily joined at the ass with Jeromy?"

Luca shrugged. "I can look, can't I?" he said, handing her the oil and turning onto his front.

"Is *that* what you're doing?" Bianca said, amused.

"You can bet that Jeromy does more than look."

"Really?" Bianca said, obligingly smoothing the sticky oil all over Luca's bronzed back.

"Yeah, really. He thinks I don't have any idea about what he gets up to, but I know everything."

"Yes?"

"Hey, it's not as if I care," Luca said casually. "Do you see me as the jealous type?"

"I'm jealous as shit," Bianca said, rolling her eyes. "If I caught Aleksandr screwing around, I'd cut off his balls and bounce them from here to Moscow."

"You're such a girl," Luca teased.

"Guilty as charged," Bianca said, putting down the bottle of oil and wiping her hands on a towel.

"So this is what true love in all its glory is like?" Luca said, still lying on his stomach.

"I suppose you could say that."

"Ah," Luca observed. "The girl who'd do anyone has finally found *the* one."

"Yep," Bianca said, nodding vigorously. "Aleksandr is *it* for me. He's so sexy, and he treats me like a queen."

"Darling," Luca objected, "*I'm* the queen. You're just a girl in lust."

"Love," Bianca corrected briskly. "True fuckin' love."

"Okay, okay, but trust me — I know you. You'll get bored eventually."

"No, I won't."

"Yes, you will."

"Don't be such a Debbie Downer."

"If you're giving me a girl's name, make it Lucia."

"Oh my *God*!" Bianca exclaimed, once more rolling her eyes. "You're too much!"

Luca sat up, picked up his drink, and took a sip. "Hey, remember when you and I nearly —"

"Don't remind me!" Bianca squealed. "Shades of *you* couldn't get it up, and I was totally insulted."

"Yeah, but then later we became best friends."

"After I discovered you were gay."

"For your information, the *reason* I couldn't get it up was 'cause I had a hard-on for one of Suga's backup dancers," Luca confessed. "That black dude with the amazing abs."

"Had him," Bianca said matter-of-factly. "All abs and no cock."

They both burst out laughing.

As soon as she'd finished servicing Cliff, Lori decided she did not wish to sit around watching him snore. He was almost fifty; he needed his rest. She was twenty-four; she needed to explore the yacht. Why waste a moment of such a once-in-a-lifetime experience?

After changing into a polka-dot bikini and a skimpy cover-up, she put her hair up in a ponytail and left the room.

A helpful steward directed her to the swimming pool, where she came upon Bianca and Luca Perez in the middle of a full-on laughter fit.

She was reluctant to disturb them; they were obviously close. But Bianca waved her over and said, "Pull up a lounger and come join us. We're catching up on old times."

Lori immediately felt at ease. Even though Bianca and Luca were both enormously famous, she didn't feel intimidated. Besides, they were way nearer to her age than Cliff.

"You're with Cliff Baxter, huh?" Luca said. "I'm a big fan."

Oh God! She was so sick of hearing those four words. Didn't anyone have anything original to say? And surely *he* could come up with better than that?

Apparently not.

"How long have you and Cliff been together?" Bianca inquired.

Another much-asked question.

"A little over a year," Lori answered, settling on a lounger.

"Hmm . . ." Bianca mused, stretching out a perfect leg. "You think he's marriage minded?"

Lori bit her bottom lip. Wasn't that a somewhat personal question coming from someone she barely knew? Besides, she was sure Bianca must read the entertainment rags, and it was a well-documented fact that Cliff Baxter had no intention of ever getting married. He was anti-marriage. He drove the point home in every interview he gave.

Before she could come up with a suitable reply, Luca saved the day. "Stop pestering the girl with questions," he said. "I want to find out if *Aleksandr* is marriage minded. That's what *I* want to know."

"Aleksandr is still married," Bianca pointed out, turning frosty. "He's in the middle of getting a divorce."

"That's what they all say."

"Don't piss me off," Bianca snapped. "You know better than that."

"I guess that means no giant ring for Bianca," Luca teased.

"And no giant ring for me either," Lori said, quickly taking the opportunity to bond with the famous supermodel. "Cliff isn't into the whole marriage bit. And quite frankly, neither am I. I'm too young."

"Oh honey," Bianca advised, nodding sagely. "A man like Cliff Baxter, you *need* to put a ring on it."

"Yeah, a cock ring," Luca said with a raucous chuckle.

Bianca dissolved into peals of laughter. "You'd better not talk like that around Aleksandr," she warned when she'd finished laughing. "He doesn't appreciate dirty talk."

"What's dirty about a cock ring?" Luca asked innocently.

"And I thought stardom might've changed

you," Bianca chided. "But no, you've still got the same old potty mouth — thank God!"

"Careful with the *old*," Luca warned. "Have you forgotten we're almost the same age?"

"I'm guessing you two have known each other a long time," Lori ventured, noting the camaraderie between them and wishing she had a friend like Luca.

"Right," Bianca said. "I was nineteen and doing a swimsuit show in Rio. Luca was one of the boys in the background. Oh my God, he was totally edible!"

"And how about you, missy," Luca said, joining in. "You were like a black Bond babe with a major kick-ass attitude."

"I couldn't *wait* to jump his luscious bones," Bianca confided. "Only he wasn't interested, even though he was supposedly straight at the time. Course, I understood immediately. Gay as a fruit fly — although he didn't come out until years later, and that was only after one marriage, one son, and a red-hot career. *Finally,* he emerged from the closet and I was vindicated."

"I love this woman," Luca said, raising his glass to toast her. "She never changes."

"And you'd better believe it," Bianca said, calling for another round of champagne.

Flynn and Xuan were shown to their stateroom together as if they were a couple. Flynn was so shocked at seeing Sierra that he didn't really notice until Xuan demanded to know why they were supposed to share a bed.

"This is ridiculous," she said, quite angry. "Did you plan this, Flynn, just to get me into bed? If you wanted to fuck me so badly, you should've said so."

"What?" He stared at her, his mind taking him on a trip that he didn't have any desire to go on.

"We must have separate cabins," Xuan said firmly. "I demand it."

"You do, huh?" Flynn said, narrowing his eyes.

"I most certainly do," she retorted. "I will call for the steward."

"No," he said quickly. "You can't do that."

"And exactly *why* can't I do that?" Xuan demanded.

"Because I'm uh . . . kind of caught in a situation," he muttered, trying to get his head straight.

"What situation?" she wanted to know.

He didn't care to tell Xuan the sad story of him and Sierra, but if he expected her to stay with him, then he'd better tell her something. And she *had* to stay with him. There was no way he could face being on this cruise alone — he had to at least give the impression he was with someone.

Why hadn't he asked who the other guests would be?

Why had he walked blindly into hell, because seeing Sierra with Hammond was exactly that. Pure hell.

He was trapped. The yacht had sailed, and it was too late to get off.

Fifteen Years Earlier

Sierra was not easy like most of the girls Flynn encountered. After getting her number, he called her several times. She blew him off. Finally, he ran into her at a frat party, and when they got to talking, she offered to fix him up with her roommate, a raucous party girl who was more than hot to do whatever he fancied.

He fancied Sierra, and only her. There was no doubt about it. Not only was she cool and smart and achingly beautiful, she apparently had old-fashioned values, and his reputation as a player had obviously reached her.

But he persevered, and when they eventually began to date, he wasn't that surprised to discover that sex wasn't on the menu. "I'm not a casual girl," she informed him. "And I do not intend to start being one now."

Surprise, surprise.

Was she a virgin? He didn't dare ask. Instead, he developed a close relationship with his right hand and kept the faith.

Sierra Snow. He would do anything for

her, and eventually she would do anything for him.

They were together six months before they had sex. And it wasn't just sex. It was a mind-blowing, loving, incredible experience of epic proportions.

Suddenly he dropped his plans of trekking around the world when he finished college. He wanted only one thing, and that was to be with Sierra forever. She told him that she felt the same way.

They swore to each other that even though they were both young, they would never allow anyone or anything to split them apart. They would drop out of college, travel the world together, and share every adventure out there.

Then one day he'd received an urgent call from his grandmother in the U.K. informing him that his grandfather had been rushed to the hospital, and that she needed him to fly to England immediately.

Sierra drove him to the airport. She hugged him tightly and pledged her undying love. He promised he would come back as soon as he could.

A week later he received a FedEx envelope marked high priority. It came from a name and address in Los Angeles he did not know. Inside the envelope were half a dozen photos of Sierra in various stages of undress with several different men. One of them was Hammond Patterson. Sierra looked dreamy, almost happy, with the little half smile on her face that Flynn knew only too well.

She was enjoying herself.

There was a typed note enclosed.

STOP BELIEVING YOUR SO-CALLED GIRLFRIEND IS PERFECT.
OPEN YOUR EYES AND SEE THE TRUTH.

He felt a sickness and rage he had never experienced before. He felt betrayed and hollow inside.

Why?

Why had she professed her undying love?

Why had she spent all those months playacting something that didn't exist?

And what was she doing with Hammond Patterson?

His fury knew no bounds. He wanted to get on the next plane to L.A. and confront her.

But he couldn't; his grandfather was not expected to live much longer, and his grandmother needed him.

He was stuck in England, and there was nothing he could do about it.

CHAPTER FORTY-ONE

When Cruz Mendoza wasn't out causing mayhem on the high seas, he was a lazy son of a bitch, spending his days lolling by Sergei Zukov's pool in Acapulco, wearing nothing more than a skimpy man thong while entertaining hookers he'd picked up the night before at some dubious club in town. It made a pleasant change from life in his guarded compound in Somalia, where he always had to tread carefully, because he had many enemies intent on taking over his lucrative business.

Although only in his early forties, Cruz appeared to be much older. He was stocky and balding, with weather-beaten skin, two prominent gold front teeth, and a pronounced limp — the result of being shot in the thigh by an irate husband who'd caught him screwing his sixteen-year-old trophy wife. Cruz had gotten his revenge by persuading the sixteen-year-old to run off with him, then dumping her when he'd had enough.

Watching Cruz play was putting Sergei on edge. Cruz had insisted that everything was set, but the way Ina's brother was sitting around bothered him.

"Relax," Cruz told him. "We strike at the right moment. My contact on the yacht tells me everything, an' here in town my men wait for me to give 'em the word. We let the rich mother-fuckers get comfortable on their fuckin' yacht trip, then we move in when I say so. I've done this a hundred times, an' believe me, surprise always works."

"So there's no way you'll fuck it up?" Sergei growled.

"No, Sergei," Cruz retorted with a slight sneer, a sneer that Sergei did not appreciate. "I'm as dependable as takin' a daily shit."

Sergei knew that Ina's brother was a slippery son of a bitch. He wouldn't put it past him to try and pull something.

Then again, Cruz wasn't stupid; he must realize that to fuck with Sergei Zukov would be beyond dumb.

Sergei was impatient, but Cruz was confident that everything was on course.

Only time would tell.

CHAPTER FORTY-TWO

Aleksandr sat alone and thoughtful on the private deck outside the master suite, smoking a cigar. He was satisfied that the long-planned-for trip was finally under way. There had been a moment in time when he'd sensed that everything might fall apart after he and Bianca had exchanged heated words. She could be so headstrong and unpredictable — who knew *what* she might do? However, once she'd seen that he'd named the yacht after her, she'd melted exactly as he'd hoped she would, and here they were, everything on track.

Bianca was like a world-class racehorse, difficult to tame, but apart from the occasional incident — such as the inappropriate photos on the Internet — all was going well.

Unfortunately, his ongoing battle with his wife continued to heat up. What a difficult and spiteful woman Rushana had turned out to be. There had been affairs before — Aleksandr would be the first to admit that

268

he'd never been a faithful husband. But in the past, Rushana had chosen to ignore his infidelities. It wasn't until Bianca had entered his life, and his request for a divorce, that Rushana had turned into a vindictive bitch. She was getting everything she wanted financially, but it seemed that wasn't enough for her. Oh no, the fact that he was with a world-famous supermodel infuriated her beyond belief. Rushana was desperate to see him single and alone, pining for the family he'd once had.

Bianca's latest escapade had only fueled the fire, giving Rushana some powerful new ammunition. "I will not have my daughters in the company of such a prostitute," she'd screamed at his lawyers, along with other insults. "Until Aleksandr stops being with that tramp, there will be no divorce. And I will not allow him to see our children."

It was not a happy situation, although he was sure that once Rushana realized that he had no intention of leaving Bianca, she would be forced to give in.

Rushana's fury and jealousy had not changed his plans. He still intended to ask Bianca to be his wife, and if he had his way, by the end of the trip they would be engaged.

Drinks at five-thirty on the top deck. The sun slowly setting in the clear sky. Champagne and canapés being served on silver trays by

Mercedes and Renee, the two stewardesses. Den, the barman, standing attentively behind the bar. Soft Brazilian music wafting from hidden speakers.

Bianca made her entrance in a white, backless Valentino dress, Aleksandr close behind her in a long-sleeved black sweater and black pants.

Although Aleksandr was twenty years older than Bianca, they made a good-looking couple. A fact that did not escape Guy, who was on hand, supervising his staff. As entertainment director, Guy was very hands-on, always there to anticipate the boss's every need. This was the first time he'd worked for Aleksandr Kasianenko, but of course he knew who the man was. Who didn't? Before hooking up with Bianca, Aleksandr had managed to keep a low profile, but once they were together, his cover was blown — the words *billionaire businessman* and *Russian oligarch* were forever attached to his name.

Poor sod, Guy thought, watching the famous couple. *It has to be a real downer, everyone knowing all your crap.*

Guy had recently viewed the raunchy and uncensored images of Bianca on his laptop. He considered her to be a feisty little minx, and he couldn't help wondering how Aleksandr felt about his famous girlfriend flashing her pussy for all the world to see. The man was probably major pissed. Guy knew he would be if it was *his* boyfriend flashing his dick for public consumption.

Luca and Jeromy appeared on deck at exactly five-thirty, both in white suits. Checking them out, Guy considered them to be an odd couple. Luca was hot, Jeromy not. What hidden talents did the gorgeous blond superstar see in the tall, skinny Englishman?

Oh well, everyone to his own. Although Guy had to admit that he wouldn't say no to a run around the track with Luca Perez. He was some Latin hottie!

Mercedes sprung into action, offering them champagne or a drink of their choice, speaking to Luca in Spanish.

Guy didn't know what Captain Dickson was so concerned about. The women on the yacht were all so bloody beautiful — why would a pretty young Mexican girl threaten any of them? Mercedes was perfectly suitable for her job. She was also appropriately dressed in a smart nautical uniform, so no one would mistake her for anything other than a hardworking and eager-to-please member of the crew. He liked Renee and Den too. They were fellow Australians, and they both seemed to know what they were doing.

The next couple to arrive for cocktails was Ashley and Taye. Aleksandr stepped forward to greet them. As a football fanatic, he wanted to spend time speaking with Taye, picking his brain about the team he was in talks to buy. He beckoned Taye toward him, and the two men moved over to a quiet corner of the deck.

Ashley immediately zeroed in on Luca. "I can't believe we've never met before," she enthused. "You being with Jeromy and all, and me being Jeromy's partner. It's so lovely to finally meet you. I'm a big fan."

Cliff and Lori approached just in time for Lori to overhear Ashley's "I'm a big fan."

Here we go again, Lori thought. *Everyone's a big fan of everyone else. What a cluster fuck!*

"Luca," Cliff exclaimed. "I was making a movie in Puerto Rico last year, an' I managed to catch your concert. That was some wild performance."

Please don't say it, Lori silently begged. *Please, please, please!*

"I'm a big fan," Cliff added.

Shit! Lori thought. *You too.*

"Oh, and this is Lori," Cliff continued, introducing her as if she was some kind of an afterthought.

"Lori an' me, we're old friends," Luca said, winking at her in a knowing way like he totally got it. "Isn't that right, *cariño?*"

"You two know each other?" Cliff said, a look of puzzlement on his face.

"We go way back," Luca explained. "We were hangin' out by the pool today, catching up."

Lori experienced a small shiver of triumph.

She wasn't just an appendage on Cliff Baxter's arm; she was a person in her own right.

At which point Ashley and her cascade of blond curls moved in big-time, grabbing Cliff by the arm and whisking him away.

"Thanks," Lori muttered to Luca, who patted her on the arm and said, "I get it, sweet thing. Been there. Done that. You should know that when I was first married to Suga, nobody knew who the hell I was. I was simply the pretty boy in the background, and unless I was attached to Suga's arm, nobody gave a fast shit."

"Then you totally understand," Lori said, relieved that at least someone was aware of exactly how she felt.

"You bet I do," Luca said. "Don't sweat it, *bonita*. We're all here to have fun and relax. You're one of us now. Enjoy."

"Enjoy what?" Bianca said, creeping up behind them.

"Everything!" Luca exclaimed, indicating the sunset. "This is spectacular."

"We aim to please," Bianca said with a Cheshire cat grin.

It is spectacular, she thought, looking around and taking everything in. *It's way over the top, and I love it!*

One thing about Aleksandr: he did not disappoint. He was a man of style, and she was looking forward to seven days of utter bliss.

■ ■ ■ ■

Meanwhile, down in their stateroom, Hammond was taking his fury out on Sierra.

"WHAT THE FUCK!" he screamed at her. "You tell me what that loser bastard is doing on this trip?"

Sierra knew better than to answer him. She merely listened to him rant on about how much he hated Flynn Hudson.

"He's nothing but a low-life scumbag!" Hammond yelled. "Why is he here? How did this happen? Why didn't you get a list of guests?" He paused to take a breath. "You know something? You're useless. You probably *wanted* the son of a bitch here, the loser you used to fuck. How I could touch you after you'd had his cock inside you is beyond me." Another pause. "Let's not forget you were damaged goods and I fucking *saved* you. I've given you a life you can be proud of, and *this* is how you repay me?"

Sierra watched him closely. His face was red with fury; his eyes were bulging. He was acting like a raving lunatic and blaming her for Flynn being aboard.

She chose to remain silent. She chose to close her mind to the broken heart she'd suffered when Flynn had betrayed her. It was all too painful to remember.

Fifteen Years Earlier

Just like that Flynn stopped calling. Sierra couldn't understand why until she received a FedEx envelope marked high priority. She opened the envelope and there they were — six graphic photos of Flynn with six different girls.

At first she couldn't believe it, but after studying the photos, she had no choice but to accept the worst. There was a typed note enclosed.

STOP BELIEVING YOUR SO-CALLED BOYFRIEND IS PERFECT.
OPEN YOUR EYES AND SEE THE TRUTH.

A week later she realized she was pregnant. Heartbroken and alone, she confided everything to Hammond Patterson, who had been coming around ever since Flynn left. Hammond had told her that Flynn had asked him to look out for her. At first she'd been surprised, for she'd not realized that Flynn and Hammond were at all close. But Hammond had turned out to be the rock she'd needed to lean on; he was there for her in every way. He even offered to pay for an abortion, insisting it was the right thing for her to do.

She'd declined his offer, but he'd persuaded her to go to a party with him that night. At the party they'd both had too much to drink — especially Hammond — and while he was driving her home in his newly acquired Ferrari (a present from his adoring mother), he'd started coming on to her. One hand on the steering wheel, the other groping her breasts and between her legs.

She had never considered Hammond anything other than a friend, and his sudden attack shocked and upset her. She slapped his hand away, but he was determined.

Neither of them saw the oncoming car. Neither of them realized the danger. The rest was a blur as the Ferrari hit the oncoming car and immediately overturned, throwing Sierra out.

She suffered a broken pelvis and lost the baby.

Hammond suffered a damaged ego and walked away without a scratch.

Rumors abounded, and it wasn't long before the whispers on campus were that Sierra had been pregnant with Hammond's baby. Hammond said nothing to deny it; in fact, he promoted the story.

Still in the U.K., Flynn heard the gossip and that was it for him. By the time he returned to the States, Sierra had dropped out of college and was back in New York with her parents.

Flynn and Sierra never spoke again.

CHAPTER FORTY-THREE

Sierra and Hammond arrived at the cocktail gathering shortly before it ended, due to the fact that Hammond could not seem to stop himself from spewing venom about Flynn and how he hated him, and questioning why he was on this supposedly exclusive trip.

Sierra had continued to remain silent while her husband paced up and down venting his fury, although she was somewhat confused as to why Hammond was so angry. Hadn't he and Flynn been friends, even roommates, at one time? Wasn't he the one that Flynn had asked to watch out for her? Was his anger due to the fact that Flynn had treated her so shabbily? And if so, why was he taking it out on her?

It didn't make sense. She was the one who should be upset, not Hammond.

When they finally left their stateroom and joined the others, Sierra made sure she had no contact with Flynn whatsoever. She stayed by Hammond's side playing her role of good wife, although her stomach was churning and she did not dare to glance in Flynn's direction.

Not that she wanted to. He was the man who'd broken her heart into a thousand little pieces, and she could never forgive him for that.

After the car accident and the loss of her baby, she'd spent time traveling across Europe visiting relatives, finally returning to her family in New York, where she'd taken up social work, counseling young victims of rape and abuse. It was hard work, but she found it to be quite fulfilling. It was exactly what she needed.

Eventually she'd moved out of her parents' home and settled into an apartment with a girl she worked with. Soon she'd started dating sporadically — nothing serious — until one day she'd run into Hammond, now an up-and-coming lawyer with big political aspirations, at a fund-raiser.

At first he'd complained that he'd tried to contact her and she'd never returned his calls. Then he'd proceeded to court her in a way she'd found hard to resist. He'd been so damn charming, honest and committed to doing all kinds of worthwhile work, which really impressed her. No longer the drunken horny student who'd been responsible for their horrific car accident, he seemed like a changed man with a definite purpose in life, and although she didn't love him in the way she'd once loved Flynn, he'd finally worn her down, and she'd said yes to his marriage proposal. "Together we can change the world," he'd promised, and naïvely she'd believed him.

They were married in Connecticut at her family's house. It was a lavish wedding, exactly the way Hammond wanted it. Her parents had influential friends, and they all turned out; so did his family. Hammond used the occasion to cement future connections.

It took a year or so before she realized she'd made a horrible mistake. By that time it was too late. She was Hammond's wife, a major political asset. And one thing she knew for sure: he would never let her go.

"Ladies and gentlemen, dinner is served," Guy announced. He had heard that very line spoken in a series of old movies and he thought it sounded perfect. It gave him the personality and identity he imagined he deserved.

Guy hoped the guests not only noticed him, but depended on him for anything they might need, because being noticed and appreciated meant a much larger tip at the end of the voyage. He always made a bet in his own mind about who would turn out to be the most generous tipper. On this trip it would be Aleksandr, although one could never be

279

too sure.

Luca, perhaps — famous singers were known for their generosity. However, Luca's miserable English partner was probably a penny-pincher.

The politician? No. Politicians raised money, but they were all notoriously stingy when it came to parting with their own.

Well then, there was always the movie star, Mr. Cliff Baxter himself. Except Guy knew from past experience that movie stars expected everything for free in exchange for their illustrious presence.

Which left Taye Sherwin, a fine working-class lad who'd done well for himself. And Flynn, the journalist — a man who probably didn't believe in tipping.

Guy made a note to himself to drop the word — maybe to the movie star's girlfriend — that all guests were expected to tip the crew for services rendered.

One of the things Guy most enjoyed on a cruise was getting to know everyone's secrets, and on a boat, secrets were hard to hide. If he didn't find out for himself, the maids or other crew members were always quick to fill him in.

Life on a luxury yacht with guests aboard was very much an *Upstairs, Downstairs* experience. With this group, Guy expected mucho gossip.

"Dinner is served," Guy announced for the

second time, repeating his words loudly because nobody seemed to be moving; they were all having too good a time.

"Thanks, Guy," Bianca responded, waving her well-toned arms in the air. "Let's go, everyone. I'm starving!"

"What a fab table setting!" Ashley exclaimed as the guests approached an elegant oval table located on the middle deck. The table was decorated with a series of cut-glass vases holding white roses — Bianca's favorite. There was also exquisite crystal stemware, gleaming silver cutlery, black and silver dishes, and tall white candles in ornate holders. The result was a picture-perfect table.

"Please all find your place cards," Bianca announced, a tad mischievously. "I placed everyone myself, 'cause I'd like you all to get to know each other. I promise to change it up every day, so look out!"

"Trust you to mix it up," Luca said, admiring his old friend's style. "Who am *I* next to tonight?"

Bianca snapped her fingers, and Guy handed her a list.

"Looks like you've got Taye on one side and Ashley on the other," she said. "Hmm, Luca, a Sherwin sandwich. Think you can handle it?"

"You *know* I can," Luca boasted.

Jeromy scowled; he did not appreciate the

thought of Luca getting too friendly with the Sherwins. "And where might I be?" he asked snippily.

Bianca consulted her list; she'd spent quite some time deciding where to seat everyone. "Let me see," she said. "You're between two beautiful women. Sierra Patterson and Lori."

"Lori?" Jeromy questioned with a slight sneer, even though he knew full well who Lori was. She was the nobody redhead attached to the movie star.

Bianca chose to ignore Jeromy because he irritated her. Surely Luca could have come up with someone more exciting than this uptight turd? She turned to Cliff Baxter. "You're sitting next to me," she said warmly. "And I expect you to tell me exactly what it's like being labeled the Sexiest Man Alive."

"Pure hell," Cliff responded with a self-deprecating grin. "Women throwing themselves at me. Guys too. It's a miracle I make it through the day."

"Ah, but I'm sure that somehow you manage," Bianca teased, licking her full lips.

"I try," Cliff said with a jaunty wink. "It's not easy."

"You're seated next to Flynn Hudson," Bianca said, turning to Sierra and taking her arm in a friendly fashion. "I thought you two might have things in common. Aleksandr says Flynn's a very smart journalist and writer, so I'm sure you'll find him interesting."

"Really," Sierra murmured, her heart skipping a beat.

"By the way," Bianca continued. "It's a pleasure to finally meet you — and your husband's charming."

Charming? Sierra thought. This woman should only know the truth.

"Yes," Bianca continued. "Aleksandr is quite a supporter. He thinks that Hammond has great potential to make big changes in America."

"Does he?" Sierra said, thinking how easy it was to fool people.

"Yes, he does, and Aleksandr is usually right."

"Good to know."

"So," Bianca said mischievously. "How would you feel about becoming the first lady?"

First lady indeed. Sierra swallowed hard. Thank God for the two Xanax she'd managed to take before leaving her cabin. The drugs had dulled her senses, leaving her in a dreamy state. Still, at the thought of sitting next to Flynn she felt her heart accelerate, and a sweep of total panic overcame her.

Stay calm! a voice screamed in her head. *Do not lose control. You can do it.*

Can I?

Can I?

Yes, you can.

Jeromy shot Lori a patronizing look. Why did he have to get seated next to the only nonentity on the boat? Would he be forced to talk to her? A word or two simply to be polite; after that she was on her own.

"How are you, dear?" he sniffed.

"I'm fine," Lori replied, thinking that it was just her luck to get stuck with Luca's uptight English boyfriend. "And you?"

"Perfect."

"Lucky you," she drawled, aware that he was as unthrilled to be sitting next to her as she was to him.

"Excuse me?" Jeromy said, not appreciating her tone.

"Well, *perfect* kind of says it all."

Jeromy's back stiffened. Was this girl screwing with him? Big mistake if she was.

"I was hoping I'd be next to you," Ashley said, leaning in to Cliff as she took her seat beside him.

"You were?" Cliff said, taking in her curvy blondness. "In that case, I'll try my best not to disappoint."

"Oh, you don't have to try," Ashley said, fluttering her fake lashes. "Just looking at you is enough for me."

Shit! Cliff thought. A boatload of interest-

284

ing people, and I get the starry-eyed fan.

"I've seen all your movies," Ashley continued, twirling a strand of her long blond hair through her fingers. "My mum used to take me when I was little. She had a *huge* crush on you."

"Did she, now?"

"Well . . . even though I was only ten, I did too," Ashley admitted coyly.

"That's flattering," Cliff said smoothly.

"I still do," Ashley said, adding a quick "But don't tell my husband. He's dead jealous."

Fuck! Cliff thought. *Where's Lori when I need her?*

Glancing down the table, Aleksandr was pleased to see his guests having an engaging time. The first course — a lobster and crab salad — was being served, and the finest of wines were flowing. He stared at Bianca seated at the other end of the table. She looked so staggeringly beautiful, her dark skin gleaming in the flickering candlelight, her green eyes flashing as she spoke with Flynn.

Aleksandr was satisfied that he had captured a prize worth having. Bianca might be famous, but being with her was worth all the drama his wife was busy creating. Soon he would be free of Rushana, and then Bianca would be totally his.

Watching her, he suddenly experienced a strong surge of sexual desire. Xuan was seated on his left, Hammond Patterson on his right, and they were having a spirited conversation across him.

Aleksandr moved his chair aside and stood up. "Excuse me for a few moments," he said. "I'll be right back." He headed straight for Bianca. "I need to show you something," he said, leaning down and whispering in her ear.

"What?" she responded.

"I need to show you now."

"Now?" Bianca said, somewhat bemused.

"Now," Aleksandr stated firmly.

Bianca rose from the table. "Two minutes," she said to her guests.

Aleksandr took her hand and led her along the side of the yacht to where it was dark and deserted, the only sound the sea lapping against the stern.

"Tell me," Bianca said. "Is something the matter?"

"Not unless you consider this something," Aleksandr said, jamming her hand against the bulge in his pants.

Bianca gave a low throaty chuckle. "Oh my!" She sighed, getting excited at the thought of what was to come. "You're kidding. In the middle of dinner?"

"Are you wearing panties?"

"As if I could in this dress . . ."

Aleksandr hurriedly unzipped, grunted, and grabbed the front of her thighs, pushing her dress up high.

She leaned back against the boat railings and lifted her long slender legs, wrapping them tightly around his waist.

Without hesitation he plunged deep inside her, and after several vigorous thrusts, he was done.

"Wow!" Bianca exclaimed as they disengaged. "What's up with *you*?"

"You didn't like it?"

"Oh, you *know* I liked it."

"I will not neglect you," Aleksandr promised, his voice a deep dark whisper. "Later I will suck your pussy like it's never been sucked before. Only right now, my dear, we have guests to attend to."

"Yes, *sir*," Bianca said obediently, deciding that Aleksandr was the sexiest man she'd ever encountered, and there had been many.

Sierra took a long deep breath. Even though they were sitting next to each other, she had not turned in Flynn's direction, and he had not acknowledged her. However, with Bianca away from the table, she felt forced to say something. After all, what had happened between them was old news, many years had passed, and Flynn had obviously never cared. It had all been a game to him. Just another conquest.

Maybe he didn't even remember her.

She decided on a light approach. Let him see that the way he'd treated her had not affected her one little bit.

"Flynn?" she said. *Keep it light. Keep it casual.* "It is you, isn't it?"

CHAPTER FORTY-FOUR

The staff cabins on the *Bianca* were quite compact, with two bunk beds in each and a communal bathroom for every three cabins to share. There was no privacy as such, which pissed off Mercedes, because she had things to do. She was sharing with the other stewardess, Renee, a tall Australian girl who had a dark blond ponytail, long legs, and horse teeth. Renee had only been on one cruise before; she'd gotten the job because her uncle had once played rugby with Guy, and her uncle had called in a favor.

"You take the top bunk," Mercedes ordered when they'd first arrived.

Renee, a somewhat timid girl, bowed down to whatever Mercedes wanted.

This suited Mercedes fine. She liked taking the boss position, and it was good to know that Renee was no threat to what she had to accomplish. And what she had to accomplish was something she'd done many times before.

Seduce the enemy.

And who was the enemy?

Kyril, Aleksandr Kasianenko's security guard.

The burly Russian was a challenge, and Mercedes was always up for a challenge. She'd learned early on that most men were easy as shit. Offer them a blow job, a fuck, a walk on the wild side, and if they didn't think it was a trap, they were all in. Even the married ones. *Especially* the married ones.

It hadn't taken Mercedes long to check Kyril out. He had his own communication room, and direct contact with Aleksandr. It seemed Aleksandr had wished to keep this trip low-key, so his security was not as stringent as it probably was on land.

It amazed Mercedes that however powerful and important people were, they always operated under the illusion that vacations were safe havens.

Crap. Vacations were the best time to strike. Everyone lying around relaxed and happy, more concerned about their suntans than anything else. Too much food, too much wine — it was all the perfect recipe for a short sharp strike, which was exactly what Cruz and his team excelled at. Take the vessel over, demand a large ransom, then as soon as it was paid, get out fast.

Yes, Cruz certainly knew what he was doing. Over the last few years he'd become quite a legend in the piracy business.

Mercedes had been working alongside him since she was eight. She was now twenty-two, and a key member of his team. The inside girl. The girl nobody ever suspected. And that's because she was good at what she did. Very good.

After serving cocktails and canapés, Mercedes had told Renee to cover for her while she slipped down to their cabin. "I have a little tummy problem," she informed Renee, who was as gullible as a virgin locked in a hotel room with a sailor on shore leave. "Keep 'em happy. I'll be quick."

"What about Guy?" Renee worried. "He won't be pleased if you're missing."

"Don't worry about Guy. He'll never notice I'm gone. An' if he does, tell him I'm checkin' on the table."

Once she got down to their cabin, Mercedes pulled out her iPad from under her mattress and sent Cruz an informative e-mail about activities on the yacht, plus a crudely drawn map of the layout.

Cruz was a stickler for details; he required information about the crew, the guests, every move they made, and it was up to her to supply it.

When she was done, she erased her message, and hurried back to tend to the esteemed guests.

Esteemed guests, my fine Mexican ass, she thought. *The women are all whores fucking men for their money. While the men are pathetic assholes.*

Mercedes did not have a very positive view of the human race, which was hardly surprising considering the life she'd led. Her mother had died in childbirth, leaving her to be raised by a series of her papa's conquests — women who came and went on a regular basis, most of them prostitutes. Cruz had put her to work at the age of eight, picking the pockets of tourists in Mexico City. It was more rewarding than school any day, and she'd soon become the best pickpocket in town. Realizing his young daughter's potential, Cruz had started using her for other jobs — after all, who better than a child to gain entry to his burglary jobs? His kid could slide through any open window, however small — and doggie doors were no problem either.

A day after Mercedes celebrated her twelfth birthday, Cruz was arrested and sent to prison. Mercedes found herself dumped into foster care. Not prepared to be the victim of some horny old foster dad, she'd run away and survived the streets, honing her criminal skills, until eventually she hooked up with a twenty-year-old man who'd thought she was sixteen. They'd taken up residence in an abandoned bus outside Mexico City, and two abortions later she'd dumped her boyfriend and was waiting patiently outside the prison gates the day Cruz was released. She was fifteen.

Cruz had learned plenty in prison — he considered his time in the joint an education. Number one on his list of things to do when he got out was to leave Mexico.

Taking his kid with him hadn't factored into his plans, but there she was, loyal as ever. He'd felt obliged to organize forged papers for the two of them, and they'd taken off for Somalia to meet up with a Somalian man Cruz had formed a strong connection with in prison.

And so Cruz's adventures in piracy had begun, with Mercedes right along for the ride.

CHAPTER FORTY-FIVE

Goddamn it, Flynn thought. *What was he supposed to do? What was he supposed to say?* The love of his life was sitting next to him and what the fuck . . .

"Hey, Sierra," he said, making out as if he'd only just noticed her. "Yeah, of course it's me. Long time no see."

Casual enough? Jesus Christ. Talk about reverting to my teenage years.

"Yes, it has been a long time," she replied, turning to him with a fixed smile. "I wasn't sure . . ."

"Do I look *that* different?" he said, keeping it cool.

"No . . . I . . . uh . . ." she stammered, lost for words.

"You what?"

"Nothing."

"You and old Ham," he said, clearing his throat. "Who'd've thought?"

"I know," she murmured, taking a hearty gulp of wine, and then holding on to her glass so tightly that she hoped it wouldn't break.

"I was kind of surprised when I heard."

Really, Flynn. Surprised? Did you just imagine I'd vanish off the face of the earth once you were done with me?

They lapsed into an uncomfortable silence.

He hasn't changed, Sierra thought. *He's still Flynn.* So handsome, with the ice-blue eyes she remembered so well. No longer a boy, he now was a man with lines on his face that revealed traces of a life lived. His hair was longer. The stubble on his chin was new — or perhaps not.

How was she to know? He was a stranger.

A stranger whose baby had grown inside her for a few short weeks. And he'd never known about the baby. How sad was *that?*

"Are you and uh . . . Xuan . . . married?" she asked, breaking the strained silence.

The moment she'd asked the question, she could've kicked herself. Why ask something so dumb? What did she care if he was married or not?

I do care, a voice screamed in her head. *I care because I still love him.*

Oh, for God's sake! You do not.

Yes, I do.

Stop thinking that way.

"Not married," Flynn said, scrutinizing her beautiful face. Was she happy? She didn't look it. Her cheeks were flushed, her eyes

295

seemed empty. And she was slurring her words ever so slightly. Was she drinking too much? Way back, one shot of anything was her limit, but now she was gulping wine like it was going out of style.

"Why not?" she managed, continuing to ask questions she didn't want to hear come out of her mouth.

Flynn shrugged. *Why not? Because you screwed up my head when it came to women. You made it impossible for me to trust in any relationship. You ruined me, Sierra. You fucking ruined me.*

"Dunno," he answered vaguely. "It's just one of those things."

"Well," she said, wishing she could close her eyes and drift off into a deep sleep and not have to deal with this. "She seems lovely."

"She is," Flynn said.

And to their relief, Bianca returned to the table, a smile on her lips as she grabbed her wineglass and took a long, lingering sip. "Did I miss anything?" she asked playfully.

"Nothing," Flynn said quickly. "Nothing at all."

After his brief and irritating few words with Lori, Jeromy turned his full attention toward Sierra Patterson. She was a beautiful and stylish woman, and rumors abounded that one day in the not-too-distant future, her husband, Hammond, might make a run for

296

president of the United States. And of course, if he did, the very serene and lovely Sierra would be by his side. So she was definitely someone on top of Jeromy's "get to know" list.

He turned to her with an ingratiating smile, exhibiting his imperfect English teeth. "Tell me, Mrs. Patterson," he said, all smarm and charm, "have you ever visited our fair city?"

Dazed and confused by her conversation with Flynn, Sierra had no desire to talk to anyone. "Excuse me?" she said politely.

Jeromy repeated his question.

"Your fair what?" she asked, still thinking about Flynn.

"London, England," Jeromy said, a tad sharply. *Why wasn't she paying him more attention? Wasn't he good enough for her?*

"Oh, are you English?" she inquired, attempting to rally.

Surely his clipped and very proper accent had given her a clue? The woman seemed somewhat out of it.

"Born and bred," he informed her. And then in case she hadn't realized that he and Luca were a couple, he quickly added, "Luca and I first met in London two years ago. We've been together ever since."

"That's nice," Sierra answered vaguely. "Is Luca here?"

Good God! Was the woman drunk? Or simply dense?

"Sitting right across from us," he said, indicating Luca, who was in the middle of an animated conversation with Taye.

"Ah, yes," Sierra murmured, signaling a stewardess to refill her wineglass.

Hardly Jackie Kennedy, Jeromy thought. *Why am I even bothering? And what the hell does Luca find so interesting about Taye Sherwin?*

Since Jeromy Milton-Gold had an obvious stick up his ass, Lori decided to work her charms on Hammond Patterson. He seemed like a friendly enough dude with his neat haircut and honest brown eyes. She needed to get something going, because Ashley, the footballer's wife, was busy fawning all over Cliff.

All Lori knew about Hammond Patterson was that he was a senator, and his wife was some kind of do-gooder socialite fashion plate. But so what? Since moving in with Cliff, Lori realized she could talk to anyone and be accepted — it was one of the main perks of being a very famous movie star's number-one girlfriend. Might as well take advantage of it while she could.

"I don't know much about politics," she said brightly, attracting Hammond's attention. "But I do know that you've got the look."

"And what look would that be?" Hammond asked, his eyes sliding down to take in his dinner partner's cleavage.

"You know," Lori said with a flirty smile, "handsome. Trustworthy. The American public totally gets off on a handsome candidate. If Cliff ran, they'd vote for him tomorrow."

"I'm not sure whether I should be insulted or flattered," Hammond said, liking what he saw. And what he saw was young and pretty with nice firm tits. He had an insatiable craving for youthful flesh. It always turned him on — it was his addiction.

"Try flattered," Lori said, noting that he was easy prey. "Because let's call it like it is, Senator: you *are* a very good-looking man. But I'm sure your wife must tell you that all the time."

"Ah, my wife . . ." Hammond said, letting the words hang in the air.

"She's beautiful," Lori remarked.

"And so are you, my dear," Hammond said, suppressing an urge to reach out and touch her tender flesh, maybe even stroke her tempting red hair.

"It's all an illusion," Lori said modestly.

"Some illusion," Hammond said, ogling her breasts.

"And they're real, too," she murmured, encouraging him.

"I'm so sorry," he said, raising his eyes. "Was I staring?"

"Only a little," she said with a bold smile.

"However, I never said I minded."

And while Lori and Hammond were embarking on a flirtatious journey, Xuan and Aleksandr were involved in a deep discussion about Russian politics and the fall of the Soviet Union in the early nineties.

"Without that happening, you would never have amassed the fortune you have today," Xuan pointed out.

"Maybe. Maybe not," Aleksandr countered. "It's all relative."

"Tell that to the people who lost everything."

"Have you ever been to Russia?" Aleksandr asked, intrigued by this opinionated and quite smart Asian woman. His old friend Flynn had picked well.

"Once," Xuan replied. "I was researching a story on a Russian pop singer, supposedly your version of Lady Gaga. We walked through Red Square in Moscow accompanied by a camera crew and her army of bodyguards."

"Ah, you must mean Masha," Aleksandr said. "She is quite the personality."

"Personality or not, her bodyguards shoved and threw people out of the way as if they were garbage. And no one objected. No one complained. It was as if they were resigned to the fact that being treated like shit was perfectly okay. I didn't like seeing that."

"In Russia, people know their place."

"You mean people without money and status."

Aleksandr shrugged. "Never judge a country until you have lived there."

"I prefer not to."

"Not to what?"

"Live there."

"I'm not sure I was inviting you," Aleksandr said, quite amused.

"And if you were," Xuan retorted, "I'm not sure I would accept your invitation."

Later, when most of the guests had gotten to know each other, liqueurs, coffee, and dessert were served on the upper deck.

Partners reunited under the starry sky. Bianca sat on Aleksandr's lap, rubbing the back of his neck, thinking of the love they would make later, and reveling in this amazing trip that was all in her honor.

"Cliff Baxter is *such* a nice guy," Ashley confided to Taye, still tingling with the pleasure of sitting next to the movie star.

"Yeah, so's that Luca bloke," Taye responded. "Knows a lot about sport, an' y'know somethin' — he doesn't come across as gay at all."

"But he's with Jeromy," Ashley said, glancing across the deck to see who Cliff was speaking to.

"So are you," Taye pointed out.

"I'm in *business* with Jeromy," Ashley insisted. "I'm not *sleeping* with him."

"That's a relief," Taye joked.

"Anyway, you know what?"

"What?"

"I've been thinking that it's about time I branched out on my own."

"C'*mon,* toots," Taye groaned. "I'm not puttin' up *more* money."

"Why not?" Ashley said, bristling. "Don't you think I'm worth it?"

Tread carefully, Taye warned himself. *If you want to get laid tonight, be mindful of what you say.*

"Course you are, sweetheart," he assured her. "You're worth every penny in my pocket."

"Then can I do it?"

"I can't give you an answer now. We gotta figure it out, talk to my business manager an' shit."

"But you're saying that you'll think about it?" she pressed.

"Sure, toots."

Ashley gave him a quick kiss on the cheek. "I have a feeling that Cliff Baxter fancies me," she said, preening.

"Why wouldn't he? You're a regular hot tamale."

"You think?" she said, going all coquettish on him.

"You heard it here first."

And yes, tonight he *would* get lucky, for Cliff Baxter had already done the groundwork for him.

Thanks, Mister Big Shot. I owe it all to you!

CHAPTER FORTY-SIX

Another spectacular morning. Clear blue skies, the Sea of Cortez calm and inviting, a light breeze wafting in the air.

Breakfast was laid out on the upper deck. Mercedes and Renee were standing by, ready to be of service. Den stood behind the bar, mimosas at the ready.

Lori was the first up, leaving Cliff snoring in their room. The Sexiest Man Alive indeed. Surely they meant the Loudest Snorer Alive?

Lori giggled to herself as she imagined the headline on the cover of *People* magazine. How many of Cliff's adoring fans would believe their icon was a major snorer? Not so many.

Lori remembered the first time she'd spent the night with Cliff. She'd been in shock at the noise he'd made. The sound emitting from his mouth was like a freight train rumbling through a station in tandem with a snorting pig. And when she'd mentioned it to him, he'd casually said, "You don't like the noise, stay out of the bedroom."

So she'd purchased extra-noise-blocking earplugs, and now she hardly noticed.

At this point in time she was filled with mixed emotions about Cliff. She resented the hell out of him for what he was about to do to her when they got back. On the other hand, she still had feelings for him. It was hard not to, because when he was nice, he was very, very nice. And there was no denying that they'd shared many wonderful times together.

Marriage would solve everything.

Fat chance. Cliff was the most vocal anti-marriage advocate on two legs.

Random thoughts. *I hate him. I love him.*

What was a girl to do?

Renee offered her coffee. Idly she watched the Australian girl fill her cup. *That could be me,* she thought. *In fact, it was me. Waitressing. Only not on a luxury yacht with a bunch of famous billionaires. More like in Vegas with a bunch of randy gamblers.*

"Morning."

Lori glanced up from her place at the breakfast table to see the Brit footballer, Taye. And what a hunky sight *he* was. Striped board shorts concealing a multitude of goodies, a sleeveless tee, glistening black skin, and arms with muscles that defied description.

Wow! Lori thought. *Sex on a stick. What a*

pleasant way to start the day.

"Any sign of my wife?" Taye inquired, helping himself to a plate of fruit from a long table where all kinds of breakfast choices were laid out.

"Haven't seen her," Lori said, still admiring his impressive physique while thinking that the magazine ads didn't do him justice. "I think I'm the first up."

"No," Taye boasted, sitting down next to her, "*I'm* the first up. Already worked out in the gym for half an hour, *and* had a dip in the pool. Forty lengths. Not bad."

"Not bad at all," Lori murmured as Mercedes poured him a glass of juice.

"You been in the gym here?" Taye inquired, thinking that she looked like the athletic type.

"Not yet."

"Try it. It's real high-tech. Lots of fine equipment."

"Sounds great."

"It is. Gets you all souped up for the day."

"I'll give it a shot tomorrow. Maybe I can persuade Cliff to join me."

"You won't regret it," Taye said, stretching his arms above his head, thinking that last night had been solid. Ashley had been as randy as he was, and they'd had a shitload of fun in bed, more than they'd had in a long time.

"Cliff is kind of lazy," Lori offered. "Although he does like to keep it all moving."

"Don't we all," Taye replied.

"I'll second that."

"So, Lori," Taye said, "what do *you* do? You a model or somethin'?"

"Actress, actually."

"Yeah? Have I seen you in anythin'?"

"Well, if you had, I hope you would've remembered," she answered, artfully dodging the question.

"We don't get out to the movies much," Taye admitted. "What with work, practice, appearances, commercials, an' the twins. They take up a ton of time an' energy."

"Twins!" Lori exclaimed. "That must be amazing."

"If you fancy goin' without sleep for a couple of years," he said ruefully. "Yeah, then it's freakin' amazin'."

"I'm sure it's worth it."

"Of course it is," he said with a wide grin. "Although I gotta tell you, they're two right little ravers. It's never dull around our house. Keeps me an' the missus in top shape."

"I can see that," Lori murmured, once again admiring his spectacular physique.

"Huh?"

"Well, you look . . . uh . . . fantastic."

"I bloody well try," he said, trying to ignore the fact that she seemed to be coming on to him. Ashley did not appreciate any woman flirting with him, so he was more than relieved when Luca put in an appearance.

Luca was enjoying himself. He'd been working hard all year on two new albums and a worldwide tour, and this short break was a welcome one before he continued his South American tour. He was impressed with the group Aleksandr had gathered. In fact, he was honored to be included.

Jeromy did not seem to be as impressed as he was. Jeromy was riding high on a major bitch-fest. He hadn't liked either of his dining companions the previous evening, whereas Luca had experienced a fine old time.

Lately, Jeromy was starting to get on his nerves. At the beginning of their relationship, things had been quite different. Luca had looked up to Jeromy as being someone who could teach him things, improve his mind, and protect him from the gay mafia who were jonesing to get a shot at him. With Jeromy — a respectable, cultured, older Englishman — as his partner, he'd believed he'd be out of reach. Not exactly on a pedestal, but hardly a boy to be trifled with.

So after bravely emerging from the closet, he'd fallen straight into a relationship with Jeromy. At the time, he'd thought it was the safest move to make, but lately he was experiencing doubts. Jeromy was not the man Luca had thought he was. He was way too promiscuous, and that side of him somewhat unnerved Luca, what with all the diseases out there. Jeromy was also a rabid social climber, and a caustic and sometimes cruel critic of people who he felt didn't live up to his impossible standards.

Luca, who was extremely easygoing, had finally come to realize that Jeromy Milton-Gold was a big snob — especially when it came to Suga. Luca adored his ex-wife; he would do anything for her. After all, it was Suga he had to thank for giving him the chance to have such a fantastic career. She'd discovered him, nurtured him, loved him, made sure she'd surrounded him with the best managers and producers in the business. And even after giving birth to his son, she'd let him go with never a cross word, no bitterness or ill will. Suga was a truly wonderful and selfless woman who genuinely cared about him.

But Jeromy didn't see it. Jeromy seemed to take great pleasure in putting her down. *Why is she so grossly fat? Her career is definitely over. She's the worst dresser I've ever seen. What's with that godawful hair? Can she even sing anymore?*

Jeromy's snide comments were endless, even though he knew Luca didn't appreciate hearing the disturbing and bitchy things he had to say about Suga.

As for Luca Junior, whenever the boy was around, Jeromy more or less ignored him. This hurt Luca a lot, because he adored his son, and he would have liked his partner to feel the same way.

"Hey," Taye said, greeting the singer.

"Hey back atcha, an' good morning, everyone," Luca responded. "I guess we're the early group."

"That we are," Lori said cheerfully. "Cliff was still asleep when I got up."

"Ashley too," Taye said, joining in. "That woman can sleep the day away."

Mercedes sprang into action, offering Luca coffee, tea, or juice.

He chose juice. "Well, isn't this a beautiful day," he exclaimed to his table companions. "How lucky are we?"

"I know," Lori agreed. "If paradise existed, this would be it."

"Very poetic," Luca said, grinning. "I think I feel a song coming on."

"Really?" Lori said.

"Just kidding," Luca said, recalling Jeromy's rant about Lori when they'd returned to their cabin the previous night. *Why the hell was I the one stuck next to that redheaded tramp? She's a nobody. Why should I even bother wasting my time? It was insulting.*

Luca actually liked Lori. He found her to be refreshing and pretty with her amazing red hair and great body. So what if she wasn't important or famous? Who cared?

Jeromy did, and that pissed Luca off.

■ ■ ■ ■

True to his promise the night before, Aleksandr had satisfied Bianca until she'd begged him to stop. Aleksandr could do more with his tongue then most men could do with a seven-inch erection.

Bianca luxuriated in bed when she finally awoke. How incredible it was to be away from it all. No phones (Aleksandr had insisted every one give up their cell phones when they'd boarded the yacht). No hovering paparazzi. No fashion fittings, photo shoots, branding meetings, or personal appearances. Just pure sheer nothing to do except nothing. She was in heaven.

Aleksandr was sitting out on their private terrace eating breakfast. Bianca slid her naked body from between the sheets and strolled out to join him.

His eyes took in every feline inch of her. "Exquisite," he observed.

"And it's all yours," she said, tossing back her blacker-than-night hair.

"To do with as I will."

"Ah, but you already have," Bianca said, licking her full lips.

"You make me want more," Aleksandr said, his voice a husky growl as he reached for her.

"Shouldn't we be joining our guests?" she ventured, taking a step back.

"They can wait. Come sit with me."

She moved closer and sat on his knee. He cupped her breasts with his large hands, caressing her nipples until she began sighing with pleasure.

"Shall I make you come?" he said. "Would you like that?"

"Only if you let me return the favor."

Aleksandr roared with laughter and stood up, tipping her off his knee.

"Later," he said. "You're right; we should be joining our guests."

"You are *such* a tit tease," she said, feigning indignation. "You're leaving me all revved up with nowhere to go."

"Take a shower and put on your bikini," Aleksandr commanded. "Today we go exploring."

"Exploring what?"

"You'll see."

On her way up to the top deck for breakfast, Ashley ran into Cliff. She had on a pink jumpsuit that showed plenty of cleavage, and her long blond hair was tied back in a jaunty ponytail.

"Oh my God, talking to you last night was such fun," she said, pouncing. "You're so down-to-earth and lovely."

"What did you expect?" Cliff asked, raising a caustic eyebrow.

"Well . . . uh . . . I thought, y'know, with

you being such a big star, that you might be full of yourself."

"I try not to be," Cliff said, faintly amused. "Lori keeps me grounded."

"Lori?" Ashley questioned.

"My girlfriend."

"Oh yes," Ashley said. "I forgot that you're with someone. I mean, in the magazines you're always referred to as being single, so . . ." She trailed off. She'd chosen to ignore the fact that he was with a girl, although this one was probably only temporary like all the rest she'd read about.

"You'd better not let Lori hear you say that," Cliff chided as they approached the breakfast deck. "She's very sensitive."

"Well, I can see that it must be difficult for her."

"She can handle it."

As if on cue, Lori jumped up to greet him, planting a kiss on his mouth, while throwing the blonde with the big tits a "keep off" look. Last night at dinner she'd observed Ashley draping herself all over Cliff. Poor Taye; he must have his hands full with his flirty wife. But not to worry, because Lori was going to make sure that Ashley didn't get anywhere near Cliff, not on her watch.

Besides, Ashley had the gorgeous footballer husband. Surely he was enough to keep her busy?

313

■ ■ ■ ■

By the time morning arrived, Flynn had a backache from hell. He'd elected to sleep on the couch, while Xuan had commandeered the comfortable double bed. "We'll take turns," she'd crisply informed him. "Tomorrow night you may have the bed."

He was grateful she'd agreed to go along with his plan that they present themselves as a couple. "I wouldn't ask if it didn't mean a lot to me," he'd assured her.

"It is interesting to see you so vulnerable for once," she'd observed. "This woman must have really hurt you."

"She did," he'd muttered.

So the couch it was. And since he was six-two, and the couch was somewhat shorter, it had not been a comfortable night. Plus his head was spinning thinking about Sierra.

He had imagined he was over her.

He had thought that if he ever saw her again, it would mean nothing.

Of course he was wrong.

Seeing her in person was not the same as seeing photos of her in magazines, the politician's stylish wife, so beautiful, so popular.

He remembered the shock he'd felt when he'd read about her and Hammond getting married. The love of his life had married his archnemesis, Hammond Patterson.

Really? How the hell had *that* happened?

Then he'd remembered the sickening photos someone had sent him of Sierra — in one of them she was in a compromising position with Hammond. *Jesus Christ.*

He'd burned the photos. Obliterated them.

Now here he was. Stuck on a yacht in the middle of the Sea of Cortez. And what he had to do was come up with a clever excuse to get himself off the boat.

Xuan was in the shower. She emerged with wet hair and a towel tied around her petite body, sarong style.

"You hungry?" he asked.

"I could be."

"Get dressed and we'll go for breakfast."

"You don't have to wait for me."

"That's okay," he said restlessly, prepared to hang out until she was ready.

He was *not* prepared to risk another one-on-one conversation with Sierra. And he certainly didn't want to run into Hammond. They'd barely spoken. A brief "How are you?" and that was it.

The thought of Hammond being in a position to make a run for the highest office in the land was the biggest joke of all time. How the hell had *that* happened?

"Turn your back while I dress," Xuan instructed.

He did as she asked, and started working on an excuse to get off the yacht.

■ ■ ■ ■

Hammond hit the breakfast deck, and immediately sat himself down next to Lori.

"You look very fresh this morning, my dear," he said. "All ready for a day of sunning?"

"I get too many freckles when I sunbathe," she explained.

"Nothing wrong with a freckle or two," Hammond said with a jovial chuckle and a quick peek at her breasts, perky in a pristine white T-shirt with no bra. He could see her nipples.

Man, Lori thought. *Like the song "It's Raining Men." And they're all wildly attractive. And I'm the only single woman on the boat apart from the Asian, and she's no competition. Too serious. And short. I am about to have major fun. A little light flirting for Cliff to observe might even change his mind about dumping me.*

"I guess us ladies can go topless when we lie out to sunbathe," Lori said, addressing the table, knowing full well that there was no way Ashley would like that.

"I don't think so," Ashley responded as expected.

"Why not?" Lori said, pushing it.

"Isn't that a decision best left to our hostess?" Ashley said, her tone quite icy.

"*I* think we should put it to a vote," Lori

said boldly. "What do *you* think, Senator? Tops on or off?"

"No objections from me," Hammond chuckled. "Off sounds like a fine plan."

"I'm always topless," Luca joked.

Before the conversation could continue, Aleksandr and Bianca appeared.

"Today we are taking a magical mystery tour on an uninhabited island," Aleksandr announced. "For all those who wish to come — and I hope that will be everyone — we gather at twelve noon. Be prepared."

CHAPTER FORTY-SEVEN

Twenty-four hours in, Mercedes already knew plenty. Observation was her strong suit. As a lowly stewardess she was invisible. Conversations took place and she heard it all. The senator was flirting with the redhead. The redhead was flirting with everyone. The Asian woman was an uptight bitch who considered herself smarter than all the other women aboard, and she was not sleeping with her boyfriend — who even Mercedes had to agree was quite a hunk — because one of the maids had informed her that he'd spent the night on the couch. Aleksandr and Bianca were fucking like rabbits, even getting it on in the middle of dinner. The footballer and his blond wife were doing it too. But not the senator and his wife, who was zonked out of her mind on an assortment of pills. Plus the senator was a screamer, berating his wife in private, while fawning over her in public. The gay boys were an odd couple. Luca Perez was a sweetheart, and the older guy was a sly fox.

And finally the movie star was just that — a dumb movie star.

So . . . in twenty-four hours, Mercedes had learned plenty about the passengers, all of which she'd reported to Cruz.

She kept a different eye on the mostly Australian crew, and she foresaw no problems there. Her roommate and fellow stewardess, Renee, was all teeth with an eager-to-please personality. Den, the barman, was no problem. Guy was all mouth and no balls. Captain Dickson was a nonentity — he'd fold as soon as Cruz and his men boarded.

Kyril presented her only problem. The burly Russian bodyguard was a hard nut to crack. She'd visited his command room on several occasions, ostensibly to take him trays of food, which he always rejected.

Kyril sat in a chair in front of an array of security monitors and barely moved. He was certainly not up for any light conversation, and trying to flirt with him had gotten her exactly nowhere.

What the hell? He had a dick, didn't he? And if *she* couldn't get it hard, who could?

Kyril was an imperative part of the plan. He was the only person aboard who could cause problems.

Cruz and his team planned to strike in a few days, so there was still time. She sensed that Kyril wasn't going to be easy, and if she couldn't divert him sexually . . . well . . .

319

drugs were her other alternative.

Fortunately, she'd come prepared. Horse tranquilizers. The only sure thing.

CHAPTER FORTY-EIGHT

"I will not be coming on the excursion," Sierra said, standing up to her husband for once.

"You haven't left our room all morning," Hammond pointed out, admiring himself in the bathroom mirror, making sure he'd combed his hair exactly the way it suited him when he appeared on TV. "What must everyone think?" he added churlishly.

"Who cares *what* they think?" Sierra replied, determined not to give in. "I have a bad migraine and I'm not moving. You'll have to go without me."

Hammond considered the possibilities. If Sierra came with him, he'd be forced to be nice to her in front of everyone and stay by her side. If Sierra didn't come, he'd be free to spend more time with the sexy redhead and the blonde with the big tits, not to mention Miss Supermodel herself with the fuck-me lips and insane body. Then there was always the Asian piece of pie. Yes, quite a tasty cornucopia of pussy.

Sierra not coming was really not so bad. After all, there was no press around, no photo opportunities, which meant who cared if she was with him or not?

"Fine," he said, tight-lipped as he emerged from the bathroom. "Have it your way. However, I do expect you to be up and dressed when I return. Headache or not, I refuse to allow you to miss dinner."

"Very well," Sierra responded.

Five minutes later he was gone and she could breathe again. His vitriol about Flynn had spilled over her like a never-ending gush of rancid oil. She'd listened, staying silent, until finally he'd run out of insults.

She'd lain awake most of the night, having not taken her usual sleeping pills, and in the morning she'd willed herself not to reach for the Xanax.

The truth was, she had no headache. She felt remarkably clearheaded for the first time in months.

Flynn Hudson. He was here on this yacht. And if not now, when would she ever have the chance to find out why he'd treated her the way he had? So callously. So cruelly and nastily. So unlike the Flynn she'd known, the man she'd given up her virginity to, the man she'd once loved with every fiber of her being.

Suddenly everything seemed very clear. If

an explanation was all she needed, then maybe she could reclaim her life and become the person she once was, not this pathetic shell of a woman who yearned for a love she could never have, a woman who lived in fear of a domineering and threatening husband.

Were Hammond's threats even real?

Who knew? He'd led her to believe that they were. But surely even *he* couldn't be such a monster.

Or could he?

It was something she might be forced to find out.

Lori was totally psyched. A visit to a mysterious deserted island — how rad was *that?*

Cliff, not so much. "If you don't mind, I think I'll sit this one out," he said. "I feel like finding a nice quiet corner and reading a script or two."

"Do you want me to stay with you?" Lori asked, although she was dying to explore the island.

"No, sweetie, you go," he said, throwing her a quizzical look. "Only you'd better watch out for the horny senator."

"Excuse me?" she said, startled.

"That randy bastard has had his eye on you ever since we got here."

"Who?" she asked, as if she didn't know.

"Aren't you listening? The senator, babe. Politicians got it goin' on. Ever since Clinton, they think they're all movie stars. Only don't forget that *I'm* the real deal. Okay?"

There were times when Cliff totally endeared himself to her, and this was one of them. He'd noticed! And he was — well — if not jealous, at least aware.

"Oh," Lori said, suppressing a smile. "I can handle him. JFK he's not."

Cliff laughed. Lori was such a good sport and so much fun to be with (not to mention the world-class blow jobs) — so much fun that he was seriously considering keeping her around for another year. Who needed the hassle of breaking in a new girlfriend when an esteemed senator seemed to get off on the one he already had? Lori was hot stuff, and she never pushed him on marriage or any of that crap.

"Go have a blast," he said, patting her on the ass. "I'm not going anywhere."

She turned around and planted a big fat kiss on his cheek. "I'll miss you," she said, genuinely meaning it.

He gave her one of his famous grins. "Try not to miss me too much."

"I'll try."

"Good girl."

"Oh, and while we're on the subject of flirting," she added, "do me a favor and steer clear of Miss Blonde Big Tits. Okay?"

"She's married!" Cliff objected.

"So's the senator."

"Get outta here," Cliff said, starting to laugh again. "The blonde's all talk and no blow. Besides, I prefer me a hot-blooded red-head."

"Hmm," Lori said, putting on a mock stern voice. "Let's make sure it stays that way."

"Yes, *ma'am!*"

"I have decided not to go," Jeromy said, pursing his thin lips.

"Why not?" Luca wanted to know.

"Because I am perfectly happy staying on the yacht and relaxing, thank you very much. I have no desire to start traipsing around some stupid island. It doesn't appeal to me."

"You're missing out," Luca said mildly.

"I think not."

Luca shrugged and gave up. Jeromy was not the outdoors type. Mr. Milton-Gold preferred indoor activities, with a martini clutched in his manicured hand and his body clad in an expensive designer outfit.

"If that's the way you want it, then I guess I'll see you later," Luca said, anxious to get going and join the others.

"You're still leaving, then?" Jeromy said, surprised and irritated that Luca didn't elect to stay with him.

"You bet your ass," Luca replied enthusiastically. "Wouldn't miss it."

Jeromy scowled. He didn't like the idea of Luca running off without him. Although the thought of sweating his way through some hideous deserted island was enough to make him stick to his original decision. This was supposed to be a leisure trip, not some screwed-up version of the TV show *Survivor*.

"Well," Jeromy said testily, making the most of an annoying situation, "try to enjoy yourself without me."

"Yeah," Luca said, looking forward to some time away from Jeromy. "I'll do that."

The *Bianca* had two luxurious tenders, each able to accommodate several crew members and eight guests.

The guests gathered, ready to disembark from the big yacht.

Guy, Renee, and Den were also on the trip, prepared to cater to the celebrity guests' every need. Guy had wanted Mercedes to come too, but when several guests had elected to stay on board, he'd had to leave someone behind to cater to them; reluctantly, he'd left Mercedes.

"You're in charge of seeing that the remaining guests have everything they need," he'd warned her. "I do not wish to hear one complaint."

"Got it covered, boss," Mercedes had said with a cheeky tilt of her chin.

"Do *not* call me boss," Guy admonished, not sure if he liked this girl or not. There was something about her he couldn't quite warm to. Maybe the captain was right, and she wasn't the perfect fit. "Mr. Guy will do nicely."

"Yes, *Mr.* Guy," she said, teetering on the edge of sarcasm.

"And don't forget to see if the captain would like you to bring him lunch," Guy said, frowning. He would not be hiring this one again. She was too fresh — and not in a physical way.

"I've got it covered, bo . . . uh, Mr. Guy."

Both tenders were loaded with supplies, including several bottles of champagne, soft drinks, snacks, and an elaborate picnic lunch.

"Where's your boyfriend?" Hammond asked as he followed Lori onto one of the tenders.

"He decided to stay on board and read," Lori said. "How about your wife? Is she coming with us?"

"Headache," Hammond answered shortly, admiring Lori's long tanned legs, no freckles in sight.

"Poor thing," Lori said, her eyes following Taye as he made his way down the ladder onto the boat, followed by Ashley, clad in some kind of flimsy leopard cover-up — which actually revealed more than it covered.

Bianca, Aleksandr, Luca, Xuan, and Flynn were already in the second tender.

As the two boats took off, Captain Dickson appeared at the side of the yacht and waved them on their way. "Have a wonderful day!" he shouted.

"We plan to!" Bianca shouted back.

And then they were off.

Cliff found a quiet corner on the top deck and settled in with a pile of scripts. A peaceful afternoon suited him just fine, since it wasn't often he had the luxury of spending time by himself. His life consisted of making movies, followed by traveling the world promoting them. There was no way he could estimate how many interviews he'd given over the last two decades, or how many photo sessions he'd posed for. Not that he was complaining, for the rewards were plentiful.

Still . . . a full afternoon where he didn't have to play Cliff Baxter, charming movie star, was sheer bliss.

Mercedes brought him an iced tea and jotted down his request for a light salad lunch.

"Will you be eating with the other guests?" she asked.

"I thought they'd all gone on the trip," Cliff replied.

"No. The senator's wife is still aboard. So is Luca Perez's companion."

"I'll stay where I am," Cliff decided, in no mood to be social.

"Yes, Mr. Baxter," Mercedes said, acting as the perfect little stewardess in her neat uniform, a practiced smile on her face.

One down, two to go. The senator's wife was still in her cabin, and Mercedes wasn't quite sure where Luca Perez's significant other was.

The truth was, she didn't much care for the gays. She considered being gay a waste of manpower, although she'd had an experience or two with girls. However, girl-on-girl action was different. Besides, Luca Perez was crazy hot, so what was he doing with some old douche who seemed to be about as much fun as a box of tampons?

With most of the guests gone, she planned on doing a quick sweep of their rooms to check out the jewelry and money stash. She'd already ascertained that the limey blonde was into diamonds, and that the footballer had several expensive watches. Nice. But the real prize would be in the main stateroom, where she'd already discovered a hidden safe.

No problem there, for among her many other talents, Mercedes knew how to crack a safe with the best of 'em.

As soon as the maids were safely out of the way, she slipped into the master suite and headed straight for the safe with her handy box of tools. Fifteen heart-stopping minutes later, she was in.

What a bonanza! A stack of cash. Papers — boring. And a small black jewel box containing the most exquisite ring she'd ever seen. A magnificent emerald surrounded by dozens of sparkling diamonds.

Mercedes almost salivated.

Oh yes, when the time came, she planned on cleaning up.

Why shouldn't she grab what she wanted? Cruz could do his thing, and she'd do hers. It was about time she seized the opportunity to make a killing and strike out by herself.

Yes, she had an agenda. No more Daddy's little helper.

Mercedes had her own plans.

CHAPTER FORTY-NINE

The deserted island was a magical place. A glorious oasis in the middle of the sea. White pristine sands, crystal-clear blue water, pockets of unusual rock formations, lush greenery, and groves of palm trees heading inland.

The captain had arranged to have a tour guide meet them on the island, and the Mexican man was waiting when they arrived.

"Wow!" Bianca exclaimed, jumping off the tender and running straight onto the sand, throwing off her T-shirt to reveal a barely-there orange bikini. "This is fanfuckin'tastic! And no hidden paparazzi. I'm in heaven!"

Aleksandr smiled. There was nothing he enjoyed more than watching Bianca indulge her childlike tendencies; he found it refreshing.

"C'mon, Ashley," Bianca called out. "Join me."

Ashley, who was gingerly stepping off the tender, trying not to get her Dolce sandals wet, nodded.

"This is like a friggin' dream," Taye said to Luca. "Jesus, man, it's a bloody long way from the old Elephant."

"You had an elephant?" Luca questioned, trying to keep his eyes away from Taye's fully stocked crotch.

"No way, man," Taye said, breaking up laughing. "The bleedin' Elephant an' Castle. That's the place I was born."

Luca was even more confused, but he shrugged it off as he helped Lori from the tender.

After checking out the view, Lori wished she'd brought her camera, because this was without a doubt the most stunning place she'd ever seen. Cliff should've come. He would've loved it.

Den, Renee, and several of the crew members were busy unloading the tenders, setting up umbrellas and giant beach towels and erecting a food and drink station while Guy supervised.

Manuel, the Mexican tour guide, watched in stoic bewilderment. Tourists. They never failed to dumbfound him with their endless extravagances. It was staggering the money they must have to throw away on nonessential things. When he'd been hired for this job, he'd been informed that these were very important people. They didn't look that important to him. The women were half naked, something that didn't seem to bother the men. He would be shamed if his wife or daughters ever exposed themselves in such a blatant fashion.

Guy approached him. "The guests will be eating lunch first," he instructed Manuel. "Then we'll start the island tour. Okay, mate?"

Manuel nodded, and walked a distance away, prepared to wait. He knew from experience that he was merely there to serve.

When Flynn realized that Sierra was not on the excursion, he was torn. Should he have stayed on the yacht?

For what? So she could practically ignore him again? Treat him like a total stranger?

He had a gnawing in his stomach that was bothering the hell out of him. Maybe it wasn't the smartest move in the world, although with Hammond on the island, surely this was the perfect opportunity to clear things up with Sierra once and for all?

He needed closure. Now that he'd seen her again, he knew in his heart that he had to find out why she'd betrayed him in such a callous fashion.

Goddammit! Now he was trapped on the island when he should've stayed on the yacht. And how was he supposed to get back? Swim?

No. The yacht was too far away, at least a ten-minute trip, and that was by tender.

What to do?

Perhaps feign some kind of stomach ailment? Act like a weakling and claim to be sick? Not the most manly of actions, but it appeared to be the only excuse he could come up with.

He glanced around at the activity. The girls were frolicking on the sand as if they were just out of grade school — all except Xuan, who'd sat herself down next to Aleksandr on one of the folding chairs and was busy engaging him in conversation. Hammond was leering at the girls — typical. Taye and Luca had plunged into the ocean.

Flynn approached Guy. "I don't want to make a big deal out of this," he said quietly. "Only I got a bad case of the runs, so I'm going to have to get back to the yacht."

"Don't fancy the bushes, eh?" Guy joked. Then, realizing he might have overstepped his mark, he hurriedly backtracked. "Sorry, mate," he said with a somber shake of his head. "Not so funny, huh?"

"Any chance of a ride?" Flynn inquired.

"Sure thing. We need more stuff from the mother ship. Hop aboard tender two; one of the boys'll take you."

"Thanks," Flynn said, thinking that he'd traveled through war zones, witnessed atrocities, interviewed terrorists, and yet now, at the thought of facing Sierra, he was more nervous than he'd ever been.

Could it get any better than this? Lori didn't think so. Here she was, a girl who'd had to struggle for most of her life, on a fabulous island in the middle of nowhere with one of the world's most famous supermodels, a mega football hero, a senator (who was definitely lusting after her), a superstar Latin singer, and a Russian billionaire.

It was all totally surreal. Nobody would believe it.

She could just imagine her mom's face if she could see her now. Oh lordy, Sherrine Walsh would have a fit.

Lori often wondered why her mom had never attempted to make contact. Yes, they'd been estranged for years, but surely when Sherrine had spotted her splashed all over the magazines on the arm of Cliff Baxter she'd been tempted to make amends? They'd parted on such bad terms. Sherrine had called her every vile word she could come up with. The word that had stung the most was *worthless*.

How worthless could she be? She was living with one of the biggest movie stars in the world. She was happy. For now. She had made something of her life.

Take that, Sherrine. Who's the worthless one now?

■ ■ ■ ■

"I can't believe that Cliff didn't come today," Ashley complained to Bianca.

Bianca raised an eyebrow. Why was Ashley bothered about Cliff Baxter when she had Taye to take care of her? After all, Bianca knew what Taye had to offer in the bedroom department, and it was all good. She shrugged and rolled over on the beach towel she'd spread out. "Movie stars dance to their own tune," she offered, allowing the silky white sand to run through her fingers. "And besides, he's no Ryan Gosling."

"He's Cliff Baxter," Ashley retorted, shocked that Bianca would even dare to compare him to Ryan Gosling. "And he's bloody gorgeous."

"Does Taye know you have the hots for him?" Bianca asked, amused.

"I so do not," Ashley said, suddenly blushing.

"Oh yes, you do," Bianca singsonged. "But that's okay — it's not as if you're about to fuck him."

Why not? Ashley wanted to say. *Just because I'm married doesn't mean I'm dead.*

"That's so rude," she managed. "He's just . . . I dunno . . . special."

"Ask Lori how special he is," Bianca said, jumping to her feet and stretching her lithe body. "They're all the same between the sheets. Given the chance, they're all up for a quick cheat, however faithful they claim to be."

"You don't mean that."

"Well . . ." Bianca mused. "I like to think that Aleksandr is different."

"So is Taye," Ashley said quickly.

Bianca shot her a disbelieving look. "*How* long have you been married?"

"Uh . . . almost seven years."

"And you're telling me that Taye has never slipped it to another woman?"

Ashley immediately flashed onto Taye's glaring indiscretion. The Page 3 bimbo with the gigantic tits. The story splashed all over the English tabloids. Did Bianca know? Had she read about it?

It was one time. One time only.

She *still* resented the crap out of him for doing it. How dare he.

How dare he!

She glanced along the beach, watching her husband in the surf with Cliff's redheaded slag.

Enough of that, thank you very much.

"Think I'll take a dip before lunch," she said, ignoring Bianca's question. "Coming?"

Hammond was making a concerted effort not to stare, but the scenery was too damn tempting. He wasn't admiring the palm trees and

337

the pure white sand — no, his full attention was directed straight at Lori, Bianca, and Ashley. Three magnificent women. Bianca, sleek and dark-skinned with a feline grace. Ashley, the definitive blond babe with big boobs and a jiggly ass. And Lori, his particular favorite — young, athletic, with that mass of flaming red hair. He found himself wondering if the pussy matched. She was wearing a white bikini, and when she emerged from the sea it appeared to be see-through. Her pert nipples were definitely on display.

He felt himself starting to get an erection, which wasn't the brightest of ideas considering he was sitting in a folding chair next to Aleksandr, and his linen shorts were not the best at concealing a burgeoning hard-on.

"The girls look good, huh?" Aleksandr said in his gruff voice.

Hammond wondered if Aleksandr had noticed his excitement. If he was on the yacht he could've gone to his cabin and masturbated, but no such luck. He was on an island, and any kind of release would have to wait.

"Very pretty," he agreed. "Especially your lady."

"She's a good girl," Aleksandr said, nodding his head like a benevolent father. "Never believe the things you might read or see on the Internet."

Cryptic, Hammond thought. Everyone knew Bianca had slept with the world. She was a tramp who happened to be a very famous tramp.

"Aleksandr," Hammond said, clearing his throat. "I was hoping we might get a moment to talk about my future plans. I have many things to discuss that could be most advantageous for both of us."

"I am sure," Aleksandr replied. "However, Senator, there is a time and a place for everything, and that time and place is not now."

"Of course," Hammond said, furious at being dismissed. *Russian peasant! Rich prick!* "Perhaps when we get back to the U.S. we should pick a time and a place," he added smoothly. "I'll make sure to slot you into my schedule anytime you find convenient."

Aleksandr nodded. "We'll see," he said in a noncommittal way.

Hammond felt his erection deflate. Even Lori couldn't coax it up now.

CHAPTER FIFTY

Back in New York, Eddie March was dealing with a crisis. A crisis that could blow up in everyone's face. He'd arrived at the office bright and early, just as he did every day. And there, sitting in reception, were Mr. and Mrs. Martin Byrne, parents of young Skylar, Hammond's latest intern.

"They've been waiting half an hour," the girl at reception had informed him. "They wanted to see Senator Patterson. I told them he's abroad, and besides, they didn't have an appointment. However, since they said it was extremely urgent, I suggested they wait for you."

Wait they did. And Eddie met with them, and suddenly it was all systems on red alert, for according to Martin Byrne, Senator Patterson had sexually molested his darling daughter.

Eddie was in shock. Christ! How could this be happening? Was it true? Would Hammond be stupid enough to do such a thing?

Eddie wasn't sure how to handle such a situation. Sex scandals involving politicians were hardly unusual. He immediately thought of John Edwards, Eliot Spitzer, Gary Hart, even ex-president Bill Clinton.

The scandal had ruined Edwards's political ambitions. Hart and Spitzer were long gone. Clinton had survived being impeached, but only just. And there were numerous others who'd fallen by the wayside because of their various sexual shenanigans.

Dammit! Eddie's initial reaction was, how could Hammond do this to Sierra? She was a beloved public figure, and a rare and special beauty. Why would Hammond even consider straying? And with a teenage intern at that.

Eddie thrust his mind into overdrive. What did these people want? Was it money? Headlines? An apology?

How could he help them and keep this under wraps?

There was only one way to find out.

CHAPTER FIFTY-ONE

On his return trip to the yacht, Flynn rehearsed exactly what he was going to say to Sierra when they finally came face-to-face.

Hey, remember me — the love of your life? Isn't that what you assured me I was?

Or:

How could you do what you did to me? Were you even aware that you smashed my heart into a thousand splintered fragments and I never got over you?

Or:

What the fuck are you doing with an asshole like Hammond Patterson? You're too smart to be with a man like him.

Hell, he didn't know what he'd say, if anything.

He'd left the island without telling anyone except Guy. No one would miss him; they were all too busy. Including Xuan, who seemed to have taken a real liking to Aleksandr. Too bad the Russian was under Bianca's spell, for Aleksandr and Xuan would've made an interesting couple.

The tender zoomed toward the yacht while Flynn desperately tried to clear his head. Thoughts were flying.

Am I making a big mistake?
Should I be doing this?
Why dredge up the past?
Hell, why not?

After a peaceful hour of solitude, Jeromy turned up, putting paid to Cliff's precious time alone.

"Ah." Jeromy sighed, flopping down on a nearby lounger. "And I thought *I* was the only smart one. Now I can see that great minds think alike."

Cliché alert, Cliff thought. *And who exactly is this?*

"Yeah," Cliff said amiably, lowering the script he was leafing through. "Just getting some reading done while I can."

"All work and no play," Jeromy admonished, wagging a bony forefinger.

Cliff frowned. *Another cliché. What a jerk.*

"It seems that everyone else has deserted us," Jeromy said, delighted to spend alone time with the movie star. Maybe Cliff Baxter could be a future client — what a coup *that* would be.

"True," Cliff said. "But reading scripts isn't really work, especially if they're worthwhile."

"I must say," Jeromy continued, warming

up, "I am an ardent admirer of your work. I'm sure I don't have to tell you that you are extremely popular in the old home country."

"Home country?" Cliff questioned, thinking that maybe he should've gone on the island trip after all.

"England," Jeromy said grandly. "Actually, I'm from London. I must assume you have graced us with your presence."

Yes, the man has just proved it: he is a walking, talking cliché.

"London's a great city," Cliff said. "I've had many a good time there. In fact, I have a cousin who lives in Sloane Square. You know it?"

"Know it!" Jeromy exclaimed. "My showroom is just around the corner."

"Showroom?"

"I hate to sound immodest," Jeromy said, sounding immodest. "However, I am regarded as one of the premier interior designers in London."

"Is that so?"

"It is."

"And you're on this cruise because of Aleksandr or Bianca?" Cliff asked, wondering how he could escape.

"Well," Jeromy lied. "They're both *dear* friends. And as I am sure you know, my significant other is Luca Perez. He and Bianca are almost like brother and sister."

"Got it," Cliff said. This was not the way

he'd planned on spending the afternoon.

Fortunately, Mercedes appeared, offering drinks and snacks.

Cliff took the opportunity to stand up and stretch. "Think I'll take a break," he said, moving toward the circular staircase. "See you later."

Jeromy frowned. Was it something he'd said? Had Cliff's nobody girlfriend complained about him because he hadn't paid her enough attention the previous evening?

Dammit! A wasted opportunity.

"Can I get you anything?" Mercedes asked.

Jeromy, in a fit of pique, ignored her. It was a big mistake.

Clarity. A feeling Sierra hadn't felt in a long time. No more drugs. Even though they were legal, they still dulled her senses, made the world a different place.

She'd once been a strong woman, opinionated and positive. Hammond had turned her into a shell of the woman she once was. Unfortunately she'd allowed it to happen, punishing herself for the past, beating herself up.

Seeing Flynn had been like standing under an icy cold shower.

Wake up, little girl. Fight the fight. Get over yourself.

It was incredible to feel so free. Just like that, the shackles were loosened and she could breathe again.

After getting dressed, she headed to one of the upper decks. It was a glorious day, just the kind of day on which to emerge from the frightening fog that had enveloped her for too many years.

Come at me with your threats, Hammond. Finally I am able to stand up to you.

And I will. Oh yes, I certainly will.

Being treated like a non ex is tent piece of shit did not thrill Mercedes. Jeromy whatever-his-dumb-name-was would pay for that. She'd already scoped out his stateroom and knew exactly what she would take when the time came. Watches, rings, gold chains, cash. Between him and the singer, there was plenty of loot. The senator and his wife, not so much. But the footballer kept a stack of cash hidden in his sock drawer, which amused her. Oh sure, like no thief worth their business would ever think of checking out a sock drawer.

Who was he hiding it from anyway? His wife, Miss Big Tits?

Mercedes was glad the guests were off the boat; it gave her time to snoop around. She was especially pleased that Guy wasn't present. He was such a fussy queen and always seemed to have his eye on her. Renee and Den were both okay — easily manipulated and a bit stupid, but if the circumstances were different, maybe they could've all been friends.

Australians. A different kind of species.

Flynn was sweating — unusual for him, but he was way out of his comfort zone.

What was he going to say to Sierra?

Small talk wouldn't cut it.

Shit! This was an impossible situation.

He decided to throw himself in the shower, get himself together, and approach Sierra in a cool and collected fashion.

Yeah, that was the way to do it.

At the door to his stateroom, he encountered one of the stewardesses emerging.

"Everything okay?" he asked. "I thought the maid was already in here."

"Checking out your wet bar," Mercedes replied, unfazed at nearly being caught.

And your computer.

And your cash.

Ninety-three dollars.

Is that all? Really?

"This place is run like a hotel," Flynn commented.

"Full service," Mercedes replied, thinking that under different circumstances she might go for this guy. He was tall and macho, a touch edgy — exactly the way she liked 'em. "Didn't you go on the island trip?"

"I did."

"Wasn't for you?" she asked, curious as to

why he was back so soon.

"Uh . . . do you know where the senator's wife might be?" Flynn said abruptly, not about to be questioned.

"I think I saw her go to the top deck," Mercedes replied, wondering what was up. "Can I get you anything?"

"No thanks," he said, entering his stateroom, slamming the door, and stripping off his clothes.

Sierra. She was all he could think about as he stood under the icy needles of the shower.

Sierra. It was definitely time they talked it out.

After her run-in with Flynn, Mercedes decided that now was the time to forge some kind of contact with Kyril. She'd already thoroughly checked out his cabin — nothing personal to discover except his spare weapon stash, which was formidable. Kyril was a man prepared. He'd even affixed a special lock on the door to his cabin — a lock Mercedes had had no problem picking. She was a talented girl. Safes, locks; she knew what she was doing.

After almost getting caught by the sexy journalist guy, she headed for the kitchen and had the chef prepare a special meal for Kyril, informing the chef that it was for Cliff Baxter, so it had better be great. What man could resist a juicy steak with french fries on the side? The smell alone was too tempting.

Unfortunately, Kyril turned out to be just such a man. When Mercedes knocked on the door to his security room carrying a tray, he waved her away with a ferocious glare.

Mercedes was not a girl to be dismissed; she persevered with the knocking until eventually he reluctantly opened the door.

"What?" he demanded, his Russian accent thick and heavy.

"Food," Mercedes replied cheerfully. "A big fat steak cooked specially for you. You need to eat, and I noticed you never do."

"No steak," Kyril said grumpily. "I no eat meat."

"Oh!" Mercedes exclaimed. "I didn't know that. Can I get you something else?"

Kyrill stared at her, perhaps noticing her for the first time. She'd unbuttoned her uniform to give him a hint of cleavage. God, he was ugly — such a big stony face with gapped yellow teeth and empty eyes.

"No," he said.

"Yes," she argued, noting he had a supply of bottled water and a stack of chocolate bars sitting on a shelf.

"No," he repeated. But she could see his empty eyes checking out her cleavage.

Yes. He would soon come around. They always did.

CHAPTER FIFTY-TWO

A tempting lunch was laid out on folding tables and served on the endless stretch of golden beach. Giant shrimp and succulent lobster dripping in melted butter, sumptuous salads, an array of delicious cold cuts, and deviled eggs with a healthy dollop of caviar atop. All the while the champagne and sangria flowed as the sun blazed down. But not to worry, for canvas covers were erected to shield the privileged travelers from the burning sun.

Renee and Den worked full out making sure everything ran smoothly, while Guy supervised.

Bianca lolled at Aleksandr's feet, running her hand casually up and down his leg, murmuring about how this trip couldn't get any better.

Xuan sat with Ashley, Taye, and Luca. Their conversation was lightweight, mostly about music and movies. Earlier Xuan had moved away from Aleksandr as soon as Bianca laid claim. It surprised her that a man as intelligent as Aleksandr would be with such a woman. However, Xuan was wise enough to realize that every man had his weaknesses, even Flynn, usually so strong and dedicated. Yet on this trip he'd lost it over some married woman, and that wasn't at all like the Flynn she knew. She'd noticed his absence, and assumed he'd returned to the yacht. Xuan had learned at an early age never to let your feelings rule your heart. It was something she never did.

Hammond suggested to Lori that since both their partners had elected not to come, they should stick together.

Why not? Lori thought. *What have I got to lose? He obviously has the hots for me. And Cliff knows it. Maybe I'll get Cliff so jealous that he'll change his mind about dumping me.*

The senator's conversation was full of double entendres.

Lori smiled politely, nodded attentively, and wondered what Cliff was up to and if he was missing her.

Hammond informed her in a smarmy way that she was the sexiest woman on the trip and that the other women had better watch out because she was capable of stealing all their men.

Lori kept smiling and nodding as she adjusted her bikini top in a vain attempt to achieve more coverage, because she could swear Hammond possessed X-ray vision. Flirting was one thing, but after a while Hammond was starting to creep her out with his sexist comments. Cliff was right: politicians were just as horny as the next man, probably even more so.

After lunch, Manuel was summoned by Guy, who requested that everyone wear shoes and a cover-up to start the island tour. Renee and Den handed out T-shirts and baseball caps with "The *Bianca*" emblazoned on them.

"I feel like we're taking off on a school trip," Ashley giggled, throwing on a T-shirt over her bikini. "This is *so* much fun!"

"I know," Bianca agreed, grabbing Aleksandr's hand and squeezing it tight. "It's an adventure. A big beautiful adventure. And you, my darling," she added, gazing up at Aleksandr, "planned it all perfectly."

And so they set off, the billionaire and his elite group of famous guests.

They were not exactly roughing it as they began exploring the scenic beauty of the idyllic island.

Manuel had conducted the tour before with other groups of extremely rich tourists. He was very aware that the stark unblemished beauty of the uninhabited island was staggering. First they passed by glorious pristine white sand dunes that led on to groves of coconut and date palms. Beyond the trees, they came upon a series of natural springs and glorious cascading waterfalls.

Bianca immediately decided that she wanted to stop and swim under the most impressive waterfall — it was too incredible to resist.

"We cannot hold our group up," Aleksandr chided. "There is more to see."

"Then get rid of everyone," Bianca whispered in his ear. " 'Cause I want to swim naked with you. Tell them we'll catch up. Go on," she urged when he hesitated. "Do it!"

Aleksandr couldn't say no. He snapped his fingers for Guy. "Have everyone move ahead," he instructed. "We will stay here."

Manuel did not like the idea of splitting the group, so Guy suggested to Aleksandr that perhaps they should all stay together.

"Why?" Aleksandr scoffed. "It's perfectly safe. I hardly need my bodyguard on a deserted island."

Guy nodded, but Manuel still seemed uneasy. The island was supposedly uninhabited, but over the years there had been rumors — sightings of mountain lions that came wandering down from the surrounding jungle-like hills, foraging for any food the tourists might have left behind. A dead body that had mysteriously washed up onshore.

Yes, the island had its own secrets.

"Maybe I should stay with you?" Guy suggested, eager to please his temporary boss.

"Go," Aleksandr replied impatiently. "Stop bothering me. We will catch up when we're ready."

Guy jumped. He was hot and sweaty, and the last thing he wanted was to annoy the man responsible for the large tip he expected at the end of the trip.

Lori and Luca had already taken off. To Manuel's consternation, the rest of the group were beginning to scatter. Manuel hated it when that happened. Didn't they realize that *he* was the tour guide? They should be following him, listening to his every word as he described the wonders of the island.

But no, it was not to be. This group had their own ideas.

The lush waterfalls made the perfect backdrop for Bianca to do a slow, sensual striptease for her Russian lover. Not that she had much to take off. Merely an oversized T-shirt and a tiny Brazilian string bikini.

But Bianca knew how to milk it, and Aleksandr appreciated every single minute of her seductive play as she stripped down for him.

They were under the impression that everyone had gone off on the tour, but unbeknownst to them, Hammond had lingered behind, loitering under cover of several lush palm trees.

Watching the enticing Bianca as she put on a show for her lover, Hammond was mesmerized by her long slinky legs, small breasts with large dark nipples, tiny waist, and glistening coffee-colored skin.

He felt himself harden as the supermodel sauntered naked into the water.

And when Aleksandr stripped off and followed her in, Hammond was mortified to discover that his host was hung like a horse.

He immediately felt woefully inadequate. Wasn't it enough that the man was a billionaire? Jesus Christ! Some men had it all.

For a moment he forgot about jerking off and concentrated on the way Aleksandr seized Bianca from behind and began pounding into her, moving her toward the cascading waterfall, both of them oblivious to anything except making love. Or fucking. Because yes, that's what they were doing: fucking like a couple of wild animals.

Hammond couldn't help himself; he came in his pants like a thirteen-year-old schoolboy.

"Shit!" he muttered under his breath, attempting to clean himself up.

What if anyone had seen him? He was a United States senator, for crissakes, not some Peeping Tom getting his rocks off in the bushes.

Humiliated and furious with himself, Hammond quickly set off to find the others.

CHAPTER FIFTY-THREE

Sierra decided that she should call her sister. They'd always been close, just not close enough for Sierra to share what was actually going on in her marriage. She wasn't about to do so now, but since Clare had been excited when she'd mentioned the trip, she knew that her sister would enjoy hearing all about the famous guests and the luxurious yacht.

With a firm step, she headed for the satellite communication center, passing the security room where Kyril, Aleksandr's fierce bodyguard, sat, surrounded by security cameras. *What a strange man,* she thought. *Quite frightening, really.*

Captain Dickson greeted her with a jovial "Good morning, Mrs. Patterson. And how are we on this very fine day?"

She gave the captain a warm smile; it was such a relief not to be operating from a fog-filled daze. "I'd like to make a call," she said. "Is that okay?"

"Certainly," Captain Dickson replied, thinking that the senator's wife appeared to be a lot more cheerful than when she'd first boarded. Sierra Patterson was a beauty, as were all the female passengers. It was nice to see her looking as if she might enjoy herself. "Allow me to escort you," he added, gallantly holding out his arm.

"Thank you, Captain," she said, dazzling him with her smile.

After standing under the shower trying to get his thoughts together, Flynn set off to find Sierra. He was more determined than ever to clear things up. Maybe that way he could finally forget about her and move on. It was quite clear that she'd experienced no difficulty doing exactly that. She'd married Hammond Patterson, for crissakes. Surely that was enough to make him forget her?

No way.

Somewhat pissed off at himself, he took the circular staircase to the middle deck, where he spotted Jeromy lounging on a chair. Immediately he did an about-face, heading back downstairs. Not that he had anything against gays — Luca seemed like a great guy — but there was something about Jeromy he couldn't stomach. You didn't have to be a genius to notice that the man was a first-class ass kisser. It was patently obvious, and if there was one type of person Flynn abhorred, it was ass kissers.

Unfortunately, Jeromy saw him and called out, "Flynn, is that you? I thought you went on the jolly old island expedition."

Why was everyone bugging him about that? Who cared?

He threw Jeromy a halfhearted wave as he hurriedly dodged out of sight.

Finding Sierra, that's all he was interested in.

While Sierra was speaking to her sister, the captain informed her that Eddie March was on the line requesting to speak with the senator.

"I'll take it," she said, saying a quick goodbye to Clare, who'd been thrilled to hear from her. "What's going on?" she asked Eddie, aware that Hammond had informed him that he was not to be bothered unless it was urgent.

"Nothing for you to be concerned about," Eddie said, trying not to sound too agitated. "I should talk to Hammond."

"He's off the yacht on a day trip. Won't be back until later." She paused for a moment. "What is it? Perhaps I can relay a message."

Not this message, Eddie thought. *Oh no, certainly not this message.*

"It doesn't matter," he said quickly. "Have him call me as soon as he can."

"If it's urgent . . ."

"Not urgent," Eddie said, feeling mighty uncomfortable about having to lie to Sierra. "Just make sure he contacts me."

"I'll do that, but it might not be today."

"Fine," Eddie said, although it wasn't fine. How long could he stall the Byrnes before they took action? They were threatening all kind of moves, such as contacting a TV news station or *The Washington Post.* Eddie had somehow or other convinced them to do nothing until they heard the senator's side of the story.

Right now he also couldn't wait to hear what Hammond would have to say about the situation. How out of control and stupid could one man be?

Pretty damn stupid.

"Hey," Flynn said, finally coming face-to-face with Sierra as she exited the communications room.

"Flynn," she murmured softly. Suddenly it all came flooding back and she couldn't help remembering all the fantastic times they'd shared in the past, the amazing love they'd once had for each other, their incredible love-making, which had resulted in her becoming pregnant.

Oh God! A pregnancy Flynn had never found out about.

What would he say if he discovered the truth? She'd lost their baby, but it wasn't her fault. She'd been in a car with Hammond, and there was the accident . . .

Guilt overcame her.

"Yeah," Flynn said with a rueful sigh. "Once again, it really is me."

"I didn't doubt it," she replied, thinking how much he would hate her if he unearthed the truth.

"You, uh . . . look lovely," he said, noting that she seemed a lot better than the previous night.

"Thank you," she said, making a determined effort to pull herself together and not fall to pieces.

"Uh . . . I was thinking that maybe we should talk," he said, clearing his throat, nervous for the first time in God knew how many years, which was odd, because he didn't get nervous — it simply wasn't on his agenda.

"I think we should," she said, nodding her head, although she wasn't sure if she wanted to talk to him; it wasn't as if it would solve anything.

"Well," he said, "since this seems like the perfect opportunity, why don't we go up to the top deck. I don't think there's anyone around up there."

She nodded again, feeling breathless, and yet strangely excited at the same time.

Closure. It was exactly what she'd been waiting for all these years. And now that it was about to happen, she wondered if she was capable of handling the situation. Thank God Hammond wasn't present to get in her way. It was just her and Flynn, exactly how it should be. So yes, she *could* handle it.

They headed upstairs, and settled on facing comfortable chairs in the all-glass atrium. For a few minutes, they made stilted conversation until he finally said, "So, Sierra, all these years later, here we are."

"Yes, here we are," she agreed, glancing out at the endless blue sea. "What a place to meet up. It's so unbelievably breathtaking."

"Better than some of the places I've experienced," he said dryly.

"I know about the places you've been," she blurted. "I've followed your career on your Web site, read your newsletters."

"You did, huh?" he said, surprised and more than a little pleased.

"Yes, Flynn," she murmured, thinking that getting older suited him. He was more handsome than ever, with his intense blue eyes and strong jawline.

"I'm flattered," he said.

"In spite of what happened," she said softly, "I always had this crazy urge to keep you in my life."

They exchanged a long, intimate look.

"Hey, I kept tabs on you too," he said at last, finally breaking the look. "But I was shocked when I read you'd married Hammond." He took a long, steady beat. "I guess it must've started between you and him when I left for London. And then I got the photos." He stared at her intently. "Tell me, Sierra, was that the only way you could think of breaking up with me? 'Cause it was pretty damn shitty."

"Excuse me?" she said, frowning. What on earth was he talking about? It was *he* who'd broken up with *her.*

"The photos," he said insistently. "Why'd you do it?"

"Funny, that's exactly what I was about to ask you," she said, her eyes burning bright. This was a crazy conversation, and she didn't like it.

"Ask me what?" he said, puzzled.

"Look, I understand we were both kids back then," she said, desperately trying to stay in control of her emotions. "But sending me those photos was such a cruel thing to do. I couldn't believe you would do something like that."

"What the fuck are you talking about?" he said, his temper rising. "*You* were the one who sent *me* photos."

"Oh, come on, Flynn," she sighed. "I didn't send you anything."

"*Somebody* sent them. And while we're on the subject," he said heatedly, "it might interest you to know that you broke my fucking heart."

362

"No, Flynn," she said, torn between tears, guilt, and anger. "You broke mine."

"Oh yeah? Photos of you making out with other guys, including Ham —"

"Are you serious? I never made out with anyone, *especially* not Hammond. He was there for me when I needed him, it was purely platonic, and let's not forget that it was *you* who asked him to watch out for me."

"Yeah? Then how do you explain the photos?" he said roughly. "What's your story?"

"How do *you*?" she said indignantly. "*You* were the one with girls draped all over you."

"*What* girls?" he said, perplexed.

"The ones in the photos."

"Now hold on," he said, realizing that they were definitely talking at cross-purposes. "Are you telling me that *you* got photos too?"

"What do you mean, 'too'?"

"I mean that someone sent *me* photos of you with other men."

"And someone sent *me* photos of you with a whole bunch of naked girls."

"Jesus Christ!" he exclaimed, smacking his forehead. "There were never any other girls after I met you. I swear it. And there were sure as hell never any photos."

"Then . . . what?" she questioned, confused and upset, wishing she were somewhere else.

"Fuck!" he said, realization dawning. "Whoever sent the photos must've been out to break us up."

"Why would anyone want to do that?"

"Jesus!" he exclaimed, shaking his head. "And here's the kicker — like a couple of morons, we both fell for it. How stupid is that?"

"I don't understand," she said, her eyes widening.

"No, but I'm beginning to," he said grimly, getting up and pacing around. "Don't you get it? We were set up."

"How is that possible?"

"Who knows? But I'm sure as hell going to figure it out. What did you do with the photos you got?"

"I destroyed them."

"Yeah, that's what I did, and you know something else? Whoever sent them *knew* that's what we'd do."

"You think?"

"I know, 'cause here's the deal: they must've been fakes."

"But you were *in* the photos, Flynn. I saw them."

"So were you, sweetheart. With several guys. Want to address *that?*"

"It's impossible."

"And in one of them you were with Ham."

As soon as he said Hammond's name, it suddenly all became clear. Ham had always been jealous of his relationship with Sierra; he'd often claimed that since he'd seen Sierra first she should've been with *him.* When that logic didn't get him anywhere, he'd taken to speaking badly about her at any opportunity, calling her all kinds of sick names. It was college guy's shit, but Flynn had made sure it never got back to her.

Then when he'd left for London, Hammond had obviously moved right in and seized his opportunity, lying to her that Flynn had asked him to watch out for her. What a low-down sneaky son of a bitch.

"You're not going to like this," Flynn said, trying to keep his anger under control. "But I think I've figured out exactly what happened."

"You have?" she said tentatively. "Please share."

"You and I were taken for one big ride. And you know who was manipulating it all?"

"Who?"

"Your future husband."

Sierra felt her heart accelerate. *Hammond* was responsible? Could this possibly be true?

She could only come up with one answer.

Yes. For Hammond had proved that he was capable of anything.

Chapter Fifty-Four

"It's time to move," Cruz announced over breakfast in Acapulco.

"Move where?" asked Ina, channeling her best Salma Hayek in a formfitting turquoise dress, her overly large breasts spilling out, nipples permanently erect — the result of her breast-enlargement surgery.

"Nothin' to do with you," Sergei said, slurping strong black coffee from a ceramic mug. "Me and your brother got business to conduct. You stay out of it."

Ina frowned; if it weren't for her, Sergei never would have met Cruz. She knew for a fact that they'd done many a deal together, so shouldn't she be getting a commission? Or, at the very least, shouldn't Sergei be dumping the American *puta* he kept stashed in his Mexico City apartment and start thinking of marrying *her*? It wasn't right. She felt insulted.

Now her brother and Sergei were planning something big, and they didn't care to tell her what it was, which infuriated her.

Fortunately, she'd learned the art of spying from her brother, and she knew their plan had something to do with a yacht they were about to hijack and hold for ransom. A yacht that was cruising the Sea of Cortez. A little off Cruz's regular beat, but she supposed he knew what he was doing. Her brother had *cojones* the size of Cuba.

Ina had always had a bit of a crush on Cruz, although he'd never paid her much attention. Her brother was more exciting than Sergei, who had a vicious temper and wasn't that adventurous in bed. Sergei had never gone down on her, and several of Cruz's conquests had confided in the past that her brother was a master in that department.

Truth was that if Cruz *wasn't* her brother, she would've definitely had the hots for him. Too bad they were related.

Forbidden love. Why was it forbidden when it seemed so right?

"We leave tonight," Cruz said.

"About time," Sergei said.

"Where we goin'?" Ina inquired.

Both men ignored her.

Sergei had arranged to rent a villa on a very large private estate outside of Cabo. A sprawling villa off the beaten track, with beach access and no neighbors. Cruz's team of misfits had already taken up residence, busily preparing for their strike against the *Bianca,* making sure they had everything they needed. Two powerful speedboats, supplies, rifles, guns.

Cruz had trained them well. His men were Somalians who spoke no English, but they sure as hell understood exactly what he wanted. Over the last few years, he'd made them richer than they could ever have imagined. He was their boss, and they did what ever they were instructed to do.

Sergei was unknown to them. However, if Cruz indicated he was the man, as long as there was money to be made, they were prepared to work for him too.

Sergei brought several of his personal bodyguards to the villa. Stoic men of Russian descent, they did not mix with the Somalians — they considered themselves way too superior.

The plan had not included taking Ina with them, but since she apparently knew more than she should, Sergei had finally agreed that it would be better if she came.

Cruz had not objected. What did he care? His sister could make herself useful; she could keep Sergei busy in the bedroom and out of his way.

When taking over a boat, everyone had to know what they were doing. Gaining control was a fast and furious thing — there could be no mistakes. Cruz did not relish the thought of taking Sergei along on the ride the day they hit the *Bianca*. Sergei wasn't a professional hijacker, which meant he could well turn out to be a liability. Unfortunately, Sergei had insisted he be present. "I yearn for the joy of watchin' Aleksandr Kasianenko's fuckin' face when we take over his yacht," he'd growled. "That bastard is responsible for my brother's death, and now I will see that he pays."

The details of exactly how Aleksandr would pay were still milling around in Sergei's head.

It would be long and painful. Of that he was sure.

CHAPTER FIFTY-FIVE

Lori was basking in her time with Luca, because even though he was a huge star and world-famous, he was so down-to-earth and so much fun. She couldn't help wondering what he was doing with the crusty uptight Englishman who had practically ignored her all through last night's dinner. What could Luca possibly see in Jeromy Milton-Gold? Jeromy was not even that attractive, with his long thin nose and small squinty eyes. And judging from the previous evening, he certainly wasn't loaded with charm.

The island was such an idyllic paradise; Lori kept on wishing that Cliff had come with her. It was an experience not to be missed. On the other hand, Luca seemed quite happy that his significant other had failed to make the effort, and she could understand why.

"Jeromy's not like us," Luca confided. "He's more into indoor activities, if you get what I mean."

"Sex?" Lori questioned, tilting her head.

"Not my kind of sex," Luca retorted, grimacing.

"You're gay," Lori said boldly. "Doesn't that mean you're up for anything?"

"Not me," Luca said quickly. "I'm a one-on-one kinda guy."

"Yet the one you've chosen is Jeromy."

"Here's the situation," Luca explained. "I fell straight out of the closet into his arms. He kind of took me over." After a meaningful pause, he added, "Lately, I've been thinking it might be time to break away."

"Why?" she asked curiously. "Have you met someone else?"

"No, but Jeromy's lifestyle's not for me."

"And you've only just realized this?"

"Y'know, Lori," he said thoughtfully, "sometimes it takes a while to figure things out."

She nodded, feeling immensely flattered that Luca felt free to reveal his true feelings to her. They barely knew each other, and it wasn't as if she was famous or anything. Obviously he liked her, and that made her feel as if she belonged. This trip was turning out to be better than she'd expected.

"I guess being away from everything is the perfect time to think things through," she offered.

Luca ran his hand through his mop of thick blond hair. "Right," he agreed. "An' that's exactly what I'm doing."

371

"Then I hope for your sake that you reach the right conclusion."

"Oh, I will," he said, nodding to himself. "And you, Lori," he added, "what's up with you and Cliff Baxter?"

"Uh . . . well," she answered hesitantly. "We've been together a year."

"Where's it going? Or should I ask, where do you *want* it to go?"

"I don't know. I'm not sure," she mumbled. "It's, uh . . . complicated."

"Marriage? Children?" Luca persisted.

"Cliff's not the marrying kind," she explained.

"That doesn't mean you can't change his mind." Luca paused for a moment. "Is it something you want?"

Before she could answer, Hammond came lumbering up to them, his T-shirt drenched in sweat, his face pink from the heat, his brown hair plastered to his forehead.

Lori was relieved to be off the hook; the conversation was getting a little too personal for her liking.

"Goddammit!" Hammond complained, swatting at a flying bug. "I need to throw myself in the ocean. Isn't it time we turned back?"

Jeromy was bored. He hadn't come on this voyage to sit by himself in solitary splendor while his boyfriend ran off to an island with most of the other guests.

Jeromy did not sunbathe. His skin and the sun did not mix, so instead of becoming a sun-burnished god like Luca, he usually ended up resembling a dried-up old lobster. Not an attractive look, and one he planned to avoid.

Mercedes, the feisty stewardess, was attentive, offering him drinks and snacks whenever he felt like it. The problem was that food and drink did not alleviate boredom.

Mercedes. What kind of a name was that anyway? A Mexican girl named after a German car. How ridiculous. It was exactly the sort of moronic name movie stars bestowed on their offspring.

Thinking of movie stars, Jeromy wondered where Cliff Baxter had vanished to. Earlier they'd enjoyed a most cordial chat — surely there was more to come? Perhaps Cliff had a house in L.A. that needed redecorating. Or a New York pent house ready for renovation. Or maybe he could use his persuasive powers to talk Cliff into purchasing a London town house.

Ah . . . Jeromy Milton-Gold, designer to the stars. It had a nice ring to it.

Mercedes appeared again. There was something about the girl that was annoying. Perhaps she wasn't subservient enough for his liking. Or perhaps she was just plain cheap.

He wondered if she screwed the passengers on the side. He wouldn't put it past her — she had that dirty girl air about her. Maybe she'd even had a go at the movie star while his cheap redheaded girlfriend was cavorting somewhere on the island with Luca.

"Where is Mr. Baxter?" Jeromy inquired, peering down his nose at her.

"Ah, you mean Señor Cliff," Mercedes said, purposely irritating him.

"No, I mean *Mr.* Baxter," Jeromy said sternly, putting her in her place. "You should *never* call guests by their first names. It's extremely rude."

Mercedes stifled a strong urge to tell him to piss off. Her time would come, and when it did, she planned to clean this one out, and maybe shove a plunger up his bony ass for good measure. Except this particular *hijo de puta* would probably enjoy it.

"Señor Cliff *asked* me to use his first name," she said innocently.

"I don't *care* what he asked you," Jeromy admonished. "It is simply not done. You are in service here. Learn, dear, it is to your advantage."

Come mierda, Mercedes thought as she smiled sweetly at Jeromy, deciding that his expensive watch might make a nice birthday present for her next conquest.

Being on the island was making Taye hornier

than ever. Getting Ashley out of London and away from it all was a major move. She wasn't all Miss Design Queen and mummy to the twins, she was more like the girl he'd fallen in love with, the free spirit who got off on sexual adventures and was never averse to giving a blow job or two. Taye had to admit that getting oral sex from his wife was his favorite activity. He relished the thought of shoving Mammoth into Ashley's delicate mouth, and holding her head in place while she sucked the life out of him. Before marriage it had been a daily occurrence. After marriage it had become a special treat. And for the last few months it hadn't happened at all, until last night, when Ashley had excelled at doing what she did better than any other girl he'd been with.

Now he wanted more, and the island seemed like the perfect setup for a quick bit of sex. Ashley looked so hot in her cover-up T-shirt, her big tits sticking out, long legs on parade. Last night he'd made love to her for as long as she could take it, then he'd gone down on her and she'd moaned her appreciation. Frankly, he couldn't keep his hands off his wife.

"Hey, toots," he whispered, grabbing her hand, "follow me. Just saw somethin' you wouldn't wanna miss."

"What?" Ashley said, marveling at a pair of giant turtles crawling along in front of them;

it was quite a sight.

"Back here," Taye said, steering her away from the others and toward a cluster of tall swaying palm trees.

"What?" Ashley repeated, slightly irritated.

Taye didn't give her time to think. He went for her nipples, playing with them in a way that never failed to turn her on.

"Taye!" she objected. "Not here!"

"Why not?" he said, squeezing and twirling.

" 'Cause the others might see." Two seconds and then — "Oh . . . my . . . *God!*"

He had her. Quick as a flash he whipped out Mammoth, still keeping up the tit action.

"Go for it, baby," he encouraged, pushing her to her knees.

"Taye . . ." she began.

He stifled her objections with Mammoth, and within two delicious minutes he'd achieved a memorable orgasm, leaving Ashley wanting more. Which was fine with him, because he'd be happy to finish the job of satisfying her later.

As far as Taye was concerned, this was turning out to be the perfect trip.

After skimming through two scripts — both of them disappointing — Cliff realized that he did indeed miss Lori. It was his loss not to have gone on the island trip. Every day shouldn't be about work, and reading scripts was actually work. Before leaving L.A. he'd had his agent, his manager, and Enid all on his case about all the scripts he should read.

"I think you should seriously consider the spy movie," his agent had said.

"We need to make decisions," his manager had informed him.

"You'll be bored with Lori before you know it," Enid had lectured. "See if you can make a dent in those scripts you've got piling up. I've packed them all for you."

Wasn't he supposed to be on vacation with his girlfriend? Why not relax and enjoy it? To hell with work.

Cliff decided that for the next few days he was going to lie back and let himself go with the flow.

"What are we going to do?" Sierra questioned.

Flynn loved the fact that she was referring to them as "we." He shrugged. "I dunno what your situation is with Ham. You've been married a long time." He paused for a moment, then gazed at her intently. "Are you happy?"

"So!" she exclaimed, refusing to meet his eyes. "Just like that, we've gone from not talking for years to whether I'm happy. I'm confused, that's what I am."

"You're not answering my question."

"Are *you* happy, Flynn?" she said pointedly, finally looking at him. "I guess you must be.

Your girlfriend seems smart enough and pretty."

"Xuan is not my girlfriend," he muttered.

"You're sharing a cabin," she was quick to remind him.

"It's a long story," he said, ridiculously pleased that she sounded vaguely jealous.

Sierra was now staring at him, unsure of what to say. Should she admit that she was miserable? Should she tell him the truth?

Oh God, she felt so vulnerable. Too much time had passed; they were both grown-ups now. Could she trust Flynn? What if the whole fake-photos thing was merely a fantasy, a convenient story he'd made up to explain the way he'd treated her?

Was Hammond responsible? At first she'd had no doubts, but why would he do such a thing? *How* could he? She realized that she would have to confront him — it was the only way to get to the real truth.

"I'm kind of tired," she said at last. "I need to spend some time alone thinking things through."

"I understand," Flynn said, realizing that pushing her was not a good idea. "It's a lot to take in. For both of us."

"Yes, it is," she answered quietly.

And where do we go from here? he felt like asking. *Just friends, lovers no more? What's the deal, Sierra? Is there a future for us?*

Was he experiencing an urge to go back in

time, rekindle the feelings they'd once had for each other?

Did he still want her?

His heart said yes.

His head said no.

Whether the photos were fake or not still didn't explain the fact that she'd been pregnant with Ham's baby when she and Ham were involved in a car accident. She'd told him that they were merely platonic friends, so how come the pregnancy? Obviously she had no idea he knew.

Jesus Christ! Why was this happening? Why was Sierra back in his life? Just when he'd gotten together with Mai in Paris and thought that maybe he was finally over Sierra, this had to happen.

Too fucking bad. He could deal with it.

He had no choice.

CHAPTER FIFTY-SIX

Muttering under his breath, Manuel led the rich ones back to the beach and the tenders that awaited them. He considered his current group of affluent tourists a bunch of low-life animals, although animals would never behave in such a disrespectful and lustful way.

Did the tall black man think that nobody noticed when he pulled the large-breasted blonde behind the palm trees and made her do something to him that only *putas* indulged in?

And the big Russian man having sex with the dark girl under the waterfall. Disgraceful. Couldn't they wait until they were home and it was nighttime like normal people?

Manuel was thankful for his wife and daughters. They were fine upstanding women; they would never behave in such a lewd and filthy fashion.

As the tourists got into the boats, Guy handed Manuel a healthy tip.

He took it, vowing to himself that he would

go back to fishing for a living rather than continue to deal with people like this. These people contaminated him with their un-bridled libidos and sexual perversions. He was a simple man, and he preferred a simple life.

Hammond jumped into the boat right behind Lori, sitting himself down beside her.

"I bet you're ready for a nice warm shower," he said, edging close. "Get all that sand out of your pretty little cooch."

"Excuse me?" Lori said, not sure she'd heard him correctly.

Hammond gave an easy chuckle. "No offense," he said smoothly. "That's what my mother used to say after a day trip to the beach. Of course, *our* beach was in the Hamptons, but that's another story."

Lori stared at him; she wasn't sure how to respond.

"You are a *very* pretty girl," Hammond continued, his eyes undressing her. "Quite the temptress."

Cliff had warned her that politicians were horny bastards, and apparently he was right. At first she'd been flattered by Hammond's attention, but now she was totally turned off; there was something off-putting about this one.

"It's too bad your wife couldn't come today," she said, putting the emphasis on the word *wife.*

"Yes," Hammond replied. "She's quite . . . delicate."

"Really?" Lori said sharply. "She doesn't look delicate."

"I know," Hammond said with a put-upon sigh. "It's a personal burden I carry." A meaningful pause, then a lowering of his voice. "Between us, Lori, Sierra has, uh . . . emotional issues. It's the sad truth I live with."

What was this? Confide in Lori Day? "Sorry to hear that," she said, brushing sand off her bare leg while not believing him at all.

Hammond leaned over, his fingers lightly touching her upper thigh.

She quickly jerked back.

"You missed a bit," he explained.

"No, I didn't," she snapped.

"I apologize," he said. "I was merely being helpful."

She was saved by Taye and Ashley, who piled into the tender. Taye was grinning as if he were eight years old and had just gotten a new bike for Christmas. Ashley seemed a bit flustered.

"Wish I'd brought a camera," Lori mused, edging away from the senator.

"Me too," said Ashley, not quite as aloof as usual.

"We could probably sell our pics to the tabloids for a fortune," Lori joked, immediately realizing it was a dumb thing to come out with.

"I don't think so," Ashley said tartly, exchanging a look with Taye as if to say *I told you she was low-rent.*

"Uh . . . I was joking, of course," Lori muttered, totally embarrassed.

"I have a hunch that our host wouldn't find it particularly funny," Ashley said as the tender took off, bouncing over the waves at a brisk pace.

"Lay off, toots," Taye whispered in Ashley's ear. "Give the kid a break."

Ashley ignored him; she was too busy thinking about what dress she would wear to dinner. Something dazzling. Something to catch Cliff Baxter's eye, because she was quite sure that he fancied her. And why not? She was certainly way sexier than his girlfriend.

Sierra was tempted to reach for the Xanax as she awaited her husband's return. She stared longingly at the bottle of vodka Hammond had so thoughtfully ordered brought to their room. Hammond preferred to see her medicated, whether it be from pills or booze. That way he felt he was in complete control.

She managed to resist both temptations. Instead, she sat by herself in their stateroom, dredging up every memory she could about the photos, and the way Hammond had attached himself to her after Flynn had left for

London, claiming that Flynn had *asked* him to look out for her. What a lie that had turned out to be. According to Flynn, he had asked no such thing.

So . . . if Hammond had lied about that, what else?

The photos, of course. She'd shown them to him, and he'd carried on about how he'd always known Flynn was a cheater, and that he hadn't wanted to upset her, but now that she'd seen the proof with her own eyes . . .

Next he'd insisted on destroying the photos, taken them from her along with the typewritten note. Then he'd tried to talk her into getting an abortion.

Oh God! Of course. If the photos *were* fakes, naturally he hadn't wanted her studying them. And if he envisioned her as his future political asset, then Flynn's baby would certainly not factor into his plans.

Had he crashed his car on purpose? Had he *wanted* her to lose Flynn's baby? She shuddered at the thought.

Now that she knew what kind of man Hammond really was, she wouldn't put anything past him. He was an evil man hiding beneath the cloak of a political do-gooder.

When Hammond returned from the island trip, she was ready to face him. He barged into their stateroom spewing complaints about the heat and the bugs and how he'd had no chance to speak privately to Aleksandr. "I deserve more respect from these people," he complained. "I am a United States senator, for crissakes. I am destined for great things. If they expect any future favors, they should be aware of who they're dealing with."

The man or the monster? she wanted to say. However, she controlled herself.

"Hammond," she said evenly.

"Sierra," he said, mocking her tone as he threw off his sweat-stained T-shirt.

"I need to ask you a question."

"Do you now?" he said, pulling down his shorts and underwear, showing not a shred of modesty.

"Seeing Flynn reminded me of those photos."

"What photos?" he snapped, absentmindedly stroking his balls as he headed toward the bathroom.

"The ones you faked in college," she said bravely. "The ones you sent to me and Flynn."

"What?" Stopping at the bathroom door, he turned around and faced her.

"I was wondering how you managed such a clever job," Sierra continued. "I mean, it was before Photoshop and all the technology we have today. Did you hire a professional to help you?"

Hammond stared her down, his eyes menacing slits of anger. "Have you been talking to that son of a bitch?" he demanded.

"What son of a bitch would that be?" she answered, remaining calm.

"Do not get smart with me, woman," he said angrily. "I warned you not to speak to him."

"You warn me about a lot of things," she said, keeping her tone even. "However, we are on a yacht in the middle of an ocean, and I think I can do whatever I like."

Hammond could not believe the change in her. What the hell was going on? She seemed sober and together, not foggy and compliant. This was unlike the woman he'd grown used to. The woman who never dared to argue. The woman he'd managed to control with his constant threats of harm to her family.

"You think you can do whatever you like, do you?" he said, his voice harsh and unforgiving. "Perhaps you're forgetting who you are. You are my wife, and *as* my wife you do what *I* tell you to do, or" — he paused momentarily, his eyes narrowing even more — "you know the consequences."

"For God's sake, Hammond. How long are you going to keep this up?"

"What's come over you, Sierra? Suddenly all brave because you talked to an old boyfriend? Do you think *he* can save you? Your family? And even more important, can Flynn save himself? Think about *that* for a moment." He paused and glared at her threateningly.

386

"One phone call, and I can make his life a nightmare. I can make sure he never works again. I can have his legs broken, his pretty face smashed in. You know I can."

"It's over, Hammond," she said, her voice steady. "The moment we get off this boat, I'm leaving you. And I will make sure everyone hears about your threats, so that if anything happens to me *or* my family, the finger will be pointed at you."

"Keep it up, dear, and we will *see* what happens," Hammond jeered.

With those words, he stalked into the bathroom and slammed the door shut.

"How was it?" Cliff asked when Lori returned to their stateroom.

"Oh my God, you were so right about the senator," she replied, flopping down on the bed. "He's a randy piece of work."

"Told you so," Cliff said. "I can spot 'em a mile off."

"But Cliff, the island was *fantastic*. I wish you could've seen it. *So* beautiful, like something out of a movie. And deserted. No houses. No people. Nothing except wildlife, greenery, and these amazing waterfalls. Oh, and giant turtles," she continued excitedly. "You would've *loved* it. I wish you'd come with us."

Cliff was pleased to see Lori so animated, like a little kid who'd just experienced her first trip to Disneyland. Sometimes he forgot how young she was. Twenty-four. A mere child. Young enough to be his daughter. Yet old enough to be his lover.

And why exactly did he think it was time to trade her in for a younger, fresher face? Because he was Cliff Baxter? Because he was a star who had to maintain a certain image? To impress his male friends and acquaintances? For his adoring public?

It was all bullshit. He liked Lori; he was comfortable with her. No need for a trade-in at this time.

"Listen, toots, have I told you lately how much I love you?" Taye said, raising his head from between his wife's thighs to take a deep breath.

"Oh, for God's sake — don't stop now!" Ashley intoned, lying spread-eagled on the bed in their stateroom, luxuriating as she experienced the expertise of her husband's talented tongue.

"But I do love you so *much,*" Taye insisted. "You're *it* for me. No other woman. Ever."

"Okay, okay, then how about you get on with the job at hand," Ashley implored impatiently. "I'm almost there."

"You got it," Taye answered, grinning.

This trip was doing their marriage nothing but good.

■ ■ ■ ■

"About time you got back," Jeromy said, his tone quite snippy.

Luca threw himself down on the bed.

"Please!" Jeromy said, curling his lip. "You're all sweaty and nasty. Can you at least take a shower before you mess up our bed?"

Luca placed his hands behind his head and stretched; he had no intention of moving. "You made a mistake not coming," he remarked, wishing he were still on the magical island.

"I think not," Jeromy replied. "Staying on board was very advantageous for me. I had quite a long chat with Cliff Baxter, and he might be on the verge of hiring me to design the interior of his next house."

"Is he buying a new house?" Luca said. "Lori never mentioned it."

"Since when are you so tight with that Lori person?" Jeromy inquired, feeling quite envious that Luca was busy making friends while he languished on the yacht.

"I saved her from the hands of the horny senator," Luca said. "And don't call her 'that Lori person.' If you took the time to get to know her, you'd realize she's a very sweet girl."

"Changing tracks, are we?" Jeromy said contemptuously. "Dying to sneak your way into her dirty little panties?"

"Try not to turn into a bitchy queen," Luca replied.

"Excuse me?" Jeromy huffed. "A bitchy queen indeed!"

"You know what I mean."

"How dare you!"

"How dare I what?" Luca said flatly.

"Call me names."

"Jeromy," Luca said, giving him a long, cool look. "We really need to talk."

The dreaded words — *we really need to talk.* Jeromy had heard them before, and more than once. First from his father, a stern civil servant who'd beaten him unmercifully when he'd first come out. Then from the college professor at Oxford he'd been desperately in love with. Next from the septuagenarian marquis who'd kept him as his pet for several years. And finally from the "closeted" businessman who'd financed his design firm until the man's wife had found out what was really going on between them and called a halt to all financial dealings.

Now from Luca.

No. This couldn't be happening. Luca was his future. They would grow old together. They would enjoy Luca's fame and money together. This *couldn't* happen. He would not allow it.

One way or another, Jeromy was determined to stop the inevitable.

CHAPTER FIFTY-SEVEN

For the night's festivities, Bianca had requested a Spanish theme. Guy was on it — he'd arranged for musicians and a well-known Spanish chef famous for his seafood paella to be boated in from the mainland, even though they were several hours out at sea. He'd been informed up front that no expense was to be spared on this trip. Only the best for Aleksandr Kasianenko and his lady. Guy was sure that if Bianca requested that Wolfgang Puck be flown in from California to prepare his famous smoked salmon pizza, Aleksandr would oblige.

At sunset, Bianca appeared on deck, a true dazzler in a flounced flamenco dress, white flowers in her jet hair. Aleksandr accompanied her. He wasn't a man to dress up — his usual black pants and a white shirt did it for him.

Guy was a tad envious, because once again they made a ferociously handsome couple. Between them they had everything. Looks, money, power, fame. It wasn't fair that two people had so much.

Still, he was used to it. Serving the privileged. Catering to their every need. Watching them at play. Hoping for a major tip at the end of the journey. It was the life he'd chosen, and it wasn't such a bad one.

At least he had a steady partner who professed true love. They shared a cozy apartment in Sydney, and whenever Guy was home — which was not that often — they were quite compatible and took pleasure in doing the same things.

Yes, Guy was satisfied, although he couldn't help having lust in his heart (not to mention his pants) for the gorgeous Luca Perez. What a true specimen of magnificent manhood. And talented too. Guy had Luca's latest song repeating on his iPod; it soothed him during times of stress.

By the time Hammond emerged from the shower, Sierra was no longer in their stateroom.

Dammit! Where was the devious bitch, his cheating wife, the slut who'd been talking to her ex-boyfriend?

His fury was dark and cold. Did Sierra honestly think she could escape from him just like that? A divorce — even a separation — would ruin his political future. No way would he ever allow that to happen.

One day he was going to run for president,

and whether she liked it or not, she *would* support him — dead or alive.

"What happened to you?" Xuan asked when she returned to their stateroom and found Flynn there. "You could've told me you were leaving the island."

"I got the runs," he answered, still thinking about his conversation with Sierra.

"You seem to be better now," Xuan remarked, opening the closet to see if she could rustle up an outfit to wear for dinner. The women on this trip were so impeccably groomed and well dressed. Her choices were limited since she traveled so light, and quite frankly she couldn't care less. Leave it to the others to prance around in their fancy clothes; she knew that she was smarter and more caring about what was going on in the world than all of them put together.

"Yeah, I am," Flynn said, frustrated that he had to share the same space with Xuan. Much as he valued her friendship, he needed to be alone to think things through. He didn't appreciate Xuan questioning him, and he was sure that she would; it was her way. "I'll see you upstairs," he added, heading for the door.

"You know, Flynn, you should be careful what you wish for," Xuan said sagely. "Wishes do not always provide the answers we crave."

"Thanks for that," he said dryly. "It makes no sense at all."

"Think about it," she called after him. "You're too clever to get caught up in your own fantasies."

Ignoring Xuan's words, Flynn ran into Taye and his blond wife, all of them on their way to the drinks deck.

"You feelin' all right, mate?" Taye inquired, friendly as usual.

"Yeah, it was nothing," Flynn answered. "Something I ate."

"Ewh, nasty!" Ashley exclaimed, clinging to her husband's arm as they made their way up the circular staircase. "Remember, Taye, that time you got the runs on the field in front of thousands of fans?"

"Don't remind me," Taye groaned. "Talk about embarrassin'."

"Had to throw all your gear away." Ashley giggled. "Even your mum wouldn't go near it!"

"Thanks," Taye said, making a face. "You certainly know how to feed a bloke's ego."

"An' that's not all I can do," Ashley said, giggling suggestively.

Taye decided that on vacation, his wife was a whole other woman. And he liked this new Ashley a lot better than he did her former self.

Bianca surveyed her guests, all present for drinks with the exception of the senator. She observed that the senator's wife seemed more social tonight. Sierra was chatting with Cliff Baxter and Lori. Bianca was delighted to note that everyone was in a more relaxed state. Ah yes, the vacation vibe was taking over, and she couldn't be happier.

Aleksandr was at ease too, talking football with Taye, politics with the Asian woman — whom Bianca had secretly christened Miss Intensity.

Luca approached and clinked glasses with her. "You and old Alek certainly know how to throw a party," he remarked. "Everyone's having a great time."

"You too?" Bianca questioned.

"Why're you askin' me?" Luca said, pushing a lock of blond hair off his forehead.

" 'Cause I know you," Bianca said, looking at him intently. "Something's on your mind. Spill."

"Okay, okay, the deal is, I'm missing my kid," he confessed. "I hate being away from him. You haven't seen him lately, Bianca. He's such a cute kid, an' I don't wanna miss anything."

"He's with Suga, right?"

"He sure is, an' she's a wonderful *mamasita*. The best. Warm and nurturing and everything she should be."

"Hmm . . . sounds as if you're missing her too," Bianca ruminated.

"Hey, I'm not missin' the sex; we gave that up pretty fast," Luca said. "But the compan-

ionship an' the fun we had together, yeah —
that's what I miss."

"Well, you have Jeromy now," Bianca said
sagely. "He seems like a laugh a minute."

"Ah . . . therein lies the problem," Luca
admitted. "Jeromy."

"Trouble in gay city, huh?" Bianca said with
a knowing nod.

"You could say there's more than trouble."

"Like what?"

"Problem is he hates Suga, an' not only
that, he never pays any attention to Luca
Junior. It's driving me loco."

"That's not good."

"No, it's not," Luca said, shaking his head.
"If you really want the truth, I think I've
finally had it with Jeromy. It's time for me to
move on."

"Oh dear." Bianca sighed.

"Oh dear what?"

"We're on this very special cruise, Luca.
Please don't ruin anything. Can you at least
wait to dump him until we get back? Is that
possible?"

"I guess I can try."

"For me," she pleaded. "No dramas."

"For you," Luca acquiesced. "Only please
realize that the moment we hit dry land . . ."

"I know, I know. And you're the best!"

Luca gave a wry smile. "I try."

"Dinner is served." Once again Guy found

himself saying the words he loved to hear himself speak.

Everyone gathered by the stairs and began making their way to the upper dining deck.

Sierra looked around and noted that Hammond was still absent. She wondered what he was doing. Busy planning another deluge of threats?

She shivered at the thought and determined to stay strong.

Flynn was there. She decided it was best not to talk to him. Hammond was too unpredictable — who knew what he was capable of? She didn't want Flynn getting involved in any way.

Fortunately, there were new seating arrangements. At the dinner table she found herself seated between Cliff and Luca, which suited her fine.

Hammond appeared before the first course was served. Barely glancing in her direction, he took his seat between Bianca and Ashley and immediately started talking to Bianca.

It seemed impossible, but was he going to accept the fact that she was moving on? Had he run out of threats? Was this the beginning of a new life for her?

She could only hope.

After dinner there were professional flamenco dancers for the guests' entertainment. Fierce-looking women with strong, sturdy thighs, and darkly rugged men exhibiting plenty of attitude.

Bianca sat close to Aleksandr, enjoying the festivities. Her hand lingered near his crotch — the sensual dancers were putting her in the mood.

Aleksandr absently removed her hand and turned to listen to Xuan, who, as far as Bianca could tell, was carrying on about something boring and political.

Bianca was irritated. Couples were now sitting next to each other in the entertainment area. How come Miss Intensity always managed to find a place next to Aleksandr?

Not that she was jealous. Oh no. The day she was jealous of another woman would be a day indeed.

Bianca possessed extreme confidence, and rightfully so. Her beauty was a given. Her looks had always taken her wherever she cared to go. No roadblocks. Green lights all the way. Covers of *Vogue, Harper's,* and *Vanity Fair.* Puff pieces in *People, Esquire,* even *Newsweek* and *Time.*

Bianca was the supermodel of all supermodels. A woman admired by women and lusted after by men.

Jealous. Ha! Although Aleksandr did seem to be quite taken with the petite Asian woman. Earlier he'd told Bianca that he found Xuan to be very interesting.

Interesting indeed! Bianca didn't like her;

she was too serious by far. And what was with Xuan and her boyfriend? They barely appeared to notice each other. As far as Bianca could tell, there was no sexual chemistry between them, and that was strange because Flynn was smokin' hot.

She decided to pay attention to Flynn, find out what his deal was. Quietly she moved away from Aleksandr, who appeared unaware that she was on the move. He was too busy solving the problems of the world with Miss Intensity.

The flamenco music was loud, the dancers even louder and overly dramatic as they snaked their way around the dance floor stamping their feet and projecting fake passion.

Bianca made her way over to Flynn, who was sitting by himself. She squeezed up next to him determined to get to know him better. "How're you feeling?" she asked, putting on her sympathetic face.

He threw her a quizzical look. "Does the whole world know I had the runs?"

"The runs?"

"I'm quoting Ashley, a very eloquent young lady."

"With enormous tits," Bianca whispered, forming a bond between them.

"Yeah," he said wryly. "I had kind of noticed."

"You'd be gay if you hadn't," Bianca said,

clicking her fingers for Mercedes or Renee, the two stewardesses who were always on duty.

Mercedes dutifully made her way over.

"Two shot glasses of limoncello," Bianca ordered, barely looking at her. "And bring the bottle."

Imperious bitch! Mercedes thought. *Puta!* She couldn't wait to see the expression on Bianca's face when Cruz's men took over the yacht. *Who'll be giving orders then?*

"I gather we're drinking," Flynn said, not averse to the thought.

"You look like you need a drink," Bianca observed.

"I do."

"Problems in paradise?" she inquired, probing gently.

"Huh?" he said, rubbing his stubbled chin.

"Well," she said casually, "you and your lady friend, you're not exactly all over each other."

For one wild moment, Flynn thought she meant Sierra. Then he realized that she was talking about Xuan. Too bad. He would have quite enjoyed relaying the saga of him and Sierra, if only to get an outside opinion. Not that he would. It was private. It was between him and the love of his life.

Yes, he was forced to admit it: Sierra was indeed still the love of his life. And it wasn't too late for them, was it?

Realization dawned like a sharp kick in the gut. He wanted her back. In spite of everything, he still loved her.

"Are you pissed that Xuan is spending so much time talking to Aleksandr?" Bianca continued, leaning toward him, keeping her voice low.

Flynn snapped back to reality. "Are you?" he countered.

"Am I what?" Bianca asked, stroking a strand of her sleek dark hair.

"Pissed that your boyfriend is all over my . . . uh . . . girlfriend?"

"Oh my God!" Bianca squealed. "I can't believe you just said that!"

"Didn't *you* say it first?"

Mercedes appeared with two shot glasses and a bottle of Lemoncello.

Bianca snatched one of the glasses and hurriedly downed the sweet liquid.

"Aren't you joining me?" she said, fixing Flynn with a challenging look.

"Tequila's more my style," he replied.

"A bottle of tequila," Bianca snapped at Mercedes. "And make it fast."

"So what's going on?" Flynn asked, sensing something was on her mind. "You seem disturbed. Is Xuan annoying you?"

"Are you kidding?" Bianca said, raising an imperious eyebrow. "No disrespect to you, but it would take a lot more woman to annoy *me*. Xuan is like one of those irritating flying bugs you can't get rid of. She's after Aleksandr to put up money for all kinds of dumb stuff."

"I guess you must mean the school she's trying to get built in Cambodia?" Flynn said dryly. "Or food and supplies for the thousands of refugees in Sierra Leone?"

"I'm not sure what exactly," Bianca said vaguely. "Only please understand that this is *our* vacation, and chasing Aleksandr for money is totally inappropriate."

"You want me to tell her to lay off, is that it?"

"Yes," Bianca said firmly. "That's exactly what I want."

"I'll make an attempt," Flynn said, thinking that only a rich, spoiled, and privileged woman would act in such an insensitive way. "Although you gotta realize that Xuan is extremely single-minded. When she believes in something, it's all the way."

"Maybe you can fuck it out of her," Bianca said caustically.

"I'll take that as a suggestion," Flynn said, reaching for the bottle of tequila Mercedes brought over.

Might as well have a drink or two — maybe it would clear his head.

Two hours later, Flynn was feeling no pain. The flamenco dancers were long gone, as were most of the guests. The only ones that remained were Bianca, Aleksandr, Hammond, and Xuan. They were all drinking too much, and as the drinking progressed, so did the animosity. Hammond kept on making pointed remarks about journalists being the scum of the earth. Journalists, he announced drunkenly, staring straight at Flynn, were lying, cheating pieces of garbage who continually made up stories — especially about upstanding, honest politicians who wanted nothing more than to make the world a better place.

Xuan took umbrage at everything Hammond said, and the two of them argued, while Bianca cozied up to Aleksandr and wished he would suggest it was time for bed.

Flynn managed to keep his cool, until eventually he could hold back no longer. "Honest politicians?" he said sharply. "That's a fuckin' joke, isn't it?"

Up until this point, he and Hammond had ignored each other. But now the floodgates opened and all bets were off.

"*You* can talk about jokes," Hammond said, rising from his seat. "Everyone knows that you're nothing but a poor-ass loser, a nobody. What have *you* ever accomplished? Fuck all as far as I can tell."

"Screw you," Flynn retaliated, also jumping up. "Jesus, Ham, you cheated your way through college, an' I got a big hunch that's exactly how you're handling your so-called

403

political career. Oh yeah, an' here's the real joke: one day you're gonna try to make a run for the presidency. My *ass.* They'll see you for what you are *way* before that."

"Y'know something," Hammond slurred. "You open your mouth an' out pours a shit-load of crap."

"Hey," Flynn said, narrowing his eyes, "talking of crap, do not think I don't know what you did way back. But then I guess you couldn't get her any other way, right? You had to cheat an' lie. Fortunately, you're an expert at that, so no problem."

"I have no idea what you're talking about."

"Sure you do," Flynn taunted. "The photos, asshole. The fake fuckin' photos you sent to me and Sierra to break us up. Well, she knows all about it now, so you're screwed."

Hammond's mouth tightened into a thin line, and his face reddened. "Whatever I did was for her own protection," he said angrily. "And let me tell you this, you dumb bastard: the truth is that she *never* loved you, and Goddammit, she *never* will."

Xuan leaped to her feet, all five feet two of her. "Enough!" she shouted sternly. "Flynn, time for bed. Let's go."

"Yes, that's right," Hammond sneered. "Run away with your Chinky piece of ass. I bet she sucks you off like a true professional."

Before anyone could stop him, Flynn hauled his fist back and socked Hammond

404

square in the face.

Hammond dropped like a dead weight.

Aleksandr was unamused. He abruptly stood up. "Come," he said to Bianca, as Kyril miraculously appeared, placing his considerable bulk between Flynn and Hammond. "It is time this evening ended."

CHAPTER FIFTY-EIGHT

Cruz's gang of Somalian pirates were a wild and dirty-looking bunch, headed by their clan leader, Amiin, the only one of them who spoke English. Amiin took his orders from Cruz, and bossed the other men accordingly. They were a motley crew of misfits who thanks to a successful pirating operation had become richer than they'd ever imagined. Half of them were former fishermen who had embraced their chosen profession with much zeal, expressing no fear when it came to boarding a vessel at sea ripe for the plucking. The fruits of their labors were plentiful, allowing them many of the luxuries in life that they never thought they'd see. As long as they had their precious khat to chew on, and a formidable supply of weapons, they were ready to face anything.

Lately, they'd been enjoying the good life while awaiting instructions from Amiin, who in turn waited for Cruz to bark his orders.

In Acapulco they'd been entertained by a

few chosen hookers. Now, in the guesthouse of the rented villa, they were starting to get restless, and most of them were ready to go home to their families.

Including Amiin, there were seven of them, ranging in age from eighteen — Cashoo, Amiin's nephew — to Basra, a tall skeletal man of indeterminate age with mahogany skin, sunken eyes, unkempt dreadlocks, and very few teeth.

Basra was a man to beware of. He had no compunction about shooting to kill if anyone got in his way. He'd done so twice, even though Amiin had lectured him that it was to their advantage not to leave a trail of dead bodies.

Basra didn't care. He was a lethal weapon, and it was best to stay on his good side.

Cashoo had been working with Amiin since he was fourteen, and he'd exhibited a fearlessness that made him a useful member of the team. He was lanky, with light mocha skin, raggedy facial hair, high cheekbones, and thin lips. Cashoo's favorite pastime was sex. He had several girlfriends back home, but Cashoo was never satisfied.

The moment Ina arrived at the villa, Cashoo's libido raged out of control. Amiin saw the look of lust in his young nephew's eyes and sternly warned him to not even glance in the woman's direction, since she belonged to the big boss, and as such was

407

untouchable.

A warning didn't stop the fearless Cashoo; he'd never seen a woman like Ina before, and he was quite smitten.

The pirates were confined to the guest-house on the property, although they were also working on stocking their high-speed boats, loading supplies and weapons, in preparation for the strike against the *Bianca.*

As soon as Ina arrived, she took up a position by the pool in a patterned orange bikini that barely covered any of her considerable assets, and they were quite considerable, given the twenty pounds she'd gained since her reign as Miss Mexico.

Cashoo lusted from afar.

Ina threw him a flirtatious smile.

Cruz noticed what was going on and ordered Ina to get back inside the house pronto.

"Since when're you the boss of me?" Ina inquired, a steely glint in her over-mascaraed eyes. "It's not as if I'm your snively kid you can boss around."

There was no love lost between Ina and Cruz's daughter. Ina was jealous that Mercedes got to work with him, while she, the sister, had never been asked. Plus Mercedes was younger and prettier, and Cruz paid her plenty of money for — as far as Ina was concerned — doing nothing.

"You cause any trouble an' I'll kick your fat ass," Cruz warned her.

"What trouble?" Ina asked innocently. "You're the one that makes trouble."

She knew that the men who worked for Cruz were watching her with lust in their hearts, and she reveled in the attention.

Meanwhile, Sergei was all business. For the last few days, he'd been mulling a decision, and now that the time to strike was almost upon him, he had to make up his mind. To hold the *Bianca* for ransom was move number one. However, was that punishment enough for the son of a bitch who'd murdered his brother? The money wouldn't bring Boris back. Besides, what did money really mean to Aleksandr Kasianenko? The man was richer than God.

So Sergei had decided on a plan that would take the hijack one step further. They would certainly hold the *Bianca* for ransom, and once the money was paid and Cruz's team relinquished the boat and its passengers, the authorities would find that one key passenger was no longer aboard.

Sergei had no doubt that kidnapping Aleksandr Kasianenko was the only true way of taking his revenge.

CHAPTER FIFTY-NINE

The talk at the breakfast table was all about last night's fight. News soon spread, and by the light of day everyone knew about it.

Bianca was somewhat put out. She'd already told Luca that she didn't want any drama on the trip, and now this had to happen. "You've got to do something," she'd informed Aleksandr the moment they got back to their stateroom the night before. "We can't have our trip ruined by some stupid fight."

"I understand," he'd assured her. "It will be dealt with."

Now it was morning and everybody was trying to figure out what was going on. Why were Hammond and Flynn such bitter enemies? And who was the "she" Hammond had mentioned?

Bianca corralled Luca and gave him a blow-by-blow account of the fracas.

Luca wanted details. Bianca supplied what she knew.

Taye was upset that he'd missed the fight — or at least the knockout punch. Ashley wasn't; she hated any kind of violence.

Jeromy was relieved that something else was taking center stage. He and Luca had yet to have "the talk." Somehow or other he'd managed to avoid it.

The previous night, Hammond had retreated to his room with a burgeoning black eye only to find Sierra sleeping. They hadn't spoken since their earlier confrontation, and when he awoke the next morning, she was gone.

Xuan had attempted to calm Flynn down, but it wasn't possible because he was boiling. He'd slept fitfully on the couch, and in the morning he headed straight to the gym, making a futile attempt to work off his raging aggression. He stayed there until Guy appeared and informed him that Mr. Kasianenko would like to see him.

Guy was loving every minute of the goings-on. One day, when he wrote his tell-all book, this would make a fine chapter. Yes, it could go right next to the chapter about the garment tycoon who one year had rented a luxury yacht, filled it with hookers, and barely got them off the day his wife and children arrived. The crew had had to hustle that day.

Ah, fond memories of life at sea . . .

"We missed all the excitement," Lori said to

Cliff over breakfast.

He smiled at her across the table, white movie-star teeth in full bloom. "Maybe we're lucky, sweetie. Wouldn't want to get involved."

"Exactly," Ashley chimed in, pushing scrambled eggs across her plate. "I'm *glad* I wasn't there. I can't stand seeing men fight."

"Me either," said Lori, taking a bite of toast.

"Does anyone know what it was all about?" Ashley asked, curious to get the details.

Jeromy shrugged his shoulders. "Extremely childish if you ask me. And most disrespectful to our host."

"What about your hostess?" Bianca said, joining the table with Luca right behind her.

"Naturally I meant you too," Jeromy said, wondering where the hell they'd been. He did not appreciate Luca running off with Bianca. Were they talking about him behind his back? He certainly hoped not.

"I'm really glad there were no paparazzi around," Cliff said, reaching for the orange juice. " 'Cause if there were, everything would've been *my* fault. I'd be splashed all over TMZ with Harvey making rude comments."

"Or if it was the bloody *English* press, *I'd* be the one to get the shitty end of it," Taye interjected, staking his claim to fame. "They get off on raggin' on me. It's a national sport."

"You're both wrong," Bianca said grandly.

412

"I can see the headline now: 'Supermodel Causes Fight Between Russian Oligarch and American Senator.' I *always* get the blame."

"Aleksandr wasn't involved, was he?" Ashley asked innocently.

"Doesn't matter," Bianca said, tossing back her long dark hair. "All they're after is a headline to sell their story. Believe me, they like nothing better than putting my photo on the front page. Preferably in a bikini."

"She's right," Luca agreed.

"How positively juvenile!" Jeromy said with a peevish toss of his head.

Mercedes listened to them all as she hovered near the table, ready to serve. She'd already figured out what was going on. The day before, she'd eavesdropped on Flynn's conversation with the senator's wife. Well, it didn't take a genius to realize there was history there. The senator had a hard-on against the journalist 'cause he figured the journalist was out to fuck his wife. It was simple, only these *cabrones* didn't get it. They were too self-obsessed.

Late last night she'd sent her latest report to Cruz. He needed to know if she thought any of the guests would put up resistance. As far as she could tell, the journalist was the only one with balls, and she'd already checked that he had no weapons. The rest of them were easy street. Although she'd discovered that Aleksandr kept a loaded gun in his

413

bedside drawer. And Kyril could be a slight problem — only slight, for Mercedes knew exactly how she would handle him when the time came.

After dinner the night before, she'd taken Kyril a mug of hot chocolate. She was working on a hunch that he might like it.

Right again. The big man had drunk it down, smacked his lips, and informed her that it was good. Then his beady eyes had inspected her cleavage once again, and she'd known she was on the right track.

Hot chocolate and a flash of tit. She had Kyril's number.

"Hey," Flynn said, walking out onto the private terrace of Alekandr's stateroom. "Nice digs."

Aleksandr put down the sheaf of papers he was reading and nodded at Flynn. "I cannot blame you for last night," he said gruffly. "I also cannot condone what you did."

"No shit?" Flynn said, thinking that he didn't give a damn what Aleksandr thought. If it weren't for Sierra, he would have gotten off the yacht as soon as possible. But no, he wasn't about to walk out of her life again, not until he knew exactly where they stood.

"In Russia we toast with vodka — make the peace," Aleksandr said. "Is that possible?"

"Sure," Flynn said, Hammond's words still ringing in his ears. *She never loved you and*

414

she never will. What a fucking piece of shit.

Aleksandr buzzed for Guy. "Bring vodka and fetch the senator," he ordered. "Now."

As usual, Guy jumped. Last night's activities had certainly broken the monotony of being on a yacht. A bit of excitement was always welcome; sometimes things went along too smoothly.

Ten minutes later, Hammond appeared, wearing dark shades and a scowl.

"Let's put this nonsense to rest," Aleksandr stated firmly as Guy handed out shot glasses filled with vodka. "We'll toast to peace and harmony."

Flynn threw his vodka back, as did Hammond. They hardly looked at each other. Hatred lingered in the air.

Aleksandr nodded sagely. "Today is the day for water sports," he said, standing up. "Come, gentlemen, we have many toys to play with."

The day passed filled with a flurry of activities, including riding the state-of-the-art Jet Skis and WaveRunners, waterskiing, and exploring the crystal-blue waters of the Sea of Cortez.

Everyone threw themselves into having fun — everyone except Jeromy, who claimed his English skin was far too delicate to be exposed to the elements.

"C'mon, mate," Taye encouraged, climbing

415

aboard after his third trip on a WaveRunner. "You dunno what you're missin'. It's a freakin' blast."

Jeromy rolled his eyes, indicating his lack of enthusiasm. "Oh, I think I do know what I'm missing," he said, with a supercilious smirk. "Extreme sunburn and aching muscles."

"Party pooper," Taye said with a good-natured shrug.

Luca hauled himself aboard next, bronzed and beautiful as usual. "Another race?" he said to Taye, shaking droplets of water from his mop of blond hair.

"You got it," Taye said, always up for a challenge.

Jeromy stared at the two specimens of manhood standing before him. They were both in perfect shape. Taye all gleaming black skin and defined muscles. Luca so edible in his tight swim shorts, leaving nothing to the imagination.

Jeromy was aroused. Random anonymous sex was as necessary to him as a full meal, and usually, on land, he could always find someone to satisfy him. Now he was trapped on a yacht, so where could he find the temporary satisfaction he craved?

The answer came to him in a flash. Guy. The entertainment director. He was gay, wasn't he? He was there to serve, right?

The women were lolling on a giant hooded inflatable pool mattress, bobbing around in the sea. It held four people, so Lori, Bianca, Sierra, and Ashley had taken up residence. Flynn and Cliff had gone snorkeling, while Hammond was at the pool, sitting with Aleksandr and Xuan.

Jeromy took advantage of everyone being occupied and approached Guy. "Kindly accompany me to my room," he said. "There is something I have been meaning to show you."

"Should I call the housekeeper?" Guy inquired, wondering what was up.

"No, no, it's something that you should see first," Jeromy said, smoothing down his beige linen shirt — Tom Ford, of course.

"Right," Guy said, following the uptight Englishman down the stairs to the stateroom he shared with Luca.

As soon as they were inside the room, Jeromy quickly turned, slammed the door shut, and placed himself in front of it.

"What can I help you with?" Guy asked, imagining complaints about cleanliness or not enough towels — which were really not his problem.

"Here's what you can help me with — *this,*" Jeromy said, unzipping his shorts while still blocking the door.

Guy took one look and was immediately horrified. A guest exposing himself was the last thing he'd expected.

Jeromy shook free his penis, a long thin weapon of destruction. "Suck it," he commanded. "You know how to do that, don't you?"

Guy recoiled. Oral sex was not part of his job description. This untoward demand was unexpected and degrading. He was shocked.

"I'm . . . I'm sorry," he stammered, almost speechless. "I . . . I . . . can't."

"Don't be sorry," Jeromy said roughly, while continuing to block the door. "Simply do it, dear boy. It's a *cock* you're looking at. You've seen one of those before, haven't you?"

"I can't —"

"Oh yes, my dear boy, you certainly can," Jeromy said, feeling the need for an urgent release. "Because if you value your job, you'll do it, and you'll do it fast. Or perhaps you would prefer me to tell Mr. Kasianenko that *you* came on to *me,* then we'll see what he does about *that.* My instinct is that he'll fire your arse, and I'm sure you know I'm right."

Yes, Guy knew that he was. Reluctantly, he fell to his knees and did what the bony Englishman required.

Sometimes a man had no choice but to put his job first.

"Tell the truth," Bianca sighed, languidly trailing her hand in the calm blue sea. "Isn't Aleksandr the sexiest man ever?"

No, Lori was tempted to say. *Cliff possesses that title — courtesy of* People *magazine.*

418

"He's pretty damn sexy," Ashley chirped, blond hair piled on top of her head, bosoms fighting to stay within the confines of her minuscule bikini top. "But then so is my Taye."

"You got that right," Bianca agreed, thinking of her one night of lust with Taye and savoring the distant memory. "Taye's a hot one. I'd hang on to him if I were you."

"I already have," Ashley said with a crazed giggle. "My husband's besotted with me, in case you hadn't noticed."

"Oh yes, I've noticed," Bianca said. "He walks around with a permanent hard-on. Or is that just his normal package?"

Ashley managed a quick blush. "I am a lucky girl, aren't I?" she said, giggling again.

"You certainly are," Bianca said, turning to Lori. "How about you?" she asked. "Getting any closer to snagging Cliff?"

Oh damn. Not again. Why was everyone questioning her about Cliff's intentions? "Didn't I tell you I'm too young to get married?" Lori answered, going for the flippant approach.

"A girl is never too young to pin the guy she wants," Bianca advised. "If he asks, you gotta say yes."

"I'll remember that," Lori said, as Bianca shifted her attention to Sierra.

"How long have you and Hammond been married?" Bianca asked the senator's wife.

Sierra was lying back, enjoying the sun

while trying not to think about the inevitable confrontation with Hammond, which was yet to come. She'd heard about last night's altercation between her husband and Flynn. No details — only something about Hammond insulting all journalists and Flynn striking back.

She wished she could talk to Flynn, find out exactly what had happened, but she couldn't do that. The two men were already at war — no need to add fuel to the fire.

"Uh . . . a few years," she answered vaguely.

"It must be *so* exciting being married to a senator," Ashley enthused. "And an attractive one at that."

Don't forget horny, Lori was tempted to say, but once again she stopped herself.

"Yes," Sierra said quietly. "It's a lot of work, though. Fundraisers, endless functions, meet and greets. It can get quite tiring."

"But there are plenty of perks, I bet," Bianca said, thinking that if Sierra ever became first lady, she wouldn't mind being best friends with her. A night at the White House sounded like a fun plan. "And of course you've got all the designers offering you incredible outfits, right?" she added.

"*And* you get to meet the president, don't you?" Lori said, slightly in awe.

"Taye an' I met the prime minister of England a couple of times," Ashley said, joining in. "We've also been to a tea party at

Buckingham Palace. Prince William *loves* Taye, goes to all his big games."

"What kind of tea party?" Lori asked curiously.

"It's a Brit thing," Ashley said. "All outrageous hats, an' tea and crumpets in the palace gardens."

"Wow!" Lori exclaimed. "Sounds fancy."

"Oh, it is," Ashley said boastfully. "Only special people get invited."

Sierra felt it was time to move on. She slid quietly off the Lilo and into the calm blue water. After a few moments, she swam to the side of the yacht, where a deckhand helped her aboard.

And there was Flynn, sitting on a bench with Cliff, the two of them having just finished snorkeling.

"How was it?" she found herself asking.

"Incredible," Cliff said. "A must-do. I've been around, and I've never seen an underwater scene like it. It's a wonderland."

Her eyes met Flynn's — the connection between them was white hot.

Flynn dragged his eyes away as he stood up and reached for a towel.

"Would you care to give it a try, Mrs. Patterson?" one of the deckhands asked.

"Why not?" she said quietly.

"I can dive with you," the eager deckhand offered, handing her a snorkel, mask, and fins.

"That's okay," Flynn said quickly. "I think

I'll go back in."

"You're gonna love it, Sierra," Cliff encouraged.

"I'm sure I will," she murmured.

"I'd come back in, but I'm going to find Lori," Cliff said. "She'll really get a thrill."

Sierra barely heard him, because now Flynn was staring at her again, and this time he held the look.

Their eyes locked, and in those few seconds she knew that everything was about to change.

She still loved him — there was no doubt about it.

CHAPTER SIXTY

Eddie March was livid that Hammond had failed to call him back. He was in the middle of handling a major crisis, and the senator could not be bothered to pick up a satellite phone, or whatever the yacht he was so busy cruising on had.

The Byrne family was getting even more restless, and to top it off, Hammond's fifteen-year-old illegitimate daughter, Radical, had been thrown out of her Swiss boarding school and was on her way back to New York.

Radical was a nightmare, and Eddie was in no mood to deal with her too. The Byrnes were enough work. Keeping them from going public was getting more and more difficult. He'd even offered them money until he could sort things out. "We do not want money," Martin Byrne had informed him with a steely glare. "We want to hear the senator's side of the story."

So do I, Eddie thought.

He tried calling the yacht again, and this

time he was told that the senator was un-reachable.

"Where is he that he's so unreachable?" Eddie demanded.

"Exploring the ocean," the first officer replied. "I will certainly see that he gets your message."

Exploring the ocean indeed! While he, Eddie March, was shoveling the shit. It wasn't right. If he didn't get a call back soon, he was telling the Byrnes to do what they liked.

Hammond had created a mess, and it was up to him to deal with it.

Chapter Sixty-One

The underwater paradise was so peaceful and unbelievably breathtaking that Sierra forgot about everything and managed to lose herself in the array of marine life. She was too busy marveling at the vivid colors and incredible shapes of the numerous fish. Although she was fully aware that Flynn was in the ocean with her — and that made everything perfect.

When they finally surfaced, he reached for her hand, and as they touched, the electricity between them was startling. They bobbed in the water facing each other.

"You okay?" he asked, wishing she would open up to him.

"I will be," she replied softly.

"We need to talk some more."

"I know," she murmured, marveling at how good it felt being near him.

They exchanged another intense look.

The spell was broken when Cliff jumped into the sea with Lori, and the two of them swam over to join Flynn and Sierra.

"Found her," Cliff crowed. "Now I'm gonna show her the wonders that lurk below."

"Boasting about your crown jewels again?" Lori quipped, treading water beside him, her red hair piled on top of her head.

"Funny girl," Cliff replied, and they smiled warmly at each other.

Lori was delighted. Things were definitely looking up.

Sierra moved away from the group and swam toward the yacht. She couldn't avoid Hammond any longer; it was time to decide how they would handle the situation. No more threats. No more cowering. With or without Flynn, she had made up her mind that once this trip was over, she would free herself of Hammond forever.

"I told Flynn to have his girlfriend lay off asking you for money," Bianca said, snuggling close to Aleksandr as they lay out by their private lap pool. It was after lunch, and they'd left their guests to their own devices.

Aleksandr pushed her away and sat up. "You did what?" he said, raising his heavy eyebrows. Bianca was interfering with something that didn't concern her, and it annoyed him.

"I simply told him to get Xuan to stop bugging you," Bianca said. "It was getting to be too much."

"Too much for whom?" Aleksandr asked,

426

his tone sharp.

"Well, for me, actually," Bianca answered, narrowing her green eyes. "This trip is supposed to be all about you and me, and every time I turn around, there's Little Miss Do-Gooder bugging you for money for another of her precious causes. I can't take it."

"You shouldn't have done that," Aleksandr said, his face darkening. "It is not for you to decide who I speak to, or what we speak about."

Bianca frowned. "Excuse me?" she said haughtily. *Was Aleksandr actually scolding her?*

"You heard me," Aleksandr said, getting up and walking inside.

Furiously, Bianca leaped to her feet and followed him. "What is it with you and that girl?" she demanded. "Do you want to fuck her? 'Cause if you do, just tell me an' I'll make out with Flynn. He's quite the hunk, in case you hadn't noticed."

Aleksandr stared her down, his eyes cold and disapproving. "What is wrong with you?" he said at last. "Are you so insecure that because I talk to another woman you think I want to be with her? What kind of nonsense is that? I do what pleases me, Bianca. Never forget it."

Bianca scowled. Her plan of getting Xuan to leave Aleksandr alone was failing dismally.

Luca and Taye decided to organize a Jet Ski

contest. Later in the afternoon they rounded up everyone who wished to participate.

"Girls against dudes," Luca suggested with a cheeky grin. "Where's Bianca?"

"I'm here," she said, joining them. She was not prepared to spend the afternoon with Aleksandr; it was about time he realized he couldn't talk to her in such a dismissive way. He'd called her insecure, and that didn't fly. *Insecure indeed. Screw him.*

"You can head the girls' team," Luca said to Bianca. "Taye, you up for playin' captain?"

"Are you friggin' kiddin' me?" Taye said, running a hand over his shaved head. "It's my job, so get ready — 'cause I'm gonna kick everyone's arse."

Soon the crew had assembled a fleet of Jet Skis and they were off.

Lori raced Ashley and, to Lori's surprise, she actually won. Then Bianca went up against Xuan — and, to Bianca's extreme annoyance, Xuan beat her.

After that it was the guys' turn. Luca and Cliff raced and Luca was the winner. Then it was Flynn and Taye, a hard battle until Flynn ruled triumphant.

Everyone threw themselves into it — except Aleksandr, who wasn't present; Jeromy, who hovered on the sidelines looking thoroughly bored; and the Pattersons, who were not around.

Guy helped the proceedings move forward,

even though he was humiliated beyond belief. At least he still had his job, no thanks to Jeromy Milton-Gold.

Guy couldn't even glance in the Englishman's direction. He hated him with a deep intensity and was starting to think about how he might get his revenge. Surely there had to be a way?

The final race was between Luca and Xuan. When Xuan lost, Bianca could hardly conceal her delight.

Karma's a bitch, bitch.

Bianca smiled her satisfaction.

The moment of reckoning was near. Sierra was well aware that it had to take place soon, and she was not avoiding it. In a perverse way, she was looking forward to it. Standing up to Hammond was something she should've done a long time ago. He'd cheated and lied his way into her life, she'd lost Flynn's baby because of him, and he'd kept her a prisoner with his dire threats against her and her family. Well, no more. It was over. She was finally ready to break free.

They met up in their stateroom. She'd gone straight there after her underwater adventure, taken a shower, dressed, and waited for him to appear.

Hammond walked in wearing dark glasses, which he immediately removed to show off a serious black eye. "This is because of you," he said accusingly. "This is what your piece-of-shit boyfriend did to me for no good reason."

"He's not my boyfriend," she said evenly. "And I'm sure you gave him an excellent reason."

"You think so, do you?" Hammond sneered.

"I understand you were both drinking."

"Where did you hear that?" he said, his tone bitter. "Did your boyfriend come running to tell you?"

"No, Hammond, he didn't," she replied, determined not to break. "And I'd appreciate it if we could conduct an adult conversation for once."

"Go ahead," he said coldly. "Say what you have to say."

She took a deep breath and went for it. "I'm sure you know how unhappy I am, and that we'd be better apart, so I've made a decision. I will stay with you for the duration of this trip, present a united front to prevent embarrassing you. And then when the trip is over, so are we." She swallowed hard. "I want a divorce, Hammond. I mean it."

"Really?" he said, surprisingly calm.

"Look," she continued, her words tumbling over each other. "I understand this has political implications for you, but surely you can see that it doesn't mean the end of your career. These things happen. Divorce is not uncommon among politicians —"

"You vapid, asinine *bitch*!" Hammond exploded, his voice filled with venom. "God almighty, I knew you were stupid, but this kind of talk goes beyond stupidity. Don't you understand that it's not possible? I repeat: divorce is *not possible*." His voice rose to a vicious shout. "One day I am going to be the fucking president of the United States, and you, my dear *wife,* are going to be right there next to me. Otherwise —"

"Otherwise what?" she said bravely, holding her ground, trying not to revert to the weak-willed Sierra who'd put up with his bullying and threats for too many years.

"Otherwise," Hammond said ominously, "you'll be dead. And so will your fucking boyfriend."

Listening outside their door, Mercedes felt a shiver of excitement. Drama on the high seas. But this drama would mean nothing in comparison to what was to come. Little did they know what was in store for them.

Guy had sent her to deliver a message to Senator Patterson about someone trying to reach him via satellite phone. Guy was in a shitty mood, barking orders as if *he* were the captain. *Idiota.* He would never make captain — he didn't have the stones. Besides, he was gay, and how many gay men made captain?

Probably this wasn't a good time to interrupt the Pattersons. She knocked on the door

431

anyway. What did she care that the *imbécil* was threatening to kill his wife? The *puta* probably deserved it, seeing that she was jumping the bones of the sexy journalist guy. Or at least it looked that way.

Hammond flung open the door. "What?" he said curtly.

Mercedes stared at his mother of a black eye, handed him the neatly typed message, and inquired if he'd like her to accompany him to the communications room.

He barely glanced at the message, said a short, sharp "No!," and slammed the door in her face.

What a cabrón, Mercedes thought, switching her allegiance to the wife, who seemed like a nice enough woman, unlike the other *putas* on the boat, who all acted as if they were better than everyone else, especially the blonde with the big tits and the hot black husband.

Yet another hot guy. If she weren't working, this could be quite a trip. However, work always came first. And at the conclusion of this particular trip she was going for it, taking everything she could get her greedy hands on.

Money and jewelry. She considered it her bonus.

CHAPTER SIXTY-TWO

On a boat at sea in close quarters — albeit extremely luxurious ones — friends are made, idle gossip abounds, and all thoughts of the real world drift away. Aleksandr's ploy of enticing everyone to give up their iPhones, BlackBerrys, iPads, and computers for a delicious uninterrupted week of lazy bliss was a solid one. For emergencies there was always satellite communication.

A successful vacation equals relaxation — and Aleksandr expected his guests to leave their everyday lives behind.

Personally, he was enjoying himself. Sex with Bianca was spectacular, although her nagging about Xuan was annoying. His conversations with the Asian woman were interesting and in a way quite challenging, and in spite of Bianca's objections he had no intention of giving them up. Trust Flynn to have come up with a woman who was not only very attractive but smart too. And he was most impressed that Xuan wasn't intimidated by him, not at all.

If he weren't with Bianca, Aleksandr realized, he might have entertained different thoughts about Xuan. Sexual thoughts. However, he was in a committed relationship with Bianca, so all fantasies of sex with Xuan were banished to the back of his mind. Besides, she was with Flynn, and he would never disrespect a man like Flynn, whom he considered a true friend.

He was disturbed that Senator Patterson had behaved so badly the night before. The man had deserved to get hit; the senator had enticed Flynn to do so with his ridiculous attack of words. Quite frankly, Aleksandr was pleased to see Hammond receive a black eye, for he'd already decided there was something about him that he didn't like. Hammond possessed a pleasant and ingratiating exterior, but lurking beneath was a hard core of something else.

Aleksandr had always considered himself to be an astute judge of character, and he didn't trust Hammond. He decided he would keep an eye on the man's further rise to power, then he would act accordingly when the inevitable request came to donate money and support to the senator's campaign.

Yes, Aleksandr knew for sure that the day would eventually come.

After the race, Bianca hung out with Luca

and Taye by the pool. She wasn't about to run back to Aleksandr's side. He could be unpredictable and bossy. It pissed her off. How dare he get mad at her? *He* was the one paying too much attention to Little Miss Intensity.

She was particularly irritated because she'd never treated a man as well as she'd treated Aleksandr. Shouldn't he be kissing her beautiful tight ass like everyone else?

Didn't Aleksandr get it? She was *Bianca.* A superstar in her field. She was not used to being lectured and told what to do.

Damn him! And damn Flynn for bringing his Asian girlfriend aboard. The two of them were hardly the same caliber as the other guests.

Bianca sighed. It was her own fault; she should've vetted the guest list more closely. Xuan and Flynn were not a good fit for the rest of the group, although she had to admit that Flynn was wildly sexy with his action-movie-star looks — not all groomed and perfect like Cliff Baxter. Flynn was more edgy, like a roughed-up Ryan Reynolds with a touch of Alex O'Loughlin, the actor who played Steve McGarrett on *Hawaii Five-O.*

Another time, another place, and she would've definitely hit that.

And talking of hitting that . . .

Mischievously, she leaned over to Taye, who was busy sunning himself, his black skin gleaming in the sunlight. "Hey, sexy," she said in a seductive whisper. "Remember way back when you and I got it on?"

Taye shot up, startled. *Oh shit.* Where was Ashley? If she even suspected that he and Bianca had done the dirty, she would have his friggin' balls for breakfast, even though it had taken place long before he and Ashley were together.

"You don't have to worry," Bianca crooned. "Wifey's in the hair salon getting all prettied up for you."

Taye breathed again.

"We would've made incredible babies," Bianca mused, having fun playing with him. "Can you imagine how gorgeous they would've been with *our* genes?"

"Jeez!" Taye muttered, totally alarmed. "It was years ago. Best kept on the down low, right?"

"If you mean would I tell Ashley, of course not," Bianca said guilelessly. "Although we were both free agents then, so we've got nothing to feel guilty about. It wasn't like we were *cheating* on anyone."

"Who's guilty?" Taye said, manning up. "Although here's the deal — my wife has a raging jealous streak you do *not* wanna mess with. She *still* gives me crap about my first girlfriend way back when I was friggin' twelve!"

Luca surfaced from his nearby lounger, a

huge grin on his tanned face. "How come you never told me?" he said, directing his words toward Bianca. "Keepin' secrets, huh?"

"Oh fuck!" Taye groaned.

"My lips are shut tight," Luca said, still grinning.

"They'd better be," Taye grumbled.

Bianca stood up and dived into the pool. Revealing other people's secrets always made her feel so much better.

What next? Flynn didn't know, and it was driving him crazy. Apart from his brief underwater interlude with Sierra — during which talking was obviously not an option — he had no idea where her head was at.

Did she feel the same way he did?

Had any of those old feelings resurfaced?

Was it even possible to go back?

He didn't know. It was up to her.

Hammond's words still reverberated in his head. *She never loved you and she never will.*

Bullshit.

Cliff was behaving like a changed man. Lori wasn't sure what had come over him, although it was definitely something. She'd never known him to be this affectionate and attentive.

Was it because of the senator's blatant flirting with her?

Was it because Cliff was on vacation and

the pressures of always playing Mister Movie Star were turned off for once?

She didn't know and she didn't care, for this was a whole new Cliff Baxter. This was the man she'd fallen in love with.

After the afternoon's water sports and the under-the-sea spectacle, Cliff had taken her by the hand and suggested they repair to their room.

Fine with her. She knew what he wanted, and she was prepared to oblige.

But no, getting blown was not what he had in mind. His intent was to please *her.*

She was shocked and surprised, because making sure she was satisfied was not high on Cliff's agenda. When it came to bedroom activities, he was always the star.

Today things were different. Today Cliff was heading in a whole other direction.

He started kissing her the moment they entered their room. The kissing was dreamy, and soon led to him removing her bikini top and caressing her breasts, paying special attention to her nipples as his mouth moved downward.

Lori shivered with the unexpected pleasure of it all, reveling in his touch. After a while she reached down to fondle his crotch. He quickly pushed her hand away. "Not yet," he said, his voice a husky drawl. "Lie down on the bed, baby. I want to look at you."

She did as he asked, feeling totally turned on.

Cliff stood over her, gazing at her taut body clad in nothing but the bottom half of her bikini. "I never get to see you like this," he said. "You have a really beautiful body."

Compliments too! This was unbelievable.

Then he bent down and began slowly peeling her bikini bottom off until she was completely naked. Next he rose and stood back, once more admiring her, his eyes taking in every inch.

Lori shivered with the intensity of it all. She'd never felt more exposed and yet filled with excitement.

She gazed up at him as his hands settled on her thighs, gently pushing her legs apart. And after that he did something that he'd only ever done to her once before, and that was the first time they'd made love. He actually began performing oral sex on her.

Lori threw her hand across her eyes and writhed across the bed.

"Keep still," he commanded. "You know you like it, baby. You know you do."

Who wouldn't? Cliff Baxter, star of a million women's fantasies, was going down on her, his tongue darting in and out of her most private places.

A mind-blowing orgasm was swift. And the moment she reached the pinnacle, he dropped his shorts and moved on top of her, lazily fucking her until she came again.

It was the best time they'd ever had in bed.

Somehow, Lori had a strong suspicion that dumping her was no longer on Cliff's mind.

CHAPTER SIXTY-THREE

Sergei grunted like a soon-to-be-satisfied pig as he screwed his ex–beauty queen girlfriend doggie style. Ina was getting fat. It didn't bother him; he got off on squeezing the rolls of flesh gathered around her waist, then digging into her giant ass with his penis, which was not as large as he would've liked. Although who needed a big cock when a man had endless drug money and a certain amount of power?

Ina was adept at providing other girls for sex when he was in the mood, which was a bonus. His skinny American cunt girlfriend, Cookie, felt that she was too special to be shared, and Sergei had always been partial to a threesome.

Lately, he'd been thinking of cutting Cookie loose. All she ever did was whine, complain about inconsequential shit, and spend his money shopping for ridiculously expensive shoes and bags.

The upside was that she was an American

girl who'd once been in a successful movie; therefore, showing up with her boosted his ego when he was invited to grand functions in Mexico City. She was the arm candy to get him noticed.

Over the years, Sergei had done "favors" for a lot of important people, including well-placed politicians and high-ranking members of the police force. In return he was invited everywhere. It was a side of his life he enjoyed. It swelled his chest with importance, and a dressed-up Cookie was the perfect girl by his side. Ina wouldn't cut it — too obvious and trampy.

After finishing the task at hand, he pulled out and favored Ina with a couple of hefty slaps on her generous butt.

"You're a sow," he growled, not unaffectionately.

" 'Scuse me?" she said, reaching for her robe.

"Big titties. Big ass," he guffawed. "I like it all."

"So does everyone else around here," she boasted, flouncing across the room, not sure she was down with his so-called compliments.

Sergei's eyes went dead. "I've warned you, and so's your brother. Stop paradin' around the pool shakin' your stuff at the workers."

"What's wrong with them looking?" Ina argued. "They can look, but they can't touch."

Sergei grabbed a fistful of her hair, causing her to cry out in pain. "*I* look. *I* touch," he spat. "You stay in the goddamn house when I tell you. Got it?"

"What's that leafy shit your guys chew on all the time?" Sergei wondered.

Cruz shrugged, a cigarette hanging precariously from his bottom lip. "Khat. It's a stimulant — keeps 'em alert an' happy."

"You want 'em happy?" Sergei snorted his disgust. "What t' fuck?"

"I want 'em ready t' do anything I tell 'em to do," Cruz replied, taking a long drag on his cigarette, his small eyes ever watchful.

Sergei nodded.

"They're dangerous men — stupid an' reckless as shit," Cruz continued, blowing out a stream of smoke. "That's t' way they get the job done."

"I should hope so," Sergei grumbled, the nerve in his left cheek starting to twitch. "This deal is costing."

"You'll get it back an' plenty more when we go for the ransom," Cruz assured him.

"I fuckin' expect so."

"Here's the deal with my men," Cruz said, taking another long drag on his cigarette. "They're driven by the money — it turns 'em into heroes when they take home the loot."

"Fuckin' heroes?" Sergei jeered.

"You got it," Cruz replied, stamping his

cigarette underfoot. "An' believe me, in the shithouse towns they come from, they *are* the fuckin' heroes, with a coupla pretty wives, a fancy car, an' as many kids as they wanna have."

"You got a wife?" Sergei asked, thinking that he didn't know much about Cruz's personal life.

"Who's dumb enough to buy the cow when y' can suck the *putas*?" Cruz chuckled. "An' Somalian *putas*?" He made a wicked smacking noise with his mouth. "Beauties, an' grateful."

Sergei liked the sound of that, although he was well aware that you took your life in your hands if you visited Somalia. It was one of the most dangerous countries in the world: lawless, with a barely functioning government. The kidnapping of foreigners was a national pastime.

"My men are scared of nothin' 'cept hunger," Cruz announced. "That's what makes 'em so fearless an' strong."

"You really fell into it, didn't you?" Sergei commented.

"You bet your ass," Cruz bragged. "Me, I live like a fuckin' king. Got in at the right time with the right connections. I'm the only foreigner they trust. An' as long as I keep makin' 'em money, they're gonna keep on trustin' me."

Sergei nodded again. He understood.

CHAPTER SIXTY-FOUR

The evening plan was dinner on another, larger island, and this time Aleksandr expected everyone to attend. Instructions were to meet on the deck by the tenders at seven P.M.

Bianca returned to the master suite and gave Aleksandr the silent treatment as she sat in front of the bedroom mirror braiding her long dark hair while wearing nothing more than a sexy leopard-print thong. She was well aware that seeing her naked always turned him on. He had a thing for her tits, so small and perfect. She'd already decided that tonight he wasn't getting anything sexual, not until he apologized. Sex was definitely off the menu.

Aleksandr needed to realize that she wasn't just another pretty face he could boss around. She was Bianca. She was a superstar, and he'd better get that into his head.

Aleksandr had no desire to continue their

argument, such as it was, although he was still determined to hold his ground as far as Xuan was concerned. Bianca could sit in front of the mirror half naked for as long as she wanted; he wasn't about to touch her until she learned that she could not tell him what to do or whom to talk to. He considered it outrageous that she thought she could, and he wasn't accepting it. Bianca had a spoiled streak, and it was his job to make her see that she could not exhibit that kind of attitude with him.

He *was* the boss, something she still had to get used to.

"What an adventure!" Ashley exclaimed, getting ready for the evening's activities.

Taye nodded his agreement. Sex with his wife on a daily basis was a hell of a lot more than he'd expected. As far as he was concerned, they could stay on the yacht for a couple more months. No problem.

"Do you like these earrings?" Ashley asked, holding a pair of diamond-studded hoops to her earlobes.

"Love 'em," Taye replied, thinking he'd love them even more when he got her naked later.

Ashley put on the earrings. She was busy thinking about Cliff Baxter. She was especially excited, as Cliff had been extremely friendly at lunch. Now she was quite sure that he fancied her. Cliff Baxter had what her mum would call "bedroom eyes," and those eyes had been all over her.

She fantasized about what she would do if he came on to her.

Well, she wouldn't turn him down, that was for sure. And as far as Taye was concerned, it would be payback time for when he'd screwed that Page 3 slag.

Careful of what you do in life, Ashley thought. *'Cause one day it can come back and bite you firmly on the ass.*

Ah yes, Ashley's fantasies were in full bloom.

A feeling of helplessness overcame Sierra as she sat in their stateroom listening to Hammond drone on about exactly how he would deal with Flynn if she ever dared to talk to him again, or repeat the word *divorce.*

"You do know that I can have him killed any way I want," Hammond crowed, sweat beading his forehead. "Skinned alive. Shot in the head. Blown up in a car. I might even give you the pleasure of choosing his fate, my dear wife. Wouldn't that be an interesting decision for you to make."

This torrent of threats had been going on for some time, and she didn't know what to do. Was Hammond completely psychotic? Had he lost his mind? Or could he actually arrange to have those threats carried out?

Was it possible?

Anything was possible.

This was exactly how he'd kept her tied to him all these years. Threats against her personally. Threats against her family. But Flynn's name had never entered into the equation, and once more, it all seemed so horribly real.

"Why are you doing this?" she managed.

"Why am *I* doing this?" Hammond replied, simmering with fury. "Why am *I* doing this?" he repeated, his bland features contorting into an angry distorted mask. "*You* are the one who is doing this to us. *You* are the one who is determined to end my political career."

"No, I'm not," she objected, swallowing hard, holding back tears because she felt so helpless against his threats. Helpless and alone. She should've known there was no way out.

"Save me the whining," Hammond said harshly. "We are going to the island for dinner with our gracious host, and it would be nice if you could try to behave like a loving wife for once. These people are my future, so try to remember that. Now get dressed. I do not care to keep anyone waiting."

Lori luxuriated under the warm shower, savoring every delicious moment of Cliff's lovemaking. What a changed man! What an unexpected delight.

Cliff had showered first and gone to one of

448

the upper decks for a drink before their island visit. This time their trip to the island would be at night, so Lori wasn't quite sure how to dress. Should she take her bikini? Would there be midnight swimming in the ocean involved? Maybe even skinny-dipping?

She was exhilarated. How about *Mrs. Cliff Baxter*? Could that elusive title possibly be in her future?

Do not get carried away, she warned herself. *One session of cunnilingus does not a marriage make.*

Although things were definitely heading in the right direction.

Yes.

Mrs. Cliff Baxter.

Who knew what the future held?

"Do I *have* to go?" Jeromy groaned like a petulant child.

"Please yourself," Luca responded, keeping his tone noncommittal as he selected a sexy black frilled shirt from the closet. As each day passed, he was getting more and more fed up with Jeromy and his condescending attitude. It seemed nothing and no one pleased him. It was quite obvious that Jeromy was not the center of attention, which pissed him off. Jeromy was used to holding court, and on this trip there was no court for him to hold.

"Don't you *want* me to go?" Jeromy asked,

trying to manipulate Luca into begging for his presence.

Luca was having none of it. After this trip, he'd definitely ease Jeromy out of his life.

Jeromy was giving him an expectant look.

Luca shrugged as he put on the shirt. "Like I said, do what you want."

"I want *you* to tell me what to do," Jeromy replied, going for the subservient role, which didn't suit him at all. There was a long silent beat, and then, realizing that Luca was not about to beg him, he added a reluctant, "All right, I'll come."

Luca would have preferred it if Jeromy had opted to stay on the yacht, but it was not to be. He pulled on a pair of white pants, added a narrow black crocodile belt, and headed for the door. "See you upstairs," he said, and exited quickly, wondering how he was going to manage another few days of Jeromy's company.

In retrospect, he realized that he should've invited Suga and Luca Junior on this trip with him. They would've loved it, and everyone would've loved them.

Too bad and too late. He was stuck with Jeromy.

Cliff Baxter was already on the upper deck when Luca appeared. Cliff was sipping a martini and looking very suave in a long-sleeved charcoal T-shirt and matching linen pants, his dark hair slicked back.

Idly Luca wondered if the movie star had ever taken a walk on the wild side — there were always rumors — or if women just did it for him.

"Hey," Cliff said, greeting him with a smile.

"What's goin' on?" Luca responded.

"Don't know about you," Cliff said, "but I think I just experienced one of the best days of my life."

"That's sayin' something, comin' from you," Luca remarked.

"Yeah," Cliff said. "I came to the conclusion that Lori is a keeper."

"And you didn't know that before?" Luca asked curiously.

"Outside influences," Cliff said vaguely.

"I get it," Luca said. "Shouldn't listen to the chorus. When I came out, none of my advisers wanted me to do it. 'You'll lose all your fans,' they warned me. Hey, you know what — I *gained* fans. So I did what *I* wanted, an' it all worked out."

"I admire that," Cliff said.

"You admire what?" Bianca asked, appearing suddenly. She had a way of inserting herself into other people's conversations as if it were a perfectly acceptable thing to do.

"Never mind," Luca chided. "Where's Aleksandr?"

"He'll be here," Bianca said, waving an impatient hand at Mercedes. "Who do you

451

have to fuck around here to get a damn drink?"

Mercedes decided that when the time came, she would take Bianca's clothes. Even though the supermodel was at least eight inches taller than her, she coveted the many outfits Bianca wore. The sexy bikinis with thong bottoms; the selection of wild T-shirts and designer jeans; the long skirts and backless dresses. And the jewelry. Diamond bangles, a white Channel watch, a large aquamarine ring surrounded by diamonds. It was all expensive and ready to be taken.

The other women's clothes were more low-key — expensive, but not flashy enough for Mercedes. When this caper was over, she planned on stepping out and enjoying herself. She was thinking of buying herself a small apartment in the Seychelles, far enough away from Daddy Cruz and his heavily guarded complex in Somalia, which she'd only visited a few times. Cruz hadn't wanted her living with him anyway. "Too dangerous," he'd informed her. But he liked having her work for him. And so far she'd always blended in as one of the crew — a crew member who'd been able to supply all the information he'd needed before conducting a successful take-over.

This hijacking was different. Who expected to get taken over by Somalian pirates while quietly cruising the Sea of Cortez? Certainly not this group.

That a man of Aleksandr Kasianenko's wealth and importance would be traveling with just one bodyguard was loco. *And* with a group of rich famous people aboard. So crazy.

Mercedes had to admit that Cruz was one smart tiger. He'd somehow or other arranged to get his entire gang out of Somalia ready to do their thing. And Cruz's team was a ruthless bunch who always got the job done.

Screw it! she thought, licking her finger, then dipping it into Bianca's martini before delivering it to her. *I'm getting impatient. I've had enough of catering to these rich spoiled* chingados.

The only one who treated her with any kind of respect was Luca Perez. He spoke to her in Spanish, and always asked how she was doing. Unlike his *imbécil* partner with his I-am-better-than-anyone-else attitude, whom she truly loathed.

Ah, if Jeromy Milton-Gold only knew how many times she'd spat in his drinks. A small satisfaction.

Meanwhile, her relationship with Kyril — such as it was — seemed to be developing nicely. Once she'd discovered his weakness for chocolate, it was all systems go. She could get into his space anytime she wanted as long as she came bearing treats. Chocolate cake, chocolate cookies, chocolate bars, and his very favorite — a full mug of hot chocolate.

He must've been deprived as a kid in Russia. Never gotten his chocolate fix.

At least he only craved chocolate; she wouldn't have to screw him or service what she imagined might be a gigantic cock. Or maybe not — sometimes it was the big men who had tiny dicks. Anyway, thankfully she wouldn't have to find out. Chocolate had paved the way, and the time would soon come to put her plan in action.

Mercedes couldn't wait.

CHAPTER SIXTY-FIVE

Another island, only this time it was night, and this time the island was not completely deserted. At the top of a steep hill stood a magnificent old Spanish castle overlooking the pristine beach. The grand balcony of the castle was the setting for dinner.

A long antique table made of fine wood held candles in ornate silver holders and different arrangements of exotic flowers. A trio of Brazilian musicians had been imported for the night, and the food was also Brazilian, everything from *caruro* — a delicious mix of dried shrimp, okra, and onions — to *feijoada,* a simmered meat and bean dish.

Normally Bianca would've been all over Aleksandr, since he knew she loved anything connected to Brazil, and these were a few of her favorite foods, but she was still not talking to him, while he impatiently waited for her to apologize.

The two of them were playing a dangerous game.

Bianca began flirting outrageously with Taye, who was mortified, because if Ashley got even the slightest hint that he and the supermodel had once had sex, she would go ape-shit.

So that Bianca could see that she had no influence over what he did or who he spoke to, Aleksandr got together with Xuan and informed her that he had been thinking about their conversations, and he would be happy to finance the school she was involved with in Cambodia, and perhaps they should talk about building an orphanage outside Moscow. He confessed that he'd thought about it often, since he was an adopted child himself.

Xuan considered it a wonderful idea.

She was delighted that this luxury trip with all these so-called celebrities was paying off. She had already asked Taye if he would be interested in sponsoring a sports program for underprivileged kids in Haiti, and he'd said yes. And Cliff Baxter had agreed to be the star attraction at an auction to raise money for the refugees of Darfur.

Xuan was fully satisfied.

Flynn was not.

What the hell was going on with Sierra? She wouldn't look at him. She seemed to be in a daze again. She did not leave Hammond's side, which he found most disturbing. It was almost as if Hammond had cast some kind of spell over her.

Jesus Christ! What was he doing allowing himself to get hung up on Sierra again? Too much time had passed.

Hammond's words were burned into his brain. *She never loved you and she never will.*

Tomorrow he was definitely coming up with an excuse to get off the boat.

"I love your dress," Lori remarked to Ashley as they took their places at the dinner table.

I love your movie-star boyfriend, Ashley was tempted to reply. *And I have a strong suspicion he fancies me back.* Instead, she said, "Thanks. It's a Stella McCartney. I always feel fab in one of her designs; she really gets me."

"Oh," Lori said. "Does she sell her stuff in L.A.?"

Ashley shot Lori a semi-scornful look. Did Cliff's girlfriend know nothing? "Actually," she said, a tad condescendingly, "Stella has a store on Beverly Boulevard. I can take you there if you want. They all know me."

"I thought you lived in England."

"We do," Ashley said, thinking it was a wise move to stay friendly with the girlfriend just in case Cliff kept her around. "Taye enjoys L.A., so we try to fly in a couple of times a year, stay at the Beverly Hills Hotel, Taye's fave. Maybe you and Cliff can join us for dinner at the Polo Lounge next time we're there."

Why is she being so friendly? Lori thought. *This is a big change in personality.*

"Love to," Lori said brightly. "I'll tell Cliff."

As far as Mercedes was concerned, the timing couldn't've been better. Almost everyone was off the yacht, including Kyril, who Aleksandr had decided should accompany him for once. Mercedes was one happy girl, having feigned painful and debilitating stomach cramps to get out of going.

Guy had been furious; his bad moods were getting worse. "What's wrong with you?" he'd yelled. "Can't you understand that we need all the help we can get?"

"It's my time of the month," she'd replied, staring him down. "It's not my fault I suffer from bad cramps."

There was nothing Guy could do except give her the stink-eye.

Too bad, Mercedes thought. *He has the ever-obliging Renee and Den to take care of everyone.*

Apparently it was a big-deal dinner, so not many of the crew were left on the yacht, which suited Mercedes just fine. Earlier in the day she'd received a cryptic message from Cruz that they were ready. It was on.

Yippee!

Servitude would soon be over!

Cruz always operated at night. It was easier

458

to board when most of the crew were sleeping.

Cruz gave her the time; Mercedes gave him the approximate location.

There was much to prepare.

Tomorrow, after midnight, it was definitely on!

Hammond was disappointed to note that redheaded Lori was cuddling up to her movie-star boyfriend like a limpet. He had hoped to further their flirtation, but it was not to be. All the other women on the trip seemed to be quite cozy with their significant others, which left him no options except the Asian. Xuan was not a prospect — too militant and too short. He didn't like his women short.

Sierra was by his side and silent. He'd brought her back in line fast. Did she honestly believe she could get away from him?

No chance. He had her exactly where he wanted her. Compliant and scared. Threatening her once-upon-a-time boyfriend seemed to affect her more than threats against her precious family.

The thought occurred to him that maybe he should arrange to have Flynn killed anyway. There were people for hire who took care of that kind of thing. Why not?

Hammond smiled grimly at the thought.

Damn! He hadn't called Eddie back. And

he'd instructed him not to call unless it was urgent.

Too late now, thanks to Sierra. He'd call Eddie first thing in the morning.

"Can I get you a drink, Senator?"

Hammond turned to inspect Renee, the stewardess with the Australian accent. She wasn't bad-looking, although a little horsey with her large teeth and generous mouth. She was tall, though, which meant long legs. He was quite partial to long legs, especially when they were wrapped around his neck while his penis was firmly tucked inside the owner of the legs.

Why hadn't he noticed this one before?

Probably because the pushy Mexican girl had taken center stage, while this one had hovered on the sidelines.

He glanced over at Sierra. She was engaged in conversation with Ashley and Cliff.

"What's your name, dear?" he asked the stewardess, turning his back on his wife.

The girl blinked like a startled deer. "Uh . . . uh . . . Renee," she stammered, blushing slightly.

Ah, she was impressed. A United States senator was asking for her name, and she was thrilled.

Of course she was.

"Where are you from?"

"Australia."

"I gathered that from your accent. Where-

460

abouts in Australia?"

"Brisbane, actually."

Hammond's eyes dipped to her breasts. Not too big, not too small. He would've liked them to be bigger, but maybe her nipples would compensate. Hammond had a thing about nipples; he preferred them erect and chewy — all the better to bite on.

"Renee is a very pretty name for a very pretty girl," he said, giving her the sincere smile that always worked.

"Thank you," she murmured, lowering her eyes.

He winked at her. "I'll have a glass of champagne, Renee."

More blushing. He was on her radar.

He would fuck her. She was ripe and ready. Better than the redhead. Better than the blonde with the big tits. Better than their hostess. And sure as hell better than the Asian piece of work.

Hammond knew a sure thing when he saw it.

CHAPTER SIXTY-SIX

Preparations were in overdrive. Cruz's men were more than ready; they were on fire and primed for action. Too much lazing around was not good for them.

Second thoughts about going along with them on their mission were plaguing Sergei. Much as he harbored a strong desire to be the first to see Aleksandr Kasianenko's expression when they boarded the *Bianca,* Cruz was right: he had no experience when it came to hijacking. What if he got shot or knifed or injured in any other way? It could all go wrong, and he might easily become a victim.

Cruz's gang of misfits were heavily armed for battle, which made Sergei seriously think about veering toward the cautious side. He didn't fully trust Cruz. If anything happened to him, Ina's brother stood to gain the full ransom, so wasn't it foolish to set himself up as a target?

He'd financed this entire operation, and it

had cost him plenty, but if Cruz got greedy, he wasn't about to have it cost him his life.

Finally he came to the conclusion that the smart thing to do was back off the actual raid, and have Cruz's men bring Kasianenko to him while he stayed at the villa and waited.

When he informed Cruz of his change of heart, he thought he noticed a flash of triumph flit across the Mexican man's weather-beaten face.

Interesting. It paid to always be alert.

"I'll be sendin' two of my men with you to grab Kasianenko," he announced. "You'll arrange to have a couple of your team bring him back on one of the boats. I'll be waiting."

"That means I'm gonna be two men short," Cruz complained, spitting on the ground. "Not possible."

Sergei had not come this far to get into a pissing match with Ina's annoying brother. "Then I suggest you make it possible," he ordered coldly. "Bring Kasianenko to me, then my men'll take over, and your men can return to you."

"Chingado," Cruz muttered under his breath.

"You should be smiling," Sergei said, a note of menace in his voice. "Now you don't got me on the boat where you didn't want me gettin' in your fuckin' way. Remember?"

Cruz's mouth twisted into a hard smile.

463

"Sure," he said. "I can work it out."

"Make certain you do that," Sergei said. " 'Cause you an' me, we wouldn't wanna screw with each other, would we?"

Cruz shrugged and groped in his pocket for a cigarette. "Never," he lied.

Ina wandered down to the dock, fully aware that both Cruz and Sergei would be furious if they caught her. So what? She was bored sitting around in the villa with nothing to do. They'd warned her not to sunbathe by the pool, but they'd never mentioned anything about not going down to the dock.

She wore high-heeled silver sandals and a white mesh cover-up over her bikini. Large black sunglasses hid her eyes.

Cruz's men were busy.

Ina stood by observing. She smiled at the youngest pirate, who wasn't bad-looking in a Johnny Depp kind of way. He wore torn jeans and a sloppy T-shirt, with a colorful scarf flowing from around his neck. She noticed his beautiful high cheekbones, and wondered what it would be like to make love to someone so young. One thing was for sure: he wouldn't call her fat and whack her on the ass. He would be honored to have the pleasure of being with her.

Now he was returning her smile.

She noticed an attractive gold tooth and threw him a little wave. Then Cruz ruined everything by creeping up on her and yanking her by the arm. "Get back in the house," he growled. "An' don't lemme see you down here again."

Ina turned and walked back toward the house, but not before giving Cashoo one last lingering look.

CHAPTER SIXTY-SEVEN

"We're going to the press," Martin Byrne announced, ruddy cheeks ablaze. "This waiting around is a travesty. Skylar is nervous and upset. My wife is hysterical. We have to resolve this."

"Talking to the press will resolve nothing," Eddie said, his voice strained as he tried to figure out what to do next. "They'll jump on the story with no facts, and your daughter will be crucified, exactly like Monica Lewinsky."

"How dare you mention that Lewinsky woman and Skylar in the same breath," Martin huffed, pacing up and down. "My daughter was sexually molested. It's time the truth came out."

"I understand your dilemma," Eddie said, attempting to stay calm and in control as he tried to reason with Skylar's father. "However, I can assure you that until I speak with the senator, you should hold off doing anything."

Lurking outside Eddie's office, Radical, Hammond's illegitimate fifteen-year-old daughter, kept her ear to the door.

Shitballs! This was, like, juicy stuff. Daddy Dearest had been fiddling with some girl called Skylar.

Did stepmom Sierra know?

Was this news fresh off the block?

Could she make money from it?

Radical was all for scoring extra bucks — money made the world go 'round, and it also meant she could stock up on grass and coke without having to blow her New York dealer, who was a Puerto Rican ass-wipe and preferred blow jobs to cash.

As it was, she'd gotten thrown out of her Swiss boarding school for making out with her French teacher, who'd gotten canned.

Now that she was back in New York, it was time to, like, live it up. And money — plenty of it — could only help.

Skylar, huh?

Radical formed a plan.

CHAPTER SIXTY-EIGHT

Yet another dinner in paradise with an array of culinary delights served in a magnificent setting. What more could anyone ask?

Taking in her surroundings, Lori had no idea how she was supposed to ease back into normal life. She was savoring every moment of this once-in-a-lifetime trip. Everything was so perfect, including Cliff. She dreaded returning to their old routine, and the daily visit from Enid when Cliff wasn't at the studio. Enid was a jealous old bag who — even though she claimed to be gay — probably had the hots for her handsome boss.

Get a life, Enid, and leave us alone.

Without Enid's interference, Lori felt that she and Cliff might have a real chance of staying together. Enid was a witch; she put the evil eye on her.

"What're you thinking?" Luca inquired, approaching her as she stood by the railing on the terrace, watching the dark waves crash on the beach below.

"I'm thinking that this is a truly wonderful experience," Lori replied. "It's . . . I don't know . . . kind of magical in a way."

"That's 'cause you're in love," Luca said, adding a wistful, "I wish I was."

"You will be," Lori assured him. "Once you're free, you'll have your pick of anyone you want."

"You think so?"

"Oh, come *on,* get with the program," Lori encouraged. "You're Luca Perez. Didn't I just read that *People en Español* magazine voted you their sexiest star of the year?"

Luca shrugged. "It makes me nervous thinking about being by myself."

"Oh my *God*!" Lori exclaimed. "If *you're* nervous, then what the hell am I? Let's not forget that you're famous, rich, *and* gorgeous. You've got nothing to be nervous about."

"And you're a sweet girl, Lori," Luca said warmly. "Your friendship means a lot to me. When we get back to the real world, we'll stay in touch, yes?"

"Nothing I'd like more."

"I can be your new gay best friend," he joked. "Every girl needs one."

"Especially me," Lori said, thinking of her lack of real friends in L.A. "I don't have many friends — gay or straight."

"How come?"

"It's just the way it is," she said with a thoughtful sigh. "I'm a movie star's girlfriend.

People can't figure out how long I'll be around."

"If Cliff's smart, it'll be a lifetime deal."

"You're the best! I think I love you!"

"What are you two up to?" Cliff questioned, joining them.

"Oh, nothing much. I was just telling Luca what a babe he is," Lori said, winking at Luca. "I think I love him."

"Should I be jealous?" Cliff asked, amused.

"No!" Lori giggled. "Anyway, I thought you were busy talking to Ashley."

"*She* was talking to *me*," Cliff explained with a rueful grin. "Or rather, her tits were talking to me while *I* was trying to escape. Got a hunch she might be a bit of a fan."

"Well, *that's* the understatement of the year," Lori exclaimed, with a quick laugh. "She's all over you every opportunity she gets. Everyone's noticed."

"Really?" Cliff said with a sly smile.

"Don't act as if you don't know," Lori scolded. "Being modest doesn't suit you."

"I feel sorry for Taye," Luca lamented. "He's such a great guy."

"Do *not* worry about Taye," Lori said. "Am I the only one to see that Bianca is practically eating him for dinner?"

"She is?" Luca said. "What about our host. He doesn't mind?"

"Our host is busy making plans with Xuan about all sorts of humanitarian causes," Lori said knowingly. "They're quite a match."

Cliff started to laugh. It pleased him to note that everyone seemed to enjoy Lori's company. "Aren't *you* the little observer," he said affectionately.

"I keep my eyes open," she responded.

"You certainly do."

"I certainly do," Lori replied, mimicking him.

They exchanged an intimate smile.

"Come, my favorite redhead," Cliff said, putting his arm around her. "Let's go take a walk on the beach."

"Will you excuse us, Luca?" Lori said, smiling happily.

"Sure," Luca said, drifting back toward the table where Jeromy was earnestly trying to talk Sierra and Hammond into purchasing a pied-à-terre in London.

"My darlings, there is nothing like a summer day in a London park," Jeromy said grandly, filled with nostalgia as he recalled his first encounter with a male sex partner behind a tree in Regent's Park. He was thirteen at the time.

"We hardly ever visit London," Sierra said, studiously trying to avoid even so much as glancing in Flynn's direction as he spoke with Xuan and Aleksandr.

It was impossible — her mind refused to be still as she imagined Flynn making love to the Asian woman. She pictured them in bed

471

together, naked and passionate, all over each other. It was all too much, and her eyes filled with tears. She was dismayed to realize that she was jealous. Hopelessly, helplessly jealous.

"I have to use the restroom," Hammond said, abruptly rising. "Would you keep my wife company, Jeromy?"

"My pleasure, Senator," Jeromy replied, catching Luca's eye and beckoning him over.

Hammond left the table. He'd noticed Renee hovering by the ornate arched doorway and he immediately approached her. "Where is the men's room?" he asked, all business.

"Oh," she said, fidgeting nervously with an escaped strand of dark-blond hair. "Let me show you, Senator. I'm supposed to escort everyone there in case they get lost. This castle is huge."

"I'm not everyone," Hammond said mildly. "Just plain old me."

"I know," Renee said with a feeble giggle. "But you're a very important you."

Hammond smiled. He was never averse to compliments.

The interior of the castle was dark and cold. Nobody lived there — it was merely a place that could be rented out for special occasions. Long winding corridors led to a series of small rooms, and finally a semi-modernized bathroom that was completely out of sync with the rest of the castle.

"I can wait outside to guide you back," Renee offered.

Hammond studied her for a moment, moving close. "You are such a pretty girl," he informed her. "So very lovely."

"Uh . . . thank you," she mumbled, flattered that an important man like Senator Patterson had even noticed her.

"Would it be presumptuous if I were to kiss you?" he asked, deciding that he had no time to waste luring her in with seductive words.

Renee was ablaze with excitement, yet at the same time quite apprehensive.

Surely he was married? And not only that, but his wife was on the trip with him.

"Uh . . ." she stuttered, unsure of what to say.

Before she could say anything at all, Hammond's lips were upon hers, his tongue pushing its way aggressively into her mouth.

She tried to gasp, but couldn't. His hands were suddenly on her breasts. Everything felt dangerous and forbidden.

Was this really happening?

What if someone came along?

What if the senator's wife caught them?

Or Guy? He would fire her for sure.

The day Guy had hired her he'd given her a strict lecture about never getting inappropriate with a guest.

Hammond's hands had snaked their way under her uniform. He began manipulating

473

her nipples through her bra, playing with them hard.

His lips left hers and this time she did gasp, a long, drawn-out gasp of pure desire.

Hammond knew he had her.

Young girls were so easy.

Chapter Sixty-Nine

By the time they got back to the yacht, Bianca and Aleksandr were still not talking. Both strong personalities, neither of them was prepared to give in.

Bianca was livid that Aleksandr had spent the majority of the evening fraternizing with the enemy. Xuan. Asian bitch. Sneaky little man-stealer. Bianca hated her, and more than anything, she wanted her off the boat.

Some of their guests had gone to the upper deck for after-dinner drinks. Bianca chose to join them. Aleksandr could do what he liked — she didn't care.

Yet the truth was that she *did* care. A lot. He was her man, and he was behaving like a stubborn asshole. Typical male behavior.

On the upper deck, Taye and Ashley were all over each other in one corner. Jeromy was boring the shit out of Flynn, who couldn't stop agonizing over Sierra, while Luca was sitting with Lori and Cliff. Everyone else had gone to bed.

Bianca chose to join the Luca group. "What's up?" she asked Luca.

"What's up with you?" he replied. "Are you an' Mr. Russia in a fight?"

Bianca tossed back her long braided hair, green eyes gleaming. "What makes you think that?"

"It doesn't take a genius to see what's going on."

"Nothing," Bianca said stubbornly. "Nothing is going on."

"Bullshit," Luca responded. "It's me you're talking to."

"I think it's time for bed," Cliff said, standing up and stretching.

Lori followed his lead and said good night to everyone, and the two of them took off.

"I wish you were straight," Bianca said wistfully, gazing at Luca.

"How would that solve anything?" he asked, never sure what kind of crazy logic Bianca would come up with.

" 'Cause then you an' I could fuck all our cares away," Bianca said with a flippant laugh. "Wouldn't *that* be fun?"

"Spoken like a true princess," Luca said dryly.

Bianca frowned. "Do you think I'm being petty?" she asked.

"I dunno what you're supposed to be being petty about," Luca said, getting a tad impatient, because as far as he could tell, Bianca had everything she could ever want — including a magnificent yacht named after her.

"Aleksandr and Miss China Doll or whatever the hell she is," Bianca snapped. "She's getting on my tits."

"Whoa!" Luca objected, rolling his eyes. "Let's not get racist here."

"Are you calling *me* a racist?" Bianca objected. "I'm black, remember? I've been called more names —"

"Okay, okay," Luca said, holding up his hand. "Tell me the problem."

"Only if you promise to dump Jeromy the moment we hit dry land," Bianca said. "Your boyfriend is a pompous prick, and I hate seeing him bring you down."

"How'd we get onto the subject of Jeromy?"

"Promise you'll *sayonara* him?"

"I already decided. It's a done deal. Your turn."

And so Bianca began to voice her complaints about Xuan and all the various projects she was trying to involve Aleksandr in.

Luca sat back and listened. It was good for Bianca to spill.

When the tenders returned to the yacht, Mercedes managed to stay out of Guy's way. If he saw her, she wouldn't put it past him to expect her to help unload the dishes and all the other crap from the boats. Let Renee and

Den deal with it; she'd accomplished everything she needed to, and now it was time to lie on her bunk bed and contemplate the adventure ahead.

She'd had a busy night making sure everything was set for Cruz's takeover the following night. She knew exactly what she had to do, and number one was making sure Kyril was out of commission. He was the only real threat, and his usual mug of hot chocolate loaded with horse tranquilizers should definitely take care of him.

She wondered what men Cruz would bring with him. Amiin for sure — he was always by Cruz's side. And maybe Cashoo. She had a bit of a soft spot for Cashoo. He was young, although sexy as hell with his permanent boner that she enjoyed teasing him about, but that's as far as it went. Cruz had taught her at an early age — *never fuck where you do business.*

Thanks, Papa. Good advice.

Mercedes wasn't nervous; she never got scared. She was looking forward to the takeover. It was always a tense and invigorating time. She'd seen people get shot or knifed for not doing what they were told, and although bloodshed wasn't her favorite thing, if it happened it was because people didn't listen.

Dumb people didn't listen. If only they'd follow orders, everything would be okay and nobody would get hurt.

Who's dumb on this trip?

All of them.

Eventually Mercedes drifted off into a semi-sleep, and did not awake until Renee came in. The Australian girl was making too much noise, which pissed Mercedes off.

"What t' fuck," she mumbled. "I'm tryin' t' sleep here."

"Sorry," Renee said, clambering into the top bunk. "It's just that —"

"What?" Mercedes grumbled. "Spit it out!"

"Well . . . uh . . ."

"Did Guy tear you a new asshole? 'Cause if he did, you gotta learn to ignore it. I do."

"One of the passengers wants to sleep with me," Renee blurted out.

"Whaaat?" Mercedes sat up and burst out laughing. "You're shittin' me. Who?"

"Oh gosh!" Renee said, blushing crimson. "I don't know if I should say anything."

"You just did," Mercedes pointed out. "Who's the *cabrón* with the hard dick? Gimme a name."

"I think he really likes me," Renee moaned. "And here's the thing: he's so sweet and nice and . . . and he's very important."

"If you don't tell me who it is, I'm going back to sleep," Mercedes threatened.

"The senator," Renee whispered. "And I think I like him back."

CHAPTER SEVENTY

"Are you Skylar?"

"Huh?" Skylar Byrne took a step back from the girl with the crazy green streaks in her short black hair and the most uncomfortable-looking piercings in her nose and eyebrows. "Who're you?"

"Name's Radical, an' I get it, 'cause I'm, like, just as pissed as you."

Skylar took another step back. Was this a case of mistaken identity? Who was this girl and what did she want?

The two of them were standing at the Fifth Avenue entrance to Central Park, Skylar dressed for jogging in yellow shorts and a pale blue T-shirt emblazoned with "I vote for puppies," Radical in ripped jeans and a gray hoodie over a red T-shirt with "Hate" splashed across the front.

"Do I know you?" Skylar asked, hopping from foot to foot.

"You don't hav'ta know me," Radical replied, squinting. " 'Cause *I* know *you.*"

"You do, huh," Skylar said, standing up a little straighter.

Radical reached into the back pocket of her jeans and pulled out a crumpled pack of cigarettes. She extracted one and offered it to Skylar.

Skylar shook her head.

"Suit yourself," Radical said, scrounging for a book of matches and lighting up with a defiant flourish. "I'd sooner have a joint," she remarked. "Only, like, not in public. You smoke grass?"

"Who *are* you?" Skylar repeated. "What do you want?"

"I *want* for us to make money. Big bucks," Radical stated matter-of-factly. "An' if you're down with it, I know *exactly,* like, how we can do it."

Skylar couldn't help herself. Common sense informed her that she should be walking away, but curiosity got the better of her. "What are you talking about?" she asked.

And Radical began to explain.

CHAPTER SEVENTY-ONE

Flynn, Taye, and Cliff spent the morning working out in the gym. Flynn because he needed to purge all the angst he was feeling. Taye because he loved keeping his ripped body in fantastic shape. And Cliff because he hadn't been in such a good mood in years. Besides, he was heading toward fifty; better keep everything in working order, especially since he had a much younger girlfriend, a girlfriend he planned to hang on to.

Taye chose the music — Tinie Tempah, Jay-Z, and Wiz Khalifa. The sounds were fast and furious, blasting and full of pounding energy.

Flynn would've preferred the Stones or a laid-back Dave Matthews. Cliff was more into old-school classics such as Sinatra or Tony Bennett. However, they both went along with Taye's choice since he seemed so into it.

The three of them had a competitive time sweating it out. Three guys with nothing else to do except work on their bodies. It was a bonding experience.

Meanwhile, Bianca, Luca, Ashley, and Lori lolled by the pool, soaking up the sun and sipping on ice-cold frozen margaritas. It was one of those lazy days, and everyone felt very relaxed. Everyone except Jeromy, who was sulking in his room, because he was acutely aware of Luca's withdrawal and yet helpless to stop the inevitable. He knew it was coming. He knew the signs.

He decided to leave his room and find Guy. He had a need to release his pent-up frustration, and Guy was the only one capable of helping him out.

Too bad if he didn't want to. Guy was the entertainment director. Let him entertain.

Aleksandr was engrossed in making plans with Xuan about the orphanage he'd decided to build outside Moscow. Xuan had many innovative and intelligent ideas, and he was interested in hearing them.

It wasn't long before he found himself revealing details of his own miserable childhood, things he'd never told anyone. It was a cathartic experience to expose so much of himself, and he found it to be most comforting. He was more and more drawn to Xuan as he shared memories of a horrific childhood — a childhood he'd not even revealed to Bianca, since she'd never shown any interest in hearing about his roots.

Now that he was talking about it, he felt a burden lifting, freeing him from his past.

In return, Xuan started telling him some of *her* early stories. He soon realized that they were even more harrowing than his. Watching her as she spoke, he was starting to feel true compassion for her. She was so different from any woman he'd ever known. She was nurturing and clever, and also very sensual in a low-key kind of way. There was nothing overt about Xuan; her sexuality was a private thing.

Aleksandr started wondering about her and Flynn, and exactly how strong their relationship was.

Not that he was thinking of doing anything about it . . . or was he?

Xuan was the first woman who'd stirred his sexual interest since he'd been with Bianca.

Why was it happening now?

Maybe because Bianca was acting like such a spoiled bitch. Over nothing.

Aleksandr was angry. At Bianca. *And* at himself.

He was planning on asking Bianca to marry him. Surely he shouldn't be thinking about another woman at such a special time?

"You stay here," Hammond ordered his wife. "I'm going to call Eddie, see what's so goddamn important that it couldn't wait until I get back."

"I should come with you," Sierra suggested, not wanting to be by herself and face the temptation of popping Xanax again.

"Why?" Hammond said harshly. "So you can make eyes at your boyfriend?"

Sierra sighed and shook her head. "For the last time, Flynn is *not* my boyfriend. I have no feelings for him whatsoever. Please believe me."

"Just remember what I told you I can arrange to have done to him," Hammond taunted. "I am *not* joking."

"I know you're not," she said dully. "What happened between Flynn and me was a long time ago. You have no need to worry."

"Me? Worry?" Hammond scoffed. "Believe me, dear, it would take a better man than Flynn Hudson to make *me* worry."

Sierra hoped she'd made it clear to Hammond that she cared nothing for Flynn. If he thought she cared one little bit, who knew what he was capable of? She had to tread carefully, maybe even warn Flynn if that was possible.

"As I said, you stay here until I get back. Then we will go to lunch and present a united front," Hammond said, opening the door and stepping out. "Perhaps you can be charming for once. Wouldn't that make a pleasant change?"

Sierra watched him go with hate in her heart. He'd trapped her once again with his vile threats.

Would she ever be free?

Deep down she knew it was up to her.

Bianca could not believe that Aleksandr was taking their stupid fight all the way, even though it was ruining what should have been a perfect trip. She was determined not to be the first to give in.

After all, she was right and he was wrong.

An apology had better be forthcoming soon.

Luca was the only one who was fully aware of what was going on, although Bianca supposed the others must have noticed that their host and hostess were not talking.

She couldn't care less. It had now become a matter of principle.

Jeromy accosted Guy on the stairs shortly before lunch. "Where's your cabin?" he demanded, holding on tightly to Guy's upper arm, his nails digging into Guy's flesh.

Guy attempted to shake the Englishman's grip, to no avail. Jeromy was determined.

"I . . . I'll be serving lunch shortly," Guy stammered.

"You'll be serving nothing if I complain to Mr. Kasianenko," Jeromy cautioned. "So I suggest that you take me to your godforsaken cabin, and do it *now*. I'll only use a minute or two of your precious time."

A thousand thoughts crashed through

Guy's head. Did he have to do this? Would Kasianenko really fire him if Jeromy Milton-Gold complained? Was it worth making a drama out of one forced blow job?

Then he decided — do it and forget it. Piss in the wanker's soup for the rest of the trip.

"Your choice?" Jeromy growled.

"Follow me," Guy said, compliant, for if he wanted to keep his job, what other way was there?

Making polite conversation with the captain while waiting for his satellite call to go through, Hammond inquired if there were any more island trips planned.

Captain Dickson was cagey; he didn't want to reveal to the senator that the final island trip was to take place the following night, because he wasn't sure how much Mr. Kasianenko had told everyone. It was to be a spectacular night with fireworks, famous surprise performers, and food flown in from three of Bianca's favorite L.A. restaurants. It was to be a lovefest for Bianca, and Captain Dickson had a strong suspicion that the billionaire Russian was planning on proposing to his mercurial ladylove.

Hammond gazed out at the calm blue sea and thought about the long-legged stewardess — Jenni or Renee or whatever her name was. He would definitely be partaking of that. Maybe later, when everyone had gone to bed.

Yes. She would know of somewhere they could be alone together. Why deprive himself?

He fantasized about her long legs locked behind his neck. About brushing his cock against those big horse teeth. She was young and not too experienced, exactly the way he liked them.

"Here's your call, Senator," Captain Dickson said, handing him the phone.

"Eddie," Hammond barked. "What the hell do you want?"

Lunch was tense. Bianca and Aleksandr were still at odds. After a not-so-satisfying dalliance with Guy, Jeromy was desperately trying to ingratiate himself with whomever he could. Hammond was in a foul mood, while Flynn was still trying to come up with a "get out of paradise" excuse.

Only Luca, Lori, Cliff, Taye, and Ashley seemed in the holiday spirit as they discussed their afternoon of more water sports. Fun and games was the order of the day. Diving, snorkeling, racing the WaveRunners. It was all on.

Bianca sat beside Aleksandr, picking at her lobster and crab salad, drinking a healthy amount of red wine, and stewing about Xuan.

"After lunch, all the girls are going topless," she suddenly announced, shooting Xuan a spiteful look. "Are you in?"

"No," Xuan answered quite simply. "I do

not believe in mass nudity."

"Mass nudity!" Bianca shrieked. "It's hardly mass nudity when you're among friends."

"I prefer not to," Xuan said, remaining polite.

"Why not?" Bianca insisted. "You got something to hide?"

Aleksandr shot her a piercing look. "Enough," he said sternly.

Bianca took another gulp of red wine. "Oh please!" she slurred. "You know you're dying to see her tiny little Chinese titties."

Aleksandr stood up and reached for Bianca's arm to pull her to her feet. She resisted, and her wineglass toppled over, spilling red wine in a little river heading straight for Xuan's lap.

"Sorry!" Bianca mumbled, dissolving into a fit of giggles. "Accident, I swear."

"Come with me," Aleksandr said, this time getting a firm grip on her arm.

"Ooh!" Bianca mocked in a singsong fashion. "Have I been a naughty girl? I thought you *liked* naughty girls, Alek, or have your tastes changed?"

Tight-lipped, Aleksandr did not answer as he maneuvered Bianca away from the table.

An embarrassed silence ensued, broken by Ashley. "Are we really going topless?" she asked, quite excited at the thought of displaying her bought-and-paid-for assets to Cliff.

Taye threw her a grim look. "Not on my watch, toots. Those titties are strictly all mine."

CHAPTER SEVENTY-TWO

"Once you get goin', how long before you reach the yacht?" Sergei inquired, the nerve in his left cheek twitching as he attempted to ferret out answers.

Cruz, a perennial cigarette dangling from his lower lip, shrugged. "Coupla hours," he said casually. "The fuckin' boat's not that far out. They're stayin' around an' cruisin' the islands."

"Then after you take off, I can expect my men back with Kasianenko in four hours?"

"Don't 'spect nothin'," Cruz said, ash falling from his cigarette onto the ground. "Nobody knows how it's gonna go down. We gotta secure the yacht before we go lookin' for Kasianenko. It takes time. We hav'ta plan for the unexpected."

Sergei kept a tight rein on his temper. All along, Cruz had assured him that taking over the *Bianca* was an easy hit, and now he was voicing doubts?

Sergei scowled impatiently. It was happening tonight, and for Cruz's sake it had better go fast and smooth.

For the last twenty-four hours, his own personal security had been putting together a safe room where he planned on keeping Kasianenko. The room was in the basement of the villa, a cold dank room generally used for storage. Sergei had arranged for the door to be reinforced, special locks fitted, and solid handcuffs attached to the stone wall.

It was designed to be Kasianenko's new home. Sergei couldn't wait for his sworn enemy to take up residence.

Boredom drove Ina to do things she knew she shouldn't. However, what Cruz didn't know . . .

She found a way to get out of the villa without Cruz noticing. Once out, she attracted Cashoo's attention, directing him via hand signals to meet her on the beach beyond a large formation of rocks.

Cashoo was hot to do whatever the boss's woman wanted him to do. He had no scruples or guilt; he was simply a young man with a raging libido.

Ina had no intention of going all the way with Cashoo. She merely wanted to play with him for her own amusement.

They did not speak a word of each other's language. But who needed words when unbridled lust was a suitable form of communication?

Cashoo circled her like a wary coyote.

She smiled and unbuttoned her blouse, shaking her large breasts at him.

Cashoo had never seen enhanced breasts before. So big and firm. He reached out to touch them with his bony fingers.

Ina slapped his hands away, then unzipped his jeans, directing his long thin hard-on toward her breasts.

He got the idea and plunged his penis between her huge breasts. Within seconds he ejaculated.

Ina smiled at him once more before shooing him away.

It made a pleasant change to own the power for once. It was her way of getting back at both Cruz and Sergei for treating her as if she didn't matter.

They thought they owned her.

Think again.

She knew everything about both of them.

CHAPTER SEVENTY-THREE

After speaking to Eddie in New York, Hammond sank into a black fury. Goddammit, he was out of town for a few short days, and all of a sudden there was a girl he barely knew accusing him of sexual harassment.

Skylar Byrne, some stupid dumb intern who — as far as he could recall — had come on to *him*.

Or had she? Whatever . . .

Bitch! Fucking bitch! They were all bitches at heart.

How *dare* she accuse him? And how dare Eddie go along with it as if the girl were telling the truth?

The truth was that she was waiting for a big payout. Eddie was just too dumb to realize what was going on.

On top of that nonsense, Eddie informed him that Radical had been expelled from her strict Swiss boarding school and was now staying at his apartment until Hammond and Sierra arrived home.

Great. Radical. Such a perfect boost for his public image with her green-streaked dyed black hair and her unbearable snotty teenage attitude.

Hammond was fully aware that he would need Sierra's help in dealing with both of these problems. The public was in love with Sierra; she was their darling and could do no wrong. This was excellent, because he needed her to shut down Skylar's accusations before he shipped Radical off to another boarding school far, far away. One thing about Sierra: she kept a clear head when it came to putting out fires. She'd know exactly how to manage this crisis.

He'd told Eddie to shut the Byrnes up by promising them a meeting the moment he got back. Sierra would have to be at that meeting, supporting him while he informed the Byrnes that it was all the fantasies of a power-struck young girl with a crush, who'd used her imagination to make up silly stories. With Sierra in the room, there was no way the Byrnes would believe their daughter. It would be his word against Skylar's, and nobody played honest, moral, and upstanding better than Hammond Patterson — especially with the lovely Sierra by his side.

Unfortunately, the timing was hardly perfect, what with Sierra getting restless because of seeing Flynn Hudson, who'd apparently fed her a mouthful of lies.

Well, not actually lies. Hammond *had* doctored the photos to break them up. Flynn had not deserved a girl like Sierra, so he'd dealt with the situation. At the time, it had cost him, but the results were well worth it.

The car accident was a happy mistake, causing Sierra to lose Flynn's baby. Good riddance to that. Although the downside was that she'd taken off, and it was a few years before he'd managed to lure her back in and marry her.

Sierra Kathleen Snow. The perfect political wife. She was his ace in the hole, and there was no way he was letting her go.

It was unfortunate that Flynn had inserted himself back into their lives again, stirring Sierra up, trying to persuade her to break free.

As usual, Hammond had managed to get her under control. She always believed his threats, and so she should, because in his mind, he knew he was capable of anything. And he was *certainly* capable of getting rid of Flynn once and for all.

When they got back to New York, the demise of Flynn Hudson was number one on his agenda.

"I think I'm ready to return to the real world," Flynn remarked to Cliff as they sat on the top deck drinking Jack and Cokes before dinner. "All this luxury, it's not for

496

me. I need to be where the action is."

"You gotta admit it's not bad, though," Cliff said, reaching for the guacamole dip. "I could get used to it. Might even buy myself a sailing boat."

"I'm going to try an' leave tomorrow," Flynn said, clinking the ice in his glass.

"It's the big birthday night tomorrow," Cliff reminded him. "Why not wait?"

"Got things to deal with," Flynn said restlessly. "Besides, I'm better off on dry land."

Cliff nodded. "I get it, but I'm happy to be taking a break. No paparazzi, no interviews, no five A.M. calls to the set."

The two of them had become quite friendly over the past few days. Cliff had enjoyed listening to Flynn's stories about his world travels.

"You know," Cliff said, signaling Renee for a refill, "you should consider writing a script."

"Why's that?" Flynn asked, thinking that there was nothing he'd like less.

" 'Cause you've had some damn fascinating adventures."

"Kinda," Flynn said modestly.

"You'll write a dynamite script, I'll star in it," Cliff said, getting into the idea. "It's about time I played a real character with integrity."

"What makes you think I've got integrity?" Flynn quipped.

Cliff laughed. "Y'know, I like you," he said. "You're an interesting guy. You should take a trip to L.A. Come stay with me and Lori for a couple of weeks, months, whatever suits you. Bring Xuan — that's if you can pry her away from Aleksandr."

"Uh . . . yeah," Flynn said, hesitating for a moment. "About Xuan — between us — she's not my girlfriend."

"You don't have to explain to me." Cliff paused, then added an expectant, "Although, if you're in the mood to talk, what's up with you and the senator?"

"I guess you heard about the fight?" Flynn said ruefully.

"Hey, this yacht is luxurious, but it's still close quarters. What goes on soon spreads around. Not to mention the shiner you gave him. Ever thought of doing stunt work?"

Flynn grimaced. "He deserved it."

"No love lost between you two?"

"We go back, all the way to college," Flynn ruminated. "Hammond was always a prick."

"He's done well for being a prick."

"An insidious, smart prick, I'll give him that," Flynn allowed. "Treacherous as a fucking snake."

"Suitable character traits for a politician," Cliff said dryly. "Believe me, I've met a few of those."

"You live in L.A. Why am I not surprised?"

Cliff cleared his throat and laughed. "So . . . the current battle?" he inquired, as Renee delivered his fresh drink.

"Long story," Flynn said, rubbing his chin.

"Aren't they all?"

"Wouldn't want to bore you."

"I'm an actor," Cliff said flashing his movie-star smile. "We live to listen to other people's stories."

"Okay, you asked for it," Flynn said, deciding that if he didn't tell his story to someone soon, it was going to suffocate him.

And so he began . . .

"Something unfortunate has taken place," Hammond announced, as he and Sierra moved around their stateroom getting ready to go up for dinner.

For a moment Sierra panicked. Had Hammond somehow or other managed to throw Flynn overboard? Was Flynn dead?

Oh God! Her face paled, and she could barely speak. "What?" she muttered.

"There's this young intern," Hammond said matter-of-factly. "A new girl at the office. She's developed what you might call an obsessive crush on me."

"Why are you telling me this?" Sierra asked, relief overcoming her.

"Because," Hammond said in a sanctimonious tone, "as my dear wife, you need to be aware of these things."

"And that would be why?" Sierra asked, eyeing him warily. Something was coming, something she wasn't going to like.

"This poor deluded girl is apparently accusing me of improper conduct toward her."

Sierra almost burst out laughing. Improper conduct indeed! Had Hammond tried to fuck her and gotten caught? She couldn't be happier.

"Oh dear," she murmured. "That *is* unfortunate."

"It's nothing earth-shattering," Hammond continued. "However, we do have to deal with it."

" 'We'?" Sierra questioned, taking pleasure in making him squirm a little.

"Yes, we," Hammond said sharply, not appreciating her attitude.

"And what if I don't care to help you out on this?" Sierra said coolly.

Hammond's jaw tightened as a venomous expression crossed his face. "I can tell you're not listening to me, my dear," he said, icy cold. "It seems you are forgetting the things I can arrange. It seems that perhaps you do not care about the well-being of a certain someone."

Threats.

Again.

Forever.

She was still caught in his trap.

"Exactly how long are you planning on keeping this up?" Aleksandr inquired when Bianca

500

awoke from a too-much-red-wine-induced sleep.

Bianca slid from the bed, glared at her lover, made her way into the bathroom, and slammed the door. "Until you apologize," she yelled from behind the closed door.

Aleksandr was frustrated. Bianca and her jealous fits were ruining their trip. She was one obstinate woman behaving badly.

Was he making a mistake proposing to her?

Did she deserve the two-million-dollar rare emerald and diamond ring he had stashed in his safe?

If she didn't come around by tomorrow, he was seriously contemplating canceling the celebratory dinner he'd organized. The dinner at the end of which he'd been planning on giving her the ring.

"I am going up to join our guests," he shouted at the closed door. "We'll see you later if you're not too hungover."

"Fuck you!" a furious Bianca retaliated.

Another fine evening in paradise.

CHAPTER SEVENTY-FOUR

Cruz dressed for business. Army fatigues. Combat boots with special rubber soles. A flak jacket with plenty of useful pockets to hold his pistols and knives. He was a walking fortress, ready for anything.

Amiin was dressed in a more colorful fashion. Although his outfit was all dark brown, on his head he wore a bright orange wool cap, and around his neck were several long flowing scarves of various colors.

Cashoo opted for jeans, two T-shirts under a heavy sweatshirt to keep out the cold, and a red bandana across his forehead.

There was no dress code for pirates. They wore whatever they chose to wear; it was the weapons that mattered. Each of the two boats was fully loaded with assault rifles, semi-automatic combat pistols, rocket blasters, machetes, and an assortment of swords — a Somalian tribal thing.

Cruz didn't care how his men operated, as long as they got the job done.

Viktor and Maksim, the two bodyguards Sergei was sending to bring Kasianenko back, were both of Russian origin. They'd been with Sergei for several years and they were loyal soldiers in Sergei's army of security. Neither of them was happy about this mission. They were not seafaring men; they were security bodyguards who preferred to operate on dry land. However, Sergei paid top dollar, so they did as they were told, whether they liked it or not.

They regarded the pirates as useless scum, way beneath them.

In turn, the pirates jeered and laughed at them with their close-cropped hair, neat clothes, and Glock guns. There was no love lost. There was certainly no respect.

Sergei lectured them both before their departure. "What you gotta do is keep your eye on Kasianenko. You bring him to me, an' you'll be well rewarded. Oh yeah, an' see that those morons don't shoot him in the head by mistake. I want him alive an' kickin' like a fuckin' wild pig. Got it?"

They got it.

Meanwhile, Cruz was busy checking the weather. There was a storm brewing, only it wasn't due to hit until four or five A.M. His goal was to reach the *Bianca* by two A.M. By the time the storm moved in, they would have already boarded and taken over the yacht, and he would be on the phone making ransom demands.

Timing was everything.

Cruz was an expert at timing.

Chapter Seventy-Five

Dinner on the *Bianca* was a casual affair. Aleksandr had informed everyone that since tomorrow was Bianca's birthday celebration, tonight would be low-key. The theme of the night was a barbecue to take place on the upper deck. Two tables of six. Checkered tablecloths. Beer and red wine. Country music on the speakers. Couples seated together. Jeans and shorts was the dress code.

Ashley wore faded cutoffs and a pink shirt tied precariously under her breasts. Taye was in jeans and a wifebeater, muscles bulging. Lori opted for cute sequined shorts and a tank top, her red hair tied in side bunches.

"You look exactly like a little kid," Cliff told her, tweaking her chin.

"And *you* look like a grizzled old cowboy," she teased.

"That's some compliment!" he said with a self-deprecating chuckle. "Not exactly the look I was going for, but I guess it'll do. However, I take umbrage at 'grizzled.' "

"That's 'cause you haven't shaved," she pointed out, running her index finger across his chin.

"Thought I'd grow a beard. I'm that re-laxed."

Lori cuddled close to him. "It's so nice to see you like this."

"Like what?"

"Like no more Mister Movie Star."

"No more Mister Movie Star, huh?" he said, amused.

"That's right. No more Mister Sexiest Man Alive."

"What? You don't think I'm sexy?" he teased.

"You know I do."

"You're cute," he said, kissing her on the forehead.

"Thanks," she purred. "I try."

"And you're pretty too. What a bonus."

"Double thanks."

"You know what, Lori?" he said, squinting at her.

"What?"

"We're damn good together."

"And you're only just discovering this?" she said breathlessly.

"Don't kick a compliment in the teeth. Just go with it, baby."

"I think I will," she said, grinning at him.

And at that moment in time she'd never felt more content. It was about to be another incredible night.

"I'm taking off in the morning," Flynn informed Xuan before they went up for dinner. "It's time for me to go."

She was silent for a moment, busy painting her toenails with a crimson polish — a very girly thing for Xuan to do.

"And that would be why?" she inquired at last.

"You know why," he said irritably. "This is fucking torture for me, watching Sierra continue to screw up her life. We finally talked, and now she won't even look at me. You've got no idea what that feels like. I have to leave."

"If you go, then what about me?" Xuan asked.

"You can do what you want. Come. Stay. Whatever. I'm sure Aleksandr enjoys having you around."

"I'm supposed to be your girlfriend, or have you forgotten?"

"Are you serious? Nobody believes we're together anymore. Not when you're hovering over Aleksandr like he's some kind of god."

"I am not," Xuan retorted, her cheeks flushing pink. "Why would you say that?"

"Listen, we're in confined quarters — nothing goes unnoticed. And for your information, Bianca is seriously pissed."

"That's ridiculous," Xuan said. "Aleksandr

is merely offering his assistance and goodwill toward the less fortunate in the world. He is an intelligent man, generous and soulful."

"Yeah, yeah, sure. And you're not jonesin' to jump into bed with him, right?"

"No, Flynn," she said solemnly. "I am not."

"Then let's both leave tomorrow," he encouraged.

"No," Xuan said, taking a long, slow beat. "You do what you want. I have decided to stay."

"Fuck it," Flynn said, marching toward the door. "Like I give a shit. I'll see you upstairs."

Mercedes reviewed the situation. Eighteen crew members. Twelve guests, including Kasianenko and his diva girlfriend. The onslaught for the big party was tomorrow, so no extra bodies aboard tonight.

She relished the evening ahead, and had prepared accordingly. Drugs were not usually her thing, but to stay alert she'd gulped down several Red Bulls and snorted a few lines of coke. Coke always kept her up and at 'em. Cruz had taught her that. Who needed school when she had a papa like Cruz to educate her?

She'd also emptied two bottles of sleeping pills into the soup for the crew that the chef always had bubbling on the stove, and for good measure she'd crushed up another batch of sleeping pills and mixed them in with the baked beans being served with the barbecue. Sleepy passengers were far less likely to cause trouble, and getting everyone to bed early was of paramount importance.

She'd left Kyril until later. The timing had to be right with him. He was such a big man that she wasn't sure what level of drugs would knock him out. Better too much than too little. She'd deliver his hot chocolate later than usual. He probably wouldn't even notice. The man was a machine, a stoic, silent machine.

Guy threw her a suspicious look as they crossed paths. "*You're* lively for someone who could barely move yesterday. Had a miraculous recovery, did we?" he asked sarcastically.

"I bet you're glad you're not a girl, and don't have to go through our monthly nightmare," she said matter-of-factly. "You'd throw a shit fit, couldn't handle it."

"You got a smart mouth on you, little missy," Guy retorted, taking out his frustration regarding Jeromy Milton-Gold, for he was still steaming. "I've decided to dock you yesterday's pay since you were unable to carry out your duties."

"Ohhh," Mercedes mocked, feigning dismay. "What'll I do . . . ?"

Guy was shocked by her insolence. Captain Dickson was right, he should not have hired her.

Never again, that was for sure. She could

whistle for a decent reference.

"I was thinking that after we leave the yacht, I might stay at our house in Miami with you for a week or two before returning to London," Jeromy ventured. "Just the two of us. Does that suit you?"

They were sitting at a table with Taye and Ashley, who had spent the majority of the evening whispering to each other like a couple of teenagers on a secret date. Also at the table were the senator and his wife, who apparently didn't talk at all.

Luca gazed longingly over at the next table, where his new best friend, Lori, was sitting with Cliff, Aleksandr, Flynn, and Xuan. Bianca had failed to put in an appearance. He wondered what they were all talking about, and wished he could simply get up, leave his table, and go fill the empty chair.

"What do you think?" Jeromy persisted, irritated that Luca appeared to be ignoring him.

Luca was not comfortable with confrontations, especially when it came to Jeromy, who could turn into a bitchy queen within seconds. However, since there was safety in numbers, and even though Taye and Ashley were doing their own thing, Luca felt brave enough to tell Jeromy the truth.

"No," he said evenly. "It doesn't suit me, Jeromy. Not at all."

Jeromy tapped the side of his wineglass and cleared his throat. "Excuse me?" he said peevishly, his long, thin nose quivering slightly. "I thought you would be delighted for us to spend more time together."

"Suga and Luca Junior are coming to stay with me before I take off on the next leg of my South American tour," Luca said. "I'm planning on spending as much quality time with them as I can."

"That's no problem. We'll spend quality time together," Jeromy responded, sensing his blond god slowly slipping out of his greedy grasp. "Me, you, the boy."

"His *name* is Luca Junior," Luca said pointedly. "And the four of us together — that doesn't work for me."

"Why not?"

"Because I need time alone with them." Luca paused, wondering how far he could push it. "Besides, you can't stand Suga. You've told me enough times."

"I might have criticized her once or twice," Jeromy admitted with a vague shrug. "That doesn't mean I don't *like* her. She's . . . uh . . ."

He trailed off. Who was he kidding? Certainly not Luca, who apparently had grown a new set of balls, because Jeromy knew how his young lover shied away from any kind of discord. Not tonight, though.

"Very well," he said, feeling his throat

tighten. "I'll fly straight to London. I wouldn't want to get in your way."

Luca was relieved. If Jeromy flew directly to London he could break up with him long-distance. He knew it was the cowardly thing to do, but a full blowout with Jeromy was not something he wished to contemplate.

Jeromy would not go quietly into the night, of that he was sure.

Bianca paced around the luxurious master suite like a caged tigress. How had she allowed one small disagreement to blossom into a full-fledged fight?

She was mad at herself. Then again, she was even more mad at the Chinese do-gooder with the compact body and shiny black hair. Was it possible that Aleksandr actually fancied her?

No. Pure fantasy. How could Aleksandr even look at another woman when he had her? Their lovemaking alone was superlative, passionate, and mind-blowing. Nobody could beat the magic they made together.

Tomorrow was her birthday, and for the last few hours, her inner voice had been giving her a stern lecture.

Forgive him or you'll lose him.

Why should I?

Because he's a man. A proud, strong man. For once, admit you're wrong.

I'm not wrong.

Who cares? Stop ruining everything.
Okay, okay, I get it.

Impulsively, she reached for a sheet of paper and scribbled Aleksandr a short note. Then she rang for someone to take it to him.

Soon he would be all hers again.

CHAPTER SEVENTY-SIX

By eleven P.M., Cruz had launched both boats. He'd heard from Mercedes that things were winding down on the *Bianca;* guests were retiring early and everything was on track.

Mercedes was a real asset. She'd turned out to be the son he'd always dreamed of having. She was tough as a boy in a female body. And she was his daughter. Mother dead. He'd raised her himself, trained her to take no shit from anybody, taught her plenty — all the tricks. Smart girl, a fast learner, sharp as a carving knife.

In a way he almost depended on her. As far as this job was concerned, it sure helped having someone on the inside, because this job was special. Major bucks were on the line. Not to mention Sergei Zukov hovering over him like a hawk. No fuckups allowed.

He fingered the hunting knife he kept close to his shin in a concealed pocket. On occasion, knives could be more intimidating than guns. People recoiled from knives, and so they should. The slash of steel cutting into flesh was never pretty, and Cruz had a few scars to prove it. He often recalled the whore in Guatemala who'd attempted to rob him after a wild night of sex. She'd drawn a carving knife across his stomach and almost killed him. Fortunately, he'd been found on the street where her pimp had dumped him, and a Good Samaritan cabdriver had rushed him to a nearby clinic. When he'd recovered, he'd tracked down the cabdriver and handed the surprised and grateful man five thousand dollars in cash. Next he'd returned to the whore's room, slit her throat, and shot her pimp in the balls. No regrets.

Then there was the skipper of the cargo ship who'd come at him with a steak knife and managed to slash his neck before Cruz had plunged his own knife into the man's heart. Death while protecting some rich oil company man's shit. *Estúpido.*

Yes, Cruz had experienced several encounters with knives. He was not afraid of violence.

Sergei's deciding not to be a part of the hijack pleased him. Having Sergei along would only have slowed things down, and there was no doubt he would've gotten in the way.

Meanwhile, after Googling him, Cruz had discovered that this Kasianenko *puta* was one

515

richer-than-shit asshole, worth billions. The joke was that all they were asking as a ransom was a measly five million dollars.

It wasn't enough. By the time he'd split the money with Sergei and paid his men their share, he'd be lucky to end up with a paltry million.

He'd attempted to explain this to Sergei, who was more interested in taking Kasianenko prisoner than walking away with a king's ransom. The problem was that Sergei was so loaded down with drug money, he didn't care. All he really cared about was getting his revenge.

After thinking about it for the past few days, Cruz had begun to realize that if he played it his way, this hijack caper could turn out to be the score of a lifetime. Forget about the five mil. How about fifty? Or even one hundred?

If he was smart, it could all be his. Enough to get him out of the piracy business once and for all. He could get the fuck out of Somalia and buy himself a fancy mansion far away, in the Bahamas, Los Angeles, Argentina — anywhere in the world. He could live a life where he wasn't forced to surround himself with armed guards and watch his back at all times lest some Somalian *chingado* decide to get rid of the foreigner who was making money from their business.

Why not? This was an opportunity that

would never come around again.

Cruz was conflicted. As the powerful speed-boat sped across the night sea, crowded with his men and one of Sergei's guards — he'd separated the two Russians — he couldn't decide what to do. If he didn't go along with what Sergei expected, he'd be saddled with a lifetime enemy.

Yet if he handled things his way, he'd have more money than he'd ever imagined.

Sergei's way.

His way.

He didn't have much time to make the right decision.

CHAPTER SEVENTY-SEVEN

"Hmm . . . y'know, I never realized making up could be this sexy," Bianca purred, twisting her long slender legs around Aleksandr's neck as the two of them lay naked and entwined on the oversized bed in the master suite.

"You took me away from our guests," Aleksandr said, shifting his body until he was able to plunge his tongue into her silky wetness.

"Umm . . ." She moaned with pleasure as he thrilled her with his skills. "Perhaps they needed an early night."

Aleksandr came up for air. "You are such a provocative woman, Bianca," he said, his voice heavy with lust. "At times you make me into a crazy man."

"Crazy with desire, I hope," she murmured, adjusting her position until she was able to take him in her mouth as he continued to pleasure her.

"Yes, my *golubushka*," he groaned. "Always desire."

After a few moments of bliss, a simultaneous orgasm occurred.

Bianca rolled over and threw her arms above her head. "That was amazing," she cooed.

"For both of us," Aleksandr said, thinking how satisfied he was that Bianca had apologized. She was truly sorry, and so was he for entertaining sexual thoughts about Xuan.

"You are without a doubt the best lover." Bianca sighed, feeling extremely content. "The best I ever had."

"You too, my sweet. And in the future, we have to make absolutely sure that petty jealousy never separates us again."

"It never will," Bianca assured him. "I promise you that."

Good-bye, Asian piece of work. He's back on my side of the court.

"I'm *so* tired," Lori said, trying to suppress a yawn as she and Cliff entered their room. "I got too much sun today. My arms are all tingly."

"You're not alone," Cliff said. "I overdid it on the WaveRunners. Too much exercise," he added, making a face. "I'm turning into an old man."

"No, you're not," she objected.

He grinned, full of movie-star charisma.

"No, I'm not," he agreed.

"So . . . no sex tonight, then?" Lori said lightly. "You don't want me to —"

"No," Cliff said quickly. "Tonight all I want to do is crawl into bed and cuddle with my girl. Is that all right with you?"

"Yes, Cliff," Lori said, glowing. "That's absolutely perfect."

Thank God these beds are king-sized, Luca thought, making sure he stuck to his side of the mattress.

Jeromy emerged from the bathroom in his pretentious silk pajamas with his initials embroidered on the pocket.

They didn't speak. There was nothing to say.

Just like that, they both knew it was over, although unbeknownst to Luca, Jeromy was not giving up without a fight.

"Who's up for a movie?" Taye asked, full of energy and ready to stay awake for another couple of hours. "There's a selection of five thousand DVDs in the screening room. Bloody hell — we can take a vote."

"Don't wanna watch a movie," Ashley said, miffed that Cliff Baxter had practically ignored her all night. "I'm off to bed."

"Me too," Sierra said, shooting a quick glance at Hammond. He didn't move. "Good night, everyone," she said, making a swift exit, wondering if she'd run into Flynn, who'd already left. Or perhaps Hammond would follow her. She prayed not.

"Dunno why everyone's such a friggin' drag tonight," Taye complained to Xuan and Hammond, the last guests left. "Aren't we supposed to be havin' fun?"

"Tomorrow is fun night," Xuan said dryly. "All the fun you could ever want." She was disappointed that Aleksandr had retired early. They had plans to make, things to discuss. Perhaps in the morning she could firm up some future meetings when they were off the yacht.

"Yeah, well I like t' have fun *every* night," Taye grumbled.

"It's almost midnight," Xuan pointed out, delicately suppressing a yawn. "It's too late for me to sit through a movie."

"Right," Hammond said, glancing at his watch and getting up. "Time to pack it in."

Taye shrugged. What was he thinking? Only a few more nights on the yacht and then it was back to Blighty and the twins and his mother-in-law. So what the hell, why was he wasting lovemaking time?

Ashley was waiting. No movie tonight.

After ten minutes of searching for Renee, Hammond discovered her on the top deck, still clearing up from the barbecue. She blushed when she saw him approaching.

Den was also there, tidying up behind the bar. Ignoring him, Hammond went straight over to Renee. "I must see you," he said in a low voice. "Where can we be together?"

Renee squirmed uncomfortably. At the beginning of the trip, her fellow Australian Den had tried to stir up a bit of a flirt. She'd shut him down, not because she didn't like him, but because she knew it would be foolish to start up something with a bloke she was working with. It was a bit embarrassing, though; she didn't want Den thinking there was anything going on between her and the senator.

"Can't talk right now," she managed in a hoarse whisper. "Can you meet me back here in an hour?"

"An hour? I can't wait that long," Hammond complained, a surly expression crossing his bland face. "Surely you understand that I've been thinking about you all day?"

Renee's stomach performed a wild somersault. She was flattered and excited all at the same time. Senator Patterson was a very important man, and he wanted to be with *her*! "You'll have to," she said, slightly desperate. "I'll be here. Promise."

"Very well." Hammond glanced over at Den. "Lost my reading glasses," he said in a loud voice. "Anyone seen them?"

"Sorry, mate," Den replied, then, remembering who he was talking to, he added, "Uh,

I mean Senator Patterson."

"Not to worry," Hammond said, walking briskly away. "I'm sure they'll turn up."

Den immediately ducked out from behind the bar and made his way over to Renee. "What's up with him?" he asked, hovering beside her.

Renee shrugged. "How would I know?" she said, trying to appear super-casual but not succeeding.

"He was all up in your face," Den accused. "What's the old geezer want?"

"You heard him," Renee said, her cheeks reddening. "His bloody reading glasses. And by the way, he's not so old."

"Maybe not, but he *is* married," Den pointed out, giving her a hard look. "An' that means you shouldn't go gettin' into somethin' you can't handle."

"Oh *please!*" Renee said, quite frustrated. "You're being a dick. Nothing's going on."

"Yeah, pull the other one," Den said sarcastically. "It's got bells on."

Keeping track of everyone was not as easy as Mercedes had thought. She'd hoped that by midnight all the guests would have retired for the night. And while most of them had, there were still stragglers. Flynn Hudson, for one. Why was he taking a midnight swim? Churning up and down the length of the pool as if he were training for the Olympics. And the senator, lurking around trying to get into Renee's pants. Mercedes decided she had to do something about that, stash them somewhere secure so they wouldn't get caught in the crossfire. If there *was* crossfire, which she doubted. They were on a private yacht cruising the Sea of Cortez, not a big old tanker chugging through the Indian Ocean loaded with oil. Nobody expected pirates to descend on them. Especially heavily armed Somalians intent on gaining immediate control.

Captain Dickson had already retired, and so had most of the crew.

The yacht was anchored near one of the deserted islands; all was quiet and peaceful, although Mercedes had checked the weather report, and she had a hunch the storm was coming earlier than expected. In another life she could've been a successful weather girl on TV. She had a knack for making accurate predictions.

Adrenaline coursed through her veins as she ran upstairs to the top deck. Den was locking up the bar and leaving.

"Where've *you* been?" he said, glaring at her. "You're supposed to help Renee clear up. Jeez! You're so friggin' lazy."

"Since when did you turn into Guy?" she said irritably.

"Since *she* always lets you take advantage of her," Den answered hotly. "Renee's a beaut — an' you're a —"

"What?" Mercedes said, challenging him, her eyes flashing danger. The last thing she needed was distractions.

"Will you two shut up about me?" Renee said, hurrying over to them. "Den, I'll see you tomorrow. Mercedes, can I talk to you about something?"

"Bet I know what *that's* about," Den said, with a curl of his lip. "Some dipstick's out to get his leg over. Maybe *you* can talk some bloody sense into her, car girl."

Den had called her "car girl" ever since they'd boarded. Insulting *hijo de su madre.* He'd better get his ass down to his cabin before he got in anyone's way; she wouldn't want him getting hurt.

Renee was looking at her with a what-am-I-gonna-do guilty expression.

Mercedes waited until Den left, then, after Renee filled her in, she said, "Take him to our cabin. It's yours. Stay all night if you like."

"What about you?" Renee questioned, wringing her hands. "It wouldn't be right to throw you out of your own room."

"That's okay," Mercedes said, adding a quick, "I got my own thing going on."

"Holy crap!" Renee gulped, quite excited. "Who with?"

"It doesn't matter," Mercedes said quickly. "Just take him to our cabin."

"You're *such* a good mate," Renee enthused.

Mercedes shrugged. "Not so much," she muttered.

It was time to get back to Kyril. She'd already taken him a full plate of brownies, heavily laced with sedatives. Now came the real deal. A steaming mug of hot chocolate, or as Mercedes referred to it in her head, the horse tranquilizer special.

Soon Kyril should be sleeping like a ninety-year-old grandma.

CHAPTER SEVENTY-EIGHT

Cashoo jabbered away in Somali about the boss's woman he'd ejaculated on. He pantomimed her big breasts with his hands and cackled with ribald laughter.

His cohorts in the boat licked their lips, chewed on their khat, and wondered if they'd ever get a chance to be as daring as Cashoo. He was their Casanova, with many girls back home. They were in awe of his sexual adventures. He entertained them with his stories, and they always asked for more.

Amiin was in charge of the second boat. He thought to himself how fortunate that Cashoo was not doing his boasting in front of Cruz, because obviously the young fool didn't realize that the big boss's woman was also Cruz's sister. If Cruz found out, he'd probably cut off Cashoo's dick with a rusty razor blade.

It wasn't Amiin's concern. He was here for the money, that's all.

Although he had to remember that Cashoo

was a relative, and if anything happened to him, his sister, Kensi — a true witch — would probably place a damn curse on his head.

There were five men crowded into each boat. In Amiin's boat were Cashoo; two other pirates, Daleel and Hani; and Viktor, the Russian. Amiin wasn't sure why Cruz had chosen to break up the two Russians, but he supposed Cruz had his reasons.

The sea was calm at first, although as the boat headed farther out, the water began getting choppy. Amiin and his men were seasoned seafarers; Viktor wasn't. He started turning green as the choppiness changed into full-on bouncing waves.

Once again the Somalians laughed and jeered at him. One of them offered him a bunch of khat to chew on. When he refused, they laughed even louder. *"Kumayo,"* they muttered. *"Guska meicheke."*

Viktor wasn't sure if he was receiving insults or sympathy. He only knew that the rougher the sea became, the more his stomach churned. This was not what he'd signed up for.

Amiin called Cruz on their two-way radio. "The Russian's getting sick," he muttered. "What should I do?"

"If he gets too sick, toss him overboard," Cruz responded.

Amiin didn't know if Cruz was joking or not. Somehow he had a hunch not.

■ ■ ■ ■

When the rain began to fall, Cruz embraced it. He'd always looked upon rain as a good-luck omen, a cleansing.

His men grumbled and began pulling well-worn sweatshirts and old stained jackets over their heads. They huddled together like a team as Basra steered the fast speedboat through the treacherous rolling seas.

Like his partner, Viktor, Maksim was becoming seriously sick. The waves were now huge, causing the Somalians to pull out their prayer beads and start chanting.

Cruz managed to force a soggy cigarette into his mouth. He couldn't get it lit, which infuriated him. Goddammit, nothing was ever easy.

Maksim was leaning over the side of the boat groaning and throwing up.

One solid shove and he would be gone.

Cruz considered the possibilities. No more henchmen looking over him. And if he *was* changing plans, that's exactly what he had to do, dump the Russian. His crew wouldn't care; there was no love between them and Sergei's men.

Cruz did not have the stomach to do it himself, so he moved next to Basra, took over driving the boat, and pantomimed what he wanted him to do.

Basra — to whom life meant nothing — didn't hesitate. He took pleasure in violence; it had been that way since, as a child, he'd witnessed his father beat his mother to death.

After maneuvering himself next to Maksim, Basra waited for the next big wave to hit, then shouldered the Russian man overboard as if he were disposing of a sack of garbage. No emotion crossed his skeletal face. Death never bothered him.

Maksim was caught unaware, his desperate screams for help was obliterated by the noise of the storm.

Cruz glanced back to see if the second boat had noticed. The night was pitch-black; it was impossible to see your hand in front of you.

Cruz reached for the two-way radio. "Get rid of the Russian," he instructed Amiin. "Do it now."

How fortuitous that he'd thought of separating them.

In their weakened state, neither of the Russians saw it coming, although burly Viktor put up more of a struggle, and almost took one of the pirates with him.

"Done," Amiin advised Cruz.

"They needed to go," Cruz shouted over the howling wind. "Change of plans. We won't be returning to the villa."

"Yes, boss," Amiin said.

His job in life was not to ask questions, merely to obey.

CHAPTER SEVENTY-NINE

And while the pirates were on their way to take over the *Bianca,* a story hit the front page of a New York tabloid with one of its usual stop-you-in-your-tracks headlines:

PATTERSON DOES A CLINTON.
HERE WE INTERN AGAIN!

The headline was accompanied by a photo of Skylar with another girl — both in skimpy tank tops with prominent nipples, both sticking their tongues out at the camera.

Radical had personally chosen the photo from a selection on Skylar's Facebook page. The fact that the photo was three years old didn't bother Radical; she was searching for provocative, and that's exactly what she got.

"My parents will kill me!" Skylar had said when Radical first approached her with the idea of selling her story.

"Yeah, but you'll be, like, a *rich*-as-shit dead teenager," Radical had slyly joked. "Like, so will I."

Radical had inherited the power of convincing people to do things her way from her father. He'd parlayed his gift into becoming a respected senator, while all Radical wanted to do was make lots of money.

So she'd convinced Skylar that her parents were screwing with her and were not about to do anything about Hammond's sexual indiscretions, and surely he would do the same to other girls, which made it Skylar's duty to get the word out there.

And so even though she was a few years younger than Skylar, Radical got her way. And the two of them had marched into the offices of the New York tabloid and sold their story for — as Radical put it — a shitload of money.

Now the the story was out there. No stopping them anytime soon.

When Eddie started getting calls at five A.M., he flipped out.

WHAT . . . THE . . . FUCK?

How could this have happened?

And with a feeling of deep dread, he knew that if anyone was about to get the blame, it would be him.

CHAPTER EIGHTY

The storm hit at one A.M. It was a tropical summer storm — the worst kind — violent and unpredictable.

Mercedes darted around the yacht taking note of who was still around. As the large yacht began to buck and roll, she was sure that some of the guests would get seasick and come staggering to the upper decks.

She wondered if Captain Dickson would surface. Probably not; he wasn't exactly hands-on.

Kyril had finally fallen into a drugged sleep, snoring like a freight train, his big body sliding down in his chair, hefty legs spread wide, mouth gaping open.

The timing was right on: if the storm didn't hold them up too much, Cruz and his men would be boarding the yacht in around twenty minutes.

It wasn't going to be as easy as they'd thought, what with the yacht bucking and rolling like crazy; getting aboard would be a struggle. Mercedes had no doubt that her papa could handle it — he always did.

She'd already unloaded Kyril's guns, rendering them useless. And earlier that day, she'd made it into the master suite and commandeered the revolver Kasianenko kept in a locked drawer by his bed. If anyone else on the yacht had weapons, she hadn't found them, and over the past few days, she'd conducted a pretty thorough search.

It was on, and she was ready. There was nothing else to do now except wait.

"You're not shy, are you?" Hammond inquired. He was getting impatient with this tall Australian girl, who was not giving up her pussy to him as fast as he would've liked. He had her top and bra off — nice breasts — and he figured if he played with them long enough, she'd be good to go. The annoying problem was that every time he attempted to make it downtown, she shied away from him like a nervous colt.

He had a strong urge to fuck her and get out of the miserable room she'd taken him to. If it didn't happen soon, he was contemplating *slapping* her into submission.

They were on an uncomfortable lower bunk bed, lying side by side. He was fully clothed and hard as a rock.

"I'm . . . I'm not shy," she whispered, shivering as he twisted one of her nipples a fraction too hard. "It's just that . . . uh . . . I know I should have told you before . . ."

"Told me what?"

"It's, uh . . . embarrassing."

"What?" he thundered, starting to lose it.

"I'm . . . a . . . virgin."

For some men those three words would deflate a hard-on quicker than a bucket of cold water. Hammond was not one of those men. Her words made him more excited than ever.

A virgin. Ripe for deflowering. Ah yes, he was just the man for the job.

The yacht began to rock, but Hammond didn't notice.

Now he *had* to have her.

No doubt about it.

"What's going on?" Ashley stuttered, sitting up with a start.

Taye was sleeping soundly. He'd had great sex with his wife for the fourth day in a row, and now he was sleeping like a satisfied stallion, dreaming about winning the World Cup, then fucking Angelina Jolie. Didn't every man dream about fucking Angelina Jolie?

Ashley vigorously shook his shoulder. He groaned and opened one eye. "Wassamatter, toots?" he mumbled.

"The boat's shaking," she said in a weak voice. "I feel sick."

Taye launched himself into an upright position. He could hear the rain pounding on the porthole, and there was a flash of bright lightning followed by loud rumbles of thunder.

"It's nothin', babe," he assured her. "A bit of a storm, that's all."

"I feel sick," she repeated.

"Want me t' hold your head over the loo?" he offered.

"No, thank you," she said crossly. "I didn't say I was going to *be* sick, I just *feel* it."

"That's 'cause the boat's churnin'," he advised. "It'll soon stop."

"How do *you* know?" she said accusingly.

" 'Cause it's a tropical storm. That's what they do, babe. Now spoon up against me and go back to bye-bye land."

For once Ashley did as she was told.

Sleep was impossible for Sierra. Her mind refused to be still.

Was there going to be some big political sex scandal when they got back to New York? Would she be forced to stand by her husband's side while he made a smarmy televised apology?

The good wife. The obedient wife. The stupid wife who puts up with her husband's indiscretions and continues to support him.

Or perhaps Hammond would summon people adept at running damage control. He would get the girl's accusations squashed before they went public. Then he'd pay off Skylar and her parents, and that would be that. No cringe-worthy TV appearances. No fake apology. All quiet on the political front.

Which left Radical to contend with, and what were they supposed to do about her? The girl was difficult, to say the least. She hated her father as much as he hated her.

Sierra sighed. There was nothing she could do to intervene. It was what it was.

Her thoughts drifted to Flynn. The man she'd always wanted, the man she could never have — not while Hammond was still around.

It was all too much.

The storm roared outside, and the yacht was in constant motion.

She barely noticed.

Where was Hammond, anyway?

She didn't know, and she didn't care. Perhaps he'd slipped and fallen overboard. What a relief *that* would be.

Jeromy's stomach flipped and flopped. He felt light-headed and quite ill. To his fury, Luca didn't care. Luca was in a deep sleep.

Jeromy staggered toward the bathroom and collapsed onto the floor by the toilet. The boat swayed back and forth. He could hear the storm outside, and it unnerved him. Once, in the South of France, he and some acquaintances had gotten caught in a storm on a sailing boat. He could still remember the nausea that had overcome him, and now it was back, that ghastly seasick sensation.

He leaned his head against the cold porcelain of the toilet and prayed for morning.

"It's okay," Cliff assured Lori when she nudged up against him. "This yacht is built to withstand anything."

"It is?" she asked tentatively. "It feels awfully rough."

"Think of it as turbulence when you're on a plane," Cliff said. "Nothing to worry about."

"You're sure?" Lori said, shivering.

Cliff held her close. "Positive."

Flynn never made it to bed. After churning fifty or so lengths in the lap pool, he'd gone to the gym and worked out with weights.

He'd made up his mind that he was leaving tomorrow. Leaving Sierra and everything she'd once meant to him. He'd finally realized there was nothing he could do about the situation. She was married to Hammond, and that's the way it was. No going back.

After a vigorous workout, he made his way up to the front of the top deck, grabbed the railing, and leaned out, gazing at the turbulent black sea, getting drenched but liking the feel of the driving rain hitting him in his face.

Lightning flashed. Thunder roared. Nature

was doing its thing.

Too bad he didn't have anyone to share it with.

Xuan pulled the covers over her head. Lightning terrified her. Too many bad memories of when she was escaping from Communist China and running, running, running.

She'd gotten raped in the middle of a raging storm. Five men. Five pigs. Five penises drilling into her until she'd passed out.

Somehow she'd survived that horrific night, but the bad memories still lingered, especially when she saw lightning and heard the roar of thunder.

Where was Flynn when she needed him?

Bianca suddenly shot up in bed. "It's a storm," she announced as if she were only just making such a startling discovery.

Aleksandr was already up, sitting in a chair smoking a cigar. "I was hoping you'd sleep through it," he said.

"Don't you know?" Bianca retorted, green eyes flashing. "Storms are my thing."

"They are?" Aleksandr said. Bianca never failed to surprise him.

"Yes, ever since I was a little kid," she said, leaping out of bed. "Storms are *so* exciting! All that thunder and lightning, it's major sexy."

"What are you doing?" Aleksandr asked.

"Getting my storm on," Bianca replied, a wicked smile playing around her lips as she wrenched the terrace doors open and raced outside.

"Are you crazy?" Aleksandr bellowed as the wind blew a deluge of rain into the room. "It's dangerous out there."

"No, it's not," Bianca yelled back at him. "It's a trip."

"You're naked," he shouted. "Put some clothes on."

"Why? There's no one to see me," she said, jumping into the churning Jacuzzi. "Come, my big bad Russian. I wanna make love. Get your ass out here an' join me."

The one person Mercedes didn't want to run into was Guy.

Yet there he was, in sweatpants, a rumpled T-shirt, and a rain slicker, checking things out on the middle deck.

Before she could dodge out of sight, he spotted her.

"What are *you* doing up?" he asked, throwing her a suspicious look.

This was not good. What if he noticed Kyril slumped in a drugged-out stupor on the job? What if he figured out something was about to go down?

She managed a concerned expression. "I was worried about the guests," she said. "Wonderin' how they're coping."

"Well, well, well," Guy said, a look of surprise on his face. "Little Miss Lazy Pants actually cares."

"You never know," Mercedes said, putting on her all wide-eyed innocence expression. "Some people get quite seasick. It's not a great feeling."

"You seen anyone around?" Guy asked. "Any of the passengers?"

Mercedes shook her head.

"You're sure?" Guy said, thinking it was quite possible that he'd misjudged this girl.

"Quite sure," she said firmly.

"Then I expect we can both go back to bed," he said, stifling a yawn.

"Yes," Mercedes said, realizing that at any moment Cruz and his team would be making their play. Two boats. One on each side of the yacht. Pirates boarding. Fast and furious.

"Good night," she said, and quickly hurried out of Guy's sight.

CHAPTER EIGHTY-ONE

The pirates were wet through and through, freezing cold, pissed off, and ready for action. They all knew what they had to do — secure the yacht — which meant herding the crew into the downstairs area so that they could be controlled, securing the guests, then keeping everyone in place until the ransom was paid and they could be on their merry way.

Amiin had supplied each of them with a crude map of the interior of the yacht. Their job was to get all of the crew into the mess hall next to the kitchen in the bowels of the boat, while Cruz took care of whoever was on the bridge — or at least in the control room, since the yacht was at anchor for the night.

The storm had held them up, but fortunately, as they got nearer to the *Bianca,* the storm had started to abate, making it easier for them to board.

Everyone had a job to do, and since the

543

two boats were approaching from both sides of the yacht, it all had to happen at top speed. The element of surprise was crucial, which is why Cruz had decided to stage the raid in the middle of the night when most of the crew and guests would be sleeping.

As they approached the *Bianca*, Cruz ordered them to cut the engines on the speedboats, allowing a stealth landing. They secured the boats to the large yacht with strong bindings before affixing sturdy rope ladders.

Within seconds, the pirates were clambering aboard.

"Don't move," Hammond instructed, his voice thick with lust. "Stay perfectly still."

Renee did as she was told, spread-eagled on Mercedes's lower bunk bed, quite naked and a tad fearful, but mostly excited as she watched Hammond strip off his clothes. She noticed that he had a small paunch — she hadn't expected that — and his manhood was not exactly impressive. But he was a UNITED STATES SENATOR, and she was a simple girl from Brisbane. This was the most thrilling thing that had ever happened to her, and if it meant giving up her virginity, so be it.

Hammond approached the bed. He was in no rush as he savored every moment.

"Relax," he said soothingly. "It might hurt for a moment or two, but trust me, dear, when I'm finished with you, you'll be *begging* for more."

Mercedes ran to meet Cruz on the starboard side. So far so good. Nobody had realized that invaders were busy slipping aboard. This was Cruz's easiest takeover yet.

He handed Mercedes a bag filled with heavy-duty padlocks, and told her to use them to lock the guests in their cabins until it was time to extract them.

"Somebody better secure Kyril," she worried. "Before the drugs wear off an' he goes on a rampage."

"I'll take care of it," Cruz answered.

She noticed he had his gun out. Was the big chocolate-loving Russian about to be terminated?

It wasn't her concern. She had a job to do.

At first Flynn thought he was hallucinating as he peered out to sea. What the hell? Boats were approaching. Boats in the middle of the night.

Was someone in trouble? What was going on?

The rain had almost stopped, and from his vantage point on the top deck, he could make out shadowy figures. Shadowy figures that were affixing ropes and then crawling up both sides of the *Bianca*.

Jesus Christ! Was it possible the *Bianca* was

being pirated?

"I'm sick," Jeromy muttered, feeling sorry for himself. "Really sick."

Luca didn't hear him, because Luca was still asleep.

Jeromy had tried to wake him, to no avail. *Selfish blond god pop star. May his next tour tank. May his success vanish overnight. May his golden cock wither and fade away.*

Jeromy made it out of the bathroom, reached for his monogrammed silk robe, put it on, left their room, and headed for the stairs, figuring that fresh air might help him recover.

As he reached the staircase, he came face-to-face with Mercedes.

"Thank God someone's up," he grumbled. "Fetch me some seasick pills and a hot cup of tea. Perhaps some plain toast too. Do it fast. I'll be upstairs."

Mercedes was speechless, but only for a moment. "You'd better get back to your room," she said brusquely. "We have a flood going on."

"I need fresh air," Jeromy said with a petulant scowl. "Forget about your stupid flood and get me what I require. I'll be on the middle deck."

"Fine," she said, brushing past him.

"Now," Jeromy called after her. "Do it now."

She was gone.

Staff. Rude and arrogant. Jeromy decided he would complain to Guy about the girl. He'd never liked her; she'd always exhibited attitude. The Australian girl was far more polite, and prettier too.

On the next deck up, Cruz surveyed the drugged Russian security guard. He was a big man — huge, in fact. A fucking giant.

Did they really want to deal with him when he woke up?

Negative on that.

Diving under the water of the Jacuzzi, Bianca surfaced between Aleksandr's strong thighs. She resembled a sleek seal, her long black hair sticking to her back, mimicking an exotic tail.

"You, my dear, are extremely inventive," Aleksandr remarked, attempting to get his breath back after a marathon session of underwater lovemaking. When Bianca was in the mood, she could be quite insatiable. But then so could he, which made them extremely compatible in the bedroom.

"I know," Bianca purred, stroking his thighs. "I told you we'd have fun."

"The storm is over. We should go back inside."

"Not before I —"

Her words were cut short by the sound of a gunshot.

Aleksandr was immediately alert.

"What was that?" Bianca asked.

On his feet, stepping out of the Jacuzzi, Aleksandr was already trying to reach Kyril, who failed to answer.

Somewhere in the distance, he heard shouting and another gunshot.

Aleksandr's survival instinct kicked into high gear.

He immediately rushed over to his bedside drawer to retrieve his gun.

It was gone.

He turned to Bianca. "Get dressed," he said urgently, reaching for his own clothes. "Something's wrong."

CHAPTER EIGHTY-TWO

"Shit!" Eddie March exclaimed. His phones in the office had not stopped ringing, and he could not get through to Hammond on the *Bianca*. It appeared all lines were down.

The office was pandemonium. Outside on the street, the press were assembling, waiting for something — anything — from Senator Patterson's camp regarding the sex scandal.

Radical had vanished. Taken her ill-gotten gains and no doubt skipped town. Where she would run to, Eddie had no clue. And quite frankly, he didn't care. Although he could imagine another lurid headline in the making: SENATOR PATTERSON'S TEENAGE DAUGHTER MISSING.

Martin Byrne had turned into a man possessed. He'd stormed into Eddie's office yelling and screaming about how he would sue the senator for everything he had.

"It was *your* daughter who sold her story," Eddie pointed out.

"Because that degenerate you work with

had *his* daughter talk her into it," Martin shouted, ready to explode with wrath.

Eddie had no sympathy for any of them. He was seriously considering resigning when Hammond returned.

How could he stay working for a man who obviously had no respect for the position he held? Let alone respect for his beautiful wife. It simply wasn't good enough.

Meanwhile, Radical had hooked up with a boy she'd known and crushed on way back in Wyoming, before her mom had died and before she'd come searching out her father.

His name was Biff. He was seventeen and a Goth.

She'd sent him a bus ticket and booked them into a hotel room off Times Square, paying for everything with her newfound newspaper money.

Radical was happy for the first time in years.

CHAPTER EIGHTY-THREE

Power. Yes, power was the ultimate aphrodisiac, and didn't Hammond know it as he gazed down at the naked virgin spread out in all her glory.

He hadn't had a virgin in a long while. Girls today seemed to get it on with their boyfriends earlier and earlier. It was a shame, a waste. Smart girls picked a man who knew what he was doing. Hammond Patterson — *Senator* Hammond Patterson — was just such a man.

A wolf-like smile spread across his bland face as he lowered himself onto the quivering girl. She was nervous. He liked that; it made him even harder. A delicate virgin waiting for her master to deflower her — what could be more inviting?

Hammond Patterson. Master of the universe. He recalled the Hollywood director James Cameron picking up an award for his movie *Titanic* and calling himself king of the world. Yes, that's what Hammond felt like right now as his penis thrust inside her, breaking the barrier, ignoring her sharp cries of sudden pain.

He was on a path to glory. He was about to fuck the life out of her. Give her something to think about, to remember.

Hammond Patterson was on fire.

Panic ensued. Panic as various crew members were dragged from their beds by a ferocious ragtag band of men who jabbered to each other in a foreign language and wielded lethal weapons such as assault rifles and knives.

There was hardly any resistance from the crew; they were too shocked and scared to do anything as they were hustled into the mess hall in various stages of undress.

Den attempted to grapple with one of the pirates and received a pistol-whipping across his forehead, causing a large gash. Blood dripped down his face as the housekeeper and the two Polish maids screamed in terror.

One of the maids handed him a dishcloth, and he held it to his head while searching around for Renee and Mercedes. Neither of them was there. Could it be because their room was more isolated?

Guy was marched in by a pistol-wielding pirate who shoved him to the ground. "What the *hell?*" Guy shouted as he landed on the floor next to Den.

"I think we're in trouble, mate," Den said

in a low voice. "Big friggin' trouble."

Guy staggered to his feet. "Where's the captain?" he said, trying to sound authoritative.

"Dunno," Den answered, stemming the flow of blood from his forehead. "They're still bringing people in."

Guy shook his head. This wasn't happening. This couldn't possibly be happening.

Unfortunately for everyone on the *Bianca,* it was.

"Here's what I want you to do," Aleksandr said to Bianca, keeping his voice low and reassuring.

She'd pulled on black leggings and a sweatshirt. "What?" she asked, wondering why Aleksandr was suddenly so serious.

"I think there might be something going on."

"Like what?" she said, gazing at him expectantly.

"I'm not sure, Bianca," he said patiently. "I need to find out."

"Was that a gunshot we heard? Was it?"

"Perhaps," he said, purposefully sounding noncommittal. "Do not worry. Just do as I say until I find out what is taking place."

"Should we go investigate?"

"I will do that while you stay here."

"Can't we call someone?"

"The internal phone system is dead, and so

are the TV monitors."

Bianca experienced a tiny shiver of apprehension. "Are we in any kind of danger?"

"I doubt it. However, in case there is a problem, I have a plan."

Settling himself in a comfortable chair in the middle deck lounge, Jeromy noted that the storm was over and the sea was almost calm again, making him feel considerably better. Once that insolent girl brought him his tea and seasick pills, he would return to bed. In the morning he would make damn sure that Luca heard all about how ill he'd been, and hopefully Luca would be filled with guilt for not waking up and ministering to him.

The room was dark — he had not bothered putting on the lights — so he did not see Cashoo until the tall, lanky boy was standing over him brandishing a lethal-looking dagger.

"Move!" Cashoo yelled, proudly using the one word of English he knew. "Move, *kumayo!*"

Jeromy almost fell off his chair. Was this some kind of joke? Some kind of bizarre plot cooked up by Suga to get him out of Luca's life?

"Move!" Cashoo yelled again, grabbing Jeromy's arm and yanking him up.

"Excuse *me,*" Jeromy said, quite affronted.

Cashoo had his eye on Jeromy's robe. He imagined himself strutting around showing it off in front of his girlfriends. He had two girlfriends at home. One of them was pregnant.

He snatched the robe off Jeromy, who was too startled to struggle. Not that Jeromy would; he'd always abhorred violence unless it was of the sexual kind. Chains, whips, cock rings — all good at the right time.

Cashoo held Jeromy's arm in a vise-like grip, and, pulling him along, he marched him downstairs to the mess hall.

Jeromy's eyes swept around the room in horror. Where were the other guests? Where were Bianca and Aleksandr? For God's sake, why was he being thrown in with the crew?

This was completely unacceptable.

Flynn had been caught in many situations. Over the years, he'd traveled through war zones, interviewed masked and hooded terrorists, almost been captured by bandits twice, survived two earthquakes and a tsunami. But this — what the hell was this?

They were cruising the Sea of Cortez, for crissakes. They were in safe waters.

Apparently *not* so safe. The *Bianca* was being taken over. And what was he supposed to do about it?

He knew the drill. A couple of years ago, he'd interviewed several Somalian pirates when he'd been thinking of maybe writing a book about the modern-day piracy industry.

555

And it *was* an industry; they shoveled in millions of ransom dollars a year.

Talking with the pirates in Eyl, the small town by the sea famous for being the center of pirate activity, accompanied by four armed bodyguards and a translator, he'd discovered that a large percentage of them were former fishermen who felt that their livelihood had been affected by illegal fishing vessels raiding their waters, so it was perfectly fine to take what wasn't theirs.

Apart from the fishermen, some of the pirates were ex-militiamen, tough as old leather, and each clan had its own technical geek to deal with satellite phones and GPS.

The pirates had enjoyed boasting about their activities, how much money they made, and how they earned respect, drove big cars, and married the most beautiful clan women.

They refused to address the violence and the weapons they amassed.

In the end, Flynn had decided against writing a book. He didn't trust any of them, and he knew that if he wasn't protected by armed bodyguards, he'd immediately be kidnapped and held for ransom. It was their way.

Usually they didn't stray far from familiar waters. So how was it possible they were running riot on the *Bianca*? This was a crazy situation.

On the top deck, Flynn knew he wouldn't be safe for long. If these intruders were indeed Somalians — and from the stray words he'd heard shouted, they were — then their next move would be securing the boat, making sure everyone was accounted for and locked away. After that it was a question of demanding the required ransom. Until then, the yacht and its occupants would remain their prisoners.

And if the ransom wasn't paid . . .

He recalled that a couple of years ago, Somalians had hijacked a yacht with four Americans aboard. Bible-thumping Americans. The pirates had killed all four of them.

Flynn had a choice. He could try to launch one of the tenders and go for help.

Or he could stay.

Sierra was aboard. He decided to stay.

CHAPTER EIGHTY-FOUR

Usually Cliff was a heavy sleeper, so much so that he would've slept through the entire storm if Lori hadn't awakened him. He could sleep through most things — including the big L.A. earthquake in 1994 — but tonight was different. After Lori nudged him awake, he couldn't get back to sleep, even though the storm had stopped and the yacht was only gently rocking.

Not wishing to disturb Lori, who was now sleeping, he got out of bed, padded into the bathroom, closed the door, put on the light, took a leak, then stood in front of the mirror above the marble sink and studied his reflection.

Cliff Baxter. Superstar.

Cliff Baxter. Soon to be fifty.

Cliff Baxter. Man alone.

His face was craggy, not as handsome as it appeared on screen. There were new lines around his eyes and jowls every day, and the gray in his hair was increasing by the week.

He refused to dye it — artificial props were not for him. No Botox, fillers, or whatever miraculous shit some famous dermatologist was forever coming up with.

Cliff was comfortable with the way he looked. Most of all, he was comfortable with Lori.

Before the trip he'd considered trading her in for a new model.

Why? Because Enid didn't like her?

Because the press felt he should change it up every year? Get himself a fresh young girlfriend for even more photo opportunities? A new spectacular body to pose beside him at industry events looking pretty while saying nothing?

What the hell. If he wasn't careful, he could easily be perceived as a dirty old man, and that was *not* the image he cared to project.

Lori had been great on this trip. Warm, fun, and sexy as hell, and everyone liked her.

So, would he ever consider making her a permanent fixture?

Hmm . . . It was not such an impossible thought.

Mercedes had been under the impression that everyone was going to be rounded up and put into the mess hall — crew and guests alike. Padlocking the rich and famous into their luxurious suites was not what she'd expected.

How was she supposed to raid their rooms and take the loot she had her eye on? This was supposed to be the trip where she made her own personal score — jewelry, cash, and the big prize: the emerald and diamond ring Aleksandr Kasianenko had stashed in his safe.

In her mind she'd already mapped out her future. Enough with being Cruz's happy helper; she yearned for her own life. And counting on the score she'd make with the jewelry and cash, she could have everything she'd ever wanted. After all, she was the only one who knew about the ring. And apart from Cruz, she was the only one who could crack a safe.

What was this padlocking them into their rooms crap? This wasn't the way it was supposed to be.

She had to persuade Cruz to gather everyone in the same place, and soon.

"This is outrageous!" Jeromy objected loudly as the lanky young pirate pushed and shoved him into the crew's dining room. "I will not stand for it!"

Was he dreaming? Was this a bizarre nightmare? If he shut his eyes, would it all go away?

Cashoo was a happy young man. He slipped Jeromy's fancy robe over his clothes and pantomimed a wild and somewhat obscene dance for Daleel and Hani, the two smirking pirates standing near the door, weapons drawn.

The shocked crew watched in horror, anticipating their fate. They'd heard stories about what pirates did to their hostages, and it wasn't pretty.

"Where are the girls?" Den whispered to Guy. "Renee and Mercedes?"

Guy didn't want to think about where they might be.

As far as Cruz was concerned, he did not believe in wasting time. Everyone had a job to do, and his job was to get the ransom demand in action as fast as possible.

He was in charge, and they'd all best listen to him or else, because the faster the money was paid, the easier it would be for all concerned.

He was in possession of a yacht full of rich, famous people. It wouldn't be long before some kind of rescue mission was launched. Also, he had no doubt that when Sergei's men failed to return with Kasianenko, Sergei would go on an angry rampage.

Cruz could only imagine Sergei's fury, which he'd probably take out on Ina.

Too bad. Unfortunately, there was nothing Cruz could do about that. He had himself to look out for. Besides, he and Ina had never been close. She might be his sister, but he didn't like her that much.

The key to getting this all done quickly was Kasianenko himself. Once he had the Russian billionaire's cooperation, everything should move smoothly.

Cruz was confident that soon he'd be richer than he'd ever dreamed of.

"What the hell is this?" Bianca questioned, staring at her Russian lover.

Aleksandr had pressed a hidden button, and the mirrored wall behind his shower slid back, revealing a secret room.

"It's a safe room," Aleksandr said matter-of-factly. "For emergencies."

"Is this an emergency?" Bianca questioned, widening her eyes.

"I have no idea until I see what's going on," Aleksandr said. "And before I do that, I must make sure you are protected."

"Oh my God!" Bianca exclaimed, beginning to experience waves of panic. "You *do* think something bad is happening."

Ever so gently, Aleksandr edged her into the compact room, which was fully equipped for any kind of situation, including with a satellite phone. "I'll make a call when I know for sure what's happening," he said.

Bianca was in semi-shock. She watched in awe as Aleksandr removed a handgun from a cupboard stocked with all kinds of emergency supplies. Then he checked that the gun was loaded, and stuck it in his belt. Talk about macho! Somehow it was reassuring that he remained so calm.

"In the meantime," Aleksandr said, "do not even *think* of coming out until I return."

"Yes," she said meekly. "Hurry back and be safe."

"Oh, I will be, *angel moy.* No need to worry about me."

CHAPTER EIGHTY-FIVE

Adventure had always been Flynn's thing. Taking risks, getting himself out of dangerous situations, knowing what to do and when to do it.

Being trapped on a billionaire's yacht with a bunch of bloodthirsty pirates was not a situation he'd imagined he'd ever encounter. Only here it was, and here *he* was, bang in the middle.

Obviously, their main prize was Aleksandr, although who knew what they'd do when they discovered who else was aboard?

Flynn recalled his conversations with the pirates he'd interviewed in Eyl. At the time, they'd been holding a large oil tanker for ransom. They'd proudly informed him that all the captives aboard were being well looked after and treated like guests at a fine hotel. It was only later he'd discovered that two of the female hostages had been raped, and one of the male captives brutally murdered, even though the ransom was eventually paid.

Flynn's mind started clicking into overdrive.

Advantages: He knew every detail of the yacht. He was into martial arts. He understood the pirate mentality. So far he had not been spotted.

Disadvantages: No weapon. No idea how many pirates there were. No form of communication with the outside world. Unsettling to say the least.

He'd heard a lot of shouting and a couple of gunshots. Not good.

His main thought was *Is Hammond capable of protecting Sierra?*

No fucking way.

It was up to him to figure something out.

Roaming the yacht searching for stragglers, waving his gun in front of him ready to shoot anyone who gave him any trouble, Basra made a frightening figure with his deep sunken eyes, lack of teeth, and unkempt, rain-soaked dreadlocks.

He passed the security room where Kyril now lay on the floor, a neat bullet hole through the middle of his forehead.

Had he done that? He couldn't remember.

After a moment he doubled back, entered the room, wrenched the watch from Kyril's wrist, and put it on his own emaciated wrist. The watch was black with a red dial. Cheap and cheerful.

Next he kicked and pushed Kyril's body out of his way, and sat himself down in the command chair facing a slew of security monitors, all of them blank, for Cruz had cut the feed.

A plate of brownies stood on the shelf in front of him. Basra snatched one up and shoved it in his mouth. Sweet and tasty. He wolfed down another one, and then a third.

Sitting back, he admired his new black watch with the smart red dial. The watch of a dead man was a fine souvenir for him to cherish, especially when he showed it off at home, making his three sons jealous.

Ah . . . his sons. Lazy *wacals.* It was time to kick some sense into them as only he could.

Perhaps he'd remember, perhaps he wouldn't.

On the first day the guests had boarded the yacht, Aleksandr had generously offered everyone the opportunity to take the full tour. Flynn had accepted his offer, and now he was glad he'd done so, for knowing the layout of the yacht was imperative.

There were four levels. The lower level consisted of staff quarters, kitchens, and the engine room. On the next level were a series of luxury suites, all with their own small terraces, plus the movie theater, spa, and other facilities. On the middle deck, there was the swimming pool, the gym, and various areas for relaxing and entertaining, plus the bridge, the communication center, and the master suite with its own large terrace. And finally the upper level was all lounges, sundecks, and more entertaining areas.

Flynn realized that he had to figure out a way to reach Aleksandr, because maybe — just maybe — Kasianenko was still in his suite.

He made a dangerous but doable decision. Before anyone discovered him, he was going over the side.

After getting Bianca into the safe room, Aleksandr headed toward the door. To his consternation, it would not open more than an inch. Bending down and peering through the crack, he soon saw why. The door had been padlocked from the outside.

He wondered where Kyril was. The big man had protected him for so many years, always at his side whenever Aleksandr needed him. Indeed, Kyril had once taken a bullet for him when an irate business associate had attempted to shoot him. Kyril was loyal through and through. If he were alive, he would be here now.

Aleksandr felt a thickness in his throat. Instinct told him that Kyril was not alive. Kyril was either dead or mortally wounded.

Reaching back, he felt the reassuring presence of his gun. Motherfuckers. Whoever was on his yacht had better beware. Aleksandr Kasianenko was not going down without a fight.

Captain Dickson was hauled unceremoniously from his bed by Amiin, who punched him in the stomach and muttered a gruff "Up, mister. This boat now ours."

Anxiety overcame the English captain as he realized what was taking place. In all his years at sea, this was the moment he'd always dreaded.

"What . . . what are you thinking?" he managed, shying away from the dark-skinned man who stood before him brandishing a gun.

"Come," Amiin said. "Follow me or I shoot you in gut."

"Can I get dressed first?"

"Quick," Amiin said, waving his gun in the air. "You do it quick."

Hurriedly the captain pulled on a pair of pants and a shirt. Then, at gunpoint, he went with Amiin upstairs to the bridge, where Cruz waited restlessly.

Captain Dickson came face-to-face with the man he assumed was the leader. He immediately attempted to assert himself. "This is outrageous," he said, sounding extremely stiff-upper-lip British. "Who are you people? What do you want?"

"Whaddya *think* we want?" Cruz retorted, rubbing the deep scar on his neck. "Wanna make a guess?"

"You won't get away with this," Captain Dickson blustered, swallowing hard. "My men have already alerted the coast guard. Help is on its way."

"Your fuckin' men were all asleep on the job," Cruz sneered. "Comin' aboard was like takin' a walk in the park."

"Where are my passengers?" Captain Dickson demanded. "If you've harmed them in any way —"

"Shut your fuckin' mouth an' listen t' me," Cruz said roughly. "You're gonna fetch the Russian mothafucker, an' bring him here. Understand?" He gestured toward Amiin. "Take him with you. He gives you any trouble, shoot him in the head."

Captain Dickson swallowed hard again. Fear coursed through his body. If he survived this, he was retiring.

The *if* hung like a neon question mark before his eyes.

Meanwhile, down in the mess hall, the pirates had discovered bottles of beer, and Daleel and Hani were swigging it down, quenching their thirst, jeering at their hostages, making lewd signs at the two petrified maids and the housekeeper.

Jeromy huddled in a corner still wearing his silk pajamas, trying to make himself as inconspicuous as possible. These men were

569

dangerous savages. God knew what they were capable of.

Guy did a quick head count. All the crew were accounted for except the captain, Mercedes, and Renee. He felt fear for the two girls. He'd heard the stories — rape was not uncommon, and Mercedes and Renee were certainly attractive enough.

Den was thinking along the same lines. In spite of his head injury, he was definitely getting his macho up. Renee was a sweet girl; she didn't deserve what might be happening to her.

"We just gonna sit here an' do nothin'?" he muttered to Guy. "These dickheads are gettin' drunker than a pig's arse. Fair go, mate, we gotta do somethin' with these drongos."

"And get ourselves shot?" Guy said, eyeing the three pirates who were supposedly in charge. "Best to sit tight and wait."

"For what?" Den said, his temper rising. "We gotta go for it."

Guy realized that Den was young — twenty-five, twenty-six. He didn't understand the danger they were in. This wasn't a TV show. This was real life. Guy knew that the smart thing to do was absolutely nothing.

If they didn't give the pirates any trouble, help would surely come. He had to keep the faith.

CHAPTER EIGHTY-SIX

The side of the boat was wet and slippery. To Flynn's relief, the rain had stopped, the storm seemed to be over, and the sea was almost calm.

Slowly and surely he lowered himself down the side of the yacht with the help of strong ropes he'd found in a utility cupboard. He kept going until he landed on the terrace that led to the master suite.

The glass doors leading inside were locked. He could see Aleksandr. Urgently he banged on the glass with his fists until Aleksandr turned around, saw him, and hurried to open the doors.

"Jesus Christ!" Aleksandr exclaimed. "What is happening, Flynn? Do you know?"

"Pirates," Flynn answered quickly. "They've taken over the boat."

"You can't be serious?"

"Dead serious, I'm afraid."

"This is a disaster," Aleksandr said, shaking his head. "What do we do?"

"Is the door to this room locked?"

"No. Someone's secured it from the outside. I can't get out of here."

"Lock it now," Flynn said sharply. "They'll be coming for you any minute."

"Why me?" Aleksandr said, frowning.

" 'Cause they'll be needing you to speak to your businesspeople. They'll want you to order them to pay the ransom immediately."

"How do you know this?"

"Trust me, I have knowledge of the way they work."

"This is some fucked-up situation," Aleksandr said, his face grim.

"It is, but we'll do our best to deal with it," Flynn said, trying to inspire confidence. "Where's Bianca?"

"I put her in the safe room," Aleksandr said, moving over to lock the door from the inside.

"Where's that?"

"Behind the shower door in my bathroom. It was a last-minute decision to incorporate it into the plans. Thank God I listened."

Flynn nodded. "How many people does it hold?" he asked.

"Five or six."

"We need to get all the women inside," Flynn said, speaking fast. "Is there a working phone in there?"

"Satellite," Aleksandr said.

"Call the coast guard. Summon help," Flynn said. "Do you have a gun?"

"Yes."

"More than one?"

"Someone took the revolver I kept by my bed."

"You think they were in here?"

"Not as far as I know."

"They might have a person on the inside. Maybe one of the crew."

"How should we handle this?" Aleksandr asked, thankful that Flynn was aboard.

"You put in a distress call to the coast guard while I try to reach the others. They've probably got no idea what's going on."

"How can you do that?"

"Same way I got in here. Who's in the suite below this?"

Aleksandr thought for a moment, his mind going stubbornly blank. "The footballer," he said at last. "Be careful."

Flynn nodded, and headed for the terrace. "I'll be back," he said confidently. "Go make that call."

"You should have put them all together in the mess hall," Mercedes complained to Cruz. "It's not safe to keep them in their rooms."

"Why not?" Cruz said, dragging on a cigarette, then spitting out fragments of tobacco. "They're secure. They don't got nowhere t' go."

"Ever think they could jump overboard and

573

swim for help?" Mercedes said. "You never know."

"My little *idiota,*" Cruz said with a benevolent chuckle, flashing his two front gold teeth while exhaling a stream of thick smoke. "Who's gonna risk swimming to a deserted island in the middle of the night? You locked 'em in. There's nothin' they can do 'cept wait."

"What if the ransom takes days?" Mercedes insisted. "You lettin' them starve to death?"

"Why you so concerned?" Cruz asked, giving her a what-are-you-hiding look.

She bit down hard on her lower lip. He knew her so well that it was difficult to hide anything from him.

"I was thinkin' I could go through their rooms, see if there's anything worth takin'," she said, keeping it casual.

"Were you now?" Cruz said with a knowing smirk. "As if you haven't already picked out what you're after."

"What if I did? I think I deserve a bonus after all the work I've put in. It's not much fun bein' stuck on this boat with a bunch of rich fuckers ordering me around."

"You spotted something good, *chiquita*?"

Cruz rarely used words of affection toward her. She kind of liked it.

"Oh, just clothes an' stuff," she answered vaguely. "These spoiled *putas* have a ton of nice things."

"Tell you what," Cruz said amiably. "Amiin took the captain to bring Kasianenko back here. Once I get the Russian to make it clear to his people they gotta pay up or he ends up on the bottom of the ocean, then we'll move 'em all downstairs. That make you happy?"

"Thanks, Papa," she said, already picturing her future.

"Don't call me that," Cruz snapped, his mood abruptly changing.

She'd forgotten for a moment that he didn't allow her to call him papa. It made him feel old in front of whatever whore he was banging.

"Sorry . . . uh . . . Cruz," she muttered. "It won't happen again."

Since he seemed to be getting nowhere with Guy, Den began canvassing other members of the crew. None of them was prepared to make a move.

"So we just sit here," Den said, staring them down. "Y'know what that makes us? Nothin' but a bunch of bloody wankers. Why stay still when we could rush 'em? C'mon, mates, there's only three of 'em against all of us."

"Yes, and get our heads blown off for the trouble," the chef — a stocky Englishman — said. "We sit here quietly and wait for the ransom to be paid. That's what we do. I got a wife and three kids to think about."

Den was frustrated. The pirates were getting drunker by the minute. If the rest of the crew cooperated, he was sure they could turn it around.

Shit! It wasn't in his nature to sit back, do nothing, and be a victim. Besides, he was still worried about Renee and Mercedes. They could be in deep trouble.

Never the heaviest of sleepers, Taye was instantly awake when he heard tapping coming from the direction of the terrace doors.

He jumped out of bed, bare-assed, which was the way he always slept, and padded over to the doors. Flynn was standing outside.

Taye opened the glass doors. "What the hell?" he mumbled, disoriented. "You fall overboard or what?"

"Boat's been taken over by pirates," Flynn said brusquely, pushing past him. "We gotta get Ashley somewhere safe. Do you think she can manage to climb a rope?"

Taye shook his head to make sure he wasn't dreaming. Nope. He wasn't dreaming. Flynn was still standing there talking about pirates.

"Are you shittin' me?" he said, confused.

"No, I'm deadly serious. You've got to get her upstairs to Aleksandr's suite right now. There's a rope outside — help her climb it. Aleksandr has a safe room up there."

"Jeez!" Taye exclaimed. "You bloody mean it, dontcha?"

"Who's next door to you?" Flynn said urgently.

"The senator," Taye said. "Never stops yellin' at that poor wife of his."

"Okay," Flynn said, tucking that information away for later. "You take care of Ashley. I gotta try to warn everyone else. I'll see you up there."

Moving fast, he took off again, not certain how he could convince Hammond to help get Sierra to safety. But he was sure as hell going to try.

Frog-marching Captain Dickson back to the bridge, Amiin passed Kyril's room, and spotted Basra asleep on a chair in front of a slew of blank monitors.

"You," Amiin warned the captain, "no move." Then he began screaming a stream of expletives at Basra in Somali. Basically telling him to move his lazy ass and continue looking for any stragglers, which was what he was supposed to be doing.

Basra forced his eyes open, mumbled a weak excuse, stood up, picked up his gun, and set off downstairs.

His job was to inspect the crew's quarters, make sure they had them all stashed in the mess hall. Yes, and if he came across anyone, he decided in his groggy state of mind, then he might as well shoot to kill.

CHAPTER EIGHTY-SEVEN

"Whaddya mean, he won't come out?" Cruz demanded, glaring at Amiin as if it was his fault. "Open the fuckin' door and *haul* him out."

"He got door locked from inside," Amiin explained.

"Jeez! What a *cabrón*," Cruz snarled. "Gettin' him up here is for his own fuckin' good."

"Why do you want him?" Mercedes piped up.

Captain Dickson stared at her in shock. Mercedes was standing there as if she were one of them.

Then it struck him: she *was* one of them. The little bitch he'd told Guy not to hire was with the pirates! She must have been working with them all along.

Guy was such a fool. Captain Dickson couldn't wait to confront his director of entertainment — if he was lucky enough for that day to ever come, because right now he had a gun stuck in his face and a strong urge to crap his pants.

Mercedes felt the hate in Captain Dickson's eyes burning into her. "Get over it," she spat.

"I need Kasianenko here," Cruz said heatedly. "To get the ransom demand started."

Time was important. He expected the money to be paid within twenty-four hours; every moment wasted ate up precious time.

"Blow a hole in the *chingado*'s door and *drag* him up here," he ordered Amiin. "Do it now."

"Yes, boss," Amiin said.

The door to the Pattersons' terrace was not locked. Flynn opened it, slid inside, and approached the bed.

Sierra was in it. Hammond was not.

Flynn checked out the bathroom. Empty. He leaned over the bed and shook Sierra awake. She opened her eyes and gasped.

"Don't be alarmed," he said, speaking fast. "There are pirates aboard."

She sat up, coppery hair tumbling around her beautiful face. "Flynn," she murmured, her eyes widening. "Pirates. Seriously?"

"Yeah, I know, it's crazy," he said. "I can hardly believe it myself."

"You're sure?"

"Yes, I'm sure. Where's Ham?"

"I . . . I don't know. He never came to bed."

"Put on something warm and grab your tennis shoes. I'm getting you to safety."

■ ■ ■ ■

Cashoo had been expecting to see gorgeous women on this luxurious yacht, but to his disappointment the three females sitting with the male hostages were nothing special.

As usual, he was feeling horny. He couldn't seem to get his mind off the big boss's woman with her huge breasts — breasts he could play with all day long given the opportunity.

He had a hunch that they might not be returning to the villa, since Cruz had disposed of the two Russian bodyguards. That was a shame, because he would've liked to have played around with the boss's woman some more. Still, Cruz always had a plan, and at the end of the plan there was always plenty of money to share, so Cashoo couldn't complain.

Once more Cashoo eyed the crew of the *Bianca*. A sorry-looking bunch.

He started wondering where Mercedes was. The two of them got along fine. Mercedes was a spitfire, up for anything. She was his kind of girl: pretty and dangerous.

Tired of guarding the hostages, he told Daleel that he had to take a piss and would be right back.

Daleel nodded, and Cashoo headed off to search out Mercedes.

As soon as Cashoo left, Den nudged Guy. "There's only two of 'em now," he muttered. "C'mon, mate, grow a pair. If we all move together, we can rush 'em."

"It's not going to happen," Guy said, wishing that Den would settle down and stop bugging him. "In case you haven't noticed, they've got guns — nobody wants to risk getting shot. We stay calm, they'll stay calm," Guy said, trying to convince himself.

"You think?" Den argued, jutting out his chin. "They're gettin' drunker by the minute. We don't do somethin', we're gonna be toast. Shove *that* in your stay-calm book."

Over in the corner it occurred to Jeromy that if everyone was murdered on the yacht, who would even remember that he was aboard? The headlines would be all about the famous people — Luca, Cliff Baxter, Taye, Bianca, the senator, and of course Aleksandr. There was a strong possibility that he might not be mentioned at all. Jeromy Milton-Gold, an also-ran.

For some obscure reason he experienced a strong burst of anger toward Luca. Where was his blond god? Why wasn't he doing anything?

Jeromy knew he was thinking in an unreasonable fashion because, unfortunately, there was nothing Luca *could* do. Stone-cold fact: there was nothing anyone could do.

He glanced over at Guy. Was he an enemy or a friend?

Jeromy hoped he was a friend, for he needed to be close to someone at this frightening time.

Moving like a sure-footed cat, Flynn jumped from terrace to terrace, alerting everyone and telling them to get up to Aleksandr's suite. The only two people missing were Hammond and Jeromy Milton-Gold. Flynn had no idea where either of them was, and right now they were the least of his worries.

The women turned out to be a hardy bunch, climbing the rope like veterans, crowding into the safe room with Bianca. The safe room was soundproof, and at the top of the panel was a one-way mirrored section that allowed whoever was inside to see what was going on outside.

Once everyone was assembled, Xuan confronted Flynn and insisted that she stay and face the pirates with the men.

Flynn was having none of it. "You will stay in here until we come get you. Do not come out for anything, and stay quiet. You'll all be safe if you do that."

Sierra gave him a long look. "How about you?" she asked softly. "Will *you* be safe?"

"I can look after myself," he said tersely. Then, gesturing toward the other men, he said, "We all can."

"What about Hammond?" she asked.

"We'll find him," Flynn assured her, wondering if she was asking because she cared.

On the other side of the door, Amiin yelled, "Out now or me shoot!"

Aleksandr slid the panel to the safe room shut.

Flynn looked around at Taye, Luca, and Cliff. "We gonna go for the bastard or be trapped as hostages?"

"No question. We'll friggin' take the bugger," Taye said, eyes gleaming.

Cliff nodded his agreement. "I've done it in movies enough times," he said wryly. "Let's put it to the test and see how I make out in real life."

"I'm ready," Luca said, nervous inside but determined to put on a strong front. He was worried about Jeromy, but there was nothing he could do about finding him now.

Aleksandr removed the gun from his belt. "We're all in this together," he said, full of steely determination. "Five men as one."

"Right," Flynn said. "Gimme the gun. I reckon I've had more practice than you."

Aleksandr didn't argue; he handed Flynn his gun.

Outside the door, Amiin yelled a final warning: "Open or I blast in!"

"Go for it, cocksucker," Flynn muttered. "We're ready an' waiting."

Thrusting into the girl with all the force he could muster, Hammond found himself riding high, in a state of total dominance.

At one point, the girl — what was her name, Gemma? Renna? Ah yes, Renee — had pleaded with him to stop. He knew she didn't mean it; he knew she was loving every second of his enormous member penetrating her virgin territory.

He heard muffled noises outside the room. He took no notice — he was on his way to the ultimate orgasm.

Building . . . building . . .

And YES! "Aargh!" Hammond's body shook with the exquisite release, while Renee trembled beneath him.

And at that exact moment, the door to the room opened, and a groggy Basra, not quite sure what he was seeing, staggered in, raised his gun, and shot the heaving naked figure on top of the girl.

Blood flowed.

And for Senator Hammond Patterson, death and orgasm happened at the exact same moment.

CHAPTER EIGHTY-EIGHT

Pacing up and down, Sergei kept consulting his watch, muttering to himself about what he would do to Kasianenko when he had him safely shackled in the basement.

After a while, Ina emerged from the bedroom wearing little more than a short baby-doll nightie and furry high-heeled mules. "When you comin' to bed?" she whined.

"When I feel like it," he snapped back at her.

He had no intention of sleeping until Kasianenko was his prisoner, chained and trussed up like a chicken ready to be put in the oven and roasted.

"I don't feel safe sleepin' alone," Ina complained, curling a loose strand of hair around her finger. "This place is scary at night. Come to bed."

Sergei shot her a look. "Stop bitchin' like a little *pizda*," he muttered. "I'll come to bed when I'm ready."

And he wouldn't be ready until Maksim

and Viktor returned with Kasianenko.

He checked his watch once more. Cruz and his men had been gone for over four hours. They should be arriving any minute now.

Sergei licked his lips in anticipation. He was more than ready.

CHAPTER EIGHTY-NINE

"You'll never get away with this," Captain Dickson warned, desperately trying to assert an air of authority as he faced the grungy-looking Mexican man with the lethal scar running across his neck and the automatic Uzi balanced precariously on his knee. "Do you even realize who this yacht belongs to?"

"I say it was okay for you to speak?" Cruz snarled, giving Captain Dickson a long hard look.

"Here's what'll happen," Captain Dickson continued, refusing to be intimidated. "You'll be caught and punished. This is treason on the high seas."

"What century you from?" Cruz sneered, wiping the back of his hand across his mouth.

"I'm warning you, if any of my crew are harmed —"

"Shut the fuck up," Cruz said, spitting on the ground. "When Kasianenko gets here, I'm sendin' you down to *be* with your fuckin' crew. How does *that* suit you?"

Captain Dickson was silent. He'd sooner be with his crew than up on the bridge with this gun-wielding maniac.

Lie still.
Don't move.
What happened?
Should I scream?

Blood trickled onto Renee's naked body as a hundred thoughts rambled through her head.

Hammond was heavy on top of her, crushing her with his full weight, his penis still inside her.

Or was it?

She didn't know.

Tears formed in her eyes and slid mournfully down her cheeks.

Something awful had happened.

She could feel Hammond's blood dripping onto her skin.

Paralyzed with fear, she found herself unable to move.

Then someone was rolling the senator off her, landing him on the floor with a thud, and she found herself staring into the eyes of the most frightening-looking man she had ever seen.

She wanted to scream. But when she opened her mouth to do so, nothing came out.

Cashoo caught Mercedes on the top stairs. She was hovering there, waiting to run down to the guest suites when Amiin got Kasianenko out. She had jewelry on her mind. And clothes. And cash, plenty of it.

Cashoo shot her a jaunty grin and gave her a quick hug. His raggedy facial hair scratched her cheek. She didn't mind; she'd always liked Cashoo, ever since they'd first worked together. He was young and handsome with his high cheekbones, piercing eyes, and smooth mocha skin, and although they didn't speak a word of each other's language, they'd always managed to communicate.

Once she'd given him a quick blow job, which had progressed to them almost having sex, until Amiin had interrupted them and screamed at his nephew to never touch her again.

Right now Cashoo was determined not to waste time. He leaned in and kissed her, his slithery tongue darting in and out of her mouth like a fast-moving snake.

Mercedes responded with equal enthusiasm. She was as horny as he was, having been on the yacht with no one to play with except herself, which wasn't easy with Renee sleeping in the bunk above her.

Cashoo touched her breasts before hurriedly pulling her shorts down, then plunging his hand between her legs.

Mercedes responded accordingly, unzipping his jeans and releasing his pulsating hard-on.

Cashoo was a big boy with plenty to offer.

Mercedes was into the distraction. She knew it would be fast and furious like the raid on the yacht. And that's exactly the way she wanted it, because she had things to get on with.

After kicking her shorts away from her ankles, she wrapped her legs tightly around Cashoo's waist, feeling him slide inside her, whereupon they proceeded to take a wild ride, both of them enjoying the ride equally.

The sound of gunfire rang out just as they were reaching the peak.

"Mierda!" Mercedes exclaimed, still managing to shudder to a satisfying climax.

Cashoo did the same.

Then, without exchanging a word, they grabbed their clothes and took off in different directions.

"This isn't exactly turning out to be the trip we'd planned," Bianca said, deciding that if she was going to be stuck in confined quarters with the other women, she might as well try to make light of it. "Beverage, anyone?" she offered, gesturing toward a shelf stocked with cans of Coca-Cola and 7-Up.

"Thanks," Lori said, determined not to

show fear. "I'll take a Coke."

"How's everyone holding up?" Sierra asked.

"Not so good," Ashley muttered, a slight tremor in her voice. "I get claustrophobic. This is freaking me out."

"You must breathe deeply," Xuan advised. "Imagine something you take pleasure in doing. Can you meditate?"

"Never done that," Ashley said, clutching her pink velour Victoria's Secret hoodie around her.

"*I* know," Lori encouraged. "Think about your twins. Taye showed me some photos of them — they're so adorable."

"What if something happens to us?" Ashley wailed, beginning to panic. "Who'll take care of my babies then?"

"We're going to be fine," Sierra assured her. "Flynn knows what he's doing. He'll get us out of this."

"You must know him pretty well, then," Bianca said, giving her a piercing look.

"We both do," Xuan interjected. "If anyone can figure a way out of this, it'll be Flynn."

"Then I guess all we gotta do is stay calm and trust him," Bianca said brightly, the perfect hostess. "Right, girls?"

"We can only try," Xuan said.

Then they were all silent as the sound of gunfire took over.

Thinking *he* was the one in control, Amiin

blasted open the door to the master suite, and was immediately set upon by several men.

Before he could even think of using his gun against them, they wrestled it away from him and pinned him to the floor. One of them sat astride him, while the others tied his ankles and wrists together with strips of sheets.

"How many of you are there?" Flynn demanded. "And don't pretend you can't understand me, 'cause I know you can."

Amiin was mortified. Cruz would blame him, although it wasn't his fault. There was only supposed to be one couple in this room and no weapons. Mercedes had given the information to Cruz. She'd made a serious mistake, and her mistake could ruin everything. *She* was the one to blame.

Amiin glared at his captors with bloodshot eyes. "No Engleesh," he muttered.

"No English, my black arse," Taye threatened. "Spit it out, moron, or you'll end up wearin' your teeth around your neck."

Basra grimaced at the naked girl.

She shrank away from him in horror and opened her mouth as if to scream.

But she didn't. Couldn't.

Basra appreciated her silence, for he was so very tired. He'd done his duty, gotten rid of a straggler who should've been in the mess hall with the others. Now he deserved to rest.

Only for a minute, he thought as he settled himself on the bed next to the naked girl and closed his eyes. *Only for a minute . . .*

Seconds later he was snoring as loudly as a snorting pig.

Cruz took stock. Where the fuck was Mercedes? He had to send her to find out why Amiin was taking so long. He'd heard the shots — surely Amiin had gotten Kasianenko by now and was bringing him up to the bridge?

It was time to alert Kasianenko's people to start getting the ransom money together. He was giving them twenty-four hours only. After that, if his demands were not met, he would put Basra to work. Basra would have no compunction about knocking off the hostages one by one. If Kasianenko could not get his people to pay the ransom, then the fuckers deserved it.

Cruz dragged on his cigarette while giving the captain the evil eye. He didn't like the man; he wanted him out of his sight. After a moment or two, he jumped to his feet and yelled, "Mercedes!"

She came running onto the bridge, looking flustered.

"What the fuck's takin' so much time?" he demanded. "Go find Amiin, an' tell him to shift his lazy ass. I want Kasianenko *here.* An' I want him here *now!*"

CHAPTER NINETY

With Amiin firmly secured, Taye had persuaded the pirate to reveal that there were at least seven more men aboard. Seven armed pirates floating around, men to whom killing meant nothing.

Flynn tried to force Amiin to reveal what locations they were at. Amiin was done. He spat a bloody tooth at him and refused to divulge more.

At least they had two weapons now. Flynn kept Aleksandr's gun, and Cliff took Amiin's. It turned out that Cliff had made several movies where he'd had to use a gun, so he assured Flynn that he knew what he was doing.

Decisions had to be made, and fast. Somehow Flynn seemed to have gotten himself the title of team leader. It didn't bother him; he was used to being in dangerous situations.

"Luca and Taye, you stay here with our prisoner," he said, taking control. "Aleksandr, Cliff, and I will go on a search mission."

"It don't need two of us to stay with this prick," Taye said hotly, not one to miss out on any action. "I'm comin' with."

Flynn made a quick judgment call. Was Luca able to handle it if one of the other pirates came looking for their comrade? He didn't think so, especially if the predators were armed.

The answer? Everyone had to stick together, and they would take the captured pirate along as a human shield.

Yeah, that was it. He should've thought of it before.

"Untie his ankles," Flynn said. "New plan. We're taking him with us."

"Why's that?" Cliff asked.

" 'Cause if anyone's getting shot, it'll be him," Flynn said grimly. "Okay, guys?"

Everyone nodded.

Renee attempted to move. She was naked on the blood-soaked bunk bed, squashed up against the wall. The man who'd shot Hammond was curled up next to her, snoring.

She was almost too frightened to struggle free. Instinctively she knew that to survive, it was what she had to do.

There was something horribly wrong with this scary man lying next to her. The smell emanating from him was noxious. His skin was the color of old cowhide and wrinkled with wear. His hair was matted into unkempt

595

dreadlocks. His eyelids were black over sunken eyes and he had no eyelashes.

Repulsive, disgusting, and a killer.

Move! her inner voice screamed.

Get out!

Run!

Gingerly she made a vain attempt to squeeze past him.

It wasn't possible; he had her wedged against the wall.

Renee realized that the only way out was to slide across him. Yet if she did that, what would happen if he awoke?

She shuddered to think.

Hardly daring to breathe, she carefully began moving over him, blood from her body dripping onto his filthy clothes.

For a moment he ceased snoring.

She immediately stopped moving, lying on top of him as if they were lovers, desperately trying to control her shaking body.

Basra grunted, farted, then resumed his noisy snoring.

Renee continued with her escape plan.

After making her way downstairs, Mercedes quickly dodged out of sight the moment she saw Amiin being frog-marched out of the master suite surrounded by several of the male passengers.

Her heart started beating at an accelerated pace. Why were the male passengers on the loose? How had *this* shit happened? Things were progressing so smoothly, and now Amiin had gotten himself *caught?* This wasn't part of the plan.

She knew she should warn Cruz immediately, but the pull of opening Kasianenko's safe was luring her in. Besides, Cruz was sitting upstairs with an Uzi and other guns. He'd blow everyone's head off at the first sign of trouble.

Before that happened she could open the safe and grab the ring and the piles of cash she knew were there. Then, with that done, she'd go find Basra, Cashoo, and the others to take care of the passengers.

At least — whatever happened — she'd have her future secured.

Screw it! The time had come to put herself first.

Down in the mess hall, the pirates were getting out of control. Daleel and Hani had been away from their homes for too long; their testosterone was raging. Plus the beer was having an effect.

Daleel didn't bother finding a bathroom. He took out his penis and pissed in the direction of his captives, jerking his cock back and forth so the stream of urine spurted in all directions.

"Friggin' wanker!" Den yelled, as a spray of urine splashed him in the face.

Daleel cackled, and reached for the assault rifle slung over his shoulder. He then waved it threateningly in the air.

"Still wanna do nothin'?" Den muttered to Guy, as Hani decided to take a shot at the ceiling.

The bullet missed the ceiling and ricocheted off the wall, hitting Jeromy in the shoulder.

Jeromy squealed like a stuck pig. To his horror, he'd been shot, actually shot. His face paled as he slumped forward clutching his wound, blood seeping through his fingers.

"I'm going to die," he moaned. "I'm going to die among you people. And no one will ever know I was here."

Then he passed out.

Cruz was not a man to be taken by surprise. Mercedes had always said that her papa had eyes in the back of his head. He was a crack shot too, so anyone coming at him had better watch out.

However, the last thing Cruz expected to see was Amiin, hands bound, a gag covering his mouth, being shoved onto the bridge with several men behind him.

"Drop your weapon," Flynn commanded. "Do it now or we shoot our hostage."

Amiin's eyes were popping out of his head. He knew what was coming, and there was nothing he could do to stop it from happening. Cruz would show no mercy.

Cruz was on his feet in a flash. Eyes blazing, he began shooting. Several bullets hit Amiin full on; another bullet grazed the top of Flynn's ear.

Captain Dickson cowered in a corner, too scared to do anything.

Cruz was acting like a madman, wielding the Uzi as if he were Al Pacino in *Scarface*.

"Back off, everyone!" Flynn yelled to the others. "We gotta take cover."

He didn't need to tell them twice.

"What's she doing?" Ashley whispered, peering at the one-way mirrored panel at the top of the safe room entry.

Bianca crowded next to her. "It's that stewardess, whatever her name is."

"Should we bring her in here with us?" Sierra questioned. "She needs to be protected."

"Hold on a minute," Bianca said. "It looks like she's trying to open Aleksandr's safe."

"Are you kidding?" Lori said.

"Holy shit!" Bianca said excitedly. "Seems like she knows the combination."

The women crowded near the panel, watching as Mercedes got the safe open and started piling the contents into a large garbage bag.

"That little bitch!" Bianca exclaimed. "She must be one of them. What can we do?"

"Nothing," Xuan said evenly. "Flynn and Aleksandr told us to stay in here until they get back, so that's what we should do."

Bianca shot Xuan a dirty look. She still didn't like her, and hearing the Asian woman mention Aleksandr's name infuriated her.

"Well," Bianca said sharply, "if you think I'm staying in here while some skank robs my man, then you are very much mistaken."

"You're not going out there, are you?" Ashley asked, alarmed. " 'Cause if you do that, they'll find out where we're hiding. We'll be caught, and who knows what will happen then."

"She's right. We shouldn't leave here," Sierra said, the voice of reason. "This is a dangerous situation. We mustn't make it worse."

Bianca hesitated. She didn't appreciate being told what to do, yet deep down she knew they were right. It was better to be safe than to risk getting captured.

"Okay," she said reluctantly. "I'll stay in here. Although believe me, I'd sooner be out there kicking that bitch's ass."

"Right on," Lori murmured.

With one last frantic push, Renee fell off Basra onto the floor, landing next to Hammond's dead body. A terrified scream rose in her throat, but once more, no sound came out of her mouth. She was traumatized. All she could think about was running away from this room of horrors.

Without thinking about anything except escape, she staggered toward the door, her feet sliding on blood — Hammond's blood — which seemed to be everywhere.

Her hand slipped on the door handle as she wrenched it open and ran naked, streaked with blood, out into the narrow hallway.

She was looking for someone — anyone — who could possibly save her.

She was looking for sanity.

CHAPTER NINETY-ONE

An Uzi was not a weapon to argue with. The man behind the automatic gun had all the power, and would use it to his advantage.

Cruz was just such a man, a man simmering with fury. One moment he was king of it all, in total control. The next, a bunch of civilians — rich motherfuckers who should have known better than to mess with Cruz Mendoza — were coming at him with threats and a trussed-up Amiin, the fool who'd allowed himself to be taken prisoner.

Cruz didn't hesitate; in his line of work he'd discovered that hesitating is what gets a man killed.

He sprayed the motherfuckers with bullets. Many of them slammed into Amiin, and maybe a couple of them hit the others before their human shield slumped to the ground and they ran like scared rabbits.

Still cowering against the wall, Captain Dickson attempted to make himself invisible, while Cruz screamed a vicious litany of swear words in his native Spanish.

The captain understood that he was trapped with a deranged man, and once more he feared for his life.

Cruz had other things on his mind. This takeover was not going as expected. At first, so smooth and easy. Now *this* complication.

Abort was the word that sprang to mind. Abort and get the hell off this boat. The passengers had guns, and that was fucked up.

He could kill 'em all. But if he did that, who would pay the ransom?

Fucking no one, that's who.

Cruz spat on the ground, a sour taste filling his mouth.

It seemed that Amiin was dead. He'd worked with him for seven years. Amiin was the clan leader, his main link to the other pirates. Amiin was the only one who spoke English, allowing him to communicate with the Somalians. Now Amiin was gone, and it was a disaster.

Cruz made a quick decision. No use thinking about what could've been.

He had to get off this boat. And he had to do it fast.

After getting the safe open, Mercedes excitedly tipped the bundles of cash into the garbage bag. She figured there had to be at least a hundred thousand dollars in bills.

She was rich at last, and best of all, everything was hers.

The ring box stood front and center, a true prize to be enjoyed.

She recalled seeing the sparkling emerald and diamond ring for the first time, so magnificent it had taken her breath away.

Time was passing, but she couldn't resist. She opened the box and once more admired the ring. It was a thing of beauty, probably worth a fortune.

A thought crossed her mind. What if she slipped it on her finger? Then it would truly be hers.

Before she could do so, gunfire erupted, and she knew there was more big trouble.

Grabbing the ring and the garbage bag stuffed full of money, she raced from the room and set off to see what was going down.

"Get in front of me," Cruz ordered Captain Dickson, waving the Uzi in the captain's face. "We're fuckin' movin'."

Captain Dickson stared in horror at the dead pirate sprawled on the ground, the man's body riddled with bullets. The captain was well aware that he could meet the same fate, although thankfully Flynn and the others were not barbarians; they wouldn't shoot him down like a dog as Cruz had done to *his* man.

Or would they?

No. They wouldn't, he was sure of it.

He wasn't so sure about this out-of-control Mexican wild man. What if the maniac put a bullet in his back simply for the hell of it?

"Move," Cruz repeated. "An' do it now, motherfucker."

As soon as Cashoo returned to the mess hall where the hostages were gathered, Daleel lashed into him, demanding to know why taking a piss took so long and what he'd really been up to.

Cashoo considered himself just as important as the other Somalians — they might be older than him, but they were certainly not smarter.

He wasn't getting into an argument about how long it took to relieve himself. Daleel was jealous of him. Back home in Eyl, Cashoo always had the prettiest girls, while Daleel was stuck with a fat wife and two whiny kids.

Hani cackled on the sidelines. He'd helped himself to a mug of hot soup, and what with the soup and too much beer, he was feeling mighty tired.

Watching the two pirates argue, Den was burning with frustration. If only he could get the crew to take action instead of sitting around like a bunch of scared girls. If he could do that, then he knew there was a fair chance they could grab control.

Guy was busy ministering to Jeromy, who had recovered consciousness and was whimpering like a wounded puppy, clinging to Guy as if Guy were a lifeboat in a storm.

In spite of their history, Guy did what he had to do and assured Jeromy that everything would be fine.

Den had maneuvered himself next to the first officer and a couple of the deckhands, and he was urgently attempting to get them motivated to take action.

The first officer, a fellow Australian, seemed up for it. The deckhands — scared of catching a bullet — not so much.

And while the pirates were bickering among themselves and Den was in full persuasion mode, an apparition entered the room.

It was Renee. Blood streaking her naked body. Hair matted with blood. A blank look in her glassy eyes. She wandered into the room, arms outstretched, walking as if she were a ghost.

For a moment, nobody moved, until, summoning his best Tom Cruise, Den leaped into action. Throwing himself at a surprised Cashoo, he wrestled the gun out of the boy's hands, hoping that the crew would follow his lead and that he wasn't alone in his bid for freedom.

CHAPTER NINETY-TWO

Six hours had passed, and Sergei was starting to get the message that something was very wrong. He couldn't reach either Maksim or Viktor, and that was infuriating enough. They both had phones. No signal. Nada. Nothing.

Had Cruz double-crossed him?

Had he dared to make the hijacking of the *Bianca* all about him?

Was he planning on keeping Kasianenko, claiming the ransom, then letting the bastard go?

If Cruz did such a thing, there was nothing to stop Sergei from ordering a hit on him, a major hit that would involve torture before death, because nobody fucked with Sergei Zukov and lived to tell the tale.

Son of a bitch!

He summoned Ina from her bed and berated her.

"It's not my fault if he's done somethin' bad," she whined. "I can't tell him what to do."

"How much does your low-life brother care about you?" Sergei demanded, his left cheek twitching out of control.

"I dunno," she said sulkily. "We have different fathers, y'know."

As if that made a difference. They'd both sprung forth from between the legs of the same whore.

"If your brother doesn't return soon," Sergei threatened, "if he's screwed me — then you can pack your shit and get out. Understand me, *pizda*?"

Ina understood.

Chapter Ninety-Three

After taking cover, Flynn tried to figure out their next move. He was dealing with a group of inexperienced men who knew nothing about combat. It wasn't as if they were in the midst of a battle in Afghanistan, but this was still dangerous territory and he didn't care to see anyone else get hurt.

A bullet had grazed the top of his ear — no big deal. He was more concerned about Aleksandr, who'd taken a bullet in the thigh and was bleeding profusely. They'd gotten Aleksandr into Kyril's room, where they'd discovered the security man's dead body.

Aleksandr had shaken his head and groaned his sorrow.

Two dead already. How many more? Flynn didn't want to think about it. As long as Sierra and the women were safe. That was his main concern.

"I'm afraid you're out of action," he informed Aleksandr. "Luca and Cliff, you stay here with him. If anyone comes visiting, don't hesitate — shoot 'em."

Cliff nodded. Shit! He was somewhat fearful. This wasn't playacting anymore, and the gun he was holding on to was making his hands slick with sweat. Not to mention Kyril's dead body, a signal that the pirates really meant business.

"I'd like to have a gun," Taye said, bouncing on the balls of his feet, full of nervous energy.

"And I'd like to have a cold beer," Flynn retaliated. "But we gotta make do with what we got. So you and I are gonna go see what's goin' on. You up for an adventure?"

Taye wasn't afraid. Being raised in a tough London suburb had taught him plenty about street smarts; he had a few moves of his own.

"I'll lead the way," Flynn said. "If I get my head blown off, take my gun an' mow 'em all to hell an' back. Right?"

"You got it," Taye said, hoping Flynn's words were his idea of a joke.

Blood was trickling down from the top of Flynn's ear, landing on his neck. As long as it stayed out of his eyes, he didn't care. He was on a hunt, ready to shoot anyone who got in his way.

A triumphant Den surveyed the scene. Finally, they had them! All three pirates and no injuries, other than to Jeromy, who'd gotten shot earlier.

One of the deckhands had fetched sturdy ropes after they had overpowered the three pirates, and they'd tied them up.

Now not only did they have three prisoners, they also had their guns, making Den feel more secure about everyone's future.

Guy had taken charge of an incoherent Renee, wrapping her in Jeromy's robe, feeding her sips of water, assuring her she was safe now.

Renee was unable to speak. Tears coursed down her cheeks while she clutched her arms around her body and rocked back and forth.

Guy led her over to Jeromy and sat her down next to him. "Look after her," Guy said tersely. "Who knows what the poor girl's been through."

Jeromy was about to object, then thought better of it. Guy had shown him kindness. Therefore, he had to reciprocate in spite of his injury, which was probably draining the life out of him, although Guy had fixed him up with a makeshift tourniquet that could quite possibly be saving his miserable life.

Jeromy was not a religious man; he'd been to church twice in all his forty-two years, and that was only to appease one of his ex-lovers.

Slumped on the floor in the mess hall of a luxury yacht, he suddenly found himself praying to a God he'd never conversed with before. A God he'd never believed in, only right now that God was all he had.

He reached over and touched Renee's arm. "There, there, dear," he said soothingly. "Everything will be all right."

Clutching her loot, Mercedes made it up to the bridge.

No Cruz.

A dead Amiin.

She was horrified. Amiin was Cruz's right arm. Who could have done this to him? Where was Cruz?

She skipped away from the bridge, and as she passed Kyril's room she was grabbed by a concerned Luca Perez, who held her arm and said to her in Spanish, "There are pirates aboard, girl. Get in here now. You'll be safe with us."

"I know," she said, thinking fast. "They haven't seen me. I'm . . . uh . . . looking for weapons."

"Are there guns? Where?"

"There's a place I know," she said vaguely.

"You have to stay," Luca said, reverting to English. "These people are bloodthirsty savages, they shot their own man."

"Amiin?" She said his name before she could stop herself.

Cliff stepped forward. "What did you say?"

"Amen," she muttered, crossing herself.

"You're a girl — if they catch you it won't be good," Luca warned.

"Thanks for your concern, Mr. Perez. Thing

is, I know this boat pretty well, so there's no way they'll catch me."

"What's in the bag?" Aleksandr asked, leaning forward from Kyril's chair.

"Oh God! I think I hear Renee," Mercedes cried out. "I'll be back with guns. Don't worry about me. I know what I'm doing."

She ran before they could stop her.

The question was, how *had* they gotten free? Were they telling the truth? *Had* Cruz shot Amiin himself?

If so, why would he do that?

She had so many questions, and no one to answer them.

The biggest question of all was, where was Cruz?

Was he abandoning ship?

Would he do that and leave her behind?

Knowing her papa, it was quite possible.

She thought quickly. There had obviously been a confrontation. The passengers had most likely used Amiin as a shield, and Cruz had blown him away to save himself. Then he'd probably decided to make a quick getaway as things were turning sour, and right now he'd be heading for one of the speedboats to whisk him away.

Mercedes's gut feeling warned her that she'd better hurry if she wanted to catch up with him. The captain knew she was one of them, so she could hardly stay on board and bluff it out.

Screw it! She was cool. She had what she wanted. The cash. The ring.

Best to run while she still could.

"I feel like I'm in *CSI* or *Law and Order,*" Taye quipped, trying to make light of a dire situation as he followed close behind Flynn, who moved stealthily with his gun drawn. "Wish *I* had a friggin' gun," Taye continued. "It'd make me feel a lot more secure."

"Here's what you do," Flynn advised. "If I start shooting, you rush 'em, tackle them at the knees, throw them off balance. Then grab whatever guns they got."

"Yeah, sure, that's if they don't shoot my balls off first," Taye said, imagining the worst.

"They won't," Flynn said with a grim smile. "We got this."

"*You* got it," Taye said, running his hand over his shaved head. "I certainly ain't."

They were doing a sweep of the top deck; it all seemed to be clear.

Taye stuck right behind Flynn, his new hero. The bloke appeared to be fearless, and Taye got off on the air of confidence Flynn exuded.

Taye wondered how Ashley was coping. If he knew his wife at all, by this time she'd be a hysterical wreck. Ashley didn't do well under pressure, although she'd managed a pretty fine job of climbing up the side of the yacht when she'd had to. He was proud of her for that.

Flynn led the way down the staircase to the middle deck. Once more, it was all clear.

"The pirates have speedboats each side of the yacht," Flynn said quickly. "One pirate guarding each boat. If we can surprise 'em, then it's two less to deal with."

"Surprise 'em? You mean kill 'em?" Taye said, trying to stay cool.

"No," Flynn answered caustically. "How about we invite them aboard for a cup of your favorite English tea?"

"Okay, okay, I get it," Taye said, duly chastised. "Where do you think the crew is?"

"My guess is they've got them all together on the lower deck. The guy upstairs was the leader. The one he shot might've been second in command. Then there's the two with the boats. That leaves four more. Two of them at least are watching the crew. The other two — that's who we gotta keep a lookout for."

Taye couldn't hold back his curiosity. "You ever shot anyone?" he asked, as once more they moved stealthily toward the stairs.

"Why don't we shut up and concentrate," Flynn muttered, feeling the sting at the top of his ear, while blood continued to drip down his neck.

"Right," Taye said quickly. "I'm way into concentrating."

"Good," Flynn said. "So let's do this thing."

CHAPTER NINETY-FOUR

Once Cruz decided something, that was it, no going back. Every fiber in his body warned him to make a fast getaway and haul his ass off the *Bianca*.

Amiin was dead. The other pirates meant nothing to him; they were merely the workforce. Amiin was the only one who'd mattered.

Dammit. His right-hand man had been dumb enough to get himself taken prisoner, giving Cruz no choice but to shoot, since he'd managed to get himself right in the line of fire.

Cruz headed for the speedboat on the left side of the boat, pushing and shoving Captain Dickson in front of him, using him as a shield, so that if any bullets came flying, they'd hit the captain and not him.

For one brief moment he thought about Mercedes and wondered where the hell she was. Then he remembered that Mercedes was a smart girl. She could look after herself; she didn't need him to babysit her. He'd taught her to be a survivor, exactly like him.

Captain Dickson was breathing heavily. Abject fear overcame him; he felt that at any moment he might succumb to a heart attack.

Cruz dug him in the back with the Uzi and yelled at him to move faster.

The captain struggled to do as he was told, but he still failed to move fast enough for Cruz's liking.

Cruz gave him a vicious kick, causing him to slip and fall down the stairs, whereupon Cruz muttered a litany of curses, came after him, and hauled him to his feet. "You do that again an' you're dead meat," Cruz growled.

As time passed, Ashley began to lose it, and no amount of consoling words could calm her down.

"I have to get out of here," she whimpered, thinking of her twins and how they couldn't possibly manage without her. "I can't stay in here. I feel sick. I'm about to faint."

"No, you're not," Xuan said sternly. "What you *are* going to do is sit down, shut up, and put your head between your legs."

"I can't do that," Ashley wailed. "Surely you understand? We've all got to get out of here. They'll find us anyway, so what are we waiting for?"

"We're waiting for Aleksandr and the others to come back," Bianca said, fast losing patience. "And you're not making the wait easy. So like Xuan said — shut up."

"Listen, I know we're all scared," Sierra said, sure that Flynn wouldn't let them down. "However, staying in control is the most important thing of all. Fighting among ourselves is not helping."

"She's right," Lori said. "We can't lose it."

"Oh, be quiet," Ashley snapped. "What do *you* know? You're here on a pass."

"Excuse me?" Lori said, bristling.

"Now, now, ladies," Bianca interjected. "This is no time to get into a bitch fest."

Ashley slumped down on the bench that ran along one side of the small room. "Oh my God!" she moaned. "I have a premonition. We're all going to die in here. We're getting raped, then murdered. I know it."

"Be quiet, you stupid woman," Xuan said with steely determination. "You're talking nonsense. And you'd better stop your nonsense before I force you to."

"We gotta go investigate, find out what's goin' on," Den insisted to Guy, once the three pirates were firmly secured.

Guy, a lot braver now that he was no longer being held at gunpoint, demurred. "Let's not forget who's in charge here," he said, asserting himself. "I'm the one with seniority. I'll decide what we do next."

"Where was all that seniority when I was

beggin' you to get the crew to do somethin'?" Den demanded.

Guy did not appreciate the younger man's tone. "We should stay put," he said. "It's safer for us to all be in one place."

"You're such a friggin' pussy," Den said in disgust. "Doncha understand what's goin' on here? You're not in charge of me or anyone else. This is a shit situation, an' I'm not sittin' around waitin' for it to get worse."

Ignoring Guy, he started talking to a few of the crew who finally seemed to have realized that they did indeed have balls, and even better, they now had guns.

Den proposed that several of them set off to find out exactly what was going on. The first officer and two of the crew agreed.

Den took the front position.

Jabrill, an emaciated man with slit eyes and a mean mouth, guarded the speedboat on the left-hand side of the boat. A former fisherman, he was not as bloodthirsty as his comrades. He preferred sitting on the sidelines, chewing on his khat while contemplating his Ethiopian girlfriend and the money he had coming to him.

Jabrill was anxious to get home. He hoped that the ransom would be paid fast, and that they could be on their way soon.

When Cruz appeared, Jabrill was pleased. It seemed things had happened quicker than expected, although he hadn't heard a helicopter overhead, and usually the ransom was paid in cash and dropped off by helicopter.

Cruz was not alone. He had an unknown white man with him, a man he shoved into the speedboat ahead of him at gunpoint.

Jabrill stared at his boss and wondered where Amiin was. Cruz never made a move without Amiin by his side. Amiin was Cruz's conduit to the pirates, the only one who could translate his orders.

"Let's go!" Cruz shouted, jumping into the boat.

Jabrill continued staring, his expression blank.

"Go!" Cruz yelled. "Fuckin' take off, you moron!"

Jabrill did not understand a word he was saying.

Fully charged with the leadership gene, Den experienced no fear as he and several members of the crew began checking out the yacht. On the upper level, they came upon Aleksandr, Cliff, and Luca, and quickly exchanged information.

Once they saw Kyril's lifeless body, they all realized the seriousness and extreme danger of the situation.

Den was on fire. They had guns. They had balls. He decided that if he got through this, he was going into the security business.

Maybe start his own firm. Yeah, no more bar-man crap; he was hot to strike out on his own.

He suggested to Cliff and Luca that they get Aleksandr down to the mess hall, pointing out that it was safer if everyone stayed together.

Luca and Cliff seemed to think it was a smart idea, and Aleksandr agreed.

"We should go find Flynn and Taye — tell them what's going on," Cliff announced, commandeering an AK rifle. "I'll do it."

"And I'll stick with you," Den said, thinking of his mum's face if she knew he was on a dangerous mission with an actual movie star.

Oh yes, his mum would have a fit! So would his married sister, who had a big crush on Cliff Baxter. She'd always considered her little brother a total loser, so screw you, big sis!

Den had never felt more alive.

The movie star and the barman set off to find Flynn and Taye, while Luca and several crew members assisted in getting Aleksandr downstairs.

Aleksandr was not happy about being a victim. He was a strong, powerful man, and not being able to walk because of his injury infuriated him.

In his mind he was going over how this could possibly have happened and who was responsible. He had enemies. Every successful businessman had enemies. And then there were his soon-to-be ex-wife's brothers. He wouldn't put it past them; they were a bunch of jealous, greedy pricks who thought he owed them a living.

He promised himself that however long it took, he would find the person who had masterminded this outrage, and they would be duly punished. Not only by the law, but by his own hand.

Aleksandr never made a promise he couldn't keep.

"He's dead!" Renee cried out, her eyes wide with fear. "A man . . . a bad bad man shot him."

"What did you say?" Jeromy asked, leaning closer to the girl. It was the first time she'd spoken, and he couldn't quite understand her; she wasn't making much sense.

"Dead," she repeated, shivering uncontrollably, her face deathly pale.

"Who is dead?" Jeromy asked, fear creeping up on him, for surely this couldn't be true?

"The senator," Renee gasped, breaking into heavy sobs. "He was on top of me . . . the man shot him . . . I could've been shot too."

Jeromy didn't like what he was hearing. He summoned Guy, who came over carrying a blanket that he wrapped around Renee.

"She's saying something about the senator being shot," Jeromy informed him. "It can't be true . . . can it?"

"God no!" Guy said. "I'm sure it isn't. She's traumatized, doesn't know what she's saying."

"There's an evil man in my cabin," Renee whispered, barely able to speak. "He's asleep on the bed. He has a gun. If he wakes up, he'll come kill us all."

Guy looked around.

Where was Den?

Moving as fast as she could, Mercedes made it to the speedboat just as Cruz was screaming at Jabrill to take off.

She shimmied down the rope ladder and jumped into the boat, clutching her garbage bag of cash, the ring stuffed into her bra for safekeeping.

"Were you leavin' without me?" she said accusingly.

"Who d'you *think* I was waitin' for?" Cruz lied. "You, of course."

"Why's *he* here?" Mercedes demanded, indicating the captain.

" 'Cause he might be useful," Cruz said gruffly. "An' when he's not so useful, I'm gonna toss him overboard. Now tell this motherfucker to start the boat an' get us the fuck outta here."

Mercedes knew a few words of Somali, enough to tell Jabrill to go.

Jabrill wasn't having it. Sensing all was not

right, he demanded to know where the others were. Cashoo, Hani, and especially Amiin.

Cruz screamed his frustration as Flynn and Taye appeared on deck.

Spotting Mercedes and Captain Dickson in the boat, Flynn figured they were both being kidnapped and instantly knew he had to do something.

"Get out of the boat with your hands up," he yelled at Cruz. "It's over. The coast guard's on the way. You may as well surrender now."

"Go fuck yourself," Cruz screamed, raising his Uzi and letting forth a barrage of bullets.

Jabrill jumped to attention. Violence was not his thing unless absolutely necessary. To hell with the other pirates; they'd be okay on the other boat.

He revved the engine, and within seconds the powerful speedboat took off.

CHAPTER NINETY-FIVE

"Get out!" Sergei screamed, wrenching the covers off the bed.

Ina opened one eye. "What?" she mumbled.

"You heard me. Out. Now! Out of my life, you conniving cunt," Sergei shouted. "You're probably in cahoots with your thieving brother. The two of you laughing at me behind my back. I should've known better than to trust either of you."

"I've done nothing," Ina whined. "Why're you taking my brother's bad deeds out on me?"

"Bad deeds, huh?" Sergei yelled, grabbing her hair and yanking her from the bed. "So you knew all along what the *pizda* had planned. You knew it!"

"No," Ina objected. "I knew nothing. What's happened? Why are you so mad?"

"As if you don't know," Sergei snarled. "I want you out of my house. *Now.*"

"It's the middle of the night, Sergei," Ina said. "If you really mean it, I'll leave tomorrow and go back to Acapulco until you calm down."

"You'll go back nowhere," Sergei assured her. "It's over. And consider yourself lucky that I'm letting you walk away."

"But Sergei —"

"Five minutes, Ina," he threatened. "And if you're not gone by then, I promise you I'll break every bone in your body."

CHAPTER NINETY-SIX

If Flynn knew anything at all, it was that he couldn't let the bastard get away with kidnapping the young stewardess and Captain Dickson. God knew what he'd do to them — the pirate had gunned down his own man, which meant he was capable of anything.

"You okay?" he said, briskly turning to Taye.

"Not a scratch," Taye retorted.

"Then we gotta go after them," Flynn said with an air of urgency. "We need to get control of their boat, take it over."

"How're we —"

Before Taye could even think of finishing his sentence, Flynn was on the move, crossing over to the far side of the yacht, motioning Taye to be quiet.

Galad, the pirate in charge of the second speedboat, was not as laid-back as Jabrill. Over the last hour, he'd heard sporadic gunshots and was on alert.

Flynn, not about to waste time, surprised the pirate with a crack shot to the man's right arm, causing Galad to drop his gun and yelp with pain.

Moving swiftly, Flynn swooped down to the boat, rendering Galad unconscious with a fast and accurate blow to the head, then quickly tipping him into the back of the boat.

Climbing down the ladder after him, Taye was shocked. It seemed Flynn had moves nobody suspected. Bloody hell! Could it be that he was a Navy SEAL in another life? Taye wouldn't be surprised.

"You coming?" Flynn shouted.

"Yeah," Taye said, still somewhat shell-shocked. "Wouldn't miss it."

Flynn tossed him the pirate's gun, and started the engine as Taye leaped in.

The chase was on.

Cashoo's mind was running riot. Hog-tied, he was angry and frustrated. How had he allowed this to happen? Hani and Daleel too. What were they all thinking?

For one second he'd lost focus, staring at a naked girl as if he'd never seen breasts before. Then a civilian had jumped him, several of the crew had rushed the others, and now the situation was reversed. Hani, Daleel, and he were prisoners.

Cruz wouldn't be happy, nor would Amiin. Any moment Cashoo expected them to come in, guns blazing, all set to free them.

He was confident this would happen, and

soon. Cruz wasn't one to put up with any delays.

Crouching down next to Renee, Guy was pretty certain that she'd been raped by a pirate, perhaps more than one. Poor girl, she was certainly in a sorry state.

"Tell me what happened to you, dear," he said sympathetically, as one of the Polish maids brought her over a mug of hot tea and squatted down beside her.

"She's been carrying on about a man with a gun," Jeromy said, clutching his shoulder, making sure everyone realized he was badly injured. "Apparently this man shot Senator Patterson."

Beginning to feel more lucid, Renee felt her head clearing and knew that she'd better get her story across before the repugnant man who'd murdered Hammond came looking for *her.*

"The senator and me — we were in my cabin," she said, taking small sips of tea with shaking hands, the hot liquid spilling over the rim of the mug.

Guy frowned. "What was Senator Patterson doing in your cabin?" he asked.

Renee lowered her head, too ashamed to tell the truth.

"I . . . I don't remember," she stammered. "He . . . he might've been running from the monster with the gun."

"Oh, you must mean the monster who raped you, and shot the senator?" Jeromy said with a sarcastic edge, beginning to think that her story sounded somewhat far-fetched, and wishing that Guy would pay more attention to *him*. After all, he was the one who'd been shot and almost killed. *He* should be the center of attention.

"That's right," Renee mumbled.

"You should know that the yacht's been taken over by pirates," Guy told her matter-of-factly. "The man who attacked you must be one of them. It's important that you tell us where you last saw him."

"I told you," Renee said, shivering uncontrollably. "He's sleeping in my cabin. And the senator is dead — he's lying on the floor."

Then, before they could get any more out of her, she burst into hysterical sobs.

Flynn drove the fast speedboat as if he'd been doing it all his life.

And he probably has, Taye thought. *Here is a dude who can apparently do anything he sets his mind to.*

They were not that far behind the other boat, and gaining fast.

"Tie up the asshole," Flynn ordered, using one hand to toss Taye a section of sturdy rope.

Taye presumed by "asshole" he meant the still-unconscious pirate.

He did as Flynn requested, using his best

slipknot technique, although he bet that Flynn had a better method.

At least Flynn hadn't killed the man. That was a relief.

"How we gonna stop 'em?" Taye yelled over the sound of the engine.

"We'll worry about that when we get closer," Flynn responded.

"Do you have a plan?"

"People who make plans end up getting fucked," Flynn shouted. "You gotta play it by instinct."

Taye could hardly believe that this was the same laid-back guy he'd spent days on the yacht with. Who knew that Flynn Hudson was a friggin' superhero?

Dawn was breaking, and they could clearly make out the boat in front of them. The sea was calm, although the boat ahead of them was causing a swell, so their boat was bouncing over the waves, spray hitting them in the face.

Flynn began covering the gap fast.

Taye was mindful of the fact that the wild man in the boat ahead of them was carrying an Uzi.

Would the pirate use it?

Bloody right he would.

Jeez! If Taye got himself shot, Ashley would never forgive him.

"It's too quiet," Lori ventured, beginning to

feel trapped in the confined space. "How long before we can get out of here?"

"Not until Aleksandr tells us we can," Bianca said, just as apprehensive as the others. She was worried about what was going on outside their safe room. She was also furious that the stewardess had robbed Aleksandr's safe. If she was not mistaken, she could've sworn she'd seen the girl open a ring box, then take the ring nestled inside, and she couldn't help wondering if it was an engagement ring.

Could it be that Aleksandr had been planning to propose?

The thought was an exciting one.

Ashley had stopped complaining. She was slumped on the bench muttering to herself.

Xuan was chanting some kind of mantra, sitting cross-legged on the floor.

Sierra was thinking that this situation was almost like a signal from God. She was not a religious person — more spiritual — however, was this a sign telling her that if they all survived, she should leave Hammond?

She would. No more excuses.

"Shitheads," Cruz snarled, as he realized the chase boat was catching up with them. "Faster!" he screamed at Jabrill. "Make this thing go faster!"

Mercedes translated to Jabrill, who wasn't happy.

Captain Dickson was hunched in the back of the boat, praying to God that he would get out of this alive and be re united with his wife of twenty years.

What did they want with him? He was useless to them.

As if reading his mind, Cruz came up with the same thought. The captain was useless to them, so why keep him around?

Flynn had his eyes fixed on the boat ahead. He figured that if he was able to pass it, maybe he could cut them off, force their engine to stall, and rescue the hostages.

He wasn't taking into account the man with the Uzi, or the driver of the boat, who was no doubt also armed. All he could think about was persuading the pirates to relinquish their two hostages: the girl and the captain. Then, as far as he was concerned, the pirates could go on their merry way.

It wasn't going to be easy — nothing ever was.

Then he thought, what if he offered an exchange? *His* trussed-up pirate for *their* two prisoners?

Seemed like a fair enough deal if he could get the fucker with the Uzi to listen.

He was thinking all of this as he powered the boat forward, intent on catching up. Then, to his utter surprise, someone on the boat in front of him hurled what appeared to be a body overboard.

Hurriedly, he swerved the boat, immediately cutting the throttle. The boat shuddered to a halt.

"Holy friggin' balls!" Taye yelled as he was thrown violently off balance. "What the *fuck*!"

Chapter Ninety-Seven

"I want you to bring me one of the prisoners," Aleksandr ordered Guy. He was now settled in the mess hall, his leg elevated.

"There's three of them, sir, and they don't speak English," Guy advised. "We gather from the looks of them that they might be Somalians."

"Then don't bother," Aleksandr said, shaking his head. "Are they well secured?" he added. "No chance of escape?"

"Absolutely no chance, Mr. Kasianenko." Guy cleared his throat. "The problem is that we don't know how many others there might be."

"The coast guard is on its way," Aleksandr said, surveying the room. "Everyone has to stay in one place until they get here. Is that understood?"

"Yes, sir," Guy said, then after hesitating a moment he added, "May I ask — where are the ladies?"

"Safe," Aleksandr replied. "However, I

regret to tell you that my bodyguard, Kyril, is no longer with us."

"I'm sorry to hear that," Guy said, wanting more details, but afraid to ask.

"So am I," Aleksandr said gravely. "He was a very loyal and fine employee."

"To fill you in, sir, we have one stewardess still missing," Guy said. "And Renee, the other stewardess" — he lowered his voice — "I fear she's been raped. She's also saying something about Senator Patterson having been shot, but this has not been confirmed."

"Jesus Christ!" Aleksandr thundered. "This is abominable."

"I know, sir. It's a terrible situation."

"Those bastards will pay for this," Aleksandr said, his face dark with fury. "You have my word."

Cliff found himself to be quite invigorated. Not that he embraced violence; however, the fact that he and the young Australian with him were prepared to defend the yacht and search out invaders — well, it was damn energizing. After all, this wasn't a movie set. He wasn't surrounded by gofers willing to accommodate his every need. This was the *real* thing, not the *reel* thing.

For once, Cliff was in charge of his own destiny. No longer the Sexiest Man Alive, a title he would like to see buried once and for all. He was living free, doing what *he* thought was the right thing, without a bevy of advisers telling him not to do anything because the press might misconstrue his actions.

Bullshit to that.

"Middle deck's all clear," Den announced. "We should go down one."

"I'm right behind you," Cliff said, holding his gun in front of him, and feeling more of a man than he had in a long time.

"I'm so sorry this had to happen to you," Luca said, commiserating with Jeromy, who was quick to tell him that he'd almost died.

"My shoulder is extremely painful," Jeromy muttered, wincing to make sure Luca realized the full extent of his suffering.

"You're being very brave," Luca said.

"It was a ghastly experience," Jeromy sniffed. "Not to mention quite humiliating." After a meaningful pause, he added, "Can you imagine being dragged down here and thrown in with the *crew*? How degrading is *that*?"

"At least we're all safe now," Luca said, attempting to be the supportive significant other.

"Are we?" Jeromy said curtly. "That girl over there says there is a man with a gun asleep in her cabin. She claims he shot Hammond."

Luca glanced over at Renee. "Well, that doesn't make sense," he said. "She's most

637

likely hallucinating after all she's been through."

"Where *is* Hammond?" Jeromy questioned. "Has anyone seen him?"

It occurred to Luca that nobody *had* seen Hammond.

"This story of a man asleep in her cabin," Luca ventured. "Did someone go check it out?"

Jeromy started to shrug, then flinched with pain instead. "Nobody wants to," he said shortly.

"Maybe *I* should," Luca suggested.

"No!" Jeromy admonished. "Leave it to one of the men."

"The 'men,' Jeromy?" Luca said, giving him an incredulous look. "What does that make me?"

"You know what I mean," Jeromy said, hurriedly backing off. "It's not your place. You're too —"

"Too what?" Luca interrupted, finally realizing what Jeromy really thought of him.

"Forget it," Jeromy said, switching to a long, deep moan. "My shoulder is *so* damn painful. What if I'm left with a disfiguring scar? Do you think I can sue Aleksandr?"

Luca shook his head in disgust. He knew now more than ever that if they survived this ordeal, then it was definitely time for him to move on.

■ ■ ■ ■

Thank God it was light out, for if it had been dark there would've been no way of finding a body in the sea.

Is that what they were looking for? Flynn wondered. A dead body? Had the pirate *shot* whoever it was he'd tossed overboard?

"Can you see anything?" he yelled at Taye.

Taye's eyes scoured the sea until finally he spotted arms waving above the swell. "I'm going in!" he shouted. "There's someone out there."

"You a good swimmer?" Flynn asked, grabbing a life preserver and tossing it overboard.

"Better than most," Taye boasted, stripping off his pants and T-shirt, then making a clean dive over the side of the boat.

The current was surprisingly strong, but it didn't stop Taye. He swam powerfully toward the flailing arms and grabbed the victim in a rescue hold.

"Thank God!" Captain Dickson gasped. Taye managed to get them both back to the boat, where Flynn helped haul them aboard.

The other speedboat was now way off in the distance. Flynn decided they had to go after it anyway to save the girl.

"What girl?" Captain Dickson managed, spluttering and coughing up seawater.

"The stewardess," Flynn said. "We can't let

them take her."

"Don't bother," Captain Dickson said, filled with relief that his prayers had been answered. "She's one of them."

Horse tranquilizers affect humans in various ways, depending on how much they have ingested.

Basra had taken enough to knock out any normal person for many hours. However, there was nothing normal about Basra.

The main drug in horse tranquilizers — ketamine — was a powerful mind-changer. After wolfing down several of the brownies Mercedes had laced with the stuff, Basra awoke with a lethal headache and a strong urge to puke.

His mind was a blank slate. He didn't know where he was or what he was supposed to be doing.

He sat up, swung his feet to the ground, and encountered the blood-soaked body of a naked man.

After coughing up a wad of phlegm, he spat it on the man.

Next he picked up his AK assault rifle, slung it over his shoulder, and set off to discover where he was.

Basra was in a killing daze.

CHAPTER NINETY-EIGHT

With Captain Dickson safely aboard, and having learned that the stewardess, Mercedes, was connected to the pirates, Flynn turned the speedboat around and headed back to the *Bianca*.

Galad was still trussed up and immobile in the back of the boat, although he'd recovered consciousness and was glaring at his captors with deep loathing. They all ignored him while Captain Dickson filled them in on everything he knew — which wasn't much. Just that the Mexican man was obviously running the operation and didn't give a damn about leaving his men behind, let alone shooting them.

Flynn tried to discover more about the girl. The captain had no further information on her, other than that Guy, his entertainment director, had hired her against his wishes.

Flynn flashed back on the day he'd caught Mercedes coming out of his room. He should've been suspicious then, but why would he be? She'd had a perfectly feasible excuse about checking out the minibar, and his mind had been on Sierra.

So, Mercedes had been the pirates' inside connection. Then who exactly was the Mexican man running the show?

As an investigative journalist and a guest on the yacht, Flynn had to find out. For his own peace of mind, he needed to know.

The big question was, who had targeted Aleksandr Kasianenko, and why.

Meanwhile, there were things to tidy up on the yacht. How many pirates were still on the loose? Maybe three or even four?

With their leader having taken flight, perhaps they'd surrendered.

Flynn sincerely hoped so; he'd had enough action for one day. Besides, he was anxious to see how Sierra was doing.

"We gotta be careful," he warned Taye and the captain as their speedboat approached the *Bianca.* "If anyone comes at you, like I told you before — shoot for the kneecaps."

The captain groaned.

Taye was totally into it.

Random thoughts crossed Cliff's mind as he and Den swept each deck, guns drawn.

How many times had he enacted a similar scene in a movie? Although in a movie, every step was choreographed, every move worked out by a professional stuntman. There was plenty of fake blood when needed. Guns that shot blanks. Actors who made it all look too real.

Cliff had the stance down. Over the years, he'd played three detectives, two cops, a renegade gunrunner, a man out to revenge his wife's murder, and a maverick cowboy.

When Cliff was six, his mother had shot his father right between the eyes. It was a secret from his past that he'd managed to hide from the world.

Oh yes, Cliff Baxter and guns were way too familiar. Yet he refused to keep one in his home lest a visitor discover it and shoot someone by accident.

So far he and Den had encountered no lurking pirates.

"Think they've run their sorry arses outta here," Den said as they finished a sweep of the lower deck. "Must've found out we caught their mates, so they pissed off."

"You think?" Cliff said, lowering his gun.

"Bunch of cowardly wankers," Den scoffed. "We're done."

"But we didn't find Flynn or Taye," Cliff pointed out.

"They're probably in the mess hall with Aleksandr," Den said, quite full of himself. "Uh . . . I mean Mr. Kasianenko."

"Right," Cliff said.

"We should go join up," Den said, wondering if anyone had a camera so he could get a

643

souvenir photo of himself with Cliff Baxter. What a coup that would be.

"Sounds like a plan to me," Cliff said.

Den started off in the other direction, and as he did so, Basra appeared.

The pirate made a grotesque sight, gaunt and haggard, with his matted dreadlocks and filthy clothes drenched in blood. His skin was cadaverous, his eyes manic; he looked like a feral animal caught in a steel trap.

Den had his back to him — he was already heading for the mess hall.

But Cliff was facing him.

Man-to-man.

There they were, the grisly murderous pirate and the handsome movie star.

They both raised their guns.

A shot rang out and one of them fell to the ground.

Den spun around. It was too late for him to do anything.

Too damn late.

Chapter Ninety-Nine

The 378-foot high-endurance coast guard cutter *Sunrise* pulled up next to the *Bianca*. Several maritime-law-enforcement officers immediately boarded the vessel, guns at the ready.

Flynn greeted them. "You're too late," he informed them with a cynical shake of his head. "Guess we did your job for you."

Captain Dickson was on deck. He led the officers straight to the captured pirates — Cashoo, Hani, Daleel, and Galad — who were put in handcuffs and taken away.

Medical personnel also boarded and began getting the wounded onto stretchers before transferring them to the cutter's helicopter.

Aleksandr insisted his guests be taken care of first. Jeromy got the star treatment, with Renee next in line, then Den, and finally Aleksandr — but not before he'd made sure that Bianca and the other women were safe.

A medic attempted to attend to Flynn, but he waved her away. "I'm fine," he said curtly.

Aleksandr personally gave Sierra the news about Hammond. Her reaction was not what he'd expected. She'd remained dry-eyed and surprisingly calm.

Then came the morbid part. The photographing and removal of the dead bodies from the yacht. First Senator Patterson, then the bodyguard Kyril, and finally the two dead pirates.

Cliff Baxter was hailed as a hero, for he was the one who'd shot and killed the man who'd brutally raped Renee, then murdered Senator Patterson.

In her mind, Renee had convinced herself that this was exactly how it had all gone down. She was a victim, and she told her story with much conviction. It was all about how she'd been in her cabin when the pirate had entered and attacked and raped her. Then Senator Patterson had burst in to try to save her, only to get himself shot.

Nobody questioned why the senator was naked. Aleksandr had spoken on the phone to certain people in power, and the investigation was cursory.

Case closed.

Nobody cared about a dead Somalian pirate.

Den, the barman, was somewhat bummed. Just his luck that the friggin' movie star had been the one to shoot the wanker. It should've been *him.* He was the person who deserved hero status.

The guests were all anxious to get off the *Bianca* as soon as possible. The crew also couldn't wait.

Captain Dickson headed back full speed ahead to Cabo, where chaos waited.

The world press were in ecstasy. What a story! One of the greatest ever. A gaggle of stars. Power. Money. Fame. Sex. Murder. Luxury.

Headlines roared across the world. The Internet blew up.

Senator Patterson's sex scandal was forgotten. Along with Cliff Baxter, the senator was now a hero. A dead hero, but a hero all the same.

Aleksandr made arrangements for an army of bodyguards to meet the *Bianca* when it docked. A fleet of private jets awaited to take his esteemed guests wherever they wished to go.

Aleksandr's personal doctor had flown in to tend to him. Fortunately, the injury to his thigh was not as serious as he'd feared, and he jetted off to Moscow with Bianca by his side.

Ashley and Taye flew back to England, where the British press descended on them in full force. So many photographers; so many flashbulbs blinding them as they stepped out of the airport.

Their two mums were waiting to greet

them, accompanied by the twins, Aimee and Wolf, in matching girl/boy outfits.

Ashley let out a yelp of pure joy as she bent down to cuddle both her children. "Mummy's home," she crooned. "And I promise you that Mummy will never leave you again."

"You got that right," said a grinning Taye.

To Jeromy's chagrin, Luca left him languishing in a hospital in Cabo while he flew back to Miami. "If I stay, the press'll drive us crazy," Luca explained. "It's better that you recover quietly without all the fuss of me being around."

Jeromy was not a happy camper.

Cliff, feted as a hero, avoided the press altogether. He and Lori returned to L.A. and holed up in his mansion while the furor died down. "I'm no hero," he kept on protesting to his inner circle.

But everyone — including Lori — knew that he was.

Xuan refused the offer of a private jet and took a commercial flight to Syria, where she had an assignment to write an in-depth piece for *The Huffington Post*.

Which left Sierra and Flynn.

And where exactly *did* it leave them?

Not in a perfect place, for although outwardly calm, Sierra was horrified at what had taken place. She might have hated her husband, but she'd certainly never wished anything like this on him.

Flynn made an attempt to comfort her.

She rejected him. Turned away from anything he had to say.

They parted ways without resolving anything.

Sierra traveled to New York.

Flynn took off to Paris.

Both understood that for now — sadly — it was not to be.

Epilogue:
Three Months Later

Scandals come and go. There is always something outrageous going on in the headlines, whether it be political, sexual, or financial. Sometimes all three combined.

The *Bianca* debacle was up there with the best of them, much as the main players involved tried to leave it in their wake.

Aleksandr Kasianenko would always be known as the Russian oligarch whose yacht was taken over by pirates.

Bianca — the famous supermodel whose name was synonymous with the scandal — would always be known as the girl after whom the infamous yacht was named.

The press never tired of writing about the pirating of the *Bianca*. Especially as the main pirate and the mystery girl who was apparently working on the inside were never captured. Their speedboat vanished, and since a second storm came in later that same day, the most popular theory was that they had been caught in the storm mid-ocean, and that possibly their boat had gone down and they'd both drowned.

Mercedes couldn't help smiling when she read the stories on the Internet. Talk about a clean getaway!

After Cruz had tossed the captain overboard — a move she considered genius — he'd disposed of Jabrill the same way, although the ill-fated Jabrill had no one to rescue him.

As soon as that business was taken care of, Cruz had landed the boat on one of the less tourist-filled islands and sold it to a local fisherman with the stipulation that he hide the speedboat until the name was changed and the boat repainted. Then he'd taken off on his own with hardly so much as a good-bye. "I'll be in touch, *cariño,*" he'd said to his one and only daughter.

Really? Where and when?

Mercedes hadn't minded. Why would she? She had the money and the ring. Cruz had been too concerned with plotting his getaway to even bother asking her what was in the garbage bag.

After making it to Madrid, where she knew people with connections, she'd gotten in touch with a man who was able to get her a new identity and passport, then she'd flown to Argentina, because it was far enough away, and she'd read about how beautiful it was in a magazine.

Now she was happily ensconced in Buenos Aires, living with a young polo player she'd met while sitting at the bar in one of the big hotels. The boy was twenty-two and his parents were major rich! Naturally, they didn't approve of her.

Did she care? No. *He* loved her. And so he should. She knew sex tricks he'd never even thought of.

Yes. Mercedes was perfectly content. On her new passport, her name was Porsche. She was a girl with a hot boyfriend, some money, and — tucked away in a safe-deposit box — the emerald and diamond ring. Her lucky prize. Her retirement fund.

Mercedes was ready for the next chapter.

Captain Dickson decided that the time had come for him to retire. He did not like the notoriety that now surrounded him; nor did his wife. Much as he'd enjoyed his many years at sea, the events that had taken place on the *Bianca* were too much for him to stomach.

He settled comfortably in his house in the Cotswolds, and never took to the sea again.

Cashoo, Daleel, Hani, and Galad were arrested and thrown into jail, where they were repeatedly questioned through an interpreter.

None of them spoke a word. They upheld

the code of silence.

In his heart, Cashoo was convinced that Cruz would come and rescue them.

Three months later he was still hoping.

Cast out in the middle of the night from the remote villa, with only the clothes on her back, Ina was burning to get her revenge on Sergei. He'd crossed the wrong girl. She wasn't her brother's keeper. It wasn't her fault that Cruz had screwed him.

Freezing cold and soaked by the storm, she'd made it to a narrow road and huddled under a tree until early in the morning, when a gardener's truck had stopped and picked her up.

She'd lost everything. Her home. Her clothes. Her life.

But Ina was not Cruz's half sister for nothing. The vengeful streak Cruz possessed ran in the family.

If she was to end up with nothing, then so was Sergei.

He was a drug lord. She knew plenty of his secrets, and she was prepared to reveal them.

With the one credit card she had concealed on her person, she purchased a ticket to Mexico City and went straight to the police.

There she went into hiding at the expense of the government, waiting to testify at Sergei's trial.

Unfortunately, this never happened, because even though she was in protective custody, an assassin managed to get past her two bodyguards, and shot her to death while she slept.

At least she never knew what hit her.

Guy returned to his hometown of Sydney and his faithful partner. He'd decided to take a month or two off before going back to work.

Guy was frankly confused. How had Renee been able to change her story and get away with it? She'd quite clearly told him *and* Jeromy Milton-Gold that Senator Patterson was on top of her when the pirate had entered her room. Then she'd switched, and said it was the *pirate* on top of her, raping her, when Senator Patterson had burst in to save her.

That's when the senator had gotten shot. In the back, no less.

Neither story made sense. And what certainly made no sense at all was Senator Patterson being naked.

Guy realized it was not for him to ask questions. He'd got a right dressing-down from Captain Dickson for having hired Mercedes in the first place. The inside girl. The insolent little twat. Who'd have thought?

Reflecting on all the drama, Guy realized that Mercedes had been a squirrely piece of work, always skiving off, never around when he needed her.

He'd done nothing about getting his revenge on Jeromy Milton-Gold. Wasn't it revenge enough that the pervert had gotten himself shot?

Karma was a right old bitch.

Den seized every opportunity he could. Returning to his native Australia, he appeared on countless TV shows, giving interviews and becoming quite a mini celebrity in the process.

Den reveled in the spotlight. So did his family. Unfortunately, it didn't last. So what next?

He took a chance and sent a letter and résumé to Aleksandr Kasianenko, reminding him of his part in the *Bianca* fiasco and requesting a job in security.

To his amazement, several weeks later he received a response with a job offer. He was currently packing up and preparing to move to Moscow.

Like Guy and Den, Renee returned to Australia, but unlike Den, she refused to do any interviews. She was still shell-shocked after all that had happened.

Before leaving the yacht, Aleksandr Kasianenko had taken her aside and handed her a check for one hundred thousand dollars. "It's best you keep your story to yourself," he'd cautioned her. "The press have a way of making things up, and you wouldn't want that, would you, dear?"

No. She wouldn't want that.

Silence was golden. Especially when it came to protecting a U.S. senator's reputation.

Cruz considered going back to his guarded compound in Eyl.

Then he reconsidered.

Sergei would know exactly where to find him. And how about the friends and relatives of the missing pirates?

Seven pirates had left. None had returned.

There would be mothers, fathers, wives, and other relatives hot to tear him into a thousand little pieces.

Cruz ran to Brazil, planning to lay low for a while. His life was in danger, so like his daughter, he forged himself a new identity and began scheming about what he would do next.

Whatever it was, he would make money. Cruz always landed right side up.

Like a snake waiting to pounce, Sergei sat back and bided his time. He could be patient when he had to. He'd waited long enough to track down his brother's killer. Now he would wait for the pond scum, Cruz, to surface, and only then would justice be done.

Just as he'd dealt with Ina, so Cruz would be next.

And sometime in the future, Aleksandr Kasianenko.

It wasn't over . . . not at all.

DATELINE: LONDON
Jeromy Milton-Gold eventually returned to London after spending a week in a hospital in Cabo. A week alone. A week during which Luca seemed to think a phone call or two would suffice.

Jeromy could not believe that Luca would dare to treat him in such a cavalier fashion after all he'd been through. Damn the trumped-up pop singer with delusions of superstardom. Luca was nothing but a lucky boy plucked from the chorus line to feed Suga's enormous ego.

Jeromy was angry. And bitter. And filled with envy that only the stars who'd been on the cruise were getting the headlines.

He was the one who'd been shot. Yet it seemed that nobody cared.

Except Lanita and Sydney Luttman, who'd come to the hospital to visit him. They'd wanted to hear *everything.*

Jeromy had obliged as best he could, digging up what ever salacious details came to mind.

The Luttmans arranged to meet up with him in London, where they'd decided to buy a town house.

"You'll be in charge of everything," Lanita had informed him, waving a diamond-encrusted wrist in the air. "Sydney pisses money. Spend what ever it takes."

Jeromy knew he was capable of doing exactly that.

Two weeks later, Sydney Luttman was felled on the tennis court by a massive heart attack. He died instantly.

A few weeks later, Lanita arrived in London, and Jeromy soon found himself spending more and more time with her. She found him to be the perfect walker, and sometime sex partner when she was up for an orgy or two. Lanita was going ahead with her town house, and was ready to spend an outrageous amount of money.

One day she'd sat herself down in Jeromy's showroom, given him a long penetrating look, then made him a proposition he couldn't refuse.

Well, he could've. But who would?

Lanita was super rich.

Lanita was a sex freak.

Lanita was generous.

Lanita wanted a husband by her side, and Jeromy was the man she had in mind.

"You do understand that I'm gay?" Jeromy said.

"Honey, gay, schmay — we can work it out."

And so — with a meticulously put-together financial agreement — Jeromy became Mr.

Lanita Luttman. A role he was most suited to.

"We should have another baby," Luca announced.

The *Bianca* debacle was long past. Jeromy was history. And recently he'd persuaded Suga to sell her Miami mansion and move into his. Luca Junior was thrilled to see his parents back together.

"I'm too old, *cariño,*" Suga responded, stroking his cheek. "Besides, you and I — our lovemaking days are over."

"That's not what I was thinking," Luca said. "I was thinking adoption."

"You were?" Suga said, noting how much more relaxed and happy Luca was since he'd finally gotten rid of Jeromy. Recently he'd been seeing a young man nearer his own age. Their partnership was a much better fit. And the best news of all was that Suga and he actually got along.

"Imagine what a blast it would be to have a baby in the house again," Luca said, full of enthusiasm. "A little girl. A little Suga."

"If it's what you want, then let's do it."

"Should we ask Luca Junior what *he* thinks?"

"Perhaps, or we could surprise him."

"Then tomorrow I'll speak with my lawyer and set everything in motion."

They smiled at each other, comfortable in a relationship that suited both of them.

Luca was happy to welcome Suga back into his life.

Suga brought the sunshine, and after Jeromy, that's exactly what he needed.

DATELINE: LONDON

"Wolf's a right talented bugger," Taye said, walking in from the garden with his six-year-old son balanced precariously on his shoulders. "One of these days this little bastard's gonna outdo me on the football field."

Father and son were both in their football gear, both grinning at Ashley with identical grins, which gave her a shiver of pleasure.

Kids. Wasn't that what life was all about? Raising them. Teaching them. Nurturing them.

Ever since their trip on the *Bianca,* Ashley had changed her outlook on life. She'd resigned from Jeromy's design firm, then shortly after that, she'd fired her children's nanny.

"All I want is to spend time with our family," she'd informed a delighted Taye.

"If it's what makes you happy, toots, then I'm all in," he'd said.

Ashley was happy. Happier than she'd ever been.

Aimee came running in wearing a pink tutu, Grandma Elise — or, as she preferred to be known, Moo-Moo — behind her.

"I'm not staying," Elise said, winking saucily at Taye. "I'm having dinner with a very fine gentleman I met on an Internet dating site."

"Get you," Taye said, raising a skeptical eyebrow. "You'd better be sure to keep your knickers on!"

"Oh, you are *awful,*" Elise responded with a coy giggle. "And in front of the children too!"

"Bye, Mum," Ashley said, kissing her on the cheek. "See you tomorrow."

"Yeah, that's if she's still alive," Taye joked. "You never know about geezers you pick up on the Internet. Could be a serial killer."

"Is Moo-Moo gonna die?" Wolf piped up.

"Of course not," Ashley said, frowning at Taye.

"Don't want Moo-Moo to die," Aimee whined.

"See what you've done," Ashley said, shaking her head.

"They know I'm only teasing," Taye said, laughing as he released Wolf from his shoulders.

"Go watch TV, kids," Ashley said crisply. "Special treat."

Aimee and Wolf raced off.

"What about me?" Taye asked, moving close and nuzzling his wife's neck. "Don't *I* get a special treat?"

Ashley smiled. A warm smile. A loving smile.

"As a matter of fact, you do," she said softly.

"What?" Taye asked, seizing the moment. "Do we get to go upstairs for a nooner? C'mon, toots. That'd be a *very* special treat."

"Even better," Ashley whispered, still smiling. "Guess what?"

"What?"

She took a long deep breath. "We're pregnant," she announced.

Taye's whoop of joy could be heard for miles.

DATELINE: LOS ANGELES

The Golden Globes. A true Hollywood night.

Cliff Baxter. A true Hollywood movie star. A true-life hero too. Handsome, charming, a fine actor, and extremely popular.

Cliff Baxter. An unmarried man.

The press loved him. The hostesses of all the popular entertainment shows creamed their thongs over him. He was *their* Cliff. His long list of girlfriends were merely along for the ride. And hopefully not too long a ride.

Until Lori.

Lori with the spectacular mane of red hair, race horse legs, and athletic body.

Lori, the girl who'd lasted longer than most. But wasn't her time about up?

Enid seemed to think so. As did Cliff's PR people, his agent, his manager, and the wives

662

of all his many friends.

It was time for Lori to go.

Or was it?

Cliff always enchanted at award ceremonies with his self-deprecating grin, his air of sophistication mixed with just that tiny sliver of bad boy.

Oh yes, Cliff Baxter was a man of the people with a sexy edge.

Tonight he was at the pinnacle of his fame, with Lori — clad in a sleek silver dress and sky-high Louboutins — by his side. It was his first public appearance since the tragedy on the *Bianca.* Expectations of what he would say and do were high. Whom would he speak to? What lucky journalist would get an exclusive?

Nobody knew.

Everyone cared.

He chose Jennifer Ward out of all of them. She was smart and feisty, and he'd always enjoyed being interviewed by her.

"So, Mr. Baxter," Jennifer said, head tilted, mildly flirting. "Want to tell us all about your summer vacation?"

Cliff smiled. Movie-star smile. Movie-star teeth.

Standing next to him, Lori felt a warm glow.

"No, Jennifer," Cliff said amiably. "I think enough has been written about that already, don't you?"

"Our viewers are dying to know more," Jennifer said, gently pushing the mic toward him. "You're quite the big hero — and yet so modest."

"I know you're anxious, so I do have something for your viewers," Cliff said, pulling Lori into the shot. "In fact, we both do."

Jennifer's eyebrows shot up. "Both?" she questioned, because usually Cliff did not include his girlfriends in his interviews.

"Yes," Cliff said. "Listen, I know I've said I would never do this, but" — he leaned into Lori and gave her a full-on kiss — "this beautiful redhead and I, we're getting married. So ladies, you can cross me off your lists. I am now well and truly taken."

DATELINE: PARIS
Bianca would always be a superstar. She did not need a billionaire Russian oligarch to give her credibility.

After the pirating of the *Bianca,* things between her and Aleksandr had not gone well. First of all, Bianca had no patience with illness. Not that Aleksandr was ill, but he *was* on crutches, and that did not sit well with her. She had a certain image to maintain, and that image did not include a bloody cripple by her side.

Harsh, yes.

But Bianca was nothing if not honest.

Back in Moscow, they fought constantly, long screaming matches about how much time he was spending with his children, and why his divorce was taking so long. They did not make love. Aleksandr was never in the mood.

The thing that really irked Bianca was that he'd never mentioned a ring, and she could've sworn she'd seen that girl on the yacht steal a ring from his safe.

One cold Moscow morning, she'd woken up and thought, *What am I doing here?*

Later that day she was on a plane to Paris. And that's where she'd been ever since.

Aleksandr never chased after her.

She didn't care.

Within weeks, she'd hooked up with an Internet nerd who'd made billions selling a series of complicated apps and Web sites.

A month later they were married in Tahiti.

Internet Nerd did not ask her to sign a prenup.

DATELINE: MOSCOW

Two weeks after Bianca left Moscow, Aleksandr called Xuan. They made polite conversation on the phone, until Aleksandr suggested that he send his plane for her to visit him in Moscow. "We have much to discuss," he said, sounding very formal.

Xuan was cagey. "We do?" she asked carefully.

"Yes, we do. The orphanage, among other matters. Where are you?"

"Vietnam."

"Of course. I'll send the plane."

"No. I'll make my own way there."

"As you please."

Xuan took her time. She arrived in Moscow ten days later and checked into a hotel. Only then did she text Aleksandr to inform him she was there.

"I'll send a car for you," he said.

"I'll walk," she said.

"Don't be so stubborn. The car will pick you up in twenty minutes."

Xuan stopped arguing and thought about all the good she could do in the world if she were with a man like Aleksandr.

But he was with Bianca.

Or maybe not. She'd heard rumors that Bianca had left him and was currently with someone else.

She prepared herself. If Aleksandr wanted more than a business relationship, could it possibly work?

He was a very attractive and intriguing man.

There was no harm in finding out.

DATELINE: NEW YORK

Sierra returned to New York and the loving arms of her family. She was no longer perceived as the good political wife. She was now the Widow. A tragic but beautiful figure, feted by all as the brave woman who'd always stood by her husband's side.

The sex scandal was long gone, wiped off the front pages in an instant.

Senator Hammond Patterson had lost his life defending the virtue of a young, innocent girl. He was an American hero.

Eddie March rallied to Sierra's side. He tracked down Radical, sent her Goth boyfriend back to Wyoming, and made sure she was front and center at her father's funeral, standing right next to Hammond's grieving widow.

Sierra went through it all in a daze. It was all too much for her to take in. Had she wished Hammond dead? Was his untimely demise her fault?

She didn't know. She was confused. She was suffused with sadness. And when Flynn tried to contact her, she told him that she needed time to get her head straight and that she would call him when she felt up to it.

In the meantime, she threw herself into her work. The rape crisis center. The battered women's homes. And anything else to keep her fully occupied.

Eddie was always there for her. Kind and understanding. The man that Hammond never was.

Sierra had no idea what her future held. She was living it day by day.

DATELINE: PARIS
Flynn returned to Afghanistan, a place where,

strangely enough, he felt safe. He was working on a story about a rebel leader and staying in a hotel with other journalists from across the world. The camaraderie was just what he needed. None of them gave a shit about the *Bianca* and what had taken place, although one female journalist did ask him what Bianca looked like in real life.

He stayed there for several weeks before returning to his Paris apartment.

Sierra had blanked him — it was painfully obvious she did not want a connection.

He was fine with it. It was her choice, and if that's what she wanted, so be it.

Enough obsessing over one woman. Finally, he was beginning to realize that the past could never be recaptured. Too much had happened. Too many roadblocks.

Aleksandr contacted him and offered him what ever amount of money it would take to track down the mastermind behind the taking of the *Bianca*.

"I don't want your money, Alek," Flynn told him. "But I will look into it, see what I can find out."

He still had his connections in Eyl, and since the pirates were probably from there, a little investigation might go a long way.

"Xuan is here," Aleksandr informed him. "Is that all right with you?"

"Perfectly all right," Flynn assured him. "I

always thought you two would be a great match."

Since getting back to Paris, he'd gotten together with Mai a couple of times.

Their relationship, such as it was, stayed on a casual level. She was exactly what he needed.

For now.

Somewhere out there was the right girl for him, and one of these days he would definitely find her.

ABOUT THE AUTHOR

Jackie Collins is the author of twenty-eight *New York Times* bestselling novels. More than 500 million of her books have sold in more than forty countries. From *Hollywood Wives* to *Lady Boss*, from *Chances* to *Poor Little Bitch Girl*, Jackie Collins has chronicled the lives of the rich and famous with "devastating accuracy" (*Los Angeles Times*). She lives in Beverly Hills.

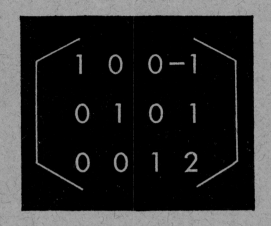

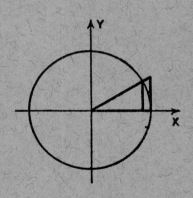

AND ONLY IF AT LEAST ONE OF ITS FACTORS IS ZERO

FUNDAMENTALS OF COLLEGE MATHEMATICS

JOHN C. BRIXEY

RICHARD V. ANDREE

The University of Oklahoma

FUNDAMENTALS

OF *College*

Mathematics REVISED

EDITION

Holt, Rinehart
and Winston *New York*

This book is affectionately dedicated to

Dorothea B. Brixey and Josephine P. Andree

without whose understanding help
it could never have been written

Preface to the Instructor

This text presents a careful integration of college algebra, trigonometry, basic statistical reasoning, analytic geometry, and the elementary calculus needed to continue with current college courses in calculus or calculus with analytic geometry. It was originally intended for a one-year, college freshman course. That it has proved highly successful in courses for which it was intended is gratifying. Your authors were, however, surprised and delighted to discover that some of the better high schools are also using the text enthusiastically with their seniors, and that several colleges are using the same material in graduate courses for the retraining of teachers. This book was *designed to be read by the student*, and we find that students *do* read it.

Many students lack skill in algebraic manipulation. Hence, the delta process is introduced early (Chapter 5) and fundamental manipulative experience is gained while applying the delta process instead of by routine drill. Concepts from algebra are reviewed as needed rather than beginning with an indiscriminate review. Since problems are the meat of a mathematics text, this book provides a variety of well-motivated problems and applications from diverse fields. The number and variety of problems are large enough to accommodate individual differences among students, classes, and instructors. Topics for outside reports of historical and mathematical nature are indicated for teachers desiring them. The function concept is used throughout the text. Inequalities as well as equations are stressed. The derivative is introduced both as the rate of change of a function and as the slope of a line tangent to a curve.

The current practice in so-called "modern" texts is to sandwich in a chapter on set theory, often including truth tables and Boolean algebra, and then to forget all about set theory from there on. Your authors disagree with this practice. Even in the first (1954) edition, the concepts of set and of inequalities were used throughout the text.

This philosophy has been preserved. The phrase *solution set* is currently popular in place of the more cumbersome "set of all values that satisfy the equation or inequality," and has been used. Various set ideas are introduced and used where needed throughout the text. When the student is ready to study *Sample Spaces* in probability (Chapter 12), he already has the principal set concepts at his disposal.

The entire book has been reworked and many improvements have resulted from the suggestions of over 500 teachers who used the first edition. Many of these teachers wrote that when they examined the first edition they considered it too advanced. When they used it in class, however, they discovered that the students not only read but understood the presentation. Moreover, the students were far better prepared for the more advanced work in calculus courses than ever before. Several colleagues have pointed out that our work with the Σ notation has prepared the student admirably to consider the integral as a limit of a sum. This is true. We have, therefore, developed the integral both as the limit of a sum (Sections 10–12 and 19–7) and also as a generalization of area (Sections 10–12, 19–5, and 19–7), as well as presenting the usual antiderivative approach. The instructor is, of course, free to pick the presentation that best fits his teaching practice. After some experience, we have concluded that it is highly worthwhile for the future development of the student to present all three views during the freshmen year. Similarly, it seems worthwhile to include brief experience with the ϵ, δ definition of limit (Section 5–4) in the first course to assist the student in his later work.

The notation of sequence unifies the chapters on progressions, permutations, combinations, and probability which climax in the mathematical statistics of the binomial distribution. The statistics does not consist of exercises in arithmetic, as beginning statistics often does, but orients the student in the general problems handled by modern statisticians and in the meaning and types of results to be expected.

The analytic portions of trigonometry (graphs, equations, inequalities) are stressed rather than the solution of triangles. The laws of sines and cosines and the expansions of $\cos (A \pm B)$ and $\sin (A \pm B)$ are obtained neatly, using methods of analytic geometry.

Throughout the text, examples, illustrations, and problems have been carefully selected to develop the understanding and the technique necessary for the student's applied work and for his later mathematical development. Many of the trigonometric identities, for example, are those that the student will encounter in further work in engineering, physics, and calculus. Intersections of polar coordinate loci are studied as problems involving trigonometric equations. Work on numerical analysis (Sections 10–9, 10–10, 10–11, 10–12, 19–8, and 19–9) is introduced with care and with an awareness of the importance of computers.

The authors feel that answers should provide additional instruction and be a vital teaching aid, rather than a mere check. With this in view, extensive skeleton solutions and over 400 sketches and graphs are included with the answers to the odd problems. Answers to the even problems and extensive comments on the text are included in a separate *Teacher's Guide* available from the publisher.

The two-semester course at The University of Oklahoma includes the unstarred sections in Chapters 1 to 22, with selected sections from Chapters 23, 24, and 25.

A one-semester course for better students has been taught using Chapters 1, 2, 5, 6, 7, 9, 10, 11, 12, 13, 17, 19, 20, 21, and part of Chapter 22.

A short course emphasizing modern trigonometry is contained in Chapters 1, 2, 8, 14, 15, and 16.

A course emphasizing college algebra, including statistics, is available in Chapters 1, 2, 3, 4, 8, 9, 10, 11, 12, and 13.

Analytic geometry may be emphasized by using Chapters 1, 2, 5, 6, 9, 17, 20, 21, 22, 23, with Chapter 24 giving the essentials of solid analytic geometry.

Several possible terminal courses, providing mathematical background desirable for a liberal (or general) education, may be selected from Chapters 1, 2, 4, 5, 6, 7, 9, 10, 11, 12, 13, and 25.

Chapter 25 is independent of the rest of the text, and provides the student with some interesting glimpses of advanced mathematics. The better students seem to relish an assignment from Chapter 25 during review periods.

The authors wish to acknowledge indebtedness to colleagues and students near and far, without whose encouragement and assistance this book could not have been written. We also thank Professor A. Gelbart, editor of *Scripta Mathematica*, for permission to use pictorial material appearing at the ends of chapters, and Keuffel & Esser Co. for illustrations of the slide rule and special graph papers.

The authors welcome your comments and suggestions concerning this text. We hope it meets your needs.

J. C. B.
R. V. A.

April, 1961
Norman, Oklahoma

Preface to the Student

The choice of text and problem material in this book was influenced by extensive interviews and correspondence with many engineers, physicists, chemists, social scientists, and mathematicians.

The material covered in this book represents more than one fourth of your first year of college study. It contains knowledge needed in more advanced courses. Your best reference book is usually the one with which you are most familiar. If you use the wide margins of this text to record points your instructor makes during his lectures, and your own related observations, you can build this text into a personal reference book that will serve you well in future years.

Throughout the text, sections and figures are numbered consecutively within each chapter. Thus, 12–3 refers to Chapter 12, Section 3. A decimal notation is used for reference equations: 5.1 indicates the first reference equation in Chapter 5.

Numerous problems in this book indicate that mathematics may be applied to other fields. Unfortunately they cannot indicate the most important role of a mathematician — that of discovery and invention. Before the planet Neptune was discovered, astronomers knew that it must exist since it had a disturbing influence on the orbit of Uranus. J. C. Adams and U. J. J. Leverrier determined the position of Neptune using purely mathematical methods. Only then were astronomers able to pinpoint their telescopes in the exact portion of the sky, and Neptune was observed. The planet Pluto was first observed in the year 1930 as a result of a similar purely mathematical discovery by Lowell and Pickering.

James Clerk Maxwell deduced the existence and nature of electromagnetic waves using differential equations. Later experiments carried out by H. Hertz confirmed Maxwell's discovery. Maxwell's equations are the basis of radio and television communication theory. Albert Einstein was a well-known mathematical physicist whose mathematical reasoning established, among other things, a connection between gravitation and the propagation of light in space.

Prior to World War II it was common engineering practice to construct test models when a new airplane or projectile was being designed. In the design of modern rockets and supersonic aircraft it is not feasible to make models and test each possible design and variation. Instead, mathematicians set up mathematical models (equations) that simulate possible significant effects, and computing machines are programmed to solve these equations. Twenty-five different rocket designs may be tested in two minutes using modern computers, once the computer has been programmed. Thus, many thousands of different designs may be completely tested in the mathematical laboratory in less time than is required to construct one model — and at much lower cost. Models are finally constructed and tested only for the few best designs.

A few remarks on **how to study** college mathematics may be appropriate. Is mathematics hard for you? If you read carefully and are willing to work, the battle is half won! In mathematics much difficulty is avoided by learning principles and not by memorizing rules. An understanding of the principles makes the rules easier to remember and apply. We, the authors, with the help of your instructor, will try to state these principles clearly, and provide you with numerous illustrative examples and with interesting problems.

For your part, read the material and study the examples before beginning to solve the problems assigned by your instructor. Please do not make the error of trying to work the assignment first, looking back at the examples only when trouble arises and finally reading the text as a last resort, if at all. That is *not* the way to study *this* course. **Read the text carefully** first. Test each statement. Study all illustrative examples, supplying any missing steps or reasons. Be sure you can solve each example without the text. Then begin to solve the problems assigned by your instructor. You will find an "Answers and Hints" section at the back of the book which should be consulted only after you have completed your solution. Self-tests have been included to help check your understanding of the material.

We sincerely hope you enjoy this book and that it will indeed meet your needs. Chapter 25 is included for *your* pleasure.

J. C. B.
R. V. A.

April, 1961
Norman, Oklahoma

Contents

1 . . . THE SET. BASIC RULES OF ALGEBRA. FIELD POSTULATES. COMBINING FRACTIONS. SPECIAL NOTATION. INEQUALITIES. ABSOLUTE VALUE. FOUR IMPORTANT NUMERICAL SETS. FUNCTIONS AND RELATIONS. SOLUTION OF EQUATIONS. MORE THEORY OF QUADRATIC EQUATIONS. AUXILIARY EQUATIONS. THE DELTA FUNCTION. SELF TEST. SUPPLEMENTARY MATERIAL TO PRESENT A WIDER POINT OF VIEW. THE MODULO 7 SYSTEM. THE MODULO 12 SYSTEM. *1*

2 . . . SOLUTION OF INEQUALITIES. COORDINATE SYSTEMS. THE DISTANCE BETWEEN TWO POINTS. EQUATIONS, INEQUALITIES, AND LOCI. SOLUTION OF INEQUALITIES OF HIGHER DEGREE. SUMMARY. SELF TEST. . . . *42*

3 . . . THE IMPORTANCE OF GRAPHING. INTERCEPTS. APPROXIMATE INTERCEPTS. DISCONTINUITIES. BEHAVIOR OF LOCI FOR LARGE VALUES OF $|x|$. DISCUSSION OF A LOCUS. SELF TEST. ROOTS OF A CONTINUOUS FUNCTION. . . . *65*

4 . . . THE REMAINDER THEOREM. SYNTHETIC DIVISION. RATIONAL ROOTS. UPPER AND LOWER BOUNDS FOR INTERCEPTS. SYMMETRY OF POINTS. SYMMETRY OF LOCI. TESTS FOR SYMMETRY. APPLICATIONS. THE QUADRATIC FUNCTION. SELF TEST. . . . *79*

5 . . . SLOPE OF A LINE. THE EQUATION OF A LINE. THE LINE TANGENT TO A CURVE AT A POINT. LIMIT OF A FUNCTION. CONTINUOUS FUNCTION. SLOPE OF A TANGENT LINE. INCREMENTS. SELF TEST. . . *103*

6 . . . THE DERIVATIVE. THE DELTA PROCESS. LABOR-SAVING GENERALIZATIONS. PRELIMINARY THEOREMS. THE DERIVATIVE OF A POLYNOMIAL. DIFFERENTIATION OF A PRODUCT. DIFFERENTIATION OF A COMPOSITE FUNCTION. IMPLICIT DIFFERENTIATON. MAXIMA AND MINIMA. THE SLOPE OF A TANGENT LINE AT A MAXIMUM OR MINIMUM POINT. TESTS FOR MAXIMUM AND MINIMUM POINTS. SELF TEST. . . *130*

7 . . . APPLICATIONS INVOLVING MAXIMA AND MINIMA. AVER-
AGE RATE OF CHANGE. INSTANTANEOUS VELOCITY. GEN-
ERAL RATE OF CHANGE. EXTREME VALUES. SELF TEST. . . *155*

8 (*Review*) NEGATIVE, FRACTIONAL, AND ZERO EXPONENTS. SCIEN-
TIFIC NOTATION. FLOATING POINT NOTATION. APPROXI-
MATION OF RESULTS. LOGARITHMS. FUNDAMENTAL
ASSUMPTIONS. LOGARITHMS TO THE BASE 8. PROPERTIES
OF LOGARITHMS. LOGARITHMS TO THE BASE 10. INTER-
POLATION. LOGARITHMIC COMPUTATION. . . *173*

9 . . . EXPONENTIAL AND LOGARITHMIC EQUATIONS. THE
NUMBER *e*. LOGARITHMS TO THE BASE *e*. DERIVATIVES
OF LOGARITHMIC AND EXPONENTIAL FUNCTIONS. HY-
PERBOLIC FUNCTIONS. SELF TEST. FALLING BODIES WITH
AIR RESISTANCE. SEMILOGARITHMIC PAPER. NOMOGRAMS.
AN ESPECIALLY USEFUL NOMOGRAM — THE SLIDE RULE. . . *195*

10 . . . SEQUENCES. A SUMMATION NOTATION. ARITHMETIC
SEQUENCES. GEOMETRIC SEQUENCES. INFINITE SE-
QUENCES. INFINITE REPEATING DECIMALS. SELF TEST.
MATHEMATICAL INDUCTION, AN AID TO THE DISCOVERY
OF NEW THEOREMS. FINITE DIFFERENCES. CURVE FIT-
TING. THE GREGORY-NEWTON INTERPOLATION FORMULA.
AREAS. . . *215*

11 . . . FUNDAMENTAL PRINCIPLE OF PERMUTATIONS AND COM-
BINATIONS. PERMUTATIONS. DISTINGUISHABLE PERMU-
TATIONS. THE BINOMIAL EXPANSION. INSTANTANEOUS
COMPOUND INTEREST LAW. COMBINATIONS. SELF TEST. . . *248*

12 . . . SETS. SAMPLE SPACES. PROBABILITY. MUTUALLY
EXCLUSIVE OR DISJOINT EVENTS. CONDITIONAL
PROBABILITY. SUMMARY. SELF TEST. . . *268*

13 . . . INTRODUCTION. ADDITIONAL APPLICATIONS OF SUMMA-
TION NOTATION. BINOMIAL DISTRIBUTIONS. MEAN AND
STANDARD DEVIATION OF THE NUMBER OF OCCURRENCES.
THE PROBABILITY OF THE NUMBER OF OCCURRENCES
LYING WITHIN STATED LIMITS. CONTROL CHART FOR
PERCENTAGE OF DEFECTIVES. CONTROL CHART FOR
DEFECTS. STATISTICAL QUALITY CONTROL. SELF TEST. . . *292*

14 . . . PLANE ANGLES. INTRODUCTION TO TRIGONOMETRIC
FUNCTIONS. STANDARD POSITION. DEFINITIONS OF TRIG-
ONOMETRIC FUNCTIONS. EXACT VALUES OF FUNCTIONS

OF ANGLES RELATED TO $45°$, $30°$, AND $60°$. TABLES. USE
OF TRIGONOMETRIC TABLES. THE LAW OF COSINES. LAW
OF SINES. THE LAW OF TANGENTS. SUMMARY. SELF TEST. . . *322*

15 . . . TRIGONOMETRIC FUNCTIONS OF A NUMBER. GRAPHS
OF $y = \sin t$ AND $y = \cos t$. THE GRAPHS $y = A \sin x$
AND $y = A \cos x$. THE GRAPHS OF $y = A \sin Bx$ AND
$y = A \cos Bx$. COMPOSITION OF ORDINATES. SKETCHING
OF OTHER TRIGONOMETRIC FUNCTIONS. SELF TEST. . . *344*

16 . . . IDENTITIES. TRIGONOMETRIC IDENTITIES. TRIGONO-
METRIC EQUATIONS. MORE IDENTITIES. FUNCTIONS OF
MULTIPLE ANGLES. FUNCTIONS OF HALF ANGLES.
FURTHER IDENTITIES. INVERSES AND INVERSE FUNC-
TIONS. INVERSE TRIGONOMETRIC RELATIONS. PRINCIPAL
VALUES. DERIVATIVES OF $\sin u$ and $\cos u$. SELF TEST. . . *356*

17 . . . POLAR COORDINATES. LINES AND CIRCLES IN POLAR
COORDINATES. THE RELATIONSHIP BETWEEN POLAR
AND RECTANGULAR COORDINATES. SKETCHING LOCI IN
POLAR COORDINATES. REMARKS ON SYMMETRY IN POLAR
LOCI. FURTHER REMARKS ON POLAR COORDINATES. A
SHORTCUT IN SKETCHING POLAR LOCI. SELF TEST. . . *394*

18 . . . COMPLEX NUMBERS. COMPLEX VECTORS IN POLAR FORM.
MULTIPLICATION AND DIVISION IN POLAR FORM. DE
MOIVRE'S THEOREM. ROOTS OF A COMPLEX NUMBER.
COMPLEX EXPONENTS. SELF TEST. SERIES RELATIONS.
HODOGRAPHS. . . *413*

19 . . . THE DERIVATIVE. THE ANTIDERIVATIVE. THE DIFFER-
ENTIAL EQUATION, $\dfrac{dy}{dx} = m$. THE DIFFERENTIAL EQUA-
TION, $\dfrac{d^2s}{dt^2} = a$. THE DEFINITE INTEGRAL AS AN AREA.
SELF TEST. THE DEFINITE INTEGRAL AS A LIMIT OF A
SUM. NEWTON'S METHOD OF APPROXIMATING ROOTS OF
AN EQUATION. APPROXIMATION OF A FUNCTION VALUE. . . *429*

20 . . . INTRODUCTION. ANGLE OF INCLINATION. PERPENDICU-
LAR LINES. ANGLE OF INTERSECTION OF TWO LINES.
NORMAL EQUATION OF A LINE. SOLUTIONS OF LINEAR
SYSTEMS USING DETACHED COEFFICIENTS. DETERMI-
NANTS. THEOREMS ABOUT DETERMINANTS. DETERMINANTS
AND SYSTEMS OF LINEAR EQUATIONS. SELF TEST. . . *455*

21 . . . A GENERAL EQUATION OF THE CIRCLE. SYSTEMS OF CIRCLES. TRANSLATIONS. THE ELLIPSE. PROPERTIES OF AN ELLIPSE. REDUCTION OF THE EQUATION TO STANDARD FORM. THE HYPERBOLA. SPECIAL PROPERTIES OF THE HYPERBOLA. REDUCTION TO STANDARD FORM. ROTATION OF AXES. MORE ABOUT THE PARABOLA. ECCENTRICITY. POLAR COORDINATE EQUATIONS OF CONICS. CONIC SECTIONS. APPLICATIONS OF FOCAL PROPERTIES OF CONICS. . . *482*

22 . . . PARAMETRIC EQUATIONS. PARAMETRIC REPRESENTATION OF THE CYCLOID AND OTHER LOCI. THE PATH OF A PROJECTILE. ADVANTAGES OF PARAMETRIC REPRE-SENTATION. SELF TEST. . . *524*

Cumulative Review Problems—Chapters 1 to 22.

23 . . . SEMILOGARITHMIC COORDINATE PAPER. THE USE OF SEMILOGARITHMIC PAPER WITH LABORATORY DATA. LOGARITHMIC PAPER. OTHER SPECIAL COORDINATE PAPERS. METHOD OF LEAST SQUARES. SELF TEST. . . *543*

24 . . . RECTANGULAR COORDINATES IN SPACE. DISTANCE FOR-MULA. CYLINDERS. GENERAL SURFACES. INTERSECTIONS. DIRECTION COSINES AND DIRECTION NUMBERS. THE ANGLE BETWEEN TWO LINES. THE PLANE. EQUATIONS OF A LINE. CYLINDRICAL COORDINATES. SPHERICAL COORDINATES. SELF TEST. . . *560*

25 . . . MATRIX MULTIPLICATION. ON PRIME NUMBERS. ANGLE TRISECTION. THE MÖBIUS STRIP — A ONE-SIDED SUR-FACE. MAGIC SQUARES. PERFECT NUMBERS. FERMAT'S "LAST THEOREM." THE NUMBER $2^{64} - 1$. THE FOUR-COLOR PROBLEM. QUATERNIONS. A FINITE GEOMETRY. CRYPTOGRAPHY. NUMBER SYSTEMS. COMPUTING MA-CHINES. . . *583*

Selected Reading List *608*

Tables *615*

Answers and Hints *635*

Index *739*

• •

The discovery of the immense power of modern mathematics can be a most rewarding and exciting experience. As a first step in this direction Chapter 1 develops certain familiar ideas in terms of what may prove to be a new technical vocabulary. It also places new emphasis on certain important concepts. The reader has been using the "basic laws of algebra" for several years, but even so may not realize that they are all derived from a simple set of postulates. He already knows how to solve equations such as $\sqrt{13x - x^2} = -6$ mechanically by squaring each member, but a more critical examination is necessary in order to determine why this equation has no solution (both $x = 4$ and $x = 9$ are extraneous values that *do not* satisfy the equation) whereas the equation $\sqrt{10x - x^2} = 4$ has two valid solutions: $x = 2$ and $x = 8$.

In short, both the new vocabulary and an understanding of the basic theory behind certain algebraic manipulations are essential to an appreciation of mathematics.

1–1. The "set." † In mathematics the word **set** is actually an undefined term, just as "line" and "point" are undefined terms in geometry. The word **set** describes any collection of objects. For example, one speaks of the set of rational numbers less than 237, the set of points inside of and on a circle, or the set of distinct letters on this page. Actually the elements of a set need have nothing in common except that they form a collection. All the sets mentioned above might be combined into a single set. The reader of this book will find a number of specific, important sets discussed — for example, the set of all solutions of a given equation or inequality (solution set), the set of continuous functions, the set of problems one can work correctly, or the set of all ways in which a seven can be thrown on a pair of dice. The word **subset** is used to describe a collection of part (or even all, or none) of the elements of a given set. Every set is a subset of itself. Another unusual, but important, concept is that of the **empty set** or **null set** which consists of a set containing no elements at all. It is reasonably easy to describe such sets; for example, the set of college freshmen who are less than 4 years old is probably an empty set. The set of pages in this text that are numbered above 900 is an empty set; and the set of negative numbers that are also perfect squares of integers (whole numbers) is an empty set. The symbol Ø is sometimes used to represent the empty set.

1–2. Basic rules of algebra. The reader is familiar with the basic concepts of high-school algebra — for example, $(a + b) \cdot x = a \cdot x + b \cdot x$. He

† A more elaborate treatment of sets appears in Chapter 12.

has worked regularly with these rules, but may never have seen them collected together. Many students know that geometry has a set of axioms or postulates from which theorems are derived, but do not realize that algebra has a similar structure. Since advanced **mathematics** involves **the study of structure,** it seems desirable to state specifically "the rules of ordinary algebra," or, in modern mathematical language, the **postulates for a field.**

Field postulates (rules of ordinary algebra). A field is defined to be a set of elements (or numbers) having two operations "+" and " · ," and having an equals † relation "=" such that the following postulates are satisfied:

1. *Closure:* For each pair x, y of elements in the set, the sum $x + y$ and the product $x \cdot y$ are in the set.

2. *Commutative:* For each pair x, y of elements in the set, $x + y = y + x$ and $x \cdot y = y \cdot x$.

3. *Associative:* For each triple x, y, z of elements in the set, $x + (y + z) = (x + y) + z$ and $x \cdot (y \cdot z) = (x \cdot y) \cdot z$.

4. *Additive Identity (zero):* There exists an element, 0, in the set such that for every x in the set $0 + x = x + 0 = x$ and $0 \cdot x = x \cdot 0 = 0$.

5. *Multiplicative Identity (one):* There exists an element, 1, in the set such that for every x in the set, $1 \cdot x = x \cdot 1 = x$.

6. *Inverses:* For each element x in the set, there is an element, $(-x)$, in the set such that $(x) + (-x) = 0$. If x is not zero, there is an element $\left(\frac{1}{x}\right)$ in the set such that $x \cdot \left(\frac{1}{x}\right) = 1.‡$ The element $(-x)$ is called the additive inverse§ of x. The element $\left(\frac{1}{x}\right)$ is called the multiplicative inverse‖ of x.

7. *Distributive:* For each triple $a, b, x,$ of elements in the set, $(a + b) \cdot x = a \cdot x + b \cdot x$ and $x \cdot (a + b) = x \cdot a + x \cdot b$.

Some typical examples of fields with which the reader is already familiar include the field of complex numbers, the field of real numbers, and the field of rational numbers.# The set of all integers is *not* a field, however, since 1 is the only nonzero integer having a multiplicative inverse that is an integer. [What does this statement mean?]

† Actually, "an equals relation" must satisfy a set of three postulates as given in Problem 14, Set 1–16, and should be "well defined," which means that $a = b$ must imply that $a + k = b + k$ and that $a \cdot k = b \cdot k$.

‡ The symbols $(-x)$ and $\left(\frac{1}{x}\right)$ represent single elements, *not* the results of a "subtraction" or of a "division."

§ Or negative of.

‖ Or reciprocal of.

A more complete discussion of real, rational, and complex numbers is given in Section 1–7.

The reader may wonder why the postulates fail to mention either subtraction or division. The omission is deliberate and not an oversight. This omission simplifies later theoretical work and, surprisingly, is no restriction. Postulate 6 guarantees the existence of an additive inverse, $(-x)$, which has the property that $x + (-x) = 0$. Subtraction really means "add the additive inverse." In a similar fashion Postulate 6 guarantees that if $x \neq 0$, then there is an element known as the multiplicative inverse $\left(\dfrac{1}{x}\right)$, which has the property that $\left(\dfrac{1}{x}\right) \cdot x = 1$. Division really means "multiplication by the multiplicative inverse." In brief, the expression $(-b)$ is the solution z, of the equation $b + z = 0$; and the expression $\left(\dfrac{1}{b}\right)$ is the solution w of the equation $b \cdot w = 1$. Clearly, $0 \cdot w = 1$ has no solution.

- **Example 1.** In the set of all decimals, the multiplicative inverse of the element 2.5 is the decimal 0.4, since $(2.5)(0.4) = 1$.

- **Example 2.** An integer (whole number) is *even* if it is an integral multiple of 2. Thus, 74, 14936, 0, -4, 2, and -768 are even integers. However, 17, 2π, and $4\sqrt{34}$ are *not* even integers.

The set of all even integers is closed under both addition and multiplication. (This follows since both the sum and the product of two even integers are even integers.) The set of even integers contains the element zero, and for each even integer x the number $(-x)$ is an even integer. Thus Postulates 1, 4, part of 6, and certain others are satisfied. There are, however, two field properties that the set of even integers does not possess. The reader should be able to determine them.

This discussion may appear as obvious to the reader. What may be new, however, is the fact that from this simple set of postulates it is possible to derive the important theorems of ordinary algebra. For example, using only the postulates for a field it is possible to derive the following theorem, which is the basic theorem used in solving equations.

Theorem. In a field, if $A \cdot B = 0$, then $A = 0$, or $B = 0$, or both $A = 0$ and $B = 0$.

PROOF: Given: A, B, elements of a field such that $A \cdot B = 0$.
　　　　　To Prove: Either $A = 0$, or $B = 0$, (or both)

If $A = 0$, the conclusion of the theorem holds.

If $A \neq 0$,† then by Postulate 6 there exists an element $\left(\dfrac{1}{A}\right)$ in the field such that $\left(\dfrac{1}{A}\right) \cdot A = 1$. We use this property in the proof.

† The symbol $\neq$ means the two members are *not* equal.

$$A \cdot B = 0 \qquad \text{Given}$$

$$\left(\frac{1}{A}\right) \cdot [A \cdot B] = \left(\frac{1}{A}\right) \cdot 0 \qquad \text{Equals relation is well defined}$$

$$\left[\left(\frac{1}{A}\right) \cdot A\right] \cdot B = \left(\frac{1}{A}\right) \cdot 0 \qquad \text{Postulate 3 (Associative Postulate of Multiplication)}$$

$$[1] \cdot B = \left(\frac{1}{A}\right) \cdot 0 \qquad \text{Postulate 6 (Multiplicative inverse)}$$

$$B = \left(\frac{1}{A}\right) \cdot 0 \qquad \text{Postulate 5 (Multiplicative identity)}$$

$$B = 0 \qquad \text{Postulate 4 (Multiplicative property of additive inverse)}$$

Hence the theorem is proved.

● **Illustration.** Find the (rational) solutions of $(x + 4)(2x - 3)(x - 2) = 0$. The theorem states that if the product $(x + 4)(2x - 3)(x - 2)$ is to be zero, then a factor must be zero. On the other hand, if a factor is zero, then the product is zero. All solutions are given by
$x + 4 = 0$, $2x - 3 = 0$, $x - 2 = 0$.
Using the distributive law $(ax + ay) = a(x + y)$ with $a = 2$, one obtains $2x - 3 = 2(x - \frac{3}{2}) = 0$. Hence $x - \frac{3}{2} = 0$. (Why?) The set of solutions is $\{- 4, \frac{3}{2}, 2\}$.

The set of postulates given is *not* the most concise set possible. For example, in Postulate 4, the statement $0 \cdot x = x \cdot 0 = 0$ can actually be proved from the remaining postulates. The purpose here is not to give an extremely brief set of postulates, but rather to give a set that conveys the idea of a field to the reader.

Section 1–16 of this text describes a simple system, which does *not* obey the theorem that "a product is zero if and only if at least one of the factors is zero." Such a system cannot be a field. (Why not?)

PROBLEM SET 1-2

1. Let S be the set of distinct letters appearing in this sentence. Which of the following are subsets of S?

(a) $\{a, b, e, t, w\}$
(b) $\{w, g, a, p, f, t\}$
(c) $\{s, t, n, c, d, p, g\}$

2. Give an example of a field. Illustrate each postulate using your example.

3. Determine exactly which field postulates are satisfied by the set of even integers.

4. The *cancellation law* states: "If $c \neq 0$, then $c \cdot a = c \cdot b$ implies $a = b$." There are mathematical systems (see p. 39, for example) in which this law does not hold. Prove that any system in which the cancellation law does not hold is *not a field*.

   [HINT: Field Postulate 6 may be helpful.]

5. The field postulates state that there exists an element 1 in the field which has the property that for each x in the set $1 \cdot x = x \cdot 1 = x$. As far as the postulates state, however, there might also be some other element, say u, in the field which also has the property that for each element t in the field $u \cdot t = t$. Prove that this is not the case by letting $t = 1$ and employing the postulate $x \cdot 1 = x$ for x to prove that any such u must actually be equal to 1.

6. Determine the set of all *integral* solutions of the equation $(2x + 6)(3x - 2)(x - 5) = 0$.

7. Pick out five different rational numbers belonging to the set S, where S is the set of all rational numbers that are greater than 6 and less than, or equal to, 8. Can you show that there is always a rational number in S between any two of the numbers you have selected?

8. Determine the set of all *rational* solutions of the equation $(2x + 6)(3x - 2)(x - 5) = 0$.

9. Pick out five different rational numbers belonging to the set S, where S is the set of all rational numbers that are greater than 5 and less than, or equal to, 8.

10. Consider two elements ϕ and I having the following rules of addition and of multiplication

+	ϕ	I
ϕ	ϕ	I
I	I	I

×	ϕ	I
ϕ	ϕ	ϕ
I	ϕ	I

Which of the postulates for a field are satisfied by the system of elements ϕ and I?

[HINT: Show the system is closed and is commutative under both + and ×. Then check the remaining postulates.]

1–3. Combining fractions. Since the reader has had experience in combining fractions, no detailed theoretical discussion will be undertaken here. Several illustrative examples are given to refresh the memory.

● *Example 1.* Simplify: $X = \frac{1}{6} + \frac{5}{14} - \frac{2}{9} + 3$.

Factoring each denominator, we obtain $X = \dfrac{1}{2 \cdot 3} + \dfrac{5}{2 \cdot 7} - \dfrac{2}{3^2} + \dfrac{3}{1}$.

The lowest common denominator is $2 \cdot 3^2 \cdot 7$. Multiply the numerator and denominator of each fraction by the quantity that will make the denominator the same as the lowest common denominator (lcd) $2 \cdot 3^2 \cdot 7$. (See Problem Set 1–4, No. 3.)

$$X = \frac{1}{2 \cdot 3} \cdot \frac{3 \cdot 7}{3 \cdot 7} + \frac{5}{2 \cdot 7} \cdot \frac{3^2}{3^2} - \frac{2}{3^2} \cdot \frac{2 \cdot 7}{2 \cdot 7} + \frac{3}{1} \cdot \frac{2 \cdot 3^2 \cdot 7}{2 \cdot 3^2 \cdot 7}$$

$$= 21 \left(\frac{1}{2 \cdot 3^2 \cdot 7}\right) + 45 \left(\frac{1}{2 \cdot 3^2 \cdot 7}\right) - 28 \left(\frac{1}{2 \cdot 3^2 \cdot 7}\right) + 378 \left(\frac{1}{2 \cdot 3^2 \cdot 7}\right)$$

$$= (21 + 45 - 28 + 378) \frac{1}{2 \cdot 3^2 \cdot 7}$$

$$= \frac{416}{2 \cdot 3^2 \cdot 7} = \frac{208}{3^2 \cdot 7} \quad \text{or} \quad \frac{208}{63}.$$

Note that the distributive postulate, $ax + bx = (a + b)x$ with $x = \frac{1}{2 \cdot 3^2 \cdot 7}$ is the basis of the above manipulations. Are the commutative postulates also used? What other postulates are used?

Essentially the same method is used in adding algebraic fractions.

● **Example 2.** $Y = \frac{2z}{z^2 - 9} + \frac{z - 4}{z^2 - 5z + 6} + \frac{3z + 4}{z^2 + z - 6}.$

Factoring each denominator, we obtain

$$Y = \frac{2z}{(z + 3)(z - 3)} + \frac{z - 4}{(z - 3)(z - 2)} + \frac{3z + 4}{(z - 2)(z + 3)}.$$

The lowest common denominator is $(z + 3)(z - 3)(z - 2)$. Multiply the numerator and denominator of each fraction by the quantity that will make the denominator of the fraction identical with the lowest common denominator.

$$Y = \frac{2z}{(z + 3)(z - 3)} \cdot \frac{(z - 2)}{(z - 2)} + \frac{z - 4}{(z - 3)(z - 2)} \cdot \frac{(z + 3)}{(z + 3)} + \frac{3z + 4}{(z - 2)(z + 3)} \cdot \frac{(z - 3)}{(z - 3)}$$

$$= \frac{[2z^2 - 4z] + [z^2 - z - 12] + [3z^2 - 5z - 12]}{(z + 3)(z - 3)(z - 2)}$$

$$= \frac{6z^2 - 10z - 24}{(z + 3)(z - 3)(z - 2)}.$$

Both algebraic and arithmetic expressions should be simplified unless some particular form is desired. Hence,

$$Y = \frac{6z^2 - 10z - 24}{(z - 3)(z + 3)(z - 2)} = \frac{2(3z^2 - 5z - 12)}{(z - 3)(z + 3)(z - 2)}$$

$$= \frac{2(3z + 4)\cancel{(z - 3)}^{1}}{\cancel{(z - 3)}_{1}(z + 3)(z - 2)} = \frac{2(3z + 4)}{(z + 3)(z - 2)}.$$

The result is usually left in factored form.

1–4. Special notation. Before giving further examples, some special mathematical notation will be introduced. The notation ax means "the quantity a multiplied by the quantity x." This is usually true for other combinations such as Bx, $(a + 3)y$, xy, etc. By special agreement, however, when an engineer, scientist, or mathematician writes the Greek letter Δ (delta) next to a letter, as, for example, Δx, it does *not* mean Δ times that letter x. The symbol Δx (read "delta x") should be thought of as a symbol representing *one single quantity*, not as a product. For example, in $\dfrac{\Delta y}{\Delta x}$ one may *not* divide out the deltas. The notation may seem peculiar at this point, but the powerful mathematical tools developed later using this notation will show the need for its introduction. At present, it should be remembered that Δx, Δy, Δt, and Δz are *single quantities*, not products.

The symbols $f(x)$, $g(x)$, and $h(t)$, read as "f of x, g of x, and h of t," may look like products, but are not used as such. They are abbreviations for formulas or more general functions. At this point such symbols will represent formulas. More general functions are considered in Section 1–8.

If the symbol $f(x)$ is used to represent the formula $3x^2 + 2x - 7$, then $f(t)$ represents the corresponding formula with x replaced by t, while $f(2)$ represents the corresponding formula with x replaced by 2. That is,

$$f(x) = 3x^2 + 2x - 7$$
$$f(t) = 3t^2 + 2t - 7$$
$$f(2) = 3(2)^2 + 2(2) - 7 = 9$$

and

$$f(4 + y) = 3(4 + y)^2 + 2(4 + y) - 7 = 3(16 + 8y + y^2) + 2(4 + y) - 7$$
$$= 3y^2 + 26y + 49.$$

● *Example 1.* If $f(t) = t^2 - 7t + 2$, then $f(x)$ represents the same formula with t replaced by x. Thus, $f(x) = x^2 - 7x + 2$, while

$$f\left(\frac{1}{y}\right) = \left(\frac{1}{y}\right)^2 - 7\left(\frac{1}{y}\right) + 2 = \frac{1 - 7y + 2y^2}{y^2}.$$

The symbol in parentheses need not be a letter; for example,

$$f(3) = (3)^2 - 7(3) + 2 = -10,$$
$$f(8) = (8)^2 - 7(8) + 2 = 10,$$
$$f(x + 3) = (x + 3)^2 - 7(x + 3) + 2 = x^2 - x - 10,$$
$$f(y + \Delta y) = (y + \Delta y)^2 - 7(y + \Delta y) + 2 = y^2 + 2y\,\Delta y + (\Delta y)^2 - 7y - 7\Delta y + 2.$$

● *Example 2.* Using $f(t) = t^2 - 7t + 2$ as before, find $f(t_1 + \Delta t) - f(t_1)$. By definition,

$$f(t_1 + \Delta t) - f(t_1) = \left[(t_1 + \Delta t)^2 - 7(t_1 + \Delta t) + 2\right] - \left[t_1^2 - 7t_1 + 2\right]$$
$$= 2t_1\,\Delta t + (\Delta t)^2 - 7\Delta t.$$

The expression $f(t_1 + \Delta t) - f(t_1)$ represents the change in the value of $f(t)$ as t changes from the value t_1 to $t_1 + \Delta t$.

● **Example 3.** If $f(t) = \dfrac{t}{t-3}$, determine $f(2)$, $f(2 + \Delta y) - f(2)$, and
$$f(2 + .01) - f(2).$$

Clearly, $f(2) = \dfrac{2}{2-3} = -2$.

$$f(2 + \Delta y) - f(2) = \frac{2 + \Delta y}{2 + \Delta y - 3} - \frac{2}{2-3} = \frac{2 + \Delta y}{\Delta y - 1} + 2$$

$$= \frac{2 + \Delta y + 2\Delta y - 2}{\Delta y - 1} = \frac{3\Delta y}{\Delta y - 1}.$$

The reader should note that both $\dfrac{3\Delta y}{\Delta y - 1}$ and $f(2 + \Delta y)$ are meaningless if $\Delta y = 1$.

In a similar fashion, $f(2 + .01) - f(2) = \cdots † = \dfrac{3(.01)}{.01 - 1} = \dfrac{.03}{-.99} = -\dfrac{1}{33}$
or approximately $-.03$. This may be obtained by setting $\Delta y = .01$ in $f(2 + \Delta y) - f(2)$ which was just computed.

Before going further you should show that if $g(z) = 3z^2 - 2z + 5$, then $g(5) = 70$ and $g(5 + \Delta x) - g(5) = 28\Delta x + 3(\Delta x)^2$.

● **Example 4.** If $f(x) = \dfrac{3}{x}$, find $f(x + \Delta x) - f(x)$.

$$f(x + \Delta x) - f(x) = \frac{3}{x + \Delta x} - \frac{3}{x} = \frac{3}{(x + \Delta x)} \cdot \frac{x}{x} - \frac{3}{x} \cdot \frac{(x + \Delta x)}{(x + \Delta x)}$$

$$= \frac{3x - 3x - 3\Delta x}{x(x + \Delta x)} = \frac{-3\Delta x}{x(x + \Delta x)}.$$

● **Example 5.** If $g(t) = \dfrac{5}{t^2}$, find $\dfrac{g(t + \Delta t) - g(t)}{\Delta t}$.

$$\frac{g(t + \Delta t) - g(t)}{\Delta t} = \frac{\dfrac{5}{(t + \Delta t)^2} - \dfrac{5}{t^2}}{\Delta t} = \frac{5}{(t + \Delta t)^2 \, \Delta t} - \frac{5}{(t)^2 \, \Delta t} = \cdots$$

$$= \frac{5t^2 - 5[t^2 + 2t\,\Delta t + (\Delta t)^2]}{(t + \Delta t)^2 \, t^2 \, \Delta t}$$

$$= \frac{-5(2t + \Delta t)\,\Delta t}{(t + \Delta t)^2 \, t^2 \, \Delta t} = \frac{-5(2t + \Delta t)}{(t + \Delta t)^2 \, t^2} \quad \text{if} \quad \Delta t \neq 0.$$

The division of numerator and denominator by Δt in the last step is valid only if Δt is not zero. If Δt is zero, the entire problem is without meaning since division by zero is not defined (see Problem 2, Set 1–4).

† As is usual in both mathematical and literary writing, the three dots indicate omission. The reader is expected to use pencil and paper and supply the missing steps.

Since $g(t + \Delta t) - g(t)$ represents the change in the function $g(x)$ as x changes from $x = t$ to $x = t + \Delta t$, it follows that $\dfrac{g(t + \Delta t) - g(t)}{\Delta t}$ is the **average rate of change** of the function $g(t)$ over the interval Δt. This concept will be used often in later chapters of this book.

● **Example 6.** $Y = \dfrac{\dfrac{3a - 2}{a - 2} - \dfrac{3}{a + 3}}{\dfrac{1}{a + 3} + \dfrac{1}{a + 1}}.$

We may combine the two fractions which form the numerator,

$$N = \frac{3a - 2}{a - 2} - \frac{3}{a + 3} = \cdots = \frac{a(3a + 4)}{(a - 2)(a + 3)},$$

and then combine the two fractions in the denominator to obtain

$$D = \frac{1}{a + 3} + \frac{1}{a + 1} = \cdots = \frac{2(a + 2)}{(a + 3)(a + 1)}.$$

Then "invert and multiply" † to obtain

$$Y = \frac{N}{D} = N \cdot \left(\frac{1}{D}\right) = \frac{a(3a + 4)}{(a - 2)(a + 3)} \cdot \frac{(a + 3)(a + 1)}{2(a + 2)} = \frac{a(3a + 4)(a + 1)}{2(a - 2)(a + 2)},$$

which is the correct answer. However, a considerable saving of effort may be made using the following technique: The lowest common denominator of the four simple fractions appearing in Y is $(a - 2)(a + 3)(a + 1)$. Multiplying both numerator and denominator of Y by this lowest common denominator quickly reduces Y to a simple fraction.

$$Y = \frac{\left\{\dfrac{3a - 2}{a - 2} - \dfrac{3}{a + 3}\right\} \cdot (a - 2)(a + 3)(a + 1)}{\left\{\dfrac{1}{a + 3} + \dfrac{1}{a + 1}\right\} \cdot (a - 2)(a + 3)(a + 1)}$$

$$= \frac{\{(3a - 2)(a + 3) - 3(a - 2)\}\,(a + 1)}{\{(a + 1) + (a + 3)\}\,(a - 2)}$$

$$= \frac{\{3a^2 - 2a + 9a - 6 - 3a + 6\}\,(a + 1)}{\{a + 1 + a + 3\}\,(a - 2)} = \frac{\{3a^2 + 4a\}\,(a + 1)}{\{2a + 4\}\,(a - 2)}.$$

The reader should verify that this answer may be factored and written in the form of the previous answer. Not only is this method often shorter, but it offers less opportunity for error.

† See Problem 17, Set 1–4

PROBLEM SET 1-4

1. Simplify $\frac{1}{12} + \frac{11}{15} - \frac{3}{16} + 4$.

2. Why is $a/0$ not defined? Consider the equation $a = 0 \cdot x$. Does this yield a definite value for x when $a \neq 0$? When $a = 0$?

3. Show that $A/D + B/D - C/D$ is equal to $(A + B - C)/D$. Note that $A/D = A \cdot \dfrac{1}{D}$; express each term of the left member in this fashion and factor out $1/D$. Which field postulate is used at each step?

4. Simplify $9(376)^3 - 14(376)^3 - \frac{11}{4}(376 \cdot 2)^2 + 5(369 + 7)^2$.

5. Simplify $\dfrac{3x}{(x+4)(x-4)} + \dfrac{x-6}{(x-3)(x-4)} + \dfrac{4x+6}{(x-3)(x+4)}$.

6. Simplify $\dfrac{y-6}{y^2 - 7y + 12} + \dfrac{3y}{y^2 - 16} + \dfrac{2(3+2y)}{y^2 + y - 12}$. Is this result related to Problem 5?

7. Simplify $\dfrac{x+1}{x^2 - 6x + 9} - \dfrac{x+2}{x^2 - 5x + 6}$.

8. If $f(x) = \dfrac{3x}{2 - 5x^2}$, find $f(3)$, $f(7)$, $f(y)$, and $f(y + \Delta y) - f(y)$.

9. If $f(x) = \dfrac{5x}{2 + x}$, find $f(-2)$, $f(2)$, $f(2y + \Delta y) - f(2y)$, and $f(2t + \Delta t) - f(2t)$.

10. If $f(x) = 3x^2 - 5x + 7$, find $f(y + \Delta y) - f(y)$.

11. If $f(t) = 2/t$, find $f(y + \Delta y) - f(y)$ and $f(3 + \Delta x) - f(3)$.

12. State which field postulates are used in each step of Problems 4 to 11.

13. If $S = -10t + 5$, find the average rate of change of S with respect to t as t changes from t to $t + \Delta t$.

14. Solve Problem 13 as t changes (a) from 3 to 3.5, (b) from 6 to 6.5.

15. If $f(x) = \dfrac{7}{x^2}$, find $\dfrac{f(z + \Delta z) - f(z)}{\Delta z}$.

16. Express as a simple fraction in lowest terms: $\dfrac{\dfrac{1}{x+3} + \dfrac{1}{x+1}}{\dfrac{3x-2}{x-2} - \dfrac{3}{x+3}}$.

17. Show that $\dfrac{A}{B} \div \dfrac{C}{D} = \dfrac{A}{B} \cdot \dfrac{D}{C}$ if $BCD \neq 0$.

[HINT: The numerator and denominator of $\dfrac{\dfrac{A}{B}}{\dfrac{C}{D}}$ may be multiplied by BD.]

18. If $f(t) = \dfrac{t}{t^2 + 1}$, find $\dfrac{f(y + \Delta y) - f(y)}{\Delta y}$.

19. Note carefully the similarity between Example 4 and Problem 11. Could you forecast the answer to Problem 11 from Example 4?

20. Same as 19 for Example 5 and Problem 15.

21. Same as 19 for Example 6 and Problem 16.

***22.** Same as 19 for Example 1, Section 1–1, and Problem 1.

23. The acceleration of protons in a betatron (a type of atom smasher) gives remarkably high velocities in a short time. Speeds in excess of 99 percent of the speed of light are possible in existing machines. If $v(t)$ is the velocity in miles per second and t is the time in seconds, where $v(t) = 100^{t/20}(1.8)$ for t between 0 and 40 sec, determine the velocity at $t = 30$ sec.

24.† The magnetic field H (in oersteds) of a solenoid containing N turns is given by the formula $H = 0.4\pi NI$ where I is the current in amperes. If a current of 2 amp produces a field of 300 oersteds, how many turns does the solenoid contain? Since there is some error in the meters used to measure H and I, would you feel justified in returning the solenoid if you had purchased it believing it contained 125 turns?

25.† If n cells of E volts each are connected in series to make a battery, a current of I amperes will be produced on a load of R ohms, if the internal resistance of each cell is r, where

$$I = \frac{nE}{R + nr}.$$

How many cells are needed in a battery that is to produce a current of 2 amperes under a load of 5 ohms? Each cell produces 2.1 volts and has an internal resistance of $\frac{1}{2}$ ohm.

26. Calvin Butterball hoes rows of onion plants in a truck garden. Calvin can hoe 4 rows in an hour. He gets paid 20¢ a row and each row is 85 ft long. (a) Find the average speed in feet per minute with which Calvin hoes. (b) Find Calvin's average rate of pay in dollars per hour.

1–5. Inequalities. The symbol $\neq$, meaning "not equal to," has already been introduced. In some cases we may wish to say more than $x \neq 5$; we may wish to say "x is less than 5." This is written $x < 5$. The statement "x is greater than minus one" can be written $x > -1$. The statement $z > t$ is read "z is greater than t." To include minus one as a possible value of x in the statement "x is greater than or equal to minus one," we write $x \geq -1$. The small ends of the symbols $<$ and $>$ point to the smaller expressions. The reader should note that $-5 < -1$, but $5 > 1$.

The expression "$-3 < t \leq 2$" indicates that t must lie between -3 and 2, including $t = 2$, but $t \neq -3$. The value of t must satisfy both of the relations $-3 < t$ and $t \leq 2$. The expression "$x > 5$ or $x \leq 1$"

---

* Problems preceded by "*" may involve an extension of theory, or may be difficult.

† This book contains many problems involving the units of engineering, chemistry, and physics, as well as some problems from other sciences. In each case it will *not* be assumed that the student is familiar with these units. Each problem contains as much information about the units as is needed to solve the problem.

indicates that either $x > 5$ or $x \leqq 1$ (*x cannot* satisfy both relations). Sections 2–1 and 2–5 are devoted to a study of inequalities.

In general, if a number axis is selected with the positive direction to the right, then $a < b$ means that a is further to the left (that is, "less positive") than b. Thus $x < -7$ means that x may be any number which is less (that is, "more negative") than -7. A few of the values of x that satisfy $x < -7$ include -10, $-\pi^2$, $-\sqrt{74}$, and -2^{17}; but the solution set for $x < -7$ would *not* include -5, or $+6$, or $+20.3$.

1–6. Absolute value. The symbol $|b|$ is read "the absolute value of b." It refers to the numerical value of b. The absolute value of a positive number or zero is the number itself. The absolute value of a negative number $-b$ is the corresponding positive number $+b$. Using the notation of the last section we may say all this by writing

$$|b| = b \text{ if } b \geqq 0; \quad |-b| = +b \text{ if } -b < 0.$$

Clearly, $|x| \geqq 0$ for all x. Examples: $|3| = 3$, $|0| = 0$, $|-7| = 7$, $|\sqrt{5} + 2| = \sqrt{5} + 2$, $|\sqrt{5} - 2| = \sqrt{5} - 2$, $|-\sqrt{5} + 2| = \sqrt{5} - 2$.

The symbol $\sqrt{5}$ designates "the positive square root of 5." If the negative root is desired, it must be indicated as $-\sqrt{5}$. Hence, $\sqrt{4} = 2$, not ± 2. Therefore, $(\sqrt{5} - 2) > 0$, while $(-\sqrt{5} + 2) < 0$.

If a number x is located on a number axis, then $|x|$ is the undirected distance between the origin and the point corresponding to x.

1–7. Four important numerical sets. The reader has already met some ideas concerning integers, rational numbers, real numbers, and complex numbers in his previous mathematical study. We shall now re-examine these systems briefly to be sure he includes the same elements in each set as are used here. No attempt is made to derive these sets. We assume the reader has used complex numbers and realizes that each of the other sets mentioned is a subset of the complex numbers.

The **set of integers** (whole numbers) includes the counting numbers (natural numbers) and their negatives (additive inverses), and zero — namely,

$$\{\cdots, -17, -16, \cdots, -4, -3, -2, -1, 0, 1, 2, \cdots, 99, 100, 101, \cdots\}.$$

It may be of interest to know that the set of integers can be derived from a set of postulates, just as geometry is derived from postulates. We shall not carry out the derivation here, but it can be found in more advanced books under the topic **Peano Postulates.**

The **set of rational numbers** consists of all quotients (**ratios**) of integers $\frac{a}{b}$ where $b \neq 0$. This includes numbers such as $\frac{13}{5}$, $\frac{2741}{8}$, 7, $-\frac{14}{1743}$, $\frac{10}{2}$ and -4, but *not* expressions such as $\frac{\pi}{2}$, $\sqrt{\frac{3}{5}}$, or $\sqrt{12}$. The *rational* numbers are, essentially, the numbers of commerce. Even the ancient Greeks, however, realized that there must exist numbers such as $\sqrt{2}$ and π which are not ratios of integers but which are essential in our discussions of geometrical lengths.

The **set of real numbers** may be thought of as being "distance numbers." A line on which a point has been selected as the zero or origin point, and with a given unit of length, and a chosen positive direction, is called a **number axis.**

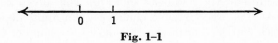

Fig. 1-1

The rational numbers may all be located on this number axis, but there will still exist points on the axis to which no rational number corresponds. Nevertheless, the distance from the origin, O, to each point on this line is a **real number.** Furthermore, for each real number r there corresponds a unique point P such that the directed distance OP is r. This establishes a correspondence between the real numbers and the points on a line. The distance to the right of O is called positive. Distance from O to P is negative if P is to the left of O.

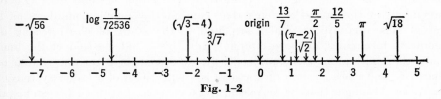

Fig. 1-2

Since every distance can be represented by a real number and every real number represents a directed distance, the reader may feel at first that here at last we have a perfect number system in which all problems can be solved. A moment's reflection, however, will remind him of several quadratic equations such as $x^2 + x + 2 = 0$ and $x^2 + 1 = 0$ which have no real solutions.

The **set of complex numbers** is the set of all numbers of the form $a + bi$, where a and b are real numbers and $i^2 = -1$. It is worthy of note that every polynomial † equation with **real** coefficients has a solution in the set of complex numbers; and, more surprising, even if the coefficients are permitted to be complex numbers, it is always possible to find a solution for a polynomial equation without going outside of the complex field.

An important theorem, which we shall not prove,‡ states that, "If $p(x)$

---

† A polynomial is an expression of the form $ax^n + bx^{n-1} + \cdots + kx + l$ where the exponents $n, n - 1, n - 2, \ldots, 1, 0$ are nonnegative integers.

‡ The reader should not feel that the proof of this theorem is beyond his comprehension. This particular proof is omitted because the authors feel that it is possible to spend the limited time available to the student more profitably in other ways than in laying the foundation needed for this proof.

is a polynomial of degree n with complex coefficients, then the equation $p(x) = 0$ has exactly n complex roots, providing multiple roots are properly counted."

The reader should not think of the number i as "a figment of the imagination" any more than he would think this of the numbers $\sqrt{3}$, π, or $\frac{277}{21638}$. Complex numbers are used in solving extremely practical problems concerning electric circuits, television, vectors, and the study of atomic energy. For the present, the number i should be considered as another number which, like $\sqrt{5}$, is used to solve equations. An approximation to $\sqrt{5}$ is given in the tables, but further interpretations of the number i do not appear until Chapter 18. If the term "imaginary number" is used, it will mean a number of the form $a + bi$ in which $b \neq 0$, and a and b are real numbers. We need not be particularly careful about distinguishing between the real number 4 and the corresponding complex number $4 + 0 \cdot i$, since we have considered already the real numbers to be a subset of the complex numbers. Later we may prefer to say that the complex numbers contain a subset that is isomorphic to (that is, behaves the same as) the real numbers, but this is not the time for such exactitude.

Although all polynomial equations with complex coefficients have complex roots, the reader ought to know that even larger systems exist. There are many mathematical systems that contain the complex numbers as a subset. The quaternions, which are used in the study of electron spin in quantum mechanics, are an example. Even this is not the end of the line, since the quaternions are contained as a subsystem of a certain system of matrices, and every system of matrices is a subsystem of a larger system of matrices. Although there is no reason to be concerned with such systems at the present moment, it is appropriate to realize that they do exist, and also that there is still much to be learned. With the exception of the Optional Sections, which appear at the ends of chapters, discussion will be confined to the complex numbers and its subsets.

PROBLEM SET 1-7

1. Some of the following sets of statements are true and some are false. Separate the set of statements into two subsets on this basis. Correct each false statement by altering the relation $(<, =, >)$.

   (a) $3 < 20$

   (b) $-7 < 1$

   (c) $14 > -21$

(d) $|2| < |-3|$
(e) $\pi^2 < \sqrt{75}$
(f) $\pi = 3.1416$
(g) $|\sqrt{14} - 5| = \sqrt{14} - 5$
(h) $\dfrac{\pi}{3} = 60$
(i) $\dfrac{1}{3+2} = \dfrac{1}{3} + \dfrac{1}{2}$
(j) $(\tfrac{1}{4})^2 > \tfrac{1}{4}$

2. Locate the 20 numbers (that is, the 10 left members and the 10 right members of the inequalities) given in Problem 1 on a number axis.
3. Write the four headings "integer," "rational number," "real number," and "complex number" on paper. Under each heading list each of the 20 numbers of Problem 1 which belongs to that set.
4. (a) Are the four subsets described in Problem 3 disjoint? Consult a dictionary if you are not sure of the meaning of the word "disjoint," then rephrase the problem as "Do the four sets of Problem 3 overlap one another?"
   (b) Is one of the four sets of Problem 3 the empty set?
   (c) Are any of the sets of Problem 3 subsets of the other sets?
5. Determine the subset of the 26 letters of the alphabet *not* contained in this sentence.

1–8 Functions and relations. It is not feasible to study all of mathematics. Even the world's best mathematician knows only a small part of the mathematics used today. As different facets of mathematics become more or less important in the scientific life of the world, the contents of college and university courses change to provide the essential background. One idea which has always been found essential is that of **function.** Recent developments have made it desirable to distinguish between a single-valued function (called a function) and a multiple-valued function (called a relation), but the basic idea is still unchanged.

Fundamentally, a function is a rule such that for each value of t taken from a given set, T, the rule determines a corresponding element $f(t)$ from a set Y.

A useful analogy represents a function f as a machine into which values of t are fed. The machine grinds out a corresponding value $f(t)$ for each t fed into the machine. It is essential that each time a given value of t, say $t = 17$, is fed into a certain function machine, the same output be obtained. Since the machine performs according to definite mathematical rules, it is impossible for it to turn out $f(17) = 3$ on one occasion and $f(17) = 5$ on another.

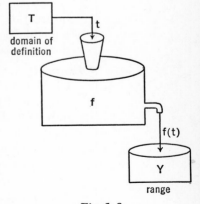
Fig. 1–3

Definition. A function consists of three things:

1. A set $T = \{t_1, t_2, t_3, \cdots\}$ called the **domain** of definition of the function.
2. A set $Y = \{y_1, y_2, \cdots\}$ called the **range** of the function.
3. A rule that assigns to each t_i of T a corresponding y_i of Y.

The reader should note that *there is nothing in the definition of function which says that a formula must exist;* nor that the y value must determine a unique t to which it corresponds. A given value y_i of Y may correspond to several different t_i's. This does not violate the definition of function. To each t_i, however, there must be **one and only one** corresponding value y_i of Y.

There is no reason to assume that the elements of T and Y are numbers. They need not be.

● *Example 1.* On most campuses, each student has a telephone number listed in a student directory. If T is the set of girls on a campus who have telephones, and Y is the set of telephone numbers, then the correspondence $y = f(t)$ where t is a girl and y is her campus phone number is a valid function, which has certain interesting applications.

The reader should restudy this section until he understands that the statement "y is a function of t" means that for any value t_i selected from a domain called T, there is a rule that assigns a corresponding value y_i taken from a range called Y.

● *Example 2.* The amount of postage P required to send a package from Los Angeles to Detroit is a function of w, the weight of the package. If the weight is known, the required postage may be computed at 3¢ for the first 2 ounces and $1\frac{1}{2}$¢ for each additional ounce or fraction thereof on packages weighing 16 ounces or less. On larger packages the postage may be computed at 64¢ for the first 2 pounds, plus 19¢ for each additional pound up to 10 pounds, and then 18¢ for each additional pound or fraction thereof. Packages weighing more than 20 pounds are not mailable between Los Angeles and Detroit; therefore the domain of definition is $0 < w \leq 20$ pounds. What is its range?

● *Example 3.* The cost C of sending 100 lb of bolts from the factory in Chicago to any terminal T in the United States via rail freight is a function of that destination. (It is not a function of distance, since rates differ.) If the terminal is known, the cost may be determined by calling the freight depot, or by consulting published tables of rates. The domain of definition is limited to those points within the United States that are rail terminals. Thus, the domain of definition may change from year to year. Note also that this is a function of a place, not a number.

The statement "y is a function of x" implies that if x is given (within the domain of definition), then y is determined. Nothing is stated about a formula connecting y and x. None need exist. Nor is it said that if y is given, then x can be determined. If the cost in Example 3 is $1.64, we may not be able to tell what the destination is.

● ***Example 4.*** The gain G on a stock market transaction is a function of the purchase price p, the selling price s, and the commissions c. In this case, if p, s, and c are known, $G = s - p - c$, and G is a function of p, s, and c.

● ***Example 5.*** The number of days, N, in a given year, Y, that the temperature was above D degrees Fahrenheit in Norman, Oklahoma, can be determined for any year for which complete records are available by consulting these records. Thus, N is a function of Y and D.

The notation $f(x)$ is commonly used to represent the value of the function F at the point x; $F(y), h(x), g(t)$ and similar symbols are also used. Example 1 becomes $y = f(t)$ while Examples 2 to 5 may be stated as $P = g(w)$, $C = h(T)$, $G = g(p, s, c)$, and $N = n(D, Y)$.

In Examples 2, 3, and 5, $g(w), h(T)$, and $n(D, Y)$ do *not* represent simple formulas. There are, of course, many functions that *can* be represented by formulas such as Example 4 in which $G = s - p - c$. We shall spend considerable time studying functions that can be so represented. Such a formula, however, is *not essential* to the idea of function. It should also be noted that the definition of function does *not* say "if t changes, $f(t)$ changes." A constant function such as $f(t) = 7$ in which the value 7 corresponds to each t is both permissible and useful.

Another pictorial representation of a function consists of two containers T and Y, where T contains elements t_i and Y contains elements y_i, and a set of strings connecting elements in the two containers such that each element t in T is connected to one and only one element y in Y, although several t's may connect to a given y.

The Function

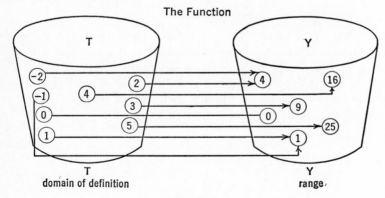

T
domain of definition

Y
range

Fig. 1–4

In Figure 1–4,
1. The domain of definition, T, consists of the numbers $t_i = -2, -1, 0, 1, 2, 3, 4, 5$, and only these numbers.
2. The range, Y, of the function f consists of the numbers $y_i = 0, 1, 4, 9, 16, 25$.

3. Can you find a rule which assigns a corresponding y_i to each t_i, as shown in the diagram? In this particular case there happens to be a formula, $y = t^2$, which is a more convenient way of giving the rule, but no such formula need exist. The essential idea of a function is the correspondence (strings) connecting the two sets of elements. It is also customary to refer to this correspondence as a "mapping" of the set T into the set Y.

In today's mathematics, the word "function" is reserved for a "single-valued function" — that is, one in which to each t there corresponds only one value of y. There are cases, however, in which one t value may give rise to several y values. On certain campuses, busy departments may have several phone numbers. For example, the University of Oklahoma directory lists three phone numbers for the computer laboratory. The word **relation** is used to describe such "multiple-valued functions."

● *Example 6.* If $y = -3 \pm 4t$, then to most real values of t there correspond two distinct values of y; for example, if

$$t = 2,\ y = f(2) = -3 \pm 4(2) = -3 \pm 8 = \begin{cases} 5 \\ \text{or} \\ -11 \end{cases}$$

Hence, $f(t) = -3 \pm 4t$ is a relation rather than a function.

● *Example 7.* Let $f(t)$ be the relation represented by the table given below.

t	1	2	3	4	5	6	7
$f(t)$	1	-1 3 2	6 1	2	5	9	11

Note that $f(2)$ and $f(3)$ each have more than one value. Is this consistent with the definition of relation? Is it consistent with the definition of function? The domain of definition is not $1 \le t \le 7$ since $f(t)$ is not defined for fractional values. The domain is the integers (whole numbers) between 1 and 7, inclusive, or merely the set $\{1, 2, 3, 4, 5, 6, 7\}$.

PROBLEM SET 1–8

1. Let A be the area of a circle and d its diameter. Then $A = f(d)$. Obtain a formula for $f(d)$.
2. Is the area of a circle a function of the circle's circumference? If possible obtain a formula for the area of a circle in terms of its circumference.

3. Make up a function $y = f(x)$ in which it is impossible to find a unique value for x if y is given. (See Example 3 if you need help.)

4. Discuss: Is a girl's telephone number a function of the room in which she lives? Give a possible domain of definition of the function for your campus.

5. If $f(x) = x^2 - 71x + 2$, find $f(-1)$, $f(2)$, $f(8)$, $f(3 + \Delta t) - f(3)$, and $f(y + \Delta y) - f(y)$.

6. If $g(t) = \dfrac{t^2 + 4}{3t}$, find $g(2)$, $g(3 + .1) - g(3)$, and $g(x + \Delta x) - g(x)$.

7. Using the $f(x)$ and $g(t)$ of Problems 5 and 6, determine $f(7) - g(3)$ and
$$\frac{f(3)}{g(2) + 1}.$$

8. Is it possible to express your age in years as a function of the number of months elapsed since your first birthday? If possible, do so. Give a possible domain of definition.

9. Express your age, in years, as a function of the number of months since you were 5 months old. State the domain of definition of this function.

10. If $g(t) = \dfrac{7}{t^2}$, find $\dfrac{g(z + \Delta z) - g(z)}{\Delta z}$. Of what variables is the result a function? Is the result multiple valued?

11. Find $\dfrac{y(t + \Delta t) - y(t)}{\Delta t}$, where $y(t) = 3g(t) + 1$ for the $g(t)$ of Problem 10.

12. If $g(x) = \dfrac{x}{x^2 + 1}$, find $\dfrac{g(y + \Delta y) - g(y)}{\Delta y}$.

13. If $p(x) = \dfrac{x^2 - 7}{3}$, find $\dfrac{p(t + \Delta t) - p(t)}{\Delta t}$.

14. If $q(x) = p(x) + g(x)$ for $p(x)$ of Problem 13 and $g(x)$ of Problem 10, find $q(2)$.

15. Discuss the similarity between Problem 10 of this set and Problem 15 of Set 1–4.

16. Discuss the similarity between Problem 12 of this set and Problem 18 of Set 1–4.

17. Is the amount of rainfall on your campus a function of the date? What is the present domain of definition? What will the domain of definition be next year at this time?

18. Discuss: Is the number of teeth T a person has a relation of his age in months? Is the relation the same for all people? Is a person's age A a function of the number of teeth T he has?

19. Make up a function that is not represented by a formula. State the domain of definition.

20. It is quite possible to have a function of several variables. In some theaters the cost of admission is a function of several variables,
$$C = F(s, t, p, a, T),$$

where s is the seat occupied, t is the time of attendance, p is the play or picture given, a is the age of the patron, and T is the amount of government tax imposed. In spite of the apparent complexity of this function many people find it possible to compute the value of C with little effort. Write out a similar function for one of your local movie houses.

21. Calvin Butterball can hoe four 85-ft rows of onions in an hour. He is paid 20¢ a row for hoeing. In addition, his parents pay him $3 a pound for each pound of weight he loses. If Calvin loses 3 ounces of weight for every 7 rows he hoes, determine his income in dollars per hour. Express the result as $I = f(t)$, where t is time in hours and I is income in dollars.

22. In Example 6, can you determine a real value of t for which only one corresponding value of $f(t)$ is obtained? Does this make $f(t)$ a (single-valued) function rather than a multiple-valued relation?

23. A "sophisticated" definition of *relation* states, "A **relation** is a set of ordered pairs $[t, f(t)]$." Show that this is in agreement with the discussion in the text.

24. The corresponding "sophisticated" definition of a *function* is "A **function** is a set of ordered pairs $[t, f(t)]$ such that if any two pairs have the same first element, then they also have the same second element."

When the reader realizes that the two definitions given in Problems 23 and 24 are the same as those given in this section, he has the basic concepts of function and relation under control. If you do not, reread this section and rethink each of the illustrative examples.

25. Let $y = g(t)$, where $g(t)$ means all real values k such that $k > t$. Is $g(t)$ a relation? Is $g(t)$ a function? Explain your answers.

1–9. Solution of equations. An equation is a sentence which states that two functions are equal. Often one of the functions is a constant function, but this is not essential. A **numerical identity** is a valid equation in which only numbers appear, for example, $3 + 2 = \frac{10}{2}$, or $\frac{5}{2} - 2 = \frac{1}{2}$. A number is said to **satisfy** an equation in one unknown or to be a **solution** of the equation if, and only if, upon substituting the number for the unknown in the equation, a numerical identity results. The word **root** is sometimes used instead of solution. A number is said to satisfy an inequality in one unknown if a valid numerical inequality results when the number is substituted for the unknown.

In an equation, or an inequality, it is always necessary to know the nature of the set from which acceptable solutions are to be found. For example: The equation $3x = 5$ has *no solution* in the set of integers (whole numbers). However, the equation $3x = 5$ does have a solution in the set of rational fractions — namely, $x = 5/3$. Hence the environment in which we seek solutions is of vital importance. If we seek "numbers" that satisfy the equation $x^2 + 1 = 0$, there are none among the set of real numbers;

but if complex solutions are permitted, it is easy to write "$x = i$ and $x = -i$ are solutions." †

We shall use the phrase "candidate set" to describe the large set from which acceptable solutions of an equation or inequality may be found. Those elements of the candidate set that satisfy the equation or inequality form the **set of solutions** or **solution set** of that equation or inequality.

- **Example 1.** (a) Let the candidate set be the set of all positive integers. The relation $x < 7$ has the solution set $\{1, 2, 3, 4, 5, 6\}$.

  (b) If, on the other hand, the candidate set had been the set of rational numbers, there would be infinitely many different elements in the solution set. [Which of the following would *not* be in the solution set for (b): $4, -31, \dfrac{\pi}{3}, \dfrac{17}{5}, -\dfrac{281}{31}, \sqrt{3}, 4 - 7i$? Why?]

- **Example 2.** Determine the solution set for the equation $(x + 1)^2 = 25$ if the candidate set is the set of rational numbers.

  The solution set consists of all rational numbers x such that $(x + 1)^2 = 25$. This set has two elements, $\{-6, 4\}$, since $x = -6$ and $x = 4$ are the only solutions of $(x + 1)^2 = 25$.

If no candidate set is specified, it will be assumed in this text that the candidate set is either the set of real numbers or the set of complex numbers, depending upon the nature of the problem. If there is any doubt, however, it should be assumed that the complex numbers are intended.

- **Example 3.** Are 4 and 3 solutions of

$$P(x) = 4x^4 - 40x^3 + 95x^2 + 10x - 24 = 0?$$

Since $P(4) = 0$, 4 is a root of $P(x) = 0$. Since $P(3) \neq 0$, 3 is not a root.

An **identity** is an equation in which both members are equal for all values of the unknown for which both members are defined. For example,

$$\frac{x^2 - 4}{x^2 - x} = \frac{(x + 2)(x - 2)}{x(x - 1)}$$

is an identity, since both members are equal for all values of x except $x = 0$ and $x = 1$. Division by zero is not defined, consequently neither member is defined for $x = 0$ or $x = 1$.

---

† Students occasionally feel that if they can give a *name* to a concept, this implies they understand the concept itself. A common answer to the question "Why does a stone fall if dropped?" is "Gravity." By uttering this word, people feel they have explained why the stone falls. This is inadequate. It is also inadequate to state that "i is a complex number, or an imaginary number" as if the mere naming of the concept explained it. Further discussion of the complex numbers will be found in Chapter 18.

Equations that are not identities are called **conditional** equations, or simply equations. For example, $x^2 - 3x = 0$ is a conditional equation since the only roots are $x = 0$ and $x = 3$.

● **Example 4.** Determine A and B such that $\dfrac{x+1}{x^2 - 5x + 6} = \dfrac{A}{x-2} + \dfrac{B}{x-3}$

is an identity.

$$\frac{x+1}{x^2 - 5x + 6} = \frac{A}{x-2} \cdot \frac{(x-3)}{(x-3)} + \frac{B}{x-3} \cdot \frac{(x-2)}{(x-2)}$$

$$= \frac{(A+B)x + (-3A - 2B)}{x^2 - 5x + 6}.$$

This will be an identity if $x + 1 = (A + B)x + (-3A - 2B)$ is an identity. (Why?) To be an identity, the last equation must be satisfied by all values of x. Upon substituting $x = -1$ and $x = 0$ (any convenient distinct values of x will do) as representative values, we find that if $x = 0$, then $1 = -3A - 2B$; and if $x = -1$, then $0 = -4A - 3B$. Solving these, we obtain $A = -3$ and $B = 4$. Examination of the original will show that $A = -3$ and $B = 4$ does give an identity.

A second method of solution follows: The two members of

$$\frac{x+1}{x^2 - 5x + 6} = \frac{(A+B)x + (-3A - 2B)}{x^2 - 5x + 6}$$

will be identical if the coefficients of x in the numerators are equal and the constant terms in the numerators are equal — that is, if $A + B = 1$ and $-3A - 2B = 1$. The solution of these last two equations is again $A = -3$ and $B = 4$. The reader should check the results by adding the two fractions on the right.

Two equations (or inequalities) are **equivalent** if they can be made identical by the addition of like terms to each member of one of the equations (or inequalities) combined with multiplication of either equation (or inequality) † by a nonzero constant. Equivalent equations (or equivalent inequalities) have the same solution set.

● **Example 5.** The equations

$$x^2 + 4x - 7 = 2 + x, \quad x^2 + 3x = 9, \quad \text{and} \quad 6 - x^2 = 3(x - 1)$$

are equivalent equations. The inequalities

$$4x - 7 < 2x + 5, \quad 2x < 12, \quad x < 6, \quad \text{and} \quad -x > -6$$

are equivalent inequalities.

A linear equation in one unknown is an equation involving only the first power of the unknown (say z) and constants. An example is

$$17z - 4 + 3z - 12 = 32z + 11.$$

† The reader should note that if an inequality is multiplied by a negative number, the inequality sign is reversed. For example, $3 < 5$, but $-3 > -5$.

The solution of this, or any other linear equation in one unknown, is obtained by arranging all terms involving the unknown (z) on one side of the equality sign and all other terms (constants) on the opposite side. This is accomplished by addition to obtain

$$17z + 3z - 32z = 11 + 4 + 12$$
$$-12z = 27.$$

Multiply both sides by the same number such that the coefficient of the unknown becomes one: (What field postulate guarantees the existence of such a number?)

$$z = \frac{27}{-12} = -\frac{9}{4}.$$

The reader should verify that $-\frac{9}{4}$ is a solution by direct substitution of $-\frac{9}{4}$ for z in the original equation.

Many quadratic equations, $Ax^2 + Bx + C = 0$, may be solved by factoring. The fundamental idea involved is that a product of factors is **zero** if, and only if, at least one of the factors is **zero.**† (Where have you seen this before?)

• *Example 6.* $x^2 - 3x = 4$. An equivalent equation is obtained by adding -4 to each member

$$x^2 - 3x - 4 = 0 \quad \text{or} \quad (x - 4)(x + 1) = 0.$$

If the elements are taken from a field, the equation holds if, and only if, either $(x - 4) = 0$ or $(x + 1) = 0$. (Why?) The two resulting linear equations may be solved to obtain $x = 4$ and $x = -1$. Either of the values 4 or -1 will satisfy the original equation, as may be shown by direct substitution.

• *Example 7.* $2x^2 + 11x - 21 = 0$.
$$(2x - 3)(x + 7) = 0.$$

Then

$$(2x - 3) = 0, \ (x + 7) = 0$$
$$x = \tfrac{3}{2}, \quad x = -7.$$

The equation $x^2 + 3x + 1 = 0$ cannot be solved directly by finding rational factors.‡ The quadratic formula will be found helpful in this and

† The reader may be interested in knowing that there exist number systems in which a product of two elements may equal zero when neither element is zero. Although such systems have important applications, we shall not discuss them here. See Sections 1–16 and 25–2.

‡ Note that we do **not** say that $x^2 + 3x + 1$ cannot be factored. Its factors are $\left[x + \dfrac{3}{2} - \dfrac{\sqrt{5}}{2}\right]$ and $\left[x + \dfrac{3}{2} + \dfrac{\sqrt{5}}{2}\right]$, but these factors are not rational since $\sqrt{5}$ cannot be expressed as a quotient of integers.

similar cases. We give two parallel derivations of this formula. A general quadratic equation, using literal coefficients, is $Ax^2 + Bx + C = 0$ with $A \neq 0$.

<table>
<tr><td>Derivation I</td><td>Derivation II</td></tr>
</table>

Derivation I	*Derivation* II

Derivation I

Divide by A and subtract the constant term from both members.

$$x^2 + \frac{B}{A} x = -\frac{C}{A}.$$

Make the left member the square of $x + \frac{B}{2A}$ by adding $\frac{B^2}{4A^2}$ to each side.

$$x^2 + \frac{B}{A} x + \frac{B^2}{4A^2} = -\frac{C}{A} + \frac{B^2}{4A^2},$$

or

$$\left(x + \frac{B}{2A}\right)^2 = \frac{B^2 - 4AC}{4A^2}.$$

Find the square root of both sides.

$$x + \frac{B}{2A} = \pm \sqrt{\frac{B^2 - 4AC}{4A^2}}.$$

Whence,

$$x = -\frac{B}{2A} \pm \frac{\sqrt{B^2 - 4AC}}{2A}$$

$$= \frac{-B \pm \sqrt{B^2 - 4AC}}{2A}.$$

Derivation II

Multiply by $4A$.

$$4A^2x^2 + 4ABx + 4AC = 0.$$

Subtract $4AC$ from both members.

$$4A^2x^2 + 4ABx = -4AC.$$

Add B^2 to both members.

$$4A^2x^2 + 4ABx + B^2 = B^2 - 4AC.$$

Then

$$(2Ax + B)^2 = B^2 - 4AC$$

$$2Ax + B = \pm \sqrt{B^2 - 4AC}.$$

Whence,

$$2Ax = -B \pm \sqrt{B^2 - 4AC}$$

$$x = \frac{-B \pm \sqrt{B^2 - 4AC}}{2A}.$$

Logically, all that has been shown is that *if* solutions exist, they must be either

$$\frac{-B + \sqrt{B^2 - 4AC}}{2A} \quad \text{or} \quad \frac{-B - \sqrt{B^2 - 4AC}}{2A}$$

or both. In the problems the student is asked to verify by direct substitution in $Ax^2 + Bx + C = 0$ that each of these possible results is actually a solution. (See Problems 1, 2, and 3, Set 1–10.) The expression

$$\frac{-B \pm \sqrt{B^2 - 4AC}}{2A}$$

is known as the **quadratic formula,** and was useful enough to merit memorizing in intermediate algebra. We rederive it here mainly to reconsider the methods of proof. Note that the formula applies only when the quadratic equation is written in the form $Ax^2 + Bx + C = 0$.

● *Example 8.* Apply the quadratic formula to $x^2 + 3x + 1 = 0$. Using $A = 1$, $B = 3$, $C = 1$ we obtain

$$x = \frac{-B \pm \sqrt{B^2 - 4AC}}{2A} = \frac{-3 \pm \sqrt{3^2 - 4 \cdot 1 \cdot 1}}{2 \cdot 1} = \frac{-3 \pm \sqrt{5}}{2}.$$

● **Example 9.** Solve $3x^2 + 7x + 2 = 0$. Using the quadratic formula with $A = 3$, $B = 7$, and $C = 2$ we obtain

$$x = \frac{-7 \pm \sqrt{49 - 4 \cdot 3 \cdot 2}}{2 \cdot 3} = \frac{-7 \pm \sqrt{25}}{6}$$

$$= \begin{cases} \dfrac{-7 + 5}{6} = -\dfrac{1}{3}. \\[2mm] \text{or} \\[2mm] \dfrac{-7 - 5}{6} = -2. \end{cases}$$

This equation can be solved by factoring.

$$3x^2 + 7x + 2 = 0$$
$$(x + 2)(3x + 1) = 0$$
$$x + 2 = 0, \qquad 3x + 1 = 0$$
$$x = -2, \qquad\qquad x = -\tfrac{1}{3}.$$

● **Example 10.** Solve $2z^2 - 5z + 4 = 0$. In this case $A = 2$, $B = -5$, $C = 4$. Hence,

$$z = \frac{-(-5) \pm \sqrt{25 - 32}}{4} = \frac{5 \pm \sqrt{-7}}{4} = \frac{5 \pm i\sqrt{7}}{4}.$$

1–10. More theory of quadratic equations. In the last section we rederived the formula for finding the solutions of a given quadratic equation. We now consider the inverse problem; namely, given the solutions of a quadratic equation, determine an equation that has these solutions. Before reading further the reader should try to solve this problem himself. Write a quadratic equation that has $\{7, -4\}$ as its solution set.

To write a quadratic equation having roots r and s, we note that $(x - r)(x - s) = x^2 - (r + s)x + rs = 0$ has the desired roots. More generally, so has $cx^2 - c(r + s)x + crs = 0$ with $c \neq 0$.

● **Example 1.** Write a quadratic equation having roots $-\tfrac{3}{2}$ and 1. Using the above method we have

$$(x - 1)\left(x - \left[-\frac{3}{2}\right]\right) = (x - 1)\left(x + \frac{3}{2}\right) = x^2 + \frac{x}{2} - \frac{3}{2} = 0.$$

Multiplying both sides by $c = 2$ we obtain $2x^2 + x - 3 = 0$. The reader should verify that this result is also obtained by forming

$$r + s = -\tfrac{1}{2} \quad \text{and} \quad rs = -\tfrac{3}{2}$$

and substituting in the formula derived above.

We offer a test for the nature of the roots of a quadratic equation. If $B^2 - 4AC = 0$, the roots of $Ax^2 + Bx + C = 0$ are equal and have the

value $x = \dfrac{-B \pm 0}{2A} = \dfrac{-B}{2A}$. On the other hand, if the roots of
$Ax^2 + Bx + C = 0$ are equal, then
$$\dfrac{-B + \sqrt{B^2 - 4AC}}{2A} = \dfrac{-B - \sqrt{B^2 - 4AC}}{2A}.$$ This implies $2\sqrt{B^2 - 4AC} = 0$
and hence $B^2 - 4AC = 0$. The reader should note the difference between
the two statements just proved. Are they converse theorems?

- **Example 2.** Determine b such that $x^2 + (mx + b)^2 = 16$ has equal roots.
  This equation is equivalent to $(1 + m^2)x^2 + 2bmx + (b^2 - 16) = 0$.
  Hence, $A = 1 + m^2$, $B = 2bm$, and $C = b^2 - 16$. Therefore,

  $$B^2 - 4AC = (2bm)^2 - 4(1 + m^2)(b^2 - 16) = \cdots = -4b^2 + 64 + 64m^2.$$

  If the roots of the original are equal, then $B^2 - 4AC = 0$. Hence,

  $$-4b^2 + 64 + 64m^2 = 0$$
  $$b^2 = 16(m^2 + 1)$$
  and $$b = \pm 4\sqrt{m^2 + 1}.$$

If A, B, and C are **real numbers** and if $B^2 - 4AC > 0$, then
$\sqrt{B^2 - 4AC}$ is real and the two roots of $Ax^2 + Bx + C = 0$ are real and
different. If A, B, and C are real and $B^2 - 4AC < 0$, then $\sqrt{B^2 - 4AC}$
is imaginary and the two roots are complex and different.

- **Example 3.** Determine the nature of the roots of (a) $4x^2 - 12x + 9 = 0$,
  (b) $4x^2 - 12x - 9 = 0$, and (c) $4x^2 - 12x + 11 = 0$.

  (a) $B^2 - 4AC = (-12)^2 - 4(4)(9) = 0$. Hence, the roots are real
  and equal.
  (b) $B^2 - 4AC = (-12)^2 - 4(4)(-9) = 288 > 0$. Hence, the roots
  are real and different.
  (c) $B^2 - 4AC = (-12)^2 - 4(4)(11) = -32 < 0$. Hence, the roots
  are complex and different.

- **Example 4.** Determine real values of k such that the roots of
  $3x^2 + kx + 5 = 0$ are (a) real and equal, (b) real and different, (c) complex and different.
      In each case $B^2 - 4AC = k^2 - 60$.

  (a) The roots are real and equal if $B^2 - 4AC = k^2 - 60 = 0$, hence,
  if $k = \pm\sqrt{60} = \pm 2\sqrt{15}$.
  (b) The roots are real and different if $B^2 - 4AC = k^2 - 60 > 0$,
  that is, if $k^2 > 60$. This happens if $k > \sqrt{60} = 2\sqrt{15}$, or if
  $k < -\sqrt{60} = -2\sqrt{15}$. Write this as $k > 2\sqrt{15}$ or $k < -2\sqrt{15}$
  in accordance with Section 1–5, or as $|k| > 2\sqrt{15}$.
  (c) The roots are complex and different if $B^2 - 4AC = k^2 - 60 < 0$.
  This implies $k^2 < 60$ which happens only if k satisfies both of the
  inequalities $k < 2\sqrt{15}$ and $k > -2\sqrt{15}$. Write this as

$-2\sqrt{15} < k < 2\sqrt{15}$ in accordance with Section 1–5 or as $|k| < 2\sqrt{15}$. A graphical representation may help to visualize these results. The roots of $3x^2 + kx + 5 = 0$ have the character indicated for the values of k shown.

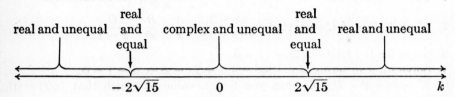

Occasionally equations in several variables must be solved for one of the variables in terms of the other variables. The next example uses the quadratic formula to accomplish this. In solving for x we consider all other variables (here y) as constants.

● **Example 5.** Solve for x in terms of y: $2x^2 - 3xy + 5y^2 - x + 7y - 6 = 0$.
Write the equation in the form $Ax^2 + Bx + C = 0$.

$$2x^2 + (-3y - 1)x + (5y^2 + 7y - 6) = 0.$$

Then $A = 2$, $B = -3y - 1$, $C = 5y^2 + 7y - 6$ and

$$x = \frac{-(-3y - 1) \pm \sqrt{(-3y - 1)^2 - 4(2)(5y^2 + 7y - 6)}}{2 \cdot 2}$$

$$= \frac{3y + 1 \pm \sqrt{-31y^2 - 50y + 49}}{4}.$$

PROBLEM SET 1–10

1. Show by direct substitution that $\dfrac{-B + \sqrt{B^2 - 4AC}}{2A}$ satisfies the equation $Ax^2 + Bx + C = 0$.

2. Show by direct substitution that $\dfrac{-B - \sqrt{B^2 - 4AC}}{2A}$ satisfies the equation $Ax^2 + Bx + C = 0$.

3. Write a quadratic equation having roots

$$\frac{-B + \sqrt{B^2 - 4AC}}{2A} \quad \text{and} \quad \frac{-B - \sqrt{B^2 - 4AC}}{2A}.$$

Is this equation equivalent to $Ax^2 + Bx + C = 0$?

4. Solve for x: $3x^2 - 5x - 12 = 0$.

5. Solve for w: $7w^2 + 54w - 16 = 0$.

6. Find A and B such that $\dfrac{x+10}{x^2-4} = \dfrac{A}{x-2} + \dfrac{B}{x+2}$ is an identity.

7. Find A, B, and C such that $\dfrac{4x+3}{x^2(x-1)} = \dfrac{A}{x} + \dfrac{B}{x^2} + \dfrac{C}{x-1}$.

8. Solve for t: $1.4t^2 - 3.2t - 11 = 0$.

9. Solve for x in terms of z: $3x^2 - 4zx + 2x - z^2 + 3z - 1 = 0$.

10. If $g(t) = t^2 - 7t + 6$, can you find a value of t such that $g(t) = 0$? Does more than one such value of t exist?

11. Determine z such that $g(z) = -4$ for the g of Problem 10.

12. Solve for z: $3z^2 - 5iz + 2z + 3 - 2i = 0$, where $i^2 = -1$.

13. If $h(b) = b^2 + 5b - 7$, can you find values of b such that $h(b) = 3$? How many? What are they?

14. Is it possible to write a quadratic equation having equal complex roots? Would it be possible if the coefficients were restricted to real numbers?

15. Solve for x: $(x-2)(x+1) = 4$.

16. Discuss the fallacy of the following attempted solution of Problem 15.
$$(x-2) = 2 \quad \text{or} \quad (x+1) = 2.$$
Then $x = 4$ or $x = 1$. Show that neither 4 nor 1 is a root.

17. An electric circuit contains three resistances in parallel. If the three resistances are R_1, R_2, and R_3, then the total resistance is R, where

$$\frac{1}{R_1} + \frac{1}{R_2} + \frac{1}{R_3} = \frac{1}{R}.$$

Determine R when $R_1 = 25$ ohms, $R_2 = 15$ ohms, and $R_3 = 42$ ohms.

18. The same as Problem 17, where $R_1 = 10$ ohms, $R_2 = 60$ ohms, and $R_3 = 35$ ohms.

19. The length of a piece of tin is 3 inches longer than its width. The piece of tin costs \$1.08 at 1¢ per sq. in. Determine the dimensions of the piece of tin. Be sure to indicate the *units* of your answer on this and other statement problems.

20. Express each of the following functions in a manner such that the quadratic expression in the denominator is a sum or a difference of squares, $A^2 \pm B^2$. For example, $\dfrac{3x+2}{4x^2+3x-1}$ is equal to

$$\frac{3x+2}{\left[4x^2 + 3x + \dfrac{9}{16}\right] + \left[\dfrac{-9}{16} - 1\right]} = \frac{3x+2}{\left(2x + \dfrac{3}{4}\right)^2 - \left(\dfrac{5}{4}\right)^2}$$

which is in the form requested. This technique is essential before tables can be used in certain calculus problems.

(a) $\dfrac{5x+2}{4x^2+5x-6}$ 　　　 (b) $\dfrac{3}{\sqrt{6x-2x^2}}$ 　　　 (c) $\dfrac{3x+1}{x^2+2x+3}$

21. Another method of completing the square is shown in this example. The method is similar to the second derivation of the quadratic formula. We begin by multiplying numerator and denominator by $4A$, as in the second derivation of the quadratic formula in Section 1–9.

$$\frac{3x + 2}{4x^2 + 3x - 1} = \frac{4 \cdot 4(3x + 2)}{4 \cdot 4(4x^2 + 3x - 1)} = \frac{48x + 32}{64x^2 + 48x + (9 - 9) - 16}$$

$$= \frac{48x + 32}{(8x + 3)^2 - (5)^2}.$$

Use this method of completing the square to express the quadratic functions as the sum or difference of two squares.

(a) $\dfrac{5x + 3}{x^2 + x + 1}$ (b) $\dfrac{13t}{9t^2 - 12t + 20}$ (c) $\dfrac{5}{2x - 3x^2}$ (d) $\dfrac{49}{ax^2 + bx + c}$

22. Prove that the sum Σ (Greek capital letter sigma) of the two roots of $Ax^2 + Bx + C = 0$ is $\Sigma = -B/A$.

23. Prove that the product Π (Greek capital letter pi) of the two roots of the above equation is $\Pi = C/A$. It is customary in science to use the Greek Σ and Π in the roles indicated in Problems 22 and 23.

24. Problems 22 and 23 provide a quick check for the correctness of the roots of a quadratic equation. Use them to check some of the problems in this list.

25. Show that if $|k| < 10$, then $2t^2 - kt + 18 = 0$ has only complex roots. Can you set a larger bound on $|k|$ such that the roots remain complex?

26. Solve for t: $t^4 - 13t^2 + 36 = 0$. If you have trouble factoring this, you might let $t^2 = x$ and first solve the resulting quadratic equation in x.

27. Solve for t: $2t^4 + 5t^2 - 12 = 0$. See suggestion in Problem 26.

28. Solve for z: $(z^4 - 4z^3 + 4z^2) - 23(z^2 - 2z) + 120 = 0$.

[HINT: let $z^2 - 2z = x$, then $x^2 = z^4 - 4z^3 + 4z^2$.]

29. Solve for x: $3.6x^2 - 2.1x - 8.5 = 0$. Equations with decimal coefficients often appear in applied problems. The quadratic formula is almost always used to determine solutions.

30. Figure 1–5 shows an electric circuit containing a resistance of $R = 10$ ohms, an inductance coil of $L = 2$ henrys, and a condenser of capacitance $C = 1/10050$ farad. To determine the current, one must solve the auxiliary equation, $Lm^2 + Rm + 1/C = 0$, for m. Using the given values of L, R, and C determine values of m. The complex value of m has an important

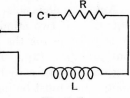

Fig. 1–5

interpretation in electrical theory. It is common practice among electrical technicians to use j rather than i to represent the number whose square is -1. Express your answer in this form.

31. Same as 30 for $R = 3$ ohms, $L = 2$ henrys, and $C = \frac{1}{200}$ farad.

32. For what integers (whole numbers) x is $3x^2 + 2x - 7 < 0$?

33. A ball bearing rolls down a track a distance s ft in t sec where $s = 4t + t^2/2$. How long does it take the ball bearing to travel 24 ft? Obtain a general formula expressing t as a function of s.

34. A circuit contains two resistors in parallel, one of 20 ohms and one of 50 ohms. How large should a third resistor be if it is also to be connected in parallel with the other two and if the total resistance is to be 6 ohms? If resistors are available in multiples of 5 ohms only, what size should be used to come as near 6 ohms as possible? See Problem 17.

35. Calvin Butterball and Phoebe Small went to an amusement park on Calvin's day off. Calvin spent $4.65 plus 40¢ carfare on the date. Phoebe packed an excellent lunch. Calvin's new job in a nice air-conditioned onion-packing plant pays 60¢ an hour plus 10¢ bonus for each box packed. Calvin averages 32 boxes per 8-hour day. Calvin is paid "time and a half" for overtime both on his base pay and on his bonus. If Calvin must finish packing a box once he starts it (that is, no fractional boxes permitted), how many hours overtime must he work to pay for the date?

1–11. Auxiliary equations. The equations

$$(1) \quad \frac{x^2 + 2x}{x - 3} = \frac{18 - x}{x - 3} \qquad \text{and} \qquad (2) \quad x^2 + 2x = 18 - x$$

are **not** equivalent equations. Equation (2) is called an **auxiliary equation** to (1) since it is useful in determining the solutions of (1). Every root of (1) is also a root of (2), but not conversely. (What does this mean?) If the auxiliary equation can be solved, its roots may be checked to see which, if any, also satisfy the original equation. The solutions of $x^2 + 2x = 18 - x$ are $x = 3$ and $x = -6$. The first of these is not a root of equation (1) since the resulting members are undefined. (Why?) The value $x = -6$ is a root, and therefore is the only root of (1). In general, if the auxiliary equation is obtained by multiplying the original equation by an expression involving the unknown, the roots of the auxiliary equation, which do *not* make that factor equal zero, will also be roots of the original equation. Roots introduced through multiplying by a factor necessarily make that factor zero.

Auxiliary equations may also be obtained by squaring both members of an equation. If two numbers are equal, their squares are also equal. However, it is possible for the squares of unequal numbers to be equal, $-2 \neq 2$, but $(-2)^2 = (2)^2$. Thus a root of an auxiliary equation obtained by squaring may not be a root of the original equation. If the original equation has roots, they must be included among the roots of the auxiliary equation.

● *Example 1.* Solve for x:
$$\sqrt{x - 2} = 3.$$
$$(\sqrt{x - 2})^2 = 9$$
$$x - 2 = 9$$
$$x = 11 \quad \text{is the only root of the auxiliary}$$

equation, hence the only possible root of the equation $\sqrt{x - 2} = 3$. Upon substituting $\sqrt{11 - 2} = \sqrt{9} = 3$ we find it is a root.

● *Example 2.* Solve for x: $2x - \sqrt{2x - 3} - 9 = 0$.

First isolate the radical, then remove it by squaring.

$$2x - 9 = \sqrt{2x - 3}$$
$$(2x - 9)^2 = (\sqrt{2x - 3})^2$$
$$4x^2 - 36x + 81 = 2x - 3$$
$$2x^2 - 19x + 42 = 0 \quad \text{(Why?)}$$
$$(2x - 7)(x - 6) = 0.$$

Therefore $x = \tfrac{7}{2}$ and $x = 6$ are the only possible roots of the original. Each must be checked.

Check $x = \tfrac{7}{2}$.

$$2(\tfrac{7}{2}) - \sqrt{2(\tfrac{7}{2}) - 3} - 9 \overset{?}{=} 0$$
$$7 - \sqrt{4} - 9 \overset{?}{=} 0 \dagger$$
$$7 - 2 - 9 \neq 0.$$

Hence, $x = \tfrac{7}{2}$ is not a root.

Check $x = 6$.

$$2(6) - \sqrt{2(6) - 3} - 9 \overset{?}{=} 0$$
$$12 - 3 - 9 = 0.$$

Consequently, the original equation has $x = 6$ as its only solution.

An extra value obtained in the process of solution, such as $\tfrac{7}{2}$ in the above example, which is not a solution of the original equation is called an **extraneous** value. The manner in which an extraneous value is introduced is more easily seen if the value $x = \tfrac{7}{2}$ is substituted in the equation in the form used just before it was squared.

$$2x - 9 = \sqrt{2x - 3}$$
$$2(\tfrac{7}{2}) - 9 \overset{?}{=} \sqrt{2(\tfrac{7}{2}) - 3}$$
$$-2 \overset{?}{=} \sqrt{4} = +2,$$

which is *not* valid.

● *Example 3.* Solve for x: $\sqrt{3x + 3} - \sqrt{2x} = \sqrt{x - 1}$. The given equation is equivalent to

$$\sqrt{3x + 3} = \sqrt{x - 1} + \sqrt{2x}.$$

Then
$$(\sqrt{3x + 3})^2 = (\sqrt{x - 1} + \sqrt{2x})^2,$$
$$3x + 3 = x - 1 + 2\sqrt{x - 1} \cdot \sqrt{2x} + 2x.$$

Upon isolating the remaining radical and dividing by 2 we obtain

$$2 = \sqrt{x - 1} \cdot \sqrt{2x}.$$

Then
$$4 = (x - 1)(2x),$$
$$x^2 - x - 2 = 0.$$

Consequently, $x = -1$ and $x = 2$ are possible roots of the original equation. We *must* check each possible value.

$\dagger$ In section 1–6 it was pointed out that $-\sqrt{4} = -2$, not ± 2.

$$\text{Check} \quad x = -1:$$
$$\sqrt{-3+3} - \sqrt{-2} \overset{?}{=} \sqrt{-2}$$
$$0 - \sqrt{-2} \neq \sqrt{-2}$$

$$\text{Check} \quad x = 2:$$
$$\sqrt{6+3} - \sqrt{4} \overset{?}{=} \sqrt{1}$$
$$3 - 2 = 1$$

Hence, $x = -1$ is extraneous.　　　Hence, $x = 2$ is a root.

- **Example 4.** Determine S and C satisfying *both* of the equations.

$$\begin{cases} (1)\ S^2 + C^2 = 1, \\ (2)\ 8S + C = 7. \end{cases}$$ Solve (1) for $C = \pm \sqrt{1 - S^2}$. If C is to be a value

common to (1) and (2), then C from (1) must satisfy (2). Consequently,

$$8S \pm \sqrt{1 - S^2} = 7$$
$$(8S - 7)^2 = (\pm \sqrt{1 - S^2})^2$$
$$64S^2 - 112S + 49 = 1 - S^2$$
$$65S^2 - 112S + 48 = 0$$
$$(13S - 12)(5S - 4) = 0.$$

$$\begin{cases} S = \frac{12}{13} \\ C = -\frac{5}{13} \end{cases} \quad \text{and} \quad \begin{cases} S = \frac{4}{5} \\ C = \frac{3}{5} \end{cases} \quad \text{are two possible solutions.}$$

Both check in each given equation. Hence, both pairs are solutions.

A second and more desirable method of solution is to solve (2) for $C = 7 - 8S$ and substitute in (1) obtaining $S^2 + (7 - 8S)^2 = 1$, or $65S^2 - 112S + 48 = 0$ again. The solution is then completed as shown in the above work. Readers familiar with trigonometric equations will see that the solution of $8 \sin \theta + \cos \theta = 7$ for $\sin \theta$ and $\cos \theta$ using the identity $\sin^2 \theta + \cos^2 \theta = 1$ is accomplished by the method of this problem.

1–12. The delta function: $\Delta f = f(x + \Delta x) - f(x)$. With each function $f(x)$, there is associated a function, called the **delta function,** which is of considerable importance in later work. Before defining the delta function, let us examine two examples.

- **Example 1.** If the distance $s(t)$ in feet which a ball falls is given by the function $s(t) = 16t^2$ for t in seconds during the interval $0 \leq t \leq 6$, determine the change, Δs, in s between $t_1 = 4$ and $t_2 = 5$. At

$$t_2 = 5, \quad s(5) = 16(5)^2 = 400.$$

While at

$$t_1 = 4, \quad s(4) = 16(4)^2 = 256.$$

Hence, the change in s is

$$\Delta s = s(5) - s(4) = 400 - 256 = 144.$$

- **Example 2.** If the distance $s(t)$ in feet which a ball falls is given by the function $s(t) = 16t^2$ for t in seconds, during the interval

$0 \leq t \leq 6$, determine the change Δs in s between $t_1 = 4$ and $t_2 = 4 + \Delta t$.

At

$t_2 = 4 + \Delta t$, $s(4 + \Delta t) = 16(4 + \Delta t)^2 = 256 + 128\Delta t + 16(\Delta t)^2$.

At

$t_1 = 4$, $s(4) = 16(4)^2 = 256$.

Hence, the change in s is

$\Delta s = s(4 + \Delta t) - s(4) = (256 + 128\Delta t + 16[\Delta t]^2) - 256 = 128\Delta t + 16(\Delta t)^2$.

Note that by placing $\Delta t = 1$ in Example 2, the result of Example 1 is obtained as a special case. However, in Example 2, it is permissible to let Δt take on other values such as $\Delta t = \frac{1}{2}$, or $\Delta t = 1.25$ to determine the Δs corresponding to different values of t_2.

We now turn our attention to the problem of determining the change in s for an arbitrary starting point t_1 and an arbitrary end point $t_2 = t_1 + \Delta t$.

At

$t_2 = t_1 + \Delta t$, $s(t_1 + \Delta t) = 16(t_1 + \Delta t)^2 = 16t_1^2 + 32t_1 \ \Delta t + 16(\Delta t)^2$.

At t_1 $s(t_1) = 16t_1^2$

Hence, the change in s is

$s = s(t_1 + \Delta t) - s(t_1) = (16t_1^2 + 32t_1 \ \Delta t + 16[\Delta t]^2) - (16t_1^2)$
$= 32t_1 \ \Delta t + 16(\Delta t)^2$.

Given any two values t_1 and $t_2 = t_1 + \Delta t$ which lie in the domain of definition of the function s, it is possible to use the formula

$$\Delta s = 32t_1 \ \Delta t + 16(\Delta t)^2$$

to determine the change in s between t_1 and t_2.

Since Δs depends upon the function s and the values t_1 and $t_1 + \Delta t$, it would be permissible to write $\Delta(s, t_1, t_1 + \Delta t)$ to represent this change. It is customary, however, to write $\Delta s(t, \Delta t)$, or more simply, Δs.

We next restate the above ideas for a general function $f(x)$.

The function $f(x + \Delta x) - f(x)$ occurs so often in mathematics that a special symbol is used to represent it. The symbol is $\Delta f(x, \Delta x)$, or sometimes merely Δf. The notation $\Delta f(x, \Delta x)$ is used since, for a given function $f(x)$,

$$\Delta f(x, \Delta x) = f(x + \Delta x) - f(x)$$

is a function of both x and Δx. It represents the change in $f(x)$ between the values at x and $x + \Delta x$.

The reader should not try to "multiply out" the function $\Delta f(x, \Delta x)$, any more than he would any function of two variables. By *definition*

$$\Delta f = \Delta f(x, \Delta x) \equiv f(x + \Delta x) - f(x).$$

- **Example 3.** Using $f(t) = t^2 - 7t + 2$, find Δf. By definition,
$$\Delta f \equiv f(x + \Delta x) - f(x)$$
$$f(x + \Delta x) - f(x) = [(x + \Delta x)^2 - 7(x + \Delta x) + 2] - [x^2 - 7x + 2]$$
$$= 2x\,\Delta x + (\Delta x)^2 - 7\Delta x.$$

The definition of Δf states that Δf is the change in $f(t)$ as t changes from x to $x + \Delta x$.

- **Example 4.** If $f(t) = \dfrac{t}{t-3}$, determine $f(2)$, and $\Delta f(2, \Delta y)$.

Clearly, $f(2) = \dfrac{2}{2-3} = -2$. From the definition of $\Delta f(2, \Delta y)$,

$$\Delta f(2, \Delta y) \equiv f(2 + \Delta y) - f(2) = \frac{2 + \Delta y}{2 + \Delta y - 3} - \frac{2}{2-3}$$
$$= \frac{2 + \Delta y}{\Delta y - 1} + 2 = \frac{2 + \Delta y + 2\Delta y - 2}{\Delta y - 1} = \frac{3\Delta y}{\Delta y - 1}.$$

Before going further, show that if
$$g(z) = 3z^2 - 2z + 5, \quad \text{then} \quad \Delta g(5, \Delta x) = 28\Delta x + 3(\Delta x)^2.$$

- **Example 5.** If $f(x) = \dfrac{3}{x}$, find $\Delta f(x, \Delta x)$.

$$\Delta f(x, \Delta x) = \frac{3}{x + \Delta x} - \frac{3}{x} = \frac{3}{(x + \Delta x)} \cdot \frac{x}{x} - \frac{3}{x} \cdot \frac{(x + \Delta x)}{(x + \Delta x)}$$
$$= \frac{3x - 3x - 3\Delta x}{x(x + \Delta x)} = \frac{-3\Delta x}{x(x + \Delta x)}.$$

- **Example 6.** If $g(t) = \dfrac{5}{t^2}$, find $\dfrac{\Delta g(t, \Delta t)}{\Delta t}$.

$$\frac{\Delta g(t, \Delta t)}{\Delta t} = \frac{\dfrac{5}{(t + \Delta t)^2} - \dfrac{5}{t^2}}{\Delta t} = \frac{5}{(t + \Delta t)^2 \Delta t} - \frac{5}{(t)^2 \Delta t} = \cdots$$
$$= \frac{5t^2 - 5[t^2 + 2t\,\Delta t + (\Delta t)^2]}{(t + \Delta t)^2\, t^2\, \Delta t}$$
$$= \frac{-5(2t + \Delta t)\Delta t}{(t + \Delta t)^2\, t^2\, \Delta t} = \frac{-5(2t + \Delta t)}{(t + \Delta t)^2\, t^2} \quad \text{if} \quad \Delta t \neq 0.$$

The division of numerator and denominator by Δt in the last step is valid only if Δt is not zero. If Δt is zero, the entire problem is without meaning since division by zero is not defined. (See Problem 2, Set 1–4.)

Since $\Delta g(t, \Delta t)$ represents the change in the function $g(t)$ corresponding to a change Δt in t, it follows that $\dfrac{\Delta g(t, \Delta t)}{\Delta t}$ is the **average rate of change** of the function $g(t)$ over the interval Δt.

Locate Δx and $\Delta f = f(x_1 + \Delta x) - f(x_1)$ in Figure 1–6. Construct similar sketches using other curves.

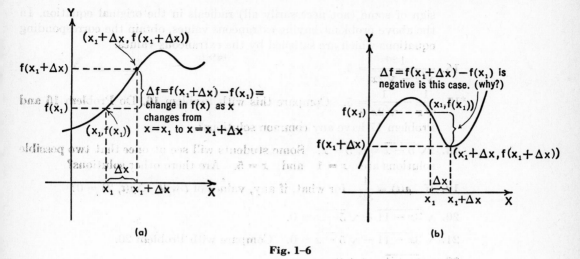

Fig. 1–6

PROBLEM SET 1–12

Solve the following equations:

1. $\sqrt{x-3} = x-5$.

2. $1 + \sqrt{3x+3} = \sqrt{6x+7}$.

3. $\sqrt{x-6} = \sqrt[3]{x-2}$.

[HINT: $x = 10$ is a root. Are there other roots?]

4. $\sqrt{3-2x} + 5 = 0$.

5. $\dfrac{x-7}{x-2} - \dfrac{3}{x} = \dfrac{3x+4}{x(x-2)}$.

6. $\dfrac{t}{t+2} - \dfrac{5}{(t-1)(t+2)} = \dfrac{1}{t^2+t-2}$.

7. $\sqrt{w+4} + w - 2 = 0$.

8. $\dfrac{3}{z+1} + \dfrac{4}{z-1} = \dfrac{5}{1-z}$.

9. $\sqrt[3]{2x^2-8} = 4$.

10. $3.5y^2 - 4.1y + 7.2 = 6.1$.

11. $4\sqrt{2x+3} + 5 = 0$.

12. $z^3 - 8 = 0$. Be sure you find all three solutions.

13. $\begin{cases} x + 2y = 12, \\ x^2 + y^2 = 29. \end{cases}$

14. Without solving, show that $\sqrt{3x^2+7} + 2 = 0$ has no roots.

15. It is not difficult to distinguish between extraneous values and values produced through arithmetical error. If the extraneous value is introduced by squaring, it will satisfy an equation obtained by changing the sign of some (not necessarily all) radicals in the original equation. In the above problems having extraneous values, obtain the corresponding equations which are satisfied by the extraneous values.

16. $\dfrac{1}{\sqrt{x} - \sqrt{2x}} = 5.$

*17. $\dfrac{1}{\sqrt{x}} - \dfrac{1}{\sqrt{2x}} = 5.$ Compare this with Problem 16. Do Problem 16 and Problem 17 have any common solutions?

18. $x\sqrt{5 - x} = \sqrt{5 - x}.$ Some students will see at once that two possible solutions are $x = 1$ and $x = 5.$ Are there other solutions?

19. If $g(t) = \dfrac{4}{3t^2}$ for what, if any, values of t will $\Delta g(t, 2) = 0$?

20. $\sqrt{3x - 11} + \sqrt{5 - x} = 0.$

21. $\sqrt{3x - 11} - \sqrt{5 - x} = 0.$ Compare with Problem 20.

22. $\sqrt{5z + 4} = 1 + 2z.$

23. (a) $\sqrt{3x + 4} - x = 0.$ (b) $\sqrt{3x + 4} + x = 0.$

24. $\sqrt{4z - 3} - \sqrt{8z + 1} = 2.$ **25.** $x - \sqrt{x} - 6 = 0.$

26. If $f(x) = \dfrac{3x}{2 - 5x^2},$ find $\Delta f(x, \Delta x).$ Compare Problem 8, Set 1–4.

27. If $f(x) = \dfrac{5x}{2 + x},$ find $\Delta f(2y, \Delta y)$ and $\Delta f(2t, \Delta t).$ Compare Problem 9, Set 1–4.

28. If $f(t) = 2/t,$ find $\Delta f(y, \Delta y)$ and $\Delta f(2t, \Delta t).$ Compare Problem 11, Set 1–4.

29. If $f(x) = \dfrac{7}{x^2},$ find $\dfrac{\Delta f(z, \Delta z)}{\Delta z}.$ Compare Problem 15, Set 1–4.

30. If $g(y) = \sqrt{y - 3},$ find $\dfrac{\Delta g(t, \Delta t)}{\Delta t},$ and rationalize the *numerator*.

*31. Draw a curve and locate Δx and $\Delta f(x, \Delta x)$ in a manner similar to that shown on page 35.

1–13. Self test. Many students can solve homework problems, but have trouble with examinations. The following self test has been prepared for *your* benefit to help you overcome this difficulty. It is suggested that you take the test in one sitting without referring to text or notes. Time yourself on the examination. You will find the solutions in the back of the text. Do *not* look there until you have completed the self test and recorded your time. After you have graded your self test you may wish to compare your score and time with that of other members of the class. You should rework some problems in the text that are similar to any you miss on the self test. Since the self test is designed for a purpose different from that of classroom tests, the reader should not expect any marked similarity between them.

SELF TEST

Record your starting time.

1. Simplify: $\dfrac{3x-1}{2x^2-7x+6} - \dfrac{2x+3}{2x^2-x-3}$.

2. Find $\dfrac{\Delta g(x, \Delta x)}{\Delta x}$ given $g(x) = \dfrac{6x}{3x+1}$.

3. Find the solution set of: $\sqrt{x-3} = 2 - \sqrt{2x-2}$.

4. Write a quadratic equation with integral coefficients having roots $\dfrac{1+\sqrt{3}}{2}$ and $\dfrac{1-\sqrt{3}}{2}$.

5. Prove that the absolute value of the difference of the two roots of

$$Ax^2 + Bx + C = 0 \quad \text{is} \quad \left| \dfrac{\sqrt{B^2-4AC}}{A} \right|.$$

6. For what values of k will the roots of $3x^2 + kx + 12 = 0$ be (a) real and equal? (b) imaginary?

7. $f(x) = \dfrac{3x-1}{2x}$. Find (a) $f(1/x)$, (b) $f(t+\Delta t) - f(t)$, (c) $f(1.2) - f(1)$.

8. Solve: $x^4 - 31x^2 + 150 = 0$.

9. Find A, B, C so that $\dfrac{-x+3}{x^3+x^2} \equiv \dfrac{A}{x} + \dfrac{B}{x^2} + \dfrac{C}{x+1}$ is an identity.

10. Express $4x^2 - 20x + 16$ as a difference of squares.

*11. (a) Without solving, find the sum and the product of the roots of $3x^2 - 2x - 2 = 0$.

(b) Solve $3x^2 - 2x - 2 = 0$, and check using (a).

12. Use the field postulates to justify a discussion of why the expression $\dfrac{x}{0}$ is without meaning in a field.

Record your time.

1–14. Supplementary material to present a wider point of view. In the belief that some readers will wish to have something which is both interesting and instructive to do while other students review, several chapters have been provided with a terminal section containing related enrichment material. We hope you enjoy this innovation, and will welcome comments and queries directly from interested students.

*1–15. The modulo 7 system. There are mathematical systems other than subsets of the complex numbers which are of considerable interest. The modulo 7 system is one. It makes use of some of the same symbols (numerals) that the integers do, but the elements (modulo 7 numbers) themselves are different since they behave differently. To remind the reader that this is a new system, a three-bar equal sign will be used. The modulo 7 system has only seven elements — namely, $\{0, 1, 2, 3, 4, 5, 6\}$.

If the system is to satisfy the field postulates given in Section 1–2, then it certainly must be closed; that is, the sum and the product of any two elements must be in the set $\{0, 1, 2, 3, 4, 5, 6\}$. A neat device enables us to redefine the meaning of addition and multiplication in such a manner as to guarantee closure. If the ordinary (integer) sum or product is one of the given elements, it is taken as the definition of the mod 7 sum or product; thus,

$$3 + 2 \equiv 5 \bmod 7, \quad \text{and} \quad 3 \cdot 2 \equiv 6 \bmod 7.$$

If, on the other hand, the integral sum or product is a number K larger than 6, then K is divided by seven, obtaining a quotient which is discarded and a remainder which is one of the elements of the set $\{0, 1, 2, 3, 4, 5, 6\}$. This remainder is used as the definition of the sum or product. Hence,

$$4 + 5 \equiv 2 \bmod 7 \quad \text{since in integers} \quad 4 + 5 = 9 = 1 \cdot 7 + 2$$
$$4 \cdot 3 \equiv 5 \bmod 7 \quad \text{since in integers} \quad 4 \cdot 3 = 12 = 1 \cdot 7 + 5$$
$$6 \cdot 5 \equiv 2 \bmod 7 \quad \text{since in integers} \quad 6 \cdot 5 = 30 = 4 \cdot 7 + 2$$

Since the only possible remainders upon division of an integer by 7 are 0, 1, 2, 3, 4, 5, 6, the procedure suggested does guarantee closure. The additive identity is 0 and the multiplicative identity is 1. The only other field postulate that does not follow from well-known properties of the integers (as a subset of the rational field) is postulate 6 which states that for each element x in the set there exists an element $(-x)$ in the set such that $x + (-x) = 0$ and if $x \neq 0$ an element $\left(\frac{1}{x}\right)$ must also exist in the set such that $x \cdot \left(\frac{1}{x}\right) = 1$. The reader can verify that the suggested correspondents have the desired properties.

x	$(-x)$	$\left(\frac{1}{x}\right)$
6	1	6
5	2 since $5 + 2 \equiv 0$	3 since $5 \cdot 3 \equiv 1 \bmod 7$
4	3	2
3	4	5
2	5	4
1	6	1
0	0	not required by postulates

Practice should continue until sums and products come easily in the mod 7 system. Briefly, $a \equiv b \pmod 7$ means $a = b + 7k$ for some integer k. (Why?)

There are no negative numbers in the mod 7 system. None are needed. The ordinary negative number -2 is the solution of the ordinary equation $x + 2 = 0$. In the mod 7 system, the number 5 is a solution of the equation $x + 2 \equiv 0 \pmod 7$, since $(5 + 2)$ has the remainder 0 when divided by 7.

In other words: 5, in the mod 7 system, plays a role similar to that of -2 in the ordinary system. In the mod 7 system, the number 6 plays a role similar to -1 in the ordinary numbers, since $6 + 1 \equiv 0$ (mod 7) and $-1 + 1 = 0$.

There are no fractions in the mod 7 system and none are needed. The ordinary fraction $\frac{5}{3}$ is the solution of the equation $3x = 5$. In the mod 7 system, the equation $3x \equiv 5$ (mod 7) has the solution $x \equiv 4$ (mod 7). (Try it and see.) The mod 7 equation $5x \equiv 2$ (mod 7) has $x \equiv 6$ (mod 7) as solution, while $4x \equiv 6$ (mod 7) has the solution $x \equiv 5$ (mod 7).

The equation $5x^3 + x^2 + 5x + 2 \equiv 0$ (mod 7) may be shown to have $x \equiv 3$ (mod 7) as a solution by direct substitution. (Try this.) Can you find two other solutions?

To reiterate, there are only seven numbers in the entire mod 7 system. There are no negative numbers and no fractions, yet equations can be solved. Best of all, since there are only seven numbers, *all* the solutions of a given equation can be found by merely substituting each of the seven numbers, in turn, for x in order to see which, if any, of them satisfy the equation.

The mod 7 system is a finite set of numbers, whereas the integers, rational numbers, and real numbers discussed in Section 1–7 are each infinite sets.

A word of warning: There exist equations, such as $x^2 \equiv 6$ (mod 7), that have no solution at all. This is not particularly surprising. The ordinary equation $x^2 = -1$ has no solution in the set of *real numbers*.

*1–16. Mod 12 system. The reader may wonder if there is anything unusual about the number 7 in the modulo 7 system. There is not. Not every modular system, however, is a field. We give an example here of a modular system which is *not* a field.

The modulo 12 system has exactly twelve elements $0, 1, 2, \ldots 10, 11$. The sum or product of two numbers in the modulo 12 system is defined to be the remainder when the corresponding integral sum or product is divided by 12. The ordinary 12-hour clock is a familiar example of a mod 12 system. If 7 hours is added to 9 o'clock, the result is 4 o'clock.

Thus $7 + 9 \equiv 4$ mod 12, $7 \cdot 5 \equiv 11$ mod 12, and $8 \cdot 6 \equiv 0$ mod 12. Field postulates 1, 2, 3, 4, 5, and 7, and part of 6 are satisfied, but it is *not* true that for each $x \neq 0$, there exists an element $\left(\dfrac{1}{x}\right)$ in the set such that $x \cdot \left(\dfrac{1}{x}\right) = 1$. For example, by trying all 12 possible values, we can show that $3 \cdot y = 1$ has no solution. Hence for $x = 3$, no modulo 12 element plays the role of $\left(\dfrac{1}{x}\right)$.

It is significant to note that in the modulo 12 system, the theorem of Section 1–2 does *not* hold (a product is zero if, and only if, at least one of the factors is zero).

Although neither 4 nor 6 is zero, $4 \cdot 6 \equiv 0$ mod 12. Finding a counter example to the theorem of Section 1–2 is fully as valid a method of showing that the modulo 12 system is not a field as showing that one of the postulates is violated. (Why?)

The reader should work out some problems in the mod 7 and the mod 12 system.

PROBLEM SET 1-16

1. Add: $4 + 3 + 6 + 5 + 2 + 4$ (mod 7).
2. Add: $1 + 2 + 3 + 4 + 5 + 6$ (mod 7).
3. Solve: $3x \equiv 5$ (mod 7).
4. Solve: $6x - 5 \equiv 3$ (mod 7).
5. Solve: $297x + 6 \equiv 0$ (mod 7).   Although 297 does *not* occur in the mod 7 system, $297x$ still has meaning, since $297x$ represents the sum of $\underbrace{x + x + \cdots + x}_{297 \text{ terms}}$. This problem emphasizes the need for distinguishing between the set from which the unknowns of the equation are taken and the set from which the coefficients of the equation are taken.
6. Solve: $x^2 \equiv 4$ (mod 7).
7. Solve: $x^2 \equiv 2$ (mod 7).
8. Solve: $x^2 \equiv 3$ (mod 7).
9. Solve: $x^3 \equiv 6$ (mod 7).
10. Solve: $x^3 \equiv 5$ (mod 7).
11. (a) Make a table listing the seven numbers in the mod 7 system. Next to each number x, place its square, x^2; cube, x^3; fourth power, x^4; fifth power, x^5; sixth power, x^6; seventh power, x^7; and eighth power, x^8; all mod 7.
    (b) Compute, using the table of part (a), the values $(5)^{236}$ (mod 7), and $(3)^{179}$ (mod 7).
    (c) Will $x^4 \equiv 5$ (mod 7) have a solution?
    (d) For what values of b will $x^5 \equiv b$ (mod 7) have solutions?
12. Solve: $4x^2 + 3x + 4 \equiv 0$ (mod 7).   Notice that in the mod 7 system the solutions are not complex.
13. Construct addition and multiplication tables for the mod 7 system.
14. If the symbol "$\equiv$" is to be an equals (or equivalence) relation in the mod 7 system, it must satisfy the following postulates:
    (1) *Reflexive:* $a \equiv a$ (mod 7).
    (2) *Symmetric:* If $a \equiv b$ (mod 7),   then $b \equiv a$ (mod 7).
    (3) *Transitive:* If $a \equiv b$ (mod 7)   and $b \equiv c$ (mod 7),   then $a \equiv c$ (mod 7).

Use the definition "$a \equiv b$ (mod 7) means $a = b + 7k$, for some integer k" to show that the mod 7 system does satisfy these requirements.

[HINT: Given: $a \equiv b$ (mod 7), to prove that $b \equiv a$ (mod 7). This means that, if one assumes that there exists a k, such that $a = b + 7k$, then one may deduce that $b = a + 7(-k)$, and hence that $b \equiv a$ (mod 7). (Why?)]

15. Show from the definition of $a \equiv b$ (mod 7) that, if $b \equiv 2$ (mod 7) and $c \equiv 5$ (mod 7), then $b + c \equiv 2 + 5 \equiv 0$ (mod 7), and that $b \times c \equiv 2 \times 5 \equiv 3$ (mod 7).

[HINT: Since $b = 2 + k \cdot 7$ and $c = 5 + j \cdot 7$, then $b + c = (2 + k7) + (5 + j7) = (2 + 5) + (k + j)7$. Also, $b \times c = (2 + k7) \times (5 + j7) = 2 \times 5 + (2j + 5k + 7jk)7$.]

16. The days of the week can be thought of as forming a mod 7 system in which the names of the days are replaced by integers mod 7. Starting with Sunday $\leftrightarrow 0$, Monday $\leftrightarrow 1, \cdots$, Saturday $\leftrightarrow 6$, solve the following problem. If Christmas, the 359th day of the year, falls on Sunday, on what day does July 4, the 185th day, fall? On what day does September 1, the 244th day, fall?

17. How many different congruences (equations) of the form $Ax \equiv B$ (mod 7) with $A \not\equiv 0$ are there?

18. Does the relation $\sim$ (is similar to) satisfy the reflexive, symmetric, and transitive postulates given in Problem 14, if the elements $(a, b, c, \cdots)$ are triangles?

[HINT: Replace "$\equiv$" by "$\sim$" and delete the phrase "(mod 7)," and see.]

19. Does the relation $\neq$ satisfy the three postulates of Problem 14, if the elements a, b, c are integers?

20. Which of the postulates of Problem 14 are satisfied if " $\equiv$ " is replaced by "$|$" (divides) and the phrase "(mod 7)" is deleted?

21. Find a relationship, other than those mentioned in the text, which satisfies the three postulates of Problem 14.

[HINT: "Is a brother or half brother of," "Is a descendant of," "Has the same parents as," "Is the same color (or age) as," "Has long blond hair like," and other similar relationships. Does it make a difference whether the relation is defined over the set of all people or merely the set of all men?]

22. to 34. Rework Problems 1 to 13 with mod 7 replaced by mod 12.

35. Divide: $5x^3 + 6x^2 + 3x + 2$ by $4x + 3$ in the mod 7 system until a constant remainder is obtained.

[HINT:

$$\frac{Qx^2 + \ ? + \ ? \ (\text{mod } 7)}{4x + 3 \ \overline{\smash{\big)}\ 5x^3 + 6x^2 + 3x + 2}}$$

where Q is the solution of the congruence $4Q \equiv 5$ mod 7.]

2
⋯⋯⋯⋯⋯⋯⋯⋯⋯⋯

2–1. Solution of inequalities. † Inequalities were introduced in Section 1–5. It is desirable to have a less intuitive definition of $a > b$ before attempting to prove the basic theorems.

Statement: If $a > b$, then $(a - b)$ is positive; ‡ if $(a - b)$ is positive, then $a > b$. A fundamental property of the real number system follows.

Property: Given any two real numbers a and b, one and only one of the following relations must hold:

$$\text{Either} \quad a = b$$
$$\text{or} \quad a > b$$
$$\text{or} \quad b > a$$

We are now ready to prove:

Theorem 1. If $a, b,$ and c are real numbers and $a > b$ then $a \pm c > b \pm c$. (An inequality remains an inequality of the same order if the same real number is added to (or subtracted from) both members.)

Given: $a > b$ that is   Given: $a - b$ is positive.
To prove: $a + c > b + c$ that is   To prove: $(a + c) - (b + c)$ is positive.
     and $a - c > b - c$ and $(a - c) - (b - c)$ is positive.

Proof: $(a + c) - (b + c) = a - b$ which is given positive.
         $(a - c) - (b - c) = a - b$ which is given positive.

Question: What field postulates have been used in the above two lines?

Since $5 > 2$, $5 + 3 > 2 + 3$ and $5 - 17 > 2 - 17$.

• **Illustration.** Similarly if $a < b$, then

$$a + 3 < b + 3 \quad \text{and} \quad a - 17 < b - 17.$$

† The terms **inequality** and **inequation** are synonymous.
‡ Of course, the "positive subset" must be defined first, but in the real number system the concept is already familiar. All that needs to be verified here is that "$a > b$ means $(a - b)$ is positive" is in full agreement with the interpretation of $a > b$ given in Section 1–5.

Theorem 2. If a, b, and c are real numbers and $a > b, c > 0$, then $ca > cb$. (An inequality remains an inequality of the same order if both members are multiplied by the same positive real number.)

The product $c(a - b) = ca - cb$ is a positive real number since $a > b$ and $c > 0$ imply that $(a - b)$ and c are both positive real numbers.

• **Illustration.** If $a > b$, then $7a > 7b$.
  Since $5 > 2$, $7 \cdot 5 > 7 \cdot 2$.

Theorem 3. If both members of an inequality are multiplied by the same *negative* real number, the order of the inequality is *reversed*. If $a > b$, then $- a < - b$, and $- ka < - kb$ if $- k < 0$.

This rule may be proved by noting that if $a > b$, then $a - b$ is positive. Hence, if $- k < 0$, then $(- k)a - (- k)b$ is *negative*. Therefore, $(- k)a < (- k)b$.

• **Illustration.** Since $4 < 9$, therefore, $(- 7)4 > (- 7)9$; i.e., $- 28 > - 63$. The latter statement may be written as

$$- 63 < - 28.$$

The subset of the real numbers which satisfies an inequality in one variable is called the **solution set** for that inequality. The solution set for $x > 5$ using the domain of definition $\{1, 2, 3, 4, 5, 6, 7, 8\}$ is the subset $\{6, 7, 8\}$.

Two inequalities are **equivalent** if and only if, they have the same solution set. The inequalities $x^2 \leq 4$ and $- 2 \leq x \leq 2$ are equivalent if the domain of definition is the integers. The solution set is $\{- 2, - 1, 0, 1, 2\}$. They are also equivalent if the domain of definition is the rational or even the real number system. (Why?)

An **unconditional inequality** has the universal set † for its solution set. The inequality $|x| > - 1$ is an unconditional inequality for the domain of all integers since its solution set is the set of all integers.

A **conditional inequality** has a subset of the universal set that is neither empty nor the entire universal set for its solution set. The inequalities used to illustrate the two preceding paragraphs are conditional inequalities.

---

† In other words, every admissible value of the unknown satisfies the inequality.

The universal set will be the real numbers except where specifically stated otherwise.

● **Example 1.** The inequalities $4<9$, $-2<1$, $4x+3<4x+7$ and $(x+1)^2 < x^2+2x+9$ are *un*conditional inequalities. The inequality $3x-4<2$ which is true only if $3x<6$, that is, if $x<2$, is a conditional inequality.

The solution of conditional inequalities plays an important role in mathematical analysis. Simple inequalities which do not involve squares or higher powers of the unknown are usually solved using the rules already discussed.

● **Example 2.** Solve the inequality $2x+7<4$. Adding -7 to each member yields

$$2x < -3.$$

Multiply each member by $\frac{1}{2}$ to obtain

$$x < -\tfrac{3}{2}.$$

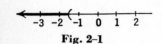

Fig. 2–1

In terms of a number axis, any x chosen from the heavily shaded portion (Fig. 2–1) will satisfy $2x+7<4$. The number $-\frac{3}{2}$ is **not** included.

● **Example 3.** What values of x satisfy the expression

$$-1 < 4x-3 \leqq 7?$$

The addition of 3 to each member, followed by multiplication by $\frac{1}{4}$, gives

$$2 < 4x \leqq 10$$
$$\tfrac{1}{2} < x \leqq \tfrac{5}{2}.$$

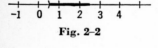

Fig. 2–2

Every value of x from the solution set shaded in Figure 2–2, including $\frac{5}{2}$ but not $\frac{1}{2}$, will satisfy the original expression.

● **Example 4.** What values of x satisfy the condition

$$\left| \frac{x-3}{2} \right| \leqq 4?$$

$$-4 \leqq \frac{x-3}{2} \leqq 4,$$
$$-8 \leqq x-3 \leqq 8,$$
$$-5 \leqq x \leqq 11.$$

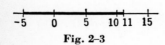

Fig. 2–3

Hence, every value of x between -5 and $+11$ including both $x=-5$ and $x=11$ satisfies the condition.

● **Example 5.** For what values of x is $|3-x|<4$? The given inequality is equivalent to $-4<3-x<4$, or

$-7 < -x < 1$. Since the coefficient of x is negative, multiply by -1, obtaining

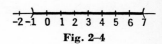

Fig. 2–4

$$+7 > x > -1 \quad \text{or} \quad -1 < x < 7.$$

● **Example 6.** For what values of t is $\,|\,t-3\,| > 1$? This is equivalent to two relationships: either

$$t - 3 > 1 \quad \text{or} \quad t - 3 < -1. \dagger$$

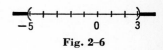

Fig. 2–5

Thus, $|\,t-3\,| > 1$ is satisfied if either $t > 4$ or if $t < 2$. The shaded portions of the axis (Fig. 2–5) indicate the t-intervals. The values $t = 2$ and $t = 4$ are excluded.

● **Example 7.** Solve $x^2 + 2x > 15$. The given inequality is equivalent to $(x + 5)(x - 3) > 0$.

A positive product $(x + 5)(x - 3)$ is obtained if, and only if, either

(1) $(x + 5)$ and $(x - 3)$ are both positive

or

(2) $(x + 5)$ and $(x - 3)$ are both negative.

The desired solution set must satisfy either

(1) both $(x + 5) > 0$ and $(x - 3) > 0$. [This implies $x > 3$. Why?]

or

(2) both $(x + 5) < 0$ and $(x - 3) < 0$. [This implies $x < -5$. Why?]

Therefore, combining these results, the solution set of $x^2 + 2x > 15$ consists of all real numbers x such that either $x < -5$ or $x > 3$.

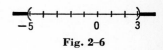

Fig. 2–6

● **Example 8.** Solve $(x + 5)(x - 3)(x - 7) \geqq 0$. Note that if $(x + 5)$ is negative, then both $(x + 3)$ and $(x - 7)$ also will be negative. Hence the product $(x + 5)(x + 3)(x - 7)$ is negative if $(x + 5)$ is negative. The solution set must either satisfy simultaneously:

(1) $x + 5 \geqq 0, x - 3 \geqq 0$ and $x - 7 \geqq 0$. [This implies $x \geqq 7$.]

or

(2) $x + 5 \geqq 0, 0 \geqq x - 3$ and $0 \geqq x - 7$. [This implies $3 \geqq x \geqq -5$.]

Hence the solution set consists of all real numbers x such that either $x \geqq 7$ or $3 \geqq x \geqq -5$.

† The reader should show that the given inequalities are *not* equivalent to $-1 < t - 3 < 1$ nor to $1 < t - 3 < -1$. There are no values of t which satisfy the latter, that is, its solution set is the empty set. (Why?)

PROBLEM SET 2-1

Determine values of the variable for which the following conditions hold. Shade each interval on a number axis.

1. $4x - 3 < 7$. **2.** $2x + 5 < 3$. **3.** $3x + 1 < 4$. **4.** $x - 1 > 11$.
5. $3 - 2x > 13$.   **6.** $3 - x < 7$.   **7.** $|x - 2| < 7$.
8. $|2x + 3| < 5$. **9.** $3 < x - 41 < 8$. **10.** $-1 < 3x + 2 < 9$.
11. $|x - 3| > 7$. **12.** $|2x + 1| > 5$.   **13.** $|3x| > -1$.
14. $|3x| < -1$.   **15.** $14x - 2 > 71$.
16. $3 - 4x > 7$.   **17.** $-2 < 13t + 2 < 100$.
18. $-7 < 4t + 2 < -1$.   **19.** $16 < 4t + 18$.
20. Show by shading on a number axis, the solution set satisfying each of the following inequalities. Which inequalities are equivalent?

     (a) $-4 < x < 4$.   (b) $|x| < 4$.   (c) $|x| > 4$.
     (d) Either $x > 4$ or $x < -4$.
     (e) Either $x < 4$ or $x > -4$.
     (f) Both $x < 4$ and $x > -4$.
     (g) $|x - 2| < 2$.   (h) $|x - 2| > 4$.

Find the real solution set and shade its locus on a number axis for each of the following sentences.

21. $(2x + 1)(x - 2) < 0$.   **22.** $(x + 3)(3x - 1) > 0$.
23. $(3x - 2)|x| \geq 0$.   **24.** $(2x + 3)|x| \leq 0$.
25. $x^2 - 3x \leq -2$.   **26.** $x^2 + 2x \geq 3$.
27. $(x - 1)x(x + 1) \leq 0$.   **28.** $(x - 1)(x - 2)(x - 3) \geq 0$.

2–2. Coordinate systems.† One way of describing the position of a point in a plane is to use two intersecting (not necessarily perpendicular) lines, called axes, as a frame of reference for the points. The point of intersection O of the reference lines is called the origin. It is usual to take one of the reference lines horizontal and to call it OX or the x-axis. The other line is called OY or the y-axis. The upward direction on a line not parallel to the x-axis is taken as positive, and the direction to the right along a horizontal (parallel to OX) line is considered positive. The four quadrants into which the axes divide the plane are numbered as indicated.

A point P may be coordinated with respect to the reference

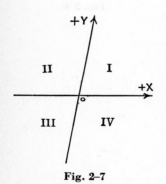

Fig. 2–7

† This reference system is known as the **Cartesian** coordinate system in honor of René Descartes ["day-cart"]. Descartes lived from 1596 to 1650, a contemporary of Shakespeare, Fermat, Galileo, and Milton. He helped introduce the coordinate system and with it the study of analytic geometry without which the calculus and hence modern physics and engineering would be almost impossible. An interesting account of Descartes' life is contained in Chapter 3 of E. T. Bell's *Men of Mathematics*.

frame by means of directed line segments through P parallel to each of the axes. In Figure 2–8, two axes are chosen with origin O and positive direction as indicated by the arrowheads. A unit of measure is chosen for each of the axes. The point P is located by directed line segments BP and AP parallel to the x- and y-axes. $BP = OA = x_1$ of the x-units, while $AP = OB = y_1$ of the y-units. The value x_1 is called the abscissa, and the value y_1 the ordinate of the point P. Together they are called coordinates of the point P and are indicated symbollically by the number pair (x_1, y_1). To each point P there corresponds just one number pair (x_1, y_1), and to each pair of real numbers there corresponds just one point P. Several points are located on the diagram. The reader should check his understanding by determining the numerical coordinates of each point. The point P_2 having coordinates (x_2, y_2) is often written with the notation $P_2(x_2, y_2)$. In a similar fashion $Q(3, -4)$ indicates that the point Q has x-coordinate 3 and y-coordinate -4.

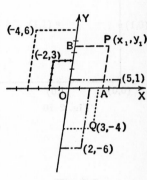

Fig. 2–8

All points having $x_1 = 0$ are on the y-axis. Furthermore, every point on the y-axis has $x_1 = 0$. For this reason $x = 0$ is called the equation of the y-axis. What corresponds to the equation $y = 0$?

All points for which $x_1 = 7$ are to be found on a line L parallel to the y-axis and $+7$ units in the x-direction to the right of the y-axis. Furthermore, every point on the line L has $x_1 = 7$. Consequently, $x = 7$ is called the equation of the line L. What corresponds to $x = -3$? To $y = 5$?

The point having coordinates $(-3, 5)$ is the point of intersection of the two lines $x = -3$, $y = 5$. The origin $(0, 0)$ is the intersection of the lines $x = 0$ and $y = 0$.

In many applied problems the axes are taken perpendicular.

* *Example 1.* Where are all points having $y > -3$? These points are the points **above** (but not on) a line parallel to the x-axis and three units below the x-axis.

* *Example 2.* Where are the points having $y = -5$? These points are the points of the line parallel to the x-axis and 5 units below the x-axis.

* *Example 3.* Where are the points having $x \neq 2$? These are all the points in the plane *except* those points on a line parallel to the y-axis and two units to the right of the y-axis.

The **graph** of an equation is the locus of all points whose coordinates satisfy the given equation, and only such points.

* *Example 4.* Graph $f(x) = 2x$ for $-2 \leq x \leq 3$, using axes which are perpendicular. See Figure 2–9.

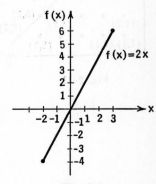

Fig. 2–9

A point in the Cartesian plane is denoted by the **ordered pair** of real numbers (x, y). If the domain of x is the set of numbers $\{0, 1\}$ and the domain of y is the set $\{0, 1, 2\}$, then the Cartesian set is the following set of six ordered pairs

$$\{(0, 0), (0, 1), (0, 2), (1, 0), (1, 1), (1, 2)\}.$$

In this case the graph of the Cartesian set consists of six points as shown in Figure 2–10.

If the domain of x and y is the set of all real numbers, then the graph of the Cartesian set of ordered number pairs (x, y) is the entire (Cartesian) plane.

A sentence involving two variables may be an equation or an inequality. The elements (x, y) that satisfy the conditions of the sentence will be called the **solution set,** and the graph of these elements is the graph of the **sentence.** A set of points is the **locus** of a given sentence if, and only if, every point of the set satisfies the sentence, and every point which satisfies the sentence is in the set. In other words, the locus of an equation or inequality is the set of points in the solution set of the equation or inequality.

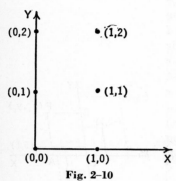

Fig. 2–10

● *Illustration.* Find and graph the solution set of the sentence $x + y \leq 7$ if the domains of both x and y are the set $\{1, 2, 3, 4, 5, 6\}$.

The solution set consists of the 21 points (x, y) having the graph indicated in Figure 2–11. Each one of the 6 points $(1, 6), (2, 5), (3, 4), (4, 3), (5, 2)$ and $(6, 1)$ satisfy the sentence $x + y = 7$. For example, $1 + 6 = 7$. The remaining 15 points $(1, 1), (2, 1), \cdots, (5, 1), \cdots, (1, 5)$ satisfy the sentence $x + y < 7$.

A sentence is called *unconditional* if every element of the universal set satisfies the conditions of the sentence. A sentence is *inconsistent* if no element of the universal set satisfies the conditions. An unconditional equation is called an *identity.*

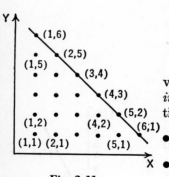

Fig. 2–11

● *Illustration.* $(x + y)^2 = x^2 + 2xy + y^2$ is an identity.

● *Illustration.* $x^2 + y^2 + 1 > 0$ is an unconditional inequality in the set of all ordered pairs (x, y) where the domain of x and y is the set of all real numbers. Is there a number system in which $x^2 + y^2 + 1 > 0$ is a conditional inequality?

[HINT: Does (i, i) satisfy $x^2 + y^2 + 1 > 0$?]

● *Illustration.* $2x = 3$ is inconsistent for x in the domain of integers, but is a conditional equation if the domain is the set of real numbers.

The following table may help the reader collate these ideas:

	Identity or Unconditional (All possible real numbers are in the solution set.)	Conditional (Some real numbers are in the solution set, some are not.)	Inconsistent (No real numbers are in the solution set.)
Equation	$x^2(x+2)=x^3+2x^2$	$3x = 4$	$x^2 + 1 = 0$
Inequality	$x^2 > -1$	$2x > 5$	$x^2 + |x+1| < 0$
Simultaneous system of two equations. The solution set will, of course, consist of pairs of real numbers (points) in this case.	$3x + 2y = 7$ $6x + 4y = 14$ All points on a line satisfy both equations.	$3x + 2y = 7$ $x - y = -1$ Only point $(1, 2)$ satisfies both equations.	$3x + 2y = 7$ $3x + 2y = 5$ No point satisfies both equations.

PROBLEM SET 2-2

Locate the following points by using a set of coordinate axes in which the angle XOY is approximately 60°. Name the quadrant in which each point lies.

1. $(3, 1)$, $(2, -5)$, $(-3, 2)$. **2.** $(3, 5)$, $(2, -1)$, $(-6, 3)$.
3. $(-1, -4)$, $(-5, 6)$, $(\pi, 2)$.
4. $(0, 1)$, $(0, 5)$, $(0, -17)$. What, if any, common property do points $(0, y_2)$ having x-coordinate zero have?
5. $(-2, 7)$, $(-2, 5)$, $(-2, -1)$, $(-2, 0)$, $(-2, -5)$. What can you state about the position of points having $x_1 = -2$?
6. $(-4, 5)$, $(-1, 5)$, $(0, 5)$, $(3, 5)$, $(7, 5)$. What can you state about the position of points having $y_1 = 5$?
7. Pretend you are working on the blackboard. Do not attempt to rule off coordinate lines, but draw two intersecting axes and mark a scale on each. Locate approximately each of the following points by eye and mark each point:
   $(3, 1)$, $(2, -5)$, $(-1, 3)$, $(-2, 4)$.

8. Same as 7 for   (1, 2),   (3, − 11),   (− 6, − 2),   (− 5, 1).

9. Locate the points $A(3, 1)$ and $B(7, 4)$ on a rectangular $(\angle XOY = 90°)$ coordinate system. (Such paper may be purchased from your bookstore.) Using another piece of paper as a measuring stick, determine the distance between the two points. Draw lines parallel to each coordinate axis in such a manner that line AB is the hypotenuse of a right triangle. How long are the legs of the triangle? From this how long would you expect the hypotenuse to be?

10. Same as 9 for $A(− 1, 2)$ and $B(7, 17)$.

11. Same as 9 for $A(4, − 1)$ and $B(9, 11)$.

On rectangular coordinate paper shade the regions represented by the following conditions:

12. $x < 3$.   **13.** $y + 4 < 0$.   **14.** $x \neq 8$.

15. $x < 3$ and at the same time $y < 5$.

16. $x > 2$ and at the same time $y > 7$.

17. $2 \leqq x < 7$.   **18.** $− 3 < y \leqq 15$.

19. $− 2 < x < 1$ and at the same time $− 5 < y < − 2$.

20. $x > 5$ and at the same time $x \neq 7$.

21. $x \neq 3$, $y + 4 < 0$.   **22.** $1 < x < 3$, $2 < y < 3$.

23. $x − 5 \neq 0$ and at the same time $x \neq − 3$.

24. $(x − 5)(x + 3) \neq 0$.   Compare with Problem 23.

25. $0 < x − 5 \leqq 3$.   **26.** $x + 3 + 4x \neq 7$.

27. $\sqrt{x + 1} < 3$,   and $\sqrt{x + 1}$ real.   **28.** $|x − 5| < 2$.

29. First-class mail costs 4¢ per ounce or fraction thereof. Make a graph showing the cost of first-class mail as a function of weight.

30. Graph $f(x) = \begin{cases} 3 & \text{for} \quad x > 7 \\ 2x & \text{for} \quad x < 7 \\ − 10 & \text{for} \quad x = 7. \end{cases}$

31. Graph $y = \begin{cases} 3x + 1 & \text{if} \quad x < 1 \\ 4 & \text{if} \quad 1 < x < 5 \\ 10 & \text{if} \quad x > 5 \\ 10 & \text{if} \quad x = 1 \\ 7 & \text{if} \quad x = 5. \end{cases}$

32. Make out a chart like that on page 49 and fill it in giving different examples.

33. Show that $x^2 + x(x − 1) = x^2$ is an identity for x in the domain $\{0, 1\}$.   Is it an identity for x in the domain of all real numbers?

34. Two coins are tossed. Represent head by 1 and tail by 0. (a) Graph (x, y) where x and y are in the domain $\{0, 1\}$. (b) What portion of the points correspond to (a) exactly 0 head, (b) exactly 1 head, (c) exactly 2 heads?

35. Two dice are tossed. What may be used for the domain of x and y? (a) Graph (x, y). (b) The point score on the two dice is the sum $S = x + y$ of the spots on the two faces that are up. Graph $x + y = 3$. (c) What portion of the points has $S=2$, $S=3$, $S=4$, $S=5$, $S=6$, $S=7$, $S=8$, $S=9$, $S=10$, $S=11$, $S=12$? (d) Find the set of all points having 2 for one of the coordinates and determine the portion of these having $S \geq 5$.

*36. Three coins are tossed. Represent head by 1 and tail by 0. (a) What may be used for the domain of x, y, z? Graph (x, y, z). (b) What portion of the points correspond to exactly two heads?

2–3. The distance between two points. In the preceding section no restriction was made on the size of the angle XOY. We shall now take the two axes perpendicular, and the same unit of length on each axis. If the axes are perpendicular, the distance between two points can be determined by constructing right triangles similar to those of Problems 9, 10, and 11 of the last section. However, it is convenient to solve this problem in general and obtain a formula much as we did in finding the general solution of the quadratic equation. Consider the case where the two points $B(x_2, y_2)$ and $A(x_1, y_1)$ lie in the first and second quadrants respectively.

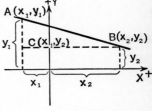

Fig. 2–12

Proceeding as in Problem 9 of the last section, we construct lines through $A(x_1, y_1)$ and $B(x_2, y_2)$ parallel to the axes so that AB is the hypotenuse of a right triangle ACB. The coordinates of C are (x_1, y_2). (Why?) The length of CA is $y_1 - y_2$ (Why?) and the length of CB is $x_2 - x_1$. (Why is $(x_1 + x_2)$ not the length of CB?) Since ACB is a right triangle, the theorem of Pythagoras gives:

$$d^2 = (CB)^2 + (CA)^2 = (x_2 - x_1)^2 + (y_1 - y_2)^2,$$

where d is the distance from $A(x_1, y_1)$ to $B(x_2, y_2)$. Then

$$d = \pm \sqrt{(x_2 - x_1)^2 + (y_2 - y_1)^2}$$

since $(y_2 - y_1)^2 = (y_1 - y_2)^2$. In speaking of the distance *from* one point *to* another, we shall select the sign as indicated in the preceding section. (In Fig. 2–12 the minus sign would be used for the directed distance AB.) Frequently one is interested in the numerical or absolute value of the distance that is spoken of as the distance *between* the two points. The formula

$$|d| = \sqrt{(x_2 - x_1)^2 + (y_2 - y_1)^2}$$

also holds when A and B are permitted to lie in other quadrants. You will be asked to show this for another choice of quadrants. Actually the formula is valid for every possible choice of A and B.

● **Example 1.** Find the distance between $(-3, 4)$ and $(2, -8)$.
$$d = \sqrt{(-3 - 2)^2 + (4 - [-8])^2} = \sqrt{25 + 144} = \sqrt{169} = 13.$$

● **Example 2.** Give an algebraic condition on (x_1, y_1) such that the distance between (x_1, y_1) and $(5, -3)$ is less than 8. Clearly, these points lie inside (but not on) a circle of radius 8 with center at $(5, -3)$. To obtain an algebraic condition let the point be (x_1, y_1). Then if and only if
$$\sqrt{(5 - x_1)^2 + (-3 - y_1)^2} < 8 \quad \text{will there be less than 8 units}$$
between (x_1, y_1) and $(5, -3)$.

PROBLEM SET 2-3

1. Show that the distance formula holds if A is taken in quadrant II and B in quadrant III.

   In Problems 2 to 10 find the distance between the given points. In each problem begin by making a quick sketch (see Problem 7, Set 2–2) showing the points and the distance found. Before using the formula to determine the distance in Problems 2 to 5, write down an estimate of the distance. This ability to estimate the answer in various problems is often the difference between an experienced engineer or scientist and a new graduate. If you always attempt to estimate the answer to a problem before working it, you too will develop this valuable skill. It takes practice.

2. $(2, -1)$, $(13, -7)$.   3. $(3, 5)$, $(2, -1)$.
4. $(-3, 4)$, $(7, 2)$.   5. $(-4, -1)$, $(-1, -4)$.
6. (h, k), $(3, 1)$.   7. $(3, r)$, $(-1, s)$.
8. $(0, 0)$, (a, b).   9. $(0, 7)$, $(5, 13)$.
10. $(17, -5r)$, $(12, 2r)$.
11. How far is the point $(3, -9)$ from the origin?
12. How far is the point $(2, 7)$ from the origin?
13. What are the lengths of the sides of a triangle with vertices $(2, 1)$, $(3, 5)$, $(4, 6)$?
14. Same as Problem 13 for $(6, 4)$, $(2, 2)$, $(-1, -5)$.
15. Same as Problem 13 for $(-1, 3)$, $(2, 6)$, $(0, -3)$.
16. Show that $(15, 4)$, $(-7, 8)$, and $(-1, -4)$ are vertices of a right triangle.

   [HINT: The converse of the theorem of Pythagoras states that a triangle is a right triangle if the sum of the squares of the lengths of the two shorter sides equals the square of the length of the longest side.]

17. Same as Problem 16 for the points   (1, 4),   (2, 1),   (3, 2).
18. Show that if three points A, B, and C have coordinates $A(0, 0)$, $B(9, -2)$ and $C(2, 4)$,   then $\angle BAC = \angle BCA$.

[HINT: Show the triangle is isosceles.]

19. Same as Problem 18 for $A(2, 1)$, $B(7, 4)$, $C(2, 7)$.
20. Show that the three points $(-2, 1)$, $(3, 11)$, $(-5, -5)$ are collinear (lie on a straight line).
21. In Problem 6 you found the distance between the point (h, k) and the point $(3, 1)$.   Set this distance equal to 2.   Make a sketch showing several possible positions of the point (h, k) so that its distance from the point $(3, 1)$ is equal to 2. Where do all such points (h, k) lie? Will there be any points (h, k) satisfying the conditions in quadrant IV? In quadrant II? In quadrant III?
22. If $A(-1, 5)$, $B(-1, -2)$,   and $C(6, -2)$ are the vertices of a triangle, show that $\angle BAC = \angle BCA$. Sketch the figure.
23. Same as Problem 22 for $A(0, 1)$, $B(3, 7)$, $C(3 + 2\sqrt{5}, 2)$.
24. Make a sketch showing the possible locations of points (a, b) such that $(a - 1)^2 + (b + 3)^2 = 4$.
25. Make a sketch showing the possible locations of points (r, s) such that $(1 + r)^2 + (4 + s)^2 = 9$.

Show in a sketch where the points (x, y) must lie to satisfy the following conditions:

26. $(1 + x)^2 + (4 + y)^2 \leq 9$.   27. $(x - 1)^2 + (y - 5)^2 > 4$.
28. $(x - 2)^2 < 4$.
29. The condition $y > 4$ and at the same time
$$(x - 3)^2 + y^2 < 25.$$

30. $x^2 + y^2 < 9$ and at the same time $(y - 2)^2 + (x + 1)^2 < 1$.
31. Write an algebraic condition such that (x, y) lies inside a circle of radius 5 with center $(3, -2)$.
32. Write an algebraic condition such that (x, y) lies in the ring determined by concentric circles with radii 2 and 7 and center $(-1, 2)$.
33. Suppose that a nonaquatic community sprang up at the edge of a river bend as in Figure 2–13. In order to get from a point x units east of the bend to a point y units north of the bend, the natives always went around the corner. What sort of distance formula might arise in such an environment?

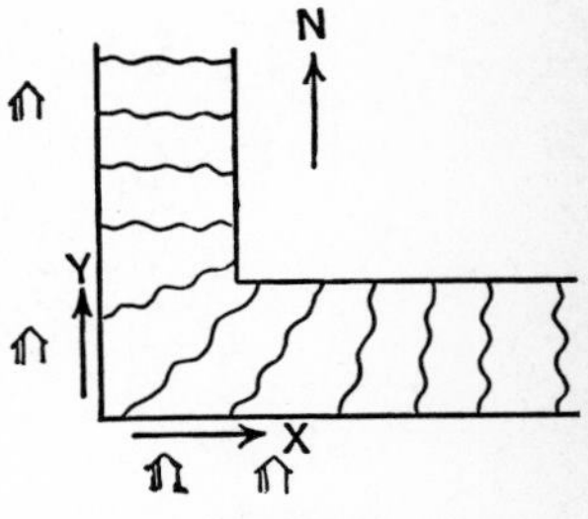

Fig. 2–13

2–4. Equations, inequalities, and loci.† We already know there is a correspondence between pairs of real numbers (a, b)

† Loci is the plural of locus.

and the points of a plane. A correspondence may also be established between certain geometrical figures and some equations in x and y. In the two preceding sections a number of examples and problems have been given to illustrate such correspondences. In general, not all points will satisfy a given equation. For example, the point $(3, 4)$ will satisfy the equation

$$x^2 - 2y + x - 4 = 0,$$

but the points $(4, 3)$ and $(-3, 4)$ will not. Verify each of these statements. The points whose coordinates do satisfy a given equation will form a geometric figure. This figure is called the **locus** of the equation. Actually the equation and the figure are so intimately linked that the usual practice is to refer to both the figure and the equation by the geometric name of the figure. The above remarks also apply to inequalities. For example, $(1, -2)$ satisfies the inequality $x^2 + y^2 < 9$ but $(-3, -4)$ does not. Hence the point $(1, -2)$ lies in the region which is the locus of $x^2 + y^2 < 9$, but the point $(-3, -4)$ does not.

The locus of an equation (or inequality) may be defined as the totality of all points whose coordinates satisfy the equation (or inequality), and only those points. This is a two-edged statement. It implies:

1. The coordinates of every point on the locus satisfy the equation (or inequality).

2. Every point whose coordinates satisfy the equation (or inequality) lies on the locus.

It may be advisable to reread the above paragraph before continuing, since the locus concept is fundamental not only for the immediate work of this chapter, but also for much of the remaining mathematical analysis.

● *Example 1.* Show that the locus of the equation

$$(x - 3)^2 + (y - 1)^2 = 4$$

is a circle † with the center $(3, 1)$ and radius 2. Let d be the distance between the point $(3, 1)$ and the point (x, y). Then, by the distance formula,

$$d = \sqrt{(x - 3)^2 + (y - 1)^2}.$$

Squaring yields

$$d^2 = (x - 3)^2 + (y - 1)^2.$$

† Here, **circle** refers to the points of the circumference — that is, to the solution set of the equation. The interior of the circle is denoted by $(x - 3)^2 + (y - 1)^2 < 4$; that is, the solution set of the inequality.

Therefore, if (x, y) is any point on the circle, then $d^2 = 4$ and the given equation is satisfied. (Does this fulfill requirement 1 or 2 of the preceding paragraph?) Furthermore, if (x_1, y_1) is a point whose coordinates satisfy the equation, we have $(x_1 - 3)^2 + (y_1 - 1)^2 = 4$, so $d^2 = 4$ and $d = 2$. Hence, the point (x_1, y_1) lies on the circle. (Which requirement does this fulfill?) Please rework Problem 21 of Set 2–3 at this point and note the relation to this example.

What is the locus of points (x, y) such that

$(x - 3)^2 + (y - 1)^2 \leqq 4$? Such that $(x - 3)^2 + (y - 1)^2 > 4$?

● *Example 2.* Obtain the equation of the perpendicular bisector of the line segment joining $(-1, 3)$ and $(2, 5)$. Make a sketch, and recall from geometry that a point is on the perpendicular bisector of a line segment if and only if it is equally distant from the endpoints of the segment. (Can you still prove this theorem? Try it. Remember that "if and only if" requires *two* proofs.)

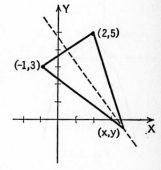

Fig. 2–14

Let d_1 be the distance between $(-1, 3)$ and (x, y) while d_2 is the distance between $(2, 5)$ and (x, y) if (x, y) is a point on the desired locus (the perpendicular bisector). Then

$$d_1 = \sqrt{(x + 1)^2 + (y - 3)^2} \quad \text{while} \quad d_2 = \sqrt{(x - 2)^2 + (y - 5)^2}.$$

Since, by geometry, $d_1 = d_2$, $(d_1)^2 = (d_2)^2$ or

(1) $$(x + 1)^2 + (y - 3)^2 = (x - 2)^2 + (y - 5)^2,$$

which simplifies to

(2) $$6x + 4y - 19 = 0.$$

(Do not believe everything that appears in print; simplify it. Putting in these missing steps is an important part of *reading* a mathematics text. Reading scientific material requires a somewhat different technique from reading literature. This is where the student can expect to learn this technique if he has not already done so. Always read with pencil and paper at hand, and supply *all* missing steps.)

Every point on the desired locus satisfies the equation (2). Furthermore, every point (a, b) which satisfies equation (2), or equation (1) since they are equivalent equations,† must have $d_1 = d_2$, and hence the point lies on the perpendicular bisector. Since both requirements are fulfilled, the desired locus is $6x + 4y - 19 = 0$.

† Equivalent equations have the same solution set.

- **Example 3.** Determine the locus of the equation $x = -2$. Every point having x-coordinate -2 is on the locus, and every point on the locus has x-coordinate -2. The locus is a straight line parallel to the y-axis and 2 units to the left of it. Please rework Problem 5 of Set 2–2 before continuing.

- **Example 4.** Sketch the locus of the equation

$$x^2 - 2x + y - 2 = 0.$$

Obtaining y as a function of x, $y = -x^2 + 2x + 2$.
Substituting various values for x, we obtain corresponding values for y. For example, if $x = 3$, $y = -(3)^2 + 2(3) + 2 = -1$. The point $(3, -1)$ therefore lies on the locus. We construct a table by giving values to x and computing the corresponding values of y.

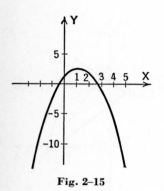

Fig. 2–15

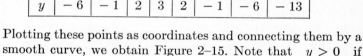

x	-2	-1	0	1	2	3	4	5
y	-6	-1	2	3	2	-1	-6	-13

Plotting these points as coordinates and connecting them by a smooth curve, we obtain Figure 2–15. Note that $y > 0$ if $-x^2 + 2x + 2 > 0$. This happens if $3 > x^2 - 2x + 1 = (x - 1)^2$. That is, if
$$-\sqrt{3} < x - 1 < \sqrt{3},$$
or $1 - \sqrt{3} < x < 1 + \sqrt{3}$,
or approximately
$$-.7 < x < 2.7.$$

Also, $y < 0$ if $-x^2 + 2x + 2 < 0$, or $3 < (x - 1)^2$.

That is, if either $x - 1 < -\sqrt{3}$, or $x - 1 > \sqrt{3}$, which is equivalent to either $x < 1 - \sqrt{3}$, or $x > 1 + \sqrt{3}$, or approximately either $x < -.7$, or $x > 2.7$.

The reader should realize that this sketch does *not* contain the entire locus, since very large values can be given to x and the corresponding y determined. He will note that we have not verified that every part of the sketch is actually part of the locus. Only eight points have been checked. Later more will be learned about this important and interesting locus. It is closely related to the path of a projectile after it is fired, or of a baseball after it is hit. The curve of water from a garden hose or a waterfall is also closely related to this locus, and one of the strongest possible bracings for a bridge follows the outline of the curve. The curve is called a parabola and will be studied in Chapters 4 and 21.

PROBLEM SET 2-4

Find the equation of and sketch each of the following loci unless otherwise instructed.

1. A circle with radius 3 and center $(-1, 2)$.
2. A circle with radius 5 and center $(4, 3)$.
3. A circle with radius 8 and center $(-3, -7)$.
4. A circle with radius 1 and center $(0, 0)$. This circle is known as a **unit** circle.
5. A circle with radius 2 and center (h, k).
6. A circle with radius r and center (h, k).
7. The perpendicular bisector of the line segment joining $(3, -1)$ and $(5, 7)$.
8. The perpendicular bisector of the line segment joining $(2, 6)$ and $(3, 5)$.
9. In Example 2 where are all points such that $d_2 > d_1$? Is this equivalent to $6x + 4y - 19 > 0$?
10. The perpendicular bisector of the segment joining $(0, 0)$ and (x_1, y_1).
11. The locus of points equidistant from the points $(2, 3)$ and $(1, 7)$.
12. The locus of points equidistant from $(0, 3)$ and $(2, -5)$.
13. A straight line parallel to the y-axis and 5 units to the right of it.
14. A straight line parallel to the y-axis and passing through the point $(5, -11)$.
15. Shade the locus of all points such that

$$(x - 1)^2 + (y + 2)^2 \leqq 9.$$

16. Shade the locus of all points such that

$$(x - 1)^2 + (y + 2)^2 < 9.$$

17. A line parallel to the x-axis and two units above it.
18. A line parallel to the x-axis and passing through $(4, -2)$.
19. A line through the origin bisecting the first quadrant into symmetric regions.
20. Determine equations of three different lines each of which passes through the point $(2, -6)$.
21. The x-axis.　　　　22. The y-axis.
*23. The locus of a point which is always as far from the x-axis as from the point $(1, 3)$.
*24. Same as Problem 23 but using the point $(-2, 5)$.
*25. Find the coordinates of all points which lie on both the locus of Problem 7 and the locus of Problem 8. Using your knowl-

edge of plane geometry, how many such points would you expect to find?

Identify the locus of each of the following equations or inequalities. Sketch the locus.

26. $(x - 4)^2 + (y + 1)^2 = 0.$ **27.** $(x - 4)^2 + (y + 1)^2 < 9.$

28. Discuss $(x - 4)^2 + (y + 1)^2 < 0.$ **29.** $x = 7.$

30. $y + 2 = 0.$ **31.** $x + 4 = 0.$ **32.** $2y - 5 = 0.$ **33.** $3x = \pi.$

Sketch each of the following loci:

34. $y - 2x + 3 = 0.$ **35.** $x^2 + y^2 - 25 = 0.$

36. $x^2 + y^2 - 25 = 0, \quad y \geq 0.$ **37.** $x^2 + (y + 9)^2 + 1 < 5.$

38. $x^2 - 6x - y + 3 = 0.$ For what x-range is $y < 0$? $y = 0$? $y > 0$?

*39. $x + 2y^2 - 3y = 0.$ For what y-range is $x > 0$? $x = 0$? $x < 0$?

*40. $y < x^2 - 2x + 1.$

The topics introduced in Problems 41 to 45 will be studied later but some students may enjoy undertaking their study as research problems now.

*41. Find the equation for and sketch the locus of a point (x, y) if the triangle having vertices (x_1, y_1), (x, y),   and (x, y_1) is similar to the triangle having vertices (x_1, y_1), (x_2, y_2), and (x_2, y_1).   What is the geometric description of the locus?

*42 Apply Problem 41 to write the equation of the line through:

(a) $(2, 3)$ and $(5, 7)$.

(b) (x_1, y_1) and $(x_1 + 1, y_1 + mx_1)$.

(c) $(0, b)$ and $(1, b + m)$.

(d) $(a, 0)$ and $(0, b)$.

*43 (a) Find a simplified equation for and sketch the locus of points (x, y) such that the distance of (x, y) from $(3, 0)$ is equal to the distance of (x, y) from the line $x = -3.$ (b) Replace $(3, 0)$ by $\left(\dfrac{P}{2}, 0\right)$ and $x = -3$ by $x = -\dfrac{P}{2}$ and solve the problem corresponding to (a).

(c) Find a geometric method for constructing such loci. These loci are called **parabolas.**

*44. Sketch the locus of points (x, y) such that $x^2 > 4y.$

*45. (a) Find a simplified equation for and sketch the locus of points (x, y) such that the sum of the distances of (x, y) from $(-3, 0)$ and $(3, 0)$ is 10. (b) Replace $(\pm 3, 0)$ by $(\pm c, 0)$ and 10 by $2a$ and solve the problem corresponding to (a). (c) Find a geometric method for constructing such loci. These loci are called **ellipses.**

2–5. Solution of inequalities of higher degree. Inequalities in which the variable is not of first degree may be solved by algebraic methods. However, graphical methods often are easier and quicker. The idea used is that $f(x) > 0$ wherever the graph of $y = f(x)$ is above the x-axis, and $f(x) < 0$ wherever the graph of $y = f(x)$ is below the x-axis. (Where does $f(x) = 0$?)

This section will be easier if sketches are made showing where functions $y = f(x)$, such as $y = (x + 10)(x + 5)^2(x - 3)$, are positive, zero, or negative. It will not be necessary to make accurate graphs for this purpose. We need to know for what x-values y will be (a) positive, (b) zero, or (c) negative. We begin by noting that each value of x determines one value of y. If $x = -10, -5$, or 3, then $y = (x + 10)(x + 5)^2(x - 3)$ has the value zero. Furthermore, if x has any other value, $y \neq 0$. (Why?) We plot these three x-intercepts on a set of coordinate axes. Now, let us check to see if $y > 0$ or $y < 0$ in each of the regions.

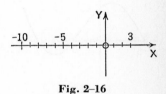

Fig. 2–16

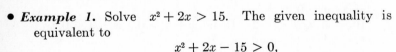

x	$x < -10$	$-10 < x < -5$	$-5 < x < 3$	$3 < x$
y	$(-)(-)^2(-) = +$	$(+)(-)^2(-) = -$	$(+)(+)^2(-) = -$	$(+)(+)^2(+) = +$

To summarize:

(a) $y > 0$ when $x < -10$ or $x > 3$,
(b) $y = 0$ when $x = -10, -5$, or 3,
(c) $y < 0$ when $-10 < x < -5$ or $-5 < x < 3$.

We note that both Figure 2–17 and the equation agree that the y-intercept is negative.

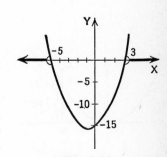

• *Example 1.* Solve $x^2 + 2x > 15$. The given inequality is equivalent to

$$x^2 + 2x - 15 > 0,$$

or

$$(x + 5)(x - 3) > 0.$$

The function $y = (x + 5)(x - 3)$ crosses the x-axis at $x = -5$ and $x = 3$.
If $x < -5$, then $x + 5 < 0$, $x - 3 < 0$, and $y > 0$.
If $-5 < x < 3$, then $x + 5 > 0$, $x - 3 < 0$, and $y < 0$.
If $x > 3$, then $x + 5 > 0$, $x - 3 > 0$, and $y > 0$.
Note that y can change sign only as the locus passes through the x-axis. A rough sketch appears in Figure 2–18. Since we are only interested in whether y is positive or negative for a given value of x, no finer details need be shown.

Fig. 2–17

Fig. 2–18

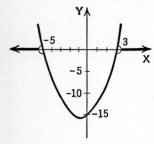

Fig. 2–18

We see from this graph, or the argument given in the preceding paragraph, that y is negative if $-5 < x < 3$. If $x < -5$ or if $x > 3$, then y is positive.

The original inequality is satisfied by values of x for which y is positive — that is, for either $x < -5$ or $x > 3$.

● **Example 2.** Solve $(x - 3)(x + 5)(x - 7) \geq 0$.

The graph of $y = (x - 3)(x + 5)(x - 7)$ has x-intercepts of 3, -5, and 7 and the y-intercept is positive. The reader can construct the rough sketch indicated in Figure 2–19 by checking a value of x in each of the intervals $x < -5$; $-5 < x < 3$; $3 < x < 7$; and $x > 7$ to see if the corresponding y value is positive or negative.

If $x < -5$, then $x + 5 < 0$, $x - 3 < 0$, $x - 7 < 0$, and $y < 0$.

If $-5 < x < 3$, then $x + 5 > 0$, $x - 3 < 0$, $x - 7 < 0$, and $y > 0$.

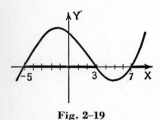

Fig. 2–19

If $3 < x < 7$, then $x + 5 > 0$, $x - 3 > 0$, $x - 7 < 0$, and $y < 0$.

If $x > 7$, then $x + 5 > 0$, $x - 3 > 0$, $x - 7 > 0$, and $y > 0$.

Thus, $y \geq 0$ and $(x - 3)(x + 5)(x - 7) \geq 0$ if either

$$-5 \leq x \leq 3 \quad \text{or} \quad x \geq 7.$$

● **Example 3.** Solve $(x - 1)^2(x + 2)(x + 5) \leq 0$. The graph of $y = (x - 1)^2(x + 2)(x + 5)$ has x-intercepts -5, -2, and 1, and a positive y-intercept. The reader should construct a rough sketch as indicated in Figure 2–20. Check to see if y is positive or negative between x-intercepts.

If $x < -5$, then $x + 5 < 0$, $x + 2 < 0$, $(x - 1)^2 > 0$, and $y > 0$.

If $-5 < x < -2$, then $x + 5 > 0$, $x + 2 < 0$, $(x - 1)^2 > 0$, and $y < 0$.

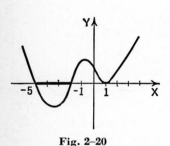

Fig. 2–20

If $-2 < x < 1$, then $x + 5 > 0$, $x + 2 > 0$, $(x - 1)^2 > 0$, and $y > 0$.

If $x > 1$, then $x + 5 > 0$, $x + 2 > 0$, $(x - 1)^2 > 0$, and $y > 0$.

Hence, $y \leq 0$ if either $-5 \leq x \leq -2$ or $x = 1$.

● **Example 4.** Find the solution set for the simultaneous inequalities $y > x^2$ and $x + y \leq 6$.

The locus of $y = x^2$ is the parabola shown in Figure 2–21. $OM = x$, $MP = y = x^2$, $MA > x^2$. Any point A above the parabola has coordinates (x, y) satisfying $y > x^2$. (Verify: For a point on or below the parabola this inequality does not hold.)

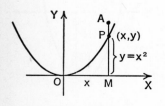

Fig. 2–21

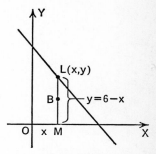

The locus of $x + y = 6$ is the line shown in Figure 2–22. $OM = x$, $ML = y = 6 - x$, $MB < 6 - x$, $x + MB < 6$. Any point L on the line $x + y = 6$ has coordinates satisfying $x + y = 6$ and any point B below the line $x + y = 6$ has coordinates satisfying $x + y < 6$. (What relation holds for points above $x + y = 6$?) Now examine Figure 2–23.

The two relations $y > x^2$ and $x + y \leq 6$ hold simultaneously for the coordinates of points inside the region OIJ bounded by the line $x + y = 6$ and the parabola $y = x^2$ and also along the segment IJ of the line $x + y = 6$. The points $I(2, 4)$ and $J(-3, 9)$ are excluded since $y > x^2$.

Fig. 2–22

● **Example 5.** Find the maximum value of $(x + y)$ if the three relations (1) $x - 2y \leq 2$, (2) $7x + 3y \leq 21$, (3) $4x - 3y \geq -12$ are all satisfied simultaneously by x and y.

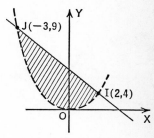

Points on or above line CA have coordinates satisfying (1). Points on or below line AB have coordinates satisfying (2). Points on or below BC have coordinates satisfying (3). The solution set of (1), (2), and (3) is the set of points inside and on the boundary of triangle ABC. Our problem is to determine the maximum value $(x + y)$ can have when (x, y) is a point inside of or on the boundary of triangle ABC (Fig. 2–24).

Fig. 2–23

To maximize $x + y$ we restrict our attention to the points inside and on the boundary of polygon $OIABJ$, since otherwise one of the terms of $(x + y)$ is negative and not a maximum. Along the line (2) $x = 3 - \frac{3}{7}y$ and $x + y = 3 + \frac{4}{7}y$ has its largest value $(\frac{65}{11})$ at B where y is largest $(\frac{56}{11})$. Similarly on any line $7x + 3y = K$ which is parallel to $7x + 3y = 21$ we find that $x + y = \frac{1}{7}K + \frac{4}{7}y$ has its largest value at the point of intersection of $7x + 3y = K$ with $4x - 3y = -12$. Verify that the values of K and y increase when moving from C to B along CB. The maximum value of $x + y = \frac{9}{11} + \frac{56}{11} = \frac{65}{11}$ occurs at point $B(\frac{9}{11}, \frac{56}{11})$. This is a simple example of linear programming, a subject of great importance in modern business and industry.

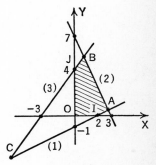

Fig. 2–24

PROBLEM SET 2–5

Determine values of the variable for which the following conditions hold. Shade the interval on a number axis.

1. $x^2 + 5x > 14$.　　　　**2.** $x^2 + 3x + 1 \geq 5$.
3. $3x + 9 < x^2 - 9$.　　　**4.** $2t^2 + 11t + 15 > 0$.

5. $5t^2 + t > t^2 - 3t.$

6. $(x - 1)^2(2x + 3) \geqq 0.$

7. $4t^3 + 12t^2 - t - 3 < 0.$

8. $7x \leqq 18 - x^2.$

9. $(t - 4)(t + 2)(t - 3) \leqq 0.$

10. $(x + 5)(x - 1)(x - 4) < 0.$

11. $(x + 3)(x + 1)x \geqq 0.$

12. $(x - 1)^2(x + 3)(x + 5) < 0.$

13. $(x + 3)^2(x - 4)^3(x + 5) < 0.$

14. $(t - 1)^2(t + 4)(t - 2) \leqq 0.$

15. $(x + 1)^2(x - 5)(x - 7)^3 < 0.$

16. $(x - 10)(x - 7)(x - 3) > 0.$

17. $|z + 4|^2 < 9.$

18. $|3 - t|^2 > 4.$

19. $|x| \cdot (x - 1)(x + 3) < 0.$

20. $x^2 - 25 < 16.$

In Problems 21 to 25 find values of x for which the given expression is real.

21. $\sqrt{x^2 - 4}.$

22. $\sqrt{3x^2 - 27}.$

23. $\sqrt{x^2 + 5x - 14}.$ Compare Problem 1.

24. $\sqrt[3]{4x + 1}.$

25. $\sqrt{4x + 35 - 4x^2}.$

Describe and sketch the sets of points (x, y) whose coordinates satisfy each of the following conditions:

26. $xy(x + y - 10) = 0.$

27. $xy \geqq 0.$

28. $(2x + 3y - 6)(4x - y + 3) = 0.$

29. $(2x + 3y - 6)(4x - y + 3) \geqq 0.$

30. $xy(x + y - 10) \leqq 0.$

31. $x^2 + y^2 \leqq 4, \quad y > x^2.$

32. Find the maximum value of $2x + 3y$ if the three relations (1) $3x - 2y \leqq 6$, (2) $x - 2y \geqq -2$ and (3) $3x + 2y \geqq -6$ are satisfied simultaneously.

2–6. Summary. Chapter 1 introduced set notation and used the field postulates to review certain concepts of elementary algebra; and it introduced the notations Δx and $\Delta f(x, \Delta x)$. Coordinate systems and a formula for the distance between two points were discussed in Chapter 2. Probably the most important ideas of the chapter are contained in Sections 2–1, 2–2, 2–3 on loci of equations and loci of inequalities. Now that you have solved Problem Set 2–5, it may be worthwhile to reread Sections 2–1, 2–2, 2–3.

PROBLEM SET 2–6

1. Example 6, Section 1–4, discusses two methods for simplifying complicated fractions. Simplify the following fraction using each method.

$$\frac{\dfrac{2x-1}{x^2-2x-35}+\dfrac{3x+5}{3x^2-15x-42}}{\dfrac{4x-3}{3x+6}-\dfrac{2x}{x^2-2x-35}}$$

2. If $g(t)=\dfrac{4t^2-12t+\sqrt{t^3+1}}{3}$, compute $g(5)$ and $g(-3)$.

3. If $h(x)=\dfrac{4x}{2x-1}$, compute $\dfrac{\Delta h(x,\Delta x)}{\Delta x}$ and simplify it until the numerator contains no Δx. What restrictions must be made on Δx?

4. Solve for x: $\sqrt{3x+1}+1=\sqrt{2x}$.

5. Solve for t: $t^3-8=0$. Find three roots.

6. Sketch the locus of points which satisfy $x^2+y^2<16$ and $x+y\geqq1$ simultaneously.

7. Find $\dfrac{\Delta f(x,\Delta x)}{\Delta x}$ if $f(x)=4\sqrt{x-3}$.

8. Solve for w: $\dfrac{1}{w^2+w-2}+\dfrac{5}{(w-1)(w+2)}=\dfrac{w}{w+2}$.

9. Sketch the locus: $\sqrt{2x+3}\leqq8$.

10. Determine the equation of the locus of points equidistant from the points $(3,1)$ and $(-2,5)$.

11. Shade the locus represented by $2x-3y+5\geqq0$.

12. Determine the equation(s) of all points 5 units from the y-axis.

13. Determine the equation of the locus of a point which is always as far from the y-axis as from the point $(2,3)$.

14. Consider points (x,y) with $y=x^2-5$. For what domain of x is $y\geqq0$?

15. Sketch: $y=\dfrac{4x}{2x-1}$.

16. Write down the integers (whole numbers) between -5 and $+10$ which satisfy the inequality $-3<x\leqq7$.

17. If possible, determine one pair of integers x and y which do *not* satisfy the inequality $x^2+y^2\leqq(x+y)^2$.

18. Solve for t: $3t^2-7t-5=0$.

19. Sketch: $y=\begin{cases}4 & \text{if } -3\leqq x\leqq3\\10-2x & \text{if } 3\leqq x\leqq5\\10+2x & \text{if } -5\leqq x\leqq-3\\-5+x & \text{if } 0\leqq x<5\\-5-x & \text{if } -5<x<0\\4-x & \text{if } 1<x<2\\4+x & \text{if } -2<x<-1\\-3+|x| & \text{if } -1<x<1\end{cases}$

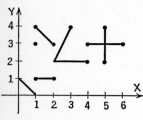

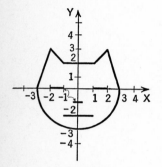

Fig. 2–25

Fig. 2–26

20. Sketch: $\begin{cases} x = \begin{cases} 1 & \text{if } 1 < y < 3 \\ 2 & \text{if } 1 < y < 3 \\ 3 & \text{if } 1 < y < 3 \end{cases} \\ y = 2 & \text{if } 1 \leqq x \leqq 2 \end{cases}$

21. For what x values do you think the function determined by the graph in Figure 2–25 is (a) undefined, (b) single valued, (c) double valued, (d) triple valued, (e) more than triple valued? The end of each line segment has integral coordinates and is part of the graph.

22. Describe the relation in Figure 2–26 in functional notation (as in Problem 19). For what values of x is the relation double valued? Triple valued? Not defined?

23. Solve: $(x - 3)^2(x + 5)(x + 9) \leqq 0$.

24. Solve: $(t + 5)(t - 3)5 < 0$.

25. Solve: $t^2 - 5t + 1 < -3$.

26. Find the solution set for $x^2 + 4 \leqq 0$ if
(a) the domain of x is the domain of real numbers.
(b) the domain of x is the domain of complex numbers of the form $a + bi$ where a and b are real and $i^2 = -1$.

2–7. Self test.

Record your starting time.

1. Shade and describe the region represented by $1 < x < 4$ and $-1 < y < 3$.

2. How far is the point $(-3, 4)$ from (a) the origin? (b) the point $(6, -8)$?

3. Shade and describe the region (locus) represented by $(x - 1)^2 + (y + 2)^2 > 9$.

4. Write the equation of the circle with center $(2, 3)$ and radius 4.

5. Sketch the locus $(x + 3)^2 + (y - 4)^2 = 25$.

6. Shade and describe the interval(s) on the x-axis satisfying $|x + 2| > 5$.

7. Determine and shade the x-intervals satisfying
(a) $(x - 1)(x - 2)(x - 3) > 0$, (b) $x^2 - 9 > 3x + 9$.

8. Sketch the locus of points satisfying both
$(x - 2)^2 + (y - 2)^2 < 4$ and $x + y > 2$.

9. Find the equation of the perpendicular bisector of the line joining $P_1(2, 3)$ to $P_2(10, 7)$.

10. $f(x) = \dfrac{3x - 1}{3x}$. Find $\dfrac{\Delta f(x, \Delta x)}{\Delta x}$.

Record your time.

Students who are having difficulties may benefit by rereading the HINTS FOR STUDY given in the Preface to the Student.

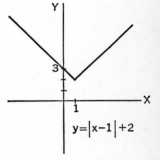

$$y = |x-1| + 2$$

Fig. 3–1

3–1. The importance of graphing. In many applications it is essential that a sketch of the locus of an equation be obtained. The word **sketch,** as used here, means a more or less quickly constructed representation of the locus, showing those important properties of the locus which can be determined readily with the tools at hand. As we derive additional tools, we will be able to give a more accurate sketch with the same effort. In general not more than three or four points should be plotted when sketching a simple locus. More points may be needed, however, if the locus is complicated.

Much of a student's success, or lack thereof, in mathematical science will depend upon his ability to sketch curves rapidly, showing the main features.

The answers to these three questions are especially helpful in discovering important features of a locus.

(a) About where does the locus cross each axis?
(b) Are there any discontinuities or sharp corners on the graph?
(c) What happens to y when x is large in absolute value?

Later we shall learn how to discover the locations of the maximum (top) and minimum (bottom) points of the "waves" in the locus, but even without this aid it is possible to gain considerable knowledge about the general shape of the graph.

3–2. Intercepts. The x-coordinates of those points at which the locus of an equation intersects the x-axis are called the **x-intercepts** of the locus (or equation). The x-intercepts are obtained by substituting zero for y in the equation of the locus and solving this resulting equation (called the x-intercept equation) for real values of x. We do not consider possible imaginary solutions since in our work only real intercepts are considered.† The coordinates of those points at which the locus of an equation intersects the y-axis are called **y-intercepts** of the locus (or equation). To obtain the y-intercepts, substitute zero for x in the equation and solve the resulting equation (y-intercept equation) for real values of y.

† It is preferable to discuss four-dimensional space before considering complex intercepts.

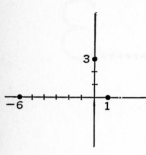

Fig. 3–2

- **Example 1.** The x-intercepts of the equation
  $x^2 - 3xy^3 + 5x + 2y - 6 = 0$ are obtained by substituting
  zero for y, giving $x^2 + 5x - 6 = 0$.   Consequently,
  $(x + 6)(x - 1) = 0$,   or $x = -6$ and   1.   Hence, the x-intercepts are -6 and $+1$. The y-intercepts are obtained by
  solving $2y - 6 = 0$.   The y-intercept is $+3$. (See Fig. 3–2.)

- **Example 2.** $y^3 - y^2x - 4x - 3x^2 - 8 = 0$.   Setting y equal to
  zero, we obtain $-4x - 3x^2 - 8 = 0$,   or $3x^2 + 4x + 8 = 0$.
  The solutions, $x = \dfrac{-4 \pm \sqrt{16 - 96}}{6}$,   are imaginary numbers. This locus does not cross the x-axis. (Why?) Setting x
  equal to zero, we obtain $y^3 - 8 = 0$.   This is factorable into

$$(y - 2)(y^2 + 2y + 4) = 0,$$

which has three solutions $y = 2$ and $y = -1 \pm i\sqrt{3}$.
The two imaginary solutions are obtained by solving the
quadratic equation $y^2 + 2y + 4 = 0$.   The only real root is
$y = 2$.   Hence, the only y-intercept is 2.

3–3. Approximate intercepts. In seeking intercepts it may
happen that when zero is substituted for one of the variables, it
is not easy, or even possible, to obtain exact solutions of the resulting equation. In such cases it is often sufficient to locate intercepts
between consecutive integers (whole numbers). For example, one
might say that $y - 2x + 5\pi = 0$ has an x-intercept between 7
and 8. In this particular example it is possible to determine the
actual intercept $5\pi/2$, but the statement "the intercept lies between 7 and 8" gives a better picture of the intercept's location
than $5\pi/2$ does unless the latter is converted into an approximate
decimal as 7.9.

- **Example 1.** Locate the intercepts of $y = -x^3 + 8x - 6$.   By
  setting $x = 0$ we obtain -6 as the only y-intercept. To
  obtain the x-intercepts we need to solve $-x^3 + 8x - 6 = 0$.
  Since the polynomial $-x^3 + 8x - 6$ is not factorable into
  a product of rational factors, we cannot, at present, solve the
  equation.

Later the reader will learn how to obtain an approximate solution accurate to any desired number of decimal places. In doing
this, the first step is to locate the roots between consecutive
integers. If one sets $p(x) = -x^3 + 8x - 6$,   then $p(0) = -6$
while $p(1) = 1$.   Assuming that $p(x)$ takes on every value between $p(a)$ and $p(b)$ at least once as x varies from a to b, then,
since $p(x)$ is negative at $x = 0$ and positive at $x = 1$,   we

conclude that $p(x)$ must equal zero for some x between $x = 0$ and $x = 1$. That there is also a root between $+2$ and $+3$, and one between -4 and -3 should be verified. Since the x-intercepts of the original equation coincide with the solutions of the x-intercept equation, we have x-intercepts located between -4 and -3, 0 and 1, and 2 and 3.

The preceding paragraph makes use of the assumption that if $p(a)$ and $p(b)$ are opposite in sign, then there exists at least one (there may be several; see Fig. 3–3) value of x, say $x = c$, lying between a and b for which $p(c) = 0$. This is a valid assumption if $p(x)$ is a polynomial.† However, if $f(x)$ is *not* a polynomial, the function $f(x)$ may be positive at one value, b, and negative for a second value, a, but it need not take on a zero value anywhere between a and b: $y = \dfrac{1}{2x - 3}$ is such a function (Fig. 3–4).

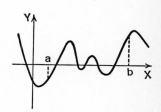

Fig. 3–3

If $p(x)$ is a **polynomial** and if $p(a)$ and $p(b)$ are of opposite algebraic sign, then there is at least one value $x = c$ such that c lies between a and b and $p(c) = 0$.

3–4. Discontinuities. Early in his mathematical career the student learns that division by zero is not permitted — that is,

$$\frac{7}{0}, \quad \frac{3x + 5}{0}, \quad \text{and} \quad \frac{2x + 7}{3x - 3x}$$

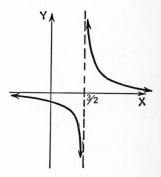

Fig. 3–4

$$y = f(x) = \frac{1}{2x - 3}$$

$f(1) = -1, \quad f(2) = 1 \quad$ **but** $f(x) = 0$ **has no solution.** (**Why?**)

are *not defined* (see Problem 2, Set 1–4). The beginner may feel it would be well to define these expressions (and perhaps certain other expressions like 0^0) and not "leave the tag ends loose." With further progress in mathematics, however, he will find these expressions are not undefined through any laziness on the part of mathematicians, but rather because *it is impossible to define them in a manner that is consistent in all, or even most, cases.* It is impossible to define $0/0$ in a consistent fashion since the expression $0/0$ would need to be defined as 3 in one problem, as 0 in another problem, and as $\sqrt{17} - 4$ in still another problem. In fact, given any number N, it is easy to construct an example such that one might *like* to define $0/0$ as N. Consider Nx/x which equals N for all values of x *except* $x = 0$. One might feel that *if* Nx/x were defined for $x = 0$, it would be nice to define it as N. Hence, $3x/x$ would be defined as 3 at $x = 0$ while $\dfrac{(\sqrt{17} - 4)x}{x}$ would be defined as $\sqrt{17} - 4$ at $x = 0$. For this and other reasons we leave division by zero undefined. A locus is said to be discontinuous for such values of x.

The notion of what happens to $y = f(x)$ when x is close to a

† Actually every **continuous** function satisfies this assumption.

value for which $f(x)$ is undefined is an important one in curve sketching. Often (but *not* always) y becomes very large and positive or very large and negative as x approaches a value for which $f(x)$ is undefined.

● **Example 1.** $y = \dfrac{1}{x - 2}$.

If $x = 2$, the denominator is zero and hence y is undefined. Let us examine y as x approaches 2 through values smaller than 2. (Say $x = 1.9$, $x = 1.98$, $x = 1.998, \cdots$ for example.) If x is less than 2, then y is negative. If x is close to 2 but less than 2, $y = \dfrac{1}{-\,|\,\text{small number}\,|} = -\,|\,\text{large number}\,|$. The closer x comes to 2 (but $x < 2$) the larger negative y becomes. This may be written in symbols $x \nearrow 2$ implies $y \searrow L^-$ (read "x approaches 2 *from below* implies y becomes large and negative"). Note that symbol $\nearrow$ indicates x is *going up* to 2. Let us examine the behavior of y as x approaches 2 through values larger than 2. If x is larger than 2, then y is positive. If x is close to 2 but greater than 2,

$y = \dfrac{1}{\text{small positive fraction}} = \text{large positive number.}$

The closer x comes to 2 (but $x > 2$) the larger y becomes. In symbols $x \searrow 2$ implies $y \nearrow L^+$. The symbol $\searrow$ suggests that x is "going down to 2."

Determine the intercepts. [Is the only intercept $y = -\frac{1}{2}$?] Note the behavior of y for large $|\,x\,|$,

$x \nearrow L^+$ implies $y \searrow 0$, $\qquad x \searrow L^-$ implies $y \nearrow 0$.

Combined with the information obtained about the behavior of the locus near its discontinuity $x = 2$ we will be able to make a reasonable estimate of the general shape of the locus of $y = \dfrac{1}{x - 2}$. We may wish to plot 3 or 4 additional points to help get the shape. Possible points are $(1, -1)$, $(3, 1)$, and $(6, \frac{1}{4})$. It is common practice to place a dotted guide line on the graph at those values that lead to undefined terms. (This dotted guide line is not a part of the locus, but is useful in drawing the sketch. The curve approaches this guide line but does not cross it.) We repeat, since y is not defined for such values of x, the curve does not cross this dotted guide line if y is a single-valued function of x. The phrase **vertical asymptote** is used to describe such a line if the curve approaches the line as y increases without bound in absolute value. Additional comments concerning asymptotes will be found in Chapter 21.

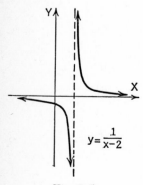

$y = \dfrac{1}{x-2}$

Fig. 3–5

● **Example 2.** $y = \dfrac{x^2 - 9}{x - 3}.$

Clearly, y is not defined if $x = 3$, since substitution gives the expression $0/0$. However, *if x does not equal 3, then*

$$y = \frac{x^2 - 9}{x - 3} = \frac{(x - 3)(x + 3)}{x - 3} = x + 3, \quad \text{if} \quad x \neq 3.$$

The locus $y = \dfrac{x^2 - 9}{x - 3}$ and $y = x + 3$ are *not* the same locus. When $x = 3$, the former is undefined and the latter is 6. The small circle and dotted line in Figure 3–6 indicate the point $(3, 6)$ is missing from this locus. The point $(3, 6)$ does not satisfy the equation. The analogy of a bridge which has been washed out and therefore leaves a break in the highway has certain mathematical disadvantages, but it may help the reader grasp the important distinction between $y = \dfrac{x^2 - 9}{x - 3}$ and $y = x + 3$. They are not the same locus and have quite different properties.

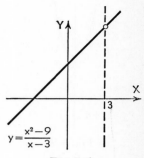

Fig. 3–6

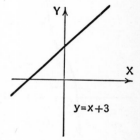

Fig. 3–7

● **Example 3.** $y^2 + |x| = 0$. This interesting locus is not discontinuous, but we take it up here for other reasons. Since both y^2 and $|x|$ are always greater than or equal to zero, the only possible points of the locus are those points at which both y^2 and $|x|$ are equal to zero. (Why?) Therefore the entire locus consists of the one point $(0, 0)$. (See Fig. 3–8.)

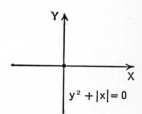

Fig. 3–8

PROBLEM SET 3–4

In Problems 1 to 6, determine the exact x-intercepts and y-intercepts where convenient. If not convenient to determine the *exact intercept*, determine an approximate intercept. Sketch the curve if you can.

1. $y = x^2 - x - 6.$ 2. $y = 4(2x - 3)(x - 5)(x + 6).$

3. $y^2 = 4 - x^2.$ 4. $y = \dfrac{6}{x + 3}.$

5. $(x - 5)(y + 2) = 4.$ 6. $y^2 = (x - 2)^2.$

In Problems 7 to 10, discuss the behavior of the locus near any discontinuities, locate the intercepts, and sketch the locus.

7. $y = \dfrac{3}{x - 5}.$ 8. $y = \dfrac{x^2 - 25}{x + 5}.$

9. $y^2 \geqq 3x + 9.$ 10. $|y| + |x| = 4.$

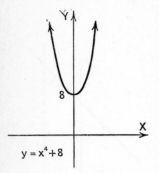

$$y = x^4 + 8$$

Fig. 3–9‡

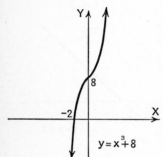

$$y = x^3 + 8$$

Fig. 3–10 ‡

3–5. Behavior of loci for large values of $|x|$. Many times, insight into the general shape of the curve can be obtained by examining what happens to y as x becomes numerically large in either the positive or negative direction. For example, in the equation $y = x^4 + 8$, as x becomes large and positive, y must also become large and positive (this may be abbreviated: if $x \nearrow L^+$, then $y \nearrow L^+$).† As x becomes large and negative we find that x^4 and hence y will become large and positive (if $x \searrow L^-$, then $y \nearrow L^+$). The symbol $\searrow$ suggests "going down" while $\nearrow$ suggests "going up."

In the equation $y = x^3 + 8$, x large and positive implies that y is large and positive (if $x \nearrow L^+$, then $y \nearrow L^+$). However, here x large and negative implies that y is large and negative (if $x \searrow L^-$, then $y \searrow L^-$). Thus, with only this information and the intercepts one can observe a fundamental difference in the loci.

A general rule for polynomials in x such as

$$y(x) = -2x^4 + 7x^3 - 3x^2 + 2x - 10$$

is that, for $|x|$ large enough, the entire polynomial behaves much the same as the term involving the highest power of x.

● **Example 1.** If x is large in absolute value, then $-2x^4$ determines the behavior of

$$y(x) = -2x^4 + 7x^3 - 3x^2 + 2x - 10 = -2x^4\left[1 - \frac{7}{2x} + \frac{3}{2x^2} - \frac{1}{x^3} + \frac{5}{x^4}\right].$$

As $|x| \nearrow L^+$, the factor in brackets becomes close to 1. (Why?) We conclude that y has the following behavior for large $|x|$:

$$x \nearrow L^+ \quad \text{implies} \quad y \searrow L^-,$$

and

$$x \searrow L^- \quad \text{implies} \quad y \searrow L^-.$$

If it should prove difficult to solve for y as a function of x, it may be feasible to solve for x as a function of y.

● **Example 2.** $y^3 - x + 3 = 0$.

In this example it is easier to solve for x than for y. Solve for x, obtaining x as a function of y, namely,

$$x = y^3 + 3.$$

† Read this as "if x becomes large and positive, then y becomes large and positive." Some instructors may prefer to use the symbols $+\infty$ and $-\infty$ to replace L^+ and L^-. However, the symbol ∞ is so easily *mis*interpreted by the beginner that it will not be used here.

‡ An arrowhead is used to suggest that the locus continues in the general fashion indicated.

The locus crosses the x-axis at (3, 0). The locus crosses the y-axis at $(0, -\sqrt[3]{3})$ or approximately $(0, -1.4^+)$.

$$y \nearrow L^+ \text{ implies } x \nearrow L^+.$$
$$y \searrow L^- \text{ implies } x \searrow L^-.$$

The sketch appears in Figure 3–11.

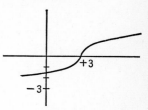

Fig. 3–11

• **Example 3.** $y^2 = \dfrac{5}{1 - x^2} - 1$

$$y^2 = \frac{4 + x^2}{1 - x^2}.$$

Since the numerator $4 + x^2$ is always positive and the denominator $1 - x^2$ is positive only if $-1 < x < 1$, it follows that the entire graph will be obtained for values of x between -1 and 1; that is, the relation $y = \pm\sqrt{\dfrac{4 + x^2}{1 - x^2}}$ has $-1 < x < 1$ as its domain of definition.

Furthermore the only discontinuities occur at $x = -1$ and at $x = +1$. (Why?)

The locus intersects the y-axis at $(0, -2)$ and $(0, +2)$ but does not cross the x-axis. (Why not?)

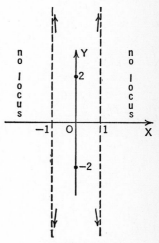

Fig. 3–12

$$x \nearrow +1 \text{ implies } \begin{array}{l} y = +\sqrt{\dfrac{4 + x^2}{1 - x^2}} \nearrow L^+ \\[2mm] y = -\sqrt{\dfrac{4 + x^2}{1 - x^2}} \searrow L^- \end{array}$$

$$\text{at } x = 0, \quad \begin{array}{l} y = +\sqrt{\dfrac{4 + x^2}{1 - x^2}} = +2 \\[2mm] y = -\sqrt{\dfrac{4 + x^2}{1 - x^2}} = -2 \end{array}$$

$$x \searrow -1 \text{ implies } \begin{array}{l} y = +\sqrt{\dfrac{4 + x^2}{1 - x^2}} \nearrow L^+ \\[2mm] y = -\sqrt{\dfrac{4 + x^2}{1 - x^2}} \searrow L^-. \end{array}$$

We have already observed that no locus exists for x outside of the region $-1 < x < 1$.

The locus is sketched in Figure 3–13.

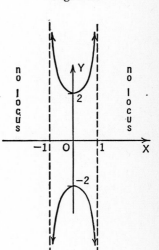

Fig. 3–13

PROBLEM SET 3–5

In Problems 1 to 10 discuss the behavior of y as $x \nearrow L^+$ and as $x \searrow L^-$.

1. $y = x^5 - 7x^2 + 3x - 10.$ **2.** $y = x^6 + 2x - 1.$ **3.** $y = \dfrac{3x + 2}{5}.$

4. $y = -2x^3 + x^2 - 7.$ $\qquad$ **5.** $y = -2x^4 + 4x + 6 + 4y + 3.$

6. $y = 5x^4 - 700.$ **7.** $y = x^6 + 3x^3 + 4x - 7.$ **8.** $y = 7x^2 - x - 1.$

9. $y = x^2 + 100x.$ $\qquad$ **10.** $y = -3x^2 + 2x + 2y - 5.$

In Problems 11 to 17 obtain x as a function of y and determine the behavior of x as $y \nearrow L^+$ and as $y \searrow L^-$.

11. $2x = y^2 - 7y + 4.$ **12.** $x = \dfrac{3y^2 - 4}{2}.$ **13.** $3x = 13x - 7y + 1.$

14. $x = -y^3 + 7.$ $\qquad$ **15.** $x = 4y^2 + 5.$

16. $x = -2y^4 + 6y^3 - 3y + 2.$ $\quad$ **17.** $x = 2y^5 - 3y + 4.$

18. Discuss $y = \dfrac{3}{x - 3}$ as $x \nearrow L^+$ and as $x \searrow L^-$.

19. Discuss $y = \dfrac{x}{x - 3}$ as $x \nearrow L^+$ and as $x \searrow L^-$.

$$\left[\text{HINT:}\ \frac{x}{x - 3} = 1 + \frac{3}{x - 3}.\right]$$

20. Discuss $y = \dfrac{4x}{x + 2}$ as $x \nearrow L^+$ and $x \searrow L^-$ using

$$y = \frac{4}{1 + \dfrac{2}{x}}, \quad \text{where } x \neq 0.$$

Discuss in writing each of the following loci for $x \nearrow L^+$ and $x \searrow L^-$, and for x near any possible discontinuities. Make a rough sketch of the curve. Do not plot more than two points in addition to the intercepts.

21. $y = \dfrac{3}{x - 3}.$

22. $y = \dfrac{x}{x - 3}.$ [See Hint, Problem 19.]

23. $y = \dfrac{2x}{x + 1}.$ $\qquad\qquad$ **24.** $y = \dfrac{3x}{2x + 5}.$

25. $y = x^2y + 3x.$ $\qquad\qquad$ **26.** $xy = 5.$

27. $y = f(x) = \dfrac{1}{5x - 6}.$ Note that $f(1) = -1$ and $f(2) = \frac{1}{4}.$

You might be tempted to say that the locus crosses the x-axis between 1 and 2, since $f(1)$ is negative and $f(2)$ is positive. This is not true. (Why?) Does this contradict the statements made in Section 3–2 about intercepts?

28. $y = \dfrac{3}{x} + 1.$ **29.** $y = \dfrac{x+3}{x}$ (Compare Problem 28.)

*30. $y = x^2 + \dfrac{-4}{x+1} + \dfrac{-8}{x-2}.$

31. Calvin Butterball receives 60¢ per hour plus a bonus of 10¢ per box for each box of onions he packs. He has learned to pack 5 boxes per hour. Since he does not earn his bonus until each box is completely packed, his income is a discontinuous function of time. (a) Plot Calvin's income as a function of time for an 8-hour day. (b) Calvin is credited with "time and a half" both on his base pay and his bonus for all time over 8 hours worked in one day. Continue the graph of part (a) to include 2 hours of overtime.

3–6. Discussion of a locus. The discussion of the locus of an equation or inequality should include as many of the following as are readily determined.

1. Is the locus likely to be a curve (that is, the locus of an equation) or is the locus likely to be a region (that is, the locus of an inequality)?

2. Intercepts. (a) x-intercepts
              (b) y-intercepts.

3. Discontinuities. In a quotient of polynomials, discontinuities occur only where a denominator is zero. Later we shall discuss other types of discontinuity. Use a dotted line to indicate the discontinuity.

4. General behavior of the locus. It is usually well to separate the x-axis (or occasionally the y-axis) into segments by marking all the intercepts and points of discontinuity and then discuss the function in each segment.† This should include a discussion of $x \searrow L^-$ and $x \nearrow L^+$, or $y \searrow L^-$ and $y \nearrow L^+$.

5. Occasionally, additional points should be plotted.

● *Example 1.* Discuss the locus $x^2 y - x - y = 0$.

    1. The equation suggests the locus is a curve rather than a region. (Why?)

    2. The origin is the only point at which the locus crosses either axis. (Prove this.)

    3. To discuss the locus further we use the form

$$y = \frac{x}{(x+1)(x-1)}.$$

† It is often convenient to consider these segments in the increasing order of size of the variable. See Example 1, Part 4.

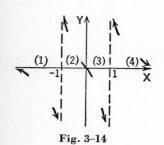

Fig. 3–14

Discontinuities occur at $x = -1$ and $x = 1$. (Why?) (In discussing y as $x \searrow L^-$ and as $x \nearrow L^+$ the form

$$y = \frac{1}{x - \frac{1}{x}} \text{ is used.)}$$

4. General behavior.

    Region

(1) $x < -1$: $y = \frac{(-)}{(-)(-)} = -.$ $\begin{cases} x \searrow L^- \text{ implies } y \nearrow 0. \\ x \nearrow -1 \text{ implies } y \searrow L^-. \end{cases}$

(2) $-1 < x < 0$: $y = \frac{(-)}{(+)(-)} = +.$ $\begin{cases} x \searrow -1 \text{ implies } y \nearrow L^+. \\ x \nearrow 0 \quad \text{ implies } y \searrow 0. \end{cases}$

(3) $0 < x < 1$: $y = \frac{(+)}{(+)(-)} = -.$ $\begin{cases} x \searrow 0 \quad \text{ implies } y \nearrow 0. \\ x \nearrow 1 \quad \text{ implies } y \searrow L^-. \end{cases}$

(4) $1 < x$: $y = \frac{(+)}{(+)(+)} = +.$ $\begin{cases} x \searrow 1 \quad \text{ implies } y \nearrow L^+. \\ x \nearrow L^+ \text{ implies } y \searrow 0. \end{cases}$

This information is sketched in Figure 3–14. The discontinuities are indicated by the vertical dotted lines and the intercept $(0, 0)$ is plotted.

    5. The points $(\frac{1}{2}, -\frac{2}{3})$ and $(2, \frac{2}{3})$ are on the locus. If symmetry is considered, this locates points on each branch of the locus. The locus is sketched in Figure 3–15. The reader should check that each statement of the discussion is consistent with the sketch. The portions of the sketch have been numbered to correspond with the subheadings of Part 4 of the discussion. This is not essential, but is convenient when discussing the curve.

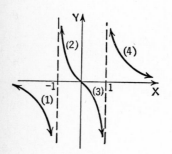

Fig. 3–15

● **Example 2.** Discuss and sketch $y = 400 + 120t - 16t^2$.

    1. The equation suggests the locus is a curve rather than a region.

    2. Intercepts. (a) The t-intercepts are obtained by solving the equation $0 \doteq 400 + 120t - 16t^2$ which is equivalent to

$$2t^2 - 15t - 50 = 0,$$
$$(2t + 5)(t - 10) = 0.$$
$$t = -\tfrac{5}{2}, \quad t = 10,$$

and the t-intercepts are $-\frac{5}{2}$ and 10.

    (b) The y-intercept is 400.

    3. There are no discontinuities.

    4. General behavior. To discuss the locus further we use the factored form $y = -8(2t + 5)(t - 10)$.

Region

(1) $t<-\frac{5}{2}$: $y=-(-)(-)=-.$ $\begin{cases} t\searrow L^- \text{ implies } y\searrow L^-. \\ t\nearrow-\frac{5}{2} \text{ implies } y\nearrow 0. \end{cases}$

(2) $-\frac{5}{2}<t<10$: $y=-(+)(-)=+.$ $\begin{cases} t\searrow-\frac{5}{2} \text{ implies } y\searrow 0. \\ t\nearrow 10 \text{ implies } y\searrow 0. \end{cases}$

(3) $10<t$: $y=-(+)(+)=-.$ $\begin{cases} t\searrow 10 \text{ implies } y\nearrow 0. \\ t\nearrow L^+ \text{ implies } y\searrow L^-. \end{cases}$

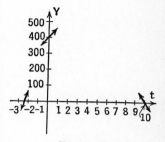

Fig. 3–16

We sketch our present knowledge on coordinate axes in Figure 3–16. Note the difference in units on the two axes. Why is this difference advantageous?

5. Apparently the locus must rise and then fall (have a maximum) for t between $-\frac{5}{2}$ and 10. We plot three points in this region, $(1, 504)$, $(3, 616)$, $(4, 624)$, and sketch the locus in Figure 3–17.

The reader should verify that the final sketch is consistent with *each* statement in the discussion. If he will make this check, he will find many of his own errors. In Chapters 4 and 6 the reader will learn to determine the peak (maximum) of this locus and study several applications of the sketching methods learned in this chapter.

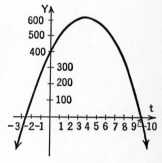

Fig. 3–17

● *Example 3.* Discuss and sketch $y \leqq 400 + 120t - 16t^2$.

1. The inequality suggests the locus is a region rather than a curve.

2, 3, 4, 5. For the portion of $y \leqq 400 + 120t - 16t^2$ represented by the $=$ sign, this is the same as Example 2, and the same curve is obtained. (See Fig. 3–17.) However, since this example also requires all points for which y is *less than* $400 + 120t - 16t^2$, the entire region *below* the curve of Figure 3–17 is also included. This is shown in Figure 3–18.

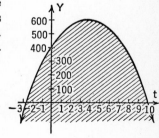

Fig. 3–18

PROBLEM SET 3–6

Discuss and sketch the locus of each sentence given below. Each locus consists of all points (x, y) satisfying the given condition.

1. $x^2 + y^2 - 2y = 0$.   2. $x^2 < 9$.
3. $x^2 + y^2 - 5x = 0$.   4. $4x - 3y = x^2y$.

5. (a) $x \leqq y$, (b) $x = y$. Note the difference in symmetry of parts (a) and (b).

6. $x^2 = y^2$. $\qquad\qquad\qquad$ **7.** (a) $x = y^2$, (b) $x^2 = y$.

8. $x = y^3$. $\qquad$ **9.** $x^2 - 3x + y = 0$. $\qquad$ **10.** $x^2 + 3y^3 = 0$.

11. $y \geqq 3x + 2$. $\qquad\qquad\qquad$ **12.** $y < 5x - 1$.

13. $y = \dfrac{7}{2x - 5}$. $\qquad\qquad$ **14.** $y = \dfrac{x - 7}{x^2 - 49}$.

15. $0 \leqq xy < 9$. $\qquad\qquad$ **16.** $x^2 - y(y - 2) = 4$.

17. $x^2 y = x + y$. $\qquad\qquad$ **18.** $(x - 1)(x - 4) = 0$.

19. $x^2 + 4 = y^2$. $\qquad\qquad$ **20.** $x^2 - 4 = -y^2 + 4y$.

21. $(x + 2)y = 4$. $\qquad\qquad$ **22.** $(x^2 + 1)y = 4$.

23. $y^2 < -x^2$. $\qquad\qquad$ **24.** $|y| = 2$.

25. $|x| + |y| = 1$. $\qquad\qquad$ **26.** $y(x^2 + 4) = 16$.

27. Determine all points (x, y) that lie in the solution set of *both* of the inequalities:

$$y \geqq x^2 - 3x + 2 \quad \text{and} \quad y \leqq 3x - 3.$$

3–7. Self test. Determine the intercepts or approximate intercepts of the loci given below. Also discuss the behavior of each locus near any possible discontinuities and for x large in absolute value and sketch the locus.

1. $y = \dfrac{3}{2x - 7}$. $\qquad\qquad$ **2.** $y = 4 - \dfrac{1}{x}$.

3. $|x| + |y| \leqq 9$. $\qquad\qquad$ **4.** $y(x) = -17x^5 + 3x^2 - 80$.

5. $y^2 = \dfrac{10}{1 - x^2} - 1$. $\qquad\qquad$ **6.** $y \leqq x^2 + 10$.

7. $y < 3x + \pi$. $\qquad\qquad\qquad$ **8.** $0 \leqq xy < 4$.

Record your time.

*3–8. Roots of a continuous function. Continuing with Section 3–3 on intercepts, we now discuss a simple repetitive method for determining certain real roots with any desired degree of accuracy. An illustrative example is given first.

● *Example 1.* Given the equation $f(x) = x^4 - x - 3 = 0$, determine one of its roots accurate to three decimal places. First note that $f(1) = -3 < 0$ and $f(2) = +11 > 0$ and that the function f is continuous in the region $1 \leqq x \leqq 2$. Hence there *must* be a root between 1 and 2. (Why?)

We now consider the value of the function for x midway between 1 and 2, namely, $f(1.5)$. Since
$$f(1.5) = (1.5)^4 - (1.5) - 3 = 5.0625 - 1.5 - 3 = +.5625 > 0,$$
we conclude there is a root between $x = 1$ and $x = 1.5$. (Why?) Next consider the sign of $f(x)$ at the midpoint of this segment, namely $f(1.25)$. A straightforward (but tedi-

ous) computation shows that $f(1.25) = -.8085937$. Thus the root lies between 1.25 and 1.50. The midpoint of this interval is 1.375 and $f(1.375) = -.8005371$.

In a similar fashion one may continue halving the interval in which the root lies until the root has been approximated to the desired degree of accuracy. If the computation is done by hand, it is usual to take the nearest "simple" value in place of the midpoint; for instance, use $f(1.2)$ or $f(1.3)$ rather than $f(1.25)$ to ease the arithmetic. This is unnecessary (and even undesirable) on a modern computer since $f(1.4526216)$ is as easy to compute as $f(1)$.

The following table presents the result of extensive computation. As x changes, the position of the entry has been moved toward the center of the page.

$$f(x) = x^4 - x - 3$$

$f(a)$	$f(b)$
$f(1) = -3.000000$	
$f(1) = -3.000000$	$f(2) = +11.00000$
$f(1.25) = -.8085937$	$f(1.5) = +.5625000$
$f(1.375) = -.8005371$	$f(1.5) = +.5625000$
$f(1.4375) = -.1674650$	$f(1.5) = +.5625000$
$f(1.4375) = -.1674650$	$f(1.5) = +.5625000$
$f(1.4375) = -.1674650$	$f(1.46875) = +.1848766$
$f(1.4453125) = -.0816915$	$f(1.453125) = +.0056125$
$f(1.4492188) = -.0382312$	$f(1.453125) = +.0056125$
$f(1.4511719) = -.0163575$	$f(1.453125) = +.0056125$
$f(1.4521485) = -.0053840$	$f(1.453125) = +.0056125$
$f(1.4521485) = -.0053840$	$f(1.453125) = +.0056125$
$f(1.4523927) = -.0026363$	$f(1.4526368) = +.0001180$
$f(1.4525148) = -.0012620$	$f(1.4526368) = +.0001180$
$f(1.4525758) = -.0005751$	$f(1.4526368) = +.0001180$
$f(1.4526063) = -.0002316$	$f(1.4526368) = +.0001180$
$f(1.4526216) = -.0000595$	$f(1.4526368) = +.0001180$

Hence the root lies between 1.45262 and 1.45264 which means that, accurate to four decimal places, the root is 1.4526. The reader should note that although the root has been determined to four decimal places (five significant digits) that the value of $f(x)$ is zero only to three decimal places. Where should the computation have stopped if three-place accuracy was desired — that is, where is $|a - b| < .0005$?

If hand computation is used, less tedious methods of determining a root are available (Newton's method, for example, which uses tools developed in Chap. 6.)

The main objection to the method just discussed is that, although the method is simple, the arithmetic is tedious. Modern high-speed computers are designed to do tedious arithmetic, so a variation of this method is often used on computers. The reader should be able to follow the flow chart given below.

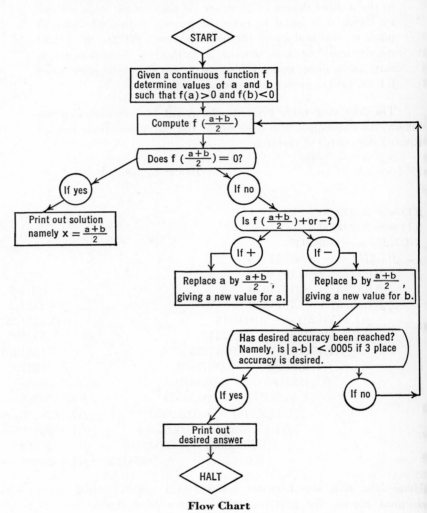

Flow Chart

4–1. This chapter discusses the remainder and the factor theorems, synthetic division, symmetry, and related additional material useful in curve sketching. The chapter concludes with an algebraic discussion of determining the vertex point of a quadratic function.

4–2. The remainder theorem. There is a very neat shortcut for computing $p(b)$ for constant b when $p(x)$ is a polynomial in x. Before explaining this shortcut, however, it is desirable to prove the remainder theorem. In this and certain other proofs we use the identity (4.2). To derive this identity, divide $x^k - h^k$ by $x - h$ using long division.

$$\frac{x^k - h^k}{x - h} \equiv x^{k-1} + hx^{k-2} + h^2x^{k-3} + \cdots + h^{k-2}x + h^{k-1}, \quad \text{if } x \neq h,$$
(4.1)

or, on multiplying both members of (4.1) by $x - h$,

$$(x - h)(x^{k-1} + hx^{k-2} + \cdots + h^{k-2}x + h^{k-1}) \equiv x^k - h^k. \quad (4.2)$$

We use this result to prove the remainder theorem. Consider polynomial†

$$p(x) = ax^n + bx^{n-1} + \cdots + sx + t. \tag{4.3}$$

Then

$$p(h) = ah^n + bh^{n-1} + \cdots + sh + t.$$

Upon subtracting and combining terms we have

$$p(x) - p(h) \equiv a(x^n - h^n) + b(x^{n-1} - h^{n-1}) + \cdots + s(x - h). \quad (4.4)$$

From (4.2) it is seen that $x - h$ is a factor of each parenthesis appearing in the right-hand member of (4.4). Moreover, the other factor in each case is a polynomial in x. Consequently, the right member of (4.4) may be written in the form $(x - h) \cdot q(x)$ where $q(x)$ is a polynomial in x. Hence, (4.4) may be written,

$$p(x) - p(h) = (x - h) \cdot q(x), \tag{4.5}$$

and

$$p(x) = (x - h)q(x) + p(h). \tag{4.6}$$

† A polynomial in x is an expression of the form (4.3), where the exponents are non-negative integers and $a, b, \cdots, s, t$ are constants.

From (4.6) which is an identity in x, it follows that if $p(x)$ is divided by $x - h$ the quotient is $q(x)$ and **the remainder is $p(h)$**. The latter statement is summarized in the

Remainder theorem. If a polynomial $p(x)$ is divided by $x - h$ until a constant remainder is obtained, this constant remainder is $p(h)$.

The remainder theorem would be an interesting curiosity if it had no further application. However, since a very neat and easy method for performing this division exists, the remainder theorem becomes a useful shortcut in computing $p(h)$ for constant h.

If, for some constant h, $p(h) = 0$, then h is a root of $p(x) = 0$. The graph of $y = p(x)$ crosses the x-axis at $x = h$ (has x-intercept h).

In more advanced mathematics it is proved that a polynomial equation $p(x) = 0$ of degree n has precisely n roots. Some of these roots may be imaginary, some may be real; some may be repeated roots. If all roots are counted, then a polynomial equation of degree n has exactly n roots. This fundamental theorem of algebra is assumed here.

- **Illustration.** $4x^4 + 12x^3 + 25x^2 + 48x + 36 = 0$
  or $(2x + 3)^2(x^2 + 4) = 0$ has four roots $-\frac{3}{2}, -\frac{3}{2}, 2i, -2i$.

Factor theorem.† If, for some constant h, $p(h) = 0$, then $x - h$ is a factor of the polynomial $p(x)$.

PROOF:

$$p(x) = (x - h)q(x) + p(h) = (x - h)q(x) \quad \text{since} \quad p(h) = 0.$$

- **Example.** Factor $p(x) = 4x^2 + 5xy - 9y^2$. Since

$$p(y) = 4y^2 + 5y^2 - 9y^2 = 0,$$

it follows that $x - y$ is a factor, and it may be verified by division that the quotient is $4x + 9y$.
   Thus, $p(x) = (x - y)(4x + 9y)$.

We need a more rapid method for dividing and are led to study a process known as synthetic division.

4–3. Synthetic division. We indicate the process by synthesizing both quotient and constant remainder when a particular

† The converse of the factor theorem is also valid. See Problem 14, Set 4–4.

polynomial $p(x) = 2x^4 - 8x^3 + 13x^2 + 40$ is divided by $x - h$. The method is capable of extension to a general proof.† From (4.4) with $p(x)$ as indicated obtain

$$\frac{p(x) - p(h)}{x - h} = \frac{2(x^4 - h^4) - 8(x^3 - h^3) + 13(x^2 - h^2) + 0(x - h)}{x - h}$$

$$= 2\frac{x^4 - h^4}{x - h} - 8\frac{x^3 - h^3}{x - h} + 13\frac{x^2 - h^2}{x - h} + 0\frac{x - h}{x - h}. \quad (4.7)$$

Using (4.1),

$$2\frac{x^4 - h^4}{x - h} = 2x^3 + 2hx^2 + 2h^2x + 2h^3$$

$$-8\frac{x^3 - h^3}{x - h} = -8x^2 - 8hx - 8h^2$$

$$13\frac{x^2 - h^2}{x - h} = 13x + 13h.$$

Add these to form

$$\frac{p(x) - p(h)}{x - h} = (2)x^3 + (2h - 8)x^2 + (2h^2 - 8h + 13)x + (2h^3 - 8h^2 + 13h + 0).$$

The coefficients of the quotient are, in order, (2), $(2h - 8)$, $(2h^2 - 8h + 13)$, $(2h^3 - 8h^2 + 13h + 0)$. The remainder, upon applying the remainder theorem, is $p(h) = 2h^4 - 8h^3 + 13h^2 + 40$. To determine this set of coefficients for the quotient and the remainder we use the following synthetic procedure.

1. Write the coefficients of the polynomial arranged in order of decreasing size of the exponent, supplying a zero for any missing term including the constant term if it is missing. In our example we write

$$h \,\big|\, 2 - 8 + 13 + 0 + 40$$

2. To divide synthetically, bring the coefficient of the term of highest degree (2 in our case) down to the third row.

3. Multiply this coefficient by h, write it under the coefficient of the term of degree one less, and add.

$$h \,\big|\, 2 \qquad -8 \qquad +13 + 0 + 40$$
$$\underline{\qquad\quad 2h \qquad\qquad\qquad}$$
$$2 + (-8 + 2h) \qquad\qquad\big|$$

4. Multiply this sum by h, write it under the coefficient of the term of degree one less, and add.

† For another method, consider the solution given for Problem 11 of Set 4–4.

5. Continue this process to derive

$$h \,\lfloor\,\begin{array}{ccccc} 2 & -8 & +\ 13 & +\ 0 & +\ 40 \\ & 2h & +(2h^2-8h) & +(2h^3-8h^2+13h) & +(2h^4-8h^3+13h^2+0) \\ \hline 2+(2h-8) & +(2h^2-8h+13) & +(2h^3-8h^2+13h+0) & | & +(2h^4-8h^3+13h^2+40) \end{array}$$

Observe that the last term of the bottom row is the remainder, while the other terms of the bottom row are the coefficients of the quotient.

● **Example 1.** Find the quotient and remainder when
$2x^4 - 8x^3 + 13x^2 + 40$ is divided by $x - 6$.
In this case $h = +6$.

$$+6 \,\lfloor\,\begin{array}{ccccc} 2 - & 8 + 13 + & 0 + & 40 \\ & +12 + 24 + & 222 & +1332 \\ \hline 2 + & 4 + 37 + & 222 | & +1372 \end{array}$$

The quotient is $2x^3 + 4x^2 + 37x + 222$, and the remainder is 1372.

● **Example 2.** Determine the quotient and remainder when
$2x^4 - 8x^3 + 13x^2 + 40$ is divided by $x + 2$.
In this case $h = -2$.   (Why?)

$$-2 \,\lfloor\,\begin{array}{ccccc} 2 - & 8 + 13 + & 0 + & 40 \\ & -4 + 24 - & 74 & +148 \\ \hline 2 - & 12 + 37 - & 74 | & +188 \end{array}$$

The quotient is $2x^3 - 12x^2 + 37x - 74$, and the remainder is 188.

Note that in division by $x + b$ the sign of b must be changed.

The remainder theorem states that if $p(x)$ is divided by $x - h$ (note minus sign) until a constant remainder is obtained, this remainder is $p(h)$.   Using this theorem in combination with synthetic division by $x - h$, we find $p(h)$.

● **Example 3.** If $p(x) = x^3 - 22x + 2$, determine $p(5)$.

$$5 \,\lfloor\,\begin{array}{cccc} 1 + 0 - & 22 & + 2 \\ & 5 + 25 & + 15 \\ \hline 1 + 5 + & 3 | & +17 \end{array}$$

Hence, $p(5) = 17$.

● **Example 4.** If $g(t) = t^5 + 6t^4 - 5t^3 + 15t^2 + 6$, find $g(-7)$.

$$-7 \,\lfloor\,\begin{array}{ccccc} 1 + 6 - & 5 + 15 + & 0 & + 6 \\ & -7 + 7 - & 14 - 7 & +49 \\ \hline 1 - 1 + & 2 + & 1 - 7 | & +55 \end{array}$$

Then $g(-7) = 55$.

It is usually easier to determine $p(0)$, $p(1)$, and $p(-1)$ by actual substitution. If $|b| \geqq 3$, it is usually easier to use synthetic division to determine $p(b)$.

4–4. Rational roots. A **rational** number can be expressed as the quotient of two whole numbers (integers). A **rational root** of an equation is a root (solution) which is a rational number.

● **Illustration.** It may be verified, by substitution, that $-\frac{2}{5}, \frac{3}{2}$, and $\frac{2}{1} = 2$ are rational roots of the equation

$$10x^3 - 31x^2 + 16x + 12 = 0.$$

Observe that, in each root, the numerator divides the constant term, 12, of the equation, and the denominator divides the coefficient, 10, of the term of highest degree. This illustrates the following theorem.

Theorem. If $ax^n + bx^{n-1} + \cdots sx + t = 0$ is a polynomial equation with *integral* coefficients and if c/d is a root of this equation, where c/d is in lowest terms, both c and d being integers, then c is a factor of t and d is a factor of a.

This is proved by noting that if c/d is a root, then

$$a(c/d)^n + b(c/d)^{n-1} + \cdots + s(c/d) + t = 0.$$

Upon multiplying through by d^n,

$$ac^n + bc^{n-1}d + \cdots + scd^{n-1} + td^n = 0. \qquad (4.8)$$

Also,

$$ac^n + bc^{n-1}d + \cdots + scd^{n-1} = -td^n,$$
$$c(ac^{n-1} + bc^{n-2}d + \cdots + sd^{n-1}) = -td^n.$$

From this we see that c is a factor of $-td^n$. Since c and d have no factors in common other than ± 1, c and d^n have no factors in common other than ± 1. Consequently, since c divides $-td^n$, c is a factor of the constant term t. Similarly, it may be argued that d is a factor of the coefficient a of the term of highest degree by first writing (4.8) in the form

$$bc^{n-1}d + \cdots + scd^{n-1} + td^n = d(bc^{n-1} + \cdots + scd^{n-2} + td^{n-1}) = -ac^n.$$

● **Example 1.** Find the rational roots of $2x^4 - x^3 - 19x^2 + 2x + 30 = 0$. If possible, determine all of the roots.

The possible choices for c are $\pm 1, \pm 2, \pm 3, \pm 5, \pm 6, \pm 10, \pm 15, \pm 30$. (Why?)

Possible choices for d are $\pm 1, \pm 2$. (Why?)

Possible values of c/d are

$$\pm 1,\ \pm\tfrac{1}{2},\ \pm 2,\ \pm 3,\ \pm\tfrac{3}{2},\ \pm 5,\ \pm\tfrac{5}{2},\ \pm 6,\ \pm 10,\ \pm 15,\ \pm\tfrac{15}{2},\ \pm 30.$$

These values for c/d may be tested by synthetic division. If no one of the possible c/d values is a root, then the equation has no rational roots. (This does not mean that the equation has no roots. Why? Consider $x^2 + x + 1 = 0$. Neither -1 nor $+1$ is a root.) In this problem $\pm 1, \pm 2$ are not roots but, upon trying 3, one finds

$$
\begin{array}{r|rrrrr}
3 & 2 & -1 & -19 & +2 & +30 \\
  &   & 6 & +15 & -12 & -30 \\
\hline
  & 2 & +5 & -4 & -10 & +0
\end{array}.
$$

Consequently, 3 is a root and the remaining roots appear in the quotient equated to zero.† (That is, in $2x^3 + 5x^2 - 4x - 10 = 0$.) We try several values only to find they are not roots, but finally

$$
\begin{array}{r|rrrr}
-\tfrac{5}{2} & 2 & +5 & -4 & -10 \\
  &   & -5 & +0 & +10 \\
\hline
  & 2 & +0 & -4 & +0
\end{array}.
$$

From this it is seen that $-\tfrac{5}{2}$ is a root, and that the remaining roots are to be found in the equation $2x^2 - 4 = 0$. Its roots are $\pm\sqrt{2}$, which are irrational. Rational factors of $2x^4 - x^3 - 19x^2 + 2x + 30$ are $(x-3)$, $(x+\tfrac{5}{2})$, (x^2-2), and 2.

In testing a candidate root, h, of a polynomial equation $f(x) = 0$, the crucial question is "Does $f(h) = 0$?"

If the remainder, $f(h)$, is 0, then h is a root, while if $f(h) \neq 0$, then h is not a root.

In testing a fractional candidate, say $h = c/d$ in a polynomial with *integral* coefficients, once a fractional entry is made in the third row, then all future third-row entries will also be fractions. The entries never vanish since they are sums of an integer and a fraction. Hence $f(c/d) \neq 0$ and c/d is not a root. We may conclude that the candidate is not a root as soon as the first fraction appears on the third line *if* the original polynomial equation has integral coefficients. *Integral candidates are often tested first.*

The reader should actually carry out the synthetic division for some fractional candidates using the above example to be sure he understands the statements. Such "paper and pencil reading" is an important part of the study of mathematics.

† This equation is sometimes called the **depressed equation.**

PROBLEM SET 4-4

1. Find the roots of $6x^3 - 11x^2 - 4x = 0$.
2. Find the roots of $6x^4 + 11x^3 + 14x^2 - 7x - 6 = 0$.
3. (a) Find rational factors of the left member of the equation given in Problem 2 and write the equation in factored form.
   (b) Find rational factors of $10x^3 - 31x^2 + 16x + 12$.
4. Find the rational factors of $x^6 - 64y^6$.
5. Determine all roots of $t^4 + t^3 + 66t^2 + 72t - 432 = 0$.
6. Determine all roots of $4x^3 - x - 3 = 0$.
7. Use synthetic division to factor $x^3 - 1$ and $x^5 + 32$. Many readers may find synthetic factoring easier than memorizing patterns.
8. Same as Problem 7 for $x^7 - 1$ and $x^4 - 81$.
9. In Problems 1 to 6, a fractional root c/d produces a depressed equation which is divisible by d. Prove that the depressed equation always has this property. Before further testing, the depressed equation should be divided by d.
10. (a) Is $x - 4$ a factor of $x^7 - 4x^3 - 2x + 1$? (b) Construct a polynomial of degree 7 with $x + 1$ and $x - 3$ as factors.
11. Divide $2x^4 - 8x^3 + 13x^2 + 40$ by $x + 2$ using long division. Compare the computation with that of Example 2. Encircle the coefficients in the long division process which also appear in the process of synthetic division. It is possible to justify synthetic division as an abbreviated form of long division.
12. The expression "monotone increasing function $f(x)$" means that as x increases, so does $f(x)$; that is, if $a < b$, then $f(a) < f(b)$. The function $f(x) = x^3 + 3x + 2$ is monotone increasing. Determine a value k such that if $x > k$, then $f(x) > 142$.
13. Calvin Butterball worked all summer for an onion grower. The onion grower's son Sebastian, who was home from college, bet Calvin \$2 that he could not find a quadratic equation in which the coefficient of x^2 was one and the constant term was seven and which had $x = 2$ as a root. Sebastian said it was impossible since the only possible roots would be $\pm \frac{1}{1}$ and $\pm \frac{7}{1}$. Calvin won the \$2 by giving the equation $x^2 - \frac{11}{2}x + 7 = 0$. What restriction did Sebastian forget? Can you find another equation which would satisfy Sebastian's conditions?
*14. A converse of the factor theorem states that if $x - h$ is a factor of $p(x)$, then $p(h) = 0$. Prove this converse and note the difference between the theorem and its converse.

In Problems 15 to 20, determine all roots of the given equations.

15. $z^3 + 4z^2 - 3z - 18 = 0.$ **16.** $2z^3 - 5z^2 - 4z + 12 = 0.$
17. $4z^4 - 2z^3 - 38z^2 + 4z = -60.$ **18.** $(z - 3)^2(z^2 + z + 1) = 0.$
19. $x^2 + x - 1 = 0.$ **20.** $(3x^2 + 3x - 7)(x - 4) = 3.$

4–5. Upper and lower bounds for intercepts. It would be very helpful when solving the intercept equation $p(x) = 0,$ (Section 3–2), if it were possible to determine a value m such that $p(x)$ would never be zero for $x > m.$ If $p(x)$ is a polynomial, such a method, which is easy to use, exists.

Consider Example 1 of Section 3–3. The x-intercept equation was $p(x) = -x^3 + 8x - 6 = 0.$ In determining $p(3)$ by synthetic substitution we obtain

$$3 \underline{\left| \begin{array}{r} -1 + 0 + 8 \quad -6 \\ -3 - 9 \quad -3 \end{array} \right.}$$
$$\overline{-1 - 3 - 1 \mid -9}.$$

Every sign in the bottom row is negative. If a value larger than 3 were used, these signs would not change. The numbers would each become larger in the negative direction. Hence, for $x > 3,$ $p(x) < 0.$ When $x > 3,$ $p(x) = 0$ has no solution. This argument can be generalized. If the signs in the quotient (third) line were all positive, similar reasoning could be used to complete the proof of Test 1.

Test 1. If every nonzero term of the bottom row obtained in the computation of $p(U)$ by synthetic division, where $U \geq 0,$ has the same sign (either all + or all −), then $p(x) = 0$ has no root greater than $U.$ In this case U is called an **upper bound** for the roots of $p(x) = 0.$

● *Example 1.* Determine an upper bound for the roots of
$$p(x) = x^3 - 2x^2 + x - 2 = 0.$$

$$2 \underline{\left| \begin{array}{r} 1 - 2 + 1 \quad -2 \\ 2 + 0 \quad +2 \end{array} \right.}$$
$$\overline{1 + 0 + 1 \mid +0}.$$

In this case $x = 2$ is a root and an upper bound. Hence, $p(x) = x^3 - 2x^2 + x - 2 = 0$ has no root larger than 2.

In Problem 23, Set 4–5, the reader will be asked to demonstrate the following similar rule on lower bounds for the roots of $p(x) = 0.$

Test 2. If the terms in the bottom row alternate in sign when $p(L)$ is obtained by synthetic division, where $L \leq 0,$ then $p(x) = 0$ has no root less than $L.$ In this case L is called a **lower bound** for the roots of $p(x) = 0.$

● **Example 2.** Determine upper and lower bounds for the roots of

$$Q(y) = y^4 - 4y^3 + 2y^2 - 28y - 5 = 0.$$

$$5 \begin{array}{|l} 1 - 4 + 2 - 28 \ - \ 5 \\ \hline 5 + 5 + 35 \ + 35 \\ \hline 1 + 1 + 7 + \ 7 \,| + 30 \end{array}.$$

All signs are positive, hence 5 is an upper bound.

$$-3 \begin{array}{|l} 1 - 4 + \ 2 - 28 \ - \ \ 5 \\ \hline - 3 + 21 - 69 \ + 291 \\ \hline 1 - 7 + 23 - 97 \,| + 286 \end{array}.$$

The signs alternate, hence -3 is a lower bound.

Thus all real (not involving i) roots of $Q(y) = 0$ must lie between -3 and 5. The student can obtain a better lower bound, and demonstrate that the roots lie between -1 and $+5$.

In applying Test 1 find the smallest positive (or zero) integer U such that the conditions are satisfied. Similarly, in Test 2 find the numerically smallest negative (or zero) integer L such that the conditions are satisfied. All real roots of $f(x) = 0$ are located in the interval $L \leq x \leq U$. In $x^3 - 2x^2 + x - 2 = 0$ we saw that 2 was both a root and an upper bound for the real roots. Since the coefficients alternate in sign, 0 is a lower bound. The depressed equation is $x^2 + 1 = 0$ which has two imaginary roots. These complex roots are $x = \pm i$.

We return to the problem of finding the rational roots (and, when possible, all of the roots) of a polynomial equation having integral coefficients. Let the equation be $ax^n + bx^{n-1} + \cdots + sx + t = 0$, where $a, b, \cdots, s, t$ are integral. To find all rational roots c/d use:

(1) The procedure indicated above for finding upper and lower bounds U and L.

(2) Consider possible choices for c/d such that $L \leq c/d \leq U$.

(3) Test, by synthetic division, these possible c/d values, testing integral values first for convenience. If the remainder is zero, the c/d value used is a root. This testing may permit the establishing of better upper and lower bounds.

(4) The remaining roots are to be found in the quotient equated to zero.

(5) Continue the process until all rational roots have been obtained.

(6) A quadratic quotient equated to zero can be solved by the formula of Section 1–9.

● **Example 3.** Find the roots of $8x^4 + 12x^3 - 6x^2 - 7x + 3 = 0$.

(1) Check $L = -2$ and $U = 1$.

(2) Choices for c/d with $-2 \leq c/d \leq 1$ are ± 1, $\pm \frac{1}{2}$, $\pm \frac{1}{4}$, $\pm \frac{1}{8}$, $-\frac{3}{2}$, $\pm \frac{3}{4}$, $\pm \frac{3}{8}$. Upon dividing by $x - \frac{1}{2}$ one finds

$$\frac{1}{2} \overline{) \begin{array}{l} 8 + 12 - 6 - 7 \ +3 \\ \ 4 + 8 + 1 \ -3 \\ \hline 8 + 16 + 2 - 6 \,|\, +0 \end{array}}.$$

Hence, $x = \frac{1}{2}$ is a root. The remaining roots are contained in the quotient set equal to zero. (Why?)

$$8x^3 + 16x^2 + 2x - 6 = 0.$$

This is equivalent to

$$4x^3 + 8x^2 + x - 3 = 0.$$

Upon testing one finds

$$\frac{1}{2} \overline{) \begin{array}{l} 4 + \ 8 + 1 \ -3 \\ \ 2 + 5 \ +3 \\ \hline 4 + 10 + 6 \,|\, +0 \end{array}}.$$

Hence, $x = \frac{1}{2}$ is again a root. The resulting quadratic $4x^2 + 10x + 6 = 0$ is easily factored.

$$2x^2 + 5x + 3 = 0,$$
$$(2x + 3)(x + 1) = 0,$$
$$x = -\tfrac{3}{2}, \quad x = -1.$$

Hence, the roots of the original equation are $\frac{1}{2}, \frac{1}{2}, -1, -\frac{3}{2}$. If instead of $\frac{1}{2}$, the integral root -1 had been used to depress the original equation, the work would have been slightly simplified.

PROBLEM SET 4–5

In Problems 1 to 5 determine all roots of each given equation.

1. $2x^4 - 3x^3 - 9x^2 + 6x + 10 = 0$.   **2.** $y^3 + 3y^2 - 2 = 0$.

3. $4t^3 - t - 3 = 0$.   **4.** $x^3 - 7x - 6 = 0$.

5. $x^4 + x^3 - 11x^2 - 9x + 18 = 0$.

In Problems 6 to 10 determine intercepts where convenient. If this is not convenient, locate each intercept between successive integers.

6. $y = x^4 - 2x^3 + x - 2$.   **7.** $y = x^3 - 6x^2 + 11x - 6$.

8. $y = x^3 - 8x + 6$.   **9.** $y = t^3 - 15t^2 - t + 16$.

10. $y = 7x^3 + 3$.

11. Divide $x^5 - 7x^3 + 5x^2 - 3x + 4$ by $x - 7$ using synthetic division.

12. Divide $x^5 - 6x^3 + 5x - 4$ by $x - 2$ using synthetic division.

13. Divide $x^7 - 4x^3 + x - 2$ by $x + 1$ using synthetic division.

14. Divide $x^4 - 3x^2 + 2x - 7$ by $x + 3$ using synthetic division.

15. In Example 2, Section 4–5, show that the roots lie between -1 and 5. Argue further that, since $Q(-1) > 0$ and $Q(5) > 0$ while $Q(0) = -5$, there must be at least one root between 0 and 5 and at least one root between -1 and 0.

16. Show that $x^3 - 8x + 6 = 0$ has a root between 2 and 3.

17. Show that $x^5 + 35 = 0$ has a root between -2 and -3. Which value is the root nearer?

18. Show that $x^3 - 2x^2 - 8x + 6 = 0$ has a root between 0 and 7.

19. Discuss the possible roots of $\dfrac{1}{3x - 5} = 0$. Why do Tests 1 and 2 *not* apply? Why can we *not* say there is a root between $x = 1$ and $x = 2$? Sketch the locus $y = \dfrac{1}{3x - 5}$.

*20. Let h be a root of the polynomial equation

$$x^n + a_{n-1} x^{n-1} + \cdots + a_2 x^2 + a_1 x + a_0 = 0.$$

Show that $|h| \leq 1 + (\text{maximum absolute coefficient } |a_i|)$.

[HINT: In synthetic division when using h larger than $[1 + (\max |a_i|)]$, every entry (including the last) will be greater than or equal to 1 in absolute value.]

*21. Is there a problem in this set to which the results of Problem 20 may be profitably applied?

*22. Show that $2x^4 - x^3 + 3x^2 - 3x + 4 = 0$ has no real roots.

[HINT: Zero is a lower bound. If the left member is multiplied by $(x + 1)$, zero may be shown to be an upper bound of the product equated to zero.]

*23. Give an argument similar to that given for Test 1 to prove Test 2 of Section 4–5.

*24. Sketch the locus of $y = 8x^4 + 12x^3 - 6x^2 - 7x + 3$. Note especially the appearance of the locus at $x = \frac{1}{2}$. See Example 3.

*25. Let $p(x) = 0$ be a polynomial equation. Show that if the sign of the coefficient of each *odd* power of x is changed, the resulting equation has roots which are opposite in sign from those of $p(x) = 0$, but the same in absolute value.

26. Find the rational roots and if possible find all roots of

$$2x^4 + 3x^3 - 6x^2 + 8x - 3 = 0.$$

27. Find the rational roots and if possible find all roots of

$$8x^3 - 12x^2 - 2x + 3 = 0.$$

28. Find all roots of $3x^4 - 4x^3 - 11x^2 - 14x + 6 = 0$.

29. Determine all roots of the equation $2x^3 + x^2 - 2x - 1 = 0$.

30. Solve and check $\sqrt{3x - 5} - \sqrt{2x + 3} + 1 = 0$.

31. The graph of $(x^2 + y^2 - 1)(x + 3) = 0$ consists of all points on the circle $x^2 + y^2 - 1 = 0$ and all points on the line $x + 3 = 0$. Every point on either piece of this locus satisfies the original equation. A point on the circle will make the first factor zero and hence the product equal to zero. A point on the line makes the second factor zero. In either case the equation is satisfied. Graph the locus,

$$[x^2 + y^2 - 9][(x - 1)^2 + (y - 1)^2 - \tfrac{1}{9}][(x + 1)^2 + (y - 1)^2 - \tfrac{1}{9}][x^2 + (y + 1)^2 - \tfrac{1}{4}] = 0.$$

32. Plot the following relation on cartesian coordinate paper. Your graph will tell you if it is correct.

$$f(x) = \begin{cases} 0 & \text{for } x < -3 \\ \pm \sqrt{9 - x^2} & \text{for } -3 \leq x < 3 \\ 0 & \text{for } 3 \leq x < 4 \\ [\text{all values from } -3 \text{ to } +3] & \text{for } x = 4 \\ \pm (x - 4) & \text{for } 4 < x < 7 \\ 0 & \text{for } x \geq 7 \end{cases}$$

4–6. Symmetry of points. Useful information concerning an equation or inequality may be determined by examining its locus. The time required to sketch certain loci may be greatly reduced by using the concepts of symmetry. We first define two types of symmetry for points and then extend these definitions to symmetry of loci. A precise statement of the meaning of symmetry is needed for further work.

Symmetry with respect to a point. Two points A and B are said to be symmetric with respect to a point M if M is the midpoint of the line segment AB. Each of the points A, B is called the symmetric point of the other with respect to M. The midpoint M is the **center of symmetry.** Every point is said to be symmetric with respect to itself.

● **Example 1.** Show that two points $A(3, 2)$ and $B(5, -4)$ are symmetric with respect to the point $M(4, -1)$. To show this we need to show that $|AM| = |MB|$ and that M lies on the line joining A and B. From the distance formula

$$|AM| = \sqrt{(3-4)^2 + (2+1)^2} = \sqrt{10},$$
$$|MB| = \sqrt{(5-4)^2 + (-4+1)^2} = \sqrt{10}.$$

Thus, $|AM| = |MB|$. Since the shortest distance between two points in a plane is a straight line, we may show that M lies on AB by showing that $|AB| = |AM| + |MB|$. (Why does this show that M lies on AB?)

$$|AB| = \sqrt{(3-5)^2 + (2+4)^2} = \sqrt{40} = 2\sqrt{10}$$

as desired. Hence, the points A and B are symmetric with respect to M. (Why?)

● **Illustration 1.** The two end points of a diameter of the circle $(x-1)^2 + (y+2)^2 = 16$ are symmetric with respect to the center $(1, -2)$ of the circle. This is true for every diameter.

● **Illustration 2.** Any two distinct points on the same diameter of the circular region $(x-1)^2 + (y+2)^2 < 16$ and each at the same distance $d < 4$ from $(1, -2)$ are symmetric with respect to $(1, -2)$. This is true for every diameter and every d such that $0 \leq d < 4$.

Symmetry with respect to a line. Two points A and B are said to be symmetric with respect to a line L if L is the perpendicular bisector of the line segment AB. Each of the points A and B is called the symmetric point of the other with respect to L. L is an **axis of symmetry.**

● **Example 2.** Determine the equation of a line L such that $A(-1, 3)$ and $B(2, 5)$ are symmetric with respect to L.

From the definition of symmetry the desired line is the perpendicular bisector of the line segment AB. This was determined in Example 2, Section 2–4, to be $6x + 4y - 19 = 0$.

PROBLEM SET 4-6

Determine the symmetric points of each of the following points with respect to the origin, each coordinate axis, the point M, and the line L indicated in the problem.

1. $(2, 3)$, $M(2, 5)$, L: $x = 4$.

2. $(1, -4)$, $M(3, 5)$, L: $y = 1$.

3. $(2, -6)$, $M(3, -1)$, L: $y = 3$.

4. $(-4, 3)$, $M(1, 2)$, L: $y = -1$.

*5. $(3, 4)$, $M(5, 5)$, L: $x = y$.

*6. Prove that symmetry with respect to both x- and y-axes implies symmetry with respect to the origin.

*7. Given two points $A(x_1, y_1)$ and $B(x_2, y_2)$ show that it is always possible to determine a point M such that A and B are symmetric with respect to M.

8. Prove or disprove: (a) If two points are symmetric with respect to the line L, then they are symmetric with respect to any point M on line L. (b) If two points are symmetric with respect to a point M, then they are symmetric with respect to any line L through M.

4-7. Symmetry of loci. A locus [meaning a curve in the case of an equation or a region in the case of an inequality] is said to be symmetric with respect to a line L (or a point M), if the symmetric point with respect to the line L (or point M) of every point of the locus also lies on the locus.

Symmetry with respect to a line implies that if the plane were folded along the line of symmetry, each point of the locus would coincide with its symmetric point. The phrase "mirror image" is descriptive.

In Illustration 1, Section 4-6, the circumference of the circle is symmetric with respect to its center. In Illustration 2, Section 4-6, the interior of the circle is symmetric with respect to its center. If L is taken as a diameter of either of these circles, then the locus (circumference in Illustration 1, interior in Illustration 2) is symmetric with respect to L.

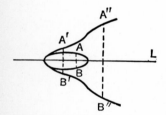

Fig. 4–1. Symmetry with respect to line L.

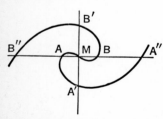

Fig. 4–2. Symmetry with respect to point M.

● **Example 1.** Consider the region of points inside and upon the perimeter of an equilateral triangle. The region of points inside and also upon the perimeter is symmetric with respect to any one of the three medians.† This may suggest reasons for calling the point of intersection of the medians the centroid (center of gravity).

† The median of a triangle is the line joining a vertex with the midpoint of the opposite side. In an equilateral triangle the median coincides with the altitude from the same vertex.

PROBLEM SET 4-7

1. Show that the locus $x^2 + y^2 = 9$ is *not* symmetric with respect to the line $x = 1$. Find a line with respect to which symmetry exists.
2. Sketch a line L and a curve C which is symmetric with respect to L and such that C crosses L at least four times.
3. Sketch a region symmetric with respect to the line $x = 5$.
4. Sketch a curve symmetric with respect to the point $(2, -1)$.
5. Problem 7, Set 4–6, states that given two points it is always possible to determine a center of symmetry. Show by a counterexample that this is not so if "two points" is replaced by "a locus."
6. Given two points A, B show that it is always possible to determine an axis of symmetry. Give a counterexample to show that if "two points" is replaced by "a locus," the theorem does not follow.
7. Find a line of symmetry for the triangle whose vertices are $(3, 1)$, $(5, 1)$, and $(4, -2)$.
8. Find a line of symmetry for the circular region

$$(x - 2)^2 + (y + 1)^2 \leqq 4.$$

Determine another line of symmetry for this region.
9. Locate a line which is symmetric to the line $x = 5$ with respect to the point $(3, 5)$.
10. Locate a line which is symmetric to the line $y = 5$ with respect to the point $(5, -1)$.

4–8. Tests for symmetry. Certain useful tests for symmetry are convenient to apply.

Symmetry with respect to the origin. If the substitution of $-x$ for x and $-y$ for y in the equation or inequality gives an equivalent equation or inequality, then the locus is symmetric with respect to the origin. To prove this we observe that if (x, y) is a point of the locus, then so is $(-x, -y)$. The origin is the midpoint of the line segment connecting (x, y) and $(-x, -y)$. If a locus is symmetric with respect to the origin, one may sketch half of the locus and draw the remaining half by symmetry. (See Fig. 4–3.)

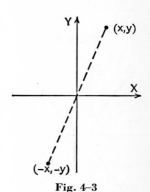

Fig. 4–3

- *Example 1.* $0 \leqq xy \leqq 4$. This locus is a region rather than a curve. Since $(-x)(-y) = xy$, the locus is symmetric with respect to the origin. If either $x = 0$ or $y = 0$, then $xy = 0$. Hence, the points on the y- and x-axes are part of the locus. The curve $xy = 4$ is also part of the locus. Let us sketch that portion of the curve $y = 4/x$ (that is, $xy = 4$) in which $x > 0$. (The curve $xy = 4$ is discontinuous at $x = 0$. Why?) At $x = 1, y = 4$. As x increases, the value of y decreases toward zero. As x decreases through positive values toward zero, the value of y increases. In symbols, $x \nearrow L^+$ implies $y \searrow 0$, and $x \searrow 0$ implies $y \nearrow L^+$. These considerations permit us to sketch the portion of the locus shown in the first quadrant. The remainder of the locus lies in the third quadrant and is sketched by symmetry with respect to the origin. Note that the locus consists of all points on the curves $xy = 4$, $y = 0$, $x = 0$, and the points in the first and third quadrants in the regions "bounded" by these curves. (See Fig. 4–4.)

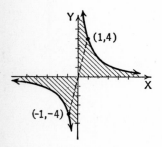

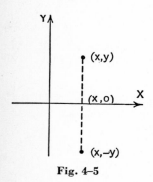

Fig. 4–4

Symmetry with respect to the x-axis. If the substitution of $- y$ for y gives an equivalent equation or inequality, then the locus is symmetric with respect to the x-axis. To prove this we observe that if (x, y) is a point on the locus, then so is $(x, - y)$. Both points lie on a line segment perpendicular to the x-axis and having the point $(x, 0)$ on the x-axis as midpoint. (See Fig. 4–5.) If a locus is symmetric with respect to the x-axis, one may sketch that part of the locus above or on the x-axis and sketch the remainder of the locus as the "mirror image."

Fig. 4–5

● *Example 2.* $|y| < 5$. The locus is symmetric with respect to the x-axis since $|-y| = |y|$. In this case the locus consists of the points in the region between the lines $y = -5$ and $y = 5$, but not on either of these lines. (See Fig. 4–6.)

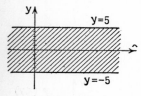

Fig. 4–6

● *Example 3.* $y^2 - x(x - 1) = 0$. Since

$$y^2 - x(x - 1) = (- y)^2 - x(x - 1),$$

the locus is symmetric with respect to the x-axis. The x-intercepts are 0 and 1. The y-intercept is 0. Let us consider the upper portion $y = + \sqrt{x(x - 1)}$. (1) If $x < 0$, $x(x - 1) > 0$ and the larger $- x$ becomes the larger y becomes. (Why?) (2) If $0 < x < 1$, $x(x - 1) < 0$ and y is imaginary. Hence, no real locus exists in this interval. (3) If $x > 1$, $x(x - 1) > 0$. The larger x becomes, the larger y becomes. (4) The portion below the x-axis is sketched using symmetry. (See Fig. 4–7.)

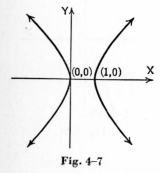

Fig. 4–7

Symmetry with respect to the y-axis. If the substitution of $- x$ for x gives an equivalent equation or inequality, then the locus is symmetric with respect to the y-axis. To prove this we observe that if $(- x, y)$ is a point on the locus, then so is (x, y). Both points lie on a line segment perpendicular to the y-axis and having the point $(0, y)$ on the y-axis as midpoint.

● *Example 4.* Find the locus of all points (x, y) where

$$0 \leqq y < x^2.$$

The locus (a region) consists of the (x, y) points between the parabola $y = x^2$ and the x-axis, including points of the x-axis but not points of the parabola. The origin is *not* part of the locus. (Why?) If (x, y) are the coordinates of any point in the region $0 \leqq y < x^2$, then $(-x, y)$ is a point in the region since $(-x)^2 = x^2$. The region is symmetric with respect to the y-axis. (See Fig. 4–9.)

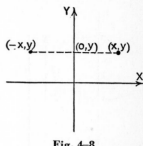

Fig. 4–8

● *Example 5.* $x^3 - 3x + xy^2 = 0.$

If y is replaced by $-y$, the resulting equation is equivalent to the original. Hence, the locus is symmetric with respect to the x-axis. If x is replaced by $-x$, the resulting equation

$$-x^3 + 3x - xy^2 = 0$$

is equivalent to the original. Since the locus is symmetric with respect to the x-axis and to the y-axis, it is also symmetric with respect to the origin. (Why?) Note that the left member of the equation is factorable: $x(x^2 + y^2 - 3) = 0$. Hence, the locus consists of *two distinct curves* — namely, the line $x = 0$ (the y-axis) and the circle $x^2 + y^2 = 3$.

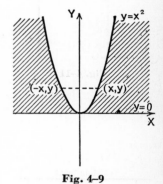

Fig. 4–9

4–9. Applications. In this chapter we are interested in the behavior of the locus in certain particular regions. It may be helpful to plot several points in these regions to obtain reasonable accuracy.

● *Example 1.* A stone is thrown vertically upward from the top of a tower 400 ft high. The height h in feet of the stone *from the ground* at any time t sec, after it is thrown until it strikes the ground, is $h = 400 + 120t - 16t^2$.

Sketch the locus of this equation, and from this sketch estimate:

(1) The time when the stone reaches its maximum height.
(2) The maximum height of the stone from the ground.
(3) The time when the stone strikes the ground.

The locus was discussed and sketched in Example 2, Section 3–6. The portion of the sketch which applies to this problem is repeated here for your convenience. The results for (1) and (2) are obtained in Example 2, Section 4–10, where it is found that the time required for the stone to reach its maximum height is $t = \frac{15}{4}$ sec, and the maximum height is $h = 400 + 120(\frac{15}{4}) - 16(\frac{15}{4})^2 = 625$ feet. (3) When

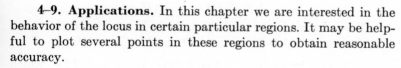

Fig. 4–10

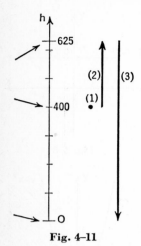

Fig. 4–11

the stone reaches the ground, the height h is zero. We see that $h = 0$ for $t = -\frac{5}{2}$ and $t = 10$. The stone was 400 ft above the ground (at the top of the tower) when $t = 0$, and hit the ground when $t = 10$. The region of interest in this problem is that portion of the parabola $h = 400 + 120t - 16t^2$ in the interval $0 \leqq t \leqq 10$.

It is convenient to study the motion using the locus just mentioned, even though the stone moves along the vertical h-axis as follows:

(1) At time $t = 0$ sec, the stone is at $h = 400$ ft.

(2) As the time increases from $t = 0$ to $t = \frac{15}{4}$ sec, the stone rises to its maximum height $h = 625$ ft.

(3) As the time increases from $t = \frac{15}{4}$ to $t = 10$ sec, the stone falls from $h = 625$ ft to the ground $h = 0$ ft.

● **Example 2.** A man has 300 linear ft of new fencing. He wishes to enclose a rectangular plot of ground using an existing fence as one side and the new fencing for the other three sides. What are the dimensions of the rectangle of largest area he may enclose?

Let x be the length in feet of each of the two sides, perpendicular to the existing fence. Then $300 - 2x$ ft is the length of the remaining side. The enclosed area is

$$A = x(300 - 2x) \text{ sq ft.}$$

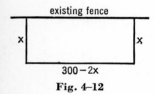

Fig. 4–12

To study this function, we examine its locus. The graph crosses the x-axis $(A = 0)$ at $x = 0$ and at $x = 150$.

When x is negative, $A = x(300 - 2x) = (-) \cdot (+)$ which is negative.

When $0 < x < 150$, $A = (+) \cdot (+)$ which is positive.

When $150 < x$, $A = (+) \cdot (-)$ which is negative.

The portion of the locus $A = x(300 - 2x)$ under consideration in this example is the part in which $A > 0$, namely, $0 < x < 150$. Since

$$\begin{aligned}
A &= x(300 - 2x) \\
&= -2(x^2 - 150x) \\
&= 11250 - 2(x^2 - 150x + 5625) \\
&= 11250 - 2(x - 75)^2,
\end{aligned}$$

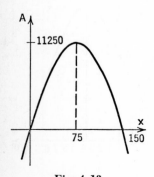

Fig. 4–13

the locus is symmetric with respect to the line $x = 75$. (Why?) The maximum area $A = 11250$ sq ft is obtained when $x = 75$ ft and $300 - 2x = 150$ ft.

The word **maximum** (or, more accurately, **relative maximum**) is used for a value of $f(x)$ at $x = a$, if $f(a)$ is greater than or equal to all other values of $f(x)$ for x close to a. More precisely, a function $f(x)$ has a (relative) maximum $f(a)$ at $x = a$ if $f(a) \geq f(a + \Delta x)$ for Δx sufficiently near to zero. The reader should notice that a function may have more than one relative maximum, and that the relative maximum is not necessarily the greatest value (absolute maximum) of $f(x)$ on the entire curve. It is the greatest value of $f(x)$ for a small segment of the curve. In a similar fashion, $f(a)$ is a **relative minimum** of a function $f(x)$ when $f(a)$ is the smallest value which $f(x)$ takes for x near a. Thus, $f(a)$ is a relative minimum of $f(x)$ if $f(a) \leq f(a + \Delta x)$ for Δx sufficiently close to zero. A more extensive discussion of relative maxima and minima is given in Sections 6–8 and 6–9.

In Figure 4–14, note that the minimum at E is actually greater than the maximum at A.

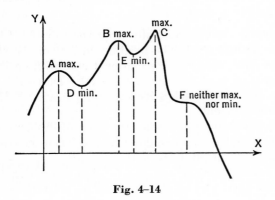

Fig. 4–14

PROBLEM SET 4–9

1. Draw a curve having three maximum and two minimum ordinates (y values).
2. Draw a curve having three minimum and three maximum ordinates. Make one of the *minimum* ordinates greater than at least one of the maximum ordinates.
3. Draw a curve which is not a straight line, and does not contain any maximum or minimum ordinates.
4. Determine the coordinates of the points of the locus $(x - 3)^2 + (y + 1)^2 = 25$ where y has a maximum or minimum value.

5. Determine the absolute maximum (greatest value) of y in the range $-1 \leqq x < 5$ for each of the curves of Problems 1, 2, 3, 4. Does x have a maximum value? At what point?

In Problems 6 to 15 discuss and sketch each locus. Estimate the maximum and minimum values for y, z, or a, as the case may be.

6. $y = x^2 + 3$.   **7.** $y = 3x^2 - 5x$.   **8.** $a = 3t^2 - 6t + 9$.

9. $z = (t - 17)^2 + 5$.   **10.** $a = 4x^4 - 3$.

11. $y = (x + 3)^2 - 1$.   **12.** $y = x^3$.   **13.** $z = (t - 7)(t + 2)$.

14. $y = \begin{cases} -3x + 1 & \text{if } x \leqq 1 \\ x^2 - 3 & \text{if } x > 1. \end{cases}$ **15.** $y = \begin{cases} x^2 & \text{if } x \leqq 2 \\ -2x + 8 & \text{if } x > 2. \end{cases}$

In each of the Problems 16 to 27, obtain a function of the variables involved and sketch its locus. Use the sketch to estimate the values called for in the problem.

16. A stone is thrown vertically from the top of a tower 80 ft above ground level. The height h in feet of the stone *from the ground* at any time t sec after it is thrown until it strikes the ground is $h = -16t^2 + 64t + 80$. Determine the time when the stone reaches its maximum height. Estimate the maximum height.

17. (a) Determine the time when the stone of Problem 16 reaches the ground. (b) Approximate the time when the stone passes a window ledge 30 ft above the ground.

18. Si Hawkins has 500 ft of new fencing. He wishes to enclose a rectangular plot of ground using an existing fence as one side and new fencing for the other three sides. What are the approximate dimensions of the rectangle of largest area he may enclose?

19. Bud Hawkins has 800 ft of new fencing. He wishes to fence a rectangular plot of ground and divide it into three pens by placing two fences parallel to one side of the rectangle. Determine the largest total area he may enclose.

20. A certain force in a machine is known to be equal to

$$F = (t - 1)(t + 3) + 2 \quad \text{for} \quad 0 \leqq t \leqq 5.$$

Determine the greatest and the least force exerted during the given time (t) interval.

21. The current I in an electrical circuit is known to obey the following law for $0 \leqq t \leqq 10$ where t is the time in seconds:

$$I = t^3 - 9t^2 + 20t - 12 = (t - 1)(t - 2)(t - 6).$$

Determine the greatest and least current during this period.

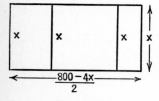

Fig. 4–15

22. A railroad trip costs 8¢ per mile. An automobile trip costs 4¢ per mile plus an additional $16 for a permit which is not needed on the rail trip. Graph the cost as a function of distance on the same set of axes for each of these modes of transportation, and determine for what distances it is cheaper to go by train and for what distances it is cheaper to go by auto.

23. (a) Determine the relative maximum and minimum values of the following function.

$$y = \begin{cases} 4x + 10 & \text{if} \quad x \leq -5 \\ x - 5 & \text{if} \quad -5 < x < 1 \\ -x - 3 & \text{if} \quad 1 \leq x < 4 \\ 5x - 27 & \text{if} \quad 4 \leq x < 10 \\ 23 & \text{if} \quad 10 \leq x. \end{cases}$$

(b) Determine the absolute maximum and absolute minimum in the range $-1 \leq x \leq 7$.

*24. A cylindrical tin can is to be constructed to contain 125 cu in. The circular top and bottom are cut from square pieces with the scraps wasted. The side is cut from a large sheet without waste. Determine the approximate dimensions of a can requiring the least total sheet metal.

HINT: First show that, since $\pi r^2 h = 125$, the total sheet metal required to construct a can (including waste) is

$$M = 2(2r)^2 + 2\pi r \left[\frac{125}{\pi r^2} \right]$$

$$= 8r^2 + \frac{250}{r}.$$

Sketch the graph in the range $0 < r < 1000$.

*25. A sheet of tin, 10 by 20 in., has equal squares cut from the corners and the edges are turned up to form a box with open top. Let x be the length of the side of the squares removed. Show that the volume of the box is

$$V = x(20 - 2x)(10 - 2x).$$

Sketch the locus, and estimate the volume of the largest box which may be so formed. For what range of values of x does the function have meaning in this problem?

26. Phoebe Small and Calvin Butterball are at the county fair. Calvin tosses a peanut from the top of the giant Ferris wheel 60 ft high. The distance $h(t)$ of the peanut from the ground at any time t sec after it is thrown until it strikes something is given by $h(t) = 60 + 8t - 16t^2$. Unfortunately, the peanut strikes the operator of the Ferris wheel on the head.

How long after Calvin throws the peanut does it strike the operator if his head is 6 ft above ground level? For what range of values of t does the function $h(t)$ represent the distance of the peanut from the ground? Does Calvin toss the peanut *up* or throw it *down* from the top of the Ferris wheel?

27. Separate 100 into two parts such that their product is a maximum.

4–10. The quadratic function. Many applied problems involve the quadratic function $y = at^2 + bt + c$ for various constant real values of a, b, c with $a \neq 0$. Examples 1 and 2 of Section 4–9 illustrate this. The locus is called a **parabola.** If $a > 0$, the curve opens upward (that is, $t \to$ either L^+ or L^- implies $y \nearrow L^+$). If $a < 0$, the curve opens downward. A good example of a segment of a parabola may be seen by noting the arch of water from a garden hose. Section 1–10 shows how to determine, by using the quadratic formula, values of t which give a fixed value for y. We now devise an algebraic method for finding the maximum, or minimum, value of y.

$$y = at^2 + bt + c$$
$$= a\left[t^2 + \frac{b}{a}t\right] + c$$
$$= a\left[t^2 + \frac{b}{a}t + \frac{b^2}{4a^2}\right] + c - \frac{b^2}{4a}$$
$$= a\left[t + \frac{b}{2a}\right]^2 + \left[c - \frac{b^2}{4a}\right].$$

There are two cases to consider: $a > 0$ and $a < 0$.

Case 1: If $a > 0$, then since $c - \frac{b^2}{4a}$ is constant and $\left[t + \frac{b}{2a}\right]^2$ is positive or zero, the minimum value of y will occur when $\left[t + \frac{b}{2a}\right]^2$ equals zero — that is, when $t = \frac{-b}{2a}$. For $t = \frac{-b}{2a}$, zero is added to $c - \frac{b^2}{4a}$ giving the minimum value, $y = c - \frac{b^2}{4a}$. There is no maximum value if $a > 0$.

Case 2: If $a < 0$, then $a\left[t + \frac{b}{2a}\right]^2$ is always negative or zero, and a maximum value is obtained when $\left[t + \frac{b}{2a}\right]^2$ is as small as possible. This occurs when $t + \frac{b}{2a} = 0$: that is, when $t = \frac{-b}{2a}$. For $t = \frac{-b}{2a}$, zero is subtracted from $c - \frac{b^2}{4a}$ and the maximum value $y = c - \dfrac{b^2}{4a}$ is obtained. There is no mini-

mum value if $a < 0$.

From the geometrical point of view it may be observed that the parabola $y = at^2 + bt + c$ is symmetrical with respect to the line $t = \dfrac{-b}{2a}$. (See Problem 8, Set 4–10.) The maximum or minimum

point $\left(\dfrac{-b}{2a}, \ c - \dfrac{b^2}{4a}\right)$ where the line of symmetry intersects the curve is called the **vertex** of the parabola.

● **Example 1.** Find the maximum or minimum value for
$$y = 3x^2 - 2x - 5.$$

Since the function is quadratic with $a = 3$, $b = -2$, $c = -5$, $|x| \nearrow L^+$ implies $y \nearrow L^+$ and no maximum exists. The minimum y occurs at $x = \dfrac{-b}{2a} = \dfrac{-(-2)}{2(3)} = \dfrac{1}{3}$, and its value is
$$y = 3(\tfrac{1}{3})^2 - 2(\tfrac{1}{3}) - 5 = -\tfrac{16}{3}.$$

● **Example 2.** Solve Example 1 of Section 4–9.
$$h = 400 + 120t - 16t^2.$$

Since
$$a = -16, \quad b = 120, \quad c = 400, \quad |t| \nearrow L^+ \text{ implies } y \searrow L^-.$$

No minimum exists. The maximum y occurs at
$$t = \frac{-b}{2a} = \frac{-120}{2(-16)} = \frac{15}{4},$$
and its value is $h = 400 + 120(\tfrac{15}{4}) - 16(\tfrac{15}{4})^2 = 625$. The time required to reach the maximum height is $t = \tfrac{15}{4}$ sec, and the actual maximum height is $h = 625$ ft.

PROBLEM SET 4–10

1. Solve Example 2 of Section 4–9 using the results of this section.
2. Solve Problem 8 of Set 4–9 using the results of this section.
3. Solve Problem 16 of Set 4–9 using the results of this section.
4. Solve Problem 19 of Set 4–9 using the results of this section.

5. Solve Problem 7 of Set 4–9 using the results of this section.
6. Solve Problem 13 of Set 4–9 using the results of this section.
7. Use the identity $x(300 - 2x) = 11250 - 2(x - 75)^2$ to show that the locus discussed in Example 2, Section 4–9, is symmetric with respect to the line $x = 75$.

*8. Complete the argument to show that $x = \dfrac{-b}{2a}$ is a line of symmetry for the parabola $y = ax^2 + bx + c$.

4–11. Self test. Record time.

1. (a) Find lower and upper bounds to the roots of
$$4x^4 - 7x^3 - 17x^2 + 3x + 9 = 0.$$
(b) Sketch $y = 4x^4 - 7x^3 - 17x^2 + 3x + 9$ using integral x-values. In finding x-intercepts, why is it unnecessary to use x-values less than the lower bound or greater than the upper bound found in (a)? (c) List all possible choices c/d for the rational roots of $4x^4 - 7x^3 - 17x^2 + 3x + 9 = 0$. (d) Eliminate from the list (c) any values that (a) and (b) show unnecessary. (e) Test for rational roots of
$$4x^4 - 7x^3 - 17x^2 + 3x + 9 = 0.$$
Use a corresponding depressed equation when a root is found.
(f) Find all roots of $4x^4 - 7x^3 - 17x^2 + 3x + 9 = 0$.
(g) Write $4x^4 - 7x^3 - 17x^2 + 3x + 9$ as a product of first-degree factors and a constant.

2. Locate the real roots between successive integers:

(a) $x^3 + 2x + 8 = 0$,   (b) $x^3 - 9x^2 - 27 = 0$.

3. Test for symmetry, find x- and y-intercepts, test for vertical and horizontal asymptotes, observe the general behavior of the locus, and sketch:

(a) $xy + 3y = 6$,   (b) $x^2y + 9y = 18$,   (c) $xy + 3y = 6x$.

4. Find the roots of $8x^4 - 12x^3 - 6x^2 + 7x + 3 = 0$.
5. Sketch: (a) $y^2 \leq 4x$,   (b) $(4 - x^2)y = 8x$.
6. Find the x- and y-intercepts of $y = 2x^3 - 5x^2 - 5x + 6$.
7. Explain the difference, if any, in the graphs of
$$y = \frac{x^2 - 25}{x + 5} \quad \text{and} \quad y = x - 5.$$

8. Find and simplify $\dfrac{\Delta f(3, \Delta x)}{\Delta x}$, where $f(t) = \dfrac{4}{3t^2}$.

9. Determine the vertex of the parabola $y = x^2 - 12x + 17$ by the method of completing the square of the right-hand member. Determine the intercepts and sketch the locus.

Record time.

5

In this chapter we define the slope of a line and the tangent line to a curve at a point P. We then devise a method for determining the slope of a line tangent to a given curve. This chapter lays the foundation for the future study of derivatives (Chap. 6). A mastery of the ideas involved in this chapter is essential for later work. The exercises should also help you gain proficiency in algebraic manipulation needed for further study.

5–1. Slope of a line. Let $C(x_1, y_1)$ and $D(x_2, y_2)$ be two distinct points on a line AB which is not parallel † to the y-axis. Construct lines through C and D parallel to the x- and the y-axes respectively. Call their point of intersection Q. The **slope** m of the line AB is the ratio of the directed distances: $\dfrac{QD}{CQ} = m$.

$$m = \frac{QD}{CQ} = \frac{y_2 - y_1}{x_2 - x_1}. \tag{5.1}$$

Why?

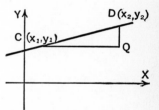

Fig. 5–1

The adjective "directed" modifying distances means the distance QD is positive if D lies above Q and negative if D lies below Q. Similarly, the distance CQ is positive if Q is to the right of C (see Section 2–2), and negative if Q is to the left of C, where it is assumed that the positive x-direction is to the right and the positive y-direction is upward.

Either the ratio $\dfrac{QD}{CQ}$ or its reciprocal would provide a quantitative measure of the "slant" of a line. The choice $\dfrac{y_2 - y_1}{x_2 - x_1}$ has the advantage that a horizontal line (level line) has the numerical slope *zero*. The definition of slope makes no numerical provision for vertical lines, however, since division by zero is not defined. The reader should note the distinction between "zero slope" and "the slope is not defined" (no slope) lest he confuse horizontal and vertical lines.

Similarly, if other points C' and D' had been chosen on the line AB instead of C and D, then CQD and $C'Q'D'$ would be similar triangles. Consequently,

$$m = \frac{QD}{CQ} = \frac{Q'D'}{C'Q'}.$$

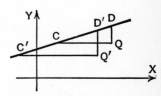

Fig. 5–2

† The slope of a line parallel to the y-axis is not defined.

Hence (excluding vertical lines), the slope of a straight line is unique. This was taken into consideration when the definition of slope was formulated.

● **Example 1.** Find the slope of the line joining $(-2, -3)$ and $(1, 2)$.

$$m = \frac{2 - (-3)}{1 - (-2)} = \frac{5}{3}.$$

If the points are considered in the opposite order, then

$$m = \frac{-3 - (2)}{-2 - (1)} = \frac{-5}{-3} = \frac{5}{3} \quad \text{as before.}$$

● **Example 2.** Assume $3x + 2y = 18$ is a line and find its slope. The intercepts provide two convenient points, $(6, 0)$ and $(0, 9)$. Then

$$m = \frac{9 - 0}{0 - 6} = \frac{9}{-6} = \frac{-3}{2}.$$

Two parallel lines have the same slope, if their slope is defined.

PROBLEM SET 5–1

In Problems 1 to 6 determine the slope of a line through the given points. Sketch the line.

1. $(2, -3)$, $(1, 5)$.   2. $(3, -1)$, $(4, -6)$.
3. $(2, 9)$, $(2, 4)$.   4. $(3, 2)$, $(1, 2)$.
5. $(1, -1)$, $(3, 7)$.   6. $(-4, 6)$, $(1, 6)$.
7. A bridge has trusses as shown. Determine the slope of the 13 trusses if the roadbed is horizontal (zero slope).

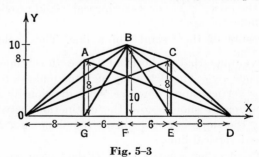

Fig. 5–3

In Problems 8, 9, 10 find the slope of each given line.

8. $3x + 2y - 5 = 0$.   9. $7x - 3y + 2 = 0$.   10. $4x + 10y = 17$.
11. Sketch the line which passes through $(2, -3)$ and has slope $m = 5$.

12. Sketch the line which passes through (1, 3) and has slope $m = 2$.

13. Sketch the line passing through $(7, -1)$ which has slope -3.

14. Sketch the line passing through $(4, -2)$ which has slope -1.

15. If $y = L(x)$ is the equation of a line, show that the slope of the line is $\dfrac{\Delta L(x, \Delta x)}{\Delta x}$.

16. Use the result of Problem 15 to solve Problems 8, 9, and 10.

17. What is the slope of the line $y = 7$?

18. Discuss the slope of the line $x = 2$.

19. Discuss the slope of the line $6x + 5 = 0$.

20. Discuss the slope of the line $4y - 3 = 15$.

21. Show that, in the usual x-, y-coordinate system, a line which rises as one goes to the right has positive slope.

22. Show that a line, in the usual x-, y-coordinate system, which falls as one goes to the right has negative slope.

23. What are the slopes of the two lines through the origin making angles of 45 degrees with the positive half of the x-axis?

24. What is the slope of a line parallel to that line of Problem 23 which lies in quadrants I and III?

25. Determine the slope of a line through the origin which divides the second quadrant into two congruent symmetric regions.

26. Determine the slope of a line parallel to the line of Problem 25.

27. Determine the slopes of the two lines through (2, 1) which make an angle of 30 degrees with the x-axis.

[HINT: Recall from geometry that in a 30-degree, 60-degree, 90-degree triangle, the short side is always half the hypotenuse.]

28. Determine the slopes of the two lines through (3, 5) which make an angle of 60 degrees with the x-axis.

29. Show that the steeper the line the larger the absolute value of the slope becomes.

30. Prove by elementary geometry that two parallel lines have the same slope.

31. Prove that the slope m of a line is the number of units that y increases (decreases if m is negative) for each unit of increase in x. Compare Problem 15.

*32. If the "slant" of a line were defined as $\dfrac{QD}{CD}$, there would be a numerical "slant" for every line, without exception. In particular, the slant of a horizontal line would be *zero* and of a vertical line *one*. Moreover, parallel lines would have the same slant. Why is "slope" superior to "slant" as a measure of the direction of a line?

33. Verify the statement given just before Problem Set 5–1.

5–2. The equation of a line. Let $P(x, y)$ be a variable point on the line joining $P_1(x_1, y_1)$ and $P_2(x_2, y_2)$. Construct P_1A and P_2B parallel to the x-axis and CP_2 and AP parallel to the y-axis. Then triangles P_1CP_2, P_2BP, and P_1AP are similar right triangles. Therefore,

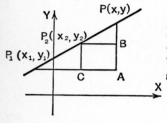

Fig. 5–4

$$\frac{y - y_1}{x - x_1} = \frac{y - y_2}{x - x_2} = \frac{y_2 - y_1}{x_2 - x_1} = m.$$

If P lies on the line joining P_1P_2, then the slope of the segment joining P to P_1 or P to P_2 is the same as the slope of P_1P_2. If a point Q, not on the line P_1P_2, is joined to P_1 or P_2, the slopes of QP_1 or QP_2 will not be the same as the slope of P_1P_2. Therefore those, and only those, points (x, y) whose coordinates satisfy

$$y - y_1 = \frac{y_2 - y_1}{x_2 - x_1} (x - x_1), \tag{5.2}$$

or

$$y - y_1 = m(x - x_1) \tag{5.3}$$

lie on the line P_1P_2. The first of these equations is the **two-point equation** of the line. The second is the **point–slope equation** of the line.

● *Example 1.* Write the equation of the line through $(-2, -3)$ and $(1, 2)$.

$$y - [-3] = \frac{2 - [-3]}{1 - [-2]} (x - [-2])$$
$$y + 3 = \tfrac{5}{3}(x + 2)$$
$$5x - 3y + 1 = 0.$$

One might, instead, first determine the slope

$$m = \frac{2 - (-3)}{1 - (-2)} = \frac{5}{3} \quad \text{and use} \quad (1, 2). \quad \text{Then, by the point-}$$

slope equation,

$$y - 2 = \tfrac{5}{3}(x - 1).$$

Show that this yields the same equation as before.

● *Example 2.* Write the equation of the line through $(0, b)$ having slope m.

$$y - b = m(x - 0),$$
$$y = mx + b. \tag{5.4}$$

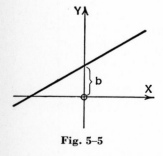

Fig. 5–5

Since b is the y-intercept of the line, this is called the **slope-y-intercept equation** of the line.

Observe that each of the preceding equations of a line may be placed in the form $Ax + By + C = 0$. In studying $Ax + By + C = 0$, two cases arise.

If $B = 0$, $A \neq 0$, then $x = -C/A$ is the equation of a line parallel to the y-axis.

If $B \neq 0$, then $y = -Ax/B - C/B$ is the equation of a line having slope $m = -A/B$ and y-intercept $b = -C/B$.

An equation of the form $Ax + By + C = 0$ is called a **linear equation** since its locus is a line.

Example 3. Find slope and y-intercept for the line $3x + 2y = 6$.

$$y = -\frac{3x}{2} + \frac{6}{2}, \quad m = -\frac{3}{2}, \quad b = 3. \quad \text{(See Fig. 5–6.)}$$

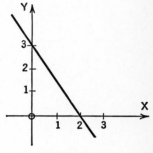

Fig. 5–6

Example 4. Show that if two lines have the same slope the lines are parallel. Consider the two lines

$$y = mx + K,$$
$$y = mx + L.$$

Clearly, if there is a point (a, b) which satisfies both equations, then $b - ma = K$ and $b - ma = L$. Hence, $K = L$. If $K = L$, the two lines have the same equation and hence are the same line. However, if $K \neq L$, the original statement is false and the two lines have no point in common. Hence, by definition, they are parallel.

Example 5. Write the equation of the line through $(-1, -2)$ parallel to the line $3x + 2y = 6$. As above, $m = -\frac{3}{2}$. Then

$$y - [-2] = -\tfrac{3}{2}(x - [-1]),$$
$$y + 2 = -\tfrac{3}{2}(x + 1),$$
$$3x + 2y + 7 = 0.$$

The phrase **family of lines** is used to describe a set of lines having some common property.

Example 6. Determine an equation of the family of lines having y-intercept 7.

The family is represented by the equation $y = mx + 7$. By assigning various values to m, different lines in the family are obtained.

Example 7. Determine an equation of the family of lines through $(3, -8)$.

This family is represented by the equation $y + 8 = m(x - 3)$ where m is the slope. The reader should note that there exists one line, namely, $x = 3$, in the family which cannot be obtained by giving a value to m. This line has no defined slope.

● **Example 8.** Find an equation of the family of lines parallel to $3x + 5y - 7 = 0$.

Since the given line has slope $-\frac{3}{5}$ the desired equation is $y = -\frac{3}{5}x + b$, where b is the y intercept.

PROBLEM SET 5-2

In each of Problems 1 to 5 determine the equation of a line having the given slope and passing through the given point p.

1. $m = 2$, $p(-1, 6)$.   **2.** $m = 3$, $p(3, 4)$.
3. $m = -1$, $p(2, -1)$.   **4.** $m = \frac{1}{2}$, $p(\frac{1}{2}, \frac{1}{3})$.
5. $m = -\frac{1}{3}$, $p(4, -2)$.

In each of Problems 6 to 9 determine the equation of a line through the given points. Use two different methods on each problem.

6. $(3, 1)$, $(2, 4)$.   **7.** $(4, -3)$, $(-1, -3)$.
8. $(1, 6)$, $(-1, -3)$.   **9.** $(-2, 0)$, $(0, 7)$.
10. Show that the equation of a line having nonzero x- and y-intercepts a and b is $x/a + y/b = 1$. Is the restriction "nonzero a and b" necessary?

In Problems 11 to 15 determine the slope and the y intercept of each given line.

11. $3x + y - 5 = 0$.   **12.** $7x - 14y + 10 = 0$.
13. $3x + 12y - 4 = 0$.   **14.** $x = 2y - 3$.   **15.** $3x + 5 = y$.

In Problems 16 to 20 find the equation of a line passing through the point p and parallel to the line L.

16. $p(3, -7)$, $L: 4x + y - 3 = 0$.
17. $p(2, 1)$, $L: x + 2y - 4 = 0$.
18. $p(3, 4)$, $L: 3x = y + 1$.
19. $p(-1, 0)$, $L: 4x + 3y = 6$.
20. $p(4, 2)$, $L: 6x - 2y + 41 = 0$.

In Problems 21 to 30 find the equation of a line having the designated properties.

21. Through $(3, -7)$ and parallel to the x-axis.
22. Through $(2, -4)$ and parallel to the x-axis.
23. Through $(-3, 1)$ and parallel to the y-axis.
24. Through $(4, -7)$ and parallel to the y-axis.
25. Through $(4, -6)$ and parallel to the line through the origin which bisects quadrant II.
26. Through $(-7, 4)$ and parallel to the line through the points $(3, 4)$ and $(2, -7)$.
27. Through the origin with slope m.
28. Through $(3, -4)$ with slope m.
29. Through $(a, 0)$ with slope 0.
30. Through the intersection of the lines $4x + y = 2$ and $x = 3$, and parallel to the line $3x - 5y + 17 = 0$.
31. In economic theory a trend line may be determined by first computing coordinates of two average points and then writing the equation of a line through these two points. Find the equation of a trend line through $(3.1, 2.6)$ and $(6.4, 9.8)$.
32. Find the equation of a trend line through $(6.1, 2.1)$ and $(9.6, 4.1)$.
33. Find the equation of a trend line through $(6.0, 9.3)$ and $(15.1, 1.4)$.
34. Determine the equation of a line which passes through $(2, -3)$ and $(5, 7)$.
35. What is the equation of a line having x intercept $\frac{3}{2}$ and y intercept 7?
36. Determine the equation of the line parallel to $3x - 7y + 5 = 0$ and passing through the intersection of $x + y = 3$ and $2x - y = 9$.
37. Determine the x and y intercepts of $3x + 7y + 5 = 2$.
38. Determine the equation of a line through $(2, -11)$ parallel to $2x - 5y + 6 = 0$.
39. Write the equation of a line parallel to the x-axis and 8 units below it.
40. What is the equation of the line passing through $(4, -3)$ and parallel to a line L, where L passes through $(-1, 6)$ and has y intercept 10?
41. Write the equation of a line parallel to the y-axis and 5 units to its right.
42. Write the equation of the locus of points equidistant from $(-3, 5)$ and $(7, 1)$.
43. Write the equation of the line through the origin which bisects that portion of the line $8x - 3y + 24 = 0$ which is included between the coordinate axes.

44. Find the member of the family $y = mx + 2$ which is parallel to $2x + y = 0$.

45. Write an equation of the family of lines parallel to the line through $(7, 1)$ and $(-3, 5)$ and select the member of the family which passes through $(4, -3)$.

46. Obtain the equation of the line through the intersection of $2x + 3y - 9 = 0$ and $x + 2y - 7 = 0$, and with slope $-\frac{1}{3}$.

47. Find c so that

$$x - y + 2 = 0, \quad 2x - 3y + 7 = 0, \quad 3x + 2y + c = 0$$

shall meet in a point.

48. The point $(5, -3)$ bisects that portion of a line which is included between the coordinate axes. Write the equation of the line.

49. Sketch the line passing through $(3, -1)$ having a slope of minus two.

50. Determine the slope of the line $y = 5x - 6$ and determine the coordinates of some one point on this line.

51. Given the triangle with vertices $A(2, -4)$, $B(6, -8)$, $C(2, 6)$. Find: (a) the equation of side AC, (b) the length of the altitude from B to side AC, (c) the length of side AC, (d) the area of the triangle.

52. Write the equation of the locus of points which are six times as far from $x = 1$ as from $x = 8$. Think carefully before you decide whether the locus consists of 1, 2, or 3 lines. Under what conditions might an answer other than the one you gave be correct?

53. A rectangular swimming pool is 75 by 20 ft at ground level. The bottom of the pool is a plane which slants uniformly from one end of the pool to the other. When the pool is full, the water is 3 ft deep at the shallow end and 10 ft deep at the deep end. Determine the volume V of water in the pool as a function of the depth h of the water at the deep end. Notice that the function has one formula for $0 \leq h \leq 7$ and another for $7 < h \leq 10$. Outside of these ranges the function is not defined. Graph V as a function of h.

54. Determine the exposed surface area of the water in the pool of Problem 53 as a function of the depth of the water at the deep end. Graph the function.

55. A rectangular box with a square base and open top is to contain 50 cu ft. Set up a formula for the area of the material used (that is, set up the function you would use to determine the box requiring the least material).

5–3. The line tangent to a curve at a point. To give a satisfactory definition it is convenient to use the idea of *limit* which is discussed in detail in later mathematical work. At this point we speak merely of a limiting geometric position.

Definition. The tangent line PT to a curve at the point P on the curve is the limiting position of the secant line PS as the point S approaches P by moving on the curve, if this limiting position exists and is unique. (An example of a curve on which the limiting position is not unique is given in Problem 10.)

Note that nothing is said about the secant line when S and P coincide. No *secant* line is determined in this case since one point does not determine a line. The reader may wish to consult the article, "What is a Geometric Tangent?" which appeared in *The Mathematics Teacher*, Vol. L, No. 7 (Nov., 1957).

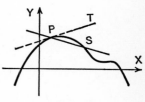

Fig. 5–7

PROBLEM SET 5-3

1. The reader will understand the definition of tangent line better if he will draw a curve on a piece of paper and locate the point P by inserting a pin or thumb tack. Rest a ruler on the paper, touching the pin. Think of the edge of the rule as the secant PS and move it in such a manner that S approaches P along the curve. Do this several times taking S on each side of P, locate what you consider the limiting position or tangent line.

2. Trace the locus of Example 1, Section 4–9 of the text. Locate the point $(t, h) = (1, 504)$. Prove this point lies on the locus by showing that it satisfies its equation. Using the ruler technique described in Problem 1 estimate the limiting position of the secant PS and draw a tangent at P. Estimate the slope of this tangent line.

3. Same as Problem 2 for $P(4, 624)$.

4. Show by the ruler technique that the line tangent to the circle $x^2 + y^2 = 25$ at the point $(3, 4)$ apparently has slope between -0.8 and -0.7, that is, $-0.8 \leq m \leq -0.7$.

5. Show that the slope of the line tangent to $x^2 + y^2 = 169$ at $(-5, 12)$ is between .4 and .5, that is, $0.4 \leq m \leq 0.5$.

6. The locus of $y^3 = 27x^2$ is shown in Figure 5–8. Show by the ruler technique that the y-axis is apparently the tangent line at the point $(0, 0)$. What is the equation of this line?

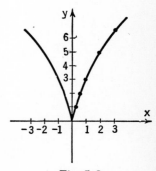

Fig. 5–8

7. Show that the line tangent to a line AB at any point on the line is the line itself.

8. The locus of $y = 2x + 3$ is a line. What is the slope of the line tangent to this line at $(4, 11)$?

9. Sketch the locus: $y = 2 \mid x \mid$. [NOTE: If $y = 2 \mid x \mid$, y never has negative values.] Determine the slope of the tangent line at the point $(3, 6)$ and at the point $(-2, 4)$.

10. Attempt to determine the tangent line to $y = 2 \mid x \mid$ at the origin. Let S be to the right of $x = 0$ and then let S be to the left of $x = 0$ and show that the two limiting positions are different. *Hence, no tangent line exists* at $(0, 0)$. Notice the distinction between this and Problem 6.

11. Discuss reasons why the phrase "a tangent line is perpendicular to the radius at the point of tangency" is not a valid definition of a tangent line unless the locus is a circle.

12. Show that the phrase "the tangent line is a line which touches the curve at only one point" is not a valid definition for a tangent line to a general curve.

13. Sketch an example of a curve which is tangent to the line $y = \frac{1}{2}x$ three times and crosses it five times.

14. Give an example showing that a line may be tangent to a curve at a point and also cross the curve at the same point. Is $y = x^3$ such a curve? What is the point?

15. Assume the slope of the tangent line of Problem 4 is $-\frac{3}{4}$, and find its equation. Solve the equation of the line and the equation of the circle simultaneously to obtain the points of intersection of the line and circle. Interpret your results.

5–4. Limit of a function. In the last section the limiting position of a secant line was considered. We now consider the limiting value of a function. We shall later associate these two ideas to determine the slope of the line tangent to a curve at a given point.

If x is near 2, $f(x) = 4x^2 - 3$ is close to 13. The closeness of $f(x)$ to 13 depends upon the nearness of x to 2. If, for example,

$$1.999 < x < 2.001,$$

then

$$4(1.999)^2 - 3 < f(x) < 4(2.001)^2 - 3$$
$$12.98 < f(x) < 13.02.$$

This could be stated as:

if $\qquad -.001 < x - 2 < .001,$

then $\qquad -.02 < f(x) - 13 < .02;$

or, using absolute value signs:

if $\qquad |x-2| < .001,$

then $\qquad |f(x) - 13| < .02.$

In words, if x is within .001 unit of 2, then $f(x)$ will be within .02 unit of 13. If x is taken nearer 2, say $|x-2| < .000001$ then $|f(x) - 13| < .000016$. This suggests that possibly the difference between $f(x)$ and 13 can be made as small as we wish by taking x sufficiently near to 2.

Consider a new function $f(x) = \dfrac{x^2 + 9x - 22}{x - 2}$. For this new $f(x)$ it will be found that if x is near to 2, *but not equal to* 2, then $f(x)$ is close to 13. Observe that $f(2)$ is meaningless (has no defined value). Consequently, x is not permitted to take the value 2. If $x \neq 2$, $\quad f(x) = \dfrac{x^2 + 9x - 22}{x - 2} = x + 11$. From this it is seen that the difference between $f(x)$ and 13 becomes numerically smaller as x becomes closer to, but not equal to, 2. In each of these illustrations $f(x)$ is said to approach 13 as a limit as x approaches 2 as a limit. In symbols, we write $\lim\limits_{x \to 2} f(x) = 13$. In the first illustration $f(2) = 13$, but in the second illustration the symbol $f(2)$ is without meaning.

More generally, we shall say a given function $f(x)$ has a limit L as x approaches b [in symbols: $\lim\limits_{x \to b} f(x) = L$] if the difference between $f(x)$ and L may be made numerically smaller than any preassigned positive number by choosing x, $\quad x \neq b$, such that the difference between x and b is sufficiently small in absolute value. The restriction $x \neq b$ takes care of difficulties appearing in the second illustration given above.

From the mathematical point of view it is desirable to frame the concept of limit with more care. It is perhaps unfortunate that the phrase "as x approaches b" has come into standard usage in mathematics, since this seems to imply *change* in the value of x. Although not precise this is a convenient misrepresentation of the basic meaning of $\lim f(x) = L$ which actually means there exists a set of values of x such that the following property is true for *every* x in the set.

Let us examine the true meaning of $\lim\limits_{x \to b} f(x)$ with care. Basically we are interested in the value of $f(x)$ for x *near* but *not equal* to b. Mathematically $\lim\limits_{x \to b} f(x) = L$ means that a value of L can be found such that for each positive number ϵ† (ϵ is a

---

† The symbol ϵ is the Greek letter "epsilon." It is often used in mathematics to denote a (small) positive constant. The symbol δ is the Greek letter "delta," the lower case form of Δ.

tolerance and indicates how near $f(x)$ must be to L) there exists a positive δ (this sets up a subset of permissible x values) such that for each value $x = x_1$ taken from the set $b - \delta < x_1 < b + \delta$, excepting possibly the value $x = b$ itself, $f(x)$ lies within ϵ units of L, that is $|f(x_1) - L| < \epsilon$ for each x_1 in this region $b - \delta < x_1 < b + \delta$ with the possible exception of $x_1 = b$.

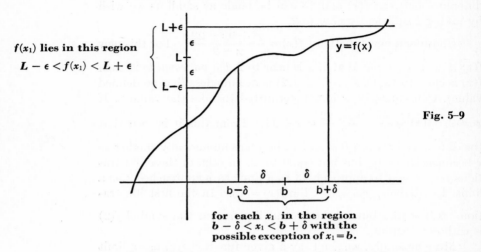

$f(x_1)$ **lies in this region**

$L - \epsilon < f(x_1) < L + \epsilon$

Fig. 5–9

for each x_1 in the region $b - \delta < x_1 < b + \delta$ with the possible exception of $x_1 = b$.

It should be noticed that the "tolerance" $\epsilon > 0$ is prescribed first and then we attempt to find a $\delta > 0$ such that our requirements are satisfied. The choice of δ depends on the ϵ chosen. The formal definition is introduced at this point so the reader may have the opportunity of becoming acquainted with it now. It is a basic tool in more advanced courses. Experience shows that the concept often takes a while to "break through." Only the reader, himself, can judge whether or not he has achieved "break through." When he does, the phraseology seems the only reasonable one to convey the idea simply. Students often remark that the epsilon-delta idea seems difficult at first, but once understood, there does not seem to be any other way to express the meaning of $\lim_{x \to b} f(x) = L$ as clearly as it does.

The basic idea is that $\lim_{x \to b} f(x) = L$ states that if x is chosen near, but not equal to, b, then $f(x)$ is near, or possibly even equal to, L. The ϵ's and δ's make the meaning of "near to" precise. The concept is important here, but will not become truly vital until later. We now state the formal mathematical definition.

Definition. The function $f(x)$ has the limit L as x approaches b, if for every positive number ϵ there is a positive number δ such that if $0 < |x - b| < \delta$ then $|f(x) - L| < \epsilon$.

Observe that the definition does *not* say that there exists a number δ such that for every $\epsilon > 0$, if $0 < |x - b| < \delta$, then $|f(x) - L| < \epsilon$. The definition states the ϵ must be chosen first, and then, no matter what $\epsilon > 0$ was chosen, there exists a δ such that if $x - b$ is smaller in absolute value than δ and $x \neq b$, then $f(x) - L$ is less in absolute value than ϵ. The ϵ is chosen *before* a δ is determined. The order of choice is important. If the ϵ is changed, then it may be necessary to determine a new δ. The reader should note that this definition does *not* say that $f(b) = L$. *The definition says nothing at all about* $f(x)$ *when* $x = b$. In fact $f(b)$ need not even be defined. The second illustration of this section is an example of this.

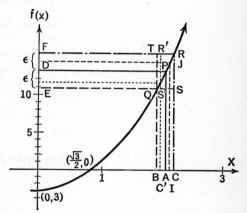

Fig. 5–10

- *Example 1.* Let $f(x) = 4x^2 - 3$ and $L = 13$. Find $\delta > 0$ such that $|(4x^2 - 3) - 13| < \epsilon$ when $0 < |x - 2| < \delta$.

To illustrate the method of solution Figure 5–10 will be used. In this example only that portion of the locus of $f(x) = 4x^2 - 3$ lying on the positive side of the $f(x)$-axis (that is, where $x > 0$) need be sketched. At $x = 2$ erect the ordinate AP intersecting the locus at P. Through P construct DP parallel to the x-axis and intersecting the $f(x)$-axis at D where $f(x) = 13$. Through $E(0, 13 - \epsilon)$ and $F(0, 13 + \epsilon)$ construct lines parallel to the x-axis and intersecting the locus in points Q and R, respectively. Through Q and R erect perpendiculars QB and RC to the x-axis. Label T the intersection of QB and FR, and S the intersection of RC and EQ. The points of the locus between Q and R lie inside the rectangle $QSRT$. The x-coordinates of B and C are found from $4x^2 - 3 = 13 - \epsilon$ and $4x^2 - 3 = 13 + \epsilon$, respectively. These equations yield

$$B\left(\sqrt{4 - \frac{\epsilon}{4}}, 0\right), \quad C\left(\sqrt{4 + \frac{\epsilon}{4}}, 0\right).$$ Now, $BA > AC$

implies $2 - \sqrt{4 - \dfrac{\epsilon}{4}} > \sqrt{4 + \dfrac{\epsilon}{4}} - 2$. If $\delta > 0$ is chosen

such that $\sqrt{4 + \dfrac{\epsilon}{4}} - 2 > \delta$, then

$$|4x^2 - 3 - 13| < \epsilon \quad \text{when} \quad 0 < |x - 2| < \delta.$$

To see this more fully, locate $C'\left(4 - \sqrt{4 + \dfrac{\epsilon}{2}}, 0\right)$ and erect a perpendicular to the x-axis at C' intersecting ES at S' and FR at R'. Any point $I(x, 0)$ on the interval $C'AC$ excluding the points C', A, and C will have x satisfying $0 < |x - 2| < \delta$ since $|AI| < AC$. $IJ = f(x)$ and $|f(x) - 13| < \epsilon$ since J lies on the locus between Q and R excluding Q, P, and R.

Students often make a serious error in their mathematical thinking at this stage. It is one which is very difficult for your instructor to detect, since, like "cancelling the 6's in $\frac{16}{64}$," the resulting answer is correct even though the method is not.

In determining L for the function $\lim_{x \to 3} f(x)$ the student soon learns that in most of the problems he encounters *at this level*, either the correct answer is obtained by substituting 3 for x, in the given function, or he can perform some algebraic manipulation on $f(x)$ before substitution which will yield the correct result. Unfortunately, this is a rather insidious procedure which masks the basic concept. The student will do well to think, "If x is close to 3, *but not* 3, does the corresponding value $f(x)$ appear near to a fixed L?

● *Example 2.* In evaluating $\lim_{x \to 3} (x^2 - 5)$ the student's reasoning might well be:

If x is close to 3 (but not 3), then x^2 is close to 9, and $(x^2 - 5)$ is near 4.

● *Example 3.* Find $\lim_{x \to 5} \dfrac{x^2 - 25}{x - 5}$.

The student who recognizes that $\lim_{x \to 5}$ specifically implies that $x \ne 5$, has a distinct advantage with this problem, since it is only if $x \ne 5$ that one may say that $\dfrac{x^2 - 25}{x - 5} = \dfrac{(x + 5)(x - 5)}{x - 5} = x + 5.$ Why?

He therefore may reason thus,

$$\lim_{x \to 5} \frac{x^2 - 25}{x - 5} = \lim_{x \to 5} \frac{(x + 5)(x - 5)}{(x - 5)}.$$

Now, since $\lim_{x \to 5}$ specifically states $x \ne 5$ we may continue

$$\lim_{x \to 5} \frac{(x + 5)(x - 5)}{x - 5} = \lim_{x \to 5} (x + 5)$$

and if x is close to 5, then $(x + 5)$ is close to 10. Hence,

$$\lim_{x \to 5} \frac{x^2 - 25}{x - 5} = 10.$$

To be precise, the student would have to show that for any $\epsilon > 0$, it would be possible to determine a corresponding δ such that if $0 < |x - 5| < \delta$, then $\left| \dfrac{x^2 - 25}{x - 5} - 10 \right| < \epsilon$. Whether or not the student is ready for this degree of sophistication at present is for his instructor to decide. The authors feel that the "suitable algebraic manipulation followed by substitution of the limiting value of x for x in the formula" which students sometimes use is *not* sufficient, but that the rigor of actually determining δ is unnecessary at this stage. The reader will be well advised to follow his instructor's dictates in this matter.

5–5. Continuous function. In the last section we pointed out that $\lim\limits_{x \to 2} f(x)$ need not equal $f(2)$. If it does, the function $f(x)$ is said to be continuous at $x = 2$. More formally:

Definition. The function $f(x)$ **is continuous at** $x = b$ if the following three conditions are **all** satisfied:

(1) $f(x)$ has a definite value $f(b)$ at $x = b$; that is, $f(b)$ is defined.

(2) $f(x)$ has a limit L as x approaches b; that is, $\lim\limits_{x \to b} f(x) = L$ exists.

(3) the limit L is equal to $f(b)$; that is, $\lim\limits_{x \to b} f(x) = f(b)$.

In symbols, we may say $f(x)$ is continuous at $x = b$ if $\lim\limits_{x \to b} f(x) = f(b)$. The reader may find it helpful to think of a continuous curve as one that can be sketched without removing the pen from the paper.

● *Example 1.* Show that $f(x) = 4x^2 - 3$ is continuous at $x = 2$.

  (1) $f(2) = 13$

  (2) $\lim\limits_{x \to 2} f(x) = 13$

  (3) $13 = 13$, thus $f(x) = 4x^2 - 3$ is continuous at $x = 2$.

● *Example 2.* Is $f(x) = \dfrac{x^2 + 9x - 22}{x - 2}$ continuous at $x = 2$?

  The $\lim\limits_{x \to 2} f(x) = \lim\limits_{x \to 2} \dfrac{x^2 + 9x - 22}{x - 2} = \lim\limits_{x \to 2} (x + 11)$† $= 13$ exists as was shown in the previous section. However, $f(2)$ is meaningless and hence, $f(x) = \dfrac{x^2 + 9x - 22}{x - 2}$ is *not* continuous at $x = 2$.

† Note that $\dfrac{x^2 + 9x - 22}{x - 2} = \dfrac{(x - 2)(x + 11)}{x - 2} = x + 11$ **if $x \neq 2$.** Since $\lim\limits_{x \to 2}$ explicitly states, in its definition, that $x \neq 2$, $[0 < |x - 2|]$ we have $\lim\limits_{x \to 2} \dfrac{x^2 + 9x - 22}{x - 2} = \lim\limits_{x \to 2} (x + 11) = 13$.

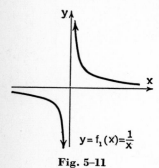

Fig. 5–11

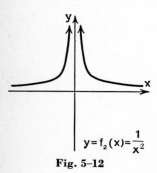

Fig. 5–12

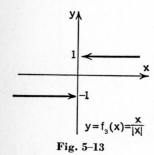

Fig. 5–13

• *Example 3.* Consider the functions

$$f_1(x) = \frac{1}{x}, \quad f_2(x) = \frac{1}{x^2}, \quad f_3(x) = \frac{x}{|x|}.$$

Each of these functions is undefined for $x = 0$ and consequently not continuous at $x = 0$. (Why?) For each of these functions we ask the question, "Does $\lim_{x \to 0} f(x)$ exist?" The sketches of these functions are helpful in understanding the reasoning involved. See Figures 5–11, 5–12, and 5–13.

In each case the function is defined everywhere except at $x = 0$. The question "Does $\lim_{x \to 0} f(x)$ exist?" asks, "Does the locus $y = f(x)$ become and remain close to some *one* point for x near, but not equal to, zero?"

In the first case, for x near zero $f_1(x)$ may be either large and positive or large and negative, and hence the locus does not approach a definite point as x approaches zero (but x not equal to zero). The $\lim_{x \to 0} 1/x$ does not exist.

The locus of $y = 1/x^2$ is always above the x-axis. If x is close to zero, then y is very large. In fact, given any y value, it is always possible to find values of x close to zero so that $1/x^2$ is much larger than the y value in question. Again, the locus does not approach a finite point as x approaches zero $(x \neq 0)$. Hence, $\lim_{x \to 0} 1/x^2$ does not exist.

The locus $y = x/|x|$ is the line $y = -1$ for $x < 0$, is undefined at $x = 0$, and is the line $y = +1$ for $x > 0$. If $x < 0$ and x approaches zero, then $y = x/|x|$ approaches $(0, -1)$. If $x > 0$ and x approaches zero, then $y = x/|x|$ approaches $(0, 1)$. There is no *one* point that $y = x/|x|$ approaches as x approaches zero. Thus $\lim_{x \to 0} x/|x|$ does not exist.

• *Example 4.* Consider the functions

$$f_4(x) = \frac{x^2}{|x|}, \quad f_5(x) = \frac{x^2 + x}{x}, \quad f_6(x) = |x|.$$

For each of these functions we ask the question "Does $\lim_{x \to 0} f(x)$ exist?" Again, we shall examine the sketches to aid our understanding of the reasoning involved. The question "Does $\lim_{x \to 0} f(x)$ exist?" asks "Does the locus of $y = f(x)$ approach (that is, become and remain close to) some one point for x near *but not equal to* zero?" Note that it makes no difference what, if any, value is given to $f(x)$ at $x = 0$. The

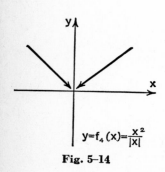

Fig. 5–14

$\lim_{x \to 0} f(x)$ is concerned with values of $f(x)$ for x near to, but *not* equal to, zero. See Figures 5–14, 5–15, 5–16.

The locus of $y = x^2/|x|$ approaches the point $(0, 0)$ as x approaches (but is not equal to) zero. Hence $\lim_{x \to 0} x^2/|x| = 0$, even though $f_4(0)$ is meaningless.

The locus of $y = (x^2 + x)/x$ is the line $y = x + 1$, with the point $(0, 1)$ removed. As x approaches zero, the locus of $y = (x^2 + x)/x$ approaches $(0, 1)$ and

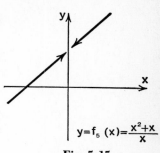

$$y = f_5(x) = \frac{x^2 + x}{x}$$

Fig. 5–15

$$\lim_{x \to 0} f_5(x) = \frac{x^2 + x}{x} = 1,$$

regardless of what value, if any, is given to $f_5(0)$.

The locus of $y = |x|$ becomes and remains arbitrarily close to $(0, 0)$ for x near to, but not equal to, zero, and $\lim_{x \to 0} |x| = 0$. Also $f_6(0) = 0$, but this does not determine $\lim_{x \to 0} f_6(x)$.

A function $f(x)$ was defined to be continuous at $x = a$ if $\lim_{x \to a} f(x) = f(a)$, where $f(a)$ must exist. Since $\lim_{x \to 0} f(x)$ does not exist in the functions of Example 3, these functions certainly are not continuous at $x = 0$.

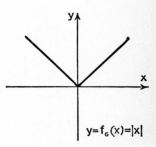

$$y = f_6(x) = |x|$$

Fig. 5–16

In the case of $f_4(x) = x^2/|x|$ and $f_5(x) = (x^2 + x)/x$, $\lim_{x \to 0} f(x)$ exists. Whether or not these $f(x)$ are continuous at $x = 0$ depends upon how $f(x)$ is defined at $x = 0$. If we define $f_4(x)$ as follows: $f_4(x) = \begin{cases} x^2/|x| & \text{if } x \neq 0 \\ 0 & \text{if } x = 0 \end{cases}$, then the function $f_4(x)$ is continuous at $x = 0$. (Why?) If $f_4(0)$ is undefined or is defined as some value other than zero, then $f_4(x)$ is discontinuous at $x = 0$.

The function $f_5(x) = (x^2 + x)/x$ must have $f_5(0) = 1$ in order to be continuous at $x = 0$. (Why?)

The function $f_6(x) = |x|$ already has

$$f_6(0) = 0 \quad \text{and} \quad \lim_{x \to 0} f_6(x) = 0.$$

Hence, $f_6(x)$ is continuous at $x = 0$.

PROBLEM SET 5–5

1. $\lim_{x \to 4} (3x^2 - 2x + 5) = ?$ **2.** $\lim_{x \to 3} \frac{x^3 - 27}{x - 3} = ?$

3. Is $f(x) = \dfrac{x^3 - 27}{x - 3}$ continuous at $x = 3$? Is it continuous at $x = 5$?

4. Show that $\lim\limits_{x \to 4} \dfrac{3x - 11}{x - 4}$ does not exist, but $\lim\limits_{x \to 4} \dfrac{3x - 12}{x - 4}$ does exist.

5. Are either of the functions of Problem 4 continuous at $x = 4$? at $x = 6$?

6. Find $\lim\limits_{t \to 5} (3t^2 + 2t - 8)$.

7. If $\epsilon = 2$ is chosen, find a corresponding δ such that if $0 < |x - 3| < \delta$, then $|f(x) - 9| < \epsilon = 2$ where

$$f(x) = 4x - 3.$$

8. If ϵ is taken as .01 in Problem 7, determine a corresponding δ.

9. Will the δ of Problem 8 also work for Problem 7? For a given ϵ, is δ unique?

*10. Does $\lim\limits_{\Delta x \to 0} f(b + \Delta x) = L$ imply that as $x \to b$, $f(x) \to L$?

*11. Does $\lim\limits_{\Delta x \to 0} |f(b + \Delta x) - f(b)| = 0$ imply $f(x)$ is continuous at $x = b$?

*12. Restate the definition of a continuous function, using delta notation.

13. $\lim\limits_{\Delta x \to 0} \dfrac{4\Delta x + (\Delta x)^2}{\Delta x} = \lim\limits_{\Delta x \to 0} (4 + \Delta x) = ?$

14. $\lim\limits_{x \to 1} \dfrac{2(x + 1)(x - 1)}{x - 1} = ?$ 15. $\lim\limits_{\Delta x \to 0} \dfrac{-3\Delta x}{(1 + \Delta x)\Delta x} = ?$

16. $\lim\limits_{x \to 2} \dfrac{\sqrt{2x + 5} - 3}{x - 2} = ?$

[HINT: Rationalize the numerator.]

17. (a) Does $\lim\limits_{x \to 3} \dfrac{x^2 - 9}{x - 3}$ exist?

(b) Is $f(x) = \begin{cases} \dfrac{x^2 - 9}{x - 3} & \text{if } x \neq 3 \\ 6 & \text{if } x = 3 \end{cases}$ continuous at $x = 3$?

(c) Is it continuous at $x = -3$?

18. (a) Does $\lim\limits_{x \to -2} \dfrac{x^2 - 4}{x + 2}$ exist?

(b) Is $f(x) = \begin{cases} \dfrac{x^2 - 4}{x + 2} & \text{if } x \neq -2 \\ 5 & \text{if } x = -2 \end{cases}$ continuous at $x = -2$?

(c) If not, what definition of $f(-2)$ will make $f(x)$ continuous at $x = -2$?

19. Give an example of a function which is not continuous at $x = 4$.

20. Is $f(x) = \begin{cases} x^2 & \text{if} \quad x \neq 10 \\ 4 & \text{if} \quad x = 10 \end{cases}$ continuous at $x = 10$?

5–6. Slope of a tangent line. In Section 5–3 the tangent line to a curve $y = f(x)$ at a point $P(a, b)$ on the curve was defined as the limiting position of the secant line PS, as the point S approaches P by moving along the curve, if a unique limiting position exists. We now show a method of determining the slope (and hence the equation) of the tangent line to the curve $y = f(x)$ at the point $P(a, b)$ on the curve. To do this a theorem is needed which will not be proved here. The theorem follows intuitively from the definition of a tangent line, but a rigorous proof is difficult with our present knowledge. We state the theorem without proof:

Theorem. If a curve has a tangent line at the point P on the curve, then the

slope of [the limiting position of the secant line PS]
$${\scriptstyle S \to P \text{ along the curve}}$$
$$= \text{limit of [the slope of the secant line } PS].$$
$${\scriptstyle S \to P \text{ along the curve}}$$

We use this theorem to determine the slope of the tangent line to a curve $y = f(x)$ at the point P on the curve.

● **Example 1.** Find the slope of the line tangent to $y = 2x^2$ at $(1, 2)$. See Figure 5–17.

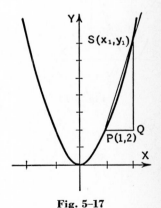

Fig. 5–17

Let $P(1, 2)$ and $S(x_1, y_1)$ be two points on $y = 2x^2$. The slope of the secant PS will be determined as in Section 5–1. The point Q has coordinates $Q(x_1, 2)$. (Why?) The directed distance $PQ = x_1 - 1$ while $QS = y_1 - 2$.

The secant line PS has slope $= \dfrac{QS}{PQ} = \dfrac{y_1 - 2}{x_1 - 1}$. Since $S(x_1, y_1)$ is on the locus $y = 2x^2$, its coordinates satisfy the equation of the locus, that is $y_1 = 2x_1^2$. Hence,

$$\text{slope of secant } PS = \frac{y_1 - 2}{x_1 - 1} = \frac{2x_1^2 - 2}{x_1 - 1} = \frac{2(x_1 + 1)(x_1 - 1)}{x_1 - 1}.$$

From the definition of tangent line and using the theorem of this section we obtain,

slope of tangent line = slope of [limiting position of secant line PS]
$${\scriptstyle S \to P \text{ along } y = 2x^2}$$

$$= \text{limit of [slope of secant line } PS]$$
$${\scriptstyle S \to P \text{ along } y = 2x^2}$$

$$= \underset{\substack{S \to P \text{ along} \\ y = 2x^2}}{\text{limit of}} \left[\frac{2(x_1 + 1)(x_1 - 1)}{x_1 - 1} \right].$$

Since $S(x_1, y_1)$ is on the curve, $S(x_1, y_1) \to P(1, 2)$ may be replaced by $x_1 \to 1$. Hence,

$$\text{slope of tangent line} = \lim_{x_1 \to 1} \left[\frac{2(x_1 + 1)(x_1 - 1)}{x_1 - 1} \right].$$

Since $\lim_{x_1 \to 1}$ specifically states $x_1 \neq 1$ (that is, $0 < |x_1 - 1|$) we have

$$\text{slope of tangent line} = \lim_{x_1 \to 1} \frac{2(x_1 + 1)(x_1 - 1)}{x_1 - 1}$$

$$= \lim_{x_1 \to 1} 2(x_1 + 1) = 2(2) = 4.$$

Hence, the line tangent to $y = 2x^2$ at $(1, 2)$ has slope 4.

● **Example 2.** Example 1 may also be solved in the following manner, which will lead to more general methods in later sections. Let $P(1, 2)$ and $S(1 + \Delta x, 2 + \Delta y)$ † be two points on the locus $y = 2x^2$. Then,

$$\text{slope of secant line } PS = \frac{\Delta y}{\Delta x}.$$

Using the theorem of this section we have

$$m = \text{slope of tangent line at } P = \lim_{\Delta x \to 0} \frac{\Delta y}{\Delta x}.$$

Since $S(1 + \Delta x, 2 + \Delta y)$ is on the locus $y = 2x^2$, we have

$$2 + \Delta y = 2(1 + \Delta x)^2$$

and

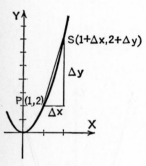

Fig. 5–18

$$\Delta y = 2(1 + \Delta x)^2 - 2$$
$$= 2 + 4\Delta x + 2\Delta x^2 - 2 \ddagger$$
$$= 4\Delta x + 2\Delta x^2.$$

Therefore,

$$m = \lim_{\Delta x \to 0} \frac{\Delta y}{\Delta x} = \lim_{\Delta x \to 0} \frac{4\Delta x + 2\Delta x^2}{\Delta x}.$$

Since $\lim_{\Delta x \to 0}$ specifically states $\Delta x \neq 0$ we have

$$m = \lim_{\Delta x \to 0} \frac{(4 + 2\Delta x)\Delta x}{\Delta x} = \lim_{\Delta x \to 0} (4 + 2\Delta x) = 4 + 0 = 4.$$

† The reader should recall that Δx and Δy are single quantities, not products.

‡ By convention the notation Δx^2 means $(\Delta x)^2$ not $\Delta(x^2)$. If the latter is intended in this book, parentheses will be used as indicated.

If the equation of the tangent line is desired, it can be written using the point-slope form of Section 5–2, with $m = 4$ and $P(1, 2)$ to obtain

$$y - 2 = 4(x - 1)$$

or

$$y = 4x - 2.$$

● **Example 3.** Determine the slope and the equation of the line tangent to $y = 3/x$ at the point $(1, 3)$.

Consider the points $P(1, 3)$ and $S(1 + \Delta x, 3 + \Delta y)$ on the graph of $y = 3/x$. Since S is on the graph, its coordinates satisfy the equation of the locus. Therefore,

$$3 + \Delta y = \frac{3}{1 + \Delta x}$$

$$\Delta y = \frac{3}{1 + \Delta x} - 3 = \frac{-3\Delta x}{1 + \Delta x}.$$

$$m = \text{slope of tangent line} = \lim_{\Delta x \to 0} \frac{\Delta y}{\Delta x} = \lim_{\Delta x \to 0} \frac{\frac{-3\Delta x}{1 + \Delta x}}{\Delta x} = \lim_{\Delta x \to 0} \frac{-3\Delta x}{(1 + \Delta x)\Delta x}.$$

Since $\lim_{\Delta x \to 0} \frac{\Delta y}{\Delta x}$ implies $\Delta x \neq 0$ we have

$$m = \lim_{\Delta x \to 0} \frac{-3\Delta x}{(1 + \Delta x)\Delta x} = \lim_{\Delta x \to 0} \frac{-3}{1 + \Delta x} = -3.$$

Note that the slope of the tangent line is negative, as you would expect from Figure 5–19.

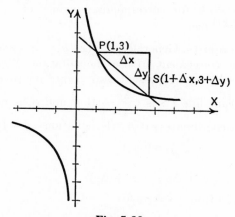

Fig. 5–19

The equation of the tangent line at $P(1, 3)$ is

$$y - 3 = -3(x - 1) \quad \text{or} \quad y = -3x + 6.$$

PROBLEM SET 5–6

1. Find the slope of the line tangent to $y = 2x^2$ at $(-1, 2)$ by the method of Example 1.
2. Find the slope of the line tangent to $y = 2x^2$ at $(3, 18)$ by the method of Example 1.
3. Solve Problem 1 by the method of Example 2.
4. Solve Problem 2 by the method of Example 2.
5. Determine the slope and equation of the line tangent to $y = 6/x$ at $(2, 3)$.
6. Carefully sketch the locus $y = 2x^2$ and the line which passes through $(1, 2)$ with slope 4. Does your sketch appear as Example 1 indicates it should?

In Problems 7 to 20 determine the slope and the equation of the tangent line to the given curve at the given point.

7. $y = 5x^2$ at $(1, 5)$.   8. $y = 2x^2 - 3x + 5$ at $(2, 7)$.
9. $y = 2/x$ at $(2, 1)$.   10. $y = 3x^3$ at $(2, 24)$.
11. $y = 5x^2 - 4$ at $(-1, 1)$.
12. $y = 2x^3 - 3x$ at $(-2, -10)$.
13. $y = -3x + 2$ at $(5, -13)$.
14. $y = x^2 - 7x$ at $(0, 0)$.   15. $y = 4x^2 + 1$ at $(1, 5)$.
16. $y = 5x^2 + 3$ at $(1, 8)$.   Compare Problem 7.
17. $y = 2x^2 - 3x + 1$ at $(2, 3)$.   Compare Problem 8.
18. $y = 2/x + 4$ at $(2, 5)$.   Compare Problem 9.
19. $y = 3x^3 - 10$ at $(2, 14)$.   Compare Problem 10.
*20. Show that lines tangent to $y = x^2$ and $y = x^2 + k$ have the same slope for corresponding values of x, no matter what value k has.

5–7. Increments. Generally, if (x_1, y_1) is a fixed point on the curve, it is convenient to use the notation $P(x_1, y_1)$ and $S(x_1 + \Delta x, y_1 + \Delta y)$ to represent two points on the locus. The slope of the secant line PS is $\dfrac{\Delta y}{\Delta x}$. If P and S lie on the locus $y = f(x)$, their coordinates satisfy the equation $y = f(x)$. Thus,

$$y_1 = f(x_1) \tag{5.5}$$

and

$$y_1 + \Delta y = f(x_1 + \Delta x). \tag{5.6}$$

Subtracting (5.5) from (5.6) yields

$$\Delta y = f(x_1 + \Delta x) - f(x_1). \tag{5.7}$$

Then,

$$\text{slope of secant line } PS = \frac{\Delta y}{\Delta x} = \frac{f(x_1 + \Delta x) - f(x_1)}{\Delta x}. \tag{5.8}$$

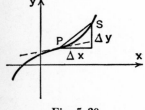

Fig. 5–20

Thus,

$$\text{slope of tangent line at } P = \lim_{\Delta x \to 0} \frac{\Delta y}{\Delta x} = \lim_{\Delta x \to 0} \frac{f(x_1 + \Delta x) - f(x_1)}{\Delta x}. \quad (5.9)$$

The reader should observe that, in the notation of Section 1–12, the slope of secant line through P is $\dfrac{\Delta f(x_1, \Delta x)}{\Delta x} = \dfrac{\Delta y}{\Delta x}.$

Actually, Δy is the same as $\Delta f(x_1, \Delta x)$ if $y = f(x).$

● **Example 1.** Find the slope of the tangent line to $y = 2x^2$ at the point (x_1, y_1) on the locus.

(1) $y_1 = 2x_1^2$

(2) $y_1 + \Delta y = 2(x_1 + \Delta x)^2$
$$= 2x_1^2 + 4x_1 \Delta x + 2\Delta x^2.$$

Subtract (1) from (2) to obtain

(3) $\Delta y = 4x_1 \Delta x + 2\Delta x^2.$

Then

(4) $\dfrac{\Delta y}{\Delta x} = \dfrac{4x_1 \Delta x + 2\Delta x^2}{\Delta x} = \dfrac{(4x_1 + 2\Delta x) \Delta x}{\Delta x}.$

If $\Delta x \neq 0$, we have $\dfrac{\Delta y}{\Delta x} = 4x_1 + 2\Delta x.$ Since $\lim\limits_{\Delta x \to 0}$ includes the restriction $\Delta x \neq 0$ in its definition, we have

(5) $m = \lim\limits_{\Delta x \to 0} \dfrac{\Delta y}{\Delta x} = \lim\limits_{\Delta x \to 0} (4x_1 + 2\Delta x) = 4x_1.$

Thus, the slope of the tangent line to $y = 2x^2$ at any point on the locus is 4 times the x-coordinate of that point.

The advantage of this method over the earlier one (Section 5–6) is that given the x-coordinates of several points on the locus one may find the slopes of the tangent lines at these points by direct substitution. Even more important, it permits one to determine points at which a curve has a given slope. This is useful in applied problems. In particular when $x_1 = 1$ in (5) we find $m = 4(1) = 4$ which is the slope found in Example 2 of Section 5–6.

● **Example 2.** Determine the slope of the tangent line to $y = x^3$ at each of the points $(1, 1)$, $(-2, -8)$, and $(3, 27)$. First determine the slope at the point $P(x_1, y_1)$ on $y = x^3$.

(1) $y_1 = x_1^3$

(2) $y_1 + \Delta y = (x_1 + \Delta x)^3$
$$= x_1^3 + 3x_1^2 \Delta x + 3x_1 \Delta x^2 + \Delta x^3.$$

Subtracting (1) from (2) one finds

(3) $\Delta y = 3x_1^2 \Delta x + 3x_1 \Delta x^2 + \Delta x^3$

(4) $\dfrac{\Delta y}{\Delta x} = \dfrac{3x_1^2 \Delta x + 3x_1 \Delta x^2 + \Delta x^3}{\Delta x}$

$\qquad = 3x_1^2 + 3x_1 \Delta x + \Delta x^2,$ if $\Delta x \neq 0.$

(5) $m =$ slope of tangent line

$\qquad = \lim_{\Delta x \to 0} \dfrac{\Delta y}{\Delta x} = \lim_{\Delta x \to 0} (3x_1^2 + 3x_1 \Delta x + \Delta x^2) = 3x_1^2.$

Hence: at $\quad(1, 1)\quad$ the tangent line has slope $\quad 3(1)^2 = 3,$
at $\quad(-2, -8)\quad$ the tangent line has slope $\quad 3(-2)^2 = 12,$
and at $\quad(3, 27)\quad$ the tangent line has slope $\quad 3(3)^2 = 27.$

● **Example 3.** Find all points of $\quad y = x^3\quad$ at which the tangent line is parallel to the line $\quad y = 48x - 15.$

Problem 33 of Set 5–1 shows that parallel lines have the same slope. Hence, the problem is reduced to finding those points at which $\quad y = x^3\quad$ has slope $\quad m = 48.$

By the last example, the tangent line has slope $\quad m = 3x_1^2$ where x_1 is the abscissa of the point. Hence, we solve

$$m = 3x_1^2 = 48$$
$$x_1^2 = 16$$
$$x_1 = \pm 4.$$

Hence, $\quad(4, 64)\quad$ and $\quad(-4, -64)\quad$ are the required points.

● **Example 4.** Determine the point or points at which the tangent line to the curve $\quad y = 3x^2 - 7x + 5\quad$ has slope 5.

Let $\quad P(x_1, y_1)\quad$ and $\quad S(x_1 + \Delta x, y_1 + \Delta y)\quad$ be points on

$$y = 3x^2 - 7x + 5.$$

(1) $y_1 = 3x_1^2 - 7x_1 + 5$

(2) $y_1 + \Delta y = 3(x_1 + \Delta x)^2 - 7(x_1 + \Delta x) + 5$

$\qquad = 3x_1^2 + 6x_1 \Delta x + 3\Delta x^2 - 7x_1 - 7\Delta x + 5.$

Subtracting (1) from (2),

(3) $\Delta y = 6x_1 \Delta x + 3\Delta x^2 - 7\Delta x$

(4) $\dfrac{\Delta y}{\Delta x} = \dfrac{6x_1 \Delta x + 3\Delta x^2 - 7\Delta x}{\Delta x}$

$\qquad = 6x_1 + 3\Delta x - 7,$ if $\Delta x \neq 0.$

Since $\quad \lim_{\Delta x \to 0} \dfrac{\Delta y}{\Delta x}\quad$ implies $\quad \Delta x \neq 0,\quad$ we have

(5) $m =$ slope of tangent $= \lim_{\Delta x \to 0} \dfrac{\Delta y}{\Delta x}$

$\qquad = \lim_{\Delta x \to 0} (6x_1 + 3\Delta x - 7) = 6x_1 - 7.$

To determine where $m = 5$, we set

$$m = 6x_1 - 7 = 5$$
$$x_1 = 2$$

and the desired point is $(2, 3)$.

PROBLEM SET 5-7

1. Find the slope of the line tangent to $y = 5x^2$ at the point (x_1, y_1) by the method of this section. Assume (x_1, y_1) lies on the locus $y = 5x^2$. At each of the points $(-2, 20)$, $(1, 5)$, and $(3, 45)$ find the slope of the tangent line.

2. Determine the slopes of the lines tangent to $y = 3x^2$ at $(-1, 3)$, $(1, 3)$, $(2, 12)$, $(5, 75)$, and $(10, 300)$. Use the method of this section.

3. Determine the slopes of the lines tangent to $y = 12/x$ at $(-1, -12)$, $(2, 6)$, $(3, 4)$, $(6, 2)$, and $(24, \frac{1}{2})$ using the method of Example 2.

4. Determine the coordinates of all points at which $y = 3x^2$ has slope 12.

5. Determine the coordinates of all points at which $y = 12/x$ has slope -3.

6. Just before Example 1 of this section the statement is made, "Actually, Δy is the same as $\Delta f(x_1, \Delta x)$ if $y = f(x)$." Explain this statement in more detail.

7. Sketch the locus $y = x^3$ and its tangent lines near $(2, 8)$ and near $(0, 0)$.

8. Show that, if the slope of the tangent line to a curve is positive at a point P, then the curve near P is rising (that is, near P, as x increases, so does y).

9. Show that, if the slope of the tangent line to a curve is negative at a point P, then the curve is falling near P (that is, near P, as x increases, y decreases).

10. Find the equation of a line tangent to $y = 2x^2 + 5x - 3$ at $(2, 15)$.

11. Find the equations of all lines tangent to $y = x^3$ and having slope 12.

12. Find the equation of the line tangent to $y = 3/x$ at $(6, \frac{1}{2})$. (Note Example 3, Section 5-6 in this connection.)

It is common practice to drop the subscripts on $P(x_1, y_1)$ and write $P(x, y)$, and similarly, $S(x + \Delta x, \; y + \Delta y)$. Solve the remaining problems using this modification. If an *equation* (in x and y) of the tangent line at (x_1, y_1) is requested, then subscripts are used to distinguish the variables, x and y, of the linear equation from the constants, x_1 and y_1, occurring in its slope.

13. Find the equations of all lines tangent to $y = 7x^2 - 6x$ and parallel to $2x - y + 5 = 0$.
14. Find the equations of all lines tangent to $y = x^3 + 2$ and parallel to $y = 3x + 5$.
15. Determine the slope of the tangent line to

$$y = 200x - 60x^2 + 4x^3$$

at the point (a, b).
16. Determine the points of $y = 200x - 60x^2 + 4x^3$ at which the tangent line is horizontal. On what intervals is the function increasing as x increases?
17. What is the slope of the line tangent to $6x^2 + 3y - 12 = 0$ at the point where it crosses the line $x = 2$?
18. Determine the points on $y = x^3 - 2x^2 - 7x + 5$ where the tangent line is horizontal. On what intervals is the function increasing as x increases?
19. At what points does $y = (x - 5)^2 + 2$ have horizontal tangent lines? Is this point a maximum or a minimum point of the curve?
*20. Sketch $y = 2x^3$. Find all points at which the line tangent to $y = 2x^3$ at $(2, 16)$ cuts the curve.

[HINT: Solve the equation of the tangent line simultaneously with the equation of the curve. The fact that $(2, 16)$ is such a point may help you solve the resulting equation.]

5–8. Self test
Record time.
1. A ball rolls on an inclined plane so that its distance s ft from the bottom of the plane at time t sec is

$$s(t) = 16t - 2t^2.$$

How far up the inclined plane does the ball roll?
2. Write the equation of the line through: (a) $(-4, 1)$ and $(2, -3)$, (b) $(-2, 3)$ with slope $-\frac{2}{3}$, (c) $(0, 0)$ and parallel to $2x - 3y + 5 = 0$.
3. (a) Write $3x + 4y - 5 = 0$ in slope-y-intercept form. (b) Write $4x - 3y = 12$ in intercept form.

4. (a) Find the coordinates of the lowest point on

$$y = 2x^2 - 6x + 4.$$

(b) Show that $y = 2x^2 - 6x + 4$ is symmetrical with respect to the line $x = \frac{3}{2}$.

5. (a) Find the slope of the tangent line to $y = x^2 - 7x$ at $(0, 0)$. (b) Write the equation of this tangent line.

6. Find the slope of $y = \dfrac{2}{x}$ at $(2, 1)$.

7. Find the coordinates of all points at which the tangent line to $y = x^3$ at $(2, 8)$ intersects the curve.

8. Given $f(x) = \begin{cases} 10 & \text{when } x = 2 \\ \dfrac{x^3 - 8}{x - 2} & \text{when } x \neq 2. \end{cases}$ Find $\lim\limits_{x \to 2} f(x)$.

9. The slope of the curve $y = f(x)$ is $m = x^2 - 6x + 8$. Find the intervals on which y increases as x increases.

10. (a) Find $\lim\limits_{x \to 1} \dfrac{x^2 + 2x - 3}{x - 1}$. (b) Is $f(x) = \dfrac{x^2 + 2x - 3}{x - 1}$ continuous at $x = 1$? Explain.

Record time.

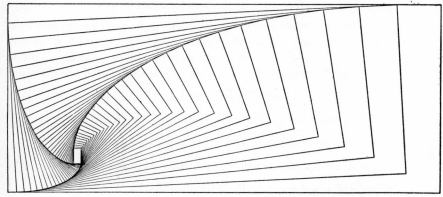

Courtesy *Scripta Mathematica*

A SEQUENCE DESIGN

To obtain this design construct a rectangle whose sides are in the ratio $\sqrt{5}$:1 and from one of its vertices draw a perpendicular to the corresponding diagonal. Rotate these two lines around their point of intersection through an angle $= 90°/32$ and construct a rectangle having three of its vertices at the intersection of the rotated lines with the sides of the exterior rectangle. Continue the rotation and construction through 32 phases. Does this suggest other limiting processes?

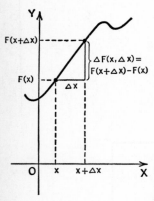

Fig. 6–1

6–1. The derivative. If the locus of $y = f(x)$ has a tangent line at the point $P(x, y)$, the slope of this tangent line is given by $\lim\limits_{x \to 0} \dfrac{f(x + \Delta x) - f(x)}{\Delta x}$. This limit is so important it is given a special name, **derivative.** The symbols† y', $f'(x)$, $\dfrac{dy}{dx}$, $D_x y$, and $\dfrac{df(x)}{dx}$ are all used to represent

$$\lim_{\Delta x \to 0} \frac{\Delta f(x, \Delta x)}{\Delta x} = \lim_{\Delta x \to 0} \frac{f(x + \Delta x) - f(x)}{\Delta x}.$$

The symbols y' and $f'(x)$ are read "y prime" and "f prime of x."

The symbols $\dfrac{dy}{dx}$ † and $\dfrac{df(x)}{dx}$ † are read "the derivative of y with respect to x" and "the derivative of f of x with respect to x."

The slope of a tangent line is only one interpretation of $y' = \dfrac{df(x)}{dx}$. Depending upon the quantities denoted by x and $f(x)$ the derivative has other interpretations such as velocity, acceleration, and various rates of change. We first interpret y' as the slope of a tangent line. Other meanings will be considered later.

Isaac Newton (1642–1727), an Englishman, used the notation $\dot{y}$ for $\dfrac{dy}{dt}$ (velocity) in his *Method of Fluxions* (1671). This notation for time derivatives remains in use today. The symbol $\dfrac{dy}{dx}$ is due to a German, Gottfried Wilhelm Leibnitz (1646–1716). In a manuscript dated October 29, 1675, Leibnitz introduced notations which culminated in symbols such as $\dfrac{dy}{dx}$. Newton and Leibnitz are considered to have been independent inventors of the calculus.

6–2. The delta process. The process of finding the derivative of y with respect to x is called **differentiation.** A function which has a derivative at a point P is said to be differentiable at P. Not all functions have derivatives at a given point P. The so-

---

† The symbols $\dfrac{dy}{dx}$ and $\dfrac{df(x)}{dx}$ are *not* fractions just as Δx is not a product. They represent a single concept. The symbol y' better emphasizes this point, but all five symbols have the same meaning.

called "delta process" used in the preceding chapter provides a method of computing $\dfrac{\Delta f(x, \Delta x)}{\Delta x}$, needed to find

$$y' = \lim_{\Delta x \to 0} \frac{\Delta f(x, \Delta x)}{\Delta x}.$$

It is summarized here and two examples are given.

To find $y' = f'(x)$ where $y = f(x)$:

1. Form $\Delta f(x, \Delta x) = f(x + \Delta x) - f(x)$.
2. Divide by Δx to obtain

$$\frac{\Delta f(x, \Delta x)}{\Delta x} = \frac{f(x + \Delta x) - f(x)}{\Delta x}.$$

3. If the limit as $\Delta x \to 0$ exists,

$$y' = \lim_{\Delta x \to 0} \frac{\Delta f(x, \Delta x)}{\Delta x} = \lim_{\Delta x \to 0} \frac{f(x + \Delta x) - f(x)}{\Delta x}.$$

● **Example 1.** Compute y' if $y = f(x) = 5x^2 - 3$.

    1. $\Delta f(x, \Delta x) = f(x + \Delta x) - f(x)$
$$= [5(x + \Delta x)^2 - 3] - [5x^2 - 3]$$
$$= [5x^2 + 10x(\Delta x) + 5\Delta x^2 - 3] - [5x^2 - 3]$$
$$= 10x(\Delta x) + 5\Delta x^2.$$

    2. Divide by Δx.

$$\frac{\Delta f(x, \Delta x)}{\Delta x} = \frac{10x(\Delta x) + 5\Delta x^2}{\Delta x} = 10x + 5\Delta x, \quad \text{if} \quad \Delta x \neq 0.$$

    3. Take the limit of $\dfrac{\Delta f}{\Delta x}$ as $\Delta x \to 0$ to determine

$$y' = \lim_{\Delta x \to 0} \frac{\Delta f(x, \Delta x)}{\Delta x} = \lim_{\Delta x \to 0} \dagger (10x + 5\Delta x) = 10x + 0 = 10x.$$

Hence,
$$y' = 10x,$$
or
$$f'(x) = 10x.$$

● **Example 2.** Compute $f'(x)$ if $f(x) = \sqrt{x + 3}$.

    1. $\Delta f(x, \Delta x) = f(x + \Delta x) - f(x) = \sqrt{x + \Delta x + 3} - \sqrt{x + 3}$.
    2. Divide by Δx.

$$\frac{\Delta f(x, \Delta x)}{\Delta x} = \frac{\sqrt{x + \Delta x + 3} - \sqrt{x + 3}}{\Delta x}.$$

    † Since $\lim\limits_{\Delta x \to 0} \dfrac{\Delta f}{\Delta x}$ specifically states $0 < |0 - \Delta x|$ (that is, $\Delta x \neq 0$), we may use the form in which numerator and denominator have been divided by Δx.

In the present form we cannot divide numerator and denominator by Δx. It will be helpful to rationalize the numerator (a process similar to rationalizing the denominator). Think of the fraction as $\dfrac{A - B}{\Delta x}$. Multiply numerator and denominator by $A + B$ to obtain

$$\frac{(A - B)(A + B)}{\Delta x(A + B)} = \frac{A^2 - B^2}{\Delta x(A + B)}.$$

In symbols this does not appear to be a simplification, but in the actual problem the reason becomes clear.

$$\frac{\Delta f(x, \Delta x)}{\Delta x} = \frac{(\sqrt{x + \Delta x + 3} - \sqrt{x + 3})(\sqrt{x + \Delta x + 3} + \sqrt{x + 3})}{\Delta x(\sqrt{x + \Delta x + 3} + \sqrt{x + 3})}$$

$$= \frac{(\sqrt{x + \Delta x + 3})^2 - (\sqrt{x + 3})^2}{\Delta x(\sqrt{x + \Delta x + 3} + \sqrt{x + 3})}$$

$$= \frac{x + \Delta x + 3 - (x + 3)}{\Delta x(\sqrt{x + \Delta x + 3} + \sqrt{x + 3})}$$

$$= \frac{\Delta x}{\Delta x(\sqrt{x + \Delta x + 3} + \sqrt{x + 3})}$$

$$= \frac{1}{\sqrt{x + \Delta x + 3} + \sqrt{x + 3}}, \quad \text{if} \quad \Delta x \neq 0.$$

It is now a simple task to find $\lim\limits_{\Delta x \to 0} \dfrac{\Delta f}{\Delta x}$. Using the previous form the task was rather ominous. This technique is often used if the numerator of $\dfrac{\Delta f(x, \Delta x)}{\Delta x}$ contains radicals.

3. Take the limit as $\Delta x \to 0$.

$$f'(x) = \lim_{\Delta x \to 0} \frac{\Delta f(x, \Delta x)}{\Delta x} = \lim_{\Delta x \to 0} \frac{1}{\sqrt{x + \Delta x + 3} + \sqrt{x + 3}}$$

$$= \frac{1}{\sqrt{x + 3} + \sqrt{x + 3}} = \frac{1}{2\sqrt{x + 3}},$$

or

$$f'(x) = \frac{1}{2\sqrt{x + 3}}.$$

The process of rationalizing the *numerator* is often very helpful.

PROBLEM SET 6-2

In Problems 1 to 8 compute the derivative of $f(x)$ with respect to x.

1. $f(x) = 5x^2$.   **2.** $f(x) = x^2 - 17$.   **3.** $f(x) = 17 - x^2$.
4. $f(x) = 3x^2 + 2$.   **5.** $f(x) = 1/x^2$.   **6.** $y = f(x) = 3x^2 + x$.
7. $y = f(x) = 7x^3$.   **8.** $y = f(x) = 2x^5$.

[HINT: $(x + \Delta x)^5 = x^5 + 5x^4\Delta x + 10x^3\Delta x^2 + 10x^2\Delta x^3 + 5x\Delta x^4 + \Delta x^5$.]

9. Let $f(x) = 7$ for all x. Determine $f'(x)$.
10. Compute y' if $y(x) = 3$.   Interpret this result graphically.
11. Prove that if $y(x) = C$ (a constant) then $y' = 0$, no matter what constant value C is given.
12. If $y(t) = -3/t$ for $t > 1$, find the slope of the curve at the point $(6, -\frac{1}{2})$.
13. If $y(x) = \sqrt{x - 5}$, compute y'.

[HINT: Rationalize the *numerator* as in Example 2.]

14. If $f(x) = \sqrt{7 - 2x}$, compute $f'(x)$.
15. If $f(t) = \sqrt{7 - 2t}$, compute $f'(t) = \lim_{\Delta t \to 0} \dfrac{\Delta f(t, \Delta t)}{\Delta t}$.
16. If $F(x)$ is a function such that $F'(x) = 3x^2 + 2$, what is the derivative of $y = F(x) + 4$?
17. If $g(x) = 3x^2 - 6x - 5$, find $\dfrac{d\,g(x)}{dx}$.
18. If $y = 2x^3$, find $\dfrac{dy}{dx}$.
19. If $f(x) = g(x) + k$, show that $f'(x) = g'(x)$.

[HINT: $\Delta f(x, \Delta x) = [g(x + \Delta x) + k] - [g(x) + k] = \cdots = \Delta g(x, \Delta x)$.]

20. If $y = 2x^3 + 27$, find $\dfrac{dy}{dx}$.   Use the results of Problems 18 and 19 to ease the computation.
21. If $y^2 = 2x + 3$, find $\dfrac{dy}{dx}$.
22. If $y = 3x + \pi^2$, find y'.
*23. If $g(x) = \dfrac{1}{\sqrt[3]{4x^2 - 1}}$, find $g'(x)$.
*24. Show that $\lim_{\Delta x \to 0} \Delta f(x, \Delta x) = 0$ if $\dfrac{df(x)}{dx}$ exists.

[HINT: Assume $\lim_{\Delta x \to 0} \Delta f(x, \Delta x) = k \neq 0$ and show that this would imply $f'(x)$ does not exist. Does this prove the theorem requested?]

*25. In Section 5–5 we defined $f(x)$ to be *continuous* at $x = b$ if $\lim_{x \to b} f(x) = f(b)$. Show that if $\dfrac{df(x)}{dx}$ exists at $x = b$, then $f(x)$ is necessarily continuous at $x = b$.

6–3. Labor-saving generalizations. Difficulty in solving certain quadratic equations by factoring led us to solve the problem *in general* (Section 1–9), obtaining the quadratic formula. Rather than construct triangles each time to find the distance between two points (Section 2–3), we again solved the problem *in general*, obtaining a distance formula. A general method of determining the derivative of a polynomial will be obtained in subsequent sections. This process for differentiating a polynomial will be a useful time saver for the reader in many applications. We first derive three preliminary theorems (or lemmas) from which the theorem on the derivative of a polynomial can be deduced.

6–4. Preliminary theorems.

Theorem 1. The derivative of a sum of two functions is equal to the sum of the derivatives of the functions. That is, if $f(x) = g(x) + h(x)$, then $f'(x) = g'(x) + h'(x)$.

We make use of the Δ process of Section 6–2.

If
$$f(x) = g(x) + h(x),$$

then
$$f(x + \Delta x) = g(x + \Delta x) + h(x + \Delta x).$$

$$\begin{aligned}
\Delta f(x, \Delta x) &= f(x + \Delta x) - f(x) \\
&= g(x + \Delta x) + h(x + \Delta x) - g(x) - h(x) \\
&= [g(x + \Delta x) - g(x)] + [h(x + \Delta x) - h(x)]. \quad (6.1)
\end{aligned}$$

$$\frac{\Delta f(x, \Delta x)}{\Delta x} = \frac{g(x + \Delta x) - g(x)}{\Delta x} + \frac{h(x + \Delta x) - h(x)}{\Delta x}. \quad (6.2)$$

$$\begin{aligned}
f'(x) &= \lim_{\Delta x \to 0} \frac{\Delta f(x, \Delta x)}{\Delta x} = \lim_{\Delta x \to 0} \left[\frac{g(x+\Delta x) - g(x)}{\Delta x} + \frac{h(x+\Delta x) - h(x)}{\Delta x} \right] \\
&= \lim_{\Delta x \to 0} \frac{g(x + \Delta x) - g(x)}{\Delta x} + \lim_{\Delta x \to 0} \frac{h(x + \Delta x) - h(x)}{\Delta x} \dagger \\
&= g'(x) + h'(x). \quad (6.3)
\end{aligned}$$

Theorem 2. The derivative of a constant is zero. That is, if $f(x) = c$, a constant, then $f'(x) = 0$ for all x.

† This step assumes that if the individual limits exist, then

$$\lim_{\Delta x \to 0} \left[\frac{\Delta g(x, \Delta x) + \Delta h(x, \Delta x)}{\Delta x} \right] = \lim_{\Delta x \to 0} \frac{\Delta g(x, \Delta x)}{\Delta x} + \lim_{\Delta x \to 0} \frac{\Delta h(x, \Delta x)}{\Delta x}.$$

This assumption is a theorem which is proved in more advanced mathematics.

This was essentially proved in Problem 11, Set 6–2. The proof is repeated here for the sake of completeness.

Let

$$f(x) = c,$$

then

$$f(x + \Delta x) = c$$

and

$$\Delta f(x, \Delta x) = f(x + \Delta x) - f(x) = c - c = 0. \qquad (6.4)$$

$$\frac{\Delta f(x, \Delta x)}{\Delta x} = \frac{0}{\Delta x} = 0, \quad \text{if} \quad \Delta x \neq 0. \qquad (6.5)$$

$$f'(x) = \lim_{\Delta x \to 0} \frac{\Delta f(x, \Delta x)}{\Delta x} = \lim_{\Delta x \to 0} [0] = 0. \qquad (6.6)$$

Theorem 3. If $f(x) = kx^n$, where k is a constant and n a positive integer, then $f'(x) = knx^{n-1}$.

The proof of this important theorem uses an identity of Section 4–2 — namely,

$$h^n - x^n = [h - x][h^{n-1} + h^{n-2}x + h^{n-3}x^2 + \cdots + hx^{n-2} + x^{n-1}]$$

with $h = x + \Delta x$.

The Δ process of Section 6–2 will be employed.

If $f(x) = kx^n$, where n is a positive integer and k is a constant, then

$$f(x + \Delta x) = k(x + \Delta x)^n,$$

and

$$
\begin{aligned}
\Delta f(x, \Delta x) &= f(x + \Delta x) - f(x) \\
&= k(x + \Delta x)^n - kx^n \\
&= k[(x + \Delta x)^n - x^n] \\
&= k[x + \Delta x - x][(x + \Delta x)^{n-1} + (x + \Delta x)^{n-2}x \\
&\qquad\qquad + \cdots + (x + \Delta x)x^{n-2} + x^{n-1}] \dagger \\
&= k[\Delta x][(x + \Delta x)^{n-1} + (x + \Delta x)^{n-2}x \\
&\qquad\qquad + \cdots + (x + \Delta x)x^{n-2} + x^{n-1}]. \quad (6.7)
\end{aligned}
$$

$$
\begin{aligned}
\frac{\Delta f(x, \Delta x)}{\Delta x} &= k[(x + \Delta x)^{n-1} + (x + \Delta x)^{n-2}x \\
&\qquad + \cdots + (x + \Delta x)x^{n-2} + x^{n-1}], \quad \text{if} \quad \Delta x \neq 0. \quad (6.8)
\end{aligned}
$$

Since the brackets $[\ ]$ contain n terms each of which has limit x^{n-1} as $\Delta x \to 0$, we find

$$
\begin{aligned}
f'(x) &= \lim_{\Delta x \to 0} k[\text{the sum of } n \text{ terms each with limit } x^{n-1} \text{ as } \Delta x \to 0] \\
&= knx^{n-1}, \qquad (6.9)
\end{aligned}
$$

where it is assumed that $\lim_{\Delta x \to 0} k\lfloor\ \rfloor = k \lim_{\Delta x \to 0} \lfloor\ \rfloor = knx^{n-1}$.

† A reader familiar with the binomial expansion (see Section 11–4) may save time here by using it to obtain $\Delta f(x, \Delta x)$ in expanded form.

Hence,

$$\frac{d(kx^n)}{dx} = knx^{n-1},$$

where k is a constant and n a positive integer.

This theorem is generalized in Problems 10, 11, 20, Set 6–6 and Problems 9, 10, Set 6–7.

● **Example.** If $y = f(x) = 7x^5$, find $f'(x)$.

In this case $k = 7$ and $n = 5$. Hence, $f'(x) = 7 \cdot 5x^4 = 35x$

PROBLEM SET 6–4

In Problems 1 to 10, use Theorem 3 of this section to determine y', or $f'(x)$, or $P'(x)$, as the case may be.

1. $y = f(x) = 17x^5$.   **2.** $f(x) = 3x^4$.   **3.** $f(x) = 127x$

4. $f(x) = 3x^5$.   **5.** $P(x) = 17x^2$.   **6.** $P(x) = 4x^{17}$.

7. $y(x) = 3x^6$.   **8.** $y(x) = P(x) = 4x^5$.   **9.** $P(x) = x$.

10. $P(x) = 3x^7$. Form $\Delta P(x, \Delta x)$ and find $\lim\limits_{x \to 0} \dfrac{\Delta P}{\Delta x}$ to see how much work was avoided by using the formula.

11. Apply Theorem 3 of this section to determine the slope of $y = x^3$ at the point $(2, 8)$.

12. Find the equation of the line tangent to $y = 4x^3$ at $(2, 32)$.

13. Determine the slope of the line tangent to $y = 3x^5$ where the curve crosses the line $x = 3$.

14. Determine the slope of the line tangent to $y = 5x^3$ where the curve crosses the line $y = 40$.

15. Determine the coordinates of a point at which $y = 7x^3$ has a slope of $\frac{21}{25}$.

The **slope of a curve** at the point (a, b) is defined as the slope of the tangent line at the point (a, b).

16. If the line $y = 9$ and the curve $y = x^2$ intersect, find the equations of the lines tangent to the curve at the points of intersection. If they do not intersect, prove this.

17. Carry out the steps of the proof of Theorem 3, using $11x^5$ for $f(x)$.

18. Find a point at which the line tangent to $3y = 5x^3$ has slope 15.

19. Find a point at which the line tangent to $y = 4x^5$ has slope $\frac{5}{4}$.

*20. Show that since $k = kx^0$ Theorem 2 also follows the general rule of Theorem 3, although the proofs are different.

6–5. The derivative of a polynomial. We are ready to put together the three theorems of the last section to derive an important theorem.

Theorem. The derivative of a polynomial is equal to the sum of the derivatives of its individual terms.

Theorem 1 of the previous section may be used repeatedly until the derivative of the polynomial is expressed as the sum of derivatives of the individual terms. The individual terms are either of the form kx^n or are constants. In each case the derivative may be determined, using Theorem 2 or 3 of the last section.

● **Example 1.** If $P(x) = 5x^3 - 7x^2 + 2x - 3$, find $P'(x)$.

$$P'(x) = \frac{d(5x^3)}{dx} + \frac{d(-7x^2)}{dx} + \frac{d(2x)}{dx} + \frac{d(-3)}{dx}$$
$$= 15x^2 - 14x + 2 + 0.$$

● **Example 2.** If $y = P(x) = 4x^3 - 7x^2 + 2x - 5$, find the slope of the curve (that is, the slope of the line tangent to the curve) at the point $(2, 3)$. Write the equation of the line tangent to the curve at this point.

$$y(x) = 4x^3 - 7x^2 + 2x - 5,$$
$$y'(x) = 12x^2 - 14x + 2.$$

The slope of the curve at $(2, 3)$ is

$$y'(2) = 12(2^2) - 14(2) + 2 = 22.$$

The equation of the tangent line may be written as

$$y - 3 = 22(x - 2) \quad \text{or} \quad 22x - y - 41 = 0.$$

● **Example 3.** Determine the coordinates of one point at which the curve $y = x^3 + 4x^2 + 7x - 5$ has slope 3.

The slope of the curve at the point (x_1, y_1) is

$$y'(x_1) = 3x_1^2 + 8x_1 + 7.$$

Setting $y'(x_1)$ equal to the desired slope 3, and solving the resulting equation for x_1, we obtain

$$3x_1^2 + 8x_1 + 7 = 3$$
$$3x_1^2 + 8x_1 + 4 = 0$$
$$(3x_1 + 2)(x_1 + 2) = 0$$
$$x_1 = -\tfrac{2}{3}, \quad x_1 = -2.$$

Since the problem requests one point, we need only determine the coordinates of the point corresponding to $x = -2$. At $x = -2$, $y = (-2)^3 + 4(-2)^2 + 7(-2) - 5 = -11$. Hence, one such point is the point $(-2, -11)$.

Problem 11 of the next set requests the coordinates of a second point at which the locus has the desired slope.

PROBLEM SET 6-5

1. If $f(x) = 3x^2 + 7x - 5$, find $f'(x)$.
2. Find y' where $y = 15x^3 - 7x^2 + 5x - 11$.
3. Find the equation of a line tangent to $y = x^3 - 2x^2 + 3x - 5$ and parallel to $y = 2x + 11$.
4. Is there a second line satisfying the conditions of Problem 3? If so, find its equation.
5. Find the equation of a line tangent to the curve $y = 5x^7 + 3x$ where the curve crosses $x = 3$.
6. Find the slope of the tangent line to the curve

$$y = f(x) = x^3 - 7x^2 + 12 \quad \text{at} \quad (2, -8).$$

7. Find the slopes of the lines tangent to the curve

$$y = x^2 - 3x + 2$$

at points where the curve crosses the x-axis.
8. Find the slope of the line tangent to the curve $y = x^5 - 7x + 4$ at the point where the curve crosses the y-axis.
9. If the line $y = 4$ and the curve $y = x^2 - 5x + 10$ intersect, determine the slopes of the lines tangent to the curve at the points of intersection. If they do not intersect, prove this.
10. Find a point at which the line tangent to $y = 3x^2 + 5x + 9$ has slope -1.

11. Determine the coordinates of a point other than $(-2, -11)$ at which the locus of Example 3 has slope 3.
12. Determine the equation of a line having slope 4 and tangent to $y = 3x^2 + 4x - 7$.
13. Find the coordinates of a point at which $y = 3x^2 - 7x + 2$ has slope -3.
14. Is the slope of $y = 5x^5 + 13$ ever negative? Is it ever zero?
15. If $p(x) = x^3 - 12x$, find the slope of the tangent line at points where $y = p(x)$ crosses the x-axis.
16. If $y = g(x) = x^3 + 3x^2 + 9x + 11$ crosses the line $x = 2$, find the equation of the tangent to $y = g(x)$ at this point. If they do not intersect, prove this.
17. Write the equations of the lines tangent to $y = 3x^2 + 4x + 5$ at the points of intersection of the curve and $y = 12$.
18. Find the point of intersection of the two tangents of Problem 17 if they intersect. If they do not intersect, prove this.

In Problems 19 to 25 determine the equation of a line tangent to the given curve at each intersection of the given line L and given curve C.

19. C: $y = 3x^2 + 6x + 5$; L: $x = 4$.
20. C: $y = 4x^3 - 7x^2 + 2x - 11$; L: $x = -3$.
21. C: $y = x^5 - 4x^2 + 9$; L: $x = 0$.
22. C: $y = -x^3 + 6x + 2$; L: $y = -3$.
23. C: $y = x^3 - 14$; L: $y = 216$.
24. C: $y = 4x^2 + 3x - 5$; L: $y = 2x$.
25. C: $y = 5x^2 - 9$; L: $y = 7x - 3$.
26. Write the equations of three curves whose slopes are (a) never positive, (b) never negative, (c) positive for $x < 3$ and negative when $x > 3$.
27. Find a point on the arc of $y = x^2 - 2x - 3$ connecting $(-1, 0)$ and $(-2, 5)$ at which the tangent line is parallel to the secant line connecting these points.
28. Determine the points at which $y = 2x^3 - x^2 - 18x + 5$ has slope 2.
29. (a) Determine the points at which $y = 6x^3 - 3x^2 - 60x + 7$ has slope zero. (b) On what domain of x values does y increase as x increases? (c) On what domain of x values does y decrease as x increases?
30. On what x domain does y (a) increase, (b) decrease as x increases if $y = 3x^2 - 7x + 5$?
31. Determine a point in the second quadrant at which $y = -3/x$ has slope 12. [Since $y = -3/x$ is *not* a polynomial, it will be necessary to use the Δ process in computing y'.]

32. Determine a point in quadrant IV at which $y = -3/x$ has slope 12. (See Problem 31.)

33. Sketch $y = -3/x$. Are there any points not found in Problems 31 and 32 at which $y = -3/x$ has slope 12? Demonstrate your reply both by considering the sketch and also by considering the algebraic solution of $y' = 12$.

*34. If $y = -x^3$ and $y = 3x^2 + 3x + 1$ intersect, determine the equation of the tangent lines to each curve at their intersection. If not, prove this.

*35. Problem 25, Set 6–2, states that if $h'(x)$ exists at a point P, then $y = h(x)$ is continuous. Use this result and the interpretation of $h'(x)$ as the slope of a tangent line to show that if $h'(x) = 0$ for all x, then $h(x)$ is constant. Is this result different from that of Problem 11, Set 6–2?

36. Use derivatives to prove that a linear function has a constant slope.

*37. Prove, using derivatives, that a linear function is the only polynomial which has constant slope. Be sure you solve this problem, not its converse, which is Problem 36.

38. The point $(2, -3)$ lies on the graph of $p(x) = 3x^2 - 7x - 1$. Determine the slope of the tangent line to $p(x)$ at the point $(2, -3)$ and make a careful sketch of the tangent line.

39. Find the equation of the tangent line to $y = 2x^3 - 5x^2 + 6$ at the point where $x = 3$.

40. Find the equation of the tangent line to $y = 2x^3 - 5x^2 + 6$ at the point where $x = 1$.

41. Find the equation of the line which passes through the point $(5, 7)$, and the intersection of the lines $7x + 11y - 12 = 0$ and $2x - 9y + 13 = 0$.

42. Determine the coordinates of each point at which the curve $y = x^3 + 2x^2 - 4x + 2$ has slope -5. How many such points exist?

*43. For a certain function $p(x)$: $p(3) = 6$, $p'(3) = 1$, and $p''(3) = -2$, where $p''(x)$ indicates the derivative of $p'(x)$. Sketch the tangent line at $(3, 6)$ and state whether the graph is above the tangent line, or below the tangent line, or both above and below the tangent line, or neither, for points of the graph near the point of tangency $(3, 6)$.

*44. Determine the slope of the curve $x^2y - yx + 10 = 0$ at the point $(2, -5)$. (See below Problem 15, Set 6–4.)

45. Determine the equation of each line which has slope equal to 2 and is tangent to the curve $y = x^3 + x^2 - 19x - 40$.

6–6. Differentiation of a product.

Theorem. If $u = u(x)$ and $v = v(x)$ are differentiable functions of x, then

$$\frac{d(u \cdot v)}{dx} = u\frac{dv}{dx} + v\frac{du}{dx}. \qquad (6.10)$$

As usual in proofs involving derivatives we use the Δ process. Let

$$f(x) = u(x) \cdot v(x),$$

then

$$f(x + \Delta x) = u(x + \Delta x) \cdot v(x + \Delta x).$$

Hence,

$$\begin{aligned}
\Delta f(x, \Delta x) &= f(x + \Delta x) - f(x) \qquad (6.11)\\
&= u(x + \Delta x) \cdot v(x + \Delta x) - u(x) \cdot v(x).
\end{aligned}$$

Now,

$$\Delta u(x, \Delta x) = u(x + \Delta x) - u(x).$$

Consequently,

$$u(x + \Delta x) = u(x) + \Delta u(x, \Delta x).$$

Similarly,

$$v(x + \Delta x) = v(x) + \Delta v(x, \Delta x).$$

Substituting in equation (6.11) we obtain

$$\begin{aligned}
\Delta f(x, \Delta x) &= [u(x) + \Delta u(x, \Delta x)][v(x) + \Delta v(x, \Delta x)] - u(x) \cdot v(x)\\
&= u(x) \cdot \Delta v(x, \Delta x) + v(x) \cdot \Delta u(x, \Delta x) + \Delta u(x, \Delta x) \cdot \Delta v(x, \Delta x).
\end{aligned}$$

Then, upon dividing by Δx, we obtain

$$\frac{\Delta f(x, \Delta x)}{\Delta x} = u(x) \cdot \frac{\Delta v(x, \Delta x)}{\Delta x} + v(x) \cdot \frac{\Delta u(x, \Delta x)}{\Delta x}$$
$$+ \frac{\Delta u(x, \Delta x)}{\Delta x} \cdot \Delta v(x, \Delta x). \quad (6.12)$$

Using

$$\lim_{\Delta x \to 0} \frac{\Delta f(x, \Delta x)}{\Delta x}$$
$$= \lim_{\Delta x \to 0} \left[u(x) \cdot \frac{\Delta v(x, \Delta x)}{\Delta x} + v(x) \cdot \frac{\Delta u(x, \Delta x)}{\Delta x} \right.$$
$$\left. + \frac{\Delta u(x, \Delta x)}{\Delta x} \cdot \Delta v(x, \Delta x) \right]$$

$$= \lim_{\Delta x \to 0} u(x) \cdot \frac{\Delta v(x, \Delta x)}{\Delta x} + \lim_{\Delta x \to 0} v(x) \cdot \frac{\Delta u(x, \Delta x)}{\Delta x}$$

$$+ \lim_{\Delta x \to 0} \frac{\Delta u(x, \Delta x)}{\Delta x} \cdot \Delta v(x, \Delta x)$$

$$= \lim_{\Delta x \to 0} u(x) \lim_{\Delta x \to 0} \frac{\Delta v(x, \Delta x)}{\Delta x} + \lim_{\Delta x \to 0} v(x) \lim_{\Delta x \to 0} \frac{\Delta u(x, \Delta x)}{\Delta x}$$

$$+ \lim_{\Delta x \to 0} \frac{\Delta u(x, \Delta x)}{\Delta x} \lim_{\Delta x \to 0} \Delta v(x, \Delta x)$$

$$= u(x) \frac{dv(x)}{dx} + v(x) \frac{du(x)}{dx} + \frac{du(x)}{dx} \cdot 0.$$

From this we obtain

$$\frac{d(u \cdot v)}{dx} = u \frac{dv}{dx} + v \frac{du}{dx}. \qquad (6.10)$$

● **Example 1.** If $\quad y = (x^3/3 - 9x + 1)(x^2 + 6x + 2), \quad$ find y'.

Using the theorem of this section with $\quad u = x^3/3 - 9x + 1$
and $\quad v = x^2 + 6x + 2, \quad$ we obtain

$$y' = u \frac{dv}{dx} + v \frac{du}{dx}$$

$$= (x^3/3 - 9x + 1) \frac{d(x^2 + 6x + 2)}{dx} + (x^2 + 6x + 2) \frac{d(x^3/3 - 9x + 1)}{dx}$$

$$= (x^3/3 - 9x + 1)(2x + 6) + (x^2 + 6x + 2)(x^2 - 9)$$

$$= (x^3/3 - 9x + 1) \cdot 2 \cdot (x + 3) + (x^2 + 6x + 2)(x - 3)(x + 3).$$

The factor $\quad x + 3 \quad$ appears in each term. Hence,

$$y' = (x + 3)[(x^3/3 - 9x + 1)2 + (x^2 + 6x + 2)(x - 3)]$$

$$= (x + 3)[5x^3/3 + 3x^2 - 34x - 4].$$

If we had multiplied the factors of y as suggested at the beginning of this section, it would not have been as apparent that $x + 3$ is a factor of y'. Since many applications require the solution of the equation $\quad y' = 0, \quad$ having y' in partially factored form is an additional advantage of this theorem.

● **Example 2.** If $\quad f(x) = (5x^2 - 3)(7x^2 + 6), \quad$ find $f'(x)$.

Setting $\quad u = 5x^2 - 3 \quad$ and $\quad v = 7x^2 + 6 \quad$ and using the theorem of this section, we obtain

† This assumes that the limit of a sum is equal to the sum of the limits if the latter limits exist, a theorem which is proved in more advanced mathematics.

‡ This assumes that the limit of a product is equal to the product of the limits if the latter limits exist, a theorem which is proved in more advanced mathematics.

$$f'(x) = u\frac{dv}{dx} + v\frac{du}{dx}$$
$$= (5x^2 - 3)(14x) + (7x^2 + 6)(10x)$$
$$= 2x[(5x^2 - 3)7 + (7x^2 + 6)5]$$
$$= 2x[70x^2 + 9].$$

Example 3. Find all points at which $\quad y = (3x^2 - 5x + 4)(2x + 3)$ has slope 9.

Since $\quad \dfrac{dy}{dx} \quad$ represents the slope, we wish to find values of x

at which $\quad \dfrac{dy}{dx} = 9.$

$$y = (3x^2 - 5x + 4)(2x + 3).$$
$$y' = (3x^2 - 5x + 4)(2) + (2x + 3)(6x - 5)$$
$$= 18x^2 - 2x - 7.$$

Values of x such that $\quad y' = 9 \quad$ will be solutions of the equation $\quad y' = 9, \quad$ that is, of

$$18x^2 - 2x - 7 = 9$$
$$18x^2 - 2x - 16 = 0$$
$$9x^2 - x - 8 = 0$$
$$(9x + 8)(x - 1) = 0,$$

are

$$x = -\tfrac{8}{9}, \; x = 1.$$

Hence, the desired points are $\quad (-\tfrac{8}{9}, \tfrac{3212}{243}) \quad$ and $\quad (1, 10).$

PROBLEM SET 6-6

1. Find y' if $\quad y = (x^3 - 1)(4x^2 - 2x + 1).$
2. If $\quad y = (x^3 - 2)(4x^2 + 5x - 7), \quad$ find y'.
3. Determine the slope of $\quad y = (3x^2 - 2x + 5)(4x^2 - 3x) \quad$ at the point on the locus where $\quad x = 2.$
4. If $\quad y = (x^5 - 1)(x^2 - 1), \quad$ find y'.

In Problems 5 to 8 compute the slope of the line tangent to the given curve at the point of intersection of the given curve C and the line L.

5. C: $\quad y = (x^3 + 7x - 4)(x + 2)$; $\quad L$: $\quad x = -2.$
6. C: $\quad y = (x^5 - 4x)(x^2 + 2)$; $\quad L$: $\quad x = 3.$
7. C: $\quad y = (x^3 + 1)(x^7 + 7x^2 + 3x - 5)$; $\quad L$: $\quad x = 1.$
8. C: $\quad y = (x^3 + 2x^2 + 4x + 5)(2x^3 + 4x^2 + 8x - 1)$; $\quad L$: $\quad x = 4.$

9. The line $x = 5$ crosses the curve $y = (3x^2 - 2x)(4x^3 - 5)$ at some point P. Determine slope of tangent to curve at P.

*10. Use the theorem of this section to prove that $\dfrac{d(x^n)}{dx} = nx^{n-1}$ for n a positive integer. Note that we have this result as a special case of Theorem 3, Section 6–4, but this proof uses a different method.

HINT: Since $x^n = x \cdot x^{n-1}$, we have

$$\frac{d(x^n)}{dx} = x\frac{d(x^{n-1})}{dx} + x^{n-1}\frac{d(x)}{dx}$$

$$= x\frac{d(x^{n-1})}{dx} + x^{n-1}.$$

Using the same method again by separating x^{n-1} into $x \cdot x^{n-2}$ we obtain

$$\frac{dx^n}{dx} = x\left[\frac{x\,d(x^{n-2})}{dx} + x^{n-2}\right] + x^{n-1} = x^2\left[\frac{d(x^{n-2})}{dx}\right] + x^{n-1} + x^{n-1}$$

$$= x^2\left[\frac{d(x^{n-2})}{dx}\right] + 2x^{n-1}.$$

Repetition leads to the desired result.

*11. Prove $\dfrac{d(kx^{-n})}{dx} = -knx^{-n-1}$, n a positive integer, k a constant.

[HINT: Let $y = kx^{-n}$. Then $x^n y = k$. Using the formula for $\dfrac{d(u \cdot v)}{dx}$ where $u = x^n$ and $v = y$, one obtains

$$\frac{d}{dx}(x^n y) = x^n\frac{dy}{dx} + nx^{n-1}y = \frac{d}{dx}(k) = 0.]$$

In Problems 12 to 17 find at least one point at which the given curve has a horizontal tangent (slope zero).

12. $y = (x^2 - 3x + 2)(x^2 + 3x + 2)$.
13. $y = (x^2 - 5x + 4)(x^2 + 6x + 9)$.
14. $y = x^7 (x^2 + 4)$.
15. $y = (ax + b)(ax - b)$.
16. $y = (3x^2 + x - 6)(6x^2 + 12x + 2)$.
17. $y = (3x^3 - 4x - 3)(3x^2 + 4x + 1)$.
18. Determine all points at which $y = (3x^2 - 5x + 4)(2x + 3)$ has slope 13.
19. Determine the slope of a line tangent to

$$y = (x^3 + 4x^2 + 2x - 3)(x^{15} - 4x^2 - 3x + 1)$$

at the point $(0, -3)$.

20. Prove that $\dfrac{d[cv(x)]}{dx} = c\dfrac{dv}{dx}$, if c is a constant.

6–7. Differentiation of a composite function. It is possible to multiply out $(t^2 - 5t + 3)^{11}$ and then differentiate the result to determine y' where $y = (t^2 - 5t + 3)^{11}$, but this is a tedious task. The theorem of this section provides a simple method for avoiding this multiplication.

Theorem. $\dfrac{d[u^n]}{dx} = nu^{n-1}\dfrac{du}{dx}$ if n is a positive integer and $u = u(x)$ is a differentiable function of x.

Let $u = u(x)$. Then, upon factoring, $u^n = u \cdot u^{n-1}$ and letting u be the u of the theorem of Section 6–6, and $u^{n-1} = v$ of the theorem of Section 6–6, we have

$$\frac{d[u^n]}{dx} = u\frac{du^{n-1}}{dx} + u^{n-1}\frac{du}{dx}.$$

Repeating the process, upon separating u^{n-1} of the first term into two factors $u^{n-1} = u \cdot u^{n-2}$, we obtain

$$\frac{d[u^n]}{dx} = u \cdot \frac{d[u \cdot u^{n-2}]}{dx} + u^{n-1}\frac{du}{dx}$$

$$= u\left[u \cdot \frac{du^{n-2}}{dx} + u^{n-2}\frac{du}{dx}\right] + u^{n-1}\frac{du}{dx}$$

$$= u^2\frac{du^{n-2}}{dx} + u^{n-1}\frac{du}{dx} + u^{n-1}\frac{du}{dx}$$

$$= u^2\frac{d[u \cdot u^{n-3}]}{dx} + 2u^{n-1}\frac{du}{dx}.$$

By repeating the process we eventually obtain the desired result,

$$\frac{d[u^n]}{dx} = n \cdot u^{n-1}\frac{du}{dx}.$$

This theorem could be derived using the Δ process in a manner similar to the derivation of Theorem 3, Section 6–4.

● **Example 1.** If $y = u^{11}$ and $u = x^2 - 5x + 3$, find $\dfrac{dy}{dx}$.

$$\frac{dy}{dx} = \frac{d[u^{11}]}{dx} = 11u^{10}\frac{du}{dx}.$$

Since

$$\frac{du}{dx} = \frac{d[x^2 - 5x + 3]}{dx} = 2x - 5$$

$$\frac{dy}{dx} = 11u^{10}(2x - 5)$$

or

$$\frac{dy}{dx} = 11[x^2 - 5x + 3]^{10}(2x - 5).$$

This method is easier than raising $x^2 - 5x + 3$ to the eleventh power and then differentiating. In addition, the result is partially factored.

● **Example 2.** Find y' where $y = (3x^2 - 7)^5$. Here $y = u^5$ if $u = 3x^2 - 7$. Then

$$y' = 5u^4 \frac{du}{dx}$$

$$= 5(3x^2 - 7)^4 \frac{d(3x^2 - 7)}{dx}$$

$$= 5(3x^2 - 7)^4(6x)$$

$$= 30x(3x^2 - 7)^4.$$

● **Example 3.** If $y = (x^2 - 5x + 3)^5(2x - 5)^3$, find $\frac{dy}{dx}$.

Since y is a product, we use $\frac{d[u \cdot v]}{dx} = u\frac{dv}{dx} + v\frac{du}{dx}$ with $u = (x^2 - 5x + 3)^5$ and $v = (2x - 5)^3$. Thus,

$$y' = (x^2 - 5x + 3)^5 \frac{d[(2x - 5)^3]}{dx} + (2x - 5)^3 \frac{d[(x^2 - 5x + 3)^5]}{dx}$$

Upon using the theorem of this section we obtain

$$y' = (x^2 - 5x + 3)^5 \cdot 3(2x - 5)^2 \cdot \frac{d[2x - 5]}{dx}$$

$$+ (2x - 5)^3 \cdot 5(x^2 - 5x + 3)^4 \cdot \frac{d[x^2 - 5x + 3]}{dx}$$

$$= (x^2 - 5x + 3)^5 3(2x - 5)^2(2) + (2x - 5)^3 5(x^2 - 5x + 3)^4(2x - 5)$$

$$= (x^2 - 5x + 3)^4(2x - 5)^2[(x^2 - 5x + 3)6 + (2x - 5)^2 5]$$

$$= (x^2 - 5x + 3)^4(2x - 5)^2[26x^2 - 130x + 143].$$

Having a polynomial partially factored may be helpful in applications.

● **Example 4.** Determine $\frac{dy}{dx}$ where $x^2 + y^2 = 16$. It is possible in this problem to solve to obtain $y = \pm \sqrt{16 - x^2}$, but a more general procedure called **implicit differentiation** which makes use of the theorem of this section will be used. Upon differentiating $x^2 + y^2 = 16$ *with respect to x*, one obtains

$$2x + 2y\frac{dy}{dx} = 0$$

which yields

$$\frac{dy}{dx} = -\frac{x}{y} = -\frac{x}{\pm\sqrt{16-x^2}}.$$

The $-\dfrac{x}{y}$ form is often preferable since the ambiguity of sign is avoided.

● **Example 5.** Derive a formula for $\dfrac{d[u(x)/v(x)]}{dx}$ where

$u = u(x)$ and $v = v(x)$ are differentiable functions of x with

$$\Delta u = u(x+\Delta x) - u(x) \quad \text{and} \quad \Delta v = v(x+\Delta x) - v(x).$$

From the basic definition of derivative:

$$\frac{d\left[\frac{u}{v}\right]}{dx} = \lim_{\substack{\Delta x \to 0 \\ \Delta u \to 0 \\ \Delta v \to 0}} \left[\frac{\frac{u+\Delta u}{v+\Delta v} - \frac{u}{v}}{\Delta x}\right]$$

$$= \lim_{\substack{\Delta x \to 0 \\ \Delta u \to 0 \\ \Delta v \to 0}} \left[\frac{uv + v\cdot\Delta u - uv - u\cdot\Delta v}{(v+\Delta v)\cdot v\cdot\Delta x}\right]$$

$$= \lim_{\substack{\Delta x \to 0 \\ \Delta u \to 0 \\ \Delta v \to 0}} \left[\frac{v\cdot\dfrac{\Delta u}{\Delta x} - u\cdot\dfrac{\Delta v}{\Delta x}}{(v+\Delta v)\cdot v}\right]$$

$$\frac{d\left[\frac{u}{v}\right]}{dx} = \frac{v\dfrac{du}{dx} - u\dfrac{dv}{dx}}{v^2}$$

PROBLEM SET 6-7

1. Carry through the proof of this section, using u^5 for u^n and $x^3 - 5x$ for $u(x)$.

2. Find $\dfrac{d[u^7]}{dx}$ where $u = x^3 - 5x + 1$.

3. Find $\dfrac{d[(x^2 - 5x + 2)^4]}{dx}$.

4. Find y' where $y = (x^2 - 5x)^7$.

5. Find y' where $y = (7x^2 - 4x + 3)^{10}$.

6. If $p(x) = (17x^3 - 3)^{15}$, find $\dfrac{dp}{dx}$.

7. If $y = (x - 3)^8$, find $\dfrac{dy}{dx}$.

8. If $y = (t^2 - 2t + 3)^3$, find $\dfrac{dy}{dt}$.

9. Prove $\dfrac{d(x^{p/q})}{dx} = \dfrac{p}{q}\, x^{(p/q)-1}$, where p and q are positive

integers. Let $y = x^{p/q}$. Then $y^q = x^p$ and

$$\frac{d}{dx}(y^q) = \frac{d}{dx}(x^p), \quad qy^{q-1}\frac{dy}{dx} = px^{p-1}.$$

The student who is unfamiliar with the meaning of fractional exponents may wish to read Section 8–1 at this point.

10. Prove $\dfrac{d}{dx}(kx^n) = knx^{n-1}$, where n is a rational number.

Apply the results of Problems 10, 11 of Section 6–6 and Problem 9 of Section 6–7.

11. If $y = (x - 3)^{\frac{1}{2}}$ find y'.

HINT: Use the results of Problem 9. $y' = \frac{1}{2}(x - 3)^{\frac{1}{2}-1}$.

*12. Prove that, if a polynomial $P(x) = (ax - b)^m \cdot q(x)$ has $(ax - b)$ as a factor of multiplicity m [that is, $(ax - b)^m$ divides $P(x)$ but $(ax - b)^{m+1}$ does not divide $P(x)$], then $P'(x)$ has $(ax - b)$ as a factor of multiplicity $m - 1$. Show also that this theorem holds *in the case of the three examples of this section* even if the factor of multiplicity m is more complicated than $(ax - b)$. For illustration, in Example 2, $(3x^2 - 7)$ is a factor of multiplicity 5 of y and of multiplicity 4 of y'.

In Problems 13 to 25 find the derivative of the given function.

13. $y = (4x - 2)^{\frac{1}{3}}$. [HINT: See Problem 11.]

14. $y = (x - 2)^8(x + 5)^7$.   **15.** $y = (3x^2 + 5x)^4(3x^2 - 4)^3$.

16. $y = (2x^3 - 4x + 1)^5$.   **17.** $y = (2x - 3)^{\frac{1}{2}}$.

18. $y = \sqrt{x^2 - 2x + 9}$.   **19.** $y = \sqrt[3]{(2x - 4)^2}$.

20. $y = (x^2 - 4x + 1)^{-3}$.   **21.** $p(x) = (x^2 + 5)^8$.

22. $p(x) = (x^3 + 9x + 6)^{11}$.   **23.** $y = (2x^3 - 5x)^{-7}$.

24. $y = \dfrac{1}{x^4}$.   **25.** $y = \dfrac{1}{(x - 3)^5}$.

Use the results of Examples 4 or 5 to determine $\dfrac{dy}{dx}$ in each of the following exercises.

26. $y = \dfrac{x^2}{5x - 3}$.

27. $y = \dfrac{\sqrt{3x - 7}}{x^2 - 5} = \dfrac{(3x - 7)^{\frac{1}{2}}}{x^2 - 5}$.

28. $3x^2 + 5y^2 = 16$.

29. $x^2 - 4y^2 + 10 = 0$.

30. $y = \dfrac{(2x - 3)^2}{x^2 - 3x + 5}$.

6–8. Maxima and minima. In Section 4–8 a (relative) maximum value of $f(x)$ is defined to be the value of $f(x)$ at $x = a$ if $f(a)$ is the largest value of $f(x)$ for x close to a. Similarly, a (relative) minimum of a function $f(x)$ is defined as the value of $f(x)$ at $x = b$ if $f(b)$ is the smallest value of $f(x)$ for x close to b. These were stated more precisely as

(1) $f(a)$ is a relative maximum of $f(x)$ if $f(a) \geqq f(a + \Delta x)$ for Δx sufficiently near zero.†

(2) $f(b)$ is a relative minimum of $f(x)$ if $f(b) \leqq f(b + \Delta x)$ for Δx sufficiently near zero.†

The function sketched appears to have relative maxima at function values corresponding to the points A, D, F, and relative minima at function values corresponding to points B, E, G. The function value corresponding to C is *neither* a maximum nor a minimum value of $f(x)$. The value of the function $f(a)$ at a relative maximum is *not* necessarily the greatest value of $f(x)$. It is true that $f(a) \geqq f(x)$ for x close to a, but not necessarily for *all* x. In Figure 6–2, we have a maximum at A which is smaller than the minimum at G. The terms (relative) maximum and (relative) minimum value refer to the greatest and least values of $y = f(x)$ in a *small* region (neighborhood) about a point. The term **maximum (or minimum) point of a locus** (graph) is used for the point on the graph corresponding to a maximum (or minimum) value of the function.

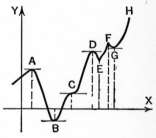

Fig. 6–2

The terms **absolute maximum** and **absolute minimum** are used for the greatest and the least values of $f(x)$ **in the entire range of the function** when these values exist. *In the range shown* in Figure 6–2, the function appears to have an absolute minimum at B and an absolute maximum at the point H. However, if the domain of definition (see Section 1–8) of $f(x)$ is increased, the absolute maximum and absolute minimum may change or even fail to exist. In many applied problems the absolute maximum or absolute minimum *in a given interval* is needed.

6–9. The slope of a tangent line at a maximum or minimum point. In this section we show that, if the graph of $y = f(x)$ has a tangent line at a maximum point $P(a, f(a))$ and if this

† Since Δx may be either positive or negative, $a + \Delta x$ may be larger or smaller than a.

line has a definite slope (that is, is not vertical) and if P is not an end point of the range of definition of $f(x)$, then the slope of the tangent line is zero. This fact is useful.

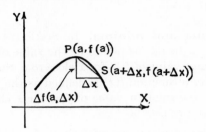

Fig. 6–3

If P is a maximum point, the slope of the secant line joining $P(a, f(a))$ and $S(a + \Delta x, f(a + \Delta x))$ is

$$m = \frac{f(a + \Delta x) - f(a)}{\Delta x} = \frac{\Delta f(a, \Delta x)}{\Delta x}.$$

If $f(x)$ has a relative maximum at P, then for sufficiently small $\Delta x \neq 0$,

$$\Delta f(a, \Delta x) = f(a + \Delta x) - f(a) \leqq 0.$$

If $\Delta f(a, \Delta x) \equiv 0$, then the slope of the tangent line is

$$\lim_{\Delta x \to 0} \frac{\Delta f(a, \Delta x)}{\Delta x} = 0.$$

If $\Delta f(a, \Delta x) < 0$ and $\Delta x > 0$, then S is to the right of P (as shown in Fig. 6–3) and

$$\frac{\Delta f(a, \Delta x)}{\Delta x} = \frac{-}{+} = -.$$

Furthermore, if $\Delta f(a, \Delta x) < 0$ and $\Delta x < 0$, then S is to the left of P and

$$\frac{\Delta f(a, \Delta x)}{\Delta x} = \frac{-}{-} = +.$$

Since $f'(a) = \lim_{\Delta x \to 0} \dfrac{\Delta f(a, \Delta x)}{\Delta x}$ and since $\dfrac{\Delta f(a, \Delta x)}{\Delta x}$ changes from negative to positive as Δx changes from positive to negative, it follows that if $\lim_{\Delta x \to 0} \dfrac{\Delta f(a, \Delta x)}{\Delta x}$ exists, it must be zero. Geometrically this requires the tangent line to be parallel to the x-axis.

The case of a relative minimum may be treated in a similar fashion.

Points A, B, D, and G of Figure 6–2 represent maximum and minimum points at which the tangent line is horizontal (has slope 0). However, there may exist points such as E and F which are maximum and minimum points but which do *not* have horizontal tangent lines. At such points the tangent line may be vertical as in Problem 6, Set 5–3, or there may be no tangent line at all, as in Problem 10, Set 5–3. Difficulties of this type do not arise if the function is a *polynomial*. It is also possible to have points at which the tangent line is horizontal (slope zero) but which are neither maximum nor minimum points of the locus. Locate such a point in Figure 6–2. In spite of these shortcomings, the determination of points at which the tangent line has zero slope is extremely helpful in many applications, as you will see.

Tests for maximum and minimum points. If $y = p(x)$, a polynomial in x, there exist four possible cases of a tangent line with slope zero. The sketches illustrate each case. Let T be a

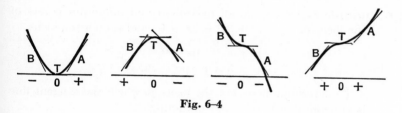

Fig. 6–4

point at which the locus has a horizontal tangent. To distinguish these four cases consider the slope of the tangent line at a point B, preceding T, and at a point A following the point T. In the case of a minimum the slope changes from negative to zero to positive as x increases. In the case of a maximum the slope changes from positive to zero to negative as x increases. In the two cases which are neither maximum nor minimum points the slope has the same sign on each side of the point where the tangent line is horizontal. For single-valued functions this provides an excellent test for distinguishing these four cases.

It is possible for a locus to have a horizontal tangent line not included in these cases as Figure 6–5 shows, but this does not occur if the function is a single-valued function of x, as is a polynomial in x.

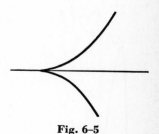

Fig. 6–5

● *Example 1.* Determine, using the derivative, the maximum and minimum points of the locus $y = x^2 - 4x + 3$ and sketch the locus.

For a polynomial, the slope of the tangent line is zero at maximum and minimum (and possibly, also at other) points. Since $x^2 - 4x + 3$ is a polynomial, we compute y' and set

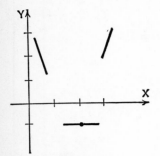

Fig. 6–6

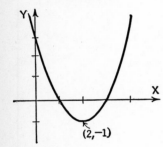

Fig. 6–7

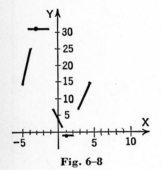

Fig. 6–8

Fig. 6–9

it equal to zero to determine values of x at which the tangent lines are horizontal.

$$y' = 2x - 4.$$

If $y' = 2(x - 2) = 0$, then $x = 2$.

Thus, $(2, -1)$ is the only point at which $y = x^2 - 4x + 3$ has a horizontal tangent line. Consider the slope of the tangent line for $x < 2$ and for $x > 2$.

If $x < 2$, then $x - 2 < 0$ and $y' = -$.
If $x > 2$, then $x - 2 > 0$ and $y' = +$.

Figure 6–6 shows the tangent lines at certain points. The point $(2, -1)$ is a *minimum point* and the locus has the sketch show in Figure 6–7.

● **Example 2.** Determine all maximum and minimum points of the locus of $y = x^3 + 3x^2 - 9x + 4$ and sketch the locus.

$$y' = 3x^2 + 6x - 9$$
$$= 3(x + 3)(x - 1).$$

To determine points of the locus at which the tangent line is horizontal, set $y' = 0$, obtaining

$$3(x + 3)(x - 1) = 0$$
$$x = -3, \quad x = 1.$$

By substitution in $y = x^3 + 3x^2 - 9x + 4$ we find the locus has horizontal tangents at $(-3, 31)$ and $(1, -1)$. The locus crosses the y-axis at $(0, 4)$.

Using the test of this section, we consider the slope

$$y' = 3(x + 3)(x - 1)$$

of the locus for $x < -3$, $-3 < x < 1$, and $1 < x$.

If $x < -3$, then $x + 3 < 0$, $x - 1 < 0$, and

$$y' = +(-)(-) = +.$$

If $-3 < x < 1$, then $x + 3 > 0$, $x - 1 < 0$, and

$$y' = +(+)(-) = -.$$

If $1 < x$, then $x + 3 > 0$, $x - 1 > 0$, and

$$y' = +(+)(+) = +.$$

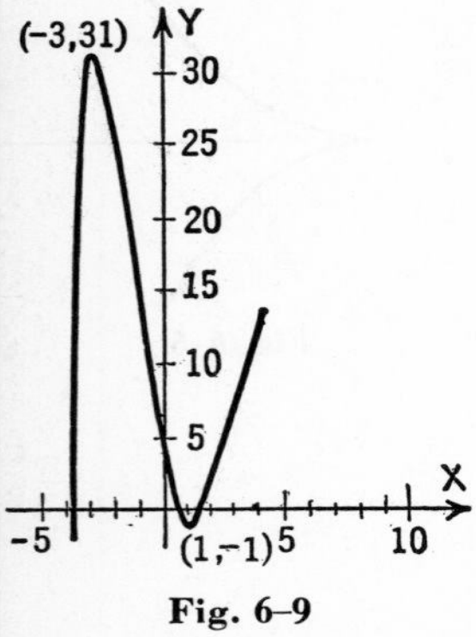

Our knowledge of the tangent lines at certain points is presented in Figure 6–8. This suggests Figure 6–9.

The function $y(x) = x^3 + 3x^2 - 9x + 4$ has a maximum value of $y(-3) = (-3)^3 + 3(-3)^2 - 9(-3) + 4 = 31$ at $x = -3$ and a minimum value of $y(1) = -1$, at $x = 1$. The maximum point is $(-3, 31)$, while the minimum point is $(1, -1)$.

● **Example 3.** Find all points at which $y = (x - 2)^3 + 5$ has horizontal tangent lines and sketch the locus.

$$y' = 3(x - 2)^2.$$

Horizontal tangent lines occur at points where $y' = 0$. This implies

$$3(x - 2)^2 = 0,$$
$$x = 2.$$

Hence, the only horizontal tangent line occurs at $(2, 5)$. Consider the slope $y' = 3(x - 2)^2$ for $x < 2$ and $x > 2$.

If $x < 2$, then $x - 2 < 0$ and $y' = + (-)^2 = +.$
If $x > 2$, then $x - 2 > 0$ and $y' = + (+)^2 = +.$

Tangent lines have positive slope except at $(2, 5)$. The point $(2, 5)$ is neither a maximum nor a minimum point of the curve. The y intercept is $(0, -3)$ (Fig. 6-10). The locus is sketched in Figure 6-11.

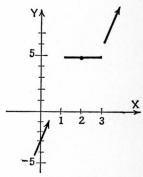

Fig. 6-10

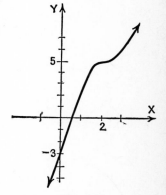

Fig. 6-11

PROBLEM SET 6-9

Determine all points at which the loci of the following equations have horizontal tangent lines and determine whether each point is a maximum, a minimum, or neither. Sketch the locus. Do *not* plot more than a few points.

1. $y = 3x^2 - 6x + 5.$ **2.** $y = x^4 - 8x + 3.$ **3.** $y = (x + 3)^3.$

4. $y = x^5 - 20x^2 + 1.$ **5.** $y = \dfrac{1}{(5x - 2)^2}.$

6. $y = (x - 3)^2(x^2 + 6x + 5).$ **7.** $y = x^4 - 32x + 6.$

8. $y = \dfrac{1}{3x - 6} + 4.$ **9.** $y = 2 - 7x + 4x^2.$

10. $h = 4t^2 - 7t + 2.$ **11.** $h = 400 + 120t - t^2.$

12. $h = x^2 - 5x + 6.$ **13.** $3y = 6x^2 + 5x - 9.$

14. $6y = x^4 - 12x^2 + 12.$ **15.** $2y = x^3 - 6x^2 + 12x.$

16. $x^4y = 2.$ **17.** $y = x^4 - 4x^3 + 8.$ **18.** $x^2(y - 1) = 11.$

19. $y(x - 2)^2 = 3.$ **20.** $8xy^3 = 1.$ **21.** $y = (3x - 3)^2(x + 2)^4.$

22. $y = (x - 3)^2(x + 2)^4 + 6.$ **23.** $h = 400 + 160t - 16t^2.$

24. $h = 64t - 16t^2.$ **25.** $t^3y = 7.$

*26. $9(x - 2)^2 + 16(y + 1)^2 = 144.$ ***27.** $y^2 = x^2(x + 3).$

6–10. Self test.

Record time.

1. Use the Δ process to find $\dfrac{df(x)}{dx}$: $f(x) = \dfrac{3}{x - 2}.$

2. Find the point on $y = x^3 + 3x^2 + 4$ at which the tangent line has slope -3. Write the equation of this tangent line.

3. (a) Find the maximum and minimum points on

$$y = 2x^3 + 6x^2 - 18x + 24.$$

   (b) For what values of x does y increase as x increases?

   (c) For what values of x does y decrease as x increases?

4. Find the derivative of: $y = (2x^3 - 4x + 1)^7.$

5. Find the derivative of: $y = \sqrt{3x^2 - 6x + 9}.$

6. Find the derivative of: $y = \dfrac{1}{(2x - 3)^5}.$

7. Find the derivative of: $y = (3x^2 + 7)^2(x + 4)^3.$

8. The sum of two numbers is 1000. Find the numbers if their product is a maximum.

9. An open box is to be made by cutting 1-in. squares from the corners of a rectangular sheet of metal and bending up the sides. If the perimeter of the base of the box must be 40 in., what is the maximum possible volume of the box?

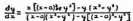

M. G. Gyllström. Courtesy *Scripta Mathematica*.

7

••••••••••••••••••••

In this chapter, the reader will see a few applications of the theory developed in the last chapter.

7–1. Applications involving maxima and minima.

● *Example 1.* A stone is thrown vertically upward from the top of a tower 400 ft high. The height, h ft, of the stone from the ground at any time t sec after it is thrown, until it strikes the ground, is $h = 400 + 120t - 16t^2$. What is the maximum height reached by the stone?

If h is graphed as a function of t, a horizontal tangent line will occur when $h' = 0$, that is, when

$$h' = 120 - 32t = 0,$$
$$t = \tfrac{15}{4} \text{ sec.}$$

The slope of the tangent line changes from $+$ to 0 to $-$ as t increases through $\tfrac{15}{4}$. Hence, $t = \tfrac{15}{4}$ corresponds to a maximum value of h. The maximum value is

$$h = 400 + 120(\tfrac{15}{4}) - 16(\tfrac{15}{4})^2 = 625 \text{ ft.}$$

This is a refinement of the technique used in Chapter 4. It often saves time and gives more precise results.

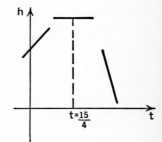

Fig. 7–1

● *Example 2.* A sluice of rectangular cross section is made from a long strip of tin 40 in. wide, by turning up the sides at right angles to the base. What width strips should be turned up to form a sluice of greatest carrying capacity?

The problem is equivalent to finding the trough of greatest cross-sectional area.

$$A(x) = x(40 - 2x)$$
$$= 40x - 2x^2.$$

Fig. 7–2

If A is graphed as a function of x, a horizontal tangent line will occur where $A' = 0$.

$$A' = 40 - 4x = 0$$
$$x = 10 \text{ inches.}$$

We show that $A(x)$ is a maximum at $x = 10$ by noting that, as x increases through 10, the slope of the tangent line changes

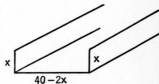

Fig. 7–3

from $+$ to 0 to $-$. $A(10) = 10(40 - 20) = 200$ is a maximum value for A. The point $(10, 200)$ is a maximum point. If a 10-in. strip is turned up on each edge, the resulting sluice will have the greatest carrying capacity.

● **Example 3.** A farm has a straight fence along one side. The owner wishes to enclose a rectangular plot of ground, using the existing fence as one side of the plot and then to divide the plot into two pens with a fence perpendicular to the existing fence. Find the largest total area he may enclose with 300 yd of additional fencing.

Fig. 7-3

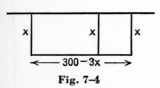

$$A = (300 - 3x)x$$
$$= 300x - 3x^2.$$
$$\frac{dA}{dx} = 300 - 6x$$
$$= 6(50 - x).$$
$$6(50 - x) = 0,$$
$$x = 50 \text{ yards.}$$

Fig. 7-4

Hence, the graph of $A = 300x - 3x^2$ has a horizontal tangent line at $x = 50$.

If $x < 50$, then $50 - x > 0$ and $\dfrac{dA}{dx} = +$.

If $x > 50$, then $50 - x < 0$ and $\dfrac{dA}{dx} = -$.

The slope changes from $+$ to 0 to $-$, indicating a maximum area.

The dimensions for the maximum area are:

$$x = 50 \text{ yd}, \quad 300 - 3x = 150 \text{ yd.}$$

The maximum area is 7500 sq yd.

PROBLEM SET 7-1

1. Determine each point at which the curve

$$y = x^3 - 8x^2 + 30x - 7$$

has slope 25.

2. Find an equation of a line which is tangent to the curve $3x^2 + 4y^2 - xy - 18 = 0$ at the point $(2, -1)$.

3. A closed rectangular box with base twice as long as it is wide is to be built to contain 72 cu ft. Determine its dimensions if the material used in the box is to be a minimum and no allowance is made for the thickness of material along the edges.

4. Find k so that $y = 4x^2 + kx + 9$ will be tangent to the x-axis.

In Problems 5 to 10 solve the given problem again, using more advanced methods learned since then.

5. Example 2, Section 4–9.   **6.** Problem 18, Set 4–9.
7. Problem 19, Set 4–9.   **8.** Problem 20, Set 4–9.
9. Problem 21, Set 4–9.   **10.** Problem 25, Set 4–9.

11. A cylindrical can is to be constructed to contain 125 cu in. Determine the dimensions of a can requiring the least total sheet metal to construct if the circular top and bottom are cut from square pieces *with the scraps wasted* and the side is cut from large sheets without waste.

12. A voltaic cell has constant emf and constant internal resistance r. The work done by this cell in sending a steady current through an external circuit of resistance x is given by

$$W = \frac{kx}{(x+r)^2} = kx(x+r)^{-2},$$

where k and r are constants. For what value of x is W a maximum?

13. John Smith has the monopoly of the sale of student pins which cost him $3 each. If the number sold varies inversely as the cube of the selling price, find what selling price will yield the greatest total profit to John.

14. The yearbook committee in a certain school estimates that 600 people will buy yearbooks if the price is $5 each. Their experience suggests that for each 5¢ the price is raised, two of the 600 people will decide not to purchase a yearbook. (a) What price will bring in the greatest total income? (b) If the yearbooks cost $3.50 each to produce, what price will bring in the greatest profit? (c) Compare the answers to parts (a) and (b) of this problem and make graphs to explain these facts to the editorial staff who may understand little mathematics.

15. A telephone answering service for doctors charges each doctor using the service a fee of $3.00 per month. They have 500 subscribers. The owners estimate that for each cent they raise the cost, one doctor will discontinue the service; that is, if the fee were raised to $3.25 per month, 25 of the 500 doctors would stop using the service; if they raised the fee to $3.30 per month, 30 doctors would drop; etc. On the basis of this assumption, what service fee will bring in the greatest monthly income?

16. A boat company agrees to transport a group of students on an outing for a charge of $6 per student if 75 or fewer students go on the outing. The boat company further agrees that for each student more than the basic 75, they will reduce the charge 5¢ per student *for all students*. What number of students will bring in the largest income to the boat company? How much will each student pay in this case?

17. Jack Trot has a 120-apartment building. His experience leads him to believe that he can rent all 120 apartments at $40 per month for each apartment. He estimates that for each dollar he raises the rent, there will be two empty apartments. That is, if he charges $41, he will be able to rent only 118 of the apartments; if he charges $42 per month, he will rent only 116 apartments; etc. What rental will bring him the greatest income?

18. Given $y = x^3 - 3x^2 - 9x + 5$. Find maximum and minimum points, and sketch.

19. Calvin Butterball wishes to enclose a rectangular area and divide it into three pens. Calvin decides to use an existing fence for one side of the rectangle and erect the cross fences perpendicular to the existing fence as shown in Figure 7–5. Find the largest total area Cal may enclose with 200 ft of additional fence.

Fig. 7–5

20. A box with a square base and open top is to be constructed to hold 4 cu ft. Determine the dimensions of such a box having the least surface area.

21. Silas Hogwinder wishes to enclose a rectangular plot of ground and divide it into four pens by erecting three fences parallel to one side of the rectangle. If Silas has a total of 300 ft of fencing, what is the largest area he can enclose?

22. If 200,000 prints are required from a press having a speed of 1200 prints per hour and costing $2 per hour to run, and if extra electrotypes cost 55¢ each, find the number of extra electrotypes, x, that should be used to secure the minimum cost, C.

$$\left[\text{HINT:} \quad C \text{ (in cents)} = \frac{200,000 \times 200}{1200(1 + x)} + 55x. \right]$$

The complete solution and a generalization of this problem appear on page 415 of Vol. 27 of the *American Mathematical Monthly*, which the reader may consult at his school library.

7–2. Average rate of change. Consider a particle P, moving in a straight line, whose distance from a fixed point O (origin) is $s = s(t)$, where $s(t)$ is some function of time t. The distance of P from O at time t_1 is $s(t_1)$ and at time $t_1 + \Delta t$ the distance is $s(t_1 + \Delta t)$. The **average velocity or average rate of change of s with respect to time** t over the interval, from $t = t_1$ to $t = t_1 + \Delta t$, is given by

$$\text{average velocity} = \frac{\Delta s(t_1, \Delta t)}{\Delta t} = \frac{s(t_1 + \Delta t) - s(t_1)}{\Delta t}.$$

● *Example 1.* A man travels south from Chicago. At 2 P.M. he is 135 miles from Chicago, while at 3:30 P.M. he is 210 miles from Chicago. Determine his average rate of change of distance with respect to time, or average velocity, during this period. Here

$$t_1 = 2, \quad t_1 + \Delta t = 3.5.$$

Hence,

$$\Delta t = 1.5,$$
$$s(t_1) = s(2) = 135$$
$$s(t_1 + \Delta t) = s(3.5) = 210.$$

$$\text{Average velocity} = \frac{s(t_1 + \Delta t) - s(t_1)}{\Delta t} = \frac{210 - 135}{1.5} = \frac{75}{1.5} = 50 \text{ mph.}$$

● *Example 2.* A ball is thrown downward from the top of a tower. One second after it is thrown, the ball is 224 ft from the ground. Three seconds after it is thrown, the ball is 76 ft from the ground. Determine the average velocity of the ball during this period.

$$t_1 = 1, \quad t_1 + \Delta t = 3, \quad \Delta t = 2,$$
$$s(t_1) = s(1) = 224 \quad \text{and} \quad s(t_1 + \Delta t) = s(3) = 76.$$

Hence,

$$\text{average velocity} = \frac{s(t_1 + \Delta t) - s(t_1)}{\Delta t} = \frac{s(3) - s(1)}{2}$$
$$= \frac{76 - 224}{2} = \frac{-148}{2} = -74 \text{ ft per sec.}$$

The reader is cautioned that this does *not* mean that the ball was falling at 74 ft per sec during the entire 2 sec. It means that *if* the ball had fallen at 74 ft per sec during the period from $t = 1$ to $t = 3$, it would have covered the same distance.

PROBLEM SET 7–2

1. Find the *average velocity* of a ball which falls 64 ft in 2 sec.
2. If the ball of Problem 1 falls 144 ft in 3 sec, find its average velocity.
3. Find the average velocity during the third second of the ball of Problems 1 and 2. Does the average velocity during the first 3 sec equal the average of the velocity during the third second and the first 2 sec?
4. If $s(t) = 8 + 10t - t^2$, find the average velocity from $t = 2$ to $t = 5$.
5. If $s(t) = 10t^2 + 4t$, find the distance $\Delta s(2, 5)$ between $t = 2$ and $t = 7$. Also, find the average velocity in this interval.
6. If $s(t) = 6t^2 + 2$, find the average velocity in the interval (a) $0 \leq t \leq 1$, (b) $10 \leq t \leq 11$.
7. If a motorist makes a trip at an average speed of 30 mph and returns over the same route at an average speed of 60 mph, what is his average speed for the entire trip? The answer is *not* 45 mph.
8. What average speed would the motorist of Problem 7 need to have on the return trip to average (a) 50 mph on the entire trip? (b) 60 mph on the entire trip?

7–3. Instantaneous velocity. In Example 1, Section 7–2, we obtained 50 mph as the *average* rate of change of distance or average velocity. This does not mean that the man was going 50 mph as he passed through the town of McLean. He may have been traveling much faster, or he may have been traveling 15 mph, or he may have stopped for dinner and hence part of the time had a speed of 0 mph. He may have traveled at each of these speeds while passing through McLean.

The last sentence uses a concept which differs from the average rate of change of distance with respect to time (average velocity) — namely, the **instantaneous** rate of change of distance with respect to time (velocity or speedometer reading). This **instantaneous rate of change** † or **instantaneous velocity,** $v(t_1)$, is defined as the limit of the **average** velocity as the intervals about t_1 approach zero. That is,

$$\text{velocity at time } t_1 = v(t_1) = \lim_{\Delta t \to 0} \frac{s(t_1 + \Delta t) - s(t_1)}{\Delta t}.$$

† One of the famous paradoxes of Zeno concerns an arrow in flight which supposedly can never move since at each instant it must be somewhere and if it is somewhere, it is not in motion. A discussion of this and other paradoxes will be found in *Mathematics and the Imagination* by Kasner and Newman, pages 37 ff.

The velocity at time $t = t_1$ may be thought of as obtained by taking the limit of smaller and smaller intervals of time Δt surrounding $t = t_1$ such that the distance $\Delta s(t, \Delta t)$ becomes smaller and smaller in size. The reader will note, however, that the right-hand member of this equation is exactly the definition of

$$\frac{d[s(t)]}{dt} \quad \text{evaluated at} \quad t = t_1.$$

Hence,

velocity at time t_1 is $\quad v(t_1) = \dfrac{d[s(t)]}{dt} \quad$ evaluated at $\quad t = t_1$.

If a point moves on an axis so that its directed distance from the origin at time t is given by $\quad s(t) = t^4 - 2t^2 + 1, \quad$ then

$$\frac{ds}{dt} = s'(t) = 4t^3 - 4t$$

is the instantaneous rate of change of the distance with respect to time. We use the word velocity for this concept. In general,

velocity at time t is $\quad v(t) = s'(t)$.

The sign of $v(t)$ determines whether $s(t)$ is increasing $(v(t) > 0)$ or decreasing $(v(t) < 0)$ as t increases. The term **speed** is used when this distinction is not made — that is, speed = | velocity |.

The velocity $v(t)$ is itself a function of t and we may compute the instantaneous rate of change $v'(t)$ of $v(t)$. The rate of change of velocity is the **acceleration.**

$$\text{Acceleration} = a(t) = \frac{d[v(t)]}{dt} = v'(t).$$

In our example $s(t) = t^4 - 2t^2 + 1,\quad v(t) = s'(t) = 4t^3 - 4t,\quad$ and $a(t) = v'(t) = 12t^2 - 4\quad$ at time t. The symbol $s''(t)$ may be used for $a(t)$ since $a(t)$ is the derivative of [the derivative of $s(t)$].

In general it is possible to determine the rate of change of $a(t)$. No special name is given to the expression $a'(t)$.

● *Example 1.* A particle moves along the s-axis. The directed distance of the particle from the origin is given by

$$s(t) = t^4 - 4t^3 + 8t - 3.$$

Determine the position, velocity, and acceleration of the particle when $t = 2$.

Since

$s(t) = t^4 - 4t^3 + 8t - 3,$
$v(t) = s'(t) = 4t^3 - 12t^2 + 8$
[$v(t)$ is *not* equal to $t^3 - 3t^2 + 2$. Why?]

and
$$a(t) = v'(t) = 12t^2 - 24t. \quad \text{(Why not} \quad t^2 - 2t \quad \text{?)}$$

At $t = 2$ we have

$s(2) = 16 - 32 + 16 - 3 = -3$ units of s from the origin.
$v(2) = 32 - 48 + 8 = -8$ units of s per t unit.
$a(2) = 48 - 48 = 0$ (units of s per t unit) per t unit.

Special attention should be given to the units in this problem and in all other supplied problems.

● **Example 2.** Determine all positions of the particle of Example 1 when the velocity is 8 units of s per t unit.
  Since
$$v(t) = 4t^3 - 12t^2 + 8,$$
we set
$$v(t) = 4t^3 - 12t^2 + 8 = 8$$
or
$$4t^3 - 12t^2 = 0$$
$$4t^2(t - 3) = 0.$$
$$t = 0, \quad t = 0, \quad t = 3.$$

At these times $v(t) = 8$. The desired positions are given by $s(0) = -3$ and $s(3) = -6$.

● **Example 3.** A stone is thrown upward into the air from the top of a tower 400 ft high [see Example 1, Section 4–9]. The height h, in feet, of the stone from the ground t sec after it is thrown is $h(t) = 400 + 120t - 16t^2$.
  (a) Determine the velocity of the stone 2 sec after it is thrown.
  (b) Determine the velocity of the stone when it strikes the ground.
  (a) Since $v(t) = h'(t) = 120 - 32t,$
$$v(2) = 120 - 32(2) = 56 \text{ ft per sec.}$$
  (b) The stone strikes the ground when $h(t) = 0$. In Section 4–9 it was shown that $t = 10$ is the desired solution of the equation $h(t) = 400 + 120t - 16t^2 = 0$. The problem requests the velocity at $t = 10$, namely,
$$v(10) = 120 - 32(10) = -200 \text{ ft per sec.}$$

The negative velocity indicates the distance from the ground $h(t)$ is decreasing, that is, the stone is going downward.

PROBLEM SET 7-3

In Problems 1 to 5 determine the position, velocity, and acceleration (at the indicated time) of a particle which moves along the s-axis and whose directed distance from the origin is given by $s(t)$. Describe the motion of the particle for $-100 \leq t \leq 100$.

1. $s(t) = t^2 - 3t + 5$ at $t = 1$, $t = 7$, and $t = 11$.
2. $s(t) = t^4 + 4t - 9$ at $t = 1$, $t = 0$, and $t = -3$.
3. $s(t) = 64t - 16t^2$ at $t = 0$, $t = 5$, and $t = 10$.
4. $s(t) = 17t$ at $t = 0$, $t = 5$, and $t = 7$.
5. $s(t) = 11$ at $t = 0$, $t = 5$, and $t = 15$.

In Problems 6 to 10 determine the times at which the particle has the given velocity or acceleration and determine the distances of the particle from the origin at these times.

6. $s(t) = 10t^3 + 7t^2 + 3$, where $a(t) = 2$.
7. $s(t) = 12t^3 - 3t + 5$, where $v(t) = 6$.
8. $s(t) = t^4$, where $v(t) = 32$.
9. $s(t) = 3t^3 - 7t + 2$, where $a(t) = 36$.
10. $s(t) = 17 + t - t^2$, where $v(t) = 9$.
11. A hockey puck is struck at time $t = 0$. The distance in feet of the puck from the spot at which it was struck is $s(t) = 72t - 3t^2$, where t is in seconds. How far did the puck travel before coming to rest? In what t interval does the function have meaning in this problem?
12. A stone is thrown upward from the top of a tower 100 ft above ground with an initial velocity of 64 ft per sec. The height h in feet of the stone above the ground t sec after throwing is given by $h(t) = -16t^2 + 64t + 100$. Determine the velocity of the stone as it passes a window ledge 20 ft above ground level.
13. From a point 1200 ft above the earth's surface a stone is thrown upward with a speed of 160 ft per sec. The height of the stone at any time t after the stone is thrown is given by $h(t) = -16t^2 + 160t + 1200$. Find the impact velocity.
14. A block of ice slides down a chute 100 ft long with an acceleration of 16 ft per sec per sec. The distance of the block from the bottom of the chute is given by $s(t) = -8t^2 - 20t + 100$. Find the velocity of the block at the bottom of the chute [when $s(t) = 0$].
15. How fast is the block of Problem 14 sliding when it has slid 4 ft [that is, when $s(t) = 96$]?
16. A ball rolls on an inclined plane so that its distance s ft from the bottom of the plane at time t sec is $s(t) = 6t - 2t^2$. How far up the inclined plane will the ball roll?

17. At what time and with what speed does the ball of Problem 16 reach the bottom of the inclined plane?

18. What is the speed of the ball of Problem 16 when it is 1 ft above the bottom of the plane?

19. John Smith is coasting down a long hill on his bike. His distance (in feet) from the top of the hill at any time t in seconds is given by $s(t) = 5t^2 + 7t$. After John has coasted 160 ft from the top of the hill he strikes a large stone and falls from his bike. Determine his velocity at the moment he strikes the stone. Express this velocity in miles per hour. Do you think it likely that John was hurt in the fall?

20. If John had fallen when he had coasted only half as far as in Problem 19, with what velocity would he have fallen?

21. A projectile is shot vertically upward from ground level. It reaches a height of 144 ft in 1 sec. How high will the projectile rise? Use $h = -16t^2 + v_0t$.

7–4. General rate of change. The remarks of Section 7–3 on rate of change are not limited to time rate of change of distance. Other rates of change are handled in a similar manner.

For example, if a spherical balloon is being inflated, then its radius and its surface area are changing. If the rate at which the volume is changing is known, then the rate of change of radius and of surface area can be computed. To accomplish this we note that if $y = f(x)$ and $x = g(t)$, then y may be considered as a function of t, since for any value of t from the domain of definition of the function g, a corresponding value of y, namely, $f[g(t)]$ is determined providing the domain of f is a subset of the range of g.†

If $y = f(x)$ and $x = g(t)$, then y may be considered to be a function of t, and $\dfrac{dy}{dt}$ may be a meaningful concept.

Theorem. If $y = f(x)$ and $x = g(t)$, then if both $\dfrac{dy}{dx}$ and $\dfrac{dx}{dt}$ exist,

$$\frac{dy}{dt} = \frac{dy}{dx} \cdot \frac{dx}{dt}.$$

If $\Delta x \neq 0$ when $\Delta t \neq 0$, then $\dfrac{\Delta y}{\Delta t} = \dfrac{\Delta y}{\Delta x} \cdot \dfrac{\Delta x}{\Delta t}$ if $\Delta t \neq 0$.

Since $\dfrac{dx}{dt}$ exists, $\Delta x \to 0$ when $\Delta t \to 0$. (See Problem 24, Set 6–2.)

† If this last sentence sounds like gibberish, reread Section 1–8, before continuing.

Thus, since $\lim\limits_{\Delta t \to 0}$ implies $\Delta t \neq 0$, we have

$$\lim_{\Delta t \to 0} \frac{\Delta y}{\Delta t} = \lim_{\Delta t \to 0} \frac{\Delta y}{\Delta x} \cdot \lim_{\Delta t \to 0} \frac{\Delta x}{\Delta t}$$

$$\lim_{\Delta t \to 0} \frac{\Delta y}{\Delta t} = \lim_{\Delta x \to 0} \frac{\Delta y}{\Delta x} \cdot \lim_{\Delta t \to 0} \frac{\Delta x}{\Delta t}$$

$$\frac{dy}{dt} = \frac{dy}{dx} \cdot \frac{dx}{dt}.$$

If the assumption $\Delta x \neq 0$ when $\Delta t \neq 0$ is not fulfilled, the theorem still holds, but a separate proof is required. The proof for this special case will be found in many calculus texts.

In Example 1 we shall use this theorem in the form $\dfrac{dV}{dt} = \dfrac{dV}{dr} \cdot \dfrac{dr}{dt}$ to determine $\dfrac{dr}{dt}$ where $V = \frac{4}{3}\pi r^3$, the volume of a sphere, and $\dfrac{dV}{dt}$ is a given constant.

• **Example 1.** Hydrogen is being forced into a spherical balloon at the constant rate of 1000 cu in. per min. How fast is the radius of the balloon increasing when the balloon is 2.0 ft in radius?

The volume, V, of a sphere is $V = \frac{4}{3}\pi r^3$. We are given $\dfrac{dV}{dt} = 1000$ cu in. per min, and are asked to find $\dfrac{dr}{dt}$ when $r = 2.0$ ft $= 24$ in. Then, since $r = r(t)$,

$$\frac{dV}{dt} = \frac{dV}{dr} \cdot \frac{dr}{dt} = \frac{d\left[\frac{4}{3}\pi r^3\right]}{dr} \cdot \frac{dr}{dt} = 4\pi r^2 \frac{dr}{dt}.$$

Substituting the known values into this equation we have

$$1000 = 4\pi(24)^2 \frac{dr}{dt}$$

$$\frac{dr}{dt} = \frac{1000}{4\pi(24)^2} \cong 0.14 \text{ in. per min.}†$$

If liquid is being poured into a rigid container, the depth of the liquid is changing. If the rate at which the liquid is being poured and the shape of the container are known, it seems reasonable that we may be able to compute the rate of change of depth at any given depth. In general, the rate of change of depth will not be constant, but will be a function of depth, as the following example illustrates.

† The symbol $\cong$ indicates approximate equality.

● **Example 2.** The horizontal V-shaped trough illustrated is 4.0 ft long with vertical ends and has a 90-degree angle between its sides. Water is poured into the trough at the rate of 500 cu in. per min. At what rate is the depth of the water increasing when the water is 5.0 in. deep?

Let V = the volume of water in the trough and $h = h(t)$ the depth of the water in inches. The *width* of the water surface is $2h$ when the depth is h (Why?). The cross-sectional area is h^2 sq in. and

$$V = 4(12)h^2 = 48h^2 \text{ cu in.}$$

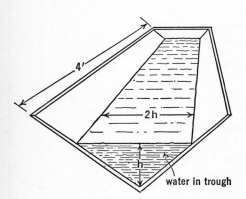

Fig. 7-6

The problem states that $\dfrac{dV}{dt} = 500$ cu in. per min and requests $\dfrac{dh}{dt}$ when $h = 5$ in.

$$\frac{dV}{dt} = \frac{dV}{dh} \cdot \frac{dh}{dt} = \frac{d[48h^2]}{dh} \cdot \frac{dh}{dt} = 96h \cdot \frac{dh}{dt}.$$

Substituting the known values we obtain

$$500 = 96(5)\frac{dh}{dt}$$

and

$$\frac{dh}{dt} = \frac{500}{96(5)} \cong 1.0 \text{ in. per min.}$$

7–5. Extreme values. If the value of $f(x)$ increases as x increases from a to b, then $f(x)$ is an **increasing function** of x. More precisely, $f(x)$ is an **increasing function** in the interval $a \le x \le b$ if

$$f(x_1) < f(x_2) \quad \text{for all} \quad x_1, x_2 \quad \text{such that} \quad a \le x_1 < x_2 \le b.$$

Similarly, $f(x)$ is a **decreasing function** in the interval

$$a \le x \le b \quad \text{if} \quad f(x_1) > f(x_2)$$

for all x_1, x_2 such that $a \le x_1 < x_2 \le b$.

The ratio

$$\frac{\Delta f(x_1, \Delta x)}{\Delta x} = \frac{f(x_1 + \Delta x) - f(x_1)}{\Delta x}$$

is the average rate of change of $f(x)$ with respect to x in the interval x_1 to $x_1 + \Delta x$.

If $f(x)$ is an increasing function, the average rate of change of $f(x)$ will be positive. If $f(x)$ is a decreasing function, the average rate of change of $f(x)$ will be negative. In the first case $\Delta f(x_1, \Delta x)$ and Δx are either both positive or both negative, while in the second case they are opposite in sign.

The **derivative of** $f(x)$ **with respect to** x **at** $x = x_1$ is defined as

$$\lim_{\Delta x \to 0} \frac{\Delta f(x_1, \Delta x)}{\Delta x} = \lim_{\Delta x \to 0} \frac{f(x_1 + \Delta x) - f(x_1)}{\Delta x}.$$

The derivative of $f(x)$ with respect to x at $x = x_1$ is represented symbolically by $f'(x_1)$, or $\dfrac{df(x)}{dx}\Big]_{x=x_1}$. The derivative $f'(x_1)$ is the rate of change of $f(x)$ with respect to x at $x = x_1$.

Geometrically, the derivative $f'(x_1)$ represents the slope of the tangent line to $y = f(x)$ at the point $(x_1, f(x_1))$. (See Sections 5–7 and 6–1.)

Since $f'(x_1) = \lim\limits_{\Delta x \to 0} \dfrac{\Delta f(x_1, \Delta x)}{\Delta x}$, it follows that:

(1) if $f(x)$ is an increasing function in an interval including x_1, then $f'(x_1) \geqq 0$;

(2) if $f(x)$ is a decreasing function in an interval including x_1, then $f'(x_1) \leqq 0$.

● **Example 1.** Discuss $f(x) = x^3 - 3x + 2$.

$$f'(x_1) = 3x_1^2 - 3 = 3(x_1 + 1)(x_1 - 1).$$

x_1	$f'(x_1)$	$f(x)$	Conclusion	
$x_1 < -1$	$(-)(-) = +$	increasing	at $x_1 = -1$	
-1	0	4	rel max	
$-1 < x_1 < 1$	$(+)(-) = -$	decreasing	$f(-1) = 4$	
1	0	0	at $x_1 = 1$ rel min	
$1 < x_1$	$(+)(+) = +$	increasing	$f(1) = 0$	

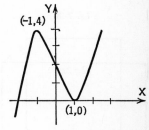

Fig. 7–7

We are now able to state another method of testing for extreme values.

1. Find x_1 such that $f'(x_1) = 0$. Such x_1 values which may † cause $f(x_1)$ to be an extreme are called **critical x values.**

Let x be another value which is closer to x_1 than the nearest critical x value, or nearest discontinuity.

2. If $f'(x) > 0$ when $x < x_1, f'(x_1) = 0$, and $f'(x) < 0$ when $x > x_1$, then $f(x_1)$ is a relative maximum. This means graphically, that $y = f(x)$ is increasing preceding $(x_1, f(x_1))$, neither increasing nor decreasing at $(x_1, f(x_1))$, and decreasing following $(x_1, f(x_1))$.

† The x_1 value may correspond to the abscissa of an inflection point.

3. If $f'(x) < 0$ when $x < x_1, f'(x_1) = 0$, and $f'(x) > 0$ when $x > x_1$, then $f(x_1)$ is a relative minimum. Graphically, $y = f(x)$ is decreasing preceding $(x_1, f(x_1))$, neither increasing nor decreasing at $(x_1, f(x_1))$, and increasing following $(x_1, f(x_1))$.

4. If the sign of $f'(x)$ is the same for $x < x_1$ as for $x > x_1$, then $f(x_1)$ is neither a maximum nor a minimum. Graphically, the curve $y = f(x)$ either continues to increase or continues to decrease after it passes through $(x_1, f(x_1))$. In this case, if $f'(x_1) = 0$, the point $(x_1, f(x_1))$ is called an **inflection point.**

● *Example 2.* Test for extreme values: $y(x) = x^3$.

As before, $y'(x_1) = 3x_1^2$ and $y'(x_1) = 0$, when $x_1 = 0$. Application of the above test shows $(0, 0)$ to be an inflection point.

The reader should note that although $f(x) = x^3$ is an everywhere increasing function, that $f'(0) = 0$. This example demonstrates why it was necessary to specify that if $f(x)$ is an increasing function $f'(x) \geqq 0$, rather than being able to say that if $f(x)$ is increasing, then $f'(x) > 0$, as one might expect.

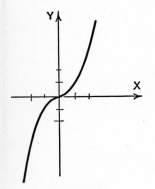

Fig. 7–8

● *Example 3.* A square sheet of metal 12 in. on a side has square pieces cut out of the corners and the edges turned up to form a box with open top. Determine the box of largest volume which may be formed.

$$V(x) = x(12 - 2x)^2$$
$$= 144x - 48x^2 + 4x^3,$$

where the dimensions of the squares to be removed are x in. by x in.

$V'(x) = 144 - 96x + 12x^2 = 12(12 - 8x + x^2) = 12(x - 2)(x - 6.)$ The critical † values are $x = 2$ and $x = 6$. Due to the physical limitations in this problem, the domain of x values is $0 \leqq x \leqq 6$. On this domain, $x = 2$ yields an absolute maximum, $V = 128$.

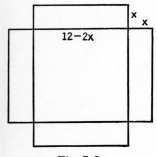

Fig. 7–9

PROBLEM SET 7–5

1. Gas is being forced into a spherical balloon at the rate of 400 cu in. per min. How fast is the radius of the balloon increasing when the radius is 5 in.?

2. Same as Problem 1 for 10-in. radius.

† Why not **necessarily** maximum or minimum values?

3. Gas is forced into a spherical balloon at the rate of 600 cu in. per min. How fast is the radius of the balloon increasing when it encloses 288π cu in. of gas?

4. At what rate is the surface area of the balloon of Problem 1 changing when $r = 5$ in.?

5. At what rate is the surface area of the balloon of Problem 3 changing at the instant in question?

6. Determine the rate at which the depth of the water is changing in the trough of Example 2, Section 7–4, when the water is 1 in. deep.

7. Determine the rate at which the depth of the water is changing in the trough of Example 2, Section 7–4, when the water is 10 in. deep.

Discuss and sketch the functions given in Problems 8 to 15. List all maximum and minimum points and the approximate intercepts.

8. $y = 2x^3 - 7x + 5$.   9. $y = 3x^2 - 4x + \dfrac{2}{x}$.   10. $y = x + \dfrac{1}{x}$.

11. $y = x^3 - 12x$.   12. $y = 4x^3 - 108$.   13. $y = 12 - x^3$.

14. $y = 5 + 3x - 10x^3$.   15. $y = -7 - 2x + x^2$.

16. A steamer is rented for an excursion for 100 passengers at $10 per passenger. The absolute minimum rental is $1000. The owners agree to reduce the fare of every passenger 5¢ per passenger for each person beyond the basic 100.

(a) How much is the maximum rental the owners may expect on the excursion?

(b) Find the number of passengers needed to obtain this maximal rental.

(c) Assuming the fire laws will not permit the steamer to carry more than 180 passengers, what will be the smallest gross income the owners may receive for a legal load?

(d) Sketch a graph of income, I, versus number of passengers, x. Notice that for $0 < x \leq 100$, I is constant.

17. An exporter can ship a cargo of 100 tons today at a profit of $5 a ton. By waiting, he can add 20 tons per week to the shipment, but the profit on all that he exports will be reduced 25¢ per ton per week. How long will it be profitable to wait?

18. The owner of a 200-apartment building can keep all 200 apartments filled at a rental of $40 per month per apartment. His experience suggests that if he raises the monthly rent $5 per apartment, one apartment will remain vacant, if he raises it $10 per month 4 apartments will remain vacant, $15 per month 9 empty apartments, etc. — that is, if he raises the rent $5x$ dollars, x^2 apartments will remain empty.

(a) What monthly rental will bring in the greatest income?

(b) What percent of the apartments will be rented at this maximum income?

(c) Over what domain of values of x does the function have meaning?

(d) Make graphs to explain your conclusions to nonmathematical friends.

19. Solve Problem 18 assuming that each empty apartment saves the owner $2 per month on janitorial expenses.

20. The amount of candy and pop an individual huckster can sell at a football game decreases as the number of hucksters increases. If 100 hucksters can average $80 each in sales at a big game, and if for each additional huckster added, the average per huckster drops 10¢, find the number of hucksters for a maximum total income for the concession owner. How much does each huckster sell at this maximum? How much larger is the maximum total income than if 100 hucksters were employed?

21. John Smith is in the hospital recovering from a bike accident. A doctor is inflating a spherical balloon to please John. If hydrogen is supplied at 100 cu in. per min, how long will it take to inflate the balloon to a radius of 10 in.? How fast is the radius increasing when the balloon is 5 in. in radius? 10 in. in radius? Just before it bursts at 12.3 in. in radius?

22. Show that $y = x^3 - 6x^2 - 15x + 8$ is neither rising nor falling at the points where $x = -1$ and $x = 5$.

23. Consider the curve of Problem 22. Tell whether the curve is rising or falling as x increases on each of the intervals (a) $x < -1$, (b) $-1 < x < 5$, (c) $5 < x$.

24. Determine the critical points and the intervals in which $y = (x + 6)(x - 1)^3$ is increasing as x increases.

25. The weight W of hot gas passing up a chimney in a given time is given by

$$W = \frac{k\sqrt{0.96T - T_0}}{T}$$

where T denotes the (variable) temperature of the gas and T_0 is the constant temperature of the outside air and k is a constant. What value of T will force a maximum weight of gas through the chimney in a given time interval?

26. An electron moves on the path $y = x^2 - \frac{9}{2}$. Determine the closest the electron comes to the origin.

27. An electron travels along the path represented by $x^2 = y$. How close does the electron come to an accelerator placed at (3, 0)?

28. A square sheet of brass, 20 in. on a side, has square pieces cut from the corners and the edges turned up to form a box with open top. Determine the dimensions of the box of largest volume which may be formed in this fashion.

29. A tin container is to be constructed in the form of a right circular cylinder containing a 27-cu-in. volume. If the top and bottom of the can are cut from square sheets and the corner pieces are wasted, find the dimensions of the container requiring the least tin.

30. Bill McFurson wishes to fence in a rectangle of ground in his pasture and then divide the rectangle into three (not necessarily equal) pens, by erecting two fences parallel to the ends of the rectangle. If the three pens enclose a total area of 1800 sq ft, determine the smallest amount of fencing Bill can use to do the job.

31. An engine cylinder has a diameter of 12 in. At what speed is the piston moving when steam is entering the cylinder at the rate of 18 cu ft per sec?

32. Sand is being poured on the ground, forming a conical pile with its altitude equal to $\frac{2}{3}$ of the radius of its base. If the sand is falling at the rate of 12 cu ft per sec, how fast is the altitude increasing at the time when the volume is 54π cu ft?

33. If $V = \frac{4}{3}\pi r^3$, where $r = r(t)$, find $\dfrac{dV}{dt}$ in terms of r and $\dfrac{dr}{dt}$.

34. If $v = s^5 + 17$, where $s = 3t^2 - 5$, find $\dfrac{dv}{dt}$ in terms of s and $\dfrac{ds}{dt}$.

35. If $W = 4H^3S$, where $H = 3S^2 - 5$, find $\dfrac{dW}{dS}$ in terms of H, S, and $\dfrac{dH}{dS}$.

36. Evaluate the derivatives in Problem 34 at $t = 2$.

37. Evaluate the derivatives in Problem 35 at $s = 3$.

38. Solve Problem 34 by substituting $s = 3t^2 - 5$ into $v = s^5 + 17$, obtaining $v = (3t^2 - 5)^5 + 17$ and then differentiating.

7–6. Self test.

Record time.

1. A particle moves in a straight line. Its distance from the origin is given by $x = t^3 - 6t^2 + 9t + 5$. For what time interval is the velocity negative? Explain.

2. The edge of a cube is increasing at the rate of 2 in. per sec. Find the rate of change of the volume when the edge is 10 in.

3. $y = (x - 5)(x - 1)^3$. Find the points where $y' = 0$. Examine these for maxima and minima, supplying reasons for conclusions.

4. $y = x + \dfrac{1}{x}$. Find maxima and minima, and sketch.

5. A piston of an engine has $\frac{1}{4}$ ft radius. How fast does it move if steam enters the cylinder at 80π cu ft per sec?

6. A ladder 20 ft long is leaning with its top against a vertical wall. How fast is the top being lowered at the instant the bottom is 12 ft from the base of the wall, if the bottom is being moved horizontally away from the base at 10 ft per sec?

7. Find the point on $y = x^2$ nearest $(18, 0)$.

8. Find the minimum cost for the material for a box with square base to contain 16 cu ft, if the material for the top and bottom costs $2 per sq ft and that for the sides costs $1 per sq ft.

Record time.

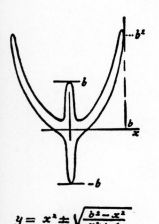

$$y = x^2 \pm \sqrt{\dfrac{b^2 - x^2}{x^2 + 1}}$$

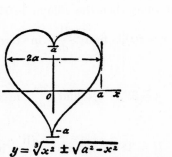

$$y = \sqrt[3]{x^2} \pm \sqrt{a^2 - x^2}$$

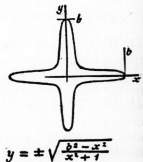

$$y = \pm \sqrt{\dfrac{b^2 - x^2}{x^2 + 1}}$$

Courtesy *El-Milick's Éléments d'Algèbre Ornementale*

Those students already familiar with the theory and use of logarithms may be able to cover this chapter rapidly. They will, however, find the text helpful, since familiarity with exponents and logarithms does not always imply understanding of the reasons behind these notations.

8–1. Negative, fractional, and zero exponents. If n is a *positive integer*, then a^n is defined as 1 multiplied n times by a. $[a^n = 1 \cdot \overbrace{a \cdot a \cdot a \cdots a}^{n\,\text{factors}}]$. Thus $2^5 = 1 \cdot 2 \cdot 2 \cdot 2 \cdot 2 \cdot 2$. Certain "laws of exponents" are derived from this definition in elementary algebra. The more important of these laws are:

   I. $a^m \cdot a^n = a^{m+n}$.

   II. $\dfrac{a^m}{a^n} = \begin{cases} a^{m-n} & \text{if} \quad m > n \\ 1 & \text{if} \quad m = n \\ 1/a^{n-m} & \text{if} \quad m < n. \end{cases}$

   III. $[a^n]^k = a^{nk}$.

   IV. $(a \cdot b)^n = a^n b^n$.

These laws may be proved for m and n positive integers directly from the definitions by counting up the factors, or, more elegantly, by the use of mathematical induction. So far we have not, on this page, defined a^n except for the case where n is a positive integer. Hence, symbols such as 3^{-2}, 5^0, $4^{\frac{1}{2}}$ which involve negative, zero, or fractional exponents have no meaning. It is desirable to define **negative, zero,** and **fractional exponents** so that the above laws hold for such new exponents. The following definitions satisfy these laws.

    $b^0 = 1$ if $b \neq 0$; 0^0 remains undefined.

    $b^{-k} = \dfrac{1}{b^k}$ if $b \neq 0$; $0^{-|k|}$ remains undefined.

$b^{n/d} = \sqrt[d]{b^n}$. If d is even, $b^{n/d}$ is defined only for non-negative b; that is, if d is even, $b \geq 0$.†

A common *misconception* seems to be that it is possible to *prove* that $3^{-2} = \dfrac{1}{3^2}$ or that $5^0 = 1$ or that $4^{\frac{1}{2}} = 2$. This is not the case. These are matters of definition. All that can be shown is that the above definitions are consistent and compatible with the four laws listed earlier in this section.

A few illustrations may be helpful.

† If $b^{n/d}$ were defined for $b < 0$,   then $[b^{1/d}]^n$ might not equal $[b^n]^{1/d}$. For example: $[(-1)^{\frac{1}{2}}]^2 = [i]^2 = -1$,   while $[(-1)^2]^{\frac{1}{2}} = [1]^{\frac{1}{2}} = 1$.

- **Example 1.** $4^{-\frac{1}{2}} = \dfrac{1}{4^{\frac{1}{2}}} = \dfrac{1}{\sqrt{4}} = \dfrac{1}{2} \cdot$ †

- **Example 2.** $(a + b)^{-2} = \dfrac{1}{(a+b)^2},$ for $a + b \neq 0.$

- **Example 3.** $\dfrac{3^{-7}}{3^4} = \dfrac{1}{3^4 \cdot 3^7} = \dfrac{1}{3^{11}},$ which may be written $3^{-11}.$

- **Example 4.** $\dfrac{\sqrt{x}\sqrt[5]{x^2}}{\sqrt[3]{x}}$ with $x > 0.$

  Fractional exponents are helpful in problems of this type.

$$\frac{x^{\frac{1}{2}} \cdot x^{\frac{2}{5}}}{x^{\frac{1}{3}}} = x^{\frac{1}{2}+\frac{2}{5}-\frac{1}{3}} = x^{\frac{15+12-10}{30}} = x^{\frac{17}{30}}, \quad \text{or} \quad \sqrt[30]{x^{17}} \quad \text{if preferred.}$$

- **Example 5.** $(x^{\frac{1}{3}} - 5^{\frac{2}{3}})(x^{\frac{2}{3}} + x^{\frac{1}{3}}5^{\frac{2}{3}} + 5^{\frac{4}{3}}).$

  [HINT: $[A - B][A^2 + AB + B^2] = A^3 - B^3.$]

  Hence, $[x^{\frac{1}{3}} - 5^{\frac{2}{3}}][x^{\frac{2}{3}} + x^{\frac{1}{3}}5^{\frac{2}{3}} + 5^{\frac{4}{3}}] = [x^{\frac{1}{3}}]^3 - [5^{\frac{2}{3}}]^3 = x - 25.$

- **Example 6.** $\dfrac{x^{-1} + y^{-2}}{(x+y)^{-2}}.$ This may be written $\dfrac{\dfrac{1}{x} + \dfrac{1}{y^2}}{\dfrac{1}{(x+y)^2}}$ ‡ and simplified

as in Section 1–4. However, negative exponents were introduced to *simplify* algebraic manipulations. The method of Section 1–4 ignores any possible advantage gained by the introduction of negative exponents. If the numerator and the denominator of the given expression are multiplied by $xy^2(x + y)^2,$ the fraction is unchanged in value. Using the definition of the zero exponent, the simplification is accomplished in two steps.

$$\frac{[x^{-1} + y^{-2}]xy^2(x+y)^2}{[(x+y)^{-2}]xy^2(x+y)^2} = \frac{y^2(x+y)^2 + x(x+y)^2}{xy^2} = \frac{(y^2+x)(x+y)^2}{xy^2}.$$

- **Example 7.** If $h(x) = 3x^{-1} + 2x^{\frac{1}{3}} - 4,$ find $h(8).$

$$h(8) = 3(8^{-1}) + 2(8^{\frac{1}{3}}) - 4 = \tfrac{3}{8} + 4 - 4 = \tfrac{3}{8}.$$

Recall that in bx^n the n operates on x only, not on $b.$ Consequently,

$$3 \cdot 8^{\frac{1}{3}} = 3(8^{\frac{1}{3}}) = 6.$$

- **Example 8.**

$$\frac{[3x + x^2]x^{-5}}{x^2} - \frac{3x^{-4}}{x} = [3x + x^2]x^{-7} - 3x^{-5} = 3x^{-6} + x^{-5} - 3x^{-5} = 3x^{-6} - 2x^{-5}.$$

† The symbol $\sqrt{4}$ means $+2,$ not $\pm 2,$ although if $x^2 = 4,$ $x = \pm 2.$

‡ The given expression does *not* equal $\dfrac{(x+y)^2}{x+y^2}.$

PROBLEM SET 8–1

1. If $h(x) = x^{-\frac{1}{2}} + 3x^2 + 4x^{-2} + 3$, find $h(1)$ and $h(4)$. Does $h(0)$ have meaning? Does $h(3)$ have meaning?

2. If $h(x) = (3x + 3)^{-\frac{1}{2}} + 17x^{-5} + 4^{-\frac{1}{2}} - 3$, find $h(2)$ and $h(26)$ accurate to two decimal places.

3. Simplify (a) $\dfrac{x^{-2} + y^2}{x^{-1} + y^{-1}}$, (b) $4^{\frac{3}{2}} + 8^{\frac{2}{3}}$, (c) $(32^{\frac{3}{2}})^{-\frac{2}{5}}$.

4. Simplify $4^{-\frac{3}{2}} + 3^2 - 7 \cdot 2^4 + 3 \cdot 9^{-\frac{1}{2}} - 16^{-2}$ and obtain an approximation accurate to two decimal places.

The expressions in Problems 5 to 10 arise when the derivatives of certain more complicated expressions are computed. The reader will learn to compute similar derivatives in calculus, but should be able to simplify these fractions now. In each case alter the expression on the left to obtain that on the right. Also, obtain one other simplification of the expression on the left.

5. $\dfrac{(x^2 - x)(2)(2x - 1)(2) - (2x - 1)^2(2x - 1)}{(x^2 - x)^2} = \dfrac{1 - 2x}{x^2(x - 1)^2}$.

6. $\dfrac{x^3 \cdot \frac{1}{3}(2x - 1)^{-\frac{2}{3}}(2) - (2x - 1)^{\frac{1}{3}}(3x^2)}{(2x - 1)^{\frac{2}{3}}} = \dfrac{2x^3 - 9x^2(2x - 1)}{3(2x - 1)^{\frac{4}{3}}}$.

7. $\dfrac{x^3(1 - x^2)^{-\frac{1}{2}}}{4x} = \dfrac{1}{4} x^2(1 - x^2)^{-\frac{1}{2}}$.

8. $\dfrac{4(\frac{1}{2})(3x^2 + 5)^{-\frac{1}{2}}(6x)}{4(3x^2 + 5)^{\frac{1}{2}}} = \dfrac{3x}{3x^2 + 5}$.

9. $\dfrac{(2x + 7)\frac{1}{2}(4x - 5)^{-\frac{1}{2}}(4) - \sqrt{4x - 5}(2)}{(2x + 7)^2} = \dfrac{24 - 4x}{(2x + 7)^2(4x - 5)^{\frac{1}{2}}}$.

10. $\dfrac{(2x + 3)(1) - (x - 3)(2)}{(2x + 3)^2} \cdot (2x + 3)^{-\frac{1}{3}} = \dfrac{9}{(2x + 3)^{\frac{7}{3}}}$.

In Problems 11 to 26 solve the given equations. Check for extraneous values.

11. $\dfrac{x^{-1} + 3x}{x} = \dfrac{13}{4}$.   **12.** $(2x - 5)^{\frac{1}{2}} + 3 = 0$.   **13.** $4(5x + 7)^{\frac{1}{3}} = 3x$.

14. $(W + 4)^{\frac{1}{2}} + W - 2 = 0$.   **15.** $3(z + 1)^{-1} + 4(z - 1)^{-1} = 5(1 - z)^{-1}$.

16. $(x - 2)^{\frac{1}{3}} = (x - 6)^{\frac{1}{2}}$.   **17.** $\dfrac{x^{-1} + 1}{x^{-1} - 1} = 1$.   **18.** $x^5 = 4x^3$.

19. $x^{-\frac{1}{2}} - (2x)^{-\frac{1}{2}} = 5$.   **20.** $[x^{\frac{1}{2}} - (2x)^{\frac{1}{2}}]^{-1} = 5$. Compare with Problem 19.

21. $x(6 - x)^{\frac{1}{2}} = (6 - x)^{\frac{1}{2}}$.   ***22.** $(x^2 - 4x + 3)^{\frac{1}{5}} + 1 = 3x^{-1}$.

23. $(x + 2)^{-\frac{1}{2}}(x + 3)^{-1} + 3 = \frac{91}{30}$.   **24.** $5x^{-1} + x^{-2} = 6$.

25. $3x^{-2} + 4x^{-1} = -1$.   **26.** $(x + 2)^{\frac{1}{2}} - 3 = 0$.

In Problems 27 to 30 show that the expression on the left may be simplified to the expression on the right. These identities arise in hyperbolic function theory which is used in solving projectile problems involving air resistance, and in electric-circuit theory.

27. $\left[\dfrac{e^x + e^{-x}}{2}\right]^2 - \left[\dfrac{e^x - e^{-x}}{2}\right]^2 = 1.$ 28. $\left[\dfrac{2}{e^x + e^{-x}}\right]^2 + \left[\dfrac{e^x - e^{-x}}{e^x + e^{-x}}\right]^2 = 1.$

29. $\dfrac{1}{2}\left[e^{\frac{x}{2}} - e^{-\frac{x}{2}}\right]^2 = \dfrac{e^x + e^{-x}}{2} - 1.$

30. $\left[\dfrac{e^x + e^{-x}}{2}\right]^2 + \left[\dfrac{e^x - e^{-x}}{2}\right]^2 = \dfrac{e^{2x} + e^{-2x}}{2}.$

Readers needing additional drill on the use of fractional and negative exponents should simplify the expressions given in Problems 31 to 35. The laws of exponents may be used to advantage. For example:

$$(32^{\frac{3}{2}})^{-\frac{2}{5}} = 32^{-\frac{3}{5}} = (2^5)^{-\frac{3}{5}} = 2^{-3} = \tfrac{1}{8}.$$

31. (a) $4^{\frac{3}{2}} + 2^{-3}$ (b) $16^{\frac{3}{4}} - (\tfrac{1}{2})^{-3}$ (c) $9^{-2} + (\tfrac{1}{4})^{\frac{1}{2}}$.

32. (a) $(a^{\frac{1}{3}} - b^{\frac{2}{3}}) \cdot (a^{\frac{2}{3}} + a^{\frac{1}{3}}b^{\frac{2}{3}} + b^{\frac{4}{3}})$ (b) $(a^{\frac{1}{4}} - b^{\frac{1}{4}}) \cdot (a^{\frac{1}{4}} + b^{\frac{1}{4}}) \cdot (a^{\frac{1}{2}} + b^{\frac{1}{2}})$.

33. (a) $(a^x - a^y)(a^x + a^y)$ (b) $(7^{2x} + 5^{3y})(5^{3y} - 7^{2x})$.

34. (a) $(-2)^{-5}$ (b) $(-2)^5$ (c) $(2)^{-5}$ (d) $(2)^{\frac{1}{5}}$.

35. (a) $\dfrac{a^{-2} + b^{-2}}{a^{-1} + b^{-1}}$ (b) $\dfrac{x^{-3} - 2^{-3}}{12x}$ (c) $\dfrac{x^4 y - x^{-1}y^{-4}}{x^{-5}y^5}$.

8–2. Scientific notation. In applied mathematics it is necessary to use and to compare numbers such as the ionization constants of boric acid, 0.00000000064, and hydrogen cyanide, 0.0000000012. This is easier if **scientific notation** is used. To write a number in scientific notation, express it as

(a number containing *exactly one* nonzero digit to the left of the decimal point) times (the appropriate power of 10).

For example: $0.00000000064 = 6.4 \times 10^{-10},$
$0.0000000012 = 1.2 \times 10^{-9}.$

Clearly, 1.2×10^{-9} is the larger.

To obtain exactly one digit to the left of the decimal point may require a shift of the decimal point. The number of places the decimal point is shifted indicates the appropriate power of 10.

This notation also indicates the accuracy (tolerance) of a number. For example, to say that the population of a certain city is 30,000 does not indicate whether the number is (a) 30,000 to the nearest 10,000, or (b) 30,000 to the nearest 1000, or (c) 30,000 to the nearest 100.

In scientific notation we can indicate this difference with ease:
(a) 3×10^4,   (b) 3.0×10^4,   (c) 3.00×10^4.

In physical problems the sizes of numbers vary over a wide range. The speed of light is 983,570,000 ft per sec while the mass of the hydrogen atom

is .$\overbrace{000000000}^{\text{23 zeros}}$ ... 016617 grams. These are more accurately (since tolerance is indicated) and more easily indicated in scientific notation as
9.8357×10^8 ft per sec and 1.6617×10^{-24} grams.

A number has k **significant digits** if, when expressed in scientific notation, there are k digits in the first factor. Thus 4.70×10^5 has three significant digits.

● *Example 1.* Arrange the numbers

$\quad$ 37, 6.6×10^{-4}, .0005, 327, 3×10^6, 0, 429000000, and
$- 141200$ in increasing order of magnitude.

$\quad$ Write each number in scientific notation and arrange, to obtain,

$\quad - 1.412 \times 10^5$, 0, 5×10^{-4}, 6.6×10^{-4}, 3.7×10, 3.27×10^2,
3×10^6, 4.29×10^8.

● *Example 2.* The larger the ionization constant, the stronger an acid is said
$\quad$ to be. A table gives the following ionization constants for weak acids.
$\quad$ (a) Which of the acids listed is the weakest? (b) Which is the strongest?

Acid	Ionization constant
Acetic	1.8×10^{-5}
Arsenic	4.5×10^{-3}
Arsenous	2.1×10^{-8}
Benzoic	6.6×10^{-5}
Boric	1.1×10^{-9}

(a) The strongest *of the acids listed* is arsenic acid since it has the largest
$\quad$ ionization constant.
(b) The weakest acid listed is boric acid since it has the smallest ioniza-
$\quad$ tion constant.

Modern high-speed computers have brought about the introduction of
another notation known as a **floating point number.** It is, essentially, an
adaptation of the scientific notation to a form suited to computer input and
output. Let us consider a computer in which the basic unit ("word") contains
ten digits and a sign. It seems reasonable in many problems to use eight of
the ten available digits for significant digits of the number and the remaining
two digits as an exponent.

Thus,

$$- 983570000 = - .98357000 \times 10^{09}$$

and

$$\overbrace{.00000000000000000000000}^{\text{23 zeros}}16617 = .16617000 \times 10^{-23}$$

(The observant reader will note that the decimal point is *before* the first nonzero value, not after it as in the scientific notation.)

There are two difficulties in using this notation which must be overcome before it is usable on a computer.

1. The computer "word" contains ten digits and *one* sign, while this notation requires two signs — one for the number and one for the exponent.

2. Computers are not built to read or to write numbers "a little above the line" as we usually write exponents.

The first of these difficulties is met by adding 50 to the exponent. Thus any number between 10^{-50} and 10^{49} can be represented without using a negative exponent since

$$10^{-50+50} = 10^{00} \quad \text{and} \quad 10^{49+50} = 10^{99}.$$

Numbers greater than 10^{50} which would now require a three digit (exponent + 50) cannot be represented in this notation.

Thus,

	Factor	Exponent plus 50
$- 983570000 = - .98357000 \times 10^{09} \rightarrow$	$- .98357000$	59

The second difficulty is resolved by noting that since the exponent always uses 10 as its base, we need not write the 10. There is also no reason to keep the decimal point, since this is always understood to be *before* the first digit. Hence,

	Factor	Exponent plus 50
$- 983570000 = - .98357000 \times 10^{09} \rightarrow$	$- 98357000$	59

● *Examples.*

Express 4721.6392 as a floating point number.

Answer   47216392   54.

Express .0000000000072316 as a floating point number.

Answer   72316000   39.

Express the floating point number 42111672   62 as a decimal.

Answer   421116720000.

Express the floating point number 87213376   21 as a decimal.

Answer $.87213376 \times 10^{-29}$

PROBLEM SET 8-2

Perform the indicated operations. Estimate your answer *before* doing the arithmetic.

1. $\dfrac{[3.6 \times 10^5][2.1 \times 10^4]}{8[2.7 \times 10^3]}$.

2. $\dfrac{[2.9 \times 10^4][6.1 \times 10^{-8}]}{\sqrt{4.0 \times 10^{-12}}}$.

3. $\dfrac{[1.1 \times 10^{-9}][2.1 \times 10^{-8}]}{4.0 \times 10^{-15}}$.

4. $\dfrac{[6.4 \times 10^{-11}][2.71 \times 10^9]}{.000000013}$.

5. Solve for y: $1.37 \times 10^5 y + 2.1 \times 10^3 = 7.1 \times 10^3$.

6. Solve for t: $2.1 \times 10^4 t + 1.6 \times 10^{-5} = 30 \times 10^{-6}$.

7. The solubility product constant k_{sp} of certain compounds, at room temperature, is given in the table below. Which compound has the largest k_{sp}? Arrange the compounds in *increasing* order of k_{sp}.

Compound	k_{sp}
Silver sulfide	4.1×10^{-52}
Barium carbonate	8.1×10^{-9}
Mercurous bromide	4.0×10^{-23}
Lead chromate	2.0×10^{-14}
Cadmium hydroxide	1.2×10^{-14}
Cupric iodate	1.4×10^{-7}

8. Will the product of the solubility products of silver sulfide and of cupric iodate be more or less than that of mercurous bromide?

9. Consult a chemical table and determine the most and the least soluble compounds of those listed. If several different temperatures are considered, use 20° C.

10. Consult a physics text or handbook to determine the speed of light and that of sound. Light moves how many times as fast as sound? Find W, where W is to the speed of sound as the speed of sound is to the speed of light.

11. Determine the concentration of hydrogen ions in 0.10-molar HCNO (cyanic acid) by solving for x:

$$\frac{x^2}{0.10 - x} = 2.00 \times 10^{-4}.$$

12. Obtain the concentration of hydrogen ions, x, in a solution containing 0.10 mole HCNO and 0.10 mole NaCNO by solving the equation

$$\frac{x(0.10 + x)}{0.10 - x} = 2.00 \times 10^{-4}.$$

Compare the results of Problems 11 and 12.

13. If 100 cc of 0.010-molar ammonium chloride solution is added to 150 cc of 0.10-molar ammonium hydroxide solution, the $(OH)^-$ ion concentration is computed by solving the equation

$$\frac{(0.040 + x)x}{0.060 - x} = 1.80 \times 10^{-5}.$$

Determine the concentration. There is no justification for obtaining your answer to more than two significant digits.

14. Solve the equation $\dfrac{x(0.10 + x)}{(0.025 - x)} = 1.85 \times 10^{-5}$ for x to determine the concentration of H^+ ion when 0.10 mole of solid ammonium hydroxide is added to 1 liter of 0.125-molar acetic acid.

15. Considerations involving the hydrogen atom permit one to compute the mass of an electron as

$$\frac{1.67 \times 10^{-24}}{1.84 \times 10^3 \times 10^3} \text{ kgm.}$$

Express this in simpler form to obtain 9.08×10^{-31} kgm.

16. The following expressions arise in computing the electric intensities due to charged particles.

$$A = 9 \times 10^9 \times \frac{12 \times 10^{-9}}{(.06)^2} \text{ newtons per coulomb.}$$

$$B = 9 \times 10^9 \times \frac{12 \times 10^{-9}}{(.04)^2} \text{ newtons per coulomb.}$$

$$C = 9 \times 10^9 \times \frac{12 \times 10^{-9}}{(.14)^2} \text{ newtons per coulomb.}$$

Show that $A \cong 3.00 \times 10^4$ newtons per coulomb,
$B \cong 6.75 \times 10^4$ newtons per coulomb,
$C \cong 0.55 \times 10^4$ newtons per coulomb.

17. In a simple diode vacuum tube of 250-volt potential, the speed with which electrons emitted from the cathode reach the anode may be computed as

$$v = \frac{2eV}{m} = \frac{2 \times 1.6 \times 10^{-19} \times 250}{9.1 \times 10^{-31}} \text{ m per sec.}$$

Show that $v \cong 8.8 \times 10^{13}$ m per sec.

18. The potential energy V required to produce the deuteron speed attained in certain cyclotrons is

$$V = \tfrac{1}{2} \times 4.8 \times 10^7 \times (1.8)^2 \times (.48)^2 \text{ volts.}$$

Show that V is approximately 18 million volts.

9. The relative permeability k of a ring of iron of certain dimensions is found to be

$$k = \frac{\left[\dfrac{2.0 \times 10^2}{32}\right]}{1.257 \times 10^{-6}}.$$

Show that $k \cong 5.0 \times 10^6$.

20. The following equation arises in obtaining the wavelength of light:

$$1/x = 1.097 \times 10^7 (\tfrac{1}{4} - \tfrac{1}{9}).$$

Show that $x \cong 6.5 \times 10^{-7}$.

21. Express the answer to each problem you worked in this set as a floating-point number.

8–3. Approximation of results. One characteristic of an experienced scientist or engineer is the ability to *estimate* results. The reader is urged to estimate answers *before* computing. Scientific notation is useful in obtaining quick estimates. Often, rough estimates are obtained by rounding off each figure used in the computation to one significant digit.

● *Example 1.* Problem 11 of the last section requires the solution of

$$\frac{x^2}{0.10 - x} = 2.00 \times 10^{-4}.$$

A chemist would know that x is small compared to 0.10, and, hence, for a quick estimate, would use 0.10 for $(0.10 - x)$. The equation becomes:

$$\frac{x^2}{0.10} \cong 2.0 \times 10^{-4}$$
$$x^2 \cong 2.0 \times 10^{-5}$$

or

$$x^2 \cong 20 \times 10^{-6}.$$
$$x \cong \sqrt{20} \times 10^{-3} \cong 4.5 \times 10^{-3}.†$$

In this example the "estimate" is almost as accurate as the original data will permit. In other problems the estimate may be quite crude, but still give a worthwhile check on a more accurately computed result.

● *Example 2.* Estimate the volume of a sphere of radius 9.

$$V = \tfrac{4}{3}\pi(9)^3.$$

To one significant digit $\pi \cong 3$.
Hence,

$$V \cong \tfrac{4}{3} \cdot 3(9)^3 \cong 4 \times 10^3,$$

which may be too large.

† Only the positive root has meaning in this example.

PROBLEM SET 8-3

In each problem *estimate* [do not compute] the result.

1. $(3784)(251)(17500) \cong (4^- \times 10^3)(2^+ \times 10^2)(2^- \times 10^4) \cong 16 \times 10^9 = 1.6 \times 10^{10}$.

2. $\frac{4}{3}\pi(17)^3$.

3. $\dfrac{(3.2 \times 10^6)(4.9 \times 10^{18})}{1.346 \times 10^{-22}}$.

4. $\frac{22}{7} \times \pi^{-1}$.

5. $3.14159 \times \pi^{-1}$.

6. $\dfrac{(3.7 \times 10^{-4})(16 \times 10^5)}{2.71}$.

7. The torque T developed in the drive shaft of an automobile whose 80-hp engine rotates it at 3600 rpm is

$$T = \frac{44000}{3600 \times 2\pi/60}.$$

Show $T \cong 1.2 \times 10^2$ lb-ft.

8-4. Logarithms. Fundamental assumptions: For every positive number N and positive base b, $b \neq 1$, there exists a unique real exponent x such that $b^x = N$. The laws of exponents (Section 8-1) hold for all real exponents.

● **Illustration.** Since $10^0 = 1$ and $10^1 = 10$, it is assumed that there is an exponent m having its value between 0 and 1 such that $10^m = 2$.

Definition of logarithm. If $N = b^x$ where $N > 0$, $b > 0$, $b \neq 1$, then x is called the logarithm of N relative to the base b. In symbols this may be written $\log_b N = x$.

To state the definition in words: the logarithm of a positive number †relative to a given positive base different from one is the exponent or the power to which the base must be raised to produce the number. This implies $b^{\log_b N} = N$.

● **Example 1.** Find $\log_2 \frac{1}{8}$.

If

$$\log_2 \tfrac{1}{8} = x,$$

then

$$2^x = \tfrac{1}{8}.$$

Since

$$\tfrac{1}{8} = 2^{-3},$$
$$2^x = 2^{-3},$$
$$\log_2 \tfrac{1}{8} = x = -3.$$

† As the reader goes further in mathematics he will need log k defined for negative (and even complex) k. This occurs, for example, in electrical theory. Such logarithms are many valued complex numbers and will not be needed in this text. The logarithm of zero is never defined.

• **Example 2.** Determine $\log_8 4$.

If
$$\log_8 4 = x,$$

then
$$8^x = 4.$$

That is,
$$2^{3x} = 2^2,$$
$$3x = 2,$$
$$x = \tfrac{2}{3}.$$

Hence,
$$\log_8 4 = \tfrac{2}{3}.$$

• **Example 3.** If $\log_t 16 = \tfrac{4}{3}$, find the base t
$$\log_t 16 = \tfrac{4}{3}$$

or
$$16 = t^{\frac{4}{3}}.$$

Then
$$2^4 = (t^{\frac{1}{3}})^4$$

and
$$t^{\frac{1}{3}} = 2$$

or
$$t = 2^3 = 8.$$

The reader may verify that $8^{\frac{4}{3}} = 16$ and hence $\log_8 16 = \tfrac{4}{3}$.

PROBLEM SET 8-4

Determine y in each problem.

1. $y = \log_2 16$.
2. $y = \log_8 4$.
3. $y = \log_4 32$.
4. $y = \log_5 625$.
5. $y = \log_3 \tfrac{1}{243}$.
6. $y = \log_4 1024$.
7. $y = \log_8 512$.
8. $y = \log_{10} 10,000$.
9. $y = \log_3 729$.
10. $y = \log_{27} 81$.
11. $\log_2 y = 3$.
12. $\log_3 y = -4$.
13. $\log_8 y = \tfrac{5}{3}$.
14. $\log_8 y = -2$.
15. $\log_4 y = \tfrac{5}{2}$.
16. $\log_{27} y = -\tfrac{4}{3}$.
17. $\log_y 81 = 2$.
18. $\log_y 128 = \tfrac{3}{7}$.
19. $\log_y 1000 = 3$.
20. $\log_y \tfrac{1}{4} = 2$.
21. $\log_y 8 = \tfrac{5}{3}$.
22. $\log_y 4 = -3$.
23. $\log_y 16 = -\tfrac{7}{2}$.
24. $\log_y 1 = 0$. Is y unique? Give three possible values and one impossible value for y.
25. $y = 7^{\log_7 15}$.

8-5. Logarithms to the base 8. From Example 2, Section 8-4, we have $\log_8 4 = \frac{2}{3}$. In a similar fashion, we obtain the table below.

N	$\frac{1}{128}$	$\frac{1}{64}$	$\frac{1}{32}$	$\frac{1}{16}$	$\frac{1}{8}$	$\frac{1}{4}$	$\frac{1}{2}$	1	2	4	8	16	32	64	128	256	512
$\log_8 N$	$-\frac{7}{3}$	-2	$-\frac{5}{3}$	$-\frac{4}{3}$	-1	$-\frac{2}{3}$	$-\frac{1}{3}$	0	$\frac{1}{3}$	$\frac{2}{3}$	1	$\frac{4}{3}$	$\frac{5}{3}$	2	$\frac{7}{3}$	$\frac{8}{3}$	3

Table 8-5

● **Example 1.** Compute $\log_8 \frac{1}{32} = x$.

Then

$$8^x = \frac{1}{32} = 2^{-5}$$
$$2^{3x} = 2^{-5}.$$

Hence,

$$x = -\frac{5}{3}.$$

● **Example 2.** Sketch the graph of $y = \log_2 x$.

By the definition of a logarithm, the equations $y = \log_2 x$ and $x = 2^y$ represent the same relationship, and hence have the same graph.

y=log₂ x or x=2ʸ

Fig. 8-1

y	L^-	-3	0	5	L^+
x	0^+	$\frac{1}{8}$	1	32	L^+

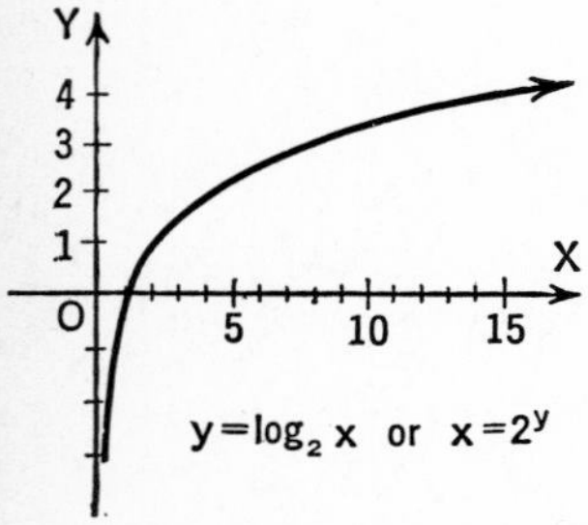

PROBLEM SET 8-5

1. Verify that Table 8-5 is correct for $N = \frac{1}{128}$, $\frac{1}{2}$, 16, and 256.

2. Sketch $y = \log_2 x$ and $y = \log_3 x$ on the same set of axes.

3. Sketch $y = \log_{10} x$ and $y = \log_2 x$ on the same set of axes.

4. Sketch $y = \log_2 |x|$.

5. Use Table 8-5 to make an estimate of $\log_8 12$. Note that 12 is halfway between $N = 8$ and $N = 16$, both of which are given in the table. Express your answer to one decimal place.

6. Estimate $\log_8 10$. Note that 10 is $\frac{1}{4}$ of the way between 8 and 16.

7. Estimate $\log_8 18$.

8. Show by direct substitution that $\log_8 2(64) = \log_8 2 + \log_8 64$.

9. Since $\log_8 2 = \frac{1}{3}$, or $8^{\frac{1}{3}} = 2$, while $\log_8 64 = 2$, or $8^2 = 64$, show that $64(2) = 8^2 \cdot 8^{\frac{1}{3}} = 8^{\frac{7}{3}}$ implies that $\log_8 (64)(2) = \log_8 8^{\frac{7}{3}} = \frac{7}{3}$.

8-6. Properties of logarithms. In multiplication of expressions with identical bases, such as $b^m \cdot b^n = b^{m+n}$, the exponents are added to obtain the resulting exponent. Since logarithms are exponents, it follows that (1) the addition of the logarithms of two numbers yields the logarithm of the product of the two numbers; (2) the subtraction of the logarithm of a second number from the logarithm of a first number yields the logarithm of the quotient of the first number by the second number; (3) the multiplication of the logarithm of a number by a constant yields the logarithm of the number raised to the constant as exponent. These three properties of logarithms are useful in shortening computations involving products, quotients, powers, and roots. Due to their importance we state and prove these three properties.

In the following $b > 0$, $b \neq 1$, $M > 0$, $N > 0$, $D > 0$, $M = b^x$, $N = b^y$, $D = b^z$. Then $\log_b M = x$, $\log_b N = y$, $\log_b D = z$.

The reader should recall that $\log_b b^x = x$, which follows directly from the definition of a logarithm.

Property 1. $\log_b MN = \log_b M + \log_b N$.

PROOF: $MN = b^x b^y = b^{x+y}$. Therefore,

$$\log_b MN = \log_b b^{x+y} = x + y = \log_b M + \log_b N.$$

REMARK: If $M_1 > 0, \cdots, M_n > 0$ it may be shown that

$$\log_b M_1 \cdots M_n = \log_b M_1 + \cdots + \log_b M_n.$$

- **Illustration.** $\log_2 [8 \cdot 32] = \log_2 8 + \log_2 32 = 3 + 5 = 8$. $\log_2 256 = 8$ since $2^8 = 256$.

Property 2. $\log_b \left[\dfrac{N}{D}\right] = \log_b N - \log_b D$.

PROOF: $\dfrac{N}{D} = \dfrac{b^y}{b^z} = b^{y-z}$. Then $\log_b \left[\dfrac{N}{D}\right] = \log_b b^{y-z} = y - z = \log_b N - \log_b D$.

- **Illustration.** $\log_2 \left[\frac{8}{32}\right] = \log_2 8 - \log_2 32 = 3 - 5 = -2$. $\log_2 \left[\frac{1}{4}\right] = -2$ since $\frac{1}{4} = 2^{-2}$.

- **Example 1.** Show that Property 2 can be proved from Property 1.

$$\log_b N = \log_b \left(\frac{N}{D} \cdot D\right) = \log_b \frac{N}{D} + \log_b D.$$

Therefore,

$$\log_b \frac{N}{D} = \log_b N - \log_b D.$$

Property 3. $\log_b N^k = k \log_b N$.

PROOF: $N^k = (b^y)^k = b^{ky}$. Consequently, $\log_b N^k = \log_b b^{ky} = ky = k \log_b N$.

- **Illustration.** $\log_2 4^3 = 3 \cdot \log_2 4 = 3(2) = 6$. $\log_2 64 = 6$ since $64 = 2^6$.

- **Illustration.** $\log_2 \sqrt[3]{512} = \frac{1}{3} \log_2 512 = \frac{1}{3} \log_2 2^9 = \frac{1}{3}(9) = 3$.

$$\sqrt[3]{512} = 8 \quad \text{and} \quad \log_2 8 = 3.$$

PROBLEM SET 8-6

1. Show that $\log_b \sqrt[r]{N} = \frac{1}{r} \log_b N$ by taking $k = \frac{1}{r}$ in Property 3.

2. Prove $\log_b \sqrt[r]{N} = \frac{1}{r} \log_b N$ directly from the definition.

$$\log_b N = x \quad \text{as} \quad N = b^x.$$

3. Show that Property 2 can be proved by using Property 1 and Property 3 with $k = -1$.

Use Table 8–5 of $\log_8 N$ to compute:

4. $\log_8 \sqrt{2}.$ **5.** $\log_8 \sqrt[3]{\frac{1}{16}}.$ **6.** $\log_8 [(512)(128)].$

7. $\log_8 \frac{1}{512}.$ **8.** Prove $\log_b \frac{P^2}{Q\sqrt{M}} = 2\log_b P - \log_b Q - \frac{1}{2}\log_b M.$

Given $\log_{10} 2 = 0.301$ and $\log_{10} 3 = 0.477$, compute the following logarithms.

9. $\log_{10} 12.$ **10.** $\log_{10} [\frac{2}{3}].$ **11.** $\log_{10} 20 = \log_{10} 10 + \log_{10} 2 = ?$

12. $\log_{10} 1.$ **13.** $\log_{10} \frac{1}{2}.$ **14.** $\log_{10} \frac{9}{8}.$

15. $\log_{10} 90.$ **16.** $\log_{10} \sqrt[5]{12}.$ **17.** $\log_{10} 9\sqrt{3}.$

18. $\log_{10} (\frac{27}{2})\sqrt[5]{12}.$ **19.** $\log_{10} 1000.$ **20.** $\log_{10} 0.001.$

21. Show that, for all k, $\log_{10} (10^k) = k$.

22. Show that $b^{\log_b x} = x$ for all $x > 0$.

23. Use $\log_{10} 2 = .301$, $\log_{10} 3 = .477$, $\log_{10} 10 = 1.000$, and the three properties of logarithms to determine the logarithms of the integers between 1 and 25. Do *not* use any tables. If you cannot find a logarithm by using the given facts, estimate it. (Log$_{10}$ 7 is an example of this type; a reasonable estimate would put $\log_{10}$ 7 halfway between $\log_{10}$ 6 and $\log_{10}$ 8, both of which can be found by the method requested.†) *Put a large circle* around and a question mark next to those answers which were estimated, and indicate on each answer, guess or not, how you arrived at your conclusion. For example:

$$\log_{10} 5 = \log_{10} \tfrac{10}{2} = \log_{10} 10 - \log_{10} 2 = 1.000 - .301 = .699.$$

24. In Problem 23 we found $\log_{10} 5 = .699$ approximately. Since $\log_{10} 100 = 2.000$, compute $\log_{10} 100 = 2\log_{10} 5 + 2\log_{10} 2$ and compare the results.

25. If $\log_{10} x < 0$, what can be said about the size of x?

26. If $\log_b x < 0$, $b > 3$, what can be said about the size of x? of x^2?

27. If $0 < \log_{10} x^2 < 10$, what can be said about the size of x?

28. If $0 < \log_b x < b$, $b > 5$, what can be said about the size of x?

29. If $3 < \log_{10} x < 5$, what can be said about the size of x?

30. If $-9 < \log_{10} x < -5$, what can be said about the size of x?

† Another method for estimating $\log_{10} 7 = \frac{1}{2} \log_{10} 49 \cong \frac{1}{2} \left[\dfrac{\log_{10} 48 + \log_{10} 50}{2} \right].$

In Problems 31 to 35 express the following logarithms as sums of the form indicated in Problem 31. This technique is used in calculus to simplify complicated differentiations.

31. $\log_e \dfrac{\sqrt{3x^2+5}\,(e^{3x})}{7x^2(2x-5)^3} = \frac{1}{2}\log_e (3x^2+5) + 3x - \log_e 7 - 2\log_e x - 3\log_e (2x-5).$

32. $\log_e \dfrac{4x^2\sqrt[3]{x^2-7}}{17(2x+5)^8}.$

33. $\log_e \dfrac{(4x+2)^{\frac{1}{3}}(2x^3+7)}{4x-9}.$

34. $2\log_e \dfrac{(4x+3)^2(-7x)}{15}.$

35. $\log_e \dfrac{(4x+7)^5\sqrt{2x^2+1}}{5(2x^2+1)^3}.$

8–7. Logarithms to the base 10. In elementary logarithmic computation it is usual to use $b = 10$ as the base. In more advanced applications another base, which will be discussed later, is more convenient. In this text, when log N is written, it means $\log_{10} N$.

A portion of a table of four-place logarithms to the base 10 is supplied below to aid in the illustrative examples. More complete tables will be found in mathematical handbooks and in this text. This table contains logarithms of numbers between 1 and 10. To compute with numbers not found in the interval from 1 to 10 such numbers are expressed in scientific notation as a number with one digit to the left of the decimal point multiplied by the appropriate power of 10. Since $\log 10^N = N$, the logarithm of a number in scientific notation is obtained by adding the integral exponent of the power of 10 used in writing the number in scientific notation to the logarithm of the number between 1 and 10 found in the table. The integral exponent is called the **characteristic.**

Logarithmic tables were first published in 1614 by their inventor, a Scot, John Napier. At that time exponents were unknown. Current tables are constructed using infinite series. Examples of such series appear in Chapter 10.

● *Example 1.*

$$\log 64100 = \log (6.41 \times 10^4)$$
$$= \log 6.41 + \log 10^4$$
$$= .8069 + 4.$$

The value $\log 6.41 = .8069$ is obtained using the table below. The method of reading this table will be described next.

Four-place Logarithms							
	0	1	2	↓3	4	5	6	
60	7782	7789	7796	7803	7810	7818	7825	...
→1	7853	7860	7868	7875	7882	7889	7896	...
2	7924	7931	7938	7945	7952	7959	7966	...
3	7993	8000	8007	8014	8021	8028	8035	...
4	8062	8069	8075	8082	8089	8096	8102	...
:	:	:	:	:	:	:	:	
7	.	.	.	.	.	.	8299	...

- **Example 2.**
$$\log 613 = \log (6.13 \times 10^2)$$
$$= \log 6.13 + \log 10^2$$
$$= \log 6.13 + 2.$$
$$= .7875 + 2.$$

The decimal part of the logarithm, which is listed in the table, is a *positive* decimal called the **mantissa.** In using a four-place table, the first two digits (here "61") are found in the left column while the third digit (here "3") is found in the top row (see arrow on table, p. 187). The mantissa is found at the intersection of row 61 and column 3, giving $\log 6.13 = .7875$. **The decimal point which precedes the mantissa must be supplied since it is not printed in the table.**

- **Example 3.** Find N if $\log N = .8299 - 3$. From the tables we find that the tabular entry 8299 corresponds to the number 676. Thus, if

$$\log N = .8299 - 3,$$

then

$$N = 6.76 \times 10^{-3}$$
$$= .00676.$$

PROBLEM SET 8-7

Use a four-place table of common logarithms to approximate:

1. $\log 3.47$.
2. $\log 34700$.
3. $\log .000347$.
4. $\log 2160$.
5. $\log 7.64$
6. $\log 87200$.
7. $\log (3.6 \times 10^{15})$.
8. $\log .00314$.
9. $\log (1.02 \times 10^{-8})$.
10. $\log (9.62 \times 10^4)$.
11. In chemistry it is usual to indicate hydrogen ion concentration as a "pH value." The pH value is defined: $pH = \log \dfrac{1}{(H^+)}$, where (H^+) indicates the concentration of the H^+ ion. Determine the pH of the solution mentioned in Problem 11, Set 8–2.
12. Same as Problem 11 for Problem 12, Set 8–2.
13. Same as Problem 11 for Problem 14, Set 8–2.
14. If $p(OH) = \log \dfrac{1}{(OH^-)}$, compute $p(OH)$ of the solution given in Problem 13, Set 8–2.
15. What approximate value do you think $\log 3.415$ will have? Why?

In Problems 16 to 24 approximate the values of N.

16. $\log N = 0.9777 - 3$.

17. $\log N = .8482 - 7$.

18. $\log N = .3118 - 4$.

19. $\log N = .5453 + 7$.

20. $\log N = .9294 + 1$.

21. $\log N = .7956 + 6$.

22. $\log N^2 = .9542 + 4$.

23. $\log N = 3.6253 = .6253 + 3$.

24. $\log N = 4.6 = .6 + 4$.

25. Determine the H^+ ion concentration in a solution having $pH = 4.6$. See Problem 11 for the definition of pH.

26. Find an approximation of $\log e$, if $e \cong 2.718$.

27. Find an approximation of $\log \pi$, if $\pi \cong 3.142$.

28. State a rule concerning the effect that moving the decimal point in a number has on the $\log_{10}$ of that number. Use the facts

$$\log_{10}(10x) = \log_{10} x + \log_{10} 10 = ?$$

and that

$$\log_{10}\left(\frac{x}{10}\right) = \log_{10} x - \log_{10} 10 = ?$$

to prove your rule.

8–8. Interpolation. The table we have been using is known as a 4-place table, since mantissas are given to 4 decimal places. Many handbooks carry 5- and 7-place tables and your school library may have 12- or 15-place tables. In using any table, and in certain problems not involving tables, interpolation must sometimes be applied. The process is essentially that used in finding log 7 in Problem 23, Set 8–6. Log 6 and log 8 were known and log 7 was to be approximated. It was assumed (incorrectly, but with reasonable closeness) that log 7 was halfway between log 6 and log 8. In a similar fashion, if log 3.768 is desired from a table listing

$$\log 3.76 = .5752$$
$$\log 3.77 = .5763$$

we may assume (again incorrectly, but with reasonable closeness) that log 3.768 is $\frac{8}{10}$ of the way between log 3.76 and log 3.77. A convenient form for this computation follows:

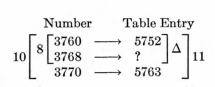

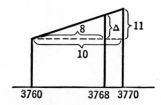

Fig. 8–2

Assuming $\dfrac{8}{10} = \dfrac{\Delta}{11}$, we find $\Delta = 8.8$ or 9 and $5752 + 9 = 5761$.

Hence $\log 3.768 = .5761$. The assumption $\dfrac{8}{10} = \dfrac{\Delta}{11}$ is close enough to

give $\log 3.768 = .5761$ with almost four-place accuracy *but not more.* Since, in general, computation cannot give results of greater accuracy than the original data, this last remark *should* be superfluous. The result of interpolation can be expected to have slightly less accuracy than the table used since interpolation assumes the locus between the two known values is a straight line, while the graph of $y = \log x$ is not linear. (See Example 2, Section 8–5, and Problem 3, Set 8–5.)

The reader should correlate the diagram of Figure 8–2 with the numerical array showing Δ given on page 189.

• *Example 1.* Approximate $\log 625.3$.

$$\log 625.3 = \log 6.253 + \log 10^2$$
$$= \log 6.253 + 2.$$

Using the tables and interpolation,†

$$
10\begin{bmatrix} 3\begin{bmatrix} 6250 & \longrightarrow & 7959 \\ 6253 & \longrightarrow & ? \end{bmatrix}\Delta \\ 6260 & \longrightarrow & 7966 \end{bmatrix}7
$$

Number   Table Entry

Now, $\dfrac{3}{10} = \dfrac{\Delta}{7}$, or $\Delta = 2.1 \cong 2$ (dropping the decimal), and

$$7959 + 2 = 7961.$$

Hence,

$$\log 6.253 = .7961$$

and

$$\log 625.3 = .7961 + 2.$$

• *Example 2.* Determine N if $\log N = .7940$.

The table lists,

Number   Table Entry

$$
10\begin{bmatrix} \Delta\begin{bmatrix} 6220 & \longleftarrow & 7938 \\ ? & \longleftarrow & 7940 \end{bmatrix}2 \\ 6230 & \longleftarrow & 7945 \end{bmatrix}7
$$

$\dfrac{\Delta}{10} = \dfrac{2}{7}$, $\Delta = \dfrac{20}{7} = 2.9 \cong 3$ (dropping the decimal),

† The use of an equals sign is not desirable since $6250 \neq 7959$. An arrow is used and is read "corresponds to." The reader should note that no decimal points are used in this array.

and

$$6220 + 3 = 6223.$$

Number	Table entry
6223 ⟵	7940

Since the characteristic is zero, we have

$$\log N = .7940,$$
$$N = 6.223 \times 10^0$$
$$= 6.223 \times 1$$
$$= 6.223.$$

8–9. Logarithmic computation. As mentioned earlier the properties of logarithms are useful in evaluating products, quotients, and roots. These properties are repeated here for convenience.

1. $\log MN = \log M + \log N$
2. $\log (N/D) = \log N - \log D$
3. $\log N^k = k \log N$

In any computation it is essential that an orderly procedure be used. For example, in general engineering practice one person does the computation, a second checks it, and a third man uses the results. It is essential that each step be indicated clearly in a systematic way.

● *Example 1.* Compute $Y = (63.50)(.0006130)$.

The reader should *always* first estimate his result roughly.

$$Y \cong (6 \times 10^1)(6 \times 10^{-4}) \cong 40 \times 10^{-3} \cong .04.$$

$$\log Y = \log 63.50 + \log .0006130$$
$$\log 63.50 = \log (6.350 \times 10^1) = .8028 + 1$$
$$\log .0006130 = \log (6.130 \times 10^{-4}) = \underline{.7875 - 4}$$
$$\log Y = 1.5903 - 3$$
$$= .5903 - 2.$$

We do not find the entry 5903 in a four-place table. We do find:

	Number		Table Entry	
	3890 ⟵		5899	
10 [Δ [	? ⟵		5903] 4	12
	3900 ⟵		5911	

$$\frac{\Delta}{10} = \frac{4}{12} = \frac{1}{3}, \quad \Delta = 3.3 \cong 3.$$

Hence, $3893 \longleftarrow 5903$ which indicates

$$\log Y = .5903 - 2,$$
$$Y = 3.893 \times 10^{-2}$$
$$= .03893.$$

This result checks with our rough estimate .04.

● **Example 2.** Compute $Z = \dfrac{625.3}{470000}$.

A rough approximation of Z is obtained using scientific notation.

$$Z \cong \frac{6 \times 10^2}{5 \times 10^5} = \frac{6}{5} \times 10^{-3} \cong 1 \times 10^{-3} = .001.$$

An outline for a more accurate logarithmic computation follows:

$$\log Z = \log (6.253 \times 10^2) - \log (4.7 \times 10^5).$$

$$
\begin{array}{lll}
& \log (6.253 \times 10^2) = . & +2 \\
(-)\dagger & \log (4.700 \times 10^5) = . & +5 \\
\hline
& \log Z = & \\
& Z = &
\end{array}
$$

Using the result of Example 1, Section 8–8, and four-place tables we fill in the missing mantissas and subtract, obtaining

$$
\begin{array}{l}
\log (6.253 \times 10^2) = .7961 + 2 \\
\log (4.700 \times 10^5) = .6721 + 5 \\
\hline
\qquad\qquad \log Z = .1240 - 3 \\
\qquad\qquad\quad Z = ?.
\end{array}
$$

$$
\begin{array}{ccc}
\text{Number} & & \text{Table Entry} \\
\end{array}
$$

$$
10\left[\Delta\begin{bmatrix}1330 & \longleftarrow & 1239 \\ ? & \longleftarrow & 1240 \\ 1340 & \longleftarrow & 1271\end{bmatrix}1\right]32
$$

$$\frac{\Delta}{10} = \frac{1}{32}, \quad \Delta = 0.3 \cong 0.$$

Hence,

$$Z = 1.330 \times 10^{-3} = .001330.$$

The estimate $Z \cong .001$ agrees with this result. This is an opportune place to point out that 1.330×10^{-3} and 1.33×10^{-3} are not the same. The former indicates an accuracy of four significant digits while the accuracy of the latter is only three significant digits.

● **Example 3.** Compute $T = (2.350)^8$.

An estimate of T may be obtained by rounding *up* part of the factors and rounding *down* the remaining factors.

$$T \cong (2)^5(3)^3 = (32)(27) \cong (3 \times 10)(3 \times 10) = 9 \times 10^2.$$

Since $\log T = 8 \log 2.350$ we have

$$
\begin{array}{r}
\log 2.350 = .3711 \\
\times 8 \\
\hline
\log T = 2.9688 \\
= .9688 + 2.
\end{array}
$$

† The small (−) indicates a subtraction is to be performed. Time is saved if the entire problem is set up *before* the tables are used.

$$10\left[\Delta\begin{bmatrix}9300 & \longleftarrow & 9685 \\ ? & \longleftarrow & 9688 \\ 9310 & \longleftarrow & 9689\end{bmatrix}3\right]4$$

Number   Table Entry

$$\frac{\Delta}{10} = \frac{3}{4}, \quad \Delta = 7.5 \cong 8.$$

Hence,

$$9308 \leftarrow 9688 \quad \text{and} \quad T = 9.308 \times 10^2 = 930.8.$$

This checks with our approximation $T \cong 9 \times 10^2$.

- **Example 4.** Compute $D = \sqrt{.8160}$.

Since $.8160 = 81.60 \times 10^{-2}$, we estimate D as

$$D \cong \sqrt{82 \times 10^{-2}} \cong 9 \times 10^{-1}.$$

Using the third principle of logarithms,

$$\log D = \tfrac{1}{2} \log (8.160 \times 10^{-1})$$
$$= \tfrac{1}{2}[.9117 - 1].$$

Since it is convenient to have integral characteristics and since the present characteristic (-1) is not an integral multiple of 2, we use an equivalent statement *in which the integral part is a multiple of 2*.

$$\log (8.160 \times 10^{-1}) = 1.9117 - 2.$$

Hence,

$$\log D = \tfrac{1}{2} \log (8.160 \times 10^{-1})$$
$$= \tfrac{1}{2}[1.9117 - 2]$$
$$= .9558 - 1.$$

A four-place table gives

Number   Table Entry

$$10\left[\Delta\begin{bmatrix}9030 & \longleftarrow & 9557 \\ ? & \longleftarrow & 9558 \\ 9040 & \longleftarrow & 9562\end{bmatrix}1\right]5$$

$$\frac{\Delta}{10} = \frac{1}{5}, \quad \Delta = 2.$$

Hence,

$$9032 \leftarrow 9558$$

and

$$\log D = .9558 - 1,$$
$$D = 9.032 \times 10^{-1} = .9032.$$

This corresponds closely with our estimate of $D \cong 9 \times 10^{-1}$.

● **Example 5.** Compute $W = \dfrac{(.000135)(41.2)}{\sqrt{.816}}$.

First, obtain an estimate of W.

$$W \cong \frac{(1 \times 10^{-4})(4 \times 10^{1})}{(82 \times 10^{-2})^{\frac{1}{2}}} \cong \frac{4 \times 10^{-3}}{9 \times 10^{-1}} = \tfrac{4}{9} \times 10^{-2} \cong .5 \times 10^{-2} = 5 \times 10^{-3}.$$

Before using tables make a complete arrangement of the problem.

$$\log W = \log(1.35 \times 10^{-4}) + \log(4.12 \times 10^{1}) - \tfrac{1}{2}\log(8.16 \times 10^{-1})$$

$$
\begin{array}{llr}
 & \log(1.35 \times 10^{-4}) = . & -4 \\
(+) & \log(4.12 \times 10^{1}) \; = . & +1 \\
\hline
 & \log(\text{numerator}) \; = & \\
(-) & \tfrac{1}{2}\log(8.16 \times 10^{-1}) = . & \\
\hline
 & \log W = & \\
 & W = &
\end{array}
$$

Using tables:

$$
\begin{array}{llr}
 & \log(1.35 \times 10^{-4}) = .1303 - 4 \\
(+) & \log(4.12 \times 10^{1}) \; = .6149 + 1 \\
\hline
 & \log(\text{numerator}) \; = .7452 - 3
\end{array}
$$

From Example 4, $\tfrac{1}{2}\log(8.16 \times 10^{-1}) = .9558 - 1$.
The following subtraction should be performed:

$$
\begin{array}{lll}
 & \log(\text{numerator}) \; = .7452 - 3 \\
(-) & \tfrac{1}{2}\log(8.16 \times 10^{-1}) = .9558 - 1 \\
\hline
 & \log W =
\end{array}
$$

If the *mantissas* were subtracted a negative decimal would result. To use logarithmic tables, the mantissa *must* be positive. This may be accomplished by using the equivalent $1.7452 - 4$ for $.7452 - 3$, obtaining

$$
\begin{array}{lll}
 & \log(\text{numerator}) \; = 1.7452 - 4 \\
(-) & \tfrac{1}{2}\log(8.16 \times 10^{-1}) = .9558 - 1 \\
\hline
 & \log W = .7894 - 3.
\end{array}
$$

Interpolation is necessary in the final step.

$$
\begin{array}{ccc}
\text{Number} & & \text{Table Entry} \\
10\left[\Delta\left[\begin{array}{l}6150 \\ ? \\ 6160\end{array}\right.\right. & \begin{array}{l}\longleftarrow \\ \longleftarrow \\ \longleftarrow\end{array} & \left.\left.\begin{array}{l}7889 \\ 7894 \\ 7896\end{array}\right]5\right]7
\end{array}
$$

$$\frac{\Delta}{10} = \frac{5}{7}, \quad \Delta \cong 7.$$

Hence,

$$6157 \leftarrow 7894$$

and

$$\log W = .7894 - 3,$$
$$W = 6.157 \times 10^{-3} = .006157.$$

This agrees with the estimate $W \cong 5 \times 10^{-3}$.

However, $W \cong 6.16 \times 10^{-3} = .00616$, since the original data have only three significant digit accuracy. This result can be obtained by using the closest table entry, and the interpolation illustrated is unnecessary.

PROBLEM SET 8-9

Make an estimate of the result of each problem. After computing, compare your estimate with your computed result. If they do not agree to within a factor of 10, find your error.

1. $\dfrac{(7.69)^2(3.25)}{4.92}$.

2. $\dfrac{(3.614)(\pi)}{(17)^3}$.

3. $\dfrac{(736200)(3.14)}{6\sqrt{4.13}}$.

4. $\dfrac{4.912 \times 10^{17}}{83.6}$.

5. $\sqrt[5]{.02798}$.

6. $\sqrt[4]{21.68}$.

7. $\dfrac{\sqrt[3]{61.4(1038)}}{1.92 \times 10^6}$.

8. $\dfrac{(4.683)^3 \times 6.192}{\sqrt[4]{8310}}$.

9. $4 \times (1.68)^{-\frac{1}{3}}$.

10. $(2.3)^2 \times (4.91)^{-\frac{1}{2}}$.

11. Compute $Z = \sqrt{(34.2)^2 + (197)^2}$ by logarithms.

Partial solution: To determine Z, let $A = (34.2)^2$ and $B = (197)^2$. Then, A is computed by logarithms. Next, B is computed by logarithms. Now, the sum $A + B = Z^2$ is obtained in the ordinary way *without use of logarithms*. Then Z is computed using logarithms.

$$A = (34.2)^2 \qquad\qquad B = (197)^2$$
$$\log A = 2 \log 34.2 \qquad \log B = 2 \log 197$$
$$A = \qquad\qquad\qquad B =$$
$$A + B = \qquad + \qquad = \qquad = Z^2$$
$$\log Z^2 =$$
$$\log Z = \tfrac{1}{2} \log Z^2 = \tfrac{1}{2} \log (A + B) =$$
$$Z =$$

Problems 12 to 17 are included to help the reader realize the limitations of logarithms in computation.

12. $\sqrt{(9.61)^2 - (3.1)^2}$.

13. $\sqrt{(14.6)^2 + (3.7)^2}$.

14. $\sqrt[3]{(16)^3 - 1}$.

15. $\sqrt{(4.98)^2 + 3164}$.

16. $\sqrt{(537)^8 - (47)^3}$.

17. $\sqrt[3]{296 - (1.43)^5}$.

*18. Consult a mathematical table for the *approximate* value of the constant e and determine which is larger, e^π or π^e.

*19. Robert, James, and David were walking on a sandy beach, speculating on possible estimates for the total number of grains of sand contained in all the beaches and deserts of the world. They knew this number was *not* "infinite." Bob suggested $2^{(4^5)}$ [that is, $2^{(1024)}$] as a possible estimate of the total number of grains. James laughed and said, "If the entire earth were composed of very fine sand (10^6 grains per cu in.), $2^{(4^5)}$ would be too high as an estimate of the total number of grains." David agreed and said, "If for every grain of sand in James' sphere, you had a pile of fine sand as big as the earth, $2^{(4^5)}$ would still be *very much* too large as an estimate of the total number of grains." Using $\log 2 = 0.301$ and scientific notation, make estimates of the sizes of the numbers involved to justify the statements of James and David.

*20. If a sphere large enough to contain the entire solar system

$$(\text{radius} = 3.67 \times 10^9 \text{ miles})$$

were filled with fine sand, how would the approximate number of grains in it compare with the three quantities in Problem 19?

$$\bullet$$

It is possible that the reader has become quite familiar with exponential and logarithmic computation without ever meeting some of the most important facets of these versatile concepts. Chapter 9, although brief, is vital to further work.

9–1. Exponential and logarithmic equations. Frequently, when the unknown is involved in the exponents, an equation may be solved using logarithms as illustrated in the following examples.

● *Example 1.*

$$17^{2x+3} = 5(4^{3x})$$
$$\log\left[17^{2x+3}\right] = \log\left[5(4^{3x})\right]$$
$$(2x+3)\log 17 = \log 5 + 3x \log 4.$$

From a table, $\log 17 = .2304 + 1$, $\log 5 = .6990$, and $\log 4 = .6021$. In problems of this type it is usual to write the characteristic first, that is, $\log 17 = 1.2304$.

Hence,

$$(2x+3)(1.2304) \cong .6990 + 3x(.6021).$$

Which becomes

$$2.4608x + 3.6912 = .6990 + 1.8063x$$
$$.6545x = -2.9922$$
$$x = -\frac{2.9922}{.6545}.$$

This division may be done on a slide rule, or by long division, or by logarithms. If logarithms are used, write
$\log(-x) = \log(2.992) - \log(.6545)$† as the first step, since logarithms have been defined for positive numbers only.

An approximate result is, $x \cong -4.6.$ [NOTE: If the integers, 2, 3, 4, 5, 17, involved in the original problem are assumed to be exact, then the result may be computed to as many significant digits as the tables permit.]

● *Example 2.* Solve for x: $29^{x^2} = 103$.

$$\log\left[29^{x^2}\right] = \log 103$$
$$x^2 \log 29 = \log 103$$
$$x^2(1.4624) = 2.0128$$
$$x^2 = \frac{2.0128}{1.4624} \qquad\qquad x = \pm\sqrt{\frac{2.0128}{1.4624}}.$$

† Numbers are rounded off to four significant digits when four-place tables are used.

Solving for $| x |$,

$$\log | x | = \tfrac{1}{2}[\log 2.013 - \log 1.462].\dagger$$

$$
\begin{array}{r}
\log 2.013 = \\
(-) \quad \log 1.462 = \\
\hline
\log x^2 =
\end{array}
$$

$$\log | x | = \tfrac{1}{2} \log x^2 =$$
$$| x | =$$

The reader may use tables to verify

$$x \cong \pm 1.2.$$

Whether or not interpolation is necessary depends upon the use of the final result. If the result need be accurate only to two significant digits, for example, then interpolation is unnecessary.

● **Example 3.** Equations of the following type occur in annuities, banking, and finance. In such equations the numbers involved are assumed to be exact.

Solve for n:

$$\frac{(1.05)^n - 1}{.05} = 24.$$

$$(1.05)^n - 1 = 24(.05)$$
$$= 1.2$$
$$(1.05)^n = 2.2$$
$$n \log 1.05 = \log 2.2$$
$$n(.0212) \cong .3424$$
$$n \cong \frac{.3424}{.0212}.$$

$$
\begin{array}{r}
\log .3424 \cong .5345 - 1 \\
(-) \quad \log .0212 \cong .3263 - 2 \\
\hline
\log n \cong .2082 + 1 \\
n \cong 16.15.
\end{array}
$$

● **Example 4.** Solve for t: $\log (3t + 1) - \log (2t + 3) = \log 2$.

If the logarithms exist, then this is equivalent to the equation

$$\log \left[\frac{3t + 1}{2t + 3} \right] = \log 2,$$

$$\frac{3t + 1}{2t + 3} = 2$$

$$3t + 1 = 4t + 6$$

$$t = -5.$$

Thus, *if* a solution exists, it must be $t = -5$. However, $\log (3t + 1)$ is *undefined* at $t = -5$. (Why?) Hence, the equation has *no solution*.

† Numbers are rounded off to four significant digits when four-place tables are used.

using our definition of a logarithm. This is another example of an extraneous value which is a root of the auxiliary equation, but not of the original. See Section 1–11.

● **Example 5.** (a) For what values of t is $\log \dfrac{3t+1}{2t+3}$ defined?

(b) For what values of t is $\log \left| \dfrac{3t+1}{2t+3} \right|$ defined?

(a) $\log \dfrac{3t+1}{2t+3}$ is defined if $\dfrac{3t+1}{2t+3} > 0$. This implies either

$$(1) \quad 3t+1 > 0 \quad \text{and} \quad 2t+3 > 0$$

or

$$(2) \quad 3t+1 < 0 \quad \text{and} \quad 2t+3 < 0.$$

Both of the inequalities (1) are satisfied if $t > -\frac{1}{3}$. Both of the inequalities (2) are satisfied if $t < -\frac{3}{2}$. Hence, $\log \dfrac{3t+1}{2t+3}$ is defined if *either* of the inequalities $t > -\frac{1}{3}$ or $t < -\frac{3}{2}$ is satisfied.

(b) $\log \left| \dfrac{3t+1}{2t+3} \right|$ is defined for all t excepting $t = -\frac{1}{3}$ and $t = -\frac{3}{2}$. (Why?)

● **Example 6.** Solve for t: $\log |3t+1| - \log |2t+3| = \log 2$.

If solutions of this equation exist, they are also solutions of

$$\log \left| \frac{3t+1}{2t+3} \right| = \log 2$$

$$\left| \frac{3t+1}{2t+3} \right| = 2$$

$$\frac{3t+1}{2t+3} = \pm 2.$$

The last two equations have solutions $t = -5$ and $t = -1$, both of which are solutions of the original equation, as can be seen by direct substitution.

PROBLEM SET 9–1

In Problems 1 to 18, solve the given equations.

1. $9^{2x} = 321$. **2.** $2^x = 65$. **3.** $4^x = \frac{1}{32}$. **4.** $(1.3)^x = 54$.
5. $2x^{15} = 1878$. **6.** $(4.69)^{3x} = 11$. **7.** $(2.1)^x = 1765$. **8.** $(2.3)^{-x^2} = .0018$.
9. $x^5 = 4\pi$. Obtain x accurate to two significant digits.

10. $\log \sqrt{x(3x-5)} = 1.$ **11.** $\log (x^2 - 3x) = 3.$ **12.** $31^{x^2} = 149$

13. $\dfrac{(1.02)^{3n} - 1}{.02} = 24.$ **14.** $\dfrac{(1.07)^k - 1}{.07} = 5000.$

15. $\log (2t + 4) - \log (3t + 1) = \log 6.$

16. $\log (2t + 3) + \log (4t - 1) = 2 \log 3.$

17. $\log (5x + 7) - \log 3x = 2.$ **18.** $\log (17x + 2) - 2 \log x = 1.$

19. (a) For what domain of x values is $\log \left(\dfrac{2x + 4}{3x}\right)$ defined? (b) For wha domain of x values is the logarithm positive?

20. For what values of x, if any, are $2 \log x$ and $\log (x^2)$ not equivalent

21. Money invested at i percent interest, compounded annually, increases according to the law $A = P(1 + i/100)^n$, where A is the amount accumulated after n years on an initial investment of P dollars. How many years will it take \$1 to grow to \$2 at 5 percent, compounded annually?

22. How long will it take \$$N$ to double itself at 4 percent, compounded annually?

23. A man invests \$1000 when his son is born. If the investment earns 6 percent, compounded annually, how much will it be worth when his son is ready for college at the age of 18?

24. P dollars, invested at interest of r percent per year compounded k times per year, increases in n years according to the law $A = P[1 + r/(100k)]^{nk}$. Solve Problem 23 if money is at 8 percent, compounded quarterly.

25. A certain piece of real estate was purchased for \$24 about 325 years ago. If this money had been invested at 12 percent interest, compounded annually [a not unusual rate at that time] to what amount would it have grown?

26. Recently P. A. Rees discovered that an ancestor of his had forgotten a \$100 deposit made in The Bank of Hamilton in the year 1780. If this sum had earned 6 percent interest, compounded annually during the intervening period, about how much could P. A. Rees expect to withdraw this year? The result of this problem may indicate why banks do not pay interest on dormant accounts — that is, on accounts on which no deposit or withdrawal has been made in 10 years.

27. The adiabatic law for confined gas states $pV^{1.4} = 976$, where p is pressure in centimeters of mercury and V is volume in cubic centimeters. (a) Find the pressure when the volume is 100 cc. (b) Find the volume when the pressure is 800 cm of mercury.

28. If $y = x^x$, find y when $x = 3.1$. Make a rough sketch of $y = x^x$ and locate the point under discussion.

29. (a) If $x = 10^{\log 17.4}$, find x. (b) If $x = 10^{\log R}$, find x in terms of R if possible.

30. Sketch $y = \log x$, $y = \log |x|$, and $y = \frac{1}{2} \log x^2$ on the same set of axes.

31. (a) Find $\log_2 10$. [HINT: Solve $2^x = 10$ for x.]
(b) Find $\log_{10} 2$. (c) How are the results of (a) and (b) related? (d) Show that

$$\log_b N = (\log_{10} N)/\log_{10} b.$$

[HINT: Let $x = \log_b N$. Solve $b^x = N$ for x.]

9–2. The number e. If asked to guess the value of

$$\lim_{z \to 0} (1 + z)^{1/z}$$

a student might feel that the limit did not exist, or he might feel that the limit was 1. Neither of these hunches is correct. The limit is a number between 2 and 3. This number is of such great importance in science that a special letter, e, is usually used to denote it:

$$\lim_{z \to 0} (1 + z)^{1/z} = e \cong 2.718 \cdots.$$

The idea of using a letter to represent a number is not new to the reader. For example, the number $\pi \cong 3.14 \cdots$ is denoted by its special letter. The number e, like the number π, is not a rational number. No decimal, no matter how long, can ever be more than an approximation of e. The reader will show in his calculus course that

$$\lim_{z \to 0} (1 + z)^{1/z} = e \cong 2.718 \cdots.$$

Additional discussion of the number e appears in Section 11–4.

9–3. Logarithms to the base e. When $\log_b N = x$ was defined to mean $b^x = N$, no value of the base b was specified. Unlikely as it seems, the use of the number $e = 2.7182818 \cdots$ as the base has many advantages in later work. For example, if $y = \log_e x$, then $dy/dx = 1/x$, but if $y = \log_{10} x$, then $\dfrac{dy}{dx} = \dfrac{\log_{10} e}{x}$. Since the latter is more complicated, and still requires the introduction of the number e, it is customary, when calculus is involved, to use logarithms to the base e. In this text, as in many other books, the abbreviation **ln x** is used in place of $\log_e x$. The symbol **ln x** is read "natural (or Napierian) logarithm of x" or "the logarithm of x to the base e."

Handbooks contain tables of logarithms to the base e. Since the characteristic cannot be determined by the method used for $\log_{10} x$, the natural logarithm tables list characteristics as well as mantissas. If $\ln N = \log_e N$ is needed for some N not in the table, we express N as $N = k \cdot 10^n$ where $\ln k$ is in the table. Then $\ln N = \ln (k \cdot 10^n) = \ln k + n \ln 10$.

● **Example 1.** Find ln 296.

If tables extensive enough to include this number are available, it may be read from the tables. If not, proceed as follows:

$$
\begin{aligned}
\ln 296 &= \ln (2.96 \times 10^2) \\
&= \ln 2.96 + 2 \ln 10 \\
&= 1.08519 + 2(2.30259) \\
&= 5.69037.
\end{aligned}
$$

Earlier in this chapter we solved equations of the type $4^x = 7$ using logarithms. A similar technique may be used to convert logarithms from one base to another base.

● **Example 2.** Convert $\log_{10} x$ to a function involving natural logarithms. Let $R = \log_{10} x$ then $10^R = x$.

Taking the natural logarithms of both members, we have

$$
\begin{aligned}
\ln 10^R &= \ln x \\
R \ln 10 &= \ln x \\
R &= \frac{\ln x}{\ln 10} \cong \frac{\ln x}{2.30259}.
\end{aligned}
$$

Hence,

$$
\log_{10} x = \frac{\ln x}{\ln 10} \cong \frac{\ln x}{2.30259}.
$$

The number $\dfrac{1}{\ln 10} \cong \dfrac{1}{2.30259} \cong .43429$ occurs so frequently that the letter μ is sometimes used to designate it. The reader should show that $\mu = \log_{10} e$.

● **Example 3.** Without using tables obtain a *rough* approximation of the following values (a) ln 0.5; (b) ln 37; (c) ln 215.

(a) If $R = \ln 0.5$
$e^R = \frac{1}{2}$.

For a rough approximation we use $e \cong 3^-$. Hence,
$(3^-)^R = \frac{1}{2}$.

If $R = 0$, $3^0 = 1 > \frac{1}{2}$. If $R = -1$, $3^{-1} = \frac{1}{3} < \frac{1}{2}$.

Hence, ln .5 appears to lie between 0 and -1, that is, $-1 < \ln 0.5 < 0$.

(b) If $R = \ln 37$
$e^R = 37$.

Since $3^3 = 27 < 37$ and $3^4 = 81 > 37$, we conclude that ln 37 is close to 3.

(c) If $R = \ln 215$
$e^R = 215$.

Since $3^4 = 81 < 215$, and $3^5 = 243 > 215$, we conclude that $\ln 215$ is close to 5. The reader may feel that $4 < \ln 215 < 5$, but this is not the case. Since $e \cong 2.718 < 3$, our estimate may be somewhat low. Actually $\ln 215 = 5.3706$, so our estimate of "close to 5" is still valid.

Estimates of the type given in Example 3 are not used to replace the more accurate results obtained by tabular computation, but rather as a quick approximate check on the reasonableness of the result. Many errors made in computation or in use of tables can be detected by an alert person who will apply the test, "Is it reasonable?"

● **Example 4.** An engineer notices that $\log_e 56.1$ has been replaced by the decimal 6.32972 in part of a computation. Since the final result of the computation does not agree with his experience, he questions the value used. Without using tables, show that $\ln 56.1 \neq 6.32972$.

If $\ln 56.1 = R$, then $e^R = 56.1$. Since $3^3 = 27$ and $3^4 = 81$, we expect $\ln 56.1$ to be close to 4, not 6.

The reader may be interested in finding N such that $\ln N = 6.32972$ to discover why this error was made.

● **Example 5.** Sketch the curve $y = e^{-x^2}$.

As $x \nearrow L^+$, $y \searrow 0^+$.
$x \searrow L^-$, $y \searrow 0^+$.
When $x = 0$, $y = 1$.

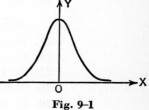

Fig. 9–1

● **Example 6.** Sketch $y = \log_{10} x$, $y = \ln x$, and $y = \log_2 x$.

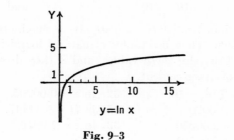

Fig. 9–2   Fig. 9–3   Fig. 9–4

PROBLEM SET 9–3

1. In the formula $e = \lim_{z \to 0} (1 + z)^{1/z}$ take $z = 1$, $\frac{1}{5}$, $\frac{1}{10}$, $\frac{1}{100}$ to obtain approximations of the number e. Logarithms may be used to perform the more difficult computations.

2. Which is larger, π or e?

3. Obtain a decimal approximation of $(e - \pi)^2$.

4. If e is used as the base of a system of logarithms in place of 10, use the definition of a logarithm to determine the value of $\log_e 1$.

5. If e is used as the base of a system of logarithms, determine the value of N such that $\log_e N = 1$.

6. Show that the method used to determine the characteristic of $\log_{10} x$ is not valid for $\log_e x$.

In Problems 7 to 10 obtain rough approximations without using tables.

7. (a) $\ln 17$.   (b) $\log_e 5$.   (c) $\ln 23.7$.

8. (a) $\ln .002$.   (b) $\log_e 1.42$.   (c) $\log_e 3760$.

9. (a) $\ln 14.2$.   (b) $\ln 13.4$.   (c) $\log_e 20.6$.

10. (a) $\ln .014$.   (b) $\ln 2.41$.   (c) $\ln .00213$.

In Problems 11 to 20 give a rough approximation of the indicated logarithm. Then use tables to obtain it with more accuracy and compare your estimate. If they do not agree, try to determine the cause of disagreement.

11. $\ln 13.9$.   **12.** $\ln 139$.   **13.** $\ln .139$.   **14.** $\log_e 346$.   **15.** $\log_e 17600$.

16. $\ln 4.42$.   **17.** $\ln .84$.   **18.** $\ln 36.5$.   **19.** $\log_e 4.6$.   **20.** $\ln .0057$.

In Problems 21 to 25 express the given number as a power of e.

21. $10^{1.3}$.   **22.** $4^{3.6}$.   **23.** $3(10^{15.1})$.   **24.** $4^{6.18}$.   **25.** $3^{-74.6}$.

26. Graph $y = \log_{10} x$ and $y = \ln x$ on the same set of axes.

27. Sketch $y = e^x$ and $y = 10^x$ on the same set of axes.

28. Sketch $y = e^x + e^{-x}$.   **29.** Sketch $y = e^x - e^{-x}$.

30. Compare the sketches of

$$y = 10^x - 10^{-x}, \quad y = e^x - e^{-x}, \quad \text{and} \quad y = 2^x - 2^{-x}.$$

In each of Problems 31 to 40, give a rough approximation of the value of the unknown. Then use tables of natural logarithms to obtain it with more accuracy. Compare these values, and if they do not agree, try to determine the cause of disagreement.

31. $\ln x = 7.96 - 10$.   **32.** $\ln z = 0.00995$.   **33.** $\ln 2t = 1.00063$.

34. $\ln y = 4.0000$.   **35.** $\ln 7t = 6.11147$.   **36.** $\ln t = 2.20937$.

37. $\ln 5x = 2.30259$.   **38.** $\ln z = 7.0076$.   **39.** $\ln t^2 = 12.8269$.

40. $\ln 7t^3 = 1.94591$.

9–4. Derivatives of logarithmic and exponential functions. We have already mentioned that $\dfrac{d \ln_e x}{dx} = \dfrac{1}{x}$ and $\dfrac{d \log_{10} x}{dx} = \dfrac{1}{x} \cdot \log_{10} e$ in Section 9–3. The proofs of these important formulas are given in Examples 1 and 2. We shall need the following lemma in this proof:

$$\lim_{\Delta x \to 0} \ln \left[\left(1 + \frac{\Delta x}{x}\right)^{x/\Delta x}\right] = \lim_{t \to 0} \ln \left[(1 + t)^{1/t}\right] \tag{9.1}$$

$$= \ln \left[\lim_{t \to 0} (1 + t)^{1/t}\right] = \ln (e) = 1.$$

The proof that $\lim\limits_{t\to 0} \ln f(t) = \ln \lim\limits_{t\to 0} f(t)$ is not given here. The remainder of the proof only requires the substitution $t = \dfrac{\Delta x}{x}$ and the definition of e.

● **Example 1.** By definition

$$\frac{d \ln x}{dx} \equiv \lim_{\Delta x \to 0} \frac{\ln (x + \Delta x) - \ln (x)}{\Delta x}$$

$$= \lim_{\Delta x \to 0} \left[\frac{1}{\Delta x} \ln \frac{x + \Delta x}{x} \right]$$

$$= \lim_{\Delta x \to 0} \left[\frac{1}{\Delta x} \ln \left(1 + \frac{\Delta x}{x} \right) \right]$$

Upon dividing and multiplying by x, this becomes

$$= \lim_{\Delta x \to 0} \left[\frac{1}{x} \cdot \frac{x}{\Delta x} \ln \left(1 + \frac{\Delta x}{x} \right) \right]$$

$$= \lim_{\Delta x \to 0} \left[\frac{1}{x} \cdot \ln \left[\left(1 + \frac{\Delta x}{x} \right)^{x/\Delta x} \right] \right]$$

Using $\lim\limits_{t\to 0} \dfrac{1}{x} \cdot f(t) = \dfrac{1}{x} [\lim\limits_{t\to 0} f(t)]$, with $t = \dfrac{\Delta x}{x}$, and $f(t) = \ln \left[(1 + t)^{1/t} \right]$,

$$\frac{d \ln x}{dx} = \frac{1}{x} \left[\lim_{\Delta x \to 0} \ln \left[\left(1 + \frac{\Delta x}{x} \right)^{x/\Delta x} \right] \right]$$

Now, taking the big step using equation 9.1, namely, that

$$\lim_{t\to 0} [\ln f(t)] = \ln [\lim_{t\to 0} f(t)] = \ln e, \quad \text{one obtains}$$

$$\frac{d \ln x}{dx} = \frac{1}{x} \ln e.$$

Hence, since $\ln e = 1$, we have, as desired,

$$\frac{d \ln x}{dx} = \frac{1}{x}.$$

More generally,

Theorem 1. $\dfrac{d \ln u}{dx} = \dfrac{1}{u} \dfrac{du}{dx}$ since $\dfrac{d \ln u}{dx} = \dfrac{d \ln u}{du} \cdot \dfrac{du}{dx} = \dfrac{1}{u} \dfrac{du}{dx}.$

Using this, it is fairly simple to obtain other derivatives.

● **Example 2.** If $y = \log_{10} x$

$$10^y = x$$
$$\ln [10^y] = \ln x$$
$$y \cdot (\ln 10) = \ln x$$
$$y = \frac{1}{\ln 10} \cdot \ln x$$

Since ln 10 *is a constant*, upon differentiating one obtains

$$\frac{dy}{dx} = \frac{1}{\ln 10} \frac{1}{x}.$$

As an exercise in exponential manipulation, the reader should verify that $\frac{1}{\ln 10} = \log_{10} e$ and hence that

$$\frac{d (\log_{10} x)}{dx} = \frac{\log_{10} e}{x}.$$

More generally,

Theorem 2. $\dfrac{d (\log_{10} u)}{dx} = \dfrac{\log_{10} e}{u} \dfrac{du}{dx}.$

● *Example 3.* If $y = e^x$, by definition of ln we have

$$\ln y = x;$$

upon differentiating, one obtains

$$\frac{1}{y} \frac{dy}{dx} = 1$$

or

$$\frac{dy}{dx} = y.$$

Hence

$$\frac{d\, e^x}{dx} = e^x.$$

More generally,

Theorem 3. $\dfrac{d\, e^u}{dx} = e^u \dfrac{du}{dx}.$

In a similar fashion,

● *Example 4.* $y = a^x$.

$$\ln y = \ln (a^x) = x \ln a$$
$$\frac{1}{y} \frac{dy}{dx} = \ln a$$
$$\frac{dy}{dx} = y \cdot \ln a$$

or

$$\frac{d\, a^x}{dx} = a^x \cdot \ln a$$

which generalizes to

Theorem 4. $\dfrac{d\, a^u}{dx} = a^u \cdot \ln a \cdot \dfrac{du}{dx}.$

PROBLEM SET 9-4

1. Derive the formula for $\dfrac{d \ln x}{dx}$ without looking back at the book's derivation. If it should be necessary to look back, however, then also derive the formula for $\dfrac{d \log_{10} x}{dx}$ directly from the definition

$$\lim_{\Delta x \to 0} \frac{\log_{10} (x + \Delta x) - \log_{10} (x)}{\Delta x}.$$

2. Derive the formula for $\dfrac{d\,e^x}{dx}$ without looking back at Section 9–4; if you need to look back, then also derive formulas for $\dfrac{d\,e^u}{dx}$ and $\dfrac{d\,a^x}{dx}$ to give yourself extra practice.

*3. In radioactive decay, it is known that the time rate of decomposition, $\dfrac{du}{dt}$, is proportional to the amount u of radium present at time t, that is, that $\dfrac{du}{dt} = ku$. Solve the differential equation $\dfrac{du}{dt} = k \cdot u$ recalling that $u = u(t)$ is a function of t and k is a constant. Transform the given equation to the form $\dfrac{1}{u}\dfrac{du}{dt} = k$. Now can you find functions $W(t)$ and $V(t)$ such that $\dfrac{d\,W(t)}{dt} = \dfrac{1}{u}\dfrac{du}{dt}$ and $\dfrac{d\,V(t)}{dt} = k$? If so, you can solve the given differential equation, and simplify the result to

$$u = e^{kt + k_2}$$

where k_2 is an arbitrary constant.

4. Use $\dfrac{d \ln x}{dx} = \dfrac{1}{x}$ and the facts that $\ln x$ is undefined if $x \le 0$ and that $\ln 1 = 0$ to sketch $y = \ln x$.

5. Both $y = \ln x$ and $y = \log_{10} x$ pass through the point $(1, 0)$. Using derivatives, show which curve is steeper:
(a) If $0 < x < 1$.
(b) If $1 < x$.

Sketch each curve in a different color on the same set of axes.

6. Derive a formula for $\dfrac{d \log_2 x}{dx}$.

7. Determine a point at which the line tangent to $y = e^x$
(a) Is parallel to the line $3x - 2y = 5$.
(b) Is parallel to the line $x - 5y = 4$.

8. If the curves $y = \ln x$ and $y = 10^{-x}$ cross, determine the point at which they cross. Otherwise prove they do not cross.

*9. Determine the slope of $y = \ln x$ and of $y = \log_{10} x$ at that point where each crosses $x = 5$. Sketch the loci.

10. Determine the slopes of $y = \ln x$, $y = e^x$, $y = 10^x$ and $y = \log_{10} x$ at the points where each crosses $x = \frac{1}{2}$. Sketch all the curves.

11. Prove Theorems 1 to 4 of this section directly.

9-5. Hyperbolic functions. The functions

$$\tfrac{1}{2}(e^x - e^{-x}) \quad \text{and} \quad \tfrac{1}{2}(e^x + e^{-x})$$

occur so often in applied mathematics that they have been given special names.

$$\tfrac{1}{2}(e^x - e^{-x}) = \sinh x = \text{the } \textbf{hyperbolic sine} \text{ of } x.$$
$$\tfrac{1}{2}(e^x + e^{-x}) = \cosh x = \text{the } \textbf{hyperbolic cosine} \text{ of } x.$$
$$\frac{e^x - e^{-x}}{e^x + e^{-x}} = \tanh x = \text{the } \textbf{hyperbolic tangent} \text{ of } x.$$

The curve $y = \cosh x$ is a **catenary**. It is similar to the curve in which a string or telephone wire hangs when suspended between two supports.

● *Example 1.* Verify the identity: $\cosh^2 x - \sinh^2 x = 1$.

$$\cosh^2 x - \sinh^2 x = \left(\frac{e^x + e^{-x}}{2}\right)^2 - \left(\frac{e^x - e^{-x}}{2}\right)^2 = \frac{e^{2x} + 2 + e^{-2x}}{4} - \frac{e^{2x} - 2 + e^{-2x}}{4} = 1.$$

PROBLEM SET 9-5

1. Sketch $y = \sinh x$.   2. Sketch $y = \cosh x$.

3. Sketch $y = \tanh x$.   (Note that $-1 < \tanh x < 1$.)

In Problems 4 to 10 prove the stated identities.

4. $\sinh(-x) = -\sinh x$.   5. $\cosh(-x) = \cosh x$.

6. $\tanh(-x) = -\tanh x$.   7. $1 - \tanh^2 x = \operatorname{sech}^2 x$.

8. $\sinh(x + y) = \sinh x \cosh y + \cosh x \sinh y$.

9. $\cosh(x + y) = \cosh x \cosh y + \sinh x \sinh y$.

10. $\sinh^2(x/2) = \tfrac{1}{2}(\cosh x - 1)$.

11. Show that $\dfrac{d \sinh x}{dx} = \cosh x$.   Also find $\dfrac{d}{dx} \sinh(-17x)$.

2. Show that $\dfrac{d \cosh x}{dx} = \sinh x$. Also find $\dfrac{d}{dx} \cosh 3x$.

3. Find $\dfrac{d}{dx} \tanh x$ in two ways.

9–6. Self test.

Record time.

1. Find x: (a) $x = \log_4 32$, (b) $\log_{27} x = -\frac{4}{3}$, (c) $\log_x \sqrt{125} = \frac{3}{2}$.

2. Sketch: $y = 3^x$.

3. Express as a sum of logarithms: $\ln \left[\dfrac{(4x + 7)^3 \sqrt{2x^2 + 1}}{5(2x^2 + 1)^5} \right].$

4. Use four-place common logarithms and compute to an appropriate number of significant figures:

   (a) $Q = \dfrac{(283)(.00352)}{.0876}$, (b) $R = \sqrt[3]{.05766}$, (c) $T = \dfrac{.24357}{\sqrt[3]{.0087534}}$.

5. Solve for x: $(2.1)^x = 1765$.

6. For what values of x is $\log \dfrac{2x - 3}{3x - 1}$ defined?

7. How long will it take for \$100 to double at 4% compounded annually? Solve using logarithms.

8. Find: (a) $\ln 2.87$, (b) $\ln 0.0287$, (c) $\ln 2870$, (d) $\dfrac{d\left[\ln (4x^2 - 3)\right]}{dx}$.

9. Determine a point at which the curves $y = 3^{-x}$ and $y = \log_{10} x$ intersect. (Use tables.)

10. Determine the slope of the line tangent to $y = 8^x$ at the point $(3, 512)$.
    Compare your time with the times of your classmates.

*9–7. Falling bodies with air resistance. In earlier discussions of falling objects, air resistance was neglected. This assumption works well for short falls of dense objects; it does not apply to objects falling from great heights such as rain, bombs, or a man on a parachute. In this case it can be shown, approximately, that

$$s = \frac{V^2}{g} \log_e \cosh \frac{gt}{V} \qquad \text{and} \qquad v = V \tanh \frac{gt}{V},$$

where g is the acceleration of gravity and V is a constant which depends upon the density of the air and the shape and density of the body.

Since $\tanh t$ approaches 1 as t increases, it will be noted that the velocity $v = V \tanh (gt/V)$ approaches a constant limiting value V. This quantity V is called the **terminal velocity** of the object.

The techniques developed for falling bodies without air resistance are still used if air resistance is considered. The resulting equations involve exponential functions rather than linear and quadratic equations, and the arithmetic of the solution is more cumbersome.

PROBLEM SET 9-7

In the following problems take $g = 32$.

1. If the terminal velocity of an object is $V = 200$ ft per sec, how far will the object fall in 5 sec? In 10 sec? In 30 sec?
2. Neglecting air resistance, compute how far an object would fall in 5 sec. In 10 sec. In 30 sec.
3. Compare the results of Problems 1 and 2.

*9–8. Semilogarithmic paper. The markings on the vertical axis (ordinates) on semilogarithmic paper correspond to logarithms of numbers rather than numbers themselves. If one considers the **distance** from the ordinate marked 1 (bottom of paper) to the ordinate marked 10 to be one unit (log 1 = 0, log 10 = 1), then the distance to the ordinate marked 2 is log 2 ≅ .301 unit, while the distance to the ordinate marked 8.5 is log 8.5 ≅ .906 unit. The distance between ordinates of successive integral powers of 10 is called a **cycle.** This paper has many practical uses. We shall study one of them in the next section, and others in Chapter 23.

PROBLEM SET 9-8

Locate the following points on a sheet of three-cycle semilogarithmic paper in which the x units run from 0 to 1, and y units run from 1 to 1000.

1. (0, 80), (0.3, 75), (0.7, 115). 2. (0, 960), (0.4, 871), (0.9, 1.6).
3. (0.4, 431), (0.7, 15), (0.9, 98). 4. (1, 15), (1, 150), (1, 1.5).
5. Construct a sheet of one-cycle semilogarithmic paper with the integral ordinates located. Locate and label a few points.

*9–9. Nomograms. In various laboratories and in industry the same general types of problems must be solved repeatedly. Such computation takes time from more profitable investigation. Graphical methods or nomograms can be used to reduce the labor involved. In fact, a mathematically trained worker often devises a nomogram to aid in an algebraic or arithmetic computation. The solution by nomogram is then turned over to a relatively untrained worker who can "run out the answers."

The simplest nomograms are those used for converting from one scale of notation to another. They are made by placing two scales, one on each side of a common line. The scales are adjusted for length of unit and position so that readings correspond. A ruler which is marked both in inches and in centimeters is a simple nomogram.

• **Example 1.** Construct a nomogram which will convert temperature reading from centigrade T_c to Fahrenheit T_f. A formula connecting these variables is $T_f = \frac{9}{5}T_c + 32$.

From this we see that each increase of 1 unit of the T_c scale corresponds to an increase of $\frac{9}{5}$ units on the T_f scale. The 0 point of T_c scale [written 0_c] corresponds to 32_f. Using this data we construct the nomogram, Figure 9–5.

This nomogram saves time if many conversions must be made. It also reduces the "opportunity for error" — an important factor.

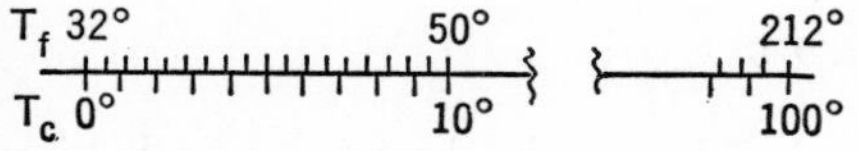

Fig. 9–5

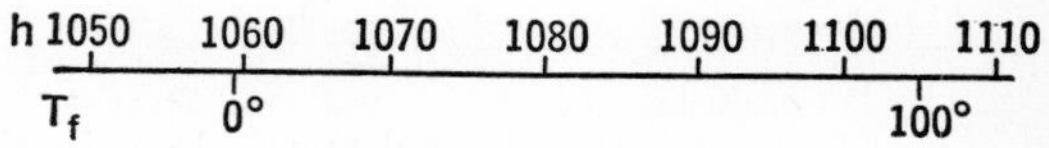

Fig. 9–6

• **Example 2.** Construct a nomogram for the formula $h = 1059 + 0.45T_f$, which gives the heat content h in BTU per pound of either saturated or superheated steam at a temperature $T_f°$ Fahrenheit.

Each unit on the T scale corresponds to .45 unit on the h scale and 0_T corresponds to 1059. Using these data we construct the nomogram, Figure 9–6.

Example 3. Make a nomogram which will convert hydrogen ion concentration to pH values (see Problem 11, Set 8–7).

$$(p\text{H}) = \log \frac{1}{(\text{H}^+)} = - \log (\text{H}^+).$$

Since the ordinates of a sheet of semilogarithmic paper are measured in logarithmic units (see Section 9–8), we use a logarithmic scale against a uniform scale. Some varieties of semilogarithmic paper already have a uniform scale indicated. On others a uniform scale may be constructed by dividing the length of each cycle into equal divisions. The nomogram below uses three-cycle paper and ranges from pH4 to pH7. A nomogram of greater range may be constructed by pasting several logarithmic scales together.

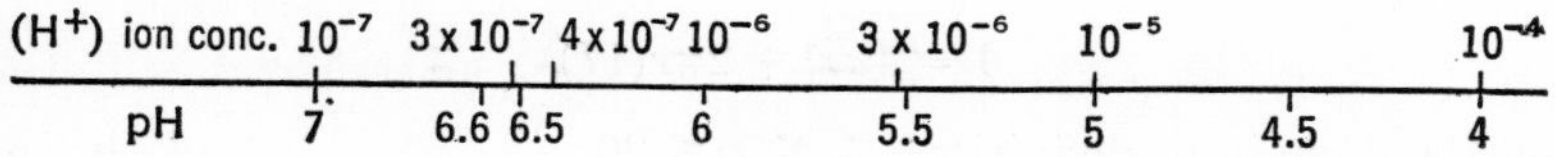

Fig. 9–7

Example 4. Construct a nomogram to evaluate $K = f(A) = A^{\frac{3}{2}}$. Also devise a method for evaluating $A = t^2$ and $K = t^3$.

If $K = A^{\frac{3}{2}}$, then $K^2 = A^3$ and $2 \log K = 3 \log A$. If we use a logarithmic scale, then two K-cycles (*not* units) must equal three A-cycles. This may be obtained by placing a sheet of two-cycle (5-in. cycle) semilogarithmic paper next to a sheet of three-cycle ($3\frac{1}{3}$-in. cycle) semi-logarithmic paper.

By placing a single cycle (10-in. cycle) t scale below these we obtain nomograms to evaluate the functions $A = t^2$ and $K = t^3$.

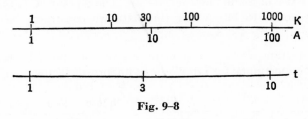

Fig. 9–8

It is hoped that when, in the course of his work, the reader finds himself doing many computations of the same type, he will recall the idea of a nomogram and either construct a nomogram or have one constructed to aid him. Several books on the construction of nomograms and alignment charts have been published. The complexity of problems solvable using nomograms seems almost unlimited.

PROBLEM SET 9–9

1. Use the nomogram of the text to determine $5^{\frac{3}{2}}$ and $9^{\frac{3}{2}}$.
2. Use the nomogram of the text to evaluate $4^{\frac{3}{2}}$, 7^3.
3. Devise a nomogram which will give the area of a circle as a function of its diameter.
4. Determine the temperature in degrees Centigrade corresponding to 54° F. Do this by nomogram and by computation and compare the work.
5. What Fahrenheit temperature corresponds to 68° C?
6. Construct a nomogram to evaluate the function $F = 10 - 4t/3$ which occurs in the study of the movement of particles through oil.
7. Construct a nomogram for the evaluation of the function

$$A = 4\pi r^2 + 2\pi r(17)$$

on the domain of definition $5 \leq r \leq 20$.

8. Construct a nomogram to evaluate $y = f(x) = 3x - 5$.
9. Construct a nomogram to evaluate $y = x^2 + 7$.
*10. Using a strip of two-cycle semilogarithmic paper and a compass to transfer distances, show that if the distance log 2 is added to the distance log 3, we obtain the distance log 6. Perform other additions and subtractions and show this is a convenient method of doing multiplication and division.

11. Examine the nomograms appearing in the April 1961 issue of the *Mathematical Log* and construct similar nomograms for use with your family.

12. Two sheets of semilogarithmic graph paper are available. Sheet A is two cycles per 10 in. Sheet B is five cycles per 10 in. A nomogram is constructed by placing the two scales side by side. Give an example of the type of equation for which such a nomogram would prove useful.

13. Construct and use the nomogram of Problem 12.

*9–10. An especially useful nomogram — the slide rule.† A logarithmic scale such as the ordinates of a sheet of semilogarithmic paper may be used to perform multiplication and division. The printed numbers on such a scale run 1, 2, 3, · · ·, 10, but the distances represented are

$$\log 1 = 0, \quad \log 2 \cong .30, \quad \log 3 \cong .48, \quad \cdots, \quad \log 10 = 1.$$

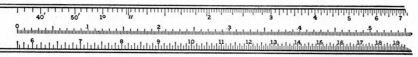

Courtesy Keuffel & Esser Co

Fig. 9–9.

If the distance corresponding to 3 is added to the distance corresponding to 2, we are adding $\log 2 + \log 3$ and should obtain log 6. (Try it.) In a similar fashion, if the distance corresponding to 2 is subtracted from the distance corresponding to 7, we obtain a distance corresponding to 3.5, since $\log 7 - \log 2 = \log \frac{7}{2} = \log 3.5$. The C and D scales of a slide rule provide convenient tools for carrying out these operations. The nomograms for squaring and cubing numbers constructed in Example 4, Section 9–9, are represented by the D, A, and K scales on a slide rule. Libraries and bookstores carry instruction manuals on the use of the slide rule.

In applied problems the use of logarithms or a slide rule will speed the solution. A problem involving moments of inertia which culminates in the solution of the equation, $x^5 = 4\pi$, would pose difficulty without logarithms.

† William Oughtred (1574–1660), an English minister, invented the circular and rectilinear slide rules. The circular rule was described in his *Circles of Proportion* (1632). Later he described his rectilinear rule in *An Addition to Circles of Proportion* (1633).

PROBLEM SET 9–10

1. Determine the dimensions of a 2-qt (115.5 cu in.) cylindrical can, having the least total surface area.

2. The material for the bottom of a 1000-gal (231,000/1728 cu ft) cylindrical tank costs twice as much per square foot as the material for the sides and top. Determine the dimensions of the most economical tank.

3. A formula for the approximate area of a segment of a circle (see any geometry text or your handbook for the definition of a segment) is

$$A = \frac{h^3}{2c} + \frac{2ch}{3},$$

where c is the length of the chord and h is the altitude of the segment. Use this formula to determine the area of a semicircle of radius 1. Would the three-place accuracy of a slide rule materially lower the accuracy of the result obtained using this approximate formula?

4. Clever use of judgment in slide-rule computation will improve the results. For example, show that more accurate decimal approximation of 265/233 is obtained if 32/233 is first computed by slide rule and then $265/233 = 1 + 32/233$ is used to obtain the approximation rather than dividing 265 by 233 on the slide rule.

5. A city needs 40,000,000 gal of water per 24 hours. Find the pumping capacity in cubic feet per second needed to supply this city if a safety capacity of one quarter the needs must be maintained.

6. 30,000 acres of irrigable land will be supplied by water from a canal. A yearly average of 3 cu ft of water per sq ft of land is required. Determine the needed capacity of the canal in cubic feet per second if the water is to be delivered uniformly during a 4-month irrigation season. There are 43,560 sq ft in an acre.

7. A box with a square base and open top is to be constructed to contain 2000 cu in. Find the dimensions of the box with the least surface area.

8. A cylindrical cistern with open top is designated to hold 1000 gal. If 1 gal = 231 cu in., determine the dimensions of the cistern having the least surface area.

9. If the bottom of the box of Problem 7 is to cost $1\frac{1}{2}$ times as much per unit area as the sides, determine the cheapest box.

10. Determine the volume of the largest box that can be made from a 9×12-in. sheet of metal by cutting out squares from the corners and turning up the edges. On what domain does the function you obtain have meaning in the problem?

Self test. See Section 9–6, page 209.

•••••••••••••••••••••

10–1. Sequences. In arranging a set of ten objects a first object may be chosen and called a_1. A second object may be chosen and named a_2, a third object a_3, and so on to the tenth object a_{10}. This sets up a correspondence between the ten objects and the ten integers $1, 2, 3, \cdots, 10$. Each object corresponds to one integer and each of the ten integers corresponds to exactly one object. A similar method may be applied to a set of n objects, for every positive integer n. In this case the "sequence" of symbol names of the objects is

$$a_1, a_2, \cdots, a_n. \tag{10.1}$$

The first object is represented by a_1, the second object by a_2, and so on to the nth object, represented by a_n. The three dots represent objects that are numbered but are not written. In the case of $a_1, a_2, \cdots, a_{10}$ the three dots represent $a_3, a_4, a_5, a_6, a_7, a_8, a_9$.

An array (10.1) of symbols is called a **sequence**. The symbols a_1, a_2, and so on are called the **terms or elements** of the sequence. The term a_i, where i may take any one of the values $1, 2, \cdots, n$, is the **typical or general term** of the sequence.

The notation

$$a_i, \quad (i = 1, 2, \cdots, n) \tag{10.2}$$

(read "a_i for i equals 1 to n") will be used to represent the sequence (10.1). The reader should note that a_i, $(i = 1, 2, \cdots, n)$ is a function of i where the domain of the variable i is the positive integers from 1 to n inclusive.

● **Example 1.** Write the first three terms and the fifteenth term of

$$a_i = 2i + 1, \quad (i = 1, 2, \cdots, 15).$$

$a_1 = 2(1)+1=3, \quad a_2 = 2(2)+1=5, \quad a_3 = 2(3)+1=7, \quad \cdots, \quad a_{15} = 2(15)+1=31.$

● **Example 2.** Write the first three terms of the sequence

$$a_i = (-1)^i \frac{3^{2i+1}}{i^2 + 1}, \quad (i = 1, 2, \cdots, n).$$

$a_1 = (-1)^1 \dfrac{3^{2+1}}{1^2+1} = -\dfrac{3^3}{2}, \quad a_2 = (-1)^2 \dfrac{3^{4+1}}{2^2+1} = \dfrac{3^5}{5}, \quad a_3 = (-1)^3 \dfrac{3^{6+1}}{3^2+1} = -\dfrac{3^7}{10}.$

● **Example 3.** Write the first three terms and the tenth term of the sequence

$a_x = x(x + 1), \quad (x = 1, 2, \cdots, n).$
$a_1 = 1(1 + 1) = 1 \cdot 2, \quad a_2 = 2(2 + 1) = 2 \cdot 3, \quad a_3 = 3(3 + 1) = 3 \cdot 4, \quad \cdots,$
$$a_{10} = 10(10 + 1) = 10 \cdot 11.$$

From the sequence a_i, $(i = 1, 2, \cdots, n)$ of elements a_i a new se quence of **partial sums** S_i, $(i = 1, 2, \cdots, n)$ can be formed where

$$S_1 = a_1, \quad S_2 = a_1 + a_2, \quad \cdots, \quad S_n = a_1 + a_2 + \cdots + a_n. \tag{10.3}$$

● *Example 4.* Form the sequence S_i, $(i = 1, 2, 3, 4, 5, \cdots, n)$ of partial sums from the sequence $a_i = 2i - 1$, $(i = 1, 2, \cdots, n)$.

$$S_1 = 1, \quad S_2 = 1 + 3 = 4, \quad S_3 = 1 + 3 + 5 = 9, \quad S_4 = 1 + 3 + 5 + 7 = 16$$
$$S_5 = 1 + 3 + 5 + 7 + 9 = 25, \quad \cdots, \quad S_n = 1 + 3 + 5 + \cdots + (2n - 1)$$

On examining this sequence one sees that $S_i = i^2$, $(i = 1, 2, 3, 4, 5)$ Does $S_i = i^2$ for $i = 1, 2, \cdots, n$? The answer to this question is given in the proof of Theorem 4, Section 10–2.

PROBLEM SET 10–1

In Problems 1 to 6 write the first five terms of the sequence.

1. $a_i = i$, $(i = 1, 2, \cdots, n)$.   **2.** $a_i = 3i$, $(i = 1, 2, \cdots, n)$.

3. $a_x = x(3x + 2)$, $(x = 1, 2, \cdots, n)$.

4. $a_k = \dfrac{(-1)^{k+1}}{2^{k+1}}$, $(k = 1, 2, \cdots, n)$.

5. $a_x = a_1 + (x - 1)d$, $(x = 1, 2, \cdots, n)$, where a_1 and d are constants.

6. $a_j = r^{j-1}a_1$, $(j = 1, 2, \cdots, n)$, where a_1 and r are constants.

In Problems 7 to 11 write the first five terms of the sequence S_i, $(i = 1, 2, \cdots, n)$ of partial sums formed from the given sequence.

7. $a_i = i$, $(i = 1, 2, \cdots, n)$.   **8.** $a_i = 2i$, $(i = 1, 2, \cdots, n)$.

9. $a_i = y^i$, $(i = 1, 2, \cdots, n)$.   **10.** $a_i = \dfrac{y^i}{2^i + 1}$, $(i = 1, 2, \cdots, n)$.

11. $p_i(x) = a_i x^i$, $(i = 0, 1, 2, \cdots, n)$.

12. Write the first six terms of $a_k = \begin{cases} \dfrac{1}{2k}, & \text{if } k \text{ is odd,} \\ 2^k, & \text{if } k \text{ is even.} \end{cases}$ $(k = 1, 2, 3, \cdots, n)$

10–2. A summation notation. In the preceding section we used $S_n = a_1 + a_2 + \cdots + a_n$. It is customary to write

$$\sum_{i=1}^{n} a_i = a_1 + a_2 + \cdots + a_n \tag{10.4}$$

(read $\displaystyle\sum_{i=1}^{n} a_i$ as "the summation of a_i from $i = 1$ to n"). The capita

Greek letter Σ corresponds to the capital Latin letter S (the first letter in the word sum). As illustrations, we see that

$$\sum_{i=1}^{4} i = 1 + 2 + 3 + 4 = 10, \quad \sum_{i=1}^{4} i^2 = 1^2 + 2^2 + 3^2 + 4^2 = 30.$$

The Σ notation is a shorthand method for indicating a sum. For example, the polynomial $a_0 + a_1x + a_2x^2 + \cdots + a_nx^n$ may be written briefly as $\sum_{i=0}^{n} a_ix^i$. Also, the S_i of the last section may be expressed in the form $S_i = \sum_{k=1}^{i} a_k = a_1 + a_2 + \cdots + a_i$. A study of the proofs of the following theorems and examples will help the reader gain familiarity with the Σ notation.

Theorem 1. If c is a constant, then $\sum_{i=1}^{n} c = nc$.

$$\sum_{i=1}^{n} c = c + c + \cdots + c = nc. \tag{10.5}$$

Theorem 2. $\sum_{i=1}^{n} cx_i = c \sum_{i=1}^{n} x_i$.

$$\sum_{i=1}^{n} cx_i = cx_1 + cx_2 + \cdots + cx_n = c(x_1 + x_2 + \cdots + x_n) = c \sum_{i=1}^{n} x_i. \tag{10.6}$$

Theorem 3. $\sum_{i=1}^{n} (x_i + y_i - z_i) = \sum_{i=1}^{n} x_i + \sum_{i=1}^{n} y_i - \sum_{i=1}^{n} z_i$.

$$\sum_{i=1}^{n} (x_i + y_i - z_i) = (x_1 + y_1 - z_1) + (x_2 + y_2 - z_2) + \cdots + (x_n + y_n - z_n)$$
$$= (x_1 + x_2 + \cdots + x_n) + (y_1 + y_2 + \cdots + y_n) - (z_1 + z_2 + \cdots + z_n)$$
$$= \sum_{i=1}^{n} x_i + \sum_{i=1}^{n} y_i - \sum_{i=1}^{n} z_i. \tag{10.7}$$

Theorem 4. The sum of the positive integers from 1 to n is $\sum_{x=1}^{n} x = \dfrac{n + n^2}{2}$.

The expression $\sum_{x=1}^{n} (x^2 - [x - 1]^2)$ will be expanded in two different ways, one of which contains the expression $\sum_{x=1}^{n} x$. The expansions are equated and the resulting equation is solved for $\sum_{x=1}^{n} x$. Now,

$$\sum_{x=1}^{n} (x^2 - [x - 1]^2) = (1^2 - 0^2) + (2^2 - 1^2) + (3^2 - 2^2) + \cdots$$
$$+ ([n - 1]^2 - [n - 2]^2) + (n^2 - [n - 1]^2) = n^2. \tag{10.8}$$

Also,

$$\sum_{x=1}^{n} (x^2 - [x-1]^2) = \sum_{x=1}^{n} (x^2 - x^2 + 2x - 1)$$

$$= \sum_{x=1}^{n} (2x - 1) \qquad (10.9)$$

$$= \sum_{x=1}^{n} (2x) - \sum_{x=1}^{n} 1$$

$$= 2 \sum_{x=1}^{n} (x) - n. \qquad (10.10)$$

From (10.8) and (10.10) we obtain $2 \sum_{x=1}^{n} (x) - n = n^2$, which has solution

$$\sum_{x=1}^{n} x = \frac{n + n^2}{2}.$$

Using (10.9) and (10.8) we find $\sum_{x=1}^{n} (2x - 1) = n^2$. This answers the question at the end of Example 4, Section 10–1.

● **Example 1.** Find $\sum_{x=1}^{5} (x^2 + 3)$.

$$\sum_{x=1}^{5} (x^2 + 3) = (1^2 + 3) + (2^2 + 3) + (3^2 + 3) + (4^2 + 3) + (5^2 + 3)$$
$$= 4 + 7 + 12 + 19 + 28 = 70.$$

● **Example 2.** Find $\sum_{k=0}^{3} \frac{\sqrt{4+k}}{2}$.

$$\sum_{k=0}^{3} \frac{\sqrt{4+k}}{2} = \frac{\sqrt{4+0}}{2} + \frac{\sqrt{4+1}}{2} + \frac{\sqrt{4+2}}{2} + \frac{\sqrt{4+3}}{2}$$
$$= \tfrac{1}{2}[2 + \sqrt{5} + \sqrt{6} + \sqrt{7}].$$

● **Example 3.** Find the smallest value of n such that $\sum_{i=1}^{n} i(i+1) > 15$.

$$\sum_{i=1}^{n} i(i+1) = 1 \cdot 2 + 2 \cdot 3 + 3 \cdot 4 + 4 \cdot 5 + \cdots + n(n+1).$$

For $n = 2$, $\sum_{i=1}^{2} i(i+1) = 1 \cdot 2 + 2 \cdot 3 = 8.$

For $n = 3$, $\sum_{i=1}^{3} i(i+1) = 1 \cdot 2 + 2 \cdot 3 + 3 \cdot 4 = 20.$

For $n < 3$ the sum is less than 15, while for $n \geq 3$ the sum is greater than 15. The desired value is $n = 3$.

Example 4. Find $\displaystyle\sum_{x=2}^{4} \frac{5 \cdot 4 \cdots (5 - x + 1)}{1 \cdot 2 \cdots x}$.

$\displaystyle\sum_{=2}^{4} \frac{5 \cdot 4 \cdots (5 - x + 1)}{1 \cdot 2 \cdots x} = \frac{5 \cdot 4}{1 \cdot 2} + \frac{5 \cdot 4 \cdot 3}{1 \cdot 2 \cdot 3} + \frac{5 \cdot 4 \cdot 3 \cdot 2}{1 \cdot 2 \cdot 3 \cdot 4} = 10 + 10 + 5 = 25.$

Example 5. Find $\displaystyle\sum_{i=1}^{4} (x_i - 2)^2$ where $x_1 = 1$, $x_2 = 5$, $x_3 = 0$, $x_4 = 8$.

$\displaystyle\sum_{=1}^{4} (x_i - 2)^2 = (1 - 2)^2 + (5 - 2)^2 + (0 - 2)^2 + (8 - 2)^2 = 1 + 9 + 4 + 36 = 50.$

PROBLEM SET 10-2

1. Find $\displaystyle\sum_{x=1}^{7} x^2$.

2. Find $\displaystyle\sum_{x=1}^{5} (2x + 1)$.

3. Find $\displaystyle\sum_{x=1}^{5} (2x) + 1$.   Compare with Problem 2.

4. Find $4 \displaystyle\sum_{n=1}^{3} n^2$.

5. Find $\displaystyle\sum_{k=0}^{4} (k + 1)^2$.

6. Find $\displaystyle\sum_{x=1}^{10} (x - 5)^2$.

7. Find $\displaystyle\sum_{x=1}^{5} (x - 3.5)^2$.

8. Find $\displaystyle\sum_{i=1}^{5} (x_i - 4)$, $x_1 = 1$, $x_2 = 7$, $x_3 = 4$, $x_4 = 2$, $x_5 = 6$.

9. Find $\displaystyle\sum_{i=1}^{5} x_i^2$ for x_i as given in Problem 8.

10. Find $\displaystyle\sum_{i=1}^{5} |x_i - 4|$ for x_i as given in Problem 8.

11. Find $\displaystyle\sum_{i=1}^{5} (x_i - 4)^2$ for x_i as given in Problem 8.

12. Find the smallest value of n such that $\displaystyle\sum_{i=1}^{n} i^2 > 20$.

13. Find the smallest value of n such that $\displaystyle\sum_{x=1}^{n} (x - 4)^2 > 30$.

14. For what values of n will $\displaystyle\sum_{x=1}^{n} x^2$ lie between 10 and 50?

15. Find $\displaystyle\sum_{x=1}^{4} \frac{4 \cdot 3 \cdots (4 - x + 1)}{1 \cdot 2 \cdots x}$.

16. Let $\displaystyle\bar{x} = \frac{1}{n}\sum_{i=1}^{n} x_i$ and prove $\displaystyle\sum_{i=1}^{n} (x_i - \bar{x}) = 0, \quad \frac{1}{n}\sum_{i=1}^{n} c x_i = c\bar{x}.$

17. Let $\displaystyle\bar{x} = \frac{1}{n} \cdot \sum_{i=1}^{n} x_i$ and prove $\displaystyle\frac{1}{n}\sum_{i=1}^{n} (x_i - \bar{x})^2 = \frac{1}{n}\sum_{i=1}^{n} x_i^2 - \bar{x}^2.$

10–3 Arithmetic sequences. From the sequence $a_i, \quad (i = 1, 2, \cdots, n$ one may define a sequence of differences

$$\Delta a_i = a_i - a_{i-1}, \quad (i = 2, 3, \cdots, n). \tag{10.11}$$

Then

$$a_i = a_{i-1} + \Delta a_i, \quad (i = 2, 3, \cdots, n).$$

The sequence $a_i, \quad (i = 1, 2, \cdots, n)$ is called an **arithmetic sequence** if, and only if, Δa_i is the same for all values of i. That is,

$$\Delta a_i = d, \quad (i = 2, 3, \cdots, n),$$

for a fixed quantity d. An arithmetic sequence may be written in the form

$$a_1, \quad a_2 = a_1 + d, \quad a_3 = a_1 + 2d, \quad \cdots, \quad a_n = a_1 + (n-1)d, \tag{10.12}$$

or

$$a_x = a_1 + (x - 1)d, \quad (x = 1, 2, \cdots, n). \tag{10.13}$$

In an arithmetic sequence, each term after the first is obtained by adding the common difference d to the preceding term. The formula for the **nth term** of the arithmetic sequence (10.12) is

$$a_n = a_1 + (n-1)d. \tag{10.14}$$

● **Example 1.** Find the 16th term of the arithmetic sequence 10, 7, 4, $\cdots$ Here, $d = 7 - 10 = -3, \quad a_1 = 10, \quad n = 16,$ and

$$a_{16} = 10 + (16 - 1)(-3) = -35.$$

Theorem 1. The sum of the first n terms of the arithmetic sequence

$$a_x = a_1 + (x - 1)d, \quad (x = 1, 2, \cdots, n)$$

is

$$S_n = \sum_{x=1}^{n} a_x = n\left[\frac{2a_1 + (n-1)d}{2}\right], \tag{10.15}$$

or

$$S_n = \sum_{x=1}^{n} a_x = n\left[\frac{a_1 + a_n}{2}\right]. \tag{10.16}$$

† Arithmetic sequences are sometimes called **arithmetic progressions**.

From (10.16) it is seen that the sum of the first n terms of the arithmetic sequence is equal to n multiplied by the average of the first and nth terms. A proof of this theorem using some results of Section 10–2 is given below. Another proof is given in Example 2.

$$S_n = \sum_{x=1}^{n} a_x = \sum_{x=1}^{n} (a_1 + [x-1]d)$$

$$= \sum_{x=1}^{n} a_1 + \sum_{x=1}^{n} (x-1)d \qquad \text{(Theorem 3, Section 10–2)}$$

$$= na_1 + \left(\sum_{x=1}^{n} x - \sum_{x=1}^{n} 1 \right) d \qquad \text{(Theorems 1, 2, 3, Section 10–2)}$$

$$= na_1 + \left(\frac{n+n^2}{2} - n \right) d \qquad \text{(Theorems 1, 4, Section 10–2)}$$

$$= n \left[\frac{2a_1 + (n-1)d}{2} \right]$$

$$= n \left[\frac{a_1 + [a_1 + (n-1)d]}{2} \right]$$

$$= n \left[\frac{a_1 + a_n}{2} \right].$$

● **Example 2.** A second proof of Theorem 1 is as follows:

$$S_n = [a_1] + [a_1 + d] + [a_1 + 2d] + \cdots + [a_1 + (n-2)d] \\ + [a_1 + (n-1)d].$$

Also,

$$S_n = [a_1 + (n-1)d] + [a_1 + (n-2)d] + [a_1 + (n-3)d] + \cdots \\ + [a_1 + d] + [a_1].$$

Add to obtain

$$2S_n = [2a_1 + (n-1)d] + [2a_1 + (n-1)d] + [2a_1 + (n-1)d] + \cdots \\ + [2a_1 + (n-1)d].$$

$$2S_n = n[2a_1 + (n-1)d],$$

$$S_n = n \left[\frac{2a_1 + (n-1)d}{2} \right] = n \left[\frac{a_1 + a_n}{2} \right].$$

● **Example 3.** Find the sum of the first 16 terms of the arithmetic sequence 10, 7, 4, $\cdots$.

$$a_1 = 10, \quad d = -3, \quad S_{16} = 16 \left[\frac{2(10) + (16-1)(-3)}{2} \right] = -200,$$

or use

$$a_{16} = -35 \quad \text{and} \quad S_{16} = 16 \left[\frac{10-35}{2} \right] = -200.$$

PROBLEM SET 10-3

1. Find the 50th term and the sum of the first 50 terms of the arithmetic sequence of positive odd integers 1, 3, 5, $\cdots$.
2. Find the 20th term and the sum of the first 20 terms of the arithmetic sequence $-6, -.5, 5.0, \cdots$.
3. Find the 25th term and the sum of the first 25 terms of the arithmetic sequence 7.0, 4.5, 2.0, $\cdots$.
4. The 5th term of an arithmetic sequence is -3. Its 21st term is -43. Find its 25th term.
5. The rungs of a ladder diminish uniformly from 28 in. in length at the base to 15 in. at the top. If there are 24 rungs, what is the total length of wood in them?
6. A man piles 150 logs in layers so that the top layer contains 3 logs and each lower layer has one more log than the layer above. How many logs will be in the lowest layer?
7. A city issued \$100,000 in 3 percent bonds to be retired beginning 1 year after issue in 25 annual installments of \$4,000.00 plus simple interest. Compute the total interest paid by the city.
8. If a mountain climber can ascend 1000 ft in the first hour and 100 ft less in each succeeding hour than in the preceding hour, how long will it take him to climb 5200 ft?
9. Write the first three terms of the sequence whose general term is $a_x = 1000 + (x-1)(.05)(1000)$, $(x = 1, 2, \cdots, n)$. Is this an arithmetic sequence?
10. If P dollars are invested for one year at a rate r percent, the interest earned will be $(r/100)P$ dollars. In computing simple interest, only the original principal invested earns interest. Write the general term which will give the total interest earned on an investment of P dollars at a rate r percent for n years. Is the sequence having this general term an arithmetic sequence?
11. Write the first three terms of the sequence

$$a_x = 3(x-5), \quad (x = 1, 2, \cdots, n).$$

Is the sequence arithmetic? Find $\sum_{x=1}^{8} a_x$, also $\sum_{x=1}^{n} a_x$.

12. Write the first four terms of the sequence $a_x = x^2$, $(x = 1, 2, \cdots, n)$. Is the sequence arithmetic?
13. Write the first eight terms of the sequence

$$a_x = 3x^2 - 2x + 1, \quad (x = 1, 2, \cdots, n).$$

Find Δa_i, $(i = 2, 3, \cdots, 8)$.
Define $\Delta^2 a_i = \Delta(\Delta a_i) = \Delta a_i - \Delta a_{i-1}$. Find $\Delta^2 a_i$, $(i = 3, 4, \cdots, 8)$.

14. A flat coil of rope has 12 complete turns. The inside turn is 4 in. long and the outside turn is 37 in. long. Find the length of the rope.

15. If you save 10¢ during the first week of January, 20¢ the second week, 30¢ the third week, and so on, how much will you save during the last (52nd) week of the year? What will be the total of the year's savings?

16. Find a formula for m such that a, m, b form an arithmetic sequence. The number m is called **the arithmetic mean** of a and b.

17. Find the arithmetic mean of -17 and 201.

10–4. Geometric sequences. The sequence a_i, $(i = 1, 2, \cdots, n)$ is called a **geometric sequence** † if, and only if, each term, after the first, is equal to the preceding term multiplied by a fixed quantity r; that is, if, and only if, $a_{i+1} = ra_i$, $(i = 1, 2, \cdots, n-1)$.

A geometric sequence may be written in the form

$$a_1, \quad a_2 = ra_1, \quad a_3 = ra_2 = r^2a_1, \quad \cdots, \quad a_n = ra_{n-1} = r^{n-1}a_1 \quad (10.17)$$

or

$$a_j = r^{j-1}a_1, \quad (j = 1, 2, \cdots, n). \quad (10.18)$$

The formula for the *nth term* of the geometric sequence is

$$a_n = r^{n-1}a_1. \quad (10.19)$$

● **Example 1.** Find the eighth term of the geometric sequence $108, -36, 12, \cdots$.

$$a_1 = 108, \quad r = -\tfrac{36}{108} = -\tfrac{1}{3}; \quad n = 8 \quad \text{and} \quad a_1 = (-\tfrac{1}{3})^{8-1}(108) = -\tfrac{4}{81}.$$

● **Example 2.** In problems involving compound interest the principal and accumulated interest both earn interest during the next period. Find the compound amount at the end of n interest periods if a principal P grows at the rate i percent for each interest period. The interest on the principal P for the first period is $P\left(\dfrac{i}{100}\right)$. The amount a_1 accumulated to the end of the first period is the principal P increased by the interest $\dfrac{Pi}{100}$, or

$$a_1 = P + \frac{Pi}{100} = P\left(1 + \frac{i}{100}\right).$$

The accumulation a_1 acts as the principal for the second period. The interest on a_1 for the second period is $a_1\left(\dfrac{i}{100}\right) = P\left(1 + \dfrac{i}{100}\right)\left(\dfrac{i}{100}\right)$. The amount a_2 accumulated to the end of the second period is the principal a_1 increased by the interest $a_1\left(\dfrac{i}{100}\right)$, or

$$a_2 = a_1 + a_1\left(\frac{i}{100}\right) = a_1\left(1 + \frac{i}{100}\right) = P\left(1 + \frac{i}{100}\right)\left(1 + \frac{i}{100}\right) = P\left(1 + \frac{i}{100}\right)^2.$$

† Geometric sequences are sometimes called **geometric progressions**.

Similarly, the amount a_3 accumulated to the end of the third period is

$$a_3 = a_2 + a_2\left(\frac{i}{100}\right) = a_2\left(1 + \frac{i}{100}\right) = P\left(1 + \frac{i}{100}\right)^2\left(1 + \frac{i}{100}\right) = P\left(1 + \frac{i}{100}\right)^3.$$

A repetition of the argument indicates that

$$a_n = a_{n-1} + a_{n-1}\left(\frac{i}{100}\right) = a_{n-1}\left(1 + \frac{i}{100}\right) = P\left(1 + \frac{i}{100}\right)^{n-1}\left(1 + \frac{i}{100}\right)$$

$$= P\left(1 + \frac{i}{100}\right)^n.$$

The sequence

$$a_1 = P\left(1 + \frac{i}{100}\right), \quad a_2 = P\left(1 + \frac{i}{100}\right)^2, \quad \cdots, \quad a_n = P\left(1 + \frac{i}{100}\right)^n, \quad (10.20)$$

or

$$a_j = P\left(1 + \frac{i}{100}\right)^j, \quad (j = 1, 2, \cdots, n), \quad (10.21)$$

is a geometric sequence with $r = 1 + i/100$. This sequence is used in solving compound-interest problems.

● **Example 3.** Find the amount due if $500 is loaned for 10 years at 6 percent compounded annually.

In this example $P = \$500$. The period is one year. The number of periods is $n = 10$. The interest rate for each period is i percent $= 6$ percent and $i = 6$. The amount a_{10} is given by

$$a_{10} = 500(1 + 6/100)^{10} = 500(1.06)^{10} \text{ dollars.}$$
$$\log a_{10} = \log 500 + 10 \log 1.06 = 2.69897 + 10(0.02531) = 2.95207.$$
$$a_{10} = \$895.50.$$

● **Example 4.** Find the compound amount at the end of t years, if the interest on a principal P is compounded k times per year, and the yearly interest rate is r percent.

In this example the period is $1/k$ year and the interest rate acting during each period is i percent $= r/k$ percent. The number of periods n in t years is $n = kt$. Consequently, the desired compound amount is

$$a_{kt} = P\left(1 + \frac{r}{100k}\right)^{kt}. \quad (10.22)$$

● **Example 5.** Find the compound amount due when $100 is invested for 10 years at 4 percent, compounded semiannually.

$$P = \$100, \quad t = 10, \quad k = 2, \quad kt = 20, \quad r = 4, \quad r/(100k) = .02 \quad \text{and}$$
$$a_{20} = 100(1 + .02)^{20} = 100(1.02)^{20} \text{ dollars.}$$

$$\log a_{20} = \log 100 + 20 \log 1.02 = 2.00000 + 20(0.00860) = 2.17200.$$
$$a_{20} = \$148.59.$$

Theorem 1. The sum of the first n terms of the geometric sequence

$$a_x = r^{x-1}a_1, \quad (x = 1, 2, \cdots, n)$$

is

$$S_n = \frac{a_1(r^n - 1)}{r - 1} = \frac{a_1(1 - r^n)}{1 - r} \tag{10.23}$$

or

$$S_n = \frac{ra_n - a_1}{r - 1}. \tag{10.24}$$

From

$$S_n = a_1 + ra_1 + \cdots + r^{n-1}a_1$$

and

$$rS_n = ra_1 + r^2a_1 + \cdots + r^{n-1}a_1 + r^na_1$$

one obtains, by subtraction,

$$rS_n - S_n = r^na_1 - a_1.$$

Solving the last equation for S_n, one finds

$$S_n = \frac{r^na_1 - a_1}{r - 1} = \frac{a_1(r^n - 1)}{r - 1} = \frac{ra_n - a_1}{r - 1}. \quad \text{[Apply (10.19).]}$$

● **Example 6.** Find the sum of the first eight terms of the geometric sequence $108, -36, 12, \cdots$.

$$a_1 = 108, \quad r = -\tfrac{1}{3}, \quad n = 8, \quad a_8 = -\tfrac{4}{81}$$

and

$$S_8 = \frac{108[(-\tfrac{1}{3})^8 - 1]}{-\tfrac{1}{3} - 1} = \frac{6560}{81},$$

or

$$S_8 = \frac{(-\tfrac{1}{3})(-\tfrac{4}{81}) - 108}{-\tfrac{1}{3} - 1} = \frac{6560}{81}.$$

● **Example 7.** A 16-qt radiator is filled with water. Four quarts are removed and replaced with antifreeze. If this is done four times, what portion of the original water is in the radiator?

After the first replacement, three quarters of the original water is in the radiator. If four replacements are made, then $(\tfrac{3}{4})^4 = \tfrac{81}{256}$ of the original water is in the radiator.

PROBLEM SET 10-4

1. Find the ninth term and the sum of the first nine terms of the geometric sequence $12, -6, 3, \cdots$.
2. A piece of real estate was bought for $30 in 1626. If the real estate doubles in value every 10 years, what should it be worth in 1956?

3. One fourth of the air remaining in a cylinder is removed on each operation. How much of the air remains in the cylinder after the fifth operation?

4. If the number of bacteria in milk doubles every 3 hours, by how much will the number be multiplied at the end of 24 hours?

5. A man wrote 3 post cards to 3 friends, with the request that each one of them write 3 post cards, one to each of 3 friends. If this continues for 6 sets of cards, how many cards will be sent out in the sixth set? How many cards will have been sent out all together?

6. A machine cost $7,250.00. At the end of any month the depreciation on the machine for that month was computed at the rate of 5 percent of its value at the beginning of the month. How much value was placed on the machine at the end of 20 months? (Use logarithms to aid in the solution.)

7. Find the compound amount of $1400 at 3 percent for 3 years, 6 months, compounded quarterly.

8. How much must be invested now at 3 percent, compounded semi-annually, to accumulate to $10,000 at the end of 20 years?

9. How long will it take for $100 to double itself, if invested at 4 percent, compounded semiannually?

10. A 10-year $1000 bond costs $750. Find the yearly interest rate, if interest is compounded semiannually.

11. A company sets aside $10,000 a year to retire a bond issue due in 25 years. If the money earns 3 percent, converted annually, find the amount of the bond issue.

12. Prove that if a_i, $(i = 1, 2, \cdots, n)$, is a geometric sequence then $l_i = \log a_i$, $(i = 1, 2, \cdots, n)$, is an arithmetic sequence.
(Comment: John Napier (1550–1617) utilized the relation between geometric and arithmetic sequences to construct his logarithms before exponents were known.)

13. Find a formula for g such that a, g, b form a geometric sequence where a, g, b are each positive. The number g is called **the geometric mean** of a and b.

14. Find the geometric mean of 9 and 225.

15. A man buys a house for $12,000 and agrees to pay the principal plus interest compounded semiannually at 4.75 percent at the end of 20 years. How much does he pay for the house disregarding taxes, insurance, upkeep, legal, and closing fees?

10–5. Infinite sequences. An **infinite sequence** is a sequence which does not terminate. Our interest in this topic will be in the study of infinite geometric sequences which have r such that $|r| < 1$. As an illustration consider the infinite geometric sequence

$$1, \tfrac{1}{2}, (\tfrac{1}{2})^2, \cdots, (\tfrac{1}{2})^{n-1}, \cdots.$$

Here, $a_1 = 1$, $r = \frac{1}{2}$, $a_n = (\frac{1}{2})^{n-1}$ and $S_n = \dfrac{1[1 - (\frac{1}{2})^n]}{1 - \frac{1}{2}} = 2(1 - (\frac{1}{2})^n)$.

As n increases 2^n increases and the fraction $(\frac{1}{2})^n$ decreases and approaches zero as a limit. Consequently, S_n approaches $2(1 - 0) = 2$ as n increases. We introduce the notation $\lim_{n \to \infty} S_n$ to represent the limit of S_n as n increases indefinitely. In our illustration: $\lim_{n \to \infty} S_n = 2$.

Theorem 1. If $S_n = \sum_{j=1}^{n} a_j$ is the sum of the first n terms of the infinite geometric sequence $a_j = r^{j-1}a_1$, $(j = 1, 2, 3, \cdots)$ having $|r| < 1$, then

$$\lim_{n \to \infty} S_n = \frac{a_1}{1 - r}. \tag{10.25}$$

If $|r| < 1$, then $1 > |r| > |r|^2 > \cdots > |r|^n$. It can be shown that $|r|^n$ decreases and approaches zero as a limit as n increases. Consequently, r^n approaches zero as a limit as n increases.

Write $S_n = \dfrac{a_1 - r^n a_1}{1 - r}$ in the form $S_n = \dfrac{a_1}{1 - r} - r^n \left(\dfrac{a_1}{1 - r}\right)$. Now, S_n approaches $\dfrac{a_1}{1 - r} - 0\left(\dfrac{a_1}{1 - r}\right) = \dfrac{a_1}{1 - r}$ as n increases. Hence,

$$\lim_{n \to \infty} S_n = \frac{a_1}{1 - r}.$$

The limit is called the **sum** of the **infinite geometric series**

$$a_1 + a_1 r + a_1 r^2 + \cdots + a_1 r^{n-1} + \cdots.$$

• **Example 1.** Find the sum of the infinite geometric series

$$9 - 6 + 4 - \cdots + 9(-\tfrac{2}{3})^{n-1} + \cdots.$$

$$a_1 = 9, \quad r = -\tfrac{2}{3}, \quad \lim_{n \to \infty} S_n = \frac{9}{1 - (-\frac{2}{3})} = \frac{27}{5}.$$

We state without proof:

Theorem 2. An infinite geometric series has a sum if and only if $|r| < 1$.

• **Example 2.** For what x values will the infinite geometric series

$$1 + \frac{1}{1 + x^2} + \frac{1}{(1 + x^2)^2} + \cdots + \frac{1}{(1 + x^2)^{n-1}} + \cdots$$

have a sum? Find the sum.

The series will have a sum if $|r| = \dfrac{1}{1 + x^2} < 1$. Then $1 < 1 + x^2$

and $x^2 > 0$. For every finite nonzero real value of x the sum of the series is given by

$$\lim_{n \to \infty} S_n = \frac{1}{1 - \dfrac{1}{1 + x^2}} = \frac{1 + x^2}{x^2}.$$

When $x = 2$ the series becomes

$$1 + \frac{1}{5} + \frac{1}{25} + \cdots + \frac{1}{5^{n-1}} + \cdots$$

and its sum is

$$\frac{1 + 2^2}{2^2} = \frac{5}{4}.$$

10–6. Infinite repeating decimals. The rational number

$$103/33 = 3.121212\cdots,$$

where the two digits 1, 2 are infinitely repeated. To indicate this unending repetition one may write $103/33 = 3.\overline{12}$. Similarly, an unending repetition in any decimal may be displayed by placing a line over the repeated digits. **Every rational number may be expressed as an infinite repeating decimal.** The argument made for positive rational numbers covers all rational numbers since $0 = 0.\overline{0}$ and each negative rational number R is equal to $(-1) |R|$. In the process of division there are only a finite number of non-negative remainders which are smaller than the divisor. Consequently, after a finite number of steps, there will be a return to a remainder that appeared earlier and a repetition of quotient digits will begin. This procedure may be repeated indefinitely. Certain numbers, such as $\frac{3}{5} = .6\overline{0}$, have repeating digit 0. If it is possible to show that **a repeating decimal represents a rational number,** then we shall have completed the proof of the following theorem.

Theorem 1. A number is rational if, and only if, it can be expressed as a repeating decimal.

Let us consider two examples instead of giving a general proof of the second part of this theorem. The methods used in solving these examples will suggest a procedure that can be used in proving the theorem.

● *Example 1.* Express $5.\overline{42}$ as a rational number.

Let

$$N = 5.\overline{42}.$$

Then

$$10^2 N = 542.\overline{42}$$

and

$$10^2 N - N = 542.\overline{42} - 5.\overline{42},$$

or

$$99N = 537.$$

Hence,

$$N = \tfrac{537}{99} = \tfrac{179}{33}.$$

● **Example 2.** Express $32.3\overline{455}$ as a rational number.

Let

$$N = 32.3\overline{455}.$$

Then

$$10^1 N = 323.\overline{455}$$

and

$$(10^{1+3} - 10^1)N = 323455.\overline{455} - 323.\overline{455}$$
$$= 323132.$$

Hence,

$$N = \tfrac{323132}{9990} = \tfrac{161566}{4995}.$$

A repeating decimal may be treated using infinite geometric series. To illustrate this consider:

● **Example 3.** Express $32.3\overline{455} = 32.3 + .0455 + .0000455 + \cdots$ as a rational number.

The infinite geometric series $.0455 + .0000455 + \cdots$ with

$$a_1 = .0455, \quad r = .001$$

has sum $\dfrac{.0455}{1 - .001} = \dfrac{455}{9990}.$ Therefore,

$$32.3\overline{455} = 32.3 + \tfrac{455}{9990}$$
$$= \tfrac{323132}{9990} = \tfrac{161566}{4995}.$$

PROBLEM SET 10-6

1. Find the sum of the infinite geometric series: $2 - \tfrac{2}{3} + \tfrac{2}{9} - \tfrac{2}{27} + \cdots$.

2. Find the sum of the infinite geometric series: $\dfrac{2}{3} + \dfrac{2\sqrt{6}}{9} + \dfrac{4}{9} + \dfrac{4\sqrt{6}}{27} + \cdots$.

3. An equilateral triangle has a perimeter of 12 in. Line segments join the midpoints of the sides to form a second triangle, then line segments join the midpoints of the sides of the second triangle to form a third triangle. If this continues indefinitely, find the sum of the perimeters of the triangles so formed.

4. Find the sum of the first n terms of the geometric series:

$$P + P\left(1 + \frac{r}{100}\right)^{-1} + P\left(1 + \frac{r}{100}\right)^{-2} + \cdots.$$

The geometric series given in this problem is used in computing the amount which must be invested now at r percent interest to yield an annuity of P dollars per year for the next n years.

5. Find the interval of r values for which the infinite geometric series

$$P + P\left(1 + \frac{r}{100}\right)^{-1} + P\left(1 + \frac{r}{100}\right)^{-2} + \cdots$$

has a sum. Find the sum.

The geometric series given in this problem is used in computing the amount of money which must be invested at r percent interest to provide a perpetual annual scholarship of P dollars per year.

6. A pendulum swings through an arc 30 in. long on its first swing. The length of each swing thereafter is four fifths of the length of the swing just preceding. Approximately how far will the pendulum swing before coming to rest?

7. Find a rational fraction which equals $2.\overline{35}$.

8. Find a rational fraction which equals $0.3\overline{41}$.

9. Find a rational fraction which equals $0.34\overline{14}$.

10. Find a rational fraction which equals $0.2\overline{315}$.

11. For what values of x will the infinite geometric series

$$1 - x + x^2 - x^3 + \cdots + (-1)^{n-1}x^{n-1} + \cdots$$

have a sum? Find the sum.

12. For what values of x will the infinite geometric series

$$1 - x^2 + x^4 - x^6 + \cdots + (-1)^{n-1}x^{2n-2} + \cdots$$

have a sum? Find the sum.

13. For what values of x will the infinite geometric series

$$1 + \frac{x-1}{2} + \left(\frac{x-1}{2}\right)^2 + \left(\frac{x-1}{2}\right)^3 + \cdots + \left(\frac{x-1}{2}\right)^{n-1} + \cdots$$

have a sum? Find the sum.

10–7. Self test.

Record time.

1. The sum of $6000 is distributed among 4 persons so that each person after the first receives $100 less than the preceding one. How much does the first one receive?

2. If one third of the air in a container is removed by each stroke of an air pump, what fractional part of the air remains after 10 strokes?

3. Find a rational fraction which equals $4.\overline{153}$.

4. The successive midpoints of the sides of a 2×2-inch square are joined by line segments and a new square is obtained. If this process is repeated using the new square and is continued indefinitely, find the sum of the perimeters of the squares.

5. Find $\displaystyle\sum_{x=1}^{12} (3x - 5)$.

6. For what values of n will $\displaystyle\sum_{x=1}^{n} x^2$ lie between 16 and 50?

7. How much must be invested now at 4 percent, compounded semiannually, to accumulate to \$20,000 at the end of 20 years?

8. For what x values will the infinite geometric series

$$-\frac{3}{x-3} + \frac{9}{(x-3)^2} - \cdots + \frac{(-3)^n}{(x-3)^n} + \cdots$$

have a sum? Find the sum.

Record time.

10–8. Mathematical induction, an aid to the discovery of new theorems. Occasionally in mathematical work we may discover a formula involving a variable n, which we have observed to be true for a few integral values of n, say $n = 1, 2, \cdots, 50$, and hopefully conjecture that the formula may be true for any integral value of n greater than or equal to 1. To establish the truth (or falsity) of the theorem or formula requires proof. Mathematical induction is based on the following fundamental postulate for the system of positive integers.

Postulate of finite induction. A set S of positive integers with the following two properties contains every positive integer:

(1) The set S contains the positive integer 1;
(2) If the set S contains the positive integer k, then S contains the positive integer $k + 1$.

(This postulate suggests that if $k = 1$ is in the set, then $k + 1 = 1 + 1 = 2$ is in the set, and $k = 2$ implies $k + 1 = 2 + 1 = 3$ is in the set, and so on.) The analogy of climbing a ladder is useful. To climb a ladder of any height only two things are needed:

(1) To get onto the lowest rung of the ladder;
(2) A procedure that will guarantee that if we are on the kth rung, we can ascend to the $(k + 1)$st rung.

To establish the validity of a statement, $f(n)$, about integers n by mathematical induction the following three steps are used:

(1) Test for the truth of the formula (or theorem) when $n = 1$. (If the formula fails for $n = 1$, then certainly the formula is not true for *all* positive integers.)

If the formula is true for $n = 1$, then

(2) Let $n = k$ be a positive integer for which the formula is assumed to be true, and

(3) Prove the formula holds when $n = k + 1$, based on the assumption (2).

If we can show that the formula is true for $n = 1$, and that assuming the formula is true for $n = k$ is sufficient to prove that the formula is true when $n = k + 1$, then the postulate of finite induction for the positive integers states that the formula is true for every positive integral value of n.

● **Example 1.** Prove: $\sum_{x=1}^{n} x^2 = \frac{1}{6} n(n + 1)(2n + 1)$.

(1) If $n = 1$, $1^2 = \frac{1}{6}(1)(1 + 1)(2 + 1)$. The formula holds for $n = 1$.

(2) Let $n = k$ be any positive integer. Assume the formula is true for $n = k$, that is,

$$\sum_{x=1}^{k} x^2 = \frac{1}{6}k(k + 1)(2k + 1) \quad \text{is true.}$$

To prove the formula holds when $n = k + 1$ we need to show

(3) $\sum_{x=1}^{k+1} x^2 \overset{?}{=} \frac{1}{6}(k + 1)(k + 2)(2k + 3)$.

Note that $\sum_{x=1}^{k+1} x^2 = \sum_{x=1}^{k} x^2 + (k + 1)^2$. This suggests the addition

of $(k + 1)^2$ to both members of the assumed relation in (2) to prove that (3) follows from (2).

$$\sum_{x=1}^{k} x^2 + (k + 1)^2 = \frac{1}{6}k(k + 1)(2k + 1) + (k + 1)^2$$

$$= \frac{1}{6}(k + 1)(2k^2 + 7k + 6)$$

$$= \frac{1}{6}(k + 1)(k + 2)(2k + 3), \quad \text{as desired.}$$

This completes the proof. (Why?)

● **Example 2.** Prove: $(x^n - h^n)$ has factor $(x - h)$ when n is a positive integer. (See Equation 4.2, p. 79 for another proof.)

(1) If $n = 1$, $(x^1 - h^1)$ has factor $(x - h)$. The theorem holds for $n = 1$.

(2) Assume the theorem is true for $n = k$; that is, $(x^k - h^k)$ has factor $(x - h)$.

(3) Show that this implies the theorem holds for $n = k + 1$; that is, that $x^{k+1} - h^{k+1}$ has factor $(x - h)$.

PROOF: Write $x^{k+1} - h^{k+1} = x^{k+1} - xh^k + xh^k - h^{k+1}$

$$= x(x^k - h^k) + h^k(x - h).$$

The final right member has factor $(x - h)$ since $(x - h)$ is a factor of each of the expressions in parentheses. Why does this prove the stated theorem? Would this observation alone, without (1) and (2) be sufficient to establish the desired theorem? Unless the reader realizes that *none* of the three steps (1), (2), and (3) can be omitted, he still does not understand mathematical induction and should reread this section before continuing.

PROBLEM SET 10-8

Use mathematical induction to prove the following problems.

1. The sum of the first n positive odd integers is n^2.

2. $\sum_{x=1}^{n} \dfrac{1}{x(x + 1)} = \dfrac{n}{n + 1}$.

3. $\sum_{x=1}^{n} x(x + 1) = \dfrac{n(n + 1)(n + 2)}{3}$.

4. $\sum_{x=1}^{n} x^3 = \dfrac{n^2(n + 1)^2}{4}$.

5. $\sum_{x=1}^{n} a_1 r^{x-1} = \dfrac{a_1 - a_1 r^n}{1 - r}$.

6. $x^{2n} - y^{2n}$ has factor $x + y$, n a positive integer.

7. $n(n^2 + 1)(n^2 + 4)$ is divisible by 5, n a positive integer.

[HINT: One of five consecutive integers is a multiple of 5.]

*10-9. Finite differences.† In numerical analysis many formulas involving finite differences are used. We shall examine a few of these formulas and hope it may arouse sufficient interest to encourage further reading on this important subject.

If a table gives values of a function $f(x)$ for regular intervals of x (see second column in table below), then the differences of these tabular values, usually called Δf, may be easily computed. In a similar fashion, the

---

† High-speed computers will play an increasingly important role in the science and engineering developments of the future. Many colleges and universities do not *require* work in numerical mathematics in their scientific and engineering programs, although most offer it. Practicing engineers and scientists, however, soon discover the desirability of such training and are often forced to "dig it out on their own." Sections 10–9, 10–10, and 10–11 are presented in the hope that a brief encounter with some basic concepts of numerical mathematical analysis will make study in this vital field easier.

differences of the Δfs, usually called $\Delta(\Delta f)$ or $\Delta^2 f$, may also be computed and also the $\Delta^3 f$s, etc. The following table presents a typical example:

Table 10–1

x	$f(x)$	Δf	$\Delta^2 f$	$\Delta^3 f$
− 5	− 870			
		458		
− 4	− 412		− 174	
		284		42
− 3	− 128		− 132	
		152		42
− 2	24		− 90	
		62		42
− 1	86		− 48	
		114		42
0	100		− 6	
		8		42
1	108		36	
		44		42
2	152		78	
		122		42
3	274		120	
		242		42
4	516		162	
		404		42
5	920		204	
		608		42
6	1528		246	
		854		42
7	2382		288	
		1142		42
8	3524		330	
		1472		
9	4996			

In general, the first, second, third, and higher differences of $f(x)$ are defined as follows:

$$\Delta f(x) = \quad f(x+h) - \quad f(x) \dagger$$
$$\Delta^2 f(x) = \quad \Delta f(x+h) - \quad \Delta f(x)$$
$$\Delta^3 f(x) = \quad \Delta^2 f(x+h) - \quad \Delta^2 f(x)$$

$$\Delta^n f(x) = \Delta^{n-1} f(x+h) - \Delta^{n-1} f(x)$$

Three simple theorems follow immediately.

Theorem 1. If c is a constant, $\Delta c f(x) = c \, \Delta f(x)$.

Theorem 2. If c is a constant, $\Delta c = 0$.

Theorem 3. $\Delta[f(x) + g(x)] = \Delta f(x) + \Delta g(x)$.

The proofs of these theorems are left to the student in Problem Set 10–11, numbers 6, 7, and 8.

High-speed computers are changing the basic way in which certain problems are attacked. It has become both important and feasible to fit polynomials to a given set of data. Several methods are in common use. In most cases the first problem to be settled is, "What *degree* polynomial will do a reasonable job of fitting the data?" The complete answer is not as simple as our illustrations suggest, but the basic ideas are still valid.

Theorem 4. If a "table of differences" like that above has a $\Delta^k f$ column in which all entries are identical (or almost identical), then it is possible to find a kth-degree polynomial $f(x) = a_0 + a_1 x + \cdots + a_k x^k$ which will pass through (or almost pass through) the points given in the x and $f(x)$ columns.

The function given in the preceding table has $\Delta^3 f = 42$ in each case. It will be fitted to a third-degree polynomial in Section 10–10.

Partially for use in the proof of the above theorem, but more as a help in the further study of numerics, we introduce an expression known as a **pseudo factorial.** The symbol $x^{[k]}$ is in wide use for this expression

$$x^{[1]} = x$$
$$x^{[2]} = x(x - h)$$
$$x^{[3]} = x(x - h)(x - 2h)$$
$$x^{[4]} = x(x - h)(x - 2h)(x - 3h)$$

$$x^{[k]} = x(x - h)(x - 2h)(x - 3h)(x - 4h)(x - 5h) \cdots (x - [k-1]h).$$

$\dagger$ If $h = \Delta x$ then $\Delta f(x) = f(x + \Delta x) - f(x)$ as usual.

It follows that $\quad \Delta x^{[k]} = khx^{[k-1]} \quad$ as is seen from

$$\Delta x^{[k]} = (x+h)^{[k]} - x^{[k]}$$
$$= (x+h)x(x-h)\cdots(x-[k-2]h)-x(x-h)(x-2h)\cdots(x-[k-1]h)$$
$$= (x+h-x+[k-1]h)x(x-h)\cdots(x-[k-2]h) = khx^{[k-1]}.$$

Similarly, using the symbol $k!$ to represent the product $1 \cdot 2 \cdot 3 \cdots k$, we have $\Delta^2 x^{[k]} = \Delta khx^{[k-1]} = kh \ \Delta x^{[k-1]} = (k-1)kh^2 x^{[k-2]}, \quad \cdots, \quad \Delta^k x^{[k]} = k!h^k, \quad \Delta^{k+1} x^{[k]} = 0.$ From this it follows that the $(k+1)$th and higher-order differences of the polynomial $P_k(x) = A_0 + A_1 x^{[1]} + A_2 x^{[2]} + \cdots + A_k x^{[k]}$ are zero where A_i, $(i = 0, 1, \cdots, k)$ are constants.

In numerical work it is often more advantageous to express a function as a polynomial in pseudo factorials, rather than directly in powers of x; that is, it may be preferable to express $\quad p(x) = 4x^3 - 3x^2 - 5 \quad$ as

$$P(x) = 4x^{[3]} + (12h - 3)x^{[2]} + (4h^2 - 3h)x^{[1]} - 5$$

even though at first glance the second form seems more complicated.

Any reader who plans to *study* mathematics should have a pencil in hand and be showing that

$$P(x) = 4x^{[3]} + (12h - 3)x^{[2]} + (4h^2 - 3h)x^{[1]} - 5$$
$$= 4 \cdot x(x - h)(x - 2h) + (12h - 3) \cdot x(x - h) + (4h^2 - 3h) \cdot x - 5$$
$$= 4x^3 - 3x^2 - 5 = p(x).$$

The more difficult problem of given $\quad p(x) \quad$ to determine the equivalent pseudo-factorial expression $\quad P(x) \quad$ will be discussed next.

Any polynomial $\quad p_k(x) = a_0 + a_1 x + a_2 x^2 + \cdots + a_k x^k \quad$ may be placed in pseudo-factorial form $\quad P_k(x)$. Suppose $\quad p_k(x) = P_k(x)$. Substituting zero for x determines $\quad p_k(0) = a_0 = A_0$. If $\quad q_1(x) \quad$ is the quotient obtained when $p_k(x)$ is divided by x until the constant remainder $\quad a_0 \quad$ is obtained, then $p_k(x) \equiv q_1(x) \cdot x^{[1]} + a_0 \equiv A_0 + A_1 x^{[1]} + A_2 x^{[2]} + \cdots + A_k x^{[k]}$, $q_1(x) \equiv A_1 + A_2(x - h)^{[1]} + \cdots + A_k(x - h)^{[k-1]}$, and $\quad q_1(h) = A_1$. The process may be continued. This suggests that synthetic division may be used to express $\quad p_k(x) \quad$ in the form $\quad P_k(x)$. The following examples illustrate the method.

● *Example 1.* Express $\quad 4x^3 - 3x^2 - 5 \quad$ in the form
$P_3(x) = A_0 + A_1 x^{[1]} + A_2 x^{[2]} + A_3 x^{[3]}$.

$$
\begin{array}{r|ccccc}
0 & 4\ - & 3 & + & 0 & -5 \\
  & +   & 0 & + & 0 & +0 \\
\hline
h & 4\ - & 3 & + & 0 & -5 = A_0 \\
  & +   & 4h & + (4h^2 - 3h) & & \\
\hline
2h & 4\ + (4h-3) & + (4h^2 - 3h) = A_1 & & & \\
   & +\ 8h & & & & \\
\hline
A_3 = 4 & + (12h - 3) = A_2 & & & &
\end{array}
$$

$$4x^3 - 3x^2 - 5 \equiv 4x^{[3]} + (12h - 3)x^{[2]} + (4h^2 - 3h)x^{[1]} - 5.$$

Example 2. Express x^2 in the form $A_2 x(x-1) + A_1 x + A_0$. In this example $h = 1$.

$$
\begin{array}{r|ll}
0 & 1 \;\; +0 \;\; +0 & \\
 & \quad\;\; +0 \;\; +0 & \\
1 & 1 \;\; +0 \;|\; +0 = A_0 & \\
 & \quad\;\; +1 & \\
\end{array}
$$
$$A_2 = 1 \;|\; +1 = A_1$$

$x^2 = x^{[2]} + x^{[1]}, \quad h = 1.$

To find $\displaystyle\sum_{x=h}^{nh} x^{[k]}$ we observe that

$$x^{[k]} = \Delta\left(\frac{x^{[k+1]}}{(k+1)h}\right) = \frac{1}{(k+1)h}\,\Delta x^{[k+1]} = \frac{1}{(k+1)h}\left\{(x+h)^{[k+1]} - x^{[k+1]}\right\}$$

and consequently

$$\sum_{x=h}^{nh} x^{[k]} = \frac{1}{(k+1)h}\left\{(nh+h)^{[k+1]} - (nh)^{[k+1]} + (nh)^{[k+1]}\right.$$
$$\left. - (nh-h)^{[k+1]} + \cdots + (h+h)^{[k+1]} - h^{[k+1]}\right\}$$

which simplifies to give

$$\sum_{x=h}^{nh} x^{[k]} = \frac{1}{(k+1)h}\,(nh+h)^{[k+1]}.$$

● ***Example 3.*** Find $\displaystyle\sum_{x=1}^{n} [a_1 + (x-1)d]$. (See Theorem 1 of Section 10–3.)

$$\sum_{x=1}^{n} [a_1 + (x-1)d] = na_1 + d\sum_{x=1}^{n}(x-1)^{[1]} = na_1 + \frac{d}{(1+1)1}\,(n-1+1)^{[2]}$$
$$= \frac{n}{2}\,[2a_1 + (n-1)d].$$

● ***Example 4.*** Find $\displaystyle\sum_{x=1}^{n} x^2$.

$$\sum_{x=1}^{n} x^2 = \sum_{x=1}^{n}(x^{[2]} + x^{[1]}) = \sum_{x=1}^{n} x^{[2]} + \sum_{x=1}^{n} x^{[1]} = \tfrac{1}{3}(n+1)^{[3]} + \tfrac{1}{2}(n+1)^{[2]}$$
$$= \frac{(n+1)^{[2]}(2[n-1]+3)}{6} = \frac{1}{6}\,n(n+1)(2n+1).$$

*10–10 Curve fitting.† Repeating the differences of Table 10–1 given in Section 10–9:

† Chapter 23 discusses other aspects of this important topic.

Table 10–1

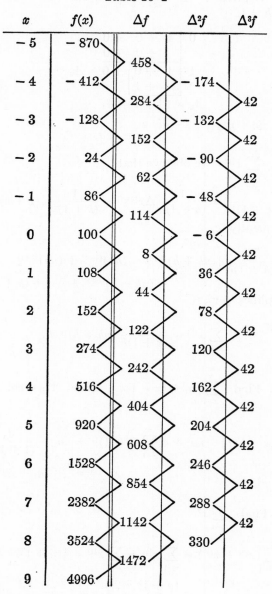

x	$f(x)$	Δf	$\Delta^2 f$	$\Delta^3 f$
− 5	− 870			
		458		
− 4	− 412		− 174	
		284		42
− 3	− 128		− 132	
		152		42
− 2	24		− 90	
		62		42
− 1	86		− 48	
		114		42
0	100		− 6	
		8		42
1	108		36	
		44		42
2	152		78	
		122		42
3	274		120	
		242		42
4	516		162	
		404		42
5	920		204	
		608		42
6	1528		246	
		854		42
7	2382		288	
		1142		42
8	3524		330	
		1472		
9	4996			

By examining the original $[x, f(x)]$ data (first two columns) it is not at all obvious what (if any) formula was used to obtain the functional correspondence. However, since the third differences, $\Delta^3 f$, are all constant, Section 10–9 assures us that there is a cubic polynomial
$f(x) = Ax^3 + Bx^2 + Cx + D$ that has the desired property for some set of

onstant coefficients A, B, C, D. We now attempt to determine this cubic polynomial. The coefficients A, B, C, D can be determined in a number of ways.

Since the third differences are all exactly equal to one another, an exact it can be guaranteed by a cubic polynomial. Hence, if we substitute any four ets of values of x and $f(x)$ from the table into

$$Ax^3 + Bx^2 + Cx + D = f(x),$$

a set of four equations involving known constants and the four unknown coefficients A, B, C, D will be obtained.

Upon substituting		One obtains
x	$f(x)$	
-2	24	$-8A + 4B - 2C + D = 24$
-1	86	$-A + B - C + D = 86$
0	100	$0 + 0 + 0 + D = 100$
1	108	$A + B + C + D = 108$

The third of these equations determines $D = 100$. Upon making the substitution $D = 100$ into the remaining three equations, the following system of three equations in three unknowns results:

$$-8A + 4B - 2C = -76$$
$$-A + B - C = -14$$
$$A + B + C = 8$$

Upon solving this system one obtains

$$A = 7 \qquad B = -3 \qquad C = 4 \qquad D = 100$$

Hence, the cubic polynomial which represents the given function is

$$f(x) = 7x^3 - 3x^2 + 4x + 100.$$

The reader should verify that the same equation is actually obtained if a different set of four points is used.

In the event that the third differences are only *approximately* equal, it is no longer true that the coefficients obtained by the above method are independent of the points chosen. In such cases it may be desirable to use the pseudo-factorial polynomial $P(x)$ to approximate the data rather than $p(x)$.

*10–11. The Gregory-Newton interpolation formula.† Frequently when data is available in tabular form, it is desirable to **interpolate** to find

† High-speed computers will play an increasingly important role in the science and engineering developments of the future. Many colleges and universities do not *require* work in numerical mathematics in their scientific and engineering programs, although most offer it. Practicing engineers and scientists, however, soon discover the desirability of such training and are often forced to "dig it out on their own." Sections 10–9, 10–10, and 10–11 are presented in the hope that a brief encounter with some basic concepts of numerical mathematical analysis will make study in this vital field easier.

values of $f(x_i)$ for x_i between some of the given tabular values. The student has already used linear interpolation in his work on logarithms. The basic assumption in all interpolation processes is that the points $[x, f(x)]$ which lie between the given points follow the same general pattern as do those given. This does not necessarily mean that if we connect two given points with a straight line, the interpolated point will lie on this line. (This was the assumption made in Section 8–8 on logarithms.) It would be more reasonable, but also a lot more work, to use finite differences to obtain the equation of a polynomial passing through the given points and use this for interpolation. The Gregory-Newton interpolation formula essentially makes use of this principle without all the work of actually constructing the polynomial. The pseudo-factorial function $P(x)$ of Section 10–9 is used to obtain the approximating polynomial.

Frequently functions $y = f(x)$ are tabulated for an arithmetic sequence of x values. Generally if the common difference h between consecutive x values is sufficiently small, $\Delta^n f(x)$ will be a nonzero constant (or approximately a nonzero constant) and higher-order differences will be zero (or approximately zero) for n sufficiently large. In such cases $f(x)$ can be approximated by $P_n(x - x_0)$. Let us form the appropriate difference table and determine $P_n(x - x_0)$ such that when $x = x_k$, we have $P_n(x_k - x_0) = y_k = f(x_k)$. This means that we are passing a polynomial of degree n through the $n + 1$ points $(x_0, y_0), \cdots, (x_n, y_n)$. We employ the notations: $x_k = x_0 + kh$, $y_k = f(x_k)$, $(k = 0, 1, 2, \cdots, n)$, $\Delta y_0 = y_1 - y_0, \Delta^2 y_0 = \Delta y_1 - \Delta y_0, \cdots,$ $\Delta^n y_0 = \Delta^{n-1} y_1 - \Delta^{n-1} y_0$.

Table 10–2

x	$y = f(x)$	$\Delta x = \Delta f(x)$	$\Delta^2 y = \Delta^2 f(x)$	$\Delta^3 y = \Delta^3 f(x)$	$\cdots$	$\Delta^n y = \Delta^n f(x)$
x_0	$y_0 = f(x_0)$					
		$\Delta y_0{'}$				
x_1	y_1		$\Delta^2 y_0$			
		Δy_1		$\Delta^3 y_0$		
x_2	y_2		$\Delta^2 y_1$		$\cdots$	$\Delta^n y_0$
		Δy_2		$\Delta^3 y_1$		
x_3	y_3					
$\vdots$	$\vdots$	$\vdots$	$\vdots$	$\vdots$		
x_n	y_n					

f $\Delta^n f(x)$ is a nonzero constant (or approximately a nonzero constant) then

$$f(x) \approx A_0 + A_1(x - x_0)^{[1]} + \quad A_2(x - x_0)^{[2]} + \quad A_3(x - x_0)^{[3]} + \cdots \\ + A_n(x - x_0)^{[n]}$$

$$\Delta f(x) \approx \quad hA_1 \quad + 2hA_2(x - x_0)^{[1]} + \quad 3hA_3(x - x_0)^{[2]} + \cdots \\ + nhA_n(x - x_0)^{[n-1]}$$

$$\Delta^2 f(x) \approx \quad 2!h^2 A_2 \quad + 2 \cdot 3h^2 A_3(x - x_0)^{[1]} + \cdots \\ + (n-1)nh^2 A_n(x - x_0)^{[n-2]}$$

$$\Delta^3 f(x) \approx \quad 3!h^3 A_3 \quad + \cdots \\ + (n-2)(n-1)nh^3 A_n(x - x_0)^{[n-3]}$$

$$\vdots \qquad\qquad\qquad\qquad \vdots$$

$$\Delta^n f(x) \approx \quad n!h^n A_n$$
$$\Delta^{n+1} f(x) \approx 0$$

n each of the above equations set $x = x_0$ and obtain

$$y_0 = A_0, \ \Delta y_0 = hA_1, \ \Delta^2 y_0 = 2!h^2 A_2, \ \Delta^3 y_0 = 3!h^3 A_3, \cdots, \ \Delta^n y_0 = n!h^n A_n.$$

On replacing A_0 by y_0, A_1 by $\dfrac{\Delta y_0}{h}$, A_2 by $\dfrac{\Delta^2 y_0}{2!h^2}, \cdots,$ A_n by $\dfrac{\Delta^n y_0}{n!h^n}$

we find

$$(x) \approx y_0 + \frac{(x - x_0)^{[1]}}{h} \Delta y_0 + \frac{(x - x_0)^{[2]}}{2!h^2} \Delta^2 y_0 + \frac{(x - x_0)^{[3]}}{3!h^3} \Delta^3 y_0 + \cdots + \frac{(x - x_0)^{[n]}}{n!h^n} \Delta^n y_0.$$

When $x = x_k = x_0 + kh,$

$(x_k) = y_k$ and

$$y_0 + \frac{(x_0 + kh - x_0)^{[1]}}{h} \Delta y_0 + \frac{(x_0 + kh - x_0)^{[2]}}{2!h^2} \Delta^2 y_0 + \cdots + \frac{(x_0 + kh - x_0)^{[n]}}{n!h^n} \Delta^n y_0$$

$$= y_0 + k\Delta y_0 + \frac{k(k-1)}{2!} \Delta^2 y_0 + \frac{k(k-1)(k-2)}{3!} \Delta^3 y_0 + \cdots + \frac{k!}{k!} \Delta^k y_0 = y_k.$$

Assuming the truth of the final equality, whose direct verification is tedious, t follows that the polynomial of degree n used to approximate $f(x)$ will pass through the $n + 1$ points $(x_0, y_0), \cdots, (x_n, y_n)$ given in the table. The polynomial

$$P_n(x - x_0) = y_0 + \frac{(x - x_0)^{[1]}}{h} \Delta y_0 + \cdots + \frac{(x - x_0)^{[n]}}{n!h^n} \Delta^n y_0,$$

which takes the values that $f(x)$ has at $x = x_0, x_1, \cdots, x_n,$ may be used to interpolate approximate $f(x)$ values for x between x_0 and x_1. The polynomial $P_n(x - x_0)$ is one of the fundamental interpolation formulas and is known as the **Gregory-Newton interpolation formula.**

• **Example 1.** Find a polynomial that will pass through the points $(x, y$
of the table:

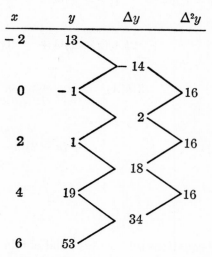

x	y	Δy	$\Delta^2 y$
-2	13		
		-14	
0	-1		16
		2	
2	1		16
		18	
4	19		16
		34	
6	53		

$x_0 = -2, \quad y_0 = 13, \quad h = 2$

$$y = 13 + \frac{-14}{2}(x - [-2]) + \frac{16}{2!2^2}(x+2)(x+2-2)$$

$$= 13 - 7(x+2) + 2(x+2)x$$

$$= 2x^2 - 3x - 1.$$

Verify by substitution that each point of the table satisfies the equation

• **Example 2.** The table lists x in degrees and the corresponding value
$y = \cot x$ † as they appear in Appendix Table VIII. Find $\cot 3° 12'$

x	$y = \cot x$	Δy	$\Delta^2 y$	$\Delta^3 y$
3° 10′	18.075			
		−.906		
3° 20′	17.169		.087	
		−.819		−.013
3° 30′	16.350		.074	
		−.745		−.010
3° 40′	15.605		.064	
		−.681		
3° 50′	14.924			

† cot x (Read: "cotangent of x") is the notation for one of the trigonometric functions. Here, if preferred, $f(x)$ may be used instead of cot x.

Form the difference table as shown. For our purposes the third differences are approximately constant. Consequently we approximate cot x near $x = 3° 10'$ by means of a Gregory-Newton polynomial of the third degree as follows:

$$y = \cot x \approx 18.075 + \frac{x - 3° 10'}{10'}(-.906) + \frac{(x - 3° 10')(x - 3° 20')}{2!(10')^2}(.087)$$

$$+ \frac{(x - 3° 10')(x - 3° 20')(x - 3° 30')}{3! \cdot (10')^3}(-.013).$$

Hence,

$$\cot 3° 12' \approx 18.075 + \frac{2}{10}(-.906) + \frac{(2)(-8)}{2!(10)^2}(.087) + \frac{(2)(-8)(-18)}{3!(10)^3}(-.013)$$

or $\cot 3° 12' \approx 18.075 - .1812 - .00696 - .000624 \approx 17.886$, which is correct to five significant figures as may be verified from more elaborate tables.

The straight-line interpolation is equivalent to stopping with first differences and using

$$\cot x \approx 18.075 + \frac{x - 3° 10'}{10'}(-.906), \quad \text{from which}$$

$$\cot 3° 12' \approx 18.075 + \frac{2(-.906)}{10} \approx 17.894.$$

This result is not as accurate as the first result.

PROBLEM SET 10–11

1. Find and simplify the Gregory-Newton polynomial that fits the table. First form the appropriate difference table.

x	y	$\Delta y \cdots$
1	-4	
3	0	
5	60	
7	224	
9	540	

Construct a difference table stopping with third differences and write the corresponding Gregory-Newton polynomial for each of the following

problems. Also interpolate to find the approximate value of the function a
the place indicated.

2.

x	$y = f(x)$
10	3.207
20	3.179
30	3.152
40	3.124
50	3.089

Find $f(13)$.

3.

x	$f(x)$
20	13.197
30	12.706
40	12.251
50	11.826
60	11.430

Find $f(26)$.

4.

x	$f(x)$
10	1.343?
11	1.384?
12	1.425?
13	1.468?
14	1.512?

Find $f(10.5)$.

5. Plot the points given in Problems 2, 3, and 4 on three sets of axes and locate
   the f value you determine.
6. Prove Theorem 1, Section 10–9.
7. Prove Theorem 2, Section 10–9.
8. Prove Theorem 3, Section 10–9.
9. Fit a curve to the data of Problem 1 by the method of Section 10–10.
10. Fit a curve to the data of Problem 2 by the method of Section 10–10.

*10–12. Areas.† The area of a regular n-sided polygon inscribed in a circle
and the area of a regular n-sided polygon circumscribed about the circle
approach a common limit called the area of the circle as n increases indefinitely.

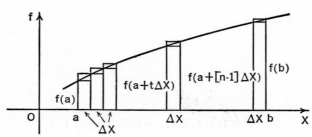

Fig. 10–1

Similarly, the area A bounded by $y = f(x)$, where $f(x) \geqq 0$ is a
continuous increasing function on $a \leqq x \leqq b$, the two ordinates $x = a$
and $x = b$, and the x-axis may be defined † as the common limit of the
sum s_n of n inscribed rectangles and the sum S_n of n circumscribed rectangles
as n increases indefinitely.‡ We need to define the sums s_n and S_n. At $x = a$,
$a + \Delta x$, $a + 2\Delta x$, $\cdots$, $a + k\,\Delta x$, $\cdots$, $a + (n-1)\,\Delta x$, $a + n\,\Delta x = b$,
where $\Delta x = \dfrac{b-a}{n}$, on the x-axis erect ordinates to $y = f(x)$.

† A further study of area is given in Section 19–5.
‡ Note that lower case s is used to denote the smaller sum and upper case S denotes
the larger sum.

(1) Construct rectangles using the ordinate at the left end of each of the n equal subintervals on the x-axis as altitude and base Δx extending to the right on the x-axis. The sum of the areas of these n rectangles is

$$s_n = f(a)\Delta x + f(a + \Delta x)\Delta x + \cdots + f(a + k\Delta x)\Delta x + \cdots + f(a + [n-1]\Delta x)\Delta x$$

or

$$s_n = \sum_{k=0}^{n-1} f(a + k\,\Delta x)\,\Delta x.$$

(2) Construct rectangles using the ordinate at the right end of each of the n equal subintervals on the x-axis as altitude and base Δx extending to the left on the x-axis. The sum of the areas of these n rectangles is

$$S_n = f(a + \Delta x)\,\Delta x + f(a + 2\Delta x)\,\Delta x + \cdots + f(a + k\,\Delta x)\,\Delta x + \cdots + f(b)\,\Delta x$$

or

$$S_n = \sum_{k=1}^{n} f(a + k\,\Delta x)\,\Delta x.$$

In the figure notice that a typical rectangle area in s_n is $f(a + t\,\Delta x)\,\Delta x$, which is smaller than the area under the curve standing on the same interval, which in turn is smaller than the corresponding rectangle area $f(a + [t+1]\,\Delta x)\,\Delta x$ in S_n. From this it appears that

$$s_n < A < S_n$$

and

$$\lim_{n \to \infty} s_n = A = \lim_{n \to \infty} S_n$$

(provided that there is a common limit).

● **Example 1.** Find the area bounded by the parabola $y = x^2$ and the lines $y = 0$ and $x = 4$. Also find the area bounded by $y = 16$ and $y = x^2$. At $x = 0$, $\dfrac{4}{n}, \dfrac{8}{n}, \dfrac{12}{n}, \cdots, \dfrac{4k}{n}, \cdots, 4$ on the x-axis erect ordinates to the parabola. (1) Construct rectangles using the ordinate at the left end of each of these n equal subintervals as altitude and base $\dfrac{4}{n}$ ex-

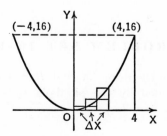

Fig. 10–2

tending to the right on the x-axis. The sum s_n of the areas of these rectangles will approximate the desired area A. This sum is

$$s_n = 0 \cdot \frac{4}{n} + \left(\frac{4}{n}\right)^2 \cdot \frac{4}{n} + \left(\frac{8}{n}\right)^2 \cdot \frac{4}{n} + \cdots + \left(\frac{4k}{n}\right)^2 \cdot \frac{4}{n} + \cdots + \left(\frac{4(n-1)}{n}\right)^2 \cdot \frac{4}{n}$$

$$= \frac{4^3}{n^3}(1^2 + 2^2 + \cdots + k^2 + \cdots + [n-1]^2)$$

$$= \frac{4^3}{n^3} \cdot \sum_{k=1}^{n-1} k^2 = \frac{4^3}{n^3} \cdot \frac{1}{6}(n-1)(n)(2n-1) = \frac{32}{3}\left(1 - \frac{1}{n}\right)(1)\left(2 - \frac{1}{n}\right).$$

$$\lim_{n \to \infty} s_n = \lim_{n \to \infty} \frac{32}{3}\left(1 - \frac{1}{n}\right)\left(2 - \frac{1}{n}\right) = \frac{32}{3}(1)(2) = \frac{64}{3}.$$

(2) Construct rectangles using the ordinate at the right end of these n equal subintervals as altitude and base $\dfrac{4}{n}$ extending to the left on the x-axis. The sum S_n of the areas of these rectangles will approximate A. This sum is

$$S_n = \left(\frac{4}{n}\right)^2 \cdot \frac{4}{n} + \left(\frac{8}{n}\right)^2 \cdot \frac{4}{n} + \cdots + \left(\frac{4k}{n}\right)^2 \cdot \frac{4}{n} + \cdots + \left(\frac{4n}{n}\right)^2 \cdot \frac{4}{n}$$

$$= \frac{4^3}{n^3}(1^2 + 2^2 + \cdots + k^2 + \cdots + n^2) = \frac{4^3}{n^3} \cdot \sum_{k=1}^{n} k^2$$

$$= \frac{4^3}{n^3} \cdot \frac{1}{6} n(n+1)(2n+1) = \frac{32}{3}(1)\left(1 + \frac{1}{n}\right)\left(2 + \frac{1}{n}\right)$$

$$\lim_{n \to \infty} S_n = \lim_{n \to \infty} \frac{32}{3}\left(1 + \frac{1}{n}\right)\left(2 + \frac{1}{n}\right) = \frac{32}{3}(1)(2) = \frac{64}{3}$$

$$s_n < A < S_n, \quad \lim_{n \to \infty} s_n = \lim_{n \to \infty} S_n = \tfrac{64}{3}, \quad A = \tfrac{64}{3} \text{ square units.}$$

The area of the segment bounded by $y = 16$ and $y = x^2$ is

$$(4 + 4)(16) - 2(\tfrac{64}{3}) = \tfrac{2}{3}(8)(16) = \tfrac{256}{3} \text{ square units.}$$

PROBLEM SET 10-12

1. Express $2x^2 + 3$ in the form $Ax^{[2]} + Bx^{[1]} + C$.
2. Find the area bounded by the parabola $y = 2x^2 + 3$ and the lines $y = 0$, $x = 1$, and $x = 3$.
3. Find $\displaystyle\sum_{x=1}^{50}(2x^2 + 3)$.

4. Express $x^2 + 2x + 5$ in the form $Ax^{[2]} + Bx^{[1]} + C$.

5. Find the area bounded by $y = x^2 + 2x + 5$ and the lines $y = 0$, $x = 0$, and $x = 2$.

6. Find $\sum_{x=1}^{20} (x^2 + 2x + 5)$.

7. Express x^3 in the form $Ax^{[3]} + Bx^{[2]} + Cx^{[1]} + D$.

8. Find the area bounded by $y = x^3$ and the lines $y = 0$, $x = 0$, and $x = 2$.

9. Express x^3 in the form $A_3x(x-1)(x-2) + A_2x(x-1) + A_1x + A_0$.

10. Find $\sum_{x=1}^{n} x^3$ and apply to $\sum_{x=1}^{10} x^3$.

11. (a) Find the area bounded by the parabola $y = \dfrac{4a}{b^2} x^2$ and the lines $y = 0$ and $x = \dfrac{b}{2}$.

(b) Find the area of the segment of the parabola bounded by the line $y = a$ and the parabola $y = \dfrac{4a}{b^2} x^2$.

11.

11–1. Fundamental principle of permutations and combinations.
In the study of problems of probability — that is, of problems of choice and
chance — one must determine the number of ways in which an event or
sequence of events can occur or can fail to occur. This may involve counting
all possible selections (combinations) or all their possible arrangements in
sequential order (permutations). The theory of permutations and combinations uses a fundamental principle which is introduced in solving the following
example.

● **Example 1.** How many different suits consisting of a jacket and a pair of
slacks may a college student wear if he has three sports jackets and four
pairs of slacks?

With any one of the three jackets he may wear any one of the four pairs
of slacks. Consequently, he may wear any one of $3 \times 4 = 12$ different
suits.

Intuitively one may see the solution to this example by means of a
figure called a "tree." (See Fig. 11–1.) The result is the number of the
uppermost branches of the tree.

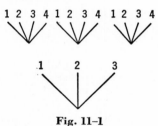

Fig. 11–1

This illustrates a

Fundamental Principle. If a first event can occur in h ways and after
it occurs, a second event can occur in k ways, then the number of ways in
which the sequence of two events can occur is hk.

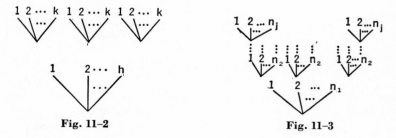

Fig. 11–2   **Fig. 11–3**

The **fundamental principle** may be stated more generally. (See Fig. 11–3.) If a first event can occur in n_1 ways and after it occurs, a second event can occur in n_2 ways, and if a third event can occur in n_3 ways, and so on to a jth event, and if the jth event can occur in n_j ways, then the number of ways in which the sequence of j events can occur is given by the product $n_1 n_2 n_3 \cdots n_j$.

- *Example 2.* In how many ways can the offices of president, vice-president, and secretary be filled by making selections from a group of twenty people?

    The office of president may be filled by any one of twenty people. Having filled the office of president any one of the nineteen people remaining may be chosen to fill the office of vice-president. Together the two offices may be filled in any one of $20 \times 19 = 380$ ways. Having filled the offices of president and vice-president any one of the eighteen people remaining may be chosen to fill the office of secretary. The three offices may be filled in any one of

$$380 \times 18 = 6840 \text{ ways.}$$

Example 3. Four different algebra texts, four different calculus texts, and five different chemistry texts are to be placed in a row on a shelf. In how many ways can the texts be arranged on the shelf if those in each subject are to be grouped together?

The algebra texts may be arranged in a row in any one of

$$4 \times 3 \times 2 \times 1 = 24 \text{ ways.}$$

Similarly, the calculus texts may be arranged in a row in any one of

$$4 \times 3 \times 2 \times 1 = 24 \text{ ways.}$$

The chemistry texts may be arranged in a row in any one of

$$5 \times 4 \times 3 \times 2 \times 1 = 120 \text{ ways.}$$

For a given subject order such as algebra, calculus, chemistry there would be $24 \times 24 \times 120 = 69,120$ ways of arranging the texts in a row such that all books on the same subject would be grouped together. But there are $3 \times 2 \times 1 = 6$ ways for ordering the three subjects. Therefore there are $6 \times 69,120 = 414,720$ ways of arranging the texts in a row such that all books on the same subject are grouped together.

PROBLEM SET 11–1

1. How many three-digit numbers can be formed from the set 1, 2, 3, 4, 5, 6 if no digit may be used more than once in the same number? How many can be formed if repetitions are allowed?

2. A teacher wishes to seat four girls and three boys alternately in a row of seven chairs. In how many ways can she seat them?

3. How many automobile finishes is it possible for a manufacturer to deliver if there is a choice of five body, three top, and two interior paints, and four upholstery materials?

4. If five coins are tossed simultaneously, in how many ways can they fall?

5. In how many ways can two dice fall? For what portion of these ways will the points of the dice total seven?

6. In how many ways can three dice fall? In how many of these ways will at least two dice show the same number of spots?

7. Seven teams belong to a basketball conference. How many games will be played if each team plays every other team at home?

8. To open a "combination" lock requires two successive settings of the pointer on a number. The dial contains twenty-four numbers and the settings are made by first turning the pointer counterclockwise to a number, then reversing the direction to a different second number. How many different "combination" locks are possible?

9. The Greek alphabet contains twenty-four letters. How many Greek-letter fraternity names, each having two or three letters, can be formed?

11–2. Permutations. Suppose we have ten different objects and we wish to select four of the objects and arrange them in a certain order (sequence). Each such arrangement (sequence) is called a permutation of the ten objects taken four at a time. The theory of permutations deals with the problem of determining the number of sequences into which a given number of objects of a finite set may be selected and arranged.

● *Example 1.* How many different sequences each containing three letters may be formed from the set a, b, c?

Any one of the three letters may be chosen as the first term of a sequence. Then either of the two remaining letters may be used as the second term of a sequence. Finally the remaining letter is used. This implies that

$$3 \times 2 \times 1 = 6 \text{ sequences}$$

may be formed using the objects a, b, c in sets three at a time. These six sequences are:

$$a, b, c; \quad a, c, b; \quad b, a, c; \quad b, c, a; \quad c, a, b; \quad c, b, a.$$

● *Example 2.* How many different sequences each containing three letters may be formed from the set a, b, c, d?

Any one of the four letters may be chosen as the first term of a sequence. Then any one of the three remaining letters may be used as the second term of a sequence. Finally either of the two remaining letters may be used as the third term of a sequence. Applying the *fundamental principle* we find the number of different sequences to be $4 \times 3 \times 2 = 24$.

A **permutation of *n* objects *x* at a time** is an arranged selection or sequence of x of the n objects. The order in which the objects are arranged is important. If the same objects are arranged in a different order, a different permutation results.

The **number** of permutations $P(n, x)$ of n distinguishable objects taken in sets x at a time is

$$P(n, x) = n(n-1) \cdots (n-x+1). \tag{11.1}$$

Any one of the n objects may be selected as the first object in a sequence. Then any one of the remaining $n-1$ objects may be selected as the second object in the sequence. From the fundamental principle it is seen that there are $n(n-1)$ possible selections for the first two terms of a sequence. After the first two terms have been selected any one of the remaining $n-2$ objects may be selected as the third object in a sequence. Consequently, there are $n(n-1) \cdot (n-2)$ selections for the first three terms of a sequence. Continuing the process, after the first $x-1$ terms have been selected any one of the remaining $n-(x-1) = n-x+1$ objects may be selected as the xth object in a sequence. From the fundamental principle it follows that there are exactly $n(n-1)(n-2) \cdots (n-x+1)$ possible selections of sequences of x of the n objects.

- *Example 3.* Three signal flags are to be run up, one above another, on a flagpole. How many different signals can be run up using five different flags three at a time?

  In this example $n = 5$ and $x = 3$. The number of different signals is

$$P(5, 3) = 5 \cdot 4 \cdot (5 - 3 + 1) = 5 \cdot 4 \cdot 3 = 60.$$

Define $0! = 1$, and $n! = 1 \cdot 2 \cdot 3 \cdots n$ for n a positive integer. The symbol $n!$ is read "n factorial." †

- *Illustrations:* $4! = 1 \cdot 2 \cdot 3 \cdot 4 = 24$, $5! = 4! \cdot 5 = 120$, $6! = 5! \cdot 6 = 720$.

Multiply both members of $P(n, x) = n(n-1) \cdots (n-x+1)$ by $(n-x)!$ and obtain

$$P(n, x) \cdot (n-x)! = [n(n-1) \cdots (n-x+1)] \cdot [(n-x) \cdots 2 \cdot 1] = n!.$$

If the preceding equation is solved for $P(n, x)$, a second formula for the number of permutations of n distinguishable objects taken in sets x at a time is obtained:

$$P(n, x) = \frac{n!}{(n-x)!}. \tag{11.2}$$

† Some writers point out that the exclamation point is used since these numbers increase at an astonishing rate!

The reader should verify that formulas (11.1) and (11.2) are equivalent. The number of permutations of n distinguishable objects taken in sets n at a time is

$$P(n, n) = n(n - 1) \cdots (n - n + 1) = n!. \tag{11.3}$$

From (11.2) and (11.3) it is seen that if formula (11.2) is to be valid for $x = n$, then we must have

$$P(n, n) = \frac{n!}{0!} = n!$$

This suggests one reason that we define

$$0! = 1.$$

● **Example 4.** How many different program arrangements beginning with a musical selection are possible using four musical numbers and three addresses, if musical numbers and addresses are to alternate?

The musical numbers can be permuted in $P(4, 4) = 4!$ ways and the addresses can be permuted in $P(3, 3) = 3!$ ways. Applying the fundamental principle it is seen that there are $4! \cdot 3! = 144$ possible program arrangements.

11–3. Distinguishable permutations. Given a set of n objects containing two or more objects that are alike, such as the set 4, 4, 5, 5, 5, 6, 8 of seven digits, one may wish to determine the number of distinguishable permutations of the n objects taken n at a time. If integers having seven digits are to be formed using the set of seven digits previously mentioned, then the permutation 4654585 is one of the resulting integers. If the two digits 4 are interchanged, the integer 4654585 is unchanged. Similarly, a permutation of the three digits 5 leaves the appearance of the seven-digit integer unchanged. A method for finding the **number of distinguishable permutations** in such cases is illustrated in the following example.

● **Example 1.** How many different seven-digit integers can be formed from the set 4, 4, 5, 5, 5, 6, 8 of seven digits?

Suppose the digits appear one each on seven different distinguishable toy blocks. If these seven blocks are placed in a row with the number faces up, then a sequence of seven digits (and a corresponding seven-digit integer) will be obtained. Let P represent the number of distinguishable seven-digit sequences. We wish to determine the number P. Since the seven blocks are distinguishable, we know that they may be permuted in 7! distinguishable ways. The two blocks with digit 4 may be permuted in 2! ways without altering the appearance of any one of the P distinguishable seven-digit integers. Similarly, the three blocks with digit 5 may be permuted in 3! ways without altering the appearance of any one of the P distinguishable seven-digit integers. Since in each of the P distinguishable permutations the digits 4 may be permuted in 2! ways and the digits 5 in 3! ways without changing the distinguishable permutation it follows that $P \cdot 2! \cdot 3!$ is the same as the total number of permutations of the blocks — namely, 7!. That is, $P \cdot 2! \cdot 3! = 7!$ and

$$P = \frac{7!}{2!3!} = \frac{7 \cdot 6 \cdot 5 \cdot 4 \cdot 3!}{2 \cdot 3!} = 420.$$

Let us return to the more general problem. Assume that a collection of n objects belong to k sets where the objects in each set are alike,† but different sets contain different objects. Let n_1 be the number of objects in a first set, n_2 the number of objects in a second set, and so on to n_k the number of objects in a kth set where $n = n_1 + n_2 + \cdots + n_k$. The number P of distinguishable permutations of the n objects taken n at a time is

$$P = \frac{n!}{n_1!n_2! \cdots n_k!}. \qquad (11.4)$$

In any one of the P distinguishable sequences of the n objects, the n_1 objects in the first set may be permuted in $n_1!$ ways without disturbing the appearance of the arrangement of the entire sequence of n objects. Similar statements may be made for the n_2 objects in the second set and on to the n_k objects in the kth set. Consequently, when the number P, the number of distinguishable sequences of the n objects, is multiplied by $n_1!n_2! \cdots n_k!$ the resulting product $Pn_1!n_2! \cdots n_k!$ is equal to $n!$, the number of permutations of n distinguishable objects. Therefore,

$$Pn_1!n_2! \cdots n_k! = n!$$

and

$$P = \frac{n!}{n_1!n_2! \cdots n_k!}, \qquad n = n_1 + n_2 + \cdots + n_k.$$

If the objects are all different then

$$n_1 = n_2 = \cdots = n_k = 1 \quad \text{and} \quad P = n! = P(n, n).$$

● **Example 2.** How many different three-digit integers can be formed from the digits 1, 2, 2?

In this example $n_1 = 1$, $n_2 = 2$ and $n = 3$. Then

$$P = \frac{3!}{1!2!} = \frac{3 \cdot 2!}{1 \cdot 2!} = 3.$$

The integers are: 122, 212, 221.

† The objects in a collection may be considered alike if they have some property in common which characterizes each set. For example, a collection of three boys and four girls could consist of the two sets: three boys alike in the property boy, and four girls alike in the property girl. The number of distinguishable sequential arrangements P of the seven objects relative to sex is

$$P = \frac{7!}{3!4!} = 35.$$

- **Example 3.** In how many ways (distinguishable as to monetary value) can two dimes, three quarters, and four half dollars be distributed, one coin to each of nine children?

  In this example $n_1 = 2$, $n_2 = 3$, $n_3 = 4$, and $n = 9$. Then

  $$P = \frac{9!}{2!3!4!} = \frac{9 \cdot 8 \cdot 7 \cdot 6 \cdot 5 \cdot 4!}{1 \cdot 2 \cdot 1 \cdot 2 \cdot 3 \cdot 4!} = 1260.$$

If there are only two sets of objects with x objects in a first set and $n - x$ objects in the second set, then formula (11.4) becomes

$$P = \frac{n!}{x!(n-x)!} = \frac{n(n-1) \cdots (n-x+1) \cdot (n-x)!}{x!(n-x)!},$$

or

$$\frac{n(n-1) \cdots (x+1) \cdot x!}{(n-x)! \cdot x!}.$$

$$P = \frac{n!}{x!(n-x)!} = \frac{n(n-1) \cdots (n-x+1)}{x!}, \quad \text{or} \quad \frac{n(n-1) \cdots (x+1)}{(n-x)!}. \quad (11.5)$$

When $x \leq n/2$ the first form of (11.5) should be used. Otherwise, use the second result. In either case, the number of factors in the numerator is the same as the number of factors in the denominator. The symbol $\binom{n}{x}$ is used to represent $\frac{n!}{x!(n-x)!}$. That is,

$$\binom{n}{x} = \frac{n!}{x!(n-x)!} = \frac{n(n-1) \cdots (n-x+1)}{1 \cdot 2 \cdots x}$$

$$= \frac{n(n-1) \cdots (x+1)}{1 \cdot 2 \cdots (n-x)}. \quad (11.6)$$

This symbol is studied further in Section 11–6.

- **Illustration.** $\binom{5}{3} = \frac{5!}{3!2!} = \frac{5 \cdot 4 \cdot 3}{1 \cdot 2 \cdot 3} = \frac{5 \cdot 4}{1 \cdot 2} = 10.$

PROBLEM SET 11–3

1. Three different mathematics texts and five different engineering texts are to be placed on a shelf. The mathematics texts are to be on the left side of the shelf, the engineering texts on the right. In how many ways may they be placed in a row on the shelf?

2. Six different red books and four different blue books are to be shelved. In how many ways can the books be arranged on a shelf if the red books are kept together and the blue books together?

3. In how many ways can twelve different books be arranged on a shelf, if a set of six books is kept together? In how many ways if the set of six books is placed in a certain order and kept together?

4. A library has seven identical copies of one book, four identical copies of another, and five of a third. In how many different ways may all sixteen books be arranged in a row?

5. A box contains five red, six white, and seven blue balls. In how many ways can four balls be drawn in succession, without replacements, such that the first is red, the second white, the third white, and the fourth blue?

6. In how many different (as to value) ways can three dimes and three nickels be distributed among six children so that each child shall receive a coin?

7. Frank Adonis knows five girls, each of whom will give him dates whenever he asks. (a) In how many different ways may Frank arrange dates for Friday evening, Saturday evening, and Sunday afternoon? (b) If Frank decides to spread his charms about a bit and refuses to date the same girl more than once during a given week end, in how many ways may he arrange dates for the above week end?

8. Frank Adonis (see Problem 7) discovers that two of the girls are roommates and decides it would be unpolitic to date more than one of the roommates on a given week end. How many ways may he now arrange dates under the conditions of Problem 7?

[HINT: Consider two cases, in one of which Frank *does* date one of the roommates and the other of which Frank *does not* date either roommate.]

9. Art Adonis, Frank's father, decides to paint his checker board with four colors. The following colors of paint are available: red, white, blue, green, black, tan, orange, yellow, purple, and grey. Art must use red and black for the squares, and any two other colors for the trim. He decides to paint the red portions first, followed by both trim colors, followed by the black. In how many different orders might he paint his checker board under these conditions?

10. A chorus consists of four girls in silver costumes and four girls in blue costumes. (a) In how many ways may the girls be lined up in a straight line facing the footlights with the colors alternating? (b) In two lines with the girls in blue behind the girls in silver?

11. How many different six-digit integers can be formed from the set 1, 1, 4, 2, 2, 3?

12. How many signals may be made with four green, three red, one blue, and one white flags by arranging them all on a mast together?

13. In how many ways (distinguishable as to monetary value) can four 1-dollar bills, three 2-dollar bills, and five 5-dollar bills be distributed, one to each of twelve children?

14. How many six-digit integers may be formed using the digits 2, 2, 2, 3, 3, 5?

15. How many of the six-digit integers of Problem 14 are divisible by 5?

16. The letter p appears on one face of each of seven toy blocks and the letter q on one face of each of four other toy blocks. Find the number of distinguishable permutations of the p's and q's if the blocks are placed in a row with the letter faces up.

17. Prove $\dbinom{n}{x} = \dbinom{n}{n-x}.$

18. Find the values of $\dbinom{n}{0}$ and $\dbinom{n}{n}.$

19. Show that if the n objects are all distinct (that is, $n_1 = n_2 = \cdots = n_k = 1$), then the formula for distinguishable permutations given in this section reduces to the formula of the previous section.

20. Find $\displaystyle\sum_{x=0}^{5} \dbinom{5}{x}.$

21. Prove (**Pascal's rule**): $\dbinom{n+1}{x} = \dbinom{n}{x-1} + \dbinom{n}{x}.$

From Pascal's rule we are able to construct the numbers $\dbinom{n}{x}$ in a triangular array called **Pascal's triangle**. Arrange the numbers in rows corresponding to $n = 0, 1, 2, \cdots$ and columns corresponding to $x = 0, 1, 2, \cdots, x \leq n$. Each table entry can be obtained from equation (11.6) for $\dbinom{n}{x}.$ However, one may construct the table row by row observing that each row begins and ends with 1 and that the intermediate entries may be found by *applying Pascal's rule*. For $n \geq 2$, to obtain an intermediate table entry $\dbinom{n}{x}$ add together the entries $\dbinom{n-1}{x}$, and $\dbinom{n-1}{x-1}$ — that is, add together the number immediately above the desired entry in the table and the number that precedes it. For example (see table): $\dbinom{4}{2} = \dbinom{3}{1} + \dbinom{3}{2} = 3 + 3 = 6.$

n \ x	0	1	2	3	4 $\cdots$
0	1				
1	1	1			
2	1	2	1		
3	1	3→3	1		
4	1	4	6	4	1

22. Construct rows $n = 5, 6, 7$ of the Pascal triangle.

11–4. The binomial expansion. In this section we obtain a simplified method of expanding $(a + b)^n$, where n is any positive integer, which avoids the tediousness of repeated multiplications and corresponding additions. Important applications of the binomial expansion will appear in studies involving numerical approximation, probability, and statistics. Write $(a + b)^n$ in the form

$$(a + b)^n = (a + b)(a + b) \cdots (a + b), \tag{11.7}$$

where there are n binomial factors $(a + b)$. To obtain each term in the expanded product one, and only one, term is selected from each of the n binomial factors in the right member. A first term, a^n, is obtained if a is selected from each of the n factors. If a is selected from $n - 1$ factors and b from the remaining factor, a term of the form $a^{n-1}b$ results. Since b may be selected from any one of the n factors, it follows that n terms $a^{n-1}b$ will appear in the expanded product. If these n terms $a^{n-1}b$ are collected together, the second term, $n \cdot a^{n-1}b$, of the desired binomial expansion is obtained. Now,

$$(a + b)^n = a^n + na^{n-1}b + \cdots,$$

where the terms represented by the dots must be determined. A general term of the expanded product in (11.7) is of the form

$$a^{n-x}b^x.$$

For, if, in forming this product, a is selected from $n - x$ of the binomial factors, then b must be selected from the remaining x binomial factors. It is necessary to determine the number of times $a^{n-x}b^x$ appears as a term in the expanded product. Consider the sequence, $a, a, \cdots, a, b, b, \cdots, b$ consisting of $(n - x)$ factors a and (x) factors b selected from the sequence of n binomial factors. The product of the terms of this sequence is $a^{n-x}b^x$. It follows that the number of times $a^{n-x}b^x$ appears in the expansion of $(a + b)^n$ is the same as the number of distinguishable n-term sequences of $(n - x)$ a's and (x) b's. This number is the same as the number of distinguishable permutations of $(n - x)$ a's and (x) b's taken n at a time, which is

$$\binom{n}{n - x} = \frac{n!}{(n - x)!x!}$$

$$= \frac{n(n - 1)(n - 2) \cdots (n - x + 1)}{1 \cdot 2 \cdot 3 \cdots x} \quad [\text{Equations (11.5), (11.6)}].$$

The addition of the terms $a^{n-x}b^x$ gives the **general term of the binomial expansion** of $(a + b)^n$. The general term is

$$\binom{n}{n - x} a^{n-x}b^x = \frac{n!}{(n - x)!x!} a^{n-x}b^x \tag{11.8}$$

$$= \frac{n(n - 1)(n - 2) \cdots (n - x + 1)}{1 \cdot 2 \cdot 3 \cdots x} a^{n-x}b^x.$$

Upon expanding $(a + b)^n$ and collecting like terms, the expansion (11.9) or (11.10), called the **binomial expansion,** is obtained.

$$(a+b)^n = a^n + na^{n-1}b + \frac{n(n-1)}{1 \cdot 2} a^{n-2}b^2 + \frac{n(n-1)(n-2)}{1 \cdot 2 \cdot 3} a^{n-3}b^3 + \cdots$$

$$+ \frac{n(n-1) \cdots (n-x+1)}{1 \cdot 2 \cdots x} a^{n-x}b^x + \cdots + \frac{n(n-1) \cdots 1}{1 \cdot 2 \cdots n} b^n. \quad (11.9)$$

$$(a+b)^n = \binom{n}{0} a^n + \binom{n}{1} a^{n-1}b + \binom{n}{2} a^{n-2}b^2 + \cdots$$

$$+ \binom{n}{x} a^{n-x}b^x + \cdots + \binom{n}{n-1} ab^{n-1} + \binom{n}{n} b^n$$

$$= \sum_{x=0}^{n} \binom{n}{x} a^{n-x}b^x. \qquad (11.10)$$

From (11.9) and (11.10) it is seen that the general term (11.8) is the $(x+1)$th term of the binomial expansion of $(a + b)^n$.

- **Example 1.** Write the expansion of $(q + p)^5$.

$$(q+p)^5 = q^5 + 5q^4p + \frac{5 \cdot 4}{1 \cdot 2} q^3p^2 + \frac{5 \cdot 4 \cdot 3}{1 \cdot 2 \cdot 3} q^2p^3 + \frac{5 \cdot 4 \cdot 3 \cdot 2}{1 \cdot 2 \cdot 3 \cdot 4} qp^4 + \frac{5 \cdot 4 \cdot 3 \cdot 2 \cdot 1}{1 \cdot 2 \cdot 3 \cdot 4 \cdot 5} p^5$$

$$= q^5 + 5q^4p + 10q^3p^2 + 10q^2p^3 + 5qp^4 + p^5.$$

- **Example 2.** Show that $2^n = \sum\limits_{x=0}^{n} \binom{n}{x}.$

In (11.10) let $a = b = 1$ and obtain $(1+1)^n = \sum\limits_{x=0}^{n} \binom{n}{x}.$

- **Example 3.** Write the expansion of $(3x^2 - \sqrt{y})^4$.

$$(3x^2 - \sqrt{y})^4 = (3x^2)^4 + 4(3x^2)^3(-\sqrt{y}) + \frac{4 \cdot 3}{1 \cdot 2} (3x^2)^2(-\sqrt{y})^2$$

$$+ \frac{4 \cdot 3 \cdot 2}{1 \cdot 2 \cdot 3} (3x^2)(-\sqrt{y})^3 + \frac{4 \cdot 3 \cdot 2 \cdot 1}{1 \cdot 2 \cdot 3 \cdot 4} (-\sqrt{y})^4$$

$$= 81x^8 - 108x^6\sqrt{y} + 54x^4y - 12x^2y\sqrt{y} + y^2.$$

- **Example 4.** Write the seventh term of the expansion of $(3/t - y/2)^9$.

Apply $\binom{n}{x} a^{n-x}b^x = \frac{n(n-1) \cdots (n-x+1)}{1 \cdot 2 \cdots x} a^{n-x}b^x$ with

$$n = 9, \quad a = 3/t, \quad b = -y/2, \quad x+1 = 7$$

and $x = 6$ to obtain

$$\frac{9!}{3!6!} \left(\frac{3}{t}\right)^{9-6} \left(-\frac{y}{2}\right)^6 = \frac{9 \cdot 8 \cdot 7 \cdot 6!}{1 \cdot 2 \cdot 3 \cdot 6!} \left(\frac{3}{t}\right)^3 \left(-\frac{y}{2}\right)^6 = 84 \left(\frac{27}{t^3}\right) \left(\frac{y^6}{64}\right) = \frac{567y^6}{16t^3},$$

or

$$\frac{9 \cdot 8 \cdot 7 \cdot 6 \cdot 5 \cdot 4}{1 \cdot 2 \cdot 3 \cdot 4 \cdot 5 \cdot 6} \left(\frac{3}{t}\right)^{9-6} \left(-\frac{y}{2}\right)^6 = 84 \left(\frac{27}{t^3}\right) \left(\frac{y^6}{64}\right) = \frac{567y^6}{16t^3}.$$

● **Example 5.** Assume that the binomial expansion applies and write the first five terms of the (series) expansion of $\sqrt{1+x} = (1+x)^{\frac{1}{2}}$.

$$(1+x)^{\frac{1}{2}} = 1+\frac{1}{2}x+\frac{\frac{1}{2}(\frac{1}{2}-1)}{1\cdot 2}x^2+\frac{\frac{1}{2}(\frac{1}{2}-1)(\frac{1}{2}-2)}{1\cdot 2\cdot 3}x^3+\frac{\frac{1}{2}(\frac{1}{2}-1)(\frac{1}{2}-2)(\frac{1}{2}-3)}{1\cdot 2\cdot 3\cdot 4}x^4+\cdots$$

$$= 1 + \tfrac{1}{2}x - \tfrac{1}{8}x^2 + \tfrac{1}{16}x^3 - \tfrac{5}{128}x^4 + \cdots.$$

In this example the binomial expansion is an unending (infinite) series. If $|x| < 1$, the first few terms may be used to obtain an approximation of $\sqrt{1+x}$. If $x = 0.1$, the approximation obtained by using the first four terms is accurate to five decimal places.

● **Example 6.** Use the first three terms of the series in Example 5 to approximate $\sqrt{95}$.

$$\sqrt{95} = \sqrt{100 - 5} = \sqrt{100}\sqrt{1 - .05} = 10(1 - .05)^{\frac{1}{2}}$$

$$= 10[1 + \tfrac{1}{2}(- .05) - \tfrac{1}{8}(.05)^2 - \cdots]$$

$$= 10[1 - .025 - .0003125 - \cdots]$$

$$\cong 10[.9747]$$

$$= 9.747.$$

● **Example 7.** Assume that the binomial expansion applies and write the first four terms and the $(k+1)$th term of the (series) expansion of $(1 + z)^{\theta/z}$.

$$(1+z)^{\theta/z} = 1+\frac{\theta}{z}\cdot z+\frac{\frac{\theta}{z}\left(\frac{\theta}{z}-1\right)}{1\cdot 2}z^2+\frac{\frac{\theta}{z}\left(\frac{\theta}{z}-1\right)\left(\frac{\theta}{z}-2\right)}{1\cdot 2\cdot 3}z^3+\cdots$$

$$+\frac{\frac{\theta}{z}\left(\frac{\theta}{z}-1\right)\left(\frac{\theta}{z}-2\right)\cdots\left(\frac{\theta}{z}-k+1\right)}{1\cdot 2\cdot 3\cdots k}z^k+\cdots$$

or

$$(1+z)^{\theta/z} = 1+\theta+\frac{\theta(\theta-z)}{1\cdot 2}+\frac{\theta(\theta-z)(\theta-2z)}{1\cdot 2\cdot 3}+\cdots$$

$$+\frac{\theta(\theta-z)(\theta-2z)\cdots(\theta-kz+z)}{1\cdot 2\cdot 3\cdots k}+\cdots. \qquad (11.11)$$

Let $z \to 0$ in (11.11). Then

$$e^\theta = \lim_{z\to 0}(1+z)^{\theta/z} = 1+\theta+\frac{\theta^2}{1\cdot 2}+\frac{\theta^3}{1\cdot 2\cdot 3}+\cdots+\frac{\theta^k}{1\cdot 2\cdot 3\cdots k}+\cdots$$

$$e^\theta = 1+\theta+\frac{\theta^2}{2!}+\frac{\theta^3}{3!}+\cdots+\frac{\theta^k}{k!}+\cdots = \sum_{k=0}^{\infty}\frac{\theta^k}{k!}.$$

The series used to evaluate the base e of the natural logarithms may be obtained as follows. The number e is defined as

$$e = \lim_{z\to 0}(1+z)^{1/z} = 1+1+\frac{1}{1\cdot 2}+\frac{1}{1\cdot 2\cdot 3}+\cdots+\frac{1}{1\cdot 2\cdots k}+\cdots$$

$$= 1+1+\frac{1}{2!}+\frac{1}{3!}+\cdots+\frac{1}{k!}+\cdots = \sum_{k=0}^{\infty}\frac{1}{k!}.$$

Decimal approximations yield:

$$
\begin{aligned}
1 + 1 &\cong 2.0000 \\
\frac{1}{2!} &\cong .5000 \\
\frac{1}{3!} = \left(\frac{1}{3}\right)\left(\frac{1}{2!}\right) &\cong .1667 \\
\frac{1}{4!} = \left(\frac{1}{4}\right)\left(\frac{1}{3!}\right) &\cong .0417 \\
\frac{1}{5!} = \left(\frac{1}{5}\right)\left(\frac{1}{4!}\right) &\cong .0083 \\
\frac{1}{6!} = \left(\frac{1}{6}\right)\left(\frac{1}{5!}\right) &\cong .0014 \\
\frac{1}{7!} = \left(\frac{1}{7}\right)\left(\frac{1}{6!}\right) &\cong .0002 \\
\frac{1}{8!} = \left(\frac{1}{8}\right)\left(\frac{1}{7!}\right) &\cong .0000 \\
\cdots \qquad\qquad & \quad \cdots \\
\hline
e \qquad\qquad\qquad & \cong 2.718.
\end{aligned}
$$

The value of e correct to eight significant figures is 2.7182818.

If one assumes, as can be proved in more advanced courses, that $\dfrac{d}{d\theta} e$ can be found by differentiating the series for e^θ termwise and adding the resulting terms then

$$
\frac{d}{d\theta} e^\theta = \sum_{k=0}^{\infty} \frac{d}{d\theta}\left(\frac{\theta^k}{k!}\right) = 1 + \theta + \frac{\theta^2}{2!} + \frac{\theta^3}{3!} + \cdots = e^\theta
$$

and

$$
\frac{d}{dx} e^\theta = e^\theta \cdot \frac{d\theta}{dx}. \qquad \text{(See Section 9–4.)}
$$

● **Example 8.** Find $\dfrac{dy}{dt}$: $y = \dfrac{1}{\sqrt{2\pi}} e^{-t^2/2}$.

$$
\frac{dy}{dt} = \frac{1}{\sqrt{2\pi}} e^{-t^2/2}(- t) = - \frac{t}{\sqrt{2\pi}} e^{-t^2/2}.
$$

Definition. If $x = e^y$ then $y = \ln x$, where $\ln x$ is the natural logarithm of x or the logarithm of x to the base e.

Now, $\dfrac{dx}{dy} = \dfrac{d}{dy} e^y = e^y = x$ and $\dfrac{d}{dx} \ln x = \dfrac{dy}{dx} = \dfrac{1}{x}$. It follows that

$$
\frac{d}{dx} \ln u = \frac{1}{u} \cdot \frac{du}{dx}.
$$

● **Example 9.** $\dfrac{d}{dx} \ln \left(\dfrac{\sqrt{2x-3}}{x^3}\right) = \dfrac{d}{dx} \left[\dfrac{1}{2} \ln (2x-3) - 3 \ln x\right]$

$$= \dfrac{d}{dx} \left[\dfrac{1}{2} \ln (2x-3)\right] - \dfrac{d}{dx} [3 \ln x]$$

$$= \dfrac{1}{2} \cdot \dfrac{1}{2x-3} \cdot 2 - 3 \cdot \dfrac{1}{x} = \dfrac{1}{2x-3} - \dfrac{3}{x}.$$

● **Example 10.** Prove: $\dfrac{d}{dx} v^n = nv^{n-1} \dfrac{dv}{dx}$, $\quad n$ a real constant.

Let $y = v^n$. Then $\ln y = n \ln v$ and $\dfrac{1}{y} \dfrac{dy}{dx} = \dfrac{n}{v} \dfrac{dv}{dx}$ (Why?)

$\dfrac{dy}{dx} = \dfrac{nv^n}{v} \dfrac{dv}{dx} = nv^{n-1} \dfrac{dv}{dx}$. This proof does not restrict n to be rational.

PROBLEM SET 11-4

1. Explain and simplify: $(t^2/2 + 3/t)^4$.

2. Write the expansion of $(2x - 3y)^5$.

3. Write the first four terms of $(2/x^3 - \sqrt{y})^7$.

4. Write the first three terms of $(2a^{\frac{1}{2}} + 3/x)^8$.

5. Find the sixth term of $\left(x - \dfrac{1}{2y}\right)^{10}$.

6. Find the fifth term of $\left(\dfrac{x^2}{y} - \dfrac{y^2}{2x}\right)^9$.

7. Expand and find the value of $(1.02)^4 = (1 + .02)^4$.

8. Find the amount of \$300 at 2 percent compounded annually for 4 years. See Section 10–4.

9. Use the first four terms of $(1 + .03)^{10}$ to approximate the value of $(1.03)^{10}$.

10. Use the first four terms of the appropriate binomial expansion to approximate the amount of \$200 compounded annually at 3 percent for 10 years. See Section 10–4.

11. Use the first three terms of the appropriate binomial expansion to find the amount of \$150 at 2.9 percent, compounded semiannually for 10 years. See Section 10–4.

12. Find $\sqrt{105} = 10(1 + .05)^{\frac{1}{2}}$. Use the first four terms of $(1 + .05)^{\frac{1}{2}}$.

13. Find $\sqrt[3]{991} = 10\sqrt[3]{1 - .009}$. Use the first three terms of $(1 - .009)^{\frac{1}{3}}$.

14. Find the sum of the coefficients in the binomial expansion of $(a + b)^8$.

*15. Show that the sum of alternate binomial coefficients in $(a+b)^n$ is 2^{n-1}.

16. Consult a handbook or tables to determine e as accurately as you can. Some students may also be interested in consulting the journal *Mathematical Tables and Other Aids to Computation*, now called *Mathematics of Computation*.

17. Use natural logarithms to help prove:

(a) $\dfrac{d}{dx} uv = v\dfrac{du}{dx} + u\dfrac{dv}{dx}$.

(b) Extend the formula in (a) to a product of four factors.

(c) $\dfrac{d}{dx}\dfrac{u}{v} = \dfrac{v\dfrac{du}{dx} - u\dfrac{dv}{dx}}{v^2}$.

18. Find the dimensions of the rectangle of maximum area having two vertices on $y = e^{-x^2}$ and a base on the x-axis.

19. Find the x values of the points on the curve

$$y = \frac{1}{\sigma\sqrt{2\pi}}\, e^{-\frac{1}{2}\left(\frac{x-\mu}{\sigma}\right)^2} \quad \text{for which} \quad \frac{d^2y}{dx^2} = 0.$$

11–5. Instantaneous compound interest law. If an amount $A(t)$ at the rate of interest r is changing continuously by instantaneous compounding, then an expression for $A(t)$ as a function of the time t is called the **instantaneous compound interest law** or the **law of growth.**

If P is the original amount invested, r is the rate of interest, t is the number of years, and k is the number of periods per year, then (Example 4, Section 10–4)

$$a_{kt} = P\left[1 + \frac{r}{100k}\right]^{kt} = P\left[\left(1 + \frac{r}{100k}\right)^{100k/r}\right]^{rt/100}.$$

Let $z = \dfrac{r}{100k}$ and obtain

$$a_{kt} = P[(1+z)^{1/z}]^{rt/100}.$$

Now, $z \to 0$ as $k \to \infty$. That is, $z \to 0$ as the number k of periods increases indefinitely. Therefore,

$$
\begin{aligned}
A(t) &= \lim_{k\to\infty} a_{kt} = \lim_{z\to 0} P[(1+z)^{1/z}]^{rt/100}\\
&= P[\lim_{z\to 0} (1+z)^{1/z}]^{rt/100}\\
&= P[e]^{rt/100}
\end{aligned}
$$

or

$$A(t) = P[e]^{rt/100}. \tag{11.12}$$

We have proved that $\dfrac{d}{dt}(e^u) = e^u\dfrac{du}{dt}$. (See pp. 206, 207.)

If this is assumed, then

$$\frac{dA(t)}{dt} = P\frac{d}{dt}(e^{rt/100}) = Pe^{rt/100}\frac{d}{dt}(rt/100) = \frac{r}{100}Pe^{rt/100} = \frac{r}{100}A(t). \quad (11.13)$$

In this case, the time rate of change of the amount is proportional to the amount.

● *Example 1.* Find the amount at the end of 10 years if a principal of $75 is placed at interest at 2.9 percent, compounded continuously.

In this example $P = \$75$, $r = 2.9$, $t = 10$ years, and

$$A(10) = 75e^{\frac{2.9}{100}(10)} = 75e^{.29} = 75(1.3364) = 100.23 \text{ dollars.}†$$

● *Example 2.* Find the simple interest rate that will yield, in one year from $1000, the same sum as $1000 at 5 percent, compounded continuously.

In this example $P = \$1000$, $r = 5$, and $A(t) = 1000e^{(5/100)t}$. The amount, compounded continuously for one year, is

$$A(1) = 1000e^{.05} \cong 1000(1.0513) = 1051.3 \text{ dollars.}$$

The interest for one year is

$$\$1051.3 - \$1000 = \$51.3.$$

Therefore, the simple interest rate is

$$100\left(\frac{51.3}{1000}\right) = 5.13 \text{ percent.}$$

● *Example 3.* Assume that bacteria in a culture increase at a rate proportional to the number present. In a bacteria culture the number present at a certain instant is 100; 4 hours later the number is 400. Approximate the number of bacteria at the end of 10 hours.

To apply (11.12) let $t = 0$ when $P = 100$. Then

$$A(t) = 100e^{(r/100)t},$$

and

$$A(4) = 100^{(r/100)(4)} = 400.$$

To find r, solve $e^{4r/100} = 4$.

$$\frac{4r}{100}\log_{10}e = \log_{10}4,$$

$$\frac{r}{100} = \frac{\log_{10}4}{4\log_{10}e} \cong \frac{0.60206}{4(0.43429)} \cong 0.345.$$

Therefore

$$A(t) \cong 100e^{0.345t},$$

and

$$A(10) \cong 100e^{3.45} \cong 3200.$$

† The value of $e^{.29}$ may be found directly in an exponential table, or may be computed using logarithms.

PROBLEM SET 11-5

1. Find the amount at the end of 10 years if a principal of $500 is placed a interest at 3 percent, (a) compounded semiannually; (b) compounde continuously.

2. Sugar in solution decomposes at a time rate proportional to the amoun $A(t)$ not decomposed. (a) Show that $A(t) = ae^{-kt}$. (b) If 25 lb of suga reduces to 10 lb in 8 hours, how long will it take for 80 percent of the suga to be decomposed?

3. A machine, when new, costs $20,000 and has a salvage value of $200 a the end of 10 years. Find the value of such a machine at the end of 5 years assuming that the time rate of depreciation is proportional to the value a the time under consideration.

4. Radium decomposes at a time rate which is proportional to the amoun present. If half the original quantity disappears in 1750 years, what por tion disappears in 50 years?

5. In a bacteria culture, the number present is 1000; 4 hours later the num ber is 4000. Find the number at the end of 15 hours assuming that th rate of increase is proportional to the number present.

6. Find $\displaystyle\lim_{x\to 0}\left(1+\frac{x}{2}\right)^{1/x}$.

7. Find $\displaystyle\lim_{\Delta u\to 0}\left(1+\frac{\Delta u}{u}\right)^{u/\Delta u}$.

8. Find $\displaystyle\lim_{x\to\infty}\left(1-\frac{2}{x}\right)^{x}$.

9. Find $\displaystyle\lim_{x\to\infty}\left(1+\frac{1}{x^2}\right)^{x^2/2}$.

11-6. Combinations. The theory of combinations is concerned with the problem of counting the number of ways in which objects of a finite set may be selected. Essentially a combination refers to the composition of a set o objects without regard to their arrangement.

- *Example 1.* How many different sets each containing three letters may be selected from a, b, c, d?

    There are four such sets: a, b, c; a, b, d; a, c, d; b, c, d. The number, 4 of these sets is the number of combinations of the four objects taken three at a time. Note that the combination a, b, c is the same as the combina tion b, a, c. Contrast this with permutations, in which the sets $a, b,$ and b, a, c form distinct permutations.

    A combination of *n* objects *x* at a time is a selection of x of the n objects.

    We shall show that if $\dbinom{n}{x}$ is the number of combinations of n dis tinguishable objects x at a time, then

$$\binom{n}{x} = \frac{n!}{x!(n-x)!} = \frac{n(n-1)\cdots(n-x+1)}{1\cdot 2\cdots x}.$$

Each of the $\binom{n}{x}$ different sets of x objects can be arranged into $x!$ different sequences. From the *fundamental principle* (Section 11–1) it is seen that $\binom{n}{x} \cdot x!$ is equal to the total number of sequences of n distinguishable objects taken x at a time. The number of sequences of n objects taken x at a time is equal to the number of permutations of n objects x at a time. Thus,

$$\binom{n}{x} \cdot x! = \frac{n!}{(n-x)!} = n(n-1) \cdots (n-x+1)$$

and

$$\binom{n}{x} = \frac{n!}{x!(n-x)!} = \frac{n(n-1) \cdots (n-x+1)}{x!}.$$

The symbol $\binom{n}{x}$ used in Section 11–3 thus represents two logically distinct ideas having identical numerical values — namely, (1) a *distinguishable permutation* of n objects x of which are of one type and $(n-x)$ of another, and (2) a *combination* of n objects taken x at a time.

Example 2. How many lines are determined by ten points no three of which are collinear?

Two points determine a line. The desired number of lines is the same as the number of combinations of ten points taken two at a time. Namely,

$$\frac{10!}{2!8!} = \frac{10 \cdot 9}{1 \cdot 2} = 45.$$

Example 3. How many different hands consisting of 5 cards could be dealt from a deck of 52 playing cards?

The number of different hands is $\dfrac{52 \cdot 51 \cdot 50 \cdot 49 \cdot 48}{1 \cdot 2 \cdot 3 \cdot 4 \cdot 5} = 2{,}598{,}960.$

Example 4. Two urns contain balls that are distinguishable. The first urn contains ten balls while the second contains eight balls. How many seven-ball selections, three balls from the first urn and four balls from the second urn, are possible?

The number of three-ball selections from the first urn is $\dfrac{10 \cdot 9 \cdot 8}{1 \cdot 2 \cdot 3}.$ The number of four-ball selections from the second urn is $\dfrac{8 \cdot 7 \cdot 6 \cdot 5}{1 \cdot 2 \cdot 3 \cdot 4}.$ Application of the fundamental principle yields the number of seven-ball selections as

$$\frac{10 \cdot 9 \cdot 8}{1 \cdot 2 \cdot 3} \cdot \frac{8 \cdot 7 \cdot 6 \cdot 5}{1 \cdot 2 \cdot 3 \cdot 4} = 120 \cdot 70 = 8400.$$

Remember: In a *permutation* the order in which the objects are arranged (permuted) is of importance, whereas in a *combination* the objects are merely selected, but not placed in any particular order after selection.

PROBLEM SET 11-6

1. An inspector is to test a sample of four parts out of fifty parts produced by an automatic machine. In how many ways can he select a sample of four parts?

2. In how many ways can three identical positions be filled by selections from eight applicants? In how many ways if the three positions are different?

3. How many planes are determined by four points which are not in the same plane?

4. In how many ways can a committee of five be selected from a group of twelve men and eight women if it is to contain three men and two women?

5. A man wishes to entertain eight friends, four at a time. In how many ways can he do it?

6. From fifteen different French books and ten different German books how many sets of six books may be chosen if exactly four are French? If at least four are French?

7. Two cards are drawn from a suit of thirteen cards. How many different sets of two cards can be drawn? In how many sets of two cards will both cards be among the five highest cards?

8. In how many different ways, distinguishable as to monetary value, can four dimes and two nickels be distributed among six children so that each child shall receive a coin?

9. A list of ten examination questions is to be chosen from fifty review questions. For each correct answer 10 percent is to be scored and only correct answers are to receive credit. In how many ways can a list of ten questions be selected such that a student who knows twenty-five of the answers will score 100 percent? So he will score 90 percent? So he will score 0 percent?

10. Five cards are dealt from an ordinary deck. In how many ways can this be done if exactly x of the five cards dealt are spades?

11. In how many ways can four men be selected from five Italians and seven Spaniards so as to include (a) exactly one Spaniard? (b) at least one Spaniard?

*12. In how many ways can twelve persons vote to fill an office for which there are three nominees? In how many of these ways will a certain one of the nominees receive a majority vote?

13. How many diagonals can be drawn in a regular polygon having n sides?

14. How many different sums can be formed from one penny, one nickel, one dime, one quarter, and one half dollar (a) using at least two coins? (b) using not more than three coins?

15. Show that, in the expansion of $(a + b)^n$, the coefficient of $a^{n-x}b^x$ may be thought of as (a) a combination of n things taken x at a time, or (b) a combination of n things taken $n - x$ at a time. See also Problem 17, Set 11-3.

11–7. Self test.

Record time.

1. Expand $(2 - \sqrt{x})^5$.

2. Find the tenth term of $\left(\dfrac{x}{2} - x^2\right)^{12}$.

3. How many signals can be made with three identical blue flags, two identical red flags, and one yellow flag by arranging them all on a mast together?

4. Find n if $\dbinom{n}{2} = 28$.

5. (a) How many different five-digit numbers can be formed using the digits 1, 2, 3, 4, 5, 6, no digit being repeated in any number? (b) How many of these five-digit numbers both begin and end with an even digit?

6. In how many ways may a committee of five be selected from six men and four women if the committee must contain either two or three women?

7. How many different bridge hands are made up of six spades and seven clubs?

8. How many different sets of five cards contain (a) three aces and two kings? (b) three aces?

9. A box contains six black and four white balls. (a) How many different sets consisting of four balls drawn simultaneously are possible? (b) How many of these sets contain exactly three white balls? (c) Find the ratio of the number of sets in (b) to the number of sets in (a).

10. A machine costs \$20,000 when new and has a value of \$10,000 at the end of 4 years. Assuming that the time rate of depreciation is proportional to the value at the time under consideration, find the value at the end of 12 years. Logarithmic tables may be used.

11. Use the binomial expansion to find the amount due on \$1000 at 6 percent, compounded semiannually for 5 years.

12. Find $\lim\limits_{x \to 0} \left(1 + \dfrac{x}{3}\right)^{2/x}$.

Record time.

12
•••••••••••••••••••••

12–1. In the study of probability theory and mathematical statistics the concept of sample space is fundamental. A sample space is a set of points on which a (probability) function is defined. Consequently we give a brief introduction to the theory of sets and then proceed to study sample spaces and probability theory.

12–2. Sets. A **set** is a definite collection of objects, things, or symbols. An item in the set is called an **element** or **member** of the set. (See Section 1–1.)

A set may be designated by specifying its elements or by listing the properties that define the set. For example, the set S consisting of the positive odd integers beginning with 3 and terminating with 11 may be designated by $S = \{3, 5, 7, 9, 11\}$, which is read "S is the set of elements 3, 5, 7, 9, 11," or by $S = \{x \mid x$ is an odd integer and $3 \leq x \leq 11\}$,† which is read "S is the set of all elements x such that x is an odd integer and $3 \leq x \leq 11$." The first of these designations names the elements of S while the second lists properties that define S. Observe that S may be defined by $S = \{2x + 1 \mid x$ is an integer and $1 \leq x \leq 5\}$, which is read "S is the set of all elements $(2x + 1)$ such that x is an integer and $1 \leq x \leq 5$."

The set of all elements that are under consideration is called the **universal set**. From the universal set U one may select subsets of elements. The **empty** or null subset $\emptyset$ contains no elements. A **finite** set contains a finite number of elements. The set $U = \{1, 2, 3\}$ has 2^3 subsets: $\{1, 2, 3\}$, $\{1, 2\}$, $\{1, 3\}$, $\{2, 3\}$, $\{1\}$, $\{2\}$, $\{3\}$, and the empty set $\emptyset$.

Two sets A and B are equal, $A = B$, if, and only if, they are identical. This requires every element of A to be in B and every element of B to be in A.

There are three especially important set operations: union, intersection, and complementation.

Let $A, B, C, \cdots$ be subsets of a universal set U.

The **union** of A and B, $A \cup B$, is the set of all elements of U that belong either to A or to B (or to both). $A \cup B = \{x \mid x$ in A or x in $B\}$. $A \cup B$ may be read "A union B."

The **intersection** of A and B, $A \cap B$, is the set of all elements of U that belong to both A and B. $A \cap B = \{x \mid x$ in A and x in $B\}$. $A \cap B$ may be read "A intersect B."

---

† This convenient notation may be unfamiliar. If so, the student should learn to use it now. The vertical bar in the notation $\{ \mid \}$ means that the statements appearing to the right of the vertical bar are conditions that the elements appearing on the left of the vertical bar must satisfy to be members of the set. Thus we may designate the set of all girls who are in a mathematics class by

$$\{g \mid g \text{ is a girl and } g \text{ is in the mathematics class}\}.$$

Two sets A and B are **disjoint** or **mutually exclusive** if they have no elements in common. If A and B are mutually exclusive, then the intersection of A and B is empty — that is, $A \cap B = \emptyset$.

The **complement** A' of A is the set of all elements in U which are not in A. $A' = \{x \mid x$ in U but not in $A\}$.

- *Illustration.* $U = \{1, 2, 3, 4, 5\}$, $A = \{1, 3, 5\}$, $A' = \{2, 4\}$, $B = \{2, 3, 5\}$, $A \cup B = \{1, 2, 3, 5\}$, $A \cap B = \{3, 5\}$, $A \cup A' = U$, $A \cap A' = \emptyset$.

The following four laws hold for sets and the operations $\cup$ and $\cap$:

(1) *Commutative:* $A \cup B = B \cup A$, $A \cap B = B \cap A$.

(2) *Associative:* $(A \cup B) \cup C = A \cup (B \cup C)$,
$$(A \cap B) \cap C = A \cap (B \cap C).$$

(3) *Intersection is distributive over union:*
$$A \cap (B \cup C) = (A \cap B) \cup (A \cap C).$$

(4) *Union is distributive over intersection:*
$$A \cup (B \cap C) = (A \cup B) \cap (A \cup C).$$

What are the analogs of the first three laws for ordinary numbers and the operations of addition and multiplication? (HINT: Let $\cup$ correspond to $+$ and $\cap$ to $\times$.) Is there an analog for the fourth law?

The proofs for the commutative and associative laws follow immediately by referring to the definitions for union and intersection. To prove the third law one may observe that any element x in $A \cap (B \cup C)$ must be in both A and B or in both A and C; that is, x is in $A \cap B$ or $A \cap C$. Therefore x is in $(A \cap B) \cup (A \cap C)$. If y is in $(A \cap B) \cup (A \cap C)$, then y is in both A and B or both A and C, which implies that y is in both A and $(B$ or $C)$. Therefore y is in $A \cap (B \cup C)$. This completes the proof that the sets $A \cap (B \cup C)$ and $(A \cap B) \cup (A \cap C)$ are equal since every element of one set is an element of the other set. If x is in $A \cup (B \cap C)$, then x is in both $A \cup B$ and $A \cup C$; that is, x is in $(A \cup B) \cap (A \cup C)$. If y is in $(A \cup B) \cap (A \cup C)$, then y is in both $A \cup B$ and $A \cup C$, which implies that y is in A or in both B and C; that is, y is in $A \cup (B \cap C)$. This completes the proof of (4). (Why?)

Venn diagrams. To aid in visualizing theorems concerning sets and properties of sets one may use Venn diagrams. In a Venn diagram a rectangle U may be used to represent the universal set U. The elements of U are represented by points in the rectangle. Sets of elements such as A and B are represented by sets of points inside the rectangle.

Let A and B be finite sets and let $n(S)$ designate the number of elements (points) in the finite set S. Now verify:†

(1) $n(A \cup B) = n(A) + n(B) - n(A \cap B)$

and for mutually exclusive sets

† A more careful proof is given in the proof of the additive set function theorem.

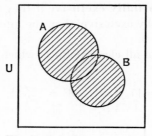

The shaded region represents
$A \cup B$.

Fig. 12–1

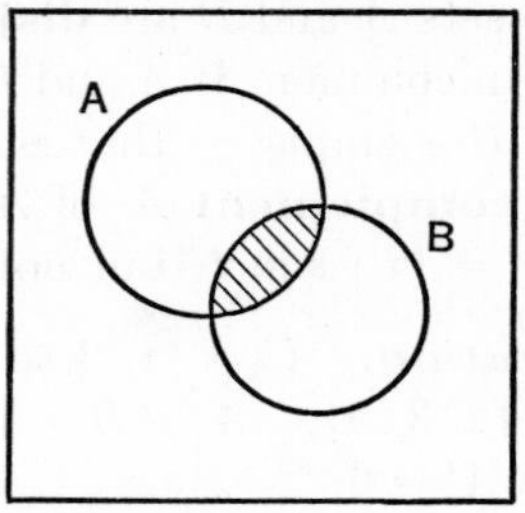

The shaded region represents
$A \cap B$.

Fig. 12–2

(2) If $A \cap B = \emptyset$ then $n(A \cap B) = 0$ and $n(A \cup B) = n(A) + n(B)$

Venn diagrams help one visualize the (1) and (2) above.

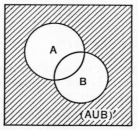

The shaded region repre-
sents $(A \cup B)'$.

Fig. 12–3

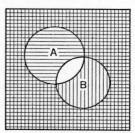

The region covered with
vertical lines repre-
sents A'.

The region covered with
horizontal lines rep-
resents B'.

The region covered by
both vertical and hori-
zontal lines represents
$A' \cap B$.

What is the totally un-
shaded region?

Fig. 12–4

Comparing $(A \cup B)'$ and $A' \cap B'$ it appears that
$(A \cup B)' = A' \cap B'$.

In the study of sample spaces we are interested in elements that have
properties which can be measured by real numbers. For example, if a set is
finite, we can count the number of elements in the set. If U is finite and has
subsets $A, B, \cdots$ and if A and B are disjoint, then
$n(A \cup B) = n(A) + n(B)$. The function n is an illustration of an additive
set function.

A function f is an **additive set function** if

(1) f is a function which assigns to any subset A of a finite set U a real number $f(A)$ and

(2) $f(A \cup B) = f(A) + f(B)$ when A and B are disjoint subsets of U.

$f(\emptyset) = 0$ since $f(A \cup \emptyset) = f(A) + f(\emptyset) = f(A)$.

The following theorem is an important additive set function theorem. It is essential in work on probability.

Theorem 1. If f is an additive set function and A and B are any two sets in the finite set U, then

$$f(A \cup B) = f(A) + f(B) - f(A \cap B).$$

PROOF: Using the distributive law (4) one may verify

$A = (A \cap B) \cup (A \cap B'), \quad B = (B \cap A) \cup (B \cap A'),$
$A \cup B = (A \cap B) \cup (A \cap B') \cup (B \cap A').$

In the three preceding equations the sets in the parentheses are disjoint. Therefore,

$$f(A) = f(A \cap B) + f(A \cap B'),$$
$$f(B) = f(A \cap B) + f(B \cap A')$$

substituted in

$$f(A \cup B) = f(A \cap B) + f(A \cap B') + f(B \cap A')$$

gives

$$f(A \cup B) = f(A) + f(B \cap A')$$
$$= f(A) + f(B) - f(A \cap B).$$

Corollary. $n(A \cup B) = n(A) + n(B) - n(A \cap B).$

In the study of probability theory and mathematical statistics we are concerned with probability functions.

A **probability function** p is an additive set function having the two properties:

(1) $p(A) \geqq 0$, A in the universal set U.
(2) $p(U) = 1$.

PROBLEM SET 12–2

1. Use Venn diagrams to check the four laws for sets and the operations $\cup$ and $\cap$.
2. Prove $(A \cup B)' = A' \cap B'$.
3. Prove $(A \cap B)' = A' \cup B'$ and check using Venn diagrams.
4. Prove $p(A) + p(A') = 1$.
5. If A is a subset of B which is a subset of a finite universal set U, show that $p(A) \leqq p(B)$.
6. If A and B are subsets of a finite universal set U, prove $p(A \cup B) = p(A) + p(B) - p(A \cap B)$ and if A and B are disjoint, $p(A \cup B) = p(A) + p(B)$.
7. If $A, B, \cdots, K$ are disjoint subsets of a finite universal set U, prove $p(A \cup B \cup \cdots \cup K) = p(A) + p(B) + \cdots + p(K)$.

8. A pack of 52 playing cards consists of four suits: thirteen spades, thirteen hearts, thirteen diamonds, thirteen clubs. There is one ace in each suit. Find the number of aces or spades.

12–3. Sample spaces. In the experiment of tossing a single coin there are two possible outcomes. The coin may fall head up or it may fall tail up. A list of the possible outcomes for an experiment is called its **sample space.** If head up is represented by 1 and tail up by 0, then these two outcomes form a sample space of two points.

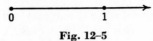

Fig. 12–5

If a coin is tossed twice there are four possible outcomes: head first, tail second represented in a two-coordinate space by $(1, 0)$; (tail, head) $= (0, 1)$; (head, head) $= (1, 1)$; and (tail, tail) $= (0, 0)$. In this case the sample space consists of four points corresponding to the four possible outcomes. The same sample space may be used to represent the possible outcomes when the experiment is a single toss of two coins. (Why?)

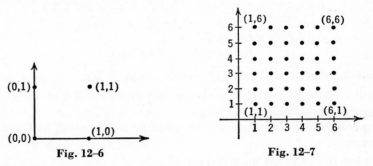

Fig. 12–6   **Fig. 12–7**

Consider the experiment: A single toss of a pair of dice consisting of one red die and one green die which yield for outcome the sample point (x, y) where x is the value that falls face up on the red die and y is the value that falls face up on the green die. There are $6 \times 6 = 36$ ordered pairs or sample points (x, y) in the sample space of possible outcomes since x and y may each take independently any one of the set of six values $\{1, 2, 3, 4, 5, 6\}$. (See Section 2–2.)

The **sample space** S or **universal set** S for an experiment is a systematic listing of all possible outcomes. Each outcome corresponds to one and only one **element** of the universal set or to one and only one **point** of the sample space. That is, the **sample space** of an experiment is a set of elements (points) such that any trial of the experiment yields an outcome which corresponds to exactly one element (point) in the set.

The notation of this section may be new to the reader. We will, therefore, expand the previous experiment to help tie the ideas of this section to a more general background.

• **Illustration.** Two dice, one red and one green, are tossed. We ask three questions.

Questions:

(1) In how many different ways could these dice land?

(2) In how many of the above ways would the sum of the spots showing be six?

(3) What is the probability of throwing a sum of six on one toss of two dice?

Answers:

(1) The green die can land in any of six ways, and so can the red die. Hence there are $6 \times 6 = 36$ ways in which the two dice could land.

(2) The only ways in which the sum of the spots would be six are

green die	1	2	3	4	5
red die	5	4	3	2	1

Hence there are exactly 5 of the 36 possible ways in which a six can be thrown.

(3) The probability of throwing a sum of six on two dice is $\frac{5}{36}$, since the events are equally likely. Unless the reader has already met probability theory, he has only intuition to assist him with the last statement.

Now we shall concentrate on expressing the three ideas given above in the important set-theoretic vocabulary of modern statistics.

(1) The **sample space** for the two dice contains 36 points representing the 36 possible outcomes of throwing the two dice. If we let the first coordinate be the number of spots shown on the green die and the second coordinate be the number of spots shown on the red die, then the points (G, R) where G and R each take on the six values 1, 2, 3, 4, 5, 6 independently are the sample space for this problem. The sample space will be represented by the 36 points as was shown in Figure 12–7.

(2) We next consider the event $E_{G+R=6}$ to be the event of throwing a sum of six points on one throw of this pair of dice. The points in the sample space which lie on the line $G + R = 6$ are the points $(G, R) = (1, 5), (2, 4), (3, 3), (4, 2), (5, 1)$, and no others. We call these five points the **event space** of $E_{G+R=6}$. The event $E_{G+R=6}$ consists of selecting a point from the sample space that is also in the event space — that is, of selecting a point in the intersection of the sample space and the event space.

(3) Before the question of the **probability** of throwing a six (that is, of selecting a point from the sample space that is also in the event space) can be determined, we must assign a numerical value (probability) to each point in the sample space. The sum of all 36 of these numerical probabilities must be 1. If we believe the dice are

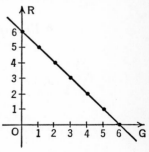

Fig. 12–8

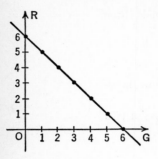

Fig. 12-8

honest, we believe any one face is as likely to be up as any other. Hence we feel all 36 points in the sample space are equally likely and therefore it seems reasonable to assign the same probabilities to each point of the sample space. If the sum of 36 equal probabilities is to be 1, each must have probability $\frac{1}{36}$.

The probability of throwing a six — that is, of selecting a point in the event space of $E_{G+R=6}$ — is determined by adding the probabilities of the points in the event space. The result is again $\frac{5}{36}$, of course.

This is the probabilistic vocabulary in which much of today's engineering, physics, psychology, and statistics is expressed. In the near future an even larger portion of the new research will be expressed in these terms. This is true of social science and business as well as of engineering and physical science.

We next ask, "What is the probability that the sum of the spots on the two dice is *not six?*" The answer may be obtained in a similar fashion. The event space $E_{G+R\neq6}$ consists of those 31 points of the sample space that are not in $E_{G+R=6}$ — that is, the complement of $E_{G+R=6}$. The probability is the sum of the probabilities of the 31 points in $E_{G+R\neq6}$, namely $\frac{31}{36}$. Since $E_{G+R\neq6} = E'_{G+R=6}$ this is an example of Theorem 1 of Section 12–4 which states $p(E) + p(E') = 1$.

12–4. Probability. To the sample space S corresponding to the possible outcomes of an experiment we assign a probability function p which has the three properties mentioned earlier:

(1) $p(A) \geqq 0$, A in S

(2) $p(S) = 1$

(3) If A and B are disjoint subsets of S, then $p(A + B) = p(A) + p(B)$.

In particular if $S = \{e_1, e_2, \cdots, e_n\}$ has a finite number of elements e_i, then to each element e_i we assign a number $p(e_i) \geqq 0$ such that $\sum_{i=1}^{n} p(e_i) = 1$. $p(e_i)$ is the probability of the element e_i.

● **Example 1.** For the experiment "toss one coin twice" the elements are $e_1 = (0, 0)$, $e_2 = (1, 0)$, $e_3 = (1, 1)$, $e_4 = (0, 1)$.† If there is reason to be-

---

† Beginning students always have trouble with the event notation when they first meet it. Probability theory is now so important in applications that subterfuge will no longer suffice. It is important that the student become familiar with this language. It is simple and useful once it is understood. This is a good opportunity to learn that e_4 refers to some "event" that was defined earlier in the problem — in this case, $e_4 = $ (tail, head) which is represented in the sample space by the point $(0, 1)$. Or one could think of a coin with 0 on the tail side and 1 on the head side.

lieve that the outcomes represented by these points are equally probable, then we may assign $p(e_i) = \frac{1}{4}$, $(i = 1, 2, 3, 4)$. Now, the probability for the experiment to yield at least one head would be

$$p(\{e_2, e_3, e_4\}) = p(e_2) + p(e_3) + p(e_4) = \frac{3}{4} = 1 - p(e_1).$$

- ***Example 2.*** Experiment: Toss one coin twice. Outcome: The number, x, of heads obtained. The sample space consists of three points $x = 0, 1, 2$. Would you assign $p(0) = p(1) = p(2) = \frac{1}{3}$? (Why not?) In Example 1 let $n(e_i)$ be the number x of heads observed in e_i. $n(e_1) = 0, n(e_2) = 1$, $n(e_3) = 2, n(e_4) = 1$. Then only one e_i has $x = 0$, two of the e_i have $x = 1$, and only one of the e_i has $x = 2$. From this it appears that if $p(e_i) = \frac{1}{4}$ (when the e_i are equally probable), then the appropriate probability assignments for $p(x)$ would be $p(0) = \frac{1}{4}$, $p(1) = \frac{2}{4}$, $p(2) = \frac{1}{4}$. (Why?) This example indicates that sample points (elements) are not necessarily equally probable.

Event. An **event** E is a subset of the sample space S. If a probability function p is defined on S, then the **probability of an event** E is $p(E)$. If $S = \{e_1, e_2, \cdots, e_n\}$ and E is a subset of S, then the probability of the event E is the sum of the probabilities of the e_i in E.

$$p(E) = \sum_i p(e_i), \quad e_i \text{ in } E.$$

An event E is a set of points in the sample space S and its probability $p(E)$ is the sum of the probabilities of its points. The probabilities of the points are not necessarily equal as was seen in Example 2.

If the points e_i in the sample space S are equally probable and there are $n(S)$ points in S and $n(E)$ points in E, then

$$p(e_i) = \frac{1}{n(S)} \quad \text{and} \quad p(E) = \frac{n(E)}{n(S)}.$$

- ***Example 3.*** In Example 1 let $E = \{e_2, e_3, e_4\}$, then $p(E) = \dfrac{n(E)}{n(S)} = \dfrac{3}{4}$.

The *event E has occurred* if a trial of the experiment results in an outcome which corresponds to a point (element) in E.

$$p(\emptyset) = 0 \quad \text{where } \emptyset \text{ is the empty set. (Why?)}$$

The set E and the complementary set E' are called **complementary events.** E occurs when the outcome of a trial of the experiment is a point E. E fails to occur when the outcome of a trial of the experiment is a point in the complementary set E'.

- ***Example 4.*** In Example 1 let $E = \{e_2, e_3, e_4\}$ then $E' = \{e_1\}$ and $p(E) = \frac{3}{4} = 1 - p(E')$.

Theorem 1. Let S be a sample space with probability function p define on S and let E and E' be any two complementary events in S. Then

$$p(E) + p(E') = 1.$$

PROOF: $E \cup E' = S, \quad p(S) = 1, \quad E \cap E' = \emptyset, \quad p(\emptyset) = 0,$
$$p(E \cup E') = p(E) + p(E') - p(E \cap E') = p(E) + p(E') = 1.$$

If the probability for an event E to occur is p, then $p(E) = p$ and $p(E') = 1 - p$ is the probability for nonoccurrence of the event.

● *Example 5.* A single toss of a die results in one of the six points 1, 2, 3, 4, 5 6. Find the probability of throwing the point 4 in a single throw of a die
  In this example an event is the throwing of a point. Hence $n(S) = 6$
  The event E is the throwing of the point 4. Hence $n(E)$ or $n(4) = 1$
  If the die is perfect † and the method of tossing is random †, then

$$p(4) = \frac{n(4)}{n(S)} = \frac{1}{6}.$$

● *Example 6.* Find the probability of failure to throw point 4 in a singl throw of a die.

$$p(\text{not } 4) = \frac{n(\text{not } 4)}{n(S)} = \frac{6 - 1}{6} = \frac{5}{6}.$$

Note that $p(4) + p(\text{not } 4) = 1.$

● *Example 7.* Find the probability of making an odd point in a single throw of a die.
  Again $n = 6$. An event E is any one of the odd points 1, 3, 5. Hence $n(E) = 3$. The desired probability is $p(E) = \dfrac{n(E)}{n(S)} = \dfrac{3}{6} = \dfrac{1}{2}.$

● *Example 8.* Find the probability of making a point greater than one and less than six in a single throw of a die.
  Of the $n = 6$ points there are $n(E) = 4$ points 2, 3, 4, 5 in the set E that have the property of being greater than one and less than six Hence, the desired probability is $p(E) = \dfrac{n(E)}{n(S)} = \dfrac{4}{6} = \dfrac{2}{3}.$

● *Example 9.* If two coins are tossed, find the probability that both will show heads.
  There are two ways in which either coin may fall. Together there are $n(S) = 2 \times 2 = 4$ mutually exclusive, equally likely events which may be indicated by the sequences: head, tail; tail, head; tail, tail; head, head. Of these events only one event E has the property that both show heads Hence, $n(E) = 1$ and $p(E) = \dfrac{n(E)}{n(S)} = \dfrac{1}{4}.$

† In the examples and problems to follow the two terms "perfect" and "random" will be implied but not always mentioned.

In order to solve many problems involving probabilities it is necessary to apply permutations and combinations to determine $n(E)$ and $n(S)$, the number of points in the event space E and sample space S.

- **Example 10.** A bag contains five white, three black, and four red balls. A single random drawing of three balls is made. Find the probability that two balls will be white and one black.

  The total number of outcomes (points in the sample space S) is the number of combinations of twelve balls taken three at a time.

  $$n(S) = \frac{12 \cdot 11 \cdot 10}{1 \cdot 2 \cdot 3} = 220.$$ A desired outcome in the event space E is a selection of two of the five white balls and one of the three black balls. The number of possible selections of two white balls from five white balls is $\frac{5 \cdot 4}{1 \cdot 2} = 10.$ The number of possible selections of one black ball from three black balls is three. From the fundamental principle it is seen that $n(E) = \frac{5 \cdot 4}{1 \cdot 2} \cdot 3 = 30.$ Therefore,

  $$p(E) = \frac{n(E)}{n(S)} = \frac{30}{220} = \frac{3}{22}.$$

  If one wishes to use combination symbols, then

  $$n(S) = \binom{12}{3}, \quad n(E) = \binom{5}{2} \cdot \binom{3}{1}$$

  and

  $$p(E) = \frac{\binom{5}{2} \cdot \binom{3}{1}}{\binom{12}{3}} = \frac{3}{22}.$$

- **Example 11.** From a deck of 52 playing cards 5 cards are selected at random. Find the probability that the 5 cards are the four aces and the king of spades.

  The total number of outcomes $n(S)$ is the number of combinations of 52 cards taken five at a time. $n(S) = \frac{52 \cdot 51 \cdot 50 \cdot 49 \cdot 48}{1 \cdot 2 \cdot 3 \cdot 4 \cdot 5} = 2{,}598{,}960.$ Only one of these events has the desired property. Therefore, the probability is $\frac{1}{2{,}598{,}960}.$

- **Example 12.** Two dice are thrown simultaneously. Find the probability that the point score on a single throw is 5.

  A single throw of two dice may result in any one of $n(S) = 6 \times 6 = 36$ outcomes since each die may show any one of its six faces. The property, point score 5, appears in $n(5) = 4$ sequences of points on the two dice.

The sequences are: 1, 4; 2, 3; 3, 2; 4, 1. Consequently,

$$p(5) = \frac{n(5)}{n(S)} = \frac{4}{36} = \frac{1}{9}.$$

● **Example 13.** Two dice are thrown simultaneously. If thrown twice, find the probability of obtaining a point score 5 followed by a point score 7.

Two throws of a pair of dice may result in one of

$$n(S) = (6 \times 6) \times (6 \times 6) = 36 \times 36 \text{ outcomes.}$$

An event E is point score 5 on the first throw followed by point score 7 on the second throw. The point score 5 may be obtained in any one of four ways as was seen in Example 12. Similarly, the point score 7 may be obtained in any one of six ways. From the fundamental principle

$$n(E) = 4 \times 6 = 24.$$

Therefore,

$$p(E) = \frac{4 \times 6}{36 \times 36} = \frac{1}{54}.$$

● **Example 14.** Two dice are thrown simultaneously. If thrown twice, find the probability of obtaining a point score 5 both times.

As in Example 13 there are $n(S) = 36 \times 36$ outcomes. An event E is point score 5 on each of the two throws. Point score 5 may occur in any one of four ways. From the fundamental principle $n(E) = 4 \times 4$. Therefore,

$$p(E) = \frac{4 \times 4}{36 \times 36} = \frac{1}{9} \times \frac{1}{9} = \frac{1}{81}.$$

PROBLEM SET 12-4

1. From the integers 1 to 40 one is chosen at random. What is the probability that it will be even? That it will be divisible by 7? Both even and divisible by 7? What is the sample space? What are the event spaces?

2. A bag contains ten balls numbered from 1 to 10. If two balls are drawn at random, what is the probability that both of the numbers on them will be odd? Describe the sample and event spaces.

3. A man is the first to draw tickets on a lottery from a group numbered 1 to 20. What is the probability that if he draws two tickets in succession, each will have a number less than 11? Describe the sample and event spaces.

4. Two cards are to be drawn in succession, without replacement, from a deck of 52 playing cards. (a) Find the probability that the first card will be an ace and the second a king. (b) Find the probability that one will be an ace and the other a king. Describe the sample and event spaces.

5. A bag contains one each of the coins 1¢, 5¢, 10¢, 25¢, 50¢, $1. (a) How many different sums of money can be obtained by drawing out three coins? (b) Find the probability that in a single random drawing of three coins the total value drawn will be less than $1. Describe the sample and event spaces.

6. (a) How many different bridge hands each containing 13 cards can be selected from a deck of 52 playing cards? (b) What is the probability of drawing at random an all spade hand? Describe the sample and event spaces.

7. Five cards are drawn from a deck of 52 playing cards. (a) What is the probability of four aces? (b) What is the probability of four aces and one king? Describe the sample and event spaces.

8. (a) In how many ways can three balls be drawn from a bag containing five black and eight white balls? (b) In how many ways can three balls be drawn if exactly two of them are to be black? (c) What is the probability of drawing at random three balls two of which are white and one black? Describe the sample and event spaces.

9. Of six eggs, two are tested and one is found to be bad. For all possible proportions of bad eggs in the original batch, calculate the probability of finding one bad out of two which are tested. Describe the sample and event spaces.

10. Find the probability of throwing an ace in the first of two successive throws of a die. Describe the sample and event spaces.

11. Which of the following bridge hands is more unusual? Explain.
   (a) Spades: 2, 3, 4, 5, 6, 7, 8, 9, 10, J, Q, K, A.
   (b) Spades: 3, 5, 7, 9, J, K, A.   Hearts: 2, 4, 6, 8, 10, Q.
   (c) Spades: 2, 3, 4, 5.   Hearts: 2, 3, 4.   Diamonds: 2, 3, 4.
       Clubs: 2, 3, 4.
   (d) All thirteen cards in the same suit.

12. In tossing two perfect coins, are you equally likely to obtain (a) two heads, or (b) one head and one tail? Describe the sample and event spaces.

13. Which of the following poker hands is more unusual? Explain.
   (a) A royal flush (that is, A, K, Q, J, 10 of the same suit).
   (b) Spades: 4.   Hearts: 5, 7.   Diamonds: 3, 7.

14. In a discussion with Calvin, Phoebe asserts that, since there are thirteen spades and four aces, $\frac{17}{52}$ is the probability for drawing either an ace or a spade from an ordinary deck of 52 playing cards. How could Calvin expose the error?

15. Later, Calvin erroneously declares that the probability for throwing two aces in a single toss of two dice is $\frac{1}{3}$. He reasons that there are three possibilities: (1) both aces, (2) one ace and the other not ace, (3) both not ace. How could Phoebe convince Calvin that he is in error?

12–5. Mutually exclusive or disjoint events. Two events E_1 and E_2 are **mutually exclusive or disjoint** if they have no common points, that is,

$E_1 \cap E_2 = \emptyset$. For example, let two dice be thrown once and the point score, the sum of the numbers that come up on the two dice, observed. The set E_1 of even points scores $\{2, 4, 6\}$ and the set E_2 of odd point scores $\{3, 5, 7\}$ are mutually exclusive events since they do not overlap. These events do not exhaust the sample space which also contains sums 8, 9, 10, 11, 12.

Theorem 1. If E_1 and E_2 are mutually exclusive events, $E_1 \cap E_2 = \emptyset$, then $p(E_1 \cup E_2) = p(E_1) + p(E_2)$.

In words, the probability for the occurrence in a single trial of one of two mutually exclusive events is the sum of their probabilities.

PROOF: $p(E_1 \cup E_2) = p(E_1) + p(E_2) - p(E_1 \cap E_2) = p(E_1) + p(E_2)$.

● **Example 1.** Find the probability for obtaining a point score of 7 or 11 in a single toss of two dice. Here E_1 is $\{7\}$ and E_2 is $\{11\}$.

$p(E_1 \cup E_2) = p(\{7\}) + p(\{11\})$. We shall assume as our mathematical model here and in the work to follow that the 36 sample points corresponding to the 36 ways a pair of dice can turn up are equally probable. This means that we assume each way has probability $\frac{1}{36}$. There are 6 points $(1, 6)$, $(2, 5)$, $(3, 4)$, $(4, 3)$, $(5, 2)$, and $(6, 1)$ that have point score 7 and two points $(5, 6)$ and $(6, 5)$ that have point score 11. From our assumption it follows that $p(\{7\}) = \frac{6}{36}$, $p(\{11\}) = \frac{2}{36}$, and $p(\{7\} \cup \{11\}) = \frac{8}{36}$. In a single toss of two dice the probability of obtaining a point score of 7 or 11 is $\frac{2}{9}$.

The theorem may be generalized.

Theorem 2. If $E_1, E_2, \cdots, E_k$ are mutually exclusive events, then $p(E_1 \cup E_2 \cup \cdots \cup E_k) = p(E_1) + p(E_2) + \cdots + p(E_k)$. In a single trial the probability for the occurrence of one of a system of mutually exclusive events is the sum of the probabilities of the events.

PROOF BY INDUCTION: By the previous theorem $p(E_1 \cup E_2) = p(E_1) + p(E_2)$. Assume the theorem true for $k - 1 \geq 1$. Then
$p(E \cup E_k) = p(E) + p(E_k) = p(E_1) + \cdots + p(E_{k-1}) + p(E_k)$,
$E = E_1 \cup E_2 \cup \cdots \cup E_{k-1}$.

● **Example 2.** A bag contains five white, three black, and four red balls. A single random drawing of one ball is made. Find the probability that the ball drawn will be either red or white.

There are $n = 12$ possible outcomes. Of these outcomes there are

$n(\text{red}) = 4$ outcomes red and $n(\text{white}) = 5$ outcomes white.

The desired probability is

$$p(\text{red or white}) = \frac{n(\text{red})}{n} + \frac{n(\text{white})}{n} = \frac{4}{12} + \frac{5}{12} = \frac{3}{4}.$$

• *Example 3.* Two cards are selected at random from a deck of 52 playing cards. Find the probability that the two cards are either both aces or both kings.

An outcome is a selection of two cards. The number of mutually exclusive outcomes possible is $n = \binom{52}{2} = \frac{52 \cdot 51}{1 \cdot 2} = 1326.$ Let E_1 be the event that both cards are aces. Then $n(E_1) = \binom{4}{2} = \frac{4 \cdot 3}{1 \cdot 2} = 6,$ since there are four aces. The probability of two aces is $p(E_1) = \frac{n(E_1)}{n} = \frac{6}{1326}.$

Let E_2 be the event that both cards are kings. Then $n(E_2) = \binom{4}{2} = 6,$ since there are four kings. The probability of two kings is $p(E_2) = \frac{n(E_2)}{n} = \frac{6}{1326}.$ On applying Theorem 1 we find

$$p(E_1 \cup E_2) = p(E_1) + p(E_2) = \tfrac{6}{1326} + \tfrac{6}{1326} = \tfrac{2}{221}.$$

PROBLEM SET 12–5

In each of the following problems describe the sample space(s) and the event space(s) before solving the problem. A thorough understanding of these spaces in each problem brings one closer to its solution.

1. A bag contains four black, three white, and two red balls. In a single random drawing what is the probability of drawing either a red or a white ball?
2. Four cards are drawn at random without replacement, from a deck of 52 cards. (a) What is the probability that they are all of the same color? (b) All of the same suit?
3. If a coin is tossed twice, find the probability of exactly one head and one tail.
4. If a pair of dice is tossed twice, find the probability of obtaining 7 on one toss and 11 on the other.
5. One bag contains five black, three white, and four red balls and a second bag contains four black, two white, and three red balls. If one ball is drawn at random from each of the bags, find the probability that neither one of the resulting pair of balls will be black.
6. Two cards are selected at random from a deck of 52 playing cards. Find the probability that they are either both face cards or both have numbers larger than 7. (An ace is not a face card nor does it have a number.)

7. Two cards are drawn at random from a suit of thirteen cards. What is the probability that both will be among the five highest cards?

8. In one throw of a pair of dice what is the probability of throwing a 7 or an 11? Of throwing a 2 or a 3 or a 12?

9. There are 100 punches on a punchboard. Ten of the punches win prizes. Twenty punches have been made resulting in one prize. If a man buys two punches, what is the probability that he will win a prize?

10. Three cards are drawn from a suit of thirteen cards. What is the probability that neither an ace nor a king is drawn? What is the probability that either the ace or the king is drawn but not both? What is the probability that the ace and king are both drawn? What is the sum of these three probabilities?

11. A box contains tickets numbered $1, 2, \cdots, 20$. Two tickets are drawn at random. What is the probability that the sum of the numbers on the two tickets will be odd?

*12. Two bags each contain four black, three white, and two red balls. A person draws a ball from the first bag, and if it is red or white he places it in the second bag, if black, he returns it to the first bag. He then draws a ball from the second bag. What is his probability of obtaining a second ball that is either red or white?

12–6. Conditional probability. A deck of 52 playing cards consists of four suits (two red suits: diamonds and hearts; two black suits: clubs and spades) of 13 cards each with designations ace, $2, 3, \cdots, 10$, and the face cards, Jack, Queen, King. If it is observed that a card is red, what is the probability that it will be a face card? This is the conditional probability for the occurrence of an event F (obtaining one of the subset of face cards) under the condition that an event R (the drawing of a red card) has already occurred. This conditional probability † may be designated $p(F \mid R)$ and read "probability for the occurrence of event F given that event R has occurred" or "probability for F given R." Assume the 52 sample points (cards) in the sample space are equally probable. The subspace R contains 26 sample points (red cards) of which 6 sample points (the subspace $F \cap R$) represent the red face cards. It follows that $p(F \mid R) = \frac{6}{26}$. (Why?) In the original sample space for all 52 cards $p(F) = \frac{12}{52}$, $p(R) = \frac{26}{52}$, $p(F \cap R) = \frac{6}{52}$.

Now, it would appear that $p(F \mid R) = \dfrac{6/52}{26/52} = \dfrac{p(F \cap R)}{p(R)}$ and

$p(F \cap R) = p(R)p(F \mid R)$. This suggests the following definition for the conditional probability $p(E_1 \mid E_2)$ of E_1 given E_2.

If E_1 and E_2 are events in a finite sample space S and $p(E_2) \neq 0$, then the **conditional probability** of E_1 given E_2 is defined by

$$p(E_1 \mid E_2) = \frac{p(E_1 \cap E_2)}{p(E_2)}.$$

† Some of the older books use $p_R(F)$ in place of $p(F \mid R)$. Both notations are still current in the literature.

- *Example 1.* Two dice are thrown. Given that the point score x is greater than 8 find the probability that x is 9 or 10.

$$p(\{9, 10\} \mid \{9, 10, 11, 12\}) = \frac{p(\{9, 10\})}{p(\{9, 10, 11, 12\})} = \frac{p(9) + p(10)}{p(9) + p(10) + p(11) + p(12)}$$

$$= \frac{n(9) + n(10)}{n(9) + n(10) + n(11) + n(12)} = \frac{4 + 3}{4 + 3 + 2 + 1} \quad \text{(Why?)}$$

$$= \tfrac{7}{10} \text{ (Why?)}$$

- *Example 2.* Two cards are drawn at random without replacement from a deck of playing cards. Find the probability of ace followed by king.

$$p(AK) = p(A)p(K \mid A) = \tfrac{4}{52} \cdot \tfrac{4}{51}.$$

This may be solved in a second way as follows. The desired probability is the ratio of the number of ace-king sequences, 4×4, to the total number of two card sequences, 52×51. From this point of view what is the sample space and what is the event space? Are they the same as required in the first method of solution?

If $p(E_1 \mid E_2) = p(E_1)$ then the occurrence of the event E_1 does not depend on the event E_2 and the events E_1 and E_2 are **independent**.

Theorem 1. If E_1 and E_2 are independent, then $p(E_1 \cap E_2) = p(E_1)p(E_2)$. If two events are independent, then the probability for their joint occurrence is the product of their probabilities.

- *Example 3.* A first bag contains four white and eight black balls. A second bag contains two white, three red, and nine black balls. One ball is selected at random from each of the bags. (a) Find the probability that both are white. (b) Find the probability that both are white or one is white and the other red.

(a) $$n_1 = 4 + 8 = 12, \; n_1(\text{white}) = 4$$

$$p(\text{white from first bag}) = \frac{n_1(\text{white})}{n_1} = \frac{4}{12} = \frac{1}{3}.$$

$$n_2 = 2 + 3 + 9 = 14, \; n_2(\text{white}) = 2$$

and

$$p(\text{white from second bag}) = \frac{n_2(\text{white})}{n_2} = \frac{2}{14} = \frac{1}{7}.$$

Note that the pairs of events are pairs of independent events. The probability that both balls are white is

$$p(\text{white from first bag, white from second bag}) = \tfrac{1}{3} \cdot \tfrac{1}{7} = \tfrac{1}{21}.$$

(b) The first bag contains no red balls. Therefore the desired result is the probability of drawing a white ball from the first bag and either a white or a red ball from the second bag. The probability of a white or a red from the second bag is $\frac{2}{14} + \frac{3}{14} = \frac{5}{14}$. The desired probability is $\frac{1}{3} \cdot \frac{5}{14} = \frac{5}{42}$.

- **Example 4.** Two cards are drawn in succession, without replacement, from a deck of 52 playing cards. Find the probability that the first card is an ace and the second a king.

    In this example $n_1 = 52$, $n_1(\text{ace}) = 4$, and

$$p(\text{ace first}) = \frac{n_1(\text{ace})}{n_1} = \frac{4}{52} = \frac{1}{13}.$$

After drawing one card $n_2 = 51$ and if an ace was drawn first, then $n_2(\text{king}) = 4$. Now $p(\text{king} \mid \text{ace})\dagger = \dfrac{n_2(\text{king})}{n_2} = \dfrac{4}{51}$. In this case the two events are not independent and $p(\text{king first}) \neq p(\text{king} \mid \text{ace})$ since

$$p(\text{king first}) = \tfrac{4}{52}.$$

The desired probability is
$p(\text{ace first, king second}) = p(\text{ace first}) \cdot p(\text{king} \mid \text{ace}) = \frac{1}{13} \cdot \frac{4}{51} = \frac{4}{663}.$
The problem may be solved by applying permutation notations. See Section 11–2.

$$p(\text{ace first, king second}) = \frac{P(4,\ 1) \cdot P(4,\ 1)}{P(52,\ 2)} = \frac{4 \cdot 4}{52 \cdot 51} = \frac{4}{663}.$$

- **Example 5.** Two balls are drawn in succession from a box containing five red, three green, and two blue balls. What is the probability that both balls are red?

    For the first drawing $n_1 = 5 + 3 + 2 = 10$, $n_1(\text{red}) = 5$, and

$$p(\text{red first}) = \frac{n_1(\text{red})}{n_1} = \frac{5}{10} = \frac{1}{2}.$$

After the first drawing there are $n_2 = 9$ balls left and, if the first ball was red, there are only $n_2(\text{red}) = 4$ red balls remaining. Hence,

$$p\ (\text{red} \mid \text{red}) = \frac{n_2(\text{red})}{n_2} = \frac{4}{9}$$

and

$$p(\text{red, red}) = p(\text{red first}) \cdot p(\text{red} \mid \text{red}) = \tfrac{1}{2} \cdot \tfrac{4}{9} = \tfrac{2}{9}.$$

This may be solved using permutations.

$$p(\text{red, red}) = \frac{P(5,\ 2)}{P(10,\ 2)} = \frac{5 \cdot 4}{10 \cdot 9} = \frac{2}{9}.$$

- **Example 6.** Find the probability of drawing a red ball first and a blue ball second under the conditions of Example 5.

    † The reader is reminded that $p(\text{king} \mid \text{ace})$ means "the probability of drawing a king on the assumption that an ace has already been drawn."

Again $p(\text{red first}) = \frac{1}{2}$. After the first drawing there are $n_2 = 9$ balls left and, if the first ball was red, there are $n_2(\text{blue}) = 2$ blue balls left. Hence, $p(\text{blue} \mid \text{red}) = \frac{2}{9}$ and

$$p(\text{red, blue}) = p(\text{red first}) \cdot p(\text{blue} \mid \text{red}) = \frac{1}{2} \cdot \frac{2}{9} = \frac{1}{9},$$

or

$$p(\text{red, blue}) = \frac{P(5, 1)P(2, 1)}{P(10, 2)} = \frac{5 \cdot 2}{10 \cdot 9} = \frac{1}{9}.$$

An induction proof similar to the proof for Theorem 2, Section 12–5, may be used to prove the next theorem.

Theorem 2. If $E_1, E_2, \cdots, E_k$ are independent events, then

$$p(E_1 \cap E_2 \cap \cdots \cap E_k) = p(E_1)p(E_2) \cdots p(E_k).$$

● *Example 7.* A card is to be drawn at random from a deck of playing cards, observed, and replaced. This is to be repeated until three cards have been observed. What is the probability of Ace, King, Queen in the order mentioned?

The three events A, K, Q are independent. (Why?)

$$p(AKQ) = p(A)p(K)p(Q) = \frac{4}{52} \cdot \frac{4}{52} \cdot \frac{4}{52}.$$

What sample space and what event spaces are used in this solution?

● *Example 8.* If three cards are drawn in sequence from a deck of playing cards without replacement, what is the probability for: (1) A, K, Q in the order stated? (2) A, K, Q in any order?

(1) This is a conditional situation. The drawings are not independent. $p(AKQ) = p(A)p(K \mid A)p(Q \mid AK) = \frac{4}{52} \cdot \frac{4}{51} \cdot \frac{4}{50}.$

There are $52 \times 51 \times 50$ different three card sequences. Included in these sequences there are $4 \times 4 \times 4$ different AKQ sequences. Therefore the desired probability is $\dfrac{4 \times 4 \times 4}{52 \times 51 \times 50}.$

(2) There are $3 \times 2 \times 1 = 6$ permutations of A, K, Q each of which has probability $\dfrac{4 \times 4 \times 4}{52 \times 51 \times 50}.$ Since a particular order excludes any different order (the six orders are mutually exclusive), it follows that the desired probability p is obtained by adding $\dfrac{4 \times 4 \times 4}{52 \times 51 \times 50}$ six times

— that is, $p = 6 \times \dfrac{4 \times 4 \times 4}{52 \times 51 \times 50}.$

A second method of solving (2) is as follows: There are $\dbinom{52}{3}$ selections (combinations) of 52 cards in sets of three (without regard to order) of which $\binom{4}{1}\binom{4}{1}\binom{4}{1}$ are sets of three consisting of one ace, one king, one queen.

$$p = \frac{\binom{4}{1}\binom{4}{1}\binom{4}{1}}{\binom{52}{3}} = \frac{6 \times 4 \times 4 \times 4}{52 \times 51 \times 50}.$$

- **Example 9.** If five dimes are tossed simultaneously, what is the probability of obtaining no head?

  For each dime the probability of no head is $\frac{1}{2}$. By Theorem 2 the probability of no head on all five times is

$$\tfrac{1}{2} \cdot \tfrac{1}{2} \cdot \tfrac{1}{2} \cdot \tfrac{1}{2} \cdot \tfrac{1}{2} = \tfrac{1}{32}.$$

- **Example 10.** If five dimes are tossed simultaneously, what is the probability of obtaining exactly one head?

  To determine the probability of exactly one head we shall use both Theorem 2, Section 12–5, and Theorem 2, Section 12–6. We may think of the five dimes arranged in a row. A head on one of the dimes and tails on the other four dimes is an event with the desired property. By Theorem 2, Section 12–6, the probability of such an event is $(\frac{1}{2})(\frac{1}{2})^4 = \frac{1}{32}$. There are as many mutually exclusive events with the desired property as there are distinct sequences of one head and four tails. The number of such sequences is the number of distinct permutations of five objects taken five at a time with four of the objects alike. Hence the number of events with the property one head and four tails is $\frac{5!}{1!4!}$. Using Theorem 2, Section 12–5 we conclude that the probability of exactly one head is

$$(\tfrac{1}{2})(\tfrac{1}{2})^4 + (\tfrac{1}{2})(\tfrac{1}{2})^4 + \cdots + (\tfrac{1}{2})(\tfrac{1}{2})^4 = \frac{5!}{1!4!}(\tfrac{1}{2})(\tfrac{1}{2})^4 = 5(\tfrac{1}{2})^5 = \tfrac{5}{32}.$$

- **Example 11.** If five dimes are tossed simultaneously, what is the probability of obtaining exactly two heads?

  Again think of the five dimes arranged in a row. Heads on two of the dimes and tails on the other three dimes is an event with the desired property. There are as many mutually exclusive events with the property as there are distinct permutations of five objects taken five at a time where the five objects belong to two distinct sets, two alike and three alike. The number of such events is $\frac{5!}{2!3!}$ and the probability of each such event is $(\frac{1}{2})^2(\frac{1}{2})^3$. Therefore the desired probability is

$$\frac{5!}{2!3!}(\tfrac{1}{2})^2(\tfrac{1}{2})^3 = \frac{5 \cdot 4}{1 \cdot 2}(\tfrac{1}{2})^5 = \tfrac{5}{16}.$$

- **Example 12.** If five dimes are tossed simultaneously, what is the probability of obtaining not more than two heads?

An event with the property not more than two heads is an event with the property no head (and five tails) or with the property exactly one head (and four tails) or with the property exactly two heads (and three tails). These events are mutually exclusive. Using Theorem 2, Section 12–5, and the results of Examples 9, 10, and 11 we find the desired probability

$$(\tfrac{1}{2})^5 + \frac{5!}{1!4!}\,(\tfrac{1}{2})^5 + \frac{5!}{2!3!}\,(\tfrac{1}{2})^5 = \tfrac{1}{32} + \tfrac{5}{32} + \tfrac{5}{16} = \tfrac{1}{2}.$$

• **Example 13.** If five dimes are tossed simultaneously, what is the probability of obtaining at least one head?

An event with the property at least one head is an event with the property exactly one head (and four tails) or exactly two heads (and three tails) or exactly three heads (and two tails) or exactly four heads (and one tail) or exactly five heads (and no tail). These events are mutually exclusive. Applying Theorem 2, Section 12–5, and methods similar to those used in Examples 9 to 12, we find the desired probability

$$p = \frac{5!}{1!4!}\,(\tfrac{1}{2})^5 + \frac{5!}{2!3!}\,(\tfrac{1}{2})^5 + \frac{5!}{3!2!}\,(\tfrac{1}{2})^5 + \frac{5!}{4!1!}\,(\tfrac{1}{2})^5 + \frac{5!}{5!}\,(\tfrac{1}{2})^5.$$

The following is a more rapid way to obtain p. To fail to get at least one head requires the complementary event no head (five tails). The probability for failure to get at least one head is

$$q = (\tfrac{1}{2})^5 = \tfrac{1}{32} \quad \text{(see Example 9).}$$

Now,

$$p = 1 - q = 1 - \tfrac{1}{32} = \tfrac{31}{32}.$$

Replacing the words "If five dimes are tossed simultaneously" with "If one dime is tossed five times" in Examples 9 to 13 will yield problems with the same solutions as the original examples.

• **Example 14.** A machine makes nails with an average of 1 percent defective. A random sample of fifty nails is examined. (a) Approximate the probability of exactly two defective nails. (b) Approximate the probability of not more than two defective nails.

In this example $p = .01$, $q = 1 - p = .99$, and $n = 50$.

(a) p(two defective nails) † $= \dfrac{50!}{2!48!}\,(p)^2(q)^{48} = \dfrac{50!}{2!48!}\,(.01)^2(.99)^{48}$

$$= \frac{50 \times 49}{1 \times 2}\,(.01)^2(.99)^{48} \cong .076.$$

† The notation p(two defective nails) means the probability of **exactly** two defective nails.

(b) p(not more than two defective nails)

$= p$(no defective nail) $+ p$(1 defective nail) $+ p$(2 defective nails)

$= (.99)^{50} + \dfrac{50!}{1!49!}(.01)(.99)^{49} + \dfrac{50!}{2!48!}(.01)^2(.99)^{48}$

$= (.99)^{50} + 50(.01)(.99)^{49} + 25(49)(.01)^2(.99)^{48} \cong .987.$

12–7. Summary. In most (but not all) of the applications that we shall study, the sample space S will consist of a finite number $n(S)$ of sample points each of which are assumed equally probable. This means that each sample point has probability $\dfrac{1}{n(S)}$ Let $n(E)$ be the number of points in S corresponding to the occurrence of the event E. The probability $p(E)$ for the occurrence of E is given by the ratio of the number $n(E)$ of points in E to the number $n(S)$ of points in S. (Why?) That is,

$$p(E) = \frac{n(E)}{n(S)}.$$

If $E_1, E_2, \cdots, E_k$ are mutually exclusive events in S, then

1. $p(E_1 \cup E_2 \cup \cdots \cup E_k) = \dfrac{n(E_1) + n(E_2) + \cdots + n(E_k)}{n(S)}$

$= \dfrac{n(E_1)}{n(S)} + \dfrac{n(E_2)}{n(S)} + \cdots + \dfrac{n(E_k)}{n(S)}$

$= p(E_1) + p(E_2) + \cdots + p(E_k).$

2. $p(E_1 \cap E_2 \cap \cdots \cap E_k) = \dfrac{n(E_1)n(E_2) \cdots n(E_k)}{n(S)n(S) \cdots n(S)}$

$= p(E_1)p(E_2) \cdots p(E_k).$

If E_1 and E_2 are events in S, then

$$p(E_1 \cap E_2) = p(E_1)p(E_2 \mid E_1) = \frac{n(E_1)}{n(S)} \cdot \frac{n(E_2 \cap E_1)}{n(E_1)}.$$

PROBLEM SET 12–7

In each problem determine the sample space(s) and event space(s) before attempting the solution.

1. In tossing a coin three times, what is the probability of:
   (a) head, head, tail? (b) head, tail, head? (c) tail, head, head? (d) exactly two heads and one tail? Construct the sample and event spaces.
2. In tossing five coins what is the probability that at least four will turn heads up?

3. In the manufacture of a certain article it is known that 2 percent of the articles are defective. What is the probability that a random sample of ten of the articles will contain not more than two defective articles?

4. On inspecting 1200 welded joints produced by a certain welding process, 120 defective joints were found. If six welded joints are inspected, what is the probability of finding two defective joints? Not more than two defective joints?

5. If two dice are tossed four times, what is the probability of obtaining a point score of 9 exactly three times? Not more than three times?

6. In tossing a coin three times, what is the probability of getting three heads?

7. If a coin has been tossed twice with heads resulting each time, what is the probability of getting heads on the next toss?

8. An old "sucker bet" states, "I'll bet (even money) that you won't get three heads and three tails if six coins are tossed." Determine the probability of getting three heads and three tails in one toss of six coins.

9. A box contains five red, six white, and seven blue balls. Four balls are drawn in succession without replacements. What is the probability that the first is red, the second and third are white, and the fourth blue?

10. If one tosses four coins simultaneously, what is the probability that he will obtain at least two heads?

11. A "piggy bank" contains ten dimes, ten nickels, and five pennies. If four coins are shaken out of the bank, what is the probability of obtaining two dimes and two pennies?

12. What is the probability that a person may throw exactly one 7 in three successive throws of a pair of dice?

13. One box contains two white and ten red balls. A second box contains six white, two red, and two green balls. A box is selected at random and then one ball selected at random from that box. Find the probability that the ball is white.

14. The probability of Calvin Butterball's receiving his party's nomination for a certain office is $\frac{1}{3}$. If he is nominated, the probability of his being elected is $\frac{6}{7}$. Determine the probability that Calvin will be nominated and elected.

15. Three G–2 men work independently at deciphering an intercepted cipher message. If the probabilities that the men will decipher the message are $\frac{1}{4}$, $\frac{2}{3}$, and $\frac{1}{2}$, what is the probability that the message will be deciphered?

[HINT: The desired probability is $1 - p$(all fail).]

16. A dice game is played as follows. A man rolls a single die until he rolls an odd number or until he has rolled the die ten times, whichever occurs first. His opponent then pays him as many dollars as he has made rolls. Find the probability that the man will win more than $3. More than $5. What is the least he may win? What is the most he may win?

17. Assume that the natural life of a transatlantic plane is 200 passages and that such planes complete 997 out of 1000 such passages safely. Find the probability that a given plane will complete its normal period of service.

18. Four equally good trains leave Central Station for a nearby town at about the same time. If two friends take one of these trains at the same time, what is the probability they will go on the same train by chance?

19. Calvin Butterball, Phoebe Small, and five other students are assigned seats, at random, in a row of seven chairs. Find the probability that Calvin and Phoebe will sit in adjacent seats.

20. At a recent bridge party attended by four couples each man was assigned a woman partner by random cuts of the cards. Each man drew his own wife. Find the probability of this happening.

21. A committee of three is chosen by lot from a group of five men and three women. Find the probability that the committee contains (a) all men, (b) two men and one woman, (c) at least one woman, (d) all women.

22. Answer the questions of Problem 21 if the group contains six men and two women.

23. Two men play a game as follows. William throws a single die. If he throws a 6, he wins. If he does not throw a 6, Joe throws the die. If Joe throws a 6 (and William does not), then Joe wins. If neither man throws a 6, the money is given to charity. Find the probabilities for each man to win.

24. Six men play as follows. Bill throws a die. If he throws a 6, he wins, and the game ends. If he does not win, Joe throws the die. If Joe throws either a 6 or a 5 he wins and the game ends. If he does not win, Tom throws the die. If he throws a 6 or a 5 or a 4, he wins and the game ends. The game continues adding one point with each throw until the sixth man wins if no previous winner has occurred and he throws a 6, 5, 4, 3, 2, or 1. Find the probability for each man to win. What is the best position to play?

25. In a bridge game North is the dummy and South observes that the ace of hearts is not in his hand or in the dummy. What is the probability that East has the ace of hearts?

26. In a card game, Calvin Butterball is dealt a hand containing: Hearts: A, K, Q, J; Spades: 3. Calvin discards the three of spades (not replaced in pack), and draws one card from the pack. What is the probability that the card Calvin drew was (a) the ten of hearts? (b) any heart? (c) any ten? (d) one of the cards mentioned in (a), (b), (c) above?

27. Prove Theorem 2, Section 12–6, by induction.

28. Show that $p(E_2 \mid E_1) = p(E_2)$ when E_1 and E_2 are independent events.

29. (a) Find the probability $p(x)$ for drawing a five-card poker hand consisting of x aces and $5 - x$ not ace. (b) Show that $\sum_{x=0}^{4} p(x) = 1$.

30. Let x be the number of the time on which a tossed coin first shows head up.

(a) Find the probability $p(x)$ for requiring x tosses to obtain the first head.

(b) Show that $\displaystyle\sum_{x=0}^{\infty} p(x) = 1.$

(c) Show that a sequence of eleven tails would be unusual.

(d) Describe and illustrate the sample space.

*31. Read and report on the two solutions given to Bertrand's paradox (Problem 3, pp. 250–51) in *Introduction to Mathematical Probability* by Uspensky.

12–8. Self test.

Record time.

1. An urn contains five pure white balls, four white balls with a red dot on each ball, and six red balls. What is the probability of drawing a ball that has some red on it? Describe the sample and event spaces.

2. Two (honest) dice have been tossed twelve times and the point 7 has not been obtained. What is the probability that point 7 will appear on a thirteenth toss?

3. A box contains six black and four white balls. Four balls are drawn simultaneously. What is the probability of drawing: (a) three white balls? (b) two black and two white balls? Describe the sample and event spaces.

4. If a four-volume set of books is placed on a shelf in random order, what is the probability that they will be arranged in the proper order?

5. A set of fifty disks is numbered 1 to 50 and placed in a bowl. If two disks are drawn at random, what is the probability that (a) both disks will have odd numbers on them? (b) the sum of the numbers on the two disks will be even? Describe the sample and event spaces.

6. If it is known that a single toss of two dice resulted in the sum of points being odd, what is the probability that the point was either 3 or 9? Describe the sample and event spaces.

7. If three cards are drawn from a suit of thirteen cards, what is the probability that the ace will be drawn? Describe the sample and event spaces.

8. (a) What is the probability, $p(x)$, that a five-card hand will contain exactly x spades?

(b) $\displaystyle\sum_{x=0}^{5} p(x) = ?,$ where $p(x)$ is defined in part (a).

Record time.

13 ••••••••••••••••••••

13–1. Introduction. The study of mathematical statistics is increasing in importance in science and engineering. Mathematical statisticians are needed in industrial and government positions. This is an appropriate place to introduce mathematical statistics. We shall discuss briefly five aspects of statistics.

I. In descriptive statistics certain **descriptive measures** such as the mean and standard deviation **are used to present a** condensed picture or **summary of** a set of existing **data.**

II. A second aspect of statistics consists of taking data on several samples from an unknown universe and **deducing from the data** within what limits **certain properties of the universe** must lie. A properly conducted survey leads to an attempt to predict certain properties, within limits, based on the data collected. A statement concerning the limits of reliability should *always* accompany the conclusion. For example: "Our survey shows 75 percent of the people in Jager County are brunette. *There are only* **3** *chances in* **1000** *that the true percentage differs from* **75** *percent by more than* **8.5** *percent.*" This last statement is important. Without such a statement, properly computed, the value of the survey is greatly diminished.

III. In a third aspect of statistics the nature of the universe is completely known in advance, and the problem is to make **predictions on the nature of a sample** taken from this known universe. The analysis of games of chance and the determination of the critical mass of an isotope of uranium for an atomic bomb are examples of this type of statistics.

IV. In the fourth aspect of statistics (quality control), **samples are taken from an unknown universe** and from these samples, **predictions are made as to the nature of forthcoming samples.** Again, without some accurate statement concerning the limits of reliability, the value of a prediction is greatly diminished.

V. Experimental design is another important phase of statistics. Often people come to a statistician with large amounts of data and ask him to interpret them. This is the wrong approach. A statistician should be consulted *before* collecting data. If he knows what you are interested in determining, he may suggest possible changes in the design of an experiment and can indicate what data should be collected in order to obtain valid results. This has a double value since it may not only eliminate unneeded data collection but may also indicate valuable data that otherwise might not be obtained. In general it permits better results with less effort.

The aspects of statistics indicated in II, III, IV, and V require extensive use of mathematics. These remarks are included so that the student will be aware of the existence and importance of **mathematical statistics in** modern science and engineering.

13–2. Additional applications of summation notation. Consider a set of N values of x:

$$\underbrace{x_1, \cdots, x_1}_{f_1 \text{ of the } x_1\text{'s}}; \quad x_2, \cdots, x_2; \quad \cdots; \quad \underbrace{x_i, \cdots, x_i}_{f_i \text{ of the } x_i\text{'s}}; \quad \cdots; \quad x_n, \cdots, x_n.$$

Let f_i denote the number of times x_i occurs in this set. The f_i are called the **frequencies** with which the x_i occur. The **total frequency** is

$$N = f_1 + f_2 + \cdots + f_n = \sum_{i=1}^{n} f_i.$$

The sum of the N values of x is

$$(x_1 + \cdots + x_1) + (x_2 + \cdots + x_2) + \cdots + (x_i + \cdots + x_i) + \cdots + (x_n + \cdots + x_n)$$
$$= x_1 f_1 + x_2 f_2 + \cdots + x_i f_i + \cdots + x_n f_n$$
$$= \sum_{i=1}^{n} x_i f_i.$$

The **average** or **mean** of the x values is defined by

$$\bar{x} = \frac{1}{N} \sum_{i=1}^{n} x_i f_i, \quad \text{where} \quad N = \sum_{i=1}^{n} f_i. \tag{13.1}$$

● **Example 1.** Five dimes were tossed simultaneously 100 times. In the table, x represents the number of heads resulting from a toss and f represents the number of tosses in which exactly x heads occurred. One sees from line three of the table that exactly two of the five coins showed heads on each of 41 tosses. In this case $x_3 = 2$ and $f_3 = 41$. Find $\sum_{i=1}^{6} x_i f_i$ and $\bar{x}$.

x	f	xf	
$x_1 = 0$	$f_1 = \quad 1$	$x_1 f_1 = 0 \cdot (1) =$	0
$x_2 = 1$	$f_2 = \quad 18$	$x_2 f_2 = 1(18) \quad =$	18
2	41	$2(41) \quad =$	82
3	19	$3(19) \quad =$	57
$x_5 = 4$	$f_5 = \quad 16$	$x_5 f_5 = 4(16) \quad =$	64
$x_6 = 5$	$f_6 = \quad 5$	$x_6 f_6 = 5(5) \quad =$	25
	$N = 100$	$\sum_{i=1}^{6} x_i f_i =$	246

To solve this example a third, xf, column has been adjoined. Its construction is indicated in the table. The total frequency is obtained by summing the second column. The result, $N = 100$, is the number of times the set of five coins was tossed. The sum of the items listed in the third column of the table, $\sum_{i=1}^{6} x_i f_i = 246$, is the total number of heads obtained in the 100 tosses. The average number of heads per toss is given by

$$\bar{x} = \frac{1}{N} \sum_{i=1}^{6} x_i f_i = \frac{246}{100} = 2.46.$$

The **deviation** of x_i from the mean $\bar{x}$ is $(x_i - \bar{x})$. The mean of the sum of the squares of the deviations from the mean is called the **variance.** The formula for the variance s_x^2 of the x_i, $(i = 1, 2, \cdots, n)$ is

$$s_x^2 = \frac{1}{N} \sum_{i=1}^{n} (x_i - \bar{x})^2 f_i. \tag{13.2}$$

The **standard deviation** of the x_i, $(i = 1, 2, \cdots, n)$ is $s_x = \sqrt{s_x^2}$.†
The standard deviation is the square root of the average of the squares of the deviations from the mean. For this reason s_x is sometimes called the "root-mean-square deviation."

Theorem 1. The variance, $s_x^2 = \frac{1}{N} \sum_{i=1}^{n} x_i^2 f_i - \bar{x}^2.$

The variance is the mean of the squares minus the square of the mean.

$$\sum_{i=1}^{n} (x_i - \bar{x})^2 f_i = \sum_{i=1}^{n} (x_i^2 f_i - 2\bar{x} x_i f_i + \bar{x}^2 f_i)$$

$$= \sum_{i=1}^{n} x_i^2 f_i - \sum_{i=1}^{n} 2\bar{x} x_i f_i + \sum_{i=1}^{n} \bar{x}^2 f_i$$

$$= \sum_{i=1}^{n} x_i^2 f_i - 2\bar{x} \sum_{i=1}^{n} x_i f_i + \bar{x}^2 \sum_{i=1}^{n} f_i$$

$$= \sum_{i=1}^{n} x_i^2 f_i - 2\bar{x}(N\bar{x}) + \bar{x}^2(N)$$

$$= \sum_{i=1}^{n} x_i^2 f_i - N\bar{x}^2.$$

$$s_x^2 = \frac{1}{N} \sum_{i=1}^{n} (x_i - \bar{x})^2 f_i = \frac{1}{N} \left(\sum_{i=1}^{n} x_i^2 f_i - N\bar{x}^2 \right) = \frac{1}{N} \sum_{i=1}^{n} x_i^2 f_i - \bar{x}^2.$$

The formula $s_x = \sqrt{\dfrac{1}{N} \sum_{i=1}^{n} x_i^2 f_i - \bar{x}^2}$ is easier to use than the definition

$$s_x = \sqrt{\frac{1}{N} \sum_{i=1}^{n} (x_i - \bar{x})^2 f_i}.$$

† The symbol σ_x is frequently used in place of s_x.

● **Example 2.** Find the standard deviation of the number x of heads in the preceding example.

It is convenient to adjoin an x^2f column to the table, constructed as indicated.

x	f	xf	$x(xf) = x^2f$
0	1	0	$x_1(x_1f_1) = \ 0(0) = \ 0$
1	18	18	$x_2(x_2f_2) = 1(18) = \ 18$
2	41	82	$2(82) = 164$
3	19	57	$3(57) = 171$
4	16	64	$4(64) = 256$
5	5	25	$5(25) = 125$
	$N = 100$	$\displaystyle\sum_{i=1}^{6} x_if_i = 246$	$\displaystyle\sum_{i=1}^{6} x_i^2f_i \qquad = 734$

The items in the fourth column are summed to obtain $\displaystyle\sum_{i=1}^{6} x_i^2f_i = 734$.

Applying Theorem 1 and the results of the preceding example we find

$$s_x^2 = \frac{1}{N} \sum_{i=1}^{6} x_i^2f_i - \bar{x}^2 = \tfrac{734}{100} - (2.46)^2 = 1.2884.$$

The standard deviation is $s_x = \sqrt{1.2884} \cong 1.14$. Observe that all of the x values lie between $\bar{x} - 3s_x = -.96$ and $\bar{x} + 3s_x = 5.88$.

Theorem 2. Tchebycheff's inequality. Let $x_1, x_2, \cdots, x_n$ be any set of real numbers. The proportion $p(|\,x_i - \bar{x}\,| \leq ks_x)$ of the x_i that lie on the interval $\bar{x} - ks_x$ to $\bar{x} + ks_x$ inclusive is greater than or equal to $1 - \dfrac{1}{k^2},\ k > 0$.

$$p(|\,x_i - \bar{x}\,| \leq ks_x) \geq 1 - \frac{1}{k^2},\quad k > 0.$$

PROOF: Let $x_1, x_2, \cdots, x_t$ be the labels of the x values that lie outside the interval $\bar{x} - ks_x$ to $\bar{x} + ks_x$. Then

$$(x_1 - \bar{x})^2 \geq k^2s_x^2,\ (x_2 - \bar{x})^2 \geq k^2s_x^2,\ \cdots,\ (x_t - \bar{x})^2 \geq k^2s_x^2. \quad \text{(Why?)}$$

Write s_x^2 in the form

$$s_x^2 = \frac{1}{n} \sum_{j=1}^{t} (x_j - \bar{x})^2 + \frac{1}{n} \sum_{i=t+1}^{n} (x_i - \bar{x})^2 \geq \frac{1}{n} \sum_{j=1}^{t} (x_j - \bar{x})^2$$

$$\geq \frac{1}{n} \sum_{j=1}^{t} k^2s_x^2 = \frac{t}{n} k^2s_x^2. \quad \text{(Why?)}$$

Therefore, $\dfrac{t}{n} \leqq \dfrac{1}{k^2}$. (Why?)

Then, $1 - \dfrac{t}{n} = p(|x_i - \bar{x}| \leqq ks_x) \geqq 1 - \dfrac{1}{k^2}$. (Why?)

Does the Tchebycheff inequality hold when $s_x = 0$? What is true about $x_1, x_2, \cdots, x_n$ when $s_x = 0$?

- **Illustration.** If $k = 2$ the inequality indicates that

$$p(|x_i - \bar{x}| \leqq 2s_x) \geqq 1 - \dfrac{1}{2^2} = \dfrac{3}{4}.$$ That is, at least $\dfrac{3}{4}$ or 75 percent of the

x values must lie within two standard deviations of their mean. Similarly, at least $\frac{8}{9}$ (almost 90 percent) of the x values must lie within three standard deviations of their mean.

The mean is a measure of location of the center of the distribution of x values. From the Tchebycheff inequality it is seen that if the standard deviation is relatively small, the x values are packed closely about their center value, the mean; while if the standard deviation is relatively large, the x values tend to be spread farther from the center. The mean locates the "center" and the standard deviation measures the variability or spread about the mean.

- **Example 3.** What portion of the set of observations 3, 5, 7, 4, 3, 2, 1 lies within two standard deviations of their mean?

$$\bar{x} = \dfrac{25}{7} \approx 3.6, \; s_x = \sqrt{\dfrac{\Sigma x^2}{n} - \bar{x}^2} = \sqrt{\dfrac{113}{7} - \dfrac{625}{49}} = \dfrac{\sqrt{166}}{7} \approx 1.84, 2s_x \approx 3.7,$$

$\bar{x} - 2s_x < 0$ and $\bar{x} + 2s_x > 7$. For this set not just three fourths but all of the numbers lie within two standard deviations of the mean.

PROBLEM SET 13-2

1. Given $N = 25$, $\Sigma xf = 6850$, and $\Sigma x^2 f = 1,878,500$. Find $\bar{x}$ and s_x.
2. Find the mean and standard deviation of 3, 8, 10, 10, 4, 5, and verify that the sum of the deviations from the mean is zero. Here $x_1 = 3, f_1 = 1$; $x_2 = 8, f_2 = 1$; $x_3 = 10, f_3 = 2$; $x_4 = 4, f_4 = 1$; $x_5 = 5, f_5 = 1$. What portion of the set lies within $2s_x$ of $\bar{x}$?
3. Four dimes were tossed simultaneously 50 times. In the table x represents the number of heads resulting from a toss, while f represents the number of tosses in which x heads occurred. Complete the unfilled items in the table.

x	f	xf	x^2f	$x - \bar{x}$	$(x - \bar{x})f$	$(x - \bar{x})^2f$
0	2					
1	14					
2	20	40	80	$2 - 2 = 0$	$0(20) = 0$	$0(0) = 0$
3	10	30	90	$3 - 2 = 1$	$1(10) = 10$	$1(1)(10) = 10$
4	4					
	$N = 50$	$\Sigma x_i f_i =$	$\Sigma x_i^2 f_i =$		$\Sigma(x_i - \bar{x})f_i =$	$\Sigma(x_i - \bar{x})^2 f_i =$

Verify $\bar{x} = 2$, $\sum_{i=1}^{5} (x_i - \bar{x})f_i = 0$. Show that (13.2) and Theorem 1 give

$s_x^2 = 0.9600$ and $s_x \cong .98$. What portion of the 50 observations lies within $2s_x$ of $\bar{x}$?

4. The four dimes in Problem 3 were tossed an additional 50 times with the combined results listed in the table. Complete the table. Find $\bar{x} = 2.05$, $s_x^2 = .9675$, $s_x \cong .98$. What portion of the 100 observations lies between

$\bar{x} - 2s_x$ and $\bar{x} + 2s_x$? Between $\bar{x} - 3s_x$ and $\bar{x} + 3s_x$?

x	f	xf	x^2f
0	3		
1	28		
2	39		
3	21		
4	9		
	$N = 100$	$\Sigma x_i f_i =$	$\Sigma x_i^2 f_i =$

5. Prove: $S(\xi) = \sum_{i=1}^{n} (x_i - \xi)^2 f_i = \sum_{i=1}^{n} x_i^2 f_i - 2\left(\sum_{i=1}^{n} x_i f_i\right)\xi + N\xi^2$ is a minimum when $\xi = \bar{x}$. Find $\dfrac{dS(\xi)}{d\xi}$, equate to zero, and solve for ξ. This result indicates why the variance is defined in terms of deviations from the mean.

6. Write the first four terms of $a_x = \dfrac{1}{x(x+1)}$, $(x = 1, 2, \cdots, n)$. $a_n = ?$

Find $\sum_{x=1}^{n} a_x$. $\left[\text{HINT: } a_x = \dfrac{1}{x} - \dfrac{1}{x+1}.\right]$

7. Find $\sum_{x=1}^{n} x^2$, the sum of the squares of the positive integers from 1 to n.

$\left[\text{HINT: Express } \sum_{x=1}^{n} (x^3 - [x-1]^3) \text{ in two ways and apply Theorem 4 of Section 10–2.}\right]$

8. Find $\sum_{x=1}^{n} x^3$.

9. Perform the following experiment. Toss six coins 50 times and record the number of tosses on which no head, exactly one head, exactly two heads, $\cdots$, exactly six heads occur. Compute $\bar{x}$, s_x, $\bar{x} - 3s_x$, and $\bar{x} + 3s_x$.

10. Combine the results found by all members of the class in Problem 9 and compute $\bar{x}$ and s_x for the combined data. Does the $\bar{x}$ of this problem lie between $\bar{x} - 3s_x$ and $\bar{x} + 3s_x$ as found in Problem 9?

11. Prove: The (algebraic) sum of the deviations of the x_i, $(i = 1, 2, \cdots, n)$ from the mean $\bar{x}$ is zero. Apply (13.1), and Theorems 3 and 2 of Section 10–2 to prove $\sum_{i=1}^{n} (x_i - \bar{x})f_i = 0$.

13–3. Binomial distributions. Let p be the probability that an event occurs in a single trial and x the number of times the event occurs in n independent trials. The probability that the event will fail to occur at a single trial is $q = 1 - p$. We wish to determine the probability of obtaining an event consisting of precisely x occurrences in n independent trials. The methods to be used have been illustrated in Examples 9 to 13 of Section 12–6. There are as many events with the property of x occurrences and $n - x$ failures in n independent trials as there are distinct permutations of n objects taken n at a time with x objects (occurrences) alike and $n - x$ objects (failures) alike. The number of such events is $\dfrac{n!}{x!(n-x)!}$. These events are equally likely and mutually exclusive. By Theorem 2 of Section 12–6, the probability of each of these events is $p^x q^{n-x}$. It follows from Theorem 2 of Section 12–5 that the probability of obtaining exactly x occurrences in n independent trials of an event, for which p is the probability of occurrence at a single trial, is

$$B(n, x, p) = \frac{n!}{x!(n-x)!} p^x q^{n-x} = \frac{n!}{(n-x)!x!} q^{n-x}p^x = \binom{n}{x} p^x q^{n-x}. \quad (13.3)$$

The function $B(n, x, p)$ is called the **Bernoulli** or **binomial distribution function.** The latter name is due to the fact that

$$(q + p)^n = q^n + \frac{n!}{(n-1)!1!} q^{n-1}p + \frac{n!}{(n-2)!2!} q^{n-2}p^2 + \cdots$$

$$+ \frac{n!}{(n-x)!x!} q^{n-x}p^x + \cdots + \frac{n!}{n!} p^n$$

$$= B(n, 0, p) + B(n, 1, p) + B(n, 2, p) + \cdots + B(n, x, p) + \cdots$$
$$+ B(n, n, p)$$

$$= \sum_{x=0}^{n} B(n, x, p). \quad (13.4)$$

Since $(q + p)^n = 1^n = 1,$ we have

$$\sum_{x=0}^{n} B(n, x, p) = 1.$$

The terms of the binomial expansion of $(q + p)^n$ give the probabilities of occurrences in the order $0, 1, 2, \cdots, n$. These results are summarized in the following theorem.

Theorem 1. If on each trial the probability that an event will occur is p and that it will not occur is q, then the probability that the event will occur exactly x times in n independent trials is

$$B(n, x, p) = \frac{n!}{(n - x)!\, x!}\, q^{n-x} p^x.$$

● *Example 1.* Five dimes are tossed simultaneously (or one dime is tossed five times). Find the probabilities of exactly 0, 1, 2, 3, 4, 5 heads.
   The probability of a head on a single trial is $p = \frac{1}{2}$. Then $q = \frac{1}{2}$ and

$$p(x \text{ heads}) = B(5, x, \tfrac{1}{2}) = \frac{5!}{(5 - x)!\, x!} \left(\frac{1}{2}\right)^5.$$

Hence,

$$p(\text{no head}) = \tfrac{1}{32}, \quad p(1 \text{ head}) = \tfrac{5}{32}, \quad p(2 \text{ heads}) = \tfrac{10}{32},$$
$$p(3 \text{ heads}) = \tfrac{10}{32}, \quad p(4 \text{ heads}) = \tfrac{5}{32}, \quad p(5 \text{ heads}) = \tfrac{1}{32}.$$

● *Example 2.* Five dimes are tossed simultaneously (or one dime is tossed five times). Find the probability of not less than two nor more than four heads.
   An event with the property not less than two nor more than four heads is an event with the property exactly two heads (and three tails) or with the property exactly three heads (and two tails) or with the property exactly four heads (and one tail). Applying Theorem 2 of Section 12–6 and Theorem 2 of Section 12–5 we find the desired probability:

$$\sum_{x=2}^{4} B(5, x, \tfrac{1}{2}) = \tfrac{10}{32} + \tfrac{10}{32} + \tfrac{5}{32} = \tfrac{25}{32}.$$

● *Example 3.* Five dimes are tossed simultaneously (or one dime is tossed five times). Find the probability of at least one head.
   This is Example 13 of Section 12–6. In our present notation we see that the desired probability is

$$p = \sum_{x=1}^{5} B(5, x, \tfrac{1}{2}).$$

From (13.4) we have

$$\sum_{x=0}^{5} B(5, x, \tfrac{1}{2}) = B(5, 0, \tfrac{1}{2}) + \sum_{x=1}^{5} B(5, x, \tfrac{1}{2}) = \tfrac{1}{32} + p = 1^5 = 1.$$

Therefore,

$$p = 1 - \tfrac{1}{32} = \tfrac{31}{32}.$$

● **Example 4.** Obtain relative frequencies for Example 1 of Section 13–2 (p. 293).

x_i	0	1	2	3	4	5
$\dfrac{f_i}{N}$	.01	.18	.41	.19	.16	.05

The relative frequency of x_i in Example 1 of Section 13–2 is obtained by dividing the corresponding frequency f_i by the total frequency $N = \sum_{i=1}^{n} f_i$. In this example $N = 100$. The results are listed in the table.

● **Example 5.** Compare the results of Example 1 of this section with those of an actual experiment which were given in Example 1 of Section 13–2 (p. 293).

x	$\dfrac{f}{N}$	$p(x \text{ heads}) = B(5, x, \tfrac{1}{2})$
0	.01	$\tfrac{1}{32} \cong .03$
1	.18	$\tfrac{5}{32} \cong .16$
2	.41	$\tfrac{10}{32} \cong .31$
3	.19	$\tfrac{10}{32} \cong .31$
4	.16	$\tfrac{5}{32} \cong .16$
5	.05	$\tfrac{1}{32} \cong .03$
	1.00	1.00

The observed relative frequencies appear in the table given in Example 4. Relative frequencies resemble probabilities in the sense that they are the ratios of the number of occurrences f_i to the number of trials N. The probabilities are listed in Example 1 of this section. For convenience we assemble all of this information in a table. A comparison indicates considerable disagreement between the relative frequencies in column 2 and the corresponding probabilities in column 3. This causes one to raise the question: Is the probability for heads one half, at each trial, in the experiment, or are the coins biased?

PROBLEM SET 13–3

1. In one toss of four coins what is the probability of at least three heads?

2. In a random drawing of 5 cards from a deck of 52 playing cards what is the probability that the 5-card hand will contain exactly two aces? At least two aces?

3. A distributor of seeds determines from extensive tests that 5 percent of a large batch of a certain expensive seed will not germinate. He sells the seeds in packets of 30 and guarantees 90-percent germination. What is the probability that a given packet will violate the guarantee?

[HINT: The desired probability is

$$1 - p(\text{not more than 10 percent fail to germinate}).]$$

4. A manufacturing process produces 5-percent defective items. In a sample of 50 items what is the probability of having from 2 to 5, inclusive, defective items?

5. Four dimes are tossed simultaneously. Find the probabilities of exactly 0, 1, 2, 3, 4 heads.

6. Obtain relative frequencies of heads for Problem 4 of Section 13–2 and compare with the theoretical results found in Problem 5.

7. In a random drawing of 3 cards from a deck of 52 playing cards, what is the probability that at least one of the 3 cards is an ace or a jack or a deuce?

8. An urn contains six white and nine black balls. Three balls are drawn and laid aside without their color being observed. A fourth ball is drawn. What is the probability that it will be black?

9. If a four-volume set of books is placed upon a shelf in random order, what is the probability that they will be arranged in the proper order?

*10. Five balls are tossed into three pockets. Each ball is equally likely to fall into any one of the three pockets. Find the probability that no pocket will be empty.

11. If it is known that at least one head appeared when five dimes were tossed, what is the probability that the exact number of heads was two?

12. An urn contains six white and nine black balls. If when three balls are drawn it is known that at least two are black, what is the probability that all three will be black?

13. Four men toss a coin to see who pays for their dinners. John Smart tosses with a second man. The loser tosses with a third man. The loser of this toss then tosses with Bob Witling and the loser buys the dinners. Compute the probability that John Smart pays for the dinners. Compute the probability that Bob Witling pays for the dinners.

14. A woman's purse contains a lipstick, a pencil stub, a box of pencil leads, a bundle containing thirteen bobby pins and a burned match, a loose cigarette, a small vial of perfume, and five hair curlers. Each of these articles is equally likely to be drawn from the purse. The purse also contains "other articles too numerous to mention." If the probability of getting one of the "other articles too numerous to mention" is two thirds, what is the probability of getting the lipstick on the first draw?

13–4. Mean and standard deviation of the number of occurrences.

Let p be the probability that an event will occur on a single trial. We wish to obtain formulas for the mean and standard deviation of the number of occurrences of the event in n independent trials. We have used $\bar{x}$ and s_x for the mean and standard deviation of a sample in Section 13–2. It is customary to use μ_x for the mean and σ_x for the standard deviation of the universe from which samples may be drawn. We wish to find formulas for the mean μ_x and the standard deviation σ_x of the number of occurrences of the event in n independent trials.

Analogous to the definition of Section 13–2 we define

$$\mu_x = \frac{\displaystyle\sum_{x=0}^{n} xB(n, x, p)}{\displaystyle\sum_{x=0}^{n} B(n, x, p)}. \tag{13.5}$$

To obtain formulas for $\displaystyle\sum_{x=0}^{n} xB(n, x, p)$ and $\displaystyle\sum_{x=0}^{n} B(n, x, p)$ we use a method†

that employs the first and second derivatives of a function $M(t) = (q + tp)^n$, where p, q, n are fixed, $q + p = 1$, and t is a variable.

$$M(t) = (q + tp)^n$$
$$= q^n + t \frac{n!}{(n-1)!1!} q^{n-1}p + t^2 \frac{n!}{(n-2)!2!} q^{n-2}p^2 + \cdots$$
$$+ t^x \frac{n!}{(n-x)!x!} q^{n-x}p^x + \cdots + t^n p^n$$
$$= B(n, 0, p) + tB(n, 1, p) + t^2 B(n, 2, p) + \cdots + t^x B(n, x, p) + \cdots$$
$$+ t^n B(n, n, p).$$

where $q + p = 1$. Setting $t = 1$ in this equation, we have

$$(q + p)^n = \sum_{x=0}^{n} B(n, x, p)$$

$$1^n = 1 = \sum_{0=x}^{n} B(n, x, p).$$

The function $M(t)$ is a polynomial in t with constant coefficients

$$B(n, x, p), \quad (x = 0, 1, 2, \cdots, n).$$

† Immediately following the derivation of μ_x by this method, a second direct method is given which some readers may prefer. Likewise a direct method is given for σ_x following the first derivation of the formula for σ_x.

The derivative of $M(t)$ with respect to t is

$$\frac{dM(t)}{dt} = np(q + tp)^{n-1}$$

$$= (0)B(n, 0, p) + 1B(n, 1, p) + 2tB(n, 2, p) + \cdots + xt^{x-1}B(n, x, p) + \cdots$$
$$+ nt^{n-1}B(n, n, p).$$

On substituting $t = 1$ in the derivatives we obtain, since $q + p = 1$,

$$\frac{dM(1)}{dt} = np$$

$$= (0)B(n, 0, p) + 1B(n, 1, p) + 2B(n, 2, p) + \cdots + xB(n, x, p) + \cdots$$
$$+ nB(n, n, p).$$

Hence,

$$np = \sum_{x=0}^{n} xB(n, x, p).$$

From the definition
$$\mu_x = \frac{\displaystyle\sum_{x=0}^{n} xB(n, x, p)}{\displaystyle\sum_{x=0}^{n} B(n, x, p)} = \frac{np}{1},$$

or

$$\mu_x = np. \tag{13.6}$$

A more direct but less typical derivation of the formula for μ_x follows:

For the binomial distribution $\binom{n}{x} p^x q^{n-x}$, $\displaystyle\sum_{x=0}^{n} \binom{n}{x} p^x q^{n-x} = (q + p)^n = 1.$

The mean number of occurrences is

$$\mu_x = \frac{\displaystyle\sum_{x=0}^{n} x \binom{n}{x} p^x q^{n-x}}{\displaystyle\sum_{x=0}^{n} \binom{n}{x} p^x q^{n-x}} = \frac{\displaystyle\sum_{x=0}^{n} x \binom{n}{x} p^x q^{n-x}}{1}$$

$$= 0 + 1 \cdot \frac{n}{1} pq^{n-1} + 2 \frac{n(n-1)}{1 \cdot 2} p^2 q^{n-2} + 3 \frac{n(n-1)(n-2)}{1 \cdot 2 \cdot 3} p^3 q^{n-3} + \cdots$$
$$+ x \frac{n(n-1) \cdots (n-x+1)}{1 \cdot 2 \cdots x} p^x q^{n-x} + \cdots + np^n$$

$$= np \left[q^{n-1} + \frac{n-1}{1} pq^{n-2} + \frac{(n-1)(n-2)}{1 \cdot 2} p^2 q^{n-3} + \cdots \right.$$
$$\left. + \frac{(n-1) \cdots (n-x+1)}{1 \cdot 2 \cdots (x-1)} p^{x-1} q^{n-x} + \cdots + p^{n-1} \right]$$

$$= np(q + p)^{n-1} = np \cdot 1 = np.$$

Since p corresponds to the proportion of occurrences, one would expect $n \cdot p$ occurrences as an average for sets of n trials.

This is a useful formula for computing the mean μ_x of the number of occurrences of an event in n independent trials.

● **Illustration.** If three coins are tossed, the probability of getting all heads is $p = \frac{1}{8}$. The formula states that, on the average, three heads will occur 75 times in 600 tosses of three coins, since $\mu_x = np = 600(\frac{1}{8}) = 75$.

Analogous to the definition of Section 13–2 we define

$$\sigma_x^2 = \frac{\sum_{x=0}^{n} (x - \mu_x)^2 B(n, x, p)}{\sum_{x=0}^{n} B(n, x, p)}. \tag{13.7}$$

We have just shown that $\mu_x = np$ and that $\sum_{x=0}^{n} B(n, x, p) = 1$. We now use the second derivative of $M(t)$ to obtain a formula for

$$\sum_{x=0}^{n} (x - np)^2 B(n, x, p).$$

$$\frac{d^2 M(t)}{dt^2} = (n - 1)np^2(q + tp)^{n-2}$$

$$= 0 \cdot B(n, 0, p) + 0 \cdot 1 \cdot B(n, 1, p) + 1 \cdot 2 \cdot B(n, 2, p) + \cdots$$
$$+ (x - 1)xt^{x-2}B(n, x, p) + \cdots + (n - 1)nt^{n-2}B(n, n, p)$$

and

$$\frac{d^2 M(1)}{dt^2} = (n - 1)np^2 = 0 \cdot B(n, 0, p) + 0 \cdot 1 \cdot B(n, 1, p) + 1 \cdot 2 \cdot B(n, 2, p) + \cdots$$
$$+ (x - 1)xB(n, x, p) + \cdots + (n - 1)nB(n, n, p)$$

$$= \sum_{x=0}^{n} (x - 1)xB(n, x, p)$$

$$= \sum_{x=0}^{n} (x^2 - x)B(n, x, p)$$

$$= \sum_{x=0}^{n} [x^2 B(n, x, p) - xB(n, x, p)]$$

$$= \sum_{x=0}^{n} x^2 B(n, x, p) - \sum_{x=0}^{n} xB(n, x, p),$$

or

$$(n - 1)np^2 = \sum_{x=0}^{n} x^2 B(n, x, p) - np. \tag{13.8}$$

On solving (13.8) for $\sum_{x=0}^{n} x^2 B(n, x, p)$ we find

$$\sum_{x=0}^{n} x^2 B(n, x, p) = np - np^2 + n^2 p^2$$

$$= np(1 - p) + (np)^2,$$

or

$$\sum_{x=0}^{n} x^2 B(n, x, p) = npq + (np)^2. \tag{13.9}$$

From the definition

$$\sigma_x^2 = \frac{\sum_{x=0}^{n} (x - np)^2 B(n, x, p)}{\sum_{x=0}^{n} B(n, x, p)} = \sum_{x=0}^{n} (x^2 - 2npx + n^2 p^2) B(n, x, p)$$

$$= \sum_{x=0}^{n} [x^2 B(n, x, p) - 2npx B(n, x, p) + n^2 p^2 B(n, x, p)],$$

or

$$\sigma_x^2 = \sum_{x=0}^{n} x^2 B(n, x, p) - 2np \sum_{x=0}^{n} x B(n, x, p) + (np)^2 \sum_{x=0}^{n} B(n, x, p). \tag{13.10}$$

Using $\sum_{x=0}^{n} B(n, x, p) = 1$, $\sum_{x=0}^{n} x B(n, x, p) = np$ and

$$\sum_{x=0}^{n} x^2 B(n, x, p) = npq + (np)^2$$

we find

$$\sigma_x^2 = npq + (np)^2 - 2np(np) + (np)^2(1),$$

or

$$\sigma_x^2 = npq. \tag{13.11}$$

Hence,

$$\sigma_x = \sqrt{npq}. \tag{13.12}$$

A more direct derivation of the formula for σ_x^2 follows:

$$\sigma_x^2 = \frac{\sum_{x=0}^{n} (x - \mu_x)^2 \binom{n}{x} p^x q^{n-x}}{\sum_{x=0}^{n} \binom{n}{x} p^x q^{n-x}} = \sum_{x=0}^{n} x^2 \binom{n}{x} p^x q^{n-x} - 2\mu_x \sum_{x=0}^{n} x \binom{n}{x} p^x q^{n-x}$$

$$+ \mu_x^2 \sum_{x=0}^{n} \binom{n}{x} p^x q^{n-x}$$

$$= \sum_{x=0}^{n} x^2 \binom{n}{x} p^x q^{n-x} - \mu_x^2$$

$$= \sum_{x=0}^{n} [x(x-1) + x] \binom{n}{x} p^x q^{n-x} - (np)^2$$

$$= \sum_{x=0}^{n} x(x-1) \binom{n}{x} p^x q^{n-x} + np - n^2 p^2$$

Now

$$\sum_{x=0}^{n} x(x-1) \binom{n}{x} p^x q^{n-x} = 0 + 0 + 2 \cdot 1 \cdot \frac{n(n-1)}{1 \cdot 2} p^2 q^{n-2} + 3 \cdot 2 \frac{n(n-1)(n-2)}{1 \cdot 2 \cdot 3} p^3 q^{n-3}$$

$$+ \cdots + x(x-1) \frac{n(n-1) \cdots (n-x+1)}{1 \cdot 2 \cdots x} p^x q^{n-x} + \cdots + n(n-1) p^n$$

$$= n(n-1) p^2 \left[q^{n-2} + \frac{n-2}{1} pq^{n-3} + \cdots + \frac{(n-2) \cdots (n-x+1)}{1 \cdot 2 \cdots (x-2)} p^{x-2} q^{n-x} \right.$$

$$\left. + \cdots + p^{n-2} \right]$$

$$= n(n-1) p^2 (q+p)^{n-2} = n(n-1) p^2.$$

Therefore,

$$\sigma_x^2 = n(n-1) p^2 + np - n^2 p^2 = np(1-p) = npq.$$

- **Example 1.** If five dimes are tossed simultaneously (or one dime is tossed five times), what are the mean and standard deviation of the number of occurrences of heads?

   In this example $p = \frac{1}{2}$, $q = \frac{1}{2}$, and $n = 5$. Hence, $\mu_x = np = \frac{5}{2} = 2.5$, and $\sigma_x^2 = npq = 1.25$. Also the standard devia-tion, $\sigma_x = \sqrt{\sigma_x^2}$, is

$$\sigma_x = \frac{\sqrt{5}}{2} \cong 1.12.$$

   The meaning of $\mu_x = 2.5$ as the average number of occurrences of heads becomes clearer if one considers the result of tossing five dimes simul-taneously a very large number of times. Although one would never obtain 2.5 heads on a single toss, nevertheless one would expect the average ob-tained on dividing the total number of heads by the total number of tosses to be near 2.5.

- **Example 2.** Compare the theoretical results found in Example 1 with those obtained from the experimental table in Example 1 of Section 13–2.

   In the experiment studied in Examples 1 and 2 of Section 13–2 it was found that, when five dimes were tossed simultaneously 100 times, the average number of heads per toss was $\bar{x} = 2.46$ and the standard deviation was $s_x \cong 1.14$. Although these results do not agree with the theoretical results obtained in Example 1, it is to be noticed that the amount of disagreement is relatively small. One would hardly expect to obtain the same results in each of two sets of 100 trials.

• **Example 3.** Using the table in Example 1 of Section 13–2 find the frequency, relative frequency, and percent frequency of the number x of heads when

(a) $\bar{x} - s_x \leq x \leq \bar{x} + s_x$, (b) $\bar{x} - 2s_x \leq x \leq \bar{x} + 2s_x$,
(c) $\bar{x} - 3s_x \leq x \leq \bar{x} + 3s_x$.

For convenience we list $\bar{x} = 2.46$, $s_x = 1.14$ and the table

x	0	1	2	3	4	5
f	1	18	41	19	16	5

(a) $\bar{x} - s_x \leq x \leq \bar{x} + s_x$
$1.32 \leq x \leq 3.60$.

The frequency of x in this interval is $41 + 19 = 60$. The corresponding relative frequency is $\frac{60}{100} = .6$ and the percent frequency is 60 percent.

(b) $\bar{x} - 2s_x \leq x \leq \bar{x} + 2s_x$
$0.18 \leq x \leq 4.74$.

The frequency of x in this interval is $18 + 41 + 19 + 16 = 94$. The corresponding relative frequency is $\frac{94}{100} = .94$ and the percent frequency is 94 percent.

(c) $\bar{x} - 3s_x \leq x \leq \bar{x} + 3s_x$
$- .96 \leq x \leq 5.88$.

The entire frequency lies in this interval. The corresponding relative frequency is 1.00 and the percent frequency is 100 percent.

PROBLEM SET 13–4

1. If four dimes are tossed simultaneously, what are the average and variance of the number of occurrences of heads? Compare the theoretical results found in this problem with those obtained from the experimental table in Problem 4 of Section 13–2.
2. Using the table in Problem 4 of Section 13–2 find the percent frequency of the number x of heads when (a) $\bar{x} - s_x \leq x \leq \bar{x} + s_x$,
(b) $\bar{x} - 2s_x \leq x \leq \bar{x} + 2s_x$, (c) $\bar{x} - 3s_x \leq x \leq \bar{x} + 3s_x$.

3. Using the data of Example 3 of Section 13–4 find the frequency, relative frequency, and per cent frequency of the number x of heads when

(a) $0 \leqq x \leqq 3$,   (b) $2 \leqq x \leqq 5$,   (c) $x \neq 2$.

13–5. The probability of the number of occurrences lying within stated limits. The results of Example 3 of Section 13–4 correspond, in part, to a more general theory which we shall state as an unproved theorem.

Let $P(a \leqq x \leqq b)$ denote the probability that x lies on the interval $a \leqq x \leqq b$.

Theorem 1. If x represents the number of occurrences in n independent trials of an event for which p is the probability of occurrence on a single trial and $npq \geqq 25$,† then

$$P(np-\sqrt{npq} \leqq x \leqq np+\sqrt{npq}) \cong .68, \quad P(x < np-\sqrt{npq}) \cong .16,$$

$$P(x > np + \sqrt{npq}) \cong .16, \tag{13.13}$$

$$P(np-2\sqrt{npq} \leqq x \leqq np+2\sqrt{npq}) \cong .95, \quad P(x < np-2\sqrt{npq}) \cong .025,$$

$$P(x > np + 2\sqrt{npq}) \cong .025, \tag{13.14}$$

$$P(np - 3\sqrt{npq} \leqq x \leqq np + 3\sqrt{npq}) \cong .997 \tag{13.15}$$

and

$$P\left(p - \sqrt{\frac{pq}{n}} \leqq \frac{x}{n} \leqq p + \sqrt{\frac{pq}{n}}\right) \cong .68, \quad P\left(\frac{x}{n} < p - \sqrt{\frac{pq}{n}}\right) \cong .16,$$

$$P\left(\frac{x}{n} > p + \sqrt{\frac{pq}{n}}\right) \cong .16, \tag{13.16}$$

$$P\left(p - 2\sqrt{\frac{pq}{n}} \leqq \frac{x}{n} \leqq p + 2\sqrt{\frac{pq}{n}}\right) \cong .95, \tag{13.17}$$

$$P\left(\frac{x}{n} < p - 2\sqrt{\frac{pq}{n}}\right) \cong .025,$$

$$P\left(\frac{x}{n} > p + 2\sqrt{\frac{pq}{n}}\right) \cong .025,$$

$$P\left(p - 3\sqrt{\frac{pq}{n}} \leqq \frac{x}{n} \leqq p + 3\sqrt{\frac{pq}{n}}\right) \cong .997. \tag{13.18}$$

For the binomial distribution the mean is $\mu_x = np$ and the standard deviation is $\sigma_x = \sqrt{npq}$.

The inequalities (13.13), (13.14), and (13.15) indicate that for binomial distributions with $npq \geqq 25$:

(a) Approximately 68 percent of the total frequency lies on the interval beginning 1 sigma (standard deviation) to the left of the mean and ending

† Experience indicates that the approximations are fairly good if $npq > 5$.

1 sigma to the right of the mean. Also, approximately 16 percent of the total frequency lies to the left of this interval and 16 percent to the right.

(b) Approximately 95 percent of the total frequency lies on the interval beginning 2 sigmas to the left of the mean and ending 2 sigmas to the right of the mean. Also, approximately 2.5 percent of the total frequency lies to the left of this interval and 2.5 percent to the right.

(c) Approximately all of the total frequency lies on the interval beginning 3 sigmas to the left of the mean and ending 3 sigmas to the right of the mean.

These statements help one appreciate the importance of the standard deviation as a measure of the spread, or variability, of the observations about the average.

The results obtained by interpolation in Example 3 of Section 13–4 compare favorably with (13.16), (13.17), and (13.18) where x/n is the relative frequency.

● *Example 1.* A fraternity has a membership of 316. One hundred members indicate that they will attend a dinner. Usually about 4 percent who have not reserved plates come without reservations. How many should be prepared for if about 1 chance in 40 of estimating too low can be risked?

On the average $216(.04) = 8.64$ members of the 216 members not making reservations would be expected to attend. Since 8.64 is an average, it may be too large or too small. Consequently a correction based on the amount of risk is needed. To obtain a suitable correction it is necessary to calculate the standard deviation and apply Theorem 1. Now

$$p = .04, \quad q = .96, \quad n = 216, \quad \mu \cong np \cong 8.64,$$
$$\sigma \cong \sqrt{npq} \cong \sqrt{216(.04)(.96)} \cong 2.88.$$

Although $npq \cong 8.3 < 25,$ experience indicates that the conclusions of Theorem 1 may apply.

A 1 to 40 risk corresponds to $\frac{1}{40} = .025.$ If 2 sigmas (usually called 2 sigma limits) are used

$$P(x > 8.64 + 2[2.88]) = P(x > 14.40) \cong .025.$$

Under the given conditions the probability of 15 or more members attending without reservations is approximately .025. Consequently, the estimate of the maximum number who will attend without reservations is 15.

The total number to prepare for is $100 + 15 = 115.$

● *Example 2.* A field house will accommodate 3000 people. On the average three fourths of the students purchasing season tickets will attend an event. How many tickets can be sold if a 1 to 6 chance of overcrowding can be taken?

In this case 1 sigma limits can be used since $\frac{1}{6} \cong .17 > .16$. A risk not exceeding 1 to 6 of overcrowding will result if the number of tickets sold does not exceed n where n satisfies

$$np + \sqrt{npq} = 3000$$

or

$$n(\tfrac{3}{4}) + \sqrt{n(\tfrac{3}{4})(\tfrac{1}{4})} = 3000$$

and

$$(\sqrt{3n})^2 + (\sqrt{3n}) - 12{,}000 = 0,$$

a quadratic equation in $\sqrt{3n}$. Hence,†

$$\sqrt{3n} = \frac{-1 + \sqrt{1 - 4(1)(-12{,}000)}}{2} \cong 109$$

and

$$n = 3960.$$

The value 3960 checks and gives the maximum number of tickets *under the assumption that a binomial distribution is to be expected, and corresponding to the risk allowed.*

● **Example 3.** A newspaper polled a random sample of 200 voters and found 104 favored while 96 opposed a city bond issue. What inference can be made about the outcome of the election?

Although we know the relative frequency of favorable votes in a random sample, $\frac{104}{200}$, we do not know the probability of a favorable vote. Let p be the probability of a favorable vote. Then, for a random sample of 200 voters, the mean and the standard deviation are $200p$ and $\sqrt{200pq}$, respectively. We shall apply (13.15), use 3 sigma limits, since we wish to be very certain about the prediction. To do this the inequalities in (13.15) must be altered. We add $3\sqrt{npq}$ to both members of

$$np - 3\sqrt{npq} \leqq x,$$

and subtract $3\sqrt{npq}$ from both members of

$$x \leqq np + 3\sqrt{npq},$$

and obtain

$$np \leqq x + 3\sqrt{npq}, \qquad x - 3\sqrt{npq} \leqq np.$$

Then

$$x - 3\sqrt{npq} \leqq np \leqq x + 3\sqrt{npq}. \tag{13.19}$$

Either np lies on the interval (13.19) or it does not. By (13.15), when n is sufficiently large, we expect that if it were possible to repeat the experiment a large number of times yielding many x values, then

† Only the positive root of the quadratic equation is used since $\sqrt{3n} > 0$.

approximately 99.7 percent of the intervals (13.19) would contain np. The interval (13.19) is called a **99.7 percent confidence interval for** np. If n is sufficiently large $\dfrac{x}{n}$ may be used to approximate p in $\sqrt{npq}$ to yield an approximate 99.7 percent confidence interval:

$$x - 3\sqrt{n\left(\frac{x}{n}\right)\left(1 - \frac{x}{n}\right)} \leq np \leq x + 3\sqrt{n\left(\frac{x}{n}\right)\left(1 - \frac{x}{n}\right)} \qquad (13.20)$$

The relative frequency $\frac{104}{200}$ or $\frac{13}{25}$ is an estimate of p. If this estimate is substituted into the first and third members of the preceding inequalities, we get

$$104 - 3\sqrt{200(\tfrac{13}{25})(\tfrac{12}{25})} \leq 200p \leq 104 + 3\sqrt{200(\tfrac{13}{25})(\tfrac{12}{25})},$$
$$104 - 21.2 < 200p < 104 + 21.2$$
$$.41 < p < .63.$$

We may conclude that an approximate 99.7 percent confidence interval for p is $.41 < p < .63$, but we are unable to predict the outcome of the election since the interval extends both below and above $\frac{1}{2}$.

● *Example 4.* To observe the effect of larger sample sizes, suppose 10,400 people favored while 9600 opposed the issue when a larger sample of 20,000 was questioned. Now, what inference can be made about the outcome of the election? Note that the percentage favoring the issue is unchanged.

$$10,400 - 3\sqrt{20,000(\tfrac{13}{25})(\tfrac{12}{25})} \leq 20,000p \leq 10,400 + 3\sqrt{20,000(\tfrac{13}{25})(\tfrac{12}{25})},$$
$$10,400 - 212 \leq 20,000p \leq 10,400 + 212,$$
$$.509 \leq p \leq .53.$$

Under these conditions the bond issue is likely to be favored by a narrow margin.

Events that happen less frequently than $np - 2\sqrt{npq}$, or more often than $np + 2\sqrt{npq}$ (that is, when $|x - np| > 2\sqrt{npq}$) are considered relatively rare. Consequently, when the frequency of occurrence of an event deviates from the expected average number of occurrences by an amount greater than 2 sigmas in size (again, $|x - np| > 2\sqrt{npq}$), it is concluded that this is not the result of chance and that *such an event does not have probability* p. It becomes even more certain that an event does not have probability p when the frequency of occurrence of the event deviates from the expected average number of occurrences by an amount greater than 3 sigmas in size ($|x - np| > 3\sqrt{npq}$), since such events occur only about 3 times in 1000. Examples 5 and 6 will serve as illustrations.

● *Example 5.* An ace came up 25 times in 100 tosses of a die. Is the die "honest"? (Does this contradict $p = \frac{1}{6}$ for probability of an ace?)

For $n = 100$, $x = 25$ and $p = \frac{1}{6}$, we find $np = 100(\frac{1}{6}) = \frac{50}{3}$,

$$x - np = 25 - \tfrac{50}{3} = \tfrac{25}{3}, \quad 2\sqrt{npq} = 2\sqrt{100(\tfrac{1}{6})(\tfrac{5}{6})} = \frac{10\sqrt{5}}{3} \cong \frac{22.36}{3}.$$

Since $x - np = \tfrac{25}{3} > \dfrac{22.36}{3} \cong 2\sigma$, we conclude that the die is not "honest." That is, the die does not have $\frac{1}{6}$ as the probability of an ace.

- **Example 6.** In a random group of 270 dark-haired persons there were 90 with blue eyes, while in a random group of 330 light-haired persons there were 260 with blue eyes. Do the two proportions of blue-eyed persons differ significantly? (Is it likely or not that the probability of blue eyes is the same for both hair types?)

  An estimate of the probability of blue eyes and dark hair is $\frac{90}{270} = \frac{1}{3}$. Using (13.20) and this estimate,

  $$\frac{90 - 3\sqrt{270(\tfrac{1}{3})(\tfrac{2}{3})}}{270} \cong \frac{67}{270} \cong .25 \quad \text{and} \quad \frac{90 + 3\sqrt{270(\tfrac{1}{3})(\tfrac{2}{3})}}{270} \cong \frac{113}{270} \cong .43.$$

  Consequently, an approximate 99.7 percent confidence interval for p is $.25 \leq p(\text{blue eyes with dark hair}) \leq .43$.

  An estimate of the probability of blue eyes and light hair is $\frac{260}{330} = \frac{26}{33}$. Using (13.20) and this estimate,

  $$\frac{260 - 3\sqrt{330(\tfrac{26}{33})(\tfrac{7}{33})}}{330} \cong \frac{238}{330} \cong .72 \quad \text{and} \quad \frac{260 + 3\sqrt{330(\tfrac{26}{33})(\tfrac{7}{33})}}{330} \cong \frac{282}{330} \cong .86.$$

  Consequently, an approximate 99.7 percent confidence interval for p is $.72 \leq p(\text{blue eyes with light hair}) \leq .86$.

  The two intervals do not overlap since the upper limit in the first case is .43 and the lower limit in the second case is .72. This suggests that the probability of blue eyes is not the same for both hair types.

13–6. The binomial distribution is useful in attacking statistical problems in which events are separated into two categories A and B such that at each one of a set of n independent trials the probability for an outcome in A is p and the probability of an outcome in B is $1 - p$, where p is a constant.

- **Example 1.** A student takes an examination consisting of 20 true-false questions. Does he possess any "real knowledge" of the material on which he was examined if he answers 15 questions correctly?

  To solve this problem we must agree on a basis for solution. (1) If the student has "real knowledge," he should do better than select by chance one of the two answers to each problem. We shall assume that if he guesses, his probability for a correct answer is $p = \frac{1}{2}$ and if he has "real knowledge," his probability for a correct answer is $p > \frac{1}{2}$. (2) The problem becomes the following: under the hypothesis $p = \frac{1}{2}$

(that the student is guessing) is the probability of 15 or more correct answers so small as to make $p = \frac{1}{2}$ unlikely? (At the same time this would rule out $p < \frac{1}{2}$. Why?) Using the initial hypothesis that $p = \frac{1}{2}$ (that is, the hypothesis that the student is guessing), how small should the probability of 15 or more correct answers be before we agree that actually $p > \frac{1}{2}$? (That is, agree that the student has "some real knowledge.")

In statistical work a usual risk in denying an initial hypothesis is .05. This means in our problem that if we assume $p = \frac{1}{2}$ and find the probability of 15 or more correct answers is less than or equal to .05, then we would reject the hypothesis $p = \frac{1}{2}$ and accept $p > \frac{1}{2}$ with the knowledge that such a decision was incorrect in not more than $100(.05) = 5$ percent of such situations where p actually was $\frac{1}{2}$.

Under the hypothesis $p = \frac{1}{2}$, 15 or more correct answers are unusual since

$$\sum_{x=15}^{20} \binom{20}{x}(\tfrac{1}{2})^x(\tfrac{1}{2})^{20-x} = \sum_{x=15}^{20} \binom{20}{x}(\tfrac{1}{2})^{20} = .02069.$$

Consequently, we reject $p = \frac{1}{2}$ and accept $p > \frac{1}{2}$. We agree that the student has "some real knowledge" of the material on which he was examined. In agreeing to this we run a risk of being incorrect in $100(.02069) = 2.069$ percent of such decisions since the probability of 15 or more correct answers when $p = \frac{1}{2}$ is .02069.†

PROBLEM SET 13-6

1. On past inspection, a manufacturer has had to reject as defective 10 percent of the items inspected. A new lot consisting of 400 items comes up for inspection. (a) How many pieces should he expect to reject? (b) From past experience what is the standard deviation of the number of rejects? (c) If he has to reject 59 pieces what can he conclude?

2. A purchaser tests a sample of 100 items from a large shipment and finds four defective items. (a) Find an approximate 99.7 percent confidence interval for p. (b) If the purchaser cannot tolerate more than 10-percent defective would he accept or reject the shipment, or test a larger sample?

† This has considerable importance in evaluating true-false examination procedures. If 1000 students take a 20-question true-false examination in which they merely fill in the answer sheet without even seeing the questions they certainly have no "real knowledge" in this case. We can expect that 2.069 percent or about 20 of the 1000 students will score 15 or more correct answers in spite of the fact that they have not even seen the questions!

3. Would it be unusual for a city of 12,000 population to have 1300 individuals in the 20 to 24 age group if about 9 percent of the nation's population is in this age group? Discuss.

4. According to Mendelian inheritance, certain crosses of peas should give yellow and green peas in the ratio 3:1. In an experiment, 168 yellow and 48 green peas were obtained. Do these results conform to theory?

5. A sample of 1000 articles from a factory is examined and found to be 3-percent defective. A sample of 1500 similar articles from a second factory is found to be only 2-percent defective. Is it reasonable to conclude that the product of the first factory is inferior to that of the second?

6. From past experience a manufacturer of parts finds that when a certain machine is functioning properly 5 percent of the parts are defective, on the average. During the course of a day's operation by a new operator 400 parts are turned out, 35 of which are defective. Is the new operator satisfactory? Comment.

7. From a study of the third edition of *American Men of Science*, H. L. Rietz observed that a group of scientists had 1705 sons and 1527 daughters. Do these data agree with the hypothesis that one half is the probability that a child will be a boy?

8. The philosopher Buffon threw a coin 4040 times obtaining 2048 heads. Was Buffon's coin "true"?

9. If a coin is tossed 100 times and comes up the same way each time, can you conclude the coin is not true?

10. If a coin is tossed 100 times giving 80 heads and 20 tails, would you be willing to conclude the coin was not true? Discuss.

11. If two dice are tossed 72 times, what is the mean number of times a point score of five would be expected? What is the standard deviation of this number? If a point score of five came up 12 times in 72 tosses are the dice "honest"?

12. A certain disease has 10-percent fatality. Out of 20 patients belonging to a certain occupational class, 5 died. Does this indicate unusual susceptibility to this disease on the part of this class?

13. If a coin turns up heads in 1000 successive tosses, is it equally likely to turn up heads or tails on the next toss? Discuss. Do you think the coin has two heads?

14. A swimming pool can accommodate a maximum of 400 people during rush hours and past experience indicates that only three fourths of all season ticket holders come during rush hours. How many season tickets can be sold if a 1 to 6 risk of overcrowding can be taken? How many can be sold if a 1 to 40 risk of overcrowding can be taken?

15. Past experience indicates that 20 percent of all college freshmen students entering a certain college take remedial mathematics. How many remedial mathematics students should be prepared for if there are 400 entering freshmen and a 1 to 6 risk of overcrowding is allowed? How many if a 1 to 40 risk of overcrowding is allowed?

6. A wine taster claims that he can distinguish between two brands of wine by taste. If he correctly identified the brands 14 times out of 20 trials, would you accept or reject his claim? Use the usual .05 risk mentioned in Example 1 of Section 13–6.

13–7. Control chart for percentage of defectives. A control chart is a quick visual aid for controlling the quality of a product. Such charts are easily constructed. They are especially useful in sampling inspection.

Consider the case in which each sample contains n items and the standard percentage of defective items, $100p$, has a predetermined value. By (13.18), Section 13–5, the percentage of defective items in any sample, $100x/n$, almost certainly satisfies

$$100 \left[p - 3\sqrt{\frac{p(1-p)}{n}} \right] \leq 100\frac{x}{n} \leq 100 \left[p + 3\sqrt{\frac{p(1-p)}{n}} \right].$$

The chart is a set of three horizontal lines drawn on graph paper at

$$100 \left[p - 3\sqrt{\frac{p(1-p)}{n}} \right], \quad 100p, \quad 100 \left[p + 3\sqrt{\frac{p(1-p)}{n}} \right]$$

on the vertical scale.† The central line is the **standard** percentage or the **process average.** The other two lines are **control limits.** Periodic samples are taken and a point plotted on the chart for each sample. We shall call such points **sample points.**

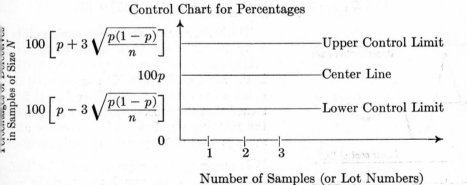

Control Chart for Percentages

Number of Samples (or Lot Numbers)

Each sample point has the number of the sample for abscissa (x value). The abscissa of the ith sample point is i. The percentage of defectives in the sample is the ordinate (y value). The process is in control as long as each sample point is between the control limits. Approximately 99.7 percent of all sample points should be between the control limits [see (13.18), Section 13–5]. It follows that on the average only 3 sample points out of every 1000 fall outside the control limits when the process is in control. Consequently

† In certain applications 2-sigma control limits are used.

a sample point outside the control limits is such a rare event that the process is considered out of control and action is taken to restore control.

- **Example 1.** From past experience a manufacturer of parts determined that on the average, when a certain machine was functioning properly 3.5 per cent of the parts produced were defective. Ten successive samples were taken from the machine and the results tabulated. Each sample contained 500 parts. Was the machine functioning properly?

Lot number	1	2	3	4	5	6	7	8	9	10
Number of defective parts	21	13	17	28	12	10	23	15	14	16
Percent defective	4.2	2.6	3.4	5.6	2.4	2.0	4.6	3.0	2.8	3.2

We shall use a control chart to help us answer this question.
The process percentage is $100p = 3.5.$ Now

$$3 \sqrt{\frac{p(1-p)}{n}} = 3 \sqrt{\frac{.035(.965)}{500}} \cong 3(.0082) \cong .025.$$

The upper control limit is

$$100 \left[p + 3 \sqrt{\frac{p(1-p)}{n}} \right] \cong 100[.035 + .025] = 6.0.$$

The lower control limit is

$$100 \left[p - 3 \sqrt{\frac{p(1-p)}{n}} \right] \cong 100[.035 - .025] = 1.0.$$

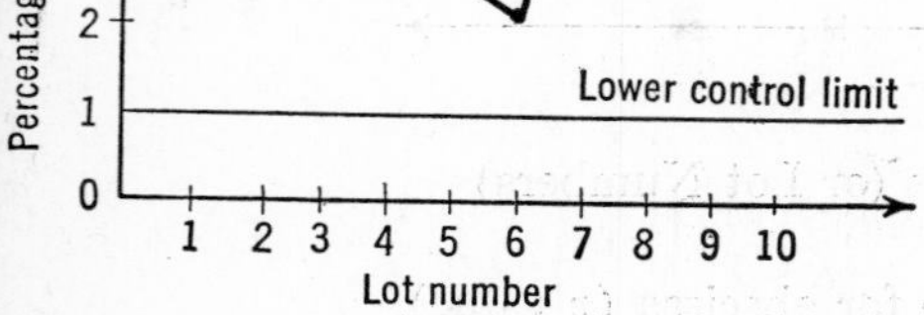

Fig. 13–1

The broken line connecting sample points is not an essential part of the chart, but it is useful in helping one visualize quality fluctuations in their historical order. No sample point falls outside the control limits. Therefore it is assumed that the process was under control and the machine was functioning properly at an average level of 3.5 percent defective parts.

It is necessary to compute control limits for each sample size when samples of various sizes are used. This is illustrated in the next example.

- **Example 2.** Ten samples were inspected and the results tabulated.

Lot number	1	2	3	4	5	6	7	8	9	10	Total
Number of units inspected	300	300	300	300	300	200	200	200	200	200	2500
Number of defective units	15	9	10	20	8	6	11	7	6	8	100
Percent defective	5	3	3.3	6.7	2.7	3	5.5	3.5	3	4	4

In this example the process percentage of defectives must be estimated. For the estimate of $100p$ we use 100 times the ratio of the total number of defective units to the total number of units inspected. That is,

$$100p \cong 100(\tfrac{100}{2500}) = 4.0.$$

For sample size $\quad n = 300,\quad 3\sqrt{\dfrac{p(1-p)}{n}} \cong 3\sqrt{\dfrac{.04(.96)}{300}} \cong .034.$ The control limits are

$$100\left[p + 3\sqrt{\dfrac{p(1-p)}{n}}\right] \cong 100[.040 + .034] = 7.4,$$

$$100\left[p - 3\sqrt{\dfrac{p(1-p)}{n}}\right] \cong 100[.040 - .034] = 0.6.$$

For sample size $\quad n = 200,\quad 3\sqrt{\dfrac{(.04)(.96)}{200}} \cong .042.$ The control limits are

$$100[.040 + .042] = 8.2,\quad 100[.040 - .042] = -0.2.$$

In this last case the lower control limit is taken as zero since the percentage of defective items is never negative. The sample points are plotted on the chart. For convenience a broken line is drawn connecting successive sample points.

Again, the sample points are between the control limits. On the basis of the given information the process is assumed to be in a state of control.

13–8. Control chart for defects. By (13.15), Section 13–5, the number of defective items x in any sample almost certainly satisfies

$$np - 3\sqrt{npq} \leqq x \leqq np + 3\sqrt{npq}.$$

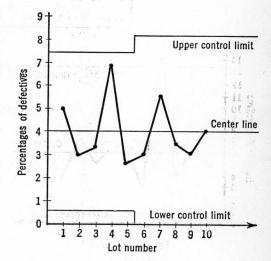

Fig. 13–2

A control chart for the **number** of defective items, rather than the percentage of defective items, can be constructed using the center line at np on the vertical scale and the control limits at $np - 3\sqrt{npq},\ np + 3\sqrt{npq}$ on the vertical scale. Observe that the control limits are 3-sigma limits. Also, the position of the center line changes as the sample size changes. The two examples of the previous section could be studied using control charts for defectives. The charts would be similar to those already shown. If p is quite small, then $q = 1 - p \cong 1$ and the control limits are

$$np + 3\sqrt{nqp} \cong np + 3\sqrt{np},$$
$$np - 3\sqrt{nqp} \cong np - 3\sqrt{np}.$$

An illustration involving very small p is given in the next example.

Control Chart for Defectives

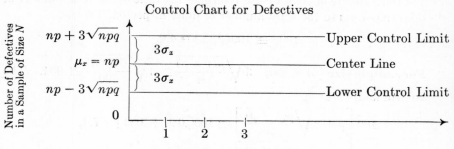

Sample (or Lot) Number

● **Example 1.** Ten successive samples of a mixed paint were tested by applying each to similar 1-foot square plane surfaces and counting the number of pinholes in the dried painted surfaces. The results appear in the table.

Sample Number	1	2	3	4	5	6	7	8	9	10	Total
Number of pinholes	5	6	4	14	3	6	6	5	7	4	60

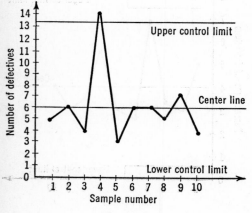

Fig. 13-3

Was the quality of the paint in a state of control?

The value of p is very small, since for any sample the ratio of the pinhole area to 1 square foot is very small. We use the average number of pinholes per sample to approximate np.

$$np \cong \tfrac{60}{10} = 6.$$

The control limits are taken as

$$np + 3\sqrt{np} \cong 6 + 3\sqrt{6} \cong 13.3$$
$$np - 3\sqrt{np} \cong 6 - 3\sqrt{6} \cong -1.3.$$

The lower control limit is zero, since the number of defects is never negative.

The fourth sample point is above the upper control limit. The quality of the paint was *not* in a state of control, as judged by the data and method of testing.

Statistical quality control is of great importance in modern manufacturing. It is usual in most universities to devote an entire course to this important subject. An engineer or a business man who understands statistical quality control is a valuable asset to any firm. We do not pretend to have presented an entire course in these few pages, but we hope the reader may have gained some insight into this facet of mathematical statistics.

PROBLEM SET 13-8

1. A class of 28 students met 64 times with the following absence record.

Student number	1 2 3 4 5	6 7 8 9 10	11 12 13 14 15	16 17 18 19 20	21 22 23 24 25	26 27 28
Absences	11 1 4 1 10	2 2 3 0 6	2 8 3 7 0	4 1 0 5 6	3 0 12 6 2	8 2 2

Construct a control chart for percentages of absences. Does the chart indicate a state of control? Were any of the absence records outside the control limits?

2. Fifteen samples of 50 items each were inspected with results as listed.

Lot number	1 2 3 4 5	6 7 8 9 10	11 12 13 14 15
Number of defectives	3 1 1 1 1	2 5 3 2 4	3 2 5 3 2

Construct a control chart for percentages of defective items. Does the chart indicate that a state of control exists?

3. According to the *World Almanac* there were 31,500 motor-vehicle deaths in the United States in 1949 and the 1950 population census was 150,697,361. From this the average motor-vehicle death rate per 100,000 population in 1949 was approximately 20.9. Use the following table based on information given in the *World Almanac* and construct a control chart for percentages of deaths. Recall that the control limits depend on sample size. Indicate any instances of lack of control.

State	1950 Population	1949 Motor-vehicle deaths
Arizona	7.5×10^5	281
California	105.9×10^5	3003
Colorado	13.3×10^5	318
Idaho	5.9×10^5	168
Montana	5.9×10^5	162
Nebraska	13.3×10^5	256
Nevada	1.6×10^5	82
New Mexico	6.8×10^5	245
North Dakota	6.2×10^5	134
Oklahoma	22.3×10^5	518
Texas	77.1×10^5	1957
Utah	6.9×10^5	174
Washington	23.8×10^5	441
Wyoming	2.9×10^5	137

4. Use the following purchaser's inspection data to construct a control chart for the number of defects found in 100-yard pieces of woolen goods. Does the chart indicate that a state of control exists?

[HINT: See Example 1, Section 13–7.]

Sample number	1 2 3 4 5	6 7 8 9 10	11 12 13 14 15	16 17 18 19 20	21 22 23 24 25	26 27 28 29
Number of defects	13 5 1 4 3	3 6 5 0 1	3 5 7 8 4	10 5 5 5 4	3 4 5 1 1	0 1 1 4

5. Read and report on one of the following booklets published by the *American Standards Association*, New York: (a) *Guide for Quality Control and Control Chart Method of Analyzing Data*, (b) *Control Chart Method of Controlling Quality During Production*.

6. Read and report on one of the following articles: (a) "Statistics" by Warren Weaver, *American Scientist*, January, 1952, p. 60. (b) "Quality Control" by A. G. Dalton, *Scientific American*, March, 1953, p. 29. (c) "Pascal and the Invention of Probability Theory" by O. Ore, *American Mathematical Monthly*, May, 1960, p. 409.

7. A purchaser tests a random sample of 100 items from a large shipment and finds 9 defective items. Past shipments received from the same manufacturer were in control at a level of 3 percent defective. (a) Does this sample indicate that the level is no longer 3 percent defective? (b) Find an approximate 99.7 percent confidence interval for the true p of the shipment. (c) If the purchaser cannot tolerate more than 8 percent defective, should he accept the shipment?

13–9. Statistical quality control offers a major contribution to manufacturing economy. A manufacturing process will produce parts that show variation from one another. If the parts vary **within the tolerance limits** established for the item, they are acceptable. Tool wear, operator carelessness, variation in raw material, fluctuating power supply, or other causes may produce parts outside of the tolerance limits. Statistical quality control makes it possible to locate such troubles quickly and to correct the process without wasting a day's or a week's production. Also, with constant sampling it is usually unnecessary to provide a costly and time-consuming final, total inspection. As soon as more than an occasional misfit is produced, quality control spots the trouble and permits correction. Moreover, the amount of risk of defective production can be computed with mathematical accuracy, and held to whatever limit best suits the economy of the situation.

In the examples discussed in this chapter, pieces were rated as either acceptable or defective. Even more effective quality control charts may be constructed if instrument readings are obtained in the testing process. For example, the amount of tension (weight) needed to produce a 1-inch deflection in a spring is easily measured for each spring in a sample. The average of the tensions may be plotted on a control chart of the type previously described, and the range (difference between the highest and the lowest tension) plotted on another (range) control chart. If either of these entries falls outside of the control limits, the process is out of control. Often an engineer or mathematician skilled in statistical quality control analysis can suggest where the trouble lies from the appearance of these control charts. For example, tool wear is apt to cause the average to exceed control limits gradually, while the range remains in control. Nonuniformity of raw material, on the other hand, may cause the range to be out of control while the average stays within the specified limits.

Recently a single order for 10,000,000 springs for use in proximity fuses was completed (including cost of springs, defects, and quality control inspection) for $51,000 by the use of quality control, while without quality control the order (including cost of springs, defects, and inspection) would have cost $81,200, a saving of $30,200 on one order. It is not surprising that engineers with training in quality control are in high demand.

13–10. Self test.

Record time.

1. In tossing two dice 10 times what is the probability for obtaining a point score of 7 (a) Exactly 2 times? (b) At least 2 times?
2. If 400 tosses of a coin resulted in 236 heads, is the "honesty" of the process in doubt?
3. A certain disease has 10 percent fatality. Out of 200 patients belonging to a certain occupational class 34 died. Does this suggest unusual lack of resistance to this disease on the part of this class?
4. A manufacturer is prepared to distribute 10,000 tubes of toothpaste free to holders of coupons received by mail. Past experience indicates that only one fifth of such coupon holders will request gifts. How many coupons should be mailed if a risk of 1 to 6 of not having enough free toothpaste is to be allowed?
5. It is expected that four fifths of those buying tickets to a benefit concert will attend. If only 500 persons can be seated and a 1 to 6 risk of having too few seats can be taken, how many tickets may be sold?

Record time.

R. Boyd.   Courtesy *Scripta Mathematica*

14

● ● ● ● ● ● ● ● ● ● ● ● ● ● ● ● ● ● ● ●

In ancient Egypt (250 B.C.) the computation of certain parts of a triangle, given the measures of other parts, was the most important problem of trigonometry. Eratosthenes calculated the earth's radius, correct to within 25 miles, by measuring the angle that the sun's rays made with a vertical rod at Alexandria and at Aswan. The solution of triangles is still of importance in astronomy and in surveying. When the headings for the 5000-foot Musconetcony tunnel were driven from opposite sides of the mountain, the error in alignment was found to be only $\frac{1}{2}$ inch, and the error in level only $\frac{1}{6}$ inch. Such precision would be impossible without computational triangulation. Nevertheless triangles and angles are of only minor importance. In the numerous applications of modern trigonometry the analytic trigonometry is of prime importance. It often comes as a surprise to the student to learn that the more important applications of trigonometry, say in electrical theory, have *nothing whatsoever to do with angles*. One example may be helpful. The demand for long-distance telephone communication has grown rapidly. It is expensive to string and to maintain additional long-distance lines. Consider the monetary value of a discovery that would enable each long-distance line to carry two conversations simultaneously! The discovery was made several years ago and has since been extended to permit modern long-distance lines to carry ten or more conversations *at the same time* on each line without intermixing. This was a mathematical discovery based on the formula for $\sin (A + B)$ given in Section 16–4. In this application A and B are not angles, but numbers corresponding to time frequencies.

The engineer of today is busy with problems that were unthought of 20 years ago. As a result of this, many shop technicians are doing work that was done by the engineer and scientist of 20 years ago. The technician who is to get ahead tomorrow must be mathematically prepared to accept some of the responsibility that previously rested on other shoulders. The scientist and engineer will be reaching toward new horizons.

14–1. Plane angles. We now discuss a more general concept of angle than the reader met in elementary geometry. If, in a plane, a half line is rotated about its end point (the vertex of the angle), the **amount of rotation** from an initial, starting, position to the terminal, final, position is known as a **plane angle** or simply as an **angle.** The rotation may be in either the clockwise, or counterclockwise direction. Since these two directions are opposite in sense, they are assigned different algebraic signs. It is customary to designate angles generated by counterclockwise rotation as positive. An angle is pictured by showing the initial and terminal positions of the rotating half line (sides of the angle) with a curved arrow indicating the direction and amount of the rotation.

The three angles of Figure 14–1 have the same initial and terminal sides. The arrows indicate the angles are *not* equal. Angles α and γ have positive (counterclockwise) rotation, while angle β has negative (clockwise) rotation. Angle γ represents one complete revolution more than angle α.

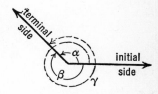

Fig. 14–1

In the degree system of angular measure, each complete rotation is subdivided into 360 equal angles called degrees. Each degree is subdivided into 60 minutes, and each minute into 60 seconds; or the degree may be broken up into tenths or hundredths of a degree. This latter "deci-trig" system of angular measure is in common use and many instruments are calibrated in hundredths of a degree.

In the radian system of angular measure each revolution is subdivided into 2π equal angles called *radians*, where $\pi = 3.14159265 \cdots$. From this it follows that a central angle of a circle is one radian if the angle subtends an arc whose length is equal to the radius of the circle. One should note that $360° = 2\pi$ radians. The calculus and its applications are simplified when radian measure is used. (See Sections 15–1 and 16–11.)

PROBLEM SET 14-1

In Problems 1 to 7 make approximate sketches of the indicated angles.

1. $30°$.
2. $300°$.
3. $-45°$.
4. $-70°$.
5. 1 radian.
6. 5 radians.
7. $390°$.
8. Are any of the angles in Problems 1 to 7 coterminal? That is, do any of these angles have the same initial and terminal sides?
9. Arrange the angles $60°$, $20°$, 1 radian, $\pi/2$ radians in order of increasing size.
10. How many degrees are there in the *smallest* positive angle that has its initial and terminal sides perpendicular?

11. How many degrees are there in the *largest* negative angle that has its initial and terminal sides perpendicular? [NOTE: $-139° < -84°$.]

12. Two fixed, intersecting half lines form the initial and terminal sides of a 47° angle. Determine two other angles between $-370°$ and $+800°$ having the same initial and terminal sides.

13. Same as Problem 12, when the smallest positive angle is 26°.

14. Same as Problem 12, when the smallest positive angle is 235°.

15. There are 360° in a revolution and 2π radians in a revolution. Show that $1° = \pi/180$ radians.

16. How many degrees are equal to $\pi/2$ radians? To $\pi/3$ radians?

17. How many radians are equal to 30°, to 45°, to $-144°$?

14–2. Introduction to trigonometric functions. The trigonometric functions may be defined in two ways. We may define the sine of θ (abbreviated sin θ) where θ is an angle,† or we may define sin θ where θ is a number; the number θ corresponds to the radian measure of an angle as will be seen from the definition given in Section 15–1. We begin by defining the trigonometric functions of angles. Later, these same functions are defined for numbers. The angular definition is used in problems concerning surveying and mensuration, while the numerical definition is used in electrical engineering, physics, chemistry, and other sciences.

14–3. Standard position. An angle is in **standard position** in a coordinate system if the vertex is at the origin, and the initial side of the angle is along the positive half of the x-axis. The terminal side may fall in any position through the vertex. Angles α, β, γ in Figure 14–1 are in standard position.

14–4. Definitions of trigonometric functions. Let θ be an angle in standard position. Select any point $P(x, y)$, other than the vertex, on the terminal side, and construct a line through P perpendicular to the x-axis (*never* to the y-axis). Since the coordinates of P are (x, y), the distance between P and the origin is $r = \sqrt{x^2 + y^2}$. The distance r is always positive; while x and y may each be positive, zero, or negative, depending upon the angle.

In Figure 14–2, $x > 0$, $y < 0$, while in Figure 14–3, $x < 0$ and $y > 0$.

Define, *if the denominator is not zero:*

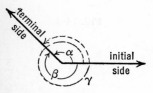

Fig. 14–1

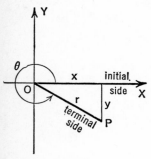

Fig. 14–2

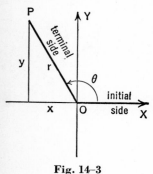

Fig. 14–3

sine of $\theta = \sin \theta = y/r$ cosecant of $\theta = \csc \theta = r/y$
cosine of $\theta = \cos \theta = x/r$ secant of $\theta = \sec \theta = r/x$
tangent of $\theta = \tan \theta = y/x$ cotangent of $\theta = \cot \theta = x/y$.

† The symbol θ is the Greek letter theta. A table of Greek letters will be found with the tables in the back of the book.

These six functions should be memorized.

Note that certain functions are not defined for some angles. For example, tan 90° is undefined. Why?

Suppose another point P' on the terminal side had been chosen instead of P. Since corresponding sides of similar triangles are proportional, $y'/r' = y/r$, $x'/r' = x/r$, and $y'/x' = y/x$. Hence, each of the six **ratios** is the same for both P' and P. This means each trigonometric function is a function of an angle and does not depend upon the point P chosen. The values are fixed for a fixed angle, and as the angle changes the values of the trigonometric functions may be expected to change. Trigonometric functions are dimensionless abstract numbers (ratios of distances measured in the same unit).

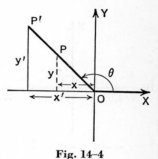

Fig. 14–4

- **Example 1.** The angle β is a positive angle of more than 2.5 and less than 3 revolutions. The point $(-3, -1)$ lies on the terminal side of the angle β when β is in standard position. Determine six trigonometric functions of β.

  Since $(-3, -1)$ lies on the terminal side, we may take $P = (-3, -1)$. Then $x = -3$, $y = -1$, $r = \sqrt{10}$.

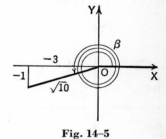

Fig. 14–5

$$\sin \theta = \frac{-1}{\sqrt{10}} = \frac{-\sqrt{10}}{10}, \qquad \csc \theta = \frac{\sqrt{10}}{-1} = -\sqrt{10},$$

$$\cos \theta = \frac{-3}{\sqrt{10}} = \frac{-3\sqrt{10}}{10}, \qquad \sec \theta = \frac{\sqrt{10}}{-3} = -\frac{\sqrt{10}}{3},$$

$$\tan \theta = \frac{-1}{-3} = \frac{1}{3}, \qquad \cot \theta = \frac{-3}{-1} = 3.$$

- **Example 2.** The sign of sec θ will remain fixed for θ in a given quadrant. Determine this sign in each quadrant. From Figures 14–6, 7, 8, 9 we see the behavior of sec θ.

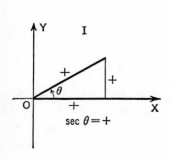

Fig. 14–6

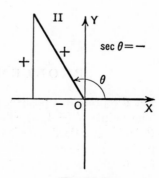

Fig. 14–7

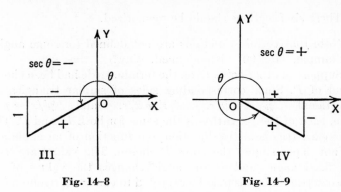

Fig. 14–8   Fig. 14–9

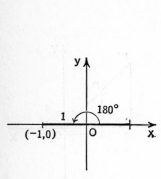

$x = -1,\ y = 0,\ r = 1.$

Hence, $\sec 180° = \dfrac{1}{-1} = -1.$

Fig. 14–10

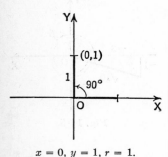

$x = 0,\ y = 1,\ r = 1.$

Hence, $\sec 90°$ is undefined. Why?

Fig. 14–11

● **Example 3.** Discuss $\sec 180°$ and $\sec 90°$. Consider Figures 14–10 and 14–11. For convenience take $r = +1$.

$$\sec 180° = 1/-1 = -1.$$
$$\sec 90° \text{ is undefined. Why?}$$

● **Example 4.** Prove that $|\sec \theta| \geqq 1$ for all θ for which $\sec \theta$ is defined. By definition

$$|\sec \theta| = \left|\frac{r}{x}\right| = \left|\frac{\sqrt{x^2 + y^2}}{x}\right| = +\sqrt{\frac{x^2 + y^2}{x^2}}.$$

Since $\dfrac{y^2}{x^2} \geqq 0,$

$$|\sec \theta| = +\sqrt{1 + \frac{y^2}{x^2}} \geqq +\sqrt{1} = 1.$$

● **Example 5.** Show that $\sin^2 \theta + \cos^2 \theta = 1$ for every θ.
[NOTE: $\sin^2 \theta$ is written for $(\sin \theta)^2$.]
From the definitions

$$\sin^2 \theta + \cos^2 \theta = \left(\frac{y}{r}\right)^2 + \left(\frac{x}{r}\right)^2 = \frac{y^2 + x^2}{r^2} = \frac{r^2}{r^2} = 1.$$

PROBLEM SET 14–4

1. Let θ represent a positive rotation of less than 1 revolution. The point $P(-4, 3)$ lies on the terminal side of θ when θ is in standard position. Sketch the angle in standard position and from this sketch determine the six trigonometric functions of θ discussed in this section.

2. Same as Problem 1 for   (a) $P(12, -5)$,   (b) $P(-6, 8)$.

3. Same as Problem 1 for (a) $P(0, -4)$, (b) $P(5, 0)$.

4. Same as Problem 1 for (a) $P(-1, -3)$, (b) $P(-5, 12)$.

5. From a sketch determine the other four functions of θ if $\sec \theta = -\frac{5}{4}$, $\tan \theta = \frac{3}{4}$.

6. The sign of $\cos \theta$ is always the same as the sign of $\sec \theta$. Why? Does any other function always have the same sign as $\cos \theta$? Find a function always having the same sign as $\tan \theta$.

7. Discuss the sign of $\tan \theta$ in each quadrant.

8. Same as Problem 7, for $\sin \theta$, $\cos \theta$, $\sec \theta$, and $\cot \theta$.

9. Show that $\tan \theta = \dfrac{1}{\cot \theta}$ whenever both are defined. Does $\cot \theta$ always equal $\dfrac{1}{\tan \theta}$?

10. Use the definitions of $\tan \theta$ and $\sec \theta$ to prove that
$$1 + \tan^2 \theta = \sec^2 \theta$$
for all θ for which the terms are defined.

11. (a) Show that $\sec \theta = \dfrac{1}{\cos \theta}$ for all θ for which both members are defined. Does $\sec \theta$ always equal $\dfrac{1}{\cos \theta}$? Does $\cos \theta$ always equal $\dfrac{1}{\sec \theta}$?

(b) Give a similar discussion for the relationship
$$\csc \theta = \frac{1}{\sin \theta}.$$

Determine from a sketch of the types given in Examples 1 and 3 the values of the six trigonometric functions of the angles listed in Problems 12 to 20.

12. $90°$.   **13.** $180°$.   **14.** $270°$.   **15.** $360°$.

16. $0°$.   **17.** $810°$.   **18.** $-90°$.   **19.** $-270°$.

20. $135°$. [NOTE: It is convenient to take $x = -1$ and $y = +1$.]

21. Prove that $-1 \le \cos \theta \le 1$.

22. Prove that $|\sin \theta| \le 1$.

23. Prove that $|\csc \theta| \ge 1$ for all θ for which $\csc \theta$ is defined.

24. Is there any restriction on the values of $\tan \theta$?

25. There are many values of β such that $\cos \beta = \sin \beta$. Find five such values.

26. Same as Problem 25 for $\cos \beta = -\sin \beta$.

*27. Approximate five values of β such that $\cos \beta = \frac{1}{2} \sin \beta$. Use a protractor to measure the angle.

28. The angles α and β are in standard position. The terminal side of α lies in quadrant III, while the terminal side of β lies in quadrant IV. Can $\sec \alpha = \csc \beta$?

29. Same as Problem 28. Can $\csc \beta = -\sec \alpha$?

30. The angles θ and δ are in standard position. The terminal side of θ lies in quadrant II, while the terminal side of δ lies in quadrant III. Can $\tan \theta = \tan \delta$? Explain your answer.

31. Other trigonometric functions are sometimes used. For example, versine $A = 1 - \cos A$ and coversine $A = 1 - \sin A$. These functions are used in navigation and astronomy. Compute versine 180° and coversine 180°.

14–5. Exact values of functions of angles related to 45°, 30°, and 60°. An angle θ has α as a **reference angle** if the positive acute angle between the terminal side of θ and the x-axis is α, when θ is in standard position. An acute angle is its own reference angle.

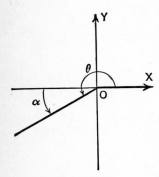

Fig. 14–12

● *Example 1.* Determine the trigonometric functions of 45°.

A 45° angle is placed in standard position, and from a point $P(x, y) \neq (0, 0)$ on the terminal side, a perpendicular is dropped to the x-axis. The triangle determined by the x-axis, the perpendicular, and the terminal side has angles 45°, 90°, 45°. (Why?) Since this triangle is isosceles, $x = y$, and

$$r = \sqrt{x^2 + y^2} = \sqrt{x^2 + x^2} = x\sqrt{2}.$$

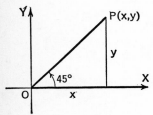

Fig. 14–13

Consequently,

$$\sin 45° = \frac{y}{r} = \frac{x}{x\sqrt{2}} = \frac{1}{\sqrt{2}} = \frac{\sqrt{2}}{2}, \qquad \csc 45° = \frac{r}{y} = \frac{x\sqrt{2}}{x} = \sqrt{2},$$

$$\cos 45° = \frac{x}{r} = \frac{x}{x\sqrt{2}} = \frac{1}{\sqrt{2}} = \frac{\sqrt{2}}{2}, \qquad \sec 45° = \frac{r}{x} = \frac{x\sqrt{2}}{x} = \sqrt{2},$$

$$\tan 45° = \frac{y}{x} = \frac{x}{x} = 1, \qquad \cot 45° = \frac{x}{y} = \frac{x}{x} = 1.$$

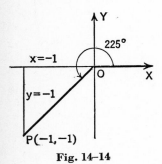

Fig. 14–14

● *Example 2.* Determine the trigonometric functions of all angles coterminal with 225°.

Each of the angles coterminal with 225° has the same functional values as 225°. Each such angle has 45° as reference angle. This implies $|x| = |y|$. Take $|x| = |y| = 1$ for convenience. The location of the terminal side gives $(-1, -1)$ as coordinates of P, $r = +\sqrt{2}$. Values of the trigonometric functions of 225° may be read directly from the sketch of Figure 14–15.

$$\sin 225° = \frac{-1}{\sqrt{2}} = -\frac{\sqrt{2}}{2}, \quad \csc 225° = -\sqrt{2},$$

$$\cos 225° = \frac{-1}{\sqrt{2}} = -\frac{\sqrt{2}}{2}, \quad \sec 225° = -\sqrt{2},$$

$$\tan 225° = +1, \qquad\qquad \cot 225° = +1.$$

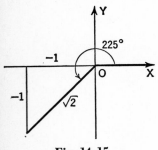

Fig. 14–15

Please observe that the trigonometric functions of an angle are the same **in absolute value** as the corresponding functions of the reference angle, but they may differ in algebraic sign.

In a 30°, 60°, 90° triangle the length of the shorter leg (opposite the 30° angle) is half the length of the hypotenuse. Observe that the bisector of one angle of an equilateral triangle (60° angles) bisects the opposite side. Applying the theorem of Pythagoras to Figure 14–16 we have $r^2 = (r/2)^2 + (\text{altitude})^2$. Hence, altitude $= \dfrac{r\sqrt{3}}{2}$. A convenient choice is $r = 2$ units.

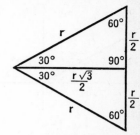

Fig. 14–16

● *Example 3.* Determine the trigonometric functions of 30°.

$$\sin 30° = \tfrac{1}{2}, \qquad \csc 30° = 2,$$

$$\cos 30° = \frac{\sqrt{3}}{2}, \qquad \sec 30° = \frac{2}{\sqrt{3}} = \frac{2\sqrt{3}}{3},$$

$$\tan 30° = \frac{1}{\sqrt{3}} = \frac{\sqrt{3}}{3}, \quad \cot 30° = \sqrt{3}.$$

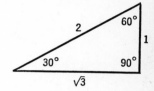

Fig. 14–17

● *Example 4.* Determine the trigonometric functions of 60°.

$$\sin 60° = \frac{\sqrt{3}}{2}, \quad \csc 60° = \frac{2}{\sqrt{3}} = \frac{2\sqrt{3}}{3},$$

$$\cos 60° = \tfrac{1}{2}, \qquad \sec 60° = 2,$$

$$\tan 60° = \sqrt{3}, \quad \cot 60° = \frac{1}{\sqrt{3}} = \frac{\sqrt{3}}{3}.$$

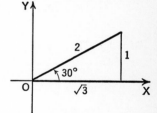

Fig. 14–18

● *Example 5.* Determine $\csc \theta$ and $\tan \theta$ if θ is an angle co-terminal with $(-60°)$. Every such angle, in standard position, has its terminal line in quadrant IV, and has 60° as reference angle.

From the previous discussion, with $r = 2$, taking care to prefix proper signs, we sketch Figure 14–20. Hence,

$$\csc \theta = \frac{2}{-\sqrt{3}} = -\frac{2\sqrt{3}}{3},$$

$$\tan \theta = \frac{-\sqrt{3}}{1} = -\sqrt{3}.$$

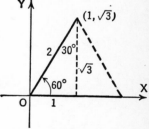

Fig. 14–19

● *Example 6.* Determine sec 150° and sin 150°. The reference angle is 30°. From Figure 14–21,

$$\sec 150° = \frac{2}{-\sqrt{3}} = -\frac{2\sqrt{3}}{3}, \quad \sin 150° = \tfrac{1}{2}.$$

Fewer errors in sign will be made if the correct sign (either $+$ or $-$) is prefixed to each numerical value of x, y, and r, in the figure for every problem.

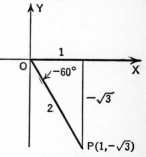

Fig. 14–20

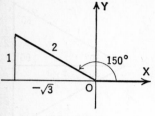

Fig. 14-21

The reader may be interested in the origin of the *co* in *co*sine, *co*secant, and *co*tangent. Two angles are called *complementary* if their sum is 90°. Thus 30° and 60° are complementary, as are 23° and 67°. The *co* in *co*function is taken from the word complementary. The *co*sine of an angle is the complementary angle's sine.

$$\text{cosine } 30° = \text{sine [complement of } 30°]$$
$$= \sin 60°.$$

In a similar fashion, $\tan 23° = \cot 67°$ and $\sec 81° = \csc 9°$. This information will be helpful to the reader in understanding the structure of the trigonometric tables used in the next section.

PROBLEM SET 14–5

Evaluate:

1. (a) sec 30°.   (b) sec 210°.

2. (a) tan 150°.   (b) cot (− 30°).

3. (a) csc 225°.   (b) cot 300°.

4. (a) sin 930°.   (b) sec (− 300°).

5. $\sin 30° \cdot \cos 300° - \sin 60° \cdot \cos 330°$.

6. $\cos 45° \cdot \sin 210° - \sin 30° \cdot \cos 135°$.

7. $\cos 180° \cdot \cos 45° - \sin 180° \cdot \sin 45°$.

8. Find the exact values of the six trigonometric functions of θ if $\csc \theta = -2$ and $\cos \theta < 0$. What is the value of θ if $90° < \theta < 450°$?

9. Construct a right triangle containing acute angles α and β. By placing α and β in standard position, show that

$$\sin \alpha = \cos (90° - \alpha) \quad \text{and} \quad \cos \alpha = \sin (90° - \alpha).$$

Note that $\beta = 90° - \alpha$.

10. Use the construction of Problem 9 to demonstrate that

$$\sec \alpha = \csc (90° - \alpha), \qquad \csc \alpha = \sec (90° - \alpha),$$
$$\tan \alpha = \cot (90° - \alpha), \quad \text{and} \quad \cot \alpha = \tan (90° - \alpha).$$

In Problems 11 to 20, find six trigonometric functions of the given angle.

11. 1035°.   **12.** − 600°.   **13.** 60°.   **14.** 150°.   **15.** − 120°.
16. − 750°.   **17.** 120°.   **18.** 240°.   **19.** − 150°.   **20.** 390°.

21. Determine   log cos 45°   and   log | sec 120° |.

22. If   log sin $\theta = 0$,   give four possible values of θ.

23. If   log cos $\theta = 0$,   give four possible values of θ.

24. Find three values of θ which satisfy   log | sin θ | $= 0$ which do *not* satisfy   log sin $\theta = 0$.

25. Show that the slope of a line that intersects the x-axis at I is equal to the tangent of the angle XIQ, where Q is a point on the line above I, and X is a point on the x-axis to the right of I.

Problems 26 to 35 refer to triangles having vertex angles A, B, C, with the length of the sides opposite these angles denoted by a, b, c, respectively. Find the missing parts, accurate to one or two significant digits.

26. $A = 90°$, $a = 6$, $b = 3$.

27. $B = 90°$, $a = 10$, $c = 10$.

28. $C = 90°$, $b = 25$, $c = 50$.

29. $B = 90°$, $A = 30°$, $a = 4$.

30. $C = 90°$, $B = 60°$, $c = 1$.

31. $A = 90°$, $b = 4$, $c = 4\sqrt{3}$.

32. $A = 90°$, $b = 10$, $c = 20$.

33. $B = 90°$, $b = 4$, $c = 2$.

34. $C = 90°$, $a = 6$, $b = 6$.

35. $A = 90°$, $B = 60°$, $b = 4$.

36. When the angle of elevation of the sun is 30°, Calvin Butterball's shadow is $9\frac{1}{2}$ feet long. How tall is Calvin?

37. Calvin Butterball is in the dentist's chair. He notes the angle of elevation of the top of a neighboring building is 30°, while the angle of elevation of the top of the flag pole that surmounts the building is 45°. If the distance from Calvin to the neighboring building is 30 feet, how tall is the flag pole?

14–6. Tables. One may obtain trigonometric functions of certain angles by relations of elementary geometry. The values of the trigonometric functions of many other angles may be obtained to two or more significant digits by construction with a vernier protractor and careful measurement. This is unnecessary since tables are available. These tables are computed by use of infinite series. Some infinite series are studied in Chapter 10. These tables consider functions of angles between 0° and 90°. After learning how to use the tables for these angles, we shall learn to determine functions of other angles as well, using the same tables. The reader may be able to suggest a method for making this extension.

14–7. Use of trigonometric tables.

● *Example 1.* Find sin 9° 10′ from the four-place table give
below.

Degrees	Radians	Sin	Csc	Tan	Cot	Sec	Cos		
9° 0′	.1571	.1564	6.392	.1584	6.3138	1.012	.9877	1.4137	81° 0
10′	600	593	277	614	1970	013	872	108	50
20′	629	622	166	644	6.0844	013	868	079	40
30′	.1658	.1650	6.059	.1673	5.9758	1.014	.9863	1.4050	30
40′	687	679	5.955	703	8708	014	858	1.4021	20
50′	716	708	855	733	7694	015	853	1.3992	10
10° 0′	.1745	.1736	5.759	.1763	5.6713	1.015	.9848	1.3963	80° 0
10′	774	765	665	793	5764	016	843	934	50
			575	823	4845				
				.1853					
30′	.3054	.3007	3.326						
40′	083	035	295	185	1397	049	528	625	20
50′	113	062	265	217	1084	050	520	595	10′
18° 0′	.3142	.3090	3.236	.3249	3.0777	1.051	.9511	1.2566	72° 0′
		Cos	Sec	Cot	Tan	Csc	Sin	Radians	Degrees

Table 1

Locate the row labeled 9° 10′. In the intersection of this row
and the column headed sin, read

$$\sin 9° 10′ \cong .1593.$$

If we need to use logarithms, log sin 9° 10′ is located similarl
in Table 2. The logarithm is obtained by subtracting 10 fro
the table entry

$$\log \sin 9° 10′ \cong 9.2022 - 10 \quad \text{or} \quad 0.2022 - 1.$$

Angle	L Sin	d 1′	L Tan	cd 1′	L Cot	d 1′	L Cos		
9° 0′	9.1943	7.9	9.1997	8.1	10.8003	.2	9.9946	81° 0′	
10′	.2022	7.8	.2078	8.0	.7922	.2	.9944	50′	
20′	.2100	7.6	.2158	7.8	.7842	.2	.9942	40′	
30′	.2176	7.5	.2236	7.7	.7764	.2	.9940	30′	
40′	.2251	7.3	.2313	7.6	.7687	.2	.9938	20′	
50′	.2324	7.3	.2389	7.4	.7611	.2	.9936	10′	
10° 0′	9.2397	7.1	9.2463	7.3	10.7537	.3	9.9934	80° 0′	
10′	.2468	7.0	.2536	7.3	.7464	.2	.9931	50′	
			.2609	7.1	.7391		.9929		
30′	.4781	4.0	.4987	4.4	.4969		.9790	20′	
40′	.4821	4.0	.5031	4.4	.4925	.4	.9786	10′	
50′	.4861	3.9	.5075	4.3		.4			
18° 0′	9.4900		9.5118		10.4882		9.9782	72° 0′	
	L Cos	d 1′	L Cot	cd 1′	L Tan	d 1′	L Sin	Angle	

Table 2

If the angle is between 0° and 45°, the desired row is locate
using an angle found in the *left-hand* margin and the function head
ings at the *top* of the table are used. If the angle is between 45
and 90°, the desired row is located using an angle found in th

ght-hand margin, and the function titles at the *bottom* of the
ble are used. The reader should note that the function title
the bottom of a given column is, in each case, the cofunction
that at its top. Thus the complementary relationships men-
oned in Section 14–5 have been used.

Using this method one obtains $\tan 72° \, 10' \cong 3.1084$.

Upon supplying the proper characteristic, we find

$$\log \tan 72° \, 10' \cong 10.4925 - 10 = 0.4925.$$

The reader should check the following tabular entries in a
milar fashion:

$$\log \tan 81° \cong 0.8003$$
$$\sin 72° \cong .9511$$
$$\log \cos 9° \, 10' \cong .9944 - 1$$
$$\log \tan 80° \, 30' \cong 0.7764.$$

Interpolation may be used to obtain values for angles between
ted sizes.

To compute a trigonometric function for an angle not in the
ble, first make a rough sketch of the angle in standard position
d determine the sign of the desired function and the reference
gle. For example, $\cos 137°$ is *negative*, and the reference angle is
$0° - 137° = 43°$. Values of the trigonometric functions of the
ference angle included between the terminal side and the x-axis
ig. 14–22) are the same as those of 137°, except possibly for
gebraic sign. Since the reference angle is 43°, we have:

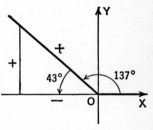

Fig. 14–22

$$\cos 137° = - \cos 43° \cong - .7314$$

d

$$\sin 137° = + \sin 43° \cong .6820.$$

a similar fashion,

$$\tan 264° = + \tan 84° \cong 9.514.$$
$$\sin(- 27°) = - \sin 27° \cong - .4540.$$

PROBLEM SET 14-7

Use tables to determine the following functional values.
ketch the angle in standard position in each example to determine
e correct sign.

1. $\sin 15° \, 20'$.   2. $\tan 35° \, 40'$.   3. $\tan 75° \, 10'$.   4. $\cos 17° \, 30'$.
5. $\cot 89° \, 10'$.   6. $\sin 135° \, 20'$.   7. $\cos 361° \, 20'$.

8. cot 43° 20′.   **9.** tan 936° 20′.   **10.** cot (− 17° 40′).

11. cos (− 22° 10′).   **12.** sin 1007°.   **13.** sec 46° 10′.

14. csc 190° 0′.   **15.** cot 46° 10′.   **16.** cos (− 1396° 40′

17. Convert 72° 10′ into radians, using a table.

18. Convert 4 radians into degrees, using a table.

19. Convert 22° 15′ into radians (use interpolation).

20. Convert 1.24 radians into degrees (use interpolation).

21. If sin θ = .6202, determine θ in degrees. Determine θ radians.

22. If tan x = .5022, determine x.

23. If log cot θ = 1.1205, find θ in degrees; in radians.

24. If log sin θ = 9.3058 − 10 and 90° < θ < 350°, find Is it unique?

25. If log | sin θ | = 9.3058 − 10 and 90° < θ < 350°, find Is it unique?

26. If log tan θ = 0.18224 and 0° < θ < 180°, find θ.

27. Find a value of θ which satisfies the equation

$$.2000 + \log \sin \theta = \log \cos \theta.$$

[HINT: Run down the log sin x and log cos x columns of table until you find where the corresponding entries for the sam value of x differ by .2000 or, consider log cot θ = .2000. Note tha log cot θ = .2000 is an auxiliary equation and has solutions whic are not solutions of the equation .2000 + log sin θ = log cos θ.]

Problems 28 to 35 refer to triangles having vertex angle A, B, C with the lengths of the sides opposite these angles de noted by a, b, c respectively. Find the missing parts as accu rately as the data permit. *Estimate* each answer *before* computin and check your result against your estimate.

28. $A = 35° 10′$, $B = 90°$, $b = 17.0$.

29. $A = 64° 10′$, $B = 90°$, $c = 100.0$.

30. $C = 42° 20′$, $B \approx 90°$, $a = 12.0$.

31. $A = 37° 10′$, $B = 52° 50′$, $a = 0.810$.

32. (a) $B = 90°$, $a = 17.0$, $b = 26.4$.

    (b) $B = 90°$, $a = 12.00$, $c = 20.00$.

33. (a) $C = 90°$, $a = 2.10$, $b = 12.3$.

    (b) $A = 90°$, $B = 12° 30′$, $b = 50.0$.

34. $A = 56° 10′$, $C = 24° 30′$, $b = 326$. Note that this is no a right triangle. If a perpendicular is dropped from C to AB the two resulting right triangles may be used to obtain a solution of the given triangle.

35. $A = 32° 10′$, $b = 12.5$, $c = 42.8$. See remarks on Problem 34

36. A flag pole casts a shadow 51.7 feet long on the level drill field surrounding it. If the angle of elevation of the sun is 31° 10′, how tall is the flag pole? If you know the length of the original pole was some integral multiple of 5 feet, and that at least 3 feet of it have been buried to anchor the pole, what is the least possible length of the original pole, and least amount actually buried?

7. An escalator in a department store moves at the rate of 300 feet per minute and is inclined at 40° to the horizontal. How long will it take to carry a shopper from one floor to the next, the height of one story being 20 feet?

8. Find   log sec 68° 10′.   **39.** Find   log csc 125° 0′.

9. Find θ, if   90° ≤ θ < 180°,   and   log csc θ = 0.80.

1. The top of a south window is 6 feet above floor level. The latitude of the house is 40° N. (a) Find how far the sun shines into the room at noon on September 21 when the angle of elevation of the sun is 50°. (b) On June 21 when the angle of elevation of the sun is 73.5°. (c) On December 21 when the angle of elevation of the sun is 26.5°.

2. If the window of Problem 41 extends down to floor level, how wide a shelf will be needed directly above the window to keep the sun out between June 21 and September 21, and still admit winter sun?

14–8. The law of cosines. Problems involving right triangles are solved by applying the definitions of the trigonometric functions. Oblique triangles may be solved using the law of cosines developed in this section, or the law of sines developed in the next section. If the vertices of a triangle are labeled A, B, and C, then the corresponding angles of the triangle are designated by A, B, and C, respectively. The length of the side opposite angle A is designated by a, the length of the side opposite angle B is designated by b, and that opposite angle C by c. Each angle of a triangle lies between 0° and 180°.

LAW OF COSINES.   In a triangle ABC,

$$a^2 = b^2 + c^2 - 2bc \cos A.$$

PROOF: Construct a coordinate system so that angle A of triangle ABC is in standard position with vertex B on the positive portion of the x-axis.

The vertices have coordinates

$$A(0, 0), \quad B(c, 0), \quad C(b \cos A, b \sin A),$$

whether A is an acute or an obtuse angle. From the distance formula, the distance between B and C is a, where

$$a^2 = (b \cos A - c)^2 + (b \sin A)^2$$
$$a^2 = b^2 \cos^2 A - 2bc \cos A + c^2 + b^2 \sin^2 A$$
$$= b^2 (\cos^2 A + \sin^2 A) + c^2 - 2bc \cos A.$$

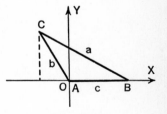

Fig. 14–23

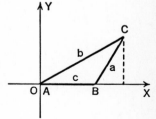

Fig. 14–24

In Example 5, Section 14–4, we showed that $\sin^2 A + \cos^2 A = 1$, hence,

$$a^2 = b^2 + c^2 - 2bc \cos A.$$

NOTE: If $A = 90°$, then $a^2 = b^2 + c^2$. This suggests wh the law of cosines is occasionally spoken of as the generalize Pythagorean theorem. By placing angles B and C, respectivel in standard position we obtain

$$b^2 = a^2 + c^2 - 2ac \cos B \quad \text{and} \quad c^2 = a^2 + b^2 - 2ab \cos C.$$

In words: The square of the length of one side of a triangle equal to the sum of the squares of the other two sides minus twi the product of the other two sides and the cosine of their include angle. Example 3 suggests a convenient form for computatio where logarithms are to be used.

- **Example 1.** Find the length of the side b opposite the ang $B = 60°$ in a triangle having sides $a = 10$, $c = 30$.

$$b^2 = a^2 + c^2 - 2ac \cos B$$
$$b^2 = 100 + 900 - 2(10)(30)(\tfrac{1}{2})$$
$$b^2 = 700$$
$$b = \sqrt{700} \cong 26,$$

which is as accurate as the data permit.

- **Example 2.** Find the smallest angle in a triangle having sid 6.0, 7.2, 4.0.
  Let $b = 4.0$. The smallest angle is opposite the shorte side.

$$b^2 = a^2 + c^2 - 2ac \cos B$$
$$(4.0)^2 = (7.2)^2 + (6.0)^2 - 2(7.2)(6.0) \cos B$$
$$16.0 = 51.8 + 36.0 - 86.4 \cos B$$
$$86.4 \cos B = 71.8$$
$$\cos B = \frac{71.8}{86.4} = 0.83.$$
$$B = 34°.$$

The original data do not permit more accuracy.

- **Example 3.** Show that $1 + \cos A = \dfrac{(b + c + a)(b + c - a)}{2bc}$.
  From the law of cosines,

$$\cos A = \frac{b^2 + c^2 - a^2}{2bc}$$
$$1 + \cos A = 1 + \frac{b^2 + c^2 - a^2}{2bc}$$

$$= \frac{b^2 + 2bc + c^2 - a^2}{2bc}$$

$$= \frac{(b+c)^2 - a^2}{2bc}$$

$$1 + \cos A = \frac{(b + c + a)(b + c - a)}{2bc}.$$

This form is convenient for logarithmic computation.

PROBLEM SET 14-8

1. (a) If $A = 60°$, $b = 10.0$, $c = 3.0$, find a.
   (b) If $a = 2\sqrt{61}$, $b = 8$, $c = 10$, find A.
2. (a) If $A = 78°$, $b = 14.2$, $c = 10.0$, find a.
   (b) If $a = 4\sqrt{3}$, $b = 2\sqrt{2}$, $c = 6$, find B.
3. (a) If $B = 48°$, $a = 12.0$, $c = 10.0$, find b.
   (b) Can you find A?
4. (a) If $a = 10.0$, $b = 12.0$, $c = 8.0$, find A.
   (b) Find C.
5. (a) If $a = 4.0$, $b = 20.0$, $c = 18.0$, find A.
   (b) Find B.
6. Find the largest angle of a triangle having sides 7.0, 8.0, and 13.0 inches. Can this problem be solved without using tables?
7. Show that the law of Pythagoras is actually a special case of the law of cosines with one angle equal to 90°. This would not be a valid proof, since Pythagoras' law was used to obtain $\sin^2 \theta + \cos^2 \theta = 1$, and also to obtain the distance formula, both of which were used in proving the law of cosines.
8. It is impossible to measure the distance BC across a lake directly. However, at a point A, the angle CAB is found to be $30° 0'$ while $AC = 121$ feet and $AB = 162$ feet. How long is BC? With what accuracy should you report your answer?
9. Show that $1 + \cos C = \dfrac{(a + b + c)(a + b - c)}{2ab}$ starting with the law of cosines involving angle C.
10. A parallelogram has two adjacent sides a, b and included angle θ. (a) Find the length of the diagonal that passes through the intersection of the given sides. (b) Find the area of the parallelogram.

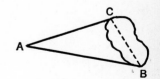

Fig. 14-25

11. A body is acted upon by a force of 85 pounds, and by another force of 70 pounds the direction of which makes an angle of 50° with the first force. Find the magnitude of the resultant force.

[HINT: This is equivalent to finding the side AC of a triangle ABC with $AB = 85$, $BC = 70$, $B = 130°$.]

12. Calvin Butterball and Phoebe Small have cottages on opposite sides of a bay in Lake Muchimuck. Calvin rows over to see Phoebe each morning, and rows back home at noon. He works on his university correspondence study course in solid geometry in the afternoon and then rows over to Phoebe's in the evening, returning home before midnight. Calvin does this each day, excepting Sundays, during the eight weeks of his vacation. On Sunday he makes one trip, going over in the morning and returning in the evening. (Phoebe still packs a good lunch.) Calvin wonders how far he has rowed. From a point 600 yards from Calvin's house and 900 yards from Phoebe's house, Calvin observes that the angle subtended by the two houses is 120°. Find the distance, in *miles*, Calvin rowed, to see Phoebe, during the eight weeks.

13. Given the triangle ABC, let the sides opposite angles A, B, and C have lengths a, b, c respectively. Show that the perpendicular from B to AC has length $c \sin A$. Use this construction to develop a proof of the law of cosines for a triangle each of whose angles is acute.

[HINT: If the perpendicular intersects AC at D, then $AD = c \cos A$ and $DC = b - AD$.]

14. Use the construction of Problem 13 to prove the law of cosines for a triangle having angle A obtuse.

[HINT: Show that if A is obtuse, $DA = - c \cos A$.]

15. Take C in quadrant II and show that the algebra of the text's proof of the law of cosines is unchanged.

16. On a quiz John Smith is unable to recall whether the sign of the term involving $\cos A$ in the law of cosines is $+$ or $-$. He guesses incorrectly and loses points on the quiz. Show John that he could have determined the correct sign by noting whether the value of a is greater or less than the hypotenuse of a right triangle with legs b and c. Make two arguments, one for the case where $A < 90°$ and one for $A > 90°$.

17. Calvin and Phoebe camp on opposite sides of Lake Nofishee. The lake shores on which they live are parallel lines $\frac{1}{2}$ mile apart. Calvin lives $\frac{1}{2}$ mile south and 1 mile west of Phoebe's home. Calvin can row at the rate of 3 miles per hour and walk at the rate of 5 miles per hour. How far along the shore from Phoebe's house should Calvin land in order to reach her home in the shortest time?

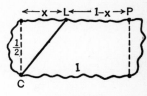

Fig. 14–26

18. Draw a figure and verify the following proof of the law of cosines.

In triangle ABC (with sides a, b, and c) draw altitudes AE, BD, and CF. Assign a positive direction to each side so that in passing counterclockwise around the triangle one is always moving in a positive direction.

$$b^2 = b(AD + DC)$$
$$= cb \cos A + ab \cos C = c(FA) + a(CE)$$
$$= c(c - a \cos B) + a(a - c \cos B)$$
$$b^2 = c^2 + a^2 - 2ac \cos B.$$

14–9. Law of sines. If two angles and a side of a triangle are given, the triangle is uniquely determined. The reader would find difficulty in determining the unknown sides using the law of cosines.† In this, and certain other cases, the law of sines is used.

LAW OF SINES: In a triangle ABC

$$\frac{\sin A}{a} = \frac{\sin B}{b} = \frac{\sin C}{c}.$$

In words: In a given triangle, the ratio of the sine of each angle to the side opposite that angle is a fixed constant.

PROOF: Construct a coordinate system so that angle A of triangle ABC is in standard position with vertex B on the positive portion of the x-axis. The altitude from side c of triangle ABC is

$$h = b \sin A.$$

Also:

$$h = a \sin B.$$

Thus,

$$b \sin A = a \sin B$$

and

$$\frac{\sin A}{a} = \frac{\sin B}{b}.$$

Similarly,

$$\frac{\sin B}{b} = \frac{\sin C}{c}.$$

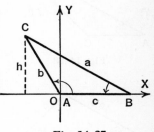

Fig. 14–27

† It is not, however, impossible, since the law of sines may be proved from the law of cosines. See v. 56, p. 550 of the *American Mathematical Monthly*.

● **Example 1.** If $A = 11°$, $B = 72°$, and $a = 10.0$, find angle C and side b.

$C = 180° - 11° - 72° = 97°$. From the law of sines, we have

$$\frac{\sin 11°}{10.0} = \frac{\sin 72°}{b}. \text{ Hence,}$$

$$b = \frac{(\sin 72°)10.0}{\sin 11°} = \cdots = 49.8.$$

● **Example 2.** If $A = 30°$, $a = 7.0$ and $c = 10.0$ inches, find angle C. The law of sines states:

$$\frac{\sin C}{10.0} = \frac{\sin 30°}{7.0}.$$

$$\sin C = \frac{(10.0)(.50)}{7.0} = \cdots = .71.$$

$$C = 45° \quad \text{or} \quad 135°.$$

Since the original data is accurate to only two significan digits, the size of angle C cannot be determined more ac curately than the nearest degree.

The reader may be surprised to find that two possible angles 45° and 135°, are listed for C. Figures 14–28 and 14–29 show tha either result is possible with the given data. The case in which two sides and the angle opposite one of these sides are given i the only possible ambiguous case.

If the law of cosines is used to determine side b,

$$a^2 = b^2 + c^2 - 2bc \cos A$$

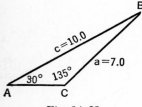

becomes

$$49 = b^2 + 100 - 2(b)(10.0)(\sqrt{3}/2)$$

and

$$b^2 - 17.3b + 51 = 0.$$

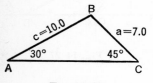

Fig. 14–28

Fig. 14–29

This quadratic equation has two distinct roots. Hence, two tri angles are indicated again.

● **Example 3.** If $A = 32°$, $a = 4.5$ and $c = 11.3$, find an gle C.

$$\frac{\sin 32°}{4.5} = \frac{\sin C}{11.3}$$

$$\frac{.53}{4.5} = \frac{\sin C}{11.3}$$

$$\sin C = \frac{(.53)(11.3)}{4.5} \simeq 1.3.$$

Since $\sin C \le 1$ for all C, there is no solution for the above equation. The sketch shows that $a = 4.5$ is too short to complete the triangle, and no such triangle exists. The perpendicular distance between B and the line AQ is

$$(11.3) \sin 32° = (11.3)(.53) > 4.5.$$

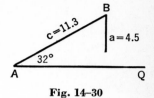

Fig. 14–30

PROBLEM SET 14–9

In Problems 1 to 10 find the parts not given.

1. $A = 45°, \quad C = 60°, \quad b = 10.0.$
2. $a = 10, \quad b = 15, \quad C = 60°.$
3. $B = 68°, \quad C = 30°, \quad c = 22.0.$
4. $A = 120°, \quad B = 20°, \quad a = 100.$
5. $A = 42°, \quad C = 61°, \quad b = 52.$
6. $B = 62°, \quad b = 14.0, \quad c = 21.2.$
7. $C = 30°, \quad b = 5.0, \quad c = 1.9.$
8. $B = 41°, \quad b = 2.1, \quad c = 7.4.$
9. $A = 20°, \quad C = 60°, \quad b = 12,000.$
10. $B = 110°, \quad a = 10, \quad b = 26.$
11. Two observation posts, A and B, are 600 feet apart. Each observer marks the angle of a shell burst at a point X in enemy territory. Angle $XAB = 60°$, angle $XBA = 73°$. Find the range of X from a gun located at B.
12. The observers of Problem 11 locate a gun, such that angle $XAB = 31° \, 10'$ while angle $XBA = 112° \, 30'$. Find the range from B to X.
13. Work Problem 12 if $\angle XAB = 32°$ and $\angle XBA = 49°$.
14. Work Problem 12 if $\angle XAB = 21°$ and $\angle XBA = 119°$.
15. Work Problem 12 if $\angle XAB = 63°$ and $\angle XBA = 81°$.
16. In a triangle ABC verify that $\sin C = \sin (B + A)$.
17. In a triangle ABC verify that $c = b \cos A + a \cos B$.
18. Use the law of sines to express b and a in Problem 17 in terms of c and obtain $\sin (B + A) = \sin B \cos A + \sin A \cos B$.
19. Use the formula of Problem 18 to obtain

$$\sin 75° = \sin (45° + 30°) = (\sqrt{6} + \sqrt{2})/4.$$

Then use six-decimal-place table values of $\sqrt{6}$ and $\sqrt{2}$ to approximate the value of $\sin 75°$ and compare with the five-place table value of $\sin 75°$.

Determine the number of triangles represented in each of the following sets of data.

20. $a = 8$, $b = 12$, $A = 34°$. **21.** $a = 12$, $c = 10$, $C = 49°$.
22. $a = 21$, $c = 21$, $A = 35°$, **23.** $b = 13$, $c = 20$, $C = 53°$.
24. $b = 7073$, $c = 7837$, $B = 60°$.
25. $a = 80$, $b = 100$, $A = 54°$.
26. $a = 49$, $b = 69$, $A = 37°$.
27. $a = 50.6$, $b = 54.3$, $A = 58° \, 40'$.
28. $a = 4993$, $b = 6258$, $A = 111° \, 20'$.
29. A slide 28 feet long makes an angle of 39° with the ground and is reached by a ladder 18 feet long. Find the angle of inclination of the ladder.
30. to 39. Solve the triangles given in Problems 20 to 29, respectively.
40. Show that if $a < b$ and $b \cdot \sin A = a$, the triangle exists and is unique.
41. Show that if $a < b$ and $b \cdot \sin A < a$, there exist two triangles satisfying the given conditions.
42. Show that if $a < b$, and if $b \cdot \sin A > a$, no such triangle exists.
43. Show that if $a \geqq b$, with A given, only one triangle exists.

*14–10. The law of tangents. Example 3, Section 14–8, gives a form of the law of cosines that is convenient for logarithmic computation. The law of tangents may be used if preferred.

LAW OF TANGENTS: In any triangle ABC

$$\frac{a - b}{a + b} = \frac{\tan\left[(A - B)/2\right]}{\tan\left[(A + B)/2\right]}$$

In words: The ratio of the difference to the sum of two sides of a triangle equals the ratio of the tangent of one half the difference to the tangent of one half the sum of the angles opposite the two given sides. The reader is asked to prove this relationship in Problems 6 and 7 of Set 16–7.

14–11. Chapter summary. In this chapter we have thought of an angle as an amount of rotation of a half line. Six trigonometric functions were defined and their exact values determined for integral multiples of 30° and 45°. Tables of trigonometric functions and of their logarithms were studied and applied to the solution of triangles using the definitions, the law of sines, and the law of cosines.

14–12. Self test.

Record your starting time.

1. In a certain triangle, two angles are 30° and 45° respectively. The side opposite the 45° angle is 12 feet long. Find, without consulting tables, the length of the side opposite the 30° angle.

2. From a point, on level ground, a surveyor finds the angle of elevation of the top of a flag pole is 45°. From a point 10 feet closer to the base of the flag pole the angle of elevation is 60°. Without consulting tables determine the height of the flag pole.

3. Given that $\cot A = \frac{4}{3}$ and $\pi < A < 2\pi$, find $\csc A$ and $\cos A$.

4. (a) A ladder 25 feet long is resting against a house. If it makes an angle of 45° with the ground, how high up does it reach?
(b) If the angle were 60°, how high would the ladder reach?
(c) What angle will the ladder make with the ground if it reaches a point 21 feet above the ground? (Use tables if you wish on part *c*.)

5. Find the exact value, if defined, of the given expression. *Do not use tables.*
(a) $\csc 210° + \cot 90° + 4$.
(b) $\sec (-120°) + \cos 750° + \sin 90°$.
(c) $4 \cos 0° + 5 \sin 90° + 7 \cos 180° + 20 \sin 180°$.

6. (a) Starting with the geometric fact that an angle bisector of an equilateral triangle is perpendicular to the base, prove that the sides of a 30°, 60°, 90° triangle are proportional to $1:\sqrt{3}:2$.
(b) From this determine the six trigonometric functions of 30° and of 60°.

7. Determine the largest angle of a triangle having sides of length 7, 8, and 13 units. It will not be necessary to use tables in this problem.

Record your time.

R. Boyd. Courtesy *Scripta Mathematica*

15.

15–1. Trigonometric functions of a number. In many applications it is desirable to define the trigonometric functions of a number. In electrical theory, for example, use is made of "phase angle." In many interpretations the phase angle is *not* an angle at all, but a displacement (distance or number). It is possible to associate the phase angle with an actual angle by considering a rotating vector field. It is possible to interpret a trigonometric function of a number t as a function of an angle of t radians.

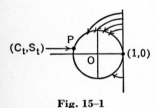

Fig. 15–1

Let us set up a correspondence between the points on the number axis and the points on a unit circle by placing the origin of a number line at the point $(1, 0)$ on the circle and then wrapping the number line tightly around the circle. For each point on the number line, there corresponds a unique point on the circle, but each point on the circle corresponds to many points on the line since the line is wrapped around the circle many times. Such a correspondence is, of course, a valid function, since to each real number t, there corresponds a point $P(C_t, S_t)$.

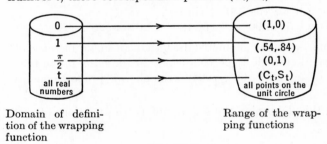

Domain of definition of the wrapping function

Range of the wrapping functions

Fig. 15–2

We now use the wrapping function to define the trigonometric functions of a real number t.

Select a real number t. Construct a circle with center $(0, 0)$ and radius 1. Starting at $(1, 0)$, measure an arc of length t around the circumference of the circle. If t is positive, measure in a counterclockwise direction; if t is negative, measure in a clockwise direction. Call the end point of this arc (C_t, S_t) as before. In other words, use the wrapping function to establish a correspondence between the real number t and the point (C_t, S_t).

We now define the cosine of the real number t, cos t, to be the x coordinate of the end point of the arc of length t, namely C_t. In similar fashion the y coordinate of the end point, namely, S_t, is defined to be sin t. Furthermore

$$\tan t = \frac{\sin t}{\cos t}, \quad \cot t = \frac{\cos t}{\sin t}, \quad \sec t = \frac{1}{\cos t}, \quad \csc t = \frac{1}{\sin t}.$$

These definitions are consistent with the definitions already given for the angle XOP in standard position. The unit circle has circumference 2π units. If the central angle subtended by an arc of length t is measured in radian measure, then the central angle contains t radians. Also

$$\sin t = \sin \text{ (of the number } t) = \sin (t \text{ radians}) = \sin \left(\frac{180t}{\pi} \text{ degrees}\right).\dagger$$

PROBLEM SET 15–1

Use the definitions of this section to show that the following relationships hold [for all t, if t is involved].

1. $\cos 0 = 1$.

2. $\sin 0 = 0$.

3. $\sin 90° = \sin (\pi/2) = 1$.

4. $\sin 180° = \sin \pi = 0$.

5. $\sin (- t) = - \sin t$.

6. $\cos (- t) = \cos t$.

7. $\sin (\pi/2 - t) = \cos t$.

8. $\cos (\pi/2 - t) = \sin t$.

9. $\sin (\pi + t) = - \sin t$.

10. $\sin^2 t + \cos^2 t = 1$.

11. $\cot (3\pi/4) = - 1$.

12. $\cos \pi = - 1$.

13. $\sin (\pi/6) = \frac{1}{2}$.

14. $\cos (7\pi/6) = - \sqrt{3}/2$.

15. $\tan (5\pi/4) = 1$.

16. $\csc (11\pi/6) = - 2$.

Using tables of trigonometric functions of numbers, or of angles in radians, find the functions indicated in Problems 17 to 23.

17. $\cos 1.25$.

18. $\sin 0.46$.

19. $\cos 2.17$.

[HINT: $\cos 2.17 = - \cos (\pi - 2.17) = - \cos 0.97 = ?$]

20. $\tan 0.82$.   **21.** $\cos 0.13$.   **22.** $\sin 4.63$.   **23.** $\tan (- 1.29)$.

24. Use the definition of this section to obtain the graph of $y = \sin t$, for $2 \leq t \leq 7$.

25. Same as Problem 24, for $y = \cos t$.

Use tables of trigonometric functions of numbers, or of angles in radians, to determine x if

26. $\cos x = .47$, $0 \leq x \leq \pi$.

27. $\sin x = .21$, $\pi/2 < x < \pi$.

28. $\sin 3x = .40$.

29. $3 \sin x = 1.92$.

30. $\cos x = - .37$, $0 < x < 3$.

31. $\sec x = 25$.

† Again, 1 radian $= 180°/\pi$, since 2π radians $= 360°$.

32. $3 \tan x = 4$. **33.** $\tan 3x = 1.2$. **34.** $3 \tan 5x = 4.7$

*35. The Gudermannian of x [written $gd(x)$] is defined as follows: If

$$x = \log \tan (\pi/4 + \theta/2), \quad \text{then} \quad \theta = gd(x).$$

Determine $gd(0)$ and $gd(.43)$.

One use of the Gudermannian is in computing rhumb lines (loxodromes) on a Mercator map of the earth. The Gudermannian is also related to the hyperbolic functions of Section 9–5.

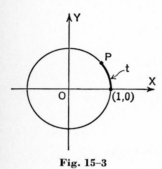

Fig. 15–3

15–2. Graphs of $y = \sin t$ and $y = \cos t$. Sketches of $y = \sin t$ and $y = \cos t$ form a foundation for more complicated sketches. These sketches are obtained by using the definitions of $\sin t$ and $\cos t$ given in Section 15–1, which involve numbers rather than angles. The distance t is laid off on the circumference of the unit circle from $(1, 0)$ as in Section 15–1. The x coordinate of the end point P of this arc is $\cos t$, while the y coordinate is $\sin t$. Since the circle has circumference $2\pi(1) = 2\pi$, the following table is obtained:

t	0	$\pi/2$	π	$3\pi/2$	2π	$5\pi/2$	etc.
$\cos t$	1	0	-1	0	1	0	$\cdots$
$\sin t$	0	1	0	-1	0	1	$\cdots$

Sketches are given in Figure 15–4.

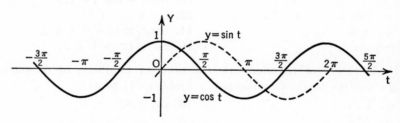

Fig. 15–4

A **cycle** is the shortest possible segment of the curve such that the entire locus is a repetition of this segment. The x distance occupied by one cycle is the **period** of the function. The functions $y = \sin t$ and $y = \cos t$ each have period 2π. More precisely, the period of a function $f(x)$ is the smallest positive value p such that for every x,

$$f(x + p) = f(x).$$

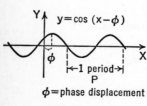

ϕ = phase displacement

Fig. 15–5

If a locus is shifted ϕ units to the right along the x-axis, this displacement is termed the **phase displacement** or in the case of trigonometric functions, the **phase angle.** We note that the graph $y = \sin x$ is similar to that of $y = \cos x$ except that $y = \sin x$

is moved $\pi/2$ radians (or 90°) to the right. The two loci are out of phase by $\pi/2$. The locus $y = \sin x$ *leads* the locus $y = \cos x$ by a phase angle of 90°, or by a phase displacement of $\pi/2$.

PROBLEM SET 15-2

1. Construct the curve $y = \sin t$, $-2\pi \leqq t \leqq 3\pi$. Use equal units in each direction.
2. Same as Problem 1 for $y = \cos t$. What is the period? Mark, in heavy lines, two cycles beginning with $t = -\pi/3$.

In Problems 3 to 16, verify from the graph each relationship in the interval $-2\pi \leqq x \leqq 3\pi$.

3. $\sin(-x) = -\sin x$.
4. $\cos(-x) = \cos x$.
5. $\sin(\pi/2 - x) = \cos x$.
6. $\cos(\pi/2 - x) = \sin x$.
7. $\sin(\pi + x) = -\sin x$.
8. $\sin(2\pi + x) = \sin x$.
9. $\cos(x - 4\pi) = \cos x$.
10. $|\sin x| \leq 1$.
11. $-1 \leqq \cos x \leqq 1$.
12. $\sin x = \cos(x - \pi/2)$.
13. $\tan(x + \pi) = \tan x$.
14. $(\sin x)^2 \leqq 1$.
15. $|\csc x| \geqq 1$.
16. $\cos(\pi - x) = -\cos x$.
17. Compare the functions $y = \cos x$ and $y = \sin x$.
18. Compare $y = \cos x$ and $y = 5\cos x$.
19. Show that $y = \cos x$ is symmetric with respect to the y-axis. See tests for symmetry, Section 4–8.
20. Does $y = \sin x$ have any of the three types of symmetry discussed in Section 4–8?
21. On a sketch of $y = \sin x$, use a straightedge to draw a tangent line at $(0, 0)$. If this is carefully done, the tangent line will pass through $(1, 1)$. What does this suggest about $\sin x$ and x (radians) for small x?
22. Replace $y = \sin x$ by $y = \tan x$ in Problem 21.
23. Write an inequality that will compare $\sin x$, x, and $\tan x$ on the interval $0 < x < \pi/2$.
24. Over what interval of small values of x does $\sin x = x$ to two significant digits? You may wish to consult a table.
25. Over what interval of small values of x does $\tan x = x$ to two significant digits? Be sure to consider negative as well as positive values of x.
26. Let the angle between two radii of a circle, of radius R, be θ radians. Show that the length L of the arc of the circle subtending the angle θ is $L = R\theta$.

    [HINT: The ratio of L to the circumference is equal to the ratio of θ to 2π radians (one revolution).]

27. Find the arc length which subtends an angle of 36° at the center of a circle of radius 10 feet.

28. Find, in radians and in degrees, the central angle which is subtended by a 3-inch arc in a circle of radius 4 inches.

29. Let the angle between two radii of a circle, of radius R, be θ radians. Show that the area A of the sector having central angle θ is $A = R^2\theta/2$. [HINT: The ratio of A to the area of the circle is equal to the ratio of θ to 2π radians (one revolution).]

30. Find the area of the sector of a circle of radius 10 inches if the central angle is 18°.

15–3. The graphs $y = A \sin x$ and $y = A \cos x$. The loci of $y = 7 \sin x$ and $y = \sin x$ rise and fall together when referred to the same coordinate system, but each ordinate (y value) of $y = 7 \sin x$ is seven times the corresponding ordinate of $y = \sin x$. Similarly, each ordinate of $y = A \sin x$ is obtained when the corresponding ordinate of $y = \sin x$ is multiplied by A. If $A = -1$, the curves $y = \sin x$ and $y = -\sin x$ are mirror images. The locus of $y = A \sin x$ is sketched in Figure 15–6 for

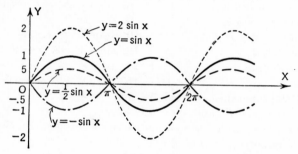

Fig. 15–6

$A = -1, \frac{1}{2}, 1, 2$. A similar discussion may be made for $y = A \cos x$. The maximum absolute value of the ordinate, namely $|A|$, is the **amplitude** of $y = A \cos x$, or of $y = A \sin x$. It represents the greatest distance between a point on the graph and the x-axis.

PROBLEM SET 15–3

Sketch the following loci:

1. $y = 4 \sin x$.
2. $y = -5 \sin x$.
3. $y = 7 \cos x$.
4. $y = 4 \cos x$.
5. $y = -2 \sin x$.
6. $y = -3 \sin x$.
7. $y = -\cos x$.
8. $y = -10 \cos x$.
9. $y = \pi \cos x$.

10. $5y = -\cos x.$ **11.** $4y = \sin x.$ **12.** $y = 3 \sin x.$
13. $7y = -3 \sin x.$ **14.** $6y = 5 \cos x.$ *****15.** $y = 4 \cos x + 3.$

*****16.** A *mental* problem. In your imagination wrap a sheet of paper around a cylindrical candle. Cut the paper and candle with a sharp knife at an angle of about 45° to the axis of the candle.

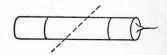

Unwrap one of the pieces of paper.

Fig. 15–7

(a) What will be the shape of the curve along the cut edge of the paper?
(b) Can you prove the curve is, or is not, a sine curve?

15–4. The graphs of $y = A \sin Bx$ and $y = A \cos Bx$. To obtain $y = \cos 3x$, we measure $3x$ units around the circle instead of x units. Thus, as x changes from 0 to 2π, $3x$ changes from 0 to 6π and $y = \cos 3x$ will have three complete cycles.† The effect upon the graph will be to "squeeze it up like an accordion." If $|B| < 1$, then the length of a cycle is increased. The locus of $y = \cos Bx$ will contain $|B|$ cycles in 2π units; hence the **period** (length of one cycle) is $2\pi / |B|$. The reciprocal of the period is the **frequency.** The graph of $y = A \cos Bx$ may be obtained from that of $y = \cos Bx$ by multiplying each ordinate (y value) by A. A similar discussion may be made for $y = A \sin Bx$.

The locus of $y = A \cos Bx$ is shown for several values of A and B in Figure 15–8.

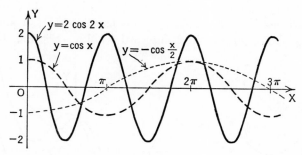

Fig. 15–8

PROBLEM SET 15–4

Sketch the following loci:

1. $y = 3 \cos x.$ **2.** $y = \cos 2x.$ **3.** $y = 3 \cos 2x.$ **4.** $y = -3 \cos 2x.$
5. $y = 5 \sin (x/2).$ **6.** $y = \frac{1}{2} \sin (x/2).$ **7.** $y = \frac{1}{2} \sin 3x.$

† The meaning of the word *cycle* is easily recalled if the numerical definition of $\cos 3x$ is used. Each cycle represents a change in $3x$ equal to the distance once around the circle. As x changes from 0 to 2π, $3x$ changes from 0 to 6π or 3 times around the unit circle.

8. $y = 100 \sin 5x$. [A suitable change of scale may be helpful.]

9. $y = 5 \cos 2\theta$. Let the horizontal axis be the θ-axis.

10. $y = (-\frac{1}{2}) \sin 3\theta$. **11.** $3y = 7 \cos (\theta/3)$. **12.** $4 \sin (\theta/2) = y$.

13. $y + 2 = 3 \cos (2x/3)$. **14.** $7y = -4 \sin 3x$.

15. $y = 3 \cos \pi x$. [In this case the x intercepts are $x = \pm \frac{1}{2},\ \pm \frac{3}{2},$ $\pm \frac{5}{2},\ \cdots.$]

16. $y = 3 \sin 4\pi x$. **17.** $y = -3 \sin (x/4)$. **18.** $4y = 6 \cos (-x/2)$.

19. The voltage E delivered by an electric generator is approximately $E = 170 \sin 120\pi t$. Sketch the graph. This is the graph of a typical 60-cycle household voltage wave. Notice that although it is usually spoken of as a 110- to 120-volt circuit, the instantaneous voltage varies from 0 to 170 volts in absolute value.

20. Make ten identical sketches of a cosine curve on plain paper. By changing the units and axes as needed, let these sketches serve to represent a sketch of each locus in turn in Problems 1 to 10. List the maximum value of y, the length of period, and the smallest positive x intercept in each problem.

21. Sketch $y = (\sin x)^2$, $-\pi \leqq x \leqq 2\pi$.

22. Sketch $y = (\cos x)^2$, $-\pi \leqq x \leqq 2\pi$.

15–5. Composition of ordinates. The process of adding the ordinates (y values) of two loci is known as **composition of ordinates.**

● *Example 1.* The sketch of $y = 4 + 3 \sin x$ is obtained by adding 4 units to each ordinate of $y = 3 \sin x$. This has the effect of moving (translating) the curve $y = 3 \sin x$ upward 4 units. See Fig. 15–9.

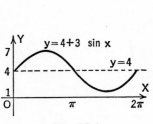

Fig. 15–9

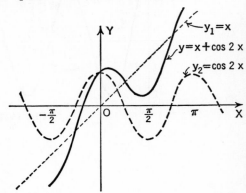

Fig. 15–10

● *Example 2.* Sketch $y = x + \cos 2x$. Sketch $y_1 = x$ and $y_2 = \cos 2x$ using the same axes. For each value of x, $y = y_1 + y_2$. This addition of ordinates may be accomplished directly on the graph by use of dividers. Distances below the x-axis must be subtracted from, rather than added to, the ordinates of the other sketch. This is algebraic addition. From such a sketch it may be possible to approximate the solution of an equation. The solutions of $x + \cos 2x = 0$ are the x values for which $y = 0$. In this case $x \cong -\pi/6$. See Fig. 15–10.

The reader should show that Example 1 can be obtained by sketching the loci $y_1 = 4$ and $y_2 = 3 \sin x$ and adding corresponding ordinates.

In electrical theory, harmony, and seismology the wave patterns studied may not be fundamental waves such as $y = A \sin Bx$ or $y = G \cos Fx$, but often include harmonic waves obtained by composition of ordinates. Such harmonics also are important in electronics, nuclear physics, and other sciences.

● **Example 3.** Sketch $y = 3 \sin x + \cos 2x$.

Let $y_1 = 3 \sin x$ and $y_2 = \cos 2x$.

Graphing these on the same axes and adding the ordinates, we obtain Figure 15–11.

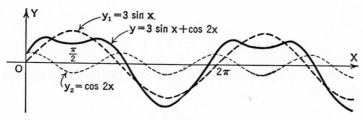

Fig. 15–11

To approximate the solutions of $3 \sin x + \cos 2x = 0$, $0 \leq x < 2\pi$, observe that the x intercepts of $y = 3 \sin x + \cos 2x$ are, approximately, $\pi + \pi/8 = 9\pi/8$, and $2\pi - \pi/8 = 15\pi/8$.

● **Example 4.** Sketch $y = 2 \cos x - \cos 2x$.

Let $y_1 = 2 \cos x$ and $y_2 = - \cos 2x$.

To approximate the solutions of $2 \cos x - \cos 2x = 0$, $0 \leq x < 2\pi$, observe that the x intercepts of $y = 2 \cos x - \cos 2x$ are, approximately, $\pi - 2\pi/5 = 3\pi/5$ and $\pi + 3\pi/5 = 8\pi/5$.

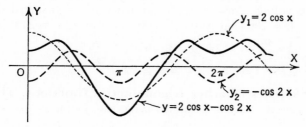

Fig. 15–12

In Problem 12, Set 15–2, and in Section 14–5 it was shown that

$$\sin x = \cos (x - \pi/2).$$

Thus the sine curve is the cosine curve shifted over (translated) $\pi/2$ units to the right. In a similar fashion, one may study the curves $y = \sin(x - \pi/3)$ and $y = \sin(x - \alpha)$, $\alpha > 0$, which are sine curves shifted $\pi/3$ and α units to the right, respectively. (If $\alpha < 0$, the curve is shifted $|\alpha|$ units to the left.) This shift is the phase angle described in Section 15–2.

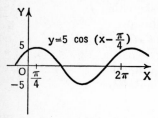

Fig. 15–13

● **Example 5.** Sketch $y = 5 \cos(x - \pi/4)$. Each value of x must be $\pi/4$ larger than in $y_1 = 5 \cos x$ to have the same ordinate; hence the curve is shifted $\pi/4$ units to the right. The wave $y = 5 \cos(x - \pi/4)$ leads the wave $y = 5 \cos x$ by $\pi/4$.

PROBLEM SET 15–5

Sketch, using composition of ordinates, and estimate the x intercepts, if any, in the interval $0 \leq x < 2\pi$.

1. $y = x + \cos 3x$.
2. $y = x - \sin 2x$.
3. $y = 7 + 4 \sin 3x$.
4. $y = 6 - 2 \sin 5x$.
5. $y = 3 + 4 \sin(x/2)$.
6. $y = 4 \sin x + \cos 2x$.
7. $y = 4 + (\sin x)^2$.
8. $y = |\sin x| + |\cos x| + 2.9$.
9. $y = (\sin x)^2 + (\cos x)^2$.
10. $y = 4 \sin \pi t + \cos 2\pi t$.
11. $y = 5 \sin x + 12 \cos x$.
12. $y = 4 \sin 3x + 3 \cos 3x$.
13. $y = \sin t - \sin 3t$.
14. $x = \sin y$.
15. $y = \sqrt{3} \cos x + \sin x$.
16. $y = x \sin x$.
17. A commutator may be arranged so that the current from a generator is switched (inverted) at the time when normal alternating current would enter the negative phase of its cycle. The voltage, E, may be represented by the locus $E = 200 |\sin 120\pi t|$. Sketch the locus.
18. The voltage of Problem 17 is pulsating (not alternating). Sketch the resulting voltage curve if a second generator is arranged out of phase so that $E = 200 |\sin 120\pi t| + 200 |\sin 120(\pi t + \pi/240)|$.

*19. Sketch $y = \dfrac{\sin x}{x}$, $-2\pi \leq x \leq 2\pi$.

*20. Sketch $y = e^{-x} \sin x$, $-2\pi \leq x \leq 2\pi$.

*15–6. Sketches of other trigonometric functions. The sketch of $y = \sec x = 1/\cos x$ may be obtained using the sketch of $y = \cos x$ as an aid.

$$\cos x \searrow 0 \text{ implies } \sec x \nearrow L^+.$$
$$\cos x \nearrow 0 \text{ implies } \sec x \searrow L^-.$$
$$|\cos x| = 1 \text{ implies } |\sec x| = 1.$$

L^+ stands for large positive values, L^- for numerically large negative values. $y = \sec x$ is discontinuous wherever $\cos x = 0$, that is, for $x = n\pi/2$, where n is an odd integer.

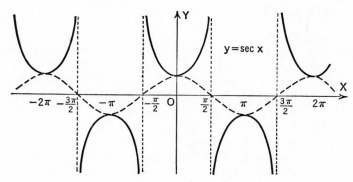

Fig. 15–14

The sketch of $y = \csc x = 1/\sin x$ is the curve $y = \sec x$ shifted $\pi/2$ units to the right.

The locus of $y = \tan x = \dfrac{\sin x}{\cos x}$ has discontinuities at points where $\cos x = 0$, and crosses the x axis for values of x such that $\sin x = 0$.

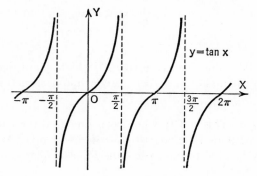

Fig. 15–15

PROBLEM SET 15–6

Sketch the following loci on the range $-\pi \leqq x \leqq 3\pi$, or $-\pi/2 \leqq \theta \leqq 2\pi$ as appropriate.

1. $y = \csc x$.   2. $y = \sec x + 5$.   3. $y = \tan x/2$.   4. $y = \cot x$.
5. $3y = 5 \csc 2x$.   6. $5y = \sec 2x$.   7. $y = -\sec \theta$.   8. $y = \tan \pi\theta$.

9. $y = \sec x + \cos x.$ **10.** $y = 4 + \tan (x/2).$ ***11.** $y = x + \tan x$

12. $y = - \csc 5x.$ **13.** $x = \sec \theta.$

14. Sketch $y = $ coversine $x = 1 - \sin x$ by addition of ordinates.

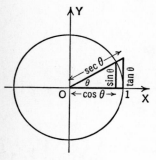

15. Sketch $y = $ haversine $x = \dfrac{1 - \cos x}{2}$ by addition of ordi

nates.

*16. The reader may find Figure 15–16 of interest. Show tha
the lengths of the line segments equal the indicated func
tions of θ if the circle is a unit circle and $0 \leqq \theta < \pi/2$
Can these functions be represented by directed line seg
ments if $\pi/2 < \theta \leqq \pi$?

*17. Using the unit circle and the areas of certain triangles anc
sector, show that
(a) $\sin \theta \cos \theta < \theta < \tan \theta,\ \ 0 < \theta < \pi/2.$
(b) $\sin \theta \cos \theta > \theta > \tan \theta,\ \ -\pi/2 < \theta < 0.$

Fig. 15–16

*18. Using the results of Problem 17, show that
(a) $\cos \theta < \theta/\sin \theta < 1/\cos \theta,$ if $-\pi/2 < \theta < \pi/2,$ and $\theta \neq 0.$

(b) $\lim\limits_{\theta \to 0} \dfrac{\theta}{\sin \theta} = 1.$

(c) $\lim\limits_{\theta \to 0} \dfrac{\sin \theta}{\theta} = 1.$

The result in 18(c) is used in showing that $\dfrac{d}{dx} (\sin x) = \cos x.$

19. (a) Sketch: $y = f(x) = \dfrac{\sin x}{x}.$

(b) What value must be given to $f(0)$, which is not defined at present,
in order to make $y = f(x)$ a continuous function? (See Section
5–5.)

15–7. Self test. This self test has been prepared for your benefit. Take
it in one sitting, without referring to your notes or text. After correcting it
yourself, you may be able to discover some topics which you need to review.

SELF TEST

Record your time.

1. A pencil compass is set for the radius 2.7 inches. How long a plane arc
is traced by rotating the pencil through an angle of 1 radian?

2. Use tables to determine (a) $\sin 37°$, (b) $\tan 2.4$, (c) $\cos 3.8$, (d) x
in radians, where $3 \sin x = 1.92$ and $-\pi \leqq x < \pi.$

3. Sketch, showing intercepts, $y = 5 \cos 2x.$

4. Sketch $y = x + \sin x.$

5. Sketch $2y = 3 - \cos (x/2).$

6. Sketch $y = 3 \sec x.$

7. Find five points of intersection of the two loci $y = 2 + \sin x$ and $2y = 3$.

8. Use a unit circle to determine whether each of the following statements is true or false:

    (a) $\cos 3 > 0$.   (b) $\sec 172 = 1$.   (c) $\tan(-5) < 0$.

Record your time.

By Herman Barovalle.   Courtesy *Scripta Mathematica*

WHAT INVERSION DOES TO A CHECKER BOARD

    The above design is obtained by inverting every point P outside of a circle into a point P' in it such that $OP \cdot OP'$ equals square of r, where O is the center and r the radius of the circle.

    This operation establishes a one-to-one correspondence between all the points in the region beyond the circle of inversion and those in it. Note that for every point exterior to the checker board there is one and only one point in the innermost white figure and as the exterior point recedes toward infinity in any direction its inverted "image" keeps on approaching the center without ever reaching it.

16

16-1. Identities. In Sections 1-9 and 2-2 we defined an identity as an equation that is satisfied by each value of the unknown for which both members are defined.

Two expressions are identical if it is possible to change one expression into the other by reversible steps.

● *Example 1.* Show that $\dfrac{3x}{x-3} - \dfrac{4}{x} = \dfrac{6x^2 - 8x + 24}{2x^2 - 6x}$ is an identity. If the equation is an identity, it will be satisfied by every value of x except $x = 3$ and $x = 0$. The two terms of the left member may be combined to obtain the right member as is shown below.

$$\dfrac{3x}{x-3} - \dfrac{4}{x}$$
$$\dfrac{3x^2 - 4(x-3)}{(x-3)x}$$
$$\dfrac{3x^2 - 4x + 12}{x^2 - 3x}$$

Multiplying numerator and denominator by 2, we obtain:

$$\dfrac{6x^2 - 8x + 24}{2x^2 - 6x}$$

$$\dfrac{6x^2 - 8x + 24}{2x^2 - 6x}$$

This proves that the two members are equal for each x value for which the left member is defined. It remains to be proved that the members are equal for each x value for which the right member is defined. Since *each step* used is reversible, we may proceed from the right member to the left by reading up the left-hand column.

In proving that an equation $A = B$ is an identity, it is logically permissible to reduce each member of $A = B$, independently, to a common form C, using steps each of which is reversible. Then, since $A \equiv C$ and $B \equiv C$, we may conclude that $A \equiv B$. Beginning students make fewer errors, especially in checking the reversibility of steps, if only one member is altered. The following example illustrates a difficulty involved if the operation is not reversible.

● *Example 2.* Is $\sqrt{x^2 - 6x + 9} = x - 3$ an identity? Upon squaring each member, we obtain

$$x^2 - 6x + 9 = (x - 3)^2$$

which is certainly an identity. However, the original equation *is not* an identity if the x domain consists of all real numbers. (Is there an x domain on which the original equation is an identity?) This may be seen by substituting any value of x that is less than 3 in the original equation and recalling that the symbol $\sqrt{}$ means the nonnegative square root. For example, if zero is substituted for x, the given relationship becomes $+3 = -3$, which is *not* valid. Why is the operation of squaring each member not reversible?

The reader may wish to ponder whether or not

$$\sqrt{x^2 - 6x + 9} = |x - 3|$$

is an identity.

In this text, only one member will be altered in proving an identity. This is partly to avoid the difficulty mentioned above. The main reason for this restriction, however, is that in later work it is desirable to start with a given trigonometric expression and reduce it to another more useful form. The technique gained in proving identities by changing only one member will help when this reduction is encountered in calculus and differential equations.

PROBLEM SET 16–1

Prove that the equations given in Problems 1 to 7 are identities on the domain of real numbers. Alter only one member of each equation.

1. $(x - 3)^2 - (x^2 + 9) = -6x.$ **2.** $\dfrac{x - 5}{x + 2} + 1 = \dfrac{2x - 3}{x + 2}.$

3. $\dfrac{x - 4}{x - 3} = \dfrac{x^2 - 7x + 12}{x^2 - 6x + 9}.$ **4.** $\dfrac{4}{x} - \dfrac{4x^2 + 1}{x^3 + 2} = \dfrac{8 - x}{x^4 + 2x}.$

5. $\log\left(\dfrac{1}{t}\right) - \log(t + 1) = \log\left(\dfrac{1}{t^2 + t}\right).$

6. $\log\left(\dfrac{10^{ax}\sqrt{2x^3 - 5}}{4x^2}\right) = ax \log 10 + \tfrac{1}{2}\log(2x^3 - 5) - 2\log x - \log 4.$

7. $x^{-1}(x + 1)^{-1} = x^{-1} - (x + 1)^{-1}.$

8. Transform $\dfrac{e^x + 1}{e^x - 1}$ into $-1 + \dfrac{2e^x}{e^x - 1}.$

9. Change $\dfrac{2}{e^x + 2}$ into $1 - \dfrac{e^x}{e^x + 2}$.

10. Show that $\dfrac{y^2}{r^2} + \dfrac{x^2}{r^2} = 1$, if $x^2 + y^2 = r^2$ and $r > 0$.

11. Use the definitions of $\sin \theta = y/r$ and $\cos \theta = x/r$ and $x^2 + y^2 = r^2$ to show that $\sin^2 \theta + \cos^2 \theta = 1$.

12. Is the following equation an identity?

$$(x - 4)^2 + 1 = x^2 - 4x + 17.$$

Prove your answer.

13. Make up two equations that are identities and two equations that are not identities. Exchange equations with another student and determine which of his equations are identities and which are not.

14. Is the following equation a numerical identity?

$$\sin 14° \tan 14° = \sec 14°.$$

Prove your answer.

15. There is an error in the following chain of reasoning which seems to suggest that 2 is equal to 1. Can you find it?

Let $a = b$. Then,

a^2	ab	(Multiply each member by a.)
$a^2 - b^2$	$ab - b^2$	(Subtract b^2 from each member.)
$(a - b)(a + b)$	$(a - b)b$	(Factor each member.)
$a + b$	b	(Divide each member by $a - b$.)
$2b$	b	($a = b$.)
$2 = 1.$		(Divide each member by b.)

16–2. Trigonometric identities. The following identities are obtained from the definitions of the trigonometric functions:

$$\csc \theta = \frac{1}{\sin \theta}. \tag{16.1}$$

$$\sec \theta = \frac{1}{\cos \theta}. \tag{16.2}$$

$$\cot \theta = \frac{1}{\tan \theta}. \tag{16.3}$$

In addition,

$$\tan \theta = \frac{y}{x} = \frac{y/r}{x/r} = \frac{\sin \theta}{\cos \theta}.$$

$$\tan \theta = \frac{\sin \theta}{\cos \theta}. \tag{16.4}$$

$$\cot \theta = \frac{x}{y} = \frac{x/r}{y/r} = \frac{\cos \theta}{\sin \theta}$$

$$\cot \theta = \frac{\cos \theta}{\sin \theta}. \tag{16.5}$$

Identities (16.6), (16.7), and (16.8) are obtained by applying the Pythagorean law. For example,

$$1 = \left(\frac{x}{r}\right)^2 + \left(\frac{y}{r}\right)^2 = \cos^2\theta + \sin^2\theta$$

leads to

$$\cos^2\theta + \sin^2\theta = 1. \qquad (16.6)$$

The expression $\sin^2\theta$ is used to mean $(\sin\theta)^2$. The expression $\sin\theta^2$ means $\sin[\theta^2]$. If $x \neq 0$, then $1 + \frac{y^2}{x^2} = \frac{r^2}{x^2}$, and

$$1 + \tan^2\theta = \sec^2\theta. \qquad (16.7)$$

Finally, if $y \neq 0$, then $\frac{x^2}{y^2} + 1 = \frac{r^2}{y^2}$, and

$$\cot^2\theta + 1 = \csc^2\theta. \qquad (16.8)$$

In applied problems it may be desirable to change from one trigonometric form to another. A few hints are listed:

1. Know the fundamental identities (16.1) to (16.8) inclusive.

2. In general, start with the more complicated member and reduce it to the simpler member.

3. Check to see that each step is reversible.

4. The expression to be obtained should be kept in mind. For example, if the member you are working with contains two terms, and the other only one term, combine the two terms. See Example 3 as an illustration.

5. If no shorter method is apparent, express each member in terms of sines and cosines.

● **Example 1.** Prove the identity $\dfrac{\sec y - \cos y}{\sec y + \cos y} = \dfrac{\tan^2 y}{\sec^2 y + 1}.$

This identity *may* be proved by expressing everything in terms of $\sin y$ and $\cos y$ and then reducing. A shorter way is to note that if the left member is multiplied by $\dfrac{\sec y}{\sec y}$, the two members have equal denominators since $\sec y \cos y = 1$.

$$\begin{array}{c|c}
\dfrac{\sec y - \cos y}{\sec y + \cos y} & \dfrac{\tan^2 y}{\sec^2 y + 1} \\[2ex]
\dfrac{\sec^2 y - \sec y \cos y}{\sec^2 y + \sec y \cos y} & \\[2ex]
\dfrac{\sec^2 y - 1}{\sec^2 y + 1} & \\[2ex]
\dfrac{\tan^2 y}{\sec^2 y + 1} \quad = & \dfrac{\tan^2 y}{\sec^2 y + 1}.
\end{array}$$

These steps are reversible and the identity is proved.

● **Example 2.** In the solution of a problem, a consulting engineer obtained $E(x) = (1 + \cos 2x)(\csc 2x - \cot 2x)$. He noticed that the graph of $y = E(x)$ looked like a sine wave. Simplify the expression for $E(x)$ [that is, reduce $E(x)$ to a form involving only the sine function, if possible].

In this problem the reduced form is not given; we suspect its existence. Perform the indicated multiplication and simplify the result.

$$E(x) = (1 + \cos 2x)(\csc 2x - \cot 2x)$$

$$\csc 2x - \cot 2x + \cos 2x \csc 2x - \cos 2x \cot 2x$$

$$\frac{1}{\sin 2x} - \frac{\cos 2x}{\sin 2x} + \cos 2x \frac{1}{\sin 2x} - \frac{\cos 2x \cos 2x}{\sin 2x}$$

$$\frac{1 - \cos^2 2x}{\sin 2x}$$

$$\frac{\sin^2 2x}{\sin 2x}$$

$$E(x) = \sin 2x.$$

The form $E(x) = \sin 2x$ is easier to use in computation than $E(x) = (1 + \cos 2x)(\csc 2x - \cot 2x)$ and more desirable.

● **Example 3.** Prove the identity

$$\frac{1}{1 + \sin x} + \frac{1}{1 - \sin x} = 2 \sec^2 x.$$

$$\frac{1 - \sin x + 1 + \sin x}{(1 + \sin x)(1 - \sin x)}$$

$$\frac{2}{1 - \sin^2 x}$$

$$\frac{2}{\cos^2 x}$$

$$2 \sec^2 x \qquad\qquad = 2 \sec^2 x.$$

PROBLEM SET 16–2

1. Compute $E(\pi/6)$ and $E(1.03)$ using each form of $E(x)$ in Example 2.

In Problems 2 to 17 prove the given identity by changing one member only, or specify a value which demonstrates that the equation is not an identity.

2. $(2 + \cos x)(2 - \cos x) = 3 + \sin^2 x.$

3. $\dfrac{\tan 5x}{\sec 5x} = \sin 5x.$

4. $\dfrac{2 + 3 \cos \theta}{\sin \theta} = 2 \csc \theta + 3 \cot \theta.$

5. $(\sin A \cos B + \cos A \sin B)^2 + (\cos A \cos B - \sin A \sin B)^2 = 1$

6. $\dfrac{\cot \theta}{\csc \theta - 1} = \dfrac{\csc \theta + 1}{\cot \theta}.$ 7. $\sec^2 t \csc^2 t = \sec^2 t + \csc^2 t.$

8. $\csc^2 x (1 - \cos^2 x) = 1.$

9. $\cot A \cot B = \dfrac{\cot A + \csc B}{\tan B + \tan A \sec B}.$

10. $\tan A + \csc A = \dfrac{\sin A + \cot A}{\cos A}.$

11. $\sin^4 \theta + 2 \sin^2 \theta \cos^2 \theta + \cos^4 \theta = 1.$

12. $3 + 3 \sin^4 x = 3 \cos^4 x + 6 \sin^2 x.$

13. $\sec^2 3\theta + \tan^2 3\theta = \sec^4 3\theta - \tan^4 3\theta.$

14. $- \log_b \cos \theta = \log_b \sec \theta.$ 15. $\log_b \sin \theta = - \log_b \csc \theta.$

16. $- \log_b (\csc \theta + \cot \theta) = \log_b (\csc \theta - \cot \theta).$

17. $\log_b (\sec \theta + \tan \theta) = - \log_b (\sec \theta - \tan \theta).$

In Problems 18 to 21 verify the identities by altering the left members only.

18. $\dfrac{\cos^3 x}{\sqrt{\sin x}} = \sin^{-\frac{1}{2}} x \cos x - \sin^{\frac{3}{2}} x \cos x.$

19. $\sin^5 x \cos^4 x = \cos^4 x \sin x - 2 \cos^6 x \sin x + \cos^8 x \sin x.$

20. $\tan^5 x = \tan^3 x \sec^2 x - \tan x \sec^2 x + \tan x.$

21. $\sin^2 \theta \cot \theta = \dfrac{1}{\tan \theta} - \cot \theta \cos^2 \theta.$ Give three values of θ for which the members are undefined.

22. Show that angles coterminal with $90°, 120°, 240°, 270°$ all satisfy the equation $2 \cot x + \cos x \cot x = 2 \cot x \sin^2 x.$

23. Show that $2 \cot x + \cos x \cot x = 2 \cot x \sin^2 x$ is *not* an identity.

24. Evaluate each of the following functions for $\theta = \pi/6$: (a) $\sin^2 \theta$, (b) $\sin 2\theta$, (c) $2 \sin \theta$, (d) $\sin \theta^2$, (e) $\sin \theta$.

25. Same as Problem 24 with "cosine" in place of "sine."

*26. Use the diagram of Problem 16, set 15–6, to verify identities (16.1) to (16.8) of this section.

In calculus and differential equations it is desirable to be able to change a trigonometric function from a given form into a more useful form. In Problems 27 to 35 use identities to change:

27. $\dfrac{1}{1 + \cos \theta}$ into $\csc^2 \theta - \csc \theta \cot \theta.$

28. $\dfrac{1}{1 - \sin \theta}$ into $\sec^2 \theta + \sec \theta \tan \theta.$

29. $\cot^4 x$ into $\cot^2 x \csc^2 x - \csc^2 x + 1$.

30. $\sin^3 x \cos^2 x$ into $\cos^2 x \sin x - \cos^4 x \sin x$.

31. $\dfrac{1 + \sin x}{1 - \sin x}$ into $2 \sec^2 x + 2 \sec x \tan x - 1$.

32. $\dfrac{\sec x}{\sec x - \tan x}$ into $\sec^2 x + \sec x \tan x$.

33. $\dfrac{\tan^3 3x}{\sec 3x}$ into $\sec 3x \tan 3x - \sin 3x$.

34. $\sec^6 ax$ into $\sec^2 ax + 2 \tan^2 ax \sec^2 ax + \tan^4 ax \sec^2 ax$.

35. $\pm \sqrt{\dfrac{1 - \sin x}{1 + \sin x}}$ into $\pm (\sec x - \tan x)$.

Problems 36 to 49 contain errors culled from student examination papers. In each case if the statement is an identity, prove it. If it is not an identity, or if it is nonsense, correct it in such a manner that a valid identity is obtained.

36. $\sin A + \cos A \overset{?}{=} 1$.

37. $\dfrac{\cos A}{\sin A} \overset{?}{=} \cot$.

38. $\sin^2 2\theta + \cos^2 2\theta \overset{?}{=} 2$.

39. $\sin 3\theta \overset{?}{=} \dfrac{1}{\cos 3\theta}$.

40. $\tan A \cot B \overset{?}{=} 1$.

41. $\sin^4 x + \cos^4 x \overset{?}{=} 1$.

42. $5 \sin (\theta^2) + 5 \cos (\theta^2) \overset{?}{=} 5$.

43. $\sin \theta \overset{?}{=} (1 - \cos^2 \theta)^{\frac{1}{2}}$.

44. $\cot^2 100° - \csc^2 100° \overset{?}{=} 1$.

45. $\sin 5t \overset{?}{=} 1 - \cos 5t$.

46. $\cos \overset{?}{=} \dfrac{1}{\sec}$.

47. $\dfrac{\sin x}{\tan x} \overset{?}{=} \dfrac{si}{ta}$.

48. $3x \cos \dfrac{2\pi}{x} \overset{?}{=} 3 \cos 2\pi \overset{?}{=} 0$.

49. $\dfrac{\sin x}{n} \overset{?}{=} 6$.

16–3. Trigonometric equations. Conditional trigonometric equations are trigonometric equations that are not satisfied by all values of the variable for which the functions are defined. Methods for the solution of conditional algebraic equations (Sec. 1–9) apply to conditional trigonometric equations.

- *Example 1.*

$$\sin^2 z = 1, \quad 0 \leqq z < 3\pi.$$
$$\sin z = \pm 1$$
$$z = \pi/2, 3\pi/2, 5\pi/2 \quad \text{since} \quad 0 \leqq z < 3\pi.$$

In degree notation $\quad z = 90°, 270°, 450°$.

- *Example 2.* $2 \sin \theta \cos \theta + \sin \theta - 6 \cos \theta - 3 = 0$,
$-\pi \leqq \theta < \pi$.

This factors as $\quad (\sin \theta - 3)(2 \cos \theta + 1) = 0$.

A product is zero if, and only if, at least one of its factors is zero. That is, if, and only if, at least one of the following equations is satisfied.

$\sin \theta = 3$	$\cos \theta = -\frac{1}{2}$
which has no real solution.	$\theta = -2\pi/3, 2\pi/3$
	since $-\pi \leqq \theta < \pi$.
	In degree notation $\theta = -120°$,
	$120°$.

● **Example 3.** $1 - \cos x = \sqrt{3} \sin x, \quad 0° \leqq x < 360°$.

Often, it is desirable to express trigonometric equations in terms of the same function before attempting a solution. We use $\sin x = \pm \sqrt{1 - \cos^2 x}$ to obtain

$$1 - \cos x = \pm \sqrt{3} \sqrt{1 - \cos^2 x}.$$

In view of the $\pm$ sign, these equations may have solutions that are not solutions of the original equation. All solutions should be checked in the original equation. Square both members as in Section 1–11 and obtain

$$1 - 2 \cos x + \cos^2 x = 3(1 - \cos^2 x).$$
$$4 \cos^2 x - 2 \cos x - 2 = 0.$$
$$2 \cos^2 x - \cos x - 1 = 0.$$
$$(2 \cos x + 1)(\cos x - 1) = 0.$$

$\cos x = -\frac{1}{2},$	$\cos x = 1$
$x = 120°, 240°$	$x = 0°$ where $0° \leqq x < 360°$.

Upon checking these values, however, only $x = 120°$ and $x = 0°$ satisfy the original equation. The value $240°$ is an extraneous value introduced by the method of solution.

● **Example 4.** Given $r = 1 + \sqrt{2} \cos \theta$. Find θ so that
(a) $r = 0, \quad 0 \leqq \theta < 2\pi$,
(b) r is a maximum, $0 \leqq \theta < 2\pi$.

(a) $1 + \sqrt{2} \cos \theta = 0, \quad \cos \theta = -1/\sqrt{2}, \quad \theta = 3\pi/4$ and $5\pi/4$.
(b) r is a maximum when $\cos \theta = 1$. The maximum value, $r = 1 + \sqrt{2}$, is obtained when $\theta = 0$.

● **Example 5.** Given $r(3 - 2 \sin \theta) = 4$ and $r(3 + 2 \sin \theta) = 2$. Find the simultaneous solutions (r, θ), with $0 \leqq \theta < 2\pi$.
Now, $r = \dfrac{4}{3 - 2 \sin \theta} = \dfrac{2}{3 + 2 \sin \theta}$ yields
$12 + 8 \sin \theta = 6 - 4 \sin \theta$, or $\sin \theta = -\frac{1}{2}, \quad \theta = 7\pi/6$ and $11\pi/6$. The simultaneous solutions are
$\left(r = \dfrac{4}{3 - 2(-\frac{1}{2})} = 1, \quad \theta = 7\pi/6 \right)$ and $(r = 1, \quad \theta = 11\pi/6)$.

PROBLEM SET 16-3

Solve the following trigonometric equations in the domain indicated.

1. $\tan^2 \theta = 1$, $0 \le \theta < 2\pi$.
2. $\sin \theta \cos \theta = 0$, $-\pi \le \theta < \pi$.
3. $\sin^2 \theta = 2$, $0 \le \theta \le 3\pi$. 4. $2 \cos x = 1$, $0 \le x \le 5\pi$.
5. $\sec \theta = 2$, $0 \le \theta \le 2\pi$. 6. $\sec \theta + 2 = 0$, $0 \le \theta < 2\pi$.
7. $\sin \theta + 1 = 0$, $0 < \theta < \pi/2$.
8. $\sec^2 \theta = \cos^2 \theta - 2 \tan^2 \theta$, $0 \le \theta \le 360°$.
9. $2 \tan^2 \theta - \sec^2 \theta = 0$, $-\pi < \theta < 3\pi$.
10. $\sin^2 \theta \cot^2 \theta - \cot^2 \theta + 3 \cos^2 \theta = 0$, $0 < \theta < 360°$.
11. $4 \cos^2 \theta = 3$, $-\pi < \theta \le \pi$.
12. $\cos 2\theta \csc \theta - 2 \cos 2\theta = 0$, $0 \le \theta \le 360°$.
13. $4 \sin^2 x = 3 \sin x$, $0 \le x < 450°$. Note that $x = 180°$ is a solution.
14. $\sin^2 \theta - \cos^2 \theta - \cos \theta - 1 = 0$, $0 \le \theta \le 2\pi$.

In Problems 15 to 23, the domain of definition is from 0° to 360°.

15. $\tan \theta - \sec \theta = 1$.

[HINT: $\sec \theta = \pm \sqrt{1 + \tan^2 \theta}$. The solution then resolves into the solution of the auxiliary equation $x \pm \sqrt{1 + x^2} = 1$. Be sure to check for extraneous values.]

16. $\tan \theta \, (\csc 3\theta - 1) = 0$. 17. $(2 \cos x - 1)(\csc x + 1) = 0$.
18. $\sin 4x = \cos 4x$. 19. $6 \tan^2 \theta + \sec \theta + 5 = 0$.
20. $\csc x = \cot x - 1$. 21. $\sec^2 t + 3 \csc^2 t = 8$.
22. $\csc^2 \theta \, (1 - \cos^2 \theta) = 1$. Does an equation of this type have a special name?
23. $\sin^2 x + \cos^2 x = 2$.
24. Given $r = 1 + 2 \sin \theta$.
    (a) Find θ so that $r = 0$, $0 \le \theta < 2\pi$.
    (b) Find θ so that r is a maximum, $0 \le \theta < 2\pi$.

In Problems 25, 26, 27, pairs of simultaneous equations in the variables r and θ are given. In each case find the solutions in the domain indicated.

25. Given $\begin{cases} r = 1 - \cos \theta, \\ r = \cos \theta. \end{cases}$ Find the simultaneous solutions (r, θ) with $0 \le \theta < 2\pi$.

26. Given $\begin{cases} r(5 - 4 \cos \theta) = 9, \\ r(1 + 2 \cos \theta) = 6. \end{cases}$ Find the simultaneous solutions (r, θ) with $0 \le \theta < 2\pi$.

27. Given $\begin{cases} r = 4 \cos \theta, \\ r = 3 \sec \theta. \end{cases}$ Find the simultaneous solutions (r, θ) with $0 \le \theta < 2\pi$.

In Problems 28 to 35 find the subintervals of $0 \le \theta < 2\pi$ on which:

28. $\sin \theta > 0$.   **29.** $0 \le \sin \theta < \frac{1}{2}$.

30. $|\sin \theta| < \frac{1}{2}$.   **31.** $\sin \theta < 1/\sqrt{2}$.

32. $\tan \theta > 1$.   **33.** $\cos^2 \theta \le \frac{3}{4}$.

34. $1/\sqrt{3} \le \cot \theta < 1$.   **35.** $\sec \theta < \frac{1}{2}$.

16–4. More identities. In calculus the reader will evaluate

$$\lim_{\Delta x \to 0} \frac{\cos (x + \Delta x) - \cos x}{\Delta x}$$

to determine $\dfrac{d}{dx} (\cos x) = - \sin x$. (See Sec. 16–11.) To prepare him for this and other important derivations we show that

$$\cos (A - B) = \cos A \cos B + \sin A \sin B. \qquad (16.9)$$

Every angle may be expressed in radian measure. Propositions proved for functions of numbers are also true for functions of angles in radian measure.

Let A and B be arc lengths on the unit circle beginning at $(1,0)$. This is the "standard position" of Sections 14–3 and 15–1. (Let P be the point of intersection of the terminal side of A and the unit circle.) Let Q be the point of intersection of the terminal side of B and the unit circle. The sketch shows

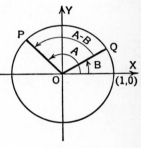

Fig. 16–1

$$0 < B < \pi/2, \quad \pi/2 < A < \pi.$$

No such restriction is included in the algebra.

The coordinates of P are $(\cos A, \sin A)$.   Why?

The coordinates of Q are $(\cos B, \sin B)$.   Why?

If d is the distance between P and Q, then, using the distance formula of Section 2–3,

$$d^2 = (\cos A - \cos B)^2 + (\sin A - \sin B)^2$$
$$= 2 - 2 \cos A \cos B - 2 \sin A \sin B.$$

Using the law of cosines, a second form for d^2 is obtained.

$$d^2 = \overline{OP}^2 + \overline{OQ}^2 - 2\overline{OP}\,\overline{OQ} \cos (A - B)$$
$$= 1 + 1 - 2 \cos (A - B).$$

Equate these two expressions for d^2

$$2 - 2 \cos (A - B) = 2 - 2 \cos A \cos B - 2 \sin A \sin B.$$

Solve for $\cos (A - B)$

$$\cos (A - B) = \cos A \cos B + \sin A \sin B. \qquad (16.9)$$

Since $\cos [- x] = \cos x$ for all x, including $x = A - B$,   it is immaterial which of A or B is larger. That is,

$$\cos (B - A) = \cos (A - B).$$

To determine $\cos(A + B)$ one may use identity (16.9) and the relations $\cos[-B] = \cos B$, $\sin[-B] = -\sin B$ as follows:

$$\begin{aligned}
\cos(A + B) &= \cos(A - [-B]) \\
&= \cos A \cos[-B] + \sin A \sin[-B] \\
&= \cos A \cos B - \sin A \sin B.
\end{aligned}$$

$$\cos(A + B) = \cos A \cos B - \sin A \sin B. \tag{16.10}$$

The relationships

$$\sin x = \cos(\pi/2 - x) \quad \text{and} \quad \cos x = \sin(\pi/2 - x)$$

will be employed with identity (16.9) to prove †

$$\sin(A + B) = \sin A \cos B + \cos A \sin B.$$
$$\begin{aligned}
\sin(A + B) &= \cos(\pi/2 - [A + B]) \\
&= \cos([\pi/2 - A] - B) \\
&= \cos[\pi/2 - A]\cos B + \sin[\pi/2 - A]\sin B \\
&= \sin A \cos B + \cos A \sin B. \tag{16.11}
\end{aligned}$$

In a fashion similar to that used in deriving (16.10)

$$\begin{aligned}
\sin(A - B) &= \sin(A + [-B]) \\
&= \sin A \cos[-B] + \cos A \sin[-B] \\
&= \sin A \cos B - \cos A \sin B.
\end{aligned}$$

$$\sin(A - B) = \sin A \cos B - \cos A \sin B. \tag{16.12}$$

In further work in analytic geometry a formula for $\tan(A - B)$ is needed to determine the angle between two lines or vectors. It may be derived as follows

$$\begin{aligned}
\tan(A - B) &= \frac{\sin(A - B)}{\cos(A - B)} \\
&= \frac{\sin A \cos B - \cos A \sin B}{\cos A \cos B + \sin A \sin B}.
\end{aligned}$$

Upon dividing numerator and denominator by $\cos A \cos B$ one obtains

$$\tan(A - B) = \frac{\dfrac{\sin A}{\cos A} - \dfrac{\sin B}{\cos B}}{1 + \dfrac{\sin A \sin B}{\cos A \cos B}}.$$

$$\tan(A - B) = \frac{\tan A - \tan B}{1 + \tan A \tan B}. \tag{16.13}$$

† See Problem 18, Set 14–9.

The derivation of a formula for $\tan (A + B)$ is left to the reader.

$$\tan (A + B) = \frac{\tan A + \tan B}{1 - \tan A \tan B}. \qquad (16.14)$$

● **Example 1.** Determine the amplitude and period of

$$y = A \cos x + B \sin x.$$

By use of identity (16.9) we shall reduce it to the form

$y = k\,[\cos \alpha \cos x + \sin \alpha \sin x] = k \cos (x - \alpha).$

$y = A \cos x + B \sin x$

$$= \sqrt{A^2 + B^2}\left[\frac{A}{\sqrt{A^2 + B^2}}\,(\cos x) + \frac{B}{\sqrt{A^2 + B^2}}\,(\sin x)\right].$$

Note that there is an angle α such that $\sin \alpha = B/\sqrt{A^2 + B^2}$ and $\cos \alpha = A/\sqrt{A^2 + B^2}$. For example, if $A > 0$ and $B < 0$, a possible angle α is shown in Figure 16–2.

Making this substitution, and using identity (16.9) with $A = x$ and $B = \alpha$ one obtains:

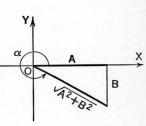

Fig. 16–2

$$y = \sqrt{A^2 + B^2}\,[\cos \alpha \cos x + \sin \alpha \sin x]$$
$$= \sqrt{A^2 + B^2} \cos (x - \alpha).$$

Letting $\theta = x - \alpha$, this becomes

$$y = \sqrt{A^2 + B^2} \cos \theta.$$

The amplitude is $\sqrt{A^2 + B^2}$, and the period is 2π. The reader should note that the phase angle is α, an angle whose sine is $B/\sqrt{A^2 + B^2}$.

● **Example 2.** Compute $\sin 195°$ from functions of 150° and 45°.

$\sin 195° = \sin (150° + 45°)$
$\qquad = \sin 150° \cos 45° + \cos 150° \sin 45°$

$$= \frac{1}{2}\left(\frac{1}{\sqrt{2}}\right) + \left(-\frac{\sqrt{3}}{2}\right)\left(\frac{1}{\sqrt{2}}\right)$$

$$= \frac{1-\sqrt{3}}{2\sqrt{2}} = \frac{(1-\sqrt{3})\sqrt{2}}{4} = \frac{\sqrt{2}-\sqrt{6}}{4} \cong \frac{1.4142-2.4495}{4}$$

$\sin 195° \cong -0.2588.$

● **Example 3.** Reduce $s = 3 \sin (2\pi t/3) + 4 \cos (2\pi t/3)$ to the form $s = A \cos (kt - \omega)$; find the amplitude, the period, and the least positive value of t for which s is a maximum.

Here, $A = 4$, $B = 3$, $\sqrt{A^2 + B^2} = 5$, and

$$s = 5\left[\left(\cos\frac{2\pi t}{3}\right)\left(\frac{4}{5}\right) + \left(\sin\frac{2\pi t}{3}\right)\left(\frac{3}{5}\right)\right]$$

$$= 5\left[\cos\left(\frac{2\pi t}{3}\right)\cos\omega + \sin\left(\frac{2\pi t}{3}\right)\sin\omega\right]$$

$$= 5\cos\left(\frac{2\pi t}{3} - \omega\right),$$

where $\cos\omega = \frac{4}{5}$ and $\sin\omega = \frac{3}{5}$. The amplitude is 5. The period is $2\pi/(2\pi/3) = 3$. The least positive value of t for which s is a maximum, 5, is obtained by solving $(2\pi t/3) - \omega = 0$. (Why?) The value of ω, in radians, is first determined using a table, by noting that $\sin\omega = \frac{3}{5} = 0.600$. Hence, $\omega = .643$, and

$$t = \frac{3\omega}{2\pi} \cong \frac{3(.643)}{2(3.14)} \cong .31.$$

PROBLEM SET 16-4

1. Use identities (16.11) and (16.10) to determine $\sin(\pi/2 + \theta)$ and $\cos(\pi/2 + \theta)$.

2. Use identities of this section to determine

   $\sin(180° - \theta)$, $\cos(\pi - \theta)$, and $\tan(180° - \theta)$.

3. Assume identity (16.11) and show that (16.10) can be derived from (16.11). Would the proof given in the text for (16.11) be valid if (16.10) had been proved using the method of this problem? Explain your answer.

4. State the quadrants in which the terminal sides of angles A and B fall given that A and B are in standard position, $\sin A < 0$, $\tan A = \frac{3}{4}$, $\cos B > 0$, and $\sin B = \frac{1}{2}$. Find $\sin(A + B)$, $\cos(A + B)$, $\tan(A + B)$, and $\cos(A - B)$.

5. Prove the identity $\sin(\alpha + 60°) - \cos(\alpha + 30°) = \sin\alpha$.

6. Reduce $\sin(4x/5)\cos(x/5) + \cos(4x/5)\sin(x/5)$ to a simpler form.

7. Find $Z = \sin 110° \cos 70° + \cos 110° \sin 70°$ first by using a table and computing Z and second by simplifying the ex-

pression for Z and then computing it. Which way is easier? Which method is more accurate?

Use the identities of this section to confirm the results stated in Problems 8, 9, 10.

8. $\sin (\theta + 90°) = \cos \theta$.

9. $\sin (\theta + 30°) + \cos (\theta + 60°) = \cos \theta$.

10. $\tan (\alpha + 45°) + 1 = \sqrt{2} \cos \alpha \sec (\alpha + 45°)$.

11. If A and B are acute angles with $\sin A = \frac{1}{3}$ and $\cos B = \frac{4}{5}$, in what quadrant does $(A + B)$, in standard position, have its terminal line?

[HINT: Consider the sign of $\cos (A + B)$ and, if necessary, of $\sin (A + B)$.]

12. In what quadrant is the terminal line of $(A - B)$, if A and B are the angles of Problem 11?

In Problems 13 to 21, prove the stated equation is an identity, or show that it is not an identity by finding values of the variables for which both members are defined, but unequal.

13. (a) $\cos (\theta + 180°) = - \cos \theta$. (b) $\cos (\theta + 180°) = \cos \theta$. Note that (a) and (b) cannot both be identities.

14. $\sqrt{2} \sin (x + 45°) = \sin x + \cos x$.

15. $\dfrac{\cos 7\theta}{\sin 2\theta} - \dfrac{\sin 7\theta}{\cos 2\theta} = \cos 9\theta \sec 2\theta \csc 2\theta$.

16. $(\sin A \cos B + \cos A \sin B)^2 + (\cos A \cos B - \sin A \sin B)^2 = 1$.

17. $\sec (A - B) = \dfrac{\sec A \sec B}{1 + \tan A \tan B}$.

18. $\tan (45° + \theta) + \tan (135° - \theta) = \cos 90°$.

19. $\tan (\theta + 135°) \tan (\theta - 315°) = \cos 180°$.

20. $(\sin x \cos \theta - \cos x \sin \theta)^2 + (\cos x \cos \theta + \sin x \sin \theta)^2 = \sin (\pi/2)$.

21. $\cos (\theta + \beta) \cos \beta + \sin (\theta + \beta) \sin \beta = \cos \theta$.

22. Compute $\sin 120°$ from the functions of $180°$ and $60°$.

23. Compute $\cos 15°$ from the functions of $45°$ and $30°$. Check, using a table.

24. Compute $\sin 15°$ from the functions of $45°$ and $30°$. Check, using a table.

25. Prove the identity $\tan (A + B) = \dfrac{\tan A + \tan B}{1 - \tan A \tan B}$.

26. Prove that $\dfrac{\cot A \cot B - 1}{\cot A + \cot B} = \cot (A + B)$.

27. Sketch $y = 5 \sin x + 12 \cos x$ using the results of Example 1.

28. Sketch $y = 4 \sin 3x + 3 \cos 3x$ using the results of Example 1. Find the period and amplitude of y.

29. Show that $A \cos x + B \sin x = \sqrt{A^2 + B^2} \sin (\alpha + x)$,

where $\sin \alpha = \dfrac{A}{\sqrt{A^2 + B^2}}$ and $\cos \alpha = \dfrac{B}{\sqrt{A^2 + B^2}}$.

Reduce the expressions in Problems 30 to 34 to the form $s = A \cos (kt - \omega)$. In each case find the amplitude, the period, and the least positive value of t for which s is a maximum.

30. $s = 4 \cos 2t - 3 \sin 2t$.   **31.** $s = \sqrt{3} \sin \pi t + \cos \pi t$.

32. $s = 8 \sin 3t - 15 \cos 3t$.   **33.** $s = 10 \sin (\pi t/2) + 10 \cos (\pi t/2)$.

34. A vertical flywheel 6 feet in diameter rotates at the constant rate of 10 revolutions per second. Find an equation defining the motion of the projection on a horizontal line, of a point on the rim of the wheel. Find the amplitude and period of the motion of the projection.

In Problems 35 to 40 find all values of the variable which satisfy the given equation in the domain $0° \leqq \theta < 360°$.

35. The nonidentity in Problem 13.

36. $\sin \theta \cos 2\theta - \sin 2\theta \cos \theta = 1$.

37. $\sin x \sin 2x + \cos x \cos 2x = 0$.

38. $\sin x \sin 30° + \cos x \cos 30° = -1$.

39. $\tan^2 (x + 17°) = 1$.

[HINT: Do *not* use the formulas of this section.]

40. $\sec^2 (x + 32°) = 4$.

41. John Smith is sure that the formula for $\cos (A - B)$ is one of $\cos A \cos B \pm \sin A \sin B$, but he is not sure of the sign of the second term. John guesses wrong and loses several points on a quiz. Show John that, since

$$\cos (A - A) = \cos 0 = 1,$$

he could have easily figured out which sign is correct and need not have guessed.

42. Can John tell which of the four formulas,
$\sin A \cos B \pm \cos A \sin B$ and $\cos A \cos B \pm \sin A \sin B$,
is correct for $\sin (A + B)$ by letting A and B take on different combinations of the values $0°$, $45°$, $90°$?

43. Let $B = A$ and show that

$$\cos (A + A) = \cos 2A = \cos^2 A - \sin^2 A.$$

Then show, by using identities, that $\cos 2A = 1 - 2 \sin^2 A$, and also that $\cos 2A = 2 \cos^2 A - 1$.

In Problems 44, 45 find the subinterval of $0 \leqq x < 2\pi$ for which:

44. $0 < \sin x \cos 30° - \cos x \sin 30° \leqq \frac{1}{2}$.

45. $|\cos x \cos 45° + \sin x \sin 45°| > 1/\sqrt{2}$.

16–5. Functions of multiple angles. Set $B = A$ in Formulas (16.10), (16.11), (16.14) to obtain

$$\cos 2A = \cos^2 A - \sin^2 A \qquad (16.15)$$
$$= 2 \cos^2 A - 1$$
$$= 1 - 2 \sin^2 A.$$

$$\sin 2A = 2 \sin A \cos A. \qquad (16.16)$$

$$\tan 2A = \frac{2 \tan A}{1 - \tan^2 A}. \qquad (16.17)$$

● **Example 1.** Solve $\sin 2x - \sqrt{3} \cos x = 0$ on the domain $0° \leqq x \leqq 360°$.

$$\sin 2x - \sqrt{3} \cos x = 0$$
$$2 \sin x \cos x - \sqrt{3} \cos x = 0$$
$$(2 \sin x - \sqrt{3}) \cdot \cos x = 0$$
$$\sin x = \sqrt{3}/2 \qquad \cos x = 0$$
$$x = 60°, \ 120°, \ 90°, \ 270°.$$

PROBLEM SET 16–5

1. What results are obtained when $B = A$ in (16.9), (16.12), (16.13)?
2. Prove $\sin^2 x \cos^2 x = (1 - \cos 4x)/8$.
3. Prove $\sin^4 x = (3 - 4 \cos 2x + \cos 4x)/8$.
4. Compute $\sin 120°$ as $\sin 2(60°)$.
5. Compute $\cos 120°$ as $\cos 2(60°)$. Is the sign correct?

In Problems 6 to 10 prove that the stated relationship is an identity.

6. $\sin 2\theta = \dfrac{2 \tan \theta}{1 + \tan^2 \theta}$.   7. $\sec 2x = \dfrac{\sec^2 x}{2 - \sec^2 x}$.

8. $\dfrac{1 - \tan^2 x}{1 + \tan^2 x} = \cos 2x$.   9. $\tan A = \dfrac{\sin 2A}{1 + \cos 2A} = \dfrac{1 - \cos 2A}{\sin 2A}$.

*10. $8 \sin^2 3t \cos^2 3t = 1 - \cos 12t$.
11. Set $B = A$ in the identity of Problem 25, Set 16–4, and use this to prove $\tan 2A = \dfrac{2 \tan A}{1 - \tan^2 A}$.
12. Divide $\sin 2A$ by $\cos 2A$ to obtain the formula for $\tan 2A$ given in Problem 11. Use, in turn, each of the three formulas for $\cos 2A$.
*13. Express $\sin^4 x \cos^2 x$ in terms of first powers of multiple angles.

14. Prove $\log_b \tan \theta = \log_b (\csc 2\theta - \cot 2\theta)$.

15. Prove the identity $\sin 3x = 3 \sin x - 4 \sin^3 x$.

[HINT: $\sin 3x$ is $\sin (x + 2x)$.]

16. Prove the identity $\cos 3x = 4 \cos^3 x - 3 \cos x$.

17. Prove the identity $\sin 4x = 8 \cos^3 x \sin x - 4 \cos x \sin x$.

*18. Use Problems 15 and 16 to show
$$\sin 6x = 32 \cos^5 x \sin x - 32 \cos^3 x \sin x + 6 \cos x \sin x.$$

19. Show that $\tan 3x = \dfrac{3 \tan x - \tan^3 x}{1 - 3 \tan^2 x}$.

In Problems 20 to 24, find all values of x which satisfy the equation in the given domain.

20. $\cos 2x - \sin x = 0$, $\quad 0° \leq x < 360°$.

21. $\cos x + \sin 2x = 0$, $\quad -\pi \leq x < \pi$.

22. $\sin 2x - \cos 2x = 0$, $\quad -90° \leq x < 270°$.

$$\left[\text{HINT:} \quad \tan 2x = \frac{\sin 2x}{\cos 2x} = ? \right]$$

23. $\tan 3x = \cot 3x$, $\quad 0° \leq x < 360°$.

24. $\sin x + \cos 2x = 0$, $\quad 0 \leq x < 2\pi$.

*25. Set $\alpha = 2A$ in $\cos 2A = 1 - 2 \sin^2 A$ to obtain $\cos \alpha = 1 - 2 \sin^2 (\alpha/2)$ and solve this equation for $\sin (\alpha/2)$ in terms of $\cos \alpha$.

26. Given $r = 5 \cos 2\theta$. Find θ so that $r = 0, 0 \leq \theta < 2\pi$.

27. Given $r = 5 \cos 2\theta$. Find all sets of (r, θ) values having $|r|$ a maximum and $0 \leq \theta < 2\pi$.

28. Given $r^2 = a^2 \cos 2\theta$.

(a) Find θ so that $r = 0, 0 \leq \theta < 2\pi$.

(b) Find θ so that r^2 is a maximum and $0 \leq \theta < 2\pi$.

29. Given $r = 2 \sin \theta$ and $r^2 = 2 \cos 2\theta$. Find the simultaneous solutions (r, θ) with $0 \leq \theta < 2\pi$.

30. Given $r^2 = a^2 \cos 2\theta$, and $r^2 = a^2 \sin 2\theta$. Find the simultaneous solutions (r, θ) with $0 \leq \theta < 2\pi$.

16–6. Functions of half angles. In solving (16.15) for $\cos^2 A$ one obtains

$$2 \cos^2 A - 1 = \cos 2A.$$

$$\cos^2 A = \frac{1 + \cos 2A}{2}. \tag{16.18}$$

From (16.18), one obtains

$$\cos A = \pm \sqrt{\frac{1 + \cos 2A}{2}}. \tag{16.18'}$$

Identities (16.19) and 16.20) may be obtained in an analogous fashion. Equivalent forms (16.19') and (16.20') are also given.

$$\sin^2 A = \frac{1 - \cos 2A}{2}. \tag{16.19}$$

$$\sin A = \pm \sqrt{\frac{1 - \cos 2A}{2}}. \tag{16.19'}$$

$$\tan A = \frac{\sin 2A}{1 + \cos 2A}. \tag{16.20}$$

$$= \frac{1 - \cos 2A}{\sin 2A}.$$

$$\tan A = \pm \sqrt{\frac{1 - \cos 2A}{1 + \cos 2A}}. \tag{16.20'}$$

In the identities (16.18'), (16.19'), and (16.20') the desired sign may be determined by considering the quadrant in which the terminal side of A lies, for A in standard position.

● **Example 1.** Determine $\cos 15°$.

Let $A = 15°$ in (16.18), then

$$\cos^2 15° = \frac{1 + \cos 2(15°)}{2} = \frac{1 + \cos 30°}{2} = \frac{1 + \sqrt{3}/2}{2} = \frac{2 + \sqrt{3}}{4}.$$

Hence,

$$\cos 15° = \pm \sqrt{\frac{2 + \sqrt{3}}{4}} = \pm \frac{\sqrt{2 + \sqrt{3}}}{2}.$$

Since $\cos 15° > 0$,

$$\cos 15° = + \frac{\sqrt{2 + \sqrt{3}}}{2}.$$

● **Example 2.** Find $\tan 105°$.

Since $2(105°) = 210°$ is an angle whose trigonometric functions are known, one may use (16.20) to determine $\tan 105°$.

$$\tan 105° = \frac{1 - \cos 210°}{\sin 210°} = \frac{1 + (\sqrt{3}/2)}{-\frac{1}{2}} = -2 - \sqrt{3} \cong 3.7.$$

PROBLEM SET 16–6

In Problems 1 to 9 compute the indicated functional values using the methods of this section.

1. $\sin 15°$.   **2.** $\tan 15°$.

3. $\cos 105°$ (Be sure to check the sign).

4. $\cos 22.5°$.   **5.** $\sec 15°$.   **6.** $\cos 165°$

7. $\tan 165°$.   **8.** $\csc (-15°)$.   **9.** $\cos 375°$

10. Find $\sin 15°$ using the relationship $\sin 15° = \sin (45° - 30°)$ and compare the result with that of Problem 1. Show these two results are identical. Take care! It does not follow immediately that the two expressions are equal just because the squares of the expressions are equal. For example, $(-2)^2 = 2^2$, but $-2 \neq 2$.

11. Show that the quadrant in which the terminal side of $\alpha/$ lies *cannot* be determined from the quadrant in which the terminal side of α lies. Consider $\alpha_1 = 150°$ and $\alpha_2 = 510°$ which are coterminal, but $\alpha_1/2$ and $\alpha_2/2$ do not have terminal sides in the same quadrant. Would the sign of $\sin (\alpha/2)$, or of $\cos (\alpha/2)$, or both, be changed if α is changed from 150° to 510°?

12. Prove $\log_b \tan \left(\dfrac{\theta}{2}\right) = \log_b (\csc \theta - \cot \theta)$.

13. Show that $\cos^2 \left(\dfrac{x}{2}\right) = \dfrac{1 + \cos x}{2}$

and that

$$\sin^2 \left(\frac{x}{2}\right) = \frac{1 - \cos x}{2}.$$

14. Given $r = 2 \sec^2 \left(\dfrac{\theta}{2}\right)$, and $r = 1 + \cos \theta$. Find the simultaneous solutions (r, θ) with $0 \leq \theta < 2\pi$.

15. Divide $\sin \left(\dfrac{\alpha}{2}\right)$ by $\cos \left(\dfrac{\alpha}{2}\right)$ and simplify to obtain

$$\tan \left(\frac{\alpha}{2}\right) = \pm \sqrt{\frac{1 - \cos \alpha}{1 + \cos \alpha}}.$$

16. Rationalize the fraction under the radical sign of Problem 15 by multiplying numerator and denominator by $(1 + \cos \alpha)$ to obtain

$$\tan \left(\frac{\alpha}{2}\right) = \pm \frac{\sin \alpha}{1 + \cos \alpha}.$$

Show further that $\tan \left(\dfrac{\alpha}{2}\right)$ and $\sin \alpha$ have the same sign, and that $\tan \left(\dfrac{\alpha}{2}\right) = \dfrac{\sin \alpha}{1 + \cos \alpha}$ since $1 + \cos \alpha \geq 0$.

17. Rationalize the fraction under the radical sign of Problem 15 by multiplying numerator and denominator by $(1 - \cos \alpha)$

and then, by considerations similar to those of Problem 16,

show that $\tan\left(\dfrac{\alpha}{2}\right) = \dfrac{1 - \cos\alpha}{\sin\alpha}$.

18. In a manner similar to that used in Problems 15, 16, and 17, show that

$$\cot\left(\frac{\alpha}{2}\right) = \frac{1 + \cos\alpha}{\sin\alpha}.$$

19. In a manner similar to that used in Problems 15, 16, 17, and 18, show that

$$\cot\left(\frac{\alpha}{2}\right) = \frac{\sin\alpha}{1 - \cos\alpha}.$$

20. Obtain the results of Problems 18 and 19 from those of 16 and 17 using $\cot x = \dfrac{1}{\tan x}$.

21. John Smith is having memory trouble again. He has forgotten whether $\sin\left(\dfrac{\alpha}{2}\right)$ is

$$\pm\sqrt{\frac{1 - \cos\alpha}{2}} \quad \text{or} \quad \pm\sqrt{\frac{1 + \cos\alpha}{2}}.$$

Show that he may determine which of these is correct by letting $\alpha = 0$.

22. Show that John might have reached the correct conclusion in Problem 21 by considering which of the two functions increases as $\alpha \searrow 0$.

23. Show that if $A = 180° - B - C$, then

$$\sin A = \sin B \cos C + \cos B \sin C,$$

and

$$\cos A = \sin B \sin C - \cos B \cos C.$$

*24. Use the identities of Problem 23 to show that

$$\sin^2 A = \sin^2 B + \sin^2 C - 2\sin B \sin C \cos A,$$

where $A = 180° - B - C$.

*25. Use Problem 24 to show that the law of cosines may be proved from the law of sines. This removes some of the objections discussed in Problem 7, Set 14–8 to proving the law of Pythagoras from the law of cosines.

26. The function $f(x) = \dfrac{\cos 10x - \cos 6x}{\sin 5x - \sin x} + \dfrac{\sin 15x + \sin x}{1 + \cos 10x - 2\sin^2 2x}$ was tabulated for various values of the number x using a modern high-speed computer. The results follow:

x	$f(x)$
0	undefined
.1	$+$ .00000007
.5	$-$ .000002
1.0	$+$ .00000021
1.5	$+$ .0000043
2.0	$+$ .00000055
2.5	
3.0	$+$ .00000075
3.5	$-$ .0000001
4.0	$+$ .00000024
4.5	$-$ .0000011

x	$f(x)$
5.0	$+$ .00000066
5.5	$+$ .000001032
6.0	$+$ .0000007
6.5	$-$ .0000101
7.0	$-$ .00000254
7.5	$-$ .00000697
8.0	$-$ .0000246
8.5	$-$ .00000366
9.0	$-$ .00025133
9.5	$+$ .00010776
10.0	$-$ .0001499

Since $f(x)$ is nearly zero for each value of x, one wonders if possibly $f(x) = 0$ is an identity and that the difference between zero and the computed values is a result of "round off and truncation error." Either prove that $f(x) = 0$ is an identity or show conclusively that it is not, as the case may be.

In Problems 27 to 35, prove the given identities, or show that they are not identities as the case may be.

27. $\tan^2 \dfrac{x}{2} - 2 \csc x \tan \dfrac{x}{2} + 1 = 0.$

28. $\cot \dfrac{x}{2} = \csc x + \cot x.$

29. $\tan \dfrac{x}{2} = \dfrac{1 + \sin x - \cos x}{1 + \sin x + \cos x}.$

30. $\log \left[\tan^2 \dfrac{x}{2} + 2 \cot x \tan \dfrac{x}{2} \right] = 0.$

31. $\sin^2 \dfrac{x}{2} = \dfrac{\sin 4x + 2 \sin 3x + \sin 2x}{4 \sin 3x}.$

32. $\dfrac{1 + \tan (x/2)}{1 - \tan (x/2)} = \dfrac{1 + \sin x}{\cos x}.$

33. $4 \sin^2 \dfrac{x}{2} \cos^2 \dfrac{x}{2} = 1 - \cos^2 x.$

34. $\tan \dfrac{\alpha + \beta}{2} = \dfrac{\sin \alpha + \sin \beta}{\cos \alpha + \cos \beta}.$

*35. $\sin \dfrac{t}{2} [\sin \theta + \sin (\theta + t) + \sin (\theta + 2t) + \cdots + \sin (\theta + mt)]$

$$= \sin \left(\theta + \dfrac{mt}{2} \right) \sin \dfrac{(m + 1)t}{2}.$$

36. Given that $x = -3 \cos^2 \theta \sin \theta$ and $y = 3 \sin^2 \theta \cos \theta$ prove that $4x^2 + 4y^2 = 9 \sin^2 2\theta.$

Solve the following equations on the range $0 \leqq \theta < 2\pi$.

37. $\sin 2\theta - 4 \cos^2 \dfrac{\theta}{2} - \sin \theta + 3 = 0$.

38. $\cos 2\theta + 2 \sin^2 \dfrac{\theta}{2} = 1$.

39. $\sin \theta - \cos \dfrac{\theta}{2} = 0$.

40. $\log \left(\sin \dfrac{\theta}{2} + \cos \theta \right) = 0$.

16–7. Further identities. Certain further identities are useful. By adding (16.11) and (16.12), we obtain (16.21)

$$\begin{array}{ll} \sin (A + B) = \sin A \cos B + \cos A \sin B. & (16.11) \\ \underline{\sin (A - B) = \sin A \cos B - \cos A \sin B.} & (16.12) \\ \sin (A + B) + \sin (A - B) = 2 \sin A \cos B. & (16.21) \end{array}$$

Upon subtracting (16.12) from (16.11) we obtain

$$\sin (A + B) - \sin (A - B) = 2 \cos A \sin B. \qquad (16.22)$$

By setting $A + B = \alpha$ and $A - B = \beta$ in (16.21) and (16.22) one obtains

$$\sin \alpha + \sin \beta = 2 \sin \tfrac{1}{2}(\alpha + \beta) \cdot \cos \tfrac{1}{2}(\alpha - \beta), \qquad (16.23)$$

$$\sin \alpha - \sin \beta = 2 \cos \tfrac{1}{2}(\alpha + \beta) \cdot \sin \tfrac{1}{2}(\alpha - \beta). \qquad (16.24)$$

The reader will be asked to derive the following relationships in a similar manner

$$\cos \alpha + \cos \beta = 2 \cos \tfrac{1}{2}(\alpha + \beta) \cdot \cos \tfrac{1}{2}(\alpha - \beta). \qquad (16.25)$$

$$\cos \alpha - \cos \beta = - 2 \sin \tfrac{1}{2}(\alpha + \beta) \cdot \sin \tfrac{1}{2}(\alpha - \beta). \qquad (16.26)$$

● **Example 1.** Solve $\sin 3x - \sin x = \cos 2x$ in the domain

$$0° \leqq x < 360°.$$

Using (16.24) with $\alpha = 3x$, $\beta = x$ the above equation becomes

$$2 \cos 2x \sin x = \cos 2x,$$
$$2 \cos 2x \sin x - \cos 2x = 0.$$
$$\cos 2x(2 \sin x - 1) = 0.$$

$$\begin{array}{l|l} \cos 2x = 0 & 2 \sin x - 1 = 0 \\ \quad 2x = 90°, 270°, 450°, 630° & \quad \sin x = \tfrac{1}{2} \\ \quad x = 45°, 135°, 225°, 315°. & \quad\quad x = 30°, 150°. \end{array}$$

Note that, if $0° \leqq x < 360°$, then $0° \leqq 2x < 720°$.

● **Example 2.** Express $4 \sin 2x \cos 3x \cos 4x$ as a sum or dif
ference of sines.

By (16.21), and using $\sin(-x) = -\sin x,$

$$\sin 2x \cos 3x = \frac{\sin(2x+3x) + \sin(2x-3x)}{2}$$

$$= \frac{\sin 5x + \sin(-x)}{2}$$

$$= \frac{\sin 5x - \sin x}{2}.$$

Now,

$$4 \sin 2x \cos 3x \cos 4x = 2[\sin 5x \cos 4x - \sin x \cos 4x]$$
$$= [\sin(5x+4x) + \sin(5x-4x)]$$
$$\quad - [\sin(x+4x) + \sin(x-4x)]$$
$$= \sin 9x + \sin x - \sin 5x - \sin(-3x)$$
$$= \sin x + \sin 3x - \sin 5x + \sin 9x.$$

● **Example 3.** Derive a formula expressing $\sin A \sin B$ as
sum or difference of sines, of cosines, or of both.

We need a formula containing the term $\sin A \sin B$. Two
such formulas are already known to us.

$$\cos(A-B) = \cos A \cos B + \sin A \sin B$$

and

$$\cos(A+B) = \cos A \cos B - \sin A \sin B$$

Upon subtracting,

$$\cos(A-B) - \cos(A+B) = 2 \sin A \sin B$$

or $\sin A \sin B = \tfrac{1}{2}[\cos(A-B) - \cos(A+B)].$

PROBLEM SET 16-7

Solve Problems 1 to 5 for values of the variable in the domain
indicated.

1. $\cos x + \sin 2x = 0,\quad 0 \leq x < 2\pi.$
2. $\sin 4\theta = \sin 2\theta,\quad -\pi < \theta \leq \pi.$
3. $\sin 2\theta = \sqrt{2} \cos \theta,\quad -180° \leq \theta \leq 360°.$
4. $\cos 3x - \sin x = \cos x,\quad 0° \leq x < 360°.$
5. $\cos x + \cos 3x + \cos 5x = 0,\quad 0° \leq x < 360°.$

6. Show that $\dfrac{\sin A - \sin B}{\sin A + \sin B} = \dfrac{a-b}{a+b}$ in triangle ABC where side a is opposite angle A, etc.

7. Use the results of Problem 6 and identities (16.23) and (16.24) to obtain the law of tangents for a triangle ABC,

$$\frac{\tan[(A-B)/2]}{\tan[(A+B)/2]} = \frac{a-b}{a+b}.$$

In Problems 8 to 15 determine whether or not the given equation is an identity. If it is an identity, prove this. If it is not an identity, find all solutions of the equation which lie between $0°$ and $360°$.

8. $\cos 6x + \sin 3x - 1 = 0.$ 9. $\sin t + \sin\left(\dfrac{t}{2}\right) = 0.$

10. $\sin 3x + \sin x = \cos x.$

[HINT: Use identity (16.23) to simplify the left member.]

11. $\dfrac{\cos 9\theta + \cos 5\theta}{\cos 9\theta - \cos 5\theta} = -\cot 7\theta \cot 2\theta.$

12. $\dfrac{\sin 80° - \sin x°}{\cos 80° - \cos x°} = -1.$ (Show it is *not* an identity by letting $x = 0°$,   then solve the equation.)

13. $\dfrac{\cos 50° + \cos 40°}{\sin 80° - \sin 10°} = \dfrac{\cos 5°}{\sin 35°}.$ 14. $\sin 50° + \cos 80° = \cos x°$

15. $(1 + 2\cos A)\sin 2A = \sin A + \sin 2A + \sin 3A.$

16. Add identities (16.9) and (16.10) to obtain

$$\cos(A+B) + \cos(A-B) = 2\cos A \cos B.$$

17. Use identities (16.9) and (16.10) to obtain

$$\cos(A+B) - \cos(A-B) = -2\sin A \sin B.$$

18. Let $\alpha = A + B$ and $\beta = A - B$ in the identity of Problem 16 and verify the identity (16.25).

19. Let $\alpha = A + B$ and $\beta = A - B$ in the identity of Problem 17 and verify the identity (16.26).

20. Solve for θ, $\sin^2 2\theta + 3\cos^2 \theta = 3,$ $-\pi < \theta < \pi.$

In Problems 21 to 25 express each of the given relationships as a sum or difference of cosines, or of sines.

21. $\sin(x - \pi/6)\sin(x + \pi/6).$

[HINT: Use Problem 17.]

22. $\sin x \cos 2x.$ 23. $\sin x \cos 2x \sin 3x.$

24. $\cos x \cos 2x.$ 25. $\cos x \cos 2x \cos 3x.$

Find the subinterval of the interval $0 \leq x < 2\pi$ on which

26. $\cos x + \sin 2x < 0$. **27.** $\sin 4x < \sin 2x$.

28. (a) Is the following equation an identity? (b) Are there any values of x which satisfy the equation? Prove your assertions.

$$2 \sin^2 x + 3 \cos^2 x = \sin^2 x + 2 \cos^2 x - 3.$$

16–8. Inverses and inverse functions. The inverse of the fraction $\dfrac{n}{d}$ is the fraction $\dfrac{d}{n}$ obtained by interchanging the numerator and denominator giving $\dfrac{d}{n} = \left(\dfrac{n}{d}\right)^{-1}$, provided $n \neq 0, d \neq 0$. In more advanced mathematics the rational numbers $\dfrac{n}{d}$ are developed as classes of ordered pairs of integers (n, d), with $d \neq 0$. The inverse of $\dfrac{n}{d} = (n, d)$ is then obtained by interchanging the elements of the ordered pair, giving $(d, n) = (n, d)^{-1}$.

Since a function is a set of ordered pairs (see Problem 24, Set 1–8) this suggests a method of defining the inverse of a function.

Definition. The **inverse of a function** is obtained by interchanging the coordinates in each of its ordered pairs.

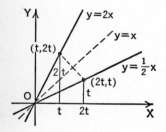

● **Illustration 1.** Consider the function $y = 2x$, that is the set of all ordered pairs $(t, 2t)$ of real numbers. This set of ordered pairs $(t, 2t)$ has for its inverse the set of ordered pairs $(2t, t)$. Note that each point $(t, 2t)$ is reflected about the line $y = x$ into the point $(2t, t)$. The pairs $(t, 2t)$ are represented by the linear function $y = 2x$ as is seen from $x = t, y = 2t$. The inverse of this function of x is $x = 2y$ or $y = \frac{1}{2}x$, which is a function of x also.

Fig. 16–3

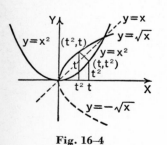

Fig. 16–4

● **Illustration 2.** The set of all ordered pairs of real numbers (t, t^2) has for its inverse the set of all ordered pairs (t^2, t). The set of all ordered pairs (t, t^2) defines y as the parabolic function $y = x^2$ of x as is seen from $x = t, y = t^2$. The ordered pairs (t^2, t) of the inverse yield $y^2 = x$ or $y = \pm \sqrt{x}$. A restriction on t is necessary if the inverse is to be a function of x. For $t \geq 0$, the function $y = x^2, x \geq 0$ will have for its inverse the function $y = \sqrt{x}, x \geq 0$. For $t \leq 0$, the function $y = x^2, x \leq 0$ will have for its inverse the function $y = -\sqrt{x}, x \geq 0$.

The second illustration helps to make the need for the next statement clear.

The *inverse of a function of x* is a *function of x* if, and only if, no line parallel to the x-axis intersects the graph of the given function in more than one point. Otherwise the inverse is a (multiple-valued) *relation* rather than a (single-valued) function.

For t in the domain of all real numbers the set of all ordered pairs $(t, \sin t)$ is the function $y = \sin x$ and has for its inverse the set of all ordered pairs $(\sin t, t)$ that yields $\sin y = x$; that is, y is a number whose sine is x. We would like to express y as the inverse sine function of x and write it in the form $y = \sin^{-1} x$ or $y = \text{Arcsin } x$ (either of which is read "inverse sine of x" or "the number whose sine is x"). Unfortunately corresponding to each x value in the interval $-1 \leq x \leq 1$ there exist infinitely many y values satisfying $\sin y = x$. For example, if $x = \frac{1}{2}$,

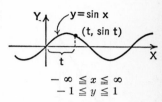

Fig. 16–5

then $y = \dfrac{\pi}{6} + 2n\pi$ or $y = \dfrac{5\pi}{6} + 2n\pi$, n an integer. How shall we define the inverse of the function $y = \sin x$ so that it too will be a function of x? The statement in the preceding paragraph suggests a method. We need to restrict the domain of x values such that no line parallel to the x-axis will intersect the graph of $y = \sin x$ in more than one point. In order to obtain an inverse sine function, $y = \sin^{-1} x$ or $y = \text{Arcsin } x$, it is customary to restrict the domain of the sine function, $\sin x$, to real values of x from $-\dfrac{\pi}{2}$ to $\dfrac{\pi}{2}$, inclusive. It may be noticed that as x traverses the interval from $-\dfrac{\pi}{2}$ to $\dfrac{\pi}{2}$, inclusive, the function $\sin x$ passes continuously through all of its values from -1 to 1, inclusive, once and only once. A line parallel to the x-axis will not intersect the graph of $y = \sin x$, $-\dfrac{\pi}{2} \leq x \leq \dfrac{\pi}{2}$ in more than one point. The function $y = \sin x$, $-\dfrac{\pi}{2} \leq x \leq \dfrac{\pi}{2}$ has for its inverse function $y = \sin^{-1} x$ or $y = \text{Arcsin } x$, $-\dfrac{\pi}{2} \leq \text{Arcsin } x \leq \dfrac{\pi}{2}$.

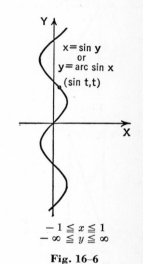

Fig. 16–6

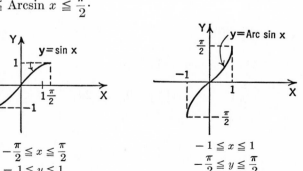

Fig. 16–7

Fig. 16–9

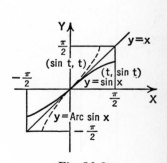

Fig. 16–8

16–9. Inverse trigonometric relations. It is desirable to have terminology indicating the x values that are solutions of $\sin x = A$. We introduce the notation   arc sin $A = x$,   which may be read *"an angle whose sine is A."*

The relationship $N = \sin x$ gives N as a trigonometric function of x, while $x = $ arc sin N is the corresponding **inverse trigonometric relation.** The trigonometric function $N = \sin x$ is a single valued function of x. To each permissible value of x there corresponds exactly one value of N. To illustrate:

If $x = \pi/6$, $N = \sin(\pi/6) = \frac{1}{2}$;
If $x = 5\pi/6$, $N = \sin(5\pi/6) = \frac{1}{2}$.

The inverse trigonometric relation $x = $ arc sin N is multiple valued, since to each permissible value of N, there correspond many x values. For example, there are many x values such that $x = $ arc sin $\frac{1}{2}$.   (Name five such x values.) In a similar fashion, we define $x = $ arc cos N and $x = $ arc tan N as equivalent to $\cos x = N$ and $\tan x = N$ respectively. In our present work, arc sec N,   arc csc N and   arc cot N will not be needed.

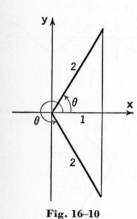

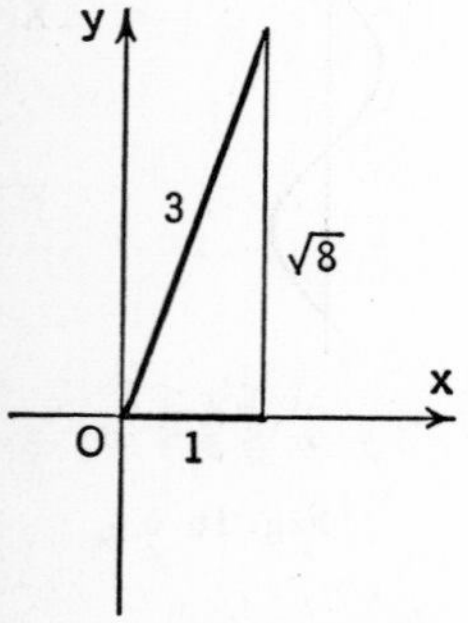

Fig. 16–10

● *Example 1.* Write in degrees, and in radians, formulas giving all values of   arc sin $(-\frac{1}{2})$.

arc sin $(-\frac{1}{2}) = -30° + n(360°) = -\pi/6 + n(2\pi)$, n an integer.

and

$$210° + n(360°) = 7\pi/6 + n(2\pi), \quad n \text{ an integer.}$$

● *Example 2.* Find $\theta = $ arc cos $\frac{1}{2}$,   where $0 \leqq \theta < 2\pi$.

If $\cos \theta = \frac{1}{2}$, $\theta = \dfrac{\pi}{3}, \dfrac{5\pi}{3}$.   See Fig. 16–10.

● *Example 3.* Find $\sin ($arc cos $\frac{1}{3})$.

From Figures 16–11 and 16–12,

$$\sin (\text{arc cos } \tfrac{1}{3}) = \pm \frac{\sqrt{8}}{3} = \pm \frac{2\sqrt{2}}{3}.$$

● *Example 4.* Find   arc cos $\left[\sin \dfrac{\pi}{2}\right]$.

arc cos $\left[\sin \dfrac{\pi}{2}\right] = $ arc cos $[1] = 0, \quad \pm 2\pi, \quad \pm 4\pi, \quad \cdots$.

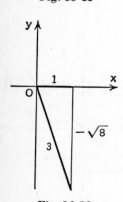

Fig. 16–11

Fig. 16–12

PROBLEM SET 16–9

If possible, find five values for each of the expressions given in Problems 1 to 15.

1. arc sin $\frac{1}{2}$.

2. arc cos $(1/\sqrt{2})$.

3. arc sin $(-1/\sqrt{2})$.

4. arc sin $(-\sqrt{3}/2)$.

5. arc tan 1.

6. arc cos (-1).

7. arc tan (-1).

8. arc sin $\sqrt{3}$.

9. arc tan $\sqrt{3}$.

10. arc cos $(.86)$.

11. sin [arc sin $\frac{1}{2}$].

12. tan [arc sin $\frac{1}{2}$].

13. sec [arc cos $(-\frac{1}{2})$].

14. arc sin [cos $(5\pi/3)$].

15. arc cos [sin $(5\pi/3)$].

*16. Write, in degrees, and in radians, formulas that will give all angles in Problems 1, 2, 6, and 9.

17. Show that for properly chosen values of the multiple-valued relations   arc sin $\frac{3}{5}$ + arc sin $\frac{5}{13}$ = arc sin $\frac{56}{65}$.

Each of the following statements is either: (a) true for all values of u; or (b) true for infinitely many, but not all, values of u; or (c) true for only a finite number of values of u; or (d) false for every value of u. Tell which of (a), (b), (c), or (d) is valid in each case and explain your reasons.

*18. arc sin $u \overset{?}{=} 1/$arc csc u.

19. arc tan $[1/\cot u] \overset{?}{=} u$.

20. arc sin $(-u) \overset{?}{=} -$ arc sin u.

21. arc cos $(-u) \overset{?}{=} -$ arc cos u.

22. arc sin $\frac{x}{a} \overset{?}{=}$ arc sin $\frac{x}{a} \overset{?}{=}$ rc sin x.

*23. arc sin $u \overset{?}{=}$ arc sec u.

24. arc tan $(\cos u) \overset{?}{=} -\pi/4$.

*25. tan (arc sec 2) $\overset{?}{=} u$.

26. What range of values of N is permissible for   (a) arc sin N, (b) arc tan N,   *(c) arc sec N?

16–10. Principal values. In certain work it is desirable to have continuous single-valued inverse trigonometric *functions*. To accomplish this, we define a *principal angle whose sine is N*. This is denoted by using an initial capital letter.

arc sin N = an angle whose sine is N.

Arc sin N = the principal angle whose sine is N.

The function sin x takes on all possible values from minus one to plus one, once, and only once, as x ranges from $-\pi/2$ to $\pi/2$. It is customary to define Arc sin N by

$$-\pi/2 \leqq \text{Arc sin } N \leqq \pi/2.\dagger$$

† Some authors use the symbol $\sin^{-1} A$ to mean the function Arc sin A, others use it to mean the relation arc sin A. In either case the symbol $\sin^{-1} A$ must not be confused with $[\sin A]^{-1} = \dfrac{1}{\sin A} = \text{csc } A$.

- **Example 1.** Arc sin $\frac{1}{2} = \pi/6$, Arc sin $(-\sqrt{2}/2) = -\pi/4$ but
    arc sin $(-\sqrt{2}/2) = \cdots$, $-3\pi/4$, $-\pi/4$, $5\pi/4$, $\cdots$.

    The function cos x takes on all of its values once, and only once, in the interval $0 \leqq x \leqq \pi$.
    Define

$$0 \leqq \text{Arc cos } N \leqq \pi.$$

- **Example 2.** Arc cos $1 = 0$; Arc cos $(-\frac{1}{2}) = 2\pi/3$; but
    arc cos $(-\frac{1}{2}) = \cdots$, $-4\pi/3$, $-2\pi/3$, $2\pi/3$, $\cdots$,

    while Arc cos 3 is not defined.

    The function tan x takes on all of its values once, and only once, in the interval $-\pi/2 < x < \pi/2$, and is not defined for $x = \pm \pi/2$. Arc tan N is defined by

$$-\pi/2 < \text{Arc tan } N < \pi/2.$$

    The choice of domain of definition for each of these functions makes it continuous and single valued. The reader should check this statement by considering appropriate graphs.

- **Example 3.** Arc tan $\sqrt{3} = \pi/3$, Arc tan $(-1) = -\pi/4$.

- **Example 4.** Evaluate
    $y = $ Arc sin $\frac{1}{2} - 2$ Arc tan $1 + 5$ Arc cos 1.

$$y = \pi/6 - 2(\pi/4) + 5(0) = -\pi/3.$$

- **Example 5.** Find tan [arc sin $\frac{2}{3}$].

    Since arc sin $\frac{2}{3}$ is an angle (or one of several possible angles) we may determine tan (arc sin $\frac{2}{3}$). Figure 16–13 will prove useful.

    Thus tan (arc sin $\frac{2}{3}$) $= \pm 2/\sqrt{5}$. We cannot tell which value is desired unless more information is given.

- **Example 6.** Sketch the relation $y = $ arc sin x and indicate the function $y = $ Arc sin x by using heavier lines.
    See Figure 16–14.

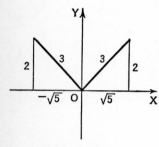

Fig. 16–13

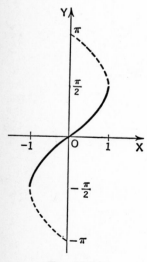

Fig. 16–14

PROBLEM SET 16–10

Evaluate:

1. Arc sin $(-\frac{1}{2})$.
2. Arc cos 0.
3. Arc tan (-1).
4. arc tan (-1).
5. Arc sin $1 -$ Arc cos $(-\frac{1}{2}) + 3$ Arc tan 1.
6. sin [Arc sin $\frac{1}{3}$]. [What is the name of a man whose name is Bill?]

7. $\tan [\text{Arc sin} (-\frac{1}{5})]$.   **8.** $\sin [\text{Arc tan} (-1)]$.

9. Arc tan (cos 0).   **10.** Arc cos $[\sin (2\pi/3)]$.

11. Sketch $y = \text{arc cos } N$ for $-2\pi \le y \le 4\pi$,   and indicate $y = \text{Arc cos } N$ by using heavier lines.

12. Sketch $y = \text{arc tan } N$ for $-2\pi \le y \le 4\pi$,   and indicate $y = \text{Arc tan } N$ by using heavier lines.

13. In certain problems in calculus it is desirable to simplify inverse trigonometric functions. Show, for example, that Arc tan $(x/\sqrt{1-x^2}) = \text{Arc sin } x$,   if $|x| < 1$.

*14. Show that   Arc tan $(x/\sqrt{1-x^2}) = \text{Arc cos } \sqrt{1-x^2}$ if $0 \le x < 1$,   but not if $x < 0$.

15. Show   that   Arc sin $(x/\sqrt{1+x^2}) = \text{Arc tan } x$.   Are   any values of x excluded?

16. Why is it impossible to use the same interval in defining all three principal inverse trigonometric functions and still obtain continuous single-valued functions?

17. Show that   Arc tan $x = \text{arc tan } x$ is not an identity, but that   tan (Arc tan x) $= x$ and $x = \tan (\text{arc tan } x)$ are always valid.

18. Arc tan $\frac{3}{4}$ + Arc tan $\frac{4}{3}$ = ?

19. Arc tan $\frac{1}{4}$ + Arc tan $\frac{3}{5}$ = ?   This leads to a numerical identity that is of the type used in computing the value of π to a large number of decimal places. The computation of π is of great interest to industrial statisticians. It sheds light on the nature of random-sample theory. The student may be interested in glancing at the journal *Mathematical Tables and Other Aids to Computation* and its successor *Mathematics of Computation* in his school library.

20. Consult a set of mathematical tables, or a mathematical handbook, to determine two identities not studied in this chapter. Prove they can be derived using the identities already studied.

21. Express   Arc sin $(\sqrt{a^2 - x^2}/a)$ as   Arc tan (?),   as Arc cos (?).

22. Express   Arc cos $\left(\dfrac{\sqrt{4x - x^2}}{2}\right)$ as   Arc sin (?),   as Arc tan (?).

23. Express   Arc tan $[(2x + 3)/\sqrt{-4x^2 - 12x}]$ as
$$\text{Arc sin (?), as Arc cos (?)}.$$

Certain of the results in the preceding exercises are of simpler form. Later, in the calculus, considerable labor may be saved in differentiating inverse trigonometric functions if the simplest form is recognized and used.

24. cos {Arc tan $[(x - 1)/2]$} = ?

25. sec (arc cos x) = ?   **26.** tan [arc sin $(x/2)$] = ?

27. Find   tan [Arc cos $\frac{4}{5}$ + Arc tan $\frac{2}{3}$].

28. Find   cos [Arc sin $\frac{3}{5}$ − Arc cos $\frac{3}{5}$].

29. Find   sec [Arc sin 0.6 + Arc cos 0.8].

30. Find   Arc tan {cos [Arc cos $\frac{2}{3}$ + Arc cos $\frac{1}{3}$]}.

31. Show that, if $x \geq 0$,   the principal value of any inverse trigonometric function of x is that value lying between 0 and $\pi/2$, inclusive.

32. Show that the principal value   Arc sin x,   or   Arc tan x, is that value which is *smallest numerically*. (This value is negative and not less than $-\pi/2$ if $x < 0$.)

33. Show that the principal value   Arc cos x,   or   Arc cot x, is the smallest positive value of the function. (This value of the function is between 0 and π inclusive.)

16–11. Derivatives of sin u and cos u. In this section the formulas for the derivatives with respect to x of sin u and cos u are derived, and examples illustrating their use are included for the benefit of those readers who need this information in their physics courses.

The delta process, combined with identity (16.24) of Section 16–7 and the limit in Problem 18(c), Set 15–6, is used to obtain Theorem 1. It is assumed that u is measured in radians.

Theorem 1. $\dfrac{d(\sin u)}{dx} = \cos u \dfrac{du}{dx}$,   where u is a differentiable function of x.

Let

$$f(x) = \sin u,$$

then

$$f(x + \Delta x) - f(x) = \sin (u + \Delta u) - \sin u.$$

Apply (16.24) with $\alpha = u + \Delta u$ and $\beta = u$.

$$f(x + \Delta x) - f(x) = 2 \cos \frac{u + \Delta u + u}{2} \sin \frac{u + \Delta u - u}{2}$$

$$= 2 \cos \left(u + \frac{\Delta u}{2}\right) \sin \frac{\Delta u}{2}.$$

Now,

$$\frac{f(x + \Delta x) - f(x)}{\Delta x} = 2 \cos \left(u + \frac{\Delta u}{2}\right) \sin \frac{\Delta u}{2} \cdot \frac{1}{\Delta x}$$

$$= \cos \left(u + \frac{\Delta u}{2}\right) \cdot \left(\frac{\sin \dfrac{\Delta u}{2}}{\dfrac{\Delta u}{2}}\right) \cdot \frac{\Delta u}{\Delta x}.$$

The last step was obtained by multiplying and dividing the preceding right member by $\dfrac{\Delta u}{2}$. The reason follows.

$$\frac{df(x)}{dx} = \frac{d(\sin u)}{dx} = \lim_{\Delta x \to 0} \frac{f(x + \Delta x) - f(x)}{\Delta x}$$

$$= \lim_{\Delta x \to 0} \cos\left(u + \frac{\Delta u}{2}\right) \cdot \left(\lim_{\Delta x \to 0} \frac{\sin \dfrac{\Delta u}{2}}{\dfrac{\Delta u}{2}}\right) \cdot \lim_{\Delta x \to 0} \frac{\Delta u}{\Delta x}$$

$$= \lim_{\Delta u \to 0} \cos\left(u + \frac{\Delta u}{2}\right) \cdot \left(\lim_{\frac{\Delta u}{2} \to 0} \frac{\sin \dfrac{\Delta u}{2}}{\dfrac{\Delta u}{2}}\right) \cdot \lim_{\Delta x \to 0} \frac{\Delta u}{\Delta x},$$

since $\Delta u \to 0$ and $\dfrac{\Delta u}{2} \to 0$ as $\Delta x \to 0$. It also follows that

$$\lim_{\Delta u \to 0} \cos\left(u + \frac{\Delta u}{2}\right) = \cos u, \quad \text{and} \quad \lim_{\frac{\Delta u}{2} \to 0} \frac{\sin \dfrac{\Delta u}{2}}{\dfrac{\Delta u}{2}} = 1$$

by Problem 18(c), Set 15–6, with $\theta = \dfrac{\Delta u}{2}$. If u is a differentiable function of x, then $\lim_{\Delta x \to 0} \dfrac{\Delta u}{\Delta x} = \dfrac{du}{dx}$.

Hence,

$$\frac{d(\sin u)}{dx} = \cos u \cdot 1 \cdot \frac{du}{dx} = \cos u \frac{du}{dx}.$$

● **Example 1.** Find (a) $\dfrac{d}{dx}(\sin x)$, (b) $\dfrac{d}{dt}(4 \sin 3t)$.

(a) $\dfrac{d}{dx}(\sin x) = \cos x \dfrac{dx}{dx} = \cos x.$

(b) $\dfrac{d}{dt}(4 \sin 3t) = 4 \dfrac{d(\sin 3t)}{dt} = 4 \cos 3t \dfrac{d(3t)}{dt} = 12 \cos 3t.$

The application of Theorem 1, and the identity $\cos u = \sin(\pi/2 - u)$ yield Theorem 2.

Theorem 2. $\dfrac{d}{dx}(\cos u) = -\sin u \dfrac{du}{dx}.$

$$\frac{d(\cos u)}{dx} = \frac{d}{dx}[\sin(\pi/2 - u)] = \cos(\pi/2 - u)\frac{d}{dx}(\pi/2 - u)$$

$$= \cos(\pi/2 - u) \cdot \left(-\frac{du}{dx}\right)$$

$$= -\sin u \frac{du}{dx}.$$

● **Example 2.** A particle is moving along the s axis such that its distance from the origin at time t is given by $s = 12 \cos (\pi t - \pi/4)$. Find (a) the velocity and (b) the acceleration of the particle at time t. (c) Describe the motion of the particle. This type of motion is called simple harmonic motion.

(a) $\displaystyle v = \frac{ds}{dt} = \frac{d}{dt}\left[12 \cos \left(\pi t - \frac{\pi}{4}\right)\right]$

$\displaystyle = -12 \sin \left(\pi t - \frac{\pi}{4}\right)\frac{d}{dt}\left(\pi t - \frac{\pi}{4}\right)$

$\displaystyle = -12\pi \sin \left(\pi t - \frac{\pi}{4}\right).$

(b) $\displaystyle a = \frac{dv}{dt} = \frac{d}{dt}\left[-12\pi \sin \left(\pi t - \frac{\pi}{4}\right)\right]$

$\displaystyle = -12\pi \cos \left(\pi t - \frac{\pi}{4}\right)\cdot \pi$

$\displaystyle = -12\pi^2 \cos \left(\pi t - \frac{\pi}{4}\right)$

$\displaystyle = -\pi^2 s.$

The last result indicates that the acceleration is proportional to the displacement of the particle from the origin, and is directed toward the origin.

(c) s has period $2\pi/\pi = 2$, and amplitude 12. When $t = 0$,

$$s = 12 \left(\frac{\sqrt{2}}{2}\right) = 6\sqrt{2}, \quad v = -12\pi\left(-\frac{\sqrt{2}}{2}\right) = 6\pi\sqrt{2},$$

$$a = -6\pi^2\sqrt{2}.$$

(1) At time $t = 0$, $s = 6\sqrt{2}$ and the particle moves in the positive direction with an initial velocity $6\pi\sqrt{2}$. The motion in the positive direction stops when $v = 0$, that is, when

$$\sin (\pi t - \pi/4) = 0$$

for the smallest positive t, $\pi t - \pi/4 = 0$, $t = \frac{1}{4}$.

When $t = \frac{1}{4}$, $s = 12$, $v = 0$, $a = -12\pi^2$.

(2) Immediately after $t = \frac{1}{4}$ the negative acceleration causes the particle to move in the negative direction until v is again zero. This occurs when $\pi t - \pi/4 = \pi$, that is, at $t = \frac{1}{4} + 1 = \frac{5}{4}$. At this instant $s = -12$, $v = 0$, $a = 12\pi^2$.

(3) Immediately after $t = \frac{5}{4}$ the positive acceleration causes the particle to move in the positive direction until v is again zero. This occurs when $\pi t - \pi/4 = 2\pi$, that is, at $t = \frac{1}{4} + 2 = \frac{9}{4}$. At this instant $s = 12$, $v = 0$, $a = -12\pi^2$ and the particle is ready to repeat its motion during the next

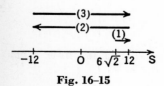

Fig. 16–15

period from time $t = \frac{9}{4}$ to time $t = \frac{9}{4} + 2 = \frac{17}{4}$. The particle shuttles forth and back between $s = 12$ and $s = -12$ inclusive during each period.

● **Example 3.** An interesting proof of the identity $\sin^2 x + \cos^2 x = 1$ may be obtained using differentiation. To begin with, we note that the expression $\sin^2 x + \cos^2 x$ is a function of x. (The reader knows that this function is actually the constant 1, but this is what we are trying to prove, so for now we observe that $\sin^2 x + \cos^2 x$ is a function of x.)

$$f(x) = \sin^2 x + \cos^2 x$$

Upon differentiating we obtain

$$\frac{df(x)}{dx} = 2 \sin x \,(\cos x) + 2 \cos x \,(- \sin x)$$

or

$$\frac{df(x)}{dx} = 0.$$

Therefore the function $f(x)$ is actually a constant. (Why?) We determine the value of the constant function $f(x)$ by setting x equal to zero.

Since $\qquad f(0) = \sin^2 0 + \cos^2 0 = 0^2 + 1^2 = 1$

and since we have established that $f(x)$ is constant for all values of x, it follows that

$$\sin^2 x + \cos^2 x = 1$$

This simple proof of a fundamental trigonometric identity by use of derivatives illustrates a technique common in mathematical proof today.

● **Example 4.** Find $\dfrac{d \tan x}{dx}$.

Since $\quad \tan x = \dfrac{\sin x}{\cos x} \quad$ and $\quad \dfrac{d\left(\dfrac{u}{v}\right)}{dx} = \dfrac{v \dfrac{du}{dx} - u \dfrac{dv}{dx}}{v^2}$

by Section 6–7 we have

$$\frac{d \tan x}{dx} = \frac{d\left(\dfrac{\sin x}{\cos x}\right)}{dx} = \frac{\cos x \cdot \dfrac{d \sin x}{dx} - \sin x \cdot \dfrac{d \cos x}{dx}}{\cos^2 x}$$

$$= \frac{\cos x \cos x - \sin x \,(- \sin x)}{\cos^2 x} = \frac{\cos^2 x + \sin^2 x}{\cos^2 x}$$

$$= \sec^2 x.$$

This generalizes to $\quad \dfrac{d \tan u}{dx} = \sec^2 u \dfrac{du}{dx}.$

A student who is having difficulty with these concepts will b
well advised to review Chapter 7 on velocity and rate of chang
before continuing.

● *Example 5.* A rotating spotlight is set up 100 feet from a lon
straight wall. The spotlight rotates in a horizontal plane a
the rate of one revolution per second (that is, 2π radians pe
second). Determine the speed at which the spot of light i
moving along the wall:

(a) When the spot of light S is passing the point P on th
wall that is nearest the rotating light.

(b) When the spot of light S is passing a point Q 400 fee
down the wall from P.

Let θ be the angle PLS. By the conditions of the problem
$\dfrac{d\theta}{dt} = 2\pi$.   The problem asks you to find $\dfrac{du}{dt}$ when $u =$ ●
and when $u = 400$, where u is the distance between th
fixed point P and the moving spot of light S.

Fig. 16–16

$$\frac{u}{100} = \tan \theta$$

$$u = 100 \tan \theta$$

Differentiating

$$\frac{du}{dt} = 100 \sec^2 \theta \frac{d\theta}{dt}$$

$$= 100 \sec^2 \theta \cdot (2\pi)$$

$$= 200\pi \sec^2 \theta$$

At $u = 0$, $\theta = 0$ and $\sec \theta = 1$,

Hence at $u = 0$, $\dfrac{du}{dt} = 200\pi \cong 628$ feet per second.

At $u = 400$, $\theta = $ Arc tan $\frac{400}{100}$ and $\sec \theta = \sqrt{17}$

Hence at $u = 400$,

$$\frac{du}{dt} = 200\pi(17) \cong 10{,}679 \text{ feet per second.}$$

PROBLEM SET 16–11

1. Find $\dfrac{d}{dx}\left(6 \sin \dfrac{x}{2}\right).$

2. Find $\dfrac{d}{dx}\left(4 \sin \dfrac{3x}{2}\right).$

3. Find $\dfrac{d}{dt}\left(15 \cos \dfrac{2t}{3}\right).$

4. Find $\dfrac{d}{dx}\left(10 \cos \dfrac{3x}{5}\right).$

5. If $s = 3 \sin \pi t + 4 \cos \pi t$, show that $\dfrac{d^2s}{dt^2} = -\pi^2 s$.

6. If $s = 5 \cos 3t - 12 \sin 3t$, show that $\dfrac{d^2s}{dt^2} = -9s$.

7. A particle is moving along the s axis such that its distance from the origin at time t is given by $s = 6 \sin (2\pi t - \pi/3)$. Find (a) the velocity and (b) the acceleration of the particle at time t. (c) Describe and sketch the motion of the particle.

8. (a) Read D. K. Pease's article in *The American Mathematical Monthly*, Vol. 60 (1953), pages 477–8, and report on the method discussed for obtaining the limits of Problem 18, Set 15–6. (b) Make a report on S. Hoffman's article in *The American Mathematical Monthly*, Vol. 67 (1960), pages 671–3.

9. Derive a formula for $\dfrac{d \cot x}{dx}$.

10. Use the fact that $\dfrac{d(1/v)}{dx} = -\dfrac{1}{v^2}\dfrac{dv}{dx}$ (proved in Sec. 6–7) to determine formulas for $\dfrac{d \sec x}{dx}$ and $\dfrac{d \csc x}{dx}$.

11. A rotating spotlight turns in a horizontal plane at a rate of 12 revolutions per minute. It shines on a long straight wall which is 100 feet from the light at the point P on the wall nearest the light. Determine the speed at which the spot of light is moving (a) as it passes P, (b) as it passes a point Q on the wall 150 feet from P.

12. Two straight roads intersect at a point P with an angle of 45° as shown in Fig. 16–17. Cars leave P simultaneously. Al drives east at 30 miles per hour on one road while Bob drives northeast at 50 miles per hour on the other road. (a) Set up functions $X_A(t)$, $Y_A(t)$, $X_B(t)$, $Y_B(t)$ which will give the location of Al (X_A, Y_A) and of Bob (X_B, Y_B) on a coordinate system having PA as x axis and P as origin.

(b) Use the results of part (a) and the distance formula to determine a formula $D(t)$ that will give the actual cross-country distance between Al and Bob at any time t under the conditions of the problem. If Al stops after driving for 90 miles, what range of t values is the domain of definition of the function $D(t)$.

(c) How fast is the distance between Al and Bob changing when $t = \frac{1}{2}$ hour? When $t = 2$ hours?

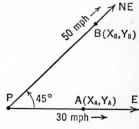

Fig. 16–17

13. A certain enzyme activity is known to take place in surges. The activity at time t is given by $A(t) = t \sin \pi t$. Make a rough sketch of $y = t \sin \pi t$ and determine the time t at which the activity begins to slow down after the first surge, and also the time at which the second surge begins (that is, find the first maximum and first minimum of $y = t \sin \pi t$).

14. An alternating current is delivered with voltage
$V(t) = 400 \sin 120\pi t + 200 \cos 60\pi t$. Determine the maximum and minimum line voltage that occurs at the delivery point.

15. Use the derivative to help you sketch some of the loci of Section 15–5.

16–12. Self test. This self test should be taken in one sitting without referring to your text or notes. The reader is reminded that he should not expect a close correlation between the problems asked on this self test and on his classroom examination.

SELF TEST

Record your time.

1. Prove the identity $\dfrac{\sec \theta - \cos \theta}{\sec \theta + \cos \theta} = \dfrac{\tan^2 \theta}{\sec^2 \theta + 1}$.

2. Solve for θ: $1 - \sqrt{3} \sin \theta = \cos \theta$, $-\pi \le \theta \le \pi$.

3. Compute $\cos 75°$ using functions of $150°$.

4. Compute $\sin 15°$ using functions of $30°$ and of $45°$.

5. Obtain $y = 5 \sin x + 12 \cos x$ in the form $y = k \cos (x - \alpha)$.

6. Prove the identity $\dfrac{1 - \cos 2\theta}{\sin 2\theta} = \tan \theta$.

7. Given that $\sin 4\theta = -\dfrac{1}{3}$, with $\pi < 4\theta < \dfrac{3\pi}{2}$, find $\cos 2\theta$ and $\cos 8\theta$.

8. Solve for x, $-\pi \le x < \pi$, if $\sec x = \tan x - 1$.

9. Solve for θ, $0 \le \theta < 2\pi$, if $\cos 2\theta = 3 \sin \theta + 2$.

10. Evaluate (a) $\sec [\text{Arc cos} (-\frac{1}{2})]$. (b) Arc tan $[\sin (3\pi/2)]$.

11. Find the subintervals of $0 \le x < 2\pi$ for which
$$| 2 \cos 3x \sin 3x | < \sqrt{3}/2.$$

12. Find $\cos [\text{Arc sin} (\frac{2}{3}) + \text{Arc cos} (-\frac{4}{5})]$.

13. Find values of r and θ which satisfy $r = 3 + \cos \theta$ and $r = 2 + 3 \cos \theta$ simultaneously.

14. Use the Δ process to derive the formula for $\dfrac{d \cos x}{dx}$ from the definition.

15. Find the greatest and the least value of the function

$$y = 2 \sin x + \cos 2x$$

on the interval $0 \leqq x \leqq 2\pi$ and sketch the function.

Record your time.

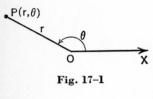

P(r,θ)

Fig. 17–1

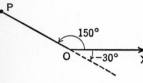

Fig. 17–2

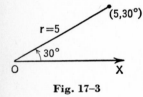

Fig. 17–3

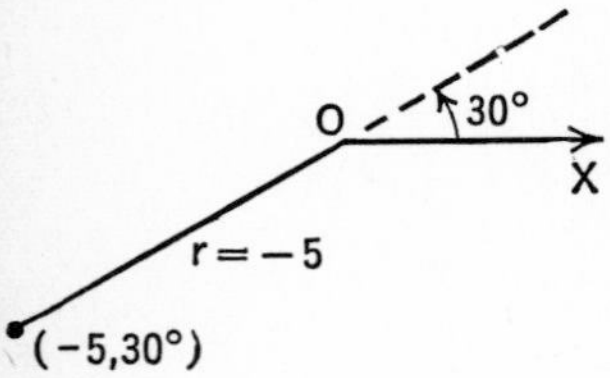

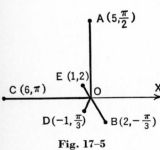

Fig. 17–4

17–1. Polar coordinates. Thus far our graphical work has been in the rectangular coordinate system. For many applications, it is more convenient to use the polar coordinate system. In the polar coordinate system one of the variables is an angle; the other is a distance measured along the terminal side of the angle.

In the coordinate plane, choose a unit of length and a horizontal half line OX, originating at O and with positive direction to the right. The line OX is the **polar axis,** and the point O is the **pole.**

To determine the coordinates of a point P, construct the line segment OP.

If P is not at the pole, it may be located by finding the distance $r = OP$, and an angle θ coterminal with XOP. The distance r is the **radius vector** or **polar distance** of P. The angle θ is a **polar angle** or **vectorial angle** of P. Together r and θ, written (r, θ), are **polar coordinates** of the point P. This system is essentially the same as that used in saying that a certain city is 38 miles (r) northwest (θ) of a particular town. For a given point P the value of θ is *not* unique. For example, the point $P(r, \theta) = (3, 150°)$ may also be represented as $(3, 510°)$, or $(3, -210°)$. In fact, every $(3, 150° \pm n \cdot 360°)$, for integral n, is a possible set of coordinates for the point $P(3, 150°)$. The radius vector, r, may be negative. If r is positive, P lies on the terminal side of θ. If r is negative, P lies on the line obtained by projecting the terminal side of θ back through the pole. For example, $(3, 150°)$ may be represented by $(-3, 330°)$ or $(-3, -30°)$.

At the pole, $r = 0$ and every value of θ is a valid choice. In Figures 17–3 and 17–4 the points $(5, 30°)$ and $(-5, 30°)$ are located.

In rectangular coordinates, each pair of coordinates represents a unique point, and each point has a unique set of coordinates. In polar coordinates, each pair of coordinates represents a unique point but, as was seen above, every point has many possible sets of polar coordinates.

● **Example 1.** Plot the points having polar coordinates $A(5, \pi/2)$, $B(2, -\pi/3)$, $C(6, \pi)$, $D(-1, \pi/3)$, and $E(1, 2)$. See Fig. 17–5.

Fig. 17–5

• **Example 2.** Plot the points having polar coordinates $(3, -\pi/2)$ and $(-2, \pi/3)$.

• **Example 3.** Give four other sets of polar coordinates for each of the points of Example 2.

$$(3, -\pi/2) = (3, 3\pi/2) = (-3, \pi/2)$$
$$= (-3, -3\pi/2) = (3, 7\pi/2).$$
$$(-2, \pi/3) = (-2, 7\pi/3) = (2, 4\pi/3)$$
$$= (-2, -5\pi/3) = (2, -2\pi/3).$$

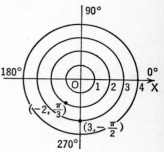

Fig. 17–6

PROBLEM SET 17–1

Locate the points having the following polar coordinates. (Several points may be plotted on the same system of axes. Label each point clearly.) Give three additional sets of coordinates for each point. In at least one set take θ and r opposite in sign from those given.

1. $(3, \pi/2)$. **2.** $(5, \pi/3)$. **3.** $(7, 11\pi/3)$.
4. $(-2, \pi/3)$. **5.** $(4, -\pi/3)$. **6.** $(-3, -10°)$.
7. $(6, 14\pi)$. **8.** $(-2, -1)$.

Where do all points (r, θ) satisfying the conditions given in Problems 9 to 13 lie? Sketch and name the locus in each case.

9. $r = 5$. **10.** $r = -5$. **11.** $\theta = 30°$.
12. $\theta = -60°$. **13.** $\theta = \pi/6$.
14. Show that if $r = 0$, a unique point is located independent of the value of θ.
15. Two sides and the included angle are determined in the triangle $(0, 0)$, $(4, \pi/2)$, $(8, \pi/6)$. The distance between the latter two points may be found using the law of cosines. Locate the points and estimate the distance. Use the law of cosines to compute it.
16. Show that the distance between the points (r_1, θ_1) and (r_2, θ_2) is

$$d = \sqrt{r_1^2 + r_2^2 - 2r_1r_2 \cos (\theta_1 - \theta_2)}.$$

17. Apply the formula of Problem 16 to obtain the polar equation of the locus of a point (r, θ) which is always at a distance of 5 units from the point $(2, \pi/3)$. Name the locus.

18. Find the distance between the points $(3, \pi/2)$ and $(5, \pi/6)$.

19. Find the distance between $(3, -\pi/6)$ and $(7, \pi/3)$.

20. Find the area of the triangle of Problem 15.

*21. Show that the area of a triangle having vertices $(0, 0)$, (r_1, θ_1), (r_2, θ_2), is $\frac{1}{2}| r_1 r_2 \sin (\theta_1 - \theta_2) |$. Give an example demonstrating that the absolute value sign is needed. [HINT: Is $\sin (\theta_1 - \theta_2)$ equal to $\sin (\theta_2 - \theta_1)$?]

In Problems 22 to 25 find the area of the triangle formed by the origin and the two points given.

22. The points of Problem 18.   23. The points of Problem 19.

24. $(7, \pi/2)$, $(4, \pi/4)$.   25. $(3, -\pi/2)$, $(5, 0)$.

26. Sketch $r = 2\theta$, $0 \le \theta \le 3\pi$.

27. Sketch $r = 2\theta$, $-3\pi \le \theta \le 0$.

17–2. Lines and circles in polar coordinates. Certain loci have simple polar coordinate equations. For example, $\theta = k$, where k is a constant, is the polar equation of a line through the pole making an angle of k radians with the polar axis. Here r may take any positive, zero, or negative value while $\theta = k$ radians. The equation $r = a$ defines a circle with center at the pole and radius $| a |$, since θ may take any positive, zero, or negative value while $| r | = | a |$. The locus $0 \le r < | a |$ consists of all points inside a circle of radius $| a |$ with center at the pole.

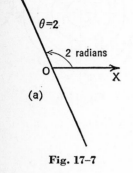

$\theta = 2$

2 radians

O

X

(a)

Fig. 17–7

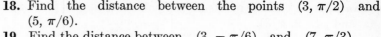

$r = 5$

O — 5 —

X

(b)

Fig. 17–8

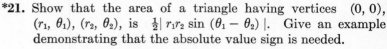

$0 \le r \le 2$

O — 2 —

X

(c)

Fig. 17–9

● **Example 1.** Sketch   (a) $\theta = 2$,   (b) $r = 5$,   (c) $0 \le r \le 2$. (See Figs. 17–7, 17–8, 17–9.)

The locus of equation

$$r \sin \theta = b \quad \text{or} \quad r = b \csc \theta, \tag{17.1}$$

is a line parallel to the polar axis and b units above (if $b < 0$, $| b |$ units below) the polar axis. This may be seen by considering Figure 17–10, where $P(r, \theta)$ may be any point on the line. Then $OP \sin \theta = OB = b$.

In a similar fashion, one may determine that

$$r \cos \theta = a \quad \text{or} \quad r = a \sec \theta, \tag{17.2}$$

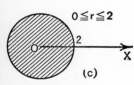

$r \sin \theta = b$

B $P(r, \theta)$

b r b

θ

O   X

Fig. 17–10

is the equation of a line perpendicular to the polar axis, crossing it a units from the pole, since $OP \cos \theta = OA = a$.

The locus of

$$r \cos (\theta - \omega) = p \quad \text{or} \quad r = p \sec (\theta - \omega), \tag{17.3}$$

for constant ω and p, may be obtained from $r \cos \theta' = p$ by noting that equivalent values of r are obtained in the two equa-

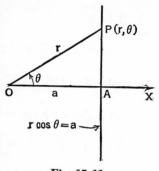

Fig. 17–11

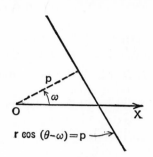

Fig. 17–12

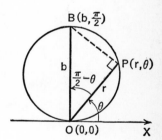

Fig. 17–13

tions if $\theta - \omega = \theta'$. Therefore, $r \cos (\theta - \omega) = p$ is the locus $r \cos \theta = p$ rotated through the angle ω about the pole.

This may be seen by considering Figure 17–13, since

$$OP \cos (\theta - \omega) = ON.$$

If $\omega = 0$ and $p = a$, (17.3) becomes (17.2). The reader should investigate how (17.1) may be obtained from (17.3), and how $\theta = k$ (a constant) may be obtained from (17.3).

The locus of

$$r = b \sin \theta, \quad \text{with } b \text{ constant}, \tag{17.4}$$

is a circle. The endpoints of a diameter, $(0, 0)$ and $(b, \pi/2)$, are obtained by letting $\theta = 0$ and $\pi/2$ respectively.

These statements should be checked by noting, in Figure 17–14, that angle BPO is a right angle if it is inscribed in a semi-circle,

$$OP = OB \cos (\pi/2 - \theta)$$
$$= OB \sin \theta,$$

or $\qquad r = b \sin \theta.$

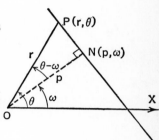

Fig. 17–14

In a similar fashion, it may be shown that

$$r = a \cos \theta \tag{17.5}$$

is the polar equation of a circle. The endpoints of a diameter are $(a, 0)$ and $(0, \pi/2)$.

The equation

$$r = a \cos (\theta - \omega), \tag{17.6}$$

for a and ω constant, is a circle. The endpoints of a diameter are $(0, \omega + \pi/2)$ and (a, ω). This may be verified by considering equations (17.5) and (17.6), analogous to the derivation of (17.3) for the line, or directly from Figure 17–15, noting that

$$OP = OA \cos (\theta - \omega), \quad \text{or} \quad r = a \cos (\theta - \omega).$$

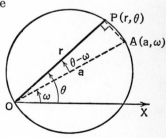

Fig. 17–15

PROBLEM SET 17-2

In Problems 1 to 8 write a polar coordinate equation of the indicated line. Sketch the locus.

1. Through the pole, and making an angle of $-120°$ with the polar axis.
2. Through the pole, and making an angle of $30°$ with the polar axis.
3. Through $(-4, 0)$, and perpendicular to the polar axis extended.
4. Through $(3, \pi)$, and perpendicular to the polar axis extended.
5. Through $(-3, 3\pi/2)$, and perpendicular to $\theta = \pi/2$.
6. Through $(4, 2\pi)$, and perpendicular to $\theta = \pi/2$.
7. Through $(-5, \pi/6)$, and perpendicular to $\theta = \pi/6$.
8. Through $(4, -\pi/3)$, and perpendicular to $\theta = \pi/2$.

In Problems 9 to 20 write a polar coordinate equation of the indicated circle and sketch the locus.

9. Center $(0, 0)$, radius 5.
10. Center $(0, 0)$, radius 10.
11. Center at the pole, radius zero.
12. Center at the pole, radius 3.
13. Center $(-4, 0)$, radius 4.
14. Center $(6, 0)$, radius 6.
15. Center $(-3, 3\pi/2)$, radius 3.
16. Center $(4, \pi/2)$, radius 4.
17. Center $(-5, \pi/6)$, radius 5.
18. Center $(41, 0)$, radius 41.
19. Center $(3, \pi)$, radius 3.
20. Center $(7, -\pi/2)$, radius 7.

In Problems 21 to 38, sketch and name the locus. If the locus is a circle find its center and radius.

21. $r = -6$.
22. $r = 5$.
23. $\theta = -4$.
24. $\theta = -\pi/3$.
25. $\tan \theta = -\frac{3}{4}$.
26. $\sin \theta = \frac{1}{2}$.
27. $r \cos \theta = -3$.
28. $r \sin \theta = 2$.
29. $r \sin \theta = 5$.
30. $r \cos \theta = -1$.
31. $r = -6 \csc \theta$.
32. $r = 10 \csc \theta$.
33. $r \cos (\theta + 45°) = -2$.
34. $r \sin (\theta + 30°) = 5$.
35. $r = -3 \cos \theta$.
36. $r = -5 \sin \theta$.
37. $r = 10 \sin \theta$.
38. $r = 6 \cos \theta$.

*39. Show that the equation $r = b \sin (\theta - \omega)$, for b and ω constant, represents a circle, and that the end points of a diameter are $(0, \omega)$ and $(b, \pi/2 + \omega)$.

40. Show that the equation of Problem 39 may be specialized to (17.4) or (17.5) by appropriate choice of constants.

41. Sketch $r = 8 \cos (\theta + 60°)$.

*42. Sketch $r (\cos \theta + \sqrt{3} \sin \theta) = 20$.

[HINT: Upon dividing by $\sqrt{1 + 3} = 2$, the given equation becomes

$$r \left(\frac{1}{2} \cos \theta + \frac{\sqrt{3}}{2} \sin \theta\right) = 10,$$

or

$$r \left(\cos \frac{\pi}{3} \cos \theta + \sin \frac{\pi}{3} \sin \theta\right) = 10.]$$

Thus the given equation is equivalent to

$$r \cos \left(\theta - \frac{\pi}{3}\right) = 10.$$

*43. The polar equation of a circle with center (r_1, θ_1) and diameter $|a|$ is

$$r^2 + r_1^2 - 2r_1 r \cos (\theta - \theta_1) = a^2/4.$$

Verify that each of equations (17.4), (17.5), (17.6), and the equation $r = a$ may be obtained by a suitable specialization of the constants r_1, θ_1, and a, in the above general equation.

17–3. The relationship between polar and rectangular coordinates.

Since some problems are handled more easily in one coordinate system than in another, it is desirable to be able to change from one to another. Let us superimpose the two systems with the origin and pole coinciding, letting the positive x-axis coincide with the polar axis as in Figure 17–16. From Figure 17–16 we see:

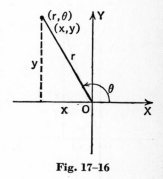

Fig. 17–16

$$\left.\begin{array}{l} x = r \cos \theta, \\ y = r \sin \theta, \\ x^2 + y^2 = r^2. \end{array}\right\} \quad (17.7)$$

$$\left.\begin{array}{l} r = \pm \sqrt{x^2 + y^2}, \\ \theta = \text{arc tan } (y/x). \end{array}\right\} \quad (17.8)$$

In (17.8) the correct sign for $r = \pm \sqrt{x^2 + y^2}$, and an appropriate value for the multiple-valued relation $\theta = \text{arc tan } (y/x)$ may be obtained from a sketch.

Equations (17.7) may be used to change from rectangular to polar coordinates.

● **Example 1.** Change $x^2 + y^2 - 6x + 4y = 0$ to polar coordinates.

Using (17.7), this becomes

$$r^2 - 6r \cos \theta + 4r \sin \theta = 0,$$

which is equivalent to the two equations

$$r = 0 \quad \text{and} \quad r - 6 \cos \theta + 4 \sin \theta = 0.$$

Since every point on the locus $r = 0$ (the locus consists of one point, the pole) is also on $r - 6 \cos \theta + 4 \sin \theta = 0$, the equation $x^2 + y^2 - 6x + 4y = 0$ and the polar equation

$$r - 6 \cos \theta + 4 \sin \theta = 0$$

have the same locus.

Equations (17.7) or (17.8) may be used to change from polar to rectangular coordinates.

● **Example 2.** Change $r(\cos \theta - \sin \theta) = 3$ to rectangular coordinates.

Using either (17.7) or (17.8), we obtain $x - y = 3$.

● **Example 3.** Obtain a set of polar coordinates for the point having rectangular coordinates (1, 3).

Using equations (17.8), one may take

$$r = \sqrt{9 + 1} = \sqrt{10} \cong 3.16, \quad \text{and} \quad \theta = \text{Arc tan } (3/1) \cong 71.5°.$$

A set of polar coordinates are $(\sqrt{10}, \text{Arc tan } 3)$, or approximately $(3.16, 71.5°)$.

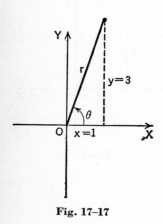

Fig. 17–17

● **Example 4.** Determine the rectangular coordinates of the point having polar coordinates $(3, 5\pi/3)$.

Using equations (17.7), we have

$$x = 3 \cos (5\pi/3) = 3(\tfrac{1}{2}) = 1.5$$
$$y = 3 \sin (5\pi/3) = 3 (- \sqrt{3}/2) \cong - 2.6.$$

The desired rectangular coordinates are $(3/2, - 3\sqrt{3}/2)$, or approximately $(1.5, - 2.6)$.

A rectangular equation is an equation connecting rectangular coordinates.

● **Example 5.** Find the polar equation of the locus having the rectangular equation

$$(x^2 + y^2)^2 = 18(x^2 - y^2).$$

Using (17.7) one obtains

$$(r^2)^2 = 18(r^2 \cos^2 \theta - r^2 \sin^2 \theta)$$
$$r^4 = 18r^2 (\cos^2 \theta - \sin^2 \theta)$$
$$r^4 = 18r^2 \cos 2\theta. \quad \text{(Why?)}$$

This is equivalent to the two equations:

$$r^2 = 0, \ r^2 = 18 \cos 2\theta.$$

The locus $r^2 = 0$, namely the pole, is included in

$$r^2 = 18 \cos 2\theta.$$

Consequently, the latter equation is the one desired.

- **Example 6.** Obtain the rectangular equation of the locus whose polar equation is $r = 5 \sec \theta$.

  Since $\sec \theta = 1/\cos \theta$, the given equation is equivalent to $r \cos \theta = 5$. Upon changing to rectangular coordinates, this becomes $x = 5$. Why? The locus is the line perpendicular to the polar axis at $(5, 0)$.

PROBLEM SET 17-3

In Problems 1 to 10, obtain the polar equation of the locus whose rectangular coordinate equation is given.

1. $x^2 + y^2 = 25$.
2. $x^2 + (y - 3)^2 = 9$.
3. $2x^2 + xy = 1$.
4. $xy = 10$.
5. $3xy = x^2 + y^2$.
6. $x^2 + y^2 + 4x + 6y = 0$.
7. $x^2 + y^2 = [\text{arc} \tan (y/x)]^2$.
8. $x^4 = x^2 + y^2$.
9. $\text{arc} \tan (x/y) = 2$.
10. $y = x \ \text{arc} \tan \sqrt{x^2 + y^2}$.

In Problems 11 to 22, obtain the rectangular coordinate equation of the locus whose polar equation is given.

11. $r \sin \theta = 5$.
12. $r \cos \theta = 2$.
13. $3r \sec \theta = 4$.
14. $2r \csc \theta = 7$.
15. $3r = \sin 2\theta$.
16. $4r (\sin \theta - \cos \theta) = 7$.
17. $2r = 7 \cos 2\theta$.
18. $3r - 4 \tan \theta = 0$.
19. $r(1 + \cos \theta) = 14$.
20. $r \cos \theta = \sin 2\theta$.
21. In $r = 4(1 + \cos \theta)$, express x and y each in terms of θ as a parameter. Thus,

$$x = r \cos \theta = 4(1 + \cos \theta) \cos \theta = 4(\cos \theta + \cos^2 \theta),$$
$$y = r \sin \theta = 4(1 + \cos \theta) \sin \theta = 4(\sin \theta + \sin \theta \cos \theta).$$

Now, eliminate the parameter θ.

22. Same as Problem 21, for $r = 3 \sin 2\theta$.

23. Find 8 or 10 points on the locus $r = 3 \sin 2\theta$ and plot them on polar coordinates. What do you think the locus looks like?

24. Same as Problem 23 for the locus $r = 1 + \cos \theta$.

25. Show, by changing from polar to rectangular coordinates, that equations (17.1), (17.2) represent the lines stated.

26. Show, by changing to rectangular coordinates, that equation (17.3) represents the line stated.

27. Show, by changing to rectangular coordinates, that equations (17.4) and (17.5) represent the circles stated.

28. Show, by changing to rectangular coordinates, that equation (17.6) and the equation $r = a$ represent the circles stated.

17–4. Sketching loci in polar coordinates. If the constants θ_1, θ_2, θ_3, $\cdots$ are the real roots of the equation $f(\theta) = 0$, then the locus of the polar coordinate equation $r = f(\theta)$ passes through the pole for $\theta = \theta_1, \theta_2, \theta_3, \cdots$. In general, the graph is tangent to the lines $\theta = \theta_1, \theta = \theta_2, \theta = \theta_3, \cdots$ at the pole. The graph of $r = f(\theta)$ often has a loop for θ between successive roots, say $\theta_2 \leqq \theta \leqq \theta_3$, for example. If the real roots θ_i of $f(\theta)$ are readily found, the corresponding tangent lines $\theta = \theta_i$ are an aid in sketching the locus. Values of θ for which r takes maximum and minimum values are also helpful. As we have seen in a previous section, values of r for $\theta = 0°, 90°, 180°, 270°$ are useful. We shall call these values of r the **polar intercepts.** It is unnecessary to apply *all* of these sketching aids to every problem. Indeed, we have already sketched many simple loci without doing so. Obtaining a sketch of a difficult polar curve, $r = f(\theta)$, is frequently simplified by the following steps:

(1) Find the real roots $\theta = \theta_1, \theta_2, \theta_3, \cdots$ of $f(\theta) = 0$.

(2) Draw the possible tangent lines $\theta = \theta_1, \theta = \theta_2, \theta = \theta_3, \cdots$.

(3) Plot at least one point (r, θ) for θ between each successive pair of roots. Values of θ which cause r to be a maximum or minimum and $\theta = 0°, 90°, 180°, 270°$ are desirable choices. Intervals of θ for which r is complex ("imaginary") should be noted. Such values of θ do not determine points on the locus.

(4) Use the above data to construct a smooth curve for θ between successive tangent lines $\theta = \theta_1, \theta = \theta_2, \cdots$. Two examples may clarify these remarks.

● *Example 1.* Sketch $r = 4 \sin 3\theta$.

(1) $4 \sin 3\theta = 0$ if $\sin 3\theta = 0$, that is, where:
$$3\theta = 0°, 180°, 360°, 540°, 720°, 900°,$$
$$\theta = 0°, 60°, 120°, 180°, 240°, 300°.$$

For these values of θ, $r = 0$.

(2) Draw the possible tangent lines:

$\theta = 0°$, $\theta = 60°$, $\theta = 120°$, $\theta = 180°$, $\theta = 240°$, $\theta = 300°$.

(3) Maximum values for r, namely, $r = 4$, occur when $\sin 3\theta = 1$, namely at:

$$3\theta = 90°, 450°, 810°,$$
$$\theta = 30°, 150°, 270°.$$

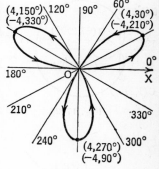

Fig. 17–18

Minimum values for r (that is, $r = -4$) occur when $\sin 3\theta = -1$, namely at:

$$3\theta = 270°, 630°, 990°,$$
$$\theta = 90°, 210°, 330°.$$

Combined with (1), this gives the following table of points:

θ	0°	30°	60°	90°	120°	150°	180°	210°	240°	270°	300°	330°
r	0	4	0	-4	0	4	0	-4	0	4	0	-4

(4) Plotting these data, we find that for $0° \leq \theta < 180°$ the entire locus is traced once, and that for $180° \leq \theta < 360°$ the locus is retraced. Note, for example, that the point of maximum r, $(4, 30°)$, is the same point as $(-4, 210°)$ which is a point of minimum r. This is not always true (see Example 2).

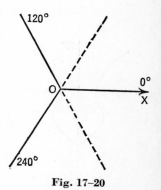

Fig. 17–19

The arrows and the tangent lines are not part of the locus but have been added to help the student. Again note that the entire curve is traced *twice* as θ changes from 0 to 2π and that a complete loop is traced as θ changes from 0 to $\pi/3$. Such facts will be needed when the integral calculus is studied.

● *Example 2.* Sketch the limaçon $r = 1 + 2 \cos \theta$.

The locus goes through the pole $(r = 0)$ when $1 + 2 \cos \theta = 0$, that is, when $\theta = 120°$ and $240°$. The curve is tangent to the lines $\theta = 120°$ and $\theta = 240°$ at the pole. We may use these tangent lines to help sketch $r = 1 + 2 \cos \theta$.

We expect a loop L_1 for θ in the intervals

$$240° \leq \theta \leq 360°, \quad 0° \leq \theta \leq 120°.$$

You may prefer to think of this as the interval $-120° \leq \theta \leq 120°$. A second loop L_2 is expected when θ is on the interval

$$120° \leq \theta \leq 240°.$$

Fig. 17–20

The maximum r value, $r = 3$, is obtained for $\cos \theta = 1$, when $\theta = 0°$ and $360°$. This locates $A(3, 0°)$ on L_1.

The minimum r value, $r = -1$, is obtained for $\cos \theta = -1$, when $\theta = 180°$. This locates $E(-1, 180°)$ on L_2.

The points $B(1, 90°)$ and $C(1, 270°)$ are on L_1. Other points on L_1 could be found by assigning values to θ on the interval $-120° \leq \theta \leq 120°$ and finding the corresponding r values.

The points $(1 - \sqrt{3}, 150°) \cong F(-.7, 150°)$ and
$$(1 - \sqrt{3}, 210°) \cong G(-.7, 210°)$$

are on L_2. Other points on L_2 may be obtained by assigning values to θ on the interval $120° \leq \theta \leq 240°$.

To complete loop L_1, join A to B to O using a smooth curve and in a similar way join O to C to A. The location of more points on L_1 may be helpful.

To complete loop L_2, join E to F to O using a smooth curve and in a similar way join O to G to E. Note that the small loop is obtained for $120° \leq \theta \leq 240°$ and the corresponding negative values of r.

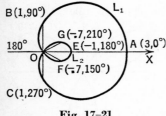

Fig. 17–21

17–5. Remarks on symmetry in polar loci. If for every point $P(r, \theta)$ on a polar locus the point $S(r, -\theta)$ is also on the locus, then the locus is symmetric with respect to the polar axis.

If $f(\theta) = f(-\theta)$, the locus $r = f(\theta)$ is symmetric with respect to the polar axis. [It *may* be symmetric with respect to the polar axis even if $f(\theta) \neq f(-\theta)$.] When using this test, it is helpful to remember that

$$\cos(-\theta) = \cos \theta \quad \text{and} \quad \sec(-\theta) = \sec \theta.$$

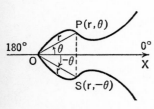

Fig. 17–22

● *Example 1.* Use the above test on the limaçon $r = 1 + 2 \cos \theta$. Here,

$$f(\theta) = 1 + 2 \cos \theta, \quad f(-\theta) = 1 + 2 \cos(-\theta) = 1 + 2 \cos \theta.$$

Since $f(\theta) = f(-\theta)$, the locus is symmetric with respect to the polar axis (see Fig. 17–21).

If for every point $P(r, \theta)$ on a polar curve, the point $Q(r, 180° - \theta)$ is also on the curve, then the curve is symmetric with respect to the vertical line $\theta = 90°$.

If $f(\theta) = f(180° - \theta)$, the locus $r = f(\theta)$ is symmetric with respect to the line $\theta = 90°$. [The locus **may** be sym-

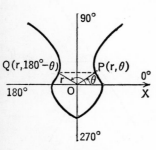

Fig. 17–23

metric with respect to $\theta = 90°$ even though
$f(\theta) \neq f(180° - \theta)$.] It is helpful to remember that

$$\sin (180° - \theta) = \sin \theta \quad \text{and} \quad \csc (180° - \theta) = \csc \theta$$

when using this test.

● *Example 2.* Use the above test on the circle $r = 4 \sin \theta$.
 Here,

$$f(\theta) = 4 \sin \theta, \quad f(180° - \theta) = 4 \sin (180° - \theta) = 4 \sin \theta.$$

Since $f(\theta) = f(180° - \theta)$, the circle is symmetric with respect to the line $\theta = 90°$.

The locus $r = 4 \sin \theta$ is a circle. The end points of a diameter are $(0, 0)$ and $(4, \pi/2)$.

Notice that $r = 0$ when $\theta = 0°, 180°$; and that $r = 4 \sin \theta$ is tangent to $\theta = 0°$ and $\theta = 180°$ (which represent the same line). The graph has one loop (a circle) on the interval $0° \leq \theta \leq 180°$. In the interval $180° \leq \theta \leq 360°$, the r values are negative and the original circle is retraced.

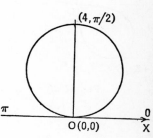

Fig. 17-24

If for every point $P(r, \theta)$ on the polar locus the point $R(-r, \theta)$ is also on the locus, then the curve is symmetric with respect to the pole.

● *Example 3.* Sketch the lemniscate $r^2 = 9 \sin 2\theta$.
 Upon substituting $(-r, \theta)$ for (r, θ), we obtain

$$(-r)^2 = 9 \sin 2\theta$$

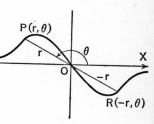

Fig. 17-25

which is equivalent to the original equation. The locus, therefore, is symmetric with respect to the *pole*. The other two suggested tests fail to demonstrate further symmetry (although it may exist). We examine values of θ for which $r = 0$, and thus determine polar tangents to the curve. Solutions of $\sin 2\theta = 0$ are

$$2\theta = 0, \pi, 2\pi, 3\pi, \cdots,$$
$$\theta = 0, \pi/2, \pi, 3\pi/2, \cdots.$$

Thus, the quadrant lines are possible tangent lines at the pole.

Furthermore, r^2 is a maximum, $r^2 = 9$, when $\sin 2\theta = 1$, that is, when

$$2\theta = \pi/2, 5\pi/2$$

or

$$\theta = \pi/4, 5\pi/4.$$

Observe that $r^2 < 0$ when $\sin 2\theta < 0$, which occurs when $\pi < 2\theta < 2\pi$ and $3\pi < 2\theta < 4\pi$. This implies

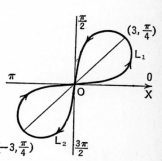

Fig. 17-26

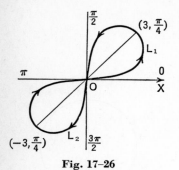

Fig. 17-26

that r is imaginary, and no real loops exist on the intervals $\pi/2 < \theta < \pi$ and $3\pi/2 < \theta < 2\pi$ (that is, for θ in quadrants II and IV). We expect a loop L_1 on the interval $0 \leq \theta \leq \pi/2$ and a second loop L_2 on the interval $\pi \leq \theta \leq 3\pi/2$. The point $(3, \pi/4)$ is on L_1. Other points on L_1 may be determined by computing $r = +3\sqrt{\sin 2\theta}$ for other values of θ on the interval $0 \leq \theta \leq \pi/2$. If one uses $r = -3\sqrt{\sin 2\theta}$ the loop L_2 will be traced, since the curve is symmetric with respect to the pole.

PROBLEM SET 17-5

Sketch, using the methods illustrated in Sections 17-4 and 17-5.

1. $r = 3 + 2 \cos \theta$.   **2.** $r = 4 \sin 2\theta$.

3. $r = 5 \cos 3\theta$.   **4.** $r^2 = 4 \sin 2\theta$.

5. $r^2 = \cos 2\theta$.   **6.** $3r = 2 \sin \theta \cos \theta$.

7. $r = 7(1 - \sin \theta)^{-1}$.   **8.** $r = 11 \cot \theta$.

9. $r = 4 \sin (\theta - \pi/3)$.   **10.** $r \cos (\theta - \pi/6) = 1$.

11. $r = 3 + 4 \cos \theta$.   **12.** $r = 4 + 3 \cos \theta$.

13. $0 \leq r \leq 1 - \sin \theta$.   **14.** $r(\sin \theta + 1) = 4$.

15. $r = 3 + \cos 3\theta$.   **16.** $r = \cos (\theta/4)$.

17. $r = 1 + \cos (\theta/3)$.   **18.** $r = 1 - \sin 5\theta$.

19. $r = 1 + \sin 4\theta$.   **20.** $r^2 \csc^2 2\theta \leq 25$.

21. Calvin Butterball dreams that he is the swashbuckling hero of a science fiction novel, and has just landed on Planet $3RX$. What essential features must he get across to the natives before he can tell them where he came from? (Consider the essentials of a polar coordinate system.)

17-6. Further remarks on polar coordinates. A study of the material in this section suggests that certain loci are more readily handled in polar coordinates, while other loci have simpler equations in rectangular coordinates. In a given problem the reader should try to discover and use the system best suited to his needs. For example, polar coordinates are useful in astronomy when studying the motion of a planet about the sun. The position of the sun is usually taken as the pole. The distance from the sun to the planet is the radius vector r, while θ is the angle between the radius vector and the radius vector of minimum length.

Similarly, in atomic physics and chemistry, polar coordinates are used when studying the motion of an electron about its nucleus. The equations of lines and circles should be recognized in each system, and the reader should be able to change from either system to the other. The eight-leaved rose $r = \cos 4\theta$ has a simple equation in polar coordinates, but its rectangular coordinate equation is complicated. The curve $(y - 5)^2 = x^3$ has a simple rectangular equation, but a complicated polar equation. The reader must determine which is more advantageous for his immediate use.

● **Example 1.** Sketch the cardioid $r = 1 + \cos \theta$.

The rectangular equation of this locus $(x^2 + y^2 = x \pm \sqrt{x^2 + y^2})$ is more complicated than the polar equation. Hence, we use the polar equation. The curve comes in to the pole when $1 + \cos \theta = 0$; that is, when $\theta = \pm \pi$. This suggests that there is only one loop on the interval $-\pi \leqq \theta \leqq \pi$. The maximum r value, $r = 2$, occurs when $\cos \theta = 1$, that is, at $\theta = 0$ or 2π. The minimum r value, $r = 0$, occurs when $\theta = \pi$. The point $A(2, 0)$ is on the loop. The points $B(1, \pi/2)$ and $C(1, 3\pi/2)$ are on the loop. Other points may be located by assigning θ values on the θ intervals. To sketch the curve, join A to B to O to C to A with a smooth curve. Notice that

$$r = 1 + \cos \theta = 1 + \cos (-\theta).$$

Consequently, the curve is symmetric with respect to the polar axis.

Since $(1 + \cos \theta)$ is periodic, further positive or negative values of θ will repeat points already on the locus. Loci of this type are called cardioids from their "heart-shaped" appearance.

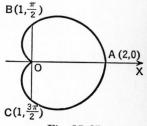

Fig. 17–27

● **Example 2.** Sketch the spiral $r = \frac{1}{2}\theta$.

Since $r = 0$ only if $\theta = 0$, the polar axis is the only tangent line at the pole. In general, as θ (in radians) increases,

θ (in radians)	-100	-10	-1	0	1	10	1000
r	-50	-5	$-\frac{1}{2}$	0	$\frac{1}{2}$	5	500

so does r. Negative values of θ give one branch of the spiral, and positive values of θ determine another branch.

Note that even though the tests for symmetry discussed in Section 17–5 do not disclose any symmetry, nevertheless the locus *is* symmetric with respect to the line $\theta = \pi/2$ (See Problem 30, Set 17–6).

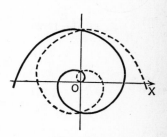

Fig. 17–28

PROBLEM SET 17-6

Sketch the locus. If the locus is a familiar geometric shape, state its name and give its location.

1. $\theta = 3$.   **2.** $r = 3$.   **3.** $r = 5 \sin \theta$.   **4.** $r \sin \theta = 5$.

5. $r \cos \theta = 8$.   **6.** $r = 8 \cos \theta$.   **7.** $0 \leq r \leq 7 \mid \sin 2\theta \mid$.

8. $r = 6 \sin \theta \cos \theta$.   ***9.** $r = 9 \sec^2 (\theta/2)$.   **10.** $r = 3\theta$.

11. $r = -2\theta$.   **12.** $r = \theta/5$.   **13.** $r\theta = 4$.

14. $r = \sin (\theta/3)$.   **15.** $r = 2 + \cos 3\theta$.   **16.** $r = 3 - \sin 2\theta$.

17. $r \csc 2\theta = 11$.   **18.** $r \sec 3\theta = 1$.   **19.** $0 \leq r \leq \mid \sin \theta \mid$.

20. $r = -5$.   **21.** $r = 1 + \sin \theta$.   **22.** $r = \mid \theta \mid$.   **23.** $\mid r \mid = \theta$.

24. $r = 2 + 3 \sin \theta$. [Note that for some θ, r is negative.]

25. $r^2 = 5 \sin 2\theta$. [Note if $\sin 2\theta < 0$, r is imaginary and does not appear on the graph.]

26. $r = 4 + \sin 3\theta$.   **27.** $r = 5 + \sin 2\theta$.

28. $r = 2^\theta$.   **29.** $r = \log \theta$.

30. Make up an additional test (not given in Section 17–5) for symmetry which will show Example 2 of this section to be symmetric with respect to the line $\theta = \pi/2$.

[HINT: Show that a locus is symmetric with respect to $\theta = \pi/2$ if for every point (r, θ) on the locus the point $(-r, -\theta)$ is also on the locus.]

31. Calvin Butterball became interested in the path traveled by a spider that he watched one day. In Calvin's classroom there was a clock with a minute hand 8 inches long. Calvin observed the spider walk along the minute hand, moving steadily from the center of the clock face to the tip of the minute hand in a 15-minute time interval. Obtain a polar coordinate equation for the locus of the spider.

32. An indicator has two hands of equal length, one of which rotates at twice the speed of the other. Use polar coordinates to find the locus of the midpoints of the line segments joining the ends of the moving hands.

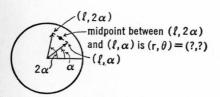

Fig. 17–29

midpoint between $(\ell, 2\alpha)$ and (ℓ, α) is $(r, \theta) = (?,?)$

*33. The base of a triangle is of length $(a\sqrt{2})$. Use polar coordinates to find the locus of the vertices of all such triangles, if the product of the lengths of the other two sides is $a^2/2$. Sketch the locus.

[HINT: Take the base along the polar axis with the pole at the center of the base. Answer: $r^2 = a^2 \cos 2\theta$ (Lemniscate).]

34. A chord through the end of a diameter of a circle is extended the length of the diameter. Use polar coordinates to find the locus of the end points of all such extended chords. Sketch the locus.

17–7. A shortcut in sketching polar loci. Time can be saved in sketching loci like

$$r = 5 \sin 3\theta, \quad r = 7 \cos 2\theta, \quad \text{and} \quad r = 4 + \sin \theta,$$

by first sketching the auxiliary graphs $y = 5 \sin 3\theta$, $y = 7 \cos 2\theta$, and $y = 4 + \sin \theta$ on a rectangular (θ, y) coordinate system. The ordinates (y values) of the auxiliary graph are the radii vectors (r values) for the corresponding θ in the polar sketch. Students of calculus and mechanics find this method of sketching polar loci especially helpful, since it permits them to determine special regions and points which are needed to solve their problems.

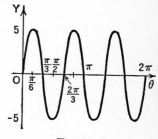

Fig. 17–30

● *Example 1.* Sketch $r = 5 \sin 3\theta$. The auxiliary equation $y = 5 \sin 3\theta$ is sketched in Figure 17–30.

The ordinates (y values) vary from 0 at $\theta = 0$ to 5 at $\theta = \pi/6$, then back to 0 at $\theta = \pi/3$, to -5 at $\theta = \pi/2$, etc. One may determine the values of θ for which $r = 0$ directly from the auxiliary graph, and sketch the polar tangents (here $\theta = 0$, $\theta = \pi/3$, $\theta = 2\pi/3$, etc.). The locus appears in Figure 17–31.

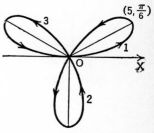

Fig. 17–31

Starting with $\theta = 0$ we trace the loop in the order indicated. This order is important in certain work in calculus. Since the equation is periodic, an extension of the range of θ will not add to the locus.

● *Example 2.* Sketch the lemniscate $r^2 = 9 \cos 2\theta$.

The auxiliary equation $y = 9 \cos 2\theta$ is sketched in Figure 17–32 using the methods of Section 15–4.

Since $r^2 = y$, r is complex if $y < 0$. Hence, no real r exists for $\pi/4 < \theta < 3\pi/4$ and $5\pi/4 < \theta < 7\pi/4$. For each $y > 0$ there will be two real values $r = \pm \sqrt{y}$. The locus is symmetric with respect to the pole. (Why?) Possible polar tangents are

$$\theta = \pi/4, \quad \theta = 3\pi/4, \quad \theta = 5\pi/4, \quad \theta = 7\pi/4.$$

The locus is sketched in Figure 17–33.

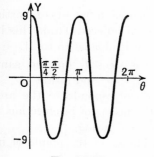

Fig. 17–32

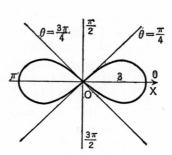

Fig. 17–33

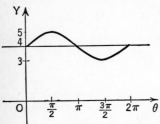

Fig. 17–34

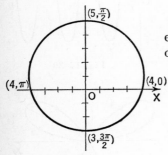

Fig. 17–35

• *Example 3.* Sketch the limaçon $r = 4 + \sin \theta$.

The auxiliary equation is $y = 4 + \sin \theta$ and has the sketch Figure 17–34.

The values of r are taken from the ordinates (y values) in the auxiliary rectangular sketch to obtain the locus shown in Figure 17–35. The locus is *not* a circle. (See Problem 24 of the next set.)

• *Example 4.* Sketch the spiral $r = 3\theta$. Even in so simple a sketch the auxiliary graph is helpful. The auxiliary graph $y = 3\theta$ is a line through the origin with slope 3.

Then $\theta \nearrow L^+$ implies $r = y \nearrow L^+$, and $\theta \searrow L^-$ implies $r = y \searrow L^-$.

This is very similar to Example 2, Section 17–6, Figure 17–28, except for the r scale. The locus $r = a\theta$ is known as a spiral of Archimedes.

PROBLEM SET 17-7

Use the method of Section 17–7 to help sketch the following loci.

1. $r = 4 \sin 3\theta$.   2. $0 \leqq r \leqq 7 \,|\cos 3\theta\,|$.   3. $r = 4 \cos 5\theta$.
4. $r = 3 \sin 2\theta$.   5. $r = 5 \cos 2\theta$.   6. $r = \cos 4\theta$.
7. $r^2 = 25 \cos 2\theta$. (Compare this with Problem 5.)
8. $r^2 \leqq 4 \,|\sin 2\theta\,|$.   9. $r = 3 + \sin \theta$.
10. $r = 3 - \sin \theta$.   11. $r = 3 + \cos \theta$.
12. $r = 3 - \cos \theta$. 13. $r = 4\theta$.   14. $r = -2\theta$.

In calculus the student will compute area, moments of inertia, and centers of gravity for certain physical objects. To do this he must be able to solve problems similar to Problems 15 to 21.

15. Sketch both loci $r = 2$ and $r = 4 \cos \theta$ on the same axes and shade the area (outside $r = 2$ and inside $r = 4 \cos \theta$). What domain of θ corresponds to the area shaded? Find the coordinates of the points of intersection.

16. Same for the area outside $r = 6$ and inside $r = 4(1 + \cos \theta)$. Find the coordinates of the points of intersection.

17. Same for area outside $r = 3 + \sin \theta$ and inside $r = 2 + 3 \sin \theta$.

18. Shade the area enclosed by the smaller loop of $r = 1 + 2 \cos \theta$. What domain of θ corresponds to the shaded area?

19. Same as 18 for $r = \sqrt{3} + 2 \sin \theta$.

20. Same as Problem 18 for $r = 10 \cos \theta/2$, for each of the smaller loops.

21. Shade the area enclosed by the lower loop of $r = \sin 3\theta$. What domain of θ corresponds to the shaded area?

22. Shade the area inside of both the circles $r = 6$ and $r = 8 \cos \theta$. Determine the domain of θ corresponding to the area shaded. You may wish to leave the result in terms of an inverse trigonometric function.

*23. Sketch the curve $r = \sin^3 (\theta/3)$. What domain of θ will generate the entire locus?

24. By changing the equation of Example 3 into rectangular coordinates, settle the question of whether or not the sketch is a circle.

25. Sketches of several polar coordinate equations have been made by M. R. E. Moritz and are reproduced here through the courtesy of *Scripta Mathematica*.

Can you identify the sketch that goes with each equation?

(a) $r = 1 + \cos \theta$.

(b) $r = \cos \theta$.

(c) $r = \cos (7\theta/2)$.

(d) $3r = 1 + 3 \cos \theta$.

(e) $r = \frac{1}{4} + \cos (7\theta/2)$.

(f) $r = 1 + \cos (7\theta/2)$.

(g) $r = \cos (9\theta/10)$.

(h) $r = \cos (9\theta/10) + \frac{1}{3}$.

(i) $r = 3 + \cos 7\theta$.

(j) $r = \cos (3\theta/10)$.

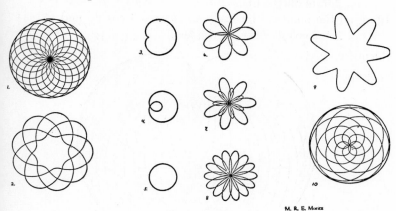

M. R. E. Moritz

Fig. 17–36

Additional material of this nature may be obtained from issues of the journal *Scripta Mathematica* at the library.

26. A tangent line drawn to a circle, whose center is the origin has its ends on the x- and y-axes. Use polar coordinates to find the locus of the midpoints of all such tangent lines. Sketch the locus.

27. Using polar coordinates find the locus of the midpoints of chords drawn from the end of a fixed diameter of a circle. Sketch the locus.

28. Each radius of a circle, whose center is at the origin, is extended a distance equal to the ordinate (y value) of the end point of that radius. Use polar coordinates to find the locus of the end points. Sketch the locus.

17–8. Self test.

Record your time.

1. Determine the coordinates of the points $P(r, \theta)$ on the locus $r = 4 + 2 \cos 3\theta$, such that the distance between P and the pole is (a) as large as possible; (b) as small as possible.

2. Shade the area which is outside of the curve $r = 1 + \cos \theta$ and inside $r \sec \theta = 3$. Label all points of intersection of the two curves.

In Problems 3 to 8 sketch the indicated loci.

3. $0 \leqq r \leqq 5 \,|\sin 2\theta\,|$.   **4.** $r = \theta/2$.

5. $r^2 = 25 \sin 2\theta$.   **6.** $r = 4 + \sin 2\theta$.

7. $r = 1/(1 - \sin \theta)$.   **8.** $(r - \sin \theta)(r + 5) = 0$.

9. (a) Determine a domain of values of θ for which the sketch of $r = 5 \sin 3\theta$ is traced just once. (b) Determine a domain of θ such that the corresponding loop of $r = 5 \sin 3\theta$ has its end points on the line $\theta = \pi/2$.

10. Find the points of intersection of $r = 4 \cos \theta$ and $r = 4 + 2 \cos \theta$. Sketch the loci.

Record your time.

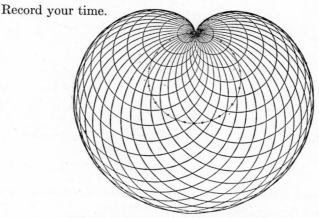

H. Barovalle. Courtesy *Scripta Mathematica*

18

18–1. Complex numbers. We have seen that the system of complex numbers $a + bi$ where a and b are real and i satisfies $i^2 = -1$ form a field. Consequently the "rules of ordinary algebra" are valid. In applying these rules it is necessary to keep in mind: Two complex numbers $a + bi$ and $c + di$ are equal $(a + bi = c + di)$ if, and only if, both $a = c$ and $b = d$. At this point we wish to establish an important geometric interpretation of the complex numbers. Just as Section 1–7 developed a correspondence between the real numbers and the points on a line, we now show a similar correspondence between the complex numbers and the points in a plane.

Let each complex number $x + yi$ correspond to the point (x, y) in the plane. To every point in the plane there corresponds a complex number, and to every complex number there corresponds a point. The real numbers, $x + 0i$, all lie on the x-axis, or **real axis.** The numbers $0 + yi$ all lie on the y-axis, or **i-axis** (in many applications called the **j-axis** — see Problem 30, Set 1–10). A plane in which the point (x, y) represents the complex number $x + yi$ is an Argand † plane, or complex plane.

Let (r, θ), $r \geqq 0$, be the polar coordinates ‡ of a point whose rectangular coordinates are (x, y). Then $r = \sqrt{x^2 + y^2}$ is the **magnitude, absolute value,** or **modulus** of the complex number $x + yi$, and any appropriate value of $\theta = \arctan(y/x)$ is the **angle** or **amplitude** of $x + yi$. The point (x, y), which corresponds to the complex number $x + yi$, is called the **point $x + yi$.**

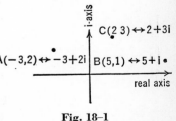

● **Example 1.** Locate the points $A(-3 + 2i)$ and $B(5 + i)$ in a complex plane, and draw lines from the origin to each point. Locate $C = A + B$ and show that C is the fourth vertex of a parallelogram, three of whose vertices are A, B, and the origin O.

Fig. 18–1

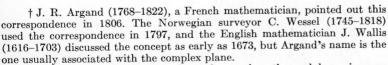

† J. R. Argand (1768–1822), a French mathematician, pointed out this correspondence in 1806. The Norwegian surveyor C. Wessel (1745–1818) used the correspondence in 1797, and the English mathematician J. Wallis (1616–1703) discussed the concept as early as 1673, but Argand's name is the one usually associated with the complex plane.

‡ In the polar representation of complex numbers the modulus, r, is never negative.

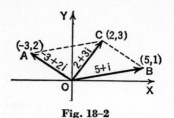

Fig. 18–2

Using the distance formula it may be verified that

$$AC = OB = \sqrt{26} \quad \text{and} \quad OA = BC = \sqrt{13},$$

hence $AOBC$ is a parallelogram.

A **plane vector** may be interpreted as a complex number. A vector joining the origin to the point (x, y) represents the complex number $x + yi$. The parallelogram law of addition, commonly used for vector addition, may be replaced by the addition of complex numbers.

Vectors are used extensively in mechanics and electronics.

The **complex product** † AB of two vectors A, B is the vector corresponding to the product of the two complex numbers A and B.

• *Example 2.* Form the complex product of $3 + 2i$ and $4 - i$.

$$(3 + 2i)(4 - i) = 12 + (8 - 3)i - 2i^2$$
$$= 12 + 5i - 2i^2$$
$$= 14 + 5i, \quad \text{since} \quad i^2 = -1.$$

PROBLEM SET 18–1

In Problems 1 and 2 form $A + B$ and plot A, B, and $A + B$ in the complex plane.

1. (a) $A(3 + 2i)$, $B(5 - 7i)$.
   (b) $A(3 - i)$, $B(4 + 2i)$.
2. (a) $A(3 + 2i)$, $B(3 + 2i)$.
   (b) $A(-4 + 8i)$, $B(5 - 3i)$.

† The complex product is not the same as either the vector dot product or the cross product of two vectors.

3. Find $z = x + iy$, where x and y are real numbers, such that

$$3 + 2i + z = 5 - 7i.$$

4. Find $z = x + iy$, where x and y are real, and

$$-4 + 8i + 2z = 5 - 3i.$$

In Problems 5 to 10, find a complex number z in the form $a + bi$ such that the given equation is satisfied.

5. $(3 - 2i)z = 5 + 10i.$

$$\left[\text{HINT:} \quad z = \frac{5 + 10i}{3 - 2i} = \frac{(5 + 10i)(3 + 2i)}{(3 - 2i)(3 + 2i)} = ?\right]$$

6. $2 - i + 3z = 17.$ **7.** $2z - 5iz + 6 = 4i - 2.$

8. $8i - 3z + 2 = (4i - 1)z.$ **9.** $16iz - 4z + 8 = 2i/(3 + i).$

10. $(1 + 3i)/(2i + 5) - 4z + 12iz = 10.$

11. Solve the equation $x^2 + xi = y^2 - 2yi + 4i$, where x and y are real numbers.

[HINT: Upon equating the real portions, one obtains $x^2 = y^2$. Upon equating the coefficients of i, one obtains $x = -2y + 4$. These equations may be solved simultaneously for x and y.]

12. Find the modulus (absolute value) r and angle θ of the number $7 - 2i$.

13. Since every real number a is a complex number $a + 0 \cdot i$, the definition of absolute value of a real number given in Section 1–6 must be a special case of the definition of absolute value of a complex number given in this section, if these definitions are to be consistent. Show that this is the case.

14. Solve the equation $3x + 4yi = 17x - 32i - 11y + 37$, where x and y are real numbers.

[HINT: Use a method similar to that discussed in Problem 11.]

15. Solve $x^2 + xy + xyi - 3 + 2i + y^2 = 0$, where x and y are real.

16. Find all values of $3/z$, where $z = x + iy$, and $x^2 + iy - 3y^2 + 2 = 16 + y - i$, and x and y are real.

If $u = -\frac{1}{2} + i\sqrt{3}/2$ and $v = -\frac{1}{2} - i\sqrt{3}/2$, show that the relations of Problems 17 to 21 hold.

17. $u^2 = v.$

18. $v^2 = u.$ (Compare Problems 17 and 18. Is this possible?)

19. $u^3 = 1.$ **20.** $v^3 = 1.$

21. $uv = 1.$

[HINT: Use the results of Problems 17 and 19 for a short method.]

22. Obtain the three solutions of $z^3 - 1 = 0$. Does this help explain the peculiar properties noted in Problems 17 to 21?

23. Find i^n for $n = 1, 2, 3, 4, \cdots, 15$. Also find i^{37} and i^{293}.

24. Find i^n for $n = 171, 186, 192, 211, 861$, and 1020.

25. If the integer N is divided by 4, the numbers $0, 1, 2, 3$ are the only possible remainders. Show that, if the remainder is R, then $i^N = i^R$.

18–2. Complex vectors in polar form. We now examine the vector form of a complex number more closely. If (x, y) and (r, θ), $r \geq 0$, each represent the coordinates of the point $x + iy$, then $x = r \cos \theta$, $y = r \sin \theta$ and

$$x + iy = r[\cos \theta + i \sin \theta].$$

In the polar form, $r[\cos \theta + i \sin \theta]$, of a vector the magnitude, r, and angle, θ, are emphasized. In the rectangular form, $x + iy$, the components, x and y, are emphasized.

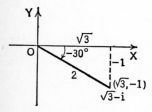

Fig. 18–3

● **Example 1.** Locate the point $\sqrt{3} - i$ in the complex plane and give its polar form. Thus,

$$r^2 = (\sqrt{3})^2 + (-1)^2 = 4.$$
$$r = +2 \quad \text{since} \quad r \geq 0,$$

and

$$\theta = \text{arc tan } (-1/\sqrt{3}) = -30°, 330°, \cdots, 330° \pm n \cdot 360°, \cdots.$$

We select

$$\theta = -30° \quad \text{as an appropriate value of } \theta.$$

Then,

$$\sqrt{3} - i = 2[\cos (-30°) + i \sin (-30°)].$$

It may be verified that the right member is equal to the left by substituting the values of $\sin (-30°)$ and $\cos (-30°)$ into the right member.

● **Example 2.** A vector V has magnitude 6 and angle 120°. Determine the polar and the rectangular forms of the vector. Since $r = 6$ and $\theta = 120°$, the polar form of V is

$$6[\cos 120° + i \sin 120°].$$

The rectangular form is obtained by substituting the values of $\cos 120°$ and $\sin 120°$ into the polar form.

$$6[\cos 120° + i \sin 120°] = 6[-\tfrac{1}{2} + i\sqrt{3}/2] = -3 + 3\sqrt{3}i.$$

It is convenient to use the mnemonic abbreviation $r \text{ cis } \theta$ to represent $r(\cos \theta + i \sin \theta)$. In this notation the polar forms of Examples 1 and 2 become:

$$2[\cos (-30°) + i \sin (-30°)] = 2 \text{ cis } (-30°)$$
$$6[\cos 120° + i \sin 120°] = 6 \text{ cis } 120°.$$

PROBLEM SET 18–2

In Problems 1 to 5, plot vectors having the indicated magnitude, r, and angle, θ, in the complex plane. Also obtain the $a + bi$ form of the given vector. In each case let the direction $\theta = 0$ be the positive x direction. Write each vector in polar and in rectangular form.

1. $r = 10$, $\quad \theta = 60°$. **2.** $r = 4$, $\quad \theta = 120°$.
3. $r = 6$, $\quad \theta = -135°$. **4.** $r = 12$, $\quad \theta = 330°$.
5. $r = 2$, $\quad \theta = 86°$.

In Problems 6 to 10 plot the indicated rectangular points in the complex plane and obtain the corresponding polar form.

6. $\sqrt{3} - i$. **7.** $1 - i$. **8.** $-4 + 4i\sqrt{3}$.
9. $-7 - 7i$. **10.** $1/(-1 - i\sqrt{3})$.

In Problems 11 to 20 find the rectangular, $a + bi$, form of the given number. Use tables only when necessary.

11. $7(\cos 0° + i \sin 0°)$. **12.** $4[\cos (2\pi/3) + i \sin (2\pi/3)]$.
13. $4(\cos \pi + i \sin \pi)$. **14.** $10[\cos (\pi/2) + i \sin (\pi/2)]$.
15. $20[\cos (7\pi/6) + i \sin (7\pi/6)]$.
16. $6[\cos (-270°) + i \sin (-270°)]$.
17. $4/(\cos 210° + i \sin 210°)$. **18.** $8(\cos 271° + i \sin 271°)$.
19. $10[\cos (-32°) + i \sin (-32°)]$.
20. $100[\cos 423° + i \sin 423°]$.

In Problems 21 to 25, if possible, determine a value of θ, $0° \leq \theta < 360°$, such that the stated equation is satisfied. If no such θ exists, state why.

21. $2(\cos \theta + i \sin \theta) = -\sqrt{3} - i$.
22. $4(\cos \theta + i \sin \theta) = 2 - 2i\sqrt{3}$.
23. $8(\cos \theta + i \sin \theta) = -2 + 2i$.
24. $(\cos \theta + i \sin \theta) = 0.3987 + 0.9171i$.
25. $4(\cos \theta + i \sin \theta) = 2 - i$.

18–3. Multiplication and division in polar form. The product of

$$X = r[\cos \alpha + i \sin \alpha] = r \text{ cis } \alpha$$

and

$$Y = s[\cos \beta + i \sin \beta] = s \text{ cis } \beta$$

is

$$\begin{aligned} XY &= r[\cos \alpha + i \sin \alpha]s[\cos \beta + i \sin \beta] \\ &= rs[\cos \alpha \cos \beta + i^2 \sin \alpha \sin \beta + i \sin \alpha \cos \beta + i \cos \alpha \sin \beta] \\ &= rs[(\cos \alpha \cos \beta - \sin \alpha \sin \beta) + i(\sin \alpha \cos \beta + \cos \alpha \sin \beta)] \\ &= rs[\cos (\alpha + \beta) + i \sin (\alpha + \beta)], \end{aligned}$$

or

$$[r \text{ cis } \alpha][s \text{ cis } \beta] = rs \text{ cis } (\alpha + \beta).$$

The **modulus** of the product of two complex numbers is the **product** of the moduli of the two complex numbers. The **angle** of the product of two complex numbers is the **sum** of the angles of the two complex numbers.

● *Example 1.* Find the product AB where

$$A = 5[\cos 210° + i \sin 210°] = 5 \text{ cis } 210°.$$
$$B = 4[\cos 60° + i \sin 60°] = 4 \text{ cis } 60°.$$

Then,

$$AB = 5 \text{ cis } 210° \cdot 4 \text{ cis } 60°$$
$$= 20 \text{ cis } 270°.$$

If the rectangular form is desired

$$AB = 20[\cos 270° + i \sin 270°]$$
$$= 20[0 + i(-1)]$$
$$= 0 - 20i.$$

● *Example 2.* Determine the product MN where

$$M = 4[\cos 10° + i \sin 10°],$$

and

$$N = 7[\cos 40° + i \sin 40°].$$

Then,

$$MN = 4 \text{ cis } 10° \cdot 7 \text{ cis } 40° = 28 \text{ cis } 50°.$$

Tables may be used to obtain the rectangular form.

● *Example 3.* Find $i(x + iy)$.

Since, $i = 1 \text{ cis } 90°$, and $x + iy = r \text{ cis } \theta$ we obtain

$$i(x + iy) = 1 \text{ cis } 90° \cdot r \text{ cis } \theta$$
$$= r \text{ cis } (\theta + 90°).$$

This shows that multiplication of $x + yi$ by i induces no change in modulus, but increases the angle by 90°.

Upon multiplying the numerator and denominator of

$$\frac{X}{Y} = \frac{r \text{ cis } \alpha}{s \text{ cis } \beta}$$

by $\text{cis } (-\beta) = \cos (-\beta) + i \sin (-\beta) = \cos \beta - i \sin \beta$, it may be verified that

$$\frac{X}{Y} = \frac{r \text{ cis } \alpha}{s \text{ cis } \beta} \cdot \frac{\text{cis } (-\beta)}{\text{cis } (-\beta)}$$
$$= \frac{r \text{ cis } (\alpha - \beta)}{s \text{ cis } 0} = \frac{r}{s} \text{ cis } (\alpha - \beta).$$

Thus

$$\frac{r \text{ cis } \alpha}{s \text{ cis } \beta} = \frac{r}{s} \text{ cis } (\alpha - \beta).$$

The **modulus** of the quotient of two complex numbers is the **quotient** of their moduli, while the **angle** of the quotient is the **difference** of the angles of the two complex numbers.

● **Example 4.** Determine X/Y where $X = 24$ cis $113°$ and $Y = 8$ cis $53°$.

$$\frac{X}{Y} = \frac{24 \text{ cis } 113°}{8 \text{ cis } 53°}$$
$$= (\tfrac{24}{8}) \text{ cis } (113° - 53°) = 3 \text{ cis } 60°.$$

In rectangular form this becomes

$$\frac{X}{Y} = 3[\cos 60° + i \sin 60°]$$
$$= 3[\tfrac{1}{2} + i\sqrt{3}/2] = \tfrac{3}{2} + 3i\sqrt{3}/2.$$

PROBLEM SET 18–3

Determine XY, X/Y, and Y/X in Problems 1 to 10, and reduce the result to rectangular form, using tables when needed.

1. $X = 3[\cos 45° + i \sin 45°]$, $Y = 5[\cos 15° + i \sin 15°]$.
2. $X = 4[\cos 25° + i \sin 25°]$, $Y = 9[\cos 20° + i \sin 20°]$.
3. $X = 2$ cis $20°$, $Y = 5$ cis $50°$.
4. $X = 10$ cis $(-27°)$, $Y = 12$ cis $27°$.
5. $X = 10$ cis $0°$, $Y = 50$ cis $30°$.
6. $X = 3$ cis $43°$, $Y = 18$ cis $17°$.
7. $X = 16$ cis $116°$, $Y =$ cis $176°$.
8. $X =$ cis $118°$, $Y = 2$ cis $73°$.
9. $X = 10$ cis $75°$, $Y = 4$ cis $165°$.
10. $X = 7$ cis $25°$, $Y =$ cis $20°$.
11. Verify that $(r \text{ cis } \alpha)/(s \text{ cis } \beta) = (r/s) \text{ cis } (\alpha - \beta)$, using trigonometric identities.
12. Show that multiplication of a vector $V = r$ cis θ by i makes no change in the absolute value of the vector, but that the vector Vi is perpendicular to the vector V.

18–4. De Moivre's theorem. The formula for the multiplication of complex numbers in polar form gives

$$[r \text{ cis } \theta][r \text{ cis } \theta] = r^2 \text{ cis } 2\theta.$$

Multiplication of this result by r cis θ yields

$$[r \text{ cis } \theta]^3 = [r \text{ cis } \theta][r^2 \text{ cis } 2\theta]$$
$$= r^3 \text{ cis } 3\theta.$$

Further multiplication leads to **De Moivre's theorem** †

$$[r \text{ cis } \theta]^n = r^n \text{ cis } n\theta.$$

De Moivre's theorem is also valid if n is a negative integer, and if n is a rational fraction.

For a negative integer $-n < 0$, we have

$$[\text{cis } \theta]^{-n} = \frac{1}{[\text{cis } \theta]^n} = \frac{1}{\text{cis } n\theta} = \frac{1}{\text{cis } n\theta} \cdot \frac{\text{cis } (-n\theta)}{\text{cis } (-n\theta)}$$

$$= \frac{\text{cis } (-n\theta)}{\text{cis } 0} = \text{cis } (-n\theta).$$

Thus, using De Moivre's theorem for the positive integer $|n|$ we have shown that it is valid for the negative integer n. The reader is asked to show in Problem 20 that De Moivre's theorem is valid when $n = 0$. Fractional exponents are studied in Section 18–5.

PROBLEM SET 18–4

In Problems 1 to 19, expand by De Moivre's theorem and, if possible, expand directly. Compare the work involved in the two methods.

1. $(1 + i)^6$.   **2.** $(\sqrt{3}/2 + i/2)^9$.   **3.** $(1 - i\sqrt{3})^4$.

4. $(-1 + i)^6$.   **5.** $(-1 - i\sqrt{3})^5$.   **6.** $(-2 + 2i)^{-3}$

7. $(7 - 7\sqrt{3}i)^{-3}$.   **8.** $(\sqrt{3}/2 - i/2)^{-5}$.   **9.** $(4 - 4i)^{-1}$.

10. $32(1 + i)^{-6}$.   **11.** $(\frac{1}{2} - i/2)^4/(\sqrt{3} + i)^6$.

12. $(-1 + i)^5/(4 - 4i)$.   **13.** $7(\text{cis } 51°)^{10} \times 4(\text{cis } 6°)^5$.

14. $4/(2 - 2i)^2$.   **15.** $(3 - i)^6$.   Use tables.

16. $(2 + 6i)^{-4}$.   Use tables.   **17.** $(\frac{1}{4})(\text{cis } 36°)^{-5}$.

18. $1/(4 \text{ cis } 36°)^5$.   Compare with Problem 17.

19. $256/(4 \text{ cis } 36°)^5$.   Is this equal to the expression given in Problem 17? In 18?

20. Show that De Moivre's theorem holds if $n = 0$.

21. Use $(\cos \theta + i \sin \theta)^2 = \cos 2\theta + i \sin 2\theta$, to find identities for $\cos 2\theta$ and $\sin 2\theta$.

22. Use $(\cos \theta + i \sin \theta)^3 = \cos 3\theta + i \sin 3\theta$ to find identities for $\cos 3\theta$ and $\sin 3\theta$.

† The French mathematician, Abraham De Moivre (1667–1754), fled from France to England when the Edict of Nantes was revoked. He settled in London, earning his living by private teaching and by solving mathematical puzzles for frequenters of the coffee houses of that era. De Moivre's principal fame is due to his work in the mathematical treatment of games of chance. It is likely that his coffee house associates spurred on his investigations in this field.

23. Use $(\cos \theta + i \sin \theta)^4 = \cos 4\theta + i \sin 4\theta$ to find identities for $\cos 4\theta$ and $\sin 4\theta$.

24. Prove De Moivre's theorem by mathematical induction: $(\cos \theta + i \sin \theta)^n = \cos n\theta + i \sin n\theta$, where n is a positive integer.

18–5. Roots of a complex number. De Moivre's theorem may be used to obtain solutions, z, of the equation,

$$z^n = a + bi = r \operatorname{cis} \theta, \qquad (18.1)$$

where n is a positive integer. If $z = m \operatorname{cis} \alpha$ is a solution of (18.1), then,

$$z^n = [m \operatorname{cis} \alpha]^n = m^n \operatorname{cis} n\alpha = r \operatorname{cis} \theta.$$

This will be satisfied if,

$$m = \sqrt[n]{r}, \quad \text{and} \quad n\alpha = \theta + 2k\pi,$$

where k is an integer. Note that the n different angles,

$$\alpha = (\theta/n) + (2k\pi/n),$$

where $k = 0, 1, 2, \cdots, n - 1$, determine n distinct roots each satisfying (18.1). Thus, the n solutions of

$$z^n = r \operatorname{cis} \theta \qquad (18.1)$$

are given by

$$z = \sqrt[n]{r} \operatorname{cis} \left(\frac{\theta}{n} + \frac{2k\pi}{n} \right), \qquad (18.2)$$

where $k = 0, 1, 2, \cdots, n - 1$.

Attention is called to the fact that **if $k \geq n$, the resulting values of α are coterminal with angles obtained for** $k = 0, 1, 2, \cdots, n - 1$. We have shown that every nonzero complex number (which includes the real numbers) has two square roots, three cube roots, and n nth roots, which may be obtained by writing the complex number in polar form and applying (18.2).

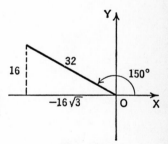

Fig. 18–4

● **Example 1.** Determine the five fifth roots of $-16\sqrt{3} + 16i$.

$$z^5 = -16\sqrt{3} + 16i = 32 \operatorname{cis} 150°. \text{ (See Fig. 18–4.)}$$

Then,

$$z = \sqrt[5]{32} \operatorname{cis} [(150/5) + (k360/5)]°.$$
$$k = 0, 1, 2, 3, 4.$$

$$z = \begin{cases} 2(\cos 30° + i \sin 30°) \\ 2(\cos 102° + i \sin 102°) \\ 2(\cos 174° + i \sin 174°) \\ 2(\cos 246° + i \sin 246°) \\ 2(\cos 318° + i \sin 318°). \end{cases}$$

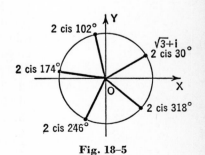

Fig. 18–5

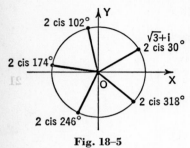

Fig. 18–5

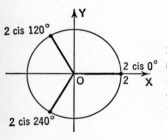

Fig. 18–6

The first of these roots is $\sqrt{3}+i$. The other four roots may be approximated in the form $a+bi$ by using tables to determine $\cos 102°$, $\sin 102°$, etc. If the answer is desired in the polar form, which indicates direction and magnitude rather than in the $(a+bi)$ form, which indicates components, this last step can be omitted.

● **Example 2.** Find the three cube roots of 8.

$$z^3 = 8 + 0i = 8(\cos 0° + i \sin 0°) = 8 \text{ cis } 0°.$$
$$z = \sqrt[3]{8} \text{ cis } [0/3 + k \cdot 360/3]°, \quad \text{for} \quad k = 0, 1, 2.$$
$$= 2[\text{cis } k \ 120°], \quad \text{for} \quad k = 0, 1, 2.$$
$$= \begin{cases} 2(\cos 0° + i \sin 0°) = 2 + 0i \\ 2(\cos 120° + i \sin 120°) = -1 + i\sqrt{3} \\ 2(\cos 240° + i \sin 240°) = -1 - i\sqrt{3}. \end{cases}$$

Each of the nth roots of a complex number has the same modulus (r value). In the complex plane the roots are equally spaced on a circle with radius r, with center at the origin. The angles of two adjacent roots differ by $360°/n$. The sum of the n nth roots is zero. This forms a convenient partial check when the rectangular form is used.

Using this partial check on Example 2, we find

$$\begin{array}{r} 2 + 0i \\ -1 + i\sqrt{3} \\ -1 - i\sqrt{3} \\ \hline 0 + 0i \end{array}$$

PROBLEM SET 18–5

In Problems 1 to 15 find the indicated roots, or solve the given equation. When possible to do so without consulting tables, obtain the answers in the form $a+bi$. Plot the roots and the given number for each problem. Use a protractor if needed.

1. The five fifth roots of $-32 + 0i$.

2. The three cube roots of -1. **3.** The sixth roots of 1.

4. The square roots of $-i$.

5. The fifth roots of $16 - 16\sqrt{3}i$.

6. The square roots of $8 + 8\sqrt{3}i$.

7. The tenth roots of $1 - i\sqrt{3}$.

8. The seventh roots of 1.   **9.** The cube roots of 8 cis 135°.

10. The fourth roots of $-i$.   **11.** Solve: $z^5 + 32 = 0$.

12. Solve: $z^4 - 81 = 0$.   **13.** Solve: $z^2 - 18 = 18\sqrt{3}i$.

14. Solve: $z^4 = -8 - 8\sqrt{3}i$.   **15.** Solve: $z^{10} + 1 = 0$.

16. Factor $z^3 + 27$ into *linear* factors.

17. Factor $z^3 - 64$ into *linear* factors.

18–6. Complex exponents. In later mathematical work, the expression $re^{i\theta}$ is used instead of r cis θ. In $re^{i\theta}$, the complex exponent obeys the usual laws of exponents. In Problem 1, you are asked to show that the r and θ of r cis θ and of $re^{i\theta}$ follow the same laws of multiplication and division. Problem 2 shows that the two expressions have the same values at $r = r$, $\theta = 0$) and at $(r = 0$, $\theta = \theta)$. Combining the results of Problems 1 and 2 we see that

$$re^{i\theta} = r(\cos \theta + i \sin \theta)$$

is a reasonable definition † for $re^{i\theta}$.

On solving

$$e^{i\theta} = \cos \theta + i \sin \theta$$
$$e^{-i\theta} = \cos \theta - i \sin \theta,‡$$

one obtains two identities

$$\cos \theta = \frac{e^{i\theta} + e^{-i\theta}}{2}, \qquad \sin \theta = \frac{e^{i\theta} - e^{-i\theta}}{2i},$$

which are useful in electrical theory and other mathematical applications.

The reader will notice a similarity between these identities and the definitions of the hyperbolic functions given in Section 9–5.

PROBLEM SET 18–6

1. Show that the laws of multiplication and of division for $re^{i\theta}$ and for r cis θ are identical.

2. Show the two expressions in Problem 1 are identical for $[r = r$, $\theta = 0]$ and for $[r = 0$, $\theta = \theta]$.

† Present-day physics, engineering, electrical theory, and atomic study use this notation.

‡ This equation is obtained by substituting $-\theta$ for θ in the first equation and recalling that $\cos(-\theta) = \cos \theta$, $\sin(-\theta) = -\sin \theta$.

3. Show that $e^{\pi i} = -1$. This relation connects four his-
torically interesting numbers π, -1, e, and i.

4 to 8. Rework Problems 4 to 8 of Set 18–3, using the exponential notation.

9. Show that $\cosh x = \cos ix$.

10. Show that $\sinh x = -i \sin ix$.

11. Prove the identity of Example 3, Section 16–2, by substitutin
the complex exponent definition for the trigonometric func
tions and simplifying.

*12. Use the $re^{i\theta}$ notation to show that De Moivre's theorem
would be obvious *if* complex exponents are assumed to obe
the same rules as real exponents.

*13. Show that for real exponents x, $e^{(x+2\pi)} \neq e^x$, while for com
plex exponents $e^{i(\theta+2\pi)} = e^{i\theta}$.

18–7. Self test.

Record your time.

1. Find

$2(\cos 117° + i \sin 117°)5(\cos 211° + i \sin 211°)/20(\cos 28° + i \sin 28°$

2. Find the fourth roots of $648 - 648\sqrt{3}i$.

3. Solve $z^5 + 16\sqrt{3}i = 16$.

4. Prove, using the identities of trigonometry, that

$$\frac{r(\cos \alpha + i \sin \alpha)}{s(\cos \beta + i \sin \beta)} = (r/s)[\cos (\alpha - \beta) + i \sin (\alpha - \beta)].$$

5. Express in the form $a + bi$: $(13 - 5i)/(\sqrt{3}/2 + i/2)^9$.

6. Find the sum and the product of the six sixth roots of 1.

7. Find the identities for $\cos 3\theta$ and $\sin 3\theta$ from
$(\cos \theta + i \sin \theta)^3$.

8. Show that there is a single constant K and a positive integer N
satisfying $(\cos \pi r + i \sin \pi r)^{N_r} = K$ where r is any rationa
number and N_r depends on r. If possible determine the actua
value of this constant K.

Record your time.

*18–8. Series relations. The student should note that e
defined formally by $e^{i\theta} = (\cos \theta + i \sin \theta)$ is in agreement wit
the results of this chapter. It is also a consequence of the forma
results on infinite series discussed in Section 11–4.

The series definition of e^x is

$$e^x = 1 + x + \frac{x^2}{2!} + \frac{x^3}{3!} + \frac{x^4}{4!} + \cdots.$$

It is possible to define $\sin x$ and $\cos x$ in terms of series. Earlier we gave two definitions for these functions in Sections 14–4 and 15–1. In advanced mathematical work, infinite series expressions for functions are extremely useful when they are available. The trigonometric tables are computed from series.

The appropriate definitions are

$$\sin x = x - \frac{x^3}{3!} + \frac{x^5}{5!} - \frac{x^7}{7!} + \cdots$$

$$\cos x = 1 - \frac{x^2}{2!} + \frac{x^4}{4!} - \frac{x^6}{6!} + \cdots$$

Since

$$e^{i\theta} = 1 + i\theta + \frac{(i\theta)^2}{2!} + \frac{(i\theta)^3}{3!} + \frac{(i\theta)^4}{4!} + \frac{(i\theta)^5}{5!} + \frac{(i\theta)^6}{6!} + \frac{(i\theta)^7}{7!} + \cdots$$

$$= 1 + i\theta - \frac{\theta^2}{2!} - \frac{i\theta^3}{3!} + \frac{\theta^4}{4!} + \frac{i\theta^5}{5!} - \frac{\theta^6}{6!} - \frac{i\theta^7}{7!} + \cdots$$

$$= \left[1 - \frac{\theta^2}{2!} + \frac{\theta^4}{4!} - \frac{\theta^6}{6!} + \cdots \right] + i \left[\theta - \frac{\theta^3}{3!} + \frac{\theta^5}{5!} - \frac{\theta^7}{7!} + \cdots \right]$$

it follows that $e^{i\theta} = \cos \theta + i \sin \theta$.

The student is not yet ready to establish trigonometry by use of infinite series, but it can be so established with complete rigor. We present this brief glimpse to help the student realize that mathematical theory is not a collection of isolated facts but rather a highly interrelated body of theory. We once again emphasize that the more important applications of trigonometry have nothing whatsoever to do with angles. The series definition makes use of x as a real number (or even a complex number), rather than an angle.

We conclude this section with two more evidences of the consistency of the familiar definitions of $\sin x$ and $\cos x$ and the series definitions just discussed. Before doing so we must make a rather wild assumption, which is well founded in this case but may be fallacious in others. Namely, if a function is represented by an infinite series, then the derivative of the function is obtained by differentiating the series term by term as if it were a polynomial. This is *not* always a valid procedure, but it is valid for the series under discussion; so we use the process here to provide additional evidence of the compatibility of series definitions with those already used. Specifically we show that $\dfrac{d \sin x}{dx} = \cos x$ and $\dfrac{d \cos x}{dx} = - \sin x$.

$$\sin x = x - \frac{x^3}{3!} + \frac{x^5}{5!} - \frac{x^7}{7!} + \cdots$$

then, if termwise differentiation of the sin x series is valid,

$$\frac{d \sin x}{dx} = 1 - \frac{3x^2}{3!} + \frac{5x^4}{5!} - \frac{7x^6}{7!} + \cdots$$

$$= 1 - \frac{x^2}{2!} + \frac{x^4}{4!} - \frac{x^6}{6!} + \cdots$$

$$= \cos x.$$

In a similar fashion

$$\cos x = 1 - \frac{x^2}{2!} + \frac{x^4}{4!} - \frac{x^6}{6!} + \frac{x^8}{8!} - \cdots$$

and, assuming termwise differentiation of the cos x series is valid,

$$\frac{d \cos x}{dx} = 0 - \frac{2x}{2!} + \frac{4x^3}{4!} - \frac{6x^5}{6!} + \frac{8x^7}{8!} - \cdots$$

$$= - \left[x - \frac{x^3}{3!} + \frac{x^5}{5!} - \frac{x^7}{7!} + \cdots \right]$$

$$= - \sin x$$

as desired.

The reader should note how easily one can conclude that *if x is near zero*, then sin x is near 0 and cos x is near 1 from the series definitions.

Perhaps one of the most interesting relations in mathematics, since it involves five basic constants, e, π, i, 1, and 2 in a simple relation is $e^{2\pi i} = 1$. The reader should have no difficulty in establishing this by putting $\theta = 2\pi$ in the basic definition

$$e^{i\theta} = \cos \theta + i \sin \theta.$$

*18–9. Hodographs. The word **hodograph** is used to describe a polar coordinate vector chart. This chart is widely used in air and sea navigation as well as in artillery spotting and meteorology. To construct hodographs, polar coordinate paper may be used. Special scales containing nomograms (see Section 9–9) in the margins have been designed for solving specific problems. Vector data which are expressed in magnitude-direction form may be represented on hodographs, while vector data in component form are more easily plotted on rectangular coordinate paper.

● *Example 1.* During World War II techniques for single-station weather forecasting were developed. A hodograph is used to construct a "winds aloft chart" by plotting the velocity (magnitude and direction) of the wind at 1000 foot levels from 1000 feet to 10,000 feet.† The directed line segments con-

† It is interesting to note that these data are often obtained by using *another* hodograph, on which the position of a balloon is plotted, at 1-minute intervals, after it is released from ground level.

necting points for successive levels are called "shear vectors."
It is known that certain shear vector patterns indicate an
approaching low pressure (storm) area.

Example 2. A force may be represented as a vector by giving its
magnitude r, and its direction θ from a fixed direction (say
north). The motors of a small airplane attempt to move it at
an angle of 20° east of north [N 20° E] with a speed of
80 mph while the wind attempts to move it at an angle of
70° east of north [N 70° E] with a speed of 30 mph. Plot
the vectors on a hodograph having 0° at the top and complete
the parallelogram to obtain the actual velocity (speed and
direction) of the plane.

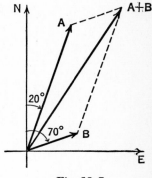

Fig. 18–7

Hence,

$$A + B = ? \text{ cis } ?.$$

The plane is moving with a speed of ? mph at an angle of ?
from north. The reader is asked to complete the computation.

*PROBLEM SET 18-9

. Complete Example 2.
. Bring to class a hodograph of the type used in navigation and
  be prepared to explain its use to the class.
. Construct a "winds aloft" hodograph for 2300 EST, January 16, Chicago, Illinois, from the data given in the accompanying table.
. Construct a "winds aloft" hodograph for 0400 EST, January 17, Chicago, Illinois, from the data given on page 428.
. Consult your local weather bureau, department of meteorology,
  or library, and obtain a set of "winds aloft" data for 1000-foot
  levels from 1000 to 10,000 feet. Plot these data on a hodograph
  and draw the shear vectors. Be certain that you connect successive levels, not nearest points.
. Can you invent a device, based on the hodograph, that a pilot
  could use to determine in what direction he should head his
  plane, when flying, in order to allow for the "drift" which
  results from the wind? Explain your device to a classmate.

Height (feet)	Chicago 2300 EST, January 16		Chicago 0400 EST, January 17	
	Direction	Velocity (mph)	Direction	Velocity (mph)
Surface	160	6	190	10
1,000	160	18	200	30
2,000	180	34	220	42
3,000	200	29	240	38
4,000	210	22	230	38
5,000	220	22	220	34
6,000	250	22	230	30
7,000	250	22	240	24
8,000	250	23	260	22
9,000	260	20	250	27
10,000	260	24	250	31

Chapters 6 and 7 discussed the derivative of a rational function. Later chapters introduced derivation of exponential, logarithmic, and trigonometric functions. Chapter 19 reviews these
concepts and introduces the important related problem of finding
functions whose derivatives are known. This leads to the vital
concept of the definite integral.

19–1. The derivative. If $y = f(x)$, then y' is defined as

$$y' = \frac{dy}{dx} = \lim_{\Delta x \to 0} \frac{f(x + \Delta x) - f(x)}{\Delta x}, \tag{19.1}$$

when this limit exists.

If $y = ku^n$, where $u = u(x)$, then $y' = knu^{n-1}(du/dx)$.

Example 1. Find y', where $y = 11(3x^2 + 5x - 4)^5$.

In this problem, $y = 11u^5$, where $u = 3x^2 + 5x - 4$.
Therefore,

$$y' = 11 \cdot 5u^4(du/dx), \quad \text{where} \quad (du/dx) = 6x + 5.$$

Thus,

$$y' = 55(3x^2 + 5x - 4)^4(6x + 5).$$

Example 2. If $f(x) = 5(x^2 - 3)^{10}$, find $f'(x)$.

Here, $f(x) = 5u^{10}$, where $u = x^2 - 3$.
Hence,

$$f'(x) = 50u^9(du/dx) = 50(x^2 - 3)^9 2x = 100x(x^2 - 3)^9.$$

In Section 6–6, a formula for the derivative of a product of two
functions was obtained. If $f(x) = u(x) \cdot v(x)$, then

$$f'(x) = \frac{d[u \cdot v]}{dx} = u\frac{dv}{dx} + v\frac{du}{dx}. \tag{19.2}$$

Example 3. If $f(x) = (x^2 - 5x + 3)(2x - x^2)$, find $f'(x)$.

Here, $f(x) = u \cdot v$, where $u = x^2 - 5x + 3$, and
$v = 2x - x^2$. Thus,

$$f'(x) = (x^2 - 5x + 3)(2 - 2x) + (2x - x^2)(2x - 5).$$

Example 4. If $y = (2x^2 - 3x)^5(3x - 5)^2$, find y'.

Here, $y = U \cdot V$, where $U = u^5$ and $V = v^2$, while
$$u = 2x^2 - 3x \quad \text{and} \quad v = 3x - 5.$$

Thus,

$$y' = \frac{d[U \cdot V]}{dx} = U\frac{dV}{dx} + V\frac{dU}{dx},$$

$$= u^5\frac{d[v^2]}{dx} + v^2\frac{d[u^5]}{dx},$$

$$= u^5 2v\frac{dv}{dx} + v^2 5u^4\frac{du}{dx},$$

$$= (2x^2 - 3x)^5 2(3x - 5)(3) + (3x - 5)^2 5(2x^2 - 3x)^4(4x - 3)$$

The derivative y' of $y = f(x)$ has several interpretations. The first interpretation of $f'(a)$ studied in this book involved the slope of a line tangent to the curve $y = f(x)$ at the point $(a, f(a))$ on the curve. This led to the observation that a $y = f(x)$ has a maximum or a minimum value, then the tangent line *may* be horizontal at the corresponding point. Examples were given (Sections 4–9, 5–3, 6–8, 6–9) of functions having a maximum value at a point at which the tangent did not even exist. Examples were given of the more common occurrence of a curve with a horizontal tangent at a point which was *neither a maximum nor minimum*. Study the examples of Chapters 6 and 7 before continuing.

The derivative was interpreted as a rate of change. Velocity is the rate of change of distance with respect to time. Acceleration is the rate of change of velocity with respect to time. Other rates of change were considered in Chapter 7. (Example 2 of Section 7– involves rates of change in volume, and in depth, of liquid in a trough with respect to time.)

● **Example 5.** A stone is thrown upward from the top of a building 560 feet tall. The height $h(t)$ of the stone *from the ground* is given by $h(t) = -16t^2 + 32t + 560$, where $h(t)$ is in feet and t is in seconds. The function represents the height above the ground from the instant the stone is thrown $(t = 0)$ until it hits the ground.

(a) What is the velocity of the stone as it strikes the ground?

(b) What is the greatest height reached by the stone?

(c) What is the velocity of the stone as it passes a window ledge 320 feet above ground level?

(a) The time at which the stone strikes the ground is obtained by solving $h(t) = 0$.

$$h(t) = -16t^2 + 32t + 560 = 0$$
$$-16(t - 7)(t + 5) = 0$$
$$t = 7, \quad t = -5.$$

The function $h(t)$ has meaning in this problem only for non-negative t. Hence, when the stone strikes the ground, $t = 7$ seconds. The velocity at this time is computed from $v(t) = h'(t)$.

$$v(t) = h'(t) = -32t + 32$$
$$v(\text{at ground}) = v(7) = h'(7) = -32(7) + 32 = -192 \text{ ft /sec.}$$

The negative sign indicates that the stone is falling.

(b) To find the maximum value of $h(t)$, determine the value of t such that $h'(t) = 0$. The problem assures us that an actual maximum is obtained. The solution of $h'(t) = -32t + 32 = 0$ is $t = 1$. The maximum height is

$$h(1) = -16(1)^2 + 32(1) + 560 = 576 \text{ feet}$$

above ground level.

(c) The stone passes a window ledge 320 feet above ground level when $h(t) = 320$. Solving $h(t) = 320$ for t, the time at which the stone passed the 320 foot level is determined.

$$\begin{aligned} h(t) = -16t^2 + 32t + 560 &= 320 \\ -16t^2 + 32t + 240 &= 0 \\ -16(t-5)(t+3) &= 0 \\ t = 5, \quad t &= -3. \end{aligned}$$

In this problem, $t = -3$ is rejected. (Why?) The velocity, at the time $(t = 5)$ when the stone passes the 320 foot level, is

$$v(\text{at 320 feet above ground}) = v(5) = h'(5) = -32(5) + 32$$
$$= -128 \text{ feet per second.}$$

PROBLEM SET 19-1

1. If $f(x) = (3x - 2)(x^2 + 5x - 1)$, find $f'(x)$.
2. If $g(t) = (t^2 - 4t + 7)^{10}$, find dg/dt.
3. Compute y' by the delta process (Section 6–2) if $y = 1/(4x)$.
4. Find dy/dx if $y = (3x^2 + 6x - 7)(4x^5 + 3x^4 - 17)$.
5. (a) Find the equation of one of the lines which is tangent to $y = x^3 - 2x^2 + 3x - 5$ and parallel to $2x - y + 11 = 0$. (See Example 3, Section 6–5, and Example 3, Section 6–6.)
   (b) Find the equation of another parallel tangent line. How many are there?

6. Find the slope of the line tangent to $y = (x^2 - 3x + 1)^{10}$ the point $(2, 1)$.

7. Find dy/dx if $y = \sqrt{2x - 3x^2 + 5}$.

8. Find all maximum and minimum points, and sketch the cur $y = x^4 - 4x^3 + 16x - 7$.

9. A cylindrical can is to be constructed to contain 1000 cub inches. Determine the dimensions of a can requiring the lea total sheet metal to construct, if the circular top and botto are cut from square pieces *and the scraps wasted*, while t side is cut from a large sheet without waste.

10. A stone is thrown upward with an initial velocity of 64 fe per second, from the top of a tower 100 feet above the groun The height h, in feet, of the stone above the ground t secon after throwing, is given by $h(t) = -16t^2 + 64t + 100$. D termine the velocity of the stone as it passes a window led 20 feet above ground level.

11. Determine a point at which $y = 2x^3 - x^2 - 23x + 50$ h slope minus three.

12. Write the equation of a line tangent to $y = 2x^2 - 5x +$ at $(1, -2)$.

13. Find the equation of a line that is parallel to $3x + y =$ and is tangent to $y = 2x^3 - x^2 - 23x + 50$. Is there mo than one such line? Compare this problem with Problem 1

14. Find the equation of one line tangent to

$$y = x^3 - 3x^2 + 5x - 7,$$

such that the tangent line is parallel to $2x - y + 5 = 0$.

15. A projectile is fired from the top of a building 225 feet hig The height from the ground, h feet, of the projectile t secon after it is fired is given by $h(t) = -16t^2 + 64t + 225$. Th function has meaning, in this problem, from $t = 0$ unt the projectile strikes the ground. Determine the veloci of the projectile when the projectile is level with a windo ledge 11 yards (33 feet) above ground level.

*16. With what approximate velocity does the projectile of Prob lem 15 strike the ground?

[HINT: Use the quadratic formula to obtain a one-decimal-pla approximation of the time when the projectile strikes the groun that is, when $h(t) = 0$.]

17. How high does the projectile of Problem 15 rise?

18. A horizontal V-shaped trough is 4 feet long with vertica ends, and has a 90-degree angle between its sides. Water poured into the trough at the rate of 500 cubic inches pe minute. At what rate is the depth of the water increasin when the water is 10 inches deep?

19. A rectangular box with an open top is to be constructed from a 10×10 inch square of sheet metal by cutting out equal squares from each corner, and turning up the edges. Determine the volume of the largest box which may be so formed.

20. A telephone answering service for doctors charges each doctor using the service a fee of $3.00 per month. It has 500 subscribers. The owners believe that for each cent they raise the cost, one doctor will discontinue the service: that is, if the fee were raised to $3.25 per month, 25 of the 500 doctors would stop using the service; if they raised the fee to $3.30 per month, 30 doctors would drop; etc. On the basis of this assumption, what service fee will bring in the greatest monthly income?

In Problems 21 to 35, find the derivative of the given function, nd evaluate this derivative at the point where $x = 2$ or $= -1$, whichever is appropriate.

21. $y = (2x - 4)^3(x^2 + 5x)^5$.   **22.** $y = (3x - x^2)^4(x^2 + 5)^3$.

23. $y = (7x^2 + 5x - 36)^3(14x + 5)^5$.

24. $y = (t^3 - 2)^{12}(t^3 - 18)$.   **25.** $z = (t^2 - 5)(4 - 3t)^{-1}$.

26. $z = (1 + 2x)^{-1}(3x + 3)^{\frac{1}{2}}$.   **27.** $w = (29t - 25)^{\frac{1}{2}}(3t + 2)^3$.

28. $s = (-16t^2 + 81t - 5)(2t + 1)^3$.

29. $D = (\sqrt{(3 - t)^2 + t^4})(1 - 4t^2)$.

30. $R = (1 - 2t)/(2t - 1)$.

31. $y = e^{2t} + \sin t$.

32. $y = e^x \cos x$.

33. $y = 5 \tan x$.

34. $y = 4 + 3 \sin 2x$.

35. $y = 5 + \ln 3x$.

36. Find the maximum value of $y = xe^{-3x}$ and sketch the curve.

37. Find the coordinates of the points at which $\dfrac{d^2y}{dx^2}$ is zero and the x intercepts of the tangent lines through these points for $y = (1/\sqrt{2\pi})e^{-x^2/2}$. Sketch the curve.

19-2. The antiderivative. The rate of change of $F(x)$ is found by differentiation. The symbol $F'(x)$ is used to represent this rate of change. In many applications one wishes to find a function, $F(x)$, whose rate of change $F'(x)$ is known. This problem is the inverse of the problem mentioned in the first sentence of this section. Can you find $F(x)$, if $F'(x) = 3x^2 + 10x$? A little thought indicates that $x^3 + 5x^2 + 2$, or $x^3 + 5x^2 - 17$, or $x^3 + 5x^2 - 3\sqrt{11}$, or $x^3 + 5x^2 + C$ for any constant C are

possible choices for $F(x)$, since in each case $F'(x) = 3x^2 + 10$
It is not surprising that $F(x)$ is not unique. It was shown
Problem 19, Set 6–2 that if $F(x)$ and $G(x)$ differ by a con
stant, then $F'(x) = G'(x)$. We shall show that if $F'(x) = G'(x$
then $F(x)$ and $G(x)$ differ, *at most*, by a constant. (Wh
is this not the same as Problem 19, Set 6–2?)

We wish to determine $F(x)$ when $F'(x)$ is known. Th
function $F(x)$ is called an **antiderivative** or **integral**
$F'(x)$. The following theorem enables us to state that poly
nomials $F(x) = x^3 + 5x^2 + C$ are the *only possible* antideriv:
tives (integrals) of the function $F'(x) = 3x^2 + 10x$.

Theorem 1. If $F(x)$ and $G(x)$ are two functions suc
that $F'(x) = G'(x)$ for every x, then $F(x)$ and $G(x)$ diffe
at most, by a constant.

Set $\qquad h(x) = G(x) - F(x).$

Then,

$$h'(x) = G'(x) - F'(x).$$

Since,

$$F'(x) = G'(x) \quad \text{by hypothesis,}$$

we have

$$h'(x) = G'(x) - G'(x) = 0 \quad \text{for all } x.$$

Problem 35, Set 6–5, shows that $h'(x) = 0$ for all x implie
$h(x) = C$, a constant. Hence, $G(x) - F(x) = h(x) = C$, a con
stant, or $G(x) = F(x) + C$. Consequently, if $F'(x) = f(x)$, the
the only possible antiderivatives (integrals) of $f(x)$ are $F(x) + C$
$F(x) + C$ is the **indefinite integral** of $f(x)$ and is written
$\int f(x)\, dx = F(x) + C$. This integral is called an indefinite integra
since the constant of integration, C, has not been determined.

Special attention is called to the fact that the symbol of in
tegration is $\int f(x)\, dx$, not just $\int f(x)$. The symbol
$\int f(x)\, dx$ represents the general antiderivative of $f(x)$.

- **Example 1.**† $\int (12t^2 - 3)\, dt = 4t^3 - 3t + C.$

- **Example 2.**† $\int (3x^4 - 4x + 6)\, dx = \frac{3}{5}x^5 - 2x^2 + 6x + C.$

- **Example 3.**† $\int (4y^7 - 3y + 2)\, dy = \frac{1}{2}y^8 - \frac{3}{2}y^2 + 2y + C.$

† These results may be checked by differentiation.

● *Example 4.* A curve has slope equal to six times its abscissa at every point on the curve. The curve passes through (3, 7). Find the equation of the curve.

The slope of $F(x)$ is $F'(x) = 6x$. Hence,

$$y = F(x) = \int 6x \, dx = 3x^2 + C.$$

This is a family of parabolas.

Since the curve passes through (3, 7), this point must satisfy the equation $y = 3x^2 + C$. Hence, $7 = 3(3)^2 + C$ or $C = -20$. The equation is $y = 3x^2 - 20$.

The following theorems may be checked by differentiation.

Theorem 2.

$$\int [f(x) + g(x) - h(x)] \, dx = \int f(x) \, dx + \int g(x) \, dx - \int h(x) \, dx$$
$$= F(x) + G(x) - H(x) + C,$$

where $F'(x) = f(x)$, $G'(x) = g(x)$, $H'(x) = h(x)$ and C is constant.

Theorem 3. $\int ax^n \, dx = a \dfrac{x^{n+1}}{n+1} + C$, where n is a rational number other than -1, and a and C are constants.

● *Example 5.* $\int (13x^5 - 7x + 2) \, dx = 13(x^6/6) - 7(x^2/2) + 2x + C.$

19–3. The differential equation. $\dfrac{dy}{dx} = m$. In Section 5–2 the equation of a line having slope m and y intercept b was obtained. We present a related development at this point.

Consider a function $y = f(x)$ such that $dy/dx = m$, a constant. Possible functions which have this property are $y = mx + 7$ and $y = mx - 2$. Theorem 1 of Section 19–2 states that two functions having the same derivative differ, at most, by a constant. Hence, we conclude that a function $y = f(x)$ which satisfies

$$\frac{dy}{dx} = m$$

must be of the form

$$y = mx + b$$

where b is a constant. Note that $(0, b)$ is the y intercept. This is a simple example of a differential equation.

PROBLEM SET 19–3

Integrate the expressions given in Problems 1 to 13.

1. $\int (10x^4 - 6x^2 + 2x - 3)\, dx.$ **2.** $\int (8x^3 + 6x^2 - 2x + 5)\, dx.$

3. $\int (3t + 2)\, dt.$ **4.** $\int dx.$ **5.** $\int (15x^2 + 2x - 11)\, dx$

6. $\int (100x^{19} - 16x^{15} + 12x^5 - 3x + 2)\, dx.$

7. Does $\int (3x + 4)$ have meaning? Discuss.

8. $\int (x^4 - 4x^2 + 3x - 8)\, dx.$ **9.** $\int (5x^6 - 7x + 1)\, dx.$

10. $\int (6t^2 - 4t + 3)\, dt.$ **11.** $\int (y^3 - 4y + 2)\, dy.$

12. $\int (8w^7 - 12w^5 + 9w^2 - 6w + 5)\, dw.$

13. $\int (z^2 - 6z^3 + 9z)\, dz.$

14. A curve has slope equal to four times its abscissa $[F'(x) = 4x]$ and passes through $(3, -6)$. Determine the equation of the curve.

15. The slope of a curve is six times the square of its abscissa. The curve has a y intercept of 5. Determine the equation of the curve.

16. Verify Theorem 3 by differentiation. Be sure to consider the case in which $n = 0$.

17. The slope of a curve at a point is always four units less than twice the abscissa of that point. Find the equation of the family of curves having this property, and pick out the member of the family which passes through $(-2, 3)$.

18. If $dy/dt = 3t^2 - 7t + 6$ and $y = 30$ when $t = -2$, find an equation expressing y as a function of t. Graph this function.

19. If $dz/dx = 8x^7 - 10x^4 + 12x^3 - 7$ and $z = 40$ when $x = 1$, find an equation relating z and x.

20. Prove, using integration, that if the derivative of a function is constant, then the function is a linear function (that is, its graph is a straight line).

21. $F(x)$ is a cubic polynomial such that $y = F(x)$ has a maximum at $(-3, 20)$ and a minimum at $(1, -12)$. Explain why the slope of $y = F(x)$ must be of the form $k(x - 1)(x + 3)$. Determine the equation of the curve.

19–4. The differential equation, $\dfrac{d^2s}{dt^2} = a.$ **Problems of**

motion. In rectilinear (straight line) motion, if the distance s

of a particle from the origin is expressed as a function of the time t, then the velocity is $v = ds/dt$, and the acceleration is $a = dv/dt = s''(t)$. Starting with either the acceleration function or the velocity function, and certain observed facts, one may derive the distance function using integration. In elementary physics, the formula $s = -\frac{1}{2}gt^2 + v_0 t + s_0$ is used to obtain the distance above ground of a body falling under gravity, if the velocity at time $t = 0$ is v_0, and the distance above ground at time $t = 0$ is s_0, and the upward direction is taken as positive. This formula is obtained by integration.

● *Example 1.* A ball is thrown *upward* from the top of a tower 400 ft high with an initial velocity of 120 ft per sec. Assuming that the acceleration due to gravity is 32 ft per sec per sec *downward*, determine the velocity with which the ball strikes the ground.

Let us take the upward direction as positive, the time of throwing as $t = 0$, and the origin at the earth's surface. Then,

$$a(t) = -32 \text{ ft per sec per sec}$$
$$v(t) = \int -32 \, dt = -32t + C.$$

The problem states $v(0) = 120$ ft per sec. Consequently,

$$120 = 0 + C,$$

and

$$v(t) = -32t + 120.$$

Now,

$$h(t) = \int v(t) \, dt = \int (-32t + 120) \, dt$$
$$= -16t^2 + 120t + k.$$

The problem states $h(0) = 400$. Hence, $400 = 0 + 0 + k$, and

$$h(t) = -16t^2 + 120t + 400.$$

From here on, the problem is the same as Example 3, Section 7–3.

In general, the differential equation

$$\frac{d^2s}{dt^2} = a, \quad \text{where } a \text{ is constant,}$$

has as its first integral

$$\frac{ds}{dt} = at + k_1$$

and as its general solution

$$s = \tfrac{1}{2}at^2 + k_1 t + k_2.$$

Problem 23 of Set 19–4 requests the solution with certain boundary conditions.

PROBLEM SET 19–4

In all problems involving gravity, assume $g = 32$ ft per sec per sec directed downward.

1. A stone is thrown upward with an initial velocity of 32 ft per sec from the top of a building 560 ft tall. Starting with the assumption that the acceleration of the stone is -32 ft per sec per sec, derive the equation for the height $h(t)$ of the stone from the ground at any time t sec after it is thrown, until it strikes the ground. From this deduce the impact velocity with which the stone strikes the ground.

2. (a) Find the velocity of the stone of Problem 1 as it passes a window ledge 320 ft above ground level. (b) How high does the stone of Problem 1 ascend?

3. A pellet is projected upward with an initial velocity of 96 ft per sec. Using the methods of this section, find an equation giving the distance of the pellet above the earth at any time t sec after it is projected. When will the pellet reach its highest point? How high will it go? When and with what velocity will it strike the ground?

4. If the pellet of Problem 3 were projected from a point 80 ft above ground level with an initial velocity of 64 ft per sec, answer the same questions.

5. A ball is dropped from rest from a point 45 ft above the ground. Simultaneously, a second ball is thrown upward from a spot on the ground directly below the first ball. If the initial velocity of the second ball is 30 ft per sec, determine whether or not the two balls will meet while they are still in the air. If they do meet find the speed, direction, and height of each ball at the moment of impact.

6. A ball is thrown upward with an initial speed of 128 ft per sec. How high above the ground is the ball 3 sec after it is thrown? In which direction is it moving? How high does the ball go? With what velocity does it strike the ground?

7. A bullet is shot upward with an initial velocity of 1600 ft per sec. How high does it go? How long does it remain in the air? Will it have sufficient velocity when it strikes the ground to be dangerous?

8. Calvin Butterball and Phoebe Small spent a day at the beach near Big Falls. Calvin notes that a piece of wood that was swept over the falls requires 4.5 sec to descend. How high are the falls?

9. Phoebe's little brother, who is interested in airplanes, guesses that the piece of wood of Problem 8 must have been going more than 70 mph as it struck the water near the base of the falls. Is his estimate a reasonable one?

10. A hockey puck travels 216 ft before coming to rest. If the deceleration of the puck is 12 ft per sec per sec, find the initial velocity of the puck at the time it was struck.

11. A package slides down a chute 60 ft long with an acceleration of 5 ft per sec per sec.

(a) Find the initial velocity of the package if it requires 4 sec to traverse the chute.

(b) How fast was the package moving when it was one third of the way down the chute?

(c) How long did it take the package to get half way down the chute?

(d) How far down the chute did the package go during the first half of the time of descent?

12. What constant acceleration is needed to increase the speed of an automobile from rest (0 mph) to 60 mph in a distance of 440 ft?

[HINT: 440 ft is what portion of 1 mile?]

13. A bullet buries itself 9 in. into a tree in 0.01 sec. Assuming that the deceleration of the bullet was constant, and that the bullet comes to rest in the indicated time, find the speed of the bullet at the moment of impact.

14. With what approximate speed would a projectile need to be hurled to just reach the top of the Empire State Building, which is 1250 ft high?

15. A long inclined plane is constructed in such a manner that objects slide down it with an acceleration of 12 ft per sec. An object is thrown *up* the incline. It travels 3750 ft up the incline before starting to slide back down. Find the initial velocity with which the object was thrown.

*16. Work may be defined as force times distance, if the force is constant. If the force is not constant, but is a function of distance (as in a stretched spring, for example), then one defines work as $W = \int_a^b f(x)\, dx$, where $f(x)$ is the force at distance x and W is the work done by $f(x)$ as x varies from a to b. If the force required to stretch a spring x in. is $f(x) = 12x$ lb, find the work required to stretch the spring (a) 3 in., (b) 6 in., (c) 12 in. In what units will the work be expressed? If $f(x) = F'(x)$, then $W = F(b) - F(a)$.

*17. Work Problem 16 if $f(x) = 4x$.

18. A balloon is rising at the rate of 15 ft per sec. A stone dropped from the balloon reached the ground in 8 sec. How high was the balloon when the stone was dropped? (The nature of the data does not merit an accuracy of more than the nearest 10 ft, if that.)

19. A ball is thrown upward and reaches a height of 80 ft in 1 sec. How high will the ball go?

20. A stone is thrown upward with an initial speed of 32 ft per sec from the top of a building 100 ft above ground level. Determine the velocity of the stone as it passes a window ledge 52 ft above ground level on its way down. Start with the assumption that $d^2s/dt^2 = -32$ ft per sec per sec and derive all relationships.

21. Consult a table of integrals and note the variety of things yet to be learned. Find three functions which we have studied, but whose derivatives and integrals we have not studied.

22. A table of integrals lists $\int \dfrac{dx}{\sqrt{1 - x^2}}$ as arc sin $x + C$.

Another table lists this integral as $-$ arc cos $x + C$. Since arc sin x and $-$ arc cos x are not, in general, equal this seems like a peculiar discrepancy. Show that if either table is correct, the other is also. Consult Section 16–9.

23. Obtain the formula $s = -gt^2/2 + v_0t + s_0$, mentioned earlier in this section. Start with the acceleration due to gravity as a constant g.

24. If a 5-lb weight stretches a helical spring from length 4 in. to 4.1 in., find the work done in stretching the spring from 4 in. to 5 in. (assuming the stretch is within the elastic limits).

25. Imagine that you are the navigator on an interplanetary rocket ship about to land on planet $X3T$. It is known that the rocket braking power needed for a safe landing is proportional to the gravitational attraction of the planet. Your ship uses one half its rocket braking power on earth. If on planet $X3T$ a ball drops 100 ft, from rest, in 2 sec, can you safely land your ship on $X3T$?

19–5. The definite integral as an area. The discussion of area presented here is partially intuitive. The problems of a more rigorous treatment are left for later study. The discussion given is valid, but is not complete. The area of a plane figure bounded entirely by straight-line segments may be computed by elementary means. A careful reader will discover that a definition of the area of a plane figure bounded by curves requires a limiting process which results in an integral.†

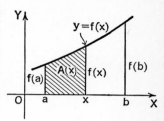

Fig. 19–1

Let $f(x)$ be a continuous, non-negative, nondecreasing function on the closed interval $a \leq x \leq b$. Let $A(x)$ be the area bounded by the x-axis, and the curve $y = f(x)$, between the ordinates at $x = a$ and $x = x$.

Consider the area $\Delta A(x, \Delta x)$ between the ordinates at x and $x + \Delta x$. The magnitude of this area, $\Delta A(x, \Delta x)$, is between the magnitudes of the areas of rectangles having altitudes $f(x)$ and $f(x + \Delta x)$ with base Δx. (See Fig. 19–3.) That is, if $\Delta x > 0$ ‡ as indicated in Figure 19–3,

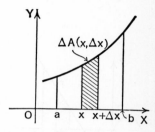

Fig. 19–2

Area of rectangle [with height $f(x)$ and width Δx] $\leq \Delta A(x, \Delta x)$
  $\leq$ Area of rectangle [with height $f(x + \Delta x)$ and width Δx].

$$f(x) \cdot \Delta x \leq \Delta A(x, \Delta x) \leq f(x + \Delta x) \cdot \Delta x.$$

Accordingly,

$$f(x) \leq \frac{\Delta A(x, \Delta x)}{\Delta x} \leq f(x + \Delta x), \quad \text{if} \quad \Delta x > 0.$$

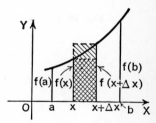

Fig. 19–3

(The reader should recall that Section 5–4 points out that $\lim_{\Delta x \to 0}$ requires $\Delta x \neq 0$. Hence, the division in the last step is permissible.) We take the limit as $\Delta x \to 0$ in these relationships.

$$\lim_{\Delta x \to 0} f(x) \leq \lim_{\Delta x \to 0} \frac{\Delta A(x, \Delta x)}{\Delta x} \leq \lim_{\Delta x \to 0} f(x + \Delta x).$$

Since $f(x)$ is continuous by hypothesis, $\lim_{\Delta x \to 0} f(x + \Delta x) = f(x)$.

Clearly, $\lim_{\Delta x \to 0} f(x) = f(x)$ (see Section 5–5). Thus,

$$f(x) \leq \lim_{\Delta x \to 0} \frac{\Delta A(x, \Delta x)}{\Delta x} \leq f(x).$$

Since the limit lies between two identical functions, it follows that the limit must equal this function. Hence,

$$\lim_{\Delta x \to 0} \frac{\Delta A(x, \Delta x)}{\Delta x} = f(x).$$

† Some students may wish to read Section 6, Chapter I, and Sections 1 and 2, Chapter II, of *Differential and Integral Calculus*, Vol. I by R. Courant, for further information on this subject. Chapters I and II are worth reading in their entirety.

‡ If $\Delta x < 0$, the inequalities are reversed, but $\Delta A(x, \Delta x)$ is still *between* the areas of the two rectangles.

By definition,

$$\frac{dA}{dx} = \lim_{\Delta x \to 0} \frac{\Delta A(x, \Delta x)}{\Delta x}.$$

Consequently,

$$\frac{dA}{dx} = f(x).$$

In words, the rate of change with respect to x of the area $A(x)$ under the curve $y = f(x)$ is equal to the ordinate $f(x)$ of the curve at that x value. The phrase "area under the curve" is often used in place of "area between the curve and the x-axis."

An example may clarify this.

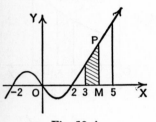

Fig. 19–4

● **Example:** Determine the area under the curve $y = x^3 - 4x$ between $x = 3$ and $x = 5$. Figure 19–4 shows the desired locus. The conditions mentioned above are satisfied, namely, if $A(x)$ is the area under $y = x^3 - 4x$ between the vertical line $x = 3$ and some arbitrary vertical line crossing the x-axis at a point x, then

$$\frac{dA(x)}{dx} = x^3 - 4x.$$

Hence, the area under $y = x^3 - 4x$ and between the two vertical lines crossing the axis at 3 and at x is

$$A(x) = \int (x^3 - 4x)\, dx = \frac{x^4}{4} - 2x^2 + C.$$

The value of C may be determined by noting that when $x = 3$, the lines MP and $x = 3$ coincide and the area is zero. Hence $A(3) = 0$.

$$A(3) = \frac{3^4}{4} - 2(3)^2 + C = 0$$
$$\tfrac{81}{4} - 18 + C = 0$$
$$C = -\tfrac{9}{4}.$$

Hence the area under $y = x^3 - 4x$ between two vertical lines — one crossing the x-axis at 3 and the other at an arbitrary point x is

$$A(x) = \frac{x^4}{4} - 2x^2 - \frac{9}{4}.$$

The desired area is given by taking $x = 5$, namely,

$$A(5) = \tfrac{625}{4} - 50 - \tfrac{9}{4} = 104 \text{ square units.}$$

This example is repeated on the next page after a desirable short-cut involving the notation $\int_3^5 (x^3 - 4x)\, dx$ is introduced.

If $dA/dx = A'(x) = f(x)$ is known, integration may be used to obtain the area bounded by the curve $y = f(x)$ and the x-axis, between the ordinates at $x = a$, $x = b$.

$$A(x) = \int A'(x)\, dx = \int f(x)\, dx = F(x) + C, \quad \text{where} \quad F'(x) = f(x).$$

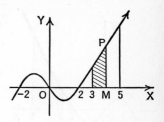

Fig. 19-4

The value of C is determined by observing that $A(x)$ is the area between the ordinates at $x = a$ and $x = x$; when $x = a$, $A(a) = 0$. Consequently,

$$0 = A(a) = F(a) + C, \quad \text{and} \quad C = -F(a).$$

Thus, in general,

$$A(x) = F(x) - F(a).$$

The desired area, $A = A(b)$, under $y = f(x)$ between the lines $x = a$ and $x = b$, is given by $A = A(b) = F(b) - F(a)$, where $F'(x) = f(x)$. If one defines the symbol

$$\int_a^b f(x)\, dx = F(x)\Big]_a^b = F(b) - F(a), \qquad (19.3)$$

then the area under $y = f(x) \geqq 0$ between $x = a$ and $x = b$, $a < b$, is given by

$$A = \int_a^b f(x)\, dx. \qquad (19.4)$$

Similar discussions may be given if $f(x)$ is a continuous non-negative, nonincreasing function over a closed interval. If $f(x)$ is a non-negative continuous function on the closed interval $a \leqq x \leqq b$, and this interval can be broken up into a finite number of subintervals on each of which $f(x)$ is either nondecreasing or nonincreasing, then the total area A is still given by $A = \int_a^b f(x)\, dx$. Corresponding discussions may be given if $f(x)$ is a nonpositive continuous function on a closed interval. In this case the formula $\int_a^b f(x)\, dx$ yields a negative number since the area is below the x-axis and $f(x)$ is negative. Area is defined as the absolute value of this quantity. Care must be taken that the function $f(x)$ has the same sign throughout the interval a, b on which the formula $A = \left| \int_a^b f(x)\, dx \right|$ is used. Example 3 shows why this is necessary.

● *Example 1.* Determine the area under $y = x^3 - 4x$ between $x = 3$ and $x = 5$.

A sketch of the locus shows that $f(x) = x^3 - 4x$ does not change sign in the interval $3 \leqq x \leqq 5$.

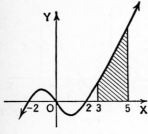

Fig. 19–5

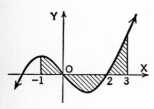

Fig. 19–6

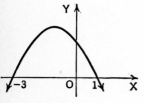

Fig. 19–7

Then,

$$A = \int_3^5 (x^3 - 4x)\, dx = \frac{x^4}{4} - 2x^2 \bigg]_3^5$$

$$= \left[\tfrac{625}{4} - 50\right] - \left[\tfrac{81}{4} - 18\right] = \tfrac{544}{4} - 32 = 104 \text{ square units.}$$

● **Example 2.** Find the area bounded by $y = -x^2 - 2x + 3$ and the x-axis.

The locus has x intercepts -3 and $+1$.

$f(x) = -x^2 - 2x + 3$ is continuous and non-negative in the interval $-3 \leqq x \leqq 1$.

$$A = \int_{-3}^1 (-x^2 - 2x + 3)\, dx = -\frac{x^3}{3} - x^2 + 3x \bigg]_{-3}^1$$

$$= \left[-\frac{1^3}{3} - 1^2 + 3\right] - \left[-\frac{(-3)^3}{3} - (-3)^2 + 3(-3)\right]$$

$$= \left[\tfrac{5}{3}\right] - \left[-9\right] = \tfrac{32}{3} \text{ square units.}$$

● **Example 3.** Determine the area bounded by the x-axis and $y = x^3 - 4x$ between the ordinates at $x = -1$ and $x = 3$. This is the function considered in Example 1, but the interval is different.

Since $f(x) = x^3 - 4x$ changes sign at $x = 0$ and at $x = 2$, within the interval $-1 \leqq x \leqq 3$, the area will be found by adding the absolute values of the integrals in the three intervals

$$-1 \leqq x \leqq 0, \quad 0 \leqq x \leqq 2, \quad 2 \leqq x \leqq 3,$$

in each of which the sign of $f(x)$ does not change.

$$A = \int_{-1}^0 (x^3 - 4x)\, dx + \left| \int_0^2 (x^3 - 4x)\, dx \right| + \int_2^3 (x^3 - 4x)\, dx$$

$$= \left(\frac{x^4}{4} - 2x^2\right)\bigg]_{-1}^0 + \left| \left(\frac{x^4}{4} - 2x^2\right)\bigg]_0^2 \right| + \left(\frac{x^4}{4} - 2x^2\right)\bigg]_2^3$$

$$= [0] - \left[\frac{(-1)^4}{4} - 2(-1)^2\right] + \left| \left[\frac{2^4}{4} - 2(2)^2\right] - [0] \right|$$

$$+ \left[\frac{3^4}{4} - 2(3)^2\right] - \left[\frac{2^4}{4} - 2(2)^2\right]$$

$$= -\left[\tfrac{1}{4} - 2\right] + \left| [4 - 8] \right| + \left[\tfrac{81}{4} - 18\right] - [4 - 8]$$

$$= -\left[-\tfrac{7}{4}\right] + \left| [-4] \right| + \left[\tfrac{9}{4}\right] - [-4]$$

$$= \tfrac{7}{4} + 4 + \tfrac{9}{4} + 4 = 12 \text{ square units.}$$

The reader should note that this area is *not* equal to

$$\int_{-1}^3 (x^3 - 4x)\, dx,$$

which has the value 4.

The integral is discussed further in Section 19–7.

PROBLEM SET 19-5

In Problems 1 to 10 determine, by integration, the area bounded by the following curves and the x-axis between the ordinates indicated. In each case, sketch the curve, and shade the area found.

1. $y = 5x$ between $x = 0$ and $x = 4$. Show that the integral gives the same value for the area of this triangle as may be found by elementary geometry.

2. $y = 5x$ between $x = 3$ and $x = 5$. Compare the result obtained upon integration with the result obtained by geometry.

3. $y = 5x$ between $x = 2$ and $x = 7$.

4. $y = 5x + 4$ between $x = 0$ and $x = 4$. Also compute the area by geometry. Compare with Problem 1.

5. $y = 5x + 7$ between $x = -2$ and $x = 3$. Also find this area by geometry.

6. $y = 3x^2$ between $x = 0$ and $x = 2$. This area cannot be found by methods usually considered in high school plane geometry.

7. $y = 3x^2$ between $x = 1$ and $x = 3$.

8. $y = x^3 + 8$ between $x = -1$ and $x = 4$.

[HINT: To aid in the sketch of $y = x^3 + 8$, consider its x and y intercepts, and also values of x for which the tangent is horizontal.]

9. $y = x^2 - 3x$ between $x = -1$ and $x = 4$.

[HINT: See Example 3.]

10. $y = 5x - x^2$ between $x = -2$ and $x = 3$.

11. Determine the area bounded by $y = -x^2 + 4x$ and the x-axis.

12. Determine the area bounded by $y = x^2 - 4x$ and the x-axis. Compare this problem, both as to sketch and as to result, with Problem 11.

13. Find the area bounded by the x-axis and the function $y = f(x)$ between $x = 0$ and $x = 3$ if

$$f(x) = \begin{cases} x^2, & \text{for } x \le 2 \\ 6 - x, & \text{for } x > 2. \end{cases}$$

[HINT: Sketch the locus and consider separate integrals over the intervals $0 \le x \le 2$ and $2 \le x \le 3$.]

14. Find the area bounded by the x-axis and $y = f(x)$ between $x = 1$ and $x = 5$, if $f(x)$ is the function defined in Problem 13.

15. Determine the area bounded by the x-axis and $y = g(x)$ between $x = 2$ and $x = 5$ if

$$g(x) = \begin{cases} 2x + 3, & \text{if } x \leq 3 \\ -x + 12, & \text{if } x \geq 3. \end{cases}$$

Also determine this area by geometry.

16. The same as Problem 15 between the ordinates $x = -2$ and $x = 7$.

17. In computing the moment of inertia of a circular disk (radius a) with respect to its center (a wheel with respect to its axle) in rectangular coordinates, we must compute the integral of an integral

$$I_0 = \int_{-a}^{a} \left[\int_{-\sqrt{a^2-x^2}}^{\sqrt{a^2-x^2}} (x^2 + y^2)\, dy \right] dx$$

$$= \int_{-a}^{a} \left[2x^2\sqrt{a^2 - x^2} + \tfrac{2}{3}(a^2 - x^2)^{\frac{3}{2}} \right] dx.$$

This is, at best, a difficult integration to perform. It is beyond our present knowledge. To compute this moment of inertia, *using polar coordinates*, we evaluate the integral

$$I_0 = \int_{0}^{a} 2\pi r^3\, dr.$$

This we may do, even with our present slight knowledge of integration. This is one illustration of the importance of polar coordinates. Evaluate the latter integral to obtain I_0.

18. (a) Consult a table of integrals to find $\int \sin x\, dx$ and $\int \cos x\, dx$.

(b) Use the appropriate integral to find the area under $y = \sin x$ from $x = 0$ to $x = \pi$.

19. Find the area above the x-axis bounded by $y^2 = x$, $x = 4$, and $y = 0$. [HINT: Use $y = x^{\frac{1}{2}}$.]

20. Find the area bounded by the parabola $x^{\frac{1}{2}} + y^{\frac{1}{2}} = 1$ and the coordinate axes. [HINT: $y = (1 - x^{\frac{1}{2}})^2$.]

19–6 Self test.

Record your time.

1. A stone is thrown upward, from the top of a building 180 ft high, with an initial velocity of 8 ft per sec. Starting with 32 ft per sec per sec downward as the acceleration due to gravity, determine a function which expresses the height of the stone above the ground, as a function of the time t in seconds, after the stone is thrown.

2. Determine the velocity of the stone of Problem 1, as it passes a window ledge 60 ft above ground level.

3. $\int (x^2 - 4x + 6)\, dx.$ **4.** $\int_2^5 (6y^3 - 4y + 11)\, dy.$

5. $\int_1^2 \sqrt{x}\, dx.$ **6.** $\int_1^8 \dfrac{dx}{\sqrt[3]{x^2}}.$

7. A curve has slope equal to $\frac{7}{2}$ times its abscissa, and passes through $(2, -1)$. Determine the equation of the curve.

8. Find the area bounded by the parabola $y + x^2 - 6x + 5 = 0$ and the x-axis. Sketch the curve, and shade the area found.

9. Find the area bounded by the x-axis and the curve $y = (x - 2)(x - 3)(x - 5)$ between the ordinates $x = 1$ and $x = 6$. Sketch the curve, and shade the area found.

10. Determine the area under $y = f(x)$, between $x = -2$ and $x = 3$, if

$$f(x) = \begin{cases} 2x + 5, & \text{for } x \leqq 1 \\ 6x^2 + 1, & \text{for } x \geqq 1. \end{cases}$$

Record your time.

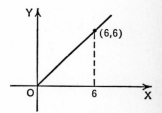

Fig. 19–8

*19–7. The definite integral as a limit of a sum. The reader has met the definite integral $\int_a^b f(x)\, dx$ as a limit in Section 19–5. At that time our consideration was restricted to area. We wish to consider the more general case of a limit of a sum. We shall use the limit of a sum process to determine the volume of a cone generated by revolving the triangle formed by the lines $y = x$, $y = 0$, and $x = 6$ about the x-axis. Each one of us has an intuitive understanding of the meaning of volume and many of us can recall a formula for the volume of a cone, given its height and base radius. The proof of this formula, like that for the area of a circle involves the use of a limit of a sum process which is frequently used without proof in earlier work.

It is not difficult to obtain numerical bounds for the volume of this cone. Figure 19–10 tells us considerably more than we pre-

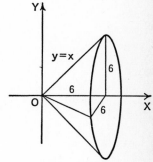

Fig. 19–9

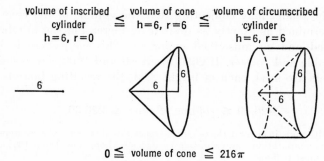

| volume of inscribed cylinder $h=6, r=0$ | $\leqq$ | volume of cone $h=6, r=6$ | $\leqq$ | volume of circumscribed cylinder $h=6, r=6$ |

$$0 \leqq \text{volume of cone} \leqq 216\pi$$

Fig. 19–10

viously knew about the volume — namely, that it lies somewhere between 0 and 669.8 cubic units. We wish to obtain closer bounds by inscribing two cylinders each half as long, and likewise circumscribing two cylinders. From Figure 19–11 the reader will note

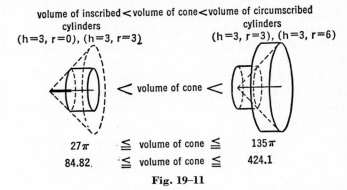

volume of inscribed < volume of cone < volume of circumscribed
cylinders   cylinders
(h=3, r=0), (h=3, r=3)   (h=3, r=3), (h=3, r=6)

< volume of cone <

$27\pi \; \leqq \;$ volume of cone $\leqq \; 135\pi$

$84.82 \; \leqq \;$ volume of cone $\leqq \; 424.1$

Fig. 19–11

the improvement in the bounds; whereas before we knew the volume of the cone was between 0 and 669.8, we now know that this volume is between 84.8 and 424.1. The range is about half of the previous range. This success may encourage us to divide the x-axis of the cone into 20 sections instead of 2 sections. If this is done we find that †

$$\sum_{i=0}^{19} \pi x_i^2 h_i \leqq \text{volume of cone} \leqq \sum_{i=1}^{20} \pi x_i^2 h_i, \quad \text{where} \quad x_i = h_i = .3i$$

$$209.5 \leqq \text{volume of cone} \leqq 243.4$$

Continuing in this way, if 200 inscribed and 200 circumscribed cylinders are used, each .03 units high, the resulting bounds will be †

$$\sum_{i=0}^{199} \pi x_i^2 h_i \leqq \text{volume of cone} \leqq \sum_{i=1}^{200} \pi x_i^2 h_i, \quad \text{where} \quad x_i = h_i = .03i$$

$$224.5 \leqq \text{volume of cone} \leqq 227.9$$

The reader may conjecture that the volume of the cone can be determined as exactly as desired by increasing the number of inscribed and circumscribed cylinders. This conjecture is both reasonable and correct. If 2000 inscribed and 2000 circumscribed cylinders are used, each of height .003, the resulting bounds will be †

$$226.19 \leqq \text{volume of cone} \leqq 226.36.$$

† Although, in general, the reader is expected to fill in any missing steps and to verify computations, an exception is suggested here since the actual arithmetic is most tedious.

By taking the limit, one obtains the definite integral

$$\lim_{n \to \infty} \sum_{i=0}^{n-1} \pi x_i^2 h_i \leq \text{volume of cone} \leq \lim_{n \to \infty} \sum_{i=1}^{n} \pi x_i^2 h_i$$

where $x_i = h_i = \dfrac{6}{n}$

$$\lim_{n \to \infty} \sum_{i=0}^{n-1} \pi \left(\frac{6}{n}\right)^3 \leq \text{volume of cone} \leq \lim_{n \to \infty} \sum_{i=1}^{n} \pi \left(\frac{6}{n}\right)^3.$$

If it happens, as it does in this case and in the case of every continuous function, that the two outside bounds approach the same limit, then the common limit is the volume.

The reader may well feel that once again coincidence has reached out and saved him, since this common limit, when it exists, is exactly the definite integral of Section 19–5.

$$\text{volume} = \int_0^6 \pi x^2 \, dx = \pi \left. \frac{x^3}{3} \right]_0^6 = 72\pi \cong 226.195 \text{ cubic units.}$$

In general, if the region bounded by a segment of a continuous positive function $y = f(x)$ and the lines $x = a$, $x = b$, and $y = 0$ is revolved about the x-axis to obtain a solid, then the volume of this solid of revolution is

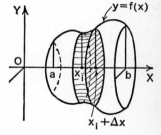

Fig. 19–12

$$\lim_{n \to \infty} \sum_{i=0}^{n} \pi y_i^2 \, \Delta x = \lim_{n \to \infty} \sum_{i=1}^{n} \pi [f(x)]^2 \, \Delta x = \int_a^b \pi [f(x)]^2 \, dx$$

where

$$\Delta x = \frac{b-a}{n} \quad \text{and} \quad x_i = a + i \, \Delta x.$$

The reader who wishes further enlightenment may consult almost any book entitled Calculus under the topics *integral* and *volume*.

At this mathematical level the two most important things to remember are:

1. An integral is actually the limit of a sum, not merely an antiderivative.

2. The fundamental theorem of the integral: If $\dfrac{dF(x)}{dx} = f(x)$

and if $\int_a^b f(x) \, dx$ exists, then $\int_a^b f(x) \, dx = F(b) - F(a)$.

*19–8. Newton's method of approximating roots of an equation. Sections 3–2, 3–8, and 4–5 each considered methods of determining approximate real roots of an equation $f(x) = 0$. The method of halving the interval given in Section 3–8 is excellent for machine computation, but involves considerable arithmetic

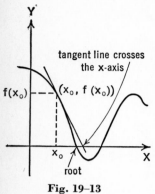

Fig. 19–13

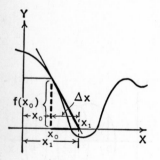

Fig. 19–14

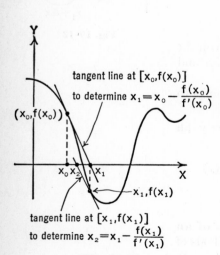

Fig. 19–15

work if more than two significant digits of accuracy is desired by hand computation.

All methods of determining approximate roots are essentially methods of refinement. First an approximate value x_0 near the root must be determined and then some systematic method be used to improve the approximation of the root. Just how near to the root x_0 must be depends upon the method used and how complicated the equation is. One of the most effective methods of improving a guess is known as **Newton's method.**†

The solution of the equation $f(x) = 0$ is the value of x at which the curve $y = f(x)$ crosses the x-axis. Let a point $x = x_0$ be selected which is near this crossing point (see Fig. 19–13). If the curve $y = f(x)$ is sufficiently steep at $[x_0, f(x_0)]$, it seems reasonable to believe that the tangent line at the point $[x_0, f(x_0)]$ will cross the x-axis at a point x_1 nearer to the root than was x_0. It would be feasible to write the equation of the tangent line and determine where it crosses the x-axis, but this really is unnecessary. What we need is the distance Δx between x_0 and x_1 (see Fig. 19–14). The slope of this tangent line is $\dfrac{-f(x_0)}{\Delta x}$ and must also equal $f'(x_0)$. (Why?)

Hence

$$\frac{-f(x_0)}{\Delta x} = f'(x_0)$$

or

$$\Delta x = -\frac{f(x_0)}{f'(x_0)}$$

and $x_1 = x_0 + \Delta x = x_0 - \dfrac{f(x_0)}{f'(x_0)}$ is a new approximation of the root. There is no reason why this process need stop after one improvement. Using x_1 as a starting guess, a similar agreement gives rise to

$$x_2 = x_1 - \frac{f(x_1)}{f'(x_1)}$$

and

$$x_3 = x_2 - \frac{f(x_2)}{f'(x_2)}$$

etc.

Newton's method. Let $f(x)$ be a continuous function (*not* necessarily a polynomial) such that the equation $f(x) = 0$ has a real root near $x = x_k$. Then

† The reader will recall that Newton was one of the coinventors of the calculus, and is also remembered for his work on the theory of gravitation.

$$x_{k+1} = x_k - \frac{f(x_k)}{f'(x_k)}$$

is apt to be a better approximation of the root than was x_k, especially if $f'(x_k)$ is larger than $f(x_k)$ in absolute value.

The reader will note some hesitation in the phrase "is apt to be." Unless rather complicated restrictions are placed on the function $f(x)$ and its derivative, this is as strong a statement as is justified. Newton's method is used in more advanced courses where a more detailed discussion is given. In practice, if the sequence of approximate roots $\{x_0, x_1, x_2, x_3, \cdots\}$ appears to converge, then very likely the sequence does converge. If it does not appear to be converging, then either a better starting approximation x_0 is needed or the function $f(x)$ is "not well behaved." The latter is apt to be the case if $f'(x_i)$ is very small, or if $f'(x_i)$ is undefined for some x_i near the root. In this case other methods of refinement should be used.

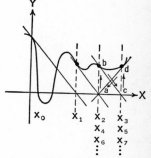

Some of the dangers involved in the mechanical use of Newton's method are apparent if the first approximation had been taken as $x = 0$ on the function sketched in Figure 19–16. In this case the "approximations" x_0, x_1, x_2, x_3 recede from the root and finally, since x_2 and x_4 are identical, the remaining approximations will shuttle back and forth between x_2 and x_3. (Why?) Even though there are two roots between x_0 and x_1, in this example they will not be found by starting with $x_0 = 0$. A choice of x_0 nearer one root could have given better results.

A few examples are given below. The arithmetic is not always easy, so concentrate on the ideas and accept the arithmetic as correct at least on your first reading.

Fig. 19–16

● *Example 1.*

Determine a root of

$$f(x) = x \sin x - 2x + 0.2 = 0$$

accurate to six decimal places.

As a first approximation we start with $x_0 = .7$.

If $x_0 = .7$, then $f(x_0) = -.7490476$, $f'(x_0) = -.8203928$, $\Delta x = .91303532$, and $x_1 = x_0 - \Delta x = -.21303532$.

The first and second approximations differ by almost a whole unit, which is large percentagewise, in this case. Nevertheless we continue:

If $x_1 = -.21303532$, then $f(x) = .67111218$, $f'(x) = -2.4196469$, $\Delta x = -.27735955$, and $x_2 = x_1 - \Delta x = +.06432423$.

Since $f'(x_1)$ is greater than one in absolute value, we feel hopeful. Let us continue:

If $x_2 = +.06432423$, then $f(x_2) = .07548914$, $f'(x_2) = -1.8714846$, $\Delta x = -.040336501$ and $x_3 = x_2 - \Delta x = .10466073$.

Continuing we obtain:

$x_3 = .10466073$, $f(x_3) = .00161242$,
$\qquad f'(x_3) = -1.7914422$, $\Delta x = -.000900068$

$x_4 = x_3 - \Delta x = .10556080$, $f(x_4) = +.0000008$,
$\qquad f'(x_4) = -1.7896619$, $\Delta x = .000000447$

$x_5 = x_4 - \Delta x = .10556125$, $f(x_5) = -.00000001$,
$\qquad f'(x_5) = -1.7896611$, $\Delta x = .00000000559$

$x_6 = x_5 - \Delta x = .10556124$, $f(x_6) = +.00000001$.

Note that x_5 and x_6 differ only in the eighth decimal place and that $f(x_5)$ is negative while $f(x_6)$ is positive. Hence, we can be certain that there is a root of $f(x) = 0$ between x_5 and x_6. Accurate to six decimal places the root is $x = .105561$. The computation was carried further than was needed in this problem to show the behavior at the next step. Newton's method is also useful in solving much simpler problems.

- **Example 2.** Use Newton's method to solve the equation $f(x) = x^2 - 7 = 0$ thus determining $\sqrt{7}$.

  We start with $x_0 = 3$ as our guess of $\sqrt{7}$. A better guess would be $x_0 = 2.5$.

$$f(x) = x^2 - 7 \qquad f'(x) = 2x$$

n	x_n	$f(x_n)$	$f'(x_n)$	Δx	$x_{n+1} = x_n - \Delta x$
0	+ 3.	+ 2.	6.	.33333333	2.6666667
1	2.6666667	+ .11111130	5.3333334	.020833368	2.6458333
2	2.6458333	+ .00043390	5.2916666	.00008199685	2.6457513
3	2.6457513	− .00000010	5.2915026	−.0000000188982	2.6457513

$x = 2.6457513$ is accurate to eight significant digits in three iterations — which is less work than the traditional "divide by 20 more than . . ." rule often taught in elementary schools.

- **Example 3.** Use Newton's method to solve the equation $f(x) = x^7 - 5 = 0$, thus determining $\sqrt[7]{5}$.

  We begin with $x_0 = 1$ as a first approximation.

$$f(x) = x^7 - 5 \qquad f'(x) = 7x^6$$

n	x_n	$f(x_n)$	$f'(x_n)$	Δx	$x_{n+1} = x_n - \Delta x$
0	1.0000000	$-$ 4.0000000	$-$ 7.	$-$ .57142857	1.5714286
1	1.5714286	18.662393	105.40520	.17705382	1.3943748
2	1.3943748	5.2483400	51.448419	.10201169	1.2923631
3	1.2923631	1.0213594	32.614299	.031316317	1.2610468
4	1.2610468	.0712755	28.150366	.0025319564	1.2585148
5	1.2585148	.0004182	27.812885	.000015036196	1.2584998
6	1.2584998	.0000132	27.810964	.00000047463295	1.2584993
7	1.2584993	.0000112	27.810964	.00000040271887	1.2584989

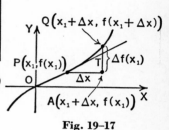

Fig. 19–17

Thus, to six significant digits (five decimal places in this case) the answer is

$$\sqrt[7]{5} = x = 1.25850 \quad \text{(note the rounding)}.$$

*19–9. Approximation of a function value. We wish to approximate $f(x_1 + \Delta x)$ when $x_1, \Delta x, f(x_1), f'(x_1)$ have known values.

At $P[x_1, f(x_1)]$ construct the tangent line to $y = f(x)$. Let T and A, respectively, be the points of intersection of the tangent line and the line $y = f(x_1)$ with the line $x = x_1 + \Delta x$.

Then

$$\frac{AT}{\Delta x} = f'(x_1) \quad \text{and} \quad AT = f'(x_1)\, \Delta x.$$

Also

$$\Delta f(x_1) = AQ = AT + TQ = f'(x_1)\, \Delta x + TQ$$
$$\Delta f(x_1) \approx f'(x_1)\Delta x$$

The smaller TQ is in absolute value, the better the approximation of $\Delta f(x_1)$ by $f'(x_1)\, \Delta x$. Frequently TQ is small in numerical value when Δx is small in numerical value. (In the figure consider what will happen to TQ as $PA = \Delta x$ gets nearer to zero.)

Now

$$f(x_1 + \Delta x) = f(x_1) + \Delta f(x_1)$$

and using our approximation $f'(x_1)\, \Delta x$ for $\Delta f(x_1)$ we obtain the approximation

$$f(x_1 + \Delta x) \approx f(x_1) + f'(x_1)\, \Delta x.$$

● *Example 1.* Approximate $\sqrt{105}$.

Here $f(x_1 + \Delta x) = \sqrt{105}$. So $f(x) = \sqrt{x}, f'(x) = \dfrac{1}{2\sqrt{x}},$

$f(x_1 + \Delta x) \approx \sqrt{x_1} + \dfrac{1}{2\sqrt{x_1}}\, \Delta x.$ The last result suggests that

x_1 be chosen as the nearest square to 105. Let $x_1 = 100$
then $100 + \Delta x = 105$ or $\Delta x = 5$ and

$$\sqrt{100 + 5} \approx \sqrt{100} + \frac{5}{2\sqrt{100}} = 10.25.$$

The approximation is correct to four significant figures.

● *Example 2.* In a right triangle A is measured as $60° \pm 0.1°$
The side adjacent to A is 100.0 ft long. Approximate the
length of the side a opposite A.

$$\frac{a}{100.0} = \tan A, \quad a = 100.0 \tan A = f(A),$$

$$f'(A) = 100.0 \frac{d \tan A}{dA} = 100.0 \sec^2 A, \quad A_1 = 60° \times \frac{\pi}{180°} = \frac{\pi}{3}$$

$$\Delta A = \pm 0.1° \times \frac{\pi}{180°} = \pm \frac{\pi}{1800}, \quad f\left(\frac{\pi}{3}\right) = 100.0 \tan \frac{\pi}{3}$$
$$= 173.2,$$

$$f'\left(\frac{\pi}{3}\right) = 100.0 \sec^2 \frac{\pi}{3} = 400.0,$$

$$a = f(A_1 + \Delta A) \approx f(A_1) + f'(A_1) \Delta A = 173.2 \pm \frac{400.0\pi}{1800}$$
$$= 173.2 \pm .7.$$

That is,

$$172.5 \leqq a \leqq 173.9.$$

PROBLEM SET 19-9

1. Approximate $\sqrt[3]{995}$.
2. Approximate $\sqrt{93}$.
3. In a right triangle the hypotenuse is measured as 500.0 to
the nearest tenth of a unit and one acute angle is $30° \pm 0.2°$.
Approximate the length of the side adjacent to the acute angle
mentioned.
4. Approximate the area of a circle if its radius is 10.0 ± 0.1.

20–1. Introduction. In Chapter 5 it was learned that $y - y_1 = m(x - x_1)$ is the equation of a line through the point (x_1, y_1) with slope m. Every straight line may be represented, in rectangular coordinates, by a linear equation of the type $Ax + By + C = 0$, and every linear equation of this type represents a straight line. It was seen that two lines have the same slope if, and only if, the lines are parallel. Some additional properties of the line will be considered, followed by a study of determinants, and of methods for solving systems of linear equations.

20–2. Angle of inclination. A line parallel to the x-axis has $0°$ for its **angle of inclination.** On a line not parallel to the x-axis, the upward direction is called the positive direction. The **angle of inclination** of a line not parallel to the x-axis is the smallest positive angle between the positive direction on the x-axis and the positive (upward) direction on the line. The angle of inclination α of a line in the xy-plane satisfies, $0° \leqq \alpha < 180°$.

Theorem 1. The slope,† m, of a line is equal to the tangent of the angle of inclination of the line.

$$m = \frac{y_2 - y_1}{x_2 - x_1} = \tan \alpha. \qquad (20.1)$$

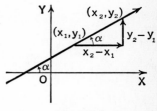

Fig. 20–1

20–3. Perpendicular lines.

Theorem 1. Two lines having nonzero slopes m_1 and m_2 are perpendicular if, and only if, $m_1 = -1/m_2$, or $m_1 m_2 = -1$.

The proof is given in two parts.
(1) We first show that if the lines are perpendicular, then $m_1 = -1/m_2$. Since the lines are perpendicular,‡ $\alpha_1 = \alpha_2 \pm 90°$, and

$$\tan \alpha_1 = \tan (\alpha_2 \pm 90°) = -\cot \alpha_2 = -1/\tan \alpha_2.$$

Hence, $m_1 = -1/m_2$.
(2) We next show that, if $m_1 = -1/m_2$, then the lines are perpendicular. If $m_1 = -1/m_2$, then,

$$\tan \alpha_1 = -1/\tan \alpha_2 = -\cot \alpha_2 = \tan (\alpha_2 \pm 90°),$$

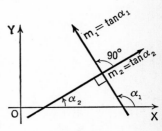

Fig. 20–2

† The slope is not defined when $\alpha = 90°$.
‡ In this paragraph, $\alpha_2 \pm 90°$ means either $\alpha_2 + 90°$ or $\alpha_2 - 90°$, but not both. Only one of the signs is correct for given α_1 and α_2, but it is unnecessary to determine which one is correct.

and $\alpha_1 = \alpha_2 \pm 90°$, since α_1 and α_2 each lie between $0°$ and $180°$. Consequently, the lines are perpendicular.

● **Example 1.** Write an equation of the line through $(3, -2)$ parallel to $5x - 4y + 7 = 0$.

The slope of a parallel line is the same as the slope of the given line, $m = \frac{5}{4}$. Using the point-slope form, a desired equation is $y + 2 = \frac{5}{4}(x - 3)$, or $5x - 4y - 23 = 0$.

● **Example 2.** Write an equation of the line through $(3, -2)$ perpendicular to $5x - 4y + 7 = 0$.

The slope of the given line is $\frac{5}{4}$. The slope of a line perpendicular to the given line is $-\frac{4}{5}$. An equation of the desired line is

$$y + 2 = (-\tfrac{4}{5})(x - 3), \quad \text{or} \quad 4x + 5y - 2 = 0.$$

Theorem 2. $Bx - Ay + k = 0$, with k an arbitrary constant, represents a family of lines perpendicular to the line $Ax + By + C = 0$.

If $A = 0$, the lines $Bx + k = 0$ and $By + C = 0$ are perpendicular, since the first line is parallel to the y-axis while the second line is parallel to the x-axis. If $B = 0$, the lines $-Ay + k = 0$ and $Ax + C = 0$ are perpendicular, since the first line is parallel to the x-axis while the second line is parallel to the y-axis. If $AB \neq 0$, the lines $Bx - Ay + k = 0$ and $Ax + By + C = 0$ have slopes B/A and $-A/B$, respectively. These slopes are negative reciprocals, and the lines are perpendicular.

● **Example 3.** Apply Theorem 2, to solve Example 2. The line $4x + 5y + k = 0$ is perpendicular to $5x - 4y + 7 = 0$. If the point $(3, -2)$ is on $4x + 5y + k = 0$, then

$$4(3) + 5(-2) + k = 0, \quad \text{and} \quad k = -2.$$

An equation of the desired line is $4x + 5y - 2 = 0$.

PROBLEM SET 20-3

1. Write an equation of the line through the point $(1, 3)$ (a) parallel to the line through the points $(-3, 1)$ and $(2, -2)$, (b) perpendicular to the line through the points $(-3, 1)$ and $(2, -2)$.

2. Find the area of the triangle having vertices

$$(1, 3), \quad (-3, 1), \quad (2, -2).$$

3. Prove that the points $(-1, 3), \quad (2, 15), \quad (-2, -1)$ lie on a line.

4. Is the triangle whose vertices are

$$(1, 0), \quad (2, 4) \quad \text{and} \quad (-3, 1)$$

a right triangle?

5. Write equations of the two tangent lines to $x^2 + y^2 = 25$ that are parallel to $3x + 4y = 50$.

6. Write an equation of the diameter that passes through the two points of tangency of Problem 5.

7. Write an equation of the line through $(-3, 4)$ that is perpendicular to $3x + 4y = 0$.

8. Write an equation of the line that passes through the point of intersection of the lines $3x - 5y + 7 = 0$ and $2x + 3y - 4 = 0$, and is perpendicular to $5x + 5y - 3 = 0$.

9. Prove: $Ax + By + k = 0$, with k an arbitrary constant, represents a family of lines parallel to the line

$$Ax + By + C = 0.$$

10. Apply the theorem of Problem 9 to solve Example 1 of Section 20–3.

11. At a point of intersection of the circles $x^2 + y^2 = 8$ and $x^2 + y^2 - 8x + 8 = 0$ there is a tangent line to each circle. Show that these tangent lines are perpendicular.

In Problems 12 to 15 consider the triangle with vertices ABC. Find (a) the equation of the side AC, (b) the length of the altitude from A to side BC, (c) the length of side AB, (d) the area of the triangle.

12. $A(2, -4), \quad B(6, -8), \quad C(4, 6)$.

13. $A(0, 0), \quad B(1, 7), \quad C(-2, 3)$.

14. $A(4, 3), \quad B(2, 4), \quad C(-6, 10)$.

15. $A(1, 3), \quad B(5, -4), \quad C(2, 3)$.

16. Find the equation of a line that passes through $(2, 5)$ and has equal intercepts. How many such lines are there?

17. Find the equation of a line passing through $(3, 4)$ and having intercepts equal in absolute value but opposite in sign. Is there more than one such line?

18. Find an equation of the perpendicular bisector of the line segment joining $(3, -1)$ and $(5, 7)$, using the method of this section. Compare Problem 7, Set 2–4.

19. Obtain the result of Problem 8, Set 2–4, using methods of this section.

The word **normal** is used in mathematics to mean "perpendicular." The **normal line** to a curve at a given point P on the curve is the line through P and perpendicular to the line tangent to the curve at P. The slope of the tangent line may be determined by differentiation. The slope of the normal line is the negative reciprocal of the slope of the tangent line. Hence the slope, and the equation, of the normal line to a given curve may be obtained at any point for which the derivative may be computed. In each of Problems 20 to 30 find the equation of the normal line to the stated curve at the indicated point P.

20. $y = x^3 - 4x + 6$, at $P(2, 6)$.
21. $y = 7x^3$, at $P(1, 7)$.
22. $3y = 4x^2 - 15$, at $P(-2, \frac{1}{3})$.
23. $5y^2 + 2x - 7x^2 = 0$, at $P(0, 0)$.
24. $3x^2 + x^3 - y^2 = -2$, at $P(-1, 2)$.
25. $3x + 7y - 6 = 0$, at $P(-5, 3)$.
26. $4x^2 + y - 67 = 0$, at $P(4, 3)$.
27. $3x^3 - x + 5y + 2 = 0$, at $P(-2, 4)$.
28. $y = \sqrt{4x - 3}$, at $P(3, 3)$.
29. $y = (x^2 - 3x + 1)^{10}$, at $P(2, 1)$.
30. $y = \sqrt{2x + 3x^2 + 6}$, at $P(3, \sqrt{39})$.

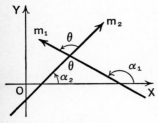

Fig. 20-3

Fig. 20-4

20-4. Angle of intersection of two lines. The angle of intersection of two parallel lines is defined to be 0°. If two lines are not parallel, let m_1 be the slope of the line having the larger angle of inclination and let m_2 be the slope of the line having the smaller angle of inclination. The **angle of intersection** is the smallest positive angle between the line of slope m_2 and the line of slope m_1.

From Figure 20-3, $\theta + \alpha_2 = \alpha_1$, $\theta = \alpha_1 - \alpha_2$. As a result,

$$\tan \theta = \tan (\alpha_1 - \alpha_2) = \frac{\tan \alpha_1 - \tan \alpha_2}{1 + \tan \alpha_1 \tan \alpha_2}$$

or

$$\tan \theta = \frac{m_1 - m_2}{1 + m_1 m_2}. \qquad (20.2)$$

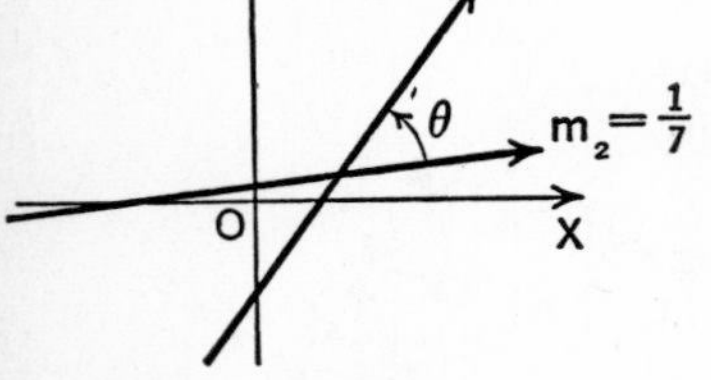

The angle of intersection is the smaller of the angles θ, $180° - \theta$.

● **Example 1.** Find the angle of intersection of $4x - 3y = 6$ and $x - 7y + 3 = 0$.

$$\tan \theta = \frac{\frac{4}{3} - \frac{1}{7}}{1 + (\frac{4}{3})(\frac{1}{7})} = 1, \qquad \theta = 45°.$$

PROBLEM SET 20-4

1. Find the angle of intersection of $3x + 2y = 5$ and $4x - 5y = 3$.

2. Find the angle of intersection of $2x + 5y - 10 = 0$ and $3x + 4y + 12 = 0$.

3. Write the equation of the line through $(2, -3)$ making an angle of intersection of $45°$ with $4x - 3y = 6$.

4. Write the equation of the line through $(-2, 1)$ making an angle of intersection of $60°$ with $2x + 3y - 5 = 0$.

5. Find the angle of intersection of the tangent lines to the circle $x^2 + y^2 = 5$ and to the parabola $y^2 = 4x$ at their point of intersection in the first quadrant.

6. Find the equation of the normal line to the parabola $y^2 = 4x$, at the point $(1, 2)$.

7. Find the point on the line $3x - 6y + 8 = 0$ that is equidistant from the points $(-7, 2)$ and $(5, 4)$.

8. Where is the center of a circle that is tangent to the line $11x + 2y = 9$ at the point $(-1, 10)$?

An angle of intersection of two curves at a point of intersection is the acute angle between lines tangent to each curve at that point. In Problems 9 to 12, find the angle of intersection of the given curves at each point of intersection.

9. $y = 3x + 5$, $y = x^2 + 1$.   **10.** $y^2 = 2px$, $x^2 = 2py$.
11. $x^2 + y^2 - 2x = 0$, $y = x^2 - 2x$.
12. $x^2 + y^2 - 2x = 0$, $x^2 + y^2 - 2y = 0$.

20-5. Normal equation of a line. In Figure 20-5 the line LN is perpendicular (normal) to the line ON. The angle of inclination of ON is ω. The distance from O to N is p. The coordinates of N are $(p \cos \omega, \ p \sin \omega)$. The slope of ON is $\tan \omega$. When $\omega \neq 0$, the slope of LN is

$m = -1/\tan \omega = -\cos \omega / \sin \omega$, since LN is normal to ON. The point-slope form of the equation of the line LN is
$y - p \sin \omega = (-\cos \omega / \sin \omega)(x - p \cos \omega)$. Then,

$$(\sin \omega)y - p \sin^2 \omega = -(\cos \omega)x + p \cos^2 \omega,$$

or $(\cos \omega)x + (\sin \omega)y - p(\sin^2 \omega + \cos^2 \omega) = 0,$

or the **normal equation**

$$(\cos \omega)x + (\sin \omega)y - p = 0. \qquad (20.3)$$

When $\omega = 0°$, the normal equation is $x - p = 0$.

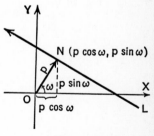

Fig. 20-5

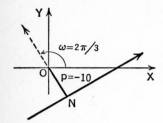

Fig. 20–6

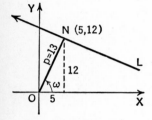

Fig. 20–7

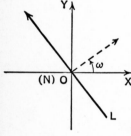

Fig. 20–8

● **Example 1.** Write the normal equation of the line, given
$$\omega = 2\pi/3, \quad p = -10.$$
$\cos \omega = \cos (2\pi/3) = -\tfrac{1}{2}, \quad \sin \omega = \sin (2\pi/3) = \sqrt{3}/2,$
$p = -10.$
The desired normal equation is
$$(-\tfrac{1}{2})x + (\sqrt{3}/2)y - (-10) = 0.$$
See Fig. 20–6.

● **Example 2.** Write the normal equation of the line through $N(5, 12)$, which is perpendicular to the line ON.
$$p = \sqrt{5^2 + 12^2} = 13, \quad \cos \omega = \tfrac{5}{13}, \quad \sin \omega = \tfrac{12}{13}.$$
The desired normal equation is
$$\tfrac{5}{13}x + \tfrac{12}{13}y - 13 = 0.$$
See Fig. 20–7.

● **Example 3.** Write the normal equation of the line through the origin, and perpendicular to $3x - 4y - 7 = 0$.
$$p = 0, \quad \tan \omega = \tfrac{3}{4}, \quad \cos \omega = \tfrac{4}{5}, \quad \sin \omega = \tfrac{3}{5}.$$
The desired normal equation is
$$\tfrac{4}{5}x + \tfrac{3}{5}y = 0.$$
See Fig. 20–8.

● **Example 4.** Write the equation of the line $Ax + By + C = 0$ in normal form.

The normal equation, $(\cos \omega)x + (\sin \omega)y - p = 0$, is equivalent to $Ax + By + C = 0$, if there is a constant k such that
$$k \cos \omega = A, \quad k \sin \omega = B, \quad k(-p) = C. \tag{20.4}$$
Now, $k^2 \cos^2 \omega + k^2 \sin^2 \omega = A^2 + B^2$. Hence, $k^2 = A^2 + B^2$, and $k = \pm \sqrt{A^2 + B^2} \neq 0$, since A and B are not both zero.

From (20.4), $\cos \omega = A/k$, $\sin \omega = B/k$, $p = -C/k$, and the normal form of $Ax + By + C = 0$ is
$$\left(\frac{A}{\pm \sqrt{A^2 + B^2}}\right)x + \left(\frac{B}{\pm \sqrt{A^2 + B^2}}\right)y - \left(\frac{-C}{\pm \sqrt{A^2 + B^2}}\right) = 0. \tag{20.5}$$

If $B \neq 0$, then $\sin \omega = B/k > 0$ and $k = +\sqrt{A^2 + B^2}$ when $B > 0$, or $k = -\sqrt{A^2 + B^2}$ when $B < 0$.
If $B = 0$, then $\cos \omega = A/k = 1$ and $k = A$.

• **Example 5.** Write $3x - 4y = 20$, in normal form. Since $B = -4 < 0$, we divide by $k = -\sqrt{3^2 + 4^2} = -5$. The normal equation is $(-\frac{3}{5})x + \frac{4}{5}y - (-4) = 0$, where $\cos \omega = -\frac{3}{5}$, $\sin \omega = \frac{4}{5}$, $p = -4$.

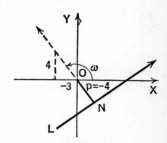

Fig. 20–9

• **Example 6.** Write the equations of the lines through the point $(7, 1)$ and tangent to the circle $x^2 + y^2 = 25$.

The equation of a line tangent to $x^2 + y^2 = 25$ may be written in one of the forms $(\cos \omega)x + (\sin \omega)y - (\pm 5) = 0$. (Why?) If $(7, 1)$ is on the line, then it satisfies the equation of the line. Hence, $7 \cos \omega + \sin \omega - (\pm 5) = 0$. The solution for $p = +5$ is left as a problem. The solution for $p = -5$ follows. In $7 \cos \omega + \sin \omega + 5 = 0$ solve for $7 \cos \omega$, and square both members of the resulting equation.

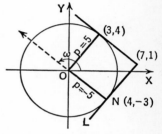

Fig. 20–10

$$7 \cos \omega = -\sin \omega - 5$$
$$49 \cos^2 \omega = \sin^2 \omega + 10 \sin \omega + 25.$$

Replace $\cos^2 \omega$ by $1 - \sin^2 \omega$, and rewrite as a quadratic equation in $\sin \omega$.

$$49(1 - \sin^2 \omega) = \sin^2 \omega + 10 \sin \omega + 25$$

$$50 \sin^2 \omega + 10 \sin \omega - 24 = 0,$$

or

$$2(5 \sin \omega + 4)(5 \sin \omega - 3) = 0.$$

The solution $\sin \omega = -\frac{4}{5}$ is impossible, since $0° \leq \omega < 180°$, (ω is an angle of inclination). Hence, $\sin \omega = \frac{3}{5}$,

$$7 \cos \omega = -\frac{3}{5} - 5, \quad \cos \omega = -\frac{4}{5},$$

and the normal equation of the desired tangent line is

$$(-\frac{4}{5})x + \frac{3}{5}y - (-5) = 0.$$

• **Example 7.** Find the distance between the point $(4, 5)$ and the line $(\cos 30°)x + (\sin 30°)y - 3 = 0$.

The normal equation of the line through $(4, 5)$ and parallel to the given line is $(\cos 30°)x + (\sin 30°)y - (3 + d) = 0$, where $|d|$ is the distance between the parallel lines. Now, $|d|$ will be the distance between $(4, 5)$ and $(\cos 30°)x + (\sin 30°)y - 3 = 0$ if the point $(4, 5)$ lies on $(\cos 30°)x + (\sin 30°)y - (3 + d) = 0$. Hence, $4 \cos 30° + 5 \sin 30° - (3 + d) = 0$, and

$$|d| = |4 \cos 30° + 5 \sin 30° - 3| = 2\sqrt{3} - \frac{1}{2}.$$

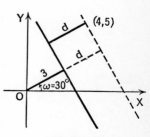

Fig. 20–11

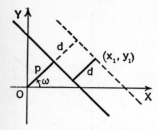

Fig. 20–12

● **Example 8.** Find the distance between the point (x_1, y_1) and the line $(\cos \omega)x + (\sin \omega)y - p = 0$.

The normal equation of the line through (x_1, y_1) and parallel to the given line is $(\cos \omega)x + (\sin \omega)y - (p + d) = 0$ where d is determined such that

$$(\cos \omega)x_1 + (\sin \omega)y_1 - (p + d) = 0.$$

Hence,

$$|\,d\,| = |\,(\cos \omega)x_1 + (\sin \omega)y_1 - p\,|.$$

The distance between (x_1, y_1) and $Ax + By + C = 0$ is

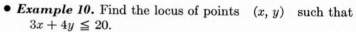

$$|\,d\,| = \left|\left(\frac{A}{\pm \sqrt{A^2 + B^2}}\right)x_1 + \left(\frac{B}{\pm \sqrt{A^2 + B^2}}\right)y_1 - \left(\frac{-C}{\pm \sqrt{A^2 + B^2}}\right)\right| = \frac{|\,Ax_1 + By_1 + C\,|}{\sqrt{A^2 + B^2}}. \qquad (20.6)$$

● **Example 9.** Find the distance between $(-8, -6)$ and $3x + 4y - 12 = 0$.

$$|\,d\,| = \frac{|\,3(-8) + 4(-6) - 12\,|}{\sqrt{3^2 + 4^2}} = 12.$$

● **Example 10.** Find the locus of points (x, y) such that $3x + 4y \leqq 20$.

Now, $\frac{3}{5}x + \frac{4}{5}y = p \leqq \frac{20}{5}$. When $p = 4$, the point (x, y) is on the line $\frac{3}{5}x + \frac{4}{5}y = 4$. When $p < 4$, the point (x, y) is on a line parallel to, and below, the line $\frac{3}{5}x + \frac{4}{5}y = 4$. The locus consists of all points on and below the line $3x + 4y = 20$.

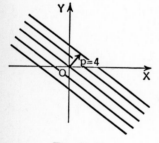

Fig. 20–13

PROBLEM SET 20–5

In each of Problems 1 to 8, write the normal equation of the line. Sketch the line.

1. $\omega = 120°$, $p = -6$.
2. $\omega = 135°$, $p = 4\sqrt{2}$.
3. $m = \frac{3}{4}$, $b = -5$.
4. $m = -\frac{5}{12}$, $b = 4$.
5. $y = -3x + 6$.
6. $y = 4x - 5$.
7. $6x - 8y - 25 = 0$.
8. $12x + 5y + 52 = 0$.
9. Find the distance between the line $6x - 8y - 25 = 0$, and the point $(6, -8)$.

0. Find the distance between the line $12x + 5y + 52 = 0$, and the point $(1, 8)$.

1. Find the distance between the lines $3x - 4y + 10 = 0$ and $3x - 4y - 20 = 0$.

2. Find the distance between the lines $5x + 12y - 39 = 0$ and $5x + 12y - 78 = 0$.

3. Write the equation of the circle that is tangent to $8x - 6y + 23 = 0$ and has the same center as $x^2 + y^2 - x + y - 5 = 0$.

4. A circle has its center at $(3, 2)$ and is tangent to $5x + 12y + 39 = 0$.
   (a) Find its radius.   (b) Write the equation of the circle.

5. Find the locus of points such that $5x - 12y \geq 39$.

6. A side of a triangle is on the line $3x + 4y = 15$. If the altitude to this side is 4, what is the locus of the opposite vertex? Find two solutions.

7. Write the equation of the line that has positive slope and bisects an angle between $3x - 4y - 5 = 0$ and $12x - 5y - 26 = 0$.

8. Complete the solution of Example 6, Section 20–5.

9. Find the equations of the tangent lines from $(3, 2)$ to the circle $x^2 + y^2 = 2$.

20–6. Solutions of linear systems using detached coefficients. A detached coefficient, or matrix, method for the solution of a system of linear equations is illustrated in this section. The rectangular array of coefficients and constant terms of a system of linear equations is called its matrix. In Example 1 this matrix is

$$\begin{bmatrix} 3 & 2 & 2 & 3 \\ 2 & -3 & 3 & 1 \\ 2 & 3 & -2 & -3 \end{bmatrix}.$$

Example 1. Solve $\begin{cases} 3x + 2y + 2z = 3 \\ 2x - 3y + 3z = 1 \\ 2x + 3y - 2z = -3. \end{cases}$

Solution using equations

$\begin{cases} (1)\ 3x + 2y + 2z = 3 \\ (2)\ 2x - 3y + 3z = 1 \\ (3)\ 2x + 3y - 2z = -3 \end{cases}$

Solution using matrices

$$\begin{bmatrix} 3 & 2 & 2 & 3 \\ 2 & -3 & 3 & 1 \\ 2 & 3 & -2 & -3 \end{bmatrix}$$

Multiply equation (1) by $\frac{1}{3}$. Add $-\frac{2}{3}$ of equation (1) to equation (2). Add $-\frac{2}{3}$ of equation (1) to equation (3). Obtain the resulting equivalent system of equations and the corresponding matrix.

Solution using equations

$$\begin{cases} (4) \ 1x + \tfrac{2}{3}y + \tfrac{2}{3}z = 1 \\ (5) \quad\ -\tfrac{13}{3}y + \tfrac{5}{3}z = -1 \\ (6) \qquad\ \tfrac{5}{3}y - \tfrac{10}{3}z = -5 \end{cases}$$

Solution using matrices

$$\begin{bmatrix} 1 & \tfrac{2}{3} & \tfrac{2}{3} & 1 \\ 2 + (-\tfrac{2}{3})(3) & -3 + (-\tfrac{2}{3})(2) & 3 + (-\tfrac{2}{3})(2) & 1 + (-\tfrac{2}{3})(3) \\ 2 + (-\tfrac{2}{3})(3) & 3 + (-\tfrac{2}{3})(2) & -2 + (-\tfrac{2}{3})(2) & -3 + (-\tfrac{2}{3})(3) \end{bmatrix}$$

or

$$\begin{bmatrix} 1 & \tfrac{2}{3} & \tfrac{2}{3} & 1 \\ 0 & -\tfrac{13}{3} & \tfrac{5}{3} & -1 \\ 0 & \tfrac{5}{3} & -\tfrac{10}{3} & -5 \end{bmatrix}$$

Multiply equation (6) by $\tfrac{3}{5}$ and write as equation (7). Ad $\tfrac{13}{5}$ of equation (6) to equation (5) and write as equation (8). O tain the resulting equivalent system of equations and the corr sponding matrix.

Solution using equations

$$\begin{cases} (4) \ 1x + \tfrac{2}{3}y + \tfrac{2}{3}z = 1 \\ (7) \qquad\ 1y - 2z = -3 \\ (8) \qquad\quad\ -7z = -14 \end{cases}$$

Solution using matrice

$$\begin{bmatrix} 1 & \tfrac{2}{3} & \tfrac{2}{3} & 1 \\ 0 & 1 & -2 & -3 \\ 0 & 0 & -7 & -14 \end{bmatrix}$$

Multiply equation (8) by $-\tfrac{1}{7}$. Add $-\tfrac{2}{7}$ of (8) to (7 Add $\tfrac{2}{21}$ of (8) to (4). Obtain the new equivalent system of equatio and the corresponding matrix.

$$\begin{cases} (9) \ 1x + \tfrac{2}{3}y \quad\ = -\tfrac{1}{3} \\ (10) \qquad\ 1y \quad\ = 1 \\ (11) \qquad\qquad 1z = 2 \end{cases} \qquad \begin{bmatrix} 1 & \tfrac{2}{3} & 0 & -\tfrac{1}{3} \\ 0 & 1 & 0 & 1 \\ 0 & 0 & 1 & 2 \end{bmatrix}$$

Add $-\tfrac{2}{3}$ of (10) to (9) and obtain a final equivalent syste of equations and the corresponding matrix.

$$\begin{cases} (12) \ 1x \qquad\quad = -1 \\ (10) \qquad 1y \quad\ = 1 \\ (11) \qquad\qquad 1z = 2 \end{cases} \qquad \begin{bmatrix} 1 & 0 & 0 & -1 \\ 0 & 1 & 0 & 1 \\ 0 & 0 & 1 & 2 \end{bmatrix}$$

The preceding systems of three equations are equivalent in th sense that the solutions of any system are the solutions of ever system. The work may be shortened by noticing that equivale systems of linear equations may be obtained by applying thr rules.

For equations	**For the coefficient array, or matrix**
1. Both members of an equation may be multiplied by the same nonzero constant.	1. The elements of a row of the coefficient matrix may be multiplied by a nonzero constant.
2. The order in which the equations are written is immaterial.	2. Any two rows of the matrix may be interchanged.
3. The members of an equation may be added to those of another equation.	3. The elements of a row of a matrix may be added to the corresponding elements of a different row of the matrix.

The detached coefficient, matrix method, applied by an efficient operator, usually yields a solution more rapidly than other methods. Large computing machines use the matrix method.

• **Example 12.** Apply the matrix method to find solutions of

$$\begin{cases} 2x + 3y + 3z = 2 \\ 4x - 3y - 6z = 2 \\ 10x - 6y + 3z = 0. \end{cases}$$

The coefficient matrix is
$$\begin{bmatrix} 2 & 3 & 3 & 2 \\ 4 & -3 & -6 & 2 \\ 10 & -6 & 3 & 0 \end{bmatrix}.$$

Add -2 times the elements of the first row to the corresponding elements of the second row. Add -5 times the elements of the first row to the corresponding elements of the third row. The new matrix is

$$\begin{bmatrix} 2 & 3 & 3 & 2 \\ 4 + (-2)(2) & -3 + (-2)(3) & -6 + (-2)(3) & 2 + (-2)(2) \\ 10 + (-5)(2) & -6 + (-5)(3) & 3 + (-5)(3) & 0 + (-5)(2) \end{bmatrix},$$

or

$$\begin{bmatrix} 2 & 3 & 3 & 2 \\ 0 & -9 & -12 & -2 \\ 0 & -21 & -12 & -10 \end{bmatrix}.$$

Multiply the elements of the first row by $\frac{1}{2}$, the second by $-\frac{1}{9}$, and the third by $-\frac{1}{21}$. The new matrix is

$$\begin{bmatrix} 1 & \frac{3}{2} & \frac{3}{2} & 1 \\ 0 & 1 & \frac{4}{3} & \frac{2}{9} \\ 0 & 1 & \frac{4}{7} & \frac{10}{21} \end{bmatrix}.$$

Subtract the elements of the second row from the corresponding elements of the third row to obtain

$$\begin{bmatrix} 1 & \frac{3}{2} & \frac{3}{2} & 1 \\ 0 & 1 & \frac{4}{3} & \frac{2}{9} \\ 0 & 0 & -\frac{16}{21} & \frac{16}{63} \end{bmatrix}.$$

Multiply the elements of the third row by $-\frac{21}{16}$ to obtain

$$\begin{bmatrix} 1 & \frac{3}{2} & \frac{3}{2} & 1 \\ 0 & 1 & \frac{4}{3} & \frac{2}{9} \\ 0 & 0 & 1 & -\frac{1}{3} \end{bmatrix}.$$

To the elements of the second row add $-\frac{4}{3}$ of the corresponding elements of the third row, and to the elements of the first row add $-\frac{3}{2}$ of the corresponding elements of the third row. The resulting matrix is

$$\begin{bmatrix} 1 & \frac{3}{2} & 0 & \frac{3}{2} \\ 0 & 1 & 0 & \frac{2}{3} \\ 0 & 0 & 1 & -\frac{1}{3} \end{bmatrix}.$$

To the elements of the first row add $-\frac{3}{2}$ of the corresponding elements of the second row and obtain

$$\begin{bmatrix} 1 & 0 & 0 & \frac{1}{2} \\ 0 & 1 & 0 & \frac{2}{3} \\ 0 & 0 & 1 & -\frac{1}{3} \end{bmatrix}.$$

The desired solution is

$$1x \qquad\qquad = \tfrac{1}{2}$$
$$1y \qquad = \tfrac{2}{3}$$
$$1z = -\tfrac{1}{3}.$$

PROBLEM SET 20-6

Use the matrix method to solve each of the following systems of equations. Check solutions by substitution.

1. $\begin{cases} A + B - C = 7 \\ 2A - 3B - C = 0. \\ 2A - 4B - 3C = 0. \end{cases}$

2. $\begin{cases} 3x - 2y + z = 4 \\ x - 5y + 3z = 18 \\ 2x - y + 4z = 12. \end{cases}$

3. $\begin{cases} x - 2y + z + t = 4 \\ 3x - y - 3z - 2t = 1 \\ x - 3y - z + t = 1 \\ x - y - 2z - 3t = -6. \end{cases}$

4. $\begin{cases} A - B + C - D = -2 \\ 2A + 3B - 4C + D = 0 \\ 5A + 8B - 10C + 3D = 3 \\ 7A + 2B - 3C + D = 6. \end{cases}$

5. $\begin{cases} 4x + y + 3t + 3 = 0 \\ 2x + 4y + 4z + t = 14 \\ 8x - z + t + 7 = 0 \\ 4x - y - 3z + 2t + 12 = 0. \end{cases}$

6. $\begin{cases} 2A + B - 3C = 4 \\ 5A - 2B - C = -2 \\ 19A - 4B - 9C = -3. \end{cases}$

7. $\begin{cases} 2A + 2B - C = 3 \\ 4A + 4B + 5C = 7 \\ A + B + 3C = 5. \end{cases}$

8. $\begin{cases} A + 2B - 5C = 0 \\ 2A + B - 2C = 0 \\ A - 4B + 11C = 0. \end{cases}$

9. $\begin{cases} 3A + B - 2C = 0 \\ 4A + 2B - C = 0 \\ A - 3B - C = 0. \end{cases}$

10. $\begin{cases} x - 3y + 2z = 0 \\ x - 2y - z = 0 \\ 2x - y + 3z = 0. \end{cases}$

11. $\begin{cases} 5x + 2y - 3z = 2 \\ 2x - y - 3z = -3. \end{cases}$

12. $\begin{cases} A + 2B + 3C = 0 \\ 2A - B + 2C = 0. \end{cases}$

13. $\begin{cases} 3A - 2B + C = 0 \\ 2A + 4B - 5C = 0. \end{cases}$

14. $\begin{cases} 3x + y + 2z - 1 = 0 \\ 2x - 4y + z - 2 = 0. \end{cases}$

15. $\begin{cases} 2x - y - z = 0 \\ 4x + y - 11z = 0 \\ x - 3y + 7z = 0 \end{cases}$

16. $\begin{cases} 2x - y - z = 1 \\ 4x + y - 11z = -2 \\ x - 3y + 7z = 2 \end{cases}$

17. $\begin{cases} x - y + 2z - 3w = 0 \\ 2x + 3y - 4z + 5w = 0 \\ 2x - y + z + 2w = 0 \\ 3x + 3y - 5z + 10w = 0 \end{cases}$

18. $\begin{cases} x - y + 2z - 3w = 0 \\ 2x + 3y - 4z + 5w = 0 \\ 2x - y + z + 2w = 0 \\ 3x + 3y - 5z + 10w = 0 \\ x + y + z + w = 0 \end{cases}$

19. Find the point on the line $6x - 3y - 8 = 0$ that is equidistant from the points $(2, -7)$ and $(4, 5)$.

20. A circle has its center at $(-\frac{1}{2}, \frac{1}{2})$ and is tangent to $6x - 8y - 23 = 0$.
    (a) Find its radius. (b) Write the equation of the circle.

21. Calvin Butterball has $2.88 in pennies, nickels, and dimes. There are 144 coins with more dimes than nickels. Can you tell how many coins of each type Calvin has, if you know that he has at least one of each type?

20–7. Determinants. Any set of n^2 elements can be arranged in a square array or square **matrix**, M_n, as follows:

$$M_1 = [a_1], \qquad M_2 = \begin{bmatrix} a_1 & b_1 \\ a_2 & b_2 \end{bmatrix}, \qquad M_3 = \begin{bmatrix} a_1 & b_1 & c_1 \\ a_2 & b_2 & c_2 \\ a_3 & b_3 & c_3 \end{bmatrix}, \cdots \qquad (20.7)$$

where the subscript indicates the row, and the letter indicates the column, in which any particular element appears.

The determinants $|M_i|$ of the square matrices M_i are represented by the following symbols †:

$$|M_1| = |a_1|, \quad |M_2| = \begin{vmatrix} a_1 & b_1 \\ a_2 & b_2 \end{vmatrix}, \quad |M_3| = \begin{vmatrix} a_1 & b_1 & c_1 \\ a_2 & b_2 & c_2 \\ a_3 & b_3 & c_3 \end{vmatrix}, \cdots \quad (20.8)$$

A **minor** of an **element** in $|M_i|$, $i \geq 2$, is the determinant remaining after removing the row and the column containing the element. For example, the minor of c_2 in $|M_3|$ is

$$\begin{vmatrix} a_1 & b_1 & c_1 \\ a_2 & b_2 & c_2 \\ a_3 & b_3 & c_3 \end{vmatrix} = \begin{vmatrix} a_1 & b_1 \\ a_3 & b_3 \end{vmatrix}.$$

The **cofactor of an element** in a determinant is the product of the minor of the element and $(-1)^{\rho+\gamma}$, where ρ is the row number or subscript of the element and γ is the column number (numbered $1, 2, 3, \cdots$ from left to right) of the element. The corresponding capital letter is used to indicate the cofactor of an element. The cofactor of c_2 in $|M_3|$ is

$$C_2 = (-1)^{2+3} \begin{vmatrix} a_1 & b_1 \\ a_3 & b_3 \end{vmatrix} = -\begin{vmatrix} a_1 & b_1 \\ a_3 & b_3 \end{vmatrix}.$$

The **determinants** $|M_i|$ **of the square matrices** M_i **are** defined by the following expansions:

$$|M_1| = |a_1| = a_1, \quad |M_2| = \begin{vmatrix} a_1 & b_1 \\ a_2 & b_2 \end{vmatrix} = a_1 A_1 + a_2 A_2,$$

$$|M_3| = \begin{vmatrix} a_1 & b_1 & c_1 \\ a_2 & b_2 & c_2 \\ a_3 & b_3 & c_3 \end{vmatrix} = a_1 A_1 + a_2 A_2 + a_3 A_3, \cdots,$$

$$|M_n| = \sum_{i=1}^{n} a_i A_i, \quad\quad\quad (20.9)$$

where A_i is the cofactor of a_i. The determinant of a numerical array is a single number.

● *Example 1.*

$$\begin{vmatrix} 3 & -4 \\ 5 & 6 \end{vmatrix} = 3(-1)^{1+1}|6| + 5(-1)^{2+1}|-4| = 3(6) - 5(-4) = 38.$$

● *Example 2.*

$$|M_2| = \begin{vmatrix} a_1 & b_1 \\ a_2 & b_2 \end{vmatrix} = a_1(-1)^{1+1}|b_2| + a_2(-1)^{2+1}|b_1| = a_1 b_2 - a_2 b_1.$$

† Here $|a_1| = a_1$, not the absolute value of a_1.

● *Example 3.*

$$\begin{vmatrix} \overset{\downarrow}{1} & 6 & 7 \\ -2 & -5 & 8 \\ 3 & 4 & -9 \end{vmatrix} = 1(-1)^{1+1} \cdot \begin{vmatrix} -5 & 8 \\ 4 & -9 \end{vmatrix}$$

$$+ (-2)(-1)^{2+1} \cdot \begin{vmatrix} 6 & 7 \\ 4 & -9 \end{vmatrix} + 3(-1)^{3+1} \cdot \begin{vmatrix} 6 & 7 \\ -5 & 8 \end{vmatrix}$$

$$= 1\{(-5)(-9) - 4(8)\} + 2\{6(-9) - 4(7)\} + 3\{6(8) - (-5)(7)\}$$
$$= 1\{13\} + 2\{-82\} + 3\{83\} = 98.$$

● *Example 4.* Show that $|M_3|$ can also be expanded as
$|M_3| = a_1 A_1 + b_1 B_1 + c_1 C_1.$

$$|M_3| = \begin{vmatrix} \overset{\downarrow}{a_1} & b_1 & c_1 \\ a_2 & b_2 & c_2 \\ a_3 & b_3 & c_3 \end{vmatrix} = a_1(-1)^2 \cdot \begin{vmatrix} b_2 & c_2 \\ b_3 & c_3 \end{vmatrix} + a_2(-1)^3 \cdot \begin{vmatrix} b_1 & c_1 \\ b_3 & c_3 \end{vmatrix} + a_3(-1)^4 \cdot \begin{vmatrix} b_1 & c_1 \\ b_2 & c_2 \end{vmatrix}$$

$$= a_1(b_2 c_3 - b_3 c_2) - a_2(b_1 c_3 - b_3 c_1) + a_3(b_1 c_2 - b_2 c_1)$$
$$= a_1 b_2 c_3 - a_1 b_3 c_2 - a_2 b_1 c_3 + a_2 b_3 c_1 + a_3 b_1 c_2 - a_3 b_2 c_1.$$

If the terms in a_1, b_1, c_1 respectively, are collected, then
$$|M_3| = a_1(b_2 c_3 - b_3 c_3) - b_1(a_2 c_3 - a_3 c_2) + c_1(a_2 b_3 - a_3 b_2)$$

$$= a_1(-1)^2 \cdot \begin{vmatrix} b_2 & c_2 \\ b_3 & c_3 \end{vmatrix} + b_1(-1)^3 \cdot \begin{vmatrix} a_2 & c_2 \\ a_3 & c_3 \end{vmatrix} + c_1(-1)^4 \cdot \begin{vmatrix} a_2 & b_2 \\ a_3 & b_3 \end{vmatrix}$$
$$= a_1 A_1 + b_1 B_1 + c_1 C_1.$$

It follows that $|M_3|$ may be obtained by using cofactors of elements either of the first column or of the first row. Similarly, it can be shown that the expansion of every determinant may be obtained by summing all products obtained on multiplying each element of the first row (rather than column) by its cofactor. We shall state, but not prove, a more general theorem.

Theorem 1. A determinant may be expanded by summing all products obtained by multiplying each element of a fixed column (or row) by its cofactor.

In the summation notation (of Section 10–2) Theorem 1 states that

$$| M_n | = \sum_{i=1}^{n} a_i A_i = \sum_{i=1}^{n} b_i B_i = \sum_{i=1}^{n} c_i C_i = \cdots = \sum_{x} x_1 X_1$$

$$= \sum_{x} x_2 X_2 = \sum_{x} x_3 X_3 = \cdots, \tag{20.10}$$

where

$$x = a, b, c, \cdots, n.$$

● **Example 5.** Expand the determinant of Example 3, using the cofactors of the elements of (a) the second column, (b) the third row.

(a) $6(-1)^{1+2} \cdot \begin{vmatrix} -2 & 8 \\ 3 & -9 \end{vmatrix} + (-5)(-1)^{2+2} \cdot \begin{vmatrix} 1 & 7 \\ 3 & -9 \end{vmatrix} + 4(-1)^{3+2} \cdot \begin{vmatrix} 1 & 7 \\ -2 & 8 \end{vmatrix}$

$= -6\{(-2)(-9)-(3)(8)\}-5\{1(-9)-3(7)\}-4\{1(8)-(-2)(7)\}$

$= -6\{-6\}-5\{-30\}-4\{22\} = 98.$

(b) $3(-1)^{3+1} \cdot \begin{vmatrix} 6 & 7 \\ -5 & 8 \end{vmatrix} + 4(-1)^{3+2} \cdot \begin{vmatrix} 1 & 7 \\ -2 & 8 \end{vmatrix} + (-9)(-1)^{3+3} \cdot \begin{vmatrix} 1 & 6 \\ -2 & -5 \end{vmatrix}$

$= 3\{6(8)-(-5)(7)\}-4\{1(8)-(-2)(7)\}-9\{1(-5)-(-2)(6)\}$

$= 3\{83\}-4\{22\}-9\{7\} = 98.$

PROBLEM SET 20-7

Expand the determinants given in Problems 1 to 9, using the cofactors of the elements of (a) the first column, (b) the second row.

1. $\begin{vmatrix} -2 & 3 \\ 3 & -5 \end{vmatrix}.$

2. $\begin{vmatrix} -2-x & 3 \\ 3 & -5-x \end{vmatrix}.$

3. $\begin{vmatrix} 4-x & -5 \\ -5 & -3-x \end{vmatrix}.$

4. $\begin{vmatrix} 0 & -2 & 3 \\ -2 & 1 & 4 \\ 3 & 4 & 2 \end{vmatrix}.$

5. $\begin{vmatrix} -2 & 4 & 1 \\ 3 & -6 & 2 \\ 4 & -8 & 5 \end{vmatrix}.$

6. $\begin{vmatrix} 3 & -4 & -1 \\ 0 & 2 & 1 \\ -15 & 20 & 5 \end{vmatrix}.$

7. $\begin{vmatrix} 1-x & 2 & -3 \\ 2 & -1-x & -2 \\ -3 & -2 & 2-x \end{vmatrix}.$

8. $\begin{vmatrix} 2-x & 0 & 2 \\ 0 & 1-x & 0 \\ 2 & 0 & 3-x \end{vmatrix}.$ **9.** $\begin{vmatrix} 1 & x & x^2 \\ 1 & y & y^2 \\ 1 & z & z^2 \end{vmatrix}.$

Solve the equations given in Problems 10 and 11.

10. $\begin{vmatrix} -2-x & 3 \\ 3 & -5-x \end{vmatrix} = 0.$ **11.** $\begin{vmatrix} 1-x & 2 & 0 \\ 2 & -1-x & -2 \\ 0 & -2 & 1-x \end{vmatrix} = 0.$

20–8. Theorems about determinants. The theorems on determinants used in this text may be proved for $i = n$. For simplicity, we shall merely exhibit examples in the case $i = 3$. The reader who is interested in a more general treatment of determinants, may consult one of the references listed in the footnote.†

Let $T(M_i)$ be the matrix obtained from M_i by interchanging the corresponding rows and columns of M_i. $T(M_i)$ is the **transpose** of M_i.

● *Example 1.*

$$T(M_3) = \begin{bmatrix} a_1 & a_2 & a_3 \\ b_1 & b_2 & b_3 \\ c_1 & c_2 & c_3 \end{bmatrix}, \quad \text{where} \quad M_3 = \begin{bmatrix} a_1 & b_1 & c_1 \\ a_2 & b_2 & c_2 \\ a_3 & b_3 & c_3 \end{bmatrix}.$$

Theorem 1. The determinant of $T(M_i)$ is equal to the determinant of M_i. In symbols, $|T(M_i)| = |M_i|$.

$$|T(M_3)| = \begin{vmatrix} a_1 & a_2 & a_3 \\ b_1 & b_2 & b_3 \\ c_1 & c_2 & c_3 \end{vmatrix} = a_1(-1)^{1+1} \begin{vmatrix} b_2 & b_3 \\ c_2 & c_3 \end{vmatrix} + b_1(-1)^{2+1} \begin{vmatrix} a_2 & a_3 \\ c_2 & c_3 \end{vmatrix}$$

$$+ c_1(-1)^{3+1} \begin{vmatrix} a_2 & a_3 \\ b_2 & b_3 \end{vmatrix}$$

$$= a_1(b_2c_3 - b_3c_2) - b_1(a_2c_3 - a_3c_2) + c_1(a_2b_3 - a_3b_2)$$
$$= a_1(b_2c_3 - b_3c_2) - a_2(b_1c_3 - b_3c_1) + a_3(b_1c_2 - b_2c_1)$$
$$= a_1A_1 + a_2A_2 + a_3A_3 = |M_3|.$$

From Theorem 1 it follows that theorems about determinants stated for columns, *may be restated for rows.*

† Andree, R. V., *Selections from Modern Abstract Algebra*, New York: Holt, Rinehart and Winston, 1958, pages 104–173. Weiss, Marie J.: *Higher Algebra for the Undergraduate*, New York: Wiley, 1949, pages 123–144.

Theorem 2. If two columns (or rows) of a square matrix are interchanged, the determinant of the resulting matrix is equal to minus one times the determinant of the original matrix.

$$\begin{vmatrix} c_1 & b_1 & a_1 \\ c_2 & b_2 & a_2 \\ c_3 & b_3 & a_3 \end{vmatrix} = c_1(-1)^{1+1}\begin{vmatrix} b_2 & a_2 \\ b_3 & a_3 \end{vmatrix} + c_2(-1)^{2+1}\begin{vmatrix} b_1 & a_1 \\ b_3 & a_3 \end{vmatrix}$$

$$+ c_3(-1)^{3+1}\begin{vmatrix} b_1 & a_1 \\ b_2 & a_2 \end{vmatrix}$$

$$= c_1(b_2a_3 - b_3a_2) - c_2(b_1a_3 - b_3a_1) + c_3(b_1a_2 - b_2a_1)$$
$$= - a_1(b_2c_3 - b_3c_2) + a_2(b_1c_3 - b_3c_1) - a_3(b_1c_2 - b_2c_1)$$
$$= (-1) \cdot \begin{vmatrix} a_1 & b_1 & c_1 \\ a_2 & b_2 & c_2 \\ a_3 & b_3 & c_3 \end{vmatrix} \cdot$$

Theorem 3. If each element of a column (or row) of a square matrix is divided by k, $k \neq 0$, then the determinant of the original matrix is equal to k times the determinant of the resulting matrix.

$$\begin{vmatrix} a_1 & b_1 & kc_1 \\ a_2 & b_2 & kc_2 \\ a_3 & b_3 & kc_3 \end{vmatrix} = kc_1(-1)^{1+3}\begin{vmatrix} a_2 & b_2 \\ a_3 & b_3 \end{vmatrix} + kc_2(-1)^{2+3}\begin{vmatrix} a_1 & b_1 \\ a_3 & b_3 \end{vmatrix} + kc_3(-1)^{3+3}\begin{vmatrix} a_1 & b_1 \\ a_2 & b_2 \end{vmatrix}$$

$$= k(c_1C_1 + c_2C_2 + c_3C_3) = k\begin{vmatrix} a_1 & b_1 & c_1 \\ a_2 & b_2 & c_2 \\ a_3 & b_3 & c_3 \end{vmatrix} \cdot$$

● *Example 2.*

$$\begin{vmatrix} 2 & 8 & 5 \\ 6 & -12 & 15 \\ -4 & 20 & 20 \end{vmatrix} = (2)(4)(5)\begin{vmatrix} 1 & 2 & 1 \\ 3 & -3 & 3 \\ -2 & 5 & 4 \end{vmatrix}$$

$$= 40(3)\begin{vmatrix} 1 & 2 & 1 \\ 1 & -1 & 1 \\ -2 & 5 & 4 \end{vmatrix}$$

$$= 120\left(1\begin{vmatrix} -1 & 1 \\ 5 & 4 \end{vmatrix} - 1\begin{vmatrix} 2 & 1 \\ 5 & 4 \end{vmatrix} - 2\begin{vmatrix} 2 & 1 \\ -1 & 1 \end{vmatrix}\right)$$

$$= 120(-4 - 5 - 8 + 5 - 4 - 2) = -2160.$$

Theorem 4. If the elements of a column (row) of a square matrix are a constant, k, times the corresponding elements of another column (row), then the determinant of the matrix is zero.

If $k = 0$, there is a column (row) of zeros. On applying Theorem 1 of Section 20–7 using the cofactors of the elements of this column (row) the value of the determinant is found to be zero.

If $k \neq 0$, then by Theorem 3

$$| M | = \begin{vmatrix} a_1 & b_1 & ka_1 \\ a_2 & b_2 & ka_2 \\ a_3 & b_3 & ka_3 \end{vmatrix} = k \begin{vmatrix} a_1 & b_1 & a_1 \\ a_2 & b_2 & a_2 \\ a_3 & b_3 & a_3 \end{vmatrix}.$$

If the first and third columns of M are interchanged, then by Theorem 2

$$(k) \cdot \begin{vmatrix} a_1 & b_1 & a_1 \\ a_2 & b_2 & a_2 \\ a_3 & b_3 & a_3 \end{vmatrix} = - (k) \cdot \begin{vmatrix} a_1 & b_1 & a_1 \\ a_2 & b_2 & a_2 \\ a_3 & b_3 & a_3 \end{vmatrix}$$

and,

$$2k \begin{vmatrix} a_1 & b_1 & a_1 \\ a_2 & b_2 & a_2 \\ a_3 & b_3 & a_3 \end{vmatrix} = 0. \quad \text{(Why?)}$$

Consequently, since $k \neq 0$,

$$\begin{vmatrix} a_1 & b_1 & a_1 \\ a_2 & b_2 & a_2 \\ a_3 & b_3 & a_3 \end{vmatrix} = 0. \quad \text{Therefore,} \quad | M | = 0.$$

● *Example 3.*

$$\begin{vmatrix} -4 & 6 & 0 \\ 6 & -9 & 8 \\ 10 & -15 & 7 \end{vmatrix} = \begin{vmatrix} -2(2) & 3(2) & 0 \\ -2(-3) & 3(-3) & 8 \\ -2(-5) & 3(-5) & 7 \end{vmatrix} = 0,$$

since the first and second columns are proportional.

Theorem 5. If k times the elements of a column (row) of a square matrix are added to the corresponding elements of a second column (row), then the determinant of the resulting matrix is equal to the determinant of the original matrix.

$$\begin{vmatrix} a_1 + kc_1 & b_1 & c_1 \\ a_2 + kc_2 & b_2 & c_2 \\ a_3 + kc_3 & b_3 & c_3 \end{vmatrix} = (a_1 + kc_1) \begin{vmatrix} b_2 & c_2 \\ b_3 & c_3 \end{vmatrix} - (a_2 + kc_2) \begin{vmatrix} b_1 & c_1 \\ b_3 & c_3 \end{vmatrix} + (a_3 + kc_3) \begin{vmatrix} b_1 & c_1 \\ b_2 & c_2 \end{vmatrix}$$

$$= a_1 \cdot \begin{vmatrix} b_2 & c_2 \\ b_3 & c_3 \end{vmatrix} - a_2 \cdot \begin{vmatrix} b_1 & c_1 \\ b_3 & c_3 \end{vmatrix} + a_3 \cdot \begin{vmatrix} b_1 & c_1 \\ b_2 & c_2 \end{vmatrix}$$

$$+ k \cdot \left\{ c_1 \cdot \begin{vmatrix} b_2 & c_2 \\ b_3 & c_3 \end{vmatrix} - c_2 \cdot \begin{vmatrix} b_1 & c_1 \\ b_3 & c_3 \end{vmatrix} + c_3 \cdot \begin{vmatrix} b_1 & c_1 \\ b_2 & c_2 \end{vmatrix} \right\}$$

$$= \begin{vmatrix} a_1 & b_1 & c_1 \\ a_2 & b_2 & c_2 \\ a_3 & b_3 & c_3 \end{vmatrix} + k \begin{vmatrix} c_1 & b_1 & c_1 \\ c_2 & b_2 & c_2 \\ c_3 & b_3 & c_3 \end{vmatrix}$$

$$= \begin{vmatrix} a_1 & b_1 & c_1 \\ a_2 & b_2 & c_2 \\ a_3 & b_3 & c_3 \end{vmatrix} + k(0).$$

● **Example 4.** Find the value of

$$D = \begin{vmatrix} 2 & 4 & -8 \\ 5 & 2 & 1 \\ 3 & 1 & 4 \end{vmatrix}.$$

(1) Divide the first row by 2, and multiply the resulting determinant by 2 (Theorem 3) to obtain

$$D = 2 \begin{vmatrix} 1 & 2 & -4 \\ 5 & 2 & 1 \\ 3 & 1 & 4 \end{vmatrix}.$$

(2) Now, add -2 times the elements of the first column to the corresponding elements of the second column (Theorem 5). (3) Add 4 times the elements of the first column to the corresponding elements of the third column. (4) Finally, expand using cofactors of elements of the first row.

$$D = 2 \begin{vmatrix} 1 & 2-2(1) & -4+4(1) \\ 5 & 2-2(5) & 1+4(5) \\ 3 & 1-2(3) & 4+4(3) \end{vmatrix} = 2 \begin{vmatrix} 1 & 0 & 0 \\ 5 & -8 & 21 \\ 3 & -5 & 16 \end{vmatrix}$$

$$= 2 \left\{ 1 \begin{vmatrix} -8 & 21 \\ -5 & 16 \end{vmatrix} - 0 + 0 \right\}$$

$$= 2 \cdot \begin{vmatrix} -8 & 21 \\ -5 & 16 \end{vmatrix} = 2(-128 + 105) = -46.$$

● **Example 5.** Evaluate:

$$D = \begin{vmatrix} 2 & 3 & -5 & 4 \\ 4 & 2 & 3 & 1 \\ -7 & 6 & 4 & 3 \\ 5 & 6 & 1 & 2 \end{vmatrix}.$$

To find the value of D one may obtain zeros in the first, third, and fourth rows of the fourth column, and expand as follows: (1) Add -4 times the elements of the second row to the corresponding elements of the first row. (2) Add -3 times the elements of the second row to the corresponding elements of the third row. (3) Add -2 times the elements of the second row to the corresponding elements of the fourth row.

$$D = \begin{vmatrix} 2-4(4) & 3-4(2) & -5-4(3) & 4-4(1) \\ 4 & 2 & 3 & 1 \\ -7-3(4) & 6-3(2) & 4-3(3) & 3-3(1) \\ 5-2(4) & 6-2(2) & 1-2(3) & 2-2(1) \end{vmatrix}$$

$$= \begin{vmatrix} -14 & -5 & -17 & 0 \\ 4 & 2 & 3 & 1 \\ -19 & 0 & -5 & 0 \\ -3 & 2 & -5 & 0 \end{vmatrix}.$$

(4) Expand, using cofactors of elements of the fourth column.

$$D = 1(-1)^{2+4} \cdot \begin{vmatrix} -14 & -5 & -17 \\ -19 & 0 & -5 \\ -3 & 2 & -5 \end{vmatrix}.$$

(5) To expand the resulting determinant, add $\frac{5}{2}$ times the elements of the third row to the corresponding elements of the first row, and (6) expand using cofactors of elements of the second column.

$$D = \begin{vmatrix} -14+(\frac{5}{2})(-3) & -5+(\frac{5}{2})(2) & -17+(\frac{5}{2})(-5) \\ -19 & 0 & -5 \\ -3 & 2 & -5 \end{vmatrix}$$

$$= \begin{vmatrix} -\frac{43}{2} & 0 & -\frac{59}{2} \\ -19 & 0 & -5 \\ -3 & 2 & -5 \end{vmatrix} = 2(-1)^{3+2} \begin{vmatrix} -\frac{43}{2} & -\frac{59}{2} \\ -19 & -5 \end{vmatrix}$$

$$= -2(215/2 - 1121/2) = 906.$$

PROBLEM SET 20-8

Verify Problems 1 to 5 without expanding.

1. $\begin{vmatrix} 3 & -6 & 9 \\ 0 & 2 & 5 \\ -2 & 4 & -6 \end{vmatrix} = 0.$

2. $\begin{vmatrix} 1 & 3 & -5 \\ 2 & 4 & 7 \\ 8 & -3 & 2 \end{vmatrix} = -\begin{vmatrix} 8 & -3 & 2 \\ 2 & 4 & 7 \\ 1 & 3 & -5 \end{vmatrix}.$

3. $\begin{vmatrix} 1 & x^2 \\ 1 & y^2 \end{vmatrix} = (y+x)(y-x)$.

4. $\begin{vmatrix} x^2 & x & 1 \\ y^2 & y & 1 \\ z^2 & z & 1 \end{vmatrix} = -(x-y)(y-z)(z-x)$.

5. $\begin{vmatrix} 2 & -4 & 6 \\ 3 & 2 & -5 \\ -2 & 3 & 7 \end{vmatrix} = 2 \cdot \begin{vmatrix} -1 & 1 & 10 \\ 3 & 2 & -5 \\ 1 & 5 & 2 \end{vmatrix}$.

Use the methods illustrated in Examples 4 and 5 of Section 20–8 to place zeros in as many positions as possible in a column (row) before expanding, and then expand and find the results for Problems 6 to 11.

6. $\begin{vmatrix} 20 & 17 & 2 \\ 15 & 12 & 8 \\ 25 & 22 & -6 \end{vmatrix}$.

7. $\begin{vmatrix} -1 & 6 & 5 \\ -2 & 3 & 3 \\ -10 & 8 & 10 \end{vmatrix}$.

8. $\begin{vmatrix} 2 & 2 & -2 \\ 3 & -2 & 4 \\ 2 & 2 & 8 \end{vmatrix}$.

9. $\begin{vmatrix} 4 & -3 & -1 & 2 \\ -1 & 2 & 2 & 4 \\ 2 & -1 & 3 & 1 \\ 3 & 0 & 10 & 5 \end{vmatrix}$.

10. $\begin{vmatrix} 3 & 5 & 4 & 2 \\ 2 & 6 & 2 & 3 \\ 1 & 4 & 1 & 2 \\ 2 & 9 & 2 & 5 \end{vmatrix}$.

11. $\begin{vmatrix} 6 & 5 & 7 & 4 \\ 0 & -2 & 1 & -1 \\ 3 & 3 & 6 & 2 \\ 3 & 1 & 7 & 1 \end{vmatrix}$.

12. Show that

$$\begin{vmatrix} x & y & 1 \\ x_1 & y_1 & 1 \\ x_2 & y_2 & 1 \end{vmatrix} = 0$$

is the equation of the line through the points (x_1, y_1) and (x_2, y_2). Discuss any necessary restrictions.

13. Write the equation of the line through $(2, -3)$ and $(-4, 5)$, in determinantal form. Expand and simplify the result.

14. Show that the area of the triangle whose vertices are

$$(x_1, y_1), \quad (x_2, y_2) \quad \text{and} \quad (x_3, y_3)$$

is the absolute value of

$$\pm \left(\tfrac{1}{2}\right) \cdot \begin{vmatrix} x_1 & y_1 & 1 \\ x_2 & y_2 & 1 \\ x_3 & y_3 & 1 \end{vmatrix} \cdot \quad \text{Discuss.}$$

[HINT: Drop perpendicular from each point to the x-axis.]

15. Use the determinantal form of Problem 14 to find the area of the triangle whose vertices are
(a) $(2, -3)$, $(-4, 5)$, $(3, 2)$,
(b) $(-1, 3)$, $(2, 15)$, $(-2, -1)$. Discuss.

16. Verify that

$$\begin{vmatrix} x^2 + y^2 & x & y & 1 \\ x_1^2 + y_1^2 & x_1 & y_1 & 1 \\ x_2^2 + y_2^2 & x_2 & y_2 & 1 \\ x_3^2 + y_3^2 & x_3 & y_3 & 1 \end{vmatrix} = 0$$

is the equation of a circle through the points (x_1, y_1), (x_2, y_2) and (x_3, y_3). Discuss any necessary restrictions.

17. Write the equation of the circle through $(2, -3)$, $(-4, 5)$, $(3, 2)$ in determinantal form. Expand and simplify the result.

18. Write the equation of the circle through $(-2, -1)$, $(2, 15)$, $(-1, 3)$ in determinantal form. Expand and simplify. Discuss.

19. Use Theorem 5 to obtain a simple proof of Theorem 4.

*20–9. Determinants and systems of linear equations. In the solution of systems of linear equations, Theorem 1 is helpful.

Theorem 1. Any sum, such as $a_1A_2 + b_1B_2 + c_1C_2$, obtained from a determinant, by adding the products of the elements of one row (column) by the cofactors of the corresponding elements of another row (column) is zero.

Such sums vanish, since they are expansions of determinants having two identical rows (columns).

● **Example 1.**

$$a_1A_2 + b_1B_2 + c_1C_2 = \begin{vmatrix} a_1 & b_1 & c_1 \\ a_1 & b_1 & c_1 \\ a_3 & b_3 & c_3 \end{vmatrix} = 0.$$

● **Example 2.** Solve: $a_1x + b_1y = k_1$, $a_2x + b_2y = k_2$.

$$b_2(a_1x + b_1y) = k_1b_2 \qquad -a_2(a_1x + b_1y) = -a_2k_1$$
$$-b_1(a_2x + b_2y) = -k_2b_1. \qquad a_1(a_2x + b_2y) = a_1k_2.$$

On adding

$$(a_1b_2 - a_2b_1)x = k_1b_2 - k_2b_1, \qquad (a_1b_2 - a_2b_1)y = a_1k_2 - a_2k_1,$$

or, using an equivalent determinantal expression,

$$\begin{vmatrix} a_1 & b_1 \\ a_2 & b_2 \end{vmatrix} x = \begin{vmatrix} k_1 & b_1 \\ k_2 & b_2 \end{vmatrix} \quad \text{and} \quad x = \frac{\begin{vmatrix} k_1 & b_1 \\ k_2 & b_2 \end{vmatrix}}{\begin{vmatrix} a_1 & b_1 \\ a_2 & b_2 \end{vmatrix}},$$

$$\begin{vmatrix} a_1 & b_1 \\ a_2 & b_2 \end{vmatrix} y = \begin{vmatrix} a_1 & k_1 \\ a_2 & k_2 \end{vmatrix} \quad \text{and} \quad y = \dfrac{\begin{vmatrix} a_1 & k_1 \\ a_2 & k_2 \end{vmatrix}}{\begin{vmatrix} a_1 & b_1 \\ a_2 & b_2 \end{vmatrix}},$$

provided $\begin{vmatrix} a_1 & b_1 \\ a_2 & b_2 \end{vmatrix} \neq 0.$

If $\begin{vmatrix} a_1 & b_1 \\ a_2 & b_2 \end{vmatrix} = 0,$ then $-a_1/b_1 = -a_2/b_2,$ and the lines represented by the two equations are parallel. If $a_1/b_1 = a_2/b_2 = k_1/k_2,$ then the lines are coincident.

- **Example 3.** Find the coordinates of the point of intersection of the lines $2x - 3y + 5 = 0, \quad 3x + 4y - 6 = 0.$

$$x = \dfrac{\begin{vmatrix} -5 & -3 \\ 6 & 4 \end{vmatrix}}{\begin{vmatrix} 2 & -3 \\ 3 & 4 \end{vmatrix}} = \dfrac{-20 + 18}{8 + 9} = \dfrac{-2}{17},$$

$$y = \dfrac{\begin{vmatrix} 2 & -5 \\ 3 & 6 \end{vmatrix}}{17} = \dfrac{12 + 15}{17} = \dfrac{27}{17}.$$

- **Example 4.** Solve: (1) $a_1x + b_1y + c_1z = k_1$
  (2) $a_2x + b_2y + c_2z = k_2$
  (3) $a_3x + b_3y + c_3z = k_3.$

Let

$$D = \begin{vmatrix} a_1 & b_1 & c_1 \\ a_2 & b_2 & c_2 \\ a_3 & b_3 & c_3 \end{vmatrix}, \quad K_1 = \begin{vmatrix} k_1 & b_1 & c_1 \\ k_2 & b_2 & c_2 \\ k_3 & b_3 & c_3 \end{vmatrix},$$

$$K_2 = \begin{vmatrix} a_1 & k_1 & c_1 \\ a_2 & k_2 & c_2 \\ a_3 & k_3 & c_3 \end{vmatrix}, \quad K_3 = \begin{vmatrix} a_1 & b_1 & k_1 \\ a_2 & b_2 & k_2 \\ a_3 & b_3 & k_3 \end{vmatrix}$$

and let A_1, A_2, A_3 be the cofactors of a_1, a_2, a_3 respectively, in D.

Multiply (1) by A_1, (2) by A_2, (3) by A_3. Then add, obtaining

$$(a_1A_1 + a_2A_2 + a_3A_3)x + (b_1A_1 + b_2A_2 + b_3A_3)y$$
$$+ (c_1A_1 + c_2A_2 + c_3A_3)z = k_1A_1 + k_2A_2 + k_3A_3.$$

The coefficients of y and z are each zero. (Why?)

$$D \cdot x + 0 \cdot y + 0 \cdot z = K_1$$

and

$$x = K_1/D, \quad \text{when} \quad D \neq 0.$$

Multiply (1) by B_1, (2) by B_2, (3) by B_3, where B_1, B_2, B_3 are the cofactors of b_1, b_2, b_3 respectively, in D. Add and get $Dy = K_2$, and $y = K_2/D$ when $D \neq 0$. Similarly, $Dz = K_3$, and $z = K_3/D$ when $D \neq 0$. It is possible to extend this method to solve n linear equations in n unknowns.

This method of solving simultaneous linear equations by determinants is often referred to as Cramer's rule in honor of the Swiss mathematician G. Cramer (1704–1752). In fairness, however, it should be noted that as early as 1100 B.C. the Chinese solved two linear equations in two unknowns by a rule equivalent to Cramer's rule. The present notation for determinants was introduced during the nineteenth century by A. Cayley (1821–1895, English). The importance of determinant theory does *not* lie in determining solutions of linear equations. The powerful tensor algebra, which is so important in the modern theory of relativity, has its roots in the theory of determinants.

PROBLEM SET 20–9

1 to 12. Use determinants to solve Problems 1 to 12 of Set 20–6.

13. Solve for x and y: $2z + 3iz = -7 - 4i$, where $z = x + iy$ and $i = \sqrt{-1}$.

14. Solve: $2^{x+y} = 3^{2x-5}$, $3^{2x-y} = 2^{3y}$.

15. Find K such that the lines
$Kx - 2y - 7 = 0$, $2x - Ky - 8 = 0$ and $x + 2y + K = 0$
intersect in a point.

16. The following puzzle recently appeared in a national magazine. The owner of a small dog and bird shop claims that his pets have a total of 36 heads and 100 feet. How many of each are there?

17. Two particles of masses M_1 and M_2 collide. The particle of mass M_1 has a velocity U_1 before collision and V_1 after collision. The particle of mass M_2 is stationary before collision and has a velocity of V_2 after collision. The law of conservation of momentum states that $M_1U_1 = M_2V_2 + M_1V_1$. The law of conservation of kinetic energy states that
$$M_1U_1^2 = M_2V_2^2 + M_1V_1^2.$$

(a) Assuming that M_1, M_2, and U_1 are known, determine the velocity of each particle after collision.

(b) What happens to each particle after collision, if $M_1 = M_2$?

(c) What happens to each particle after collision, if M_1 is very small in comparison to M_2?

[HINT: Take $M_2 = 1$ and let $M_1 \to 0$.]

(d) What happens to each particle if M_2 is very small in comparison to M_1?

*18. Discuss: (a) the relative positions of the lines and (b) the number of solutions of the system $a_1x + b_1y = k_1$, $a_2x + b_2y = k_2$, when $a_1b_2 - a_2b_1 = 0$ but $a_1k_2 - a_2k_1 \neq 0$. Make a similar discussion if both determinants are zero.

19. $\begin{cases} a_1x + b_1y + c_1z = 0 \\ a_2x + b_2y + c_2z = 0 \\ a_3x + b_3y + c_3z = 0 \end{cases}$ If $\begin{vmatrix} a_1 & b_1 & c_1 \\ a_2 & b_2 & c_2 \\ a_3 & b_3 & c_3 \end{vmatrix} = 0$

show that $x = A_1t$, $y = B_1t$, $z = C_1t$ give a solution of the homogeneous system of equations for each value assigned to t. Does this set of solutions give all solutions? Can you extend the method (a) by using A_i, B_i, C_i? (b) to homogeneous systems of n equations in n unknowns?

20. Apply the method of Problem 19 to solve the systems:

(a) $\begin{cases} 2x - y - z = 0 \\ 4x + y - 11z = 0 \\ x - 3y + 7z = 0 \end{cases}$ (b) $\begin{cases} x - y + 2z - 3w = 0 \\ 2x + 3y - 4z + 5w = 0 \\ 2x - y + z + 2w = 0 \\ 3x + 3y - 5z + 10w = 0 \end{cases}$

20–10. Self test.

Record your time.

1. Find the distance between the lines $4x + 3y + 25 = 0$ and $4x + 3y = 10$.

2. Use the matrix method to solve the system of equations:

$$3x + 4y - 2z = 15, \quad x - y + 3z = -7, \quad x + 2y - z = 7.$$

3. Evaluate: $\begin{vmatrix} 1 & 3 & 2 & 5 \\ 1 & 9 & 3 & 6 \\ 2 & 1 & 4 & 1 \\ 0 & 1 & 3 & 2 \end{vmatrix}$.

4. Find the angle of intersection of $y^2 = 8x$ and $x^2 = 8y$ at each point of intersection.

5. Find the distance between the point $(2, -3)$ and the line $5x - 12y = 26$.

6. Write the equations of the lines tangent to the circle $x^2 + y^2 = 16$ and passing through $(0, 5)$.

7. Find z such that $\begin{vmatrix} z & -6 & 4 \\ 2 & 3 & 1 \\ -7 & 2 & 9 \end{vmatrix} = 0$.

8. Find the equation of the line normal to $3x^2 - 7y + 9 = 0$ at (2, 3).

***9.** Solve the system using determinants:

$$\begin{cases} 2x + 3y - 5z = 0 \\ 3x - 4y + 3z = 0 \\ 5x - y - 2z = 0 \end{cases}$$

Record your time.

21

21–1. A general equation of the circle. The reader has learned (Section 2–3) that the equation of a circle with center (h, k) and radius $r \geqq 0$ † may be written in the **standard form** $(x - h)^2 + (y - k)^2 = r^2$. If the squared terms are expanded, and like terms combined, an equation of the form

$$x^2 + y^2 + Dx + Ey + F = 0$$

is obtained. We now show that every equation of the form ‡ $x^2 + y^2 + Dx + Ey + F = 0$ either represents a circle or has no real locus. This is done by completing the square in the x terms, and in the y terms.

$$(x^2 + Dx \qquad) + (y^2 + Ey \qquad) = -F$$
$$(x^2 + Dx + D^2/4) + (y^2 + Ey + E^2/4) = -F + D^2/4 + E^2/4,$$
$$(x + D/2)^2 + (y + E/2)^2 = \frac{D^2 + E^2 - 4F}{4}.$$

This corresponds to the standard form of the equation of a circle. If $(D^2 + E^2 - 4F)/4$ is positive, a real circle results. If it is zero, a "point circle," namely $(-D/2, -E/2)$, results. If $(D^2 + E^2 - 4F)/4$ is negative, there are no real points on the locus since the sum of two real squares is never negative. The term "imaginary circle" is sometimes used to describe this situation.

● *Example 1.* Reduce $4x^2 + 4y^2 - 8x + 24y + 4 = 0$ to standard form. If the locus is real, find its center and radius.

Dividing each member by 4 and transposing the constant term yields

$$x^2 - 2x + \qquad y^2 + 6y \qquad = -1$$
$$(x^2 - 2x + 1) + (y^2 + 6y + 9) = -1 + 1 + 9$$
$$(x - 1)^2 + (y + 3)^2 = 9.$$

This is a real circle with center $(1, -3)$ and radius 3.

● *Example 2.* Reduce $x^2 + y^2 + 4x - 6y + 17 = 0$ to standard form. If the locus is real, find its center and radius.

† A circle with radius $r = 0$ is a single point, in this case the point (h, k).

‡ If $A' \neq 0$, an equation of the form $A'x^2 + A'y^2 + D'x + E'y + F' = 0$ may be transformed into the above form by dividing each member by $A' \neq 0$.

$$x^2 + 4x + \qquad y^2 - 6y \qquad = -17$$
$$(x^2 + 4x + 4) + (y^2 - 6y + 9) = -17 + 4 + 9$$
$$(x + 2)^2 + (y - 3)^2 = -4.$$

There are no real points which satisfy this equation. (Why?)

21–2. Systems of circles. If $f(x, y) = 0$ and $g(x, y) = 0$ are equations of two loci, then

$$f(x, y) + kg(x, y) = 0 \quad \text{and} \quad k_1 f(x, y) + k_2 g(x, y) = 0$$

each represents † loci passing through all points of intersection of $f(x, y) = 0$ and $g(x, y) = 0$. Let (X, Y) be a point of inter-section, then $f(X, Y) = 0$ and $g(X, Y) = 0$. Consequently, $f(X, Y) + kg(X, Y) = 0$ and $k_1 f(X, Y) + k_2 g(X, Y) = 0$. Hence, the point of intersection (X, Y) lies on $f(x, y) + kg(x, y) = 0$ and on $k_1 f(x, y) + k_2 g(x, y) = 0$. Thus every point of intersec-tion (X, Y) of $f(x, y) = 0$ and $g(x, y) = 0$ lies on

$$f(x, y) + kg(x, y) = 0 \quad \text{and on} \quad k_1 f(x, y) + k_2 g(x, y) = 0.$$

Let
$$x^2 + y^2 + D_1 x + E_1 y + F_1 = 0$$
and

$$x^2 + y^2 + D_2 x + E_2 y + F_2 = 0$$

represent nonconcentric circles. Then

$$k_1[x^2+y^2+D_1x+E_1y+F_1]+k_2[x^2+y^2+D_2x+E_2y+F_2]=0 \qquad (21.1)$$

or

$$(k_1+k_2)x^2+(k_1+k_2)y^2+(k_1D_1+k_2D_2)x+(k_1E_1+k_2E_2)y+k_1F_1+k_2F_2=0$$

is a curve passing through the points of intersection (if any) of the two given circles. Why?

If $k_1 + k_2 \neq 0$, the resulting Equation (21.1) is a real circle, a point circle, or an imaginary circle. Why?

If $k_1 + k_2 = 0$, the squared terms of (21.1) vanish and the resulting equation is that of a line. Why? This line is the **radical axis** of the two circles. If the circles intersect in two points, the radical axis passes through these two points and contains the common chord of the circles. If the two circles are tangent, then the radical axis is the common tangent line. The radical axis exists even if the circles do not have points in common. In any case, it may be shown that the radical axis includes all points from which tangent line segments drawn to the two given circles have equal lengths.

---

† If both k_1 and k_2 are zero, the identity $0 = 0$ results. Every point in the plane satisfies this identity.

To determine the points of intersection (if any) of the two non-concentric circles, it is convenient to determine the equation of the radical axis and solve this equation simultaneously with the equation of either circle.

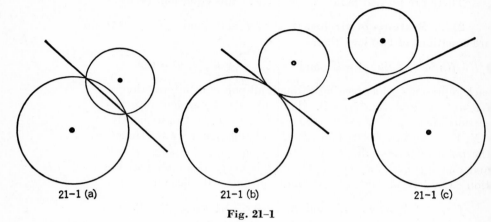

21–1 (a)   21–1 (b)   21–1 (c)

Fig. 21–1

A quadratic equation results upon eliminating one variable. The roots of this quadratic are:

(a) real and different if the circles intersect in two points;

(b) real and equal if the circles are tangent;

(c) complex (imaginary) if the circles do not intersect.

The reader is asked to investigate what happens if the circles are concentric.

- **Example 1.** Find the equation of a system (family) of circles passing through the points of intersection of

$$x^2 + y^2 = 4 \quad \text{and} \quad (x-1)^2 + y^2 = 5.$$

The equation of the desired system is

$$k_1[x^2 + y^2 - 4] + k_2[(x-1)^2 + y^2 - 5] = 0.$$

- **Example 2.** Determine the equation of the circle of the family given in Example 1 which passes through (6, 8).

If k_2 were zero, then (6, 8) would have to satisfy the equation $x^2 + y^2 - 4 = 0$. It does not. Hence $k_2 \neq 0$. Let us, therefore, divide the equation of the family by k_2. Replacing the constant k_1/k_2 by k we obtain

$$k[x^2 + y^2 - 4] + [(x-1)^2 + y^2 - 5] = 0.$$

If (6, 8) lies on this locus, it must satisfy the equation of the locus.

$$k[6^2 + 8^2 - 4] + [(6-1)^2 + 8^2 - 5] = 0$$
$$k[96] + [84] = 0,$$

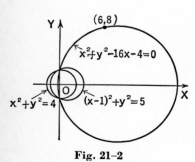

Fig. 21–2

and
$$k = (-\tfrac{84}{96}) = -\tfrac{7}{8}.$$

The desired equation is
$$(-\tfrac{7}{8})[x^2 + y^2 - 4] + [(x-1)^2 + y^2 - 5] = 0$$
$$-7[x^2 + y^2 - 4] + 8[(x-1)^2 + y^2 - 5] = 0$$
$$x^2 + y^2 - 16x - 4 = 0.$$

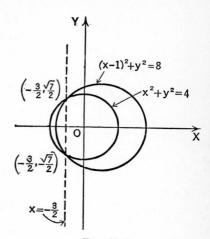

Fig. 21-3

- **Example 3.** Find the points of intersection of
$$x^2 + y^2 = 4 \quad \text{and} \quad (x-1)^2 + y^2 = 8.$$

The radical axis of the two circles is
$$[x^2 + y^2 - 4] - [(x-1)^2 + y^2 - 8] = 0, \quad \text{or} \quad 2x + 3 = 0.$$

The equation of the radical axis is solved simultaneously with the equation of either one of the circles, say $x^2 + y^2 = 4$, to obtain
$$(-\tfrac{3}{2})^2 + y^2 = 4$$
$$y^2 = 4 - \frac{9}{4} = \frac{7}{4}, \quad \text{and} \quad y = \pm \frac{\sqrt{7}}{2}.$$

Hence the points of intersection of the given circles are
$$\left(-\frac{3}{2}, \pm \frac{\sqrt{7}}{2}\right).$$

- **Example 4.** *First Method.* Determine the equation of a line that passes through the point $(0, 5)$ and is tangent to the circle $x^2 + y^2 = 16$.

The equation of such a family of lines is $y = mx + 5$. The x-coordinates of the intersections of the line and circle are the solutions of $x^2 + (mx + 5)^2 = 16$. The line will be tangent to the circle if, and only if, the line and circle intersect in exactly one point. That is, if, and only if,
$$x^2 + (mx + 5)^2 = 16$$
$$(m^2 + 1)x^2 + 10mx + 9 = 0$$

has two equal roots. If
$$A = m^2 + 1, \quad B = 10m, \quad C = 9,$$
then
$$B^2 - 4AC = 100m^2 - 4(m^2 + 1)9 = 64m^2 - 36.$$

Hence, $B^2 - 4AC = 0$ implies $m = \pm \sqrt{\tfrac{36}{64}} = \pm \tfrac{3}{4}$. Two such lines exist, namely, $y = \tfrac{3}{4}x + 5$ and $y = -\tfrac{3}{4}x + 5$. Another method of solution is given in Example 6, Section 20-5.

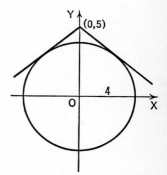

Fig. 21-4

Second Method. Using the method of Section 6–7 we obtain the slope of the line tangent to $x^2 + y^2 = 16$ at any point (x_1, y_1) on the circle. See page 147.

$$x^2 + y^2 = 16$$

$$2x + 2y \frac{dy}{dx} = 0$$

$$\frac{dy}{dx} = -\frac{x}{y}.$$

The slope of the tangent at (x_1, y_1) on circle is $m = -\dfrac{x_1}{y_1}$.

The equation of a line through $(0, 5)$ with slope $m = \dfrac{-x_1}{y_1}$ is

$$y = \frac{-x_1}{y_1} x + 5.$$

If this line is to be tangent to the circle $x^2 + y^2 = 16$ at (x_1, y_1) then (x_1, y_1) must satisfy the equation of the line and also the equation of the circle.

(x_1, y_1) satisfies equation of line:

$$y_1 = -\frac{x_1}{y_1} x_1 + 5 \quad \text{or} \quad x_1^2 + y_1^2 = 5y_1$$

(x_1, y_1) satisfies equation of circle: $x_1^2 + y_1^2 = 16$

Hence, $\quad 5y_1 = 16$
$$y_1 = \tfrac{16}{5}$$

$$x_1 = \pm \sqrt{16 - y_1^2} = \pm \sqrt{16 - \frac{16^2}{5^2}} = \pm \frac{12}{5}$$

Substituting these into the equation $y = -\dfrac{x_1}{y_1} x + 5$ produces

$$y = -\tfrac{3}{4}x + 5 \quad \text{and} \quad y = \tfrac{3}{4}x + 5$$

the equations of the desired tangent lines.

● **Example 5.** Find an equation of the circle with center $(3, 5)$ and passing through $(2, -1)$.

A family of circles with center $(3, 5)$ and radius r has the equation $(x - 3)^2 + (y - 5)^2 = r^2$.

If $(2, -1)$ lies on the circle, then the coordinates $(2, -1)$ satisfy the equation of the circle. Substituting $(2, -1)$ in $(x - 3)^2 + (y - 5)^2 = r^2$ gives $1 + 36 = r^2$, $37 = r^2$. The desired equation is $(x - 3)^2 + (y - 5)^2 = 37$.

This result could have been obtained using the distance formula of Section 2–3. The above procedure illustrates another method which is useful in a wide variety of problems.

● **Example 6.** Find the points of intersection of $x^2 + y^2 - 10x = 0$ and $x + 7y - 30 = 0$. At one of these points find the acute angle between the circle and the line.

Substitute $y = \dfrac{30 - x}{7}$ into $x^2 + y^2 - 10x = 0$ and obtain $x^2 - 11x + 18 = 0$. Then $(x = 2, y = 4)$ or $\left(x = 9, y = \dfrac{30 - 9}{7} = 3\right)$ are the desired points of intersection. From the equation for the circle we obtain

$2x + 2y\dfrac{dy}{dx} - 10 = 0$ or $\dfrac{dy}{dx} = \dfrac{5 - x}{y}$. The line has constant slope $\dfrac{dy}{dx} = -\dfrac{1}{7}$. At $(2, 4)$ we have $\dfrac{5 - 2}{4} = \dfrac{3}{4}$ as the slope of the circle. The angle θ between the circle and the line at $(2, 4)$ is found from

$$\tan \theta = \frac{\frac{3}{4} - (-\frac{1}{7})}{1 + \frac{3}{4}(-\frac{1}{7})} = \frac{\frac{25}{28}}{\frac{25}{28}} = 1. \quad \theta = \text{Arctan } 1 = \frac{\pi}{4}.$$

PROBLEM SET 21–2

In each of Problems 1 to 12 write the equation of a circle with center C and either having radius R or passing through the point P, whichever is given. Sketch each locus.

1. $C(3, -5)$, $R = 4$.   **2.** $C(1, 3)$, $R = 5$.

3. $C(2, 11)$, $R = 1$.   **4.** $C(-6, 5)$, $R = 13$.

5. $C(4, -2)$, $P(2, 1)$.   **6.** $C(-1, 7)$, $P(3, 11)$.

7. $C(5, -2)$, $P(0, 0)$.   **8.** $C(0, 11)$, $P(41, 0)$.

9. $C(4, 6)$, $P(-1, 3)$.   **10.** $C(6, -1)$, $P(1, -1)$.

11. $C(3, -5)$, $P(17, 2)$.   **12.** $C(10, 1)$, $P(9, 0)$.

13. The circles of Problems 1 and 11 have the same center. Which circle is larger?

14. Are the circles of Problems 3 and 9 concentric? Which is larger? Do they intersect? If so, where?

15. Let two circles be $A: \quad x^2 + y^2 - 4x - 2y + 1 = 0,$
$$B: \quad x^2 + y^2 - 8x - 4y + 11 = 0.$$

(a) Does the center of A lie inside circle B? (b) Does the center of B lie inside circle A? (c) Make a careful sketch and find the distance between the centers of A and B. (d) Do A and B have a common chord? If so, what is its equation? Be sure it is a common chord, not merely the radical axis. (e) Write the equation of a system of circles passing through the points of intersection of these two circles. (f) Find a member of the system (e) which also passes through $(0, 0)$. (g) Find a member of the system (e) which passes through $(2, 3)$. Sketch.

16. Write the equation of a circle concentric with
$$C: \quad (x - 4)^2 + (y + 1)^2 = 121, \quad \text{and entirely inside } C.$$

17. Write the equation of a circle concentric with the circle of Problem 6, and entirely outside it.

18. Write the equation of a circle *not* concentric with the circle of Problem 6, and entirely inside it.

19. Write the equation of a circle not concentric with the circle of Problem 6, and such that all of the circle of Problem 6 is inside it.

20. Write the equation of a circle that has points in common with the circle of 6, but such that each circle also contains points not in common with the other. Could such circles be concentric?

21. Determine the equation of a line that passes through the point $(0, 11)$ and is tangent to the circle $x^2 + y^2 = 9$.

22. Find the equation of a line that passes through $(5, 0)$ and is tangent to $x^2 + y^2 = 16$.

23. Determine the points of intersection of the line $y = 3x + 5$ and the circle $x^2 + (y - 4)^2 = 9$.

24. Determine the points of intersection of the circles
$$x^2 + y^2 = 9 \quad \text{and} \quad x^2 + (y - 1)^2 = 16.$$

25. A tank, 20 feet deep, with plane vertical sides, is three quarters full of oil. The bottom of a circular opening one foot in *diameter* is located in a side 2 feet above the base of the tank. (a) Find the equation of this circle when the x-axis is taken at the level of the top of the tank and the y-axis passes through the center of the circle. Let the x and y units each be in feet. (b) Determine the equation of the circular opening if the y-axis is unchanged but the x-axis is taken at the level of the top of the oil. Often computations of this type must be made before calculus may be used to solve problems of hydrodynamics.

26. A circular plate 2 feet in diameter is lowered in a vertical position into Lake Superior [the port on a bathysphere, for example]. (a) Determine the equation of the circle when the center of the plate is 1000 feet below the surface with the x-axis taken at water level and any convenient y-axis. (b) Make a similar determination with the x-axis level with the deepest portion of Lake Superior, 1290 feet below the surface.

*27. Investigate what line is obtained as the radical axis when the circles do *not* intersect and have (a) equal radii, (b) unequal radii. Show that, in each case, the radical axis includes all points from which tangent line segments drawn to the two given circles have equal lengths.

28. Find the points of intersection of $x^2 + y^2 + 20y = 0$ and $x - 7y - 20 = 0$. At one of these points find the acute angle between the circle and the line.

29. Use trigonometric identities to verify that $(x = h + a \cos \theta, y = k + a \sin \theta)$ are the coordinates of a point on a circle. Obtain center, radius, and equation of the circle.

30. The point $(x = -2 + a \cos \theta, \quad y = 3 + a \sin \theta)$ is on a circle. Find its equation. If time rate of change of a, $\dfrac{da}{dt}$, is 5 units per sec, how fast is the area of the circle changing?

31. (a) Find the equation of the circle on which the coordinates of P at time t sec are $P(5 \cos \pi t, \quad 5 \sin \pi t)$. (b) How fast is the x-coordinate of the point P changing and in what direction when P is at the highest point on the circle?

32. (a) Find by differentiation the slope of the tangent line to $x^2 + y^2 = a^2$ at any point (x_1, y_1) on the circle. (b) Write and simplify the equations of the tangent and normal lines through (x_1, y_1).

33. The delivery charge for an article delivered from $A(6, 0)$ in a straight line to $P(x, y)$ is 30 cents per unit distance. The delivery charge on the same article from $B(0, 10)$ to P is 50 cents per unit distance. In what region are the delivery charges from B cheaper? Sketch the region.

21–3. Translations. If y is replaced by $y - k$ in a given equation, the effect is to move the locus up k units. [If $k < 0$, the locus is moved $|k|$ units downward.] In a similar fashion, if $x - h$ is substituted for x, the locus is moved h units to the right. [If $h < 0$, the locus is moved $|h|$ units to the left.] A sliding movement, without rotation, is a **translation.**

- *Example 1.* $x^2 + y^2 = 16$ is the equation of a circle of radius 4 with center $(0, 0)$. The locus of $(x - 5)^2 + (y + 2)^2 = 16$ is a circle of radius 4 with center $(5, -2)$.

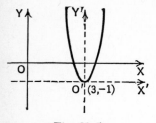

Fig. 21–5

• Example 2. The curve $y = 4x^2$ is a parabola of the typ studied in Sections 4–10 and 21–10. It has its vertex at th origin. Obtain an equation of a congruent parabola obtaine by translating the given curve so that its vertex is $(3, -1)$ The desired equation is $y + 1 = 4(x - 3)^2$.

It is often convenient to think of a new set of (dotted x'-, y'-axes parallel to the original axes such that the locu has a simple equation in the x'-, y'-system. In this case if the ne origin is taken at the vertex of the parabola, the equation referre to the new axes becomes $y' = 4x'^2$.

• Example 3. Determine a substitution (translation) which wi eliminate the first degree terms in the equation obtained fron $xy - 3x + 2y - 5 = 0$. Sketch the locus.

Substitute $x = x' + h$, $y = y' + k$ for x and y and de termine values of h and k which yield the desired simplifica tion.

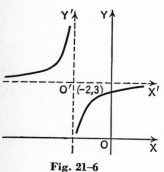

Fig. 21–6

$$(x' + h)(y' + k) - 3(x' + h) + 2(y' + k) - 5 = 0$$
$$x'y' + hy' + kx' + hk - 3x' - 3h + 2y' + 2k - 5 = 0$$
$$x'y' + (k - 3)x' + (h + 2)y' + (hk - 3h + 2k - 5) = 0.$$

The problem requires that the coefficients of x' and of y' eacl be zero. Consequently, $k - 3 = 0$, $h + 2 = 0$, and $k = 3$ $h = -2$.

The equation $x'y' = -1$ is obtained upon substituting $x = x' - 2$ and $y = y' + 3$ into $xy - 3x + 2y - 5 = 0$. If the coordinates of a point are $(x', y') = (0, 0)$, then the x-, y-coordinates of the same point are $(x, y) = (0 - 2, 0 + 3) = (-2, 3)$. A set of x'-, y'-axes may be constructed parallel to the original x-, y-axes and having the new origin $(x', y') = (0, 0)$ at the old point $(x, y) = (-2, 3)$. The curve $x'y' = -1$ may be sketched using the methods of Chapter 3. If the x'-, y'-axes are ignored, the sketch of $xy - 3x + 2y - 5 = 0$ referred to the x-, y- axes remains.

21–4. The ellipse. Let F_1 and F_2 be two fixed points. Let P be a point such that the sum $|F_1P| + |F_2P|$ is a constant. The plane locus of all such points P, in a plane containing the fixed points, is an **ellipse.**

• Example 1. Let $F_1(1, -3)$ and $F_2(1, 5)$ be two fixed points. Determine the equation of the locus of points $P(x, y)$, such that $|F_1P| + |F_2P| = 10$. See Fig. 21–7.

$$\sqrt{(x - 1)^2 + (y + 3)^2} + \sqrt{(x - 1)^2 + (y - 5)^2} = 10.$$

Transposing:

$$\sqrt{(x-1)^2 + (y+3)^2} = 10 - \sqrt{(x-1)^2 + (y-5)^2}.$$

Squaring:

$$(x-1)^2 + (y+3)^2 = 100 - 20\sqrt{(x-1)^2 + (y-5)^2}$$
$$+ (x-1)^2 + (y-5)^2$$
$$16y - 116 = -20\sqrt{(x-1)^2 + (y-5)^2}$$
$$4y - 29 = -5\sqrt{(x-1)^2 + (y-5)^2}.$$

Squaring again:

$$16y^2 - 232y + 841 = 25(x^2 - 2x + 1 + y^2 - 10y + 25),$$

or

$$25x^2 - 50x + 9y^2 - 18y - 191 = 0.$$

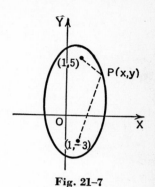

Fig. 21-7

PROBLEM SET 21-4

In each of Problems 1 to 10 determine the locus of points $P(x, y)$ having $|F_1P| + |F_2P| = d$.

1. $F_1(1, 5)$, $F_2(1, -3)$, $d = 10$.
2. $F_1(2, 6)$, $F_2(2, -2)$, $d = 16$.
3. $F_1(0, 3)$, $F_2(0, -3)$, $d = 8$.
4. $F_1(3, 4)$, $F_2(-1, 4)$, $d = 6$.
5. $F_1(13, 0)$, $F_2(0, 0)$, $d = 15$.
6. $F_1(12, -1)$, $F_2(8, -1)$, $d = 10$.
7. $F_1(1, 3)$, $F_2(2, 3)$, $d = 8$.
8. $F_1(1, 2)$, $F_2(3, 4)$, $d = 6$.
9. $F_1(-1, 3)$, $F_2(4, -2)$, $d = 10$.
10. If both F_1 and F_2 are taken as the same point $(3, -4)$ and $d = 10$, find the equation of the locus so obtained. What is the locus?
11. Two pins are inserted in a drawing board and a loop of string placed over the pins. Show that the curve traced by running a pencil around the loop keeping the string taut is an ellipse. This is a standard engineering drawing construction for an ellipse.
12. Determine a substitution that will eliminate the first degree terms in the equation obtained from

$$x^2 + y^2 - 6x + 4y - 12 = 0.$$

Sketch the locus in the new coordinate system.

13. Determine a substitution such that $y^2 - 20x - 10y + 5 = 0$ will take the form $y'^2 = cx'$. Sketch the locus in the new coordinate system.

14. Determine a substitution such that the simultaneous system of equations $2x - 3y - 7 = 0$, $3x + 2y - 4 = 0$ will take the form $2x' - 3y' = 0$, $3x' + 2y' = 0$. Sketch relative to the new coordinate system.

21–5. Properties of an ellipse. Certain important concepts related to an ellipse will be defined now.

Focus. The points F_1 and F_2 are the **foci** of the ellipse.

Vertex. The points V_1, V_2, in which a line through F_1 and F_2 intersects the ellipse, are the **vertices** of the ellipse.

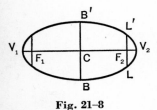

Fig. 21–8

Center. The midpoint C of the line segment F_1F_2 is the **center** of the ellipse. It is a point of symmetry.

Major axis. The line segment V_1V_2 through the foci is the **major axis** of the ellipse. The length of the semimajor axis $|V_1C| = |V_2C|$ is designated by a.

Minor axis. The line segment BB' perpendicular to the major axis V_1V_2 at the center C, where B and B' lie on the ellipse, is the **minor axis** of the ellipse. The length of the semiminor axis $|BC| = |B'C|$ is designated by b.

Latus rectum. A line segment LL' perpendicular to the major axis at a focus and which terminates on the ellipse is a **latus rectum** † of the ellipse.

Theorems 1 to 4 are proved in this section and in Problem Set 21–5.

Theorem 1. The distance between the center C and either focus of an ellipse is $|CF_1| = |CF_2| = \sqrt{a^2 - b^2}$.

Theorem 2. The length of the latus rectum is $2b^2/a$.

Theorem 3. If P is a point on the ellipse and MP is perpendicular to the major axis at M, then the distances $|CM|$ and $|MP|$ satisfy the following relationship:

$$\frac{(CM)^2}{a^2} + \frac{(MP)^2}{b^2} = 1.$$

Theorem 4. If an ellipse has center (h, k) and semiaxes a and b, then its equation is

$$\frac{(x - h)^2}{a^2} + \frac{(y - k)^2}{b^2} = 1, \tag{21.2}$$

† Latin meaning, "right chord."

if the major axis is parallel to the x-axis. If the major axis is parallel to the y-axis, the equation is

$$\frac{(x-h)^2}{b^2} + \frac{(y-k)^2}{a^2} = 1. \tag{21.3}$$

Each of the Equations (21.2) and (21.3) is said to be in standard form. In either case $a \geq b$.

- **Example 1.** Derive the equation of an ellipse having center $(0, 0)$, semiaxes a and b with the major axis along the x-axis.

The foci are taken as $F_1(c, 0)$ and $F_2(-c, 0)$ where c is to be determined later. The vertices are $(a, 0)$ and $(-a, 0)$. The coordinates of each point P on the ellipse must satisfy the condition $|F_1P| + |F_2P| =$ some constant.

Since $V(a, 0)$ is a point on the ellipse,

$$|F_1V| + |F_2V| = \text{some constant}, \quad |a - c| + |a + c| = 2a.$$

Hence, the constant is $2a$, the length of the major axis, and

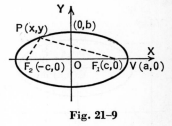

Fig. 21–9

$$|F_1P| + |F_2P| = 2a.$$

$$\sqrt{(x-c)^2 + y^2} + \sqrt{(x+c)^2 + y^2} = 2a$$
$$\sqrt{(x-c)^2 + y^2} = 2a - \sqrt{(x+c)^2 + y^2}$$
$$(x-c)^2 + y^2 = 4a^2 - 4a\sqrt{(x+c)^2 + y^2} + (x+c)^2 + y^2$$
$$-4cx - 4a^2 = -4a\sqrt{(x+c)^2 + y^2}$$
$$cx + a^2 = a\sqrt{(x+c)^2 + y^2}.$$

Then,

$$c^2x^2 + 2a^2cx + a^4 = a^2x^2 + 2a^2cx + a^2c^2 + a^2y^2$$
$$(a^2 - c^2)x^2 + a^2y^2 = a^2(a^2 - c^2)$$

$$\frac{x^2}{a^2} + \frac{y^2}{a^2 - c^2} = 1.$$

Since the point $(0, b)$ lies on the ellipse, it must satisfy the equation, giving

$$\frac{0}{a^2} + \frac{b^2}{a^2 - c^2} = 1,$$

or

$$b^2 = a^2 - c^2.$$

Hence the equation becomes

$$\frac{x^2}{a^2} + \frac{y^2}{b^2} = 1.$$

Theorem 1 is a corollary, since

$$|CF_1| = |CF_2| = c = \sqrt{a^2 - b^2}. \quad \text{Also} \quad a \geq b. \quad \text{The equality}$$
holds if, and only if, the locus is a circle.

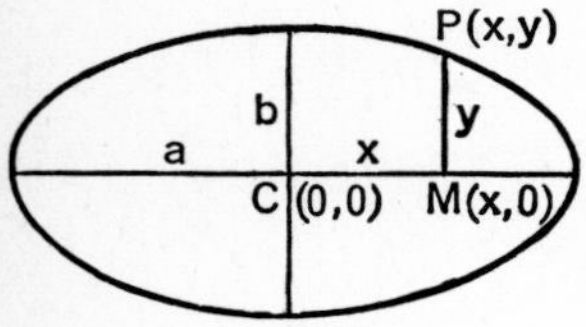

The derivation of Example 1 provides a proof for Theorem 3. If P is a point on the ellipse, then $CM = x$ and $MP = y$.

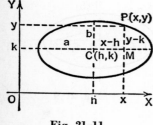

Fig. 21–10

Since the coordinates of each point on the ellipse satisfy the equation of the ellipse, $\dfrac{(CM)^2}{a^2} + \dfrac{(MP)^2}{b^2} = 1$. This is a geometric property of the ellipse itself and does not depend upon the choice of coordinate axes.

The reader may find it useful to note that a circle of radius a with center at either end of the minor axis will cut the major axis at the foci, since $|CF| = c = \sqrt{a^2 - b^2}$. (See Problem 34, Set 21–5.)

● **Example 2.** Find the equation of the ellipse having center (h, k), major axis parallel to the x-axis and semiaxes a and b (that is, Theorem 4, Part 1).

We shall use Theorem 3 which states that

$$\frac{(CM)^2}{a^2} + \frac{(MP)^2}{b^2} = 1.$$

Since $CM = x - h$ and $MP = y - k$, Theorem 3 yields

$$\frac{(x - h)^2}{a^2} + \frac{(y - k)^2}{b^2} = 1.$$

The reader should note that the second part of Theorem 4 may be proved in a similar fashion (see Problem 33, Set 21–5), or by interchanging the roles of the x- and y- axes.

Fig. 21–11

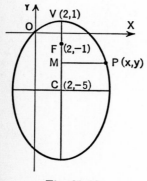

● **Example 3.** Determine the equation of the ellipse having center $C(2, -5)$, focus $F(2, -1)$, and vertex $V(2, 1)$.

We begin by sketching the known data

$$a = |CV| = 6$$
$$c = |CF| = 4$$
$$b^2 = a^2 - c^2 = 36 - 16 = 20$$
$$|CM| = |y + 5|$$
$$|MP| = |x - 2|.$$

By Theorem 3: $\dfrac{(CM)^2}{a^2} + \dfrac{(MP)^2}{b^2} = 1.$

The desired equation is

$$\frac{(y + 5)^2}{36} + \frac{(x - 2)^2}{20} = 1.$$

Fig. 21–12

● **Example 4.** Find the equation of the ellipse having center $C(-3, 1)$, vertex $V(5, 1)$ and such that the point $(1, -1)$ lies on the ellipse. See Fig. 21–13.

$$a = |CV| = 8$$
$$|CM| = |x+3|$$
$$|MP| = |y-1|$$
$$\frac{(CM)^2}{a^2} + \frac{(MP)^2}{b^2} = 1.$$

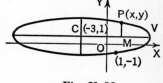

Fig. 21–13

Hence,

$$\frac{(x+3)^2}{64} + \frac{(y-1)^2}{b^2} = 1.$$

Since the point $(1, -1)$ lies on the ellipse, its coordinates must satisfy the equation of the ellipse.

$$\frac{(1+3)^2}{64} + \frac{(-1-1)^2}{b^2} = 1$$

$$\frac{4}{b^2} = \frac{3}{4}$$

$$b^2 = \tfrac{16}{3}.$$

The desired equation is

$$\frac{(x+3)^2}{64} + \frac{(y-1)^2}{\frac{16}{3}} = 1.$$

• **Example 5.** Sketch the locus $4x^2 - 8x + 9y^2 + 90y + 193 = 0$.

Complete the square on the terms involving x and also on those involving y. First factor out the coefficients of the squared terms to obtain

$$4(x^2 - 2x \quad) + 9(y^2 + 10y \quad) = -193.$$

In completing the squares add 1 to $x^2 - 2x$ and 25 to $y^2 + 10y$. Then, $4(1) + 9(25)$ must be added to the right member. (Why?)

$$4(x^2 - 2x + 1) + 9(y^2 + 10y + 25) = -193 + 4 + 225$$
$$4(x-1)^2 + 9(y+5)^2 = 36$$
$$\frac{(x-1)^2}{9} + \frac{(y+5)^2}{4} = 1.$$

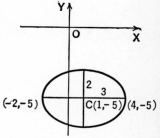

The locus is an ellipse with center $C(1, -5)$, semimajor axis $a = 3$, semiminor axis $b = 2$. The major axis is parallel to the x-axis. The vertices are $(4, -5)$ and $(-2, -5)$. Each focus is $c = \sqrt{a^2 - b^2} = \sqrt{9-4} = \sqrt{5}$ units from the center $(1, -5)$. Thus, the foci are $(1 \pm \sqrt{5}, -5)$.

Fig. 21–14

The student should study the five examples given above with care before attempting to work the problems in the next problem set. *Always* read the text *first*, then work *each* illustrative example with the text solution covered to be sure you understand the concepts *before* you start the homework assignment. This is the way to study your text.

PROBLEM SET 21-5

In each of Problems 1 to 20 sketch the locus and, if it is an ellipse, determine the coordinates of the center, vertices, and foci and the lengths of semimajor axis, semiminor axis, and the latus rectum.

1. $\dfrac{x^2}{9} + \dfrac{y^2}{25} = 1.$ **2.** $\dfrac{x^2}{9} + \dfrac{y^2}{4} = 1.$

3. $\dfrac{x^2}{4} + \dfrac{y^2}{4} = 1.$ **4.** $\dfrac{x^2}{25} + \dfrac{(y-7)^2}{4} = 1.$

5. $x^2 + \dfrac{(y+2)^2}{9} = 1.$ **6.** $\dfrac{(x-4)^2}{9} + \dfrac{(y+1)^2}{25} = 1.$

7. $\dfrac{(x+2)^2}{16} + \dfrac{(y-5)^2}{4} = 1.$ **8.** $\dfrac{(x+1)^2}{25} + (y+2)^2 = 1.$

9. $x^2 + 4y^2 = 36.$ **10.** $4x^2 + 25y^2 = 400.$

11. $4(x-3)^2 + 25(y+1)^2 = 400.$

12. $25(x+7)^2 + 100(y-2)^2 = 100.$

13. $4(x-11)^2 + 4(y+2)^2 = 10.$

14. $3x^2 + 12y^2 = 75.$ **15.** $(x+3)^2 + 4(y+1)^2 = 1.$

16. $100x^2 + y^2 - 2y = 0.$ **17.** $xy = 5.$ (Is this an ellipse?)

18. $x^2/4 + y = 1.$ (Is this an ellipse?)

19. $4(x+1)^2 + (y-3)^2 = 36.$ (Compare with Problem 9.)

20. $50(x-4)^2 + 18(y+1)^2 = 450.$

21. $4x^2 + 9y^2 = 0.$ (Is this an ellipse?)

22. $16x^2 + 9y^2 + 144 = 0.$ (Is this an ellipse?)

23. Show that $x = a \cos t,$ $y = b \sin t,$ where t may take any value, will represent an ellipse in the x-, y-plane.

[HINT: Use $\sin^2 t + \cos^2 t = 1.$]

24. Find the equation of an ellipse with center $(3, -1),$ semimajor axis 6, and semiminor axis 3, if the major axis of the ellipse is parallel to the y-axis.

25. Find the equation of an ellipse with center $(5, 2),$ vertex $(5, 6),$ and semiminor axis $b = 1.$

In Problems 26 to 32 sketch and write the equations of ellipses having the given properties.

26. $C(4, 3),$ $V(4, 9),$ $F(4, 7).$

27. $C(5, -1),$ $V(11, -1),$ $F(3, -1).$

28. $C(4, 1),$ $V(-1, 1),$ $F(2, 1).$

29. $V(-3, 1),$ $V(3, 1),$ $F(1, 1).$

30. $F(7, -6),$ $V(4, -6),$ $V(13, -6).$

31. $F(-7, 5),$ $F(-7, -1),$ $V(-7, -3).$

32. $V(3, -1),$ $C(-2, -1),$ and $(1, 1)$ lies on the ellipse.

33. Give an argument similar to that given in Example 1 for the case of an ellipse with major axis parallel to the y-axis.

4. Show that a circle of radius a with center at either end point of the minor axis of an ellipse will cut the major axis of the ellipse at the foci.

5. Joe Benson read in his garden book that if you drive two stakes into the ground and throw a loop of rope over the two stakes, the outline of an elliptical flower bed can be marked by moving a third stick in such a manner that the rope is kept taut. If Joe wishes his elliptical flower bed to measure 6 feet by 4 feet, how far apart should the stakes be placed and how long should the loop of rope be?

6. Show that $(x = -2 + 3 \cos \theta, \quad y = 1 + 5 \sin \theta)$ are the coordinates of a point on an ellipse. Find the center, semiaxes, and equation of the ellipse.

7. Use differentiation to find the slope of the tangent line at a point (x_1, y_1) on the ellipse $b^2x^2 + a^2y^2 = a^2b^2$.

8. Write and simplify the equations of the tangent and normal lines through a point (x_1, y_1) on the ellipse $b^2x^2 + a^2y^2 = a^2b^2$.

9. **A diameter of an ellipse,** $b^2x^2 + a^2y^2 = a^2b^2$, is the segment cut off by the ellipse on any line through the center of the ellipse. Prove that tangent lines to the ellipse at the ends of a diameter are parallel.

10. Use differentiation to find the slope of $9(x - 1)^2 + 16(y + 2)^2 = 100$ at $(3, -4)$. Write the equations of the tangent and normal lines through $(3, -4)$ and sketch the figure.

11. Show that the locus of the midpoints of all the ordinates (y values) of a circle $x^2 + y^2 = a^2$ is an ellipse.

12. Show that if the length of each ordinate of a circle is multiplied by a constant $k \neq 0$, the resulting locus is an ellipse.

13. Prove that the length of the latus rectum of an ellipse is $2b^2/a$.

21-6. Reduction of the equation to standard form. The equation $Ax^2 + Cy^2 + Dx + Ey + F = 0$, with $AC > 0$ may be reduced (by completing the squares in x and y) to the equation of an ellipse with axes parallel to the coordinate axes.†

● **Example 1.** Sketch the locus

$$25x^2 + 16y^2 - 100x + 96y - 156 = 0.$$

Before completing the square it is convenient to group the terms in the same letter and factor out the coefficient of the squared term. This leads to

$$25(x^2 - 4x \quad) + 16(y^2 + 6y \quad) = 156.$$

† The ellipse may be a "point" ellipse of type $x^2/a^2 + y^2/b^2 = 0$, or an "imaginary" ellipse of type $x^2/a^2 + y^2/b^2 = -1$.

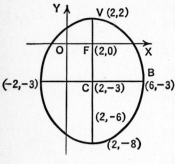

Fig. 21–15

Upon completing the squares by adding appropriate constants to each member of the equation we have

$$25(x^2 - 4x + 4) + 16(y^2 + 6y + 9) = 156 + 100 + 144,$$
$$25(x - 2)^2 + 16(y + 3)^2 = 400.$$

In standard form

$$\frac{(x - 2)^2}{16} + \frac{(y + 3)^2}{25} = 1.$$

The locus is an ellipse with center $(2, -3)$, having $a = 5$, $b = 4$ and the major axis parallel to the y-axis.

● **Example 2.** Determine the locus of

$$x^2 + 36y^2 + 6x - 144y + 144 \leqq 0.$$

Proceeding as in Example 1

$$x^2 + 6x \quad\quad + 36(y^2 - 4y \quad) \leqq -144$$
$$x^2 + 6x + 9 + 36(y^2 - 4y + 4) \leqq -144 + 9 + 144$$
$$(x + 3)^2 \quad\quad + 36(y - 2)^2 \quad\quad \leqq 9$$

or, in the standard form,

$$\frac{(x + 3)^2}{9} + \frac{(y - 2)^2}{\frac{1}{4}} \leqq 1.$$

The locus consists of all points inside and on an ellipse with center $(-3, 2)$, $a = 3$, $b = \frac{1}{2}$ and having major axis parallel to the x-axis.

PROBLEM SET 21–6

In Problems 1 to 10 determine the coordinates of the center, vertices, foci, and end points of the minor axis of the given ellipses. Sketch the loci.

1. $x^2 + 36y^2 + 6x - 144y + 144 = 0.$
2. $25x^2 - 50x + 4y^2 + 56y + 121 = 0.$
3. $x^2 + 4y^2 - 4x + 8y = 8.$
4. $9x^2 + 16y^2 - 36x + 128y + 148 = 0.$
5. $9x^2 + 4y^2 + 54x - 40y < -37.$
6. $9x^2 + 4y^2 = 24y.$
7. $16x^2 + 99y^2 + 80x - 132y + 100 \leqq 0.$

8. $4x^2 - 8x + y^2 + 8y + 20 = 0$.

9. $4x^2 + 9y^2 - 24x + 200 = 0$.

10. $25x^2 + 16y^2 - 128y + 100x \geq 44$.

11. A semielliptical arch is 40 feet across the base and 16 feet from the base to the highest point on the arch. Find the height of the arch (a) 4 feet from an end of the base, (b) 5 feet from the center of the base.

12. Write the equation of the locus of a particle which moves so that its distance from the point $(1, 1)$ is always equal to one half its distance from the point $(-2, 0)$. Identify the locus.

13. Write the equation of the locus of a particle which moves so that its distance from $(2, 2)$ is always equal to one half its distance from the line $x = -2$. Identify the locus.

14. Find the equation of an ellipse with vertices $(\pm 5, -4)$ and foci $(\pm 3, -4)$.

15. A road bed 24 feet wide is centered under the span of a semielliptical arch. The arch is 30 feet wide at ground level. The highest point on the semielliptical arch is 15 feet above the center of the road. How high is the arch above the edge of the road?

16. (a) Could a truck 8 feet wide and 14 feet high pass under the bridge of Problem 15?

(b) Could it pass under without crossing the middle line of the road?

17. Show that a circle is obtained as a special case of the ellipse when the foci are coincident.

18. Sketch $x^2 + 2x = y - 2y^2$.

19. Sketch $(x - 3)^2 - 4 < 21 - (y + 2)^2$.

20. Find all solutions (x, y) of the system

$$y - x + 10 = 0, \quad 3x^2 + 9y^2 = 252$$

and check graphically.

21. (a) Find the coordinates of the points of intersection of $9x^2 + 16y^2 = 100$ and $16x^2 + 9y^2 = 100$.

(b) Find the acute angle between the two ellipses at one of their points of intersection.

22. Find the equations of the tangent and normal lines to $x^2 + 4y^2 - 2x + 4y = 24$ through $(2, 2)$. Sketch.

23. Verify that for all values of t, $(2 + 3 \cos \pi t, \ 3 + 4 \sin \pi t)$ is on an ellipse. Find center, semiaxes, and equation of the ellipse.

24. In Problem 23 find $\dfrac{dx}{dt}$ and $\dfrac{dy}{dt}$ at the highest point on the ellipse.

25. Find the slope of the tangent line to the ellipse

$$x = 2 + 3 \cos \pi t, \quad y = 3 + 4 \sin \pi t \quad \text{at} \quad t = \tfrac{1}{3}.$$

$$\left[\text{HINT:} \ \frac{dy}{dx} = \frac{dy/dt}{dx/dt} \right].$$

26. How fast is the distance from the center to a point on the ellipse $(x = 5 \cos t, \quad y = 4 \sin t)$ changing at the instant

$$t = \frac{\pi}{6}?$$

*27. The inside edge of a race track is an ellipse having major axis 400 feet and minor axis 200 feet. The track is 6 feet wide (measured perpendicular to the inside edge) at every point. Prove that the outside edge of the track is *not* an ellipse. For a hint, see Problem E 753, *American Mathematical Monthly*, p. 414, Vol. 54 (1947).

28. Determine the ratio $b:a$ for the ellipse of Problem 2 by inspection.

21–7. The hyperbola. Let F_1 and F_2 be two fixed points. Let P be a point such that $\big| \, |F_1P| - |F_2P| \, \big|$ is a constant. The locus of all points P, in a plane containing the fixed points, is a **hyperbola.**

● **Example 1.** Given $F_1(1, -3)$ and $F_2(1, 5)$. Determine the equation of the locus of points $P(x, y)$ such that

$$\Big| \, |F_1P| - |F_2P| \, \Big| = 2,$$

$$\left| \sqrt{(x-1)^2 + (y+3)^2} - \sqrt{(x-1)^2 + (y-5)^2} \right| = 2.$$

Hence,

$$\sqrt{(x-1)^2 + (y+3)^2} - \sqrt{(x-1)^2 + (y-5)^2} = \pm 2.$$

Transposing,

$$\sqrt{(x-1)^2 + (y+3)^2} = \pm 2 + \sqrt{(x-1)^2 + (y-5)^2}.$$

Squaring,

$$(x-1)^2 + (y+3)^2 = 4 \pm 4\sqrt{(x-1)^2 + (y-5)^2} + (x-1)^2 + (y-5)^2.$$

This simplifies to

$$16y - 20 = \pm 4\sqrt{(x-1)^2 + (y-5)^2},$$

or

$$4y - 5 = \pm \sqrt{(x-1)^2 + (y-5)^2}.$$

Squaring again

$$16y^2 - 40y + 25 = (x-1)^2 + (y-5)^2,$$

or

$$x^2 - 2x - 15y^2 + 30y + 1 = 0,$$

the required hyperbola.

PROBLEM SET 21–7

In each of Problems 1 to 6, find the equation of the locus of points $P(x, y)$ having $\big|\,|F_1P| - |F_2P|\,\big| = d.$

1. $F_1(3, 5)$, $F_2(3, 13)$, $d = 6$.
2. $F_1(-1, 5)$, $F_2(-1, -8)$, $d = 10$.
3. $F_1(0, 4)$, $F_2(0, -4)$, $d = 6$.
4. $F_1(-4, 2)$, $F_2(-4, -6)$, $d = 5$.
5. $F_1(4, 0)$, $F_2(0, 3)$, $d = 4$.
6. $F_1(7, 1)$, $F_2(-1, 1)$, $d = 6$.

21–8. Special properties of the hyperbola. Certain terms will be defined to aid in the study of the hyperbola.

Focus. The two fixed points F_1 and F_2 are the **foci** of the hyperbola.

Center. The midpoint C of the line segment F_1F_2 is the **center** of the hyperbola. It is a point of symmetry.

Vertices. The points of intersection V_1 and V_2 of the line F_1F_2 with the hyperbola are the **vertices** of the hyperbola.

Transverse axis. The line segment V_1V_2 is the **transverse axis** of the hyperbola. The length of the semitransverse axis, $|V_1V_2|/2$, is denoted by a.

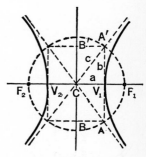

Fig. 21–16

Conjugate axis.† The **conjugate axis** is a line segment BB' through C perpendicular to the transverse axis V_1V_2. The length of the semiconjugate axis, $|BB'|/2$, is

$$b = \sqrt{(CF_1)^2 - (CV_1)^2}.$$

Asymptotes. The hyperbola has two **asymptotes** which intersect at C and pass through points A and A' located b units from V_1 on a line perpendicular to the transverse axis V_1V_2 at V_1. The hyperbola becomes and remains arbitrarily close to these asymptotes at points sufficiently far from the center C.

† The reader who is familiar with the meaning of transverse as "to cross" can easily distinguish the two axes.

Latus rectum. The **latus rectum** is a line segment terminating on the hyperbola, and perpendicular to the transverse axis at a focus.

Theorems 1 to 4 are proved in this section and in Problem Set 21–8.

Theorem 1. The distance between the center C and either focus of a hyperbola † is $\quad | CF_1 | = | CF_2 | = \sqrt{a^2 + b^2}$.

Theorem 2. The length of a latus rectum is $\quad 2b^2/a$.

Theorem 3. If P is a point on the hyperbola and MP is perpendicular to the extended transverse axis at M, then the distances $| CM |$ and $| MP |$ satisfy the following relationship

$$\frac{(CM)^2}{a^2} - \frac{(MP)^2}{b^2} = 1.$$

Theorem 4. If a hyperbola has center (h, k), semiaxes a and b, and transverse axis parallel to the x-axis, then its equation is

$$\frac{(x - h)^2}{a^2} - \frac{(y - k)^2}{b^2} = 1. \tag{21.4}$$

If the transverse axis is parallel to the y-axis, the equation is

$$\frac{(y - k)^2}{a^2} - \frac{(x - h)^2}{b^2} = 1. \tag{21.5}$$

In the hyperbola the a is associated with the positive term in the standard form regardless of size, while in the ellipse the a is the larger of a and b.

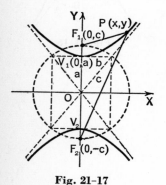

Fig. 21-17

● **Example 1.** Derive the equation of a hyperbola with center at the origin and vertices $(0, -a)$, $(0, a)$.

The foci may be taken as $F_1(0, c)$ and $F_2(0, -c)$. Each point $P(x, y)$ on the hyperbola satisfies $\big| | F_1P | - | F_2P | \big| =$ some constant. The point $V_1(0, a)$ is on the hyperbola and must satisfy the above relationship. Consequently,

$$\big| | F_1V_1 | - | F_2V_1 | \big| = \big| | c - a | - | -c - a | \big|$$
$$= | c - a - c - a | = 2a.$$

Hence,

$$\big| | F_1P | - | F_2P | \big| = 2a.$$

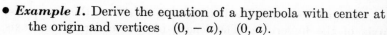

† Contrast this with the ellipse, where a similar distance equals $\sqrt{a^2 - b^2}$. On which curve is the distance $a = | CV_1 |$ less than $c = | CF_1 |$?

Use the distance formula (Section 2–3) to compute

$$|F_1P| \quad \text{and} \quad |F_2P|$$

to obtain

$$\left|\sqrt{x^2 + (y - c)^2} - \sqrt{x^2 + (y + c)^2}\right| = 2a,$$
$$\sqrt{x^2 + (y - c)^2} - \sqrt{x^2 + (y + c)^2} = \pm\, 2a,$$
$$\sqrt{x^2 + (y - c)^2} = \pm\, 2a + \sqrt{x^2 + (y + c)^2}.$$

Upon squaring:

$$x^2 + y^2 - 2cy + c^2 = 4a^2 \pm 4a\sqrt{x^2 + (y + c)^2} + x^2 + y^2 + 2cy + c^2.$$

This simplifies to

$$-\,4cy - 4a^2 = \pm\, 4a\sqrt{x^2 + (y + c)^2},$$

or,

$$cy + a^2 = \pm\, a\sqrt{x^2 + (y + c)^2}.$$

Squaring again

$$c^2y^2 + 2a^2cy + a^4 = a^2(x^2 + y^2 + 2cy + c^2).$$

This simplifies to

$$(c^2 - a^2)y^2 - a^2x^2 = a^2(c^2 - a^2).$$

Hence,

$$\frac{y^2}{a^2} - \frac{x^2}{c^2 - a^2} = 1.$$

Since $b^2 = c^2 - a^2 > 0$, this becomes †

$$\frac{y^2}{a^2} - \frac{x^2}{b^2} = 1.$$

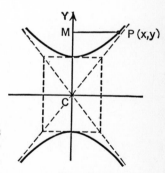

Fig. 21–18

Since $|CF_1| = |CF_2| = c = \sqrt{a^2 + b^2}$, Theorem **1** follows as a corollary. The derivation of Example 1 provides a proof for Theorem 3. If P is a point on the hyperbola, then $CM = y$ and $MP = x$. Since the coordinates of every point on the hyperbola satisfy the equation, we have $\dfrac{(CM)^2}{a^2} - \dfrac{(MP)^2}{b^2} = 1$. This is a geometric property of the hyperbola itself, and does not depend upon the choice of coordinate axes.

A circle of radius $c = \sqrt{a^2 + b^2}$ with center C will intersect the transverse axis at the foci (see Problem 37, Set 21–8.) It is convenient to sketch a rectangle with center C, having sides of length $2a$ parallel to the transverse axis and sides of length $2b$ parallel to the conjugate axis. The hyperbola is tangent to this

† $2c > 2a$ since the difference between two sides of a triangle is smaller than the third side.

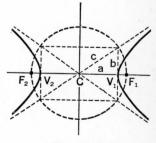

Fig. 21–19

rectangle and the asymptotes of the hyperbola pass through the diagonally opposite vertices ("corners") of the rectangle.

● **Example 2.** Find the equation of the hyperbola having center (h, k), transverse axis parallel to the y-axis and semiaxes a and b (that is, Theorem 4, Part 2).

We use Theorem 3 which states that

$$\frac{(CM)^2}{a^2} - \frac{(MP)^2}{b^2} = 1.$$

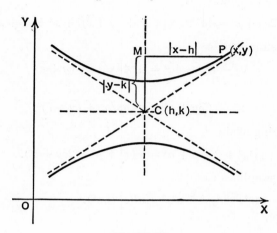

Fig. 21–20

Since $CM = y - k$ and $MP = x - h$, Theorem 3 yields

$$\frac{(y - k)^2}{a^2} - \frac{(x - h)^2}{b^2} = 1,$$

as desired.

● **Example 3.** Find the semiaxes, center, vertices, foci and sketch the hyperbola, $9(x - 3)^2 - 4(y + 1)^2 = 144$.

The equation in standard form is

$$\frac{(x - 3)^2}{16} - \frac{(y + 1)^2}{36} = 1.$$

The locus is a hyperbola with semiaxes $a = 4$, $b = 6$ and center $C(3, -1)$. The transverse axis is parallel to the x-axis. (Why?) The distance from center to focus is

$$|CF| = c = \sqrt{a^2 + b^2} = \sqrt{16 + 36} = \sqrt{52} \cong 7.2.$$

The sketching is simplified by constructing the reference rectangle and the asymptotes. See Fig. 21–21.

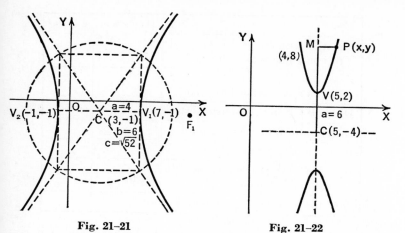

Fig. 21–21   Fig. 21–22

● **Example 4.** Determine the equation of a hyperbola with center
$(5, -4)$, vertex $(5, 2)$ and passing through the point
$(4, 8)$. From $|CM| = |y + 4|$, $|MP| = |x - 5|$,
$a = |CV| = 6$ and

$$\frac{(CM)^2}{a^2} - \frac{(MP)^2}{b^2} = 1,$$

obtain

$$\frac{(y + 4)^2}{36} - \frac{(x - 5)^2}{b^2} = 1,$$

where the value of b^2 is to be determined. The coordinates of
the point $(4, 8)$ must satisfy the equation of the hyperbola.
Making this substitution and solving the resulting equation
for b^2, one obtains,

$$\frac{(8 + 4)^2}{36} - \frac{(4 - 5)^2}{b^2} = 1, \quad b^2 = \tfrac{1}{3}.$$

The desired equation is

$$\frac{(y + 4)^2}{36} - \frac{(x - 5)^2}{\tfrac{1}{3}} = 1.$$

PROBLEM SET 21–8

1. Complete the following table, comparing properties of the
ellipse and the hyperbola.

	Hyperbola	Ellipse
Equation with center (h, k) and foci on a line parallel to x-axis		
Equation with center (h, k) and foci on a line parallel to y-axis		
Distance CV from center to vertex		
Distance CF from center to focus		
Length of latus rectum		
Into how many regions does the locus divide the plane?		
Does the locus have asymptotes?		

In each of Problems 2 to 20 sketch the locus and if it is a hyperbola or an ellipse determine the coordinates of the center, vertices, and foci, and the lengths of the semiaxes and latus rectum.

2. $\dfrac{x^2}{9} - \dfrac{y^2}{4} = 1.$ **3.** $\dfrac{y^2}{9} - \dfrac{x^2}{4} = 1.$ **4.** $\dfrac{y^2}{25} - x^2 = 1.$

5. $\dfrac{(y-7)^2}{25} - \dfrac{(x-2)^2}{9} = 1.$ **6.** $\dfrac{(x+2)^2}{9} - \dfrac{(y-3)^2}{25} = 1.$

7. $\dfrac{x^2}{4} + (y-1)^2 = 1.$ **8.** $\dfrac{(x-1)^2}{25} - \dfrac{(y+3)^2}{100} = 1.$

9. $25y^2 - 100(x+1)^2 = 100.$ **10.** $(x-6)^2 - (y+5)^2 = 1.$

11. $3x^2 - 12y^2 = 75.$ **12.** $4(x+5)^2 - (x+2)^2 = 36.$

13. $50(x-4)^2 - 18(y+1)^2 = 450.$ **14.** $4x^2 - 9y^2 + 36 = 0.$

15. $36(y-6)^2 - 4(x+1)^2 = 81.$ **16.** $36(x+1)^2 - 9(y+2)^2 = 576.$

17. $y^2 - x^2 = 1.$ **18.** $(x-2y)(x+2y) = 36.$

19. $9x^2 - 4y^2 = 0.$ **20.** $4(x-1)^2 - 12(y-3)^2 = 25.$

21. Find the equation of a hyperbola with center $(3, -5)$ semi-transverse axis 5, semiconjugate axis 7, if the transverse axis of the hyperbola is parallel to (a) the x-axis, (b) the y-axis.

In Problems 22 to 30 determine the equation of an ellipse or hyperbola having the stated properties.

22. Hyperbola: $C(2, 1)$, $V(2, 5)$, $F(2, 6)$.

23. Hyperbola: $a = 4$, $b = 3$, center $(2, 1)$, transverse axis parallel to $x = 7$.

24. Focus $(-3, 0)$, vertex $(5, 0)$, center $(0, 0)$. [Is this an ellipse or hyperbola? Why?]

25. Center $(0, 3)$, vertex $(5, 3)$, asymptote $5(y-3) = 4x$.

26. Focus on x-axis, asymptotes $y = \pm 3x/2$, latus rectum of length 18.

27. Center $(7, 1)$, focus $(7, -5)$, $a = 2$.

28. Ellipse: vertices $(\pm 4, 3)$, $b = 1$.

29. Hyperbola: center $(-4, 7)$, vertex $(2, 7)$, $b = 4$.

30. Center $(-2, 2)$, focus $(3, 2)$, asymptote $2x - 3y + 10 = 0$.

31. Find the locus of the midpoints of the abscissas drawn to the hyperbola $9x^2 - 16y^2 = 144$.

32. Prove that the length of the latus rectum of a hyperbola is $2b^2/a$.

33. Find the equation of the locus of the vertex of a triangle whose vertices are $(-a, 0)$ and $(a, 0)$ and for which the product of the tangents of the base angles is b^2/a^2.

34. Prove that the minor axis of an ellipse is a mean proportional between the major axis and the latus rectum.

35. Find the locus of the midpoints of the ordinates drawn to the hyperbola $4x^2 - 9y^2 = 36$.

36. Given, $x = a \sec t$, $y = b \tan t$. Show that these are x-, y-equations of a hyperbola.

[HINT: Use $\sec^2 t - \tan^2 t = 1$.]

37. Prove that a circle of radius $c = \sqrt{a^2 + b^2}$, with center C, intersects the transverse axis of the hyperbola at the foci.

38. Use differentiation to find the slope of $b^2x^2 - a^2y^2 = a^2b^2$ at a point (x_1, y_1) on the hyperbola.

39. Write and simplify the equations of the tangent and normal lines through the point (x_1, y_1) on the hyperbola $b^2x^2 - a^2y^2 = a^2b^2$.

40. Consider a line through the center of the hyperbola $b^2x^2 - a^2y^2 = a^2b^2$ and its points of intersection with the hyperbola. Are the tangent lines at these points parallel?

41. A point $P(x, y)$ is moving along the hyperbola $x^2 - y^2 = 21$ such that $\dfrac{dx}{dt} = 4$. Find $\dfrac{dy}{dt}$ if $x = 5$ and $y > 0$.

21–9. Reduction to standard form. The equation

$$Ax^2 + Cy^2 + Dx + Ey + F = 0,$$

with

$$A \cdot C < 0\dagger$$

may be reduced (by completing the squares in x and in y) to the equation of a hyperbola with axes parallel to the coordinate axes.‡

† Contrast this with the first statement of Section 21–6.
‡ The hyperbola may degenerate into two intersecting lines

$$\frac{(x - h)^2}{a^2} - \frac{(y - k)^2}{b^2} = 0.$$

● **Example 1.** Sketch $9x^2 - 4y^2 - 90x - 8y + 185 = 0$.

$$9(x^2 - 10x \qquad) - 4(y^2 + 2y \qquad) = -185$$
$$9(x^2 - 10x + 25) - 4(y^2 + 2y + 1) = -185 + 225 - 4$$
$$9(x - 5)^2 \qquad - 4(y + 1)^2 \qquad = 36$$
$$\frac{(x - 5)^2}{4} \qquad - \frac{(y + 1)^2}{9} \qquad = 1.$$

Hence, the locus is a hyperbola with center

$$(5, -1), \quad a = 2, \quad b = 3,$$

and transverse axis parallel to the x-axis.

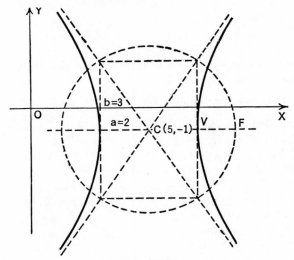

Fig. 21–23

21–10. Rotation of axes. The sine of a sum and cosine of a sum identities (Section 16–4) can be used to derive the rotation of axes equations. In an equation such as $x^2 + xy\sqrt{3} + 2y^2 = \frac{5}{2}$ it is possible to apply a rotation of axes and transform to a new equation of the type $Ax'^2 + Cy'^2 = K$ where the $x'y'$ term is missing. The curve may be identified more easily from this equation since the rotation of axes transformation does not change either shape or size. The sketch may be made relative to the $x'y'$-axes and the xy-axes copied in. Think of a set of axes coinciding with the xy-axes at the outset and then rotated in the xy-plane about the origin through an angle α to obtain the new $x'y'$-axes as shown in the figure. Any point P in the plane has coordinates (x, y) referred to the xy-axes and (x', y') referred to the $x'y'$-axes. Using the figure and the appropriate identities one may verify:

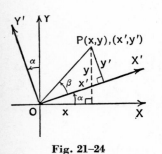

Fig. 21–24

$$x = OP \cos(\beta + \alpha) = OP \cos\beta \cos\alpha - OP \sin\beta \sin\alpha,$$
$$y = OP \sin(\beta + \alpha) = OP \cos\beta \sin\alpha + OP \sin\beta \cos\alpha.$$

On substitution of $x' = OP \cos \beta$, $y' = OP \sin \beta$ we obtain the desired *rotation of axes equations*:

$$x = x' \cos \alpha - y' \sin \alpha,$$
$$y = x' \sin \alpha + y' \cos \alpha.$$

• **Example 1.** Transform $x^2 + xy\sqrt{3} + 2y^2 = \frac{5}{2}$ to a new $x'y'$ system by rotating through $\alpha = \frac{\pi}{3}$.

$$x = x' \cos \frac{\pi}{3} - y' \sin \frac{\pi}{3} = \frac{x' - y'\sqrt{3}}{2}, \quad y = \frac{x'\sqrt{3} + y'}{2}.$$

$$x^2 + xy\sqrt{3} + 2y^2 = \left(\frac{x' - y'\sqrt{3}}{2}\right)^2 + \left(\frac{x' - y'\sqrt{3}}{2}\right)\left(\frac{x'\sqrt{3} + y'}{2}\right)\sqrt{3}$$

$$+ 2\left(\frac{x'\sqrt{3} + y'}{2}\right)^2$$

$$= \frac{10x'^2 + 2y'^2}{4} = \frac{5}{2}.$$

$5x'^2 + y'^2 = 5$, an ellipse (see Section 21–5). Its sketch is given in Figure 21–25.

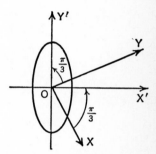

Fig. 21–25

• **Example 2.** Transform $x^2 - 2xy + y^2 - 2x - 2y = 0$ by rotation of axes such that $x'y'$ is missing.

This requires that we find the coefficient of $x'y'$ after substituting $x = x' \cos \alpha - y' \sin \alpha$, $y = x' \sin \alpha + y' \cos \alpha$ for x and y in the given equation and then equate the coefficient to zero. Then solve the resulting equation for α or find $\cos \alpha$ and $\sin \alpha$. Finally simplify.

$x^2 - 2xy + y^2 - 2x - 2y$
$= (x' \cos \alpha - y' \sin \alpha)^2 - 2(x' \cos \alpha - y' \sin \alpha)(x' \sin \alpha + y' \cos \alpha)$
$\quad + (x' \sin \alpha + y' \cos \alpha)^2 - 2(x' \cos \alpha - y' \sin \alpha)$
$\quad - 2(x' \sin \alpha + y' \cos \alpha)$
$= (\cos^2 \alpha - 2 \sin \alpha \cos \alpha + \sin^2 \alpha)x'^2$
$\quad - 2(\sin \alpha \cos \alpha + \cos^2 \alpha - \sin^2 \alpha - \sin \alpha \cos \alpha)x'y'$
$\quad + (\sin^2 \alpha + 2 \sin \alpha \cos \alpha + \cos^2 \alpha)y'^2 - 2(\cos \alpha + \sin \alpha)x'$
$\quad - 2(- \sin \alpha + \cos \alpha)y'$
$= (1 - \sin 2\alpha)x'^2 - 2(\cos 2\alpha)x'y' + (1 + \sin 2\alpha)y'^2$
$\quad - 2(\cos \alpha + \sin \alpha)x' - 2(- \sin \alpha + \cos \alpha)y' = 0.$

Let $\cos 2\alpha = 0$ and use $2\alpha = \frac{\pi}{2}$, $\alpha = \frac{\pi}{4}$. Then the transformed equation is

$$2y'^2 - 2x'\sqrt{2} = 0 \quad \text{or} \quad y'^2 = x'\sqrt{2},$$

a parabola (see Section 21–11). Its sketch is shown in Figure 21–26.

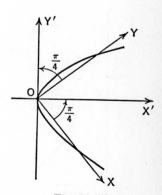

Fig. 21–26

PROBLEM SET 21–10

Reduce each equation to standard form and sketch. If the locus is a hyperbola, dot the asymptotes before sketching the locus.

1. $x^2 - 2x - y^2 + 4y - 4 = 0.$

2. $16x^2 - 9y^2 + 128x + 90y - 113 = 0.$

3. $4y^2 - x^2 + 8x - 28 = 0.$ **4.** $y^2 - x^2 - 4y = 0.$

5. $10x^2 + y^2 + 60x - 8y + 96 = 0.$

6. $25x^2 - 9y^2 + 50x + 36y + 214 = 0.$

7. $9y^2 - 16x^2 - 128x - 90y + 113 = 0.$

8. $2y^2 - 3x^2 - 4y - 12x - 16 = 0.$

9. $x^2 - y^2 - 6x - 4y + 1 = 0.$ **10.** $4x^2 - 2y^2 + 2x + y - 6 = 0.$

11. Sketch showing foci and vertices:

$$9x^2 - 54x - 4y^2 + 8y + 41 = 0.$$

12. Determine the coordinates of one focus and one vertex of $9(x - 4)^2 + 25(y + 7)^2 = 900$ and sketch the curve.

13. Transform $x^2 + y^2 = 16$ by rotation of axes using $\alpha = \dfrac{\pi}{6}.$ Sketch.

14. Transform $x^2 + y^2 - 4x - 4y = 0$ by rotation of axes using $\alpha = \dfrac{\pi}{4}.$ Sketch.

15. Solve Problem 14 using $\alpha = -\dfrac{\pi}{4}.$ Sketch.

16. Transform $xy = 8$ by rotation of axes and selecting α such that the $x'y'$ term is missing. Sketch.

17. Find the equations of the tangent and normal lines to $x^2 - 2xy + y^2 - 2x - 2y = -5$ at $(2, 1).$

$$\left[\text{HINT: } \frac{d}{dx} (-2xy) = -2x \frac{dy}{dx} - 2y. \right]$$

21–11. More about the parabola. The reader has seen (Problem 23, Set 2–4, also Sections 2–4, 4–10) that a parabola is a plane curve which is the locus of a point equidistant from a given line and a given point.

The given line is the **directrix** of the parabola. The given point is the **focus** of the parabola. A line through the focus and perpendicular to the directrix is the **axis** of the parabola. The axis is a line of symmetry. The point of intersection of the parabola and the axis is the **vertex** of the parabola. Since every point of the parabola including the vertex is equidistant from the focus and the directrix, it follows that the vertex is midway between the focus and the directrix.

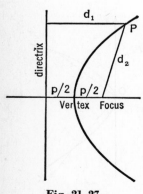

Fig. 21–27

● **Example 1.** Determine the equation of a parabola having vertex $V(0, 0)$ and focus $F(p/2, 0)$.

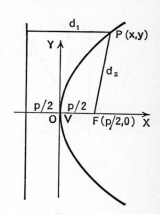

Each point on the parabola is equidistant from the focus and the directrix line. Since V is a point on the parabola and $VF = p/2$, the equation of the directrix is $x = -p/2$. In this case the directrix is perpendicular to the x-axis. (Why?) We seek the locus of points $P(x, y)$ whose absolute distance d_1 from the line $x = -p/2$ is equal to the distance d_2 between $P(x, y)$ and $F(p/2, 0)$.

$$d_2 = d_1$$
$$\sqrt{(x - p/2)^2 + y^2} = |x + p/2|$$
$$x^2 - px + p^2/4 + y^2 = x^2 + px + p^2/4$$
$$y^2 = 2px. \tag{21.6}$$

Fig. 21–28

If the roles played by x and y are interchanged, a parabola opening in the y direction is obtained. In this case the equation becomes $x^2 = 2py$.

Theorem. If from a point P on a parabola a perpendicular PM is dropped to the axis of the parabola, then $(MP)^2 = 2p(VM)$.

The parabola opens in a positive direction (that is, the direction from V to F is positive) if p is positive. The parabola opens in a negative direction if p is negative.

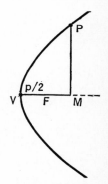

In a manner similar to that used in obtaining standard equations of the ellipse and hyperbola, we may obtain standard equations of a parabola with vertex (h, k) and $VF = p/2$ as

$$(y - k)^2 = 2p(x - h)$$

when VF is parallel to the x-axis or as

Fig. 21–29

$$(x - h)^2 = 2p(y - k)$$

when VF is parallel to the y-axis.

● **Example 2.** Find the equation of a parabola with vertex

$$V(3, -2) \quad \text{and focus} \quad F(-4, -2).$$

The directed distance $VF = -7 = p/2$. (Why not $+7$?) Therefore, $p = -14$. Since

$$VM = x - 3, \quad MP = y + 2 \quad \text{and} \quad (MP)^2 = 2p(VM),$$

the desired equation is

$$(y + 2)^2 = 2(-14)(x - 3), \quad \text{or} \quad y^2 + 28x + 4y - 80 = 0.$$

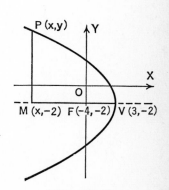

Fig. 21–30

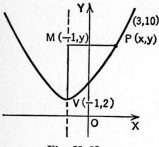

Fig. 21–31

● *Example 3.* A parabola has vertex $(-1, 2)$ and focus on the line $x = -1$. If the parabola passes through the point $(3, 10)$, determine an equation of the parabola.

Since the focus and vertex are both on the line $x = -1$, this is the axis of the parabola. The x must appear squared in the final equation. The equation has the form

$(MP)^2 = 2p(VM)$ with $MP = x + 1$, $VM = y - 2$.

Hence, $(x + 1)^2 = 2p(y - 2)$.

Since the point $(3, 10)$ is on the curve, its coordinates must satisfy the equation of the curve.

$$(3 + 1)^2 = 2p(10 - 2), \quad \text{or} \quad 16 = 2p(8), \quad 2p = 2.$$

Thus, the equation is,

$$(x + 1)^2 = 2(y - 2), \quad \text{or} \quad x^2 + 2x - 2y + 5 = 0.$$

PROBLEM SET 21-11

In each of Problems 1 to 10 determine an equation of a parabola having the given vertex V and focus F.

1. $V(3, -1)$, $F(5, -1)$.   2. $V(2, 4)$, $F(2, -1)$.
3. $V(4, 5)$, $F(-1, 5)$.   4. $V(7, -2)$, $F(7, 3)$.
5. $V(4, 6)$, $F(4, 4)$.   6. $V(3, 1)$, $F(3, 3)$.
7. $V(-2, 3)$, $F(-2, -1)$.   8. $V(2, 6)$, $F(3, 6)$.
9. $V(9, -2)$, $F(7, -2)$.   10. $V(8, -7)$, $F(-1, -7)$.

In Problems 11 to 14 determine an equation of a parabola having its vertex V as given, its focus on the given line L, and passing through the point P.

11. $V(3, -2)$; $L: x = 3$; $P(4, 4)$.
12. $V(7, 2)$; $L: y = 2$; $P(0, 0)$.
13. $V(4, -6)$; $L: y = -6$; $P(1, 1)$.
14. $V(3, 2)$; $L: x = 3$; $P(-1, -5)$.

In each of Problems 15 to 20 determine an equation of a parabola having vertex V, directrix D.

15. $V(0, 1)$, $D: y = -3$.   16. $V(3, 5)$, $D: x = -1$.
17. $V(2, -1)$, $D: x = 5$.   18. $V(1, 4)$, $D: y = 0$.
19. $V(-7, -6)$, $D: y = 1$.   20. $V(9, 2)$, $D: x = -7$.

21. A line segment perpendicular to the axis of the parabola at its focus and terminated by the parabola is called the **latus rectum.** (Similar definitions were given for the ellipse and hyperbola.) Show that the length of the latus rectum of a parabola is two times the distance between the directrix and the focus, that is, $|2p|$.

22. In a parabolic reflector it is desirable to place the source of light at the focus. Locate the focus if the reflector is 10 inches across the opening and 6 inches deep.

23. The cable of a suspension bridge hangs in the shape of an arc of a parabola. The supporting towers are 70 feet high and 200 feet apart and the lowest point on the cable is 20 feet above the roadway. Find the length of a supporting rod 50 feet from the middle of the bridge.

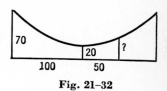

Fig. 21–32

24. A parabolic gate in a dam has its vertex downward. The vertex is located 12 feet above the base of the dam. When the water level is 15 feet above the base of the dam, the gate is 4 feet wide at the water level. Taking the base of the dam as the x-axis and any convenient y-axis, determine an equation of the gate's outline.

25. Same as Problem 24, but take the x-axis 2 feet above the water level mentioned.

26. Write the equations of the following loci:
    (a) Parabola with vertex $(2, 3)$ and focus $(6, 3)$.
    (b) Ellipse with vertices $(\pm 5, -4)$ and foci $(\pm 3, -4)$.

27. Find (a) center, (b) vertices, (c) foci, (d) equations of asymptotes, and (e) sketch $4x^2 - 9y^2 + 8x - 54y - 113 = 0$.

28. The base of a parabolic arch is 20 feet wide at road level. How high must the arch be to have a clearance of 8 feet at a point 6 feet from the center of the base?

29. Find the points of intersection of

$$x^2 + y^2 = 9 \quad \text{and} \quad y^2 = 2x - 6,$$

and check graphically.

30. Show that $x = 2/m^2$, $y = 2/m$ represent a parabola in the xy plane as m is permitted to take on all nonzero values.
    [HINT: Solve for m in terms of y and substitute in the expression for x.]

31. (a) Find the equation of the locus of the points of intersection of the line $x = R - \dfrac{p}{2}$ and the circle having center $\left(\dfrac{p}{2}, 0\right)$ and radius R where R may be any value greater than or equal to $\dfrac{p}{2}$. Show that the locus is a parabola with focus

$\left(\dfrac{p}{2}, 0\right)$ and directrix $x = -\dfrac{p}{2}.$ Does this give a method for constructing a parabola?

(b) Discuss what happens if $0 \leqq R < |p/2|$.

32. Find the area of a segment of a parabola that has its vertex at the origin, axis the y-axis, passes through $(10, 2)$ and has base $y = 10$.

33. Find the area bounded by the parabola $y^2 = 4(x + 2)$ and the line $x = 7$.

34. Let P be any point on the parabola $y = \dfrac{x^2}{2p}.$ Prove that the normal through P bisects the angle between the vertical line through P and the line joining P to the focus. This verifies the reflector property of the parabola.

35. Show that the point $(x = 2p \cot^2 \theta, \ y = 2p \cot \theta)$ is on a parabola and write the equation of the parabola.

36. Use differentiation to find the slope at a point (x_1, y_1) on $y^2 = 2px$ and write and simplify the equations of tangent and normal lines through (x_1, y_1).

37. A point P moves along the parabola $x^2 = 14y$ such that $\dfrac{dy}{dt} = 3.$ Find $\dfrac{dx}{dt}$ when $x = 7$.

21–12. Eccentricity. In this section a definition is given which yields an ellipse, a parabola, or a hyperbola by a suitable choice of a constant appearing in the definition.

Eccentricity definition. Given a fixed point F and fixed line L. If P is a point such that the distance $|d_1|$ between F and P is equal to some constant $e \geqq 0$ times the distance $|d_2|$ between † P and the line L, then for

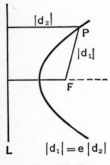

$|d_1| = e\,|d_2|$

Fig. 21–33

(1) $0 \leqq e < 1,$ the locus is an ellipse ‡.
(2) $e = 1,$ the locus is a parabola.
(3) $1 < e,$ the locus is a hyperbola.

The constant e is the **eccentricity** of the curve. The point F is a **focus** and the line L a **directrix** of the curve.

● *Example 1.* Show that if $e = 1,$ the curve is a parabola.

This follows directly from the definition of a parabola as the locus of points P equidistant between a point F and a line L.

---

† Distance between a point and a line is measured perpendicular to the line.
‡ This constant e should not be confused with, $e \cong 2.72,$ the base of the natural logarithms. For ellipses and hyperbolas the eccentricity is a measure of the amount the focus is "off center" since $e = c/a.$ In a circle, the foci and center are identical, therefore a circle is said to have eccentricity zero.

● **Example 2.** Show that if $0 \leqq e < 1$ the locus is an ellipse.

Take the point F as the origin and the line through F perpendicular to the given line L as the x-axis. Let the distance between F and L be p units.

Then,

$$|d_1| = e |d_2|$$
$$\sqrt{x^2 + y^2} = e |p - x|$$
$$x^2 + y^2 = e^2(p^2 - 2px + x^2)$$
$$(1 - e^2)x^2 + 2pe^2x + y^2 = p^2e^2.$$

If $0 \leqq e < 1$, then $(1 - e^2) > 0$, and the coefficients of x^2 and y^2 are both positive. The equation is that of an ellipse. When $e = 0$, the locus is a point circle. The equation may be placed in the form $\dfrac{(x - h)^2}{a^2} + \dfrac{y^2}{b^2} = 1.$

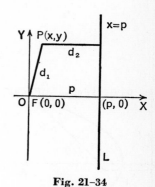

Fig. 21–34

PROBLEM SET 21–12

In each of Problems 1 to 8 use the eccentricity definition to determine the equation of the locus having the indicated focus F, directrix L, and eccentricity e.

Name and sketch each curve.

1. $F(3, 0)$; L: $x = 1$; $e = 1$.
2. $F(0, 0)$; L: $x = 12$; $e = \frac{1}{2}$.
3. $F(4, 0)$; L: $4x = 25$; $e = \frac{4}{5}$.
4. $F(0, -4)$; L: $4y = -25$; $e = \frac{4}{5}$.
5. $F(0, 5)$; L: $5x = 16$; $e = \frac{5}{4}$.
6. $F(15, 0)$; L: $13x = 144$; $e = \frac{13}{12}$.
7. $F(3, 2)$; L: $x = 5$; $e = 1$.
8. $F(0, 13)$; L: $13y = 144$; $e = \frac{13}{12}$.
9. Show that, if $1 < e$ the resulting locus is a hyperbola.
10. Show that, if the locus is an ellipse or a hyperbola, the distance from the center (a) to a focus is ae, (b) to a directrix is a/e.
11. Use the result of Problem 10 to show that, $e = \sqrt{a^2 - b^2}/a$ for an ellipse.
12. Use the result of Problem 10 to show that, $e = \sqrt{a^2 + b^2}/a$ for a hyperbola.

21–13. Polar coordinate equations of conics. In many applications of the ellipse, parabola, and hyperbola to astronomy, chemistry, and physics it is useful to have an expression for the distance between the focus and a point on the conic. If a polar coordinate equation of the locus is used, with the focus at the pole, the desired distance is the radius vector r.

We apply the eccentricity definition of a conic with eccentricity e, a focus at the pole (origin), and directrix perpendicular to the polar axis extended and p units from the pole.

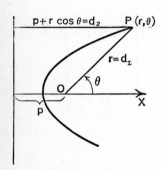

$$| d_1 | = e | d_2 |$$
$$r = e | p + r \cos \theta |$$
$$= \pm e(p + r \cos \theta)$$
$$r = \pm ep \pm er \cos \theta$$
$$r(1 \mp e \cos \theta) = \pm ep$$
$$r = \frac{\pm ep}{1 \mp e \cos \theta}. \qquad (21.7)$$

In Figure 21–35,

$$r = \frac{ep}{1 - e \cos \theta}.$$

Fig. 21–35

If a focus is at the pole and the directrix is parallel to the polar axis, the resulting equation has the form

$$r = \frac{\pm ep}{1 \mp e \sin \theta}. \qquad (21.8)$$

The eccentricity may be determined by examination of the denominator when the equation is in one of the **standard forms** (21.7) or (21.8).

● *Example 1.* Identify and sketch the curve $\quad r = \dfrac{16}{2 + 5 \sin \theta}.$

To obtain this equation in standard form, divide numerator and denominator by 2.

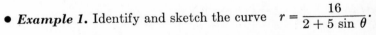

$$r = \frac{8}{1 + (\frac{5}{2}) \sin \theta}$$

The eccentricity $e = \frac{5}{2} > 1,$ and the locus is a hyperbola. The intercepts are

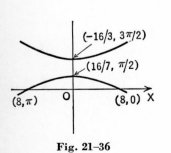

θ	0	$\pi/2$	π	$3\pi/2$
r	8	$\frac{16}{7}$	8	$-\frac{16}{3}$

Fig. 21–36

Remember: A focus of the locus of equations (21.7) or (21.8) is the pole, and every conic bends around its focus.

● **Example 2.** Identify and sketch

$$r = \frac{17}{3 - 2 \cos \theta}.$$

In standard form,

$$r = \frac{\frac{17}{3}}{1 - \frac{2}{3} \cos \theta}.$$

The eccentricity $e = \frac{2}{3} < 1$, and the locus is an ellipse. The intercepts are

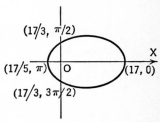

θ	0	$\pi/2$	π	$3\pi/2$
r	17	$\frac{17}{3}$	$\frac{17}{5}$	$\frac{17}{3}$

Since the pole is a focus, the length of the latus rectum is $\frac{34}{3}$ units, and the major axis is $17 + \frac{17}{5}$ units long. If desired, the center and length of the minor axis could be computed using relationships obtained earlier in this chapter.

Fig. 21–37

● **Example 3.** Identify and sketch $r(3 - 3 \sin \theta) = 14$.
In standard form,

$$r = \frac{\frac{14}{3}}{1 - 1 \sin \theta}.$$

The eccentricity $e = 1$, and the locus is a parabola. Its intercepts are:

θ	0	$\pi/2$	π	$3\pi/2$
r	$\frac{14}{3}$	none	$\frac{14}{3}$	$\frac{7}{3}$

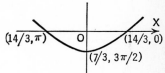

Fig. 21–38

● **Example 4.** Sketch $r = 10 \sec^2 (\theta/2)$.
By use of trigonometric identities,

$$r = 10 \sec^2 (\theta/2) = \frac{10}{\cos^2 (\theta/2)} = \frac{10}{(1 + \cos \theta)/2} = \frac{20}{1 + \cos \theta}.$$

The sketch of $r = \dfrac{20}{1 + \cos \theta}$ is a parabola, since $e = 1$.

It has polar intercepts

θ	0	$\pi/2$	π	$3\pi/2$
r	10	20	none	20

● **Example 5.**
A stationary cam in the shape of the cardioid $r = 2 + 2 \cos \theta$ inches has a point follower E that moves around the perimeter with constant angular velocity of 6 revolutions per minute.
(a) Determine the vertical velocity of the follower at $(4, 0)$.

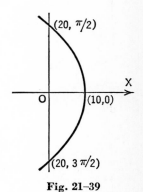

Fig. 21–39

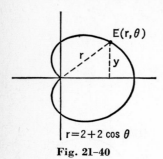

$r = 2 + 2 \cos \theta$

Fig. 21-40

(b) Determine the maximum displacement of the follower from the polar axis.

(a) An angular velocity of 6 revolutions per minute is equivalent to 12π radians per minute

Hence,

$$\frac{d\theta}{dt} = 12\pi.$$

Since,

$$y = r \sin \theta$$
$$= (2 + 2 \cos \theta) \sin \theta$$
$$= 2 \sin \theta + \sin 2\theta.$$

The problem asks for $\dfrac{dy}{dt}$ when $(r, \theta) = (4, 0)$.

$$\frac{dy}{dt} = \frac{dy}{d\theta} \cdot \frac{d\theta}{dt}$$

$$= (2 \cos \theta + 2 \cos 2\theta) \cdot \frac{d\theta}{dt}$$

$$= (2 \cos \theta + 2 \cos 2\theta)(12\pi)$$

Hence,

$$\frac{dy}{dt}\Big]_{\theta=0} = 48\pi \text{ inches per minute.}$$

(b) The expression

$$y = 2 \sin \theta + \sin 2\theta$$

gives y as a function of θ. We wish to determine the maximum value of y. From the solutions of $\dfrac{dy}{d\theta} = 0$ one can obtain the desired result. (Why?)

$$\frac{dy}{d\theta} = 2 \cos \theta + 2 \cos 2\theta$$

$$4 \cos^2 \theta + 2 \cos \theta - 2 = 0$$

$$2(2 \cos \theta - 1)(\cos \theta + 1) = 0$$

$$\cos \theta = \tfrac{1}{2}, \quad \cos \theta = -1.$$

From the sketch it is clear that the desired maximum is obtained at $\theta = \text{Arccos } \dfrac{1}{2} = \dfrac{\pi}{3}$. The corresponding maximum y value is

$$y = 2 \sin \frac{\pi}{3} + \sin \frac{2\pi}{3} = \sqrt{3} + \frac{\sqrt{3}}{2} = \frac{3\sqrt{3}}{2}.$$

PROBLEM SET 21-13

Identify and sketch the following loci.

1. $r = \dfrac{4}{1 - \sin \theta}.$ **2.** $r = \dfrac{3}{1 + \cos \theta}.$ **3.** $r = \dfrac{6}{2 - \cos \theta}.$

4. $r = \dfrac{15}{3 + 4 \cos \theta}.$ **5.** $r = \dfrac{10}{5 + \sin \theta}.$ **6.** $r = \dfrac{-4}{2 - 7 \sin \theta}.$

7. $r = \dfrac{3}{8 + \cos \theta}.$ **8.** $r = \dfrac{5}{1 - 2 \sin \theta}.$ **9.** $r = \dfrac{10}{10 + 7 \sin \theta}.$

10. $r = \dfrac{1}{2 - \cos \theta}.$ **11.** $r = \dfrac{15}{3 + 8 \sin \theta}.$ **12.** $r = \dfrac{13}{4 - 2 \cos \theta}.$

13. $r = 12 \sec^2 (\theta/2).$ **14.** $r = 6 \csc^2 (\theta/2).$ **15.** $r = 20 \csc^2 (\theta/2).$

16. $r = 2 - \cos \theta.$ **17.** $r = 1 - 2 \sin \theta.$ **18.** $r = 1 - \sin \theta.$

19. If $\dfrac{d\theta}{dt} = 3$ find $\dfrac{dr}{dt}$ at the vertex of $r = \dfrac{4}{1 - \sin \theta}.$

20. If $\dfrac{dr}{dt} = 2$ and $r = \dfrac{3}{1 + \cos \theta}$ find $\dfrac{d\theta}{dt}$ when $\theta = \dfrac{\pi}{3}.$

21. If $r = 1 - \sin \theta$, then $x = r \cos \theta = (1 - \sin \theta) \cos \theta,$ $y = r \sin \theta = (1 - \sin \theta) \sin \theta.$ Now find (r, θ) and (x, y) coordinates of the point on the cardioid that is farthest to the right by making x a maximum.

22. Use $x = (1 - \sin \theta) \cos \theta,$ $y = (1 - \sin \theta) \sin \theta$ and find the slope of the cardioid when $\theta = \dfrac{\pi}{4}.$

$$\left[\text{HINT:} \frac{dy}{dx} = \frac{dy/d\theta}{dx/d\theta}\right].$$

21-14. Conic sections. Greek geometers studied curves obtained as plane sections of a (double-napped) right circular cone.† It was not until René Descartes applied algebra to geometry in 1637 that the study of these **conic sections** became a part of elementary mathematics.

Three general classes of curves are obtained as the intersection of a plane and a cone.

1. A plane section that cuts only one nappe of a cone and that is not parallel to an element of the cone is an ellipse (a circle is obtained as a special ellipse). [A single point (the vertex) is obtained as a limiting case.]

2. A parabola is obtained as a plane section parallel to an element of the cone. [A line (an element) is obtained as a limiting case.]

† A double-napped right circular cone is generated by a moving line (element or generator) that moves in space making a constant angle with a fixed line (axis) and intersecting the fixed line in a point called the vertex of the cone.

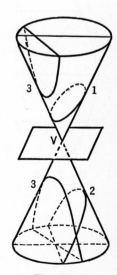

Fig. 21-41

3. A hyperbola is a plane section of both nappes of a cone. [Two intersecting lines (elements) are obtained as a limiting case.]

21–15. Applications of focal properties of conics. Many applications of the ellipse, parabola, and hyperbola depend upon special focal properties of the curve. In astronomy it is convenient to use polar coordinates to represent the paths of planetary motions in the solar system, since the paths of the planets are elliptical, with the sun as focus. Some comets describe approximately parabolic paths with the sun as focus, since $e \cong 1$. Computations are made using polar equations which accurately predict eclipses hundreds of years in advance. If a rocket with sufficient power to reach the moon were fired *at* the moon, it would almost certainly miss it since the earth and the moon rotate at different speeds on different axes. Nevertheless, the mathematics of space travel is already known. Given the speed and other conditions about the projectile, it is possible to compute the precise times and directions of firing needed to reach the moon. Polar equations of the conic sections are also used in the study of atomic reactions.

In the language of geometry the reflector property of the parabola states that if F is the focus of a parabola and P is a point on the parabola, then the line PJ through P parallel to the axis of the parabola and the line PF make equal angles with the tangent to the parabola at P. If a reflector is constructed in the form of a paraboloid of revolution and a light is placed at the focus, the light will be reflected in parallel rays. This principle is used in locomotive headlights and large search lights. It may also be used in beamed television, radar, and sonar for producing a directional beam. If light comes from a distant source (say a star) the rays of light are essentially parallel. If these rays are collected using a parabolic reflector, they will be concentrated at the focus (hence the name **focus**). Astronomical telescopes use this property. Parabolic mirrors are used to collect and focus light from the stars. For convenience in observing, an additional mirror is placed at the focus to reflect the image to an eyepiece outside the telescope tube. A similar reflecting surface may be used to collect and magnify sound waves. Such a parabolic receiver in addition to magnifying reception has the advantage of being highly selective in direction.

The dark field microscope is used in modern science and medicine for examining objects too small or too transparent to show up under direct light. Condensers, which are parabolas or cardioids in cross section, are used to produce a dark field with the concentration (focus) of light on the object from the sides. The object then appears luminous against a dark field.

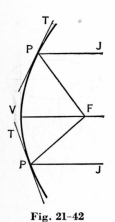

Fig. 21-42

Engines using the sun's heat have been proposed in which a large reflecting surface is bent into a parabolic cylinder. A pipe placed along the line of foci will have the sun's rays focused on it. Steam may be so generated at low fuel cost.

Solar stoves are used for household cooking in some parts of the world. India, for example, is producing about 1000 solar stoves per month for domestic use, each with a parabolic reflector.

Solar ovens using parabolic reflectors have become high-temperature research tools, producing the highest controlled temperatures yet attained by man. This intense heat, in which flame-proof fire bricks melt in seconds, is used in research involving metals for jet and rocket engines. *Life* magazine carried articles on solar ovens in its November 6, 1950, and March 2, 1953, issues.

The ellipse has interesting focal properties. If the foci of an ellipse are F_1 and F_2, and P is a point on the ellipse, then F_1P and F_2P make equal angles with the tangent line to the ellipse at P. Hence if sound, light, or a billiard ball starts or crosses at one focus, it will pass through the other focus if reflected by the ellipse. Some whispering galleries (the Mormon Tabernacle, Salt Lake City) make use of this focal property of the ellipse. The Museum of Science and Industry (Chicago), for example, has constructed a large ellipsoidal room. People standing at the two foci of the ellipsoid may converse in whispers, but a person standing between them cannot overhear the conversation since the concentration of sound is below the audible range except near the foci.

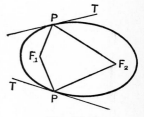

Fig. 21–43

Two elliptical gears may be made to mesh on shafts through a focus. If one shaft is turned at a constant rate, the other shaft turns in an eccentric manner with the speed of rotation varying periodically.

The navigational aid LORAN uses properties of the hyperbola. A hyperbola is the locus of all points the difference of whose distances from two given foci is constant. Consider two sending stations, of known location, which transmit simultaneous signals at regular intervals (the reader may think of these as blasts of sound on horns of different pitch). An observer in a ship will not hear these two signals simultaneously. This will locate his ship somewhere on a hyperbola with the two stations as foci. If a third station that also sends a simultaneous signal is now added, stations two and three (or one and three) may be considered in a similar fashion to locate the ship somewhere on another hyperbola. The ship is thus pinpointed at the intersection of hyperbolas. In present use LORAN makes many of these computations automatically.

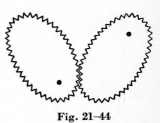

Fig. 21–44

The pressure-volume equation for a gas under constant temperature, $pv = k$, is the equation of a hyperbola in the pv-plane.

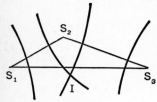

Fig. 21–45

The equations of magnetic characteristics are also hyperbolic. The interference pattern seen in a glass plate under compression strain may consist of families of conjugate pairs of hyperbolas with common asymptotes. Much economic theory is based on the assumptions that certain variables are connected by equations that are hyperbolic.

Like other conics, the hyperbola has a reflector property. The tangent line at a point on a hyperbola makes equal angles with the two lines joining the foci and the point of contact. The reader may be able to relate this property to the "virtual image" discussed in a course on optics.

PROBLEM SET 21–15

1. Make sketches to illustrate and be able to discuss each application of the parabola mentioned in this section.

2. Make sketches to illustrate and be able to discuss each application of the ellipse mentioned in this section.

3. Make sketches and be able to discuss the method in which LORAN uses properties of the hyperbola.

4. Show, from the definitions of an ellipse, that congruent elliptical gears may be made to mesh. What should the distance between shafts be if the major axis is 6 inches and the minor axis 4 inches long? If one shaft is driven at a uniform rate, what position will the gears have when the speed of the other shaft is a maximum?

*5. Prove the focal property of the ellipse.

21–16. Self test. These self tests have been included for the student's benefit. He should use them to the best advantage.

SELF TEST

Record your time.

1. The vertex of a parabola is $(2, -5)$. The axis of symmetry is the line $x = 2$. The parabola passes through the point $(1, 3)$. Determine an equation of the parabola.

2. Put the equation in standard form, give the coordinates of one vertex, and of one focus. Sketch the curve, including asymptotes, if any.

$$25x^2 + 100x - 144y^2 + 1440y + 100 = 0.$$

3. Find the equation of the circle which has its center at the point $(4, 11)$ and which is tangent to the line $3x - 5y + 9 = 0$.

4. Write the equation of the locus of a point which moves so that its distance from the point $(1, 1)$ is always equal to one half its distance from the point $(-2, 0)$. Identify the locus.

5. Given the conic: $25x^2 - 50x + 4y^2 + 56y + 121 = 0$:

  (a) Sketch the curve.
  (b) Determine the coordinates of the foci.
  (c) Determine the coordinates of the vertices.
  (d) Determine the eccentricity of the curve.

6. Determine the coordinates of the foci and of the vertices of $25x^2 + 250x + 9y^2 - 36y + 436 = 0$.

7. The cables on a suspension bridge hang in a parabolic curve between two supports. The point attachment of a cable to the supports is 70 feet above the water level. The supports are 100 feet apart. The lowest point on the cable (vertex of the parabola) is 40 feet above the water level. Take the x-axis at water level and the y-axis as the right-hand supporting tower. Determine an equation of the locus of the cable.

8. If a conic has its foci at $(7, 3)$ and $(7, -5)$ and one vertex is $(7, 2)$, determine its equation.

9. Reduce to type form and sketch carefully. Show the coordinates of the vertices and foci, and sketch the asymptotes, if any, with care.

$$16y^2 - 9x^2 - 96y + 72x - 144 = 0.$$

10. Sketch $r(3 - 5\cos\theta) = 15$.

11. The endgate of a dam is in the shape of a parabola with the vertex down. The water level is 2 feet above the bottom (vertex) of the gate. The gate is 4 feet across at water level.

  (a) Determine an equation of the gate.
  (b) Use integration to determine the wet area of the gate.

12. Find the area bounded by $x^2 = 6(y - 3)$ and $y = 9$.

13. Find the equations of the tangent and normal lines to $3x^2 - 2xy + y^2 = 3$ at $(1, 2)$.

Record your time.

22

22–1. Parametric equations. Many times data are obtained in terms of an auxiliary variable. The auxiliary variable is a **parameter,** and the equations involving the auxiliary variable are **parametric equations.** For example, in a laboratory, values of x and y may be obtained by taking readings every second. In this case the values of x and y may be expressed as functions of time, t, say $x = x(t)$, and $y = y(t)$. To obtain a relationship $f(x, y) = 0$ connecting x and y, it is necessary to eliminate t between $x = x(t)$ and $y = y(t)$. It is often desirable to use parametric equations. This is especially true for complicated functions in which it may be difficult to eliminate t. In preparation for the study of more difficult parametric equations, simple loci which may be obtained in either parametric or nonparametric form will be examined using parametric methods. Discussions of these loci will be based on the parametric form, and the nonparametric representation will be obtained only after the discussions are complete.

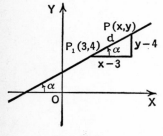

Fig. 22–1

● **Example 1.** Obtain parametric equations of a line through the point $P_1(3, 4)$ making an inclination angle α. Use the distance along the line from $(3, 4)$ as the parameter.

From Figure 22–1, $(x - 3)/d = \cos \alpha$, and $(y - 4)/d = \sin \alpha$. In parametric form this becomes,

$$x = 3 + d \cos \alpha$$
$$y = 4 + d \sin \alpha,$$

where α is a constant and d is the parameter.

Notice that the following nonparametric form may be obtained,

$$\frac{x - 3}{\cos \alpha} = \frac{y - 4}{\sin \alpha} \quad (= d)$$

This form is related to one that will be obtained in Chapter 24, where analytic geometry of three dimensions is discussed.

● **Example 2.** The parametric equations $x = 3t$, $y = 2t + 1$ are given. Sketch y as a function of x.

The abbreviations L^+ and L^- are used to represent "large and positive" and "large and negative," respectively.

t	L^-	-10	-5	-1	0	1	5	L^+
x	L^-	-30	-15	-3	0	3	15	L^+
y	L^-	-19	-9	-1	1	3	11	L^+

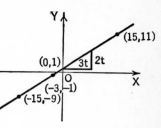

Fig. 22-2

The locus seems to be a straight line. That this is the case may be verified by solving $x = 3t$ for $t = x/3$, and substituting into the equation $y = 2t + 1$, obtaining the non-parametric linear equation $y = \frac{2}{3}x + 1$.

● **Example 3.** Sketch the locus having parametric equations,
$x = \sin t$, $y = 2 + \cos t$.

Note that, for all values of t, $-1 \leq x \leq 1$ and $1 \leq y \leq 3$. Thus the locus must be entirely inside the rectangular region

$$\begin{cases} -1 \leq x \leq 1 \\ 1 \leq y \leq 3. \end{cases}$$

The periodic nature of $\sin t$ and of $2 + \cos t$ implies that, for t greater than 2π, the same curve will be traced as for $0 \leq t < 2\pi$. Negative values of t give points already found. We locate several points obtained from values of the parameter t in the interval $0 \leq t \leq 2\pi$.

Fig. 22-3

t	0	$\pi/6$	$\pi/3$	$\pi/2$	$2\pi/3$	π	$4\pi/3$	$3\pi/2$	$5\pi/3$	2π
x	0	$\frac{1}{2}$	$\frac{1}{2}\sqrt{3}$	1	$\frac{1}{2}\sqrt{3}$	0	$-\frac{1}{2}\sqrt{3}$	-1	$-\frac{1}{2}\sqrt{3}$	0
y	3	$2+\frac{1}{2}\sqrt{3}$	$\frac{5}{2}$	2	$\frac{3}{2}$	1	$\frac{3}{2}$	2	$\frac{5}{2}$	3

The locus appears to be a circle with radius 1 and center $(0, 2)$. That this is so, may be seen by eliminating t. The given equations, $x = \sin t$, $y = 2 + \cos t$, are equivalent to the equations

$$x = \sin t, \quad y - 2 = \cos t.$$

Upon squaring and adding the latter equations one obtains

$$x^2 + (y - 2)^2 = \sin^2 t + \cos^2 t = 1.$$

This is the equation of a circle of radius 1, with center $(0, 2)$. It is also feasible to compute the distance, d, between $(0, 2)$ and (x, y). Since $d^2 = 1$ for every point (x, y) on the locus, the desired result is obtained.

● **Example 4.** Sketch the cycloid represented by the parametric equations

$$x = \phi - \sin \phi$$
$$y = 1 - \cos \phi.$$

Although x may take any real value, y is restricted to the range $0 \leqq y \leqq 2$. The locus of y as a function of x lies in a band of width two units having the x-axis as base (that is, $0 \leqq y \leqq 2$). Using a table of trigonometric functions of angles in radians we find:

ϕ	0	.5	1	$\pi/2$	2	π	$3\pi/2$	2π	
x	0	.02	.16	.57	1.09	3.14	3.71	6.28	as ϕ increases x increases
y	0	.13	.46	1	1.42	2	1	0	as ϕ increases y repeats the cycle just completed.

The locus is sketched in Figure 22–4.

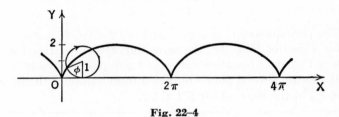

Fig. 22–4

Cycloids will be studied in greater detail in the next section.

PROBLEM SET 22–1

Discuss and sketch each of the following loci. Obtain an equation relating x and y. If a familiar equation is obtained, use it to check your sketch.

1. $x = 5t + 2, \quad y = t - 3.$ 2. $x = 2t, \quad y = -3t + 5.$
3. $x = 4t + 1, \quad y = t^2.$ 4. $x = t^2, \quad y = -2t + 1.$
5. $x = 4 + \sin t, \quad y = 3 + \cos t.$ 6. $x = 2 + \cos t, \quad y = 3 + \sin t.$
7. (a) $x = 5 \cos t, \quad y = 2 + 5 \sin t.$
    (b) $x = 5 \cos t, \quad y = 2 + 5 \cos t.$
8. $x = 4/t, \quad y = 3t.$ 9. $x = 3 \sin t, \quad y = 5 \cos t.$
10. $x = 2 + 3 \sin t, \quad y = 7 + 4 \cos t.$
11. $x = \cos^3 t, \quad y = \sin^3 t.$ 12. $x = 3 \sec t, \quad y = 3 \tan t.$

13. $x = 1000t$, $y = 1000\sqrt{3}t - 16t^2$. [NOTE: If air resistance is neglected, the locus is that of a projectile fired at an angle of 60 degrees with the horizontal and an initial velocity of 2000 feet per second.]

14. The folium of Descartes, $x = \dfrac{t}{1+t^3}$, $y = \dfrac{3t^2}{1+t^3}$.

15. $x = 3^t$, $y = 7 + 2^{-t}$.

16. Eliminate the parameter ϕ in the equation of Example 4 to obtain the equation $y + \cos(x \pm \sqrt{2y - y^2}) = 1$.

Note that the parametric representation may be easier to use in this case.

22–2. Parametric representation of the cycloid and other loci.

Example 1. If a circle of radius a rolls on a straight line, the path of a point P upon the circumference of this circle is called a **cycloid**. The rolling circle and point P are shown in several positions in Figure 22–5.

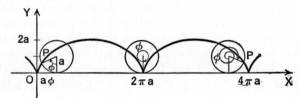

Fig. 22–5

To obtain parametric equations for this curve, let the line be the x-axis, and a point at which P is on the x-axis be the origin. As the circle rolls along the x-axis, the arc PA rolls along the line segment OA. Hence,

$$\text{arc } PA = OA.$$

If the angle PCA, through which the circle has rotated, is denoted by ϕ radians then,

$$\text{arc } PA = a\phi = OA.$$

From the sketch, $PB = a \sin \phi$ and $BC = a \cos \phi$.

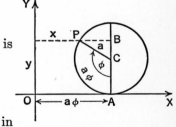

Fig. 22–6

We wish to find the coordinates of the point $P(x, y)$ in terms of ϕ. From the sketch, $x = OA - PB$, and $y = a - BC$. [*Directed* line segments are used. Hence $CB = -BC$ and $y = a - BC$.]

It follows that,

$$x = a\phi - a \sin \phi, \quad \text{or} \quad x = a(\phi - \sin \phi)$$
$$y = a - a \cos \phi, \qquad\qquad y = a(1 - \cos \phi).$$

Note that the cycloid is symmetric with respect to the y-axis and also with respect to the line $x = \pi a$ through maximum point. It is symmetric with respect to the line $x = n\pi a$ for every integer n, since the curve is periodic.

Example 4 of Section 22–1 is a cycloid. The radius of the rolling circle is 1.

The reader may be interested in a few properties of the cycloid. If a particle is permitted to slide along a curve from point A to a lower point B (not directly below A) under the influence of gravity alone, the time required for the descent depends upon the shape of the curve along which the particle slides. It is reasonable to ask, "Which curve requires the shortest time of descent?" A straight line joining A to B provides the shortest path between A and B, but does *not* give the quickest journey. It can be shown that the curve of quickest descent (brachistochrone) is a cycloid in the position shown in Figure 22–7.

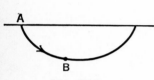

A

B

Fig. 22–7

Another interesting problem concerning a particle sliding from A to B along a curve follows. Since the acceleration of the particle after it is released, is dependent upon the steepness of the curve near the point of release, it is possible that some curve (a tautachrone) joining A to B may exist such that the time required for the particle to reach B is the same no matter where on the curve the particle is released. There is such a curve, and, surprisingly enough, it is again a cycloid. Cycloids are discussed in references given in the reading list at the end of Chapter 25.

● *Example 2.* Eliminate the parameter ϕ in the equations of the cycloid:

$$x = a(\phi - \sin \phi)$$
$$y = a(1 - \cos \phi).$$

The second equation is equivalent to $\cos \phi = 1 - y/a$, or $\phi = \text{arc cos } (1 - y/a)$. If this is substituted into the parametric equation for x, one obtains,

$$x = a[\text{arc cos } (1 - y/a) - \sin (\text{arc cos } (1 - y/a))],$$

which reduces to

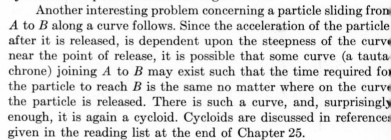

$$x = a[\text{arc cos } (1 - y/a) - \sqrt{2y/a - (y^2/a^2)}],$$

or

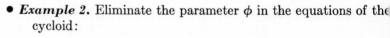

$$x = a \text{ arc cos } (1 - y/a) - \sqrt{2ay - y^2}.$$

● *Example 3.* Let B move on the circumference of a circle of radius 2. Let $P(x, y)$ be a point that slides on the radius OB in such a manner that OP is equal to the absolute value of

the ordinate of the point B. $OP = |MB| = |$ ordinate of $B|$.
Determine parametric equations of the locus of P. Two positions of $P(x, y)$ are shown in Figure 22–8.

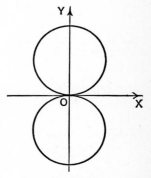

To obtain parametric equations of the locus of P, note that
$OP = |MB|$, $OB = 2$, $MB = 2 \sin \theta$.   Use $\theta = \angle LOP$
as a parameter. From $\sin \theta = LP/OP$ and $\cos \theta = OL/OP$
one obtains,

$$x = OL = OP \cos \theta = |MB| \cos \theta, \quad \text{or} \quad x = |2 \sin \theta| \cos \theta,$$

and

$$y = LP = OP \sin \theta = |MB| \sin \theta, \quad \text{or} \quad y = |2 \sin \theta| \sin \theta.$$

Hence, parametric equations of this locus are

$$x = 2 |\sin \theta| \cos \theta, \quad y = 2 |\sin \theta| \sin \theta.$$

The locus is sketched in Figure 22–9.

Fig. 22–8

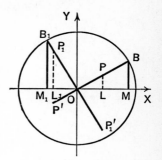

Fig. 22–9

● ***Example 4.*** If a circle of radius b/n rolls inside a fixed circle
of radius b, the locus of a point P on the circumference of the
rolling circle is called a hypocycloid of n cusps. Obtain parametric equations for a hypocycloid of four cusps.

From Figure 22–10, we can express α in terms of ϕ. Since the
small circle rolls on the larger circle,   arc $AT = $ arc PT.   The

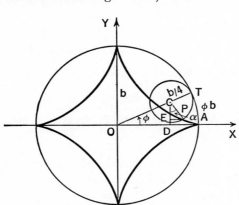

Fig. 22–10

length of the arc of a circle is equal to the radius times the
number of radians in the central angle subtended. Hence,

$$\phi b = (\angle PCT)b/4, \quad \text{and} \quad \angle PCT = 4\phi.$$

Since

$$\angle DCT = \pi/2 + \phi \quad \text{and} \quad \angle DCT = \alpha + \angle PCT = \alpha + 4\phi,$$

we have

$$\pi/2 + \phi = \alpha + 4\phi \quad \text{or} \quad \alpha = \pi/2 - 3\phi.$$

The following trigonometric relations are useful in obtaining the desired parametric equations.

$$OD = \left(\frac{3b}{4}\right) \cos \phi, \quad EP = \left(\frac{b}{4}\right) \sin \alpha;$$

$$DC = \left(\frac{3b}{4}\right) \sin \phi, \quad EC = \left(\frac{b}{4}\right) \cos \alpha.$$

The coordinates of $P(x, y)$ are

$$x = OD + EP, \quad \text{or} \quad x = \tfrac{3}{4}b \cos \phi + \tfrac{1}{4}b \sin \alpha$$
$$y = DC - EC, \quad \text{or} \quad y = \tfrac{3}{4}b \sin \phi - \tfrac{1}{4}b \cos \alpha.$$

Since

$$\alpha = \pi/2 - 3\phi, \quad \sin \alpha = \sin (\pi/2 - 3\phi) = \cos 3\phi,$$

and

$$\cos \alpha = \cos (\pi/2 - 3\phi) = \sin 3\phi.$$

The desired parametric equations of the hypocycloid of four cusps are,

$$x = (b/4)(3 \cos \phi + \cos 3\phi), \quad y = (b/4)(3 \sin \phi - \sin 3\phi).$$

Using the identities

$$\sin 3\phi = 3 \sin \phi - 4 \sin^3 \phi \quad \text{and} \quad \cos 3\phi = 4 \cos^3 \phi - 3 \cos \phi,$$

these equations may be reduced to

$$x = b \cos^3 \phi, \quad y = b \sin^3 \phi,$$

where the radius of the fixed circle is b and that of the rolling circle is $b/4$.

● **Example 5.** Write the equation of the hypocycloid of Example 4 in rectangular coordinates.

Substituting

$$\cos \phi = (x/b)^{\frac{1}{3}} \quad \text{and} \quad \sin \phi = (y/b)^{\frac{1}{3}}$$

into the identity $\cos^2 \phi + \sin^2 \phi = 1$, one obtains,

$$(x/b)^{\frac{2}{3}} + (y/b)^{\frac{2}{3}} = 1, \quad \text{or} \quad x^{\frac{2}{3}} + y^{\frac{2}{3}} = b^{\frac{2}{3}}.$$

● **Example 6.** A long straight rod rotates counterclockwise in a plane at 60 revolutions per minute. A bead moves outward along the rod at the rate of 3 centimeters per minute, starting at the center of rotation. Use the center of rotation as pole, and the position of the rod at the instant the bead is at the pole as polar axis. Use the time t, in minutes after the bead was in starting position, as parameter. (a) Obtain polar parametric equations for the locus of the bead. (b) Eliminate the parameter and identify the locus.

(a) The rod rotates at 60 revolutions per minute, or $60(2\pi) = 120\pi$ radians per minute. In t minutes the rod rotates $120\pi t$ radians. Therefore, $\theta = 120\pi t$. In 1 minute, the bead is 3 centimeters from the pole. In t minutes, the bead is $3t$ centimeters from the pole. Therefore, $r = 3t$. Parametric equations of the locus are,

$$r = 3t, \quad \theta = 120\pi t.$$

(b) Eliminating the parameter, $t = \dfrac{\theta}{120\pi}$, yields,

$$r = 3\left(\frac{\theta}{120\pi}\right) = \frac{\theta}{40\pi}.$$

The locus is a spiral of Archimedes.

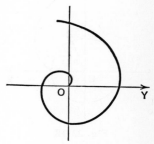

Fig. 22–11

PROBLEM SET 22–2

1. Determine parametric equations of a cycloid in the position of Example 1, with greatest ordinate (y value) 6.
2. The line segment AB, of fixed length four units, moves with its end points on the x- and y-axes, respectively. Determine parametric equations of the locus of the midpoint M of AB.
3. Determine parametric equations of the locus of a point P, whose movement is described in Example 3, except that the restriction $OP = |MB|$ is replaced by the restriction $OP = |OM|$.
4. A circle of radius 5 rolls on the line $y = 3x + 2$. Determine parametric equations of the locus of the center of the circle.
5. In Problems 1 to 6 of Set 22–1, find values of t which locate the following points on the curve: in Problem 1, $(7, -2)$; Problem 2, $(4, -1)$; Problem 3, $(1, 0)$; Problem 4, $(1, 3)$; Problem 5, $(4, 2)$; Problem 6, $(2, 4)$; Problem 6, $(2, 2)$.
6. A circle of radius 1 rolls on the inside of a circle of radius 4. Determine parametric equations of the locus of a point on the circumference of the rolling circle. Name the locus.

7. A circular wheel of radius 1 rolls along the line $y = x$. Determine parametric equations of the locus of the point on the circumference of the wheel which makes contact with the origin as the wheel passes over it.

8. An involute of a circle is a plane curve described by the end of a piece of thread that is kept taut as it is unwound from the circle. Involutes play an important role in the tooth designs for high-speed gears. Determine parametric equations of the involute of a unit circle, if the end of the thread is initially on the x-axis, using the sketch shown (Fig. 22–12). Note that arc $AB = PB = \theta \cdot 1$ in length, and that the line PB is tangent to the circle at B. Also $\theta = \measuredangle\, CBP$, since their sides are mutually perpendicular. Hence,

$$x = OC + DP$$
$$y = CB - DB.$$

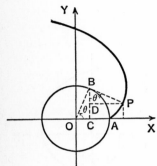

Fig. 22–12

9. As the point P of Figures 22–5 and 22–6 traces the cycloid, the point B traces a curve known as the companion of the cycloid. (a) Determine its parametric equations. (b) Eliminate the parameter.

10. If a circle of radius 1 rolls on the *outside* of a fixed circle of radius 1, a point P on the circumference of the rolling circle traces a cardioid. (a) Obtain parametric rectangular equations of this locus, by taking the initial position such that the point P is on the x-axis at the point of tangency of the two circles. (b) Obtain parametric polar equations of this locus. (c) Eliminate the parameter in (b) to show the locus is a cardioid.

11. Complete the trigonometric substitutions to show that the equations of the hypocyloid in Example 4 reduce to

$$x = b \cos^3 \phi, \quad y = b \sin^3 \phi.$$

12. Read one of the references mentioned in the discussion of cycloids and write a short report on your reading.

13. Determine a set of parametric equations of the brachistochrone having cusp $A(0, 3)$ and minimum $B(3\pi/2, 0)$.

22–3. The path of a projectile. We use parametric equations to study the path of missiles projected at any angle α with the horizontal. If the position $P(x, y)$ of a projectile at time t is given by parametric equations

$$x = x(t), \qquad y = y(t),$$

then the x and y components of the velocity are given by

$$v_x = \frac{dx}{dt}, \qquad v_y = \frac{dy}{dt},$$

and the x and y components of the acceleration are

$$a_x = \frac{dv_x}{dt} = \frac{d^2x}{dt^2}, \quad a_y = \frac{dv_y}{dt} = \frac{d^2y}{dt^2}.$$

If gravity is the only force † acting on the projectile while it is in motion, then since gravity acts entirely in the y direction, we may derive the equations of the path of motion beginning with

$$a_x = 0, \qquad a_y = -g.$$

Upon integrating,

$$v_x = c_1, \qquad v_y = -gt + c_2.$$

The constants c_2 and c_1 may be determined from the given conditions. Then $x = x(t)$ and $y = y(t)$ are obtained by further integration. The determination of the y component is essentially the same as that used, in Chapter 19, in the discussion of missiles projected vertically.

● **Example 1.** A projectile is shot with an angle of elevation of 60 degrees and an initial velocity of 200 feet per second. Determine parametric equations of the path of motion of the projectile.

The initial velocity is $v_0 = 200$ feet per second at an angle of 60 degrees to the horizontal x-axis. The x and y components of this initial velocity are

$$v_{x_0} = 200 \cos 60° \quad \text{and} \quad v_{y_0} = 200 \sin 60°$$
$$= 100 \text{ ft per sec} \qquad\qquad = 100\sqrt{3} \text{ ft per sec}$$

If the origin is taken at the initial (gun) position, then the given conditions are summarized in the following table:

t	x	y	v_x	v_y
0	0	0	100	$100\sqrt{3}$

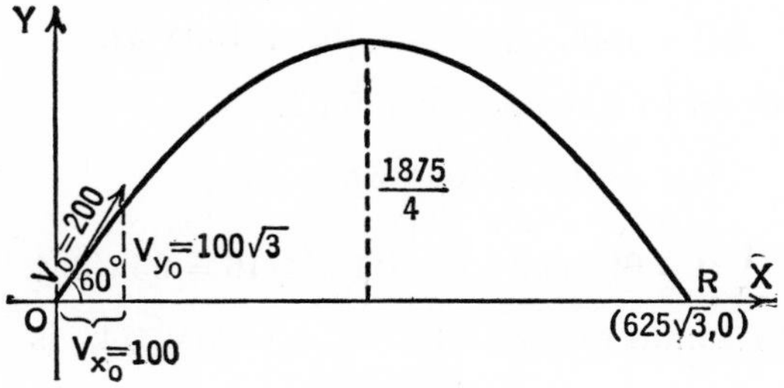

Fig. 22-13

† If air resistance is not neglected, similar equations hold, except that the additional retarding force, expressed in terms of hyperbolic functions is included in equations for a_x and a_y. The resulting equations for v_x, v_y, $x(t)$ and $y(t)$ cannot, in general, be handled using the quadratic formula. Each problem, thus, takes longer to solve. However, the general method of solution of projectile problems with air resistance is similar. (See Section 9–7.)

Using $g \cong 32$ ft per sec per sec one obtains,

$$a_x = 0, \qquad\qquad a_y = -32$$
$$v_x = c_1, \qquad\qquad v_y = -32t + c_2.$$

Upon substituting data from our table, one has at $t = 0$, $v_x = 100$, and $v_y = 100\sqrt{3}$. Whence,

$$100 = c_1, \qquad\qquad 100\sqrt{3} = 0 + c_2.$$

The velocity equations are,

$$v_x = 100, \qquad\qquad v_y = -32t + 100\sqrt{3}.$$

After integrating again, one obtains,

$$x = 100t + c_3, \qquad\qquad y = -16t^2 + 100\sqrt{3}\,t + c_4.$$

Since at $t = 0$, $x = 0$, and $y = 0$, upon substituting one determines that,

$$0 = 0 + c_3, \qquad\qquad 0 = 0 + 0 + c_4.$$

Thus, for any value of t while the projectile is in flight, its location is given by the parametric equations

$$x = 100t, \qquad\qquad y = -16t^2 + 100\sqrt{3}\,t.$$

● **Example 2.** Determine (a) the horizontal range of the projectile of Example 1, and (b) the maximum height to which the projectile rises.

(a) The horizontal range (distance from the gun to the striking point of the projectile on level ground) is the distance OR in Figure 22–13. The y-coordinate of the point R is zero, hence we wish to determine a nonzero value of x for which $y = 0$. Using the equations of Example 1, we have,

$$x(t) = 100t, \quad y(t) = -16t^2 + 100\sqrt{3}\,t.$$

Set y equal to zero and solve for t:

$$0 = -16t^2 + 100\sqrt{3}\,t$$
$$0 = t(-16t + 100\sqrt{3})$$
$$t = 0, \quad \text{and} \quad t = 100\sqrt{3}/16 = 25\sqrt{3}/4.$$

The horizontal range $x(t)$ at $t = 25\sqrt{3}/4$ is

$$x(25\sqrt{3}/4) = 625\sqrt{3} \cong 1100 \text{ feet}$$

to the nearest 100 feet (that is, 1.1×10^3 feet).

(b) To determine the maximum height of the projectile, we note that $dy/dt = 0$ at the maximum value of y.

$$dy/dt = v_y = -32t + 100\sqrt{3}.$$

This will be equal to zero if $t = \dfrac{100\sqrt{3}}{32} = \dfrac{25\sqrt{3}}{8}$. The height $y(t)$ at $t = \dfrac{25\sqrt{3}}{8}$ is given by,

$$y(25\sqrt{3}/8) = -16(25\sqrt{3}/8)^2 + 100\sqrt{3}(25\sqrt{3}/8)$$
$$= \cdots \cong 4.7 \times 10^2 \text{ ft.}$$

● **Example 3.** The gun of Example 2 is located 150 feet from the base of a cliff whose top is 200 feet above the level of the gun. Will the projectile clear the top of the cliff, if the direction of fire is toward the cliff?

In terms of parametric equations, this problem asks if $y(t_1)$ is greater than 200, when $x(t_1) = 150$.

Solve $x(t_1) = 100t_1 = 150$, and find $t_1 = 3/2$. Then,

$$y(3/2) = -16(3/2)^2 + 100\sqrt{3}(3/2) = \cdots \cong 2.2 \times 10^2 \text{ feet.}$$

Since this is greater than 200, the projectile will clear the cliff.

PROBLEM SET 22-3

1. (a) Would the projectile of Example 1 clear a hilltop whose summit is 250 feet above the level of the gun, and in the line of fire, 1000 feet horizontally from the gun?
   (b) By how much will the projectile of Problem 1 clear, or fail to clear, the hilltop?
2. A projectile is shot with an angle of elevation of 30 degrees and an initial velocity of 600 feet per second.
   (a) Determine parametric equations of the path of motion.
   (b) Find the horizontal range.
   (c) Find the maximum height of the projectile.
   (d) How high a hill will the projectile clear, if the hill is 1000 feet horizontally from the gun, with its base at the level of the gun?
3. A stone is projected with an initial velocity of 48 feet per second at an angle of elevation of 30 degrees. Determine the length of time the stone is in the air, and the horizontal range.
4. If the starting position of Problem 3 is 16 feet above the level ground, determine the distance from a spot on the ground below the starting position to the point where the stone strikes the ground.

5. (a) Calvin Butterball works in a third-floor office. Phoebe Small works in the neighboring building on the sixth floor. Calvin's window is 30 feet above the ground, while Phoebe's window is 62 feet above the ground. The horizontal distance between the buildings is 72 feet. Calvin uses a catapult to send a note to Phoebe. What must the initial velocity of the projectile be if it is to reach Phoebe's window and if it is launched at an angle of $\alpha = \text{Arc tan}\ (\frac{4}{3})$ to the horizontal?

(b) Is the note traveling in a generally upward or downward direction as it goes through Phoebe's window?

*(c) With what velocity and at what angle should Phoebe launch a return missile, assuming it returns over the same path?

6. A projectile has an initial velocity of 80 feet per second. Find the angle of elevation needed so that the projectile will hit an object which is 160 feet horizontally away from and 20 feet above the initial position. If you obtain two answers, explain how this is possible, and sketch the two paths to show their difference.

7. A bomber flies horizontally at an elevation of 14,400 feet and at a speed of 180 miles per hour. (?? feet per second). If a bomb is released, how far will it travel horizontally before striking the ground?

8. Work Problem 7 if the bomber flies at an elevation of 3000 feet at the same speed. Compare with Problem 7.

9. Show that, if a missile is projected at an angle α from the horizontal, with an initial velocity v_0 and, $g = 32$ ft per sec per sec, its position at any time t while in flight is given by

$$x = tv_0 \cos \alpha, \quad y = tv_0 \sin \alpha - 16t^2,$$

if the origin is the point from which the missile is projected.

10. Eliminate the parameter t in the equation of Problem 9, to show that the xy equation of the path of the projectile is the parabola $(2v_0^2 \cos^2 \alpha)y = (v_0^2 \sin 2\alpha)x - 32x^2$.

22-4. Advantages of parametric representation. Parametric representation has advantages other than those discussed in the preceding sections. The ranges of the x and y variables are often easily determined in parametric form. Certain relations, in which y is a multiple-valued function of x, have both $x = x(t)$ and $y = y(t)$ as single-valued functions of t.

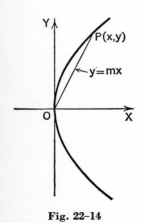

Fig. 22–14

● *Example 1.* $y^2 = 2px$.

Since $y = \pm \sqrt{2px}$, the function y is double valued. If the slope m of the line OP (Fig. 22–14) is used as a parameter, then

$$y/x = m, \quad \text{or} \quad y = mx, \quad \text{and} \quad (mx)^2 = 2px,$$

from which $x = 2p/m^2$, $y = 2p/m$ are parametric equations of the parabola. Here x and y are single-valued functions of m. Does this representation include the vertex?

Translations of a locus are simple, when a parametric representation is used.

● **Example 2.** If $x = x(t)$, $y = y(t)$ is a parametric representation of a curve, then $x = x(t) + 5$, $y = y(t) - 2$ is a parametric representation of a congruent curve obtained by translating the original curve 5 units to the right and 2 units down.

It may be desirable to find dy/dx from a parametric representation $x = x(t)$, $y = y(t)$. If $\Delta x(t, \Delta t) = x(t + \Delta t) - x(t)$, and $\Delta y(t, \Delta t) = y(t + \Delta t) - y(t)$, then as $\Delta t \to 0$, $\Delta x \to 0$, $\Delta y \to 0$.

Hence,

$$\frac{dy}{dx} = \lim_{\Delta x \to 0} \frac{\Delta y}{\Delta x} = \lim_{\Delta t \to 0} \frac{\Delta y(t, \Delta t)}{\Delta x(t, \Delta t)}$$

$$= \lim_{\Delta t \to 0} \frac{\dfrac{\Delta y(t, \Delta t)}{\Delta t}}{\dfrac{\Delta x(t, \Delta t)}{\Delta t}} = \frac{\lim\limits_{\Delta t \to 0} \dfrac{\Delta y(t, \Delta t)}{\Delta t}}{\lim\limits_{\Delta t \to 0} \dfrac{\Delta x(t, \Delta t)}{\Delta t}}$$

$$= \frac{\dfrac{dy}{dt}}{\dfrac{dx}{dt}} \quad \text{if each of the limits exists.}$$

● **Example 3.** Find the equation of the tangent line to

$$x = 4t^2 + 3, \quad y = t^3 - 2, \quad \text{when} \quad t = 1.$$

The point $(7, -1)$ is determined by the parametric value $t = 1$.

$$\frac{dy}{dx}\bigg]_{(7, -1)} = \frac{\dfrac{dy}{dt}\Big]_{t=1}}{\dfrac{dx}{dt}\Big]_{t=1}} = \frac{3t^2}{8t}\bigg]_{t=1} = \frac{3}{8}.$$

The tangent line at $(7, -1)$ has slope $\frac{3}{8}$, and equation

$$y + 1 = \tfrac{3}{8}(x - 7), \quad \text{or} \quad 3x - 8y = 29.$$

Problems involving loci in polar coordinates frequently present a more convenient appearance when written in a rectangular parametric form using the polar angle θ for parameter.

● **Example 4.** Find the points on $r = 1 + \cos \theta$ where the tangent lines are horizontal.

Now, $y = r \sin \theta = (1 + \cos \theta) \sin \theta$. Since $\dfrac{dy}{dx} = \dfrac{\dfrac{dy}{d\theta}}{\dfrac{dx}{d\theta}}$,

it follows that $\dfrac{dy}{dx} = 0$ when $\dfrac{dy}{d\theta} = 0$. Using

$$\frac{d(\sin \theta)}{d\theta} = \cos \theta, \quad \frac{d(\cos \theta)}{d\theta} = - \sin \theta, \quad \frac{d(uv)}{d\theta} = u \frac{dv}{d\theta} + v \frac{du}{d\theta},$$

we obtain

$$\frac{dy}{d\theta} = (1 + \cos \theta)(\cos \theta) + \sin \theta \, (- \sin \theta)$$
$$= 2 \cos^2 \theta + \cos \theta - 1$$
$$= (2 \cos \theta - 1)(\cos \theta + 1).$$

Hence, $\dfrac{dy}{d\theta} = 0$ when $\theta = \pi/3$, π, and $5\pi/3$.

The points on the cardioid $r = 1 + \cos \theta$, where the tangent lines are horizontal, are $(r = \frac{3}{2}, \ \theta = \pi/3)$, $(r = 0, \ \theta = \pi)$ and $(r = \frac{3}{2}, \ \theta = 5\pi/3)$.

PROBLEM SET 22–4

1. What are the x and y ranges of the locus having parametric representation $x = 5 + 4 \sin t$, $y = 1 - \cos t$?
2. What are the x and y ranges of the locus having parametric representation $x = 7 - e^t$, $y = \cos t$?
3. Determine approximate y-coordinates (accurate to two significant digits) of all points on the locus of Problem 1 having x-coordinate 1.5.
4. Same as Problem 3, for the locus of Problem 2.
5. Translate the locus of Problem 1, so that it goes through the origin. Is the translation obtained unique?
6. Translate the locus of Problem 2, so that it passes through the origin. Is the translation obtained the only possible translation which will do this?
7. Obtain three possible translations of the locus of Problem 1, for which it will pass through the point $(7, -4)$.

8. Obtain two translations which will make the locus of Problem 2 pass through (1, 3).

*9. What is the equation of the tangent line to

$$x = t^3 + 5, \quad y = 3t^2 - 7 \quad \text{at} \quad (4, -4)?$$

*10. What is the equation of the line tangent to

$$x = t^2 - 4t + 1, \quad y = 2t^3 + 1 \quad \text{at} \quad (-3, 17)?$$

Use a method similar to that shown in Example 1 to find a parametric representation for each of the loci in Problems 11 to 13 such that the calculation of a table of values for (x, y) will not involve the extraction of roots, and sketch:

11. The semicubical parabola, $y^2 = x^3$.
12. The cissoid, $y^2(2 - x) = x^3$.
13. Maclaurin's trisectrix, $x^3 + xy^2 + y^2 - 3x^2 = 0$.
14. As in Example 4, find the points on $r = 1 + \sin \theta$ where the tangent lines are horizontal.

22–5. Self test.

Record your time.

1. A projectile is thrown upward from the top of a 256-foot building with an initial velocity of 192 feet per second and an initial angle of 30 degrees to the horizontal. Start with the assumption that $g = 32$ feet per second per second and derive parametric equations of the path of flight. Use these equations to determine the distance from the base of the tower to the point where the stone strikes the level ground.

2. A point P moves so that the square of its distance from (3, 5) is twice the absolute distance between the line $5x - 12y + 13 = 0$ and the point P. Determine an equation of the locus of P, and simplify the equation.

3. Graph the locus having the parametric equations,

$$x = 3t/(1 + t^3), \quad y = 3t^2/(1 + t^3).$$

4. Eliminate the parameter from the equations of the locus of Problem 3. Answer: $x^3 + y^3 - 3xy = 0$.

5. A man holds the nozzle of a garden hose inclined at an angle of 30 degrees to the horizontal and 4 feet above the ground. Water from the hose falls on a plant 25 feet from the man's feet. Find the velocity of the water as it leaves the nozzle.

6. A circle with 2-foot radius has its center at the origin. A radius OR is extended through R to Q such that $RQ = 2$ feet. Through R draw a line parallel to the x-axis and through Q draw a line parallel to the y-axis. Label the intersection of these two lines P. Find parametric equations of the locus of P.

Review Problems

Before continuing it seems wise to review Chapters 11 through 22 so that the student may undertake any needed review well in advance of his final examination period.

1. Two cards are to be drawn from a deck of 52 playing cards What is the probability that the first card is an ace and the second card is a king? Describe the sample and event spaces.
2. A single die is tossed 100 times. The three spot came up 25 times. Do you feel the die is honest? Defend your answer in terms of 2σ limits and explain your defense in three or four well-stated sentences.
3. Sketch $y = 5 + 3 \cos 2x$ in the interval $-\pi \leqq x \leqq 2\pi$.
4. Solve for all x with $0 \leqq x < 2\pi$: $\tan x \csc 3x = \tan x$.
5. Prove the following relationship is an identity if it is. If it is not an identity, state this.

$$\frac{\tan^2 \theta}{\sec^2 \theta + 1} = \frac{\sec \theta - \cos \theta}{\sec \theta + \cos \theta}.$$

6. Sketch the polar locus $r = 1 + \sin 2\theta$.
7. Find the cube roots of $0 + 27i$. Express your answers in the form $a + bi$ where possible without using tables.
8. Given the triangle $A(2, -4)$, $B(4, 6)$, $C(6, -8)$; find the length of the altitude from C to AB.
9. Find the equation of a circle such that $(-2, 3)$ and $(5, -2)$ will be end points of a diameter. Do not bother to expand the resulting equation.
10. Reduce to type form and graph, showing the coordinates of center, vertices, foci (and one additional point on each asymptote if the locus has asymptotes):

$$16y^2 - 9x^2 - 96y + 72x - 144 = 0.$$

11. The vertices of a conic are $(7, 3)$ and $(-3, 3)$. One focus is $(5, 3)$. Identify the locus and write its equation.
12. A hockey puck travels 100 feet before coming to rest. If the deceleration of the puck is 8 feet per second per second, find the initial velocity of the puck at the time it was struck.
13. Find the area bounded by $y = 5 + 4x - x^2$ and the x-axis.
14. Use the detached coefficient (matrix) method to solve

$$2x + y + z = 3.$$
$$y - z = 4.$$
$$4x + y \quad\;\; = 5.$$

15. Graph the locus having parametric equations

$$x = \sin t$$
$$y = 2^{-t}$$

What range of values will x have? What range of values will y have?

16. A parabolic arch is 20 feet wide at road level. How high must the arch be at its center to have a clearance of 7 feet at a point 8 feet from the axis of symmetry of the arch?

17. A block of ice slides down a chute with an acceleration of 16 feet per second per second. The block is observed to be traveling 6 feet per second at a certain instant. How fast is it traveling when it is 5 feet beyond the observed position?

18. An elliptical plane is submerged in a lake in such a manner that the major axis of the ellipse is perpendicular to the surface of the water, and the vertices of the ellipse are 10 feet and 18 feet below the water surface. The ellipse has a maximum width of 2 feet (at the end points of the minor axis). Find an equation of the ellipse taking the x-axis at water level and the y-axis along the major axis.

19. Prove the identity $\dfrac{1 - \cos 2\theta}{\sin 2\theta} = \tan \theta$, if true, or show it is not an identity.

20. A triangle has vertices $(0, 0)$, $(2, 3)$, $(4, 1)$. Find its area.

21. A flagpole is mounted on the top of a wall. At a point level with the base of the wall and 30.0 feet away, the angle of elevation of the bottom of the pole is 45 degrees, and of the top is 60 degrees. What is the height of the pole?

22. (a) Find an angle θ, $\pi/2 < \theta < 3\pi/2$, if $\sin \theta = -\frac{1}{2}$.
(b) Find an angle θ, $-\pi < \theta < 0$, if $\sec \theta = \sqrt{2}$.
(c) Write the values of the other five trigonometric functions given $\sin \theta = -\frac{1}{2}$, $\pi/2 < \theta < 3\pi/2$.

23. Find $\sin (\text{Arc sin } \frac{4}{5} + \text{Arc sin } \frac{3}{5})$.

24. (a) Sketch $y = 3 \cos 2x$ for x on the domain 0 to 2π.
(b) Sketch $y = \text{arc sin } x$ using the y range from $-\pi$ to π.

25. Prove the identities:
(a) $\tan^3 \theta \sec \theta = (\sec^2 \theta - 1) \sec \theta \tan \theta$.
(b) $4 \cos^4 \theta = 1 + 2 \cos 2\theta + \cos^2 2\theta$.
(c) $\sin (30° - \theta) + \cos (60° - \theta) = \cos \theta$.

26. Solve for θ between 0 degrees and 360 degrees:
$\sqrt{3} \cos \theta - \cos \theta \tan \theta = 0$.

27. Reduce to functions of angles between 0 degrees and 90 degrees
(a) $\cos 150°$, (b) $\tan (-260°)$, (c) $\sin 120°$, (d) $\csc (-480°)$.

28. Find the area of triangle ABC given
$$b = 8\sqrt{3}, \quad c = 10, \quad A = 120°.$$

29. Find b given $A = 45°$, $B = 120°$, $a = 10\sqrt{6}$.

30. Find a given $b = 8$, $c = 5$, $A = 120°$.

31. Find the area under $y = \sin x$ from $x = 0$ to $x = \pi$.

32. Given the cardioid $r = 1 - \cos\theta$. Use $x = r\cos\theta$, $y = r\sin\theta$ and express the rectangular coordinates of a point on the cardioid in terms of θ alone. Find the r, θ, x, y values of the highest point on the cardioid by making the function y of θ a maximum.

33. A point P is located on a parabola by $(x = 20t^2, \quad y = 20t)$ at time t. How fast is the point moving away from the focus at time $t = 1$?

34. Find the slope and write the equation of the tangent line to $2x^2 - 2xy + 3y^2 = 7$ at $(2, 1)$.

35. Find area bounded by $y = 12(x + 2)x(x - 3)$ and the x-axis.

36. A point P starts at $(4, 0)$ and moves counterclockwise around a circle with center at the origin such that the angle joining the point to the origin is changing at the rate of 3 revolutions per second. Find $\dfrac{dx}{dt}$ and $\dfrac{dy}{dt}$ when the angle has made $\frac{1}{8}$ revolution.

37. A point P is moving along $y = \cos\dfrac{x}{3}$ such that $x = 3t$. Find $\dfrac{dy}{dt}$ when $t = \dfrac{\pi}{2}$.

38. Find $\dfrac{dy}{dx}$: $y = \ln\left[\dfrac{x^2\sqrt{3x - 5}}{\cos 2x}\right]$.

39. Use logarithms and then differentiate to find $\dfrac{dy}{dx}$:
$$y = \frac{e^{3x}\sqrt{x^2 - 4}}{(\sin x)(x^2 + 3x - 5)}.$$

40. If it is known that at least two heads occurred when five coins were tossed, find the probability that exactly three of the five coins showed heads. Describe the sample and event spaces.

[HINT: This is a conditional probability.]

41. Five disks are numbered 0, 1, 2, 3, 4. From this set a disk is drawn at random and its number noted and the disk returned to the set. A second such drawing is made. Find the probability that the sum of the squares of the two numbers drawn is a multiple of 5. Describe the event and sample spaces.

42. How many times should a coin be tossed so that the probability of getting at least one head is greater than or equal to $\frac{3}{4}$?

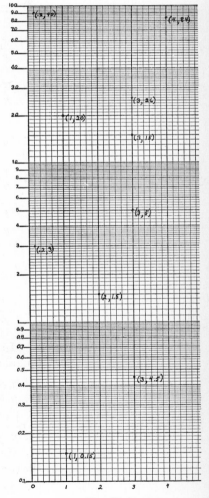

$$\large 23$$

In this chapter several types of special coordinate paper are discussed. These coordinate papers are designed to ease the work of the scientists and engineers who need to apply graphical techniques, and every student should be familiar with them.

23–1. Semilogarithmic coordinate paper. Functions such as $y = 3(5^x)$, $y = 2(e^x)$ and $y = e^{3x}$ appear in problems involving natural growth, radioactive decay, electrical theory, compound interest, and other applications. The construction of accurate graphs for these equations is time consuming. Given appropriate laboratory data, it is difficult to determine which function of the form $y = a(b^x)$ will approximate the data. To simplify such problems, a special type of graph paper has been developed.

Consider

$$y = a(b^x). \qquad (23.1)$$

Equating the logarithms of each member, one obtains

$$\log y = x \log b + \log a. \qquad (23.2)$$

If a capital letter is substituted for the logarithm of the corresponding lower case letter, Equation (23.2) reduces to a linear form

$$Y = Bx + A.$$

This is the equation of a straight line in an (x, Y) coordinate system. If a paper is designed so that $Y = \log y$ is used as the ordinate, the equation $y = a(b^x)$ will be represented on this paper as a straight line having slope $B = \log b$ and Y intercept $A = \log a$. Paper of this type is known as semilogarithmic paper.

If a function is known to be of exponential form $y = a(b^x)$, then it may be sketched on semilogarithmic paper by plotting points on the corresponding line (two to determine the line, a third as a check point). Several points are plotted in Figure 23–1 on a sheet of 3-cycle † semilogarithmic paper to help the reader become familiar with the scales.

† See Section 9-8.

Fig. 23–1

PROBLEM SET 23-1

1. The range of the y data is from .03 to 235. How many cycles in the y direction must be used if all points are to be plotted on semilogarithmic paper?

2. The range of the y data is from 181 to 965. How many cycles in the y direction must be used if all points are to be plotted on semilogarithmic paper?

In each of Problems 3 to 10, plot the given data on rectangular coordinate paper and also on semilogarithmic paper.

3.

x	0	$\frac{1}{3}$	$\frac{1}{2}$	1	2
y	3	3.8	4.2	6	12

4.

x	0	0.2	0.4	0.6	0.8	1.0	1.2
y	1.3	2.5	5.4	14	26	56	96

5.

x	0	1	2	3	4	5	6	7	8	9	10
y	80	66	56	46	35	28	23	19	15	13.5	10.0

6.

x	4	5	7	8	9
y	1.9	2.3	3.5	4.6	5.6

7.

x	30	31	32	32.5	33
y	1000	230	54	25	14

8.

t	0	2	4	6	8
y	10.0	11.5	13.0	15.5	17.5

9.

t	1	3	5	7	9
Z	0.17	0.32	0.61	1.15	2.30

10.

t	60	70	80	90	100
Z	120	65	35	19	10

In each of Problems 11 to 20, sketch the given locus on rectangular coordinate paper and also on semilogarithmic paper.

11. $y = 3(2^x)$.   **12.** $y = e^x$.

13. $y = e^{3+x}$.

[HINT: $e^{3+x} = e^3 \cdot e^x \cong 20.1e^x$.]

14. $y = 7(2^x)$.   **15.** $2y = 3(10^x)$.   **16.** $y = 7 \cdot 10^x$.

17. $y^2 = 4 \cdot e^{2x}$.   **18.** $y = (1.03)^{2x}$.

19. $y = 1000(1.06)^x$.   **20.** $y = x$.

23–2. The use of semilogarithmic paper with laboratory data. Data obtained from laboratory experiments or industrial practices suspected of being of the form $y = a(b^x)$ may be plotted on semilogarithmic paper. If the graph on semilogarithmic paper is approximately a straight line, a functional equation of the form $y = a(b^x)$ may be obtained from the graph. Often, a line is drawn using a transparent straight edge, although more refined techniques are available when needed.

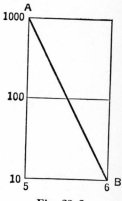

Fig. 23–2

- **Example 1.** Assume the line of Figure 23–2 has been obtained on semilogarithmic paper. Determine a functional equation representing this locus.

    Two points on the locus are $(x, y) = (5, 1000)$ and $(6, 10)$. Use the form

    $$Y = Bx + A,$$

    where $Y = \log y$. The **slope** (B) is

    $$B = \frac{\log 1000 - \log 10}{5 - 6} = \frac{3 - 1}{-1} = -2.$$

    The equation becomes

    $$Y = -2x + A$$
    $$\log_{10} y = -2x + A.$$

    The corresponding exponential form is

    $$y = 10^{-2x+A}.$$

    The point $(x, y) = (6, 10)$ may be substituted and the value of A determined.

    $$10^1 = 10^{-12+A}$$
    $$1 = -12 + A$$
    $$13 = A.$$

    The desired equation is

    $$y = 10^{-2x+13},$$

    or

    $$y = 10^{13}(10^{-2x}).$$

The same value of A is obtained if the point $(x, y) = (5, 1000)$ is substituted in $y = 10^{-2x+A}$.

- **Example 2.** Data are found to cluster about the line of Figure 23–3 when plotted on semilogarithmic paper. Determine a function that will approximate the data.

    An approximate equation is of the form

    $$Y = Bx + A, \quad \text{where} \quad Y = \log y.$$

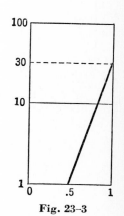

Fig. 23–3

In this case the slope,

$$B = \frac{\log 30 - \log 1}{1 - 1/2} = \frac{1.477 - 0}{1/2} = 2.954.$$

The equation becomes

$$Y = 2.95x + A,$$

or

$$\log_{10} y = 2.95x + A.$$

Upon converting to exponential form this becomes

$$y = 10^{2.95x+A}.$$

Since $(x, y) = (\frac{1}{2}, 1)$ is a point on the locus, A may be determined by substitution.

$$1 = 10^{(2.95)(\frac{1}{2})+A}, \quad \text{or} \quad 10^0 = 1 = 10^{1.48+A},$$

which implies,

$$A = -1.48.$$

Whence,

$$y = 10^{2.95x-1.48},$$

is an equation which approximates the data. One of the following equivalent forms may be preferable, depending upon the use to be made of the data:

$$y = 10^{2.95x-1.48}, \quad y = 0.033(10^{2.95x}), \quad y = e^{6.78x-3.40}, \quad y = 0.033e^{6.78x}$$

It should be verified that each of these is equivalent to the form previously obtained.

● **Example 3.** Data are found to cluster about the line of Figure 23–4, when plotted on semilogarithmic paper. Determine a function that will approximate the data within the indicated range. Note that the length of the units in the x direction has been changed.

$$Y = Bx + A,$$

where

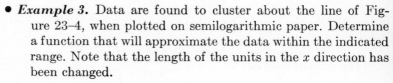

$$B = \frac{\log 10 - \log .01}{8 - 0} = \frac{1 - (-2)}{8} = \frac{3}{8}.$$

$$Y = \tfrac{3}{8}x + A$$
$$\log_{10} y = \tfrac{3}{8}x + A$$
$$y = 10^{\frac{3}{8}x+A}.$$

Since $(0, .01)$ is a point on the locus, its coordinates satisfy the equation of the locus, and $.01 = 10^A$, or $A = -2$. Whence,

$$y = 10^{\frac{3}{8}x-2}, \quad \text{or} \quad y = .01(10^{.37x}).$$

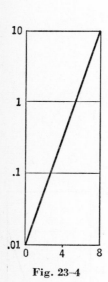

Fig. 23–4

PROBLEM SET 23-2

In each of the following problems, data are found to lie close to the indicated line when plotted on semilogarithmic paper. Determine a function that will approximate the data. For each problem write two equivalent answers using bases e and 10.

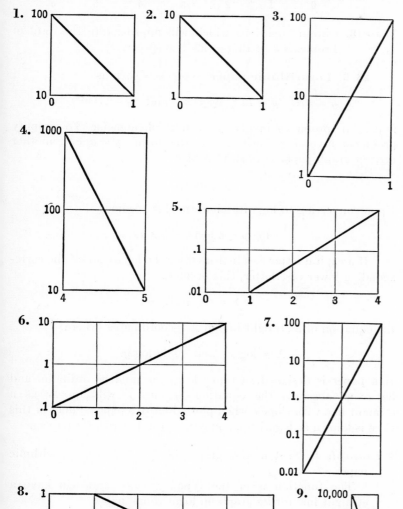

10.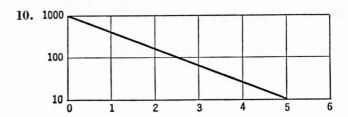

11 to 18. Obtain equations which will approximate the data of Problems 3 to 10, Set 23–1, respectively.

23–3. Logarithmic paper. Functions such as

$$y = 3x^2, \quad y = 7x^{15}, \quad y = x, \quad \text{and} \quad y = .1(x^{.28})$$

appear in problems involving natural phenomena. To simplify problems involving functions of the form $y = a(x^c)$ another type of graph paper is used. Consider

$$y = a(x^c).$$

Upon converting to logarithmic form this becomes

$$\log y = c \log x + \log a.$$

If a capital letter is substituted for the logarithm of the corresponding lower case letter, this becomes

$$Y = cX + A,$$

the equation of a straight line in XY-coordinates, where

$$X = \log x \quad \text{and} \quad Y = \log y.$$

If a paper is designed so that $\log y$ is used as ordinate, and $\log x$ as abscissa, the equation $y = a(x^c)$ will appear as a straight line with slope c when plotted on this paper. Paper of this type is known as logarithmic paper (or full logarithmic paper).

● *Example 1.* Sketch the graph of $y = 3x^5$ on logarithmic paper.

The function is of the type $y = ax^c$ and will have a straight line for its graph on logarithmic paper.

x	1	2	3
y	3	96	729

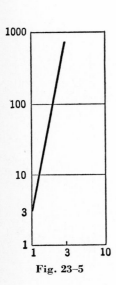

Fig. 23–5

Notice that while the point $(x, y) = (0, 0)$ satisfies the equation, it will not appear on the graph, since $\log_{10} 0$ does not exist.

● **Example 2.** Data plotted on logarithmic paper are found to lie
close to the line indicated in Figure 23–6. Determine a function
that will represent the data.

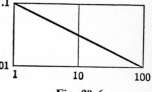

Fig. 23–6

The data are approximated by a straight line on logarithmic
paper. Hence the data are approximated by a function of
the form

$$Y = cX + A, \quad \text{where} \quad Y = \log y, \quad X = \log x, \quad \text{and} \quad A = \log a.$$

The slope c is determined by using the points $(1, .1)$ and
$(100, .01)$ which lie on the xy graph. Since XY-coordinates
are used, logarithms must be taken in order to determine
the slope,

$$c = \frac{\log .01 - \log .1}{\log 100 - \log 1} = \frac{-2 - (-1)}{2 - 0} = \frac{-1}{2}.$$

Whence,

$$Y = (-\tfrac{1}{2})X + A$$
$$\log y = (-\tfrac{1}{2}) \log x + \log a$$
$$\log y = \log (x^{-\frac{1}{2}}) + \log a, \quad \text{or} \quad \log y = \log [a(x^{-\frac{1}{2}})].$$

Equating antilogarithms of each member gives, $y = a(x^{-\frac{1}{2}})$.

The point $(1, .1)$ on the graph must satisfy the equation.
This may be used to determine a. Upon substituting, one obtains
$0.1 = a(1)$, whence $y = .1(x^{-\frac{1}{2}})$. The same value of a is obtained if the point $(100, .01)$ is used in place of $(1, .1)$.

● **Example 3.** Determine the equation of the locus shown on
logarithmic paper in Figure 23–7.

$$Y = cX + A$$
$$c = \frac{\log 100 - \log .1}{\log 100 - \log 10} = \frac{2 - (-1)}{2 - 1} = 3.$$
$$Y = 3X + A$$
$$\log y = 3 \log x + \log a$$
$$\log y = \log x^3 + \log a$$
$$\log y = \log ax^3$$
$$y = ax^3.$$

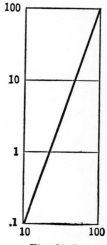

Fig. 23–7

The value of a is determined by substituting the point
$(10, .1)$, which lies on the locus.

$$.1 = a10^3 \quad \text{or} \quad .0001 = a,$$

whence,

$$y = .0001x^3, \quad \text{or} \quad y = 10^{-4}x^3.$$

PROBLEM SET 23-3

In each of Problems 1 to 5, plot the given data on logarithmic paper.

1.

x	1	1.5	2	3	4	5
y	1.3	2.1	3.0	5.0	7.2	9.5

2.

x	1	2	3	4	5	6	7	8	9	10
y	20	28	35	40	44	49	53	56	60	64

3.

x	0.1	0.3	0.9	1.2	2.5	6.9	10
y	1.1	6.0	12.8	44	130	600	1000

4.

x	1	1.5	2	2.5	3
y	99	42	23	14	9.5

5.

x	1.0	2.0	3.0	4.0	7.0	10
y	9800	1300	400	170	30	10

In each of Problems 6 to 10, sketch the locus of the given function on logarithmic paper.

6. $y = 5x^2$.   **7.** $y = 5x^7$.   **8.** $y = 2\pi x$.

9. $y = 4x^3$.   **10.** $y = 10x^6$.

In each of Problems 11 to 20, data have been plotted on logarithmic paper and found to lie close to the line indicated. Determine functions which will approximate the data.

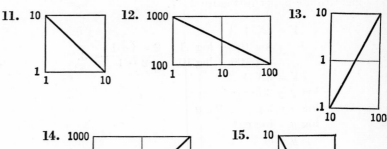

11.   **12.**   **13.**

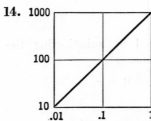   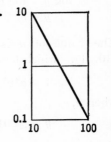

14.   **15.**

16.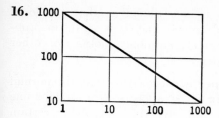

17.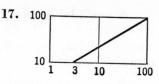

18.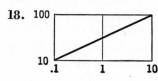

19.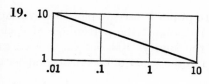

20.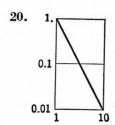

21 to 25. Determine functions which will approximate the data of Problems 1 to 5 of this set.

Plot the data given in Problems 26 to 29 both on logarithmic and on semilogarithmic paper. Decide on which paper the data are more nearly represented by a straight line, and obtain a formula which approximates the data.

26.

x	0.8	2.0	2.4	4.0	5.2	7.2	8.0	9.0	10.0
y	2.8	4.5	5.0	9.0	14.0	28.0	37.2	53.0	80.0

27.

x	1	1.5	2	2.5	3
y	10	4.2	2.3	1.4	.95

28.

x	1	2	3	4
y	100	23	5.4	2.5

29.

x	2	4	6	8	10
y	5.6	3.5	2.3	1.5	1.0

*23–4. Other special coordinate papers. The reader has used rectangular coordinate paper, polar coordinate paper, semi-logarithmic paper, and logarithmic paper. Many other coordinate papers are available. Often, time can be saved by using these papers, especially if many problems of similar type must be solved. Brief descriptions of several additional papers follow.

Sinusoidal paper. This is constructed so that the locus $y = \sin A(x - k)$ graphs as a straight line. It is useful in problems involving alternating current, harmonic motion, or other sinusoidal variation.

Normal probability paper is designed so that the normal probability curve $y = (1/\sqrt{2\pi})e^{-t^2/2}$ appears as a straight line graph. The use of this paper will save time in solving certain problems involving approximately normal distributions of a single variable. Such problems occur in the application of chemistry, physics, and psychology.

Triangular coordinate paper is used to plot three variables having a constant sum. For example, the percentage of each of three metals in an alloy (the sum is 100 percent). Triangular coordinate paper is also used in the study of chemical composition.

Power emission, fidelity, and sensitivity charts are used in modern electronic studies.

PROBLEM SET 23-4

1. Using tables of sines of angles, construct a graph paper on which $y = \sin x$ will graph as a straight line. Use a uniform x scale, and a $Y = \sin y$ ordinate scale. Plot values of Y for 5-degree intervals of y.
2. Will $y = \sin 3x$ graph as a straight line on the sheet of special paper constructed in 1?
*3. Obtain samples of as many types of specialized graph paper as you can, and explain one use for each type.
4. Using tables, construct a graph paper on which

$$y = (1/\sqrt{2\pi})e^{-\frac{x^2}{2}}$$

will graph as a straight line.

23-5. Method of least squares. In analyzing experimental data, one is frequently confronted with the problem of finding a convenient formula that will summarize the data contained in a table. We shall consider a two-variable case where the corresponding points, when plotted on an appropriate rectangular coordinate system, lie approximately along a line. Suppose the points (x_1, y_1), (x_2, y_2), $\cdots$, (x_k, y_k), $\cdots$, (x_n, y_n) lie approximately on a line, and that it is desired to "fit" this set of points with an equation of the form $y = mx + b$. Consider the accompanying table and figure.

observed x	observed y	calculated $y = mx + b$
x_1	y_1	$mx_1 + b$
x_2	y_2	$mx_2 + b$
$\cdot$	$\cdot$	$\cdot$
$\cdot$	$\cdot$	$\cdot$
x_k	y_k	$mx_k + b$
$\cdot$	$\cdot$	$\cdot$
$\cdot$	$\cdot$	$\cdot$
x_n	y_n	$mx_n + b$
Σx_k †	Σy_k	$\Sigma(mx_k + b)$ $= m\Sigma x_k + nb$

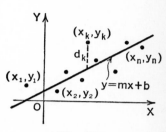

Fig. 23–8

Let $d_k = y_k - (mx_k + b) = y_k - mx_k - b$ be the distance measured in the y direction from the line $y = mx + b$ to the point (x_k, y_k), $(k = 1, 2, \cdots, n)$. A line of "best fit," the **line of regression of y on x,** is obtained by determining the unknown constants (parameters) m and b so that Σd_k^2 is a minimum.†

Now

$$\Sigma d_k^2 = \Sigma([y_k - mx_k] - b)^2 = \Sigma([y_k - mx_k]^2 - 2b[y_k - mx_k] + b^2)$$

and

$$\Sigma d_k^2 = \Sigma[y_k - mx_k]^2 - 2b\Sigma[y_k - mx_k] + nb^2. \qquad (23.3)$$

Also

$$\Sigma d_k^2 = \Sigma([y_k - b] - mx_k)^2 = \Sigma([y_k - b]^2 - 2mx_k[y_k - b] + m^2 x_k^2)$$

and

$$\Sigma d_k^2 = \Sigma[y_k - b]^2 - 2m\Sigma x_k[y_k - b] + m^2\Sigma x_k^2. \qquad (23.4)$$

The right member of (23.3) is a quadratic function of b. Consequently if Σd_k^2 is a minimum, then (see Section 4–10)

$$b = -\frac{-2\Sigma[y_k - mx_k]}{2n} = \frac{\Sigma y_k - m\Sigma x_k}{n}$$

or

$$nb + m\Sigma x_k = \Sigma y_k. \qquad (23.5)$$

† In this section the Σ summation is understood to be on k from $k = 1$ to $k = n$, unless indicated otherwise.

Similarly, the right member of (23.4) is a quadratic function of m. If Σd_k^2 is a minimum, then

$$m = -\frac{-2\Sigma x_k[y_k - b]}{2\Sigma x_k^2} = \frac{\Sigma x_k y_k - b\Sigma x_k}{\Sigma x_k^2}$$

or

$$b\Sigma x_k + m\Sigma x_k^2 = \Sigma x_k y_k. \qquad (23.6)$$

Conditions (23.5) and (23.6) are sufficient for Σd_k^2 to be a minimum although this will not be shown. If (23.5) and (23.6) are solved for b and m we obtain

$$b = \frac{\begin{vmatrix} \Sigma y_k & \Sigma x_k \\ \Sigma x_k y_k & \Sigma x_k^2 \end{vmatrix}}{\begin{vmatrix} n & \Sigma x_k \\ \Sigma x_k & \Sigma x_k^2 \end{vmatrix}}, \qquad m = \frac{\begin{vmatrix} n & \Sigma y_k \\ \Sigma x_k & \Sigma x_k y_k \end{vmatrix}}{\begin{vmatrix} n & \Sigma x_k \\ \Sigma x_k & \Sigma x_k^2 \end{vmatrix}}. \qquad (23.7)$$

The values of b, m in (23.7) when used in $y = mx + b$ give the desired equation. The method of fitting a line to a two-variable table illustrated in this section is the **least square method** since it makes Σd_k^2 a minimum.

● *Example 1.* Fit a line of regression of y on x to the table:

x	-1	0	2	4	5
y	-1	2	2	3	5

Solution

x^2	x	y	xy
1	-1	-1	1
0	0	2	0
4	2	2	4
16	4	3	12
25	5	5	25
$\Sigma x^2 = 46$	$\Sigma x = 10$	$\Sigma y = 11$	$\Sigma xy = 42$

$$5b + 10m = 11$$
$$10b + 46m = 42$$

$$b = \frac{\begin{vmatrix} 11 & 10 \\ 42 & 46 \end{vmatrix}}{\begin{vmatrix} 5 & 10 \\ 10 & 46 \end{vmatrix}} = \frac{86}{130} = \frac{43}{65}$$

$$m = \frac{\begin{vmatrix} 5 & 11 \\ 10 & 42 \end{vmatrix}}{130} = \frac{100}{130} = \frac{10}{13}.$$

The desired line is $y = \frac{10}{13}x + \frac{43}{65}$. Note that the line passes through $\left(\bar{x} = \frac{\Sigma x}{n} = \frac{10}{5} = 2, \quad \bar{y} = \frac{\Sigma y}{n} = \frac{11}{5}\right)$ but may fail to pass through any of the points given in the table.

Data in a two-variable table may not lie along a line when plotted using rectangular coordinates but may lie approximately along a line when plotted in semilogarithmic coordinates, or logarithmic coordinates.

(1) If the data lie along a line in semilogarithmic coordinates, a regression equation of the form $Y = Bx + A$ with $Y = \log y$ may be obtained where B and A are determined by the method of least squares. The regression equation may be written in the form $y = ab^x$ where $\log a = A$ and $\log b = B$.

(2) If the data lie along a line in logarithmic coordinates, a regression equation of the form $Y = cX + A$ with $Y = \log y$ and $X = \log x$ may be obtained where c and A are determined by the method of least squares. The regression equation may be written in the form $y = ax^c$ where $\log a = A$.

- **Example 2.** The excess temperature $\theta°$ C of a heated body while cooling in air was taken at 2-minute intervals and the results tabulated.

time t	0	2	4	6	8
excess temp θ	64.9	55.0	47.2	41.9	37.6

Find a regression line $T = \log \theta = Bt + A$.

t^2	t	T	tT
0	0	1.8122	0
4	2	1.7404	3.4808
16	4	1.6739	6.6956
36	6	1.6222	9.7332
64	8	1.5752	12.6016
120	20	8.4239	32.5112

$5A + 20B = 8.4239$
$20A + 120B = 32.5112$
$A = 1.8032, B = -.0296$
$\log \theta = -.0296t + 1.8032$
$\theta = 63.6 \times 10^{-.0296t} = 63.6e^{-.0682t}$.

PROBLEM SET 23–5

1. The specific heat S of ice was observed by Nernst to vary with temperature $T°$ C as follows:

T	-180	-140	-100	-60	-20
S	.199	.262	.325	.392	.480

(a) Plot in rectangular coordinates and obtain an equation of the form $S = mT + b$.

(b) Find a regression equation of the form $S = mT + b$. Compare with (a). Answer: $S = .00173T + .505$.

(c) Estimate the specific heat of ice at $-10°$ C. The experimental result was 0.530. Does this suggest that extrapolation is to be used with caution?

2. The table lists the grams w of sugar dissolved in 100 grams of water at the temperature C in degrees centigrade.

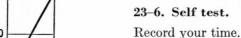

C	0	20	40	60
w	179.2	203.9	238.1	287.3

(a) Plot in semilogarithmic coordinates and obtain an equation of the form $w = ae^{kC}$.

(b) Find a regression equation of the form $W = BC + A$ with $W = \log w$ and from this equation obtain $w = ae^{kC}$. Compare with (a). Answers: $\log w = .003412C + 2.24709$,
$w = 176.6e^{.007856C}$.

(c) Estimate the amount of sugar in solution at $50°$ C. The experimental result was 260.4 grams.

3. Fit the data of Problem 1, Set 23–3, with a regression equation of the form $Y = cX + A$ with $Y = \log y$ and $X = \log x$. Also write the equation in the form $y = ax^c$. Compare with Problem 21, Set 23–3.

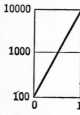

Fig. 23–9

23–6. Self test.

Record your time.

1. In an experiment concerning the number of bacteria, N, in a culture after t hours, it is found that the data cluster close to the line sketched on semilogarithmic paper in Figure 23–9. Determine an equation which will approximate the data.

2. Data in an experiment concerning the lubricating value of oil are found to cluster close to the line indicated in Figure 23–10, when plotted on logarithmic paper. Obtain a function which will approximate the data.

In Problems 3 and 4 an equation is given. State whether each equation will have a straight line graph on logarithmic, or on semi-logarithmic paper, or neither. If the graph is a straight line on one of these papers, make a sketch showing its graph on that paper. Be sure to indicate the intercepts.

3. $y = 7x^5$.   4. $y = 3(7^{2x})$.

5. (a) Describe the construction of a sheet of paper on which $y = \sin x$, x in degrees, will graph as a straight line.

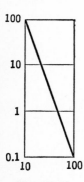

Fig. 23–10

(b) Will the x scale have uniform intervals?

(c) Will the y scale have uniform intervals?

(d) Sketch a sheet of "2-cycle" paper. State the value of a point that is approximately at the midpoint of the cycle. (On a logarithmic cycle, the point 3.16 is about midway in the cycle from 1 to 10.)

6. Identify, and give one use for each of the coordinate papers on pages 557–559.

(a)

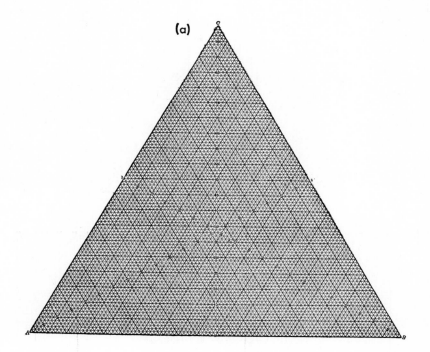

(b)

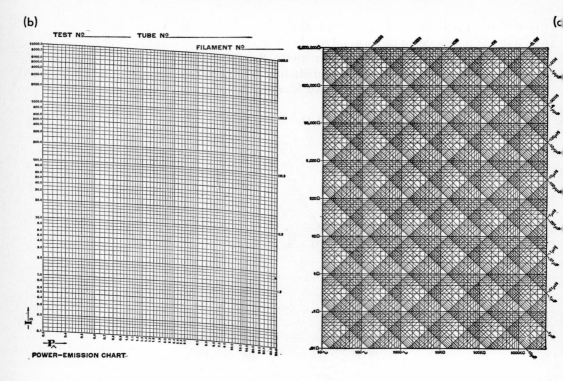

(d)

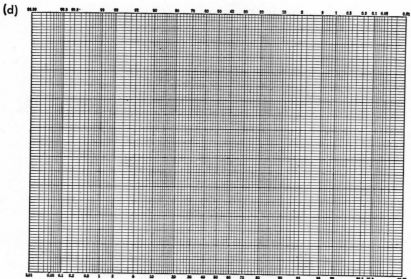

(e)

FIDELITY

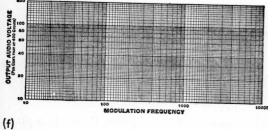

(f)

SENSITIVITY

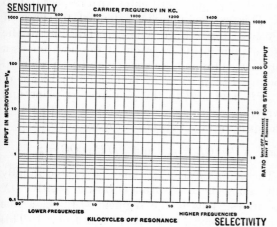

(g)

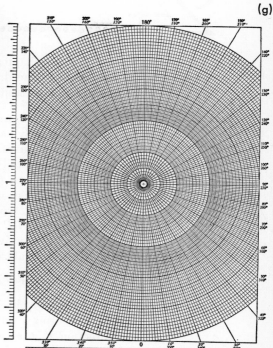

24

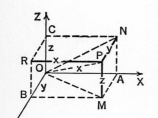

Fig. 24-1

In this chapter the analytic geometry of three-dimensional space is introduced. The loci and equations of surfaces and curves needed in later applications, are obtained.

24–1. Rectangular coordinates in space. Points in a plane are conveniently located by giving coordinates with respect to two perpendicular axes. This system may be extended to space of three dimensions by inserting a third axis perpendicular to the other two axes at their point of intersection. If the new axis is a z-axis, then the coordinates of a point in space may be represented by (x, y, z). A point $P(x, y, z)$ may be located by means of perpendiculars RP, NP, and MP to the yz plane, xz plane and xy planes, respectively.

In the parallelepiped, or box, $OAMBCNPR$ we have

$$RP = OA = x, \quad NP = OB = y, \quad \text{and} \quad MP = OC = z$$

units respectively. The point $P(x, y, z)$ may be located rapidly by measuring x units along the x-axis from O (in the positive OX direction if x is positive). This is the segment OA. On a line through A, parallel to the y-axis, measure y units from A. This is the segment AM. On a line through M, parallel to the z-axis, measure z units from M. This is the segment MP. The point P has coordinates (x, y, z). In some sketches it is desirable to reverse the directions of the axes. It is customary to indicate the positive direction of each axis on the sketch.

Using the law of Pythagoras, one finds the **distance**

$$|OP| = \sqrt{(\sqrt{x^2 + y^2})^2 + (z)^2} = \sqrt{x^2 + y^2 + z^2}.$$

The locus of points having a constant distance r from the origin is $r^2 = x^2 + y^2 + z^2$. This locus is a spherical surface with center $(0, 0, 0)$ and radius r. The interior of the sphere satisfies the relation $x^2 + y^2 + z^2 < r^2$.

● **Example 1.** Locate the points $P(3, 7, -2)$ and $Q(-4, 6, 5)$. Find $|OP|$ and $|OQ|$.

$$|OP| = \sqrt{3^2 + 7^2 + (-2)^2} = \sqrt{62}$$

and

$$|OQ| = \sqrt{(-4)^2 + 6^2 + 5^2} = \sqrt{77}.$$

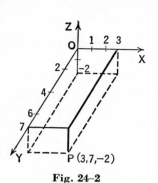

Fig. 24–2

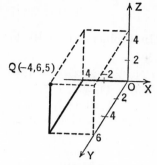

Fig. 24–3

● **Example 2.** Determine an equation of the spherical surface with center $(0, 0, 0)$ and radius 5.

The locus of points 5 units from $(0, 0, 0)$ is

$$\sqrt{x^2 + y^2 + z^2} = 5,$$

or

$$x^2 + y^2 + z^2 = 25.$$

24–2. Distance formula. The distance between points

$$P_1(x_1,\ y_1,\ z_1) \quad \text{and} \quad P_2(x_2,\ y_2,\ z_2)$$

may be obtained by constructing a parallelepiped with edges parallel to the coordinate axes and P_1P_2 as diagonal.

$$|P_1Q| = \sqrt{(x_2 - x_1)^2 + (y_2 - y_1)^2}$$
$$|P_1P_2| = \sqrt{(P_1Q)^2 + (QP_2)^2}$$
$$= \sqrt{(x_2 - x_1)^2 + (y_2 - y_1)^2 + (z_2 - z_1)^2}.$$

The distance between two points

$$P_1(x_1,\ y_1,\ z_1) \quad \text{and} \quad P_2(x_2,\ y_2,\ z_2)$$

is

$$d = |P_1P_2|$$

$$d = \sqrt{(x_2 - x_1)^2 + (y_2 - y_1)^2 + (z_2 - z_1)^2}. \qquad (24.1)$$

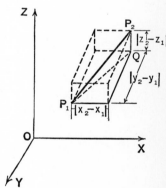

Fig. 24–4

The algebraic formula is quite general, although the points P_1 and P_2 appear in specific octants in Figure 24–4 (not quadrants, since space is divided into eight parts by the coordinate planes).

● **Example 1.** Find the distance between $P(4, -1, 2)$ and $Q(1, 3, -4)$.

$$d = |PQ| = \sqrt{(4 - 1)^2 + (-1 - 3)^2 + (2 + 4)^2}$$
$$= \sqrt{9 + 16 + 36}$$
$$= \sqrt{61} \cong 7.8 \text{ units.}$$

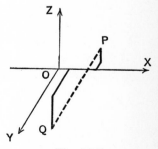

Fig. 24–5

PROBLEM SET 24-2

In Problems 1 to 10, locate the given points on coordinate systems.

1. $P(1, 3, -2)$, $Q(4, -1, 6)$.   2. $P(1, 1, -4)$, $Q(3, 7, 2)$.
3. $P(3, 4, 1)$, $Q(2, -7, 6)$.   4. $P(4, 1, 3)$, $Q(7, 2, 3)$.
5. $P(6, -1, 2)$, $Q(7, -4, -1)$.   6. $P(3, 4, 0)$, $Q(1, 4, -8)$.
7. $P(-1, -3, 4)$, $Q(-3, 1, 1)$.   8. $P(3, -4, -1)$, $Q(0, 0, 12)$.
9. $P(1, 7, 2)$, $Q(-1, 4, 9)$.   10. $P(1, 3, 8)$, $Q(7, -1, 5)$.

11 to 20. Determine the distance $|PQ|$ between the points P and Q given in Problems 1 to 10 respectively.
21. Locate five points having x-coordinate -4.
22. Locate five points having z-coordinate 2.
23. Show that $(3, 2, -3)$, $(5, 8, 6)$ and $(-3, -5, 3)$ are vertices of a right triangle.
24. Show that the triangle of Problem 23 is an isosceles triangle.
25. Show that $(13, 6, 4)$, $(-7, -7, 7)$, $(5, -6, -5)$ are vertices of an isosceles right triangle.
26. Show that $(0, -2, -3)$, $(-4, -9, 1)$, $(1, 2, 5)$ are vertices of an isosceles right triangle.
27. Are $(0, 0, 0)$, $(8, -4, 1)$, $(1, 4, 8)$ vertices of a triangle? Is it a right triangle? Is it isosceles?
28. Show that the points $(1, 2, -1)$, $(2, 6, 2)$, $(4, 14, 8)$ are collinear.
29. What common property do the coordinates of points on the z-axis have?
30. What common property do the coordinates of points in the yz plane have?
31. Find the locus of all points having $z = 3$.
32. Find three points having y-coordinate three and z-coordinate -1. Explain where these points lie.
33. Show that the equation of the locus of all points at a distance 4 units from $(2, -1, 5)$ is

$$(x - 2)^2 + (y + 1)^2 + (z - 5)^2 = 16,$$

What is the locus?
34. (a) Find the equation of the locus of all points whose distance from $(2, -5, 3)$ is 7. What is the locus?
(b) Find the locus of all points whose distance from $(2, -5, 3)$ is less than 7.
(c) Find the locus of all points whose distance from $(2, -5, 3)$ is greater than, or equal to, 7.
35. What is the nature of the locus $x^2 - 2x + y^2 - 10y + z^2 = 10$?
36. Derive the equation of the surface of a sphere with center (h, k, l) and radius r.

37. Show that the equation $z = k$ for any constant k is the equation of a plane. Describe the position of the plane.

38. Same as Problem 37 for $x = k$.

39. Same as Problem 37 for $y = k$.

40. Find the equation of a spherical surface of radius 7 and center $(0, 3, -1)$.

41. Find the equation of a spherical surface of radius 5 and center $(-3, 11, -9)$.

24–3. Cylinders. A cylinder is a surface generated by lines (generators) that pass through a given plane curve (directrix) and are parallel to a fixed line. A cylinder need not be closed or consist of one piece, for we may have sinusoidal cylinders, parabolic cylinders, and hyperbolic cylinders, as well as circular cylinders. Here we study cylinders whose generating lines are parallel to one of the coordinate axes. Such cylinders are named for their directrix curves in a coordinate plane. A cylinder is called a parabolic cylinder if its directrix in a plane perpendicular to its elements is a parabola.

● **Example 1.** Find the locus of points 3 units from the x-axis. Show that the locus is a circular cylinder.

Let $P(x, y, z)$ be a typical point of the locus. The distance between P and the x-axis † is

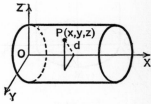

$$d = (\sqrt{x - x})^2 + (y - 0)^2 + (z + 0)^2 = \sqrt{y^2 + z^2}.$$

The desired equation is

$$\sqrt{y^2 + z^2} = 3, \quad \text{or} \quad y^2 + z^2 = 9.$$

This is the equation of a circular cylinder having as directrix the circle $x = 0$, $y^2 + z^2 = 9$ in which the surface cuts the yz plane. A line through this circle and parallel to the x-axis is a generator. Through a point $(0, y, z)$ satisfying

Fig. 24–6

$$x = 0, \quad y^2 + z^2 = 9,$$

draw a line parallel to the x-axis. The coordinates of a point (x, y, z) on this line will satisfy $y^2 + z^2 = 9$. Although only two variables appear, the equation is the equation of a *surface*, not of a curve.

If a cylinder has elements parallel to one of the coordinate axes, the variable corresponding to this axis will not appear in the equation of the cylinder. This is analogous to the fact that, in two-dimensional (plane) analytic geometry, the equation of a line parallel to one of the coordinate axes does not contain that variable.

† The distance between a line and a point is measured along the perpendicular from the given point to the given line.

For example, in two-dimensional space, $y = 4$ is the equation of a line parallel to the x-axis and 4 units above it. In three-dimensional space, $y = 4$ is the equation of a *plane* parallel to both the x- and the z-axes (hence, to the xz plane) and 4 units in the positive y direction from it.

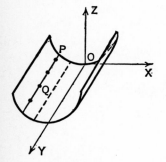

Fig. 24–7

● **Example 2.** Sketch the locus $x^2 = 4z$.

Since the variable y does not appear in the equation, y may take any value, while the x- and z-coordinates satisfy the equation. For example, the point $(2, y, 1)$ lies on the locus for all values of y. Thus $(2, y, 1)$ generates an element (generating line) of the cylinder. In the xz plane $(y = 0)$ the trace $y = 0$, $x^2 = 4z$ is a parabola.

The locus is a parabolic cylinder.

Through any point $P(x, 0, z,)$ on the parabola in the xz-plane, draw a line parallel to the y-axis. A point Q on this line has coordinates (x, y, z) satisfying $x^2 = 4z$.

● **Example 3.** Determine the equation of the cylinder with generating elements parallel to the z-axis and intersecting the xy plane in the curve $(x - 1)^2 + y^2 = 1$, $z = 0$. Sketch the locus.

The coordinates of any point $Q(x, y, z)$ on the cylindrical surface are $x = ON$, $y = NM$, and $z = MQ$. Since $M(x, y, 0)$ is on the given circle

$$(ON - 1)^2 + (MN)^2 = 1$$

holds for, and only for, each point on the desired surface. Therefore, the equation of the locus is $(x - 1)^2 + y^2 = 1$.

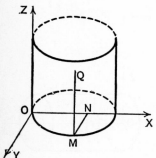

Fig. 24–8

PROBLEM SET 24–3

Name and sketch the cylinders given in Problems 1 to 15.

1. $x^2 + z^2 = 4$.   2. $4x^2 + 9y^2 = 144$.   3. $x^2 - y^2 = 4$.
4. $xy = 1$.   5. $z + 11 = 0$.   6. $z^2 = 4y$.
7. $z = 5 \sin 3x$.   8. $3x^2 - 9y^2 = 100$.   9. $x = 4 \sin z \cos z$.
10. $3z - 5x = 0$.   11. $4x + z^2 = 0$.   12. $3x - 1 = z^2 + 5$.
13. $4(y - 3)^2 + 9(z + 1)^2 = 81$.   14. $9(x - 2)^2 + (y + 1)^2 = 36$.
15. $(x - 5)(y + 2) = 100$.

In Problems 16 to 19, find the equation of the cylinder having elements parallel to the given axis A, and as directrix, the given curve D.

16. A: the x-axis. D: $z^2 - 4y = 7$, $x = 0$.
17. A: the z-axis. D: $(x - 1)^2 + (y + 2)^2 = 4$, $z = 0$.
18. A: the y-axis. D: $x^2 - 4z^2 = 36$, $y = 0$.
19. A: the line through $(2, 7, -1)$ and $(4, 7, -1)$.
$$D: z^2 + y^2 = 4, x = 0.$$

20. Determine the equation of the circular cylinder having the z-axis as axis of symmetry and radius 10.
21. Find the equation of the parabolic cylinder that is the locus of points equidistant from the y-axis and the plane $z = 4$.
22. Determine the equation of a plane (a linear cylinder) that passes through the points $(3, 0, 0)$ and $(0, 0, 5)$ and is parallel to the y-axis.
23. Determine the equation of a plane passing through the x-axis and the point $(3, 4, -1)$. Note that a line and a point not on the line determine a plane.
24. The line through $(3, -7, 2)$ and $(3, -7, -1)$ is parallel to one of the coordinate axes. Find the equation of the plane determined by these two points and the point $(4, 0, 6)$. Does the point $(-7, 1, -5)$ lie on this plane?
25. Determine the coordinates of three noncollinear points that lie on the plane $3y - 2z + 12 = 0$.

24–4. General surfaces. The curve in which a surface intersects a plane is called a **trace**. The plane † $3x + 2y - 5z = 10$

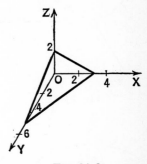

Fig. 24–9

has the line $\begin{cases} 3x + 2y = 10 \\ z = 0 \end{cases}$ as trace in the xy plane, the line

$\begin{cases} 3x - 5z = 10 \\ y = 0 \end{cases}$ as trace in the xz plane, and the line

$\begin{cases} 2y - 5z = 10 \\ x = 0 \end{cases}$

as trace in the yz plane. Observe that a line is determined by the intersection of a pair of planes. The observation that the trace in each coordinate plane is a straight line does *not* prove that $3x + 2y - 5z = 10$ is a plane. (Why?)

● **Example 1.** Sketch the surface $x^2 + y^2 = 9z$.

The trace in the xy plane is $\begin{cases} x^2 + y^2 = 0 \\ z = 0 \end{cases}$, a single point,

the origin.

† In Section 24–8, it is shown that $Ax + By + Cz + D = 0$ is the equation of a plane.

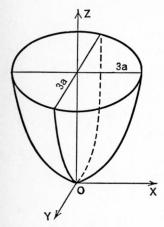

Fig. 24–10

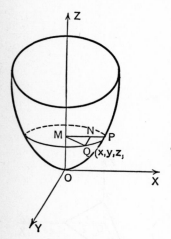

Fig. 24–11

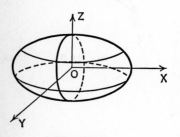

Fig. 24–12

The trace in the xz plane is $\begin{cases} x^2 = 9z, \\ y = 0 \end{cases}$ a parabola.

The trace in the yz plane is $\begin{cases} y^2 = 9z, \\ x = 0 \end{cases}$ a parabola.

The trace in the plane $z = a^2$ is $\begin{cases} x^2 + y^2 = 9a^2, \\ z = a^2 \end{cases}$, a circle of radius $3a$ with center on the z-axis.

The larger a becomes, the larger is the radius of the circle. There is no trace in a plane $z = -a^2$, $a \ne 0$. Why? The surface is a paraboloid of revolution. It is generated by revolving the parabola $x^2 = 9z$, $y = 0$ about the z-axis. To verify this, consider a point $P(MP, 0, OM)$, on the parabola, which revolves into $Q(x, y, z)$.

Construct QN perpendicular to MP. Now $x = MN$, $y = NQ$, $z = OM$.

Also $MQ = MP$ (radii of the same circle). The desired equation is found by obtaining the relation satisfied by the coordinates (x, y, z) of the point Q.

$$(MN)^2 + (NQ)^2 = (MQ)^2 = (MP)^2, \quad \text{or} \quad x^2 + y^2 = (MP)^2.$$

The point P lies on the parabola. Consequently, its coordinates MP and $OM = z$ satisfy $(MP)^2 = 9(OM) = 9z$. The desired equation is $x^2 + y^2 = 9z$.

● **Example 2.** Sketch the locus $x^2/25 + y^2/9 + z^2/4 = 1$.

The trace in each coordinate plane is the ellipse obtained by setting in turn $x = 0$, $y = 0$, and $z = 0$. No traces are obtained for planes $z = k$ with $|k| > 2$. (Why?) The traces in planes $z = \pm 2$ are single points. (Why?) The traces in planes $z = k$ with $|k| < 2$ are ellipses. (Why?) The reader should construct similar statements for

$$|x| > 5, \quad |x| = 5, \quad |x| < 5,$$

and for

$$|y| > 3, \quad |y| = 3, \quad |y| < 3.$$

In each of these cases, when a trace exists, it is either a single point or an ellipse. The surface is called an **ellipsoid**. The ellipsoid in this example is not an ellipsoid of revolution. The surface

$$\frac{x^2}{9} + \frac{y^2}{9} + \frac{z^2}{4} = 1$$

is an ellipsoid of revolution. (Why?)

● **Example 3.** Describe the locus

$$\frac{(x-1)^2}{25} + \frac{(y+2)^2}{9} + \frac{(z-3)^2}{4} = 1.$$

If one sets $x' = x - 1$, $y' = y + 2$, $z' = z - 3$ one finds that the surface is congruent to the ellipsoid obtained in Example 2, but it has been translated one unit in the positive x direction, two units in the negative y direction, and 3 units in the positive z direction.

● **Example 4.** Sketch the surface

$$100x^2 + 225y^2 - 36z^2 = 900.$$

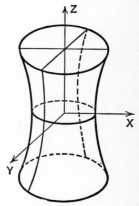

The given equation is equivalent to $x^2/9 + y^2/4 - z^2/25 = 1$. Setting $z = k$ (k positive, negative, or zero), elliptical traces are obtained in planes parallel to the xy plane. If either x or y is set equal to zero, the resulting yz or xz trace is a hyperbola with center at the origin. The surface is called an **elliptic hyperboloid of one sheet.**

The designation "of one sheet" is used to distinguish between this surface and a hyperboloid of two sheets, an example of which may be obtained by rotating a hyperbola about its transverse axis.

Fig. 24–13

● **Example 5.** Sketch the locus $4x^2 + z^2 = 36y^2$.

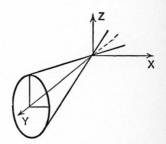

The given equation is equivalent to $x^2/9 + z^2/36 = y^2$. Setting $y = k$ (k positive, negative, or zero), elliptical traces are obtained in planes parallel to the xz plane. If either x or z is zero, the resulting yz or xy trace is a pair of lines intersecting at the origin. The surface is an elliptic cone.

● **Example 6.** Describe the locus

$$4(x+2)^2 + (z-1)^2 = 36(y+10)^2.$$

Fig. 24–14

The surface is congruent to that of Example 5, with the vertex of the cone at the point $(-2, -10, 1)$ and the axis of the cone parallel to the y-axis.

Remark: Cylinders are named by considering their directrices (see Section 24–3). Surfaces studied in the present section are named by considering their traces on three mutually perpendicular planes, at least two of which are planes of symmetry. If one trace is an ellipse and two others are hyperbolas, the surface is called an elliptic hyperboloid. The noun "hyperboloid" denoting that two traces are hyperbolas while the adjective "elliptic" indicates the other trace is an ellipse. The phrase "of revolution" may be used to replace the adjective "circular."

PROBLEM SET 24-4

In Problems 1 to 15, sketch and name the indicated surfaces.

1. $\dfrac{x^2}{4} + \dfrac{y^2}{9} + \dfrac{z^2}{4} = 1.$ **2.** $x^2 + z^2 = 4y.$ **3.** $4x^2 + 2y^2 - 3z = 24.$

4. $\dfrac{x^2}{9} + \dfrac{y^2}{16} - \dfrac{z^2}{25} = 1.$ **5.** $y^2 + 4z^2 = 144x.$ **6.** $\dfrac{x^2}{4} - \dfrac{y^2}{1} - \dfrac{z^2}{1} = 1.$

7. $3x^2 + 9z = 100.$ **8.** $\dfrac{x^2}{25} + \dfrac{y^2}{4} - \dfrac{z^2}{9} = 0.$ **9.** $\dfrac{x^2}{25} + \dfrac{y^2}{4} - \dfrac{z^2}{9} = 1.$

10. $9x^2 + (y-5)^2 + 4(z-2)^2 = 36.$ **11.** $3x + y^2 = 15.$

12. $4y^2 + 36x^2 + 144z = 0.$ **13.** $\dfrac{(x-5)^2}{4} + \dfrac{(y+9)^2}{9} + \dfrac{z^2}{4} = 1.$

14. $(x+1)^2 + (y-8)^2 = z - 3.$ **15.** $(x-5)(x+2) = -6.$

In Problems 16 to 20, sketch the given surfaces, indicate the regions, and give a rough estimate of the volumes bounded by the surfaces. Accurate determinations of such volumes are obtained in calculus courses using integration.

16. $x^2 + y^2 = 4$, $z = 1$, and $x + z = 7.$ **17.** $x^2 + 4y^2 = 4z^2$, $y + z = 12.$
18. $x = 0$, $z^2 = 4y$, $3x + y = 21.$ **19.** $z = 0$, $x^2 + y^2 = 4$, $x^2 + y^2 = 4z.$
20. $y = 0$, $x^2 + z^2 = 4(y + 3).$
21. Find the equation of the surface of revolution obtained by revolving the line $y = 2x$, $z = 0$ about the x-axis.
22. Find the equation of the surface of revolution obtained by revolving the circle $(x - 2)^2 + y^2 = 16$, $z = 0$ (a) about the x-axis, (b) about the z-axis.
23. Find the equation of the surface of revolution obtained by revolving the parabola $y^2 = 4x$, $z = 0$ about the x-axis.

24–5. Intersections. In plane analytic geometry, the point of intersection of two lines is obtained by considering the system of equations of the lines. The points of intersection of the circle $x^2 + y^2 = 16$, and the parabola $6y = x^2$, may be represented as a system of equations $\begin{cases} x^2 + y^2 = 16 \\ 6y = x^2 \end{cases}.$ The system represents all points which lie on both loci. This system may be reduced (solved) to the system $\begin{cases} x = \pm 2\sqrt{3} \\ y = 2 \end{cases}.$

In a similar fashion, the two surfaces $x^2 + y^2 + z^2 = 4$ and $(x - 1)^2 + y^2 = 1$, intersect in a **space curve**. The space curve, consisting of all points common to the two surfaces (points whose coordinates satisfy both equations), may be represented by

$$\begin{cases} x^2 + y^2 + z^2 = 4 \\ (x - 1)^2 + y^2 = 1. \end{cases}$$

The upper heavy curve in Figure 24–15 represents the portion in the positive octant of the space curve described.

A line in space may be represented as the intersection of two planes.

Often it is convenient to represent a space curve parametrically, in terms of a single auxiliary variable. Later, in Section 24–9, we shall see that equations of a line through (x_1, y_1, z_1) having "direction angles" α, β, γ may be expressed parametrically in t as follows: $x = x_1 + t \cos \alpha$, $y = y_1 + t \cos \beta$, $z = z_1 + t \cos \gamma$. For the present, as an illustration, we shall consider

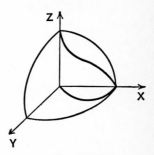

Fig. 24–15

● **Example 1.** (a) Sketch and discuss the locus of

$$x = t \cos t, \quad y = t \sin t, \quad z = t.$$

(b) Obtain a pair of nonparametric rectangular equations representing surfaces intersecting in the given space curve.

(a) The locus is a helix wrapped around a cone whose vertex is the origin and whose axis is the z-axis (the helix has a spiral shape). When $t = 0$, $x = y = z = 0$ and the curve passes through the origin. As $t > 0$ increases, the curve winds around the z-axis moving outward from it and at the same time moving upward. If $t < 0$ decreases, the curve winds around the z-axis moving outward from it and at the same time moving downward.

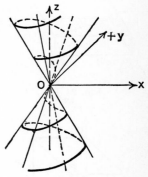

Fig. 24–16

(b) $\dfrac{y}{x} = \tan z$, $x^2 + y^2 = z^2$. The second equation indicates that the locus lies on a cone.

PROBLEM SET 24-5

Sketch the surfaces involved, and indicate with a heavy curve the space curve represented by the system.

1. $\begin{cases} x^2 + y^2 = 4 \\ x + 2z = 1. \end{cases}$ 2. $\begin{cases} x^2 + y^2 = 4 \\ z^2 = y. \end{cases}$ 3. $\begin{cases} x^2 = 4z \\ y^2 + z^2 = 1. \end{cases}$

4. $\begin{cases} x^2 + y^2 = 4 \\ y^2 + z^2 = 4. \end{cases}$ 5. $\begin{cases} x^2 - y^2 = 16 \\ x + z = 1. \end{cases}$ 6. $\begin{cases} (x - 1)^2 + y^2 = 1 \\ y^2 + z^2 = x. \end{cases}$

7. **Solid angle** is a term used, for example, when the intensity of radiation on a surface is considered. If a cone (not necessarily a circular cone) has its vertex at the center of a sphere, then the ratio of the portion of the sphere's surface area en-

closed by the cone to the square of the sphere's radius, is a measure of solid angle. Solid angle is measured in units called **steradians.** One steradian is that solid angle which encloses r^2 units on the sphere's surface where r is the radius of the sphere. Draw a diagram illustrating the above concept.

8. How many steradians are there in a solid angle which encloses one fourth the area of a sphere (a) of radius 6 units? (b) of radius 10 units?

9. Sketch and discuss the locus of $x = 2 \cos t$, $y = 2 \sin t$, $z = t$.

10. Sketch and discuss the locus of
$$x = 2t^{\frac{1}{2}} \cos t, \quad y = 2t^{\frac{1}{2}} \sin t, \quad z = t.$$

24–6. Direction cosines and direction numbers. Let L be the directed line segment from the origin $O(0, 0, 0)$ to $P(l, m, n)$. Let α be the angle L makes with the positive x-axis. Let β be the angle L makes with the positive y-axis and γ be the angle L makes with the positive z-axis. The angles α, β, γ are called **direction angles** of the directed line L. A directed line parallel to L, having the same direction as L, is said to have the same direction angles α, β, γ. A line parallel to L, having the

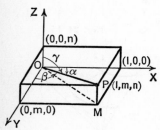

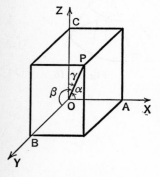

Fig. 24–17

Fig. 24–18

opposite direction (the line $\overrightarrow{PO}$, for example), has direction angles

$$\pi - \alpha, \quad \pi - \beta, \quad \pi - \gamma.$$

In many problems it is immaterial which direction along the line is considered, as long as the direction considered remains unchanged throughout the problem.

● **Example 1.** Determine a set of direction angles of the line through the origin and $P(1, 1, \sqrt{2})$.

The distance $|OP| = d = \sqrt{1 + 1 + 2} = 2$. The distance $OA = OB = 1$, while $OC = \sqrt{2}$. Hence

$$\cos \alpha = \frac{OA}{d} = \frac{1}{2}, \qquad\qquad \alpha = 60°.$$

$$\cos \beta = \frac{OB}{d} = \frac{1}{2}, \qquad\qquad \beta = 60°.$$

$$\cos \gamma = \frac{OC}{d} = \sqrt{2}/2 = 1/\sqrt{2}, \qquad \gamma = 45°.$$

If the direction PO had been used in place of OP, the resulting direction angles would be supplements of those determined above.

The method of Example 1 may be generalized to give **direction cosines,** $\cos \alpha$, $\cos \beta$, $\cos \gamma$, of a line through points

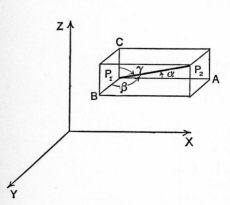

Fig. 24–19

$$P_1(x_1, y_1, z_1), \quad P_2(x_2, y_2, z_2),$$

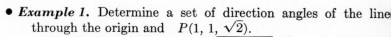

or of a directed line from P_1 to P_2. Construct a parallelepiped with edges parallel to the coordinate axes and P_1P_2 as diagonal. Then

$$|P_1P_2| = d = \sqrt{(x_2 - x_1)^2 + (y_2 - y_1)^2 + (z_2 - z_1)^2},$$

$$\begin{cases} \cos\alpha = \dfrac{P_1A}{d} = \dfrac{x_2 - x_1}{d} \\[2mm] \cos\beta = \dfrac{P_1B}{d} = \dfrac{y_2 - y_1}{d} \\[2mm] \cos\gamma = \dfrac{P_1C}{d} = \dfrac{z_2 - z_1}{d}. \end{cases} \qquad (24.2)$$

The three direction cosines are not independent since they satisfy the identity $\cos^2\alpha + \cos^2\beta + \cos^2\gamma = 1$. This is proved by noting that,

$$\cos^2\alpha + \cos^2\beta + \cos^2\gamma = \frac{(x_2 - x_1)^2}{d^2} + \frac{(y_2 - y_1)^2}{d^2} + \frac{(z_2 - z_1)^2}{d^2}$$

$$= 1. \qquad (24.3)$$

● **Example 2.** Determine a set of direction angles of the line through $(1, 2, 3)$ and $(2, 1, 3 + \sqrt{2})$.

$$d = \sqrt{(2 - 1)^2 + (1 - 2)^2 + (3 + \sqrt{2} - 3)^2} = \sqrt{1 + 1 + 2} = 2$$
$$\cos\alpha = (2 - 1)/2 = \tfrac{1}{2}, \qquad\qquad \alpha = 60°$$
$$\cos\beta = (1 - 2)/2 = -\tfrac{1}{2}, \qquad\qquad \beta = 120°$$
$$\cos\gamma = (3 + \sqrt{2} - 3)/2 = \sqrt{2}/2, \qquad \gamma = 45°.$$

The supplements of these angles form another set of direction angles. Three numbers, not all zero, which are proportional to the direction cosines of a line, are called **direction numbers** of the line. A set of direction numbers for the line of Example 2 is $[1: -1:\sqrt{2}]$. Another set is $[-3:3: -3\sqrt{2}]$. If a set of direction numbers $[l:m:n]$ of a line is known, then direction cosines may be obtained as

$$\cos\alpha = l/\sqrt{l^2 + m^2 + n^2}, \quad \cos\beta = m/\sqrt{l^2 + m^2 + n^2}$$

and

$$\cos\gamma = n/\sqrt{l^2 + m^2 + n^2}.$$

If the line is a directed line, the direction cosines are either those given, or their negatives. The reader is asked to prove this in Problem 9, Set 24–6.

● **Example 3.** Find direction angles α, β, γ of a line having direction numbers $[2: -3:6]$.

$$\cos\alpha = 2/\sqrt{4 + 9 + 36} = 2/7 \cong .29, \qquad \alpha \cong 73°.$$
$$\cos\beta = -3/7 \cong -.43, \qquad\qquad\qquad \beta \cong 116°.$$
$$\cos\gamma = 6/7 \cong .86, \qquad\qquad\qquad\quad \gamma \cong 59°.$$

PROBLEM SET 24-6

In Problems 1 to 8, sketch lines determined by the given points and obtain a set of direction cosines and three sets of direction numbers for each line.

1. $(0, 0, 0)$, $(1, \sqrt{2}, -1)$.   2. $(1, 2, -1)$, $(4, 3, -1)$.
3. $(3, 1, 7)$, $(4, 6, 3)$.   4. $(-1, 2, 5)$, $(4, 1, -6)$.
5. $(1, 2, 3)$, $(3, 1, -2)$.   6. $(4, -1, 1)$, $(-1, 6, 2)$.
7. $(4, 3, 5)$, $(2, 1, 4)$.   8. $(6, 1, 2)$, $(4, 2, 1)$.
9. Prove the formulas, giving direction cosines in terms of direction numbers, given just before Example 3.
10. Determine direction angles of a line having direction numbers $[3: -3:3/\sqrt{2}]$.
11. Find $\cos \alpha$ if $\beta = 60°$, $\gamma = 45°$. Find two possible values of α.
12. Determine direction cosines for each coordinate axis.
13. Show that the line through the origin and (a, b, c) has direction numbers $[a:b:c]$.
14. Show that the line through (x_1, y_1, z_1) and (x_2, y_2, z_2) has direction numbers $[x_2 - x_1:y_2 - y_1:z_2 - z_1]$. The quantities $x_2 - x_1$, $y_2 - y_1$, and $z_2 - z_1$ are called x, y, and z **components.**

24-7. The angle between two lines. The acute or right angle θ between two lines in space is defined as the acute or right angle between two lines through the origin, one parallel to each of the given lines. If direction numbers of two lines are

$$[l_1:m_1:n_1] \quad \text{and} \quad [l_2:m_2:n_2],$$

then the acute angle θ between these two lines is given by

$$\cos \theta = \frac{|\, l_1l_2 + m_1m_2 + n_1n_2\,|}{\sqrt{l_1^2 + m_1^2 + n_1^2}\sqrt{l_2^2 + m_2^2 + n_2^2}}. \qquad (24.4)$$

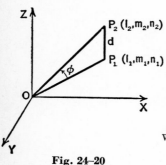

Fig. 24-20

Let L_1 and L_2 be lines with direction numbers $[l_1:m_1:n_1]$ and $[l_2:m_2:n_2]$, respectively. Then OP_1 is parallel to L_1 and OP_2 is parallel to L_2 for $P_1(l_1, m_1, n_1)$ and $P_2(l_2, m_2, n_2)$. Let $\phi = \angle P_1OP_2$.

The law of cosines states that in triangle OP_1P_2,

$$(P_1P_2)^2 = (OP_1)^2 + (OP_2)^2 - 2\,|\,OP_1\,||\,OP_2\,|\cos \phi,$$

where $\phi = \theta$, or $\phi = 180° - \theta$.

Using the distance formula this becomes,

$$(l_2 - l_1)^2 + (m_2 - m_1)^2 + (n_2 - n_1)^2 = l_1^2 + m_1^2 + n_1^2 + l_2^2 + m_2^2 + n_2^2$$

$$- 2\sqrt{l_1^2 + m_1^2 + n_1^2}\sqrt{l_2^2 + m_2^2 + n_2^2}\cos \phi.$$

Hence,

$$\cos \theta = \frac{|\, l_1 l_2 + m_1 m_2 + n_1 n_2\, |}{\sqrt{l_2^2 + m_2^2 + n_2^2}\sqrt{l_1^2 + m_1^2 + n_1^2}}$$

where θ is restricted to lie in the range $\quad 0° \leq \theta \leq 90°$.

● **Example 1.** Find the acute angle between lines having direction numbers $\quad [1\!:\!3\!:-2]\quad$ and $\quad [2\!:\!1\!:\!5]$.

$$\cos\ \theta = \frac{|\, 1\cdot 2 + 3\cdot 1 + (-2)5\, |}{\sqrt{1^2 + 3^2 + 2^2}\sqrt{2^2 + 1^2 + 5^2}} = \frac{|-5|}{\sqrt{14}\sqrt{30}} = \frac{\sqrt{105}}{42} \cong 0.24.$$

Using tables, one finds $\quad \theta \cong 76°$.

● **Example 2.** Show that two lines having direction numbers $[l_1\!:\!m_1\!:\!n_1]$ and $[l_2\!:\!m_2\!:\!n_2]$ are perpendicular if, and only if, $\quad l_1 l_2 + m_1 m_2 + n_1 n_2 = 0$.

If the two lines are perpendicular, then $\quad \theta = 90°\quad$ and $\cos \theta = 0$. Hence, $\quad l_1 l_2 + m_1 m_2 + n_1 n_2 = 0$. Conversely, if $l_1 l_2 + m_1 m_2 + n_1 n_2 = 0$, then $\quad \cos \theta = 0\quad$ and $\quad \theta = 90°$, so the lines are perpendicular.

The reader should note that skew lines may be perpendicular.

In Problem 9 of the next set, the reader is asked to show that two lines are parallel, if the direction numbers of one line are proportional to the direction numbers of the second line.

PROBLEM SET 24–7

1 to 8. Determine the acute angle between a line having direction numbers $\quad [1\!:-2\!:\!3]\quad$ and the lines of Problems 1 to 8, Set 24–6, respectively.

9. Show that two lines are parallel if their direction numbers are proportional.

[HINT: Assume $\quad l_1 = k l_2,\quad m_1 = k m_2,\quad n_1 = k n_2\quad$ and show that under this assumption $\quad \cos \theta = 1\quad$ and hence $\quad \theta = 0°$.]

10. Prove the converse of Problem 9.

11 to 18. Find a set of direction numbers of a line perpendicular to each line given in Problems 1 to 8, Set 24–6, respectively.

24–8. The plane. A line is said to be a **normal,** or perpendicular, to a plane if it is perpendicular to every line in the plane passing through the intersection † of the given line and the plane.

Theorem 1. If the normals (perpendiculars) to a plane have direction numbers $[l:m:n]$ and the plane passes through the point (x_1, y_1, z_1), then

$$l(x - x_1) + m(y - y_1) + n(z - z_1) = 0 \qquad (24.5)$$

is the equation of the plane. Conversely, an equation of this type represents the described plane.

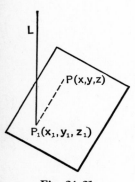

Fig. 24–21

Let L be a line through $P_1(x_1, y_1, z_1)$ having direction numbers $[l:m:n]$. Let $P(x, y, z)$ be a point different from P_1.

A set of direction numbers of P_1P is $[x - x_1:y - y_1:z - z_1]$. Line P_1P is perpendicular to line L if, and only if, P lies in the plane perpendicular to L at P_1. Then the sum of the products of their corresponding direction numbers is zero by Example 2, Section 24–7. Hence, $l(x - x_1) + m(y - y_1) + n(z - z_1) = 0$ if P is a point in the plane perpendicular to L at P_1. Conversely, if $l(x - x_1) + m(y - y_1) + n(z - z_1) = 0$, then P_1P is perpendicular to L.

● *Example 1.* Find an equation of the plane through $(9, -1, 5)$ and perpendicular to the line joining $A(4, 7, 2)$ and $B(2, 6, -1)$.

Normals to the plane have the direction numbers of the line AB, namely $[2:1:3]$. The plane has the equation

$$2(x - 9) + 1(y + 1) + 3(z - 5) = 0, \text{ or } 2x + y + 3z - 32 = 0.$$

Theorem 2. The locus of an equation $Ax + By + Cz + D = 0$ (with at least one of A, B, C not equal to zero) is a plane whose normals have direction numbers $[A:B:C]$.

Since not all of A, B, C are zero, we may, for convenience, assume $C \neq 0$. Then by Theorem 1,

$$Ax + By + C(z + D/C) = 0$$

is the equation of a plane through $(0, 0, -D/C)$ whose normals have direction numbers $[A:B:C]$.

If direction cosines are used in place of direction numbers, the equation of Theorem 2 becomes

$$(\cos \alpha)x + (\cos \beta)y + (\cos \gamma)z - p = 0. \qquad (24.6)$$

† In our extended definition of "perpendicular," a line which is normal to a plane is perpendicular to *every* line in the plane. Why?

This is the **normal form of the equation of a plane.** The distance between the origin and the plane, measured along the perpendicular to the plane from the origin, is $|p|$. The reader is asked to show this and a more general distance formula in Problem Set 24–9. Note the close connection between the normal form of the equation of a plane and the normal form of the equation of a line studied in Section 20–5 by letting $\gamma = 90°$ in the equation of the plane and recalling that $\cos(90° - \beta) = \sin \beta$.

The equation $Ax + By + Cz + D = 0$ may be put into normal form by dividing by $\pm \sqrt{A^2 + B^2 + C^2}$.

● **Example 2.** Find a set of direction cosines of the normal to the plane $3x + 5y - 2z + 12 = 0$.

Normalizing this equation one obtains

$$(3/\sqrt{38})x + (5/\sqrt{38})y + (-2/\sqrt{38})z + 12/\sqrt{38} = 0.$$

The direction cosines are $\pm [3/\sqrt{38},\ 5/\sqrt{38},\ -2/\sqrt{38}]$.

24–9. Equations of a line. Let L be a line through the point $P_1(x_1, y_1, z_1)$ with direction numbers $[l:m:n]$. If $P(x, y, z)$ is another point on this line, then a set of direction numbers of P_1P is $[x - x_1 : y - y_1 : z - z_1]$. Since these components are proportional to $[l:m:n]$ we have,

$$x - x_1 = tl; \quad y - y_1 = tm; \quad z - z_1 = tn.$$

Therefore,

$$x = x_1 + tl; \quad y = y_1 + tm; \quad z = z_1 + tn \qquad (24.7)$$

are a set of parametric equations of a line through (x_1, y_1, z_1) having direction numbers $[l:m:n]$. As t takes on all real values, the entire line is obtained. The value of t is proportional to the distance of the variable point $P(x, y, z)$ from the point $P_1(x_1, y_1, z_1)$.

● **Example 1.** Find parametric equations of a line through $(3, 1, -5)$ having $[2: -1:7]$ as a set of direction numbers.

$$x = 3 + 2t; \quad y = 1 - t; \quad z = -5 + 7t.$$

The parameter t may be eliminated to obtain,

$$t = \frac{x - 3}{2} = \frac{y - 1}{-1} = \frac{z + 5}{7}.$$

This form of equations of a line is known as the **symmetric form of the equations of a line.** In general, a line in space may be represented as the intersection of two planes.

This system of equations represents the line as the intersection of the planes $\dfrac{x-3}{2} = \dfrac{y-1}{-1}$ and $\dfrac{y-1}{-1} = \dfrac{z+5}{7}$.

● **Example 2.** The two planes

$$x + 3y - 5z + 1 = 0 \quad \text{and} \quad 2x - y - z + 4 = 0$$

intersect in a straight line. Find the equations of this line in symmetric form.

For every value of k, the equation

$$x + 3y - 5z + 1 + k(2x - y - z + 4) = 0$$

represents a plane through the desired line. Choosing $k = 3$ and $k = -5$, we obtain the two planes

$$7x - 8z + 13 = 0 \quad \text{and} \quad -9x + 8y - 19 = 0$$

which pass through the desired line and are each perpendicular to a coordinate plane. (Why were the values $k = 3$ and $k = -5$ chosen? Would another plane of the desired form be obtained by letting $k = -\frac{1}{2}$?) Solving each of the latter equations for their common variable x we find,

$$x = \frac{8z - 13}{7} \quad \text{and} \quad x = \frac{8y - 19}{9}.$$

A set of equations in symmetric form for the given line is

$$\frac{x}{1} = \frac{y - \frac{19}{8}}{\frac{9}{8}} = \frac{z - \frac{13}{8}}{\frac{7}{8}}, \quad \text{or} \quad \frac{x}{8} = \frac{y - \frac{19}{8}}{9} = \frac{z - \frac{13}{8}}{7}.$$

The given line passes through the point $(0, \frac{19}{8}, \frac{13}{8})$, and has direction numbers $[8:9:7]$.

A similar set of equations may be obtained by finding two points on the line, determining direction numbers of a line through these points, and then following the method of Example 1.

PROBLEM SET 24-9

1 to 8. Write the equation of a plane passing through the first point, and normal to the line joining the two points, given in Problems 1 to 8, Set 24–6, respectively.

Obtain the normal form of the equations given in Problems 9 to 15. Sketch each plane showing the length of its normal from the origin, and a set of direction cosines of this normal.

9. $3x + 2y - 6z - 21 = 0.$

10. $x - 8y + 4z + 72 = 0.$

11. $2x + 6y - 9z + 22 = 0.$

12. $4x - 7y = 4z - 9.$

13. $x - 2z = 12 - 2y.$

14. $9x - y + 6z = 33 + y.$

15. $12x - 18y + 36z = 7.$

16. Find the equation of the plane that has equal intercepts, and passes through $(1, 3, -5)$.

Sketch the lines given in Problems 17, 18, 19, 20. Find the direction cosines of each line.

17. $x = 5 - 2t, \quad y = 4 + 3t, \quad z = -1 - 6t.$

18. $\dfrac{x-3}{4} = \dfrac{y+1}{7} = \dfrac{z-2}{4}.$ **19.** $\dfrac{x+9}{4} = \dfrac{y-1}{2} = \dfrac{z-11}{4}.$

20. $\dfrac{x-5}{7} = \dfrac{y+6}{3} = \dfrac{z+1}{9}.$

21 to 28. Write parametric equations of the lines of Problems 1 to 8, Set 24–6, respectively.

Find symmetric equations of the lines determined by the pairs of planes given in Problems 29 and 30.

29. $4x + 3y - 2z = 5, \quad x - y + 2z = 4.$

30. $3x + 4y - z = 2, \quad 3x - y + z = 0.$

31. (a) Show that the distance between the point (x_1, y_1, z_1) and the plane $(\cos \alpha)x + (\cos \beta)y + (\cos \gamma)z - p = 0$ is $|(\cos \alpha)x_1 + (\cos \beta)y_1 + (\cos \gamma)z_1 - p|$. Compare Example 8, Section 20–5.

(b) Verify that the distance between the origin and the plane given in (a) is $|p|$.

(c) Show that the distance between the point (x_1, y_1, z_1) and the plane $Ax + By + Cz + D = 0$ is

$$|Ax_1 + By_1 + Cz_1 + D|/\sqrt{A^2 + B^2 + C^2}.$$

32. (a) Determine the distance between the plane $3x + 2y - 5z = 30$ and the point $(4, 2, -1)$.

(b) Find the coordinates of some point that *is on* the plane.

24–10. Cylindrical coordinates. In Chapter 17 we found that certain loci have simpler equations in polar coordinates than in rectangular coordinates. This is also true in three (and higher) dimensional space. We shall study two coordinate systems in addition to rectangular coordinates. The first of these, called **cylindrical coordinates,** may be thought of as replacing one of the coordinate planes, say, the xy plane, by the $r\theta$ plane of polar coordinates. Then the coordinates of a point in space are given by (r, θ, z). The following relations connect the rectangular (x, y, z) and cylindrical (r, θ, z) coordinates.

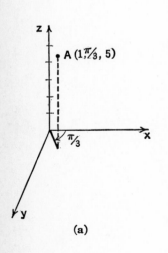

Fig. 24–22

Rectangular   Cylindrical

$$\begin{cases} x = r \cos \theta \\ y = r \sin \theta \\ z = z. \end{cases} \tag{24.8}$$

Also,

$$x^2 + y^2 = r^2.$$

It is usual to make the following restrictions on the ranges of values permitted in cylindrical coordinates: $r \geqq 0, \quad 0 \leqq \theta < 2\pi.$

In rectangular coordinates, the surfaces x equal to a constant, y equal to a constant, z equal to a constant, are planes parallel to the yz, xz, and xy planes, respectively. In cylindrical coordinates, the surface r equal to a constant is a circular cylinder with the z-axis as its axis. A plane containing the z-axis is obtained for θ equal to a constant. The locus z equal to a constant is a plane parallel to the $r\theta$ plane. The equations of cylinders (not necessarily circular) having directrix curves which are simple in polar coordinates will have simple surface equations in cylindrical coordinates. (Why?)

● **Example 1.** Locate the following points (r, θ, z) in a cylindrical-coordinate system:

$$A \left(1, \frac{\pi}{3}, 5\right), \quad B \left(2, \frac{\pi}{2}, -1\right), \quad C(3, 0, 4).$$

See Figure 24–23, (a), (b), and (c).

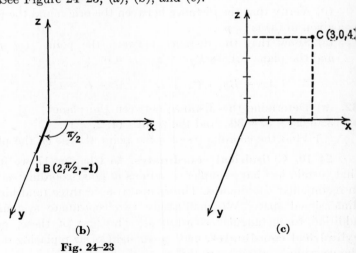

(a)   (b)   (c)

Fig. 24–23

● **Example 2.** Determine the cylindrical coordinate equation of a right circular cylinder of radius 2 having the z-axis as an element, and which is bisected by the xz plane.

Since the directrix in the $r\theta$ plane is $r = 4 \cos \theta$, the cylindrical surface also has the equation $r = 4 \cos \theta$. (Why?)

• **Example 3.** Find the equation, in cylindrical coordinates, of the locus having the rectangular coordinate equation

$$(x^2 + y^2)^2 = x^2 - y^2.$$

Upon substituting and reducing by use of identity (16.15) of Section 16–5 we obtain

$$r^4 = r^2 \cos^2 \theta - r^2 \sin^2 \theta$$
$$r^4 = r^2 \cos 2\theta$$

or

$$r^2(r^2 - \cos 2\theta) = 0.$$

The locus of $r^2 = 0$ is the z-axis. These points are also represented on the locus $r^2 = \cos 2\theta$.

• **Example 4.** Obtain cylindrical coordinates of a point having rectangular coordinates $(\sqrt{3}, 1, 5)$.

Either by substitution or directly from a sketch one obtains $(2, \pi/6, 5)$.

In a study of the calculus, certain problems that are very difficult in rectangular coordinates are more easily handled using cylindrical coordinates.

24–11. Spherical coordinates. In another useful coordinate system, called **spherical coordinates,** the point P has spherical coordinates (ρ, θ, ϕ), where ρ is the distance from the origin to the point P, $\theta = \angle XOQ$; where X is any point on the positive end of the x-axis and Q is the foot of the perpendicular from P to the xy plane; and ϕ is the plane angle from the positive z-axis to OP. The following relations may be verified from the figure.

$$x = \rho \sin \phi \cos \theta, \quad y = \rho \sin \phi \sin \theta, \quad z = \rho \cos \phi. \quad (24.9)$$

In spherical coordinates the locus of ρ equal to a constant is a sphere with center at the origin. A plane containing the z-axis is obtained for θ equal to a constant. The locus of ϕ equal to a constant is a cone with vertex at the origin and axis along the z-axis. The following restrictions are made on the ranges of values permitted in spherical coordinates: either

$$\rho \geqq 0, \quad 0 \leqq \theta < 2\pi, \quad 0 \leqq \phi \leqq \pi, \text{ or}$$

ρ any real value, $\quad 0 \leqq \theta < 2\pi, \quad 0 \leqq \phi \leqq \pi/2.$

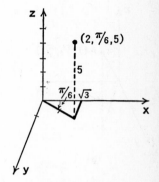

Fig. 24–24

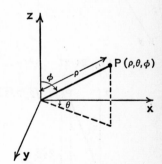

Fig. 24–25

● **Example 1.** Locate the following points (ρ, θ, ϕ) in a spherical-coordinate system

$$A(1, \pi/3, \pi/4), \quad B(2, \pi/2, \pi/6), \quad C(3, \pi/4, 2\pi/3).$$

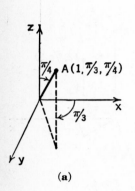
(a)

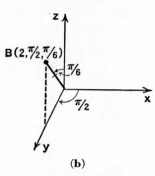
(b)

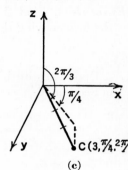
(c)

Fig. 24–26

● **Example 2.** Determine the spherical-coordinate equation of a cone having its axis along the z-axis, its vertex at the origin and such that a plane perpendicular to the axis of the cone and 4 units from the origin intersects the cone in a circle of radius 1.

In this case all points on the surface (and only such points) satisfy the condition $\phi = \arctan \frac{1}{4}$ and the desired equation is either $\phi = \arctan \frac{1}{4}$, or $\tan \phi = \frac{1}{4}$.

● **Example 3.** Obtain spherical coordinates for the points having rectangular coordinates $P(\sqrt{2}, \sqrt{2}, 2\sqrt{3})$.

By considering Fig. 24–28 we conclude that P has spherical coordinates $(4, \pi/4, \pi/6)$. (Why isn't $\phi = \pi/3$?)

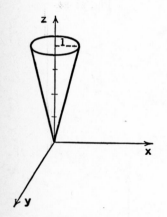

Fig. 24–27

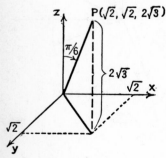

Fig. 24–28

PROBLEM SET 24–11

1. Locate the following points in a cylindrical-coordinate system and determine the rectangular coordinates of each point

$$A(7, \pi/2, 5), \quad B(4, \pi/3, -1), \quad C(0, \pi, 0), \quad D(1, 1, 1).$$

2. Locate the following points in a spherical-coordinate system and determine the rectangular coordinates of each point.

$$A(4, \pi/2, \pi/3), \quad B(2, \pi/3, \pi/2), \quad C(1, 0, \pi/6), \quad D(1, 1, 1).$$

In Problems 3 to 9 determine the equations of the given locus:
(a) rectangular coordinates, (b) cylindrical coordinates, (c) spherical coordinates.

3. A plane parallel to the xy plane and 5 units above it.

4. A sphere of radius 4 with center at the origin.

5. A right circular cylinder with the z-axis as axis of the cylinder, and radius 2.

6. Each coordinate plane   (that is, $x = 0$, $y = 0$, $z = 0$).

7. A sphere of radius 17, center at the origin.

8. A cone with vertex angle 30 degrees, vertex at the origin and axis along the z-axis.

9. An elliptical cylinder having an element along the z-axis, and such that its directrix is an ellipse having major axis 10 units and minor axis 6 units.

10. Name as many as possible of the surfaces given in Problems 11 to 15.

11. Sketch the volume common to

$$r^2 + z^2 = 16 \quad \text{and} \quad r = 4 \cos \theta.$$

12. Sketch the volume common to $r^2 + z^2 = 9$ and $r^2 = 9z$.

13. Sketch the volume common to $\phi = \dfrac{\pi}{4}$ and $\rho = 3$.

14. Sketch the volume bounded by

$$\theta = 0, \quad \theta = \frac{\pi}{4}, \quad \phi = 0, \quad \phi = \frac{\pi}{2}, \quad \rho = 2, \quad \rho = 3.$$

15. Sketch the volume bounded by

$$\theta = 0, \quad \theta = \frac{\pi}{4}, \quad r = 2, \quad r = 3, \quad z = 0, \quad z = 4.$$

In Problems 16 to 19, t is a parameter.

16. Sketch and discuss the locus of $r = 2$, $\theta = t$, $z = t$.
17. Sketch and discuss the locus of $r = 2t$, $\theta = t$, $z = t$.
18. Sketch and discuss the locus of $\rho = 2$, $\theta = t$, $\phi = t$.
19. Sketch and discuss the locus of $\rho = 2t$, $\theta = t$, $\phi = t$.

24–12. Self test.

Record your time.

1. Show that $(0, -2, -3)$, $(-4, -9, 1)$ and $(1, 2, 5)$ are vertices of an isosceles right triangle. What is the length of the altitude from the unequal side of the triangle?

2. Write a relationship which is satisfied by all points inside of and on a sphere with center $(2, 1, 5)$ which passes through $(1, 4, 9)$.

In Problems 3 to 7, sketch the surface whose equation is given. Name the surface.

3. $9x^2 - 4z^2 = 144$.

4. $4x^2 + 2y^2 - 3z = 24$.

5. $(x - 5)^2 + 4(y - 3)^2 + 25(z + 1)^2 = 900$.

6. $(y - 4)(z + 1) = 0$.

7. $9x^2 - y^2 - 36z^2 = 144$.

8. Sketch the surfaces $x^2 + y^2 + z^2 = 36$, $y^2 + (z - 3)^2 = 9$ and indicate their curve of intersection by a heavy curve.

9. Determine a set of direction cosines of a line passing through $(1, 3, -6)$ and $(-1, 8, -8)$.

10. Determine the equation of a plane perpendicular to the line of Problem 9, if the plane passes through $(2, -1, 3)$.

11. Change to cylindrical coordinates, and sketch the volume inside both surfaces: $x^2 + y^2 + z^2 = 100$, $x^2 + y^2 + 10x = 0$.

12. (a) Sketch the volume inside both surfaces:

$$\rho = 6, \quad \tan \phi = \tfrac{1}{2}.$$

(b) Find the rectangular-coordinate equations of these surfaces.

Record your time.

25–1. Chapter 25 deals with selected topics from more advanced mathematics. Each of these topics may be pursued further by consulting the references given in the reading list.

It is the sincere hope of the authors that the student of this book does *not* stop his mathematical education when his classroom education stops. If he will read books and subscribe to and read one of the less technical mathematical journals, his mathematical knowledge will continue to grow throughout his life. Many students find it helpful to read library copies of certain books and journals.

25–2. Matrix multiplication. To most students it may never have occurred that there exist algebras in which $A \cdot B$ and $B \cdot A$ are not the same thing. There are many such algebras. Portions of modern physics and chemistry are based on such "noncommutative" systems, as they are called.

The following simple experiment may convince doubters that, in the physical world in which we live, it does make a difference in what order things are done; that is, AB and BA are not always identical.

Place two closed books on the table in front of you with their faces upward and their spines (bound edge) on the left. This is the normal position in which a book might lie before it is opened. The books will remain closed throughout the experiment.

Rotate the first book through 90 degrees (a right angle) about its bottom edge. [It will now be standing upright on the table.] Now rotate the same book through 90 degrees about its spine. Leave the book in this position.

Rotate the second book through 90 degrees about its spine. [If the book were released at this point it would fall open in reading position.] Now rotate it through 90 degrees about its bottom edge.

Note that the two books are *not* in the same final position. Each book has been rotated through 90 degrees about its bottom edge and 90 degrees about its spine, but the order was not the same and the results are different. It is possible to use matrix theory to forecast the results of these and much more complicated problems involving rotations in three-dimensional, four-dimensional, or higher-dimensional space.

A matrix is a square array of numbers (elements) that has its multiplication defined in a special way. It should not be confused with a determinant, which is a single number or value associated with such a square array. A matrix is the array itself, not a single number. Two matrices are said to be equal if, and only if, elements in corresponding positions are identical. If

$$M = \begin{bmatrix} a & b \\ c & d \end{bmatrix} \quad \text{and} \quad N = \begin{bmatrix} w & x \\ y & z \end{bmatrix}$$

are two matrices, then their **product** $M \cdot N$ is

$$M \cdot N = \begin{bmatrix} a & b \\ c & d \end{bmatrix} \cdot \begin{bmatrix} w & x \\ y & z \end{bmatrix} = \begin{bmatrix} aw + by & ax + bz \\ cw + dy & cx + dz \end{bmatrix}.$$

The element in the first (horizontal) row and second (vertical) column of the product $M \cdot N$ is a sum of elements each of which is the product of an element from the first row of M multiplied by a corresponding element from the second column of N. Thus

$$\begin{bmatrix} a & b \\ * & * \end{bmatrix} \cdot \begin{bmatrix} * & x \\ * & z \end{bmatrix} = \begin{bmatrix} * & ax + bz \\ * & * \end{bmatrix}.$$

In a similar fashion the element in row R and column C of the product $M \cdot N$ is the sum of the products of the elements of the Rth row of M multiplied by the corresponding elements of the Cth column of N. If

$$A = \begin{bmatrix} 1 & -1 \\ 3 & 2 \end{bmatrix} \quad \text{and} \quad B = \begin{bmatrix} 7 & 4 \\ 5 & 8 \end{bmatrix},$$

then

$$A \cdot B = \begin{bmatrix} 1 & -1 \\ 3 & 2 \end{bmatrix} \cdot \begin{bmatrix} 7 & 4 \\ 5 & 8 \end{bmatrix} = \begin{bmatrix} (1)(7)+(-1)(5) & (1)(4)+(-1)(8) \\ (3)(7)+(2)(5) & (3)(4)+(2)(8) \end{bmatrix}$$

$$= \begin{bmatrix} 2 & -4 \\ 31 & 28 \end{bmatrix}.$$

However,

$$B \cdot A = \begin{bmatrix} 7 & 4 \\ 5 & 8 \end{bmatrix} \cdot \begin{bmatrix} 1 & -1 \\ 3 & 2 \end{bmatrix} = \begin{bmatrix} (7)(1) + (4)(3) & (7)(-1) + (4)(2) \\ (5)(1) + (8)(3) & (5)(-1) + (8)(2) \end{bmatrix}$$

$$= \begin{bmatrix} 19 & 1 \\ 29 & 11 \end{bmatrix}.$$

Thus, in 2 by 2 matrices, $A \cdot B$ and $B \cdot A$ are *not* the same

The reader may check his understanding of matrix multiplication by showing that

$$\begin{bmatrix} 3 & -5 \\ 1 & 2 \end{bmatrix} \cdot \begin{bmatrix} 7 & 4 \\ 6 & 10 \end{bmatrix} = \begin{bmatrix} -9 & -38 \\ 19 & 24 \end{bmatrix}.$$

In this article we have described 2 by 2 matrices, but larger matrices containing hundreds of elements are also used in practical applications. At the Naval Ordnance Testing Laboratories, matrices are used in computation concerning rocket and projectile flight. Matrices are used in modern economic theory. The branch of psychology known as **factor analysis** applies matrix methods. Systems of 35 (or more) equations in 35 (or more) unknowns which arise in industrial research may be neatly solved using matrix methods. Competent biologists and geneticists find matrix methods helpful in the study of the more complex interrelations of heredity. Large laboratories and oil refineries often ask universities for graduates who are dexterous in the use of matrices. *Elementary Matrices* by Frazer, Duncan, and Collar gives an idea of the extensive use of matrix theory in aeronautical engineering. The Pauli matrices, used in the study of electron spin in quantum mechanics, have an interesting arithmetic. The matrices are:

$$I = \begin{bmatrix} 1 & 0 \\ 0 & 1 \end{bmatrix}, \quad A = \begin{bmatrix} -i & 0 \\ 0 & i \end{bmatrix}, \quad B = \begin{bmatrix} 0 & 1 \\ -1 & 0 \end{bmatrix}, \quad C = \begin{bmatrix} 0 & -i \\ -i & 0 \end{bmatrix},$$

$$D = \begin{bmatrix} -1 & 0 \\ 0 & -1 \end{bmatrix}, \quad E = \begin{bmatrix} i & 0 \\ 0 & -i \end{bmatrix}, \quad F = \begin{bmatrix} 0 & -1 \\ 1 & 0 \end{bmatrix}, \quad G = \begin{bmatrix} 0 & i \\ i & 0 \end{bmatrix}.$$

The Pauli matrices form a **closed set** under matrix multiplication, in the sense that **the product of two or more Pauli matrices is again a Pauli matrix.** (Try it and see.)

The theory of composite functions is also more readily approached using matrix theory. For example,

	Equations	*Coefficient Matrices*
if	$W = 3U - 5V$ $Z = 1U + 2V,$	$\begin{bmatrix} 3 & -5 \\ 1 & 2 \end{bmatrix}$
where	$U = 7x + 4y$ $V = 6x + 10y,$	$\begin{bmatrix} 7 & 4 \\ 6 & 10 \end{bmatrix}$
then	$W = 3(7x+4y)-5(6x+10y)=-9x-38y$ $Z=1(7x+4y)+2(6x+10y)=19x+24y.$	$\begin{bmatrix} -9 & -38 \\ 19 & 24 \end{bmatrix}$

We noted above that,

$$\begin{bmatrix} 3 & -5 \\ 1 & 2 \end{bmatrix} \begin{bmatrix} 7 & 4 \\ 6 & 10 \end{bmatrix} = \begin{bmatrix} -9 & -38 \\ 19 & 24 \end{bmatrix}.$$

This is an example of a substitution of one equation into another, which can be performed using the coefficient matrices.

PROBLEM SET 25–2

In problems 1 to 5, find the matrix products indicated, where

$$A = \begin{bmatrix} -2 & 7 \\ -1 & 4 \end{bmatrix}, \quad B = \begin{bmatrix} -3 & 1 \\ 2 & 9 \end{bmatrix}, \quad C = \begin{bmatrix} 1 & 8 \\ 4 & 11 \end{bmatrix}, \quad D = \begin{bmatrix} 2 & 1 \\ 3 & 9 \end{bmatrix}.$$

1. AB, BA.   **2.** CB, BC.   **3.** AC, CA.   **4.** $A(CD), (AC)D$.
5. $B(DC), D(CB), C(BD)$.

6. Find a matrix $M = \begin{bmatrix} x & y \\ u & v \end{bmatrix}$, such that $MA = \begin{bmatrix} 1 & 0 \\ 0 & 1 \end{bmatrix}$.

Verify that, in this case, $AM = \begin{bmatrix} 1 & 0 \\ 0 & 1 \end{bmatrix}$.

7. Make a multiplication table for the Pauli matrices.

25–3. On prime numbers. A prime is an integer (whole number) greater than one that has no positive factors other than itself and one. The question of whether there are infinitely many primes, or whether there are only a finite number of primes (and hence a largest prime) was asked and answered in Euclid's time (circa 325 B.C.). The proof is interesting even today, and is reproduced here in slightly modified form. First, let us examine a few numbers.

$$\begin{aligned}
(2 + 1) &= 3 && \text{is a prime} \\
(2 \cdot 3 + 1) &= 7 && \text{is a prime} \\
(2 \cdot 3 \cdot 5 + 1) &= 31 && \text{is a prime} \\
(2 \cdot 3 \cdot 5 \cdot 7 + 1) &= 211 && \text{is a prime} \\
(2 \cdot 3 \cdot 5 \cdot 7 \cdot 11 + 1) &= 2311 && \text{is a prime}
\end{aligned}$$

but

$$(2 \cdot 3 \cdot 5 \cdot 7 \cdot 11 \cdot 13 + 1) = 30{,}031 = 59 \cdot 509 \text{ is } not \text{ a prime.}$$

However, all is not lost. If $N = (2 \cdot 3 \cdot 5 \cdot 7 \cdots p_k + 1)$ is one more than the product of all the primes less than or equal to a given prime p_k, then it is certainly true that none of the primes $2, 3, 5, 7, \cdots, p_k$ is a factor of N since if N is divided by one of these primes, there will always be a remainder of one. (Why?) We can*not* conclude that N will always be prime. (Why not?) We can conclude, however, that if N is factored into prime factors, each of its prime factors will be greater than p_k. [For example, in $(2 \cdot 3 \cdot 5 \cdots 13 + 1) = 30{,}031 = 59 \cdot 509$ each of the prime factors of 30,031 is greater than 13. Similarly the prime 2311 is greater than 11.] We use this observation, and the indirect method of proof (reductio ad absurdum) to prove:

Theorem 1. There is no largest prime.

Assume there is a largest prime. Call it p_k.

$$\text{Form } N = (2 \cdot 3 \cdot 5 \cdot 7 \cdots p_k + 1).$$

Since N does not have p_k nor any smaller prime as a factor, either N is a prime larger than p_k or the prime factors of N must each be larger than p_k. In either case our assumption that p_k was the largest prime is false. Our conclusion is that **there is no largest prime** — that is, that **there exist infinitely many primes.**

In spite of the antiquity of this proof, and the generations of mathematicians who have studied primes, the primes hold their secrets well. Given a prime, Euclid's proof will enable you to produce a larger prime, but even today no one has developed a formula that, given a prime, will produce the *next largest* prime.

Given the prime 5, Euclid's method produces $(2 \cdot 3 \cdot 5 + 1) = 31$, which is a prime larger than 5, but the next larger prime is 7, not 31.

It has been shown that there is no algebraic formula that will produce all of the primes and only primes.

In 1742 Goldbach made two conjectures,

(1) Every even number $K \geq 6$ is the sum of two odd primes.

(2) Every odd number $K \geq 9$ is the sum of three odd primes.

Both conjectures have been shown to be true for $K \leq 100{,}000$ and in 1937 Vinogradov proved that there exists an integer M such that for all odd $K > M$ the second conjecture is valid, but no one has been able to determine how large M is. V. Brun recently showed that every even integer K can be written as the sum of two odd integers, each of which has *nine or fewer factors*, but "nine or fewer factors" is a long way from "prime." Even more recently the "nine" in the statement was reduced to "four." Goldbach's conjectures, however, are still unproved.

● **Problem.** *Prove:* If a positive integer $N > 1$ has no prime factor less than or equal to $\sqrt{N}$, then n is a prime. Apply the method to test 2857 for primeness.

It is known that every set of nonnegative integers contains a least integer which is in the set.

The set of integers $xa + yb$ where a and b are fixed integers and are not both zero and x and y are arbitrary integers contains both a and b as well as $-a$ and $-b$. How could you choose x and y to show this? One of the four integers $\pm a, \pm b$ is positive. Therefore, the set contains a least positive integer g which implies there exist $x = s$ and $y = t$ such that $sa + tb = g$.

If d is a common divisor of a and b, then d divides $sa + tb$ that is, d divides g.

We wish to show that g divides both a and b. Write a in the form $a = kg + r$ where k and r are integers with $0 \leqq r < g$. (Is this always possible?) Using $g = sa + tb$, $r = a - kg = (1 - ks)a - kt$ is in the set. Now $r = 0$, since $r > 0$ would contradict being the *least* positive integer in the set. Hence, $a = kg$. Similarly it can be shown that g divides b.

A greatest common positive divisor g of two integers a and b not both zero, is defined by

(1) If d divides both a and b then d divides g.
and
(2) g divides both a and b.

The preceding work derives

Theorem 2. The greatest common positive divisor g of two integers a and b, not both zero, can be expressed as a linear combination of a and b in the form

$$sa + tb = g, \quad \text{where } s \text{ and } t \text{ are integers.}$$

Now we can prove

Theorem 3. If a prime p divides a product of integers $a \cdot b$ then p divides a, or p divides b.

Proof: If p divides a we are through. If p does not divide a then p and a have greatest common positive divisor 1. (Why?) From the preceding theorem there exist integers s and t such that

$$sa + tp = 1$$

Now

$$sab + tpb = b$$

Since p divides both ab and pb, it follows that p divides $sab + tpb$ that is, p divides b.

- **Problem.** Prove that a positive integer N can be expressed uniquely in the form

$$N = p_1^{e_1} \, p_2^{e_2} \cdots p_k^{e_k} \quad \text{where} \quad p_1 < p_2 < \cdots < p_k \quad \text{are primes.}$$

25–4. Angle trisection. A problem originally proposed by the ancient Greeks was solved completely or rather disposed of in 1837 by P. L. Wantze at the age of 23, but it remains a perennial favorite among amateur mathematicians. The problem is this: Given an arbitrary angle, construct an angle exactly (*without theoretical error*) equal to one third the size of the given angle *using a Euclidean straight edge, a Euclidean compass, and only those constructions permitted in Euclidean geometry.* A Euclidean straight edge is capable of only one operation — namely, constructing a line through two given points. It has no markings on it and may not be used to transfer distances or "snuggle up tangent to a curve." A Euclidean compass is also capable of only one operation — namely, drawing a circle (or an arc of a circle) having a given radius and a given center. These are the only tools and the only operations permitted in the classical problem of trisecting an angle. Excellent *approximate* trisections have been known using these tools since before the time of Christ. Exact trisections using constructions that are not permitted with the Euclidean straight edge and Euclidean compass have also been known for generations.

Large universities receive letters and personal visits each year from people who have devised methods of trisecting an angle. These people *do not realize* that they have not solved the classical problem of trisecting exactly a general angle using only Euclidean constructions. Their "angle trisections" fall into one or more of four classes. (1) Some of these proposed trisections contain errors. We shall say no more about this classification. (2) A method of determining an angle one third the size of some special angle of known size is sometimes given. This is not of much interest. Any student of geometry can construct an angle equal to one third of a right angle. (How?) A little thought shows how to construct an angle equal to one third of a 45-degree angle. Many other such constructions are easily obtained and well known. (3) Some of the proposed constructions use the tools permitted in the classical problem to obtain an *approximate* trisection of a general angle of unknown size. Excellent approximate constructions have been known since the time of Euclid. These constructions are interesting, but have nothing to do with the classical problem. Furthermore they are of little practical value since a good protractor permits an approximate trisection with more accuracy and less effort. (4) The fourth classification contains methods of obtaining an **exact trisection of a general angle.** Many trisections of this

type are known, but none use only Euclidean constructions. Some
use an auxiliary curve such as a parabola, limaçon, or the conchoid
of Nicomedes to help determine the trisections. A trisection of
particular interest was discovered by Archimedes. It uses a
Euclidean compass and a straight edge upon which *one mark has
been placed*. (It is, therefore, no longer a Euclidean straight edge.)
We present it here for your interest.

Angles larger than 90 degrees may be considered as the sum of
an acute angle and a multiple of 90 degrees. Since $(90°)/3 = 30°$
is easily constructed, we need only trisect acute angles. Suppose
AOB is an acute angle to be trisected.

Draw a circle of convenient radius, r, with center O. Let I
be the intersection of the circle with OB. Extend AO through O.
A mark M is placed r units from one end R of a straight edge.
(This violates a rule of Euclidean construction.) Place the straight
edge with its end R on the line AO extended, and mark M on the
circle, slide the straight edge until it passes through I. (This is
not a difficult feat to accomplish, but neither the sliding nor the
mark on the straight edge are permissible Euclidean constructions.)
Draw the line IMR. Angle IRO is one third of the given angle AOB.
This is an *exact* trisection using only a marked ruler and compass,
but it is *not* a Euclidean construction. The proof that angle IRO
is actually one third of angle AOB is left as a problem for the
reader.

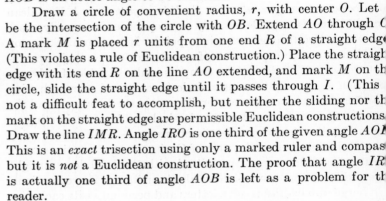
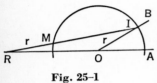

Fig. 25–1

One of the most interesting things about the angle trisection
problem is that the problem no longer exists. It has actually been
proved that it is *impossible* to trisect a general angle *using only
a Euclidean straight edge and Euclidean compass and those constructions permitted in Euclidean geometry*. It is *not* a case of no
one yet having found such a construction; it is actually impossible.
There is a close connection between algebra and geometry. (We
have already written the equation of a straight line and a circle.)
Using this connection it can be shown that the trisection of an
angle is equivalent to solving the equation $4x^3 - 3x + k = 0$
where the value of k depends upon the angle to be trisected. If
this equation has a solution that *does not involve cube roots* (it is
all right if the solution involves square roots but *not* cube roots)
then the angle can be trisected by Euclidean methods. Otherwise
it cannot. If $k = 0$ or $k = \pm 1$, then the equation has solutions of the desired type, but if $k = \frac{1}{2}$ the solutions involve cube
roots. Therefore there exist angles that cannot be trisected by
Euclidean constructions. Since this has been known for more than
100 years, it seems strange that people who are interested in the
problem do not take the trouble to find out what is already known.
Geometry is, after all, a game that must be played according

its rules. Changing the rules changes the game. No one argues that the new game is not also interesting, but it is a different game. It is fairly easy to prevent your opponent from scoring at basketball if one of your men climbs up and sits on your basket, but this is not the way the game is played under present rules.

25–5. The Möbius strip — a one-sided surface. Most surfaces have two sides. A sheet of paper, a cylinder, and a spherical surface each has two sides. It is possible to paint the two surfaces different colors, say red and green, to distinguish them. The colors will not meet except at the edge of the surface. If a line or curve is drawn from a point on the red surface to a point on the green surface, it must either cross an edge or pierce the surface.

Although it is difficult to think of a surface as having only one side, there are such things.

The German mathematician Möbius discovered one that is simple to make. Take a long rectangular strip of paper (adding-machine tape will do admirably, or a 2-inch strip of newspaper). The two ends may be pasted together in such a manner that a short cylinder is formed. This surface has two sides. However, if a half twist is given to the strip before pasting the ends together, a one-sided Möbius surface results. Think of one side of the two-sided flat strip as being sticky (like gummed tape). To form a cylinder the sticky surface is pasted to the nonsticky surface. To form a Möbius surface the tape is given a half twist and ends pasted together with the sticky surfaces touching. It is easy to see that the resulting surface is actually one-sided by attempting to color only one side.

If a line is drawn between the "parallel edges" of a Möbius surface, it will take a line twice as long as the original strip to return to the starting position. (Try it!) Before performing the next experiment, try to forecast the result. Take a strip of paper 2 inches wide and about 3 feet long. Draw a pencil line the full length of one side of the strip, halfway between the edges. Make a Möbius surface with a half twist, by pasting the ends together so that the ends of the unlined surfaces are stuck to one another. Now cut the Möbius surface apart along the pencil line. It takes excellent geometric insight to predict the result if you are unfamiliar with the Möbius surface. It is even more difficult to predict what will happen if this resulting surface is again cut along its middle, or if another Möbius surface is cut along lines parallel to the edge and one third of the distance across the strip.

It seems strange that a single half twist can so completely change the nature of a surface. In this case, a two-sided surface is changed into a one-sided surface. The Möbius surface also has

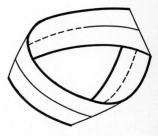

Fig. 25–2

Fig. 25-3

only one edge. (Color the edge and see.) If a cylinder is cut down the middle, two cylinders result. If a Möbius strip is cut down its middle, a single loop is obtained. If this loop is again cut along its middle, two separate, but intertwined, loops are obtained. If the Möbius strip is cut along a line parallel to the edge and one third of the distance across the strip, a large and a small intertwined loop are obtained.

A university collection of mathematical models may contain a Klein bottle, an interesting one-sided surface. The Klein bottle will hold water, yet it has neither inside nor outside. The Möbius strip and Klein bottle could provide an interesting talk or discussion for a speech class or mathematics club.

The study of surfaces arises naturally in mathematics. In order to be certain that the results are general, we are forced to study **all types** of surfaces. In this way one is led to such special surfaces as the Möbius surface and the Klein bottle.

25–6. Magic squares. A "magic square" is a square array of numbers having the property that the sum of the numbers in any row, or any column, or either main diagonal is the same. For example,

$$
\begin{array}{ccc}
1 & 12 & 7 & 14 \\
8 & 13 & 2 & 11 \\
10 & 3 & 16 & 5 \\
15 & 6 & 9 & 4
\end{array}
$$

$$
\begin{array}{ccc}
8 & 1 & 6 \\
3 & 5 & 7 \\
4 & 9 & 2
\end{array}
\quad \text{or} \quad
\begin{array}{ccc}
17 & 3 & 13 \\
7 & 11 & 15 \\
9 & 19 & 5
\end{array}
$$

In the 4 by 4 magic square, the horizontal rows each have sum 34, the vertical columns each have sum 34, as do the diagonals

$$1 + 13 + 16 + 4 = 34 \quad \text{and} \quad 15 + 3 + 2 + 14 = 34.$$

Magic squares appear in the earliest mathematical writings of the Hindus and Arabs and were known to the Chinese much earlier than this (2200 B.C.). No one knows when they actually originated.

It is possible to construct magic squares having fractional and negative entries but nothing is really gained from this. If the same number is added to (or subtracted from) each element of a magic square, the result is still a magic square. Thus negative numbers need not be considered as elements. A magic square also remains a magic square if each element is multiplied by the same constant; hence any square containing fractions may be changed into a magic square of whole numbers.

Magic squares (and even magic cubes) have long been a favorite pastime of great thinkers. They appear in the background of several famous paintings, in Dürer's "Muse," for example. Benjamin Franklin constructed a 16 by 16 magic square of which he was very proud. For years the study of magic squares was purely

16	3	2	13
5	10	11	8
9	6	7	12
4	15	14	1

From Dürer's "Muse."

Fig. 25–4

recreational. Now, however, they are used extensively in sample theory and testing. If a biologist wishes to test several types of seed under similar growing conditions, he cannot divide his field into strips and plant one strip in each crop since a natural soil fertility gradient, effect of topography, or other factor may influence one strip more than another. The field is divided into a large magic square, and the seeds sown according to a predetermined schedule. In this way a more equitable distribution is obtained. Magic squares are used extensively in statistical studies. In mathematics, the new theory of loops and certain portions of combinatorial topology may be introduced using magic squares. Thus an ancient mathematical pastime once again proves useful to modern man.

25–7. Perfect numbers. In this discussion the word *integer* will mean a *positive whole number* such as 1, 2, 3, 4, $\cdots$.

If a positive integer R divides a positive integer N, then R is called a divisor of N. For example, the divisors of 18 are 1, 2, 3, 6, 9, and 18. An integer is said to be an improper divisor of itself. All other divisors are called **proper divisors.** The proper divisors of 18 are 1, 2, 3, 6, and 9 (not 18).

An integer N is said to be **perfect** if the sum of the proper divisors of N is N. For example, the proper divisors of 6 are 1, 2, and 3; and since $1 + 2 + 3 = 6$, six is a **perfect number.** The number 28 is a perfect number, since the proper divisors of 28 are 1, 2, 4, 7, and 14; with sum $1 + 2 + 4 + 7 + 14 = 28$. The four smallest perfect numbers are 6, 28, 496, and 8128. The fifth perfect number is 33,550,336. The eighth perfect number contains 19 digits.

Perfect numbers were studied by the ancient Greeks and are still of interest today. They hold their secrets well.

No one knows whether an odd integer can be perfect. None has been found, yet no one has proved they do not exist. Since 1949 it has been shown that if an odd perfect number exists, it must be greater than 10 billion and must be equal to either $12m + 1$ or to $36m + 9$ for some whole number m. Still no odd perfect number has been discovered.

More is known about even perfect numbers. For example, *every* even perfect number must end in either 28 or 6. Another interesting fact is that the sum of the reciprocals of the divisors of an even perfect number must equal 2. The perfect number 6 has divisors 1, 2, 3, 6, and their reciprocals total $1 + \frac{1}{2} + \frac{1}{3} + \frac{1}{6} = 2$. In a similar fashion, the divisors of 28 are 1, 2, 4, 7, 14, 28 and their reciprocals total $1 + \frac{1}{2} + \frac{1}{4} + \frac{1}{7} + \frac{1}{14} + \frac{1}{28} = 2$. This fact has been proved true for *every* even perfect number.

An integer P, greater than 1, is said to be **prime** if its only positive divisors are 1 and P. Examples of prime numbers are 2, 3, 5, 7, 11, 13, 17, 19, $\cdots$. An important theorem on perfect numbers states that $2^{P-1}(2^P - 1)$ is an even perfect number if *and only if* $2^P - 1$ is prime, and that every *even* perfect number is of this form. If, for example, $P = 2$, then $2^2 - 1 = 3$ is prime. Thus $2^{2-1}(2^2 - 1) = 2(3) = 6$ is perfect. If $P = 3$, then $2^3 - 1 = 7$ is prime, and $2^{3-1}(2^3 - 1) = 2^2(7) = 28$ is perfect. If $P = 4$, $2^4 - 1 = 15$ is not prime and hence $P = 4$ does not lead to a perfect number.

The first four perfect numbers were discovered by the end of the first century. By 1870 only four more had been found. Between 1870 and 1950 four additional even perfect numbers were discovered. Considering all the facts and formulae known about perfect numbers, it is surprising to realize that in the 2000 years prior to 1951 only 12 perfect numbers had been discovered. Since then five more perfect numbers have been found, using the SWAC (giant brain) computing machine at the National Bureau of Standards Institute for Numerical Analysis at U.C.L.A. They are $2^{520}(2^{521} - 1)$, $2^{606}(2^{607} - 1)$, $2^{1278}(2^{1279} - 1)$, $2^{2202}(2^{2203} - 1)$, $2^{2280}(2^{2281} - 1)$. This last number contains 1372 digits.

Now it is known that $N = 2^{P-1}(2^P - 1)$ is perfect for $P = 2, 3, 5, 7, 13, 17, 19, 31, 61, 89, 107, 127, 521, 607, 1279, 2203$ and 2281, and that N is not perfect for any other P less than 2300. However, the principal problems, namely, "How many perfect numbers are there?" and "Do odd perfect numbers exist?" are still unsolved mysteries which await you, or one of your contemporaries.

PROBLEM SET 25-7

1. Prove that the non-Euclidean construction given in Section 25-4 does trisect angle AOB.
2. Construct several Möbius strips and cut them as described in Section 25-5.
3. Prepare a 5- or 10-minute talk on one of the articles in this chapter.
4. Construct a 3 by 3 and a 4 by 4 magic square.
5. Show that 8128 is a perfect number.

6. Estimate the number of digits contained in the largest perfect number mentioned in Section 25–7. Use logarithms.

7. Prepare a report on an article from one of the following journals: *American Mathematical Monthly, Mathematics Magazine, Mathematics Teacher, Scripta Mathematica, School Science and Mathematics.*

8. Prepare a book report on one of the books given in the Reading List at the end of this chapter.

25–8. Fermat's "last theorem." Fermat was a mathematician of considerable renown. Probably the most famous problem of Fermat is the one known as **Fermat's "last theorem."** The theorem is easy to state, and seems to be true, but in spite of 300 years of work by expert and amateur mathematicians it remains unproved. Fermat wrote (in the margin of a book) that he had discovered a remarkable proof of the theorem, but he died before he completed the manuscript in which he planned to record his proof. It is easy to find positive integers (whole numbers) x, y, z such that $x + y = z$. There are also many triples of positive integers x, y, z such that, $x^2 + y^2 = z^2$. The triples 3, 4, 5 and 5, 12, 13 are examples. Many others also exist. You may be surprised to discover that it is impossible to find positive integers x, y, z such that $x^3 + y^3 = z^3$ or such that $x^4 + y^4 = z^4$. These facts are proved in a course in Number Theory. Fermat's Last Theorem (still unproved) states that, if n is an integer greater than 2, then it is impossible to find positive integers x, y, z, such that $x^n + y^n = z^n$.

Some people wonder if Fermat really had a proof, or if he made some error. The truth or falsity of the theorem is of little real importance today, but *some extremely profound modern mathematics has been developed as a result of attempts to prove this theorem.* Kummer's theory of ideal divisors, which is used extensively in current research in mathematics and physics, was developed in an attempt to prove Fermat's last theorem.

In Germany a prize of 100,000 marks was offered in 1908 for a general proof to be given before the year 2007 (the German inflation of 1920 made the prize worthless). By 1857 it had been shown that Fermat's theorem holds for all exponents n between 3 and 100. Since then it has been shown that the theorem holds (that is, that there are no positive integers x, y, z such that $x^n + y^n = z^n$) for n between 3 and 616. The use of modern high-speed computing machines may eventually lead to the discovery of a counter example. Huge numbers will be involved.

25–9. The number $2^{64} - 1$. According to an old legend, Sissa Ben Dahir was granted a boon by King Shirhâm for inventing the game of chess. Sissa asked if the king would be willing to give him enough wheat so that he had one grain for the first square of the chess board, two for the second square, four for the third square, and so on, doubling each time, for the entire 64 squares of the chess board. The king agreed and even chided Sissa for making so modest a request. Actually Sissa asked for more wheat than the entire world would grow during his lifetime.

At the present rather advanced rate of wheat production it would take more than 20,000 years for the United States to produce the grains that were promised Sissa Ben Dahir. The student should show that the number of grains is $2^{64} - 1$, and that this is as large as the above statement implies.

25–10. The four-color problem. Maps are usually constructed so that countries having a common boundary line are shown in distinct colors. If each country had a distinctive color then the geographer would need as many colors as countries. Yet a checkerboard map requires only two colors, and for more general maps it is economical to use as few colors as possible. When several countries meet at a point, like the wedge-shaped pieces of a pie, it is considered necessary only for neighboring wedges to have distinctive hues. With three concurrent wedges, three colors are needed, but for four wedges (or any even number) two will do (say red and green alternately), and for an odd number of wedges a third color must be used at least once. If a circle is divided into three such sectors, and the whole surrounded by another region, this map will require four distinct colors.

One might suspect that as more complex maps are studied more and more colors will be needed. It can be proved mathematically that no map, no matter how complex, will ever require more than five colors. The Kempe-Heawood proof uses Euler's polyhedral theorem which states that for any solid polyhedron the total number of faces and vertices together exceed the number of edges by two: $F + V = E + 2$. On the other hand, no map on plane or sphere has ever been found that required more than four colors. Are maps requiring five colors possible? This is the famous "four-color problem" which has been studied since 1840, but so far without a clearcut solution. At least one authority on the four color problem believes that eventually a map that requires five colors will be found. Some authorities believe otherwise.

The reader may be interested in the general method used in attacking this problem. If there are maps that require five colors then there will be a simplest example, such that any map of fewer countries can certainly be colored with four colors. Such a simplest counter example to the four-color "theorem" is called

minimal map. If two adjacent countries of any minimal map are united into one country, the modified map would be four colorable, since it is below the minimum that requires five.

Many properties are known for minimal maps. For instance, there will be no points at which four or more countries meet (as do the states Utah, Colorado, Arizona, and New Mexico). In other words, all vertices are triple; that is to say, all pies are cut in precisely three sectors. It is also readily shown that a minimal map must contain at least 12 countries with exactly 5 neighbors, and that no country has fewer than 5 neighbors. Whoever draws a minimal map will have to use at least 38 countries.

Linear equations involving 274 unknowns may be used in this research. They are studied using chromatic matrices having magic square properties.

We conclude with the rather surprising observation that although this problem has *not* been solved for maps drawn on a plane or sphere, it has been completely solved for more complicated surfaces like the torus or doughnut (seven colors are required and sufficient), and for a sugar-bowl surface with two handles. More about the four-color problem can be found in *Mathematics and the Imagination* by Kasner and Newman, *What Is Mathematics?* by Courant and Robbins, or a pamphlet on *The Four-color Problem* by Philip Franklin, published by Scripta Mathematica.

25–11. Quaternions. Section 25–2 describes a system of 2 by 2 matrices. It was found that in this system $A \cdot B$ and $B \cdot A$ were not necessarily equivalent — that is, the system is noncommutative. Another, much simpler, noncommutative system is formed by quaternions.

A complex number is a number $a + bi$, where a and b are real numbers, and $i^2 = -1$. All the usual laws of algebra hold.

A quaternion is a number $a + bi + cj + dk$, where a, b, c, and d are real numbers, and $i^2 = j^2 = k^2 = ijk = -1$. Here $\pm i$, $\pm j$, and $\pm k$ are considered to be six different numbers. All the usual laws of algebra except the commutative law hold. From this definition it follows that

$$ij = k, \quad jk = i, \quad ki = j,$$

but

$$ji = -k, \quad kj = -i, \quad ik = -j.$$

Thus, if

$$\alpha = 2i + k \quad \text{and} \quad \beta = 1 + j,$$

then

$$\alpha\beta = (2i + k)(1 + j) = 2i + 2ij + k + kj = i + 3k,$$

but

$$\beta\alpha = (1 + j)(2i + k) = 2i + k + 2ji + jk = 3i - k.$$

Hence $\alpha\beta$ is not equal to $\beta\alpha$. The quaternions were discovered 100 years ago by Sir William Rowen Hamilton. His courage in discarding the commutative law (that $AB = BA$) was the first step in a new mathematics. Hamilton's discovery of quaternion algebra helped J. W. Gibbs to develop the theory of vectors and rotations in three-dimensional space. Today, the theory of electron spin in quantum mechanics employs, essentially, the same quaternions discovered by Hamilton. Without quaternions as a steppingstone, it is doubtful if the vector analysis of three dimensions or matrix theory would have been discovered as soon as they were (circa 1885), and much of today's physics, chemistry, and engineering would not exist.

25–12. A finite geometry. The possiblity of a geometry that contains only a few points is a stimulating thought. Several such finite geometries are known. We shall examine one. We must, however, agree to drop conventional ideas of what are meant by "point" and "line" (undefined objects in geometry) and adopt the meanings given by a set of postulates. Although many sets of postulates might be formulated, the set that follows has been selected for its fruitfulness in interesting theorems. This set of postulates allows many of the theorems of ordinary plane geometry to be proved. The reader may find it interesting to construct a different set of postulates and definitions and see how many theorems may be proved using them.

Postulates

A	B	C	D	E
F	G	H	I	J
K	L	M	N	O
P	Q	R	S	T
U	V	W	X	Y

A	I	L	T	W
S	V	E	H	K
G	O	R	U	D
Y	C	F	N	Q
M	P	X	B	J

A	X	Q	O	H
R	K	I	B	Y
J	C	U	S	L
V	T	M	F	D
N	G	E	W	P

1. There are exactly 25 points in the geometry, and these points are designated by the 25 letters $A, B, C, \cdots, Y$.
2. A line consists of five points located either in a row, or in a column of one of the three blocks at the left. Thus, there are exactly 30 lines in the geometry. Examples of lines are $ABCDE$, $CHMRW$, $YCFNQ$, and $ASGYM$. The points A, B, and J do *not* lie on the same line.
3. A line segment (point pair) is congruent to another line segment when *both* of the following conditions hold:
   (a) Both pairs occur in row lines, or both in column lines as in the table at the left.
   (b) The number of (directed) steps between the points is the same in each pair. In counting directed steps between points we shall always count to the right in rows, and down in columns; and the first letter of a row or column will be considered as following the last. Thus, in line $ABCDE$ there are two steps from B to D, one from B to C, and another from C to D. There are three steps from D to B (D to E

E to A, A to B). So AC and XJ and CS are all congruent, but AK is not congruent to AC. (Why not?) The number of steps between two points is the **distance** between the points. Either the directed or the undirected distances may be considered, but they should not be confused. It is sometimes desirable to count in the mod 5 system (see Section 1–15).

4. Two lines are parallel if they have no point in common.
5. A line l_1 is perpendicular to a line l_2 if, and only if, there exist two points z_1 and z_2 on l_1 such that for each point z on l_2, the absolute distance $|z_1 z|$ is equal to the absolute distance $|z_2 z|$. Thus the two lines $ABCDE$ and $AFKPU$ are perpendicular since we may take $z_1 = E$ and $z_2 = B$.

A	B	C	D	E
F	G	H	I	J
K	L	M	N	O
P	Q	R	S	T
U	V	W	X	Y

A	I	L	T	W
S	V	E	H	K
G	O	R	U	D
Y	C	F	N	Q
M	P	X	B	J

A	X	Q	O	H
R	K	I	B	Y
J	C	U	S	L
V	T	M	F	D
N	G	E	W	P

It is of interest to discover how many theorems of ordinary geometry may be obtained in this 25-point geometry. It is easily shown by examination, and hence need not be postulated, that two distinct points determine a line, and that two distinct lines either intersect in one point, or are parallel. Three points not on the same line determine a "triangle." The points R, V, A all lie in the first column of block three, and are collinear. The points J, C, B determine a triangle. Furthermore, by postulate 3, the segments JC and BJ are congruent (each has "length" one step and both lie in rows). Hence the triangle JCB is an isosceles triangle. The triangle AST is scalene; the triangle HRL is equilateral.

Here are some of the theorems that hold both in ordinary Euclidean geometry and in this 25-point geometry.

1. The three altitudes of a triangle meet at a point α.

2. The perpendicular bisectors of the three sides of a triangle meet at a point β.

3. The three medians of a triangle meet at a point μ.

4. The point of concurrence μ of the three medians of a triangle lies on a line joining the points α and β mentioned above, and divides it in the ratio of 2:1.

It is possible to develop an extensive theory of parallelograms and quadrilaterals in this geometry.

If, as in ordinary geometry, a circle is defined as the locus of all points at a given distance from a fixed point (center), many theorems may be obtained. A circle of radius AB and center A contains the six points B, E, I, W, X, H, and no others. The point F, for example, is *not* on this circle. The number of steps from A to F is 1, just as in AB, but the distances are not equal (that is, the segments are not congruent) since AB lies in a row but AF lies in a column (see Postulate 3).

The ellipse, hyperbola, and parabola all have counterparts in this geometry. Theorems such as "the locus of midpoints of a system of parallel chords of a parabola is a line perpendicular to the directrix," and "at the point where this locus meets the parabola, the tangent to the parabola is parallel to the system of chords" can be proved. It is even possible to work out a rigorous theory of area in this 25-point geometry.

An interesting 121-point geometry is given in the paper "A Finite Geometry" by Alonzo Church, available from the Galois Institute of Mathematics at Long Island University, Brooklyn, New York. Finite geometries have applications in group theory, number theory, and lattice theory.

PROBLEM SET 25-12

1. (a) Draw a map containing ten regions such that the map can be colored with two colors in such a manner that two regions having a common boundary line are colored differently (b) Draw a map containing ten regions which can*not* be colored with two colors. (c) Draw a map containing as few regions as you can (that is, a minimal map) such that four colors are required to color it in such a manner that regions having a common boundary line are colored differently.

2. Solve the quaternion equations: (a) $(4 + 7i + 4k)X = 3 + 2j$ (b) $X(4 + 7i + 4k) = 3 + 2j$.

3. Can you find a relationship between the Pauli Matrices discussed in Section 25-2 and the quaternions discussed in Section 25-11?

4. Verify two of the assertions made about the finite geometry given in Section 25-12. Can you find other theorems?

5. Everyone loves a good puzzle. Here is one which you may enjoy. Hold a piece of solid glass rod about $\frac{1}{4}$-inch above the phrase

DECIDED MYSTERY! CHECK UNUSUAL CHOICE PUZZLE

and read the phrase through the glass rod.

You will note that some words appear to be inverted while others do not. Why? A striking display model of this puzzle may be made by using red and black ink for alternate words. It illustrates a principle discussed in Section 4-7.

6. Read and report on the article "Geometry and Intuition" by Hans Hahn, *Scientific American*, Vol. 190, No. 4 (April 1954) pp. 84–91.

25–13. Cryptography. Many people have become interested in writing secret messages in cipher. Neophytes often use the word *code* when they mean *cipher*. If the reader wishes to know the distinction, he should read one of the articles mentioned at the end of this section. The first type of cipher that may suggest itself is the substitution of a cipher-symbol or letter for each letter in the original plain-text message. For example, A may become T, B may become X, etc. This is actually a mapping (correspondence) of the 26 letters onto itself or some other set of 26 symbols. The beginner soon finds he can "break" — that is, solve without the key — this type of cipher. It provides an interesting pastime.

The thoughtful person may increase the security of his cipher by letting the most common letters (E, A, T, O, ⋯ in English) have several alternate symbols (variants) to reduce their relative frequency. When the student learns that Mary, Queen of Scots, was beheaded in 1587 as a result of information Walsingham obtained by breaking a simple substitution cipher with variants, as such ciphers are called, he becomes less certain of the security of his innovation.

This section introduces the ingenious Playfair cipher for the reader's consideration. It was used during World War I as a field cipher by both the British and American armies. The Playfair is certainly superior to simple substitution with variants, yet it is not, at present, considered secure. It is written as follows:

A key word or phrase (here the phrase "LAZY BONES") is selected. A large square divided into 25 smaller squares (or cells) is constructed and the letters of the key phrase are inserted, beginning at the upper left-hand corner. If any letter is repeated in the key it is used only the first time it occurs. The remaining letters of the alphabet are used to fill up the square. In English the letters I and J are considered as one letter and written together in the same square.

```
L A Z Y B
O N E S C
D F G H IJ
K M P Q R
T U V W X
```

The text of the message is then broken up into pairs of letters and equivalents are found for each pair. When any pair comes out a double letter, TT for example, it is replaced by TXT before further breaking of the message into pairs.

Case I. If both letters appear in the same column, each letter is replaced by the letter directly below it, with the convention that the bottom letter of a column is to be replaced by the letter at the top of that column. In our example FU is represented by MA.

Case II. If both letters appear in the same row, each letter is replaced by the letter directly to the right of it, with the convention that the first letter of the row is the successor of the last. In our example AB becomes ZL.

Case III. If the letters appear at opposite corners of a rectangle, each letter of the pair is represented by the letter in the other corner of the rectangle in the same column with it. In our example HR becomes QI, while HN becomes SF. All possible combinations may be enciphered in this fashion.

L	A	Z	Y	B
O	N	E	S	C
D	F	G	H	IJ
K	M	P	Q	R
T	U	V	W	X

The message "CIPHERS ARE FUN"

Message	CI	PH	ER	SA	RE	FU	NX
Cipher	IR	GQ	PC	YN	CP	MA	UC

when transmitted by telegraph in groups of 5 letters (to reduce errors in transmission) becomes

IRGQP CYNCP MAUCX.

Nulls are added where needed to complete a group. A mathematician may think of this as a mapping of the set of 600 (I and J are one letter, no doubles) letter pairs onto itself. Thought of from this viewpoint the Playfair is again a substitution cipher, and frequency charts (of pairs) are available which will help him to break this cipher. An expert cryptanalyst with two clerks to assist him can usually break a Playfair cipher in 3 or 4 hours *if sufficient material is available.* Under war conditions it takes somewhat longer — perhaps 5 or 6 hours, on the average. As an army field cipher, however, the Playfair functions well, since it is sufficient if the enemy be kept from deciphering the order until the order has been carried out.

One of the most used ciphers during World War II was a small machine in which the sender first sets a key number on a series of setting wheels, and then "types" out the message; the machine does the rest. These machines (C–38 and BC–38) were invented in Sweden before World War II and were sold on the open international market as Hagelin converters. *Both the Allies and the Axis used the same machine for secret communication during the war, yet provided considerable security for each.* The entire machine is much smaller than a portable typewriter and can easily be carried in the field. Even if the enemy captures the machine, it is of little help to him *as long as the key number is not left on the setting wheels.* If an enemy discovers the key being used on a given day, he can read that day's intercepted messages. The next day, however, when the key number is changed, he is no better off than he was before. A photograph and further description of the Hagelin converter are contained in the *Scripta Mathematica* article mentioned below.

An excellent and still remarkably secure cipher was devised by Lester Hill using matrix multiplication.

The reader who wishes to learn more about cryptography and cryptanalysis may read the articles "Cryptanalysis" in *Scripta Mathematica*, Vol. 18, No. 1 (March 1952) and "Cryptography as a Branch of Mathematics" in *The Mathematics Teacher*, Vol. 45, No. 7 (November 1952). Chapter 14 of the revised edition of *Mathematical Recreations and Essays* by Ball and Coxeter is another easily available source of information which the interested reader should consult.

25–14. Number systems. The reader has probably heard that our number system is "positional, based on 10," and may even know what this means. The idea is simple. The number **476** really means $4 \times 10^2 + 7 \times 10 + 6$ while

$$20395 = 2 \times 10^4 + 0 \times 10^3 + 3 \times 10^2 + 9 \times 10 + 5.$$

In general, only the *coefficients* of the powers of 10 are listed and the *position* tells to what power of 10 the coefficient belongs. It may be of interest to note why 10 was chosen as a base. The answer lies in fact that man has 10 fingers. Primitive man showed "5 double-hands and 3 fingers" meaning 53. Some of the primitive tribes still use this system, and in English the word "digit" means both "a finger" and "one of the fundamental blocks on which our counting system is based."

We shall use a subscript in parentheses to indicate the base. Thus:

$$13_{(10)} = 1 \times 3^2 + 1 \times 3 + 1 = 111_{(3)}.$$

The Binary System with base 2 is one of the easiest, and most important systems.

● *Illustration.* $101_{(2)} + 111_{(2)} = 1100_{(2)} = 2^3_{(10)} + 2^2_{(10)} = 12_{(10)}$,

$$101_{(2)} \times 111_{(2)} = 100011_{(2)} = 2^5_{(10)} + 2_{(10)} + 1_{(10)} = 35_{(10)},$$

where

$101_{(2)} = 2^2_{(10)} + 1_{(10)} = 5_{(10)}$ and $111_{(2)} = 2^2_{(10)} + 2_{(10)} + 1_{(10)} = 7_{(10)}$.

This system is of great importance today since many of the new high-speed computing machines use the base 2 for all computations. An electrical switch has only 2 positions (open, and closed) and the binary system needs only 2 digits (0, and 1). Thus, they are well suited to work together. The main disadvantage of the binary system is that binary expressions are *long*. For example, $6895_{(10)} = 1,101,011,101,111_{(2)}$. Note that $101_{(2)} = 5_{(8)}$, $11_{(2)} = 3_{(8)}$, $111_{(2)} = 7_{(8)}$ etc. To overcome the difficulty of length and still have the electronic advantages of the binary notation, many modern computers use the octal (base 8) system externally and base 2 internally.

$$6895_{(10)} = 1,101,011,101,111_{(2)} = 15357_{(8)}$$

There are desk calculators that use the base 8 system, and most large-scale computer installations have one for checking purposes.

Number systems with bases other than 10 can afford many interesting puzzle problems. An interesting application of the binary system is found in the game of Nim. (See *Mathematical Recreations* by Maurice Kraitchik or *Selections from Modern Abstract Algebra* by R. Andree.) The theory of Nim has been completely analyzed using the binary system.

The student who wishes to acquire a greater understanding of number systems is urged to work a few examples in the base 8 system.

$$\begin{array}{r} 472_{(8)} \\ +\ 135_{(8)} \\ \hline 627_{(8)} \end{array}$$

Note that in the second column $7_{(8)} + 3_{(8)} = 12_{(8)}$. Hence we write down the 2 and "carry" the 1. Check your understanding by carrying out the following problems. Do *not* convert to base 10, operate in the base 8 system.

$547_{(8)}$	$462_{(8)}$	$364_{(8)}$	$472_{(8)}$	$763_{(8)}$
$+\ 215_{(8)}$	$+\ 176_{(8)}$	$+\ 516_{(8)}$	$-\ 15_{(8)}$	$-\ 65_{(8)}$
$764_{(8)}$	$660_{(8)}$	$1102_{(8)}$	$455_{(8)}$	$676_{(8)}$

Make up some additional problems of your own.

25–15. Computing machines. Desk calculators have been in use for years, but it was not until World War II that large automatic calculators came into existence. The first of these Mark I, went into operation in August 1944. Industry has demanded more and better machines until today there are thousands and thousands of automatic computers, in hundreds of designs, operating in businesses throughout the United States. There may be one in your home town — certainly there are several in the nearest large city.

A modern computer is certainly one of the wonders of the age. Consider, for example, a column of 60,000 ten-digit numbers

$$\left.\begin{array}{l} + \ 4728361954 \\ + \ 8731825961 \\ - \ 6969823754 \\ + \ 1987681009 \\ \qquad \cdot \\ \qquad \cdot \\ \qquad \cdot \end{array}\right\} 60{,}000 \text{ of them,}$$

some of which are positive and some negative. How long would it take you to total this column of 60,000 ten-digit signed numbers? How much would you charge to sum them, and guarantee accuracy? The IBM 650 is a modern medium-speed computer. It can easily do this task in 1 *minute* at a cost of about $1.50. The University of Oklahoma Research Computer, NORMAN 1066, which was completed in 1961, can do this problem in less than $\frac{1}{2}$ *second* at a cost of about 2 cents. The bigger the computer, the more it costs per hour, but the less it costs per job is the usual rule.

Modern computers have phenomenally fast arithmetic and storage (memory) facilities which use diodes, transistors, television tubes, magnetic tape recordings, magnetic core, and magnetic drums. Those of the future will probably use cryostats.

These then are the secrets of the so-called "Giant Brains." They are unbelievably fast and phenomenally accurate. They do what they are told to do, and some machines are so fast they can be told to do a million different things every minute. It is not surprising that the Sunday newspaper supplements refer to these machines as "Giant Brains" and yet they are *not* brains. Indeed a six-month-old baby has a more competent brain than the most advanced machine. Fundamentally, all the machine can do is to recognize the presence or the absence of a mark or hole in a piece of paper. A six-month-old child can recognize this and much more. He also recognizes his parents and differentiates between friends and strangers. He knows cold from warm and will respond to a smile. What then is the advantage of the computing machine? The advantage is that the computer is *fast and accurate*, and that it can be depended upon to do what it is told to do. There is the rub too! The machine *must* be told what to do. It must be programmed. The Sunday supplement says that in 7 minutes this machine can compute a problem which would take over a year to compute using desk machines. This is true, but what the Sunday supplement fails to relate is that it may take a highly paid mathematician as many as 2500 man-hours (that's more than a working year) to program the machine to do this 7-minute calculation. The question then arises, "What is gained by using the machine?" The answer is that if you are solving only *one* problem of a given type, you may waste time by using a big computer. In modern industry, however, it is usual to solve thousands of problems of the same type involving different numbers. Each of these may be solved using the same program. Thus once a program is set up for a particular problem, additional problems of the same type may be solved in short order.

Furthermore, very ingenious programs have been written which will take mathematical statements of a typical problem and translate them into a machine program. This is what is meant when people say, "That machine can write its own programs."

In the design of modern rockets and supersonic aircraft, it is not feasible to make models and test each possible design and variation. Instead, mathematicians now set up mathematical equations that consider all possible significant effects, and computing machines are programmed to solve these equations. Thus, by changing one or two input numbers, the machine will accurately predict the final behavior of the rocket. Twenty-five different rocket designs may be tested in 2 minutes using these computers, *once the computer has been programmed*. Thus, many thousands of different designs may be completely tested in the mathematical laboratory in less time than it requires to construct one model — and at much lower cost. Friends ask if these large-scale computers will not put the professional mathematicians out of business. This question displays a lack of basic knowledge about mathematics. Let us say that mathematics has *nothing* to do with arithmetical computation. By the time computation begins, the *mathematics* of the problem is already completed. It is not unusual for a mathematician to work for weeks or months without encountering a number in the usual sense of the word. He works with ideas and logic. Since the time of the Babylonians, the bugbear of the mathematician has been the long hours he must set aside from his fascinating mathematics to perform the drudgery of arithmetic. When arithmetical computation begins, the mathematics has already been completed. The fact that machines developed in the last ten years can now relieve man of computational drudgery means that the mathematician has more time for creative thinking. You may easily recognize the spectacular increase in the demand for trained mathematicians by noting that big industries now employ thousands of mathematicians, men and women with master's degrees and with Ph.D. degrees in mathematics. The demand for competent mathematicians is growing each year, and industrial salaries are so attractive that there is a great shortage of competent people to train future mathematicians. One industrial authority refers to the century from 1850 to 1950 as the age of the engineer and predicts that the century beginning in 1950 will be known as the age of the mathematician. Judging by the number of research engineers who are returning to obtain advanced degrees in mathematics, he may well be correct.

PROBLEM SET 25–15

1. Make up a message using the Playfair square given in Section 25–13 and trade messages with a classmate.
2. Read the references given in Section 25–13 and prepare an oral report for your English or speech class.
3. Express the following numbers in the base 10 system: (a) $132_{(3)}$, (b) $11010_{(2)}$.
4. Express the numbers $297_{(10)}$ and $34_{(10)}$ in each of the following bases: (a) 2, (b) 3.
5. Show that if a number (base 10) is divisible by 3, the sum of its digits is divisible by 3.
6. A merchant has a two-pan balance and the five weights of 1, 3, 9, 27, 81 ounces, respectively. Show that he can weigh any amount in ounces up to 121 ounces since weights may be placed in either pan. [HINT: Consider base 3 system.]
7. Make up a set of rules for addition and multiplication in the base 2 system, and carry out the following:
   (a) $1101_{(2)} + 101101_{(2)} + 10110_{(2)}$, (b) $(101001_{(2)}) \times (101_{(2)})$,
   (c) $1011_{(2)} - 110_{(2)}$.
8. Visit the computer laboratory at your college, university, or some nearby university. Report on your findings to the class.

Suggested Reading List

The following books and journals are suggested for further reading. Some a serious reading, others are pure entertainment, but all are worthwhile. Mo of them are available in school libraries.

Adler, I., *New Mathematics* (Day, 1958)
> With elementary algebra and plane geometry as tools, Adler ski) fully builds up many interesting concepts of modern mathematics.

Andree, R. V., *Programming the IBM Magnetic Drum Computer an Data-Processing Machine* (Holt, Rinehart and Winston, 1958)
> Basic programming for modern computers. This clearly written boo has been used in both high school and college-level courses.

Andree, R. V., *Selections from Modern Abstract Algebra* (Holt, Rineha) and Winston, 1958)
> A college-level book which includes congruences (modular algebra) Boolean algebra (set theory), groups, fields, matrices, etc.

Ball, W. W. R., and **Coxeter, H. S. M.,** *Mathematical Recreations an Essays* (Macmillan, 1953)
> A classic book on recreational mathematics which should be o every library shelf. Very enjoyable.

Begle, E. G., *Introductory Calculus with Analytic Geometry* (Holt, Rine hart and Winston, 1954)
> Covers topics usually treated in a first course in calculus; include analytic geometry through the conics. Carefully written and authori tative. Fine supplementary reading.

Bell, E. T., *Mathematics, Queen and Servant of Science* (McGraw-Hil) 1951)
> A fine book.

Bell, E. T., *Men of Mathematics* (Simon & Schuster, 1937)
> Another well-written book with a historical slant.

Boehm, G. A. W., *New World of Math* (Dial, 1959)
> An excellent, inexpensive book derived from three articles in Fortun magazine. Highly recommended.

Brixey and **Andree,** *Fundamentals of College Mathematics* (Holt, Rinehart and Winston, 1961)
> This lively book carefully integrates introductory calculus and statistical inference with college algebra, trigonometry, and analytica geometry. You have it in your hands now, why not read it?

Carnap, R., *Foundations of Logic and Mathematics* (Univ. of Chicago 1939)
> Basic logic.

Carroll, L., *Pillow Problems and a Tangled Tale* (Dover, 1959)
> "Pillow Problems" (1893) contains 72 mathematical puzzles, all

typically ingenious. The problems in "A Tangled Tale" (1895) are in story form. Carroll not only gives the solutions, but uses answers sent in by readers to discuss the wrong approaches and misleading paths, and grades them for insight.

Cell, J. W., *Engineering Problems Illustrating Mathematics* (McGraw-Hill, 1943)

Some fine problems here having an engineering slant.

CEEB, Commission on Mathematics, College Entrance Examinations Board, *Introductory Probability and Statistical Inference for Secondary Schools* (CEEB, 1959)

Introduction to probability concepts and to the mathematics involved in them; illustration of how these concepts apply to certain common statistical problems. This was written by people who really know statistics, and is not just a rehash of averages and deviations.

Courant, R., and **Robbins, H.,** *What Is Mathematics?* (Oxford, 1941)

Not an easy book, but well worth the effort. Contains excellent work on basic mathematical analysis. Portions can be read and enjoyed by all, but some parts require mature cogitation.

Court, N. A., *College Geometry* (Barnes and Noble, 1952)

Probably the best known of all advanced plane geometry texts. Has even been translated into Chinese. Requires no background beyond the usual high school course.

Court, N. A., *Mathematics in Fun and Earnest* (Dial, 1958)

An entertaining book which illustrates Dr. Court's thesis that mathematics in earnest should be fun; mathematics in fun may be in earnest. Requires little background, but will prove to be an exercise of reasoning power.

Cundy, H. M., and **Rollett, A. P.,** *Mathematical Models* (Oxford, 1952)

A discussion of the construction of various mathematical models.

Dadourian, H. M., *How to Study; How to Solve* (Addison-Wesley, 1958)

This is a book designed to help students who are having trouble with mathematics. An excellent volume, and well worth the modest price.

Dantzig, T., *Number; The Language of Science* (Macmillan, 1954)

Subtitled "A Critical Survey Written for the Cultured Non-Mathematician," this is a historical treatment of the number concept and its importance in modern life. Well written.

Dresden, A., *An Invitation to Mathematics* (Holt, Rinehart and Winston, 1940)

A fine and enjoyable book.

Dubisch, R., *Nature of Number; An Approach to Basic Ideas of Modern Mathematics* (Ronald Press Co., 1952)

A direct and understandable way to gain an over-all view of what mathematics is about, and an insight into the nature of its theory.

Dudeney, H. E., *Amusements in Mathematics* (Dover, 1959)

A selection of over 400 mathematical puzzles. Everyone will enjoy this book. Many book stores stock it.

Eves, H., and **Newsom, C. V.,** *Introduction to the Foundations and Fundamental Concepts of Mathematics* (Holt, Rinehart and Winston, 1957)
A sound book which students will enjoy reading.

Freeman, M. B. and **I. M.,** *Fun With Figures* (Random, 1946)
Following the "do-it-yourself" idea, the authors show in this book how to have fun with geometric figures. Not much math, but worth the price for fun.

Gaines, H. F., *Cryptanalysis: A Study of Ciphers and their Solutions* (Dover, 1955)
This introductory intermediate-level text is the best book in print on cryptograms and their solutions.
Gamow, G., *One, Two, Three · · · Infinity* (Mentor Books, 1954)
Problems of mathematics, physics, and astronomy clarified for the layman. This paperback should be available in book stores.
Gamow, G., and **Stern, M.,** *Puzzle-Math* (Viking, 1958)
Interesting brain-twisters and puzzles based on everyday situations that can be untangled by mathematical thinking.
Gardner, M., *Best Mathematical Puzzles of Sam Loyd* (Dover, 1959)
A delightful collection of puzzles by one of the greatest puzzle makers of all time. A classic. Book stores have a hard time keeping this in stock.
Gardner, M., *Mathematics, Magic and Mystery* (Dover, 1955)
Another interesting, inexpensive paperback by the mathematical editor of *Scientific American.* Well worth the price.
Gehman, *Opportunities in Mathematics* (Vocational Guidance Manuals, 1961)
If mathematics interests you, find out about the many employment opportunities available.

Hoel, P. G., *Elementary Statistics* (Wiley, 1960)
An excellent elementary presentation of basic statistics.
Huff, D., and **Geis, I.,** *How to Lie with Statistics* (Norton, 1955)
Humorous, but penetrating and authoritative explanation of the basic conceptions and misconceptions of statistics. Vivid illustrations in cartoon style fully capture and even extend the content.
Huff, D., and **Geis, I.,** *How to Take a Chance* (Norton, 1959)
Entertaining but soundly exact discussions of various aspects of chance, probability, and error, especially as applied to everyday life.
Hunter, J. A. H., *Figurets: More Fun with Figures* (Oxford, 1958)
More mathematical puzzles, these problems are cast in the form of entertaining anecdotes.

NCTM, *Paper Folding for the Mathematics Class* (NCTM, 1957)
Illustrated directions for folding the basic constructions, geometric concepts, circle relationships, products and factors, polygons, knots, polyhedrons, symmetry, conic sections, recreations.

Johnson and Glenn, *Topology; Pythagorean Theorem; and Sets — Sentences and Operations* (Webster, 1961)

>Three well-written, inexpensive booklets of what promises to be an excellent series of twelve.

Jones, B. W., *Elementary Concepts of Mathematics* (Macmillan, 1947)

>Designed for the nonmath student, this text clarifies such concepts of everyday importance as compound interest, averages, probability, games of chance, graphs, etc.

Kasner, E., and **Newman, J.,** *Mathematics and the Imagination* (Simon & Schuster, 1940)

>An outstanding book which can be read and enjoyed by all. Not merely a "puzzle book"; this volume contains some excellent mathematical ideas.

Kline, M., *Mathematics in Western Culture* (Oxford, 1953)

>This book gives a remarkably fine account of the influence mathematics has exerted on the development of philosophy, the physical sciences, religion, and the arts in Western life.

Kokomoor, F. W., *Mathematics in Human Affairs* (Prentice-Hall, 1942)

>Another interesting book with historical overtones.

Kraitchik, M., *Mathematical Recreations* (Dover, 1953)

>One of the most thorough compilations of recreational mathematical problems. Highly recommended.

Kramer, E. E., *Mainstream of Mathematics* (Oxford, 1952)

>A historical treatment of mathematical thought from primitive numbers to relativity.

Levinson, H. C., *The Science of Chance: From Probability to Stastistics* (Holt, Rinehart and Winston, 1950)

>Compact, highly readable survey of chance and statistics, covering many forms of speculation and risk in business, as well as the odds in games of chance.

Lieber, H. G., and **L. R.,** *Non-Euclidean Geometry* (Galois Institute, 1940)

>Various geometries needed for different surfaces, treated postulationally, making Euclidean and non-Euclidean geometries easier and interesting. Very readable.

Lieber, H. G., and **L. R.,** *The Education of T. C. Mits* (Norton, 1944)

>A delightful, easy to read book that contains some interesting philosophy as well as mathematics.

McCracken, D. D., *Digital Computer Programming* (Wiley, 1957)

>An excellent book on advanced computer programming using a mythical machine TYDAC.

Menger, K., *YOU Will Like Geometry* (Museum of Science and Industry, 1948)

>A delightful and inexpensive little pamphlet which discusses unusual curves. Needs little or no mathematical background.

Mott-Smith, G., *Mathematical Puzzles for Beginners and Enthusiasts* (Dover, 1954)

>Another collection of 188 interesting mathematical puzzles in an inexpensive edition.

Ore, O., *Number Theory and Its History* (McGraw-Hill, 1948)
> One of the most readable books on elementary number theory with many interesting historical references.

Polya, G., *Mathematics and Plausible Reasoning* (Princeton University Press, 1954)
> This is a guide to the practical art of plausible reasoning; the first volume deals with induction and analogy in mathematics, the second with patterns of plausible inference.

Rademacher, H., and **Toeplitz, O.,** *The Enjoyment of Mathematic* (Princeton University Press, 1956)
> Probably the most outstanding "popular" mathematics book. Each chapter starts with simple observations easily within the grasp of all and smoothly catapults the reader into the heart of a genuine research-type problem. Highly recommended for good students.

Ringenberg, L. A., *A Portrait of 2* (NCTM, 1956)
> Written to enlarge the reader's concept of number, this pamphlet discusses the number 2 as an integer, a rational number, a real number and a complex number. Lays an excellent foundation for modern mathematical ideas.

Sawyer, W. W., *Mathematician's Delight* (Penguin, 1943)
> A well-written popular volume, dispelling the fear that surround mathematics.

Sawyer, W. W., *Prelude to Mathematics* (Penguin, 1955)
> A delightful account of some stimulating and surprising branches of mathematics. Highly recommended. Some book stores stock the with their paperbacks.

Steinhaus, H., *Mathematical Snapshots* (Oxford, 1950)
> Pictures help visualize mathematics; the simple text and clear illustrations make this a book to be enjoyed by anyone with a knowledge of algebra. Many interesting suggestions for models and projects.

Waerden, B. L., *Science Awakening* (Stechert-Hafner, 1954)
> Published by Noordhoff in Holland, but available in the United States as indicated above. This is the finest history of mathematics book known to your authors and is warmly recommended.

Whitehead, A. N., *An Introduction to Mathematics* (Oxford, 1948)
> A highly recommended book by a well-known English mathematician.

Wilder, R. L., *Introduction to the Foundations of Mathematics* (Wiley, 1957)
> A fine book which stresses set theory and logic. Not always easy to read, but well worth the effort.

Williams, J. D., *The Compleat Strategyst* (McGraw-Hill, 1954)
> An excellent book on the theory of game strategy. Although written in a light vein, it provides a sound introduction to this fast-growing field of modern mathematics.

Wylie, C. R., *101 Puzzles in Logic and Reasoning* (Dover, 1957)
> Brand new problems requiring no special knowledge to solve. Introduction with simplified explanation of general scientific method and

puzzle solving. A fine book to stimulate logical thinking. Most book stores stock this one.

23rd Yearbook of National Council of Teachers of Mathematics (NCTM, 1957)

Provides background and reference material for both the content and spirit of modern mathematics. Not always easy reading, but an excellent reference book for better students.

24th Yearbook of National Council of Teachers of Mathematics, The Growth of Mathematical Ideas Grades K-12 (NCTM, 1959)

An excellent book not only for teachers, but also for students interested in modern concepts.

PUBLISHER'S ADDRESSES

The mailing address of a given publisher may be obtained from local libraries and book stores, but a list is included for the reader's convenience.

Addison-Wesley Publishing Co., Inc., Reading, Mass.

Barnes and Noble, Inc., 105 Fifth Ave., New York 3, N.Y.

Commission on Mathematics, College Entrance Examination Board, P.O. Box 592, Princeton, N.J.

CRC, 2310 Superior Ave., N.E., Cleveland, Ohio

John Day Co., 210 Madison Ave., New York 3, N.Y.

Dial Press, Inc., 461 4th Ave., New York 16, N.Y.

Dover Publications, Inc., 920 Broadway, New York 10, N.Y.

E. P. Dutton and Co., 300 Fourth Ave., New York 10, N.Y.

Holt, Rinehart and Winston, Inc., 383 Madison Ave., New York 17, N.Y.

Macmillan Co., 60 Fifth Ave., New York 11, N.Y.

McGraw-Hill Book Co., Inc., 330 W. 42nd St., New York 36, N.Y.

Mentor Books, New American Library of World Literature, Inc., 501 Madison Ave., New York 22, N.Y.

Museum of Science and Industry, E. 57th St. and S. Shore Drive, Chicago, Ill.

National Council of Teachers of Mathematics, 1201 16th St. N.W., Washington 6, D.C.

W. W. Norton and Co., 55 Fifth Ave., New York 3, N.Y.

Oxford University Press, 1600 Pollitt Dr., Fair Lawn, N.J.

Penguin Books Inc., 3300 Clipper Mill Road, Baltimore 11, Md.

Prentice-Hall, Inc., Englewood Cliffs, N.J.

Princeton University Press, Princeton, N.J.

Random House, Inc., 457 Madison Ave., New York 22, N.Y.

Ronald Press Co., 15 E. 26th St., New York 10, N.Y.

Simon & Schuster, Inc., 136 W. 52nd St., New York 19, N.Y.

Stechert-Hafner, Inc., 31 E. 10th St., New York 3, N.Y.

University of Chicago Press, 5750 Ellis Ave., Chicago 37, Ill.

D. Van Nostrand Co., Inc., 120 Alexander St., Princeton, N.J.

Viking Press, 625 Madison Ave., New York 22, N.Y.

Vocational Guidance Manuals, 212 48th Ave., Bayside 64, N.Y.
Webster Publishing Co., 108 Washington Ave., St. Louis 3, Mo.
John Wiley and Sons, Inc., 440 Fourth Ave., New York 16, N.Y.

PERIODICALS

The Mathematics Teacher, NCTM, 1201 Sixteenth St., N.W., Washington 6, D.C.

Scientific American, 415 Madison Ave., New York 17, New York

University of Oklahoma Mathematics Letter, Mathematics Department The University of Oklahoma, Norman, Oklahoma

Scripta Mathematica, 186th St. and Amsterdam Ave., New York 33 New York

Mathematics Student Journal, NCTM, 1201 Sixteenth St., N.W., Washington 6, D.C.

Pi Mu Epsilon Journal, St. Louis University, St. Louis, Missouri

School Science and Mathematics, P.O. Box 408, Oak Park, Illinois

Mathematical Log (Journal of the National High School and Junior College Mathematics Club, Mu Alpha Theta), Box 1155, The University of Oklahoma, Norman, Oklahoma.

Mathematics Magazine, R. E. Horton, L. A. City College, 855 N. Vermont St., Los Angeles 29, California.

American Mathematical Monthly, Mathematical Association of America University of Buffalo, Buffalo 14, New York.

Tables

I. The Greek Alphabet 616

II. Constants and Their Logarithms 616

III. Compound Amount $(1 + i)^n$ 617

IV. Four-place Logarithms of Numbers . . . 618

V. Five-place Natural Logarithms 620

VI. Exponential and Hyperbolic Functions . . 622

VII. Powers, Roots, Recriprocals 624

VIII. Four-place Functions and Radians 625

IX. Logarithms of Trigonometric Functions . 630

I. THE GREEK ALPHABET

Letters		Names	Letters		Names	Letters		Names
A	α	Alpha	I	ι	Iota	P	ρ	Rho
B	β	Beta	K	κ	Kappa	Σ	$\sigma\ s$	Sigma
Γ	γ	Gamma	Λ	λ	Lambda	T	τ	Tau
Δ	δ	Delta	M	μ	Mu	Υ	υ	Upsilo
E	ϵ	Epsilon	N	ν	Nu	Φ	ϕ	Phi
Z	ζ	Zeta	Ξ	ξ	Xi	X	χ	Chi
H	η	Eta	O	o	Omicron	Ψ	ψ	Psi
Θ	θ	Theta	Π	π	Pi	Ω	ω	Omega

II. CONSTANTS AND THEIR LOGARITHMS

Constant	Value	Common Logarithm
π	3.1415 9265	0.4971 4987
e	2.7182 8183	0.4342 9448
$\mu = \log_{10} e$	.4342 9448	9.6377 8431 − 10
$\dfrac{1}{\mu} = \log_e 10$	2.3025 8509	0.3622 1569
1 radian $= \dfrac{180}{\pi}$ degrees	$57°.2957\ 7951$ $= 57°\ 17'\ 44.8''$	1.7581 2263
1 degree $= \dfrac{\pi}{180}$ radians	0.0174 5329	8.2418 7737 − 10
1 minute $= \dfrac{\pi}{10,800}$ radians	0.0002 9089	6.4637 2612 − 10
1 second $= \dfrac{\pi}{648,000}$ radians	0.0000 0485	4.6855 7487 − 10
$\sqrt{\pi}$	1.7724 5385	0.2485 7494
$\dfrac{1}{\pi}$	.3183 0989	9.5028 5013 − 10
$\dfrac{1}{\sqrt{\pi}}$	0.5641 8958	9.7514 2506 − 10
$\dfrac{1}{\sqrt[3]{\pi}}$	0.6827 8406	9.8342 8338 − 10
$\sqrt{e}$	1.6487 2107	.2171 4724
$\dfrac{1}{e}$	0.3678 7944	9.5657 0552 − 10
g	$32.16\ \dfrac{\text{ft.}}{\text{sec.}^2} = 981\ \dfrac{\text{cm.}}{\text{sec.}^2}$	
weight 1 cubic foot water	62.425	1.7953 586
cubic inches in 1 gallon	231	2.3636 120

n	$1\frac{1}{2}\%$	2%	$2\frac{1}{2}\%$	3%	$3\frac{1}{2}\%$	4%	5%	6%	n
1	1.0150	1.0200	1.0250	1.0300	1.0350	1.0400	1.0500	1.0600	1
2	1.0302	1.0404	1.0506	1.0609	1.0712	1.0816	1.1025	1.1236	2
3	1.0457	1.0612	1.0769	1.0927	1.1087	1.1249	1.1576	1.1910	3
4	1.0614	1.0824	1.1038	1.1255	1.1475	1.1699	1.2155	1.2625	4
5	1.0773	1.1041	1.1314	1.1593	1.1877	1.2167	1.2763	1.3382	5
6	1.0934	1.1262	1.1597	1.1941	1.2293	1.2653	1.3401	1.4185	6
7	1.1098	1.1487	1.1887	1.2299	1.2723	1.3159	1.4071	1.5036	7
8	1.1265	1.1717	1.2184	1.2668	1.3168	1.3686	1.4775	1.5938	8
9	1.1434	1.1951	1.2489	1.3048	1.3629	1.4233	1.5513	1.6895	9
10	1.1605	1.2190	1.2801	1.3439	1.4106	1.4802	1.6289	1.7908	10
11	1.1779	1.2434	1.3121	1.3842	1.4600	1.5395	1.7103	1.8983	11
12	1.1956	1.2682	1.3449	1.4258	1.5111	1.6010	1.7959	2.0122	12
13	1.2136	1.2936	1.3785	1.4685	1.5640	1.6651	1.8856	2.1329	13
14	1.2318	1.3195	1.4130	1.5126	1.6187	1.7317	1.9799	1.2609	14
15	1.2502	1.3459	1.4483	1.5580	1.6753	1.8009	2.0789	2.3966	15
16	1.2690	1.3728	1.4845	1.6047	1.7340	1.8730	2.1829	2.5404	16
17	1.2880	1.4002	1.5216	1.6528	1.7947	1.9479	2.2920	2.6928	17
18	1.3073	1.4282	1.5597	1.7024	1.8575	2.0258	2.4066	2.8543	18
19	1.3270	1.4568	1.5987	1.7535	1.9225	2.1068	2.5270	3.0256	19
20	1.3469	1.4859	1.6386	1.8061	1.9898	2.1911	2.6533	3.2071	20
21	1.3671	1.5157	1.6796	1.8603	2.0594	2.2788	2.7860	3.3996	21
22	1.3876	1.5460	1.7216	1.9161	2.1315	2.3699	2.9253	3.6035	22
23	1.4084	1.5769	1.7646	1.9736	2.2061	2.4647	3.0715	3.8197	23
24	1.4295	1.6084	1.8087	2.0328	2.2833	2.5633	3.2251	4.0489	24
25	1.4509	1.6406	1.8539	2.0938	2.3632	2.6658	3.3864	4.2919	25
26	1.4727	1.6734	1.9003	2.1566	2.4460	2.7725	3.5557	4.5494	26
27	1.4948	1.7069	1.9478	2.2213	2.5316	2.8834	3.7335	4.8223	27
28	1.5172	1.7410	1.9965	2.2879	2.6202	2.9987	3.9201	5.1117	28
29	1.5400	1.7758	2.0464	2.3566	2.7119	3.1187	4.1161	5.4184	29
30	1.5631	1.8114	2.0976	2.4273	2.8068	3.2434	4.3219	5.7435	30
31	1.5865	1.8476	2.1500	2.5001	2.9050	3.3731	4.5380	6.0881	31
32	1.6103	1.8845	2.2038	2.5751	3.0067	3.5081	4.7649	6.4534	32
33	1.6345	1.9222	2.2589	2.6523	3.1119	3.6484	5.0032	6.8406	33
34	1.6590	1.9607	2.3153	2.7319	3.2209	3.7943	5.2533	7.2510	34
35	1.6839	1.9999	2.3732	2.8139	3.3336	3.9461	5.5160	7.6861	35
36	1.7091	2.0399	2.4325	2.8983	3.4503	4.1039	5.7918	8.1473	36
37	1.7348	2.0807	2.4933	2.9852	3.5710	4.2681	6.0814	8.6361	37
38	1.7608	2.1223	2.5557	3.0748	3.6960	4.4388	6.3855	9.1543	38
39	1.7872	2.1647	2.6196	3.1670	3.8254	4.6164	6.7048	9.7035	39
40	1.8140	2.2080	2.6851	3.2620	3.9593	4.8010	7.0400	10.2857	40
41	1.8412	2.2522	2.7522	3.3599	4.0978	4.9931	7.3920	10.9029	41
42	1.8688	2.2972	2.8210	3.4607	4.2413	5.1928	7.7616	11.5570	42
43	1.8969	2.3432	2.8915	3.5645	4.3897	5.4005	8.1497	12.2505	43
44	1.9253	2.3901	2.9638	3.6715	4.5433	5.6165	8.5572	12.9855	44
45	1.9542	2.4379	3.0379	3.7816	4.7024	5.8412	8.9850	13.7646	45
46	1.9835	2.4866	3.1139	3.8950	4.8669	6.0748	9.4343	14.5905	46
47	2.0133	2.5363	3.1917	4.0119	5.0373	6.3178	9.9060	15.4659	47
48	2.0435	2.5871	3.2715	4.1323	5.2136	6.5705	10.4013	16.3939	48
49	2.0741	2.6388	3.3533	4.2562	5.3961	6.8333	10.9213	17.3775	49
50	2.1052	2.6916	3.4371	4.3839	5.5849	7.1067	11.4674	18.4202	50

n	0	1	2	3	4	5	6	7	8	9
10	0000	0043	0086	0128	0170	0212	0253	0294	0334	0374
11	0414	0453	0492	0531	0569	0607	0645	0682	0719	0755
12	0792	0828	0864	0899	0934	0969	1004	1038	1072	1106
13	1139	1173	1206	1239	1271	1303	1335	1367	1399	1430
14	1461	1492	1523	1553	1584	1614	1644	1673	1703	1732
15	1761	1790	1818	1847	1875	1903	1931	1959	1987	2014
16	2041	2068	2095	2122	2148	2175	2201	2227	2253	2279
17	2304	2330	2355	2380	2405	2430	2455	2480	2504	2529
18	2553	2577	2601	2625	2648	2672	2695	2718	2742	2765
19	2788	2810	2833	2856	2878	2900	2923	2945	2967	2989
20	3010	3032	3054	3075	3096	3118	3139	3160	3181	3201
21	3222	3243	3263	3284	3304	3324	3345	3365	3385	3404
22	3424	3444	3464	3483	3502	3522	3541	3560	3579	3598
23	3617	3636	3655	3674	3692	3711	3729	3747	3766	3784
24	3802	3820	3838	3856	3874	3892	3909	3927	3945	3962
25	3979	3997	4014	4031	4048	4065	4082	4099	4116	4133
26	4150	4166	4183	4200	4216	4232	4249	4265	4281	4298
27	4314	4330	4346	4362	4378	4393	4409	4425	4440	4456
28	4472	4487	4502	4518	4533	4548	4564	4579	4594	4609
29	4624	4639	4654	4669	4683	4698	4713	4728	4742	4757
30	4771	4786	4800	4814	4829	4843	4857	4871	4886	4900
31	4914	4928	4942	4955	4969	4983	4997	5011	5024	5038
32	5051	5065	5079	5092	5105	5119	5132	5145	5159	5172
33	5185	5198	5211	5224	5237	5250	5263	5276	5289	5302
34	5315	5328	5340	5353	5366	5378	5391	5403	5416	5428
35	5441	5453	5465	5478	5490	5502	5514	5527	5539	5551
36	5563	5575	5587	5599	5611	5623	5635	5647	5658	5670
37	5682	5694	5705	5717	5729	5740	5752	5763	5775	5786
38	5798	5809	5821	5832	5843	5855	5866	5877	5888	5899
39	5911	5922	5933	5944	5955	5966	5977	5988	5999	6010
40	6021	6031	6042	6053	6064	6075	6085	6096	6107	6117
41	6128	6138	6149	6160	6170	6180	6191	6201	6212	6222
42	6232	6243	6253	6263	6274	6284	6294	6304	6314	6325
43	6335	6345	6355	6365	6375	6385	6395	6405	6415	6425
44	6435	6444	6454	6464	6474	6484	6493	6503	6513	6522
45	6532	6542	6551	6561	6571	6580	6590	6599	6609	6618
46	6628	6637	6646	6656	6665	6675	6684	6693	6702	6712
47	6721	6730	6739	6749	6758	6767	6776	6785	6794	6803
48	6812	6821	6830	6839	6848	6857	6866	6875	6884	6893
49	6902	6911	6920	6928	6937	6946	6955	6964	6972	6981
50	6990	6998	7007	7016	7024	7033	7042	7050	7059	7067
51	7076	7084	7093	7101	7110	7118	7126	7135	7143	7152
52	7160	7168	7177	7185	7193	7202	7210	7218	7226	7235
53	7243	7251	7259	7267	7275	7284	7292	7300	7308	7316
54	7324	7332	7340	7348	7356	7364	7372	7380	7388	7396

n	0	1	2	3	4	5	6	7	8	9
55	7404	7412	7419	7427	7435	7443	7451	7459	7466	7474
56	7482	7490	7497	7505	7513	7520	7528	7536	7543	7551
57	7559	7566	7574	7582	7589	7597	7604	7612	7619	7627
58	7634	7642	7649	7657	7664	7672	7679	7686	7694	7701
59	7709	7716	7723	7731	7738	7745	7752	7760	7767	7774
60	7782	7789	7796	7803	7810	7818	7825	7832	7839	7846
61	7853	7860	7868	7875	7882	7889	7896	7903	7910	7917
62	7924	7931	7938	7945	7952	7959	7966	7973	7980	7987
63	7993	8000	8007	8014	8021	8028	8035	8041	8048	8055
64	8062	8069	8075	8082	8089	8096	8102	8109	8116	8122
65	8129	8136	8142	8149	8156	8162	8169	8176	8182	8189
66	8195	8202	8209	8215	8222	8228	8235	8241	8248	8254
67	8261	8267	8274	8280	8287	8293	8299	8306	8312	8319
68	8325	8331	8338	8344	8351	8357	8363	8370	8376	8382
69	8388	8395	8401	8407	8414	8420	8426	8432	8439	8445
70	8451	8457	8463	8470	8476	8482	8488	8494	8500	8506
71	8513	8519	8525	8531	8537	8543	8549	8555	8561	8567
72	8573	8579	8585	8591	8597	8603	8609	8615	8621	8627
73	8633	8639	8645	8651	8657	8663	8669	8675	8681	8686
74	8692	8698	8704	8710	8716	8722	8727	8733	8739	8745
75	8751	8756	8762	8768	8774	8779	8785	8791	8797	8802
76	8808	8814	8820	8825	8831	8837	8842	8848	8854	8859
77	8865	8871	8876	8882	8887	8893	8899	8904	8910	8915
78	8921	8927	8932	8938	8943	8949	8954	8960	8965	8971
79	8976	8982	8987	8993	8998	9004	9009	9015	9020	9025
80	9031	9036	9042	9047	9053	9058	9063	9069	9074	9079
81	9085	9090	9096	9101	9106	9112	9117	9122	9128	9133
82	9138	9143	9149	9154	9159	9165	9170	9175	9180	9186
83	9191	9196	9201	9206	9212	9217	9222	9227	9232	9238
84	9243	9248	9253	9258	9263	9269	9274	9279	9284	9289
85	9294	9299	9304	9309	9315	9320	9325	9330	9335	9340
86	9345	9350	9355	9360	9365	9370	9375	9380	9385	9390
87	9395	9400	9405	9410	9415	9420	9425	9430	9435	9440
88	9445	9450	9455	9460	9465	9469	9474	9479	9484	9489
89	9494	9499	9504	9509	9513	9518	9523	9528	9533	9538
90	9542	9547	9552	9557	9562	9566	9571	9576	9581	9586
91	9590	9595	9600	9605	9609	9614	9619	9624	9628	9633
92	9638	9643	9647	9652	9657	9661	9666	9671	9675	9680
93	9685	9689	9694	9699	9703	9708	9713	9717	9722	9727
94	9731	9736	9741	9745	9750	9754	9759	9763	9768	9773
95	9777	9782	9786	9791	9795	9800	9805	9809	9814	9818
96	9823	9827	9832	9836	9841	9845	9850	9854	9859	9863
97	9868	9872	9877	9881	9886	9890	9894	9899	9903	9908
98	9912	9917	9921	9926	9930	9934	9939	9943	9948	9952
99	9956	9961	9965	9969	9974	9978	9983	9987	9991	9996

This table contains logarithms of numbers from 1 to 10 to the base e. To obtain the natural logarithms of other numbers use the formulas:

$$\log_e (10^r N) = \log_e N + \log_e 10^r$$

$$\log_e \left(\frac{N}{10^r}\right) = \log_e N - \log_e 10^r$$

$$\log_e 10 = 2.302585 \qquad \log_e 10^4 = 9.210340$$
$$\log_e 10^2 = 4.605170 \qquad \log_e 10^5 = 11.512925$$
$$\log_e 10^3 = 6.907755 \qquad \log_e 10^6 = 13.815511$$

N	0	1	2	3	4	5	6	7	8	9
1.0	0.0 0000	0995	1980	2956	3922	4879	5827	6766	7696	8618
1.1	0.0 9531	*0436	*1333	*2222	*3103	*3976	*4842	*5700	*6551	*7395
1.2	0.1 8232	9062	9885	*0701	*1511	*2314	*3111	*3902	*4686	*5464
1.3	0.2 6236	7003	7763	8518	9267	*0010	*0748	*1481	*2208	*2930
1.4	0.3 3647	4359	5066	5767	6464	7156	7844	8526	9204	9878
1.5	0.4 0547	1211	1871	2527	3178	3825	4469	5108	5742	6373
1.6	0.4 7000	7623	8243	8858	9470	*0078	*0682	*1282	*1879	*2473
1.7	0.5 3063	3649	4232	4812	5389	5962	6531	7098	7661	8222
1.8	0.5 8779	9333	9884	*0432	*0977	*1519	*2078	*2594	*3127	*3658
1.9	0.6 4185	4710	5233	5752	6269	6783	7294	7803	8310	8813
2.0	0.6 9315	9813	*0310	*0804	*1295	*1784	*2271	*2755	*3237	*3716
2.1	0.7 4194	4669	5142	5612	6081	6547	7011	7473	7932	8390
2.2	0.7 8846	9299	9751	*0200	*0648	*1093	*1536	*1978	*2418	*2855
2.3	0.8 3291	3725	4157	4587	5015	5442	5866	6289	6710	7129
2.4	0.8 7547	7963	8377	8789	9200	9609	*0016	*0422	*0826	*1228
2.5	0.9 1629	2028	2426	2822	3216	3609	4001	4391	4779	5166
2.6	0.9 5551	5935	6317	6698	7078	7456	7833	8208	8582	8954
2.7	0.9 9325	9695	*0063	*0430	*0796	*1160	*1523	*1885	*2245	*2604
2.8	1.0 2962	3318	3674	4028	4380	4732	5082	5431	5779	6126
2.9	1.0 6471	6815	7158	7500	7841	8181	8519	8856	9192	9527
3.0	1.0 9861	*0194	*0526	*0856	*1186	*1514	*1841	*2168	*2493	*2817
3.1	1.1 3140	3462	3783	4103	4422	4740	5057	5373	5688	6002
3.2	1.1 6315	6627	6938	7248	7557	7865	8173	8479	8784	9089
3.3	1.1 9392	9695	9996	*0297	*0597	*0896	*1194	*1491	*1788	*2083
3.4	1.2 2378	2671	2964	3256	3547	3837	4127	4415	4703	4990
3.5	1.2 5276	5562	5846	6130	6413	6695	6976	7257	7536	7815
3.6	1.2 8093	8371	8647	8923	9198	9473	9746	*0019	*0291	*0563
3.7	1.3 0833	1103	1372	1641	1909	2176	2442	2708	2972	3237
3.8	1.3 3500	3763	4025	4286	4547	4807	5067	5325	5584	5841
3.9	1.3 6098	6354	6609	6864	7118	7372	7624	7877	8128	8379
4.0	1.3 8629	8879	9128	9377	9624	9872	*0118	*0364	*0610	*0854
4.1	1.4 1099	1342	1585	1828	2070	2311	2552	2792	3031	3270
4.2	1.4 3508	3746	3984	4220	4456	4692	4927	5161	5395	5629
4.3	1.4 5862	6094	6326	6557	6787	7018	7247	7476	7705	7933
4.4	1.4 8160	8387	8614	8840	9065	9290	9515	9739	9962	*0185
4.5	1.5 0408	0630	0851	1072	1293	1513	1732	1951	2170	2388
4.6	1.5 2606	2823	3039	3256	3471	3687	3902	4116	4330	4543
4.7	1.5 4756	4969	5181	5393	5604	5814	6025	6235	6444	6653
4.8	1.5 6862	7070	7277	7485	7691	7898	8104	8309	8515	8719
4.9	1.5 8924	9127	9331	9534	9737	9939	*0141	*0342	*0543	*0744
5.0	1.6 0944	1144	1343	1542	1741	1939	2137	2334	2531	2728
N	0	1	2	3	4	5	6	7	8	9

N	0	1	2	3	4	5	6	7	8	9
5.0	1.6 0944	1144	1343	1542	1741	1939	2137	2334	2531	2728
5.1	1.6 2924	3120	3315	3511	3705	3900	4094	4287	4481	4673
5.2	1.6 4866	5058	5250	5441	5632	5823	6013	6203	6393	6582
5.3	1.6 6771	6959	7147	7335	7523	7710	7896	8083	8269	8455
5.4	1.6 8640	8825	9010	9194	9378	9562	9745	9928	*0111	*0293
5.5	1.7 0475	0656	0838	1019	1199	1380	1560	1740	1919	2098
5.6	1.7 2277	2455	2633	2811	2988	3166	3342	3519	3695	3871
5.7	1.7 4047	4222	4397	4572	4746	4920	5094	5267	5440	5613
5.8	1.7 5786	5958	6130	6302	6473	6644	6815	6985	7156	7326
5.9	1.7 7495	7665	7843	8002	8171	8339	8507	8675	8842	9009
6.0	1.7 9176	9342	9509	9675	9840	*0006	*0171	*0336	*0500	*0665
6.1	1.8 0829	0993	1156	1319	1482	1645	1808	1970	2132	2294
6.2	1.8 2455	2616	2777	2938	3098	3258	3418	3578	3737	3896
6.3	1.8 4055	4214	4372	4530	4688	4845	5003	5160	5317	5473
6.4	1.8 5630	5786	5942	6097	6253	6408	6563	6718	6872	7026
6.5	1.8 7180	7334	7487	7641	7794	7947	8099	8251	8403	8555
6.6	1.8 8707	8858	9010	9160	9311	9462	9612	9762	9912	*0061
6.7	1.9 0211	0360	0509	0658	0806	0954	1102	1250	1398	1545
6.8	1.9 1692	1839	1986	2132	2279	2425	2571	2716	2862	3007
6.9	1.9 3152	3297	3442	3586	3730	3874	4018	4162	4305	4448
7.0	1.9 4591	4734	4876	5019	5161	5303	5445	5586	5727	5869
7.1	1.9 6009	6150	6291	6431	6571	6711	6851	6991	7130	7269
7.2	1.9 7408	7547	7685	7824	7962	8100	8238	8376	8513	8650
7.3	1.9 8787	8924	9061	9198	9334	9470	9606	9742	9877	*0013
7.4	2.0 0148	0283	0418	0553	0687	0821	0956	1089	1223	1357
7.5	2.0 1490	1624	1757	1890	2022	2155	2287	2419	2551	2683
7.6	2.0 2815	2946	3078	3209	3340	3471	3601	3732	3862	3992
7.7	2.0 4122	4252	4381	4511	4640	4769	4898	5027	5156	5284
7.8	2.0 5412	5540	5668	5796	5924	6051	6179	6306	6433	6560
7.9	2.0 6686	6813	6939	7065	7191	7317	7443	7568	7694	7819
8.0	2.0 7944	8069	8194	8318	8443	8567	8691	8815	8939	9063
8.1	2.0 9186	9310	9433	9556	9679	9802	9924	*0047	*0169	*0291
8.2	2.1 0413	0535	0657	0779	0900	1021	1142	1263	1384	1505
8.3	2.1 1626	1746	1866	1986	2106	2226	2346	2465	2585	2704
8.4	2.1 2823	2942	3061	3180	3298	3417	3535	3653	3771	3889
8.5	2.1 4007	4124	4242	4359	4476	4593	4710	4827	4943	5060
8.6	2.1 5176	5292	5409	5524	5640	5756	5871	5987	6102	6217
8.7	2.1 6332	6447	6562	6677	6791	6905	7020	7134	7248	7361
8.8	2.1 7475	7589	7702	7816	7929	8042	8155	8267	8380	8493
8.9	2.1 8605	8717	8830	8942	9054	9165	9277	9389	9500	9611
9.0	2.1 9722	9834	9944	*0055	*0166	*0276	*0387	*0497	*0607	*0717
9.1	2.2 0827	0937	1047	1157	1266	1375	1485	1594	1703	1812
9.2	2.2 1920	2029	2138	2246	2354	2462	2570	2678	2786	2894
9.3	2.2 3001	3109	3216	3324	3431	3538	3645	3751	3858	3965
9.4	2.2 4071	4177	4284	4390	4496	4601	4707	4813	4918	5024
9.5	2.2 5129	5234	5339	5444	5549	5654	5759	5863	5968	6072
9.6	2.2 6176	6280	6384	6488	6592	6696	6799	6903	7006	7109
9.7	2.2 7213	7316	7419	7521	7624	7727	7829	7932	8034	8136
9.8	2.2 8238	8340	8442	8544	8646	8747	8849	8950	9051	9152
9.9	2.2 9253	9354	9455	9556	9657	9757	9858	9958	*0058	*0158
10.0	2.3 0259	0358	0458	0558	0658	0757	0857	0956	1055	1154
N	0	1	2	3	4	5	6	7	8	9

For values of x not given in the table the exponential function e^x may be found approximately by the use of a table of common logarithms in connection with the relation $\log e^x = 0.43429x$.

When x is beyond the limits of the table (that is, when $x > 6.5$) sinh x and cosh x may be obtained to five significant figures by the formula sinh $x =$ cosh $x = \frac{1}{2}e^x$ where e^x is found by using the relation above; furthermore, for such values of x tanh $x = 1.0000$.

x	e^x	e^{-x}	sinh x	cosh x	tanh x	x
0.0	1.0000	1.0000	.00000	1.0000	.00000	0.0
0.1	1.1052	.90484	.10017	1.0050	.09967	0.1
0.2	1.2214	.81873	.20134	1.0201	.19738	0.2
0.3	1.3499	.74082	.30452	1.0453	.29131	0.3
0.4	1.4918	.67032	.41075	1.0811	.37995	0.4
0.5	1.6487	.60653	.52110	1.1276	.46212	0.5
0.6	1.8221	.54881	.63665	1.1855	.53705	0.6
0.7	2.0138	.49659	.75858	1.2552	.60437	0.7
0.8	2.2255	.44933	.88811	1.3374	.66404	0.8
0.9	2.4596	.40657	1.0265	1.4331	.71630	0.9
1.0	2.7183	.36788	1.1752	1.5431	.76159	1.0
1.1	3.0042	.33287	1.3356	1.6685	.80050	1.1
1.2	3.3201	.30119	1.5095	1.8107	.83365	1.2
1.3	3.6693	.27253	1.6984	1.9709	.86172	1.3
1.4	4.0552	.24660	1.9043	2.1509	.88535	1.4
1.5	4.4817	.22313	2.1293	2.3524	.90515	1.5
1.6	4.9530	.20190	2.3756	2.5775	.92167	1.6
1.7	5.4739	.18268	2.6456	2.8283	.93541	1.7
1.8	6.0496	.16530	2.9422	3.1075	.94681	1.8
1.9	6.6859	.14957	3.2682	3.4177	.95624	1.9
2.0	7.3891	.13534	3.6269	3.7622	.96403	2.0
2.1	8.1662	.12246	4.0219	4.1443	.97045	2.1
2.2	9.0250	.11080	4.4571	4.5679	.97574	2.2
2.3	9.9742	.10026	4.9370	5.0372	.98010	2.3
2.4	11.023	.09072	5.4662	5.5569	.98367	2.4
2.5	12.182	.08208	6.0502	6.1323	.98661	2.5
2.6	13.464	.07427	6.6947	6.7690	.98903	2.6
2.7	14.880	.06721	7.4063	7.4735	.99101	2.7
2.8	16.445	.06081	8.1919	8.2527	.99263	2.8
2.9	18.174	.05502	9.0596	9.1146	.99396	2.9

x	e^x	e^{-x}	sinh x	cosh x	tanh x	x
3.0	20.086	.04979	10.018	10.068	.99505	**3.0**
3.1	22.198	.04505	11.076	11.122	.99595	3.1
3.2	24.533	.04076	12.246	12.287	.99668	3.2
3.3	27.113	.03688	13.538	13.575	.99728	3.3
3.4	29.964	.03337	14.965	14.999	.99777	3.4
3.5	33.115	.03020	16.543	16.573	.99818	3.5
3.6	36.598	.02732	18.285	18.313	.99851	3.6
3.7	40.447	.02472	20.211	20.236	.99878	3.7
3.8	44.701	.02237	22.339	22.362	.99900	3.8
3.9	49.402	.02024	24.691	24.711	.99918	3.9
4.0	54.598	.01832	27.290	27.308	.99933	**4.0**
4.1	60.340	.01657	30.162	30.178	.99945	4.1
4.2	66.686	.01500	33.336	33.351	.99955	4.2
4.3	73.700	.01357	36.843	36.857	.99963	4.3
4.4	81.451	.01228	40.719	40.732	.99970	4.4
4.5	90.017	.01111	45.003	45.014	.99975	4.5
4.6	99.484	.01005	49.737	49.747	.99980	4.6
4.7	109.95	.00910	54.969	54.978	.99983	4.7
4.8	121.51	.00823	60.751	60.759	.99986	4.8
4.9	134.29	.00745	67.141	67.149	.99989	4.9
5.0	148.41	.00674	74.203	74.210	.99991	**5.0**
5.1	164.02	.00610	82.008	82.014	.99993	5.1
5.2	181.27	.00552	90.633	90.639	.99994	5.2
5.3	200.34.	.00499	100.17	100.17	.99995	5.3
5.4	221.41	.00452	110.70	110.71	.99996	5.4
5.5	244.69	.00409	122.34	122.35	.99997	5.5
5.6	270.43	.00370	135.21	135.22	.99997	5.6
5.7	298.87	.00335	149.43	149.44	.99998	5.7
5.8	330.30	.00303	165.15	165.15	.99998	5.8
5.9	365.04	.00274	182.52	182.52	.99998	5.9
6.0	403.43	.00248	201.71	201.72	.99999	**6.0**
6.1	445.86	.00224	222.93	222.93	.99999	6.1
6.2	492.75	.00203	246.37	246.38	.99999	6.2
6.3	544.57	.00184	272.29	272.29	.99999	6.3
6.4	601.85	.00166	300.92	300.92	.99999	6.4
6.5	665.14	.00150	332.57	332.57	1.0000	6.5

n	n^2	n^3	$\sqrt{n}$	$\sqrt[3]{n}$	$1/n$	n	n^2	n^3	$\sqrt{n}$	$\sqrt[3]{n}$	$1/n$
1	1	1	1.000	1.000	1.0000	51	2,601	132,651	7.141	3.708	.0196
2	4	8	1.414	1.260	.5000	52	2,704	140,608	7.211	3.733	.0192
3	9	27	1.732	1.442	.3333	53	2,809	148,877	7.280	3.756	.0189
4	16	64	2.000	1.587	.2500	54	2,916	157,464	7.348	3.780	.0185
5	25	125	2.236	1.710	.2000	55	3,025	166,375	7.416	3.803	.0182
6	36	216	2.449	1.817	.1667	56	3,136	175,616	7.483	3.826	.0179
7	49	343	2.646	1.913	.1429	57	3,249	185,193	7.550	3.849	.0175
8	64	512	2.828	2.000	.1250	58	3,364	195,112	7.616	3.871	.0172
9	81	729	3.000	2.080	.1111	59	3,481	205,379	7.681	3.893	.0169
10	100	1,000	3.162	2.154	.1000	60	3,600	216,000	7.746	3.915	.0167
11	121	1,331	3.317	2.224	.0909	61	3,721	226,981	7.810	3.936	.0164
12	144	1,728	3.464	2.289	.0833	62	3,844	238,328	7.874	3.958	.0161
13	169	2,197	3.606	2.351	.0769	63	3,969	250,047	7.937	3.979	.0159
14	196	2,744	3.742	2.410	.0714	64	4,096	262,144	8.000	4.000	.0156
15	225	3,375	3.873	2.466	.0667	65	4,225	274,625	8.062	4.021	.0154
16	256	4,096	4.000	2.520	.0625	66	4,356	287,496	8.124	4.041	.0152
17	289	4,913	4.123	2.571	.0588	67	4,489	300,763	8.185	4.062	.0149
18	324	5,832	4.243	2.621	.0556	68	4,624	314,432	8.246	4.082	.0147
19	361	6,859	4.359	2.668	.0526	69	4,761	328,509	8.307	4.102	.0145
20	400	8,000	4.472	2.714	.0500	70	4,900	343,000	8.367	4.121	.0143
21	441	9,261	4.583	2.759	.0476	71	5,041	357,911	8.426	4.141	.0141
22	484	10,648	4.690	2.802	.0455	72	5,184	373,248	8.485	4.160	.0139
23	529	12,167	4.796	2.844	.0435	73	5,329	389,017	8.544	4.179	.0137
24	576	13,824	4.899	2.884	.0417	74	5,476	405,224	8.602	4.198	.0135
25	625	15,625	5.000	2.924	.0400	75	5,625	421,875	8.660	4.217	.0133
26	676	17,576	5.099	2.962	.0385	76	5,776	438,976	8.718	4.236	.0132
27	729	19,683	5.196	3.000	.0370	77	5,929	456,533	8.775	4.254	.0130
28	784	21,952	5.292	3.037	.0357	78	6,084	474,552	8.832	4.273	.0128
29	841	24,389	5.385	3.072	.0345	79	6,241	493,039	8.888	4.291	.0127
30	900	27,000	5.477	3.107	.0333	80	6,400	512,000	8.944	4.309	.0125
31	961	29,791	5.568	3.141	.0323	81	6,561	531,441	9.000	4.327	.0123
32	1,024	32,768	5.657	3.175	.0312	82	6,724	551,368	9.055	4.344	.0122
33	1,089	35,937	5.745	3.208	.0303	83	6,889	571,787	9.110	4.362	.0120
34	1,156	39,304	5.831	3.240	.0294	84	7,056	592,704	9.165	4.380	.0119
35	1,225	42,875	5.916	3.271	.0286	85	7,225	614,125	9.220	4.397	.0118
36	1,296	46,656	6.000	3.302	.0278	86	7,396	636,056	9.274	4.414	.0116
37	1,369	50,653	6.083	3.332	.0270	87	7,569	658,503	9.327	4.431	.0115
38	1,444	54,872	6.164	3.362	.0263	88	7,744	681,472	9.381	4.448	.0114
39	1,521	59,319	6.245	3.391	.0256	89	7,921	704,969	9.434	4.465	.0112
40	1,600	64,000	6.325	3.420	.0250	90	8,100	729,000	9.487	4.481	.0111
41	1,681	68,921	6.403	3.448	.0244	91	8,281	753,571	9.539	4.498	.0110
42	1,764	74,088	6.481	3.476	.0238	92	8,464	778,688	9.592	4.514	.0109
43	1,849	79,507	6.557	3.503	.0233	93	8,649	804,357	9.644	4.531	.0108
44	1,936	85,184	6.633	3.530	.0227	94	8,836	830,584	9.695	4.547	.0106
45	2,025	91,125	6.708	3.557	.0222	95	9,025	857,375	9.747	4.563	.0105
46	2,116	97,336	6.782	3.583	.0217	96	9,216	884,736	9.798	4.579	.0104
47	2,209	103,823	6.856	3.609	.0213	97	9,409	912,673	9.849	4.595	.0103
48	2,304	110,592	6.928	3.634	.0208	98	9,604	941,192	9.899	4.610	.0102
49	2,401	117,649	7.000	3.659	.0204	99	9,801	970,299	9.950	4.626	.0101
50	2,500	125,000	7.071	3.684	.0200	100	10,000	1,000,000	10.000	4.642	.0100

Degrees	Radians	Sin	Csc	Tan	Cot	Sec	Cos		
0° 0′	.0000	.0000	——	.0000	——	1.000	1.0000	1.5708	90° 0′
10′	029	029	343.8	029	343.8	000	000	679	50′
20′	058	058	171.9	058	171.9	000	000	650	40′
30′	.0087	.0087	114.6	.0087	114.6	1.000	1.0000	1.5621	30′
40′	116	116	85.95	116	85.94	000	.9999	592	20′
50′	145	145	68.76	145	68.75	000	999	563	10′
1° 0′	.0175	.0175	57.30	.0175	57.29	1.000	.9998	1.5533	89° 0′
10′	204	204	49.11	204	49.10	000	998	504	50′
20′	233	233	42.98	233	42.96	000	997	475	40′
30′	.0262	.0262	38.20	.0262	38.19	1.000	.9997	1.5446	30′
40′	291	291	34.38	291	34.37	000	996	417	20′
50′	320	320	31.26	320	31.24	001	995	388	10′
2° 0′	.0349	.0349	28.65	.0349	28.64	1.001	.9994	1.5359	88° 0′
10′	378	378	26.45	378	26.43	001	993	330	50′
20′	407	407	24.56	407	24.54	001	992	301	40′
30′	.0436	.0436	22.93	.0437	22.90	1.001	.9990	1.5272	30′
40′	465	465	21.49	466	21.47	001	989	243	20′
50′	495	494	20.23	495	20.21	001	988	213	10′
3° 0′	.0524	.0523	19.11	.0524	19.08	1.001	.9986	1.5184	87° 0′
10′	553	552	18.10	553	18.07	002	985	155	50′
20′	582	581	17.20	582	17.17	002	983	126	40′
30′	.0611	.0610	16.38	.0612	16.35	1.002	.9981	1.5097	30′
40′	640	640	15.64	641	15.60	002	980	068	20′
50′	669	669	14.96	670	14.92	002	978	039	10′
4° 0′	.0698	.0698	14.34	.0699	14.30	1.002	.9976	1.5010	86° 0′
10′	727	727	13.76	729	13.73	003	974	981	50′
20′	756	756	13.23	758	13.20	003	971	952	40′
30′	.0785	.0785	12.75	.0787	12.71	1.003	.9969	1.4923	30′
40′	814	814	12.29	816	12.25	003	967	893	20′
50′	844	843	11.87	846	11.83	004	964	864	10′
5° 0′	.0873	.0872	11.47	.0875	11.43	1.004	.9962	1.4835	85° 0′
10′	902	901	11.10	904	11.06	004	959	806	50′
20′	931	929	10.76	934	10.71	004	957	777	40′
30′	.0960	.0958	10.43	.0963	10.39	1.005	.9954	1.4748	30′
40′	989	987	10.13	992	10.08	005	951	719	20′
50′	.1018	.1016	9.839	.1022	9.788	005	948	690	10′
6° 0′	.1047	.1045	9.567	.1051	9.514	1.006	.9945	1.4661	84° 0′
10′	076	074	9.309	080	9.255	006	942	632	50′
20′	105	103	9.065	110	9.010	006	939	603	40′
30′	.1134	.1132	8.834	.1139	8.777	1.006	.9936	1.4573	30′
40′	164	161	8.614	169	8.556	007	932	544	20′
50′	193	190	8.405	198	8.345	007	929	515	10′
7° 0′	.1222	.1219	8.206	.1228	8.144	1.008	.9925	1.4486	83° 0′
10′	251	248	8.016	257	7.953	008	922	457	50′
20′	280	276	7.834	287	7.770	008	918	428	40′
30′	.1309	.1305	7.661	.1317	7.596	1.009	.9914	1.4399	30′
40′	338	334	7.496	346	7.429	009	911	370	20′
50′	367	363	7.337	376	7.269	009	907	341	10′
8° 0′	.1396	.1392	7.185	.1405	7.115	1.010	.9903	1.4312	82° 0′
10′	425	421	7.040	435	6.968	010	899	283	50′
20′	454	449	6.900	465	6.827	011	894	254	40′
30′	.1484	.1478	6.765	.1495	6.691	1.011	.9890	1.4224	30′
40′	513	507	6.636	524	6.561	012	886	195	20′
50′	542	536	6.512	554	6.435	012	881	166	10′
9° 0′	.1571	.1564	6.392	.1584	6.314	1.012	.9877	1.4137	81° 0′
		Cos	Sec	Cot	Tan	Csc	Sin	Radians	Degrees

Degrees	Radians	Sin	Csc	Tan	Cot	Sec	Cos	Radians	Degrees
9° 0′	.1571	.1564	6.392	.1584	6.314	1.012	.9877	1.4137	81° 0′
10′	600	593	277	614	197	013	872	108	50′
20′	629	622	166	644	6.084	013	868	079	40′
30′	.1658	.1650	6.059	.1673	5.976	1.014	.9863	1.4050	30′
40′	687	679	5.955	703	871	014	858	1.4021	20′
50′	716	708	855	733	769	015	853	1.3992	10′
10° 0′	.1745	.1736	5.759	.1763	5.671	1.015	.9848	1.3963	80° 0′
10′	774	765	665	793	576	016	843	934	50′
20′	804	794	575	823	485	016	838	904	40′
30′	.1833	.1822	5.487	.1853	5.396	1.017	.9833	1.3875	30′
40′	862	851	403	883	309	018	827	846	20′
50′	891	880	320	914	226	018	822	817	10′
11° 0′	.1920	.1908	5.241	.1944	5.145	1.019	.9816	1.3788	79° 0′
10′	949	937	164	.1974	5.066	019	811	759	50′
20′	978	965	089	.2004	4.989	020	805	730	40′
30′	.2007	.1994	5.016	.2035	4.915	1.020	.9799	1.3701	30′
40′	036	.2022	4.945	065	843	021	793	672	20′
50′	065	051	876	095	773	022	787	643	10′
12° 0′	.2094	.2079	4.810	.2126	4.705	1.022	.9781	1.3614	78° 0′
10′	123	108	745	156	638	023	775	584	50′
20′	153	136	682	186	574	024	769	555	40′
30′	.2182	.2164	4.620	.2217	4.511	1.024	.9763	1.3526	30′
40′	211	193	560	247	449	025	.757	497	20′
50′	240	221	502	278	390	026	750	468	10′
13° 0′	.2269	.2250	4.445	.2309	4.331	1.026	.9744	1.3439	77° 0′
10′	298	278	390	339	275	027	737	410	50′
20′	327	306	336	370	219	028	730	381	40′
30′	.2356	.2334	4.284	.2401	4.165	1.028	.9724	1.3352	30′
40′	385	363	232	432	113	029	717	323	20′
50′	414	391	182	462	061	030	710	294	10′
14° 0′	.2443	.2419	4.134	.2493	4.011	1.031	.9703	1.3265	76° 0′
10′	473	447	086	524	3.962	031	696	235	50′
20′	502	476	4.039	555	914	032	689	206	40′
30′	.2531	.2504	3.994	.2586	3.867	1.033	.9681	1.3177	30′
40′	560	532	950	617	821	034	674	148	20′
50′	589	560	906	648	776	034	667	119	10′
15° 0′	.2618	.2588	3.864	.2679	3.732	1.035	.9659	1.3090	75° 0′
10′	647	616	822	711	689	036	652	061	50′
20′	676	644	782	742	647	037	644	032	40′
30′	.2705	.2672	3.742	.2773	3.606	1.038	.9636	1.3003	30′
40′	734	700	703	805	566	039	628	1.2974	20′
50′	763	728	665	836	526	039	621	945	10′
16° 0′	.2793	.2756	3.628	.2867	3.487	1.040	.9613	1.2915	74° 0′
10′	822	784	592	899	450	041	605	886	50′
20′	851	812	556	931	412	042	596	857	40′
30′	.2880	.2840	3.521	.2962	3.376	1.043	.9588	1.2828	30′
40′	909	868	487	.2994	340	044	580	799	20′
50′	938	896	453	.3026	305	045	572	770	10′
17° 0′	.2967	.2924	3.420	.3057	3.271	1.046	.9563	1.2741	73° 0′
10′	996	952	388	089	237	047	555	712	50′
20′	.3025	.2979	357	121	204	048	546	683	40′
30′	.3054	.3007	3.326	.3153	3.172	1.048	.9537	1.2654	30′
40′	083	035	295	185	140	049	528	625	20′
50′	113	062	265	217	108	050	520	595	10′
18° 0′	.3142	.3090	3.236	.3249	3.078	1.051	.9511	1.2566	72° 0′
		Cos	Sec	Cot	Tan	Csc	Sin	Radians	Degrees

Degrees	Radians	Sin	Csc	Tan	Cot	Sec	Cos		
18° 0'	.3142	.3090	3.236	.3249	3.078	1.051	.9511	1.2566	72° 0'
10'	171	118	207	281	047	052	502	537	50'
20'	200	145	179	314	3.018	053	492	508	40'
30'	.3229	.3173	3.152	.3346	2.989	1.054	.9483	1.2479	30'
40'	258	201	124	378	960	056	474	450	20'
50'	287	228	098	411	932	057	465	421	10'
19° 0'	.3316	.3256	3.072	.3443	2.904	1.058	.9455	1.2392	71° 0'
10'	345	283	046	476	877	059	446	363	50'
20'	374	311	3.021	508	850	060	436	334	40'
30'	.3403	.3338	2.996	.3541	2.824	1.061	.9426	1.2305	30'
40'	432	365	971	574	798	062	417	275	20'
50'	462	393	947	607	773	063	407	246	10'
20° 0'	.3491	.3420	2.924	.3640	2.747	1.064	.9397	1.2217	70° 0'
10'	520	448	901	673	723	065	387	188	50'
20'	549	475	878	706	699	066	377	159	40'
30'	.3578	.3502	2.855	.3739	2.675	1.068	.9367	1.2130	30'
40'	607	529	833	772	651	069	356	101	20'
50'	636	557	812	805	628	070	346	072	10'
21° 0'	.3665	.3584	2.790	.3839	2.605	1.071	.9336	1.2043	69° 0'
10'	694	611	769	872	583	072	325	1.2014	50'
20'	723	638	749	906	560	074	315	1.1985	40'
30'	.3752	.3665	2.729	.3939	2.539	1.075	.9304	1.1956	30'
40'	782	692	709	.3973	517	076	293	926	20'
50'	811	719	689	.4006	496	077	283	897	10'
22° 0'	.3840	.3746	2.669	.4040	2.475	1.079	.9272	1.1868	68° 0'
10'	869	773	650	074	455	080	261	839	50'
20'	898	800	632	108	434	081	250	810	40'
30'	.3927	.3827	2.613	.4142	2.414	1.082	.9239	1.1781	30'
40'	956	854	595	176	394	084	228	752	20'
50'	985	881	577	210	375	085	216	723	10'
23° 0'	.4014	.3907	2.559	.4245	2.356	1.086	.9205	1.1694	67° 0'
10'	043	934	542	279	337	088	194	665	50'
20'	072	961	525	314	318	089	182	636	40'
30'	.4102	.3987	2.508	.4348	2.300	1.090	.9171	1.1606	30'
40'	131	.4014	491	383	282	092	159	577	20'
50'	160	041	475	417	264	093	147	548	10'
24° 0'	.4189	.4067	2.459	.4452	2.246	1.095	.9135	1.1519	66° 0'
10'	218	094	443	487	229	096	124	490	50'
20'	247	120	427	522	211	097	112	461	40'
30'	.4276	.4147	2.411	.4557	2.194	1.099	.9100	1.1432	30'
40'	305	173	396	592	177	100	088	403	20'
50'	334	200	381	628	161	102	075	374	10'
25° 0'	.4363	.4226	2.366	.4663	2.145	1.103	.9063	1.1345	65° 0'
10'	392	253	352	699	128	105	051	316	50'
20'	422	279	337	734	112	106	038	286	40'
30'	.4451	.4305	2.323	.4770	2.097	1.108	.9026	1.1257	30'
40'	480	331	309	806	081	109	013	228	20'
50'	509	358	295	841	066	111	.9001	199	10'
26° 0'	.4538	.4384	2.281	.4877	2.050	1.113	.8988	1.1170	64° 0'
10'	567	410	268	913	035	114	975	141	50'
20'	596	436	254	950	020	116	962	112	40'
30'	.4625	.4462	2.241	.4986	2.006	1.117	.8949	1.1083	30'
40'	654	488	228	.5022	1.991	119	936	054	20'
50'	683	514	215	059	977	121	923	1.1025	10'
27° 0'	.4712	.4540	2.203	.5095	1.963	1.122	.8910	1.0996	63° 0'
		Cos	Sec	Cot	Tan	Csc	Sin	Radians	Degrees

Degrees	Radians	Sin	Csc	Tan	Cot	Sec	Cos		
27° 0′	.4712	.4540	2.203	.5095	1.963	1.122	.8910	1.0996	63° 0′
10′	741	566	190	132	949	124	897	966	50′
20′	771	592	178	169	935	126	884	937	40′
30′	.4800	.4617	2.166	.5206	1.921	1.127	.8870	1.0908	30′
40′	829	643	154	243	907	129	857	879	20′
50′	858	669	142	280	894	131	843	850	10′
28° 0′	.4887	.4695	2.130	.5317	1.881	1.133	.8829	1.0821	62° 0′
10′	916	720	118	354	868	134	816	792	50′
20′	945	746	107	392	855	136	802	763	40′
30′	.4974	.4772	2.096	.5430	1.842	1.138	.8788	1.0734	30′
40′	.5003	797	085	467	829	140	774	705	20′
50′	032	823	074	505	816	142	760	676	10′
29° 0′	.5061	.4848	2.063	.5543	1.804	1.143	.8746	1.0647	61° 0′
10′	091	874	052	581	792	145	732	617	50′
20′	120	899	041	619	780	147	718	588	40′
30′	.5149	.4924	2.031	.5658	1.767	1.149	.8704	1.0559	30′
40′	178	950	020	696	756	151	689	530	20′
50′	207	.4975	010	735	744	153	675	501	10′
30° 0′	.5236	.5000	2.000	.5774	1.732	1.155	.8660	1.0472	60° 0′
10′	265	025	1.990	812	720	157	646	443	50′
20′	294	050	980	851	709	159	631	414	40′
30′	.5323	.5075	1.970	.5890	1.698	1.161	.8616	1.0385	30′
40′	352	100	961	930	686	163	601	356	20′
50′	381	125	951	.5969	675	165	587	327	10′
31° 0′	.5411	.5150	1.942	.6009	1.664	1.167	.8572	1.0297	59° 0′
10′	440	175	932	048	653	169	557	268	50′
20′	469	200	923	088	643	171	542	239	40′
30′	.5498	.5225	1.914	.6128	1.632	1.173	.8526	1.0210	30′
40′	527	250	905	168	621	175	511	181	20′
· 50′	556	275	896	208	611	177	496	152	10′
32° 0′	.5585	.5299	1.887	.6249	1.600	1.179	.8480	1.0123	58° 0′
10′	614	324	878	289	590	181	465	094	50′
20′	643	348	870	330	580	184	450	065	40′
30′	.5672	.5373	1.861	.6371	1.570	1.186	.8434	1.0036	30′
40′	701	398	853	412	560	188	418	1.0007	20′
50′	730	422	844	453	550	190	403	.9977	10′
33° 0′	.5760	.5446	1.836	.6494	1.540	1.192	.8387	.9948	57° 0′
10′	789	471	828	536	530	195	371	919	50′
20′	818	495	820	577	520	197	355	890	40′
30′	.5847	.5519	1.812	.6619	1.511	1.199	.8339	.9861	30′
40′	876	544	804	661	501	202	323	832	20′
50′	905	568	796	703	1.492	204	307	803	10′
34° 0′	.5934	.5592	1.788	.6745	1.483	1.206	.8290	.9774	56° 0′
10′	963	616	781	787	473	209	274	745	50′
20′	992	640	773	830	464	211	258	716	40′
30′	.6021	.5664	1.766	.6873	1.455	1.213	.8241	.9687	30′
40′	050	688	758	916	446	216	225	657	20′
50′	080	712	751	.6959	437	218	208	628	10′
35° 0′	.6109	.5736	1.743	.7002	1.428	1.221	.8192	.9599	55° 0′
10′	138	760	736	046	419	223	175	570	50′
20′	167	783	729	089	411	226	158	541	40′
30′	.6196	.5807	1.722	.7133	1.402	1.228	.8141	.9512	30′
40′	225	831	715	177	393	231	124	483	20′
50′	254	854	708	221	385	233	107	454	10′
36° 0′	.6283	.5878	1.701	.7265	1.376	1.236	.8090	.9425	54° 0′
		Cos	Sec	Cot	Tan	Csc	Sin	Radians	Degrees

Degrees	Radians	Sin	Csc	Tan	Cot	Sec	Cos		Degrees
36° 0'	.6283	.5878	1.701	.7265	1.376	1.236	.8090	.9425	54° 0'
10'	312	901	695	310	368	239	073	396	50'
20'	341	925	688	355	360	241	056	367	40'
30'	.6370	.5948	1.681	.7400	1.351	1.244	.8039	.9338	30'
40'	400	972	675	445	343	247	021	308	20'
50'	429	.5995	668	490	335	249	.8004	279	10'
37° 0'	.6458	.6018	1.662	.7536	1.327	1.252	.7986	.9250	53° 0'
10'	487	041	655	581	319	255	969	221	50'
20'	516	065	649	627	311	258	951	192	40'
30'	.6545	.6088	1.643	.7673	1.303	1.260	.7934	.9163	30'
40'	574	111	636	720	295	263	916	134	20'
50'	603	134	630	766	288	266	898	105	10'
38° 0'	.6632	.6157	1.624	.7813	1.280	1.269	.7880	.9076	52° 0'
10'	661	180	618	860	272	272	862	047	50'
20'	690	202	612	907	265	275	844	.9018	40'
30'	.6720	.6225	1.606	.7954	1.257	1.278	.7826	.8988	30'
40'	749	248	601	.8002	250	281	808	959	20'
50'	778	271	595	050	242	284	790	930	10'
39° 0'	.6807	.6293	1.589	.8098	1.235	1.287	.7771	.8901	51° 0'
10'	836	316	583	146	228	290	753	872	50'
20'	865	338	578	195	220	293	735	843	40'
30'	.6894	.6361	1.572	.8243	1.213	1.296	.7716	.8814	30'
40'	923	383	567	292	206	299	698	785	20'
50'	952	406	561	342	199	302	679	756	10'
40° 0'	.6981	.6428	1.556	.8391	1.192	1.305	.7660	.8727	50° 0'
10'	.7010	450	550	441	185	309	642	698	50'
20'	039	472	545	491	178	312	623	668	40'
30'	.7069	.6494	1.540	.8541	1.171	1.315	.7604	.8639	30'
40'	098	517	535	591	164	318	585	610	20'
50'	127	539	529	642	157	322	566	581	10'
41° 0'	.7156	.6561	1.524	.8693	1.150	1.325	.7547	.8552	49° 0'
10'	185	583	519	744	144	328	528	523	50'
20'	214	604	514	796	137	332	509	494	40'
30'	.7243	.6626	1.509	.8847	1.130	1.335	.7490	.8465	30'
40'	272	648	504	899	124	339	470	436	20'
50'	301	670	499	.8952	117	342	451	407	10'
42° 0'	.7330	.6691	1.494	.9004	1.111	1.346	.7431	.8378	48° 0'
10'	359	713	490	057	104	349	412	348	50'
20'	389	734	485	110	098	353	392	319	40'
30'	.7418	.6756	1.480	.9163	1.091	1.356	.7373	.8290	30
40'	447	777	476	217	085	360	353	261	20'
50'	476	799	471	271	079	364	333	232	10'
43° 0'	.7505	.6820	1.466	.9325	1.072	1.367	.7314	.8203	47° 0'
10'	534	841	462	380	066	371	294	174	50'
20'	563	862	457	435	060	375	274	145	40'
30'	.7592	.6884	1.453	.9490	1.054	1.379	.7254	.8116	30'
40'	621	905	448	545	048	382	234	087	20'
50'	650	926	444	601	042	386	214	058	10'
44° 0'	.7679	.6947	1.440	.9657	1.036	1.390	.7193	.8029	46° 0'
10'	709	967	435	713	030	394	173	.7999	50'
20'	738	.6988	431	770	024	398	153	970	40'
30'	.7767	.7009	1.427	.9827	1.018	1.402	.7133	.7941	30'
40'	796	030	423	884	012	406	112	912	20'
50'	825	050	418	.9942	006	410	092	883	10'
45° 0'	.7854	.7071	1.414	1.000	1.000	1.414	.7071	.7854	45° 0'
		Cos	Sec	Cot	Tan	Csc	Sin	Radians	Degrees

Angle	L Sin	d 1′	L Tan	cd 1′	L Cot	d 1′	L Cos	Angle
0° 0′	———		———		———	.0	10.0000	90° 0′
10′	7.4637	301.1	7.4637	301.1	12.5363	.0	.0000	50′
20′	.7648	176.0	.7648	176.1	.2352	.0	.0000	40′
30′	7.9408	125.0	7.9409	124.9	12.0591	.0	.0000	30′
40′	8.0658	96.9	8.0658	96.9	11.9342	.0	.0000	20′
50′	.1627	79.2	.1627	79.2	.8373	.0	10.0000	10′
1° 0′	8.2419	66.9	8.2419	67.0	11.7581	.1	9.9999	89° 0′
10′	.3088	58.0	.3089	58.0	.6911	.0	.9999	50′
20′	.3668	51.1	.3669	51.2	.6331	.0	.9999	40′
30′	.4179	45.8	.4181	45.7	.5819	.0	.9999	30′
40′	.4637	41.3	.4638	41.5	.5362	.1	.9998	20′
50′	.5050	37.8	.5053	37.8	.4947	.0	.9998	10′
2° 0′	8.5428	34.8	8.5431	34.8	11.4569	.1	9.9997	88° 0′
10′	.5776	32.1	.5779	32.2	.4221	.0	.9997	50′
20′	.6097	30.0	.6101	30.0	.3899	.1	.9996	40′
30′	.6397	28.0	.6401	28.1	.3599	.0	.9996	30′
40′	.6677	26.3	.6682	26.3	.3318	.1	.9995	20′
50′	.6940	24.8	.6945	24.9	.3055	.0	.9995	10′
3° 0′	8.7188	23.5	8.7194	23.5	11.2806	.1	9.9994	87° 0′
10′	.7423	22.2	.7429	22.3	.2571	.1	.9993	50′
20′	.7645	21.2	.7652	21.3	.2348	.0	.9993	40′
30′	.7857	20.2	.7865	20.2	.2135	.1	.9992	30′
40′	.8059	19.2	.8067	19.4	.1933	.1	.9991	20′
50′	.8251	18.5	.8261	18.5	.1739	.1	.9990	10′
4° 0′	8.8436	17.7	8.8446	17.8	11.1554	.1	9.9989	86° 0′
10′	.8613	17.0	.8624	17.1	.1376	.0	.9989	50′
20′	.8783	16.3	.8795	16.5	.1205	.1	.9988	40′
30′	.8946	15.8	.8960	15.8	.1040	.1	.9987	30′
40′	.9104	15.2	.9118	15.4	.0882	.1	.9986	20′
50′	.9256	14.7	.9272	14.8	.0728	.1	.9985	10′
5° 0′	8.9403	14.2	8.9420	14.3	11.0580	.2	9.9983	85° 0′
10′	.9545	13.7	.9563	13.8	.0437	.1	.9982	50′
20′	.9682	13.4	.9701	13.5	.0299	.1	.9981	40′
30′	.9816	12.9	.9836	13.0	.0164	.1	.9980	30′
40′	8.9945	12.5	8.9966	12.7	11.0034	.1	.9979	20′
50′	9.0070	12.2	9.0093	12.3	10.9907	.2	.9977	10′
6° 0′	9.0192	11.9	9.0216	12.0	10.9784	.1	9.9976	84° 0′
10′	.0311	11.5	.0336	11.7	.9664	.1	.9975	50′
20′	.0426	11.3	.0453	11.4	.9547	.2	.9973	40′
30′	.0539	10.9	.0567	11.1	.9433	.1	.9972	30′
40′	.0648	10.7	.0678	10.8	.9322	.1	.9971	20′
50′	.0755	10.4	.0786	10.5	.9214	.2	.9969	10′
7° 0′	9.0859	10.2	9.0891	10.4	10.9109	.1	9.9968	83° 0′
10′	.0961	9.9	.0995	10.1	.9005	.2	.9966	50′
20′	.1060	9.7	.1096	9.8	.8904	.2	.9964	40′
30′	.1157	9.5	.1194	9.7	.8806	.1	.9963	30′
40′	.1252	9.3	.1291	9.4	.8709	.2	.9961	20′
50′	.1345	9.1	.1385	9.3	.8615	.2	.9959	10′
8° 0′	9.1436	8.9	9.1478	9.1	10.8522	.1	9.9958	82° 0′
10′	.1525	8.7	.1569	8.9	.8431	.2	.9956	50′
20′	.1612	8.5	.1658	8.7	.8342	.2	.9954	40′
30′	.1697	8.4	.1745	8.6	.8255	.2	.9952	30′
40′	.1781	8.2	.1831	8.4	.8169	.2	.9950	20′
50′	.1863	8.0	.1915	8.2	.8085	.2	.9948	10′
9° 0′	9.1943		9.1997		10.8003	.2	9.9946	81° 0′
	L Cos	d 1′	L Cot	cd 1′	L Tan	1 d′	L Sin	Angle

† Subtract 10 from each entry in this table to obtain the proper logarithm of the indicated trigonometric function.

Angle	L Sin	d 1'	L Tan	cd 1'	L Cot	d 1'	L Cos	Angle
9° 0'	9.1943		9.1997		10.8003		9.9946	81° 0'
10'	.2022	7.9	.2078	8.1	.7922	.2	.9944	50'
20'	.2100	7.8	.2158	8.0	.7842	.2	.9942	40'
30'	.2176	7.6	.2236	7.8	.7764	.2	.9940	30'
40'	.2251	7.5	.2313	7.7	.7687	.2	.9938	20'
50'	.2324	7.3	.2389	7.6	.7611	.2	.9936	10'
10° 0'	9.2397	7.3	9.2463	7.4	10.7537	.2	9.9934	80° 0'
10'	.2468	7.1	.2536	7.3	.7464	.3	.9931	50'
20'	.2538	7.0	.2609	7.3	.7391	.2	.9929	40'
30'	.2606	6.8	.2680	7.1	.7320	.2	.9927	30'
40'	.2674	6.8	.2750	7.0	.7250	.3	.9924	20'
50'	.2740	6.6	.2819	6.9	.7181	.2	.9922	10'
11° 0'	9.2806	6.6	9.2887	6.8	10.7113	.3	9.9919	79° 0'
10'	.2870	6.4	.2953	6.6	.7047	.2	.9917	50'
20'	.2934	6.4	.3020	6.7	.6980	.3	.9914	40'
30'	.2997	6.3	.3085	6.5	.6915	.2	.9912	30'
40'	.3058	6.1	.3149	6.4	.6851	.3	.9909	20'
50'	.3119	6.1	.3212	6.3	.6788	.2	.9907	10'
12° 0'	9.3179	6.0	9.3275	6.3	10.6725	.3	9.9904	78° 0'
10'	.3238	5.9	.3336	6.1	.6664	.3	.9901	50'
20'	.3296	5.8	.3397	6.1	.6603	.2	.9899	40'
30'	.3353	5.7	.3458	6.1	.6542	.3	.9896	30'
40'	.3410	5.7	.3517	5.9	.6483	.3	.9893	20'
50'	.3466	5.6	.3576	5.9	.6424	.3	.9890	10'
13° 0'	9.3521	5.5	9.3634	5.8	10.6366	.3	9.9887	77° 0'
10'	.3575	5.4	.3691	5.7	.6309	.3	.9884	50'
20'	.3629	5.4	.3748	5.7	.6252	.3	.9881	40'
30'	.3682	5.3	.3804	5.6	.6196	.3	.9878	30'
40'	.3734	5.2	.3859	5.5	.6141	.3	.9875	20'
50'	.3786	5.2	.3914	5.5	.6086	.3	.9872	10'
14° 0'	9.3837	5.1	9.3968	5.4	10.6032	.3	9.9869	76° 0'
10'	.3887	5.0	.4021	5.3	.5979	.3	.9866	50'
20'	.3937	5.0	.4074	5.3	.5926	.3	.9863	40'
30'	.3986	4.9	.4127	5.3	.5873	.4	.9859	30'
40'	.4035	4.9	.4178	5.1	.5822	.3	.9856	20'
50'	.4083	4.8	.4230	5.2	.5770	.3	.9853	10'
15° 0'	9.4130	4.7	9.4281	5.1	10.5719	.4	9.9849	75° 0'
10'	.4177	4.7	.4331	5.0	.5669	.3	.9846	50'
20'	.4223	4.6	.4381	5.0	.5619	.3	.9843	40'
30'	.4269	4.6	.4430	4.9	.5570	.4	.9839	30'
40'	.4314	4.5	.4479	4.9	.5521	.3	.9836	20'
50'	.4359	4.5	.4527	4.8	.5473	.4	.9832	10'
16° 0'	9.4403	4.4	9.4575	4.8	10.5425	.4	9.9828	74° 0'
10'	.4447	4.4	.4622	4.7	.5378	.3	.9825	50'
20'	.4491	4.4	.4669	4.7	.5331	.4	.9821	40'
30'	.4533	4.2	.4716	4.7	.5284	.4	.9817	30'
40'	.4576	4.3	.4762	4.6	.5238	.3	.9814	20'
50'	.4618	4.2	.4808	4.6	.5192	.4	.9810	10'
17° 0'	9.4659	4.1	9.4853	4.5	10.5147	.4	9.9806	73° 0'
10'	.4700	4.1	.4898	4.5	.5102	.4	.9802	50'
20'	.4741	4.1	.4943	4.5	.5057	.4	.9798	40'
30'	.4781	4.0	.4987	4 4	.5013	.4	.9794	30'
40'	.4821	4.0	.5031	4.4	.4969	.4	.9790	20'
50'	.4861	4.0	.5075	4.4	.4925	.4	.9786	10'
18° 0'	9.4900	3.9	9.5118	4.3	10.4882	.4	9.9782	72° 0'
	L Cos	d 1'	L Cot	cd 1'	L Tan	d 1'	L Sin	Angle

† Subtract 10 from each entry in this table to obtain the proper logarithm of the indicated trigonometric function.

Angle	L Sin	d 1'	L Tan	cd 1'	L Cot	d 1'	L Cos	Angle
18° 0'	9.4900		9.5118		10.4882		9.9782	72° 0'
10'	.4939	3.9	.5161	4.3	.4839	.4	.9778	50'
20'	.4977	3.8	.5203	4.2	.4797	.4	.9774	40'
30'	.5015	3.8	.5245	4.2	.4755	.4	.9770	30'
40'	.5052	3.7	.5287	4.2	.4713	.5	.9765	20'
50'	.5090	3.8	.5329	4.2	.4671	.4	.9761	10'
19° 0'	9.5126	3.6	9.5370	4.1	10.4630	.4	9.9757	71° 0'
10'	.5163	3.7	.5411	4.1	.4589	.5	.9752	50'
20'	.5199	3.6	.5451	4.0	.4549	.4	.9748	40'
30'	.5235	3.6	.5491	4.0	.4509	.5	.9743	30'
40'	.5270	3.5	.5531	4.0	.4469	.4	.9739	20'
50'	.5306	3.6	.5571	4.0	.4429	.5	.9734	10'
20° 0'	9.5341	3.5	9.5611	4.0	10.4389	.4	9.9730	70° 0'
10'	.5375	3.4	.5650	3.9	.4350	.5	.9725	50'
20'	.5409	3.4	.5689	3.9	.4311	.4	.9721	40'
30'	.5443	3.4	.5727	3.8	.4273	.5	.9716	30'
40'	.5477	3.4	.5766	3.9	.4234	.5	.9711	20'
50'	.5510	3.3	.5804	3.8	.4196	.5	.9706	10'
21° 0'	9.5543	3.3	9.5842	3.8	10.4158	.4	9.9702	69° 0'
10'	.5576	3.3	.5879	3.7	.4121	.5	.9697	50'
20'	.5609	3.3	.5917	3.8	.4083	.5	.9692	40'
30'	.5641	3.2	.5954	3.7	.4046	.5	.9687	30'
40'	.5673	3.2	.5991	3.7	.4009	.5	.9682	20'
50'	.5704	3.1	.6028	3.7	.3972	.5	.9677	10'
22° 0'	9.5736	3.2	9.6064	3.6	10.3936	.5	9.9672	68° 0'
10'	.5767	3.1	.6100	3.6	.3900	.5	.9667	50'
20'	.5798	3.1	.6136	3.6	.3864	.6	.9661	40'
30'	.5828	3.0	.6172	3.6	.3828	.5	.9656	30'
40'	.5859	3.1	.6208	3.6	.3792	.5	.9651	20'
50'	.5889	3.0	.6243	3.5	.3757	.5	.9646	10'
23° 0'	9.5919	3.0	9.6279	3.6	10.3721	.6	9.9640	67° 0'
10'	.5948	2.9	.6314	3.5	.3686	.5	.9635	50'
20'	.5978	3.0	.6348	3.4	.3652	.6	.9629	40'
30'	.6007	2.9	.6383	3.5	.3617	.5	.9624	30'
40'	.6036	2.9	.6417	3.4	.3583	.6	.9618	20'
50'	.6065	2.9	.6452	3.5	.3548	.5	.9613	10'
24° 0'	9.6093	2.8	9.6486	3.4	10.3514	.6	9.9607	66° 0'
10'	.6121	2.8	.6520	3.4	.3480	.5	.9602	50'
20'	.6149	2.8	.6553	3.3	.3447	.6	.9596	40'
30'	.6177	2.8	.6587	3.4	.3413	.6	.9590	30'
40'	.6205	2.8	.6620	3.3	.3380	.6	.9584	20'
50'	.6232	2.7	.6654	3.4	.3346	.5	.9579	10'
25° 0'	9.6259	2.7	9.6687	3.3	10.3313	.6	9.9573	65° 0'
10'	.6286	2.7	.6720	3.3	.3280	.6	.9567	50'
20'	.6313	2.7	.6752	3.2	.3248	.6	.9561	40'
30'	.6340	2.7	.6785	3.3	.3215	.6	.9555	30'
40'	.6366	2.6	.6817	3.2	.3183	.6	.9549	20'
50'	.6392	2.6	.6850	3.3	.3150	.6	.9543	10'
26° 0'	9.6418	2.6	9.6882	3.2	10.3118	.6	9.9537	64° 0'
10'	.6444	2.6	.6914	3.2	.3086	.7	.9530	50'
20'	.6470	2.6	.6946	3.2	.3054	.6	.9524	40'
30'	.6495	2.5	.6977	3.1	.3023	.6	.9518	30'
40'	.6521	2.6	.7009	3.2	.2991	.6	.9512	20'
50'	.6546	2.5	.7040	3.1	.2960	.7	.9505	10'
27° 0'	9.6570	2.4	9.7072	3.2	10.2928	.6	9.9499	63° 0'
	L Cos	d 1'	L Cot	cd 1'	L Tan	d 1'	L Sin	Angle

† Subtract 10 from each entry in this table to obtain the proper logarithm of the indicated trigonometric function.

Angle	L Sin	d 1'	L Tan	cd 1'	L Cot	d 1'	L Cos	Angle
27° 0'	9.6570	2.5	9.7072	3.1	10.2928	.7	9.9499	63° 0'
10'	.6595	2.5	.7103	3.1	.2897	.6	.9492	50'
20'	.6620	2.4	.7134	3.1	.2866	.7	.9486	40'
30'	.6644	2.4	.7165	3.1	.2835	.6	.9479	30'
40'	.6668	2.4	.7196	3.0	.2804	.7	.9473	20'
50'	.6692	2.4	.7226	3.1	.2774	.7	.9466	10'
28° 0'	9.6716	2.4	9.7257	3.0	10.2743	.6	9.9459	62° 0'
10'	.6740	2.3	.7287	3.0	.2713	.7	.9453	50'
20'	.6763	2.4	.7317	3.1	.2683	.7	.9446	40'
30'	.6787	2.3	.7348	3.0	.2652	.7	.9439	30'
40'	.6810	2.3	.7378	3.0	.2622	.7	.9432	20'
50'	.6833	2.3	.7408	3.0	.2592	.7	.9425	10'
29° 0'	9.6856	2.2	9.7438	2.9	10.2562	.7	9.9418	61° 0'
10'	.6878	2.3	.7467	3.0	.2533	.7	.9411	50'
20'	.6901	2.2	.7497	2.9	.2503	.7	.9404	40'
30'	.6923	2.3	.7526	3.0	.2474	.7	.9397	30'
40'	.6946	2.2	.7556	2.9	.2444	.7	.9390	20'
50'	.6968	2.2	.7585	2.9	.2415	.8	.9383	10'
30° 0'	9.6990	2.2	9.7614	3.0	10.2386	.7	9.9375	60° 0'
10'	.7012	2.1	.7644	2.9	.2356	.7	.9368	50'
20'	.7033	2.2	.7673	2.8	.2327	.8	.9361	40'
30'	.7055	2.1	.7701	2.9	.2299	.7	.9353	30'
40'	.7076	2.1	.7730	2.9	.2270	.8	.9346	20'
50'	.7097	2.1	.7759	2.9	.2241	.7	.9338	10'
31° 0'	9.7118	2.1	9.7788	2.8	10.2212	.8	9.9331	59° 0'
10'	.7139	2.1	.7816	2.9	.2184	.8	.9323	50'
20'	.7160	2.1	.7845	2.8	.2155	.8	.9315	40'
30'	.7181	2.0	.7873	2.9	.2127	.7	.9308	30'
40'	.7201	2.1	.7902	2.8	.2098	.8	.9300	20'
50'	.7222	2.0	.7930	2.8	.2070	.8	.9292	10'
32° 0'	9.7242	2.0	9.7958	2.8	10.2042	.8	9.9284	58° 0'
10'	.7262	2.0	.7986	2.8	.2014	.8	.9276	50'
20'	.7282	2.0	.8014	2.8	.1986	.8	.9268	40'
30'	.7302	2.0	.8042	2.8	.1958	.8	.9260	30'
40'	.7322	2.0	.8070	2.8	.1930	.8	.9252	20'
50'	.7342	1.9	.8097	2.7	.1903	.8	.9244	10'
33° 0'	9.7361	1.9	9.8125	2.8	10.1875	.8	9.9236	57° 0'
10'	.7380	2.0	.8153	2.8	.1847	.8	.9228	50'
20'	.7400	1.9	.8180	2.7	.1820	.9	.9219	40'
30'	.7419	1.9	.8208	2.8	.1792	.8	.9211	30'
40'	.7438	1.9	.8235	2.7	.1765	.8	.9203	20'
50'	.7457	1.9	.8263	2.8	.1737	.9	.9194	10'
34° 0'	9.7476	1.8	9.8290	2.7	10.1710	.8	9.9186	56° 0'
10'	.7494	1.9	.8317	2.7	.1683	.9	.9177	50'
20'	.7513	1.8	.8344	2.7	.1656	.8	.9169	40'
30'	.7531	1.9	.8371	2.7	.1629	.9	.9160	30'
40'	.7550	1.8	.8398	2.7	.1602	.9	.9151	20'
50'	.7568	1.8	.8425	2.7	.1575	.9	.9142	10'
35° 0'	9.7586	1.8	9.8452	2.7	10.1548	.8	9.9134	55° 0'
10'	.7604	1.8	.8479	2.7	.1521	.9	.9125	50'
20'	.7622	1.8	.8506	2.7	.1494	.9	.9116	40'
30'	.7640	1.8	.8533	2.7	.1467	.9	.9107	30'
40'	.7657	1.7	.8559	2.6	.1441	.9	.9098	20'
50'	.7675	1.8	.8586	2.7	.1414	.9	.9089	10'
36° 0'	9.7692		9.8613		10.1387		9.9080	54° 0'
	L Cos	d 1'	L Cot	cd 1'	L Tan	d 1'	L Sin	Angle

† Subtract 10 from each entry in this table to obtain the proper logarithm of the indicated trigonometric function.

Angle	L Sin	d 1'	L Tan	cd 1'	L Cot	d 1'	L Cos	
36° 0'	9.7692		9.8613		10.1387		9.9080	54° 0'
10'	.7710	1.8	.8639	2.6	.1361	1.0	.9070	50'
20'	.7727	1.7	.8666	2.7	.1334	.9	.9061	40'
30'	.7744	1.7	.8692	2.6	.1308	.9	.9052	30'
40'	.7761	1.7	.8718	2.6	.1282	1.0	.9042	20'
50'	.7778	1.7	.8745	2.7	.1255	.9	.9033	10'
37° 0'	9.7795	1.7	9.8771	2.6	10.1229	1.0	9.9023	53° 0'
10'	.7811	1.6	.8797	2.6	.1203	.9	.9014	50'
20'	.7828	1.7	.8824	2.7	.1176	1.0	.9004	40'
30'	.7844	1.6	.8850	2.6	.1150	.9	.8995	30'
40'	.7861	1.7	.8876	2.6	.1124	1.0	.8985	20'
50'	.7877	1.6	.8902	2.6	.1098	1.0	.8975	10'
38° 0'	9.7893	1.6	9.8928	2.6	10.1072	1.0	9.8965	52° 0'
10'	.7910	1.7	.8954	2.6	.1046	1.0	.8955	50'
20'	.7926	1.6	.8980	2.6	.1020	1.0	.8945	40'
30'	.7941	1.5	.9006	2.6	.0994	1.0	.8935	30'
40'	.7957	1.6	.9032	2.6	.0968	1.0	.8925	20'
50'	.7973	1.6	.9058	2.6	.0942	1.0	.8915	10'
39° 0'	9.7989	1.6	9.9084	2.6	10.0916	1.0	9.8905	51° 0'
10'	.8004	1.5	.9110	2.6	.0890	1.0	.8895	50'
20'	.8020	1.6	.9135	2.5	.0865	1.1	.8884	40'
30'	.8035	1.5	.9161	2.6	.0839	1.0	.8874	30'
40'	.8050	1.5	.9187	2.6	.0813	1.0	.8864	20'
50'	.8066	1.6	.9212	2.5	.0788	1.1	.8853	10'
40° 0'	9.8081	1.5	9.9238	2.6	10.0762	1.0	9.8843	50° 0'
10'	.8096	1.5	.9264	2.6	.0736	1.1	.8832	50'
20'	.8111	1.5	.9289	2.5	.0711	1.1	.8821	40'
30'	.8125	1.4	.9315	2.6	.0685	1.1	.8810	30'
40'	.8140	1.5	.9341	2.6	.0659	1.0	.8800	20'
50'	.8155	1.5	.9366	2.5	.0634	1.1	.8789	10'
41° 0'	9.8169	1.4	9.9392	2.6	10.0608	1.1	9.8778	49° 0'
10'	.8184	1.5	.9417	2.5	.0583	1.1	.8767	50'
20'	.8198	1.4	.9443	2.6	.0557	1.1	.8756	40'
30'	.8213	1.5	.9468	2.5	.0532	1.1	.8745	30'
40'	.8227	1.4	.9494	2.6	.0506	1.2	.8733	20'
50'	.8241	1.4	.9519	2.5	.0481	1.1	.8722	10'
42° 0'	9.8255	1.4	9.9544	2.5	10.0456	1.1	9.8711	48° 0'
10'	.8269	1.4	.9570	2.6	.0430	1.2	.8699	50'
20'	.8283	1.4	.9595	2.5	.0405	1.1	.8688	40'
30'	.8297	1.4	.9621	2.6	.0379	1.2	.8676	30'
40'	.8311	1.4	.9646	2.5	.0354	1.1	.8665	20'
50'	.8324	1.3	.9671	2.5	.0329	1.2	.8653	10'
43° 0'	9.8338	1.4	9.9697	2.6	10.0303	1.2	9.8641	47° 0'
10'	.8351	1.3	.9722	2.5	.0278	1.2	.8629	50'
20'	.8365	1.4	.9747	2.5	.0253	1.1	.8618	40'
30'	.8378	1.3	.9772	2.5	.0228	1.2	.8606	30'
40'	.8391	1.3	.9798	2.6	.0202	1.2	.8594	20'
50'	.8405	1.4	.9823	2.5	.0177	1.2	.8582	10'
44° 0'	9.8418	1.3	9.9848	2.5	10.0152	1.3	9.8569	46° 0'
10'	.8431	1.3	.9874	2.6	.0126	1.2	.8557	50'
20'	.8444	1.3	.9899	2.5	.0101	1.2	.8545	40'
30'	.8457	1.3	.9924	2.5	.0076	1.3	.8532	30'
40'	.8469	1.2	.9949	2.5	.0051	1.2	.8520	20'
50'	.8482	1.3	9.9975	2.6	.0025	1.3	.8507	10'
45° 0'	9.8495	1.3	10.0000	2.5	10.0000	1.2	9.8495	45° 0'
	L Cos	d 1'	L Cot	cd 1'	L Tan	d 1'	L Sin	Angle

† Subtract 10 from each entry in this table to obtain the proper logarithm of the indicated trigonometric function.

ANSWERS AND HINTS

Neither answer nor hint should be consulted until the solution has been attempted. The hints are not intended to be complete solutions. Many of the illustrations will be rough sketches.

SET 1–2

1. (c).

3. Postulates (1), (2), (3), (4), (7), and the first part of (6).

5. Assume "u" is an element such that $u \cdot t = t$ for all "t" in the field. Then $u \cdot 1 = 1$ since 1 is in the field. Also, $u \cdot 1 = u$ since 1 is a multiplicative identity. Hence, $u = 1$.

7. See Section 1–7 for the definition of rational number, $\{\frac{25}{4}, \frac{13}{2}, \frac{27}{4}, 7, \frac{29}{4}\}$ is such a set.

9. See answer to Problem 7.

SET 1–4

1. $\dfrac{1111}{240}$.

3.

$$\frac{A}{D} + \frac{B}{D} - \frac{C}{D} = A \cdot \frac{1}{D} + B \cdot \frac{1}{D} - C \cdot \frac{1}{D} \qquad \text{Definition of multiplication of fractions and postulate 3.}$$

$$= A \cdot \frac{1}{D} + B \cdot \frac{1}{D} + (-C) \cdot \frac{1}{D} \qquad \text{Postulate 6. (See also the discussion following the postulates.)}$$

$$= (A + B) \cdot \frac{1}{D} + (-C) \cdot \frac{1}{D} \qquad \text{Postulate 7.}$$

$$= (A + B + (-C)) \cdot \frac{1}{D} \qquad \text{Postulate 7.}$$

$$= \frac{A + B + (-C)}{D} \qquad \text{Same as step 1.}$$

$$= \frac{A + B - C}{D} \qquad \text{Same as step 2.}$$

5. $\dfrac{8x^2 - 21x - 48}{(x - 3)(x - 4)(x + 4)}$.

6. $\dfrac{8y^2 - 21y - 48}{(y - 3)(y - 4)(y + 4)}$.

7. $\dfrac{4}{(x - 2)(x - 3)^2}$.

8. $f(3) = -\dfrac{9}{43}, f(7) = -\dfrac{7}{81}, f(y) = \dfrac{3y}{2 - 5y^2}, f(y + \Delta y) = \dfrac{3y + 3\Delta y}{2 - 5y^2 - 10y\Delta y - 5\Delta y^2}$.

$$f(y + \Delta y) - f(y) = \frac{3y + 3\Delta y}{2 - 5(y + \Delta y)^2} - \frac{3y}{2 - 5y^2} = \frac{6\Delta y + 15y^2\Delta y + 15y\Delta y^2}{(2 - 5y^2 - 10y\Delta y - 5\Delta y^2)(2 - 5y^2)}.$$

9. $f(-2)$ is undefined; $f(2) = \frac{5}{2}; f(2y + \Delta y) - f(2y) = \dfrac{5\Delta y}{(2 + 2y + \Delta y)(1 + y)}$.

10. $(6y - 5)\Delta y + 3\Delta y^2$.

11. $\dfrac{-2\Delta y}{y(y + \Delta y)}, \dfrac{-2\Delta x}{3(3 + \Delta x)}$.

13. -10.

15. $-\dfrac{14z + 7\Delta z}{z^2(z + \Delta z)^2}$.

17. By Postulate 6 and the discussion following the postulates, $\dfrac{A}{B}$ divided by $\dfrac{C}{D}$ means $\dfrac{A}{D}$ multiplied by the inverse of $\dfrac{C}{D}$, and the inverse of $\dfrac{C}{D}$ is $\dfrac{D}{C}$ since $\dfrac{C}{D} \cdot \dfrac{D}{C} = 1$.

21. Example 6 is the multiplicative inverse of Problem 16 if "a" is replaced by "x".
23. 1800 mph   **25.** 9.

SET 1–7

1. $T: \{a, b, c, d\};$ $F: \{e, f, g, h, i, j\}.$
   (e) $\pi^2 > \sqrt{75}.$ **(f)** $\pi < 3.1416.$
   (g) $|\sqrt{14} - 5| > \sqrt{14} - 5.$ **(h)** $\dfrac{\pi}{3} < 60.$

   (i) $\dfrac{1}{3+2} < \dfrac{1}{3} + \dfrac{1}{2}$ **(j)** $(\tfrac{1}{4})^2 < \tfrac{1}{4}.$

3. Integers: 3, 20, -7, 1, 14, -21, $|2|$, $|-3|$, 60.

Rational Numbers: All the integers and 3.1416, $\dfrac{1}{3+2}, \dfrac{1}{3} + \dfrac{1}{2}, \left(\dfrac{1}{4}\right)^2, \dfrac{1}{4}.$

Real Numbers: All the integers and rational numbers and π^2, $\sqrt{75}$, π, $|\sqrt{14} - 5|$,
$$\sqrt{14} - 5, \dfrac{\pi}{3}.$$

Complex Numbers: All of the twenty numbers.
5. $\{g, j, k, q, v, w, x, y, z\}.$

SET 1–8

1. $A = \dfrac{\pi d^2}{4}.$ **2.** $A = \dfrac{c^2}{4\pi}.$

5. $f(-1) = 74,$ $f(2) = -136,$ $f(8) = -502,$ $f(3 + \Delta t) - f(3) = -65\Delta t + \Delta t^2,$
$f(y + \Delta y) - f(y) = (2y - 71)\Delta y + \Delta y^2.$

6. $g(2) = \tfrac{4}{3}, g(3 + .1) - g(3) = \tfrac{53}{2790} \approx .02, g(x + \Delta x) - g(x) = \dfrac{(x^2 - 4 + x\Delta x)\Delta x}{3x(x + \Delta x)}.$

7. $f(7) - g(3) = -447\tfrac{4}{9} \approx -447.4, \dfrac{f(3)}{g(2) + 1} = -\dfrac{606}{7} \approx -86.6.$ **9.** $A = \dfrac{n + 5}{12}$

10. See 15 of Set 1–4.   **11.** $\dfrac{-21(2t - \Delta t)}{t^2(t + \Delta t)^2}.$ **13.** $\dfrac{\Delta t + 2t}{3}.$

17. Yes. The set of all dates that occur during the year.   **21.** $I = \tfrac{157}{140}t.$
23. A set of ordered pairs could contain elements such as [3, 5], [3, 6], in which case
more than one value $f(t)$ corresponds to a given t.
25. $y = g(t)$ is a relation since for a given t, more than one $g(t)$ corresponds to it.

SET 1–10

3. $x^2 + \dfrac{B}{A}x + \dfrac{C}{A} = 0,$ yes, $A\left(x^2 + \dfrac{B}{A}x + \dfrac{C}{A}\right) = 0.$ **5.** $\tfrac{2}{7}, -8.$

6. $A = 3, B = -2.$ **7.** $A = -7, B = -3, C = 7.$
9. $\tfrac{1}{3}(2z - 1 \pm \sqrt{7z^2 - 13z + 4}).$ **11.** $z = 5; z = 2.$
12. $\tfrac{1}{6}(5i - 2 \pm \sqrt{4i - 57}).$ **13.** $b = \tfrac{1}{2}(-5 \pm \sqrt{65}).$
15. $-2, 3.$ **17.** $\tfrac{1050}{137} \approx 7.7.$ **19.** 9 in. by 12 in.

20. (a) $\dfrac{5x + 2}{(2x + \tfrac{5}{4})^2 - (\tfrac{11}{4})^2},$ **(b)** $\dfrac{3}{\sqrt{\left(\dfrac{3}{\sqrt{2}}\right)^2 - \left(\sqrt{2}\left[x - \dfrac{3}{2}\right]\right)^2}},$

   (c) $\dfrac{3x + 1}{(x + 1)^2 + (\sqrt{2})^2}.$

21. (a) $\dfrac{20x + 12}{(2x + 1)^2 + (\sqrt{3})^2}$, (b) $\dfrac{13t}{(3t - 2)^2 + (4)^2}$, (c) $\dfrac{-15}{(3x - 1)^2 - (1)^2}$,

(d) $\dfrac{196a}{(2ax + b)^2 + (\sqrt{4ac - b^2})^2}$ if $b^2 \leqq 4ac$, $\dfrac{196a}{(2ax + b)^2 - (\sqrt{b^2 - 4ac})^2}$ if $b^2 \geqq 4ac$.

25. $|k| < 12$.   **27.** $\pm\dfrac{\sqrt{6}}{2}, \pm 2i$.   **28.** $-2, 4, -3, 5$.   **29.** $-1.3, 1.9$.

31. $\frac{1}{4}(-3 \pm j\sqrt{1591})$.   **33.** $4, t = -4 + \sqrt{16 + 2s}$.   **35.** 3 hrs, 30 min over.

SET 1-12

1. 7.   **2.** $-1, \frac{1}{3}$.   **3.** 10.   **4.** No solution.   **5.** $\frac{1}{2}(13 \pm \sqrt{161})$.

6. 3.   **7.** 0.   **8.** $-\frac{1}{2}$.   **9.** ± 6.   **10.** $\dfrac{41 \pm \sqrt{141}}{70} \approx \begin{cases} .76 \\ .42 \end{cases}$

11. No solution.   **13.** $(x = 2, y = 5), (x = \frac{14}{5}, y = \frac{23}{5})$.

15. $-\sqrt{x - 3} = x - 5$ has solution $x = 4$. $-\sqrt{3 - 2x} + 5 = 0$ has solution $x = -11$. $-\sqrt{w + 4} + w - 2 = 0$ has solution $w = 5$. $-4\sqrt{2x + 3} + 5 = 0$ has solution $x = -\frac{23}{32}$. $-\sqrt{3x^2 + 7} + 2 = 0$ has solutions $x = \pm i$.

16. No solution.   **17.** $x = \dfrac{3 - 2\sqrt{2}}{50} = \dfrac{(\sqrt{2} - 1)^2}{50}$.   **19.** -1.

21. $x = 4$.   **23.** (a) $x = 4$, (b) $x = -1$.   **25.** $x = 9$.

27. $\Delta f(2y, \Delta y) = \dfrac{5\Delta y}{(1 + y)(2 + 2y + \Delta y)}; \Delta f(2t, \Delta t) = \dfrac{5\Delta t}{(1 + t)(2 + 2t + \Delta t)}$.

29. $\dfrac{\Delta f(z, \Delta z)}{\Delta z} = \dfrac{-7(2z - \Delta z)}{z^2(z + \Delta z)^2}$.

SELF TEST 1-13

1. $\dfrac{x^2 + 3x + 5}{(2x - 3)(x - 2)(x + 1)}$.   **2.** $\dfrac{6}{(3x + 3\Delta x + 1)(3x + 1)}$ if $\Delta x \neq 0$.

3. $x = 3$.   **4.** $2x^2 - 2x - 1 = 0$.

5. $\left| \dfrac{-B + \sqrt{B^2 - 4AC}}{2A} - \dfrac{-B - \sqrt{B^2 - 4AC}}{2A} \right| = ?$.

6. (a) $k = \pm 12$,   (b) $-12 < k < 12$.   **7.** (a) $\dfrac{3 - x}{2}$, (b) $\dfrac{\Delta t}{2t(t + \Delta t)}$.

8. $x = \pm 5; x = \pm\sqrt{6}$.   **9.** $B = 3; C = 4; A = -4$.

10. $4(x - \frac{5}{2})^2 - 9$.   **11.** (a) $-\dfrac{B}{A} = +\dfrac{2}{3}, \dfrac{C}{A} = -\dfrac{2}{3}$ (b) $\dfrac{1 \pm \sqrt{7}}{3}$.

SET 1-16

1. $24 = 3 + 3 \cdot 7 \equiv 3 \pmod 7$.

3. The only *possible* solutions are 0, 1, 2, 3, 4, 5, 6.   By substitution, 4 is the only solution.

5. Write $297 = 7 \cdot 42 + 3$.   The equation then becomes $(7 \cdot 42 + 3)x + 6 \equiv 0 \pmod 7$.   But $7 \cdot 42 \cdot x \equiv 0 \pmod 7$ for all x.   Hence, solutions to the equation will be those that satisfy $3x + 6 \equiv 0 \pmod 7$.   By substitution, 5 is the only solution.

7. By substitution, 3 and 4 are the only solutions.   Notice that the equation could be written $x^2 - 2 \equiv 0 \pmod 7$ or $(x - \sqrt{2})(x + \sqrt{2}) \equiv 0 \pmod 7$.   Since the (mod 7) system is a field, $x - \sqrt{2} \equiv 0$ (mod 7) or $(x + \sqrt{2}) \equiv 0$ (mod 7), or both. Therefore, $x = \sqrt{2} \equiv 3$, since $2 \equiv 3^2$ (mod 7), and $x = -\sqrt{2} \equiv -3 \equiv 4$ (mod 7).

9. By substitution, 3, 5, and 6 are the solutions.

11. (a)

x	x^2	x^3	x^4	x^5	x^6	x^7	x^8
0	0	0	0	0	0	0	0
1	1	1	1	1	1	1	1
2	4	1	2	4	1	2	4
3	2	6	4	5	1	3	2
4	2	1	4	2	1	4	2
5	4	6	2	3	1	5	4
6	1	6	1	6	1	6	1

11. (b) $5^{236} = 5^{6 \cdot 39 + 2} = 5^{6 \cdot 39} \cdot 5^2 = (5^6)^{39} \cdot 5^2$. But, $(5^6)^{39} \cdot 5^2 \equiv (1)^{39} \cdot 4$ (mod 7)
$$\equiv 4 \text{ (mod 7)}$$

$3^{179} = 3^{6 \cdot 29 + 5} = (3^6)^{29} \cdot 3^5 \equiv 5$ (mod 7).

(c) No, since 5 does not appear in the column under x^4.

(d) Any value in the (mod 7) system since all values appear in the column under x^5.

13.

+	0	1	2	3	4	5	6
0	0	1	2	3	4	5	6
1	1	2	3	4	5	6	0
2	2	3	4	5	6	0	1
3	3	4	5	6	0	1	2
4	4	5	6	0	1	2	3
5	5	6	0	1	2	3	4
6	6	1	1	2	3	4	5

·	0	1	2	3	4	5	6
0	0	0	0	0	0	0	0
1	0	1	2	3	4	5	6
2	0	2	4	6	1	3	5
3	0	3	6	2	5	1	4
4	0	4	1	5	2	6	3
5	0	5	3	1	6	4	2
6	0	6	5	4	3	2	1

15. (a) If $b \equiv 2$ (mod 7), then $b = 7k + 2$ and if $c \equiv 5$ (mod 7), then $c = 7j + 5$. Hence, $b + c = 5 + 2 + 7(k + j)$. Therefore, by definition, $b + c \equiv 5 + 2$ (mod 7).

(b) Similarly, $b \cdot c = 7k \cdot 7j + 2 \cdot 7j + 5 \cdot 7k + 2 \cdot 5 = 7(7kj + 2j + 5k) + 2 \cdot 5$. By definition, $b \cdot c \equiv 2 \cdot 5$ (mod 7).

17. A can take any one of six different values and with each choice for A, there are seven choices for B. Thus, there are $6 \cdot 7 = 42$ different congruences of the given form.

19. No. Postulates 1 and 3 are not always satisfied. It is never true that $a \neq a$. Also, if $a \neq b$ and $b \neq a$, it is not true that $a \neq a$.

23. $1 + 2 + 3 + 4 + 5 + 6 = 21 \equiv 9$ (mod 12).

25. $6x - 5 \equiv 3$ (mod 12) is equivalent to $6x \equiv 8$ (mod 12). There are no solutions.

27. $x^2 \equiv 4$ (mod 12) has solutions 2, 4, 8, 10.

29. $x^2 \equiv 3$ (mod 12) has no solution.

31. $x^3 \equiv 5$ (mod 12) has 5 as a solution.

33. $4x^2 + 3x + 4 \equiv 0$ (mod 12) has no solution.

35.

$$
\begin{array}{r}
3x^2 + x \\
4x + 3 \overline{\smash{\big)}\ 5x^3 + 6x^2 + 3x + 2} \\
\underline{5x^3 + 2x^2} \\
4x^2 + 3x + 2 \\
\underline{4x^2 + 3x} \\
2.
\end{array}
$$

SET 2–1

1.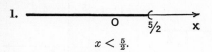

$x < \frac{5}{2}.$

3.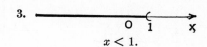

$x < 1.$

5.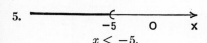

$x < -5.$

7.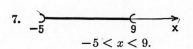

$-5 < x < 9.$

9.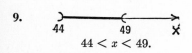

$44 < x < 49.$

11.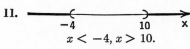

$x < -4, x > 10.$

13. All real x values.
14. No x value satisfies.

15.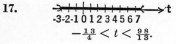

$x > \frac{73}{14}.$

17.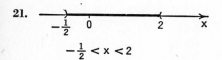

$-\frac{13}{4} < t < \frac{98}{13}.$

19.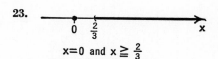

$t > -\frac{1}{2}.$

21.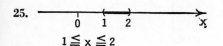

$-\frac{1}{2} < x < 2$

23.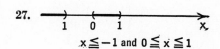

x=0 and x $\geq \frac{2}{3}$

25.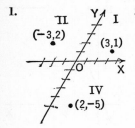

$1 \leqq x \leqq 2$

27.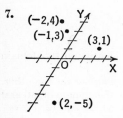

.x $\leqq -1$ and $0 \leqq x \leqq 1$

SET 2–2

1.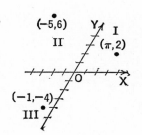

3.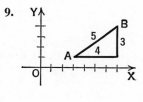

4. On the x-axis.
5. On a line, $x = -2$, parallel to the y-axis and 2 units to the left of the y-axis.
6. On a line, $y = 5$, parallel to the x-axis and 5 units above the x-axis.

7.

9.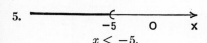

11.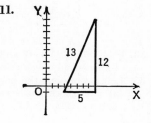

12.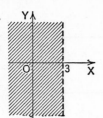

13.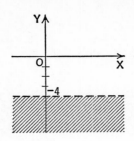

15.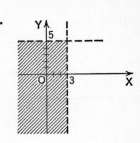

17.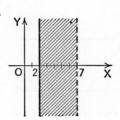

19.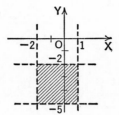

21.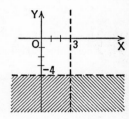

23.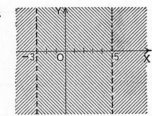

25.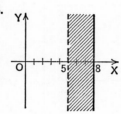

27.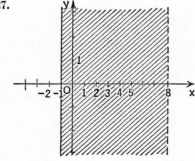

31.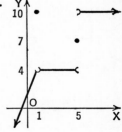

33. $0^2 + 0(0 - 1) = 0^2$ and $1^2 + 1(1 - 1) = 1^2$. It is not an identity in the domain of all real numbers since for $x = 2$, $2^2 + 2(2 - 1) \neq 2^2$.

35. Let x represent the number of spots up on one die, y the number on the other. (a) The graph consists of 36 points (x, y) where x and y take the domain of integral values 1, 2, 3, 4, 5, 6. (b) The graph consists of the points $(1, 2)$ and $(2, 1)$.

(c) $S = 2$ for 1 point. $S = 3$ for 2 points.
  $S = 4$ for 3 points. $S = 5$ for 4 points.
  $S = 6$ for 5 points. $S = 7$ for 6 points.
  $S = 8$ for 5 points. $S = 9$ for 4 points.
  $S = 10$ for 3 points. $S = 11$ for 2 points.
  $S = 12$ for 1 point.

(d) The set of all points would be those with $y = 2$ or $x = 2$. There are 11 such points. Eight of them have $S \geqq 5$.

SET 2–3

2. $\sqrt{157} \approx 12.5$. **3.** $\sqrt{37} \approx 6.1$. **4.** $2\sqrt{26}$. **5.** $3\sqrt{2}$.

6. $\sqrt{(h-3)^2 + (k-1)^2}$. **7.** $\sqrt{16 + (r-s)^2}$. **9.** $\sqrt{61}$.

11. $3\sqrt{10}$. **13.** $\sqrt{17}, \sqrt{29}, \sqrt{2}$. **15.** $3\sqrt{2}, \sqrt{37}, \sqrt{85}$. **17.** $d_1 = \sqrt{10}, d_2 = \sqrt{2}, d_3 = \sqrt{8}$.

21. The point (h, k) will lie on a circle having center $(3, 1)$ and radius 2.
25. The point (r, s) will lie on a circle having center $(-1, -4)$ and radius 3.

27. 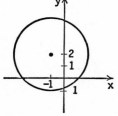 **29.** 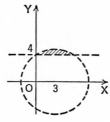 **31.** $(x-3)^2 + (y+2)^2 < 25$.
33. $d = x + y$.

SET 2–4

1. 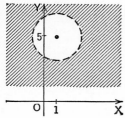 **2.** $x^2 + y^2 - 8x - 6y = 0$. **3.**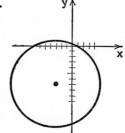

$(x+1)^2 + (y-2)^2 = 9$
or
$x^2 + y^2 + 2x - 4y - 4 = 0$.

$x^2 + y^2 + 6x + 14y - 6 = 0$.

5. $x^2 + y^2 - 2hx - 2ky + h^2 + k^2 - 4 = 0$.
6. $(x-h)^2 + (y-k)^2 = r^2$ or
  $x^2 + y^2 - 2hx - 2ky + (h^2 + k^2 - r^2) = 0$.

7.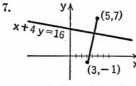

$x + 4y - 16 = 0$.

8. $x - y + 3 = 0$.

9.

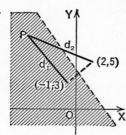

$d_2 > d_1$ implies
$-6x - 4y + 19 > 0$ or
$6x + 4y - 19 < 0$.
All points P with $d_2 > d_1$
lie below the line
$6x + 4y - 19 = 0$.

10. $2x_1 x + 2y_1 y = x_1^2 + y_1^2$.
11. $2x - 8y + 37 = 0$.
13. $x = 5$.

15.

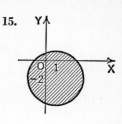

17. $y = 2$.

19. $y = x$.

21. $y = 0$.

23. $y^2 = \left(\sqrt{(x-1)^2 + (y-3)^2}\right)^2$ or $y = \dfrac{x^2}{6} - \dfrac{x}{3} + \dfrac{5}{3}$

25. $(\frac{4}{5}, \frac{19}{5})$.

27.

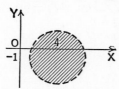

All points inside the circle $(x-4)^2 + (y+1)^2 = 9$ having center $(4, -1)$ and radius 3.

29. Line parallel to the y-axis and 7 units to the right of the y-axis.

31. Line parallel to the y-axis and 4 units to the left.

33. Line parallel to the y-axis and $\dfrac{\pi}{3}$ units to the right.

35. Circle with center $(0, 0)$ and radius 5.

37.

All points inside the circle
$$x^2 + (y+9)^2 = 4$$
having center $(0, -9)$ and radius 2.

39.

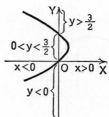

Write $x = -2y(y - \frac{3}{2})$. Then $x > 0$, if $-2y(y - \frac{3}{2}) > 0$ or $y(y - \frac{3}{2}) < 0$ implies $0 < y < \frac{3}{2}$. Also $x = 0$ when $y = 0$ and $y = \frac{3}{2}$. Finally $x < 0$ when $y(y - \frac{3}{2}) > 0$, that is, when $y < 0$ and $y > \frac{3}{2}$.

41.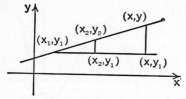

$$\frac{y - y_1}{y_2 - y_1} = \frac{x - x_1}{x_2 - x_1} \quad \text{or}$$

$$y - y_1 = \frac{y_2 - y_1}{x_2 - x_1}(x - x_1).$$

The locus is a straight line passing through the points (x_1, y_1) and (x_2, y_2).

43. (a)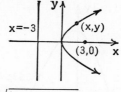

$$\sqrt{(x - 3)^2 + y^2} = x + 3$$
or $y^2 = 12x$.

(b) $y^2 = 2px$.

(c) See Problem 31, Set 21–11.

45. (a) $\dfrac{x^2}{25} + \dfrac{y^2}{16} = 1.$

(b) $\dfrac{x^2}{a^2} + \dfrac{y^2}{a^2 - c^2} = 1.$

(c) See Problem 11, Set 21–4 and Problem 35, Set 21–5.

SET 2–5

1.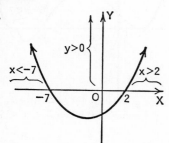

Let $y = x^2 + 5x - 14$. Then $y > 0$ when $x < -7$ and $x > 2$.

3.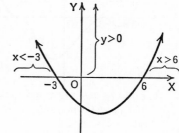

Let $y = x^2 - 3x - 18 = (x - 6)(x + 3)$. Then $y > 0$ when $x < -3$ and $x > 6$.

5.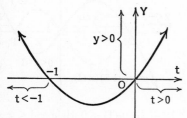

Let $y = 4t(t + 1)$. Then $y > 0$ when $t < -1$ and $t > 0$.

7.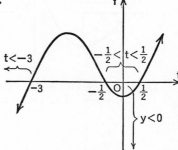

Let $y = 4(t + 3)(t + \frac{1}{2})(t - \frac{1}{2})$. Then $y < 0$ when $t < -3$ and $-\frac{1}{2} < t < \frac{1}{2}$.

9.

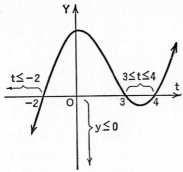

Let $y = (t + 2)(t - 3)(t - 4)$. Then $y \leqq 0$ when $t \leqq -2$ and $3 \leqq t \leqq 4$.

11.

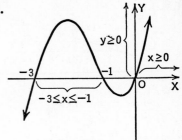

Let $y = (x + 3)(x + 1)x$. Then $y \geqq 0$ when $-3 \leqq x \leqq -1$ and $x \geqq 0$.

13.

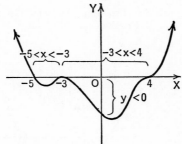

Let $y = (x + 3)^2 (x - 4)^3 (x + 5)$. Then $y < 0$ when $-5 < x < -3$ and $-3 < x < 4$.

15.

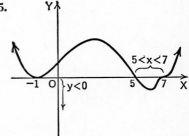

Let $y = (x + 1)^2 (x - 5)(x - 7)^3$. Then $y < 0$ when $5 < x < 7$.

17.

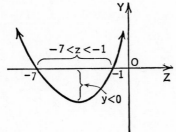

Let $y = (z + 7)(z + 1)$. Then $y < 0$ when $-7 < z < -1$.

19.

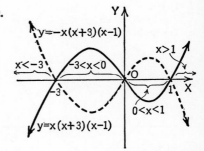

$(x + 3)(x - 1) < 0$ when $-3 < x < 1$. Hence, $|x| (x + 3)(x - 1) < 0$ when $-3 < x < 0$ and when $0 < x < 1$. Why is $x = 0$ excluded?

21. $x^2 - 4 \geqq 0$ if $x \leqq -2$, $x \geqq 2$.

23. Let $y = (x - 2)(x + 7)$. Then $y \geqq 0$ when $x \leqq -7$, $x \geqq 2$.

25. Let $y = 4x^2 - 4x - 35$. Then $y \leqq 0$ when $-\frac{5}{2} \leqq x \leqq \frac{7}{2}$.

27.

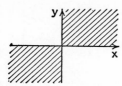

$xy \geqq 0$ All points in the first or third quadrants including the axes.

31.

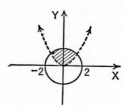

$x^2 + y^2 \leqq 4,\ y > x^2$
All points within the shaded region including the boundary above the region.

SET 2–6

1. $\dfrac{9x^2 + 29x + 19}{4x^3 - 17x^2 - 146x + 105}.$

3. $-\dfrac{4}{(2x - 1)(2x + 2\Delta x - 1)},\ \Delta x \neq 0.$

5. $(t - 2)(t^2 + 2t + 4) = 0,\ \ t = 2,\ \ t = -1 \pm i\sqrt{3}.$

6.

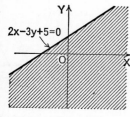

7. $\dfrac{4}{\sqrt{x + \Delta x - 3} + \sqrt{x - 3}},\ \Delta x \neq 0.$

9. $0 \leqq 2x + 3 \leqq 64\ \ \text{or}\ \ -\tfrac{3}{2} \leqq x \leqq \tfrac{61}{2}.$

11.

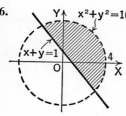

13. $x^2 = (x - 2)^2 + (y - 3)^2$ or $x = \tfrac{1}{4}y^2 - \tfrac{3}{2}y + \tfrac{13}{4}.$

15.

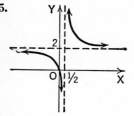

17. The given conditions imply $xy \geqq 0$. If x and y are of opposite algebraic signs, the inequality will not be satisfied.

19.

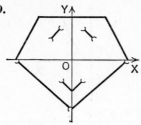

23.

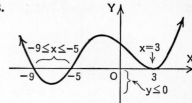

Let $\quad y = (x - 3)^2(x + 5)(x + 9)$.
Then $y \leqq 0$ when $-9 \leqq x \leqq -5$,
$x = 3$.

25.

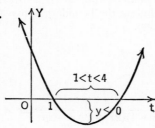

Let $y = (t - 1)(t - 4)$. Then $y < 0$ when $1 < t < 4$.

SELF TEST 2–7

1.

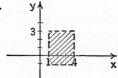

The interior of a rectangle.

2. (a) 5 units.
(b) 15 units.

3.

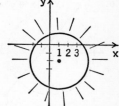

The exterior of a circle of radius 3 and center $(1, -2)$.

4. $(x - 2)^2 + (y - 3)^2 = 16.$

5.

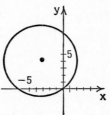

6.

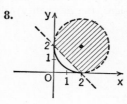

For $x > 3$ and $x < -7$.

7. (a)

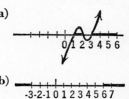

(b)

8.

9. $2x + y - 17 = 0.$

10. $\dfrac{1}{3x(x + \Delta x)} \cdot$ If $\Delta x \neq 0.$

SET 3–4

1.

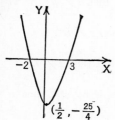

$y = x^2 - x - 6$
y intercept $= -6$
x intercepts $= -2, 3$

3.

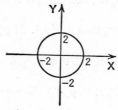

$y^2 = 4 - x^2$
y intercepts $= \pm 2$
x intercepts $= \pm 2$

5.

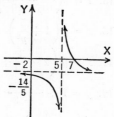

$(x - 5)(y + 2) = 4$
y intercept $= -\frac{14}{5}$
x intercept $= 7$.

7.

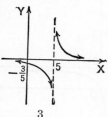

$y = \dfrac{3}{x - 5}$
$x \searrow 5$ implies $y \nearrow L^+$
$x \nearrow 5$ implies $y \searrow L^-$
no x intercept
y intercept $= -\frac{3}{5}$.

9.

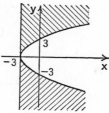

$y^2 \geq 3x + 9$
x intercept $= -3$
y intercepts ≥ 3 or ≤ -3.
The locus is represented by the shaded regions
including the point s on the parabola $y^2 = 3x + 9$
and the line $x = -3$.

SET 3–5

1. $y = x^5\left(1 - \dfrac{7}{x^3} + \dfrac{3}{x^4} - \dfrac{10}{x^5}\right).$

If $x \searrow L^-$, then $y \searrow L^-$ since $x^5 \searrow L^-$ and $1 - \dfrac{7}{x^3} + \dfrac{3}{x^4} - \dfrac{10}{x^5} \to 1.$

If $x \nearrow L^+$, then $y \nearrow L^+$ since $x^5 \nearrow L^+$ and $1 - \dfrac{7}{x^3} + \dfrac{3}{x^4} - \dfrac{10}{x^5} \to 1.$

3. $y = x\left(\dfrac{3}{5} + \dfrac{2}{5x}\right).$ If $x \searrow L^-$, then $y \searrow L^-$. If $x \nearrow L^+$, then $y \nearrow L^+$.

5. $y = x^4\left(\dfrac{2}{3} - \dfrac{4}{3x^3} - \dfrac{3}{x^4}\right).$

If $x \searrow L^-$, then $y \nearrow L^+$ since $x^4 \nearrow L^+$ and $\dfrac{2}{3} - \dfrac{4}{3x^3} - \dfrac{3}{x^4} \to \dfrac{2}{3}.$ Similarly, if $x \nearrow L^+$, then $y \nearrow L^+$.

7. $y = x^6\left(1 + \dfrac{3}{x^3} + \dfrac{4}{x^5} - \dfrac{7}{x^6}\right).$ If $x \searrow L^-$, then $y \nearrow L^+$. If $x \nearrow L^+$, then $y \nearrow L^+$.

9. $y = x^2\left(1 + \dfrac{100}{x}\right).$ If $x \searrow L^-$, then $y \nearrow L^+$. If $x \nearrow L^+$, then $y \nearrow L^+$.

11. $x = y^2\left(\dfrac{1}{2} - \dfrac{7}{2y} + \dfrac{2}{y^2}\right).$ If $y \searrow L^-$, then $x \nearrow L^+$. If $y \nearrow L^+$, then $x \nearrow L^+$.

13. $x = y\left(\dfrac{7}{10} - \dfrac{1}{10y}\right)$. If $y \searrow L^-$, then $x \searrow L^-$. If $y \nearrow L^+$, then $x \nearrow L^+$.

15. $x = y^2\left(4 + \dfrac{5}{y^2}\right)$. If $y \searrow L^-$, then $x \nearrow L^+$. If $y \nearrow L^+$, then $x \nearrow L^+$.

17. $x = y^5\left(2 - \dfrac{3}{y^4} + \dfrac{4}{y^5}\right)$. If $y \searrow L^-$, then $x \searrow L^-$. If $y \nearrow L^+$, then $x \nearrow L^+$.

19. $y = 1 + \dfrac{3}{x-3}$. If $x \searrow L^-$, then $y \nearrow 1$ since $\dfrac{3}{x-3} \nearrow 0$. If $x \nearrow L^+$, then $y \searrow 1$

since $\dfrac{3}{x-3} \searrow 0$.

21.

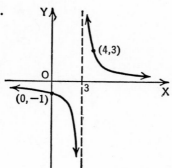

$y = \dfrac{3}{x-3}$. If $x \searrow L^-$, then $y \nearrow 0$. If $x \nearrow L^+$, then $y \searrow 0$. If $x \nearrow 3$, then $y \searrow L^-$. If $x \searrow 3$, then $y \nearrow L^+$.

23.

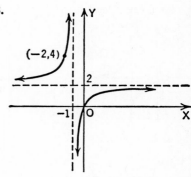

$y = 2 - \dfrac{2}{x+1}$. If $x \searrow L^-$, then $y \searrow 2$. If $x \nearrow L^+$, then $y \nearrow 2$. If $x \nearrow -1$, then $y \nearrow L^+$. If $x \searrow -1$, then $y \searrow L^-$.

25.

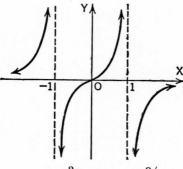

$y = \dfrac{-3x}{(x+1)(x-1)} = \dfrac{-3/x}{1 - 1/x^2}$.
If $x \searrow L^-$, then $y \searrow 0$. If $x \nearrow L^+$, then $y \nearrow 0$. If $x \nearrow -1$, then $y \nearrow L^+$. If $x \searrow -1$, then $y \searrow L^-$. If $x \nearrow 1$, then $y \nearrow L^+$. If $x \searrow 1$, then $y \searrow L^-$.

27.

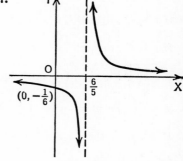

$y = \dfrac{1}{5\left(x - \frac{6}{5}\right)}$. If $x \searrow L^-$, then $y \nearrow 0$. If $x \nearrow \frac{6}{5}$, then $y \searrow L^-$. If $x \searrow \frac{6}{5}$, then $y \nearrow L^+$. A discontinuity at $x = \frac{6}{5}$. If $x \nearrow L^+$, then $y \searrow 0$.

29.

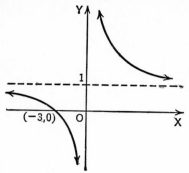

$y = 1 + \dfrac{3}{x}, x \neq 0$. If $x \searrow L^-$, then $y \nearrow 1$.
If $x \nearrow L^+$, then $y \searrow 1$. If $x \nearrow 0$, then $y \searrow L^-$. If $x \searrow 0$, then $y \nearrow L^+$.

31.

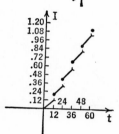

This represents the graph of Calvin's income function for 1 hour. What would it look like for 8 hours? How would his overtime change its appearance?

SET 3–6

1. $x^2 + y^2 - 2y = 0$.

(1) Intercepts: (**a**) $x = 0$; (**b**) $y = 0, y = 2$.

(2) $x^2 + (y^2 - 2y + 1) = 1$ or $(x - 0)^2 + (y - 1)^2 = 1^2$.

The locus is a circle with center $(0, 1)$ and radius 1.

2. The locus consists of all points between (but not on) the lines $x = -3$ and $x = 3$.

3. $x^2 - 5x + \frac{25}{4} + y^2 = \frac{25}{4}$ or $(x - \frac{5}{2})^2 + (y - 0)^2 = (\frac{5}{2})^2$. The locus is a circle with center $(\frac{5}{2}, 0)$ and radius $\frac{5}{2}$.

4.

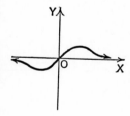

$$y = \frac{4x}{x^2 + 3} = \frac{\dfrac{4}{x}}{1 + \dfrac{3}{x^2}}.$$

(1) Symmetry: with respect to the origin.

(2) Intercepts: (**a**) $x = 0$, (**b**) $y = 0$.

(3) No discontinuities.

(4) General behavior:

(**a**) $x < 0: y = \dfrac{-}{+} = -$. $x \searrow L^-, \dfrac{4}{x} \nearrow 0$,

$1 + \dfrac{3}{x^2} \searrow 1, y \nearrow 0$.

(**b**) $x = 0, y = 0$.

(**c**) $x > 0: y = \dfrac{+}{+} = +$. $x \nearrow L^+, \dfrac{4}{x} \searrow 0$,

$1 + \dfrac{3}{x^2} \searrow 1, y \searrow 0$.

5.

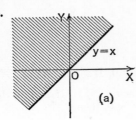

(a)

(a) $x \leq y$. The locus consists of all points on and to the left of the line $y = x$.

(b) The locus $x = y$ is a line through the origin making an angle of 45 degrees with the positive x direction.

6. The locus consists of the two lines $y = x$ and $y = -x$.

7.

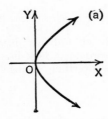

(a) $x = y^2$. (1) Symmetry: with respect to the x-axis. (2) Intercepts: (a) $x = 0$, (b) $y = 0$. (3) No discontinuities. (4) General behavior: (a) $y < 0$: $x = +$. $y \searrow L^-$, $x \nearrow L^+$. (b) $y = 0$, $x = 0$. (c) $y > 0$: $x = +$. $y \nearrow L^+$, $x \nearrow L^+$.

(b) $x^2 = y$. (1) Symmetry: with respect to the y-axis. (2) Intercepts: (a) $x = 0$, (b) $y = 0$. (3) No discontinuities. (4) General behavior: (a) $x < 0$: $y = +$. $x \searrow L^-$, $y \nearrow L^+$. (b) $x = 0$, $y = 0$. (c) $x > 0$: $y = +$. $x \nearrow L^+$, $y \nearrow L^+$.

9.

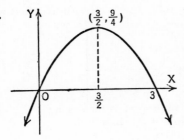

$y = -x(x - 3) = -(x - \frac{3}{2})^2 + \frac{9}{4}$.

(1) Symmetry: none of the types mentioned.

(2) Intercepts: (a) $x = 0$, $x = 3$; (b) $y = 0$.

(3) No discontinuities.

(4) General behavior:

(a) $x < 0$: $y = -(-)(-) = -$. $x \searrow L^-$, $y \searrow L^-$.

(b) $x = 0$, $y = 0$.

(c) $0 < x < 3$: $y = -(+)(-) = +$.

(d) $x = 3$, $y = 0$.

(e) $x > 3$: $y = -(+)(+) = -$. $x \nearrow L^+$, $y \searrow L^-$. The locus is a parabola with vertex $(\frac{3}{2}, \frac{9}{4})$, opening downward, and symmetrical with respect to the line $x = \frac{3}{2}$.

11.

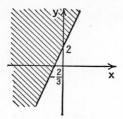

$$y \geqq 3x + 2$$
The locus consists of all points on or
above the line $y = 3x + 2$. The
intercepts are $y \geqq 2$, $x \leqq -\frac{2}{3}$.

13.

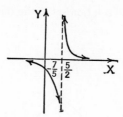

$$y = \frac{7}{2x - 5}$$
discontinuous at $x = \frac{5}{2}$.
$x \searrow \frac{5}{2}$ implies $y \nearrow L^+$; $x \nearrow \frac{5}{2}$ implies
$y \searrow L^-$.
$x \nearrow L^+$ implies $y \searrow 0$; $x \searrow L^-$ implies
$y \nearrow 0$.
y intercept $= -\frac{7}{5}$; no x intercept.

15.

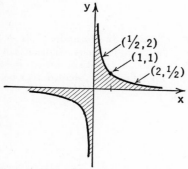

Symmetric with respect to origin.
$x \nearrow L^+$, $y \searrow 0$; $x \searrow L^-$, $y \nearrow 0$.
x-axis, y-axis, and curve are
boundaries. (All points are in
first and third quadrants, that is,
$xy \geqq 0$.)

17.

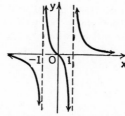

Symmetric with respect to origin.
Discontinuities at $x = \pm 1$.
$x \nearrow L^+$, $y \searrow 0$; $x \searrow L^-$, $y \nearrow 0$;
$x \searrow -1$, $y \nearrow L^+$; $x \nearrow -1$,
$y \searrow L^-$; $x \nearrow 1$, $y \searrow L^-$; $x \searrow 1$,
$y \nearrow L^+$.
Intercepts are $x = 0$, $y = 0$.

19.

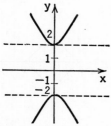

Symmetric with respect to origin,
x-axis, y-axis.
Intercepts at $y = 2$, $y = -2$.
For all $|y| \geqq 2$.
$x \searrow L^-$, $y \nearrow L^+$, and $y \searrow L^-$;
$x \nearrow L^+$, $y \nearrow L^+$, and $y \searrow L^-$.

21.

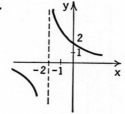

Discontinuous at $x = -2$.
Intercept: $y = 2$.
$x \nearrow L^+$, $y \searrow 0$; $x \searrow L^-$, $y \nearrow 0$;
$x \searrow -2$, $y \nearrow L^+$; $x \nearrow -2$, $y \searrow L^-$.

23. The solution set of the inequality $y^2 < -x^2$ is empty. Hence, there is no locus.

25.

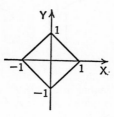

$|x| + |y| = 1$
x intercepts $= \pm 1$
y intercepts $= \pm 1$
$-1 \leqq x \leqq 1, -1 \leqq y \leqq 1$
The equation may be written as
$y = \pm(1 - |x|)$ where $|x| \leqq 1$

27.

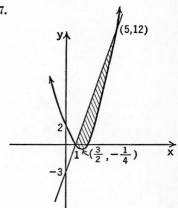

$y \geqq x^2 - 3x + 2$ and $y \leqq 3x - 3$
The simultaneous solutions of the two inequalities consist of those points in the shaded regions.

SELF TEST 3–7

1.

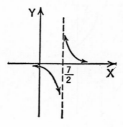

$y = \dfrac{3}{2x - 7}$ discontinuous at $x = \frac{7}{2}$
no x intercept y intercept $= -\frac{3}{7}$
As $x \searrow \frac{7}{2}, y \nearrow L^+$; as $x \nearrow \frac{7}{2}, y \searrow L^-$.
As $x \nearrow L^+, y \searrow 0$; as $x \searrow L^-, y \nearrow 0$.

3.

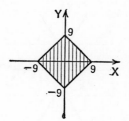

$|x| + |y| \leqq 9$
  $-9 \leqq x$ intercepts $\leqq 9$
  $-9 \leqq y$ intercepts $\leqq 9$
Locus consists of all points within or on the square.

5.

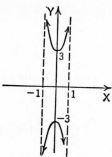

$$y^2 = \frac{10}{1 - x^2} - 1$$

   (1) Discontinuous at $x = \pm 1$
   (2) No x intercepts
   (3) y intercepts $= \pm 3$
   (4) Locus symmetric to both axes.
   (5) Locus defined only for
      $-1 < x < 1$.
   (6) As $x \nearrow 1$, $y \nearrow L^+$ and $y \searrow L^-$
   (7) As $x \searrow -1$, $y \nearrow L^+$ and $y \searrow L^-$

7.

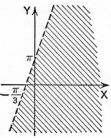

$y < 3x + \pi$, x intercepts $> \dfrac{-\pi}{3}$, y intercepts $< \pi$. Locus consists of all points below the line $y = 3x + \pi$, not including the boundary.

SET 4–4

1. $x = 0$; $x = \dfrac{11 \pm \sqrt{217}}{12}$.

2. $-\frac{1}{2}, \frac{2}{3}, -1 \pm i\sqrt{2}$.

3. (a) $6(x + \frac{1}{2})(x - \frac{2}{3})(x^2 + 2x + 3) = 0$.   (b) $(x - 2)(2x - 3)(5x + 2)$.

4. $(x + 2y)(x^2 - 2xy + 4y^2)(x - 2y)(x^2 + 2xy + 4y^2)$.   **5.** $-3, 2, \pm 6i\sqrt{2}$.

7. $x^3 - 1 = (x - 1)(x^2 + x + 1)$, $x^5 + 32 = (x + 2)(x^4 - 2x^3 + 4x^2 - 8x + 16)$.

9. The sum of a fraction and an integer cannot be an integer (assuming the fraction has been reduced to lowest terms and the denominator is not one). Therefore, if such a fraction is introduced in the second line in the process of synthetic division, every number in the second line thereafter will be a fraction and the last number in the third line will not be zero. Hence, if $\dfrac{c}{d}$ is to be a root, each number in the second line must be an integer. This means that each number in the third line must be divisible by d.

11. $\dfrac{2x^4 - 8x^3 + 13x^2 + 40}{x + 2} = 2x^3 - 12x^2 + 37x - 74 + \dfrac{188}{x + 2}$.

  (a) Use detached coefficients.

$$
\begin{array}{r}
2 - 12 + 37 - 74 \\
\hline
1 + 2 \,\underline{)\, 2 - 8 + 13 + 0 + 40} \\
2 + 4 \\
\hline
-12 + 13 \\
-12 - 24 \\
\hline
37 + 0 \\
37 + 74 \\
\hline
-74 + 40 \\
-74 - 148 \\
\hline
188
\end{array}
$$

  (b) Delete repetitions and telescope.

$$
\begin{array}{r}
2 - 12 + 37 - 74 \\
\hline
1 + 2 \,\underline{)\, 2 - 8 + 13 + 0 + 40} \\
4 - 24 + 74 - 148 \\
\hline
188
\end{array}
$$

(c) Omit the coefficient 1 of x in $x + 2$ and write the coefficients of the quotient on the third line.

$$2 \,|\, \begin{array}{r} 2 - \ 8 + 13 + \ 0 \ + \ 40 \\ 4 - 24 + 74 \ - 148 \\ \hline 2 - 12 + 37 - 74 \,|\, + 188 \end{array}$$

(d) Replace the 2 of $x + 2$ by -2 and add the resulting second line to the first line.

$$-2 \,|\, \begin{array}{r} 2 - \ 8 + 13 + \ 0 \ + \ 40 \\ - \ 4 + 24 - 74 \ + 148 \\ \hline 2 - 12 + 37 - 74 \,|\, + 188 \end{array}$$

12. $x^3 + 3x + 2 = 142$ has $x = 5$ as its only real solution. Then $x^3 + 3x + 2 > 142$ when $x > 5$.

13. Integral coefficients.

15. $z = 2; z = -3; z = -3$.

17. $z = 3; z = -\frac{5}{2}; z = \pm\sqrt{2}$.

19. $x = \dfrac{-1 \pm \sqrt{5}}{2}$.

SET 4–5

1. $-1, \frac{5}{2}, \pm\sqrt{2}$. 　　　2. $-1, -1 \pm \sqrt{3}$. 　　　3. $1, \frac{1}{2}(-1 \pm i\sqrt{2})$.

5. $-3, -2, 1, 3$. 　6. $(-1, 0), (2, 0), (0, -2)$. 　7. $(1, 0), (2, 0), (3, 0), (0, -6)$.

9. $(0, 16)$. Crossing points on t-axis: (a) between $t = -2$ and $t = -1$, (b) between $t = 1$ and $t = 2$, (c) between $t = 14$ and $t = 15$.

11. $7 \,|\, \begin{array}{r} 1 + 0 - \ 7 + \ 5 - \ \ \ 3 \ + \ \ \ \ 4 \\ 7 + 49 + 294 + 2093 \ + 14630 \\ \hline 1 + 7 + 42 + 299 + 2090 \,|\, + 14634 \end{array}$

$$\frac{x^5 - 7x^3 + 5x^2 - 3x + 4}{x - 7} = x^4 + 7x^3 + 42x^2 + 299x + 2090 + \frac{14634}{x - 7}.$$

13. $x^6 - x^5 + x^4 - x^3 - 3x^2 + 3x - 2$.

15. The conclusion follows since the function is a polynomial and therefore continuous. See Section 3–3.

17. Let $y = f(x) = x^5 + 35$. Then $f(-3) = -208$ and $f(-2) = 3$. The root is nearer $x = -2$.

19.

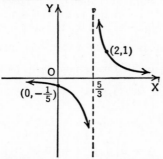

The solutions are all pairs of x and y values which satisfy the equation $3xy - 5y = 1$. Examples: $(x = 2, y = 1)$, $(x = 0, y = -\frac{1}{5})$. Since $y = \dfrac{1}{3x - 5}$, when $x \neq \frac{5}{3}$, a value of y may be found corresponding to a given x value excepting $x = \frac{5}{3}$. Tests 1 and 2 apply to polynomials in one unknown.

23. Let $p(x) \equiv a_n x^n + a_{n-1} x^{n-1} + \cdots + a_1 x + a_0$
$= (x + h)(a_n x^{n-1} - A_{n-1} x^{n-2} + A_{n-2} x^{n-3} + \cdots + [-1]^{n-1} A_0) + (-1)^n A$
where $h, a_n, A_{n-1}, A_{n-2}, \ldots, A_0$, and A are all positive numbers. This implies that in the synthetic division of $p(x)$ by $-h$ the terms in the third line alternate in sign. If $k > h$, then $p(-k) = a_n(-k)^n + a_{n-1}(-k)^{n-1} + \cdots + a_1(-k) + a_0$
$= (-k + h)(a_n[-k]^{n-1} - A_{n-1}[-k]^{n-2} + \cdots + [-1]^{n-1} A_0) + (-1)^n A$. The terms of $a_n[-k]^{n-1} - A_{n-1}[-k]^{n-2} + \cdots + [-1]^{n-1} A_0$ are all positive if n is odd and all negative if n is even. $-k + h < 0$. Consequently
$(-k + h)(a_n[-k]^{n-1} - A_{n-1}[-k]^{n-2} + \cdots + [-1]^{n-1} A_0)$

and $(-1)^n A$ are both negative if n is odd and both positive if n is even. In either case $p(-k) \neq 0$ and $-k$ is not a root of $p(x) = 0$.

25. Let $u = -x$. Then $x = -u$ and $p(x) = p(-u) = a_n(-u)^n + a_{n-1}(-u)^{n-1} + \cdots + a_1(-u) + a_0 = 0$. When simplified each odd power of u will have its coefficient opposite in sign to that of the corresponding power of x. The roots of the polynomial equation in u are equal to the corresponding roots of $p(x) = 0$ each multiplied by -1.

27. $-\frac{1}{2}, \frac{1}{2}, \frac{3}{2}$.

29. $-1, -\frac{1}{2}, 1$.

30. 3.

31.

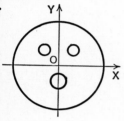

SET 4–6

1.

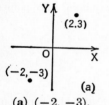

(a) $(-2, -3)$,

(b) $(2, -3)$,

(c) $(-2, 3)$,

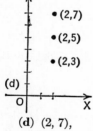

(d) $(2, 7)$,

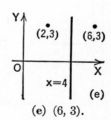

(e) $(6, 3)$.

3.

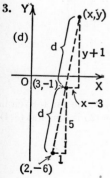

(a) $(-2, 6)$, (b) $(-2, -6)$, (c) $(2, 6)$, (d) $(4, 4)$, (e) $(2, 12)$.

$$\frac{x - 3}{1} = \frac{d}{d} = 1, x = 4$$

$$\frac{y + 1}{5} = \frac{d}{d} = 1, y = 4.$$

5.

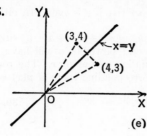

(a) $(-3, -4)$, **(b)** $(3, -4)$, **(c)** $(-3, 4)$, **(d)** $(7, 6)$, **(e)** $(4, 3)$.

7.

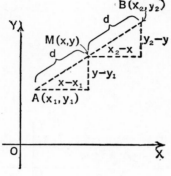

$$\begin{cases} x - x_1 = x_2 - x \\ y - y_1 = y_2 - y \end{cases} \text{ and } \begin{cases} x = \dfrac{x_1 + x_2}{2} \\ y = \dfrac{y_1 + y_2}{2} \end{cases}$$

The last two equations give formulas for finding the coordinates of the *midpoint M of a line segment* joining two points A and B.

SET 4–7

1. The point symmetric to $(3, 0)$ with respect to $x = 1$ is $(-1, 0)$ which is not on the circle. $x = 0$ is a line of symmetry.

3.

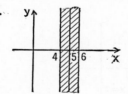

The region: $4 \leqq x \leqq 6$. Are there others?

5. Consider the locus consisting of the three noncollinear points $(0, 0)$, $(0, 5)$, $(3, 3)$.
7. $x = 4$ is a line of symmetry.   **9.** $x = 1$.

SET 4–9

4.

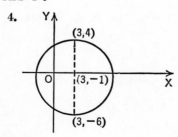

5. The absolute max y value on the circle $(x - 3)^2 + (y + 1)^2 = 25$ is $y = 4$ at $(3,4)$.

7.

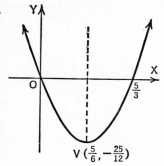

$y = 3(x - \frac{5}{6})^2 - \frac{25}{12}$.   The absolute min $y = -\frac{25}{12}$ occurs at the vertex $V(\frac{5}{6}, -\frac{25}{12})$ of the parabola. The parabola is symmetrical with respect to its axis $x = \frac{5}{6}$.

9.

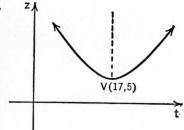

Absolute min $z = 5$ when $t = 17$.

11. Absolute min $y = -1$ when $x = -3$.
13. $z = (t - \frac{5}{2})^2 - \frac{81}{4}$ has min $z = -\frac{81}{4}$ when $t = \frac{5}{2}$.

15.

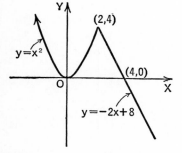

y has min $y = 0$ when $x = 0$ and max $y = 4$ when $x = 2$.

16.

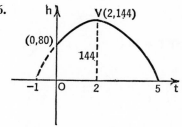

$h = -16(t - 2)^2 + 144$.   Max $h = 144$ at time $t = 2$.

17. (a) $h = 0$, $t = 5$.   **(b)** Solve $8t^2 - 32t - 25 = 0$. $t = 2 + \frac{1}{4}\sqrt{114} \cong 4.7$.
19. Let x and $400 - 2x$ be the dimensions. Then $A = x(400 - 2x)$. Max $A = 20,000$ when $x = 100$.

21.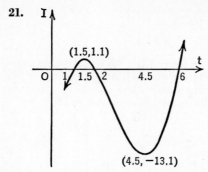

Max $I \cong 1.1$ when $t \cong 1.5$. Min
$I \cong -13.1$ when $t \cong 4.5$.

23.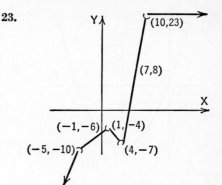

(a) Max $y = -4$ when $x = 1$.
   Min $y = -7$ when $x = 4$.
   Max $y = 23$ when $x \geq 10$.
(b) Abs max $y = 8$ when $x = 7$.
   Abs min $y = -7$ when $x = 4$.

25.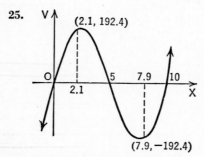

$V = 4x(10 - x)(5 - x)$. V has meaning for
 $0 \leq x \leq 5$.
Max $V \cong 192.4$ when $x \cong 2.1$.

27. Separate into 50 and 50.

SET 4–10

3. At $t = -\dfrac{64}{2(-16)} = 2$ have max $h = 144$.

5.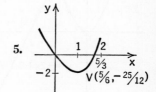

7.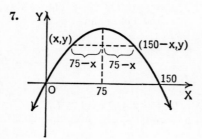

Given (x, y) satisfies
$$y = -2(x - 75)^2 + 11250.$$
To prove $(150 - x, y)$ satisfies the same
 equation.
$$-2([150 - x] - 75)^2 + 11250$$
$$= -2(75 - x)^2 + 11250 = y.$$

8.

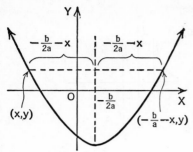

For convenience assume $a > 0$. Given (x, y) satisfies

$$y = a\left(x + \frac{b}{2a}\right)^2 + c - \frac{b^2}{4a}.$$

To prove $\left(-\dfrac{b}{a} - x, y\right)$ satisfies the same equation.

$$a\left(\left[-\frac{b}{a} - x\right] + \frac{b}{2a}\right)^2 + c - \frac{b^2}{4a}$$

$$= a\left(-\frac{b}{2a} - x\right)^2 + c - \frac{b^2}{4a} = y.$$

SELF TEST 4–11

1. (a) $L = -2;\ U = 4.$

(b)

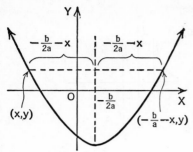

(c) $\pm 1;\ \pm 3;\ \pm 9;\ \pm\frac{1}{2};\ \pm\frac{3}{2};\ \pm\frac{9}{2};\ \pm\frac{1}{4};\ \pm\frac{3}{4};\ \pm\frac{9}{4}.$

(d) Eliminate $\pm 9;\ \pm\frac{9}{2};\ -3;\ -9;\ -\frac{9}{4}.$

(f) $3,\ -1,\ -1,\ \frac{3}{4}.$

(g) $4(x - 3)\,(x + 1)^2\,(x - \frac{3}{4}).$

2. (a) $-2 < r_1 < -1$ **(b)** $9 < r_1 < 10.$

3. (a)

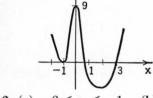

Not symmetric with respect to origin, x-axis, y-axis.
Vertical asymptote: $x = -3$, horizontal: $y = 0$.
Intercept: $y = 2$.
$x \nearrow L^+,\ y \searrow 0;\ x \searrow L^-,\ y \nearrow 0;\ x \searrow -3,\ y \nearrow L^+;$
$x \nearrow -3,\ y \searrow L^-.$

(b)

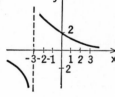

Symmetric with respect to y-axis.
Intercept: $y = 2$.
$x \nearrow L^+,\ y \searrow 0;\ x \searrow L^-,\ y \searrow 0.$

(c)

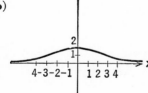

No symmetry with respect to origin, x-axis, y-axis.
Discontinuous at $x = -3$.
Intercepts: $y = 0;\ x = 0$.
$x \nearrow L^+,\ y \nearrow 6;\ x \searrow L^-,\ y \searrow 6;\ x \nearrow -3,\ y \nearrow L^+;$
$x \searrow -3,\ y \searrow L^-.$

4. $x = \frac{3}{2}$; $x = 1$; $x = -\frac{1}{2}$; $x = -\frac{1}{2}$.

5. (a) **y** 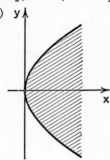   (b)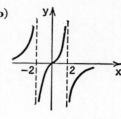

6. y intercept: $y = 6$, x intercept: $x = 3$; $x = \dfrac{-1 \pm \sqrt{17}}{4}$.

7. The point $(-5, -10)$ is on the locus $y = x - 5$ and not on the locus $y = \dfrac{x^2 - 2}{x + 5}$

8. $\dfrac{-4(6 + \Delta x)}{27(3 + \Delta x)^2}$.

9.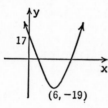

$y = x^2 - 12x + 17 = (x - 6)^2 - 19$.
Vertex: $(6, -19)$. y intercept: 17. x intercept
$6 \pm \sqrt{19}$.

SET 5–1

1. $m = \dfrac{5 - (-3)}{1 - 2} = -8$.   **3.** No slope.   **4.** $m = 0$.   **5.** $m = 4$

7. Illustrations: Slope $GB = \dfrac{10}{6} = \dfrac{5}{3}$. Slope $DA = \dfrac{8}{-6 - 6 - 8} = -\dfrac{2}{5}$.

9. Intercepts: $(-\frac{2}{7}, 0)$, $(0, \frac{2}{3})$. $m = \dfrac{\frac{2}{3} - 0}{0 - (-\frac{2}{7})} = \dfrac{7}{3}$.

11.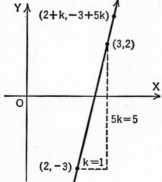

$m = \dfrac{5k}{k} = 5$, $k \neq 0$. Note that any point on
the line is given by
$$(x = 2 + k, y = -3 + 5k).$$
If the *parameter* k is eliminated, the equation
of the line is found:
$$y = -3 + 5(x - 2) \quad \text{or} \quad 5x - y - 13 = 0$$

13.

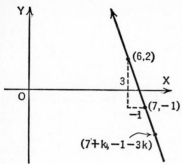

$$m = \frac{-3k}{k} = -3, k \neq 0.$$
$(x = 7 + k, y = -1 - 3k).$
$y = -1 - 3(x - 7)$ or
$3x + y - 20 = 0.$

15.

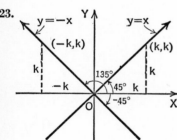

$$m = \frac{L(x + \Delta x) - L(x)}{(x + \Delta x) - (x)}$$
$$= \frac{\Delta L(x, \Delta x)}{\Delta x}.$$

16. Illustration No. 8: $y = -\frac{3}{2}x + \frac{5}{2}$. **(a)** $y + \Delta y = -\frac{3}{2}(x + \Delta x) + \frac{5}{2}$.

  (b) $\Delta y = -\frac{3}{2}\Delta x$. **(c)** $m = \frac{\Delta y}{\Delta x} = -\frac{3}{2}$.

17. $m = 0$.   **18.** No defined slope.   **19.** Same as 18.

21. See figure for No. 15. Since $\Delta L(x, \Delta x)$ and Δx have the same sign, their ratio
  $m = \frac{\Delta L(x, \Delta x)}{\Delta x}$ is positive.

22. Here $\Delta L(x, \Delta x)$ and Δx are opposite in sign and their ratio is negative.

23.

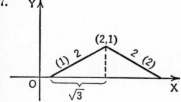

  (1) $m = \frac{k}{k} = 1,$

  (2) $m = -\frac{k}{k} = -1, k \neq 0.$

25. See (2) of No. 23.
26. $m = -1$.

27.

  (1) $m = \frac{1}{\sqrt{3}} = \frac{\sqrt{3}}{3}.$

  (2) $m = -\frac{\sqrt{3}}{3}.$

29. For given $|\Delta x|$ the steeper the line the larger the value of $|\Delta L(x, \Delta x)|$.

31. $m = \frac{\Delta L(x, \Delta x)}{\Delta x}$ where ΔL is the change in the vertical direction and Δx is the change in the horizontal direction. Hence, $m\Delta x = \Delta L$, and when $\Delta x = 1$, $\Delta L = m$.

SET 5–2

1. $y - 6 = 2(x - [-1])$ or $2x - y + 8 = 0$.

3. $x + y - 1 = 0$.

5. $y - [-2] = -(\frac{1}{3})(x - 4)$ or $x + 3y + 2 = 0$.

7. $m = 0, y + 3 = 0$.

9. $m = \frac{7}{2}, 7x - 2y + 14 = 0$.

10. $m = -\dfrac{b}{a}$.

11. $y = -3x + 5, m = -3, b = 5$.

13. $y = -\frac{1}{4}x + \frac{1}{3}, m = -\frac{1}{4}, b = \frac{1}{3}$.

15. $y = 3x + 5, m = 3, b = 5$.

16. $m = -4$. Parallel lines have the same slope.

17. $m = -\frac{1}{2}, y - 1 = -\frac{1}{2}(x - 2)$.

19. $m = -\frac{4}{3}, y = -(\frac{4}{3})(x + 1)$.

21. $m = 0, y + 7 = 0$.

23. $x + 3 = 0$.

25. $m = -1, y + 6 = -(x - 4)$.

27. $y = mx$.

29. $y = 0$.

31. $m = \dfrac{24}{11}, y = \dfrac{(24x - 45.8)}{11}$.

33. $m = -\dfrac{79}{91}, y = \dfrac{(-79x + 1320.3)}{91}$.

35. Use No. 10. $a = \dfrac{3}{2}, b = 7, \dfrac{2x}{3} + \dfrac{y}{7} = 1$.

37. $(x = -1, y = 0), (x = 0, y = -\frac{3}{7})$.

39. $y = -8$.

41. $x = 5$.

43. Intercepts: $A(-3, 0), B(0, 8)$. Midpoint of AB is $M\left(\dfrac{-3 + 0}{2}, \dfrac{0 + 8}{2}\right)$. Use No. 7, Set 4–6. Slope of line $OM: m = -\frac{8}{3}$. Apply No. 27 and obtain desired line $y = -\dfrac{8x}{3}$.

44. Use $m = -2$.

45. $m = -\dfrac{2}{5}, y = -\dfrac{2x}{5} + b, -3 = -\dfrac{2(4)}{5} + b, b = -\dfrac{7}{5}, y = \dfrac{(-2x - 7)}{5}$.

47. The solution $(x = 1, y = 3)$ of the first and second equations must satisfy the third equation. $c = -9$.

49.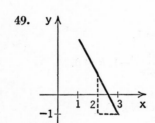

51. (a) $x = 2$.
    (b) 4 units.
    (c) 10.
    (d) 20 sq units.

53.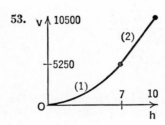

(1) $V = \frac{1}{2}(h)\left(\dfrac{75h}{7}\right)(20) = \dfrac{50h^2}{7}, 0 \leq h \leq 7$;

(2) $V = \frac{1}{2}(7)(75)(20) + (h - 7)(75)(20)$
    $= 1500h - 5250, 7 \leq h \leq 10$.

55. $A = x^2 + \dfrac{200}{x}$.

SET 5-3

4.

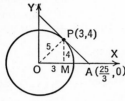

Right triangle OPA is similar to right triangle OMP.
$\dfrac{|MP|}{|AM|} = \dfrac{|OM|}{|MP|}$, $|MA| = \frac{16}{3}$, $|OA| = \frac{25}{3}$. The
slope of the tangent line AP is $m = -\frac{3}{4}$. Note that
this is the negative reciprocal of the slope of the
radius OP.

5. Use the method of Problem 4.
9. $y = 2\,|\,x\,|$ or $y = 2x$, $x \geq 0$; $y = -2x$, $x \leq 0$. $m = 2$ is the slope at $(3, 6)$.
$m = -2$ is the slope at $(-2, 4)$. At $(0, 0)$ no definite slope is determined.
15. $3x + 4y - 25 = 0$. The line and the circle meet in two coincident points.

SET 5-5

1. 45.
2. 27. **3.** (1) $f(x)$ is continuous at $x = 5$. Why? (2) $f(x)$ is not continuous at $x = 3$.
Why?
5. Neither is continuous at $x = 4$. Why? Both are continuous at $x = 6$. Why?
7. Choose $\delta \leq .5$ and $|\,x - 3\,| < \delta \leq .5$. Then $|\,4x - 12\,| < 2$.
9. For a given ϵ, δ is not unique.
11. $f(b)$ must be defined (otherwise it wouldn't be used in a mathematical sentence),
and $\lim\limits_{\Delta x \to 0} |\,f(b + \Delta x) - f(b)\,| = 0$ implies that as x takes on values which are close
to b, $f(x)$ takes on values which are close to $f(b)$. That is, $\lim\limits_{x \to b} f(x) = f(b)$.

13. 4. **15.** $\lim\limits_{\Delta x \to 0} \dfrac{-3}{1 + \Delta x} = -3$. **17.** (a) Yes. (b) Yes. (c) Yes. **19.** $y = \dfrac{4}{x - 4}$.

SET 5-6

1.

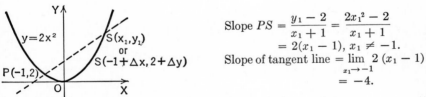

Slope $PS = \dfrac{y_1 - 2}{x_1 + 1} = \dfrac{2x_1{}^2 - 2}{x_1 + 1}$
$= 2(x_1 - 1)$, $x_1 \neq -1$.
Slope of tangent line $= \lim\limits_{x_1 \to -1} 2\,(x_1 - 1)$
$= -4$.

3. $2 + \Delta y = 2(-1 + \Delta x)^2$, $\Delta y = -4\Delta x + 2\Delta x^2$.
Slope $PS = \dfrac{\Delta y}{\Delta x} = \dfrac{-4\Delta x + 2\Delta x^2}{\Delta x} = -4 + 2\Delta x$, $\Delta x \neq 0$.

Slope of tangent line at P is $\lim\limits_{\Delta x \to 0} \dfrac{\Delta y}{\Delta x} = \lim\limits_{\Delta x \to 0} (-4 + 2\Delta x) = -4$.
5. $P(2, 3)$, $S(2 + \Delta x, 3 + \Delta y)$. Slope $PS = \dfrac{\Delta y}{\Delta x} = \dfrac{-3\Delta x}{\Delta x(2 + \Delta x)} = \dfrac{-3}{2 + \Delta x}$, $\Delta x \neq 0$.

Slope of tangent line at $P = \lim\limits_{\Delta x \to 0} \dfrac{\Delta y}{\Delta x} = -\dfrac{3}{2}$.
7. $P(1, 5)$, $S(1 + \Delta x, 5 + \Delta y)$.
Slope $PS = \dfrac{\Delta y}{\Delta x} = \dfrac{10\Delta x + 5\Delta x^2}{\Delta x} = 10 + 5\Delta x$, $\Delta x \neq 0$.
Slope of tangent line at $P = 10$. Equation of tangent line: $10x - y - 5 = 0$.

9. $P(2, 1)$, $S(2 + \Delta x, 1 + \Delta y)$. $\dfrac{\Delta y}{\Delta x} = -\dfrac{1}{2 + \Delta x}$, $\Delta x \neq 0$.

Slope of tangent line $= -\frac{1}{2}$. Equation of tangent line: $x + 2y - 4 = 0$.

11. Slope of tangent line $= -10$. Equation of tangent line: $10x + y + 9 = 0$.

13. $m = -3$; tangent line $3x + y - 2 = 0$.

15. $m = 8$, $8x - y - 3 = 0$.   **16.** $m = 10$; tangent line $10x - y - 2 = ($

17. $m = 5$, $5x - y - 7 = 0$.

19. $P(2, 14)$, $S(2 + \Delta x, 14 + \Delta y)$. $\dfrac{\Delta y}{\Delta x} = \dfrac{36\Delta x + 18\Delta x^2 + 3\Delta x^3}{\Delta x} = 36 + 18\Delta x + 3\Delta x$

$\Delta x \neq 0$. $m = 36$, $36x - y - 58 = 0$.

20. Use $\displaystyle\lim_{\Delta x \to 0} \dfrac{\Delta y(x_1, \Delta x)}{\Delta x}$.

SET 5–7

1. $m = \displaystyle\lim_{\Delta x \to 0} \dfrac{\Delta y}{\Delta x} = \lim_{\Delta x \to 0} (10x_1 + 5\Delta x) = 10x_1$. Slopes are: -20, 10, 30.

3. $\dfrac{\Delta y}{\Delta x} = \dfrac{-12}{x(x + \Delta x)}$, $\Delta x \neq 0$; $m = \displaystyle\lim_{\Delta x \to 0} \dfrac{\Delta y}{\Delta x} = -\dfrac{12}{x^2}$. -12, -3, $-\frac{4}{3}$, $-\frac{1}{3}$.

5. $-\dfrac{12}{x^2} = -3$. $(-2, -6)$, $(2, 6)$.

6. $\Delta y = f(x + \Delta x) - f(x) = \Delta f(x, \Delta x)$, $y = f(x)$.

7. Slope at $(0, 0) = 0$. Tangent line is $y = 0$. Slope at $(2, 8) = 12$. Tangent lin
is $12x - y - 16 = 0$.

8. If the curve is rising as x increases, Δx and Δy have the same sign and $\dfrac{\Delta y}{\Delta x}$ is positive

Therefore $\displaystyle\lim_{\Delta x \to 0} \dfrac{\Delta y}{\Delta x} > 0$.

9. If the curve is falling as x increases, Δx and Δy have opposite signs and $\dfrac{\Delta y}{\Delta x}$ i

negative. Therefore $\displaystyle\lim_{\Delta x \to 0} \dfrac{\Delta y}{\Delta x} < 0$.

11. $3x_1^2 = 12$. The tangent line at $(-2, -8)$ is $12x - y + 16 = 0$. The tangen
line at $(2, 8)$ is $12x - y - 16 = 0$.

13. $14x - 6 = 2$. The tangent line at $(\frac{4}{7}, -\frac{8}{7})$ is $14x - 7y - 16 = 0$.

15. Slope at $(a, b) = 200 - 120a + 12a^2$.

16. $12x^2 - 120x + 200 = 12\left(x - 5 + \dfrac{5\sqrt{3}}{3}\right)\left(x - 5 - \dfrac{5\sqrt{3}}{3}\right)$. Slope is zero when

$\left(x = 5 - \dfrac{5\sqrt{3}}{3} \cong 2.1, y \cong 192.4\right)$, $\left(x = 5 + \dfrac{5\sqrt{3}}{3} \cong 7.9, y \cong -192.4\right)$. y is

increasing when $12x^2 - 120x + 200 > 0$. That is, when $x < 5 - \dfrac{5\sqrt{3}}{3}$ or

$x > 5 + \dfrac{5\sqrt{3}}{3}$.

17. $\displaystyle\lim_{\Delta x \to 0} \dfrac{\Delta y}{\Delta x} = -4x$. The slope of the tangent line at $(2, -4)$ is -8.

18. $3x^2 - 4x - 7 = 3(x + 1)(x - \frac{7}{3})$. Slope is zero at $(-1, 9)$ and $(\frac{7}{3}, -\frac{257}{27})$. y is
increasing when $3x^2 - 4x - 7 > 0$. $x < -1$, $x > \frac{7}{3}$.

19. $\displaystyle\lim_{\Delta x \to 0} \dfrac{\Delta y}{\Delta x} = 2x - 10$. At minimum point $(5, 2)$ the slope is zero.

SELF TEST 5–8

1. 32 ft.

2. (a) $2x + 3y + 5 = 0$.
   (b) $2x + 3y - 5 = 0$.
   (c) $2x - 3y = 0$.

3. (a) $y = -\frac{3}{4}x + \frac{5}{4}$.
   (b) $\dfrac{x}{3} + \dfrac{y}{-4} = 1$.

4. (a) $(\frac{3}{2}, -\frac{1}{2})$.

5. (a) $m = -7$ at $(0, 0)$.
   (b) $y + 7x = 0$.

6. $m = -\frac{1}{2}$ at $(2, 1)$.

7. $(2, 8); (2, 8); (-4, -64)$.

8. 12.

9. y increases for $x < 2$; $x > 4$.

10. (a) $\lim\limits_{x \to 1} \dfrac{x^2 + 2x - 3}{x - 1} = 4$.
    (b) Not defined at $x = 1$.

SET 6–2

1. $10x$.

3. $-2x$.

5. $\dfrac{\Delta f(x, \Delta x)}{\Delta x} = \dfrac{-2x\Delta x - \Delta x^2}{(x + \Delta x)^2 x^2 \Delta x}, f'(x) = -\dfrac{2}{x^3}$.

7. $\dfrac{\Delta f(x, \Delta x)}{\Delta x} = \dfrac{21x^2\Delta x + 21x\Delta x^2 + 7\Delta x^3}{\Delta x}, f'(x) = 21x^2$.

9. 0.

11. $\dfrac{\Delta y(x, \Delta x)}{\Delta x} = \dfrac{0}{\Delta x}, y' = 0$.

13. $\dfrac{\Delta y(x, \Delta x)}{\Delta x} = \dfrac{\Delta x}{(\sqrt{x + \Delta x - 5} + \sqrt{x - 5})\Delta x}, y' = \dfrac{1}{2\sqrt{x - 5}}$.

14. See 15.

15. $\dfrac{\Delta f(t, \Delta t)}{\Delta t} = \dfrac{-2\Delta t}{(\sqrt{7 - 2t - 2\Delta t} + \sqrt{7 - 2t})\Delta t}, f'(t) = -\dfrac{1}{\sqrt{7 - 2t}}$.

17. $6x - 6$.

21. $(y + \Delta y)^2 = 2(x + \Delta x) + 3, (2y + \Delta y)\Delta y = 2\Delta x, \dfrac{\Delta y}{\Delta x} = \dfrac{2\Delta x}{(2y + \Delta y)\Delta x}$,

$\lim\limits_{\Delta x \to 0} \dfrac{\Delta y}{\Delta x} = \dfrac{1}{y}$.

23. Let $A = \sqrt[3]{4x^2 - 1}, B = \sqrt[3]{4(x + \Delta x)^2 - 1}$. Then

$\dfrac{\Delta g(x, \Delta x)}{\Delta x} = \dfrac{A - B}{AB\,\Delta x} = \dfrac{(A - B)(A^2 + AB + B^2)}{AB(A^2 + AB + B^2)\Delta x} = \dfrac{A^3 - B^3}{AB(A^2 + AB + B^2)\Delta x}$

$= \dfrac{-8x\Delta x - 4\Delta x^2}{AB(A^2 + AB + B^2)\Delta x}$,

$g'(x) = \dfrac{-8x}{3(\sqrt[3]{4x^2 - 1})^4}$.

25. Verify that (1), (2), (3) of definition in Section 5–5 hold.

SET 6–4

1. $17(5)x^4 = 85x^4$.

3. $127(4)x^3 = 508x^3$.

5. $34x$.

7. $18x^5$.

9. 1.

11. $y'(x) = 3x^2, m = y'(2) = 12$.

13. $y'(x) = 15x^4, m = y'(3) = 1215$.

14. $y'(x) = 15x^2, x^3 = 8, m = 60$.

15. $y'(x) = 21x^2 = \frac{21}{25}$. $(-\frac{1}{5}, -\frac{7}{125}), (\frac{1}{5}, \frac{7}{125})$.

19. $y'(x) = 20x^4 = \frac{5}{4}$. $(\frac{1}{2}, \frac{1}{8})$ and $(-\frac{1}{2}, -\frac{1}{8})$.

SET 6–5

1. $f'(x) = 3(2)x + 7 + 0 = 6x + 7$.

3. $y' = 3x^2 - 4x + 3 = 2$. Tangent line at $(\frac{1}{3}, -\frac{113}{27})$ is $54x - 27y - 131 = 0$. Tangent line at $(1, -3)$ is $2x - y - 5 = 0$.

5. $y'(x) = 35x^6 + 3$, $y - 10944 = 25518(x - 3)$.

7. $y'(x) = 2x - 3$, $y'(1) = -1$, $y'(2) = 1$.

9. $x^2 - 5x + 6 = 0$. $y'(2) = -1$, $y'(3) = 1$.

11. $(-\frac{2}{3}, -\frac{221}{27})$.

13. $(\frac{2}{3}, -\frac{4}{3})$.

15. $p'(0) = -12$, $p'(\pm 2\sqrt{3}) = 24$.

17. Points of intersection: $(1, 12)$, $(-\frac{7}{3}, 12)$. $y'(1) = 10$, $y'(-\frac{7}{3}) = -10$. Tangent lines: $y - 12 = 10(x - 1)$, $y - 12 = -10(x + \frac{7}{3})$.

19. $y - 77 = 30(x - 4)$.　　**21.** $y = 9$.　　**23.** $y - 216 = 3(\sqrt[3]{230})^2(x - \sqrt[3]{230})$.

25. Points of intersection: $(-\frac{3}{5}, -\frac{36}{5})$, $(2, 11)$. $y'(-\frac{3}{5}) = -6$, $y'(2) = 20$. Tangent lines: $y + \frac{36}{5} = -6(x + \frac{3}{5})$, $y - 11 = 20(x - 2)$.

27. Slope of secant is -5. Point: $(-\frac{3}{2}, \frac{9}{4})$.

29.

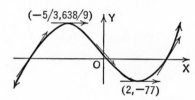
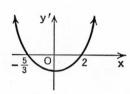

$y' = (3x + 5)(x - 2)$. **(a)** $(-\frac{5}{3}, \frac{638}{9})$, $(2, -77)$. **(b)** y increases as x increases when $y' > 0$. $x < -\frac{5}{3}$, $x > 2$. **(c)** y decreases as x increases when $y' < 0$. $-\frac{5}{3} < x < 2$.

30. See 31.

31. $\dfrac{\Delta y(x, \Delta x)}{\Delta x} = \dfrac{3\Delta x}{(x + \Delta x)x\Delta x}$. $y' = \dfrac{3}{x^2} = 12$. Points: $(-\frac{1}{2}, 6)$, $(\frac{1}{2}, -6)$.

33.

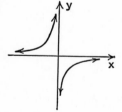

$y = \dfrac{-3}{x}$

$y' = \dfrac{3}{x^2} = 12$ implies $x = \pm\frac{1}{2}$, $y = \mp 6$.

35. Note that for a curve that is continuous and differentiable it is geometrically apparent that for any two numbers x_1 and x_2 there is at least one number $x_1 < x < x_2$ such that the slope of the tangent line to the curve at $(x, h(x))$ is equal to the slope of the secant through $(x_1, h(x_1))$ and $(x_2, h(x_2))$. That is, $h'(x) = \dfrac{h(x_2) - h(x_1)}{x_2 - x_1}$. [This is a theorem of calculus known as a mean value theorem.] Since $h'(x) = 0$ for all x by hypothesis, $h(x_2) = h(x_1)$ for all x_1 and x_2. Thus $h(x)$ is constant.

37. If a polynomial is neither a constant function nor a linear function, then it has at least one term of the form cx^n with $n > 1$. Therefore, the derivative of the polynomial has a term ncx^{n-1} with $n - 1 > 0$ since $n > 1$. Hence, the value of the slope changes as x changes and is not constant.

39. $24x - y - 57 = 0$.　　　　**40.** $4x + y - 7 = 0$.

41. (1) For each value of k the equation $7x + 11y - 12 + k(2x - 9y + 13) = 0$
represents a line through the point of intersection of the two given lines.
Since the desired line passes through $(5, 7)$,
$$7(5) + 11(7) - 12 + k[2(5) - 9(7) + 13] = 0 \text{ and } k = \tfrac{5}{2}.$$
The desired line is
$$7x + 11y - 12 + \tfrac{5}{2}(2x - 9y + 13) = 0 \text{ or } 24x - 23y + 41 = 0.$$
(2) **Second Solution.** The point of intersection of the given lines is $(-\tfrac{7}{17}, \tfrac{23}{17})$.
The slope of the desired line is $\tfrac{24}{23}$. Its equation is $24x - 23y + 41 = 0$.

43.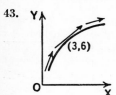

$p'(x)$ is positive and decreasing as x increases through $x = 3$
since $p''(3)$ is negative. The curve is below the tangent
line at $(3, 6)$.

45. $3x^2 + 2x - 21 = 0$. Points: $(-3, -1)$, $(\tfrac{7}{3}, -\tfrac{1787}{27})$.
Tangent lines: $2x - y + 5 = 0$, $y + \tfrac{1787}{27} = 2(x - \tfrac{7}{3})$.

SET 6–6

1. $y' = (x^3 - 1)(8x - 2) + (4x^2 - 2x + 1)(3x^2) = 20x^4 - 8x^3 + 3x^2 - 8x + 2$.
3. $y'(x) = (3x^2 - 2x + 5)(8x - 3) + (4x^2 - 3x)(6x - 2) = 48x^3 - 51x^2 + 52x - 15$,
$y'(2) = 269$.
5. $y'(x) = 4x^3 + 6x^2 + 14x + 10$, $y'(-2) = -26$.
7. $y'(x) = 10x^9 + 7x^6 + 35x^4 + 12x^3 - 15x^2 + 14x + 3$, $y'(1) = 66$.
9. $y'(x) = 60x^4 - 32x^3 - 30x + 10$, $y'(5) = 33360$.
13. $y'(x) = (x + 3)(4x^2 - 9x - 7)$. Points:
$$(-3, 0), \left(\frac{9 - \sqrt{193}}{8}, -\frac{7787 + 2123\sqrt{193}}{512}\right), \left(\frac{9 + \sqrt{193}}{8}, \frac{-7787 + 2123\sqrt{193}}{512}\right).$$
15. $y' = 2a^2x$. Point: $(0, -b^2)$.
17. $(15x^2 + 21x + 8)(3x + 2)(x - 1) = y'$. Points: $(-\tfrac{2}{3}, \tfrac{11}{27})$, $(1, -32)$.
19. $y'(0) = 11$.

SET 6–7

1. $5(x^3 - 5x)^4(3x^2 - 5)$.   **3.** $4(x^2 - 5x + 2)^3(2x - 5)$.
5. $10(7x^2 - 4x + 3)^9(14x - 4) = 20(7x^2 - 4x + 3)^9(7x - 2)$.   **7.** $8(x - 3)^7$.

8. $6(t^2 - 2t + 3)^2(t - 1)$.   **11.** $\tfrac{1}{2}(x - 3)^{-\frac{1}{2}} = \dfrac{1}{2\sqrt{x - 3}}$.

13. $\tfrac{1}{3}(4x - 2)^{\frac{1}{3}-1}(4) = \tfrac{4}{3}(4x - 2)^{-\frac{2}{3}} = \dfrac{4}{3\sqrt[3]{(4x - 2)^2}}$.

15. $(3x^2 + 5x)^4(3)(3x^2 - 4)^2(6x) + (3x^2 - 4)^3(4)(3x^2 + 5x)^3(6x + 5)$
$$= 2(3x^2 + 5x)^3(3x^2 - 4)^2(63x^3 + 75x^2 - 48x - 40).$$

16. $10(2x^3 - 4x + 1)^4(3x^2 - 2)$.

17. $\tfrac{1}{2}(2x - 3)^{-\frac{1}{2}}(2) = (2x - 3)^{-\frac{1}{2}} = \dfrac{1}{\sqrt{2x - 3}}$.

18. $y = (x^2 - 2x + 9)^{\frac{1}{2}}$, $y' = \tfrac{1}{2}(x^2 - 2x + 9)^{-\frac{1}{2}}(2x - 2) = \dfrac{x - 1}{\sqrt{x^2 - 2x + 9}}$.

19. $y = (2x - 4)^{\frac{2}{3}}$, $y' = \tfrac{2}{3}(2x - 4)^{-\frac{1}{3}}(2) = \dfrac{4}{3\sqrt[3]{2x - 4}}$.

21. $16x(x^2 + 5)^7$.

23. $-7(6x^2 - 5)(2x^3 - 5x)^{-8}$.

25. $y = (x - 3)^{-5}$, $y' = -5(x - 3)^{-6} = \dfrac{-5}{(x - 3)^6}$.

27. $y' = \dfrac{-9x^2 + 28x - 15}{2(x^2 - 5)^2 \sqrt{3x - 7}}$.

29. $y' = \dfrac{x}{4y}$ or $y' = \pm \dfrac{x}{2\sqrt{x^2 + 10}}$.

SET 6–9

1.

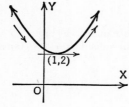

$y'(x) = 6(x - 1)$.

x	y	y'	Conclusions
$x < 1$		$-$	
1	2	0	Min
$x > 1$		$+$	$y = 2$ at $x = 1$.

3.

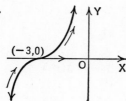

$y' = 3(x + 3)^2$.

x	y	y'	Conclusions
$x < -3$		$+$	Neither max nor min
-3	0	0	
$x > -3$		$+$	Inflection point $(-3, 0)$.

5.

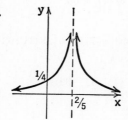

$y' = \dfrac{-10}{(5x - 2)^3}$. y and y' not continuous at $x = \frac{2}{5}$. y intercept is $\frac{1}{4}$. $x \nearrow L^+$, $y \searrow 0$; $x \searrow L^-$, $y \searrow 0$; $x \nearrow \frac{2}{5}$, $y \nearrow L^+$; $x \searrow \frac{2}{5}$, $y \nearrow L^+$. If $x < \frac{2}{5}$, then $y' > 0$. If $x > \frac{2}{5}$, then $y' < 0$.

7. $y' = 4(x^3 - 8)$. Min at $(2, -42)$.

9. $y' = 8(x - \frac{7}{8})$. Min $y = -\frac{17}{16}$ at $x = \frac{7}{8}$.

11. $h' = -2(t - 60)$. Max $h = 4000$ at $t = 60$.

13. $y' = 4(x + \frac{5}{12})$. Min $y = -\frac{241}{72}$ at $x = -\frac{5}{12}$.

15. $y' = \frac{3}{2}(x - 2)^2$. Neither max nor min. Inflection point: $(2, 4)$.

17.

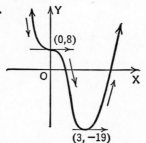

$y' = 4x^2(x - 3)$.

x	y	y'	Conclusions
$x < 0$		$-$	Neither max nor min.
0	8	0	Inflection $(0, 8)$.
$3 > x > 0$		$-$	
3	-19	0	Min
$x > 3$		$+$	$y = -19$ when $x = 3$.

19. Compare no. 5.

20.

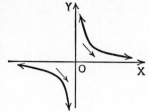

$4xy^3 = 1$, $y^3 = \dfrac{1}{4x}$. Discontinuous at $x = 0$.

If $x \searrow L^-$, then $y \nearrow 0$. If $x \nearrow 0$, then $y \searrow L^-$.
If $x \searrow 0$, then $y \nearrow L^+$. If $x \nearrow L^+$, then $y \searrow 0$.

$$\frac{d}{dx}(4xy^3) = 4x\frac{d}{dx}(y^3) + y^3\frac{d}{dx}(4x)$$

$$= 4x\left(3y^2\frac{dy}{dx}\right) + 4y^3 = \frac{d(1)}{dx} = 0.$$

Therefore $\dfrac{dy}{dx} = -\dfrac{y}{3x}$. If $x < 0$, then $y < 0$ and $y' < 0$. If $x > 0$, then $y > 0$ and $y' < 0$.

21.

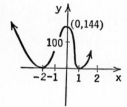

$y' = 18x(3x - 3)(x + 2)^3$

x	y	y'	Conclusions
$x < -2$		$-$	
-2	0	0	min
$-2 < x < 0$		$+$	
0	144	0	max
$0 < x < 1$		$-$	
1	0	0	min
$x > 1$		$+$	

23. $h' = -32(t - 5)$. Max $h = 800$ when $t = 5$.

25.

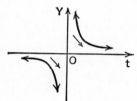

$y = 7t^{-3}$. $y' = -\dfrac{21}{t^4} < 0$ when $t \neq 0$ and finite.

y and y' discontinuous at $t = 0$.
If $t \searrow L^-$, then $y \nearrow 0$. If $t \nearrow 0$, then $y \searrow L^-$.
If $t \searrow 0$, then $y \nearrow L^+$. If $t \nearrow L^+$, then $y \searrow 0$.

27.

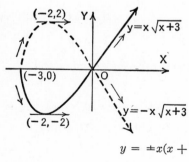

$y = \pm x(x + 3)^{\frac{1}{2}}$. $y' = \pm\dfrac{3(x + 2)}{2\sqrt{x + 3}}$.

x	$y = x\sqrt{x + 3}$	$y' = \dfrac{3(x + 2)}{2\sqrt{x + 3}}$	Conclusions
$-3 < x < -2$		$-$	Min
-2	-2	0	$y = -2$ at $x = -2$.
$x > -2$		$+$	

x	$y = -x\sqrt{x+3}$	$y' = -\dfrac{3(x+2)}{2\sqrt{x+3}}$	Conclusions
$-3 < x < -2$		$+$	Max
-2	$+2$	0	$\begin{cases} \text{Max} \\ y = 2 \text{ at } x = -2. \end{cases}$
$x > -2$		$-$	

SELF TEST 6–10

1. $\dfrac{-3}{(x-2)^2}$.

2. $(-1, 6); 3x + y - 3 = 0$.

3. (a) Max $(-3, 78)$; Min $(1, 14)$.
   (b) As x increases, y increases for $x < -3$ and $x > 1$.
   (c) As x increases, y decreases for $-3 < x < 1$.

4. $7(6x^2 - 4)(2x^3 - 4x + 1)^6$.

5. $\dfrac{3(x-1)}{\sqrt{3x^2 - 6x + 9}}$.

6. $\dfrac{-10}{(2x-3)^6}$

7. $3(3x^2 + 7)(x + 4)^2(7x^2 + 16x + 7)$.   **8.** The two numbers are 500 and 500.

9. 100 cu in.

SET 7–1

1. $y' = 3x^2 - 16x + 30 = 25$. Points: $(\tfrac{1}{3}, \tfrac{58}{27})$, $(5, 68)$.

3. Let the dimensions of the box be x ft $\times$ $2x$ ft $\times \dfrac{36}{x^2}$ ft. The surface area

$$A = 4x^2 + \frac{216}{x} \text{ sq ft} \quad A' = \frac{8(x^3 - 27)}{x^2}.$$

If $0 < x < 3$, then $A' < 0$. If $x = 3$, then $A' = 0$. If $x > 3$, then $A' > 0$.
Min $A = 108$ sq ft when $x = 3$ ft. Dimensions: 3 ft $\times$ 6 ft $\times$ 4 ft.

11. $A = 8r^2 + \dfrac{250}{r}$. $A' = \dfrac{(16r^3 - 250)}{r^2}$. Min A when $r = \dfrac{5}{2}$ in. and $h = \dfrac{20}{\pi}$ in.

13. $N = \dfrac{k}{s^3}$. $T = N(s - 3) = k(s^{-2} - 3s^{-3})$. $T' = -\dfrac{k(2s - 9)}{s^4}$. Max T when

$s = \$4.50$.

15. $I = (500 - x)(300 + x)$. Max I when $x = 100$. Monthly rate \$4.00.

17. \$50.00.   **19.** 2500 sq ft.   **21.** Max area 2250 sq ft.

SET 7–2

1. 32 ft per sec.   **3.** 80 ft per sec for third second.

5. $\Delta s(2, 5) = 470$, $\dfrac{\Delta s(2, 5)}{5} = 94$.

7. If D is the distance one way, then the time required for the round trip is
$\dfrac{D}{30} + \dfrac{D}{60} \equiv \dfrac{D}{20}$. Now $R\left(\dfrac{D}{20}\right) = 2D$ and $R = 40$ mph., the average rate.

SET 7–3

1. $v(t) = 2t - 3$, $a(t) = 2$. $v(7) = 11$, $a(7) = 2$. $v(11) = 19$, $a(11) = 2$. If
$-100 \leq t < \tfrac{3}{2}$, then $v(t) < 0$. If $t = \tfrac{3}{2}$, then $v(\tfrac{3}{2}) = 0$. If $\tfrac{3}{2} < t \leq 100$, then
$v(t) > 0$. When $t = -100$, $s = 10305$, $v = -203$. As t increases from $t = -100$
to $t = \tfrac{3}{2}$ the particle moves from $s = 10305$ to $s = \tfrac{11}{4}$. As t increases from $t = \tfrac{3}{2}$
to $t = 100$ the particle moves from $s = \tfrac{11}{4}$ to $s = 9705$.

3. $v(t) = 64 - 32t$, $a(t) = -32$. $v(0) = 64$, $v(5) = -96$, $v(10) = -256$. As t increases from $t = -100$ to $t = 2$ the particle moves from $s = -166400$ to $s = 64$. As t increases from $t = 2$ to $t = 100$ the particle moves from $s = 64$ to $s = -153600$.

5. $v = 0$, $a = 0$. The particle is at rest at $s = 11$.

7. $36t^2 - 3 = 6$. $s(-\frac{1}{2}) = 5$, $s(\frac{1}{2}) = 5$. **9.** $18t = 36$. $s(2) = 12$.

11. At rest when $72 - 6t = 0$. $s(12) = 432$. Interval: $0 \leq t \leq 12$.

13. $v(t) = -32t + 160$, $v(15) = -320$ ft per sec.

15. $v(t) = -16t - 20$. $-8t^2 - 20t + 100 = 96$, $t = \dfrac{-5 + \sqrt{33}}{4}$.

$v\left(\dfrac{-5 + \sqrt{33}}{4}\right) = -4\sqrt{33} \cong -23.0$ ft per sec.

17. $v(3) = -6$ ft per sec.

19. $v(t) = 10t + 7$. $5t^2 + 7t = 160$.

$v\left(\dfrac{-7 + \sqrt{3249}}{10}\right) = \sqrt{3249} = 57$ ft per sec $\cong 39$ mph.

21. $h = 400$ ft.

SET 7–5

1. $V = \dfrac{4\pi R^3}{3}$, $\dfrac{dR}{dt} = \dfrac{\dfrac{dV}{dt}}{4\pi R^2}$, $\dfrac{dR}{dt}\bigg]_{R=5} = \dfrac{400}{4\pi(5)^2} = \dfrac{4}{\pi}$ in. per min.

3. $\dfrac{4\pi R^3}{3} = 288\pi$, $R = 6$ in., $\dfrac{dR}{dt}\bigg]_{R=6} = \dfrac{600}{4\pi(6)^2} = \dfrac{25}{6\pi}$ in. per min.

5. $S = 4\pi R^2$, $\dfrac{dS}{dt} = 8\pi R\dfrac{dR}{dt}$, $\dfrac{dS}{dt}\bigg]_{R=6} = 8\pi(6)\left(\dfrac{25}{6\pi}\right) = 200$ sq in. per min.

7. $\dfrac{dh}{dt} = \dfrac{\dfrac{dV}{dt}}{96h}$, $\dfrac{dh}{dt}\bigg]_{h=10} = \dfrac{500}{96(10)} = \dfrac{25}{48}$ in. per min.

9.

$y = 3x^2 - 4x + 2x^{-1}$, $y' = \dfrac{2(3x^2 + x + 1)(x - 1)}{x^2}$.

x	y	y'	Conclusions
$x < 0$		$-$	
$0 < x < 1$		$-$	
1	1	0	Min $y = 1$ at $x = 1$
$x > 1$		$+$	

If $x \searrow L^-$, then $y \nearrow L^+$. If $x \nearrow 0$, then $y \searrow L^-$. Curve crosses x-axis between $x = -1$ and $x = 0$. If $x \searrow 0$, then $y \nearrow L^+$. If $x \nearrow L^+$, then $y \nearrow L^+$.

11.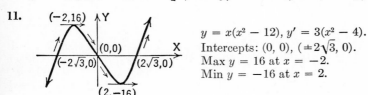

$y = x(x^2 - 12)$, $y' = 3(x^2 - 4)$.
Intercepts: $(0, 0)$, $(\pm 2\sqrt{3}, 0)$.
Max $y = 16$ at $x = -2$.
Min $y = -16$ at $x = 2$.

13.

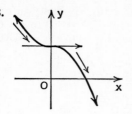

$y = 12 - x^3, y' = -3x^2.$

x	y	y'	Conclusions
$x < 0$		$-$	
$x = 0$	12	0	neither
$x > 0$		$-$	

15. $y' = 2(x - 1)$. Min $y = -8$ at $x = 1$. Intercepts: $(1 \pm 2\sqrt{2}, 0)$.

17. $P = (100 + 20w)(500 - 25w)$. $w = 7\frac{1}{2}$ weeks.

19. $P = (200 - x^2)(40 + 5x) - (E - 2x^2)$, E is a constant. $x \cong 6$. **(a)** $40 + 5(6) = \$70$.

21. $\dfrac{40\pi}{3}$ min, $\dfrac{1}{\pi}$ in. per min, $\dfrac{1}{4\pi}$ in. per min, $\dfrac{25}{\pi(12.3)^2}$ in. per min.

23. $y' = 3(x + 1)(x - 5)$. Consider x increasing. If $x < -1$, then $y' > 0$ and y is increasing. If $x = -1$, $y = 16$, then $y' = 0$. If $-1 < x < 5$, then $y' < 0$ and y is decreasing. If $x = 5$, $y = -92$, then $y' = 0$. If $x > 5$, then $y' > 0$ and y is increasing.

25. $\dfrac{25T_0}{12}$. **27.** Point: $(1, 1)$. Min distance: $\sqrt{5}$. **29.** See No. 11 of Set 7–1.

31. $V = \dfrac{\pi}{4} h$, $\dfrac{dh}{dt} = \dfrac{72}{\pi}$ ft per sec. **33.** $\dfrac{dV}{dt} = 4\pi r^2 \dfrac{dr}{dt}$, $V = \dfrac{4}{3}\pi r^3$.

35. $\dfrac{dW}{dS} = 4H^3 + 12H^2 S \dfrac{dH}{dS} = 4H^3 + 72H^2 S^2 = 4(3S^2 - 5)^2(21S^2 - 5)$, $\dfrac{dH}{dS} = 6S$.

37. $\dfrac{dH}{dS} = 18$, $\dfrac{dW}{dS} = 356{,}224$.

SET 7–6

1. Velocity is negative for $1 < t < 3$. At $t = 1$ sec velocity $= 0$. Then particle moves in negative direction until $t = 3$ when velocity $= 0$, then moves in positive direction.

2. 600 in.³ per sec.

3. $y' = 0$ for $x = 1$, $x = 1$ and $x = 4$. $(4, -27)$ is a min. $(1, 0)$ point of inflection.

4.

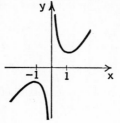

Min at $(1, 2)$ max at $(-1, -2)$.

5. 1280 ft per sec. **6.** -7.5 ft per sec.

7. $(2, 4)$ min. **8.** \$48.00.

SET 8–1

1. $h(1) = 11$, $h(4) = 51.75$, $h(0)$ is meaningless (Why?), $h(3) = \dfrac{274 + 3\sqrt{3}}{9}$.

3. (a) $\dfrac{y + x^2 y^3}{xy + x^2}$. **(b)** 12. **(c)** $\frac{1}{8}$. **11.** ± 2. **13.** 4. **15.** $-\frac{1}{2}$.

17. No solution. **19.** $\dfrac{(3 - 2\sqrt{2})}{50}$. **21.** 1, 6. **23.** 7. **25.** $-3, -1$.
31. (a) $\frac{6.5}{8}$. (b) 0. (c) $\frac{5}{6}$. **33.** (a) $a^{2x} - a^{2y}$. (b) $5^{6y} - 7^{4x}$.

35. (a) $\dfrac{b^2 + a^2}{ab(b + a)}$. (b) $\dfrac{8 - x^3}{96x^4}$. (c) $\dfrac{x^4(x^5y^5 - 1)}{y^9}$.

SET 8–2

1. 3.5×10^5. **3.** 5.8×10^{-3}. **5.** $y = 3.6 \times 10^{-2}$. **7.** Cupric iodate.
11. $x = 4.4 \times 10^{-3}$. **13.** 2.7×10^{-5}.
21. $3.5 \times 10^5 \quad \rightarrow 35000000 \quad 56.$
$5.8 \times 10^{-3} \quad \rightarrow 58000000 \quad 48.$
$9.08 \times 10^{-31} \quad \rightarrow 90800000 \quad 20.$
$8.8 \times 10^{13} \quad \rightarrow 88000000 \quad 64.$

SET 8–3

3. Approx 1.15×10^{47}. **5.** Approx 1.

SET 8–4

1. $2^y = 2^4$, $y = 4$. **3.** $2^{2y} = 2^5$, $y = \frac{5}{2}$. **5.** $3^y = 3^{-5}$, $y = -5$. **7.** 3.
9. 6. **11.** $y = 2^3 = 8$. **13.** $y = 8^{\frac{5}{3}} = 32$. **15.** 32. **17.** 9.
18. $y = 2^{\frac{4.9}{3}}$. **19.** 10. **21.** $y^{\frac{5}{3}} = 8$, $y = 8^{\frac{3}{5}} = 2\sqrt[5]{16}$.
23. $y^{-\frac{7}{2}} = 16$, $y = 16^{-\frac{2}{7}}$. **25.** 15.

SET 8–5

3.

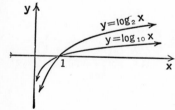

5. $\log_8 12$
$\cong \log_8 8 + \frac{1}{2}(\log_8 16 - \log_8 8) \cong 1.2.$
7. $\log_8 18$
$\cong \log_8 16 + \frac{1}{8}(\log_8 32 - \log_8 16) \cong 1.4.$

SET 8–6

3. $\log_b \dfrac{N}{D} = \log_b N \cdot D^{-1} = ?$ **5.** $\frac{1}{3}\log_8 \frac{1}{16} = \frac{1}{3}(-\frac{4}{3}) = -\frac{4}{9}.$ **7.** $-3.$
9. $2\log_{10} 2 + \log_{10} 3 = 1.079.$ **11.** 1.301. **13.** $-.301.$ **15.** 1.954.
17. $\log_{10} 9\sqrt{3} = 1.192.$ **19.** 3. **21.** $\log_{10} 10 = ?$ **25.** $0 < x < 1.$
27. $1 < x^2 < 10^{10}$, $1 < |x| < 10^5.$ **29.** $10^3 < x < 10^5.$
33. $\frac{1}{3}\log_e (4x + 2) + \log_e (2x^3 + 7) - \log_e (4x - 9).$
35. $5\log_e (4x + 7) + \frac{1}{2}\log_e (2x^2 + 1) - \log_e 5 - 3\log_e (2x^2 + 1) =$
$5\log_e (4x + 7) - \log_e 5 - \frac{5}{2}\log_e (2x^2 + 1).$

SET 8–7

1. .5403.	**3.** .5403 − 4.	**5.** .8831.	**7.** .5563 + 15.
9. .0086 − 8.	**11.** −(.6435 − 3).	**15.** .5334.	**17.** 7.05×10^{-7}.
19. 3.51×10^7.	**21.** 6.246×10^6.	**23.** 4.22×10^3.	**25.** $H^+ \approx 2.51 \times 10^{-5}$.
27. 0.4972.			

SET 8–9

1. 39.1 **3.** 1.895×10^5 or 1.9×10^5 or 2×10^5. **5.** 4.891×10^{-1}.
7. 2.08×10^{-5}. **9.** 3.365 or 3.4 or 3. **11.** 2.00×10^2.
13. 15.06. **15.** 56.47 approx. **17.** 6.6193 approx.
19. Bob's number $\approx 1.67 \times 10^{308}$, James's number $\approx 6.65 \times 10^{31}$, David's number $\approx 4.42 \times 10^{63}$.

SET 9–1

1. $x = \dfrac{2.5065}{1.9084} = 1.314$ or 1.31. **3.** $2^{2x} = 2^{-5}, x = -\frac{5}{2}$.

5. $x = 1.578$ or 1.6 **7.** $x \cong 10$. **9.** $x \cong 1.7$.

11. $x^2 - 3x - 1000 = 0, x = -30.16, x = 33.16$. **13.** $n \cong 6.6$.

15. $\dfrac{2t + 4}{3t + 1} = 6, t = -\dfrac{1}{8}$. **17.** $\dfrac{5x + 7}{3x} = 100, x = \dfrac{7}{295}$.

19. (a) $x < -2$ or $0 < x$; (b) $0 < x < 4$.

21. $n = \dfrac{.3010}{.0212} = 14.20$ years. **23.** $\$2.854 \times 10^3 = \$2854$.

25. $(2.3807)10^{17}$ dollars. **27.** (a) 1.5478 cm mercury. (b) 1.15 cc.

29. (a) $x = 17.4$; (b) $x = R$. **31.** (a) $x \cong 3.3$; (b) 0.30103.

SET 9–3

3. .1797 . . . . **5.** $N = e$. **7.** (a) 2.5. (b) 1.2. (c) 2.7.
9. (a) 2.4. (b) 2.3. (c) 2.6. **11.** 2.63189. **13.** −1.97329.
15. 9.77565. **17.** −.17436. **19.** 1.52606.
21. 2.993. **23.** 35.768. **25.** −81.956.

27.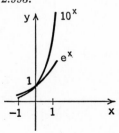

29.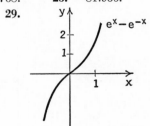

31. Approx: 0.1. Table: 0.13. **33.** Approx: 1.5. Table: 1.36.
35. Approx: 104. Table: 64. **37.** Approx: 1.8. Table: 2.
39. Approx: 700. Table: 610.

SET 9–5

1.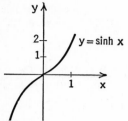

3.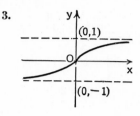

7. By definition, sech $x = \dfrac{1}{\cosh x}$. Use the result of Example 1.

9. Use the definitions of the functions on the right to transform the right side into the left.

11. $-17 \cosh(-17x)$.

13. $\dfrac{d(\tanh x)}{dx} = \dfrac{d\left[\dfrac{e^x - e^{-x}}{e^x + e^{-x}}\right]}{dx} = ?$ and $\dfrac{d(\tanh x)}{dx} = \dfrac{d\left[\dfrac{\sinh x}{\cosh x}\right]}{dx} = ?$

Answer: $\mathrm{sech}^2\ x$.

SELF TEST 9–6

1. (a) $x = 2.5$. (b) $x = \frac{1}{81}$. (c) $x = 5$.

2.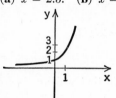

3. $3 \log(4x+7) + \frac{1}{2}\log(2x^2+1) - \log 5 - 5 \log(2x^2+1)$.

4. (a) $Q = 11.37$. (b) $R = .3863$. (c) 1.182.

5. $x = 10.08$. **6.** $x < \frac{1}{3}$ and $x > 1\frac{1}{2}$.

7. Slightly less than 18 yrs.

8. (a) 1.054. (b) -3.551. (c) 7.9620.

9. $x \approx 1.53$, $y \approx .185$. **10.** 1075.

SET 9–7

1. (a) 365 ft. (b) 587 ft. (c) 1454 ft.

SET 9–9

3.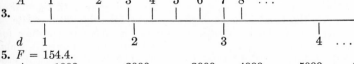

5. $F = 154.4$.

7.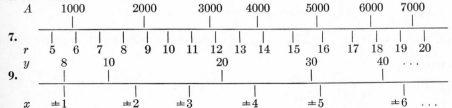

9.

SET 9–10

1. radius ≈ 3.8, height ≈ 7.6 **3.** 1.58.   **5.** 69.61 ft³ per sec.
7. Side of base $\cong 15.9$, height $\cong 7.8$.   **9.** Side of base $\cong 13$, height $\cong 12$.

SET 10–1

1. 1, 2, 3, 4, 5.   **2.** $3(1) = 3$, $3(2) = 6, 9, 12, 15$.
3. $1(3 \cdot 1 + 2) = 5$, $2(3 \cdot 2 + 2) = 16$,   33, 56, 85.   **5.** $a_1, a_1 + d, a_1 + 2d$.
6. $a_1, ra_1, r^2 a_1, r^3 a_1, \ldots r^9 a_1, \ldots$.   **7.** 1, 3, 6, 10, ...
9. $y, y + y^2, y + y^2 + y^3, y + y^2 + y^3 + y^4, y + y^2 + y^3 + y^4 + y^5, \cdots$.
11. $a_0, a_0 + a_1 x, a_0 + a_1 x + a_2 x^2, a_0 + a_1 x + a_2 x^2 + a_3 x^3$,
     $a_0 + a_1 x + a_2 x^2 + a_3 x^3 + a_4 x^4$.

SET 10–2

1. 140.   **3.** 31.   **5.** 55.   **7.** 11.25.
9. 106.   **11.** 26.   **13.** $n = 8$.   **15.** 15.

17. Hint: $\dfrac{1}{n} \displaystyle\sum_{i=1}^{n} (-2x_i \overline{x}) = -2\overline{x} \cdot \dfrac{1}{n} \sum_{i=1}^{n} x_i = ?$

SET 10–3

1. $a_{50} = 99$, $s_{50} = 2500$.   **3.** $a_{25} = -53$, $s_{25} = -575$.   **5.** 43 ft.
7. $(1 + 2 + 3 + \cdots + 25)(.03)(4000) = \cdots = \$39,000$.
9. 1000, 1050, 1100, yes.

11. $-12, -9, -6, \cdots$ yes. $\displaystyle\sum_{x=1}^{8} a_x = -12$, $\displaystyle\sum_{x=1}^{n} a_x = n(3n - 27)/2$.

13.

x	1	2	3	4	5	6	7	8
a_x	2	9	22	41	66	97	134	177
Δa_x		7	13	19	25	31	37	43
$\Delta^2 a_x$			6	6	6	6	6	6

Note that while a_x is not an arithmetic sequence, Δa_x is.

15. $a_{52} = \$5.20$, $s_{52} = \$137.80$ **17.** 92.

SET 10–4

1. $a = 12$, $r = -\frac{1}{2}$. Hence $a_9 = 12(-\frac{1}{2})^8 = \frac{3}{64}$, $S_9 = \frac{513}{64}$.
3. $(\frac{3}{4})^5 = \frac{243}{1024} \cong .24$.   **5.** $a_6 = 3^6 = 729$, $S_6 = 1092$.
7. $1400(1.0075)^{14} \cong \$1554.38$.   **9.** 17.5 years.
11. If the company sets aside \$10,000 today and \$10,000 each year until the end of the 25th year, when the bond issue is due, they have set aside 26 deposits of \$10,000 each. One of these deposits draws interest for 25 years, another for 24 years, . . ., another for 1 year, the last deposit earns no interest. Then $\$10,000[(1.03)^{25} + (1.03)^{24} + \cdots + (1.03) + 1] = R$. The bond issue is therefore approximately $R \cong \$385,500$. Since bonds are issued in round lots, only an approximate figure can be given.
13. $g = \sqrt{ab}$.   **15.** The man pays more than \$30,990 for his \$12,000 house.

SET 10–6

1. $a = 2$, $r = -\frac{1}{3}$, $S = \frac{3}{2}$.
2. $a = \frac{2}{3}$, $r = \sqrt{6}/3$, and $S = 2/(3 - \sqrt{6}) = 2(3 + \sqrt{6})/3$.

3. The perimeters form a geometric sequence 12, 6, 3, ... in which $a = 12$ and $r = \frac{1}{2}$. Then $S = 24$ inches.

5. The series has a sum if $\left|\left(1 + \dfrac{r}{100}\right)^{-1}\right| < 1$. Thus, if $-1 < \left(\dfrac{100 + r}{100}\right)^{-1} < 1$ or $-1 < \dfrac{100}{100 + r} < 1$. This implies either $r > 0$ or $r < -200$.

7.
$$x - 2 = .\overline{35}$$
$$100(x - 2) = 35 + (x - 2)$$
$$x = 2 + \tfrac{35}{99}.$$

9.
$$x = .34\overline{14}$$
$$100(x - .34) = .\overline{14}$$
$$100[100(x - .34)] = 14 + 100(x - .34)$$
$$x = \tfrac{34}{100} + \tfrac{14}{9900} = ?$$

11. $S = \dfrac{1}{1 + x}$ for $-1 < x < 1$. **13.** $S = \dfrac{2}{3 - x}$ for $-1 < x < 3$.

SELF TEST 10–7

1. $1650. **2.** If $x =$ amount of air to begin with, there is $\left(\frac{2}{3}\right)^{10}x \approx .017x$ air left.

3. $\frac{461}{111}$. **4.** $16 + 8\sqrt{2}$. **5.** 174.

6. $16 < S < 50$ for $n = 4$. **7.** $9058. **8.** $x > 6$ and $x < 0$, $S = \dfrac{-3}{x}$.

SET 10–8

1. Hint: The sum of the first k positive odd integers is $1 + 3 + 5 + \cdots + 2k - 1$ which equals k^2 by hypothesis.

3. Hint: Show that under the induction hypothesis,
$$\sum_{x=1}^{k+1} x(x + 1) = \frac{(k + 1)(k + 2)(k + 3)}{3}.$$

5. Hint: Show that $\displaystyle\sum_{x=1}^{k+1} a_1 r^{x-1} = \frac{a_1 - a_1 r^{k+1}}{1 - r}$ using the hypothesis that
$$\sum_{x=1}^{k} a_1 r^{x-1} = \frac{a_1 - a_1 r^{k}}{1 - r}. \quad \text{(What must precede this?)}$$

7. The induction hypothesis states that $k(k^2 + 1)(k^2 + 4)$ is divisible by 5, which can be true only if at least one of the three factors is divisible by 5. Consider three cases and show that in each case $(k + 1)(k^2 + 2k + 2)(k^2 + 2k + 5)$ is divisible by 5. (For example, if k is divisible by 5, then $k^2 + 2k + 5$ is divisible by 5.)

SET 10–11

1.

x	y	Δy	$\Delta^2 y$	$\Delta^3 y$	$\Delta^4 y$
1	-4				
		4			
3	0		56		
		60		48	
5	60		104		0
		164		48	
7	224		152		
		316			
9	540				

$P_4(x - 1) = x^3 - 2x^2 - 3x.$

3.

x	$f(x)$	Δf	$\Delta^2 f$	$\Delta^3 f$
20	13.197			
		$-.491$		
30	12.706		$+.036$	
		$-.455$		$-.006$
40	12.251		$+.030$	
		$-.425$		$-.001$
50	11.826		$+.029$	
		$-.396$		
60	11.430			

$$P_3(x - 20) = 13.197 + \frac{(x - 20)}{10}(-.491) + \frac{(x - 20)(x - 30)}{2 \times 10^2}(+.036) +$$
$$\frac{(x - 20)(x - 30)(x - 40)}{6 \times 10^3}(-.006) +$$
$$f(26) = 12.898.$$

5. $\Delta cf(x) = cf(x + h) - cf(x) = ?$

7. $\Delta[f(x) + g(x)] = [f(x + h) + g(x + h)] - [f(x) + g(x)] = ?$

9. $(-3.400 \times 10^{-7})x^3 + (2.500 \times 10^{-5})x^2 - (3.316 \times 10^{-3})x + 3.238 = f(x).$

SET 10–12

1. $2x^2 + 3 = 2x^{[2]} + 2hx^{[1]} + 3.$

3. Use results of Example 1, Set 10–8 to find $\sum_{x=1}^{50}(2x^2 + 3) = 86000.$

5. $A = \frac{50}{3}.$ **7.** $x^3 = x^{[3]} + 3hx^{[2]} + h^2x^{[1]}.$

9. $x^3 = x(x - 1)(x - 2) + 3x(x - 1) + x.$ **11. (a)** $A = \dfrac{ab}{6}$ **(b)** $A = \dfrac{2ab}{3}.$

SET 11–1

1. (a) $6 \cdot 5 \cdot 4 = 120.$ **(b)** $6 \cdot 6 \cdot 6 = 216.$

2. 144. **3.** $5 \cdot 4 \cdot 3 \cdot 2.$ **4.** $2^5 = 32.$

5. 36 total ways, 6 ways for total to be 7.

6. $6^3;\ 216 - 120 = 96.$ **7.** 42 games. **9.** $(24)^3 + (24)^2 = 14400.$

SET 11–3

1. $3! \cdot 5! = 720.$

2. If the red books are on the right, there exist $6!4! = 17{,}280$ ways. An equal number of ways exist with the blue books on the right. Hence 34,560 possible arrangements.

3. (a) Consider the set of books as a unit. The seven units may be arranged in 7! ways. The unit containing the set of 6 books may be arranged in 6! ways. Hence $7!6! = 3{,}628{,}800$ ways. **(b)** 7!

5. $5 \cdot 6 \cdot 5 \cdot 7 = ?$ ways. **6.** 20. **7. (a)** $5 \cdot 5 \cdot 5 = 125.$ **(b)** 60.

8. (a) $4^3 + 4^3 - 3^3 = 101$ or $125 - (18 + 6) = 101.$ **(b)** Under the additional assumption of 7b there are 42 possible arrangements.

9. $1 \cdot 8 \cdot 7 \cdot 1 = 56$ orders which result in 28 different color schemes.

11. $\dfrac{6!}{2!2!} = 180.$ **13.** $\dfrac{12!}{4!3!5!} = ?$ **15.** $\dfrac{5!}{3!2!} = 10.$

18. $\dbinom{n}{0} = 1 = \dbinom{n}{n}$

21. Multiply numerator and denominator of $\dbinom{n}{x - 1}$ by x and the numerator and denominator of $\dbinom{n}{x}$ by $(n - x + 1)$. Add and simplify.

SET 11–4

1. $\dfrac{t^8}{16} + \dfrac{3t^5}{2} + \dfrac{27t^2}{2} + \dfrac{54}{t} + \dfrac{81}{t^4}.$

3. $\left(\dfrac{2}{x^3} - y^{\frac{1}{2}}\right)^7 = \left(\dfrac{2}{x^3}\right)^7 - 7\left(\dfrac{2}{x^3}\right)^6 (y^{\frac{1}{2}}) + \dfrac{7 \cdot 6}{1 \cdot 2}\left(\dfrac{2}{x^3}\right)^5 (y^{\frac{1}{2}})^2 - \dfrac{7 \cdot 6 \cdot 5}{1 \cdot 2 \cdot 3}\left(\dfrac{2}{x^3}\right)^4 (y^{\frac{1}{2}})^3 + \cdots.$

5. $\dfrac{10 \cdot 9 \cdot 8 \cdot 7 \cdot 6}{1 \cdot 2 \cdot 3 \cdot 4 \cdot 5}(x)^5 \left(\dfrac{-1}{2y}\right)^5 = ?$

7. $1^4 + 4 \cdot 1^3 (.02) + 6 \cdot 1^2 \cdot (.02)^2 + 4 \cdot 1 (.02)^3 + (.02)^4 = 1.08243216.$

9. $(1 + .03)^{10} = 1^{10} + 10 \cdot 1^9 (.03) + \dfrac{10 \cdot 9}{1 \cdot 2} \cdot 1^8 \cdot (.03)^2 + \dfrac{10 \cdot 9 \cdot 8}{1 \cdot 2 \cdot 3} \cdot 1^7 \cdot (.03)^3$

    $+ \cdots \cong 1.344.$

10. Use the results of Problem 9.

11. $150(1 + .0145)^{20} = 150[1 + 20(.0145) + 190(.0145)^2 + \cdots] \cong 150[1.33] \cong \$200.$

13. $10(1 - .009)^{\frac{1}{3}} = 10\left[1 + \dfrac{1}{3}(-.009) + \dfrac{(\frac{1}{3})(-\frac{2}{3})}{2}(-.009)^2 + \cdots\right] \cong 9.96991,$

    which is correct to 6 significant digits.

15. Expand $(a + b)^n$ twice, once with $a = b = 1$ and again with $a = 1$, $b = -1$.

17. (a) Let $y = u \cdot v$, $\ln y = \ln u + \ln v$. $\dfrac{dy}{dx} = ? = \dfrac{d(u \cdot v)}{dx}.$

    (c) $y = \dfrac{u}{v}$, $\ln y = \ln u - \ln v.$

19. $x = \mu \pm \sigma.$

SET 11–5

1. (a) $500(1 + .015)^{20} = \$673.43.$ (b) $500(e)^{.03(10)} = 500e^{.3} = \$674.95.$

3. $A(t) = ke^{rt/100}.$ Solving $A(0) = 20{,}000$ and $A(10) = 200$ for k and r one obtains $k = 20{,}000,$ $e^{r/10} = .01$ or $r/10 = \log_e .01 = 5.395 - 10 = -4.605.$ Thus $r = -46.05$ and $A(t) \cong 20{,}000e^{-.46t}.$ We now compute $A(5) \cong \$2000.$

5. $A(15) \approx 1.811 \times 10^5.$

6. Let $\dfrac{x}{2} = z$, then $\lim\limits_{x \to 0}\left(1 + \dfrac{x}{2}\right)^{1/x} = \lim\limits_{z \to 0}[(1 + z)^{1/z}]^{1/2} = \sqrt{e}.$

7. Let $\dfrac{\Delta u}{u} = z$ for fixed u, then $\lim\limits_{\Delta u \to 0}\left(1 + \dfrac{\Delta u}{u}\right)^{u/\Delta u} = \lim\limits_{z \to 0}(1 + z)^{1/z} = e.$

9. Let $\dfrac{1}{x^2} = z$, then $\lim\limits_{x \to \infty}\left(1 + \dfrac{1}{x^2}\right)^{x^2/2} = \lim\limits_{z \to 0}(1 + z)^{1/2z} = e^{1/2}.$

SET 11–6

1. $\dfrac{50 \cdot 49 \cdot 48 \cdot 47}{1 \cdot 2 \cdot 3 \cdot 4} = 230{,}300.$ 2. (a) $\dfrac{8 \cdot 7 \cdot 6}{1 \cdot 2 \cdot 3} = 56.$ (b) 336.

3. 4.   4. $\dfrac{12 \cdot 11 \cdot 10}{1 \cdot 2 \cdot 3} \cdot \dfrac{8 \cdot 7}{2} = 6160.$ 5. $\dfrac{8 \cdot 7 \cdot 6 \cdot 5}{1 \cdot 2 \cdot 3 \cdot 4} \cdot \dfrac{4 \cdot 3 \cdot 2 \cdot 1}{1 \cdot 2 \cdot 3 \cdot 4} = 70.$

7. (a) $\dfrac{13 \cdot 12}{1 \cdot 2} = 78.$ (b) $\dfrac{5 \cdot 4}{2} = 10.$

9. (a) $\binom{25}{1} = 3{,}268{,}760.$ (b) $\binom{25}{9}\binom{25}{1} = ?$ (c) $\binom{25}{10}.$

10. If $x = 3$, the answer is $\binom{13}{3}\binom{39}{9} = ?$ The reader should compute this as well as $\binom{13}{x}\binom{39}{5-x}$ for other values of x.

11. (a) $\dfrac{5 \cdot 4 \cdot 3}{1 \cdot 2 \cdot 3} \cdot \dfrac{7}{1} = 70.$

    (b) $\dfrac{5 \cdot 4 \cdot 3}{1 \cdot 2 \cdot 3} \cdot \dfrac{7}{1} + \dfrac{5 \cdot 4}{1 \cdot 2} \cdot \dfrac{7 \cdot 6}{1 \cdot 2} + \dfrac{5}{1} \cdot \dfrac{7 \cdot 6 \cdot 5}{1 \cdot 2 \cdot 3} + \dfrac{7 \cdot 6 \cdot 5 \cdot 4}{1 \cdot 2 \cdot 3 \cdot 4} = 490.$

13. $\binom{n}{2} - n.$

SELF TEST 11-7

1. $2^5 - 80\sqrt{x} + 80x - 40x\sqrt{x} + 10x^2 - x^2\sqrt{x}.$ **2.** $\dfrac{-55}{2}x^{21}.$ **3.** 60.

4. $n = 8.$ **5.** (a) 6! ways. (b) 144 ways.   **6.** $120 + 60 = 180$ ways.

7. $(1716)^2.$ **8.** (a) 24. (b) $\binom{4}{3}\binom{48}{2}.$ **9.** (a) 210. (b) 24. (c) $\frac{12}{105}.$

10. $k = 20{,}000,\ r = -17.5,\ A(12) = 2600.$ **11.** \$1,344.   **12.** $e^{\frac{2}{3}}.$

SET 12-2

1.

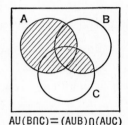

$$A \cup (B \cap C) = (A \cup B) \cap (A \cup C)$$

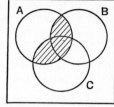

$$A \cap (B \cup C) = (A \cap B) \cup (A \cap C)$$

3. Let x be an element in $(A \cap B)'$. Then x is not in $A \cap B$ and hence is either not in A or not in B or is in neither A nor B. Thus, it is in A' or B' or both and is, therefore, in $A' \cup B'$. Conversely, if x is an element in $A' \cup B'$, then it is an element in at least one of the two sets A' and B'. Therefore, it cannot be in at least one of the two sets A and B and thus is not in $A \cap B$. Hence, it is in $(A \cap B)'$.

5. $B = A \cup (B \cap A')$ where $A \cap (B \cap A') = \phi$. Thus, $P(B) = P(A) + P(B \cap A')$ by Corollary 1. Hence $P(A) \le P(B)$.

7. By Theorem 1, the relationship is valid for one union. Assume that it is valid for K unions and prove that it is then valid for $K + 1$ unions.

SET 12-4

1. (a) $\frac{1}{2}$. (b) $\frac{1}{3}$. (c) $\frac{1}{20}$.   **2.** $\binom{5}{2}/\binom{10}{2} = \frac{2}{9}$.

3. $\binom{10}{2}/\binom{20}{2} = \frac{9}{38}$.   **4.** (a) $4 \cdot 4/(52 \cdot 51) = \frac{4}{663}$. (b) $\frac{8}{663}$.

5. (a) $\binom{6}{3} = 20$. (b) $\frac{1}{2}$.   **7.** $\frac{48}{2598960} = ?\quad \frac{4}{2598960} = ?$

9. Let the original batch contain x bad eggs and let p_x be the probability that if 2 eggs are selected from the x bad and $6 - x$ good eggs, exactly 1 will be bad. $p_0 = 0$, since if $x = 0$, no eggs are bad.

$$p_1 = 5/\binom{6}{2} = \tfrac{1}{3}.\quad p_2 = \tfrac{8}{15},\ p_3 = \tfrac{9}{15},\ p_4 = \tfrac{8}{15},\ p_5 = \tfrac{1}{3},\ p_6 = 0.$$

Probabilities of this type are used in drawing conclusions concerning the probable nature of a set from which a sample has been selected and tested.

10. $\frac{1}{6}$.

11. Each of hands (a), (b), (c) has probability $1/\binom{52}{13}$. Hands (a), (b), (c) are equally probable, although from the standpoint of the bridge player one may be more desirable than another. Hand (d) is four times as likely. Why?

12. $p(2\ \text{heads}) = \frac{1}{4}$, $p(1\ \text{head and 1 tail}) = \frac{1}{2}$. The reader should note that $p(1\ \text{head and 1 tail})$ is *not* the same as the $p(\text{head on first coin, tail on second})$.

13. Hand b is more unusual — to explain, examine the probabilities for drawing each hand.

15. Review the concepts of a sample space and a probability function defined on a sample space.

SET 12-5

1. $p(\text{red or white}) = p(\text{red}) + p(\text{white}) = \frac{2}{9} + \frac{3}{9} = \frac{5}{9}.$

3. $\frac{1}{2}.$ **5.** $\frac{35}{108}.$ **7.** $\frac{5}{39}.$

9. There remain 9 prizes in 80 punches. The number of (ordered) ways in which he may win are

$$N = n(\text{win, lose}) + n(\text{lose, win}) + n(\text{win, win}) = 9 \cdot 71 + 71 \cdot 9 + 9 \cdot 8.$$

Then $p = N/(80 \cdot 79)$.

11. $p(\text{odd sum}) = p(\text{odd, even}) + p(\text{even, odd}) = \dfrac{10 \cdot 10}{20 \cdot 19} + \dfrac{10 \cdot 10}{20 \cdot 19} = \dfrac{10}{19} > \dfrac{1}{2}.$

12. Consider two cases: Case 1: A red or white ball is drawn from the first bag and either red or white from the (now) 10 balls in the second bag. Case 2: A black ball is drawn from the first bag and either a red or a white ball is drawn from the 9 balls in the second bag. The first case may occur in any of $5 \cdot 6 = 30$ ways, and has probability $p_1 = \frac{30}{90} = \frac{1}{3}$. The second case can occur in $4 \cdot 5 = 20$ ways, and has probability $p_2 = \frac{20}{81}$. Thus $p = p_1 + p_2 = \frac{47}{81}$.

SET 12–7

1. (a) $\frac{1}{8}$. (b) $\frac{1}{8}$. (c) $\frac{1}{8}$. (d) $\frac{3}{8}$.

2. $p(\text{at least 4 heads}) = p(\text{4 heads}) + p(\text{5 heads}) = \frac{5}{32} + \frac{1}{32} = \frac{3}{16}$.

3. $p(\text{not more than 2 defectives}) = p(\text{no def.}) + p(\text{1 def.}) + p(\text{2 def.}) =$
$(.98)^{10} + 10(.98)^9(.02) + 45(.98)^8(.02)^2 \cong ?$

5. (a) $4(\frac{4}{36})^3(\frac{32}{36}) \cong ?$ (b) $1 - p(\text{all nines}) = 1 - (\frac{4}{36})^4 \cong ?$

7. If the coin is honest, $p(\text{heads on any toss}) = \frac{1}{2}$. A coin has no memory.

9. $p(\text{red, white, white, blue}) = \frac{5}{18} \cdot \frac{6}{17} \cdot \frac{5}{16} \cdot \frac{7}{15} = ?$

11. $p(\text{2 dimes and 2 pennies, in some order}) = 6 \cdot p(\text{dime, dime, penny, penny}) =$
$6(\frac{10}{25})(\frac{9}{24})(\frac{5}{23})(\frac{4}{22}) \cong ?$

13. $p(\text{white}) = p(\text{box 1 is selected})p_1(\text{white}) + p(\text{box 2})p_2(\text{white}) = \frac{1}{2}(\frac{2}{10}) + \frac{1}{2}(\frac{6}{10}) = ?$

15. $1 - (\frac{3}{4})(\frac{1}{3})(\frac{1}{2}) = \frac{7}{8}$. **17.** $(.997)^{200} \cong ?$ (Use logarithms.) **19.** $\frac{2}{7}$.

21. (a) $(\frac{5}{8})(\frac{4}{7})(\frac{3}{6}) = \frac{5}{28}$. (b) $3(\frac{5}{28}) = \frac{15}{28}$. (c) $1 - p(\text{all men}) = \frac{23}{28}$.
(d) $(\frac{3}{8})(\frac{2}{7})(\frac{1}{6}) = ?$

22. (d) zero, since only 2 women. **23.** $p(W \text{ wins}) = \frac{1}{6}$, $p(J \text{ wins}) = \frac{5}{36}$.

25. $p = \frac{1}{2}$. **29.** (a) $p(x) = \dfrac{\binom{4}{x}\binom{48}{5-x}}{\binom{52}{5}}.$

SELF TEST 12–8

1. $\frac{2}{3}$. **2.** $\frac{1}{6}$. The dice have no memory.

3. (a) Exactly 3 white: $\frac{4}{35}$. At least 3 white: $\dfrac{24 + 1}{210} = \dfrac{5}{42}$. (b) $\frac{3}{7}$. **4.** $\frac{1}{24}$.

5. (a) $\frac{12}{49}$. (b) $\frac{24}{49}$. **6.** $\dfrac{2 + 4}{2 + 4 + 6 + 4 + 2} = \dfrac{1}{3}$. **7.** $\frac{3}{13}$.

8. (a) $p(x) = \dfrac{\binom{13}{x}\binom{39}{5-x}}{\binom{52}{5}}.$ (b) $\displaystyle\sum_{x=0}^{5} p(x) = 1.$

SET 13–2

1. $\bar{x} = 274$, $s_x = \sqrt{75140 - 75076} = 8$.

2.

x	f	xf	$x(xf) = x^2f$
3	1	3	9
8	1	8	64
10	2	20	200
4	1	4	16
5	1	5	25
$N = 6$		40	314

Thus $\bar{x} = \frac{40}{6} = 6.7$.
$s_x = \sqrt{\frac{314}{6} - (\frac{20}{3})^2} \cong \sqrt{7.9} \cong 2.8$.

3.

x	f	xf	x^2f	$x - \bar{x}$	$(x - \bar{x})f$	$(x - \bar{x})^2f$
0	2	0	0	-2	-4	8
1	14	14	14	-1	-14	14
2	20	40	80	0	0	0
3	10	30	90	1	10	10
4	4	16	64	2	8	16
	50	100	248		0	48

$$\bar{x} = 2$$
$$s_x = \sqrt{.9600} \cong .98.$$

5. $S(\xi) = \sum_{i=1}^{n} x_i^2 f_i - 2\left(\sum_{i=1}^{n} x_i f_i\right)\xi + N\xi^2.$ $\dfrac{dS(\xi)}{d\xi} = 0 - 2\left(\sum_{i=1}^{n} x_i f_i\right) + 2N\xi.$

Which equals zero if $\xi = \dfrac{\sum_{i=1}^{n} x_i f_i}{N} = \bar{x}.$

7. $\sum_{x=1}^{n} (x^3 - [x - 1]^3) = \cdots = 3\sum_{x=1}^{n} x^2 - 3(n + n^2)/2 + n$

$\sum_{x=1}^{n} (x^3 - [x - 1]^3) =$

$1^3 - 0^3 + 2^3 - 1^3 + 3^3 - 2^3 + \cdots + (n - 1)^3 + (n - 2)^3 + n^3 - (n - 1)^3 = n^3.$

Equating these, one obtains $\sum_{x=1}^{n} x^2 = \dfrac{2n^3 + 3n^2 + n}{6} = \dfrac{n(n + 1)(2n + 1)}{6}.$

9. Why look here? Work it out. Perform the experiment.

11. $\sum_{i=1}^{n} (x_i - \bar{x})f_i = \sum_{i=1}^{n} x_i f_i - \bar{x}\sum_{i=1}^{n} f_i = N\bar{x} - \bar{x}N = 0.$

SET 13–3

1. $p(\text{at least } 3H) = p(3H) + p(4H) = 4(\tfrac{1}{2})^3\tfrac{1}{2} + (\tfrac{1}{2})^4 = \tfrac{1}{4} + \tfrac{1}{16} = \tfrac{5}{16}.$

3. $1 - [p(\text{all germinate}) + p(1 \text{ fails}) + p(2 \text{ fail}) + p(3 \text{ fail})]$
$= 1 - [(.95)^{30} + 30(.05)(.95)^{29} + 435(.05)^2(.95)^{28} + 4060(.05)^3(.95)^{27}] \cong ?$

5. $p(0H) = (\tfrac{1}{2})^4 = \tfrac{1}{16}, p(1H) = 4(\tfrac{1}{2})(\tfrac{1}{2})^3 = \tfrac{1}{4}, p(2H) = \tfrac{3}{8}, p(3H) = \tfrac{1}{4}, p(4H) = \tfrac{1}{16}.$
Note that the sum of these p's is one. Is this to be expected?

7. $1 - (\tfrac{40}{52})(\tfrac{39}{51})(\tfrac{38}{50}) \cong ?$ **8.** $\tfrac{3}{5}.$ **9.** $\tfrac{1}{24}.$

10. May use $\left(\dfrac{1}{3} + \dfrac{1}{3} + \dfrac{1}{3}\right)^5 = \sum \dfrac{5!}{x!y!(5 - x - y)!}\left(\dfrac{1}{3}\right)^5.$ **11.** $\tfrac{10}{31}.$

13. (a) $\tfrac{1}{8}.$ (b) $\tfrac{1}{2}.$

SET 13–4

1. $\mu = 2$, $\sigma_x = 1$, each of which is close to the result of Problem 4, Set 13–2.
2. (a) $f(1.07 \le x \le 3.03) = 39 + 21 = 60.$ Per cent def. = 60 per cent.
3. (a) $f(0 \le x \le 3) = 79$, rel. fr. = .79, per cent fr. = 79 per cent.
  (b) $f(2 \le x \le 5) = 81.$ (c) $f(x \neq 2) = 59.$

SET 13–6

1. (a) $p = .1$, expected value = $np = 40.$ (b) $\sigma = \sqrt{npq} = 6.$
  (c) Since $np + 3\sigma = 58 < 59$, the manufacturer may conclude that, almost certainly $(p \cong 1)$, this lot contains more defective items than would result from chance.

3. Although, in this case $np + 3\sigma \cong 1174 < 1300$, still we can*not* conclude this is unusual since, in general, an urban population in a specific locale will *not* be a random sample of the nation's population. It may well be that most cities have a high proportion of the 20- to 24-year age group, or the city may contain a small college, or any one of many factors. A nonrandom sample is apt to deviate sharply from the universe from which it was selected.

5. No. Even if the first factory had been operating at a 2 percent defective rate, $30 - 3\sqrt{30 \times .97} < 1000p < 30 + 3\sqrt{30 \times .97}$, $1.38 < p < 4.62$ and quite possibly a single sample might contain 30 defectives.

7. $\sigma \cong \sqrt{npq} = \sqrt{3232 \cdot \frac{1}{2} \cdot \frac{1}{2}} \cong 28.4$. Thus
$$np + 3\sigma \cong 1616 + 3(28.4) \cong 1701 < 1705.$$
This suggests that, in this case, the hypothesis that the probability that a child will be a boy is not $\frac{1}{2}$. More extensive tests on the general population also suggest that a child is slightly more likely to be male.

9. No, since $.5 - 3(.7) < 2 < .5 + 3(.7)$.

11. $p(5) = \frac{1}{9}$. Expected mean $= np = 8$. $\sigma = \sqrt{npq} = \frac{8}{3}$. Since
$$np - 3\sigma = 0 < 12 < np + 3\sigma = 16$$
we can*not* conclude the dice are dishonest from this experiment. They may or may not be dishonest.

13. Since $p(1000 \text{ heads}) = \dfrac{1}{2^{1000}} = \dfrac{1}{(\text{a number with 302 digits})}$ and
$$\sigma = \frac{1}{(\text{a number with 150 digits})}$$
it is indeed unlikely that this should happen with a normal coin. A 2-headed coin seems quite likely, especially if the method of tossing has been random. However, if it did happen to a normal coin, and it *could*, then the probability of a head on the next toss is $\frac{1}{2}$. A coin has no memory.

15. (a) $np + \sigma = 400(.2) + \sqrt{400(.2)(.8)} = 88$. (b) $np + 2\sigma = 96$.

SET 13–8

1. There were 111 absences during the $28 \cdot 64 = 1792$ student meetings, giving $p = \frac{111}{1792} \cong .06$, $n = 64$. Then
$$100[p \pm 3\sqrt{p(1-p)/n}] = 100[.06 \pm 3\sqrt{.0009}] = 100[.06 \pm .09].$$
Hence the 3 sigma percent control limits are 0 percent and 15 percent. Students 1, 5, and 23 are out of control, hence the class is not in control.

3. The data may be presented in the following table from which control charts could be constructed over several years' time.

	Ariz.	Calif.	. . .	Nev.	. . .
	156.7	2213	. . .	33	. . .
$\sigma = \sqrt{npq} \cong \sqrt{np}$	12.5	47	. . .	5.7	. . .
$np + 3\sigma$	194	2354	. . .	50	. . .
# of deaths	281	3003	. . .	82	. . .
$np - 3\sigma$	?	?	. . .	?	. . .
Within limits?	No	No	. . .	No	. . .

The student should compute other table entries.

SELF TEST 13–10

1. (a) $\dfrac{3^2 \cdot 5^9}{6^{10}}$. **(b)** $1 - \sum\limits_{x=0}^{1} \binom{10}{x} (\frac{1}{6})^x (\frac{5}{6})^{10-x}$. **2.** Yes. (Why?)

3. Since $np + 3\sigma < 34$ the answer is "yes" it *suggests* an unusual susceptibility. However, other causes may be affecting members of the class selected.

4. $n = 49,555$. **5.** $n \leqq (\frac{198}{8})^2$ or $n \leqq 612$.

SET 14–1

1.   **3.**   **5.**   **7.**

9. $20°$, 1 radian, $60°$, $\pi/2$ radian.

11.   **13.**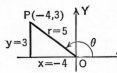

15. 2π radians $= 360°$.

17. $30° = 30(\pi/180) = \pi/6$, $45° = \pi/4$, $-144° = -144(\pi/180) = -4\pi/5$.

SET 14–4

1.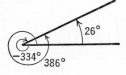

$\sin \theta = \frac{3}{5}$ $\csc \theta = \frac{5}{3}$
$\cos \theta = -\frac{4}{5}$ $\sec \theta = -\frac{5}{4}$
$\tan \theta = -\frac{3}{4}$ $\cot \theta = -\frac{4}{3}$

3. (a)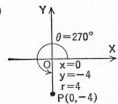

$\sin 270° = -1$ $\csc 270° = -1$
$\cos 270° = 0$ $\sec 270°$ is not de-
$\tan 270°$ is not de-   fined.
fined. $\cot 270° = 0$

3. (b)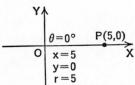

$\sin 0° = 0$ $\csc 0°$ is not defined.
$\cos 0° = 1$ $\sec 0° = 1$
$\tan 0° = 0$ $\cot 0°$ is not defined.

5.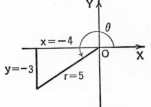

$\sin \theta = -\frac{3}{5}$ $\csc \theta = -\frac{5}{3}$
$\cos \theta = -\frac{4}{5}$ $\cot \theta = \frac{4}{3}$

7. $\tan \theta > 0$ in I and III. $\tan \theta < 0$ in II and IV.

9. $\tan \theta = \dfrac{y}{x} = \dfrac{y/y}{x/y} = \dfrac{1}{\cot \theta}$, when $x \neq 0$ and $y \neq 0$. $\tan \theta$ is not defined when $x = 0 (\theta = \pm 90°, \pm 270°, \cdots)$, and $\cot \theta$ is not defined when $y = 0$ $(\theta = 0°, \pm 180°, \cdots)$.

11. (a) $\sec \theta = \dfrac{r}{x} = \dfrac{1}{x/r} = \dfrac{1}{\cos \theta}$, when $x \neq 0 (\theta \neq \pm 90°, \pm 270°, \cdots)$.

  (b) $\csc \theta = \dfrac{r}{y} = \dfrac{1}{y/r} = \dfrac{1}{\sin \theta}$, when $y \neq 0 (\theta \neq 0°, \pm 180°, \cdots)$.

13.

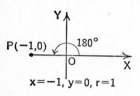

$x = -1, y = 0, r = 1$

$\sin 180° = 0$ $\sec 180° = -1$
$\cos 180° = -1$ $\csc 180°$ and $\cot 180°$
$\tan 180° = 0$ are not defined.

15.

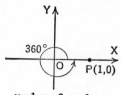

$x = 1, y = 0, r = 1$

$\sin 360° = 0$ $\csc 360°$ is not defined.
$\cos 360° = 1$ $\sec 360° = 1$
$\tan 360° = 0$ $\cot 360°$ is not defined.

17.

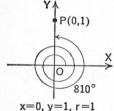

$x = 0, y = 1, r = 1$

$\sin 810° = 1$ $\csc 810° = 1$
$\cos 810° = 0$ $\sec 810°$ is not defined.
$\tan 810°$ is not defined. $\cot 810° = 0$

19. Compare with results of No. 17.

20.

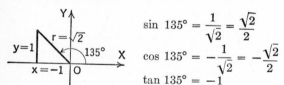

$\sin 135° = \dfrac{1}{\sqrt{2}} = \dfrac{\sqrt{2}}{2}$ $\csc 135° = \sqrt{2}$

$\cos 135° = -\dfrac{1}{\sqrt{2}} = -\dfrac{\sqrt{2}}{2}$ $\sec 135° = -\sqrt{2}$

$\tan 135° = -1$ $\cot 135° = -1$

21. $|x| \leq \sqrt{x^2 + y^2}, \; -1 \leq \dfrac{x}{\sqrt{x^2 + y^2}} \leq 1$.

23. $|y| \leq \sqrt{x^2 + y^2}, \; \dfrac{\sqrt{x^2 + y^2}}{|y|} \geq 1$.

25. $\beta = 45°, 225°, 45° + 360° = 405°, 45° - 360° = -315°, 225° + 360° = 585°,$
225° - 360° = -135°, \cdots.

27. $\beta \cong 63.5°, 243.5°, \cdots$.

29.

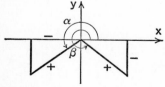

$\csc \beta \neq -\sec \alpha$, since $\csc \beta < 0$, $\sec \alpha < 0$.

31. versine $180° = 1 - \cos 180° = 1 - (-1) = 2$.
coversine $180° = 1 - \sin 180° = 1 - 0 = 1$.

SET 14–5

1. (a)

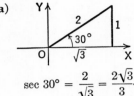

$$\sec 30° = \frac{2}{\sqrt{3}} = \frac{2\sqrt{3}}{3}.$$

(b)

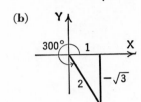

$$\sec 210° = \frac{2}{-\sqrt{3}} = -\frac{2\sqrt{3}}{3}.$$

3. (a)

$$\csc 225° = \frac{\sqrt{2}}{-1} = -\sqrt{2}.$$

(b)

$$\cot 300° = \frac{1}{-\sqrt{3}} = -\frac{\sqrt{3}}{3}.$$

5. $\left(\dfrac{1}{2}\right)\left(\dfrac{1}{2}\right) - \left(\dfrac{\sqrt{3}}{2}\right)\left(\dfrac{\sqrt{3}}{2}\right) = -\dfrac{1}{2}.$ **7.** $(-1)\left(\dfrac{\sqrt{2}}{2}\right) - (0)\left(\dfrac{\sqrt{2}}{2}\right) = -\dfrac{\sqrt{2}}{2}.$

9. 10.

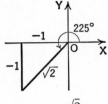

$\sin \alpha = y/r = \cos \beta = \cos (90° - \alpha)$
$\cos \alpha = x/r = \sin \beta = \sin (90° - \alpha)$
$\tan \alpha = y/x = \cot \beta = \cot (90° - \alpha)$
$\csc \alpha = r/y = \sec (90° - \alpha)$
$\sec \alpha = r/x = \csc (90° - \alpha)$
$\cot \alpha = x/y = \tan (90° - \alpha)$

11. $\sin 1035° = -\sin 45° = -\dfrac{\sqrt{2}}{2},\ \cos 1035° = \cos 45° = \dfrac{\sqrt{2}}{2},$

$\tan 1035° = -\tan 45° = -1, \cdots .$

13.

$$\sin 60° = \frac{\sqrt{3}}{2},\ \cos 60° = \frac{1}{2},\ \tan 60° = \sqrt{3},$$

$$\csc 60° = \frac{2\sqrt{3}}{3},\ \sec 60° = 2,\ \cot 60° = \frac{\sqrt{3}}{3}.$$

15. $\sin (-120°) = -\sin 60° = -\dfrac{\sqrt{3}}{2},\ \cos (-120°) = -\cos 60° = -\tfrac{1}{2},$

$\tan (-120°) = \tan 60° = \sqrt{3}, \cdots .$

17. $\sin 120° = \sin 60° = \dfrac{\sqrt{3}}{2},\ \cos 120° = -\cos 60° = -\tfrac{1}{2},$

$\tan 120° = -\tan 60° = -\sqrt{3}, \cdots .$

19.

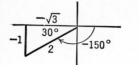

$\sin(-150°) = -\sin 30° = -\frac{1}{2},$

$\cos(-150°) = -\cos 30° = -\frac{\sqrt{3}}{2},$

$\tan(-150°) = \tan 30° = \frac{\sqrt{3}}{3}, \cdots.$

21. $\log \cos 45° = \log \dfrac{1}{\sqrt{2}} = \log 1 - \dfrac{1}{2}\log 2 = 0 - \dfrac{1}{2}(.30103)$

$= 10.00000 - .15051 - 10 = 9.84949 - 10.$

$\log |\sec 120°| = \log |-2| = \log 2 = 0.30103.$

23. $\log \cos \theta = 0, \cos \theta = 1, \theta = 0°, \pm 360°, \pm 720°, \cdots.$

25.

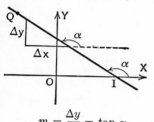

$m = \dfrac{\Delta y}{\Delta x} = \tan \alpha.$

27.

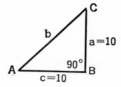

$\tan A = \dfrac{a}{c} = \dfrac{10}{10} = 1, \ A = 45°,$

$C = 90° - 45° = 45°,$

$b = \sqrt{10^2 + 10^2} = 10\sqrt{2} \cong 14.$

29.

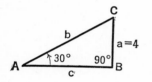

$C = 90° - 30° = 60°, \dfrac{c}{4} = \cot 30° = \sqrt{3},$

$c = 4\sqrt{3} \cong 7, \dfrac{b}{4} = \csc 30° = 2, \ b = 8.$

31.

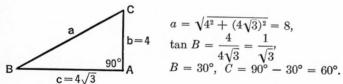

$a = \sqrt{4^2 + (4\sqrt{3})^2} = 8,$

$\tan B = \dfrac{4}{4\sqrt{3}} = \dfrac{1}{\sqrt{3}},$

$B = 30°, \ C = 90° - 30° = 60°.$

33. $a = \sqrt{4^2 - 2^2} = 2\sqrt{3} \cong 3, \ \cos A = \frac{2}{4}, \ A = 60°, \ C = 90° - 60° = 30°.$

35. $C = 90° - 60° = 30°, \ \dfrac{c}{4} = \cot 60°, \ c = \dfrac{4\sqrt{3}}{3}, \ \dfrac{a}{4} = \csc 60°, \ a = \dfrac{8\sqrt{3}}{3} \cong 4.$

37.

$\dfrac{y}{30} = \tan 30°, \ y = 10\sqrt{3}, \ \dfrac{(h + y)}{30} = \tan 45°,$

$h + y = 30, \ h = 30 - 10\sqrt{3} \cong 13.$

SET 14–7

1. $\sin 15° 20' = .2644.$
5. $\cot 89° 10' = .0145.$

3. $\tan 75° 10' = 3.776.$
7. $\cos 361° 20' = \cos 1° 20' = .9997.$

9. $936° \ 20' - 2(360°) = 216° \ 20'$, $216° \ 20' = 180° + 36° \ 20'$,
$\tan 936° \ 20' = \tan 216° \ 20' = \tan 36° \ 20' = .7355$.

11. $\cos (-22° \ 10') = \cos 22° \ 10' = .9261$.

13. $\sec 46° \ 10' = 1.444$.   **15.** $\cot 46° \ 10' = .9601$.

17. $72° \ 10' = 1.2595$ radians.

19. $22° \ 15' = 22° \ 10' + \frac{1}{2}(10') = .3869 + \frac{1}{2}(.0029) = .3883$ radian.

21. $\sin \theta = .6202$. The solutions with $0° \leqq \theta < 360°$ are $\theta = 38° \ 20' = .6690$ radian
and $\theta = 179° \ 60' - 38° \ 20' = 141° \ 40' = \pi - .6690 = 3.1416 - .6690 = 2.4726$
radians.

23. $\log \cot \theta = 1.1205$. The solutions with $0° \leqq \theta < 360°$ are $\theta = 4° \ 20' = .0756$ radian and $\theta = 180° + 4° \ 20' = 184° \ 20' = 3.2172$.

25. $\log | \sin \theta | = 9.30398 - 10$, $90° < \theta < 350°$. Reference angle is $11° \ 37'$. $\theta = 180° - 11° \ 37' = 168° \ 23'$, $180° + 11° \ 37' = 191° \ 37'$, $360° - 11° \ 37' = 348° \ 23'$.

27. $.2000 + \log \sin \theta = \log \cos \theta$ has solution $\theta = 32° \ 15'$.

29. $C = 89° \ 60' - 64° \ 10' = 25° \ 50'$, $\dfrac{a}{100.0} = \tan 64° \ 10'$,

$a = 100.0(2.066) = 206.6$, $\dfrac{b}{100.0} = \sec 64° \ 10'$, $b = 100.0(2.295) = 229.5$.

31. $C = 90°$, $\dfrac{b}{.810} = \tan 52° \ 50'$, $b = .810(1.319) = 1.068$, $c = 1.341$.

32. (b) $b = \sqrt{(12.00)^2 + (20.00)^2} \cong 23.32$, $\tan A = \dfrac{12.00}{20.00}$, $A = 30° \ 57' \cong 31°$,

$C = 59° \ 3' \cong 59°$.

33. (a) $c = \sqrt{(2.10)^2 + (12.3)^2} \cong 12.5$,

$\tan B = \dfrac{12.3}{2.10}$, $B = 80° \ 20' \cong 80°$, $A = 9° \ 40' \cong 10°$.

(b) $C = 77° \ 30'$, $\dfrac{c}{50.0} = \cot 12° \ 30'$, $c \cong 226$, $\dfrac{a}{50.0} = \csc 12° \ 30'$, $a \cong 231$.

35.

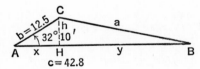

$x = 12.5 \cos 32° \ 10' \cong 10.58 \cong 10.6$
$y = 32.2$,
$h = 12.5 \sin 32° \ 10' \cong 6.65$,
$\tan B = \dfrac{6.65}{32.2}$, $B \cong 11° \ 40'$,
$C \cong 136° \ 10'$,
$a \cong 32.2 \sec 11° \ 40' \cong 32.9$.

37.

$d = 20 \csc 40°$, $t = \dfrac{d}{300} = \dfrac{20(1.556)}{300} \cong .1$ minute.

39.

$\log \csc 125° = -\log \sin 125° = -\log \sin 55° = 10.00000$
$-10 - (9.91336 - 10) = 0.08664$.   Reference angle
$180° - 125° = 55°$.

41.

(a) $x/6 = \cot 50°$, $x \cong 5$.
(b) $x/6 = \cot 73° \ 30'$, $x \cong 2$.
(c) $x = 6 \cot 26° \ 30' \cong 12$.

SET 14–8

1.

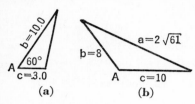

(a)
(b)

(a) $a^2 = (10.0)^2 + (3.0)^2 - 2(10.0)(3.0)(\frac{1}{2})$
$= 100 + 9 - 30 = 79,$
$a = \sqrt{79} \cong 8.9.$

(b) $\cos A = \dfrac{(8)^2 + (10)^2 - (2\sqrt{61})^2}{2(8)(10)}$

$= -\frac{1}{2},$

$A = 180° - 60° = 120°.$

3.

(a) $b^2 = 144 + 100 - 240(.6691) = 83.42,\ b \cong 9.1.$
(b) $h = 9.1 \sin A = 12.0 \sin 48°,\ A \cong 78° \ 30' \cong 78°.$

5. (a) $\cos A = (400 + 324 - 16)/720 = .9833,\ A = 10° \ 30'.$
(b) $\cos B = -.4167,\ \cos(180° - B) = .4167,\ 180° - B \cong 65° \ 20',$
$B \cong 114° \ 40' \cong 115°.$

10.

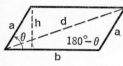

(a) $d^2 = a^2 + b^2 - 2ab \cos(180° - \theta)$
$= a^2 + b^2 + 2ab \cos \theta.$
$d = \sqrt{a^2 + b^2 + 2ab \cos \theta}.$
(b) $h = a \sin \theta,\ \text{area} = bh = ab \sin \theta.$

11.

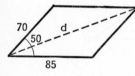

$d = \sqrt{(70)^2 + (85)^2 + 2(70)(85)\cos 50°} \cong 141.$

13.

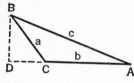

$AD = c \cos A,\ DC = b - AD$ (note directions).
$c^2 = (DB)^2 + (AD)^2$
$a^2 = (DB)^2 + (DC)^2$
$\overline{c^2 - a^2 = (AD)^2 - (b - AD)^2 = -b^2 + 2bAD}$
$= -b^2 + 2bc \cos A.$
$a^2 = b^2 + c^2 - 2bc \cos A.$

17.

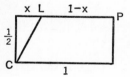

$T = \frac{1}{3}(x^2 + \frac{1}{4})^{\frac{1}{2}} + \frac{1}{5}(1 - x)$
$\dfrac{dT}{dx} = \dfrac{1}{3}\left(\dfrac{1}{2}\right)\dfrac{2x}{(x^2 + \frac{1}{4})^{\frac{1}{2}}} - \dfrac{1}{5} = 0,\ 5x - 3\sqrt{x^2 + \frac{1}{4}} = 0,$
$25x^2 - 9x^2 = \frac{9}{4},\ x^2 = \frac{9}{64},\ x = \frac{3}{8},\ 1 - x = \frac{5}{8}$ mile.

SET 14–9

1.

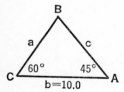

$B = 180° - (60° + 45°) = 75°$
$a/10.0 = \sin 45°/\sin 75° = \sin 45° \csc 75°$
$a = 10.0(.7071)(1.035) \cong 7.3.$
$c/10.0 = \sin 60°/\sin 75° = \sin 60° \csc 75°$
$c = 10.0(.8660)(1.035) \cong 9.0.$

3.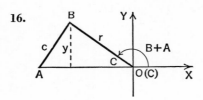

$$A = 180° - (68° + 30°) = 82°$$
$$a/22.0 = \sin 82°/\sin 30° = 2 \sin 82°$$
$$a = 44.0(.9903) \cong 43.6.$$
$$b/22.0 = 2 \sin 68°, \quad b = 44.0(.9272) \cong 40.8.$$

5. $B = 77°, \quad a = 52 \sin 42° \csc 77° \cong 35.7, \quad c = 52 \sin 61° \csc 77° \cong 46.7.$

7.

$$h = 5 \sin 30° > 1.9.$$
Impossible.

9. $B = 100°, \quad a = 12{,}000 \sin 20° \csc 100°$
$$= 12{,}000 \sin 20° \csc 80° \cong 4166,$$
$$c = 12{,}000 \sin 60° \csc 100°$$
$$= 12{,}000 \sin 60° \csc 80° \cong 10{,}550.$$

11. $X = 47°, \quad a = 600 \sin 60°/\sin 47° \cong 710.4 \cong 710.$

13. $X = 99°, \quad a = 600 \sin 32° \csc 99°$
$$= 600 \sin 32° \csc 81° \cong 322.$$

15. $X = 36°, \quad a = 600 \sin 63° \csc 36° \cong 909.$

16. 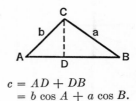 **17.**

$$c = AD + DB$$
$$= b \cos A + a \cos B.$$

$$\sin C = \frac{y}{r} = \sin (B + A).$$

18. $c = c \dfrac{\sin B}{\sin C} \cos A + c \dfrac{\sin A}{\sin C} \cos B$
$$\sin C = \sin B \cos A + \sin A \cos B = \sin (B + A).$$

19. $\sin (45° + 30°) = \sin 45° \cos 30° + \sin 30° \cos 45° = \dfrac{\sqrt{2}}{2} \cdot \dfrac{\sqrt{3}}{2} + \dfrac{1}{2} \cdot \dfrac{\sqrt{2}}{2} \cong .96593.$

21. $12 > 10, 49° < 90°, \sin A = 12 \sin 49°/10 = .9056.$ Therefore, two solutions.
$$A_1 \cong 64° 55' \cong 65°, \quad B_1 = 180° - (A_1 + C) \cong 66° 5' \cong 66°,$$
$$b_1 = 10 \sin 66° 5'/\sin 49° \cong 12.11 \cong 12.$$
$$A_2 = 180° - A_1 \cong 115° 5' \cong 115°, \quad B_2 = 180° - (A_2 + C) \cong 15° 55' \cong 16°,$$
$$b_2 = 10 \sin 15° 55'/\sin 49° \cong 3.63 \cong 4.$$

23. $20 > 13, 53° < 90°.$ Therefore, one solution. $\sin B = 13 \sin 53°/20 = .5191.$
$$B \cong 31° 16' \cong 31°, A \cong 95° 44' \cong 96°, a \cong 20 \sin 95° 44'/\sin 53° \cong 24.91 \cong 25.$$

25. $80 < 100, \sin B = 100 \sin 54°/80 > 1.$ No solution.

27. $50.6 < 54.3$ but $50.6 > 54.3 \sin 58° 40'.$ Therefore, two solutions.
$$B_1 = 66° 25', C_1 = 54° 55', c_1 = 48.49.$$
$$B_2 = 113° 35', C_2 = 7° 45', c_2 = 7.99.$$

28. $4993 < 6258, 111° 20' > 90°.$ No solution.

29. $\sin B = 28 \sin 39°/18 = .9789, B \cong 78° 13' \cong 78°.$ One solution. Why?

31. See No. 21. **33.** See No. 23. **35.** See No. 25. **37.** See No. 27. **38.** See No. 28.
39. See No. 29.

41.

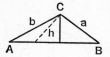

$a < b,\ h = b \sin A < a.$

SELF TEST 14–12

1.

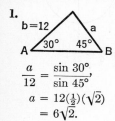

$$\frac{a}{12} = \frac{\sin 30°}{\sin 45°},$$

$$a = 12(\tfrac{1}{2})(\sqrt{2})$$
$$= 6\sqrt{2}.$$

2.

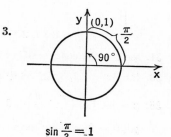

$h = x + 10$

$45°$ $60°$

10 x

$$\frac{x + 10}{x} = \sqrt{3},$$

$$x = 5(\sqrt{3} + 1) \cong 14.$$

3.

Y A

-4

-3 O X

5

$$\cot A = \tfrac{4}{3},$$
$$\csc A = -\tfrac{5}{3},$$
$$\cos A = -\tfrac{4}{5}.$$

4.

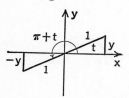

25 h

$45°$

(a) $h = \dfrac{25\sqrt{2}}{2} \cong 18.$ **(b)** $h = \dfrac{25\sqrt{3}}{2} \cong 22.$

(c) $\sin A = \tfrac{21}{25} = .84,\quad A \cong 57°.$

5. **(a)** $-2 + 0 + 4 = 2.$ **(b)** $-2 + \dfrac{\sqrt{3}}{2} + 1 = \dfrac{\sqrt{3} - 2}{2}.$ **(c)** $4 + 5 - 7 + 0 = 2.$

6. $\sin 60° = \cos 30° = \dfrac{\sqrt{3}}{2},\quad \cos 60° = \sin 30° = \tfrac{1}{2},\quad \tan 60° = \cot 30° = \sqrt{3}, \cdots.$

7. $\cos \theta = (49 + 64 - 169)/112 = -\tfrac{1}{2},\quad \theta = 180° - 60° = 120°.$

SET 15–1

1.

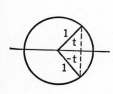

1 t

$-t$

1

y

1 y

t x

$-t$ $-y$

1

x

3.

y $(0,1)$

$\dfrac{\pi}{2}$

$90°$

x

$\sin \dfrac{\pi}{2} = 1$

5. $\sin(-t) = -\dfrac{y}{1} = -\sin t.$

6. $\cos(-t) = \dfrac{x}{1} = \cos t.$

7.

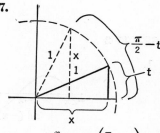

$\dfrac{\pi}{2} - t$

1 x

1

t

x

$$\cos t = \frac{x}{1} = \sin\left(\frac{\pi}{2} - t\right).$$

9.

y

$\pi + t$ 1

$-y$ t y

1 x

$$\sin(\pi + t) = -\frac{y}{1} = -\sin t.$$

11.

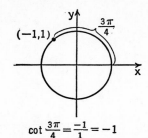

$$\cot \frac{3\pi}{4} = \frac{-1}{1} = -1$$

13.

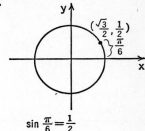

$$\sin \frac{\pi}{6} = \frac{1}{2}$$

15.

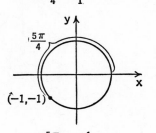

$$\tan \frac{5\pi}{4} = \frac{-1}{-1} = 1$$

17. $\cos 1.25 = .3153.$
19. $-\cos 0.97 = -.5653.$

21. $\cos 0.13 = .9916.$

23. $\tan(-1.29) = -3.467.$

25.

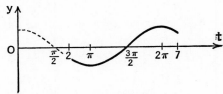

$$y = \cos t, \ 2 \leqq t \leqq 7.$$

27. $\sin x = .21, \frac{\pi}{2} < x < \pi.$
$x \cong \pi - .21 \cong 3.14 - .21 = 2.93.$
29. $3 \sin x = 1.92, \sin x = .64,$
$x \cong .69 + 2n\pi,$
$\pi - .69 + 2n\pi \cong 2.45 + 2n\pi.$
n an integer.

31. $\sec x = 25, \cos x = .04, x \cong 1.53.$

33. $\tan 3x = 1.2, 3x \cong .88 + n\pi, x \cong .29 + \dfrac{n\pi}{3}, n$ an integer.

35. $x = \log \tan \left(\dfrac{\pi}{4} + \dfrac{\theta}{2} \right). \quad \theta = gd(x).$

$gd(0) = 2n\pi, n$ an integer.
$gd(.43) = .86 + 2n\pi.$

SET 15–2

1.

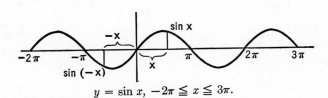

$$y = \sin x, \ -2\pi \leqq x \leqq 3\pi.$$

3. $\sin(-x) = -\sin x$ from graph.

5.

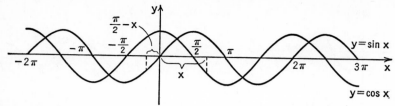

7. From graph in Problem 1. **9.** Extend graph of cos x in Problem 5.

11. See graph in Problem 5.

13.

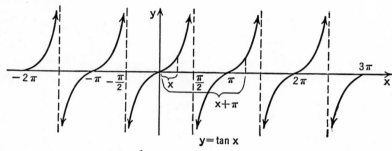

$y = \tan x$

15. $|\csc x| \geqq 1$, $|\csc x| = \dfrac{1}{|\sin x|} \geqq 1$, $1 \geqq |\sin x|$.

19. If $y = \cos x$, then $\cos(-x) = \cos x = y$.

20. If $y = \sin x$, then $-y = -\sin x = \sin(-x)$ and the locus is symmetrical with respect to the origin.

21. $\lim\limits_{x \to 0} \dfrac{\sin x}{x} = 1$, $\sin x \cong x$ for $|x|$ near zero.

23.

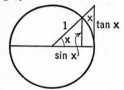

$\sin x < x < \tan x$.

25. $\tan x \cong x$ to 2 sig. digits $- .25 < x < .25$ rad.

27. $36° = 36 \times \dfrac{\pi}{180} = \dfrac{\pi}{5}$, $L = 10\left(\dfrac{\pi}{5}\right) = 2\pi \cong 6.3$ ft.

30. $(10^2)\left(\dfrac{18\pi}{180}\right)\left(\dfrac{1}{2}\right) = 5\pi$ sq in. area.

SET 15–3

1.

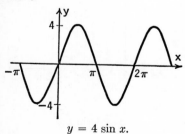

$y = 4 \sin x$.

3.

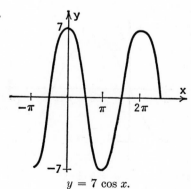

$y = 7 \cos x$.

5.

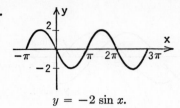

$$y = -2 \sin x.$$

7.

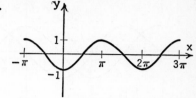

$$y = -\cos x.$$

9.

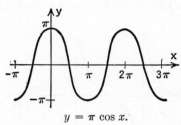

$$y = \pi \cos x.$$

11.

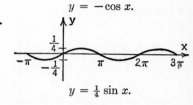

$$y = \tfrac{1}{4} \sin x.$$

13.

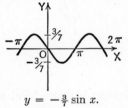

$$y = -\tfrac{3}{7} \sin x.$$

15.

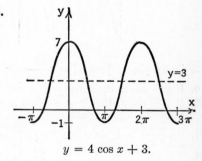

$$y = 4 \cos x + 3.$$

SET 15–4

1.

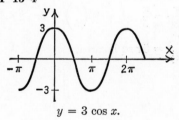

$$y = 3 \cos x.$$

3.

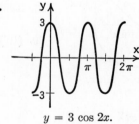

$$y = 3 \cos 2x.$$

5.

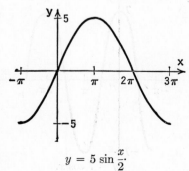

$$y = 5 \sin \frac{x}{2}.$$

7.

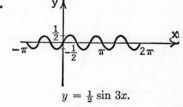

$$y = \tfrac{1}{2} \sin 3x.$$

9.

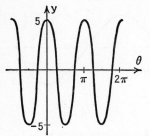

$y = 5 \cos 2\theta.$

11.

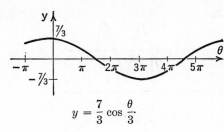

$y = \dfrac{7}{3} \cos \dfrac{\theta}{3}.$

13.

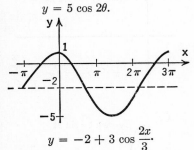

$y = -2 + 3 \cos \dfrac{2x}{3}.$

15.

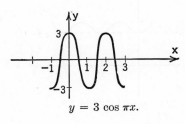

$y = 3 \cos \pi x.$

17.

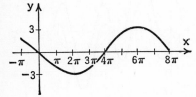

$y = -3 \sin \dfrac{x}{4}.$

19.

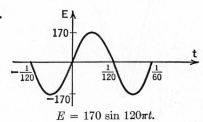

$E = 170 \sin 120\pi t.$

21.

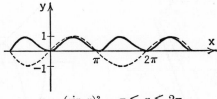

$y = (\sin x)^2, \; -\pi \leqq x \leqq 2\pi.$

SET 15–5

1.

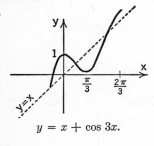

$y = x + \cos 3x.$

2.

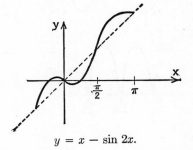

$y = x - \sin 2x.$

3.

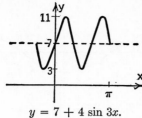

$y = 7 + 4 \sin 3x.$

5.

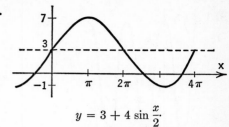

$y = 3 + 4 \sin \dfrac{x}{2}.$

7.

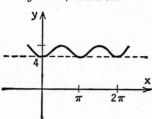

$y = 4 + (\sin x)^2.$

9. $y = (\sin x)^2 + (\cos x)^2 = 1$

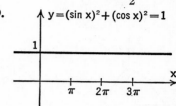

11.

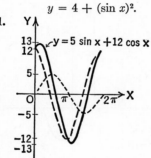

$y = 5 \sin x + 12 \cos x$

13.

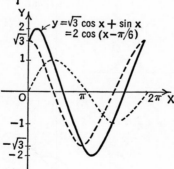

$y = \sin t - \sin 3t$

15.

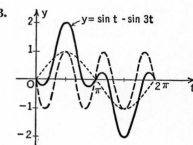

$y = \sqrt{3} \cos x + \sin x = 2 \cos (x - \pi/6)$

16.

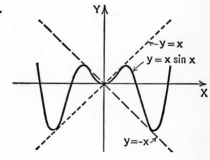

$y = x$
$y = x \sin x$
$y = -x$

17.

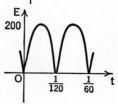

19.

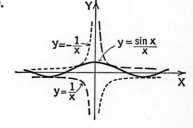

$y = -\dfrac{1}{x}$ $y = \dfrac{\sin x}{x}$

$y = \dfrac{1}{x}$

SET 15–6

1.

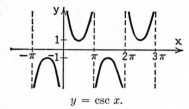

$$y = \csc x.$$

3.

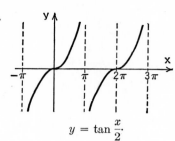

$$y = \tan \frac{x}{2}.$$

5.

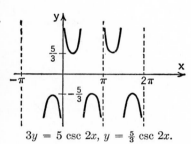

$$3y = 5 \csc 2x, \quad y = \tfrac{5}{3} \csc 2x.$$

7.

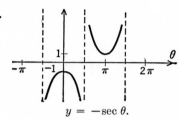

$$y = -\sec \theta.$$

9.

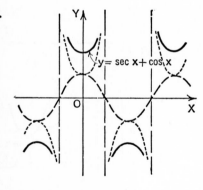

$y = \sec x + \cos x$

11.

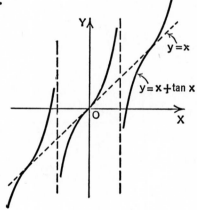

$y = x$

$y = x + \tan x$

13. Compare Fig. 15–10.

15.

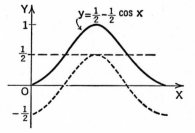

$y = \tfrac{1}{2} - \tfrac{1}{2} \cos x$

17. (a)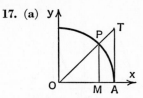

2 $\triangle OMP < 2$ sector OAP
$< 2 \triangle OAT$.

(b)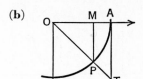

Similarly: $-\sin \theta \cos \theta < -\theta$
$< -\tan \theta$.
$\therefore \sin \theta \cos \theta > \theta > \tan \theta$.

19. (a) See Problem 19, Set 15–5.
    (b) Define $f(0) = 1$.

SELF TEST 15–7

1. $r = 2.7$ in.
2. (a) 0.60182. (b) $\tan 2.4 = -\tan (\pi - 2.4) = -\tan .74 = -0.91$.
   (c) $\cos 3.8 = -\cos 0.66 = -.79$. (d) $x = 0.7, 2.4$.

3.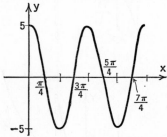

$y = 5 \cos 2x$.

4.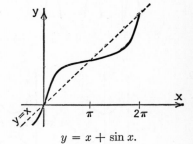

$y = x + \sin x$.

5.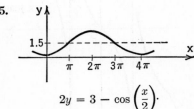

$2y = 3 - \cos \left(\dfrac{x}{2}\right)$.

6.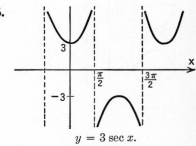

$y = 3 \sec x$.

7.

x	$\dfrac{-5\pi}{6}$	$\dfrac{-\pi}{6}$	$\dfrac{7\pi}{6}$	$\dfrac{11\pi}{6}$	$\dfrac{19\pi}{6}$
y	$\frac{3}{2}$	$\frac{3}{2}$	$\frac{3}{2}$	$\frac{3}{2}$	$\frac{3}{2}$

8. Note that problem requests conclusions drawn from the *unit circle* diagram, not from general knowledge.
   (a) false. (b) false. (c) false.

SET 16–1

In general hints will be given for proving identities, rather than the complete solution. Do not look at the hints until you have made a sincere attempt to work a problem.

5. $\log (1/t) - \log (t + 1) = \log [1/(t^2 + t)]$

$$\log \left[\left(\frac{1}{t} \right) \left(\frac{1}{t+1} \right) \right]$$

$$\log \left[\frac{1}{t^2 + t} \right].$$

7. Combine the terms of the right-hand member and simplify.

9. $\dfrac{2}{e^x + 2} = \dfrac{e^x + 2 - e^x}{e^x + 2} = 1 - \dfrac{e^x}{e^x + 2}.$

15. Hint: if $a = b$, then $a - b = 0$.

SET 16–2

1. $E(\pi/6) = \sqrt{3}/2.$ $E(1.03) = \sin (2.06) = \sin (\pi - 2.06) = \sin (1.08) = 0.882.$
3. Use hint 5, p. 359. **5.** Expand, combine, and simplify.
7. Use hint 4, p. 359.
9. Multiply numerator and denominator of right member by $\sin A \sin B \cos A \cos B$
and factor to obtain $\dfrac{\cos A \cos B (\sin B \cos A + \sin A)}{\sin A \sin B (\sin B \cos A + \sin A)} = ?$
11. $A^4 + 2A^2B^2 + B^4 = (A^2 + B^2)^2.$
13. $S^4 - T^4 = (S^2 + T^2)(S^2 - T^2).$ **15 and 17.** $-\log x = \log (1/x).$
19. $\sin^5 x \cos^4 x = \sin^4 x \sin x \cos^4 x = (1 - \cos^2 x)^2 \sin x \cos^4 x = ? = ?$
21. (a) Use Hint 4, p. 359, and Hint 5, if necessary.
  (b) $\theta = 0, \pm \pi/2, \pm \pi, \cdots.$
23. $x = 30°$ does not satisfy the given relationship. Find another value which does not satisfy it. Note Problem 22.
24. (d) $\sin (\pi/6)^2 = \sin (0.524)^2 = \sin (0.274) = 0.2706.$
25. (a) $\frac{3}{4}$. (b) $\frac{1}{2}$. (c) $\sqrt{3}$. (d) $0.9627.$
27. $[1/(1 + \cos \theta)] \cdot [(1 - \cos \theta)/(1 - \cos \theta)] = ?$
29. $\cot^4 \theta = \cot^2 \theta (\csc^2 \theta - 1) = \cot^2 \theta \csc^2 \theta - (\csc^2 \theta - 1) = ?$
31. $\dfrac{(1 + \sin x)}{(1 - \sin x)} \cdot \dfrac{(1 + \sin x)}{(1 + \sin x)} = \cdots = \sec^2 x + 2 \tan x \sec x + (\sec^2 x - 1) = ?$
33. $\dfrac{\tan 3x (\sec^2 3x - 1)}{\sec 3x} = \cdots = \tan 3x \sec 3x - \dfrac{\sin 3x}{\cos 3x} \cdot \cos 3x = ?$
35. $\pm \sqrt{\dfrac{(1 - \sin x)}{(1 + \sin x)} \cdot \dfrac{(1 - \sin x)}{(1 - \sin x)}}.$ **37.** $\cot A$ not cot.
  38. $= 1$, not 2.
39. sec 3θ not sin 3θ, or else write csc 3θ not cos 3θ.
40. Not unless $A = B$. **41.** $= 1 - 2 \sin^2 x \cos^2 x.$ (Why?)
42. $5 \sin^2 \theta + 5 \cos^2 \theta = 5$, but not as stated.
43. $= \pm (1 - \cos^2 \theta)^{\frac{1}{2}}.$ **44.** $= -1.$ **45.** $\sin^2 5t = 1 - \cos^2 5t.$
46. $\cos \theta = 1/\sec \theta.$ **47, 48,** and **49** are nonsense.

SET 16–3

1. $\pi/4, 3\pi/4, 5\pi/4, 7\pi/4.$ **3.** No solution, since $|\sin \theta| \leq 1.$ **5.** $\pi/3, 5\pi/3.$
7. There are no solutions in the domain $0 < \theta < \pi/2.$
9. $\theta = -3\pi/4, -\pi/4, \pi/4, 3\pi/4, 5\pi/4, 7\pi/4, 9\pi/4, 11\pi/4.$
11. $-5\pi/6, -\pi/6, \pi/6, 5\pi/6.$
13. $\sin x = 0, 4 \sin x - 3 = 0; x = 0°, 180°, 360°, x = 48° 35', 131° 25', 408° 35'.$
15. $\theta = \pi$ is a root. $\theta = 0$ is an extraneous value.

17. $\cos x = \frac{1}{2}$; $x = 60°, 300°$.
     $\csc x = -1$; $x = 270°$.
19. Use $\tan^2 \theta = \sec^2 \theta - 1$ to obtain a factorable quadratic equation in $\sec \theta$.
21. Express each function in terms of $\cos t$ to obtain a quadratic equation in terms of $\cos t$.
22. Identity is satisfied for all θ for which the functions are defined.
23. No such x exists since $\sin^2 x + \cos^2 x = 1$ for all x.
25. $(\frac{1}{2}, \pi/3), (\frac{1}{2}, 5\pi/3)$.
27. $(2\sqrt{3}, \pi/6), (-2\sqrt{3}, 5\pi/6), (-2\sqrt{3}, 7\pi/6), (2\sqrt{3}, 11\pi/6)$.
29. $0 \leqq \theta < \pi/6, \dfrac{5\pi}{6} < \theta \leqq \pi$.   31. $0 \leqq \theta < \pi/4$ and $3\pi/4 < \theta < 2\pi$.
33. $\pi/6 \leqq \theta \leqq 5\pi/6$ and $7\pi/6 \leqq \theta \leqq 11\pi/6$.
35. $\pi/2 < \theta < 3\pi/2$. In this domain $\sec \theta$ is negative, hence $< \frac{1}{2}$.

SET 16–4

1. $\sin (\pi/2 + \theta) = \sin \pi/2 \cos \theta + \cos \pi/2 \sin \theta = \cos \theta$.
3. $\cos (A + B) = \sin [\pi/2 + (A + B)] = \sin [(\pi/2 + A) + B] =$
    $\sin (\pi/2 + A) \cos B + \cos (\pi/2 + A) \sin B = \cos A \cos B - \sin A \sin B$. Yes.
7. (b) $\sin (110° + 70°) = \sin 180° = 0$. The second method is easier.
11. A and B are each acute and $\cos (A + B) > 0$. Hence quadrant I.
13. (b) It is not an identity.   15. Use hint 4, p. 359.
17.
$$\sec (A - B) =$$
$$\dfrac{\dfrac{1}{\cos A \cos B + \sin A \sin B}}{\dfrac{\sec A \sec B}{\sec A \sec B (\cos A \cos B + \sin A \sin B)}} = ?$$

19. Note that $\cos 180° = -1$.
21. Use equation (9).
23. $\cos (45° - 30°) = \dfrac{\sqrt{3} + 1}{2\sqrt{2}}$
    $= .966$.

25. $\tan x = \dfrac{\sin x}{\cos x}$, or use (13).
29. Compare Example 1.
31. $s = 2\left[\dfrac{\sqrt{3}}{2} \sin \pi t + \dfrac{1}{2} \cos \pi t\right]$
    $= 2 \cos \pi(t - \frac{1}{3})$.
    Amplitude $= 2$, period $= 2$, max at $t = \frac{1}{3}$.
33. $s = 10\sqrt{2} \cos \dfrac{\pi}{2} (t - \frac{1}{2})$.
    Amplitude $= 10\sqrt{2} \approx 14$, period $= 4$, max at $t = \frac{1}{2}$.

27.

y=13 cos (x−α) where
sin $\alpha = \frac{5}{13}$, $\alpha \cong 22°$.

34.

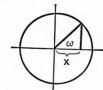

$\dfrac{d\omega}{dt} = 10$ rps $= 20\pi \dfrac{\text{rad}}{\text{sec}}$
$\omega = 20\pi t$
$x = 3 \cos \omega = 3 \cos 20\pi t$.

35. $-\cos \theta = \cos \theta$, $2 \cos \theta = 0$, $\theta = 90°, 270°$.
37. $\cos (x - 2x) = 0$, $x = 90°$, $x = 270°$.
39. $(x + 17°) = 45°, 135°, 225°, 315°$.

45. $\cos (x - 45°) > \dfrac{1}{\sqrt{2}}$ $\qquad$ $\cos (x - 45°) < -\dfrac{1}{\sqrt{2}}$

$\quad -45° < x - 45° < 45°$ $\qquad$ $135° < x - 45° < 225°$

$\quad 0 < x < 90°$ $\qquad\qquad\quad$ $180° < x < 270°$

$\quad 0 < x < \pi/2$ $\qquad\qquad\quad$ $\pi < x < 3\pi/2.$

SET 16–5

1. Try it and see.

3. $\sin^4 x = \left(\dfrac{1 - \cos 2x}{2}\right)^2 = \dfrac{1}{4}\,(1 - 2\cos 2x + \cos^2 2x)$

$\qquad = \dfrac{1}{4}\left(1 - 2\cos 2x + \dfrac{1 + \cos 4x}{2}\right).$

5. $\cos 2(60°) = \cos^2 60° - \sin^2 60° = \dfrac{1}{4} - \dfrac{3}{4} = -\dfrac{1}{2}.$ Yes.

7. $\sec 2x = \dfrac{1}{2\cos^2 x - 1} = ?$

9. $\dfrac{2\sin A \cos A}{1 + (1 - 2\sin^2 A)} = \dfrac{2\sin A \cos A}{2(1 - \sin^2 A)} = ?$

13. Equations (15) yield $\sin^2 A = \dfrac{1}{2}(1 - \cos 2A).$ Hence $\sin^4 x \cos^2 x =$

$\quad \sin^2 x \dfrac{(2\sin x \cos x)^2}{4} = \dfrac{1 - \cos 2x}{2} \cdot \dfrac{\sin^2 2x}{4} = \dfrac{1}{16}(1 - \cos 2x)(1 - \cos 4x).$

17. $\sin 4x = 2\sin 2x \cos 2x = ?$

19. $\tan 3x = \tan (x + 2x) = ?$

21. $\cos x + 2\cos x \sin x = 0,$ $\cos x(1 + 2\sin x) = 0,$ $\cos x = 0,$ $\sin x = -\dfrac{1}{2},$

$\quad x = -\dfrac{\pi}{2}, \dfrac{\pi}{2}, x = -\dfrac{\pi}{6}, -\dfrac{5\pi}{6}.$

23. $\tan^2 3x = 1,$ $x = \pm\dfrac{11\pi}{12}, \pm\dfrac{9\pi}{12}, \pm\dfrac{7\pi}{12}, \pm\dfrac{5\pi}{12}, \pm\dfrac{\pi}{4}, \pm\dfrac{\pi}{12}.$ You finish it.

25. $\sin\left(\dfrac{\alpha}{2}\right) = \pm\sqrt{\dfrac{1 - \cos \alpha}{2}}.$

27. $(5, 0), (-5, \pi/2), (5, \pi), (-5, 3\pi/2).$

29. $4\sin^2 \theta = 2\cos 2\theta$

θ	$\pi/6$	$5\pi/6$	$7\pi/6$	$11\pi/6$
r	1	1	-1	-1

SET 16–6

1. $\sqrt{\dfrac{1 - \sqrt{3}/2}{2}} = \dfrac{1}{2}\sqrt{2 - \sqrt{3}}.$

3. $-\sqrt{\dfrac{1 + (-\sqrt{3}/2)}{2}} = -\dfrac{1}{2}\sqrt{2 - \sqrt{3}}.$ Did you expect this answer, 3, to be the negative of 1?

5. $\dfrac{1}{\cos 15°} = \dfrac{2}{+\sqrt{2 + \sqrt{3}}}.$ $\qquad$ **7.** $-\sqrt{\dfrac{2 - \sqrt{3}}{2 + \sqrt{3}}}.$ $\qquad$ **9.** $\dfrac{1}{2}\sqrt{2 + \sqrt{3}}.$

11. Both. $\qquad$ **13.** Use 16.18 and 16.19. $\qquad$ **15.** Use 16.18′ and 16.19′.

17. $\tan \dfrac{\alpha}{2} = \pm\sqrt{\dfrac{(1 - \cos \alpha)^2}{\sin^2 \alpha}} = \dfrac{1 - \cos \alpha}{\pm\sqrt{\sin^2 \alpha}}$ since $1 - \cos \alpha \geqq 0$ for all $\alpha.$

Also, $\tan \dfrac{\alpha}{2} = \dfrac{\sin \dfrac{\alpha}{2}}{\cos \dfrac{\alpha}{2}} = \dfrac{\sin \alpha}{2\cos^2 \dfrac{\alpha}{2}}.$ Hence, $\tan \dfrac{\alpha}{2}$ and $\sin \alpha$ always have the same sign.

19. See Problem 17.

23. $\sin A = \sin (180° - B - C) = \sin (B + C) = ?$

25. $k^2a^2 = k^2b^2 + k^2c^2 - 2kbkc \cos A$, $a^2 = b^2 + c^2 - 2bc \cos A$.

27. Write $\csc x$ as $\dfrac{1}{2 \sin \dfrac{x}{2} \cos \dfrac{x}{2}}$, express tangents in terms of sines and cosines and

simplify.

29. Use the results of Problems 16 and 17 with the fact that $\dfrac{a}{b} = \dfrac{c}{d} = \dfrac{a + c}{b + d}$.

31. Not an identity.

33. $4 \sin^2 \dfrac{x}{2} \cos^2 \dfrac{x}{2} = \left(2 \sin \dfrac{x}{2} \cos \dfrac{x}{2} \right)^2 = ?$

35. (1) Prove that $\sin \dfrac{t}{2} [\sin \theta + \sin (\theta + t)] = \sin \left(\theta + \dfrac{t}{2} \right) \sin t$ is an identity.

   (2) Assume that $\sin \dfrac{t}{2} [\sin \theta + \cdots + \sin (\theta + kt)] = \sin \left(\theta + \dfrac{kt}{2} \right) \sin \dfrac{(k + 1)t}{2}$
   is an identity.

   (3) Use (2) to prove that
   $$\sin \dfrac{t}{2} \left[\sin \theta + \cdots + \sin [\theta + (k + 1)t] \right] = \sin \left[\theta + \dfrac{(k + 1)t}{2} \right] \sin \dfrac{(k + 2)t}{2}$$
   is an identity.

37. Not an identity.   39. Not an identity.

SET 16–7

1. $\cos x(1 + 2 \sin x) = 0$; $x = \pi/2, 3\pi/2, 7\pi/6, 11\pi/6$.

3. $-90°, 90°, 270°, 45°, 135°$.

5. Show that: $\cos A + \cos B = 2 \cos \left(\dfrac{A + B}{2} \right) \cos \left(\dfrac{A - B}{2} \right)$. Then:
$$\left[2 \cos \dfrac{x + 5x}{2} \cos \dfrac{x - 5x}{2} \right] + \cos 3x = 0$$
$2 \cos 3x \cos (-2x) + \cos 3x = 0$, $\cos 3x[2 \cos 2x + 1] = 0$
$\cos 3x = 0$, $\cos 2x = -\frac{1}{2}$, $x = 30°, 90°, 150°, 210°, 270°, 330°$,
$x = 60°, 120°, 240°, 300°$.

9. Not an identity.
$$\sin t + \sin \dfrac{t}{2} = 0$$
$$2 \sin \dfrac{t}{2} \cos \dfrac{t}{2} + \sin \dfrac{t}{2} = 0$$
$$\sin \dfrac{t}{2} \left(2 \cos \dfrac{t}{2} + 1 \right) = 0$$
$$\sin \dfrac{t}{2} = 0, \quad \cos \dfrac{t}{2} = -\dfrac{1}{2}$$
$$t = 0 \qquad t = 240°.$$

11. Use identities (25) and (26).

13. $\dfrac{\cos 50° + \cos 40°}{\sin 80° - \sin 10°} = \dfrac{2 \cos 45° \cos 5°}{2 \sin 45° \cos 35°}$
$= \dfrac{\cos 5°}{\cos 35°}$.

15. $(1 + 2 \cos A) \sin 2A$
$\sin 2A + 2 \cos A \sin 2A$
$\sin 2A + (\sin A + \sin 3A)$ by equation (23).

21. The reader may wish to show first that
$$\sin A \sin B = -\tfrac{1}{2} \cos (A + B) + \tfrac{1}{2} \cos (A - B).$$

23. $[\sin x \sin 3x] \cos 2x$
$[-\frac{1}{2} \cos 4x + \frac{1}{2} \cos 2x] \cos 2x$ ←{See answer 21.
$-\frac{1}{2} \cos 4x \cos 2x + \frac{1}{2} \cos^2 2x$
$-\frac{1}{4} \cos 6x - \frac{1}{4} \cos 2x + \frac{1}{4}(1 + \cos 4x)$
Note: This process is essential in later work in the calculus.

25. $\frac{1}{4}(1 + \cos 2x + \cos 4x + \cos 6x)$.

27. Graphical methods will be used.

Sketch $y = \sin 4x$ and $y = \sin 2x$. Note that the curves intersect when

$$\sin 4x = \sin 2x$$
$$2 \sin 2x \cos 2x = \sin 2x$$

$$\sin 2x = 0, \qquad \cos 2x = \frac{1}{2}$$
$$2x = ? \qquad 2x = ?$$

$$x = 0, \frac{\pi}{2}, \pi, \frac{3\pi}{2} \qquad x = \frac{\pi}{6}, \frac{5\pi}{6}, \frac{7\pi}{6}, \frac{11\pi}{6}.$$

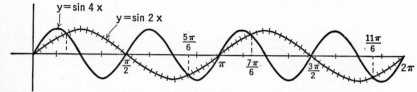

Thus $\sin 4x < \sin 2x$ on the following subintervals of the interval from 0 to 2π:

$$\frac{\pi}{6} < x < \frac{\pi}{2}, \ \frac{5\pi}{6} < x < \pi, \ \frac{7\pi}{6} < x < \frac{3\pi}{2}, \ \frac{11\pi}{6} < x < 2\pi.$$

SET 16–9

1. $-210°, 30°, 150°, 390°, 510°$. **3.** $-135°, -45°, 225°, 315°, 585°$.

5. $45°, 225°, -135°, -315°, -495°$. **7.** $\frac{3\pi}{4} + 2\pi n$ and $-\frac{\pi}{4} + 2\pi n$.

11. $\frac{1}{2}$. **12.** $\pm 1/\sqrt{3}$. **13.** -2.

15. arc cos $\left(\dfrac{-\sqrt{3}}{2}\right) = \pm\dfrac{5\pi}{6}, \pm\dfrac{7\pi}{6}, \pm\dfrac{17\pi}{6}$.

17. Verify that the sum of the *acute* angles $\theta_1 = $ arc sin $\frac{3}{5}$ and $\theta_2 = $ arc sin $\frac{5}{13}$ has a sine of $\frac{56}{65}$.

19. True for all values for which the functions are defined, but so is $u + 2\pi k$ for all integers k.

21. (b). **23.** (d). **25.** (c). **26.** (a) $|N| \leqq 1$, (b) $|N| \geqq 0$, (c) $|N| \geqq 1$.

SET 16–10

1. $-30°$. **3.** $-45°$. **5.** $7\pi/12$. **7.** $-1/\sqrt{24}$. **9.** Arc tan $(1) = 45°$.

11. Sketch in the form cos $y = N$.

13. If $\theta = $ Arc sin x, then $\sin \theta = x$. Verify $\tan \theta = x/\sqrt{1 - x^2}$.

15. If $\theta = $ Arc tan x, then $\tan \theta = x$. Verify $\sin \theta = x/\sqrt{1 + x^2}$.

17. When $x = 1$, $\dfrac{\pi}{4} \neq \dfrac{5\pi}{4}$.

19. Verify tan $\left(\text{Arc tan } \dfrac{1}{4} + \text{Arc tan } \dfrac{3}{5}\right) = \tan \dfrac{\pi}{4}$.

21. Arc sin $(\sqrt{a^2 - x^2}/a) = $ Arc tan $(\sqrt{a^2 - x^2}/x) = $ Arc cos $\left(\dfrac{x}{a}\right)$.

23. Arc sin $\dfrac{2x + 3}{3}$, Arc cos $\dfrac{\sqrt{-4x^2 - 12x}}{3}$.

25. $\dfrac{1}{x}$. **27.** $\frac{17}{6}$. **29.** sec $\dfrac{\pi}{2}$, not defined.

31. Consult the definitions.

SET 16–11

1. $6\left(\cos\dfrac{x}{2}\right)\left(\dfrac{1}{2}\right) = 3\cos\dfrac{x}{2}.$

3. $15\left(-\sin\dfrac{2t}{3}\right)\left(\dfrac{2}{3}\right) = -10\sin\dfrac{2t}{3}.$

5. $\dfrac{d^2s}{dt^2} = -3\pi^2\sin\pi t - 4\pi^2\cos\pi t = -\pi^2 s.$

6. $\dfrac{d^2s}{dt^2} = -45\cos 3t + 108\sin 3t = -9s.$

7. **(a)** $v = 12\pi\cos(2\pi t - \pi/3).$ **(b)** $a = -24\pi^2\sin(2\pi t - \pi/3) = -4\pi^2 s.$

9. $\dfrac{d(\cot x)}{dx} = -\csc^2 x.$ (See Example 3.)

11. **(a)** 2400π ft per min.   **(b)** 7800π ft per min.

13.

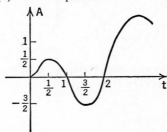

The values of t for which $A(t)$ has a relative maximum or minimum value are found from the equation $\tan(\pi t) + \pi t = 0$, or $\tan u + u = 0$ where $u = \pi t$. Using a table of trigonometric functions of angles in radians, the first two values of $u > 0$ which satisfy the equation are $u = 2.029$ and $u = 4.913$ accurate to four significant figures. Hence, A has a relative maximum value at $t = 0.645$ and a relative minimum at $t = 1.564$.

SELF TEST 16–12

1. Multiply numerator and denominator of the left member by $\sec\theta$.

2. $-\sqrt{3}\sqrt{1 - \cos^2\theta} = \cos\theta - 1$

$2\cos^2\theta - \cos\theta - 1 = 0$

$\cos\theta = -\tfrac{1}{2}, \quad \cos\theta = 1.$

$\theta = -\dfrac{2\pi}{3}$ extraneous, $\dfrac{2\pi}{3}, \theta = 0.$

3. $\cos 75° = \sqrt{\dfrac{1 + \cos 150°}{2}}$

$= \tfrac{1}{2}\sqrt{2 - \sqrt{3}}.$

4. $\sin(45° - 30°) = \sin 45°\cos 30° - \cos 45°\sin 30° = \dfrac{\sqrt{3} - 1}{2\sqrt{2}} = \dfrac{\sqrt{6} - \sqrt{2}}{4}.$

5. $y = 13[\tfrac{5}{13}\sin x + \tfrac{12}{13}\cos x] = 13[\sin\alpha\sin x + \cos\alpha\cos x] = 13\cos(x - \alpha),$ where $\sin\alpha = \tfrac{5}{13}, \cos\alpha = \tfrac{12}{13}.$

6. $\dfrac{1 - (1 - 2\sin^2\theta)}{2\sin\theta\cos\theta}.$

7. Since $\dfrac{\pi}{2} < 2\theta < \pi$

8. $\pm\sqrt{1 + \tan^2 x} = \tan x - 1$

$1 + \tan^2 x = \tan^2 x - 2\tan x + 1.$

$\tan x = 0, \quad x = -\pi,$

0 (extraneous).

$\cos 2\theta = -\sqrt{\dfrac{1 + \cos 4\theta}{2}} =$

$\cos 8\theta = 1 - 2\sin^2 4\theta = \tfrac{7}{9}.$

9. $\sin\theta = -\tfrac{1}{2}, \sin\theta = -1.$

$\theta = \dfrac{7\pi}{6}, \dfrac{11\pi}{6}, \theta = \dfrac{3\pi}{2}.$

10.

(a) $-2.$

(b) Arc tan $(-1) = -\dfrac{\pi}{4}.$

11.

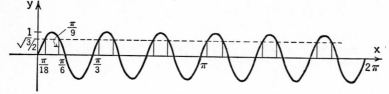

$$\frac{-\sqrt{3}}{2} < \sin 6x < \frac{\sqrt{3}}{2}.$$

The required subintervals of $0 \le x < 2\pi$ are:

$$0 \le x < \frac{\pi}{18}, \quad \frac{\pi}{9} < x < \frac{2\pi}{9}, \quad \frac{5\pi}{18} < x < \frac{7\pi}{18}, \quad \frac{4\pi}{9} < x < \frac{5\pi}{9},$$

$$\frac{11\pi}{18} < x < \frac{13\pi}{18}, \quad \frac{7\pi}{9} < x < \frac{8\pi}{9}, \quad \frac{17\pi}{18} < x < \frac{19\pi}{18}, \quad \frac{10\pi}{9} < x < \frac{11\pi}{9},$$

$$\frac{23\pi}{18} < x < \frac{25\pi}{18}, \quad \frac{13\pi}{9} < x < \frac{14\pi}{9}, \quad \frac{29\pi}{18} < x < \frac{31\pi}{18}, \quad \frac{16\pi}{9} < x < \frac{17\pi}{9}$$

$$\frac{35\pi}{18} < x < 2\pi.$$

12. $\dfrac{\sqrt{5}}{3}\left(-\dfrac{4}{5}\right) - \dfrac{2}{3}\left(\dfrac{3}{5}\right) = -\dfrac{4\sqrt{5} + 6}{15}.$ **13.** $\theta = \dfrac{\pi}{3}, \dfrac{5\pi}{3}; r = \dfrac{7}{2}.$

SET 17–1 **9–13.**

1–7.

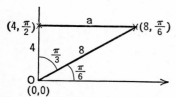

$\times (3, \frac{\pi}{2})$

$(6, 14\pi)$

$O \quad \times$

$\times (4, -\frac{\pi}{3})$

$\times (7, \frac{11\pi}{3})$

15.

$(4, \frac{\pi}{2}) \times \underset{a}{\quad\quad} \times (8, \frac{\pi}{6})$

$4 \quad \frac{\pi}{3} \quad 8$

$\frac{\pi}{6}$

O
$(0,0)$

$a^2 = 4^2 + 8^2 - 2(4)(8) \cos \dfrac{\pi}{3}$

$\quad = 16 + 64 - 2(4)(8)(\tfrac{1}{2}) = 48$

$a = 4\sqrt{3}.$

(Note: It might have been seen that this is a right triangle.)

17. $5 = d = \sqrt{r^2 + 2^2 - 2(2)r \cos\left(\theta - \dfrac{\pi}{3}\right)}$

$r^2 - 4r \cos\left(\theta - \dfrac{\pi}{3}\right) - 21 = 0.$ Locus is a circle.

19. $d = \sqrt{9 + 49 - 2(3)(7) \cos\left(\dfrac{\pi}{3} + \dfrac{\pi}{6}\right)} = \sqrt{58}.$

21. Area $= \frac{1}{2}ab \sin C$ for two sides and included angle. Here $A = \frac{1}{2}|r_1 r_2 \sin(\theta_1 - \theta_2)|$ in order to be positive (since we do not know whether $\theta_1 > \theta_2$ or $\theta_2 > \theta_1$). Thus, $A = \frac{1}{2}|r_1 r_2 \sin(\theta_1 - \theta_2)|.$

23. $A = \dfrac{1}{2}\left| (3)(7) \sin\left(\dfrac{\pi}{3} + \dfrac{\pi}{6}\right) \right| = \dfrac{1}{2}(3)(7)(1) = 10\tfrac{1}{2}.$

25. $A = \frac{1}{2}\left|(3)(5)\sin\left(0 + \frac{\pi}{2}\right)\right| = \frac{1}{2}(3)(5)(1) = 7\frac{1}{2}$.

27.

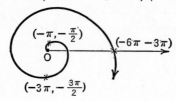

SET 17–2

1. $\theta = -\frac{2\pi}{3}$.

3.

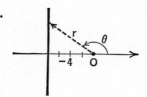

$-\frac{4}{r} = \cos\theta$

$r = -4\sec\theta$.

5. $\frac{3}{r} = \sin\theta$, or $r = 3\csc\theta$.

7. $r\cos\left(\theta - \frac{\pi}{6}\right) = -5;\ r = -5\sec\left(\theta - \frac{\pi}{6}\right)$.

9. $r = 5$. **11.** $r = 0$. **13.** $r = -8\cos\theta$.

15. $r = 6\sin\theta$. **17.** $r = -10\cos\left(\theta - \frac{\pi}{6}\right)$. **19.** $r = -6\cos\theta$.

21, 23.

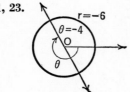

25.

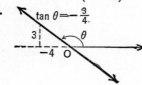

27.

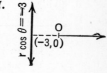

29.

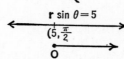

31.

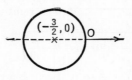

33.

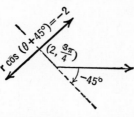

35.

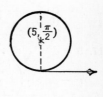

37.

39. Hint: Find the value of θ which makes r a maximum. This point with $(0, \omega)$ should determine a diameter and will locate the center. Use the definition of a circle and show that the distance of this point to any point on the locus $r = b\sin(\theta - \omega)$ is constant. $\left(\theta = \frac{\pi}{2} + \omega \text{ for max } r.\right)$

41.

43. For (4), $r_1 = \dfrac{a}{2}$ leaves only two terms,

$$r = a \cos (\theta - \theta_1).$$

Then choose $\theta_1 - \dfrac{\pi}{2}$, for

$$\cos \left(\theta - \frac{\pi}{2}\right) = \sin \left(\theta - \frac{\pi}{2} + \frac{\pi}{2}\right).$$

You do the other parts!

SET 17–3

1. $x^2 + y^2 = r^2 = 25;\ r = 5.$

3.

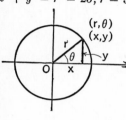

Since $x = r \cos \theta$ and $y = r \sin \theta$,
$2r^2 \cos^2 \theta + r^2 \sin \theta \cos \theta = 1.$

5. $3r^2 \sin \theta \cos \theta = r^2$, or $3 \sin \theta \cos \theta = 1.$

7. Since $y/x = \tan \theta$ or $\theta = \arctan y/x$, $r^2 = \theta^2.$

9. If $\tan \theta = \dfrac{y}{x}$, then $\dfrac{x}{y} = \tan \left(\dfrac{\pi}{2} - \theta\right).$ (Draw a diagram.) $\dfrac{\pi}{2} - \theta = 2$ or $\theta = \dfrac{\pi}{2} - 2.$

11. Since $\sin \theta = y/r$, $r \sin \theta = 5$ becomes $y = 5.$

13. $3r \cdot \dfrac{r}{x} = 4$ or $3(x^2 + y^2) = 4x.$

15. $3r = \sin 2\theta = 2 \sin \theta \cos \theta$; thus $3r = 2 \cdot y/r \cdot x/r$, $3r^3 = 2xy$ or $3(x^2 + y^2)^{\frac{3}{2}} = \pm 2xy.$

17. $2r = 7 \cos 2\theta = 7(\cos^2 \theta - \sin^2 \theta)$; $2r = 7(x^2/r^2 - y^2/r^2)$; $2(x^2 + y^2)^{\frac{3}{2}} = \pm 7(x^2 - y^2).$

19. $r(1 + x/r) = 14$; $r + x = 14$; $\pm\sqrt{x^2 + y^2} + x = 14$; $y^2 = 196 - 28x.$

21. $x^2 + y^2 - 4x = 4\sqrt{x^2 + y^2}.$

23.

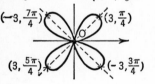

25. $r \sin \theta = b$ becomes $y = b$,
$r \cos \theta = a$ becomes $x = a.$

27. $r = b \sin \theta$ becomes $r = b \cdot y/r$, or
$x^2 + y^2 = by.$
$r = a \cos \theta$ becomes $x^2 + y^2 - ax = 0.$

SET 17–5

1.

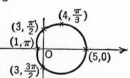

The curve does not pass through the pole since $3 + 2 \cos \theta = 0$ causes $\cos \theta = -\frac{3}{2}$, whereas $|\cos \theta| \leq 1.$ Max r when $\theta = 0$, min r when $\theta = \pi.$

3.

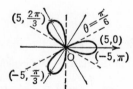

(The straight lines are tangents and axes of symmetry.)

$$\cos 3\theta = 0 \text{ for } \theta = \frac{\pi}{6}, \frac{\pi}{2}, \frac{5\pi}{6}, \frac{7\pi}{6},$$

$\dfrac{3\pi}{2}, \dfrac{11\pi}{6}.$ $|r|$ is a maximum for

$$\theta = 0, \frac{2\pi}{3}, \frac{4\pi}{3}, \text{ and a minimum}$$

for $\theta = \dfrac{\pi}{6}, \dfrac{\pi}{2}, \dfrac{5\pi}{6}.$

5.

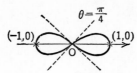

$r = \pm\sqrt{\cos 2\theta}$. Here we have symmetry with respect to the pole. We notice imaginary values for r when $\dfrac{\pi}{4} < \theta < \dfrac{3\pi}{4}$ and $\dfrac{5\pi}{4} < \theta < \dfrac{7\pi}{4}$.

7.

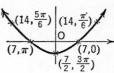

$r(1 - \sin\theta) = 7$. We cannot let $r = 0$, so the curve is not tangent to a line through the pole. Also, r is undefined for $\sin\theta = 1$ $\left(\text{or } \theta = \dfrac{\pi}{2}\right)$.

9.

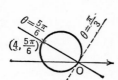

r is a maximum when $\theta = \dfrac{5\pi}{6}$. $r = 0$ when $\theta = \dfrac{\pi}{3}$.

11.

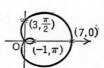

13.

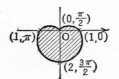

15.

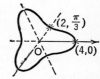

17.

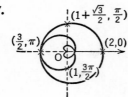

19.

21. *You* think about it!

SET 17–6

1. Line through pole making angle of 3 radians with polar axis.

3. Circle with diameter 5, center at $\left(\dfrac{5}{2}, \dfrac{\pi}{2}\right)$.

5. Line through (8, 0) perpendicular to polar axis.

7.

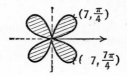

9.

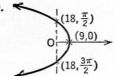

11.

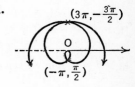

13.

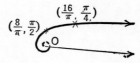

At the pole as θ increases by multiples $\dfrac{n\pi}{4}$, r decreases as $\dfrac{16}{\pi}, \dfrac{1}{2} \cdot \dfrac{16}{\pi}, \dfrac{1}{3} \cdot \dfrac{16}{\pi}, \dfrac{1}{4} \cdot \dfrac{16}{\pi}, \ldots$. r is undefined for $\theta = 0$ but $r \to \infty$ as $\theta \to 0$.

15.

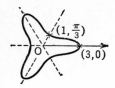

17.

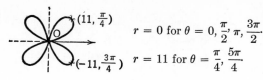

$r = 0$ for $\theta = 0, \dfrac{\pi}{2}, \pi, \dfrac{3\pi}{2}$.

$r = 11$ for $\theta = \dfrac{\pi}{4}, \dfrac{5\pi}{4}$

19.

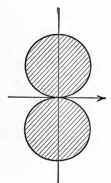

21.

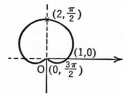

23.

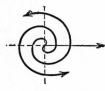

For $\theta > 0, r$ can be $+$ and $-$.

25.

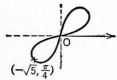

r is imaginary for $\dfrac{\pi}{2} < \theta < \pi$

and $\dfrac{3\pi}{2} < \theta < 2\pi$.

27.

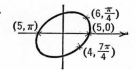

29.

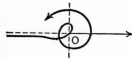

As $\theta \to 0 (\theta > 0), r \to -\infty$. When $\theta = 1, r = 0$.

31. $r = -\dfrac{16}{\pi} \theta.$

SET 17–7

1. Setting $y = 4 \sin 3\theta$, we see that as θ ranges from 0 to 2π, 3 cycles of the sine curve are made. Note: For $\theta > \pi$, the figure is simply retraced.

3.

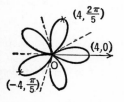

Here we would expect 5 cycles of the cosine curve with amplitude 4.

5.

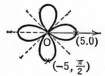

7.

Here r is imaginary for $\frac{\pi}{4} < \theta < \frac{3\pi}{4}$ and $\frac{5\pi}{4} < \theta < \frac{7\pi}{4}$. The $\pm$ value for r maps the entire figure as θ describes π radians.

9.

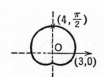

11.

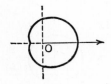

13.

15.

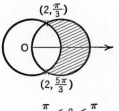

$$-\frac{\pi}{3} < \theta < \frac{\pi}{3}$$

17.

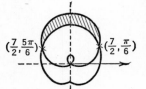

$$3 + \sin\theta = 2 + 3\sin\theta$$
$$\sin\theta = \frac{1}{2};\ \theta = \frac{\pi}{6},\ \frac{5\pi}{6}.$$

19.

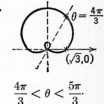

$$\frac{4\pi}{3} < \theta < \frac{5\pi}{3}.$$

21.

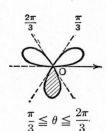

$$\frac{\pi}{3} \leqq \theta \leqq \frac{2\pi}{3}.$$

23.

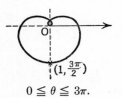

$$0 \leqq \theta \leqq 3\pi.$$

25. The following equations and figures correspond: a — 3; b — 5; c — 8; d — 4; e — 7; f — 6; g — 1; h — 2; i — 9; j — 10.

27.

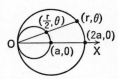

Relate given circle with diameter $2a$ to the polar axis by the equation $r = 2a\cos\theta$. Since for every value of r on the large circle the value of r for the small circle is $\frac{1}{2}$ as much, its equation is $r = \frac{1}{2}(2a\cos\theta) = a\cos\theta$, a circle.

28.

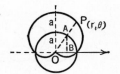

$$AP = AB = a\sin\theta$$
$$OP = r = a + a\sin\theta$$
$$r = a(1 + \sin\theta).$$

29. The Cartesian equation of a circle is of the second degree. $r = 4 + \sin\theta$ is of the fourth degree when written in rectangular form.

SET 17–8

1. (a) For $|r|$ to be as large as possible, $\cos 3\theta = 1$ or $3\theta = 0$, 2π, 4π.

Thus $\theta = 0$, $\dfrac{2\pi}{3}$, $\dfrac{4\pi}{3}$.

(b) For $|r|$ to be as small as possible, $\cos 3\theta = -1$ or $3\theta = \pi$, 3π, 5π so that

$$\theta = \frac{\pi}{3}, \pi, \frac{5\pi}{3}.$$

2.

$\left(\dfrac{3}{2}, \dfrac{\pi}{3}\right)$

$\left(\dfrac{3}{2}, \dfrac{5\pi}{3}\right)$

$1 + \cos\theta = 3\cos\theta$

$\cos\theta = \dfrac{1}{2}$

$\theta = \dfrac{\pi}{3}, \dfrac{5\pi}{3}$

$r = \dfrac{3}{2}$.

3.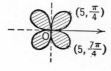

$\left(5, \dfrac{\pi}{4}\right)$

$\left(5, \dfrac{7\pi}{4}\right)$

4.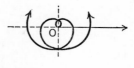

5.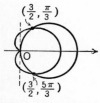

6.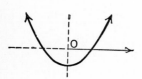

7.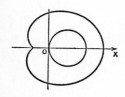

8.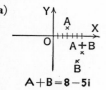

$\left(-5, \dfrac{3\pi}{2}\right)$

$\left(1, \dfrac{\pi}{2}\right)$

By graphing the factors together as $r = \sin\theta$ and $r = -5$.

9.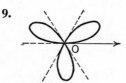

(a) $0 \leq \theta \leq \pi$.

(b) $\dfrac{\pi}{3} \leq \theta \leq \dfrac{2\pi}{3}$.

10.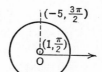

$\cos\theta = 2$ impossible. No points of intersection.

SET 18–1

1. (a)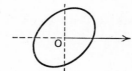

$A + B = 8 - 5i$

(b)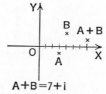

$A + B = 7 + i$

3. $2 - 9i$.

5. $z = \dfrac{5 + 10i}{3 - 2i} = \dfrac{(5 + 10i)(3 + 2i)}{(3 - 2i)(3 + 2i)} = \dfrac{15 - 20 + 40i}{9 + 4} = -\dfrac{5}{13} + \dfrac{40}{13}i.$

7. $z = \dfrac{-8 + 4i}{2 - 5i} = \dfrac{(-8 + 4i)(2 + 5i)}{(2 - 5i)(2 + 5i)} = -\dfrac{36}{29} - \dfrac{32}{29}i.$

9. $8iz - 2z = \dfrac{i - 4(3 + i)}{3 + i} = \dfrac{-12 - 3i}{3 + i},$

$z = \dfrac{3}{2} \cdot \dfrac{4 + i}{(3 + i)(1 - 4i)} = \dfrac{3}{2} \dfrac{4 + i}{7 - 11i}.$

11. $x^2 = y^2$; $x = -2y + 4$; $4y^2 - 16y + 16 = y^2$, $(3y - 4)(y - 4) = 0$, $y = 4, \frac{4}{3}$; $x = -4, \frac{4}{3}$. Hence $(-4, 4)$ and $(\frac{4}{3}, \frac{4}{3})$.

12. $r = \sqrt{7^2 + 2^2} = \sqrt{53}$; $\theta = \arctan\left(-\frac{2}{7}\right)$.

15. $x^2 + xy + y^2 - 3 = 0$, $xy + 2 = 0$; substituting $y = -\dfrac{2}{x}$ into the first equation,

$x^4 - 5x^2 + 4 \equiv (x + 1)(x - 1)(x + 2)(x - 2) = 0 \quad$ whence $\quad x = \pm 1, \pm 2$; $y = \mp 2, \mp 1$.

17–21. Do the *algebra!*

22. $z^3 - 1 \equiv (z - 1)(z^2 + z + 1) = 0$ has solutions $z = 1$, $z = -\dfrac{1}{2} \pm i\dfrac{\sqrt{3}}{2}$. Note: $z^3 = 1$ and $z = \sqrt[3]{1}$ so that these are the three cube roots of 1!

23. $i, -1, -i, 1, \cdots$.

25. Hint: $i^N = i^{4Q+R}$.

SET 18–2

1. $10(\cos 60° + i \sin 60°) = 5 + 5i\sqrt{3}$.

3. $6[\cos(-135°) + i \sin(-135°)] = -3\sqrt{2} - 3i\sqrt{2}$.

5. $2(\cos 86° + i \sin 86°) \cong .1396 + 1.9952i$.

7. $\sqrt{2}\left(\dfrac{1}{\sqrt{2}} - \dfrac{i}{\sqrt{2}}\right) = \sqrt{2}(\cos 315° + i \sin 315°)$.

9. $7\sqrt{2}(\cos 225° + i \sin 225°)$.   **11.** $7 + 0i = 7$.

13. $-4 + 0i = -4$.   **15.** $-10\sqrt{3} - 10i$.

17. $4(\cos 210° - i \sin 210°) = -2\sqrt{3} + 2i$.

19. $8.480 - 5.299i$.

21. $\cos \theta = -\sqrt{3}/2$, $\sin \theta = -\frac{1}{2}$, $\theta = 210°$.

23. $\cos \theta = -\frac{1}{4}$, $\sin \theta = \frac{1}{4}$. $\left(\frac{1}{4}\right)^2 + \left(-\frac{1}{4}\right)^2 \ne 1$. Impossible?

25. $\cos \theta = \frac{1}{2}$, $\sin \theta = -\frac{1}{4}$. $\left(-\frac{1}{4}\right)^2 + \left(\frac{1}{2}\right)^2 \ne 1$. Impossible?

SET 18–3

1. $15(\cos 60° + i \sin 60°) = \frac{15}{2} + 15i\sqrt{3}/2$,

$\frac{3}{5}(\cos 30° + i \sin 30°) = 3\sqrt{3}/10 + 3i/10$,

$\frac{5}{3}(\cos[-30°] + i \sin[-30°]) = 5\sqrt{3}/6 - 5i/6$.

3. $10 \text{ cis } 70° \cong 3.420 + 9.397i$,

$\frac{2}{5} \text{ cis}(-30°) = \sqrt{3}/5 - i/5$,

$\frac{5}{2} \text{ cis } 30° = 5\sqrt{3}/4 + 5i/4$.

5. $500 \text{ cis } 30° = 250\sqrt{3} + 250i$,

$\frac{1}{5} \text{ cis}(-30°) = \sqrt{3}/10 - i/10$,

$5 \text{ cis } 30° = 5\sqrt{3}/2 + 5i/2$.

7. $16 \text{ cis } 292° = 16(\cos 68° - i \sin 68°) \cong 5.994 - 14.84i$,
$16 \text{ cis}(-60°) = 8 - 8i\sqrt{3}$,
$\frac{1}{16} \text{ cis } 60° = 1/32 + i\sqrt{3}/32$.

9. $40 \text{ cis } 240° = -20 - 20i\sqrt{3}$,
$\frac{5}{2} \text{ cis } (-90°) = -5i/2$,
$\frac{2}{5} \text{ cis } 90° = 2i/5$.

SET 18–4

1. $(\sqrt{2})^6(1/\sqrt{2} + i/\sqrt{2})^6 = 8(\text{cis } 45°)^6 = 8 \text{ cis } 270° = -8i$.

3. $(2)^4(1/2 - i\sqrt{3}/2)^4 = 16(\text{cis } 300°)^4 = 16 \text{ cis } 120° = -8 + 8i\sqrt{3}$.

5. $32(\text{cis } 240°)^5 = 32 \text{ cis } 120° = -16 + 16i\sqrt{3}$.

7. $14^{-3} (\text{cis } 300°)^{-3} = 14^{-3} \text{ cis } 180° = -14^{-3}$.

9. $\dfrac{\text{cis}(-315°)}{4\sqrt{2}} = 1/8 + i/8$.

11. $2^{-8} (\text{cis } 315°)^4(\text{cis } 30°)^{-6} = 1/256$.

13. $28 \text{ cis } 540° = -28$.

15. $10^3 (\text{cis } 341° \ 34')^6 = 10^3 \text{ cis } 249° \ 24' \cong 10^3(-.3518 - .9360i)$.

17. $-\frac{1}{4}$.   **19.** $-\frac{1}{4}$.

21. Multiply out and apply definition of equality of complex numbers.

23. Same as 21.

SET 18–5

1. $z^5 = 32 \text{ cis } 180°$. $z = 2 \text{ cis}(36° + 72°k)$, $k = 0, 1, 2, 3, 4$.

3. $z^6 = \text{cis } 0°$. $z = \text{cis}(0° + 60°k)$, $k = 0, 1, 2, 3, 4, 5$.
$\text{cis } 0° = 1$, $\text{cis } 60° = 1/2 + i\sqrt{3}/2$, $\text{cis } 120° = -1/2 + i\sqrt{3}/2$, $\text{cis } 180° = -1$,
$\text{cis } 240° = -1/2 - i\sqrt{3}/2$, $\text{cis } 300° = 1/2 - i\sqrt{3}/2$.

5. $z^5 = 32 \text{ cis } 300°$. $z = 2 \text{ cis}(60° + 72°k)$, $k = 0, 1, 2, 3, 4$.

7. $z^{10} = 2 \text{ cis } 300°$. $z = \sqrt[10]{2} \text{ cis}(30° + 36° \ k)$, $k = 0, 1, \cdots, 9$.

9. $z = 2 \text{ cis}(45° + 120° \ k)$, $k = 0, 1, 2$.

11. See Problem 1.

13. $z^2 = 36 \text{ cis } 60°$. $z = 6 \text{ cis}(30° + 180° \ k)$, $k = 0, 1$.
$6 \text{ cis } 30° = 3\sqrt{3} + 3i$, $6 \text{ cis } 210° = -3\sqrt{3} - 3i$.

15. $z^{10} = \text{cis } 180°$. $z = \text{cis}(18° + 36° \ k)$, $k = 0, 1, \cdots, 9$.

17. $z^3 - 64 \text{ cis } 0° = 0$ has roots $z = 4 \text{ cis}(0° + 120° \ k)$, $k = 0, 1, 2$.
Therefore, $z^3 - 64 = (z - 4)(z - 4 \text{ cis } 120°)(z - 4 \text{ cis } 240°)$.

SET 18–6

1. $r_1 e^{i\theta_1} \cdot r_2 e^{i\theta_2} = r_1 r_2 e^{i\theta_1 + i\theta_2}$
               $= r_1 r_2 e^{i(\theta_1 + \theta_2)}$.

5. $500 e^{30°i} = ?$

9. $\cos ix = \dfrac{e^{i(ix)} + e^{-i(ix)}}{2} = ?$

13. $e^{x+2\pi} = e^x \cdot e^{2\pi}$; $e^{i(\theta+2\pi)} = \text{cis}(\theta + 2\pi) = ?$

SELF TEST 18–7

1. $\dfrac{1}{2} \text{ cis } 300° = \dfrac{1 - i\sqrt{3}}{4}$.

2. $z^4 = 1296 \text{ cis } 300°$. $z = 6 \text{ cis}(75° + 90° \ k)$, $k = 0, 1, 2, 3$.

3. See Problem 5, Set 18–5.

5. $(13 - 5i)/\text{cis } 270° = (13 - 5i)\,\text{cis}(-270°) = 5 + 13i.$

6. Sum $= 0$, product $= 1$.   **7.** See answer to Problem 21, Set 18–4.

8. Consider r to be of the form $\dfrac{a}{b}$, $b \neq 0$.   Let $N_r = 2\,|\,b\,|$. $K = 1$.

SET 19–1

1. $f'(x) = (3x - 2)(2x + 5) + (x^2 + 5x - 1)(3) = 9x^2 + 26x - 13.$

3. $y' = \lim\limits_{\Delta x \to 0} \dfrac{f(x + \Delta x) - f(x)}{\Delta x} = \lim\limits_{\Delta x \to 0} \dfrac{-1}{4x(x + \Delta x)} = \dfrac{-1}{4x^2}.$

5. $y' = 3x^2 - 4x + 3 = 2$, $x = 1, \frac{1}{3}$. $y + 3 = 2(x - 1)$, and $y + \frac{113}{27} = 2(x - \frac{1}{3})$.

7. $y' = \frac{1}{2}(2x - 3x^2 + 5)^{-\frac{1}{2}}(2 - 6x).$

9. $V = \pi r^2 h = 1000.$ $M = 2\pi rh + 2(2r)^2 = 2\pi r\left(\dfrac{1000}{\pi r^2}\right) + 8r^2.$

Solve, test for max: $r = 5$ in. $h = \dfrac{40}{\pi}$ in.

11. $y' = 6x^2 - 2x - 23 = -3.$ $x = -\frac{5}{3}, 2.$ point $(2, 16)$.

13. $y_2' = 6x^2 - 2x - 23 = -3$, $x = -\frac{5}{3}$ or 2, $y = 16$.
$y_1' = -3.$ $y_1 = -3x + c = 16$; $c = 22$ so $y = -3x + 22.$
$y - \frac{2060}{27} = -3(x + \frac{5}{3}).$

15. $-16t^2 + 64t + 225 = 33.$ $t = -2$ or $6.$ $h'(6) = -128$ ft per sec.

17. $h'(t) = -32t + 64 = 0.$ $t = 2.$ $h(2) = 289$ ft.

19. $x = \frac{5}{3}$, max. $V = \frac{2000}{27}.$

21. $y' = (2x - 4)^3 5(x^2 + 5x)^4(2x + 5) + (x^2 + 5x)^5 3(2x - 4)^2(2).$ $y'(2) = 0.$

23. $y' = (7x^2 + 5x - 36)^3 5(14x + 5)^4(14) + (14x + 5)^5 3(7x^2 + 5x - 36)^2(14x + 5).$
$y'(2) = (33)^4 560 + (33)^6 12.$

25. $z' = (t^2 - 5)(-1)(4 - 3t)^{-2}(-3) + (4 - 3t)^{-1}(2t).$ $z'(-1) = -\frac{26}{49}.$

27. The original function and its derivative are both complex numbers for $t = -1.$

29. $D' = \sqrt{(3 - t)^2 + t^4}(-8t) + (1 - 4t^2)\frac{1}{2}[(3 - t)^2 + t^4]^{-\frac{1}{2}}[2(3 - t)(-1) + 4t^3].$
$D'(-1) = 154/\sqrt{17}.$

31. $y' \approx 0.8122.$ **33.** $y' \approx 5.774.$ **35.** $y' = \frac{1}{2}.$

37.

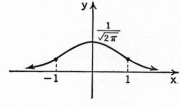

$\dfrac{d^2y}{dx^2} = 0$ at $(1, 0.242)$ and $(-1, 0.242).$

x intercepts of tangent lines are -2 and 2.

SET 19–3

1. $2x^5 - 2x^3 + x^2 - 3x + c.$ **3.** $\frac{3}{2}t^2 + 2t + c.$

5. $5x^3 + x^2 - 11x + c.$ **7.** Has no meaning; dx missing.

9. $\dfrac{5x^7}{7} - \dfrac{7x^2}{2} + x + c.$ **11.** $\dfrac{y^4}{4} - 2y^2 + 2y + c.$

13. $\dfrac{z^3}{3} - \dfrac{3z^4}{2} + \dfrac{9z^2}{2} + c.$ **15.** $y = 2x^3 + c$, at $(0, 5)$ $c = 5,$
                                                  equation $y = 2x^3 + 5.$

17. $y' = 2x - 4.$ $y = x^2 - 4x + c$ at $(-2, 3)$ $c = -9.$ $y = x^2 - 4x - 9.$

19. $z = x^8 - 2x^5 + 3x^4 - 7x + 45.$

21. $y' = k(x - 1)(x + 3).$ $y = \dfrac{k}{3}x^3 + kx^2 - 3kx + c.$ $k = 3$, $c = -7.$

SET 19–4

1. $h(t) = -16t^2 + 32t + 560$ if $0 \leq t \leq 7$. $v(7) = -192$ ft per sec.
3. $h(t) = -16t^2 + 96t$. Reaches highest point when $v(t) = 0$, that is, at $t = 3$ sec.
   $h(3) = 144$ ft. At ground level $h(t) = 0$, $t = 0$, $t = 6$. $v(6) = -96$ ft per sec.
5. *Ball 1.* $v_1(t) = -32t$ *Ball 2.* $v_2(t) = -32t + 30$
              $h_1(t) = -16t^2 + 45$. $h_2(t) = -16t^2 + 30t$.
   If the balls meet, $h_1(t) = h_2(t)$, that is, $t = \frac{3}{2}$.
   $v_1(\frac{3}{2}) = -48$ ft per sec. $v_2(\frac{3}{2}) = -18$ ft per sec.
   $h_1(\frac{3}{2}) = 9$ ft above ground. $h_2(\frac{3}{2}) = 9$ ft above ground.
   The student should note that *both* balls are going down when they meet.
7. $h(50) = 40,000$ ft, max ht. Remains in air 100 sec.
   $v(100) = -1600$ ft/sec, which is dangerous.
8. $h = 16(\frac{9}{2})^2 = 324$ ft.   9. $v = 32(\frac{9}{2}) = 144$ ft per sec $\cong 98$ mph.
11. (a) $D(t) = \frac{5}{2}t^2 + v_0 t$. $D(4) = 40 + 4v_0 = 60$, $v_0 = 5$ ft per sec.
    (b) $D(t) = \frac{5}{2}t^2 + 5t = \frac{60}{3}$, $t = 2$, $v(2) = 15$ ft per sec. Note that although $\frac{1}{2}$ the
    time has elapsed, only $\frac{1}{3}$ the distance is covered.
    (c) $D(t) = \frac{5}{2}t^2 + 5t = \frac{60}{2}$, $t = -1 + \sqrt{13} \cong 2.6$ sec.
    (d) $D(2) = 20$ or $\frac{1}{3}$ the length of the chute in $\frac{1}{2}$ the time.
12. $a = \dfrac{v^2}{2s}$. $a = 21,600$ mph.
13. $v = -kt + v_0$. $D = -kt^2/2 + v_0 t$.
    $\left.\begin{array}{l} D(.01) = -k(.01)^2/2 + v_0(.01) = .75 \text{ ft} \\ v(.01) = -k(.01) + v_0 = 0 \end{array}\right\} k = 15,000.$ $v_0 = 150$ ft per sec at moment of impact.
15. $v = -12t + v_0$. $D = -6t^2 + v_0 t$. When $v = 0$, $D = 3750$.
    $\left.\begin{array}{l} 0 = -12t + v_0 \\ 3750 = -6t^2 + v_0 t \end{array}\right\} v_0 = 300$ ft per sec.
17. (a) $\displaystyle\int_0^3 4x\,dx = 2x^2 \Big|_0^3 = 18$ in.-lbs. (b) 72 in.-lbs. (c) 288 in.-lbs.
19. $v = -32t + v_0$. $h = -16t^2 + v_0 t$. $h(1) = -16 + v_0 = 80$ ft, $v_0 = 96$ ft per sec.
    Hence $v(t) = -32t + 96 = 0$ at $t = 3$ and $h(3) = 144$ ft.
23. $a = -g$. $v = -gt + v_0$. $s = -\dfrac{g}{2}t^2 + v_0 t + s_0$.
24. $f(x) = kx$. $5 = k(4.1 - 4)$, $k = 50$, $f(x) = 50x$. $w = \displaystyle\int_0^1 50x\,dx = 25$ in-lbs.
25. Assuming $F = ma$ is valid on the planet, $a = -50$ ft per sec². The braking power needed is approximately 0.8 of the power available.

SET 19–5

1.
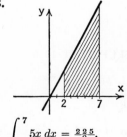

$y = 5x$.
$\displaystyle\int_0^4 5x\,dx = \dfrac{5x^2}{2} + c \Big|_0^4 = 40.$
$A = \frac{1}{2} \cdot 4 \cdot 20 = 40.$

3.

$\displaystyle\int_2^7 5x\,dx = \dfrac{225}{2}.$

5.

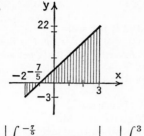

$$\left| \int_{-2}^{-\frac{7}{5}} (5x + 7)dx \right| + \left| \int_{-\frac{7}{5}}^{3} (5x + 7)\, dx \right| =$$
$$\left| -\tfrac{9}{10} \right| + \left| \tfrac{484}{10} \right| = 49.3.$$

7.

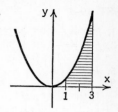

$$\int_{1}^{3} 3x^2\, dx = 26.$$

9.

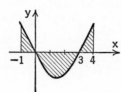

$$\int_{-1}^{0} (x^2 - 3x)\, dx + \left| \int_{0}^{3} (x^2 - 3x)\, dx \right|$$
$$+ \int_{3}^{4} (x^2 - 3x)\, dx = \tfrac{49}{6}.$$

11.

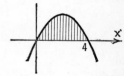

$$\int_{0}^{4} (-x^2 + 4x)\, dx = \tfrac{32}{3}.$$

13.

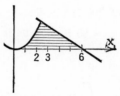

$$\int_{0}^{2} x^2\, dx + \int_{2}^{3} (6 - x)\, dx = \tfrac{37}{6}.$$

15.

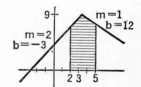

$$\int_{2}^{3} (2x + 3)\, dx$$
$$+ \int_{3}^{5} (-x + 12)\, dx = 24.$$

17. $I_0 = \int_{0}^{a} 2\pi r^3\, dr = \dfrac{\pi a^4}{2}.$

19. $\int_{0}^{4} x^{\frac{1}{2}}\, dx = \tfrac{16}{3}.$

SELF TEST 19–6

1. $h(t) = -16t^2 + 8t + 180.$
3. $x^3/3 - 2x^2 + 6x + c.$
5. $(4\sqrt{2} - 2)/3.$
6. $\int_{1}^{8} x^{-\frac{2}{3}}\, dx = 3x^{\frac{1}{3}} \Big|_{1}^{8} = 3.$

2. $v(3) = -88$ ft per sec.
4. $\tfrac{1809}{2}.$

7. $y = \tfrac{7}{4}x^2 - 8.$

8.

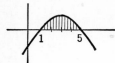

$$A = \int_1^5 (-x^2 + 6x - 5)\, dx = \tfrac{3\,2}{3}.$$

9.

$$A = \left| \int_1^2 (x^3 - 10x^2 + 31x - 30)\, dx \right|$$
$$+ \int_2^3 (x^3 - 10x^2 + 31x - 30)\, dx$$
$$+ \left| \int_3^5 (x^3 - 10x^2 + 31x - 30)\, dx \right|$$
$$+ \int_5^6 (x^3 - 10x^2 + 31x - 30)\, dx = ?$$

Note the answer is *not* $\int_1^6 f(x)\, dx$. Why not?

10.

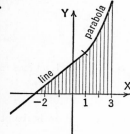

$$A = \int_{-2}^1 (2x + 5)\, dx + \int_1^3 (6x^2 + 1)\, dx = 66.$$

SET 19–9

1. 9.98.   **3.** $432.25 \le a \le 433.75$.

SET 20–3

1. (a) $m = \dfrac{-2 - 1}{2 + 3} = \dfrac{-3}{5}$: $y - 3 = (-\tfrac{3}{5})(x - 1)$.

   (b) $m = \dfrac{-1}{m_a} = \dfrac{5}{3}$: $y - 3 = (\tfrac{5}{3})(x - 1)$.

3. $(-2, -1)$ satisfies equation of line joining other points, namely $y - 3 = 4(x + 1)$.

5.

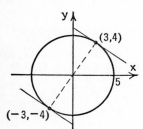

$\dfrac{dy}{dx} = -\dfrac{x}{y}$ at point (x, y) on the circle.

$y - 4 = (-\tfrac{3}{4})(x - 3)$.

$y + 4 = (-\tfrac{3}{4})(x + 3)$.

7. $m = \dfrac{-1}{(-\tfrac{3}{4})} = \dfrac{4}{3}$: $y - 4 = (\tfrac{4}{3})(x + 3)$.

9. See Example 4, Section 5-2.

11. Intersections $(2, 2)$, $(2, -2)$. Slope of the first circle $= -\dfrac{x}{y} = \begin{cases} -1 \\ +1. \end{cases}$

Slope of the second circle $= \dfrac{4 - x}{y} = \begin{cases} 1 \\ -1. \end{cases}$

Product of slopes is -1, hence lines are perpendicular.

13.

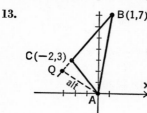

   (a) $y = (-\tfrac{3}{2})x.$
   (b) Altitude intersects BC at $(-\tfrac{68}{25}, \tfrac{51}{25})$ $QA = \tfrac{17}{5}.$
   (c) $AB = 5\sqrt{2}.$ (d) $\tfrac{17}{2}$ sq units.

15.

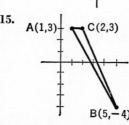

   (a) $y = 3.$

   (b) Altitude intersects BC at $(\tfrac{107}{58}, \tfrac{195}{58})$, length is $\dfrac{7}{\sqrt{58}}.$

   (c) $AB = \sqrt{65}.$ (d) $\tfrac{1}{2}\left(\dfrac{7}{\sqrt{58}}\right)\sqrt{58} = \dfrac{7}{2}.$

17. Equation of family of lines: $y - 4 = m(x - 3)$. $m = \tfrac{4}{3}$ or 1. Lines are $x - y = -1$, $3y = 4x$. [Zero intercepts.]

19. For perpendicular bisector, $m = 1$. Midpoint $(\tfrac{5}{2}, \tfrac{11}{2})$. $x - y - 3 = 0$.

21. $y' = 21x^2 \,|\, {}_{(1,7)} = 21.$ $y - 7 = (-\tfrac{1}{21})(x - 1).$

23. $10y\, dy/dx + 2 - 14x = 0.$ At $(0, 0)$ tangent vertical. Normal is horizontal. $y = 0.$

25. $m = -\tfrac{3}{7}.$ $y - 3 = (\tfrac{7}{3})(x + 5).$

27. $5\, dy/dx = [1 - 9x^2]_{(-2,4)} = -35.$ $m = \tfrac{1}{7}.$ $7(y - 4) = x + 2.$

29. $dy/dx = 10(x^2 - 3x + 1)^9(2x - 3)\,|_{(2,1)} = -10.$ $y - 1 = \tfrac{1}{10}(x - 2).$

SET 20–4

1. $m_1 = -\tfrac{3}{2}$, $m_2 = \tfrac{4}{5}$, $\tan \theta = \dfrac{-\tfrac{3}{2} - \tfrac{4}{5}}{1 + (-\tfrac{3}{2})(\tfrac{4}{5})} = 11.5$, $\theta \cong 85° 2' \cong 85°.$

3. If $\theta = +45°$ and m is the slope of the desired line, then $\dfrac{m - \tfrac{4}{3}}{1 + (\tfrac{4}{3})m} = 1$, $m = -7$, and $y + 3 = -7(x - 2)$. If $\theta = -45°$ and m is the slope of the desired line, then $\dfrac{\tfrac{4}{3} - m}{1 + (\tfrac{4}{3})m} = 1$, $m = \tfrac{1}{7}$, and $y + 3 = (x - 2)/7.$

5. Intersect at $(1, 2)$. $m_1 = -\dfrac{x}{y}\Big]_{(1,2)} = -\dfrac{1}{2}$, $m_2 = \dfrac{2}{y}\Big]_{(1,2)} = 1.$

$\tan \theta = \dfrac{-\tfrac{1}{2} - 1}{1 + (-\tfrac{1}{2})(1)} = -3$, $\tan(180° - \theta) = 3$, $180° - \theta \cong 71° 34' \cong 72°.$

7. The perpendicular bisector, $y - 3 = -6(x + 1)$, of the line segment joining $(-7, 2)$ and $(5, 4)$ intersects the given line in the desired point $(-\tfrac{2}{3}, 1)$.

9. At $(4, 17)$: $\tan \theta = \dfrac{8 - 3}{1 + 8(3)}.$ At $(-1, 2)$: $\tan \theta = \dfrac{-2 - 3}{1 + (-2)(3)}.$

11. Intersections: $(0, 0)$, $(1, -1)$, $(2, 0)$.
Slope formulas: $y' = (1 - x)/y$, $y' = 2x - 2.$

SET 20–5

1.

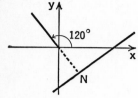

$(-\frac{1}{2})x + (\sqrt{3}/2)y = -6.$

3.

$y = (\frac{3}{4})x - 5.$
$(-\frac{3}{5})x + (\frac{4}{5})y = -4.$

5. $(3/\sqrt{10})x + (1/\sqrt{10})y = 6/\sqrt{10}.$

7. $(-\frac{3}{5})x + (\frac{4}{5})y = -\frac{5}{2}.$

9. $\left|\dfrac{6(6) - 8(-8) - 25}{-10}\right|.$

11. $(0, -5)$ lies on the second line.
$\left|\dfrac{3(0) - 4(-5) + 10}{-5}\right|.$

13. radius $= \left|\dfrac{8(\frac{1}{2}) - 6(-\frac{1}{2}) + 23}{-10}\right|.$ $(x - \frac{1}{2})^2 + (y + \frac{1}{2})^2 = 9.$

15.

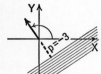

$(-\frac{5}{13})x + (\frac{12}{13})y \leqq -3.$ Region of points on and below the line $(-\frac{5}{13})x + (\frac{12}{13})y = -3.$

17. $77y - 99x + 669 = 0.$

19. $42y - 59x + 93 = 0$ and $193y - 26x - 308 = 0.$

SET 20–6

1. $\begin{bmatrix} 1 & 1 & -1 & 7 \\ 2 & -3 & -1 & 0 \\ 2 & -4 & -3 & 0 \end{bmatrix} \rightarrow \begin{bmatrix} 1 & 1 & -1 & 7 \\ 0 & 1 & 2 & 0 \\ 2 & -4 & -3 & 0 \end{bmatrix} \rightarrow \begin{bmatrix} 1 & 0 & -3 & 7 \\ 0 & 1 & 2 & 0 \\ 2 & 0 & 5 & 0 \end{bmatrix} \rightarrow$

$\begin{bmatrix} 1 & 0 & -3 & 7 \\ 0 & 1 & 2 & 0 \\ 0 & 0 & 11 & -14 \end{bmatrix} \rightarrow \begin{bmatrix} 1 & 0 & 0 & \frac{35}{11} \\ 0 & 1 & 0 & \frac{28}{11} \\ 0 & 0 & 1 & -\frac{14}{11} \end{bmatrix}.$

3. $x = 3, y = 1, z = 1, t = 2.$ **5.** $x = -\frac{1}{2}, y = 2, z = 2, t = -1.$

7. $\begin{bmatrix} 1 & 1 & 3 & 5 \\ 2 & 2 & -1 & 3 \\ 4 & 4 & 5 & 7 \end{bmatrix} \rightarrow \begin{bmatrix} 1 & 1 & 3 & 5 \\ 0 & 0 & -7 & -7 \\ 0 & 0 & -7 & -13 \end{bmatrix} \rightarrow \begin{bmatrix} 1 & 1 & 3 & 5 \\ 0 & 0 & 1 & 1 \\ 0 & 0 & 0 & -6 \end{bmatrix}.$ $0 \neq -6.$
No solution?

9. Only solution: $A = 0, B = 0, C = 0.$

11. $x = z - \frac{4}{9}, y = -z + \frac{19}{9}, z = z.$

13. $A = (\frac{3}{8})C, B = (\frac{17}{16})C, C = C,$ or $A:B:C = 6:17:16.$

15. $x = 2z, y = 3z, z = z.$

17. $x = -\frac{6}{7}w, y = \frac{31}{7}w, z = \frac{29}{7}w, w = w.$

19. $(1, -\frac{2}{3}).$ **21.** 123 pennies, 9 nickels, 12 dimes.

SET 20–7

1. (a) $(-2)(-5) - (3)(3) = 1.$ (b) $(-3)(3) + (-5)(-2) = 1.$

3. (a) $(4 - x)(-3 - x) - (-5)(-5) = x^2 - x - 37.$

   (b) $-(-5)(-5) + (-3 - x)(4 - x) = x^2 - x - 37.$

5. (a) $(-2)\begin{vmatrix} -6 & 2 \\ -8 & 5 \end{vmatrix} - (3)\begin{vmatrix} 4 & 1 \\ -8 & 5 \end{vmatrix} + (4)\begin{vmatrix} 4 & 1 \\ -6 & 2 \end{vmatrix} = 0.$

   (b) $-(3)\begin{vmatrix} 4 & 1 \\ -8 & 5 \end{vmatrix} + (-6)\begin{vmatrix} -2 & 1 \\ 4 & 5 \end{vmatrix} - (2)\begin{vmatrix} -2 & 4 \\ 4 & -8 \end{vmatrix} = 0.$

7. (a) $(1 - x)\begin{vmatrix} -1 - x & -2 \\ -2 & 2 - x \end{vmatrix} - (2)\begin{vmatrix} 2 & -3 \\ -2 & 2 - x \end{vmatrix}$

   $+ (-3)\begin{vmatrix} 2 & -3 \\ -1 - x & -2 \end{vmatrix} = ?$

   (b) $-(2)\begin{vmatrix} 2 & -3 \\ -2 & 2 - x \end{vmatrix} + (-1 - x)\begin{vmatrix} 1 - x & -3 \\ -3 & 2 - x \end{vmatrix}$

   $-(-2)\begin{vmatrix} 1 - x & 2 \\ -3 & -2 \end{vmatrix} = ?$

9. (a) $(1)\begin{vmatrix} y & y^2 \\ z & z^2 \end{vmatrix} - (1)\begin{vmatrix} x & x^2 \\ z & z^2 \end{vmatrix} + (1)\begin{vmatrix} x & x^2 \\ y & y^2 \end{vmatrix} = ?$

   (b) $(-1)\begin{vmatrix} x & x^2 \\ z & z^2 \end{vmatrix} + (y)\begin{vmatrix} 1 & x^2 \\ 1 & z^2 \end{vmatrix} - (y^2)\begin{vmatrix} 1 & x \\ 1 & z \end{vmatrix} = ?$

11. $D = (1 - x)(x^2 - 9) = 0, \ x = 1, \pm 3.$

SET 20–8

7. 4.   9. 4.   11. 0.

12. The equation is linear and is satisfied by (x_1, y_1) and by (x_2, y_2), since the resulting determinants have identical rows. The points must be distinct.

13. $\begin{vmatrix} x & y & 1 \\ 2 & -3 & 1 \\ -4 & 5 & 1 \end{vmatrix} = 0,$ or $4x + 3y + 1 = 0.$

15. (a) $-\frac{1}{2}\begin{vmatrix} 2 & -3 & 1 \\ -4 & 5 & 1 \\ 3 & 2 & 1 \end{vmatrix} = 19.$ (b) Area is zero. Points are collinear.

17. $\begin{vmatrix} x^2 + y^2 & x & y & 1 \\ 13 & 2 & -3 & 1 \\ 41 & -4 & 5 & 1 \\ 13 & 3 & 2 & 1 \end{vmatrix} = 0,$ or $19(x^2 + y^2) + 70x - 14y - 429 = 0.$

SET 20–9

1. $A = \dfrac{\begin{vmatrix} 7 & 1 & -1 \\ 0 & -3 & -1 \\ 0 & -4 & -3 \end{vmatrix}}{\begin{vmatrix} 1 & 1 & -1 \\ 2 & -3 & -1 \\ 2 & -4 & -3 \end{vmatrix}} = \frac{35}{11},$ etc.

13. $2(x + iy) + 3i(x + iy) = -7 - 4i.$ Equating the real and the pure imaginary numbers $\begin{cases} 2x - 3y = -7 \\ 3x + 2y = -4. \end{cases}$ $x = -2, y = 1.$

15. $k = 1, 3, -4.$

17. (a) $v_1 = \dfrac{m_1 - m_2}{m_1 + m_2} u_1,$ $v_2 = \dfrac{2m_1}{m_1 + m_2} u_1.$

(b) m_1 stops and m_2 acquires the velocity which m_1 had.

(c) m_1 moves with nearly the same speed but in the opposite direction. m_2 acquires a very small velocity.

(d) m_1 continues in the same direction with nearly the same velocity. m_2 acquires a velocity nearly twice that of m_1.

19. Substitute x, y, and z into each of the equations. A_1 is the cofactor of a_1 etc.

SELF TEST 20–10

1.

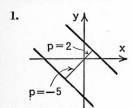

p = 2

p = −5

7 units.

2. $\begin{bmatrix} 1 & 0 & 0 & 1 \\ 0 & 1 & 0 & 2 \\ 0 & 0 & 1 & -2 \end{bmatrix}.$ **3.** $D = 148.$

4. Intersections are $(0, 0)$ at which $\theta = 90°$, and $(8, 8)$ at which $\tan\theta = \dfrac{2 - \frac{1}{2}}{1 + 2(\frac{1}{2})} = .75, \theta \cong 37°.$

5. $\left| \dfrac{5(2) - 12(-3) - 26}{-13} \right|.$

6. $(\pm\frac{3}{5})x + (\frac{4}{5})y = 4.$ **7.** $z = -10.$
   $m = -\frac{7}{12}.$
   $12(y - 3) = -7(x - 2).$ $\Big\}$

8. $y' = (6x)/7 \big|_{(2,3)} = \frac{12}{7},$

9. $x = \dfrac{\begin{vmatrix} 5z & 3 \\ -3z & -4 \\ 2 & 3 \\ 3 & -4 \end{vmatrix}}{} = ?,$ $y = \dfrac{\begin{vmatrix} 2 & 5z \\ 3 & -3z \\ 2 & 3 \\ 3 & -4 \end{vmatrix}}{} = ?,$ $z = z.$

SET 21–2

1. $(x - 3)^2 + (y + 5)^2 = 4^2$ or $x^2 + y^2 - 6x + 10y + 18 = 0.$

3. $(x - 2)^2 + (y - 11)^2 = 1.$

5. $(x - 4)^2 + (y + 2)^2 = r^2; (2 - 4)^2 + (1 + 2)^2 = r^2; r^2 = 13;$
   $(x - 4)^2 + (y + 2)^2 = 13.$

7. $(x - 5)^2 + (y + 2)^2 = r^2; (0 - 5)^2 + (0 + 2)^2 = r^2 = 29;$
   $(x - 5)^2 + (y + 2)^2 = 29.$

9. $(x - 4)^2 + (y - 6)^2 = (-5)^2 + (-3)^2 = 34.$

12. $(x - 10)^2 + (y - 1)^2 = 2.$

13. Of Problems 1 and 11 the circle of Problem 11 has the larger radius.

15. $A: C_1(2, 1), r = 2.$ $B: C_2(4, 2), r = 3.$

(a) $\overline{C_1 C_2} = \sqrt{(4 - 2)^2 + (2 - 1)^2} = \sqrt{5} < 3,$ and center of circle A is inside circle B.

(b) However, $\sqrt{5} > 2$ and center of B is not within A.

(d) $A - B: 4x + 2y - 10 = 0;$ solve with A. $5x^2 - 20x + 16 = 0; b^2 - 4ac = 20(20) - 16(20) > 0,$ unequal real values for x indicate intersection in 2 points. Chord is $2x + y - 5 = 0.$

(e) $x^2 + y^2 - 8x - 4y + 11 + k(x^2 + y^2 - 4x - 2y + 1) = 0.$

(f) Substitute $(0, 0)$ in (e); $k = -11; 5x^2 + 5y^2 - 18x - 9y = 0.$

(g) $4 + 9 - 16 - 12 + 11 + k(4 + 9 - 8 - 6 + 1) = -4 + k \cdot 0$ indicates that $(2, 3)$ lies on circle A?

17. In 6, $r^2 = 32.$ Let $r^2 > 32,$ say 33; $(x + 1)^2 + (y - 7)^2 = 33.$

19. Use $(0, 7)$ as center and $r > \sqrt{32} + 1$ (since we "moved" center 1 unit nearer circumference); for example, $x^2 + (y - 7)^2 = 16$.

21. Use slope-y-intercept form $y = mx + 11$ and solve with $x^2 + y^2 = 9$; $(m^2 + 1)x^2 + 22mx + 112 = 0$. Now demand only one point of intersection (tangency); thus $b^2 - 4ac = 0$ or $9m^2 - 112 = 0$ (simplified) or $m = \pm\dfrac{4\sqrt{7}}{3}$. Equations of two tangents are $y = \pm\dfrac{4\sqrt{7}}{3} x + 11$.

23. $x^2 + (3x + 5 - 4)^2 = 9$; $10x^2 + 6x - 8 = 0$;
$x = \dfrac{-3 \pm \sqrt{89}}{10}$, $y = \dfrac{41 \pm 3\sqrt{89}}{10}$.

25. (a) $C(0, -17.5)$; $r = \frac{1}{2}$; $x^2 + (y - 17.5)^2 = \frac{1}{4}$.
(b) Center is 5 ft nearer origin, $C(-12\frac{1}{2}, 0)$; $(x + \frac{25}{2})^2 + y^2 = \frac{1}{4}$.

27. Take the equations of the circles to be $(x - h_1)^2 + (y - k_1)^2 = r_1^2$ and $(x - h_2)^2 + (y - k_2)^2 = r_2^2$ where $r_1 + r_2 > \sqrt{(h_1 - h_2)^2 + (k_1 - k_2)^2}$.
(a) When $r_1 = r_2$, the radical axis is
$y = -\dfrac{h_2 - h_1}{k_2 - k_1}x + \dfrac{k_2^2 - k_1^2}{2(k_2 - k_1)} + \dfrac{h_2^2 - h_1^2}{2(k_2 - k_1)}$ which is the perpendicular bisector of the line segment joining the centers of the circles.
(b) When $r_1 \neq r_2$, $y = -\dfrac{h_2 - h_1}{(k_2 - k_1)}x + \dfrac{k_2^2 - k_1^2 + h_2^2 - h_1^2 + r_1^2 - r_2^2}{2(k_2 - k_1)}$ which is a line perpendicular to the line of centers.
(c) Verify that the distance from a point $(x_1 y_1)$ to the circle $(x - h_1)^2 + (y - k_1)^2 = r_1^2$ measured along the tangent is $(x_1 - h_1)^2 + (y_1 - k_1)^2 - r_1^2$ and similarly for the other circle. If the distances are equal, $(x_1 - h_1)^2 + (y_1 - k_1)^2 - r_1^2 - [(x_1 - h_2)^2 + (y_1 - k_2)^2 - r_2^2] = 0$. Hence, the point is on the radical axis.

29. $(x - h)^2 + (y - k)^2 = a^2$.

31. (a) $x^2 + y^2 = 25$. (b) $\dfrac{dx}{dt} = -5\pi$ units per sec. In the negative x direction.

33. The region of points which lie inside the circle $(8x + 27)^2 + (8y - 125)^2 = 7650$.

SET 21-4

1. $\sqrt{(x - 1)^2 + (y - 5)^2} + \sqrt{(x - 1)^2 + (y + 3)^2} = 10$;
$25x^2 + 9y^2 - 50x - 18y - 191 = 0$.

3. $\sqrt{x^2 + (y - 3)^2} + \sqrt{x^2 + (y + 3)^2} = 8$; $16x^2 + 7y^2 = 112$.

5. $56x^2 + 225y^2 - 728x - 784 = 0$.

7. $252x^2 + 256y^2 - 756x - 1536y - 1161 = 0$.

9. $3x^2 + 2xy + 3y^2 - 10x - 6y - 41 = 0$.

11. For simplicity, let the origin be midway between the pins and the pins on the x-axis c units from the origin. Denote the length of string from pin to pin by $2a$ and the positive y intercept by b. Then $\sqrt{(x - c)^2 + y^2} + \sqrt{(x + c)^2 + y^2} = 2a$.
Using $b^2 = a^2 - c^2$, we obtain the equation $\dfrac{x^2}{a^2} + \dfrac{y^2}{b^2} = 1$.

12. $x'^2 + y'^2 + (2h - 6)x' + (2k + 4)y' + (h^2 + k^2 - 6h + 4k - 12) = 0$, $h = 3$, $k = -2$, $x'^2 + y'^2 = 25$.

13. $y'^2 - 20x' + (2k - 10)y' + (k^2 - 20h - 10k + 5) = 0$, $k = 5$, $h = -1$, $y'^2 = 20x'$.

SET 21–5

1.

The form is $\dfrac{(x-0)^2}{3^2} + \dfrac{(y-0)^2}{5^2} = 1$. $a = 5, b = 3$,

$c = \sqrt{5^2 - 3^2} = 4, \dfrac{2b^2}{a} = \dfrac{18}{5}, C(0,0), V(0, \pm 5), F(0, \pm 4)$.

3. Circle with $C(0,0)$, $r = 2$.

5.

$\dfrac{(x-0)^2}{1^2} + \dfrac{(y+2)^2}{3^2} = 1$. $a = 3, b = 1, c = 2\sqrt{2}, \dfrac{2b^2}{a} = \dfrac{2}{3}$,

$C(0, -2), V(0, -2 \pm 3), F(0, -2 \pm 2\sqrt{2})$.

7.

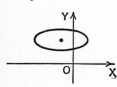

$a = 4, b = 2, c = 2\sqrt{3}, \dfrac{2b^2}{a} = 2, C(-2, 5)$,

$V(-2 \pm 4, 5), F(-2 \pm 2\sqrt{3}, 5)$.

9.

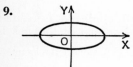

$\dfrac{x^2}{6^2} + \dfrac{y^2}{3^2} = 1$. $a = 6, b = 3, c = 3\sqrt{3}, \dfrac{2b^2}{a} = 3$,

$C(0,0), V(\pm 6, 0), F(\pm 3\sqrt{3}, 0)$.

11.

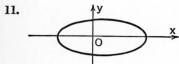

$\dfrac{(x-3)^2}{10^2} + \dfrac{(y+1)^2}{4^2} = 1$. $a = 10, b = 4$,

$c = 2\sqrt{21}, \dfrac{2b^2}{a} = \dfrac{16}{5}, C(3, -1)$,

$V(3 \pm 10, -1), F(3 \pm 2\sqrt{21}, -1)$.

13. $(x-11)^2 + (y+2)^2 = \dfrac{5}{2}$.

Circle, $C(11, -2), r = \dfrac{\sqrt{10}}{2}$.

15.

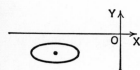

$\dfrac{(x+3)^2}{1^2} + \dfrac{(y+1)^2}{(\frac{1}{2})^2} = 1$. $a = 1, b = \frac{1}{2}$,

$c = \dfrac{\sqrt{3}}{2}, \dfrac{2b^2}{a} = \dfrac{1}{2}, C(-3, -1)$,

$V(-3 \pm 1, -1), F\left(-3 \pm \dfrac{\sqrt{3}}{2}, -1\right)$.

17.

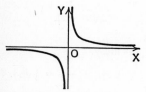

$xy = 5$.

19. $a = 6, b = 3$; same ellipse as in No. **9** but $C(-1, 3)$ and rotated 90°.

21. $4x^2 + 9y^2 = 0$ defines only one real point $(0, 0)$. It may be considered a point ellipse.

23. $\dfrac{x^2}{a^2} + \dfrac{y^2}{b^2} = \sin^2 t + \cos^2 t = 1.$

25. $a = 6 - 2 = 4$, along y-axis. $\dfrac{(x-5)^2}{1} + \dfrac{(y-2)^2}{16} = 1.$

27. $a = 11 - 5 = 6$, $c = 5 - 3 = 2$, $b^2 = 36 - 4 = 32$; $\dfrac{(x-5)^2}{36} + \dfrac{(y+1)^2}{32} = 1.$

29. C is midpoint of $(-3, 1)$, $(3, 1)$, so $C(0, 1)$. $a = 3$, $c = 1 - 0 = 1$,
$b^2 = 9 - 1 = 8$, major axis on x-axis; $\dfrac{x^2}{9} + \dfrac{(y-1)^2}{8} = 1.$

31. $c = \dfrac{5 - (-1)}{2} = 3$, $C\left(-7, \dfrac{5-1}{2}\right)$ or $(-7, 2)$, $a = 2 - (-3) = 5$,
$b^2 = 25 - 9 = 16$, major axis parallel to y-axis; $\dfrac{(x+7)^2}{16} + \dfrac{(y-2)^2}{25} = 1.$

33. Hint: Take $F_1 = (0, c)$ and $F_2 = (0, -c)$ with vertices $(0, a)$ and $(0, -a)$.

35. $a = \frac{6}{2} = 3$, $b = \frac{4}{2} = 2$, $c = \sqrt{9-4} = \sqrt{5}$, $2c = 2\sqrt{5}$, $2a = 6$; stakes $2\sqrt{5}$ ft apart,
rope 6 ft from stake to stake. Total rope $= 2\sqrt{5} + 6 \cong 10.5$ ft.

37. Slope $= -\dfrac{b^2 x_1}{a^2 y_1}.$

39. Hint: A line through the center intersects the ellipse in points (x_1, y_1) and
$(-x_1, -y_1)$. Why? What are the slopes of the tangent lines at the two points?

41. The equation of the locus is $x^2 + 4y^2 = a^2.$

42. Let circle have equation $x^2 + y^2 = a^2$. Locate points with ordinates twice that
of circle. For the point (x, y) on the locus, the corresponding point on the circle is
$(x, y/2)$. Thus $x^2 + (y/2)^2 = a^2$ or $\dfrac{x^2}{a^2} + \dfrac{y^2}{(2a)^2} = 1$ is the equation of the locus.

43. Coordinates of end point (c, y) of latus rectum satisfy $\dfrac{c^2}{a^2} + \dfrac{y^2}{b^2} = 1$, or $y = \pm\dfrac{b^2}{a}.$

Length $= \dfrac{2b^2}{a}.$

SET 21-6

1. $(x^2 + 6x + 9) + 36(y^2 - 4y + 4) = -144 + 9 + 144$ or
$\dfrac{(x+3)^2}{3^2} + \dfrac{(y-2)^2}{\left(\frac{1}{2}\right)^2} = 1.$ $a = 3$, $b = \frac{1}{2}$, $c = \frac{1}{2}\sqrt{35}$, $C(-3, 2)$, $V(-3 \pm 3, 2)$,
$F(-3 \pm \frac{1}{2}\sqrt{35}, 2)$, $M(-3, 2 \pm \frac{1}{2})$.

3. $(x^2 - 4x + 4) + 4(y^2 + 2y + 1) = 8 + 4 + 4$; $\dfrac{(x-2)^2}{4^2} + \dfrac{(y+1)^2}{2^2} = 1.$
$a = 4$, $b = 2$, $c = 2\sqrt{3}$, $C(2, -1)$, $V(2 \pm 4, -1)$, $F(2 \pm 2\sqrt{3}, -1)$,
$M(2, -1 \pm 2)$.

5. $\dfrac{(x+3)^2}{16} + \dfrac{(y-5)^2}{36} < 1.$ Region of points inside an ellipse.

7. $a = \frac{1}{2}\sqrt{11}$, $b = \frac{2}{3}$, $c = \frac{1}{6}\sqrt{83}$, $C(-\frac{5}{2}, \frac{2}{3})$, $V(-\frac{5}{2} \pm \frac{1}{2}\sqrt{11}, \frac{2}{3})$, $F(-\frac{5}{2} \pm \frac{1}{6}\sqrt{83}, \frac{2}{3})$.
Locus is all points on and within this ellipse.

9. $\dfrac{(x-3)^2}{41} + \dfrac{y^2}{\frac{164}{9}} = -1$, an imaginary ellipse.

11. $2a = 40$, $a = 20$, $b = 16$. Choose $C(0, 0)$ and equation is $\dfrac{x^2}{400} + \dfrac{y^2}{256} = 1$. Let

$x = 20 - 4 = 16$. $\dfrac{256}{400} + \dfrac{y^2}{256} = 1$ and $y = \frac{48}{5}$.

13. Let $P(x, y)$. $\sqrt{(x - 2)^2 + (y - 2)^2} = \pm\frac{1}{2}(x + 2)$, ($+$ or $-$ as $x + 2$ is positive or negative). $3x^2 + 4y^2 - 20x - 16y + 28 = 0$.

15. $a = 15$, $b = 15$, so arch is a semicircle with $r = 15$. With $C(0, 0)$, $x^2 + y^2 = 225$. If $x = 12$, $y = \sqrt{225 - 144} = 9$.

17. Choose ellipse located so that $\dfrac{x^2}{a^2} + \dfrac{y^2}{b^2} = 1$. If F_1 and F_2 are coincident, $c = -c$,

$c = 0$, and $b = \sqrt{a^2 - c^2} = \sqrt{a^2} = a$. Then $\dfrac{x^2}{a^2} + \dfrac{y^2}{a^2} = 1$ or $x^2 + y^2 = a^2$, a circle.

19. The region of points within the circle $(x - 3)^2 + (y + 2)^2 = 25$.

21. (a) $(2, 2)$, $(2, -2)$, $(-2, 2)$, $(-2, -2)$.
(b) $31° 17'$. See Section 20–4.

23. $\dfrac{(x - 2)^2}{9} + \dfrac{(y - 3)^2}{16} = 1$.   **25.** Slope $= \dfrac{-4\sqrt{3}}{9}$.

27. Hint: Take the equation of the ellipse to be $\dfrac{x^2}{200^2} + \dfrac{y^2}{100^2} = 1$. Then, if the out-

side edge is an ellipse, it must have the equation $\dfrac{x^2}{(206)^2} + \dfrac{y^2}{(106)^2} = 1$. Consider the point $(100, 50\sqrt{3})$ on the given ellipse. Since the slope of the normal there is $2\sqrt{3}$, a point on the outside edge must have coordinates

$$\left(100 + \dfrac{6}{\sqrt{13}},\ 50\sqrt{3} + \dfrac{12\sqrt{3}}{\sqrt{13}}\right).$$

Show that these do not satisfy the second equation.

SET 21–7

1. $\sqrt{(x - 3)^2 + (y - 5)^2} - \sqrt{(x - 3)^2 + (y - 13)^2} = \pm 6$;
$9x^2 - 7y^2 - 54x + 126y - 423 = 0$.

3. $\sqrt{(x - 0)^2 + (y - 4)^2} - \sqrt{(x - 0)^2 + (y + 4)^2} = \pm 6$; or $9x^2 - 7y^2 + 63 = 0$.

5. $\sqrt{(x - 4)^2 + y^2} - \sqrt{x^2 + (y - 3)^2} = \pm 4$; $28y^2 + 96xy - 144x - 276y + 495 = 0$.

SET 21–8

1. (a) Ellipse: (1) $\dfrac{(x - h)^2}{a^2} + \dfrac{(y - k)^2}{b^2} = 1$,   (2) $\dfrac{(x - h)^2}{b^2} + \dfrac{(y - k)^2}{a^2} = 1$,

(3) $CV = a (a > b)$,   (4) $CF = c = \sqrt{a^2 - b^2}$,   (5) $\dfrac{2b^2}{a}$,   (6) two,   (7) no.

(b) Hyperbola: (1) $\dfrac{(x - h)^2}{a^2} - \dfrac{(y - k)^2}{b^2} = 1$,   (2) $\dfrac{(y - k)^2}{a^2} - \dfrac{(x - h)^2}{b^2} = 1$,

(3) $CV = a (a \lesseqgtr b)$,   (4) $CF = c = \sqrt{a^2 + b^2}$,   (5) $\dfrac{2b^2}{a}$,

(6) three,   (7) yes.

3.

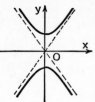

$a = 3, b = 2, c = \sqrt{13},$
$C(0, 0), \quad V(0, \pm 3),$
$F(0, \pm\sqrt{13})$
$\dfrac{2b^2}{a} = \dfrac{8}{3}.$

5.

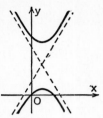

$a = 5, b = 3, c = \sqrt{34},$
$C(2, 7), V(2, 7 \pm 5),$
$F(2, 7 \pm \sqrt{34}),$
$\dfrac{2b^2}{a} = \dfrac{18}{5}.$

7.

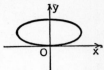

$a = 2, b = 1, c = \sqrt{3},$
$C(0, 1), \quad V(\pm 2, 1),$
$F(\pm\sqrt{3}, 1),$
$\dfrac{2b^2}{a} = 1.$

9.

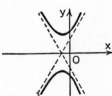

$a = 2, b = 1, c = \sqrt{5}, C(-1, 0),$
$V(-1, \pm 2), \quad F(-1, \pm\sqrt{5}),$
$\dfrac{2b^2}{a} = 1.$

11.

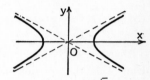

$a = 5, b = \dfrac{5}{2}, c = \dfrac{5\sqrt{5}}{2}, C(0, 0),$
$V(\pm 5, 0), F(\pm\dfrac{5\sqrt{5}}{2}, 0),$
$\dfrac{2b^2}{a} = \dfrac{5}{2}.$

13. $a = 3, b = 5, c = \sqrt{34}, C(4, -1),$
$V(4 \pm 3, -1), \dfrac{2b^2}{a} = \dfrac{50}{3},$
$F(4 \pm \sqrt{34}, -1).$

15.

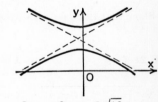

$a = \dfrac{3}{2}, b = \dfrac{9}{2}, c = \dfrac{3\sqrt{10}}{2},$
$C(-1, 6), V(-1, 6 \pm \tfrac{3}{2}),$
$\dfrac{2b^2}{a} = 27, F\left(-1, 6 \pm \dfrac{3\sqrt{10}}{2}\right).$

17.

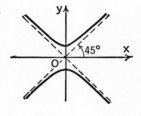

$a = 1, b = 1, C(0, 0), V(0, \pm 1), F(0, \pm\sqrt{2}),$
$\dfrac{2b^2}{a} = 2.$ (Equilateral hyp.)

19. $(3x - 2y)(3x + 2y) = 0.$ A pair of intersecting lines.

21. (a) $\dfrac{(x - 3)^2}{25} - \dfrac{(y + 5)^2}{49} = 1.$

(b) $\dfrac{(y + 5)^2}{25} - \dfrac{(x - 3)^2}{49} = 1.$

23. $\dfrac{(y - 1)^2}{16} - \dfrac{(x - 2)^2}{9} = 1.$

25. Axis parallel to x-axis; slope of asymptote is $\dfrac{4}{5} = \dfrac{b}{a}$ (since a is parallel to the abscissa 5). But $a = CV = 5$, so that $b = 4$. $\dfrac{x^2}{25} - \dfrac{(y-3)^2}{16} = 1$.

27. Axis parallel to y-axis. $c = CF = 6$, $a = 2$, $b^2 = 32$. $\dfrac{(y-1)^2}{4} - \dfrac{(x-7)^2}{32} = 1$.

29. Axis parallel to x-axis, $a = CV = 6$, $b = 4$. $\dfrac{(x+4)^2}{36} - \dfrac{(y-7)^2}{16} = 1$.

31. Let point on locus have coordinates (x, y), then corresponding point on $9x^2 - 16y^2 = 144$ would have coordinates $(2x, y)$ which must satisfy the equation. Thus $9(2x)^2 - 16y^2 = 144$ or $9x^2 - 4y^2 = 36$.

33.

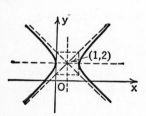

$\tan\theta_1 = \dfrac{y}{a+x}$, $\tan\theta_2 = \dfrac{y}{a-x}$. (Denominators had to be chosen carefully to be correct for all positions of P.)

$\left(\dfrac{y}{x+a}\right)\left(\dfrac{-y}{x-a}\right) = \dfrac{b^2}{a^2}$ or $\dfrac{x^2}{a^2} + \dfrac{y^2}{b^2} = 1$.

35. Replace y by $2y$; then $4x^2 - 9(2y)^2 = 36$ or $4x^2 - 36y^2 = 36$. (See **31.**)

36. $\dfrac{x^2}{a^2} - \dfrac{y^2}{b^2} = \sec^2 t - \tan^2 t = 1$.

37. See Theorem 1.

39. $a^2 y_1 y - b^2 x_1 x = a^2 y_1^2 - b^2 x_1^2$.
$b^2 x_1 y + a^2 y_1 x = (a^2 + b^2) x_1 y_1$.

41. 10.

SET 21–10

1.

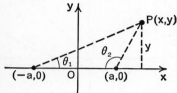

$(x^2 - 2x + 1) - (y^2 - 4y + 4) = 1$
or $(x-1)^2 - (y-2)^2 = 1$.

3.

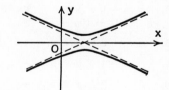

$4y^2 - (x^2 - 8x + 16) = 28 - 16$
$\dfrac{y^2}{3} - \dfrac{(x-4)^2}{12} = 1$.

5.

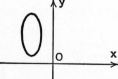

$10(x^2 + 6x + 9) + (y^2 - 8y + 16)$
$= -96 + 90 + 16$
$\dfrac{(x+3)^2}{1} + \dfrac{(y-4)^2}{10} = 1$.

7.

$\dfrac{(x+4)^2}{9} - \dfrac{(y-5)^2}{16} = 1$.

9.

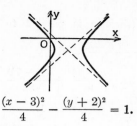

$$\frac{(x-3)^2}{4} - \frac{(y+2)^2}{4} = 1.$$

11.

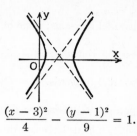

$$\frac{(x-3)^2}{4} - \frac{(y-1)^2}{9} = 1.$$

13.

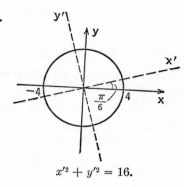

$$x'^2 + y'^2 = 16.$$

15.

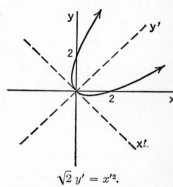

$$\sqrt{2}\, y' = x'^2.$$

17. $y = 1, x = 2.$

SET 21-11

1. $\overrightarrow{VF} = 5 - 3 = 2 = p/2, p = 4.$ $(y+1)^2 = 2(4)(x-3), y^2 - 8x + 2y + 25 = 0.$

3. $\overrightarrow{VF} = -1 - 4 = -5 = p/2, p = -10;$ $(y-5)^2 = 2(-10)(x-4),$
$y^2 + 20x - 10y - 55 = 0.$

5. $\overrightarrow{VF} = -2 = p/2, p = -4;$ $(x-4)^2 = 2(-4)(y-6), x^2 - 8x + 8y - 32 = 0.$

7. $\overrightarrow{VF} = -4 = p/2, p = -8;$ $(x+2)^2 = 2(-8)(y-3), x^2 + 4x + 16y - 44 = 0.$

9. $\overrightarrow{VF} = -2 = p/2, p = -4;$ $(y+2)^2 = 2(-4)(x-9), y^2 + 8x + 4y - 68 = 0.$

11. $(x-3)^2 = \frac{1}{6}(y+2)$ or $6x^2 - 36x - y + 52 = 0.$

13. $(y+6)^2 = 2p(x-4), (1+6)^2 = 2p(1-4), 2p = -49/3,$
$(y+6)^2 = -49(x-4)/3.$

15. $\overrightarrow{VF} = \overrightarrow{DV} = 4 = p/2, 2p = 16;$ $x^2 = 16(y-1)$ or $x^2 - 16y + 16 = 0.$

17. $\overrightarrow{VF} = \overrightarrow{DV} = -3 = p/2, 2p = -12;$ $(y+1)^2 = -12(x-2)$ or
$y^2 + 12x + 2y - 23 = 0.$

19. $\overrightarrow{VF} = \overrightarrow{DV} = -7 = p/2, 2p = -28;$ $(x+7)^2 = -28(y+6)$ or
$x^2 + 14x + 28y + 217 = 0.$

21. Let equation of parabola be $y^2 = 2px$ where $\overrightarrow{VF} = p/2, V(0, 0), F(p/2, 0).$ Find
coordinates $(p/2, y); y^2 = 2p(p/2) = p^2, y = \pm p;$ length $= 2p.$

22. Write equation of intersection of parabola with plane containing vertex and focus
of reflector, $y^2 = 2px.$ $P(6, 5)$ is on it so $25 = 2p(6), p/2 = \frac{25}{24}, VF = \frac{25}{24}$ in.

23. 32.5 ft.

25.

$x^2 = 2p(y + 5)$, $P(2, -2)$,
$4 = 2p(-2 + 5)$, $2p = \frac{4}{3}$,
$x^2 = \frac{4}{3}(y + 5)$.

27.

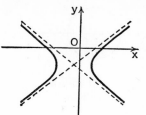

$a = 3$, $b = 2$, $c = \sqrt{13}$,
$C(-1, -3)$, $V(-1 \pm 3, -3)$,
$F(-1 \pm \sqrt{13}, -3)$, asymptotes
$y + 3 = \pm \frac{2}{3}(x + 1)$.

Substitute for y^2: $x^2 + 2x - 6 = 9$;
$x = 3, -5$; $y^2 = 6 - 6 = 0$, $y = 0$;
$y^2 = -10 - 6 = -16$, y imaginary. Only
real intersection is $(3, 0)$ (tangency).

31. Circle: $(x - p/2)^2 + y^2 = R^2$. Substitute $R = x + \dfrac{p}{2}$ for R, $(x - p/2)^2 + y^2 =$
$(x + p/2)^2$ or $y^2 = 2px$. The points of intersection determine a parabola.

29.

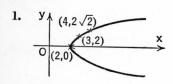

33. $A = 4 \displaystyle\int_{-2}^{7} \sqrt{x + 2}\, dx = 72$ sq units.　　　**35.** $y^2 = 2px$.　　　**37.** 3.

SET 21–12

1.

$d_1 = \sqrt{(x - 3)^2 + y^2}$, $d_2 = x - 1$. $d_1 = ed_2$,
$\sqrt{(x - 3)^2 + y^2} = x - 1$ or $y^2 = 4(x - 2)$, a
parabola.

3. $\sqrt{(x - 4)^2 + y^2} = \frac{4}{5}(x - \frac{25}{4})$, $9x^2 + 25y^2 = 225$,
ellipse.

5. $\sqrt{x^2 + (y - 5)^2} = \frac{5}{4}(x - \frac{16}{5})$, $9x^2 - 16y^2 - 160x + 160y - 144 = 0$, hyperbola.

7. $\sqrt{(x - 3)^2 + (y - 2)^2} = x - 5$ or $y^2 + 4x - 4y - 12 = 0$, parabola.

9. Let $F(0, 0)$, L: $x = c$. $\sqrt{x^2 + y^2} = e(x - c)$ or $(1 - e^2)x^2 + y^2 + 2e^2cx - c^2e^2$
$= 0$. If $e > 1$, $1 - e^2$ is negative and the equation can be written in the form
$\dfrac{y^2}{a^2} - \dfrac{(x - h)^2}{b^2} = 1$ (right member is $+$ since $c^2e^2 > 0$).

11. $CF = c$ and from Problem 10, $CF = ae$. Thus $ae = c = \sqrt{a^2 - b^2}$ or
$$e = \frac{\sqrt{a^2 - b^2}}{a} \left(= \frac{c}{a} \right).$$

SET 21–13

1.

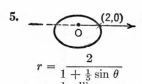

$e = 1$; parabola.

3.

$r = \dfrac{3}{1 - \frac{1}{2}\cos\theta}$
$e = \frac{1}{2}$, ellipse.

5.

$r = \dfrac{2}{1 + \frac{1}{5}\sin\theta}$
$e = \frac{1}{5}$, ellipse.

7.

$$r = \frac{\frac{3}{8}}{1 + \frac{1}{8}\cos\theta}$$
$e = \frac{1}{8}$, ellipse.

9.

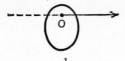

$$r = \frac{1}{1 + \frac{7}{10}\sin\theta}$$
$e = \frac{7}{10}$, ellipse.

11.

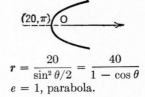

$$r = \frac{5}{1 + \frac{8}{3}\sin\theta}$$
$e = \frac{8}{3}$, hyperbola.

13.

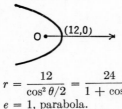
(12,0)

$$r = \frac{12}{\cos^2\theta/2} = \frac{24}{1 + \cos\theta}$$
$e = 1$, parabola.

15.

$(20, \pi)$ O

$$r = \frac{20}{\sin^2\theta/2} = \frac{40}{1 - \cos\theta}$$
$e = 1$, parabola.

17. Compare with Example 2, Section 17–4.

19. $\dfrac{dr}{dt} = 0$.   **21.** Both sets of coordinates are $(1, 0)$.

SET 21–15

5.

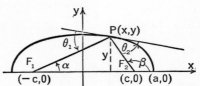

Use $\dfrac{x^2}{a^2} + \dfrac{y^2}{b^2} = 1$. Solve for slope of tangent at $P(x, y)$, $\dfrac{dy}{dx} = -\dfrac{b^2 x}{a^2 y}$.

$$\tan\alpha = \frac{y}{x + c}, \quad \tan\beta = \frac{y}{x - c}.$$

$$\tan\theta_1 = \frac{\dfrac{y}{x + c} + \dfrac{b^2 x}{a^2 y}}{1 - \dfrac{b^2 x}{a^2 y}\dfrac{y}{x + c}}, \quad \tan\theta_2 = \frac{-\dfrac{b^2 x}{a^2 y} - \dfrac{y}{x - c}}{1 - \dfrac{b^2 x}{a^2 y}\dfrac{y}{x - c}}.$$

Simplifying and substituting $b^2 x^2 + a^2 y^2 = a^2 b^2$ and $c^2 = a^2 - b^2$, you should get $\tan\theta_1 = \dfrac{b^2}{cy}$ and $\tan\theta_2 = \dfrac{b^2}{cy}$ so that $\tan\theta_1 \equiv \tan\theta_2$.

SELF TEST 21–16

1. $(x - 2)^2 = 2p(y + 5)$. Use $(1, 3)$; $(1 - 2)^2 = 2p(3 + 5)$, $2p = \frac{1}{8}$; $(x - 2)^2 = \frac{1}{8}(y + 5)$ or $8x^2 - 32x - y + 27 = 0$.

2.

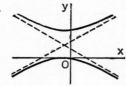

$$\frac{(y - 5)^2}{25} - \frac{(x + 2)^2}{144} = 1. \quad a = 5, b = 12, c = 13,$$
$C(-2, 5)$, $V(-2, 5 \pm 5)$, $F(-2, 5 \pm 13)$.
3. $(x - 4)^2 + (y - 11)^2 = 34$.

4. $\sqrt{(x-1)^2+(y-1)^2} = \frac{1}{2}\sqrt{(x+2)^2+y^2}$, $3x^2+3y^2-12x-8y+4=0$, a circle.

5.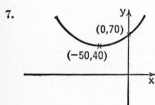

$\dfrac{(x-1)^2}{4} + \dfrac{(y+7)^2}{25} = 1.$ $a = 5,\ b = 2,\ c = \sqrt{21},$

$C(1,-7),\ V(1,-7 \pm 5),\ F(1,-7 \pm \sqrt{21}),$

$e = \dfrac{\sqrt{21}}{5}.$

6. $\dfrac{(x+5)^2}{9} + \dfrac{(y-2)^2}{25} = 1.$ $C(-5,2),$

$V(-5, 2 \pm 5),\ F(-5, 2 \pm 4).$

7.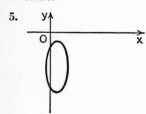

$(x+50)^2 = 2p(y-40).$ Use $(0, 70).$
$(0+50)^2 = 2p(70-40),\ 2p = \frac{250}{3};$
$(x+50)^2 = \frac{250}{3}(y-40).$

8. Hyperbola (has vertex between foci).
$C(7,-1),\ a = 3,\ c = 4,\ b^2 = 7;$
$\dfrac{(y+1)^2}{9} - \dfrac{(x-7)^2}{7} = 1.$

9.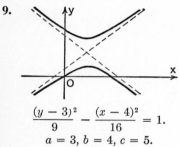

$\dfrac{(y-3)^2}{9} - \dfrac{(x-4)^2}{16} = 1.$
$a = 3,\ b = 4,\ c = 5.$

10.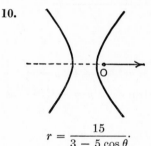

$r = \dfrac{15}{3 - 5\cos\theta}.$

11.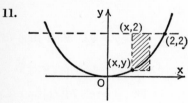

(a) $x^2 = 2py,\ (2, 2),$
$4 = 2p(2),\ 2p = 2,\ x^2 = 2y.$

(b) $dA = (2-y)\,dx = \left(2 - \dfrac{x^2}{2}\right)dx,$

$A = 2\displaystyle\int_0^2 \left(2 - \dfrac{x^2}{2}\right)dx = 4x - \dfrac{x^3}{3}\Big]_0^2$
$= 8 - \frac{8}{3} = \frac{16}{3}.$

12. $A = \frac{1}{3}\displaystyle\int_0^6 (36 - x^2)\,dx$
$= 48$ sq units.

13. $y + x = 3$ and $y - x = 1.$

SET 22–1

1. $x = 5(y+3) + 2.$

3. $y = \left(\dfrac{x-1}{4}\right)^2.$

5. $(x-4)^2 + (y-3)^2 = \sin^2 t + \cos^2 t = 1.$

7. (a) $x^2 + (y-2)^2 = 25(\cos^2 t + \sin^2 t) = 25.$
  (b) A segment of the line $y = 2 + x$?

9. $x^2/9 + y^2/25 = \sin^2 t + \cos^2 t = 1.$

11. $x^{\frac{2}{3}} + y^{\frac{2}{3}} = \cos^2 t + \sin^2 t = 1.$

13. $y = x\sqrt{3} - 0.000016x^2$.

14. Use $3t = y/x$ to eliminate t from either given equation and find $27x^3 + y^3 = 9xy$.

15. Use $t = \dfrac{\ln x}{\ln 3}$ and find $y = 7 + 2^{-\frac{\ln x}{\ln 3}}$.

SET 22–2

1. Use $2a = 6$.

3. $x = 2\,|\cos\theta|\cos\theta,\ y = 2\,|\cos\theta|\sin\theta$.

5. $1, 2, 0, -1, \pi, \pi/2, 3\pi/2$.

7.

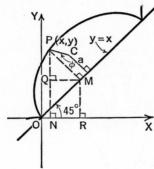

$OM = a(\phi - \sin\phi),\ MP = a(1 - \cos\phi)$.

$x = OM\cos 45° + MP\cos(45° + 90°)$

$\quad = a(\phi - \sin\phi - 1 + \cos\phi)/\sqrt{2}$.

$y = OM\sin 45° + MP\sin(45° + 90°)$

$\quad = a(\phi - \sin\phi + 1 - \cos\phi)/\sqrt{2}$.

9. $x = a\phi,\ y = a(1 - \cos\phi);\ y = a\left(1 - \cos\dfrac{x}{a}\right)$.

13. $x = 3(\phi - \sin\phi)/2,\ y = -3(1 - \cos\phi)/2 + 3$.

SET 22–3

1. (a) No. At $x = 1000$, $y \approx 130$.   (b) Approx 120 ft.

3. $t = \frac{3}{2}$, range $= 36\sqrt{3} \cong 62$ ft.

5. (a) Use $x = 3v_0t/5,\ y = 4v_0t/5 - 16t^2$ and $x = 72$ when $y = 32$. Find time of flight $t = 2$ sec and $v_0 = 60$ ft per sec.

(b) $v_x = 36,\ v_y(2) = -16$ indicates falling, $|v| = 4\sqrt{97} \cong 39,\ v_y/v_x]_{t=2} = -\frac{4}{9}$.

(c) Use results of (b).

7. Use $x = 264t,\ y = -16t^2$. Find $t = 30$ when $y = 14,400$. Travels 7,920 ft.

9. Follow the pattern of Example 1 with $60°$ replaced by α and 200 replaced by v_0.

SET 22–4

1. $1 \le x \le 9,\ 0 \le y \le 2$.

3. $\sin t = -.8750,\ \cos t = \pm.4841,\ y \cong .52$ or 1.48.

5. $x' + h = x = 5 + 4\sin t,\ y' + k = y = 1 - \cos t$,

$(x' + h - 5)^2/16 + (y' + k - 1)^2 = 1$. Through $(x' = 0,\ y' = 0)$ if

$(h - 5)^2/16 + (k - 1)^2 = 1$. Example: $h = 1,\ k = 1$.

7. $(7 + h - 5)^2/16 + (-4 + k - 1)^2 = 1$. Example: $h = 2,\ k = 5$.

9. $\dfrac{dy}{dt}\Big/\dfrac{dx}{dt}\bigg]_{t=-1} = -2,\ y + 4 = -2(x - 4)$.

11.

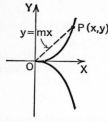

$y^2 = m^2x^2 = x^3$,
$(x = m^2, y = m \cdot m^2$
$= m^3)$.

13.

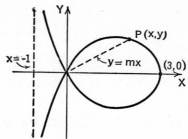

$x^3 + m^2x^3 + m^2x^2 - 3x^2 = 0$,
$\left(x = \dfrac{3 - m^2}{1 + m^2}, y = \dfrac{3m - m^3}{1 + m^2} \right)$.

14. $y = (1 + \sin\theta)\sin\theta$, $dy/d\theta = \cos\theta + 2\sin\theta\cos\theta$. $(r = 2, \theta = \pi/2)$, $(\frac{1}{2}, 7\pi/6)$, $(\frac{1}{2}, 11\pi/6)$. Why not use $\theta = 3\pi/2$?

SELF TEST 22–5

1. $x = (96\sqrt{3})t$, $y = -16t^2 + 96t$. $x(8) \cong 1330$ ft.

2. $(x - 3)^2 + (y - 5)^2 = 2\left| \dfrac{5x - 12y + 13}{-13} \right|$.

3.

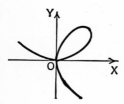

4. Use $t = y/x$.   **5.** 27 ft per sec.
6. $x = 4\cos\theta$, $y = 2\sin\theta$, $\theta = \angle XOR$.

SET 23–2

1. $y = 10^{-x+2}$, $y = e^{-2.3x+4.6}$.   **3.** $y = 10^{2x}$, $y = e^{4.7x}$.
5. $y = 10^{(2x-8)/3}$, $y = e^{1.5x-6.1}$.   **7.** $y = 10^{0.2x-2}$, $y = e^{0.46x-4.6}$.
9. $y = 10^{-3x+4}$, $y = e^{-6.9x+9.2}$.   **11.** $y = 3(2^x)$.
13. $y = 80(8^{-0.1x})$.   **15.** $y = 10^{-.62x+21.5}$.   **17.** $z = 17(10^{0.14t-2.1})$.

SET 23–3

11. $y = 10/x$.   **13.** $y = .001x^2$.   **15.** $y = 1000/x^2$.
17. $y = 10(x/3)^{0.66} = 4.8x^{0.66}$.   **19.** $y^3 = 10/x$.   **21.** $y = 1.3x^{1.2}$.
23. $y = 1000(.1x)^{1.5} = 33x^{1.5}$.   **25.** $y = 9800x^{-3.0}$.
27. $y = 10x^{-2.1}$.   **29.** $y = 10^{-.094x+.94}$.

SET 23–5

3. $Y = 1.2X + .11$
$\log y = 1.2 \log x + .11$
$\qquad = 1.2 \log x + \log 1.3$
$\quad y = 1.3\, x^{1.2}$.

SELF TEST 23–6

1. $N = 10^{2t+2}$.

2. $y = 0.1x^3$.

3. Logarithmic paper.

4. Semilogarithmic paper.

5. (a) The points on the x-axis actually correspond to sin x; that is, the point labeled $x = 10°$ will actually denote sin 10°. One half-cycle will be an interval one unit long on the x-axis (say, from sin 0° = 0 to sin 90° = 1).

   (b) No.

   (c) Yes.

   (d) A point at the midpoint of the cycle from 0° to 90° would have the value 30°.

SET 24–2

11. $\sqrt{89}$. 13. $\sqrt{147}$. 15. $\sqrt{19}$. 17. $\sqrt{29}$. 19. $\sqrt{62}$.

23. The sides are 11, 11, and $11\sqrt{2}$. The triangle is an isosceles right triangle.

25. See method of Problem 23.

27. See method of Problem 23.

29. $x = 0$, $y = 0$.

31. A plane parallel to the xy plane and 3 units above the xy plane.

33. The surface of a sphere with center $(2, -1, 5)$ and radius 4.

35. $(x - 1)^2 + (y - 5)^2 + (z - 0)^2 = 36$. The surface of a sphere with center $(1, 5, 0)$ and radius 6.

36. $(x - h)^2 + (y - k)^2 + (z - l)^2 = r^2$.

37. A plane parallel to the xy plane and k units above or below it.

39. A plane parallel to the xz plane and k units away from it.

41. $(x + 3)^2 + (y - 11)^2 + (z + 9)^2 = 25$.

SET 24–3

1. Circular cylinder with elements parallel to the y-axis.

3. Hyperbolic cylinder with elements parallel to the z-axis.

5. Plane parallel to xy plane.

7. Sinusoidal cylinder with elements parallel to the y-axis.

9. $x = 4 \sin z \cos z$. Similar to 7.

11. Parabolic cylinder. 13. Elliptical cylinder. 15. Hyperbolic cylinder.

17. $(x - 1)^2 + (y + 2)^2 = 4$. 19. $y^2 + z^2 = 4$.

21. $x^2 + 8z = 16$. 23. $y + 4z = 0$.

25. Choose any three distinct values for x and z. Determine corresponding values of y from the equation.

SET 24–4

1. Ellipsoid of revolution. Circular trace: $x^2 + z^2 = 4$, $y = 0$.
   Elliptical traces: $9x^2 + 4y^2 = 36$, $z = 0$ and $4y^2 + 9z^2 = 36$, $x = 0$.

3. Elliptical paraboloid. Elliptical trace: $2x^2 + y^2 = 12$, $z = 0$.
   Parabolic traces: $4x^2 - 3z = 24$, $y = 0$ and $2y^2 - 3z = 24$, $x = 0$.

5. Elliptical paraboloid.

7. Parabolic cylinder. Elements are parallel to y-axis.
   Directrix parabola: $3x^2 + 9z = 100$, $y = 0$.

9. Compare with example 4. 11. Parabolic cylinder.

13. Compare with 1. 15. Planes: $x = -1$ and $x = 4$.

17.

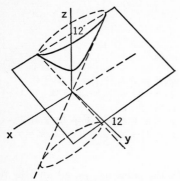

No volume is determined.

19.

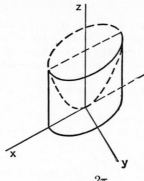

Volume $= \dfrac{2\pi}{3}$.

21. $z^2 + y^2 = 4x^2$.

23. $y^2 + z^2 = 4x$.

SET 24–5

1. A right circular cylinder of radius 2 and axis along the z-axis intersected by a plane parallel to the y-axis whose trace in the xz plane is the line $x + 2z = 1$.

3. A parabolic cylinder whose generator is parallel to the y-axis and whose directrix is the parabola $x^2 = 4z$ in the xz plane intersected by a right circular cylinder of radius 1 and axis along the x-axis.

5. A hyperbolic cylinder whose generator is parallel to the z-axis and whose directrix is the hyperbola $x^2 - y^2 = 16$ in the xy plane intersected by a plane parallel to the y-axis and whose trace in the xz plane is the line $x + z = 1$, $y = 0$.

9. A helix wrapped around the cylinder $x^2 + y^2 = 4$.

SET 24–6

1. Direction numbers: $[1:\sqrt{2}:-1]$. Direction cosines: $\left[\dfrac{1}{2}:\dfrac{\sqrt{2}}{2}:-\dfrac{1}{2}\right]$.

3. Direction numbers: $[1:5:-4]$. Direction cosines: $[1/\sqrt{42}:5/\sqrt{42}:-4/\sqrt{42}]$.

5. Direction numbers: $[2:-1:-5]$.
   Direction cosines: $[2/\sqrt{30}:-1/\sqrt{30}:-5/\sqrt{30}]$.

7. Direction numbers: $[2:2:1]$. Direction cosines: $[\tfrac{2}{3}:\tfrac{2}{3}:\tfrac{1}{3}]$.

11. $\cos \alpha = \pm\tfrac{1}{2}$. $\alpha = 60°, 120°$.

13. They are proportional to the direction cosines which are

$$\frac{a}{\sqrt{a^2 + b^2 + c^2}}, \frac{b}{\sqrt{a^2 + b^2 + c^2}}, \frac{c}{\sqrt{a^2 + b^2 + c^2}}.$$

SET 24–7

1. Arc $\cos \dfrac{1 + \sqrt{2}}{\sqrt{14}} \cong 49° \, 49' \cong 50°$.

3. Arc $\cos \dfrac{\sqrt{3}}{2} = 30°$.

5. Arc $\cos \dfrac{11}{2\sqrt{105}} \cong 57° \, 32' \cong 58°$.

7. Arc $\cos \dfrac{1}{3\sqrt{14}} \cong 84° \, 53' \cong 85°$.

11. $1l + \sqrt{2}m - 1n = 0$. Example: $l = 1$, $m = 0$, $n = 1$.

13. $[-1:1:1]$.

15. $[6:7:1]$.

17. $[-3:2:2]$.

SET 24–9

1. $1(x - 0) + \sqrt{2}(y - 0) - 1(z - 0) = 0.$
3. $1(x - 3) + 5(y - 1) - 4(z - 7) = 0.$
5. $2(x - 1) - 1(y - 2) - 5(z - 3) = 0.$
7. $2(x - 4) + 2(y - 3) + 1(z - 5) = 0.$
9. $\frac{3}{7}x + \frac{2}{7}y - \frac{6}{7}z - 3 = 0.$
11. $\frac{2}{11}x + \frac{6}{11}y - \frac{9}{11}z + 2 = 0.$
13. $\frac{1}{3}x + \frac{2}{3}y - \frac{2}{3}z - 4 = 0.$
15. $\frac{2}{7}x - \frac{3}{7}y + \frac{6}{7}z - \frac{1}{6} = 0.$
17. $[-\frac{2}{7}:\frac{3}{7}:-\frac{6}{7}].$
19. $[\frac{2}{3}:\frac{1}{3}:\frac{2}{3}].$
21. $x = t, \ y = \sqrt{2}t, \ z = -t.$
23. $x = 3 + t, \ y = 1 + 5t, \ z = 7 - 4t.$
25. $x = 1 + 2t, \ y = 2 - t, \ z = 3 - 5t.$
27. $x = 4 - 2t, \ y = 3 - 2t, \ z = 5 - t.$
29. $\dfrac{x - \frac{17}{7}}{-\frac{4}{7}} = \dfrac{y + \frac{11}{7}}{\frac{10}{7}} = \dfrac{z}{1}.$

31. (a) Consider the line segment determined by the point (x_1, y_1, z_1) and the point $\left(\dfrac{p}{\cos \alpha}, 0, 0\right)$ in the plane. The desired distance D is the projection of this line segment on to the normal. $D = L \cos \theta$ where L is the length of the line segment and θ is the angle between the line and the normal to the plane.

Hence, $D = \sqrt{\left(x_1 - \dfrac{p}{\cos \alpha}\right)^2 + y_1^2 + z_1^2} \times$

$$\dfrac{\left| \left(x_1 - \dfrac{p}{\cos \alpha}\right) \cos \alpha + \cos \beta \, y_1 + \cos \gamma \, z_1 \right|}{\sqrt{\left(x_1 - \dfrac{p}{\cos \alpha}\right)^2 + y_1^2 + z_1^2} \ \sqrt{\cos^2 \alpha + \cos^2 \beta + \cos^2 \gamma}},$$

$$= |\cos \alpha \, x_1 + \cos \beta \, y_1 + \cos \gamma \, z_1 - p|.$$

(c) Use the results of (a) with Theorem 2.

SET 24–11

1. $A(0, 7, 5), \ B(2, 2\sqrt{3}, -1), \ C(0, 0, 0), \ D(\cos 1, \sin 1, 1).$
2. $A(0, 2\sqrt{3}, 2), \ B(1, \sqrt{3}, 0).$
3. (a) $z = 5,$ (b) $z = 5,$ (c) $\rho \cos \phi = 5.$
5. (a) $x^2 + y^2 = 4,$ (b) $r = 2,$ (c) $\rho \sin \phi = 2.$
7. (a) $x^2 + y^2 + z^2 = 289,$ (b) $r^2 + z^2 = 289,$ (c) $\rho = 17.$
9. (a) $9(x - 5)^2 + 25y^2 = 225,$ (b) $9(r \cos \theta - 5)^2 + 25r^2 \sin^2 \theta = 225.$
   (c) $9(\rho \sin \phi \cos \theta - 5)^2 + 25\rho^2 \sin^2 \phi \sin^2 \theta = 225.$
11. The surfaces are a sphere with center at the origin and radius 4, and a circular cylinder with elements parallel to the z-axis and whose trace in the xy plane is a circle of radius 2 with center at $(2, 0, 0)$.
13. A right circular cone whose axis is along the z-axis cut by a sphere of radius 3, center at the origin.

15.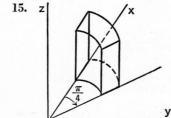

17. A helix wrapped around the cone $x^2 + y^2 = 4z^2$. See Example 1, Section 24–5.

19.

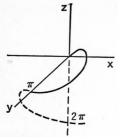

The restriction $0 \leqq t \leqq \pi$ is implied since $0 \leqq \phi \leqq \pi$. The locus is the twisting space curve shown.

SELF TEST 24–12

1. $9/\sqrt{2}$.   **2.** $(x-2)^2 + (y-1)^2 + (z-5)^2 \leqq 26$.

3. Hyperbolic cylinder. Elements are parallel to y-axis.

4. Compare with Problem **3**, Set 24–4.

5. Ellipsoid. Center $(5, 3, -1)$. Let $x' = x - 5$, $y' = y - 3$, $z' = z + 1$. Sketch $x'^2 + 4y'^2 + 25z'^2 = 900$.

6. Planes: $y = 4$ and $z = -1$.

7. Hyperboloid of two sheets.   **9.** $[2/\sqrt{33} : -5/\sqrt{33} : 2/\sqrt{33}]$.

10. $2(x-2) - 5(y+1) + 2(z-3) = 0$.

11. $r^2 + z^2 = 100$, $r = -10 \cos \theta$.

12. **(b)** $x^2 + y^2 + z^2 = 36$, $4(x^2 + y^2) = z^2$.

SET 25–2

1. $AB = \begin{bmatrix} 20 & 61 \\ 11 & 35 \end{bmatrix}$; $BA = \begin{bmatrix} 5 & -17 \\ -13 & 50 \end{bmatrix}$.

3. $AC = \begin{bmatrix} 26 & 61 \\ 15 & 36 \end{bmatrix}$; $CA = \begin{bmatrix} -10 & 39 \\ -19 & 72 \end{bmatrix}$.

5. $B(DC) = \begin{bmatrix} 21 & 42 \\ 363 & 1161 \end{bmatrix}$; $D(CB) = \begin{bmatrix} 36 & 249 \\ 129 & 1146 \end{bmatrix}$;

$C(BD) = \begin{bmatrix} 245 & 670 \\ 329 & 937 \end{bmatrix}$.

7.

	I	A	B	C	D	E	F	G
I	I	A	B	C	D	E	F	G
A	A	D	C	F	E	I	G	B
B	B	G	D	A	F	C	I	E
C	C	B	E	D	G	F	A	I
D	D	E	F	G	I	A	B	C
E	E	I	G	B	A	D	C	F
F	F	C	I	E	B	G	D	A
G	G	F	A	I	C	B	E	D

SET 25–15

3. **(a)** 20. **(b)** 26.

5. Since $10 \equiv 1 \pmod 3$,

$a_n \cdot 10^n + a_{n-1} \cdot 10^{n-1} + \cdots + a_1 \cdot 10 + a_0 \equiv a_n + a_{n-1} + \cdots + a_1 + a_0$ (mod 3). But $a_n \cdot 10^n + \cdots + a_1 \cdot 10 + a_0 \equiv 0 \pmod 3$ by hypothesis. Therefore, $a_n + a_{n-1} + \cdots + a_0 \equiv 0 \pmod 3$, which implies that the sum of the digits of the number is divisible by 3. (Review Sections 1–15 and 1–16.)

7. **(a)** 111010. **(b)** 11001101. **(c)** 101.

INDEX

INDEX

INDEX

Absolute maximum or minimum, 149
Absolute value, 12, 413
Acceleration, 161
Accuracy, 181
Addition vector, 414
Additive identity (zero), 2
Additive set function, 270
Adler, I., 608
Advantage of computers, 605
Algebra, rules of (field postulates), 2
Algebraic identities, 356
Amount, compound, 223
Amount of rotation, 322
Amplitude, 348, 413
Analysis
    factor, 585
    numerical, 233
Andree, R. V., 471, 608
Angle, 322, 413
    between two lines, 458, 572
        in a plane, 322
        in space, 572
    complementary, 330
    direction, 570
    function of half, 372
    function of multiple, 371
    of inclination, 455
    of intersection, 458
    phase, 346
    plane, 322
    polar, 394
    reference, 328
    solid, 570
    standard position, 324
    trisection, 589
    vectorial, 394
Antiderivative, 433
Approximate intercepts, 66
Approximation
    of a function value, 453
    of results, 181
    of roots by Newton's Method, 449
arc sin, and other arc functions, 382
Archimedes, spiral of, 410, 531
Area, 244, 396, 443
    as a definite integral, 441
    of a triangle, 476
Argand, J. R., 413
Argand plane, 413
Arithmetic mean, 220, 223, 293
Arithmetic modular, 37, 39
Arithmetic progressions, 220
Arithmetic sequence, sum of, 220
Associative, 2
Assumptions, fundamental logarithm, 182
Asymptotes
    hyperbola, 501
    vertical, 68
Auxiliary equations, 30

Average
    mean of x, 293
    process, 315
    rate of change, 9, 34, 158
    velocity, 159
Axis
    conjugate of the hyperbola, 501
    of ellipse, 492
    of hyperbola, 501
    i-, 413
    j-, 413
    number, 13
    of parabola, 510
    polar, 394
    radical, 483
    real, 413
    rotation of, 508
    of symmetry, 91

Ball, W. W. R., 608
Ball and Coxeter, 603
Baranalli, H., 412
Begle, E. G., 608
Behavior
    of loci for large values of $|x|$, 70
Bell, E. T., 608
Bernoulli function, 298
Binary System, 603
Binomial distribution, 298
    expansion, 257
        for fractional exponents, 259
    function, Bernoulli, 298
    mean of, 303
    variance of, 305
Boehm, G. A. W., 608
Book list, 608
Bounds
    on intercepts, tests for, 86
    upper and lower, for intercepts, 86
Brachistochrone, 528
Brixey, J. C., 608
Brun, V., 587

Cancellation law, 5
Candidate set, 21
Cardioid, 407
Carnap, R., 608
Carroll, L., 608
Cartesian coordinates, 46
Cartesian graph, 48
Cartesian plane, 48
Cartesian set, 48
Catenary, 208
Cayley, A., 479
Cell, J. W., 609
Center
    of circle, 52, 482
    of ellipse, 492
    of hyperbola, 501
    of symmetry, 91

Characteristic of a logarithm, 187
Chart
    control, 315
    for defects, control, 317
    flow, 78
Church, Alonzo, 600
Cipher, 601
Circle
    equation of, 52, 54, 57, 477, 482
        in determinantal form, 477
        in standard form, 482
    functions, 354
    polar coordinates, 396
    polar equation of, 397, 399
    systems of, 483
    unit, 57
Cissoid, 539
Closure, 2
Code, 601
Cofactor, 468
Cofunction, 330
Collar, 585
Color problem, 596
Combinations, 264
Common divisor, greatest, 588
Commutative, 2
Complement of a set, 269
Complementary angle, 330
Complementary events, 275
Complex exponents, 423
Complex numbers, 13, 14, 413
    multiplication of, 419
    roots of, 421
Complex products, 414
Complex vectors, 416
Components, direction, 572
Composition of ordinates, 350
Compound amount, 223
Compound interest law, 262
Computation, logarithmic, 191
Computers, 177, 233, 239, 604
    use of, 76
Conditional, 49
Conditional equations, 22
Conditional inequality, 43
Conditional probability, 282
Confidence interval, 311
Congruence
    modulo 7, 37
    modulo 12, 39
Conics
    focal properties of, 520
    polar coordinate equations, 516
    sections, 519
Conjugate axis of hyperbola, 501
Consecutives, Goldbach's, 587
Continuous function, 117
    roots of, 76
Control
    chart, 315, 317
    chart for defectives, 315
    chart for defects, 317
    limits, 315, 317
    statistical quality, 320
Converse of the factor theorem,
    85
Coordinate paper, 543

Coordinates
    Cartesian, 46
    cylindrical, 577
    polar, 394
    relationship between polar and rec-
        tangular, 399
    spherical, 579
Coordinate systems, 46
cosh x, 208
cosine
    $(A + B)$, 366
    derivative of, 387
    direction, 570
    graph of, 346
    law of, 335
    series, 425
cotangent, definition, 324, 344
Courant, R., 441, 597, 609
Court, N. A., 609
Cramer's rule, 479
Critical x-values, 167
Cryptography, 601
Cundy, H. M., 609
Curve
    fitting, 237
    slope of, 136
    space, 568
Cycle, 346
Cycloid, 528
    parametric, 527
Cylinders, 563
Cylindrical coordinates, 577

Dadourian, H. M., 609
Dantzig, L., 609
Decimal, infinite repeating, 228
"Deci-trig," 323
Decreasing function, 166
Definite integral, 441, 443, 447
    as an area, 441
    as a limit of a sum, 447
Delta
    function, 32
    process, 130
De Moivre's Theorem, 419
Depressed equation, 84
Derivative, 130, 429
    of a composite function, 145
    of logarithmic and exponential func-
        tions, 204
    of a polynomial, 137
    of a product, 429
    of a quotient, 146
    of sin u and cos u, 386
    of sum of two functions, 134
    with respect to x, 167
Descartes, René, 519
Descriptive statistics, 292
Design, experimental, 292
Detached coefficients, 463
Determinants, 467, 471
    expanded, 469
    systems of linear equations, 477
    theorems about, 471
Deviation, 294
    standard, 294
        of the number of occurrences, 302

Diagrams, Venn, 269
Difference
    equations, 240
    finite, 233
Differential equation, 207, 435, 436
Differentiation, 130
    of a composite function, 145
    implicit, 147
    of a product, 141
Digit, 603
    significant, 177
Direction
    angles, 570
    components, 572
    cosine, 570
    numbers, 570, 571
        of a normal to a plane, 574
Directrix, 563
    of a conic section, 514
    of a cylinder, 563
    of a parabola, 510, 514
Discontinuities, 67
Discontinuous function, 118
Disjoint, 15
    events, 279
    sets, 269
Displacement, phase, 346
Distance, 395, 560, 577
    between two points, 51, 395, 560
    formula, 51, 395, 561
    polar, 395
Distinguishable permutations, 252
Distribution, binomial, 298
    mean of, 303
    variance of, 305
Distributive, 2
Division
    in polar form, 417
    synthetic, 80, 85, 236
    by zero, 8, 10, 67
Divisor
    greatest common positive, 588
    proper, 593
Domain
    correspondence, 16
    of function, 15
Dresden, A., 609
Dubisch, R., 609
Dudeny, H. E., 609
Duncan, 585
Dürer's "Muse," 592

e, 201
    evaluation of, 259, 260
Eccentricity, 514
Economic theory, trend line, 109
Element
    cofactor of, 468
    minor of, 468
    of a sequence, 215
    of a set, 268
Ellipse, 59, 490, 519
    center of, 492
    focal properties of, 521
    focus, 492
    latus rectum of, 492
    major axis of, 492

Ellipse (*continued*)
    minor axis of, 492
    in polar coordinates, 516
    properties of, 492
    reduction to standard form, 495, 497
    standard form of equation, 492, 493
    vertex of, 492
Ellipsoid, 566
Elliptic hyperboloid of one sheet, 567
Elliptical gears, 521
Empty set, 1, 15, 268
Engines, solar, 521
Epsilon, 113
Equals relation in modular systems, 37, 39, 40
Equations, 53
    auxiliary, 30
    of a circle, 52, 54, 57, 397, 477, 482
        in standard form, 482
    conditional, 49
    of a cylinder, 563
    depressed, 84
    difference, 240
    differential, 207, 435, 436
    exponential, 197
    graph of, 48, 54
    identity, 48
    inconsistent, 48
    of a line, 106, 396, 459, 476, 575
    linear, 107
    locus of, 48, 54
    logarithmic, 197
    parametric, 524
    of a plane, normal form, 574
    point-slope, 106
    polar, 396, 516
    quadratic, 24
    rectangular, 400
    slope-y-intercept, 106
    solution, 20
        candidate set, 21
        set, 21
    trigonometric, 362
    two-point, 106
    unconditional, 48
Equivalence
    equals in the mod 7 system, 40
    relations, 41
Equivalent, 43
Equivalent equations or inequalities, 22, 43
Eratosthenes, 322
Error, truncation, 376
Estimate results, 181
Euclid's proof, 587
Euler's polyhedral theorem, 596
Eves, H., 610
Events, 275
    complementary, 275
    independent, 283
    mutually exclusive, 279
    probability of, 275
    space, 274
Exact values of functions, 328
Examinations, true-false, 313
Expansion
    binomial, 257
    series, 259

Experimental design, 292
Exponent
    complex, 423
    negative, fractional and zero, 173
Exponential equations, 197
Exponential functions, derivation of, 204
Exponential logarithmic equations, 197
Extraneous value, 31, 199
Extent of locus, 71, 73
Extreme values, 166

Factor
    analysis, 585
    multiplicity of, 80, 148
    rational, 23
    theorem, 80
        converse of, 85
Factorial, 236
    pseudo, 235
Falling bodies with air resistance, 209
False, true explanations, 313
Family of lines, 107
Fermat's "Last Theorem," 595
Field postulates, 2, 5
Finite differences, 233
Finite geometry, 598
Finite induction, 231
Finite set, 268
Floating point number, 177
Flow chart, 78
Focal properties of conics, 520
Focus
    of an ellipse, 492
    of an hyperbola, 501
    of a parabola, 510
Formula
    for distance between two points, 51, 561
    interpolation, Gregory-Newton, 241
    quadratic, 24
    slope of line, 103
Four-color problem, 596
Fractional exponents, 173
Franklin, Benjamin, 592
Franklin, Philip, 597
Frazer, 585
Freeman, I. M., and M. B., 610
Frequency, 349
    relative, 300
    total, 293
    trigonometric, 349
Function, 15, 17, 20, 344
    additive set, 271
    circular, 354
    composite, differentiation of, 145
    continuous, 117
    correspondence, 16
    decreasing, 166
    delta, 32
    derivative of, 130
    discontinuous, 118
    hyperbolic, 208
    increasing, 166
    inverse trigonometric, 383
    limit of, 112, 114
    monotone increasing, 85
    multiple valued, 18
    ordered pairs, 20

Function (*continued*)
    probability, 271
    quadratic, 100
    roots of a continuous, 76
    of several variables, 17
    single-valued, 18
    trigonometric, 324
    value, approximation of, 453
Functions
    of angles related to 30°, 45°, and 60°, 328
    of half angles, 372
    of multiple angles, 371
    of a number, trigonometric, 344
    wrapping, 344
Fundamental assumptions, logarithm, 182

Gaines, H. L., 610
Gamow, G., 610
Gardener, M., 610
Gehman, 610
Geis, I., 610
General surfaces, 565
General term of a sequence, 215
Generators, 563
Geometric mean, 226
Geometric progression, 223
Geometric sequences, 223
    sum of, 225
Geometry, finite, 598
Gibbs, J. W., 598
Goldbach's consecutives, 587
Graph
    of the Cartesian set, 48
    by composition of ordinates, 350
    of an equation, 48
    of the sentence, 48
    trigonometric, 349–353
Graphing, 65
Growth, law of, 262
Greatest common positive divisor, 588
Gregory-Newton
    interpolation, 243
        formula, 239, 241
Gudermannian, 346

Hagelin converters, 602
Hahn, Hans, 601
Half angles, functions of, 372
Hall, Lester, 603
Hamilton, Sir William R., 598
Heawood-Kempe proof, 596
Hodograph, 426
Hoel, P. G., 610
Hoffman, S., 391
Huff, D., 610
Hunter, D. A. H., 610
Hyperbola, 500, 520
    asymptotes, 501
    center of, 501
    conjugate axis of, 501
    focal properties of, 520
    focus of, 501
    latus rectum of, 502
    in polar coordinates, 516
    properties of, 501, 502
    reduction to standard form, 507
    standard form, 502

Hyperbola (*continued*)
 transverse axis of, 501
 vertices of, 501
Hyperbolic functions, 208, 346
Hyperboloid of one sheet, elliptic, 567
Hypocycloid, 529

i-axis, 413
Identities, 21, 48, 49, 356, 358, 365, 377
 additive (zero), 2
 algebraic, 22, 356
 general hints on, 359
 numerical, 20
 multiplicative (one), 2
 trigonometric, 358
Imaginary, 13, 14, 413, 423
 numbers, 13, 14, 413
 roots, 24, 421
Implicit differentiation, 147
Inclination, angle of, 455
Inconsistent, 48
 sentence, 48
Increasing function, 166
Increments, 124
Indefinite integral, 434
Independent events, 283
Induction, mathematical, 231
Inequalities, 11, 53
 conditional, 43, 48
 of first degree, 44
 of higher degree, 59
 inconsistent, 48
 locus of, 48, 54
 manipulation of, 43
 solutions of, 42
 Tchebycheff's, 295
 unconditional, 43, 49
Inequations, 42
Inertia, moment of, 446
Infinite geometric sequences, 227
Infinite repeating decimals, 228
Infinite sequence, 226
Infinitely many primes, 587
Inflection point, 168
Instantaneous compound interest law, 262
Instantaneous rate of change, 160
Instantaneous velocity, 160
Integers, set of, 12
Integral, 434
 definite, 441, 443, 447
 indefinite, 434
Intercepts, 65
 approximate, 66
 polar, 402
 upper and lower bounds for, 86
Interest law, instantaneous compound, 262
Interpolation, 189
 Gregory-Newton, 243
 formula, 239, 241
 straight-line, 243
Interpretation of imaginary number, 14
Intersection, 268, 568
 angle of, 458
Interval confidence, 311
Inverse, 2, 380
 functions, 380
 trigonometric relations, 382

j-axis, 413
Johnson and Glenn, 611
Jones, B. W., 611

Kasner, E., 611
Kasner and Neuman, 597
Kempe-Heawood proof, 596
Klein bottle, 592
Kline, M., 611
Kokomoor, F. W., 611
Kramer, E. E., 611
Kratchik, M., 611
Kummer's theory, 595

"Last Theorem" of Fermat, 595
Latus rectum
 of an ellipse, 492
 of a hyperbola, 502
 of a parabola, 513
Law
 cancellation, 5
 of cosines, 335
 of growth, 262
 of sines, 339
 of tangents, 342
Laws of ordinary algebra, field postulates, 2
Least squares, 552
Leibnitz, Gottfried W., 130
Lemniscate, 408, 409
Levinson, H. C., 611
Lieber, H. G., 611
Lieber, L. R., 611
Limacon, 403
Limit, 113
 control, 315, 317
 of a function, 112, 114
 of a sum, definite integral, 447
 tangent to a curve at a point, 110
 tolerance, 320
Linear equation, 107
 determinants and systems of, 477
Linear systems, solutions of, 463
Line
 equation of, 106, 575
 in determinantal form, 476
 normal, 458
 equation, 459
 to plane, 574
 slope of, 103
 symmetric equations of, 575
 tangent, 111
Lines
 angle of intersection, 458
 family of, 107, 456, 457
 in polar coordinates, 396
 regression, 553
 slope of parallel, 104
 slope of perpendicular, 455
Locus, 54
 behavior for large values of $|x|$, 70
 definition, 48, 54
 discontinuous, 118
 discussion of, 73
 extent of, 71
 of given sentence, 48
 graph of, 48, 54, 71

Locus (*continued*)
    in polar coordinates, 402
    polar sketching, 402, 409
    symmetry of, 92, 404
Logarithmic computation, 191
Logarithmic equations, 197
Logarithmic functions, derivatives of, 204
Logarithmic interpolation, 189
Logarithmic paper, 548
Logarithms
    to base
        e, 201
        8, 184
        10, 187
    change of base, 202
    characteristic of, 187
    conversion from base to base, 202
    definition of, 182
    fundamental assumptions, 182
    mantissa, 188
    properties of, 184
LORAN, 521
Lower and upper bounds for intercepts, 86
Lower sum, 244

Machines, computing, 604
Magic squares, 592
Magnitude of complex number, 413
Major axis of an ellipse, 492
Mantissa, 188
Mapping
    correspondence, 16
    of the set, 602
    wrapping, 344
Mathematical induction, 231
Matrices, Pauli's, 585
Matrix, 467, 472, 583
    methods, 585
    multiplication, 583
    product, 584
Maxima, 149
    applications involving, 155
Maximum, 96
    absolute, 97, 149
    applications, 154
    and minimum points, test for, 151
    point of a locus, 149
    relative, 96
Mean
    arithmetic, 223, 293
    geometric, 226
    and standard deviation, 293, 294, 302
    of x, 293
Member of a set, 268
Menger, K., 611
Mercator map, 346
Method of least squares, 552
Minimal map, 597
Minimum
    absolute, 97, 149
    applications involving, 154
    and maximum points, test for, 149, 151
    point of locus, 149
    relative, 97
Minor axis of an ellipse, 492
Minor of an element, 468
Mobius strip, 591

Modular arithmetic, 37, 39
Modulus, complex, 413, 418, 419
Moment of inertia, 446
Monotone increasing function, 85
Moritz, M. R. E., 411
Motion, problem of, 95, 160, 437, 532, 536
Mott-Smith, G., 611
Multiple angles, functions of, 371
Multiplication
    of complex numbers, 419
    matrix, 583
    in polar form, 417
Multiplicative identity (one), 2
Multiplicity of a factor, 80, 148
"Muse," Dürer's, 592
Mutually exclusive events, 279
Mutually exclusive sets, 269

Napier, John, 187
Nature of roots, quadratic, 26
Negative exponents, 173
Nernst, 555
Newman, J., 611
Newsom, C. V., 610
Newton-Gregory interpolation, 243
    formula, 239, 241
Newton, Isaac, 130
Newton's method of approximating roots, 449
Nomograms, 210, 213
Noncommutative, 583, 597
Normal, 458, 574
    equation of a line, 459
    form of the equation of a plane, 575
    line, 458
    to a plane, 574
    probability paper, 552
Notation, scientific, 176
    summation, 216, 293
Null set, 1, 268
Number
    axis, 13
    complex, 13, 413
    direction, 571
    floating point, 177
    perfect, 593
    prime, 586
    rational, 12, 228
    real, 13
    set of rational, 12
    systems, 603
    trigonometric functions of a, 344
Numerical analysis, 233
Numerical identity, 20
Numerical sets, 12

(One), Multiplicative Identity, 2
Ordinary algebra, rules of, field postulates, 2
Ordinates, composition of, 350
Ore, O., 612
Oughtred, William, 213

Paper, semilogarithmic, 210, 543
Parabola, 58, 100, 510, 519
    axis of, 510
    directrix of, 510
    focal properties of, 514, 520

Parabola (*continued*)
  focus of, 510
  latus rectum, 513
  in polar coordinates, 516
  reflector property of, 520
  standard form of, 511
  semicubical, 539
  vertex of, 101, 510
Parabolic cylinder, 563
Parabolic reflectors, 521
Paraboloid of revolution, 566
Parallel lines
  family of, 457
  slope of, 404
Parameter, 401, 524
Parametric equations, 524
Parametric representation, 536
  advantages of, 536
  of Archimedes' spiral, 531
  of the cycloid, 527
  of the hypocycloid of 4 cusps, 529
  of path of projectile, 532
Pascal's rule, 256
Pascal's triangle, 256
Path of a projectile, 532
Pauli's matrices, 585
Peano Postulates, 12
Peases, D. K., 391
Perfect number, 593
Period, 349
Periodical list, 614
Permutations, 248, 250
  distinguishable, 252
  fundamental principle, 248
  $P(n, x)$, 251
Perpendicular lines, 455
  family of, 456
Phase angle or displacement, 346
Plane, 574
  angles, 322
  Argand, 413
  equation of, 574
    normal form, 574
  vector, 414
Playfair cipher, 601
Point
  inflection, 168
  sample, 315
  sample space, 272
Point-slope equation, 106
Polar
  angle, 394
  axis, 394
  coordinate vector chart, 426
  coordinates, 394
  distance, 395
  equation, 396
    of a circle, 397, 399
    of conics, 516
  forms, 416
  intercepts, 402
  loci, sketching, 402, 409
  loci, symmetry, 404
Pole, 394
Polya, G., 612
Polynomial, 13
Polynomial, derivative of, 137

Polynomial, roots of, 14, 83
Polynomial, zeros of, 67
Position, standard, 324
Postulates
  field, 2, 5
  Peano, 12
Prediction, statistical, 309
Prime, 594
Prime infinitely, 587
Prime numbers, 586
Principal values, 383
Probability, 274
  addition theorem, 280
  conditional, 282
  of an event, 275
  function, 271
  of number of occurrences within limits, 308
  paper, normal, 552
  product theorem, 283, 285
  summary, 288
Problems, review, 62
Process average, 315
Product
  complex, 414
  derivative of, 429
  differentiation of a, 141
  matrix, 584
  two complex numbers, 418
Progressions
  arithmetic, 220
  geometric, 223
Projectile
  parametric equations of path, 536
  path of, 532
Proper divisor, 593
Properties
  of an ellipse, 492
  of a hyperbola, 501
Pseudo factorial, 235

Quadratic equations
  formula, 24
  function, 100
  nature of roots, 26
  sum and product of roots, 29
Quality control, statistical, 320
Quaternions, 597
Quotient, 419

Rademacher, H., 612
Radians, 323
Radical axis, 483
Radius vector, 394
Range
  correspondence, 16
  of function, 15, 17
Rate of change
  average, 9, 34, 159
  general, 164
  instantaneous, 160
Ratio, 12
Rational factors, 23
Rational numbers, 83, 228
  set of, 12
Rational roots, 83
Real axis, 413

Real numbers, set of, 13
Rectangular coordinates in space, 560
Rectangular equation, 400
Reduction, standard form, 497, 507
Reference angle, 328
Reflectors, parabolic, 520, 521
Reflexive, 40
Regression, line of, 553
Relations, 15, 18, 20
    equivalence, 40, 41
    inverse trigonometric, 382
    polar and rectangular coordinates, 399
    series, 424
Relative frequency, 300
Relative maximum, 96
Relative minimum, 97
Remainder, 80
    theorem, 79, 80
Repeating decimal, infinite, 228
Revolution, paraboloid of, 566
Ringenberg, L. A., 612
Robbins, A., 609
Rollett, A. D., 609
Root, 20
    of a complex number, 421
    continuous function, 76
    Newton's method of approximating, 449
    polynomial equation, 14
        upper and lower bounds for, 86
    rational, 83
    upper and lower bounds, 89
Rotation
    amount of, 322
    of axes, 508
Rules of algebra, 1
Rules of ordinary algebra, field postulates, 2

Sample
    points, 315
    size, 317
        survey, 311
    spaces, 272, 288
    point of, 272
Satisfy an equation, 20
Sawyer, W. W., 612
Scientific notation, 176
secant, graph of, 353
Semicubical parabola, 539
Semilogarithmic coordinate paper, 210, 543
Sentence
    graph of, 48
    locus of a given, 48
    unconditional, 48
Sequences, 215
    arithmetic, 220
        sum of, 220
    geometric, 223
        sum of, 225
    infinite, 226
Series
    e^θ, 259
    expansion, 259
    geometric, sum of, 227
    relations, 424
    $\sin x$, 425
Set, 1, 268

Set (continued)
    candidate, 21
    Cartesian, 48
        graph of, 48
    of complex numbers, 13
    empty, 1, 15, 268
    function, additive, 271
    of integers, 12
    null, 1, 268
    numerical, four important, 12
    of rational numbers, 12
    of real numbers, 13
    solution, 21, 48
    universal, 268, 272
Significant digits, 177
sin
    derivative of, 386
    graph of, 346
    law of, 339
$\sinh x$, 208
Sinusoidal, cylinder, 563
Sinusoidal paper, 552
Sissa, Ben, 595
Size and sample survey, 311
Sketch, 65
Sketching loci in polar coordinates, 402
Sketching polar loci, 409
Slide rule, 213
Slope
    of a curve, 136
    of a line, 103
    of tangent line, 121
        at a maximum or minimum point, 149
Solar stoves, 521
Solid angle, 569
Solubility products, 179
Solution
    of equations, 21
        candidate set, 21
    of inequalities, 42
        of higher degree, 59
    of linear systems, 463
    set, 21, 48
        for that inequality using domain of definition, 43
    using matrices, 464
Space
    coordinates, 560
    curve, 568
    event, 274
    point of sample, 272
    rectangular coordinates in, 560
    sample, 272, 288
Special symbols, 7
Speed, 161
Spherical coordinates, 579
Spiral, 407
Spiral of Archimedes, 410, 531
Spread about the mean, 296, 309
Square roots and higher roots of complex numbers, 421
Squares
    least, 552
    magic, 592
Stancliff, F., 412
Standard, 315

Standard (*continued*)
  deviation, 294
    of the number of occurrences, 302
  forms, 516
    equation of a circle, 482
    equation of an ellipse, 492, 493
    reduced to, 507
  position, 324
Statistical prediction, 292, 309
Statistical quality control, 320
Statistical survey, 310
Statistics, descriptive, 292
Steinhaus, H., 612
Steradian, 570
Sterm, M., 610
Straight-line interpolation, 243
Structure, the study of advanced mathematics, 2
Subset, 1
Substitution cipher, 601
Sum
  of an arithmetic sequence, 220
  of a geometric sequence, 225
  of a geometric series, 227
Summation notation, 216, 293
Summation theorems, 217
Survey
  sample and size, 311
  statistical, 292, 310
Symmetric, 40, 404
  form, 576
  with respect to the pole, 405
Symmetry
  axis of, 91
  of loci, 92
  of points, 90
  polar loci, 404
  with respect to a line, 91
  with respect to a point origin, 93
  with respect to x-axis, y-axis, 94
  tests for, 93
Synthetic division, 80, 85, 236
Systems
  of circle, 483
  linear, solutions of, 463, 477
  of linear equations and determinants, 477
  number, 603

Tables, trigonometric functions, 331
Tangent
  graph of, 353
  law of, 342
  line, slope of, 121
    to a curve at a point, 110
tanh x, 208
Tchebycheff's inequality, 295
Terminal velocity, 209
Tests for symmetry, 93
Theorem, 3
  See specific entries
Tolerance limits, 320
Torus, 597
Total frequency, 293
Trace, 565
Transitive, 40
Translation, 489

Transpose, 471
Transverse axis of the hyperbola, 501
"Tree," 248
Trend line, economic theory, 109
Triangle
  area of, 476
  Pascal's, 256
  solution of by sine, cosine, and tangent laws, 335–342
Triangular coordinate paper, 552
Tricotomy, 42
Trigonometric equations, 362
Trigonometric functions, 324
  of an angle in radians, 344
  definition of, 324, 344
  of half angles, 372
  inverse, 383
  of multiple angles, 371
  of a number, 344
  tables, 331
Trigonometric identities, 356, 358, 365, 377
Trigonometric relations, inverse, 382
Trigonometric tables, use of, 332
Trigonometry, 322
Trisection of an angle, 589
Trisectrix, 539
True-false examinations, 313
Truncation error, 376

Unconditional, 49
Unconditional inequality, 43
Unconditional sentence, 48
Union, 268
Unit circle, 57
Universal set, 268, 272
Upper sum, 244
Upper and lower bounds for intercepts, 86

Value
  absolute, 12, 413
  approximation of a function, 453
  extraneous, 199
  extreme, 166
  of functions of angles related to 30°, 45°, and 60°, 328
  principal, 383
  x, critical, 167
Variability about the mean, 296, 309
Variance, 294
Variants, 601
Vector(s)
  addition, 414
  analysis, 598
  complex, 416
  complex product, 414
  plane, 414
  radius, 394
Vectorial angle, 394
Velocity
  average, 159
  instantaneous, 160
  terminal, 209
Venn diagrams, 269
Vertex, of a parabola, 101, 510
Vertical asymptote, 68

Vertices, of an ellipse, 492
    of the hyperbola, 501
Vinogradon, 587

Waerden, B. L., 612
Wallis, J., 413
Wantze, P. L., 589
Weiss, Marie J., 471
Wessel, C., 413
Whitehead, A. N., 612

Whole numbers, set of integers, 12
Wilder, R. L., 612
Williams, E. D., 612
Wrapping function, 344
Wylie, C. R., 612

(Zero), Additive identity, 2
Zero
    division by, 8, 10, 67
    exponents, 173

Index of Symbols

$|x|$, absolute value, 12

$\neq$, 11

$<, >, \leqq, \geqq$, 11

L^-, L^+, 68

$+\infty, -\infty$, 70

$\triangle x^2$, 122

$\triangle x$, 124

$b^0, b^{-k}, b^{r/d}, 0^{-k}$, 173

Σ, 216, 217, 232, 233, 293, 297

$\triangle x^{(k)}$, 236

$\triangle 2_x(h)$, 236

$K!$, 236, 240, 251

S_n, 245

$n!$, 251

$0!$, 251

$P(n, x)$, 251

e^θ 259, 260

$(a + b)^n$, 257

$\dfrac{du^n}{dx}$, 261

$\dfrac{de^\theta}{d\theta}$, 260

e, 260

$(a \times b)^n$, 266

$\approx, \cong$, approximately equal, 181

$\left(\dfrac{n}{x}\right)$, 254, 264

$A \cap B$, 268

$A \cup B$, 268

$n(s)$, 269, 275

$p(E_1 \cup E_2)$, 280

$p(E_1 \cap E_2), = p$, 283

$p(f \mid r)$, 282

$P_r(F)$, 282

$p(E)$, 275

s_x, 294

$B(n, x, p)$, 298

$\lim\limits_{\theta \to 0} \dfrac{\sin \theta}{\theta}$, 354

ϕ, 1

σ_x, 302

m_x, 302

$f(x), y(x)$, 17

Σ, π, 29

y', 130

δ, 113

$D_x u^n$, 145

$D_x y$, 130

$\dfrac{dy}{dx}$, 130

ϵ, 113

$0/0$, 67, 173

0°, 67, 173